KENZIE KIRSCH MEDICAL THRILLERS

KENZIE KIRSCH MEDICAL THRILLERS

BOOKS 1 - 4

P.D. WORKMAN

ISBN: 9781774682555 (IS Hardcover)

ISBN: 9781774682548 (IS Paperback)

ISBN: 9781774682524 (KDP Paperback)

ISBN: 9781774682531 (Kindle)

ISBN: 9781774682562 (ePub)

pdworkman

Virtually Harmless

Cowritten with D. D. VanDyke
California Corwin P. I. Mystery Series
The Girl in the Morgue

Stand Alone Suspense Novels
Looking Over Your Shoulder
Lion Within
Pursued by the Past
In the Tick of Time
Loose the Dogs

YOUNG ADULT FICTION:

Stand Alone YA novels
Stand Alone
Don't Forget Steven
Those Who Believe
Cynthia has a Secret
Questing for a Dream
Darkness before the Dream (prequel story)
Once Brothers
Intersexion
Making Her Mark
Endless Change
Gem, Himself, Alone

AND MORE AT PDWORKMAN.COM

UNLAWFUL HARVEST

A KENZIE KIRSCH MEDICAL THRILLER

*For those who speak for the voiceless
and for the rights of all who are vulnerable*

1

MacKenzie reached for the ringing phone, trying to drag herself from sleep, but her hand encountered only the empty base of the phone, the wireless handset missing.

She pried her eyes open while feeling for it on the bedside table, knocking off keys and a glass and an empty bottle and other detritus. She swore and blinked and tried to focus. Where had she left the handset and who was calling her so early in the morning? The phone rang five times and went to her voicemail. Too late to answer it. She sank back down onto her pillow and closed her eyes. Whoever it was would have to wait.

But no sooner had it gone to voicemail than it started ringing again. MacKenzie groaned. "Are you serious? Come on!"

She turned her head and squinted at the clock next to her. It was hard to see the red LED display in the bright sunlight. It was almost eleven o'clock. Certainly not too early for a caller, even one who knew that she would sleep in after a party the night before. She rubbed her temples and scanned the room for the wireless handset.

There was a man in the bed next to her, but she ignored him for the time being. He wasn't moving at the sound of the phone, so he'd probably had more to drink than she had. She slid her legs out of the bed and grabbed a silk kimono housecoat to wrap around herself. The caller was sent to voicemail a second time. MacKenzie took another look around the bedroom without spotting the phone, then went out to her living room, also bright with sunlight streaming in the big windows. Outside, the pretty

Vermont scenery was covered with a fresh layer of snow, which reflected back the sunlight even more brilliantly. MacKenzie groaned and looked around. The newspaper was on the floor in a messy, well-read heap. The remains of some late-night snack were spread over the coffee table. Some of their clothing had been left there, scattered across the floor, but no phone.

It started ringing again. Now that she was out of the bedroom and away from the base, she could hear the ringing of the handset, and she kicked at the newspaper to uncover it. She bent down and scooped up the handset. She glanced at the caller ID before pressing the answer button and pressing it to her ear, but she knew very well who it was going to be.

No one else would be so annoying and call over and over again first thing in the morning. She couldn't just leave a message and wait for MacKenzie to get back to her, she had to keep calling, forcing MacKenzie to get up and answer it. Her mother didn't care how late MacKenzie might have been up the night before or how she might be feeling upon rising. It was a natural consequence of MacKenzie's own choices. MacKenzie dropped into the white couch.

"Mother."

"MacKenzie. Thank goodness I got you. Where have you been?"

Her mother had been calling for all of two minutes. Where had MacKenzie been? She could have been in the bathroom, having a shower, talking to someone else on the phone, or at some event. Granted, she didn't go to a lot of events at eleven o'clock in the morning, but it *could* happen. Mrs. Lisa Cole Kirsch had a pretty good idea where MacKenzie had been. In bed, like most any other morning.

"What is it, Mother?"

"It's Amanda. She's sick."

MacKenzie nodded to herself and scratched the back of her head. One of the things that would definitely set Lisa into a tizzy was Amanda being sick. She worried over every little cough or twinge that Amanda suffered. She had good reason, but it still made MacKenzie roll her eyes.

"What's wrong with Amanda?"

"I don't know. Maybe it's just the flu, but I'm really worried, MacKenzie. The doctors said to just wait and see, but they don't understand how frail Amanda is. They think that I'm just overreacting and being a hypochondriac. You know that I'm not just a hypochondriac."

"I know. So, how is she?"

MacKenzie had to admit that even though her mother worried about Amanda, her worry was well-justified. Amanda's health could get worse very quickly, and with the anti-rejection drugs suppressing her immune system, she was prone to picking up anything that went around.

"She's not good. She was up all night, throwing up, high fever, she's just not herself. I called an ambulance at eight o'clock. She just can't keep anything down and I don't like the way she's acting. So… weak and listless."

MacKenzie felt the first twinge of worry herself. Amanda had spent much of her life sick, but she was a fighter. She usually did her best to look like nothing was wrong, not letting on unless she was feeling really badly. She would laugh and brush it off as just a bug and smile and encourage MacKenzie to tell her about what was going on in her far-more-interesting life. MacKenzie closed her eyes, focusing on Lisa's words.

"But the doctors don't think that there's anything to worry about?"

"No, but you know… they never do. She has to be at death's door before they'll admit that there might be a problem."

"Have they given her anything or did they just send her back home again?"

"They've got her on an IV and have said that they'll keep an eye on her. But you know they don't really think there's anything wrong. They're just humoring me."

"Yeah. Do you want me to come?"

"Would you? I'm really worried."

"Okay. I'll need a few minutes to get myself together. I'll be there as soon as I can."

"Thank you, MacKenzie. I don't know what I would do without you."

The sad thing was, Lisa would do just fine without MacKenzie. Even though she said that she needed MacKenzie, MacKenzie wouldn't really be able to do anything that Lisa couldn't do herself. She'd been dealing with doctors for a lot of years, and though she didn't pick up on the medical jargon as quickly as MacKenzie did, she could hold her own very well and was stubborn as a mule when it came to Amanda's care. She would protect her baby at all costs, and Amanda would get the best of care whether MacKenzie were there or not.

But if Lisa wanted the extra comfort of having MacKenzie around, who was she to argue? She didn't have anything else going on that prevented her attendance, and even if she did, it was easy enough to beg off of any event with an excuse, especially if the excuse were that Amanda was sick. MacKenzie had used it as an excuse even when it wasn't true. Although technically, even when Amanda was feeling well, she was still sick, so it wasn't really a lie.

MacKenzie hung up the phone and put it down on the brass and glass side table. She scrubbed her eyes with her fists, and when she opened them again, Liam was standing in the front of her.

"What's up?" he asked. "Everything okay?"

He hadn't yet recovered anything more than his boxers and, for a minute, MacKenzie just let her eyes rove over the piece of eye candy, remembering the night before through a slight haze of alcohol. They had gone to the Cancer Society fundraiser, had made the rounds there and let themselves be seen, and then had returned to MacKenzie's apartment for more drinks, some real food, and private entertainment.

"MacKenzie? What's up?"

"Amanda. She's in the hospital and Mother wants me to go over there and reassure her." MacKenzie yawned.

Liam bent over to pick up the various items of clothing he had dropped the night before. "Is she okay?"

"I'm sure both Amanda and Mother will be just fine. But she sounded pretty worried, and she said that Amanda was listless, which isn't like her. A really bad flu, maybe. I hope that's all it is."

"I was going to have a shower before heading out. Do you want it?"

MacKenzie weighed the options. Amanda was in the hospital, so she would be getting the best of care. Did it really matter whether MacKenzie had to wait an extra ten minutes for Liam to shower before she got herself ready?

"Or," Liam suggested, a dimple appearing in his cheek, "we could shower together and be done twice as fast."

"I have a feeling I wouldn't be out of here very quickly if we did that," MacKenzie laughed. They could easily be another hour, and Lisa would be on the phone again, ringing insistently, demanding to know where MacKenzie was and why she wasn't at her sister's side yet.

"Okay," Liam agreed. "So, do you want it?"

"Yes. I guess so. I need to pull myself together even if I am just going to the hospital." Lisa would not want her to show up looking bedraggled. She'd expect MacKenzie to be well turned-out even if it were the middle of the night, which it wasn't.

Liam nodded agreeably. He pulled on his white shirt from the night before, but didn't put on the pants or the rest of his outfit. "Shall I make you some breakfast while you're in there so that you can get out more quickly?"

"Would you? Just a couple of pieces of toast and some juice," MacKenzie requested, heading toward the bathroom. She looked back over her shoulder at him. "And coffee."

He smiled. "I think I know by now that you don't start any morning without coffee."

"Well, I need to fortify myself with *something* this morning before facing my mother."

She had a quick breakfast while Liam got into the shower, but he wasn't out by the time she was finished. She poked her head into the bathroom.

"Will you be much longer?"

She could see his shadow through the shower curtain as he turned his head toward her. "Oh… I can just lock up when I leave. You can go ahead."

MacKenzie shook her head. "I don't like to leave people here when I'm not around. Sorry. Can you be quick?"

"Yeah, sure." His tone was agreeable, but clipped. He obviously didn't appreciate that she didn't trust him enough to leave him alone in her apartment. But MacKenzie had been burned in the past by people who didn't respect her privacy, and she wasn't about to leave him there without supervision. She didn't know him well enough. Just because she could go with him to an event, and maybe bring him home afterward, that didn't mean she knew enough about his essential character to leave him there alone. She valued her privacy and there were a few things around the apartment that were quite valuable. Not that she thought Liam Jackson was going to steal them. She knew where to find him if he did. But it just wasn't good policy. If she didn't notice that something was missing right away, she might never be able to track it down again.

"I'll just be two more minutes," Liam promised.

"Thanks."

She went back to the bedroom and, since she had the time and couldn't leave until he was finished, she actually went ahead and pulled her bed into some semblance of order. It didn't look as good as when the maid did it, but it was better than leaving it all rumpled. She would appreciate it when she got home later.

If Lisa could only see her now. Twenty-seven years old and actually making her own bed. On a roll, she went into the living room and picked up the newspaper, which she threw in the garbage, and her clothes, which she threw in the laundry. Liam was out of the shower but not yet out of the bathroom. She threw a random assortment of dishes into the dishwasher and had the place looking pretty tidy when Liam made an appearance, dressed, hair wet but neatly combed, and his face still stubbly, not having taken the time to shave. She stood on her tip-toes to give him a kiss. "Thanks. Sorry about having to rush you out of here. It's my sister. Mother wants me there, so I have to make sure she's okay."

Liam nodded, looking down at her and letting his fingers linger on her jaw for a moment. "That, or you got one of your girlfriends to call to break up the party so that you could get rid of me."

"Ugh. I wouldn't do that when I was still in bed."

He smiled. "Give me a call later, then. Let me know how it goes. And we'll see each other again… soon."

They didn't have anything lined up, no dates, no fundraisers, nothing on the horizon. Liam was a nice guy, good looking, and MacKenzie might add him to her regular coterie of admirers, but she hadn't made up her mind yet. She wasn't one hundred percent sure that he was her type. Whatever that was.

After seeing him out the door, she put on her coat and winter gear and headed for the hospital.

When she managed to find her way to Amanda's hospital room, not in the renal unit where she usually was, Amanda was asleep. Lisa sat next to the bed, watching her sleep. Not reading a book. Not looking at her schedule for the week. Just watching her sleep. MacKenzie would have gone crazy. She couldn't stand to have people staring at her.

"Hi, Mom," she said softly.

Lisa looked over at her, automatically making a motion for her to be quiet before she evaluated MacKenzie's voice and the deepness of Amanda's sleep and decided that she probably wasn't being too loud after all.

"How is she doing?" MacKenzie looked over her kid sister. Amanda was twenty years old, but when she was asleep, she looked about ten. She was shorter than MacKenzie, and MacKenzie wasn't exactly an Amazon herself. Amanda was small and elfin, and people often mistook her for a kid if they weren't paying attention. She had a beautiful face, when she was feeling well. She wasn't looking too bad. Her weight was good, her cheeks round rather than sunken like they had been when she'd been through her worst times. She had long, dark hair that got tangled if she didn't take care of it, which was hard to do when she was in a hospital bed all day, but she didn't like to cut it short so that it would be easier to take care of. She said she needed her strength, like Samson.

Amanda was pale, and that bothered MacKenzie. But if she had the flu and had been throwing up for hours, then of course she was going to be pale. It was just a virus. She would be feeling better soon.

"She's sleeping," Lisa stated the obvious. "She's been so sick all night… I'm glad she was finally able to drift off. Maybe she's on her way to feeling better."

"Probably just a bug."

"Yes. Hopefully."

There was an IV hanging, but Lisa had said that Amanda needed it to stay hydrated. It didn't necessarily mean that she was back on some treatment again.

MacKenzie pulled the other chair in the room closer to her mother's and sat down. Amanda had been given a private room, of course. There was no way she was going to be left in some hallway or emergency room curtain. Lisa would see to that.

"Do you want to go get something to eat?" MacKenzie suggested.

"Well…" Lisa's eyes flicked over to Amanda. "I don't know. I don't want to leave her alone."

"I'm here. And you haven't had anything to eat, have you? You've been with her since last night?"

"Yes, you're right."

"Well, you're not going to be any good to her if you're fainting from hunger or all angry and irritable from low blood sugar. So go. I'll be with her if she wakes up. She's not going to be alone."

"Are you sure?"

"Why don't you take advantage of the fact that I'm here, because I'm not going to be here all day. Go have something to eat."

"Okay," Lisa agreed, but she still made no movement to get up, watching Amanda with worried eyes.

"She'll be fine for now. I'll have them page you if something happens."

"Would you?" Lisa brightened at that suggestion. She could go have something to eat and still be sure that Amanda hadn't taken a turn for the worse. She clutched her purse on her lap, then nodded and got up. "Thank you so much, MacKenzie, I appreciate you coming and being here for your sister."

"And for you," MacKenzie reminded her. "Don't you try saying that I never do anything for you."

"I would never say that."

MacKenzie raised her eyebrows as her mother left. She might say it and she might not. But she would certainly imply it the next time she wanted

MacKenzie to do something for her and MacKenzie had something else going on or didn't want to be there.

Lisa's heels clicked sharply as she walked away. MacKenzie watched her go. She leaned back in her chair and looked over Amanda once more. The hospital chair was far from comfortable. She was going to have to get used to it if she were going to be there for a few hours.

"I should have brought a book," she murmured to Amanda. She hadn't thought to bring anything with her. She'd just gotten herself together and headed over. And she couldn't go down to the gift shop to pick something up. Not after dismissing her mother and saying she'd stay with Amanda while Lisa was eating. MacKenzie sighed and resigned herself to just sitting there and napping while she waited either for Amanda to wake up, or for Lisa to return from lunch.

2

She had nodded off, and when she opened her eyes and rubbed the stickiness away, she realized that Amanda was awake, her head turned to look at MacKenzie.

"Oh, hey sleepyhead," MacKenzie greeted.

"Hi," Amanda said in a soft little voice. MacKenzie waited for the rejoinder about how MacKenzie had been falling asleep in her chair. But Amanda didn't tease her. MacKenzie bit her lip. That was what Lisa was so worried about. Amanda might look like she was just a little tired, but that shouldn't change her personality. Her lassitude suggested that there was something more wrong, not just a twenty-four-hour flu bug. She shouldn't have been experiencing that level of fatigue with just a virus.

"How are you feeling?"

"I think I'm better now," Amanda said faintly.

MacKenzie waited for her to go on, but she didn't. "I guess you had a pretty rough night of it,"

Amanda nodded. She turned away from MacKenzie again and her eyes closed. MacKenzie frowned watching her. It was just the flu. Just a fever and throwing up. It could be any number of viruses. They had her on IV. She was going to be just fine.

Lisa returned, and looked worriedly over to Amanda lying in the bed, as if she had expected her to be sitting up talking by the time she got back.

"She was awake for a minute," MacKenzie said. "She didn't throw up, so that's good news."

"I think they put something in the IV to stop her."

"Oh. Well, that's good. At least they're taking it seriously."

"She really does need to sleep," Lisa said, but MacKenzie knew she was trying to reassure herself. They were all used to Amanda's high energy level. Even when she was sick, she still joked and teased and tried to keep everyone around her in a good mood. She didn't like long faces around her hospital bed.

"If she was up all night throwing up? She sure does. I was up half the night and I could still use a few more hours of sleep. And I wasn't throwing up."

"You were up late?"

"I was at the fundraiser."

"Oh, the one at the Phelps's house?"

"Yeah. That one."

"Who did you take?"

"Liam Jackson."

"He's a nice boy."

"He seems that way," MacKenzie agreed. She focused on looking out the window on the opposite side of the room. She didn't want to blush and have Lisa detect it. MacKenzie smiled and raised her eyebrows as if she weren't thinking immoral thoughts about Liam Jackson.

"How is Daddy?"

"You know your father. Always occupied with very important meetings with very important people."

MacKenzie nodded, smiling. Lisa hadn't said it in a way that was sarcastic or critical, but with a little bit of humor, as other women might talk about their husbands' interest in cars or collectibles. *Boys and their toys.* Was that how her mother saw Walter's lobbying? As a hobby that occupied her husband and kept him out from underfoot?

"Does he have anything interesting going on right now?"

"I'm not sure what he's working on. I don't really pay much attention, unless it is something that could have an impact on one of my causes."

Lisa always had plenty of causes on her agenda. There were an infinite number of foundations, societies, and fundraisers that needed her attention and support. Lobbying kept her father busy and fundraising kept her mother happy. MacKenzie just didn't know what it was that kept *her* happy. When was she going to find her way in life? She didn't want to be a lawyer, lobbyist, or politician. But she didn't want to be a socialite or drum-beater either. She had done well enough in school and had taken enough classes in college to get herself a degree, but that hadn't helped her to find her place in the world. She wasn't passionate about anything.

Lisa's eyes were quick and perhaps took in more than MacKenzie had expected. She reached over and patted MacKenzie's hand. "You'll find something," she said. "You're just a late bloomer. You need to be patient and give yourself some time."

"When you were a kid, what did you think you would be when you grew up? Did you have any dreams?"

Lisa shrugged and looked away from MacKenzie. "I don't know. I wanted to be a wife and mother. I was never really interested in a job. I felt like children were my avocation." She shrugged. "I know that's not a very popular answer these days. We're supposed to think big and take the bull by the horns, to make our mark on the world. But I can't help but think… that the marks being made on the world wouldn't amount to very much if it weren't for the mothers."

MacKenzie gave her a smile. "The hand that rocks the cradle, and all that?"

"Yes. Exactly. Mothers shape the thinkers and the soldiers. The scientists and the astronauts and the Nobel laureates. They all had mothers. They all had people to help them along the way and give them support at various parts of their lives, like a mother would, even if they didn't have a mother. I happen to think that's a very important position."

"Of course," MacKenzie agreed. "I never thought that you should be required to give up your family and have a high-power job."

"I could have, you know," Lisa said. She obviously didn't want MacKenzie thinking that she had only stayed home to be a mother because she couldn't do anything else. She had chosen to be there and not to hire a nanny to raise them. That had been her choice, not a fallback position.

"I know, Mother. You have a brain. You're very organized and I'm always amazed at what you can accomplish. I know you could have chosen to do other things."

Lisa nodded, satisfied.

MacKenzie looked back at Amanda. They had been lucky to have a mother who stayed home to look after them. Amanda probably wouldn't have survived without a strong, proactive mother watching over her. How many times had Lisa been the one to take her to the hospital and insist to the doctors that something was wrong, and she wasn't taking Amanda home until they had figured out what it was? She had insisted that Amanda wasn't just a whiner or a hypochondriac, but that she was really ill. She could have died if they hadn't been forced to dig deeper for the answers.

MacKenzie and Amanda hadn't really been playmates. MacKenzie had been too much older than Amanda to consider her a real friend and peer. Instead, Amanda had been MacKenzie's baby as much as she had been Lisa's. MacKenzie had been fascinated with her care and had happily fed and changed her. It was like having a living doll. MacKenzie had never even liked dolls. But she liked having stewardship over the tiny new person in their home. Lisa had encouraged her interest rather than shooing her off to go play or insisting that she diaper her dolls instead of her sister.

At first, no one had known that anything was wrong. Amanda got sick a lot, but children picked up viruses everywhere, it wasn't really that unusual. As she got older, she didn't outgrow it, and MacKenzie realized that she was sick a lot more often than MacKenzie or her friends, or little Amanda's other friends. She remembered the day when she had been out at the playground with Amanda, about nine years old by then, and MacKenzie a teen. Amanda had been playing tag or grounders or some other schoolyard game on the climbing equipment with her friends, but she had to sit down at the edge of one of the platforms, her face white, trying to catch her breath and get up the energy to go back to the game. The other girls teased her for calling timeout too often and told her that she couldn't be safe, but there wasn't any point in tagging her while she sat out, because she wouldn't run after the rest of them and the game would grind to a halt.

MacKenzie walked over to Amanda.

"Mandy-Candy," she singsonged, "what's wrong? Don't you want to play anymore?"

Amanda was breathing shallowly, too fast. "I want to play," she protested, her arms folded across her stomach, "I'm just too tired. I need a break."

"Do you want to go home?"

Amanda looked at the other girls still playing and having a fun time on the playground equipment around her. She looked sad. Not just sad, but desolate, as if they had all run away and left her behind where she could not follow.

"I guess so," she said finally. "I can read, I guess."

"Do you really want to?" MacKenzie pressed. "I'm not saying you have to. If you want to stay and play…"

Amanda shook her head. "I can't," she said hopelessly. "I don't know how they can run around all day."

MacKenzie sat looking at her as the seconds ticked by, a knot growing in her stomach. She walked home slowly with Amanda, back to the big house on the hill. It was a long way for a child who didn't have any energy left. Partway there, MacKenzie boosted Amanda up onto her back and carried her piggy-back to the house. Amanda lay against her, body limp, arms around MacKenzie's neck.

When they got home and MacKenzie settled Amanda in bed with a book, she went looking for Lisa. Lisa was, luckily, home for the evening and not on her way out to some fundraiser.

"Mother… I think something's wrong with Amanda. I mean… really wrong."

Lisa looked at her for a long time, then finally nodded. "I do too. And I think it's time we found out what."

So many doctors had said that Amanda was just a girly girl, that she didn't want to participate in activities and was overly sensitive to every little ache and pain that came along with growing up and roughhousing with friends. There wasn't really anything wrong.

But when they had insisted that it was time to figure out what was really wrong with Amanda and that they weren't going away until they got some answers, everything changed.

And it would never be the same again.

3

hronic kidney disease?" MacKenzie repeated what her mother had
told her after the doctor met with her to discuss all of the tests that
Amanda had been through. Anyone who thought that she was
attention-seeking in order to get those countless vials of blood drawn and all
kinds of imaging and poking and prodding should have their own head
examined. Amanda didn't want to be sick. She wanted them to find out why
she was sick so that she could get better. "What does that mean?" She understood the individual words, but not the impact that it would have on their
lives. Not what it would really mean for Amanda and her future.

"It means that her kidneys are not working the way they're supposed to,"
Walter said. He was looking very serious and using his 'bad meeting' voice.
Things always happened when he used that voice. People went out of their
way to fix things when Walter Kirsch said that there was a problem in that
grave tone. "In fact… at this point they're barely functioning at all. She needs
to go on dialysis, so that a machine can do the job that her kidneys are
supposed to be doing, cleaning her blood. That's why she hasn't had much
energy and is always getting sick… her body just isn't working the way it's
supposed to."

"But dialysis won't make her better, will it?" MacKenzie asked. She was
no idiot. She wasn't the one who was nine years old. She was old enough to
know that kidneys didn't just suddenly get better after dialysis, and that a
machine couldn't do the job of a person's real kidneys forever.

"No. At some point in the future, they're going to have to get Amanda a new kidney. If she can get a new, functioning kidney, then she won't have to be on dialysis. But until then… It's going to take a lot of time. She'll have to be on dialysis for several hours per session three times a week. She'll need to be quiet and still, and it's pretty boring. We're going to have to be understanding and flexible in our schedules. It isn't Amanda's fault. We're going to need to reshape our lives for her."

MacKenzie nodded, but didn't really understand what that was going to mean to them. How it meant spending so much time at the hospital, and traveling back and forth, and finding things for Amanda to do to entertain herself when she became so bored she threatened to disconnect herself and go home. MacKenzie spent her time at school and at the hospital and didn't have much time for friends or dating.

They didn't have too far to look for a kidney donor, since MacKenzie was a good match. But Lisa and Walter didn't want to rush into anything. They searched for any other solution. They didn't want to put both of their girls through surgery if there was any other option. There was talk of artificial kidneys being pioneered by some medical supply company. There were non-related donors and there was continuing dialysis so that they didn't have to risk MacKenzie's health for Amanda's. They put Amanda on a special kidney diet. They tried herbal cures that were supposed to improve kidney function. Vitamins and minerals. Drugs that were being trialed.

And things did improve. With some of the load being taken by dialysis, Amanda's kidneys were no longer so stressed and recovered to some degree. All of the little things that they were doing helped, and to begin with, her function inched up.

But then an infection had turned one kidney to mush, and things were getting critical.

When MacKenzie turned eighteen, she announced that she was donating one of her kidneys to Amanda. As a legal adult, Lisa and Walter no longer had any say in MacKenzie's medical decisions. She could donate without their permission. MacKenzie couldn't stand to see Amanda suffering any longer.

MacKenzie was eighteen and Amanda was twelve. Old enough and experienced enough with kidney disease to know that she wasn't like the other little girls and that the illnesses that had dogged her all of her life weren't going to go away. Old enough to understand that MacKenzie didn't have to take the risk. They were both fully informed about the surgeries and risks that they were facing and were prepped for surgery. Then they lay on gurneys, waiting, as the team assembled and did whatever last-minute jobs and briefing they needed to do before beginning. Amanda reached over the raised sides of her gurney to take MacKenzie's hand. For a while they just lay there in silence, overwhelmed by emotion, unable to find the words to say to each other.

"Thank you, MacKenzie," Amanda said softly. "This is… really nice of you to do. Thank you."

"I would do anything for you, Mandy-Candy." MacKenzie hadn't called her by the nickname for a long time, a name intended for a much younger child. "Anything I have is yours."

"I'm a little scared."

MacKenzie was a little scared too. And she wasn't the one who was facing the greatest danger. She was strong and healthy and would be left with one fully functioning kidney. Amanda was the one who was weak and would need to take anti-rejection drugs for the rest of her life, the one who could be pushed over the edge by an infection or by the doctors making a mistake in reattaching one of the tiny vessels. She was so young, and so small. MacKenzie wanted to pull Amanda onto her lap and rock her, like she had when Amanda was a little girl. She knew Amanda must be terrified.

"It's okay to be scared," MacKenzie assured her. "I am too."

"What if something goes wrong? What if they make a mistake or it just doesn't work? What if my body rejects it right away?"

MacKenzie squeezed her hand. "I don't know. We have to focus on the positive. On how great it is going to be when it works. No more dialysis!"

Amanda made a little moan. "That would be so great. I can't imagine what I'll do with all that extra time!"

"You can do things with your friends. Have a social life."

"Get my homework done," Amanda said with a little laugh.

While MacKenzie had originally thought that Amanda would be able to do her homework during the dialysis sessions, since she was sitting there with nothing to do anyway, it hadn't worked out that way. The nurses advised against doing anything stressful during that time. If Amanda tried to do too much, she would end up feeling sick during or after the dialysis.

"Yeah. It won't be so hard for you to keep up. You'll have more time for yourself."

"Maybe I'll take up a sport," Amanda said.

Turning her head to look at her sister, MacKenzie could see Amanda closing her eyes as she daydreamed.

"Tennis, maybe. Or speed cycling."

MacKenzie shuddered at the thought of her frail sister racing around a tennis court or a track, something tearing loose inside her because she was being so rambunctious. She knew Amanda was just fantasizing and would never take up something that would put her transplant in danger, but it still made her queasy and anxious.

"You can do whatever you want," she promised Amanda. She wasn't the one who would have to tell Amanda to curtail her activities. She would leave that to the doctors. "It's going to be so nice for you not to have to be in hospital anymore, to be able to just live a normal life."

"Yeah."

They lay in silence, waiting for someone to take them into the surgical theater. MacKenzie had butterflies in her stomach, worried about how everything would go and if it would all turn out right like they all hoped. What if Amanda *did* reject the kidney right away?

<hr>

"What if Amanda is rejecting her graft?" MacKenzie blurted.

Dr. Proctor, seated to her right at the dining table in the event room of the Resort Inn, looked over at her in surprise. "Sorry?" He looked at her as if she had two heads.

MacKenzie was impatient. She had taken her mother's place at the charity auction, since Lisa wanted to stay with Amanda until they were sure she was going to be okay. She had already explained to Dr. Proctor, a friend of the family who was also in attendance, why it was that she was there instead of Lisa. He wasn't a transplant surgeon, but he was one of the top doctors at the hospital and knew more than MacKenzie ever would about such matters.

"What if Amanda is rejecting her kidney? What if it isn't the flu? What would the symptoms be?"

He laid down his fork and considered her seriously, giving her his full attention. "If she was rejecting her kidney, she would probably have a high fever, vomiting, and decreased urine output. Very similar to flu symptoms to start with."

"Then how would we know? What if the doctors all just say it is the flu, but it isn't? Is there a test to see if she is rejecting the kidney?"

"I'm sure that her doctors are being very careful to watch her kidney function and all of her bloodwork to make sure that she is not. They know her history. Your mother wouldn't let them forget; I can promise you that."

"But it happens all the time. Doctors overlook symptoms and think that someone isn't really sick when they are. People get sent home from the hospital, told that they're just fine, and then die in the night. People die in the emergency room because the triage nurses think they aren't really sick."

"You can ask her doctors or the nursing staff if they have done the tests to make sure she's not rejecting her kidney. They would be very aware of her situation, but that doesn't mean you can't ask."

"They won't think that I'm just being a worrywart or interfering? I'm sure Mother is already driving them crazy."

"Does it matter?"

MacKenzie shook her head. "Amanda's health? Of course it does."

"No, I mean, does it matter what anyone thinks? Why does it matter if her doctors think you're being a worrier? Are you concerned about your sister's health care or about what they think of you?"

"Her care. Making sure they treat her properly if it's not just the flu." MacKenzie considered. "I guess it doesn't matter what anyone thinks, does it?" She had been raised by Lisa to always consider how others perceived her, how to do the right thing socially and make sure people saw her in a good light. If people stopped inviting her to events, she wouldn't have the opportunities to advance herself and to help the causes and charities that she wanted to. She wouldn't make a good marriage. She wouldn't be happy in life. And while she had often rebelled against her mother's viewpoint, it was deeply ingrained. It had been repeated so many times that it was part of her thinking. Her default.

But Dr. Proctor was right. It was Amanda's health that was important in this case, not what the medical staff at the hospital thought of MacKenzie. She needed to get her priorities straight.

"So just ask them if they have tested to see if she's rejecting her kidney?" she asked.

"They should have done basic blood panels and be monitoring her urine output levels. From that, they should be able to tell whether she is rejecting the kidney or whether it is something else, just a virus or something that she will get over quickly."

"Okay. I'm going to ask. She wouldn't reject it this late, would she? I mean, after eight years, why would her body suddenly reject it?"

He opened his mouth to answer her, his brows drawing down, and then he stopped himself. His lips pressed together and he considered her question and formulated his answer. MacKenzie waited. There were other conversations going on around them. Other people talking about the weather and local events and issues, about things that really didn't matter. It seemed strange to MacKenzie that life should just go on for the rest of the world when, for MacKenzie and her family, everything revolved around Amanda's health and what she needed from them.

"A transplant can fail at any time," Dr. Proctor said. "It isn't predictable. Immediately, one year, ten years. Or it can lose function suddenly, and we don't always know why. We just do the best we can to treat a patient who is in crisis."

"What if she needs another transplant?" MacKenzie asked. "I can't give her another one."

"No," Dr. Proctor agreed with a smile. "You need to hang on to the one that you've got. If there are no other compatible donors in your biological family, then they will need to look for a compatible donor in the database. A stranger donation. They don't have the same success rate as a familial donation, but they can be successful. And, of course, she could survive on dialysis for a while, as they tried to track down another compatible donor. It's not easy, as your family knows, but the chance of finding a match is still good, on a three- or four-year scale."

"Three or four years," MacKenzie repeated. She remembered those years that Amanda had been on dialysis before. It had been a long time, and Amanda's quality of life had not been good. She rubbed her temples. "I don't know if she can handle going through that again."

"Amanda is stronger than you think. She's always had a good attitude. She's a fighter."

MacKenzie thought of how listless Amanda had been when she had weakened. Her mother's alarm was justified. MacKenzie felt the same panic when she looked at her sister and worried that she had given up the fight. She shook her head at Dr. Proctor, unable to put it into words.

Dr. Proctor looked at her, frown lines between his brows, then shook his head. "I'm sorry, MacKenzie… I'm sure it's just the flu. It can affect a person emotionally more than we think. I'm sure she'll be back to her usual self within a day or two. Right now, her kidney is fine, as far as we know. It's just a matter of nursing her through this virus. Lots of rest and fluids, and she'll be feeling better before you know it."

4

And it seemed that Dr. Proctor was right. MacKenzie slept restlessly that night, and after a few hours got up and drove to the hospital, worrying over Amanda and ready to quiz the medical staff about her condition and to demand to see the blood tests that would prove that she wasn't rejecting the grafted organ. Instead of finding Amanda asleep or listless, MacKenzie walked into the hospital room to find Amanda sitting up, eating her breakfast and talking to Lisa. MacKenzie stopped in the doorway, looking at them for a few minutes and was smiling when Amanda looked up from her breakfast tray to see her standing there.

"Well, good morning," MacKenzie greeted. "You're looking a lot better today."

"Just a twenty-four-hour bug, I guess," Amanda said, shrugging. "I'm still feeling it a little this morning… but it's not so bad." She gestured at the bowl of green Jell-O with her spoon. "I'm not ready to try pizza, but I've been able to have a few bites without throwing it back up again."

Lisa beamed at MacKenzie. "I guess it was just the flu after all. Chalk one up against the overly concerned mother. It's a case where I'm glad to be proven wrong."

MacKenzie walked the rest of the way into the hospital room and sat down in the other chair. "I'm glad too. I was ready to do battle with the doctors this morning. Quizzed Dr. Proctor all evening on what they should be doing and whether it could be something to do with Amanda's kidney."

Lisa sat back in her chair, smiling. "How was the auction?"

MacKenzie thought back over the evening. "I… don't really have any idea. Everybody seemed happy, so I assume they raised the money they were hoping to. I was too worried about Amanda to really pay attention to anything else."

"I'll have to make some calls to apologize again and find out how it went," Lisa said, pulling out her agenda to make a note of the fact. "I appreciate you going to stand in for me. Did you find someone to go with you?"

MacKenzie shook her head. "I just went myself. I didn't really have the time to chase down a date. And I wasn't in much of a mood to be good company, worrying about my kid sister here."

"You don't want to be seen at these things without a plus-one too often," Lisa advised. "People will talk. And they won't include you if they have to worry about pairing you up with another… single. It causes all kinds of complications with the fundraising when it is all focused so much on couples. The seating, the catering, dances, all kinds of things are impacted if you have odd numbers and unaccompanied guests."

"I'm sure they'll understand that I was only standing in for you. They'll be happy that I was able to make it so that at least your dinner didn't go to waste."

Lisa nodded. "Of course. I'm just saying… you don't want to be seen alone too often."

"People will talk," Amanda chimed in.

MacKenzie glared at her. "This is all your fault. You'd better be careful what you say. Next time, I'll be sick, and you'll have to go out to be on display."

Amanda smiled.

MacKenzie felt warm and comfortable. Everything was right with the world. They would keep Amanda in hospital for one or two days, to make sure she was stable and everything was in working order, and then she'd be back home again and things would fall back into their usual routine.

She couldn't have been more wrong.

***

It was the nightmare she had imagined at the auction while talking to Dr. Proctor. The hospital cleared Amanda, saying that it had obviously just been a virus and she was fine as long as she just didn't try to do too much too soon. She went home with Lisa and everybody was happy. And then sometime in the night, Amanda had suddenly taken another bad turn. Once more, she spiked a fever and was sluggish and unresponsive, complaining of hot and cold and that she hurt all over. Lisa again called an ambulance and had her taken in. She called MacKenzie in the night, startling her out of a sound sleep.

"I'm at my wits' end, MacKenzie. I don't know what's wrong. She was just fine. Everything seemed to be just fine. And it isn't like she did too much and tired herself out. She was just sleeping!"

"What do the doctors think?" MacKenzie asked groggily, trying to marshal her thoughts. "Are they still saying it's just the flu?"

"Yes. I told them she was doing better; she was back to normal. But they're saying it's perfectly normal to have a relapse. I don't know what to do!"

"Did you ask them to do any tests? Or to call Dr. Proctor? What about her nephrologist?"

"They'll do all of the consults tomorrow… tonight there isn't anyone available. Don't people ever get sick during the night? Why aren't any of these people in until morning?"

"I don't know. I guess if they thought it was an emergency, they would get someone out of bed, so it's good, isn't it? It means that they don't think it's too serious."

"But I do. This isn't normal for Amanda. You know how she usually gets sick. This isn't her usual pattern."

"No," MacKenzie admitted. While Amanda frequently came down with whatever was going around, she was usually unwell for several days, getting gradually worse, before a virus really hit her. Then she kept a good attitude, ordered her family around, and kept a smiling, brave face throughout the course of the illness. These sudden attacks in the night, bouncing back again, and then suddenly coming up sick once more, so lethargic and apathetic were not like her. "But this is probably just a virus she hasn't had before. One that has more of an emotional impact on her. Sometimes bugs are like that."

"I hope that's all it is," Lisa sighed. "I'm sorry for bugging you in the middle of the night. I didn't know who else to talk to."

"Where is Daddy?"

"He's in Montpelier. He had some people to talk to, and we thought that Amanda was on the mend again."

Even if he was away, MacKenzie thought he should still be answering the phone when his wife called. He had a cell phone, even if he was out having late drinks with some other lobbyist. Had Lisa called him and he hadn't answered? Or had she just automatically called MacKenzie because he wasn't in Burlington? MacKenzie liked that Lisa felt like she could call her, but she worried about the relationship between her parents. Was Walter really on a business trip? Or was he seeing another woman? It seemed like he was away from home an awful lot and was too often unavailable even though she should be able to reach him on his cell phone.

How could he be away when Amanda was so sick?

MacKenzie knew she was being unfair. As far as he knew, Amanda was fine, just like the rest of them had thought. When you had a chronically ill person in the family, you had to make the most of the times when they were feeling better.

"Is everything okay between you and Daddy?"

They didn't have an ideal relationship, but who did? They pursued their separate lives, and MacKenzie wasn't sure how often he was actually home. He kept busy with his business and lived out of business suites in hotels. She knew he had a modest apartment in Montpelier for those times when he couldn't leave the capital while something was going on.

"Why do you ask?" Lisa returned.

MacKenzie frowned at the phone. That wasn't an answer, but at the same time, it was. If there were no problems between Lisa and Walter, she would have just said so straight out. Instead, she wanted to know what it was MacKenzie suspected, so as not to give away anything she didn't have to.

"Are you and Daddy having problems?" she persisted.

"You know your father and I have different interests. We're not always together, like some couples."

"I know that."

Lisa hesitated and MacKenzie waited, not willing to leave it at just that vague comment.

"It doesn't affect you and Amanda. Nothing has changed in our relationships with you."

Their father had never been that big of a presence in their day to day lives anyway. They loved him and made sure to stay in contact, but he had frequently been absent when they were growing up. No *Father Knows Best*.

"Have you… separated?"

"We haven't actually been together for quite some time."

Kenzie's grip tightened on the phone. She hadn't lived at home for years, but Amanda had, and she had never hinted to MacKenzie that anything had changed in their parents' relationship.

"Mother… can you just give me a direct answer? I don't understand why you're beating around the bush."

Lisa sighed. "You always did want everything to be black and white. No shades of gray for our MacKenzie."

MacKenzie didn't laugh or agree. She didn't accept a segue to her childhood and the many times she had insisted on knowing the exact parameters of some story or principle. She preferred to think of herself as detail-oriented rather than demanding.

"Mother."

"MacKenzie… we restructured our affairs three years ago."

"You separated."

"We had not been living as husband and wife for some time before that."

"And I'm just hearing about it now? That's crazy! What's the big secret?"

"We prefer not to have the details of our private life out there for everyone to gossip about. Especially not when Amanda was still a minor. It can be very hurtful to hear people speculating on your parents' lives. We tried to protect you children from any… negative consequences of our relationship."

"So, you've been legally separated for more than three years. And this restructuring you're talking about…?"

"That would have been when you were in Europe. A lot was going on at the time."

MacKenzie felt the stirrings of guilt over that comment. She had been convinced that she would never be able to truly find herself unless she went away. And not just on a vacation, but really living away from her family, cutting off all of their influences. Which meant cutting off most of their communications. She had still made weekly phone calls so that they knew she was still alive, but it had been her attempt to break away and really become her own person. And during that time, her parents had done what, exactly? Her father had moved out of the house for good? Had transferred his business operations to the apartment in Montpelier? And what else?

"We divorced, MacKenzie," Lisa finally said. "It was all very quiet. We divided our assets, worked with the lawyers on a fair division of all of our property and affairs, and then signed the papers to legally sever our relationship."

"You're divorced," MacKenzie said in disbelief.

"Legally, yes. But we're still friends. And he still has a room here and stays here when he has business in town. It isn't like I have lied to you."

"No… not at all… you got divorced three years ago, when I was out of the country, and didn't bother to tell me."

"That's… yes… that's how it worked out."

"And what about Amanda? Does she know?"

"She's been with me the whole time. She couldn't exactly not know."

"She never said anything about it to me."

"We don't talk about it."

"Why not?"

"It's private. I prefer not to be discussed."

"I really think…" MacKenzie was having difficulty putting her stuttering thoughts into words. "I wish you would have told me."

"I tried, dear… but you cut yourself off. You were very remote. You didn't want to talk about it."

MacKenzie tried to remember what her mother might have said in trying to bring the subject up.

Your father and I met with our lawyers this week…

Daddy is moving his business to Montpelier…

Since your father left…

How many hints had she missed, so focused on herself and her own satisfaction and personal growth? She'd blocked the family out and refused to listen to anything they might have to tell her. What else had she missed?

"I'm sorry, Mom…"

"There's nothing to be sorry about. It's all for the best. We each wanted to be free to make decisions on our own. This way, we could operate independently."

"I mean for not being there for you. Not even paying any attention to what was going on."

"You had your own concerns, dear. I expect you girls to have your own lives. To pursue your own dreams."

If only MacKenzie actually had a dream to follow. And what about Amanda? She was still living at home and if she kept getting so ill, she wouldn't ever be able to be fully independent. She would always need someone checking in on her, dealing with emergencies, making sure she was taken care of.

They both had trust funds and, as far as MacKenzie knew, they hadn't been restructured during the divorce. Not that she'd heard.

But then, that obviously didn't mean anything.

"Do you want me to come to the hospital?"

"Not tonight. Go back to sleep, if you can. I'm sorry for waking you up. I'll sit up with Amanda tonight, and tomorrow if you feel like coming by the hospital, I could use a sounding board… if you think I'm overreacting… I just don't know what to think. They said she was fine to go home."

"They don't always know. Hospitals and doctors make mistakes all the time. That's why they have malpractice insurance. If you feel like Amanda needs to be in the hospital, then you're probably right. I think you have a pretty finely-honed sense of what she needs the most. You've had twenty years with her. The doctors spend all of five minutes asking questions and taking her temperature."

"You're right. I'll ask them to re-run the blood tests tomorrow. Make sure they didn't miss anything the first time. Maybe it's just something that takes a while to show up."

"Okay. I'll come by and see how she's doing in a few hours then."

"Thank you, MacKenzie. I always feel better if it's not just me. It's good to have a second opinion, just like with the doctors."

5

MacKenzie knew that her mother could be a bit of a hypochondriac. She did tend to worry about Amanda more than was necessary, worrying about the smallest cough or pallor. She did work for so many of the disease-specific charities that she often worried about MacKenzie or Amanda getting cancer or diabetes or having a stroke.

But she had been right about Amanda being sick back before she was diagnosed. Lisa had taken her to doctor appointment after doctor appointment, just to be told that she was worrying too much and needed to give her daughter a chance to learn from her bumps and bruises and to develop a strong immune system by being exposed to other children regularly. She had been told so many times that she was just overreacting that she questioned herself and her motives even when it was obvious that Amanda was ill. She hated to take Amanda to the doctor or hospital when she was sick, for fear of being accused of being overly involved and attention-seeking.

But Lisa wasn't one of those moms who infantilized her children and got stuck in the role of a martyr. She didn't say that Amanda had a high fever when she didn't, or make up the bouts of vomiting.

MacKenzie stopped at the nursing station before going in to see Amanda and her mother.

"Can you tell me how Amanda Kirsch is doing?"

The stout nurse at with a purple smock looked up at her from the computer. "Are you family?"

"Yes. Her older sister. I was just going in for a visit, but I thought I would find out what I could before I see her. You know, reassure our mom that you're doing everything you can for her."

That last little gem seemed to put it over the edge. The nurse nodded.

"She's resting comfortably right now. We put her back on an IV and anti-emetics. Probably just released her a little too early."

"It seemed like she was doing fine. Her fever was gone, and she went a couple of days without throwing up or having any other issues. I actually thought she might have stayed a little too long last time. She seemed like she was back to normal."

"Transplant patients can be more fragile. She probably just pushed a little too hard. Did too much too soon."

"Okay. What about the fever?"

"She's still feverish, but that's her body's own natural defenses. We don't want to bring it down just for the sake of bringing it down. Give her body a chance to fight it off and produce antibodies so that she doesn't get it back again."

MacKenzie nodded her thanks. "Alright. Thanks so much." She walked down the hall to the room with Amanda's name beside the open door.

"Hello, Mother." She bent down to give Lisa a kiss on the cheek, wanting to reassure her that everything was fine. "The nurse said she's resting comfortably."

Lisa's lips pressed together. "I don't know if I would agree with that assessment," she said. "She's not throwing up right now, so that's an improvement."

MacKenzie looked down at Amanda to see for herself. Amanda's face was shiny with sweat, little tendrils of hair pasted to her damp forehead. Her pillow and sheets were mussed. She'd obviously had a restless night.

MacKenzie didn't want to wake Amanda, so she sat down on the other chair and took Lisa's hand, giving it a quick squeeze.

"The nurse said that they don't want to bring down her fever artificially."

"Yes," Lisa agreed. "They told me that. But she's so uncomfortable. And it's not just a mild fever. You know how it is when she's sick and she just gets warm. You have to take her temperature to actually be sure that she even has one. Not like this. She's burning up."

"It's just her body fighting the flu. It's a good thing. That means her body is doing what it's supposed to."

Lisa shook her head slowly. She sat there, watching Amanda, waiting for some change.

"Did you talk to the doctors about getting blood tests?"

"The ER doctor ordered some more. I'm still waiting to hear if anything showed up."

MacKenzie hadn't been able to talk her mother into going for breakfast and had eventually broken down herself to find Lisa some coffee and a granola bar she could consume while she was beside Amanda's bed. They didn't talk much, not wanting to wake Amanda up. She needed her sleep while she could get it. At lunch, Lisa made MacKenzie go get herself something to eat, and as five o'clock approached, MacKenzie finally managed to convince her mother to head down to the hospital cafeteria to get herself some real food. It was at that point that MacKenzie managed to get through to her father on his cell phone to report to him that Amanda was back in the hospital again.

"I'll try to get back as soon as I can, sweetheart," Walter assured her. "Tell Amanda and your mother both that I'll be there tomorrow sometime. How is Lisa holding out?"

"Daddy... why didn't you ever tell me that you and Mother got divorced?"

There was silence at the other end of the phone line. After a few awkward seconds, Walter cleared his throat uncomfortably. "Did Lisa tell you that?"

"Yes. When I pressed her. I don't understand why the two of you were keeping it a secret. Or how you thought you could!"

"Well... up until now, we've been pretty successful in keeping it under wraps. We didn't want to be in the spotlight, sweetie. That's all. And you were going through kind of a tough time. We didn't want to burden you with it. We were already pursuing our own separate courses, so nothing really changed... except on paper."

"You could have told me. I shouldn't have to find out by accident."

"I didn't think it would really make that much difference to you," he confessed. "It's like the difference between a common law relationship and getting married... does it really make any difference?"

"It obviously did to you."

He grunted an acknowledgment to this point.

MacKenzie heard voices and footsteps approaching in the hallway. "I think maybe the doctor is here. I'll call you back later, okay?"

"Sounds good. Leave me a message if you can't get through. I always pick them up."

She murmured another goodbye and hung up. A doctor in a white coat entered, followed by several other doctors, all looking too young to be the real thing and very intense. The head of the pack gave MacKenzie a reassuring smile of greeting.

"How's our patient?" he asked, in a hearty voice that MacKenzie was afraid would waken Amanda. But then, he was probably going to wake her up to examine her anyway. She wanted to know that they were paying attention to Amanda's condition and understood what was going on with her.

"She's mostly been sleeping... but she's still very hot and restless."

The doctor picked up the chart at the foot of the bed and looked over it. "Hasn't been throwing up since they started anti-emetics. Good fluid output. No signs of dehydration," he summarized quickly. He turned to his students. "Here we have a patient with a grafted kidney who has been admitted for observation. Fever and chills, achy, throwing up, general malaise. What are your observations and orders?"

Several of the students offered their opinions. The doctor nodded and shot back questions and made suggestions. He looked down at the clipboard at the suggestion of one of the young doctors that she might be rejecting her transplant.

"What is the average length of time that a kidney transplant will last?" he asked. "With the proper anti-rejection regimen in place, of course."

Several numbers were thrown around. MacKenzie was relieved to hear numbers longer than ten years. It had only been eight since Amanda's transplant, so she should still have a few good years left.

"In this case, it has only been a year since the graft, so we are very early on in the process, and if the tissues were a good match and the anti-rejection protocol is working, then we should still have—"

"Eight years," MacKenzie interrupted, amused. "It's been eight, not one!"

He looked back down at the clipboard. "Eight? No, I don't think so. It only says one year here."

"Then someone wrote it down wrong. I should know, I was her donor."

"You?" He looked down again. "According to the notes here, it was a non-related living donor. I just assumed..." He looked from MacKenzie to Amanda, studying the similarities in their features. They were pretty obviously sisters. Anyone who saw them together recognized the fact.

"I'm her sister," MacKenzie agreed. "They must have mixed up her history with someone else's."

He tapped the board with his thumb as he looked down at it. "I will follow up with the staff and we'll get it straightened out. At any rate, if she was rejecting her graft, whether after one year or eight, what would be the signs and symptoms?" he asked his little brood of doctors.

There was an ensuing discussion. He eventually put the clipboard back, nodded to MacKenzie, and headed out again. He didn't examine Amanda even to just check her pulse or her temperature. Then he was off and running again. As they left, MacKenzie saw that Lisa was standing outside the door waiting for them to leave. Once they were out of the way, moving down the hall to the next room, Lisa entered. She handed MacKenzie a cup of coffee and sighed.

"Did you hear that?" MacKenzie demanded, not sure how long Lisa had been waiting there. "They've got her history all screwed up. We need to talk to the nurses and get them to enter the right details. They can't make a good diagnosis and treatment plan when they don't even know her history."

"He probably just misread it," Lisa said with a shrug. "That was when she had her surgery."

MacKenzie was nonplussed at first, but then remembered the trip to a private clinic that was pioneering some new technique. Amanda had not been doing well prior to the clinic, and MacKenzie was pleased when Amanda had come back with much improved kidney function. She had not been sure about experimental treatments, thinking they should just stick to what was tried and proven, but she had to admit that they had made the right choice. Amanda had been on a dangerously steep downward slope, but the experimental surgery, whatever it was, had managed to stall the deterioration and improve her kidney function again.

"What exactly was it she had done?" MacKenzie asked, trying to remember the details. "They really did turn things around, didn't they?"

"It was a lifesaver," Lisa agreed. "I don't know if she would have lasted more than a few months without it."

Amanda had been back on dialysis at that point, and they had been talking about the need for another transplant. Whatever groundbreaking research that private clinic had been doing had been well worth whatever price her parents had paid.

***

Amanda had been shifting around restlessly for a while, and MacKenzie looked over at her, wondering whether she was hallucinating because of her fever, or getting closer to consciousness. Amanda had been babbling a few times during the hours that MacKenzie had been there, incoherent, rarely even forming words that MacKenzie could understand. She sweated with the fever, alternating with bouts of cold that left her shivering no matter how many blankets they piled onto her. Nurses came and went, taking her vital signs and pursing their lips and refusing to speculate on how she was doing or if the doctor would order a change in her treatment protocol. They were too full of assurances that Amanda was just fine and would get over this little bout of flu in no time. Fluids and time were all that she needed.

Amanda's eyes were open. MacKenzie leaned closer to her, turning her face sideways so that it would be right-side-up for Amanda.

"Hey, Mandy. How are you doing?"

Amanda's eyes went over MacKenzie's face, not appearing to recognize her at first. Then she gave a weak smile.

"MacKenzie. I didn't know you were here."

"Yeah. Just keeping an eye on you and making sure you don't go running down to the cafeteria or something. How are you doing?"

There was a delay while Amanda apparently thought this through and audited what she was feeling. "Good. I think I'm doing better." Amanda reached up and pushed hair away from her face. "Ugh. I feel like I need a shower."

"I'm sure you do. You've been sweating like you ran a marathon."

Amanda nodded. "I think I just did."

MacKenzie brushed hair back from Amanda's forehead, checking her temperature while she did so. "I think your fever finally broke. That was kind of scary."

Amanda frowned, wrinkles appearing on her forehead. "I thought I was doing better. Didn't I go home?"

"Yeah. But I guess you weren't quite over it yet, because you decided to come back here again."

"I did?"

MacKenzie smiled slightly at Amanda's confusion. "I mean you just weren't quite over it yet. The fever came back, and you ended up here again. I guess there are some nasty flu bugs going around right now."

"I should have gotten a shot. They said that I should, but they always end up making me feel so wiped out. I guess I should have."

"Your immune system just isn't very strong. I don't know if the flu shot would have prevented this from happening. They never really know which strain is going to be going around. They just guess."

Amanda nodded. She looked around the room. "Can I have a drink? My mouth is so dry."

"You've been sweating through everything. I'm not surprised. They should be giving you more fluids than they are."

"I'm sure it's fine," Amanda said, gazing up at the clear IV hanging above her. "I just breathe with my mouth open."

MacKenzie gave her a sip of the tepid water from the side table. "Do you want ice? I can go get you some."

"This is okay. Ice makes me shiver."

"Are you cold again? Do you want another blanket?"

"No, this is good, thanks."

Lisa returned and saw that Amanda was awake. "Hello, sweetie." She bent down and kissed Amanda on the forehead. "How are you feeling? Better?" She looked over at MacKenzie. "Didn't I tell you she'd wake up as soon as I left? I should have stayed here."

"If you knew she'd wake up when you left, then maybe you should have left earlier," MacKenzie teased. "You needed to get some rest. You aren't a help to Amanda if you let yourself get run down."

"Yes, you're right," Lisa agreed. She sat down on the other chair and gazed at Amanda.

MacKenzie too studied Amanda's wan face. "We'll make sure they don't release you so quickly this time. I want to make sure that you're really over this bug so that you don't end up right back here again."

"Okay," Amanda agreed, her voice barely louder than a whisper. "Sounds good."

MacKenzie glanced at her mother. Amanda was usually quite vocal about wanting to get out of the hospital and back home as quickly as she could after an admission. She insisted that she would recover faster in her own bed and didn't run the danger of getting a dangerous hospital infection there. MacKenzie didn't like that she was being so cooperative about extending her stay at the hospital. But then, she'd just barely woken up, and MacKenzie supposed she needed time to get her strength back before she would start to complain.

Lisa's eyes reflected MacKenzie's own concerns. Neither of them said anything, but they didn't need to.

6

MacKenzie pondered over her list of acquaintances, considering who she wanted to call. She was tired from the amount of time she was spending at the hospital, but it wasn't the kind of tired where she just wanted to go home and go to sleep. She wanted to go out and shake off the stresses of the hospital and the worry over Amanda's mysterious illness and to let loose. Maybe go dancing or clubbing, go home for a nightcap and further stress relief, and then sleep away what was left of the morning.

The problem wasn't that she couldn't find a man who would be happy to pursue this agenda with her, but that she wanted to keep it casual. Despite the common perception that men were happy to have a physical relationship without commitment, MacKenzie found that too many of them thought that one or two dates meant they were on a surefire track toward marriage. Whether they thought that the pot of gold at the end of the rainbow was her, her social standing, or her trust fund was sometimes difficult to discern. And it was harder than she would have thought to pick out which men were going to be interested in a more committed relationship and which would be happy to keep things casual and fun.

She settled on Roger, who had recently broken up with Anita, his fiancée of three years. MacKenzie figured he would be up for some rebound action without being ready to get back into another long-term relationship, which fit perfectly with her plans. A quick phone call to him brought a positive response, and she dressed and fixed her makeup while she waited for him to pick her up.

Their conversation was stilted at first, both of them smiling and talking about the weather and unimportant things that were going on in their lives while feeling each other out. They danced a little before dinner and then sat down to order. Getting more comfortable with her, Roger became more voluble, but his conversation all seemed to run along one track. Anita.

She hadn't figured in that he would fill the evening with Anita stories. Usually, when a guy had been recently dumped, he wanted to focus on just about anything but his ex. He could talk about her to his guy friends, but he should know better than to fill the ears of a new prospect with tales of the old.

MacKenzie did the best she could to change the subject, but he kept returning to Anita. He was ranting about the new guy she was seeing. How stupid he was, how lazy and undesirable a character he was, how inferior to Roger in every way. Why would she dump him just to go out with someone like that? It didn't make any sense.

MacKenzie cocked her head and put her hand over his on the table. "Roger."

He stopped and looked at her, almost as if he had forgotten she was there.

"Oh… yes? What is it?" He seemed slightly embarrassed. "Was I doing it again?"

"Doing what?"

"Uh… talking about Anita?" His blush showed even in the dim lighting of the restaurant. "I'm sorry. I'm over her, I really am."

"Uh-huh."

"No, really. I just forget myself sometimes, get carried away. Forget Anita, she's in the past."

MacKenzie watched his face and didn't believe it for a minute. "You're still in love with her."

"No. Goodbye and good riddance. I don't need someone like that in my life."

"Someone like what? You clearly cared about her. You were engaged for three years."

"We never got along that well. I was just lying to myself. I didn't know how to get out of the relationship, even when it obviously wasn't doing anything for me. I was just… too comfortable to get myself out. That's all."

His lips twitched as if there were more to say. Or as though his face didn't agree with his words.

"Then why are you mad at her for dating this other guy? Why aren't you happy she's out of your life?"

"I am. That's just the point. I'm glad we broke up so that we could both move on and find the right person."

"Then why do you care who she's dating?" MacKenzie persisted.

He scowled at her. "I don't care who she's dating, obviously"

She shook her head. People lied to themselves, so maybe he didn't actually know the truth, but it was plain to her. "You just spent ten minutes telling me all of the ways that this guy is inferior to you. Why would you do that if you were happy with her seeing someone else? You're mad at her for looking at someone who is not you. You still want her back."

"That's not why."

"Then explain to me why you care who she's dating now. What difference does it make to you?"

"It doesn't, obviously. She can date whoever she wants, it doesn't have anything to do with me and doesn't have any impact on my life. We're through."

MacKenzie let go of his hand and took a drink.

"Then show me."

In spite of how badly the evening was going, MacKenzie didn't have the heart to boot the already-injured Roger to the curb by the end of dinner. She continued with her plan, taking him back to her apartment for a nightcap. But the more he drank, the worse he got, and eventually he ended the night by crying himself to sleep over his memories of all the good times he'd had with Anita.

Not exactly the finale that MacKenzie had been hoping for.

Worse than that, the guy snored. Maybe he was just congested after crying so much and he didn't normally sound like a buzz saw, but MacKenzie was not at all impressed. She was awake much earlier than she wanted to be, unable to sleep with the racket he was making. She shook his shoulder.

"Roger. Roger, come on, wake up." She was not gentle about it, and it took several minutes of shaking to get him even partially awake. She was starting to consider the use of ice cubes. "Roger. Hey. You've got to go. Get up."

"What is it?" he mumbled.

"It's MacKenzie. You've got to go. If you still want to sleep, go home and sleep there."

He put both hands over his eyes, pressing into them. "I feel like crap. I've got a killer hangover. Just let me sleep it off."

"No. You have to go."

She suspected he was more hung over from crying than from drinking. She had not had enough sleep and was very irritable. He wasn't going to stay there and keep her up after she'd put up with his whining for the entire night. She could understand why Anita had dumped him. Why they had stayed together for so long and even gotten engaged was a mystery, but she wasn't going to pursue it. She wasn't spending any more time on the man. As much as she liked sensitivity in a man, she didn't like whining.

It took some more encouragement to get Roger sitting up, his eyes open a slit as he examined his surroundings and tried to remember the details of the night before. MacKenzie expected an apology when he realized that he'd talked about Anita all night long and then cried himself to sleep, but no such apology was forthcoming.

She shuffled into the kitchen to make some coffee. What she really wanted to do was to go back to sleep, but she had awakened herself even more than she had awakened him, and she probably wasn't going to be able to shut her brain off again. In the meantime, she needed some high-octane coffee to get Roger kickstarted and out of there.

"What time is it?" Roger groaned when she returned to the bedroom with a mug for him. He rubbed his eyes and squinted at his Rolex. "MacKenzie, it's only seven o'clock. We were up until dawn. I need more sleep. We both need more sleep."

"Then you can go home and sleep. Neither of us is going to get any more sleep while you're here."

She handed him the coffee. Roger sipped the scalding liquid. "Why are you being so hard-nosed? I thought we had a good time together."

"You tell me. You're the one who's been whining and crying all night. If you're looking for a good time, leave the tears at home."

"I didn't—" he started to protest, then stopped himself. He snuffled, apparently realizing how congested he was. He rubbed the puffy bags under his eyes and the middle of his forehead. "Did I really? Oh man. I must have really been sloshed. Not the way to make a good impression on a pretty girl."

"No," MacKenzie agreed. "And this girl needs some real sleep before she's going to even put on a semblance of pretty by the fundraiser tonight. So hit the road, Jack."

He grunted and drank more of the coffee.

"I wouldn't have such a problem with Anita if she hadn't started up dating as soon as we broke up," he growled. "She could at least have waited a decent interval."

"Don't start that again."

"But it's true! She was seeing someone the next week. How do I know they weren't already seeing each other before we broke up? While we were engaged and talking about wedding plans?"

"She probably was." MacKenzie was brutal. "And she's not even given you a second thought, so why are you still pining after her? Give it up."

"I'm not pining," he said sharply. "I'm glad she's out of my life and that I can pursue other avenues. I'm glad I broke up with her." He reached for MacKenzie, but she avoided his grasp. He was too late if he thought the date was going to lead to intimacy now. That ship had sailed.

"Come on! I'll show you," Roger protested. "She doesn't mean anything to me anymore." His face was red with anger rather than embarrassment this time. MacKenzie didn't care. He could think her a tease if he liked. She wasn't about to be a target for him to work out his frustration on.

"It's time for you to go, Roger," she said firmly, staying out of his reach.

"You accuse me of still being in love with her? I'll prove it to you. I'll show you that I'm not."

"No."

He threw his coffee mug across the room. He didn't aim it at MacKenzie, but it was still half-full, and she ducked out of the way to avoid the arc of liquid that sprayed across the room. The mug shattered on the wall. MacKenzie looked at the dent in the wall, the pieces of the shattered mug, and the coffee trail across her bedroom in shock and disbelief.

"MacKenzie, I'm sorry—" Roger started.

"You've got thirty seconds to get out of here before I call the cops."

"MacKenzie…"

"Twenty-nine, twenty-eight, twenty-seven…"

At first, he didn't move, trying to intimidate her with his glare. When it became obvious that she wasn't going to be pushed around and she kept counting down, he decided he didn't want to have to explain to the police what he had done. He was still fully dressed, so there wasn't any delay for him to get his clothes on. He got up and stalked out of the bedroom. MacKenzie heard him getting his coat and boots, and then the door slammed and he was gone. She shook her head.

"Good riddance."

She picked up the splintered pieces of the mug. She'd probably be finding bits of it through the room for months to come. She'd get the maid in to clean up the coffee and vacuum thoroughly in the hopes she would get all of the sharp slivers that were left in the carpet. And she'd have to get the handyman in to repair and repaint the wall. And Roger Milford would not be getting a return invitation.

7

MacKenzie arrived in Amanda's hospital room and greeted her mother, who was waiting for Amanda to finish changing into her street clothes in the bathroom so that she could, once again, head for home. The nurse came in with the discharge papers for Amanda to sign when she came back out.

"Now try to encourage her not to do too much right away," the nurse advised, giving Lisa a sage nod. "You don't want her to turn around and be back here again. She's been stable for a couple of days, no fever and no vomiting, so she appears to be in the clear now, but just be extra careful for a little while. She's not as strong as she would like to think she is."

Lisa sighed. "If I could tell her something and be sure that she would follow my advice, that would be one thing, but you know how daughters are." She gave MacKenzie a look that made them all laugh. MacKenzie gave a wide shrug.

"What are you talking about, Mother? Don't I always do exactly what you tell me to?"

Lisa shook her head and made a noise of disgust that clearly answered MacKenzie's query.

The mood was light. MacKenzie was glad that Amanda was in the clear once again and could safely go home. If she could stay quiet for a couple more days and not try to just pick up where she'd left off, MacKenzie was sure she would be fine.

"I'll just leave that with you, then," the nurse told Lisa, and took two steps toward the door.

From the bathroom, they all heard the unmistakable sounds of vomiting.

For what seemed like a long time, they just all looked at each other, not wanting to believe it. MacKenzie was the first to take a step toward the bathroom.

"Amanda? Are you okay?"

She wasn't sure why she asked that. It was obvious from the noises within that everything was not okay. Amanda was not throwing up just for something to do. After her two hospitalizations, one right on the heels of the other, Amanda was sure to want to go home, not to be wanting to throw up again. She didn't want to be sick.

Lisa dashed past MacKenzie and knocked on the door. "Amanda? I'm coming in."

Amanda knew from past experience not to lock the bathroom door. Of course, the nurse would be able to unlock it to get in, but locking it would cause a delay to Amanda getting help from her mother while she went to find someone who could unlock it. Lisa made the slightest hesitation before opening the door, as if waiting to see if Amanda would object or wishing that she didn't have to face this problem yet again, one more time. Then she turned the handle and swung the door outward. MacKenzie didn't get closer, not wanting to get in the way or to have to watch Amanda being sick if she wasn't yet finished. Lisa went into the bathroom.

"It's okay, baby. It's going to be okay."

MacKenzie could hear Amanda sobbing between heaves. Lisa swore. "Her temperature is back up again," she called out to the nurse. And she swore again, angry at the recurring fever, God, fate, or whatever kept making Amanda sick again.

The nurse looked at the IV, which she had just removed from Amanda's arm half an hour before, shaking her head. They were all too stunned to believe it. How could Amanda be sick again, when she had been perfectly well for two days? She hadn't done anything strenuous. She hadn't been exposed to anyone new. They had all been careful not to cough near her.

When the bout of vomiting was finally over, Lisa helped Amanda to wash up and rinse out her mouth, then she and the nurse walked Amanda back over to the bed to lie back down. MacKenzie picked up the discharge papers and put them to the side, a wave of despair washing over her. How could

Amanda be sick again? Why couldn't they figure out what it was that was making her sick? Food? A virus? An infection? It should show up in her bloodwork. It couldn't be that much of a mystery.

"What have you done to make yourself sick again?" the nurse demanded as she settled Amanda into bed. "Everything was going along just swimmingly. You were going to go home."

Amanda wept. "I know. I want to go home."

"It's not her fault," MacKenzie told the nurse, raising her voice in anger. "Don't you get after her for getting sick. She didn't choose to be sick!"

The nurse shook her head, looking as if she would argue with this statement. Did she really think that Amanda wanted to be sick? That she would have done something to herself to make herself sick again?

MacKenzie had heard of such things. Usually about mothers making their children sick. But Lisa hadn't done this either. It wasn't anything that any of them had any control over. Lisa wanted her daughter to get better more than anyone else did. She would never have done anything to put her daughter in danger.

The nurse said nothing as she reinserted Amanda's IV and made sure that everything was in order.

"I'll let the doctor know," she said curtly, and walked back out. MacKenzie and Lisa fell into the chairs, still unable to believe the sudden setback. Lisa was looking for something in her purse, and MacKenzie leaned closer, curiosity aroused by Lisa's frantic search.

"What is it, Mother What are you looking for?"

"I can't find my… it's just not here…"

Eventually, Lisa pulled a small cell phone out of her purse. Folded up to the size of a compact, MacKenzie could see how it could have been easily missed. Lisa opened it up and punched in the numbers for Walter's cell phone. MacKenzie thought fleetingly that she needed to show Lisa how to set up speed dial numbers so that she didn't have to remember everybody's numbers. But she suspected that Walter and MacKenzie were probably the only ones that she ever called on her cell. Anyone else could wait until her business hours, when she dealt with all of her social appointments and issues.

As Lisa waited for the phone to ring through to Walter, MacKenzie stroked the back of her mother's neck, hoping it would help to soothe her.

As soon as Walter answered, Lisa started crying.

She normally did not cry in front of the girls, and particularly not in front of Amanda. They were supposed to keep a stiff upper lip in front of Amanda. Never give away any doubts they had about her ability to fight for her life and survive. MacKenzie glanced over at Amanda. She was lying back, eyes closed, face shining, giving no sign that she heard her mother's weeping.

"MacKenzie," Lisa thrust the phone at her, gasping for breath. "Tell him."

MacKenzie took the phone, not sure what she was supposed to tell her father. Just what was going on, she supposed. So that he could make the decision as to whether to turn around and return home. Then she resolved not to leave it up to her father.

"Daddy."

"MacKenzie, what's going on?" His voice was heavy with concern. "Amanda was fine when I left. What happened?"

"I don't know. She just suddenly took another turn. I just can't understand it. She'll be sick for a day or two, and then better for two days, and then it comes back again. It's cyclical. But I can't figure out why. I don't know what's causing it."

"I'll be there as soon as I can. Is she okay for now? I'm worried."

"She's resting right now. They put her back on an IV, and I hope that means back on the anti-emetics again too. So that she won't be throwing up again. It just doesn't make any sense to me."

"I'll be back as soon as I can be. What about your mother? Can you calm her down?"

MacKenzie looked at her mother, a lump in her throat. Lisa was always so cool, always calm and rational and prepared to do just the right thing. It wasn't like her to get hysterical over a change in Amanda's condition. MacKenzie reached over and took her mother's hand and squeezed it.

"She's going to be okay, Mother. She's going to be fine."

But as MacKenzie took in Amanda's waxy pallor, fear gripped her chest. Would she be? Would she really be alright?

8

It was another longday and when she went home, MacKenzie was lonely and wishing for once that she had a companion, someone who would be there when she got home at the end of the day to rub her feet and cuddle in front of the TV and maybe get her a drink and a bite to eat so that she didn't have to think about it.

But from what she had seen of marriage, she would be the one who was expected to do those things, rather than her partner. And she didn't know how anyone could have the energy at the end of such a day as she had just been through.

She didn't want Roger this time, or any of his ilk. She wanted a real partner or best friend, but she didn't have anyone to call. While she'd had friends in school, most of them had gone in different directions, and she didn't have a crowd that she hung around with. She went out to some of the social events that her mother set up or asked her to go to. She spent time with Amanda, having nice long talks with her when she was better. She was pretty focused on her family.

So she did the next best thing she could think of. She didn't want to watch some inane show on TV. She didn't have the energy to read a book. She was worried about Amanda and wanted to help her. There was nothing she could do, but she was desperate for answers.

She booted up her computer and started typing search strings into Google. Recurring fevers. Cyclical fevers. Flu-like symptoms. Kidney transplant rejection. Unexplained fevers. For each search, she clicked on all of the possibly relevant links on the first page of results, and sometimes the second or even further. She looked for patterns, for diseases or disorders that fit with Amanda's symptoms. The doctors might still think that she just had the flu, but MacKenzie was on the warpath. They were obviously not giving her proper treatment, or she wouldn't keep coming back down with the same symptoms over and over again.

Her eyes burned from staring at the screen and she made an effort to blink more often. She took a break and put a cold cloth over her eyes for a few minutes to try to reduce the swelling. She started making some notes of the things that she was seeing repeatedly, frowning and trying to wrap her mind around the various possibilities.

She'd always had an aptitude for biology. She hadn't taken medicine in college, but when she'd been in high school, she'd gotten good marks and always been very interested in how bodies worked. She was one of the only girls who hadn't been grossed out or pretended to be grossed out by dissections. She loved dissection days and would participate whenever she could, even doing extra modules for more credit. Maybe it had started with her interest in Amanda's medical care and in understanding what was happening to her, and in her desire to donate her own kidney to Amanda even when her parents were leery of the idea. She hadn't fantasized about being a doctor, but she had imagined what it would be like to cure a fatal illness, especially Amanda's kidney disease. Someday, someone would find a way to reverse kidney failure, and the world would change, just like it had when insulin, antibiotics, or vaccines were discovered. She wanted to be there when it happened.

But she hadn't pursued science or medicine after secondary school. She'd done arts and other programs that were more suited to young ladies. The women who attended the social functions that Lisa prized so highly were not highly-trained and did not have an interest in dissecting things. They were students of the arts and maybe of business if they were expected to take over after their parents retired.

MacKenzie tapped her pen on the desk, looking at the screen. She looked at her watch and considered the time. It was late. But would that matter to a doctor? Doctors were used to being paged or woken up to take care of emergencies, weren't they? MacKenzie wanted to get done everything she could as quickly as she could. She didn't know how long Amanda would be able to last without the proper treatment.

Eventually, she bit the bullet. She might not be in the doctor's good books after this, but she had to at least try. She looked up his number and tapped it into her phone.

The phone rang a few times before it was answered. "Dr. Proctor," he growled.

"Dr. Proctor," MacKenzie used her most reasonable, more charming voice, "this is MacKenzie Kirsch."

"MacKenzie Kirsch," he repeated. "What's wrong? I do hope you're not calling to tell me that… something has happened to your sister."

"It is about Amanda. So far, she's hanging in there, but I'm really worried. We need to figure out what is going on with her before it's too late."

She could hear him moving around, the creaking of bedsprings, and the noise of cloth rubbing over the phone.

"How can I help?"

"I'm really sorry for calling you so late at night. I didn't know who else to talk to. Amanda just keeps cycling through these high fevers. But it's not the flu. I'm sure of it."

"What most people call the flu isn't even the flu," he provided unhelpfully.

"I know. But… I've been doing some research, and I was wondering about malaria."

There was a short bark of laughter from Dr. Proctor. "Malaria? My dear… I think it's time to go to bed."

"I know it's not likely. No one would look for it. And maybe that's why they haven't been able to figure out what she has."

"No one in America comes down with malaria. If they do, it's something that they picked up on a trip. Amanda isn't exactly a world traveler. She's been sheltered and coddled, she hasn't been anywhere there are mosquitoes that could be carrying malaria."

"She had surgery last year. I'm not sure where it was, but they went out of the country. To some kind of private clinic that performs an experimental procedure not approved in the US."

Proctor was silent for a moment, considering this. "Are you sure?"

"Yes."

"And you don't know what kind of procedure it was or where it was performed?"

"No. I can ask Mother and Daddy. They haven't said much to me about it because it's private, you know. Amanda's health and personal care are her business, not mine. But I know Amanda had to get a passport. And I know they went somewhere warm, because I helped to pack her suitcase, and it was all light summer clothing."

"Somewhere warm doesn't necessarily mean a tropical country. It could just mean that she would be indoors the whole time and wouldn't need to pack anything warm."

"I'll ask them. But if she did go to a country where there were mosquitoes infected with malaria, then could that be what she has?"

"I don't know. Tell me about her symptoms."

"She gets a high fever, throws up until they give her drugs to stop it. She's tired and listless. Then after she gets through it, she starts to feel better, like her old self. She goes a few days without any symptoms, and then it is back again. High fever, throwing up, tired. Flu-like symptoms, but it's not the flu."

"Surely they've done basic blood tests and would have found any parasitic infections."

"I know… but I don't know for sure if they've been looking for anything but a virus, and maybe they could miss it. Especially if they think that Lisa was just being a hypochondriac."

"It is possible to miss it. It might not show up in a smear, or it might be easily missed… sometimes it takes two or three tests before something like that shows up. If the person testing hasn't seen malaria before…"

"And they wouldn't, living here in the States, would they? They would hardly ever see a case of it."

"It's possible, MacKenzie. If she had this procedure somewhere tropical."

"So, what do I tell the doctors? How do I get them to test her for it?"

"You'll have to ask for a CBC panel and to check a blood smear for parasites."

"What if they don't want to do it?"

"You're going to have to be strong about it. You'll have to insist. Explain that she has been somewhere tropical and recurring fevers could mean malaria. Talk to your father. Tell him to insist."

"Okay. Thanks, Dr. Proctor. I really appreciate it."

"Good luck, Miss Kirsch."

"MacKenzie."

"MacKenzie, then. I hope it works out."

———

MacKenzie had not foreseen that her parents would present a bigger roadblock than the doctors. She drove over to the hospital early in the morning, having only had a couple of hours of sleep, to present them with her findings and Dr. Proctor's confirmation that Amanda could be dealing with a malaria infection. Walter shook his head adamantly.

"Malaria? No one gets malaria anymore, MacKenzie, it's a dead disease."

"A dead disease?" MacKenzie challenged. "Millions of people get it every year!"

"Not in civilized countries. Not in the US."

"But she wouldn't have gotten it in the US. Where was it she went for her surgery?"

He glared at her and didn't answer the question. "You have to be bitten by an infected mosquito to get malaria. Amanda was never bitten by a mosquito. She wasn't ever even outside."

"She must have been outside to get from the plane to the clinic," MacKenzie muttered grumpily. She had expected her parents to be happy to have a possible solution to Amanda's mysterious illness. They could stop the cyclical fevers.

"Don't be flippant, MacKenzie. It's not attractive."

MacKenzie gave him a glare as good as she was getting, and turned to appeal to her mother. "If it's malaria, it's treatable. We can get her out of the hospital and back home again."

Lisa looked at Walter, then back at MacKenzie again. "But I really don't see how she could have gotten it. We were very careful not to expose her to anything."

"I'm sure you were. I'm not saying that it was because you did something wrong. You can't foresee everything."

"I really don't think that's what this is."

"The symptoms fit. I asked Dr. Proctor and he agreed. He said to pursue it."

"If it was malaria, don't you think the doctors here would have figured that out already? It can't be."

"They wouldn't ever guess that's what it was if they didn't know she was in a tropical country."

The two of them continued to frown and shake their heads. MacKenzie was frustrated. "What's the harm in ruling it out?"

"Chasing after zebras instead of horses," Walter said. "Haven't you ever heard of Occam's razor? We need to keep the doctors focused on the likely causes of this fever, not rare tropical diseases that she could never have contracted."

"It's one test," MacKenzie insisted. "Maybe two. That's not distracting them. And maybe something else will show up in those tests. You never know."

"I'm going to have to put my foot down," Walter said stubbornly.

"Amanda can decide for herself." MacKenzie looked over at her sleeping sister. "I'll ask her when she wakes up."

"You don't need to be getting her hopes up with wild theories."

"It's not a wild theory. It's a logical hypothesis. It fits the facts."

"The facts are, she was never bitten by a mosquito. I can guarantee you that."

MacKenzie stared into his angry, unwavering eyes, at a loss as to how to deal with his certainty.

When the doctor came around, MacKenzie excused herself from the room to let her parents deal with him. She saw the relief in Walter's eyes that she wasn't going to stay there and cause problems. She waited in the hallway by the nursing station for when the doctor left Amanda's room to go on to the next one. He didn't have a group of students with him this time, and he didn't stay long in Amanda's room. Not long enough to examine her or to figure out what was really making her sick.

"Dr. Brady?"

He turned and looked at her as he left the room and headed away from her to the next one. "Yes?"

"I'm Amanda's sister. MacKenzie."

He nodded. "Yes, what can I do for you? I just talked with your parents. I have other patients to see."

"Well, they didn't want me to bring this up, so I waited until I could catch you alone."

He looked around, impatient to be on his way.

"I don't really have time for individual consults. If you want to talk to me, you should be in the room when I'm there to see your sister."

"I think she might have malaria."

He blinked at her. Then he shook his head. "Malaria is a tropical disease. We don't see much of it here in the States."

"I know that. But she was out of the country a year ago."

"Did she get malaria a year ago?"

"She didn't show any symptoms back then, as far as I know, but the stuff I read online said that it doesn't always show up right away. It can stay dormant for a few years."

Dr. Brady considered this. His dark brows drew down. He looked again toward Amanda's room.

"My father doesn't think it could be," MacKenzie confirmed. "He didn't want me to bring it up with you."

"He's right, you know."

"Nobody knows until you test for it."

"It would have shown up on the tests that we already ran."

"It never gets missed? You wouldn't have overlooked it if you didn't know that she'd been in a tropical country?"

"It would still have shown up."

"I read that they can do several tests and not see it."

He gave a small shrug, conceding the point. "That is very rare, though. And with a patient like your sister, who has so many other things going on with her health… It's far more likely to be related to her transplant than anything else."

"I know that's the most likely, but these recurring fevers… they sound just like malaria. If they're not malaria, then what are they being caused by?"

"An infection of unknown origin. Maybe hiding in her kidney."

"But then wouldn't her white blood cell count be up? It isn't, is it?"

"Her white blood cell should be up if she has a bacterial infection. But her immune system is suppressed, she might not be producing white blood cells like she should."

"What else is showing up in her blood tests? Is there anything to show that she's rejecting the kidney?"

"Not yet. We're watching pretty closely."

"So do one more test for malaria. Just to be sure. Looking for that specifically."

He pressed his thin lips together, thinking about it. Then he finally nodded. He turned to the nurse at the nursing station and gave her instructions on the blood to be drawn for the tests. He looked sideways at MacKenzie. "It might be best to do it while the parents are out of the room, if they go for supper."

MacKenzie nodded. "I'll try to get them to take a break while I sit with her."

The nurse looked from one to the other, raising an eyebrow. "You're going against the wishes of the next of kin?"

"See if you can get the patient's permission. That will override anything they can say. I don't want this to become a legal battle."

The nurse was hesitant, but finally nodded. "Alright. if you say so."

MacKenzie blew out her breath in a sigh. "Good. Thank you. I appreciate it."

"We want to find out what's wrong with your sister just as much as you do," the nurse said. "We don't like not knowing what's going on with a patient or how to treat it. Her parents should have mentioned that she's been out of the country. That makes a difference."

MacKenzie returned to the hospital room. Amanda was still sleeping. Her parents were talking in low voices, but stopped when MacKenzie entered the room. Lisa gave a strained smile. "Are you sure there isn't somewhere else you need to be?" she asked. "You don't need to sit with her, with both of us here."

"Just the opposite," MacKenzie said. "It's you two who need a break. You've been here all night and I'm here to give you a break. Go get something to eat and have a rest. Amanda will be okay with me here."

"Oh, you don't need to do that MacKenzie. You have other things to do."

"I don't know of anywhere more important than with my sister right now. Go get something to eat. Maybe find somewhere you can close your eyes for a while. Get some rest."

"We really can't do that."

"Of course you can. You can't sit by her bed twenty-four hours a day. Give me a chance to contribute."

Lisa looked at Walter, raising her eyebrows in a question. Walter finally nodded.

"I have my cell phone," he told MacKenzie. "You can call me if there is any change in her condition. Do you have your phone with you?"

MacKenzie checked her purse and nodded.

"Yeah, I've got it right here. I'll let you know if anything changes, but right now she's resting peacefully, so you guys go and get something to eat and take a breather."

They took a few more minutes to get on their way, but then finally left the room. MacKenzie flopped into one of the uncomfortable guest chairs and tried to relax. Whether her parents thought it could be malaria or not, she was still going to get it checked out. And she didn't need their permission to do it. If it turned out to be negative, there were still other things on her list that were less likely, but she'd keep looking. If it did turn out to be malaria, then her parents would forgive her for going ahead and having the tests done behind their backs. She was just a concerned sister making sure that Amanda got the best chance she could possibly get.

The nurse from the nursing station poked her head into the room to confirm that both parents were gone. She smiled at MacKenzie and shook her head. "Let's wake her up for a minute and get this done, then."

9

There was a sudden uptick in activity. MacKenzie had been keeping her ears pricked, on pins and needles while she wondered how long it would take for the tests to come back so that she would know whether her guess had been right or wrong. They were just blood tests, not ones that required any cultures to be grown or other long, involved processes. Just looking at a blood panel and looking at a single droplet of blood under the microscope. What if the parasite load wasn't large enough for them to see anything in the blood? What if it was a new lab tech who looked at the blood and didn't see anything or didn't know what he was seeing? What if they did a thin smear instead of a thick smear and there just weren't enough parasites for them to make a finding? So many things could go wrong, she didn't dare get her hopes up.

But it started as a murmur at the nursing station outside the door. There were low voices, gradually getting louder and more excited. There were people being paged and walking back and forth at an increased rate. Even Walter and Lisa started to sit up and look back toward the hallway, wondering what was going on.

She hadn't actually expected Dr. Brady to come in himself. She thought that the news would come from one of the nurses, casually mentioning that they had found something new and would be starting a new treatment. But she heard his voice at the nursing station, and it wasn't time for his rounds. She looked over her shoulder, waiting, praying silently that they finally knew what was wrong with Amanda and would be able to treat her and send her home. It was so simple. If it was malaria, they just had to treat the parasites, and she would get better. Of course, she would still have chronic kidney disease and be on anti-rejection drugs, but that was normal for Amanda. MacKenzie just wanted to get back to that normal.

Dr. Brady came in. He was looking at a clipboard, a pair of glasses perched on the end of his nose that MacKenzie hadn't seen him wearing before. Did he not need them the rest of the time? Did he not like the way that they looked on him? Maybe he thought he looked more authoritative with them on and this was one of those times when he needed to convince her parents of the veracity of what he was about to tell them.

He looked over his glasses at MacKenzie and then took them off, as if he'd just remembered he was wearing them and didn't actually want to be seen in them. He folded the arms in and put them into his breast pocket.

"There have been developments," he announced.

Lisa and Walter were both looking at him eagerly, waiting for the details. Finding something was good. Finding something meant that this new condition could be treated.

"Amanda *does* have malaria," Dr. Brady confirmed.

MacKenzie breathed out a sigh of relief. Her parents both looked stunned. They looked from the doctor to MacKenzie and back again, shaking their heads and trying to understand what was going on.

"Malaria? She can't possibly have malaria," Lisa said in disbelief.

"The slides are clear. She does have malaria. I'm not sure how it was missed on the earlier blood tests, but these things do happen. Maybe the parasitic load wasn't high enough to show up before, but it was enough to make Amanda sick, with her compromised immune system. Sometimes we just don't know why it doesn't show up. But now that we know, we can begin to treat."

"You'll put her on ACT?" MacKenzie asked.

Walter glared at her, like she had farted in public or done something else to sully their reputation. How could it be bad that they had figured out what Amanda's mysterious illness was? It means that she could be cured. Treating malaria was fairly simple.

"Yes, we'll start her on ACT and some other helper drugs. She should start to show improvement pretty quickly. It's a good thing that we caught it now. Malaria can be pretty devastating in someone with a compromised immune system. Millions die from malaria every year, and someone like Amanda is particularly susceptible."

"How could this happen?" Walter demanded. "I thought people don't get it here."

"She was out of the country for her transplant?"

Walter's eyes shifted sideways to MacKenzie and then away. His lips pressed tightly together and he didn't answer at first. "She has been out of the country for surgery," he admitted. "But that was a year ago. More than that. How could it just be showing up now? Are you telling me that she had it this whole time and we never knew it?"

"It can be dormant for long periods of time. Years, even. We don't know all of the reasons it hides. But we know what to do once it rears its head. She must have gotten infected when she was out of the country. Where was the surgery performed?"

"On an island," Walter said evasively. "But we were very careful of her exposure to anything that could have harmed her. We went to great lengths. She was never bitten by a mosquito; I can promise you that."

"There are other insects that can carry it. And she might not have even known she was bitten. She has a lot of health issues to be concerned about and might not have noticed a bite. With a compromised immune system, her body might not show the typical reaction. She might not get the usual bump and itching. Those are signs that your body is protecting you against a foreign invader."

"She was indoors at all times. The hospital was very clean. We would never have gotten the surgery done if there was any question of patient care."

"I don't doubt it," Dr. Brady agreed, though there was something in his manner that suggested he wasn't quite as confident of the conditions as Walter. It was beside the point. How his patient had gotten malaria was not as important as treating it and getting her healthy again.

"This is good news, Daddy," MacKenzie said, unable to stand their upset expressions any longer. "It means they can treat her."

He shook his head, scowling. "This is not good news," he argued. "And I was very clear that you were not to talk to the doctors about this and to distract them from their jobs."

"This is their job. They're supposed to find out what she has and treat it. They needed to know that it was malaria, or they couldn't give her the right treatment. I don't understand what you're so upset about. This is good news. This means that they can make Amanda better."

Dr. Brady nodded. "It is good that we figured out what is going on with Amanda at this point. Malaria can be fatal, and for someone like her..." he shook his head. "I want to be sure that she gets the best care possible, and I'm grateful to Miss Kirsch for pointing us in the right direction. I wasn't aware that she had been out of the country for her surgery." He took his glasses out of his pocket again and perched them on his nose to look at the information on the clipboard, flipping back several pages to look for some reference he had previously missed. "This gives the name of a *local* private clinic."

Lisa and Walter exchanged glances.

"It was facilitated by a local," Walter said slowly. "They are the ones who set everything up and supervised her care and all of the arrangements. It's just the surgery itself that is done out of the country. It isn't approved here, so…"

Dr. Brady took off his glasses and tucked them back into his pocket again. "The paperwork should have been filled out properly. You should have made it clear that she had been out of the country. You can't expect us to know when you are lying."

"It wasn't a lie," Walter protested angrily.

"You deliberately misled the staff into thinking that your daughter had not been out of the country. Wherever this private island is where the surgery was performed, you should have told us about it. Not obfuscated it saying that it was performed locally."

Walter clearly intended to intimidate Dr. Brady with his glare, but Dr. Brady wasn't having any of it. "We'll be starting the anti-malaria protocol immediately. You can look forward to your daughter regaining her full health soon."

Lisa put her hand over Walter's, and he kept quiet.

Dr. Brady gave MacKenzie a brief nod before he left, acknowledging her role in the diagnosis. He walked out of the room.

MacKenzie turned to her father. "Why does he think that the surgery Amanda had was a transplant?"

She was greeted with silence from Lisa and Walter. Lisa looked at her ex-husband for guidance, then dropped her eyes and said nothing. MacKenzie stared at the two of them.

"Are you telling me it's true? She had another kidney transplant?"

The silence ticked by. It was Walter who finally broke it. "Your kidney failed," he said finally. "That's not your fault; I don't ever want you thinking that your kidney should have been stronger and lasted longer. It gave her eight really good years."

"I… I don't care that my kidney failed. Why wouldn't you tell me that? Why would you keep something like this a secret from me? Why not tell me what was going on?"

"We thought you would be upset," Lisa said. "We didn't want you blaming yourself. And you couldn't give her another kidney, so there was no reason you had to be told."

"We did what we had to do," Walter said.

"You did what you had to do… I don't understand what that means. Why did she have to go out of the country to have a transplant? And why did it have to be such a big secret?"

"There is a shortage of transplant organs in America," Walter explained. "Other countries do not have the same restrictions and problems that we do. If we waited here, it could have been three or four years before she had the opportunity for a transplant. And in that time… well, you know that even with dialysis, kidney patients don't last forever. We couldn't take the chance that she would die while she was waiting for a transplant. We saw to it that she could get one right away."

"Some people think there is something wrong with going to another country to get a transplant," Lisa contributed. "We didn't want to have to deal with the stigma attached to transplant tourism, so we kept it quiet."

"But there isn't anything wrong with it. It's legal, right?" MacKenzie asked. "This isn't some black-market organ trade."

"You know better than that," Walter snapped. "You know there is no such thing as a black market for transplant organs. You've seen the statements put out by world health organizations. That stuff that you see on TV or hear repeated as an urban legend is just that, urban legend. There is no way that an organization performing black-market transplants could exist." He ticked points off on his fingers. "They need highly-trained medical professionals. This isn't something that can be performed by a regular doctor. They need specialized equipment and modern medical facilities. It would cost millions of dollars to run an organization like that. Maybe billions. There's just no way that it is feasible."

MacKenzie nodded. She had heard statements from the UN or WHO or local regulators assuring the public that there was no black-market organ trade. People didn't have to worry about getting drugged at the bar and having their organs stolen while they were unconscious, left in a bathtub filled with ice to bleed out. Such a crime had never been reported anywhere in the world. Certainly not in the United States.

10

MacKenzie held her breath as the ACT cocktail was started. She knew that nothing was going to happen immediately. No drug was instantaneous, and she wasn't going to be able to see the results right away. Amanda wasn't just going to awaken, sit up, and be her old self again. It would take time. A few hours or days—MacKenzie wasn't sure how long—and they would start to see improvements. But she still couldn't help holding her breath and watching Amanda for some sign that the ACT was working.

The nurse smiled and nodded at them cheerfully. "Well, that should do it, then. Just a matter of waiting for it to have effect now."

They were all there when Amanda woke up. She opened her eyes and stared up at the ceiling. Lisa, her eyes fixed on her younger daughter, was the first to notice. She stood up and leaned over Amanda.

"Hi, sweetie. How are you feeling?"

Amanda stared up at her, not responding immediately. She blinked and made a small movement with her head. Then she nodded a little and licked her lips.

"Mother."

"Yes. How are you doing?"

"Don't feel good."

"No, I guess not. But they're giving you a new drug, they've got it all sorted out now. You'll feel better soon."

"New drug?"

"You have malaria."

Amanda lay there looking up at Lisa, her face still slack.

"What's that?" she asked eventually.

Lisa laughed and smoothed Amanda's hair back from her face. "You pick it up in tropical climates. They think you must have somehow gotten it when you had your surgery."

"When? Back then?"

"It's been dormant until recently. Now it's making you sick with these fevers. But they're giving you the right medication now, so it won't come back."

Amanda nodded and closed her eyes, falling back asleep. Lisa continued to stand over her, stroking her hair and watching her sleep.

"She's looking better, don't you think? I think it's already helping."

Walter looked at her briefly, then back at his Blackberry. "I can't tell, Lisa. But I'm sure she'll be doing better soon."

"She woke up, that's a good sign." Lisa put her hand over Amanda's forehead. "Her fever is down… but of course, it's gone down on its own the last two times too. I just hope this is really the solution." Lisa turned her head to look at MacKenzie. "Whatever made you think of it?"

"Just searching the internet, looking for something that matched."

"Amazing. You really can find anything on the internet, can't you?"

MacKenzie shrugged. "I don't know about anything, but you can find a lot of things."

"Maybe you can find Amanda her next kidney on the internet," Walter grumbled without looking up.

MacKenzie saw her own frown reflected on her mother's face. "Walter. That's really not appropriate. And I don't like you talking about her needing another kidney. I don't want to…"

"Jinx this one?" Walter gave a chuckle. "But you're not superstitious, are you?"

"What do you know about this kidney?" MacKenzie asked after a while, looking over at Amanda. It seemed unbelievable to her that for the past year, Amanda had had someone else's kidney doing the work of cleaning her blood instead of MacKenzie's, and no one had told her. A stranger's kidney in her sister. And MacKenzie's donated kidney no longer functional. She'd somehow always thought that once Amanda got her kidney, it would work forever. She had never anticipated it failing and needing to be replaced.

Lisa didn't say anything. Walter sat up, stretched, and looked questioningly at MacKenzie. "What do you mean, what do we know about it?"

"I don't know… I mean, do you know anything about the donor? Who it was? Where he or she came from? Was it… a live donor?"

"We have a profile somewhere," Lisa said. "They gave us a picture and a little write-up about her. I thought it was nice that they would do that. Makes you feel a little better about going through with it if you feel like you know the donor. Around here, they still refuse to tell you anything about the donor, afraid that you'll contact the donor's family and make trouble."

"What did they say about her?"

"She was a young woman, thirties. She was… where did it say she was from, Walter, do you remember?"

Walter made a face as he tried to recall details. "Germany, Sweden, somewhere like that. Blond girl. Very pretty."

"From Germany? But the transplant wasn't in Germany."

"No. They make matches all around the world, and you pay to have the donor flown in, pay all of their expenses."

"And that's legal?"

"Why wouldn't it be?"

MacKenzie had an uneasy feeling that her parents would have done anything, quasi-legal or not, to get Amanda her transplant. If it had been completely above-board, then why would they not have told her? She wasn't buying that it was just because they didn't want to break it to her that her donated kidney had failed.

***

MacKenzie had broken down and bought a couple of paperbacks at the hospital gift store, unable to entertain herself while she sat with Amanda and her parents, but unwilling to go home until she was sure that Amanda was better and wasn't just going to get sick again as soon as she left the room. Visiting with her parents was proving to be impossible, and Lisa didn't want them talking in the room and possibly waking Amanda up. She needed her sleep.

MacKenzie looked up from her book over at Amanda. She had started to snore a little as she slept. MacKenzie listened to her critically. She sounded like she had a bit of a cold. Was she getting something else on top of the malaria because her immune system was so fragile? Or was MacKenzie just worrying too much, jumping to conclusions?

Lisa caught MacKenzie's look and smiled. "Cute," she pronounced. "Like a little puppy snoring away."

MacKenzie smiled at the picture it brought to mind. She went back to reading her book.

But over the next hour, Amanda's breathing got progressively louder, until MacKenzie could no longer ignore it and pretend that she was just making cute noises while she slept. She put down her book and went out to the nursing station.

"Would you look in on Amanda, please? Her breathing is really loud."

The nurse sitting at the desk gave a sigh and hoisted herself to her feet. She went into Amanda's room without any sense of hurry. But she cocked her head as she heard the noise that Amanda was making.

"Sounds like she might have picked up a bit of a cold," she observed.

Lisa nodded. "It figures. You just get one thing under control, and something else pops up."

The nurse put on her stethoscope and placed the diaphragm on Amanda's chest. She listened for a minute, moving it around a few times as Amanda breathed steadily in and out.

"She is sounding pretty congested," she said neutrally. "I'm going to get her on oxygen, and I'll let the doctor know."

They watched while she hooked up an oxygen cannula to Amanda's nose and recorded her observations on the patient chart.

"It's just a cold, though, right?" Lisa asked.

"I'm not sure. We'll have the doctor take a look."

She left the room again. MacKenzie sat back down slowly, looking at her mother. Lisa's eyes were round, wide with worry. She had been through so many crises with Amanda that she was not going to be reassured by anything MacKenzie said, especially since MacKenzie would only be guessing anyway. MacKenzie bit her tongue to keep from assuring her mother that Amanda would be alright and picked up her paperback. She wasn't going to read anything else. Not with Amanda breathing so heavily, now on oxygen, with the doctor being paged. They all knew that Amanda's condition could turn on a dime.

11

Amanda's breathing seemed to be growing faster and more labored. The doctor had not yet put in an appearance, but the nurse had been checking in on her regularly, her mouth a straight, uncommunicative line.

MacKenzie stood up. She didn't know what to do, but she felt like she should be doing something. Lisa apparently felt the same way. She shook Amanda's shoulder to wake her up.

"Amanda? I want you to talk to me, sweetie. Can you tell me if it's hurting? Amanda? Wake up for just a minute, sweetie."

Amanda's eyes opened. Not just slits this time, but wide with alarm. Her gasps became even more panicked. She reached for the oxygen cannula. Lisa grasped her hand so that she couldn't pull the oxygen out.

"They're giving you oxygen, sweetie. It's okay. Just leave it be. They'll make sure you're getting enough air."

Amanda gave a couple of deeper breaths. "Can't… breathe…" Another wrenching breath. "Mommy… can't…"

Lisa smoothed Amanda's hair, trying to quiet her. MacKenzie hurried back out to the nursing station. "Please. She's really bad. She needs help."

This time, the nurse's movements were swift. She came at a run. She didn't put on her stethoscope, but immediately adjusted the flow of the oxygen. Her fingers went to Amanda's pulse.

"Calm down, Amanda. I want you to try to take long, slow breaths for me. I know you're scared, but it's going to be okay. Let me hear a nice deep breath."

Amanda wasn't able to calm her stentorious breathing. The nurse hovered over her for a moment, trying to calm her. She readjusted the bed, raising the head. It gave MacKenzie a better view of Amanda's panicked expression, which she really didn't want. She tried to look at Amanda calmly rather than turning away and giving away how worried she was.

"Let's get you turned over," the nurse told Amanda, repositioning her arms and legs. "I'm just going to roll you to your front. You might find it easier to breathe that way." Once she got Amanda settled into the new position, without much change in her breathing, she hurried out of the room, calling to other nurses and giving instructions.

In a minute or two, she was back, filling in a young doctor who looked like he'd just been pulled from a nap. He blinked at Amanda, checked her pulse and listened to her breathing, and nodded at what the nurse had done to make her more comfortable. A couple of other nurses wheeled in a gurney, forcing MacKenzie and her parents to abandon their chairs and move out of the way.

"Mom and Dad, we're going to take Amanda to ICU where we can help her with her breathing. Once we've got her stable, we'll bring you up to speed."

Lisa opened her mouth to ask a question, but the doctor wasn't stopping to chat. Amanda was moved to the gurney for transport, and in a minute he and one of the nurses were wheeling her out of the room.

"What's happening?" Lisa demanded. "Somebody tell me what's going on."

The nurses who had stayed behind tried to calm her down. "They're just going to make sure she's getting enough oxygen. They'll take good care of her. Once she's stabilized, you'll be able to see her again."

"But why is she having such trouble breathing? Is it a cold?"

"We can't answer that, ma'am," the other nurse said. "The doctor will talk to you when he can."

The hardest thing was waiting. They had done it many times before with Amanda and her illness, but MacKenzie found it the hardest part. Waiting to find out what she had. Waiting to find out if they could do anything about it. Waiting for a donor. For the transplant. Waiting to see if it would take. Waiting to see if the malaria treatment would work. MacKenzie liked to be in control of things. She hated not being able to direct or predict the outcome.

But Amanda had always pulled through. She was a fighter, and she had always managed to rally and get through whatever life had thrown at her. She wasn't going to be kept down by a chest cold.

MacKenzie tried to focus on her book, but was not getting anywhere. She kept turning pages forward and back and could not pick up the thread of the story. Her mind kept going back to how pale and listless Amanda had been lately. Like something was gone out of her.

It was just the malaria. Once they got her over that, their dynamic, cheerful Amanda would be back again. She'd get the energy and the will to fight off whatever other viruses or infections got to her. She'd be able to keep her new kidney for another ten years. She'd be able to live the life that she had been—a darling of the socialites, her mother's favorite, Daddy's little girl, and MacKenzie's beloved baby. Even if MacKenzie had only been six at the time, she had fed and changed Amanda and considered Amanda to be her own, as much as if she'd been MacKenzie's daughter. She'd always sort of resented the fact that as Amanda's real mother, Lisa had the say in Amanda's medical care and how she was raised. She felt like she should at least have an equal say.

MacKenzie closed her book and held it between her hands, head bowed low, mentally urging Amanda to get better and the doctors to come talk to them and tell them she was okay.

They were shunted from one waiting area to another without being told why. Without being told how Amanda was doing or when they would be able to see her.

Then, at long last, Dr. Brady was there. He pulled up a chair and sat close to them. He spoke in a careful, measured voice about something called acute respiratory distress syndrome. "It does sometimes occur in malaria cases, even after the malaria has been treated and the infection is reduced or eliminated. It isn't because anybody did anything wrong."

"What is the treatment for this respiratory distress syndrome?" Walter demanded.

"As you saw, giving Amanda oxygen, repositioning her, admitting her to ICU so that she could be put on a ventilator to help her to breathe. Doing everything we could to help her lungs oxygenate her blood."

MacKenzie swallowed. There was a lump in her throat. 'Doing everything they could' made it sound like they were no longer helping Amanda. Like the life-giving measures had failed and been abandoned.

"Is she stable now?" Lisa asked.

Dr. Brady looked at his hands. He took a couple of breaths and then looked at their faces, meeting each of their eyes. Connecting with them like he had been taught to do when delivering bad news.

"We did everything we could for Amanda. But in the end, our best wasn't good enough. I'm sorry to have to inform you that Amanda has passed."

MacKenzie choked. Her eyes burned with tears and a rushing sound filled her ears. She felt like she couldn't breathe herself, like Dr. Brady had just pulled all of the air from the room.

"What?" Lisa said in disbelief, her voice breaking. She looked at Walter. "What? No!"

He put out both arms and enfolded his ex-wife, almost pulling her out of her chair.

"No," Lisa repeated. "It isn't true. He didn't say that. Amanda is going to get better."

Walter held her close and rubbed her back. MacKenzie thought he was sobbing, but that couldn't be true, because her father never cried. Never.

She sat there, beside them and yet separate from them, her stunned brain still trying to take it in and to believe that what the doctor said was true.

12

The rest of the day was lost from MacKenzie's memory. As were many hours and days afterward. She had only spotty recollections of helping Lisa with the obituary and arrangements for the funeral.

Her sister's funeral. Her baby's funeral. They'd had so many close calls with Amanda in the past and she had always pulled through. While MacKenzie had always feared the worst, she had never really believed that Amanda was going to die and she would be left an only child, helping her mother choose the food to serve at the reception following the funeral.

They had to pick out the clothes to dress Amanda in, discussing which were her favorites and which would look best for the open casket viewing. MacKenzie excused herself and went into the bathroom to cry, holding a cold cloth over her eyes afterward to take down the swelling, as if it were important to maintain the fiction that she was strong and holding it all together even with her mother.

Poems on the funeral program. Pallbearers. Seating plans. It was a nightmarish mix of all of the event planning they had done in the past, cruelly twisted into a celebration of what could never be celebrated.

She went home at night alone, wrung out and exhausted, only to cry into her pillow and be unable to sleep for hours. She remembered how irritated she'd been at Roger crying himself to sleep and wished she could take it back. She could have been more compassionate than that.

Her brain was far away from her body during the funeral, graveside, and reception. There was no way she could face all of the sympathetic faces and words if she had to be present and feel her feelings. So she nodded and smiled sad little smiles and shook hands and hugged and received kisses on the cheeks from old, powdered ladies, and pretended that she was accepting their comfort. That it was meaningful for her and made her feel better.

And when it was all done and she again went home alone, she stared at her computer and wanted to know why.

Her parents had been too secretive about the transplant. MacKenzie knew that there was no such thing as a black-market transplant. That there were no organized crime gangs stealing people's organs. That everything was tightly regulated and required highly-trained surgeons and an illegal organ trade was impossible. Everybody said so. All of the authorities.

Then what were her parents hiding?

She started searching for more information. If the industry was tightly regulated, then that meant that there were people breaking the regulations. There would be no rules or laws about how organ donations could be handled if there were not people who were trying to profit from them. And not just the surgeons who were performing the transplants and being paid for their services.

To begin with, all she could find were *those* stories. The urban legends that the regulators talked about. Businessmen in Vegas waking up to find out that they'd been roofied by hookers and had their organs removed while they were unconscious. Full of dramatic details about waking up in a tub full of ice with a note taped to them. Responses from the regulators saying how ridiculous the stories were and how people should not believe or be concerned about them.

But then there were other stories, ones that appeared in small columns in the news. A mother whose son had died in a tragic accident who discovered that some of her son's organs had been removed after he was declared dead, the body cavity repacked with newspaper. Bodies in dumpsters or washed up on the beach that were mysteriously missing organs, attributed to some cannibalistic serial killer. They were harder to find and were always responded to by the authorities who said that people were letting their imaginations get away from them, but MacKenzie made note of them and wondered. The more the regulators objected, the more she wondered what they had to hide. If the stories were ridiculous, then why did they find it necessary to make any defense at all?

She went back to her emails from Amanda and Lisa during the time that they were preparing for Amanda's surgery and scoured them for any details. She had been completely oblivious at the time to the secret they were keeping from her, but now that she knew, she re-examined every word and every sentence for details that they might have let slip or that were intended to hide something.

She wanted to know the truth.

MacKenzie called Dr. Proctor and made an appointment to see him. She tried to make it clear that it wasn't a medical appointment and wasn't a date, but she needed to talk to someone about Amanda, and she wasn't sure who else to call. He'd been kind to her and had put up with her questions in the past. He'd talked to her in the middle of the night about malaria without treating her like she was a child or criticizing her for disturbing her sleep. She felt like she could trust him to help her to separate the lies from the truth.

At first, she made a reservation at her favorite restaurant in Burlington, but then decided she might not want to be seen talking with Dr. Proctor or have friends interrupt her or overhear what she was talking about. It wasn't exactly polite dinner conversation, and she didn't want it getting back to her parents. They had been through enough already, without thinking that she was questioning their decision to take Amanda out of the country for a new kidney.

So instead she arranged to meet with Dr. Proctor at an out-of-the-way sandwich shop. Not a high-end place, not somewhere she had ever been before. Not an up-and-coming new kid on the block that she or her friends thought was going to become the next Starbucks. There were no reservations required, she just made sure that she was there before Dr. Proctor to get them a table so that he wouldn't have to stand around waiting for her.

She waved at him as he stood in the doorway. Not that she was hard to find. There were only a few other patrons there, most of them eating alone while reading the newspaper or a paperback they had brought with them for the purpose. MacKenzie looked around at them, speculating on why they were alone and what kind of quiet lives of desperation they were living. Did any of them have friends or relatives who had been through an organ transplant? They were all working people and she didn't think they would be able to afford the money it took to get such a procedure. Organs were supposed to be free, but like any other medical service in the USA, the procedure and stay at the hospital were not. And the working class certainly wouldn't have the resources to go to some island in the South Pacific to get a kidney from some donor flown in from Germany.

"MacKenzie, how are you doing?" Dr. Proctor held her hand for a few seconds longer after shaking it, looking into her face and inquiring in a tone that imparted that he really did want to know how she was handling Amanda's loss; he wasn't just looking for a social "fine, thanks."

She gave his hand a squeeze back, then pulled away. "I don't know. It's difficult. In spite of how sick she always was, I wasn't really prepared to lose her."

Dr. Proctor nodded sympathetically, and they both drifted up to the sandwich counter to place their orders. They sat back down at MacKenzie's table.

"And how are your parents? I have been worried about Lisa. So much of her life was about Amanda and taking care of her, I'm worried about what she'll do now with all of that extra time on her hands."

"She's been doing surprisingly well," MacKenzie admitted. Maybe that was part of what was bothering her. Seeing her mother throw herself into charities work and busy herself with other people's causes so soon after the funeral felt wrong to her. What did MacKenzie expect? Did she expect Lisa to lock herself at home in mourning and to wear black for five years? Lisa had always been social, had always been involved in charitable causes. She needed something to fill the void, and it hadn't taken her long to find it. MacKenzie, meanwhile, didn't feel like going out to any of the events she had previously committed to, let alone anything new. She didn't want to hear about anyone else's suffering and the ills and injustices of the world. She just wanted to think about Amanda. And she didn't want to think about Amanda. "I think she'll be okay. As long as she has something to do, it seems like she'll be happy. I mean, not happy happy, but… okay. Able to go on."

Dr. Proctor nodded. He was an older man. When MacKenzie had been little, she had thought him old, but looking at him with the eyes of an adult, she realized that he wasn't as ancient as she had once thought. Yes, he was balding, with only a tonsure of white hair left, and he wore wire frame glasses when he was reading or doing close work, but he probably wasn't older than sixty, which meant that when she was a child and he used to come to the house to see one of her parents or look in on Amanda, he would only have been in his forties. That didn't seem quite as old to her as it once had. Where would she be when she was forty? Would she have finally decided what it was that she wanted to do with her life? Would she be a clone of Lisa, working with her charities? Would she be political like her father, trying to right the wrongs of the world, or at least the state? Or would she have her own passion, something completely different that she wasn't even aware of yet?

"Lisa is a strong woman. She can be driven. As long as she is still working with her causes… I imagine she'll be able to hold it together."

MacKenzie took a drink of her water. She noticed that Dr. Proctor didn't ask about her father. Was that just because he was a man, and men were supposed to stuff their feelings, expected to go on with and bury themselves in their work, even if they had just lost a daughter? It was expected that he wouldn't feel it as keenly as Lisa, who had been by Amanda's side daily?

"I guess you're probably wondering why I wanted to meet with you today."

He studied her. "I did wonder… I thought maybe you wanted some advice on school. What program to pursue."

MacKenzie was surprised. She was done with school. School had always bored her, and she hadn't found anything she was interested enough in to pursue for another year, let alone another degree.

"No, actually. I wanted to talk to you about Amanda."

"She wasn't my patient. I talked to your mother sometimes when she was wondering about whether to take Amanda to the hospital or to pursue one course of treatment or another, but I was just a sounding-board. Not her physician."

"That's okay. You might be able to help me out more that way anyway. If she was your patient, you wouldn't be able to talk about her, would you?"

He smiled and nodded. "You're right about that. As a friend of the family, I'm not bound to any kind of confidentiality. If she was my patient… well, I'd love to help you, but there are standards of confidentiality that even I have to follow."

"How would I get her records? I mean, I don't know if I qualify as next of kin, and if I'd be able to get anything if I asked. Could I?"

"That would probably fall to your parents. What is it you're looking for?"

"I don't know." MacKenzie studied a chip in one of her nails, hiding from his gaze. A woman behind the counter brought their sandwiches around to them, and she and Dr. Proctor took a few initial bites, exclaiming on how fresh the ingredients were and how the shop was a diamond in the rough, just waiting to be discovered.

"I want to know more about Amanda's transplant," MacKenzie explained. "I want to know what happened. If something went wrong."

He raised his brows. "Well, you were there, my dear. You were part of all of that."

"No, not that transplant. The one a year ago."

He stopped with his mouth open, about to take another bite. Then he put his sandwich down on the plate and looked at her, frowning. "Her transplant a year ago?"

"You didn't know?"

He shook his head. He ate a slice of pickle, considering. "Like I said, I wasn't her physician. There's no reason for them to tell me about a second transplant."

"They didn't tell me about it either."

He frowned. For a few minutes, they ate in silence. MacKenzie watched Dr. Proctor covertly, trying to be patient and not look like she was hovering over him, waiting for his answer. Even though she was.

"How could they keep a transplant from you? You would have known she was in the hospital. It's a pretty big thing. A complicated procedure with a lot of hospital time. I'm sure you would have been there, waiting to know the outcome. Weren't you? Was that when you were in Europe?"

"No. I was home. They told me that she was having surgery to try to improve her kidney function. Some new procedure. They never told me it was a transplant."

"Why would that be a secret?"

"That's what I want to know. I think… I know that there's not really a black market for organ procurement, but I wonder whether it was something… a little bit shady." She grimaced. "I don't even want to say that. It all sounds so dramatic, and I'm sure everything was just routine, but…"

Dr. Proctor didn't say anything. Most notably, he didn't deny that there was a black-market trade in organs. He waited for MacKenzie to go on.

"Can you think of any reason they would keep it quiet?" MacKenzie asked.

Maybe it was a new trend. Reducing stress on the patient by not telling the public that they were going through a transplant. Maybe transplantation was getting some kind of social stigma, some ghoulish, Frankenstein's monster reputation. Multiple organ donations could be seen as something cannibalistic. Or it could be something to do with social standing, something that only the ultra-privileged could take part in, and Lisa and Walter had wanted to keep it quiet so that their friends or Amanda's friends wouldn't think that she was being greedy or taking more than her share.

"I'm afraid I would have the same concerns as you," Dr. Proctor admitted. "I would want to know whether everything was aboveboard. It seems very odd that they would keep it quiet, at a time when Amanda needed extra support."

"Yeah." MacKenzie picked at the crust of her sandwich. Should she have asked for them to cut the crust off? Was that something that only a diva would do? Or was it socially acceptable in a specialty sandwich shop? "I would have been there, if they had let me. I could have gone with everybody to this clinic, wherever it was. But they said that they were supposed to limit Amanda's exposure to possible pathogens, that they didn't want anyone extra around. Even Mother and Daddy had to stay in a separate housing facility. They weren't allowed to stay with her in her room, like they do here."

"Someone whose immunity is suppressed is very susceptible to every little thing."

"Right. So that could have been legitimate. Or… it might have just been an excuse to keep me out of it. But why would they want to keep me out of it? I was family. I was Amanda's sister. Even if they didn't want a whole lot of people visiting and possibly infecting her, I wasn't a whole lot of people… just one. Just one more person. They could have at least let me visit her. Or wave at her through the glass. Something…"

"You're searching for answers, but there may not be any logical answers. We do what seems best at the time, and sometimes we make wrong decisions, based on fear or someone's advice at the time."

"I guess." MacKenzie motioned to one of the sandwich shop workers, indicating her glass, and the man drifted over to refill it from a glass jug, then walked away again.

"Can I ask… I didn't hear the details of what it actually was that Amanda died from," Dr. Proctor said slowly. "Did she reject the kidney?"

MacKenzie shook her head. She was happy to discuss the medical details she knew rather than why her parents had kept the transplant a secret.

"She did have malaria. They did the tests like you said and found it, and they put her on the anti-malaria drugs, but she got something called acute respiratory distress syndrome."

Dr. Proctor nodded his understanding. "Nasty thing, ARDS. Very dangerous, very difficult to reverse once it has started."

"They did everything they could, I guess, but she still couldn't get enough oxygen."

"Even when they are able to save the patient, it is very damaging. She probably would never have been off of supplemental oxygen again."

MacKenzie pictured Amanda having to lug an oxygen canister everywhere she went.

Her lively, vibrant sister would not have liked that.

13

"Mother, could I help you by going through Amanda's things?" MacKenzie asked, segueing from the discussion of upcoming events over lobster bisque at the house. "I could sort through what should be donated and what we want to keep, go through her papers to see what the accountants need for her final tax filing, that kind of thing."

Lisa scratched at an invisible mark on her spoon. "I can do that, dear. You really don't need to do that. I'll get to it."

"I'd like to help, and that's something I could do."

"I don't like the thought of you doing it by yourself. We could do it together," there was a moment of hesitation, "when I'm ready."

MacKenzie was glad to see that she was correct and that it was something her mother did not really want to do. "I can do it," she repeated. "I want to. And I can do it while you're out doing something else, so you don't have to be around and thinking about it."

Lisa stirred her bisque. "You don't want to do that all by yourself. It's a big job."

"What else do I have to do?"

"There's the big cancer fundraiser at the Main Street Landing. You said that you would help out with it." This had already been repeated several times over the previous few days, and MacKenzie had already made it clear that she was not going.

"I can't do that right now. I told you that. And I already called them to beg off. They didn't mind. They know about Amanda, so they were very understanding."

"You know I don't like you not following through on your obligations like that. That's not the way you were raised."

"Would you be understanding if one of your volunteers had just lost a family member and said she was not up to doing an event?"

"Of course, but that's not the point."

"You want to lose yourself in good works. I understand that. But I don't feel the same way. I want to think about Amanda. I want to do something for her, and for you."

Lisa nodded slowly and finally had another spoonful of her bisque. "You are so like your father."

MacKenzie was surprised. "Like Daddy?"

Walter had already gone back to his apartment in Montpelier. MacKenzie thought that, like Lisa, he just wanted to get on with his life and block out the pain.

"He's a much more passionate person than I am," Lisa explained. "He feels things so much more deeply. I know he is hurting. And he wants to do something in Amanda's memory. Something that will show what she meant to him."

"Like what?"

"I don't know. He doesn't have much to say. But I know him. When you've been married to someone for thirty years—" she stopped herself, "—even if you've been divorced for a couple of years—you understand each other on another level. One that doesn't always require words. I know him inside. What he doesn't say."

Someday, maybe MacKenzie would have a relationship like that. Someone that she could get to know on a deeper level, not just the superficial relationships she had with the men in her life so far. Someone who had passions, and wasn't just a playboy, looking for the next opportunity for a good time or to get his hands on her trust fund. She needed to get to know a man who, like her father, had a passion for the causes he was involved with.

"So, when would be a good time for me to work on Amanda's things? Are you out tomorrow?"

"For the half-marathon. Yes. They start quite early," she advised, giving MacKenzie an amused look, "And then I'll be booked up at least until six o'clock. There is a lot to go through, but if you make an early start, you might be able to get most of it done by then."

An early morning. Not just early for MacKenzie, forever sleeping the morning away, but early even for regular people. The kind of people who got up before dawn to run in the cold. MacKenzie shuddered.

"Okay. I'll plan to be up with the birds tomorrow."

It wasn't very ladylike to snort at one's daughter, but that didn't stop Lisa.

MacKenzie didn't manage to get to the family home quite as early as she had planned, but she was still there before the staff, which was quite good for her. She went up the stairs to Amanda's room. It was the house she had grown up in, so she felt perfectly comfortable there, not like she was intruding on someone else's privacy.

But she wasn't prepared for the flood of emotions and memories to hit her when she opened Amanda's door. It was the room that Amanda had had when she and MacKenzie were growing up. The room that she had started in as a baby lying in a crib that was hard for MacKenzie to reach into, because she was still a child herself and the sides were tall.

She could remember what the room had looked like then, blue with fluffy white clouds painted on the walls, white furniture, colorful mobiles and pictures, and a rocking chair in the corner where she could sit and give her baby a bottle and rock her just like a grown up.

Over the years, the decorations and the furniture had changed. A toddler bed and then a grown-up bed. Playing on the floor with Amanda and her dolls, having tea parties and fundraising events and whatever else the two of them had done to mimic their own mother's life.

It was the same bedroom as had been the sick room when Amanda was doing poorly, trapped by her disease and not able to go out to the dances and dates and other things that the kids her age were doing. The room where they had exchanged stories and secrets and grown closer and closer together as sisters.

And then Amanda as an adult. But just barely. She had been hardly more than a child and she was taken away from them. It was unfair that she wasn't allowed to get older and marry and have babies and a family of her own. She should have been allowed to have her own family. She had wanted them so much. Even when they were little, she had talked about being a mommy. She had always planned to have a dozen children and to spoil them rotten and raise them to become doctors and presidents. MacKenzie's chest hurt as she looked around the little room. Amanda would never return there. They would never share secrets and girl talk there again.

MacKenzie had thought that going through Amanda's things would be pretty easy. She had collected a lot over the year, hanging on to possessions when her grip on life itself was so tenuous. She had tried to live out her whole life in those few short years, trying everything, living life fully. MacKenzie had pictured herself sorting everything efficiently into boxes. These one for charity, these ones for keepsakes. These ones just junk to be disposed of. But it wasn't going to be that easy. Not by a long shot.

She sat down on the end of Amanda's bed and closed her eyes. She felt the room around her. Amanda was everywhere. Her smell and sense of style permeated the room. The memories and the grief were almost overwhelming.

She allowed herself thirty breaths. Thirty breaths to feel the grief and to move on and get herself under control. It wasn't long. Then she forced herself to get to her feet and go to Amanda's closet.

The rod was jammed with clothes of every color and description. MacKenzie looked over them with an unemotional eye. She picked out a few of Amanda's favorite things and laid them on the bed, smoothing out the wrinkles and tidying them up. The rest of the clothes could go. She descended to the storerooms and looked around for boxes. There were a few that seemed to be made for the job, so she carried them back upstairs and set them on the floor and removed all of the clothing that remained in the closet. It looked very empty, but it was easier to focus on what else needed to be organized.

Most of Amanda's old toys had been packed away in boxes. Amanda didn't want to let anything go and had insisted that she might want them for her own children. MacKenzie just piled the boxes to the side. The ones that had really been precious to Amanda were already out on her shelves. MacKenzie left them there.

The thing that she had really wanted to do was to look at Amanda's papers. There were a few journals and art portfolios in the closet. There were files in the drawer of her writing desk. And there was a computer.

MacKenzie sat down to go through them.

14

She felt like she was invading Amanda's privacy by opening up the journals. But Amanda was gone, and who were the journals for now that she was gone? She didn't have any children to pass them on to. MacKenzie was her family. MacKenzie was her sister, and that was who Amanda would have wanted to have the journals. Still, she felt like a peeper opening them up.

She skimmed through the entries, looking at the dates and trying to find the pages that covered the time when Amanda had her last transplant. She was sure that Amanda would not have gone on a trip without bringing a journal along with her. She always had a book near her side to make notes in when she didn't have the energy to do anything else.

She tried not to look for her own name. She didn't want to hear that Amanda had been disappointed with her or that she'd held bitter feelings toward her able-bodied sister. The one who could do whatever she wanted without ever being slowed down by a body that was constantly sick and tired. Amanda had spent so much time in the hospital and MacKenzie had continued to go to parties and events and to volunteer for fundraisers that her sister was too sick to attend even as an honored guest.

MacKenzie found a series of entries leading up to the secret transplant. Amanda was excited and scared, hoping that things would turn out alright but terrified of what conditions she would find and whether she would catch an infection or reject the stranger's organ. They had been given glossy brochures showing pictures of the spotless, shining hospital. White floors and mint green walls, and windows that looked out onto a gleaming white beach and azure blue sea.

"I can't believe that I'm going there for a kidney," Amanda's voice spoke to her from the pages. "It looks like a spa as much as a hospital. Somewhere you go on vacation and relax where everybody dotes on you and spoils you with massages and five-star meals. It is a beautiful place. I really couldn't ask for more."

Amanda had read the profile of her kidney donor that her mother had mentioned, the young woman who was coming from Germany (not Sweden) to give Amanda the gift of life. She was a young person with an amazing giving heart. "Or a giving kidney." Amanda's words brought a giggle from MacKenzie's lips. There was a margin doodle of a kidney, fat and red and healthy looking. Amanda's new kidney, to replace the one that MacKenzie had given her, which had failed before it should have. MacKenzie had been so wrapped up in her own life that she hadn't even known how poorly Amanda had been doing. MacKenzie should have known. She should have been aware that her baby sister was again sitting for hours in the hospital beside a machine, just so she could survive from one week to the next.

Her eyes were caught by her own name on the page. "It's so hard not to talk about it with MacKenzie. But Mother says she would worry too much, and that it's best to just let her live her own life. She doesn't need to know that the graft failed. Pretty soon I'll have a brand-new kidney and she'll never know the difference. But I do wish she could come. It won't be the same without her there."

MacKenzie closed her eyes and let herself remember when they had been in the hospital before, recovering from the donation. MacKenzie couldn't believe how sore she was. It looked so simple on the videos and in the written descriptions. Just open her up, gently remove the kidney, pass it to the team working on Amanda, suture the dead-end vessels, and sew MacKenzie up again. The work done on Amanda's side was much more complicated, making sure that all of the vessels and ducts were connected together so that she would have good blood flow and the kidney could do its job.

But MacKenzie had felt like they had thrown her down the stairs. She was convinced the first few days that they must have dropped her when transferring her from the gurney to her bed. Every movement hurt. The anesthesia had made her throw up and every time she retched, it hurt like someone was trying to rip the missing kidney from her body with their bare hands. Or claws. Amanda had seemed to recover from it more quickly than MacKenzie, in spite of all of the drugs they had to give her to make sure she didn't reject the organ.

"We'll get Mother to read to us when she comes," Amanda promised, when MacKenzie was bored to tears, but too sore and scatterbrained to do anything about it. Even television seemed too difficult, her brain sluggish after the procedure, either because of the anesthesia or because her body was in shock and trying to heal, stealing blood and life force from her brain. "Only we'll get her to read Cosmo instead of Trixie Belden."

MacKenzie remembered cuddling with Amanda at bedtime while Lisa read to them, trying to find books that would entertain them both in spite of the six-year gap in their ages. The adventures of the girl sleuth Trixie Belden had been a good choice. MacKenzie liked her better than Nancy Drew, but could never seem to solve the mystery before the solution was presented.

After the transplant, Lisa had read to them, sitting between their two beds and first holding MacKenzie's hand and stroking her hair while she read, and then switching to Amanda.

"My two sweet girls. I'm so proud of both of you."

***

MacKenzie put Amanda's journals to the side and went to her desk. She opened the file drawer and looked through the file folders neatly labeled in Amanda's careful, round printing. It would be easy to pull out what the accountant would need for Amanda's terminal tax return. There was also a file labeled "Will" and it took only a glance to see that it was, in fact, Amanda's last will and testament. MacKenzie didn't take it out to look at it. She knew that Amanda didn't have any of her own wealth. She had been supported by a trust fund, like Amanda, but that trust had ended when she died and wasn't hers to give to anyone else. The only thing that Amanda had to divide up were her personal effects. She didn't even have her own car. MacKenzie promised herself that she would look at the will before throwing anything out. She didn't want to get rid of any personal items that Amanda had meant for someone else.

She continued to look through the files, and she found a series of thin folders that appeared to pertain to Amanda's medical care. She drew them out and laid them on the desk.

Forsberg Transplant Care Clinic.

MacKenzie opened the folder and saw the glossy brochure that Amanda had referred to. Thick, shiny pages showing the beautiful, spa-like hospital where Amanda would get her new kidney. It did look like paradise. Somewhere that MacKenzie might consider taking a vacation if she wanted to pamper herself rather than getting away from all of the suffocating attention she already faced in her day-to-day life. MacKenzie's eyes skimmed over the flowery description of the transplant hospital. She turned the pages, looking for information on the doctors and the owners of the clinic. There was an office in New Jersey. The names she did find were unfamiliar to her.

Eventually, she turned the advertising brochure over to look at the other documents in the folder. Instructions on the logistics of going to the island. Travel documents needed, what to pack, what procedure to follow once Amanda got there. Everything was very detailed and orderly, reassuring the reader that they knew what they were doing and were professional and cared about the patient's health. She had at first pictured a third-world shack with flies buzzing around, lines of people waiting, and an inexperienced back-woods doctor butchering the patients, but the brochure and other documents were reassuring. It was a professionally-run organization, not just a fly-by-night scam job.

She leafed through the other documents in the folder and found a page about the donor.

Her name was given as Katrina. No last name, because the organ dona-tion industry didn't give identifying information for donors. Apparently not even foreign transplants that took place on remote tropical islands. There was a handwritten form filled in with her answers to questions about her back-ground, family, and why she wanted to donate an organ to a stranger she would never meet. Clipped to the front of it was a photograph. A beautiful blond young woman smiling at the camera. She exuded health and vitality and the unselfish love she had for the recipient of her organ donation.

On one hand, MacKenzie could understand why the woman would do what she had done. After all, MacKenzie had done the same thing herself. But on the other, MacKenzie hadn't been donating to a stranger. She had been giving life to her sister. It wasn't unselfish. It wasn't anonymous. She didn't travel halfway around the world to a third-world country to give up a piece of herself. The recovery from donation had not been easy or without complications, and she was sure that Katrina must have been given the same warnings about the hazards as MacKenzie had. It could fail. She could get an infection. She could react to the anesthesia. There was a risk that she would die while trying to give life to her sister, and there was the possibility that it wouldn't even take, but instead Amanda's body would simply reject it as a foreign object and refuse to support it.

It had all worked out in the end, as had Amanda's second transplant. And they owed it all to a stranger named Katrina.

15

MacKenzie decided to takethe files on the transplant home with her. She could examine them in more detail there, and look up the various doctors and contacts that she could find associated with the clinic on Google. No one would miss the papers. They weren't needed for anything else now that Amanda was gone. She poked through the other files for anything else that might be helpful. Then there was Amanda's computer.

It was a laptop, the only thing that was practical for Amanda, since she spent so much time in bed and in the hospital. With a laptop computer, she could entertain herself wherever she was.

MacKenzie booted it up. She typed her own name into the password box and the Windows desktop arranged itself on the screen. Colorful icons for a number of games were arranged in neat columns. Amanda had a lot of time to while away, and she didn't always have the energy to put into anything requiring brainpower. MacKenzie opened the File Explorer and looked through the folders. Some more journal entries, little bits of poetry, notes that Amanda had written to remind herself of upcoming events. Lists of things to do when she got home or things that she wanted Lisa to buy for her or bring her from home when she was in the hospital.

A little slice of her life.

When MacKenzie left for the day, everything was neatly arranged and awaiting Lisa's return. Boxes were labeled. The files that were needed for Amanda's estate were laid out on the desk. Amanda's favorite things were still on the shelves and in the closet, but ninety-five percent of her possessions were ready to be donated or otherwise disposed of. Lisa could decide what she wanted to do with the rest in due time.

MacKenzie took the files with her. And Amanda's computer. Her mother wasn't going to use it, after all. No one had any use for it, and it was not mentioned in Amanda's will. So MacKenzie might as well take it and get some use out of it. She could play solitaire in bed and remember Amanda.

She said goodbye to the kitchen and cleaning staff that she passed on her way out of the house and drove herself back to her apartment.

It seemed cold and lonely after being in the warm, bustling house that she had grown up in. She needed some company, and she didn't really care who it was.

Well, not Roger. Other than that, pretty much anyone would do.

MacKenzie awoke to her ringing phone. At first, she was thrown back to the period of time before Amanda's death, back before the malaria attacks, and for a blissful instant she didn't remember what had happened since. But never again would it be her mother calling to let her know that they were on their way to the hospital, or asking whether MacKenzie would have time to meet with Amanda at the park or some other place where she could visit and get some time outside the house without it being too taxing on her system. MacKenzie had always said yes.

At least she had that. She didn't have to face the guilt of having turned Amanda away and pursued other occupations, interests, or relationships. She had always come to the call to support Amanda. She had always been there when Amanda asked for her, and many times when she hadn't.

At least she had that.

MacKenzie lay there for a minute without moving, trying to get back that instant of comfortable innocence before she had remembered Amanda's death. She reached over to her bedside table and found the phone handset resting in the base where it belonged. She picked it up and pressed the button to answer it.

"Hello?"

"MacKenzie." Her mother. Who else would be calling her so early in the morning? All of her friends knew she didn't get up before noon if she could help it. There was a note of worry in Lisa's voice. A little bit of panic that MacKenzie didn't quite understand. Amanda was dead, after all. Lisa couldn't be worrying about her. And any concerns over Amanda's estate could wait. She didn't need to rush into anything. "I wanted to thank you for doing all of that work in cleaning out Amanda's room."

For that, Lisa needed to wake her up? But MacKenzie knew that wasn't the reason. This was just the small talk. The real request would come after. When they were both comfortable.

"You're welcome. I'm just glad there was something I could do for you."

"It was a big help."

"Good, I'm glad."

"There's just one thing, MacKenzie. There were some files missing…"

"Files?"

"Some medical files. Did you take those with you?"

MacKenzie considered her answer. Her brain was still groggy with sleep, but she sensed the worry behind Lisa's words. Almost panic. Why would she be panicking about MacKenzie taking Amanda's medical files?

"I picked some stuff up," she admitted slowly, feeling her way through the explanation. "Just some stuff about the clinic that she went to. For the second transplant. I wanted to learn a little bit more about them. We really should consider making a donation to them in Amanda's name, don't you think?"

"What? Yes, of course, that's certainly something to consider. I need you to bring those files back, MacKenzie. That's personal medical information of Amanda's and it really shouldn't be out of our hands."

"Why not? It isn't like she needs it anymore. I just wanted to learn more about what happened. I don't understand why you kept it a secret from me."

"It wasn't a secret; we just didn't want to upset you."

"Then why won't you talk about it now?"

"We thought it would give her another ten years. Now it seems like… what was the point? If you're right and she was bitten by a mosquito because we took her to that clinic… I just can't talk about it, MacKenzie. It's too upsetting. But I need those files back."

"Why? Why do you need them?"

"There is information in there that the accountant will need. Those expenses need to be documented. We put a lot of money into that trip and the surgery. He needs all of those files to justify it."

MacKenzie sighed. She was too tired and full of grief to find any argument. She hadn't thought that anyone would miss the files. But in truth, she didn't have any right to them and if her parents needed them, she had no excuse not to give them back. "Okay. I'll drop them by later today."

"I need them right away."

"I need a few more hours of sleep. Then I'll bring them by."

There were a few seconds of silence from Lisa. "Fine. Please make sure you bring them today. Don't forget."

MacKenzie grunted. "Love you, Mother. I'll see you later."

She ended the call. Beside her, the covers stirred as the man next to her shifted his weight and turned toward her.

"MacKenzie."

"What?"

Christopher Marsh cleared a raspy throat. "Everything okay?"

MacKenzie put the handset into the base and turned to cuddle up against his warm body. "Yeah. It's fine."

"That Lady Cole-Kirsch?"

"Yes. Just need to take her some papers later today."

"You don't need to do it now?"

"No."

"Good." He pulled her closer, and she snuggled her face against the warm smooth skin in the hollow of his neck. He'd been a lot more fun than Roger Milford. Considerate too. A winning combination. She closed her eyes and breathed in his scent, seeking the return of sleep.

<hr>

It was late when she woke up, and she knew it. She had planned to be up by noon, but without having an alarm set, and warm and cozy in bed with Christopher, she had just kept sleeping. She could still get the files back before Lisa got home from her regular spa appointment, but MacKenzie had wanted to copy them before she returned them. It was the best of both worlds. Lisa could have the files back right away for her accountant, but MacKenzie could still review them at her leisure and refer back to anything she needed to later on down the line as her research progressed.

"Where can I get something photocopied quickly?" she asked Christopher as he sat down on the couch to tie his shoes.

"Library is always a possibility. There's one not too far away from here."

MacKenzie remembered the dim library she had used while in high school and the monstrous old photocopiers there. She shook her head. She'd be there all day if she were forced to use one of those persnickety old machines. She'd end up with the librarian breathing down her back and people waiting for her, and some of her copies were bound to get jammed up in the machine, which became a privacy risk if she needed someone to help her to clear them or if she threw them in the garbage there.

"No?" Christopher considered. "What about a business services store? Kinko's, UPS, something like that."

"Yeah. They'd be quick and have state-of-the-art equipment, wouldn't they? In and out of there in a few minutes…"

"Sure. They want to get people through as quickly as they can, they've always got top-line machines."

"That's what I'll do, then." MacKenzie hauled out the Yellow Pages directory and flipped through the ads for the business services stores, looking for one that was close to her, or at least between her apartment and the family home.

She paused for a moment as she thought about the family home. The only person who was left there was Lisa, bouncing around the empty house like she was in a pinball machine. Walter was no longer there. Amanda was gone. MacKenzie had moved out early on. So now it was just Lisa and the staff in that big, empty house. Did Lisa mind? She must feel the loneliness of it. Or maybe if she worked hard enough, it would eat up the time and she would just go to bed exhausted at the end of the day, unable to worry about anything because she passed out as soon as her head hit the pillow.

"Do you think she's lonely?" she asked Christopher.

"Who?"

"My mother."

He pulled his winter coat on thoughtfully. "Well… I would imagine so. With your dad out of town so much…"

"He's not living there anymore."

"Not at all?" Christopher considered it. "Sounds like it might be a good time for her to start seeing someone."

"A therapist?"

"No… a date." He gave her a knowing smile. "Having a man around can be very comforting when you are lonely, you know."

She gave him a little swat as he headed toward the door. He turned to pull her into a bear hug, lifted her off her feet for a moment, then gave her a vigorous kiss.

"Give me a call next time you're feeling lonely, Mistress Kirsch."

He gave her another quick squeeze, and then he was gone. MacKenzie stood there with a stupid, sloppy grin on her face for a minute, still feeling the tingle of his touch, then gathered together the files to take back to Lisa.

16

MacKenzie left her copy of Amanda's files in her car and took the originals into the house to give to her mother. She had not managed to beat Lisa back to the house after her spa appointment, and Lisa was apparently watching for her arrival. She was at the door to let MacKenzie in even before she got up the front walkway.

She didn't look well and relaxed after her spa treatment. She was usually pink and happy after an appointment, but she didn't look like any of that. Her face seemed dry and mapped with lines that hadn't been there before. She was pale, almost ashen in appearance. MacKenzie hadn't seen her look so bad since Amanda's death. She'd always looked presentable and healthy and as if she were in control of everything. Maybe it was just because she had been wearing makeup before, but it had been cleaned off during her spa treatment and she hadn't yet reapplied it, letting her pores breathe for a while. Maybe this was what she had looked like under the layers of makeup ever since Amanda had gone back into the hospital.

"Mother." MacKenzie put one arm around her, the one that was not holding a stack of file folders. "Are you okay?" She bussed Lisa's cheek. "You look like… you've had a rough day."

Lisa looked at her for a minute as if she didn't know what to say at first. Then she shook her head. "No, it's been fine. I just wanted to make sure that you got everything back to me today."

"You look worried. Did you really think that I wouldn't?"

Lisa used both hands to pull the files from MacKenzie's grasp. "Thank goodness. I'll just go put these away."

She turned and walked away from MacKenzie, hurrying across the front hall and up the grand staircase toward the bedrooms. MacKenzie stood watching her, stunned by Lisa's brusque manner. It would appear that she had, in fact, believed that MacKenzie would not bring the files back. Why? Was she so concerned about whatever deductions the accountant would be able to claim on the terminal tax return? Was she worried about having to pay? There was plenty of money left in the trust account. So why was Lisa so concerned about the money?

Lisa returned a few minutes later, running her hands down the front of her skirt. MacKenzie wasn't sure whether her was smoothing out wrinkles in the skirt or wiping something off of her hands. Lisa still seemed stressed, but she made an attempt at natural conversation.

"Are you able to stay for a visit? Not off to anything right away?"

MacKenzie looked back toward her car. She actually wanted to spend some more time going through the copies of Amanda's files. Lisa's behavior was making her more curious about what exactly had happened.

"Why don't we have a drink?" she suggested, motioning to the sitting room off of the hall, where there was a well-stocked sideboard.

Lisa wasn't much of a drinker, but she acquiesced. "Yes, certainly."

It wasn't yet five o'clock, the generally accepted hour for drinking to begin. And Lisa always observed the five o'clock rule. MacKenzie made no comment on this. It would be rude to point it out, especially when it was so obvious that Lisa was worried about something. They sat down in the sitting room after pouring out their preferred drinks.

They didn't talk about Amanda or the files.

***

MacKenzie did not tell her mother that she was flying to New Jersey to check out the transplant clinic. After seeing her nearly melt down over the files, she wasn't about to tempt fate by offering the information that she was digging deeper into the clinic to satisfy herself that everything was being done honestly and aboveboard. If they were everything they appeared to be on the surface, maybe she could put it to bed and stop worrying about it. But until she saw it for herself, she just wasn't sure that she was going to be able to sleep at night. She kept seeing Amanda in her mind, gasping for breath, so pale and exhausted from the recurring fevers. Could they have avoided that? Were there warning signs that Lisa and Walter should have seen and not jumped into the foreign transplant with both feet? They had wanted Amanda to be better and to have good quality of life, but had they moved too quickly and been too eager to take what appeared to be a good solution? They could afford to throw whatever money they needed to at the problem, jumping ahead of those who were patiently waiting in line in the US. Unethical, maybe, but they obviously hadn't believed it to be illegal or dangerous.

A year later, Amanda was dead, when she should have had more time.

But who could predict what twists and turns her health would take? It wasn't like her path had ever been particularly straight and predictable.

It was a ninety-minute flight, which gave her time to look through the files to get everything cemented into her memory. She needed to be able to talk like she had been aware of everything that was going on at the time it had happened, not like she was a latecomer, just catching up on it now.

She was good at social talk. She was sure she could pull it off.

She realized looking at the time that she wasn't going to be able to get to the clinic before it closed, so she was going to have to find a hotel and the sundries that she needed for an overnight stay, and then visit the clinic the next day when there was plenty of time to talk to the bigwigs, get a tour, and whatever else she could convince them to do. She was going to be a big fish, and she was sure that they were not above being persuaded by the promise of a large endowment.

<hr>

Not knowing a lot of people in New Jersey, she was going to have a lonely night. She couldn't think of anyone she could call on the spur of the moment like she could in Burlington. And however much she didn't want to have to face the darkness alone, she wasn't going to stoop to picking up strangers in a strange town.

She went to bed early, got very little sleep, and rose at a decent hour to get herself ready for her appearance. She was going to use every devious trick she knew to get their attention and convince them that she was the answer to their fundraising prayers. Even if they didn't know that they needed any more funding, she was going to convince them that they did.

She pulled up in front of the clinic in a shiny black town car with a uniformed chauffeur. They didn't have any way of knowing that he was just an hourly hire rather than her own personal driver. She waited while he walked around the car to open the door for her. MacKenzie slid gracefully out of the big car and minced her way toward the big front doors of the Forsberg clinic. It was a nice place, but she could make it better. Classier.

Serving an even more prestigious clientele. She fixed these goals in her mind and stopped at the door, waiting for either her chauffeur or one of the clinic's staff to jump in and open it for her. A receptionist stared at her for a moment in consternation, then jumped up and trotted around her desk to get to the front doors and open them for MacKenzie. MacKenzie deigned to nod and smile at her. She swept the waiting room with a glance and did not choose to sit down. Instead, she stood stiffly a few feet from the reception desk, waiting for the receptionist to sit back down and serve her.

"Welcome to the Forsberg Transplant Care Clinic," the young lady said brightly. "How can we help you today?"

MacKenzie was wearing white gloves. She pulled each of the fingertips in turn to inch the gloves off of her fingers. "I would like to speak to the Executive Director."

"I don't know if Dr. Dutton is going to be in this morning. Did you have an appointment?"

"I do not," MacKenzie said succinctly, as if that had no bearing on the situation and they should have known that she was going to show up and been ready for her anyway.

"I see… can I get your name, ma'am? I'll see what I can do."

"Miss MacKenzie Kirsch."

The receptionist wrote it down and looked nervously up at MacKenzie, wondering if it was a name that she should know. She swallowed strenuously. "And will Dr. Dutton know you? Are you a friend or a patient?"

"My sister was one of his patients. I am considering a substantial endowment for the clinic in her name. I assume he'll want to hear what I have to say about that."

"I'm sure she will," the receptionist agreed quickly. "Could I… get you a coffee and… show you to a conference room, where you'll be more comfortable?"

MacKenzie gave an imperious nod and was shown to a somber boardroom furnished with heavy dark wood furnishings. She sank into one of the well-padded chairs and indicated that the receptionist should place her coffee *there.*

The little receptionist must have been working frantically once MacKenzie was out of the way. It was only half an hour later that a tall, blond woman knocked lightly on the door of the boardroom and glided in to talk to her.

"Miss Kirsch, I can't tell you how delighted I am to see you. I am Dr. Mildred Dutton and I'm the Executive Director of the Forsberg Clinic."

MacKenzie didn't stand up to greet her. And she didn't shake Dr. Dutton's hand, but merely held out a limp hand as if she expected Dr. Dutton to kiss it. Dr. Mildred Dutton gave it an awkward squeeze and let it go. She seated herself at the end of the table, at an angle to MacKenzie rather than across from her in a position that might be taken as adversarial.

"Do tell me how Amanda is doing," Dr. Dutton encouraged, giving MacKenzie a brilliant smile.

MacKenzie didn't say anything. She let the silence draw out uncomfortably long. She readjusted the position of her white gloves and then finally answered.

"Amanda recently passed away."

Dr. Dutton's face expressed shock. She covered her hand. "Oh, dear! I'm so sorry, I had no idea. Please accept my deepest condolences."

MacKenzie gave a single nod.

"I am considering giving the clinic an endowment in Amanda's name. A rather sizable endowment, if everything seems to be in order. I believe that the clinic can do great things, if only they are well-funded. Our organ donation system here in the US is sadly lacking and in terrible need of reform. In the meantime, I believe that only by making foreign donations available to more people can we get rid of the bottleneck here in the States and make surgery a viable option for everybody who needs it."

"Yes, yes," Dr. Dutton agreed enthusiastically. "That is exactly what we believe here at the Forsberg Clinic. You can't know how much a donation like that would mean to us. There are so many people who are in need of a transplant."

"It is an untenable situation," MacKenzie agreed with a slight shudder.

"How can I help you? You must have questions for me. I don't know how involved you were at the time that Amanda received her… uh… kidney?"

"Kidney," MacKenzie agreed with a stern nod. "This was her second one. Of course, the waiting list here was three or four years, and there was no way that we could wait for that long."

"Oh, of course, I understand. No one who has the means should have to sit around waiting to be called up from a list when there are organs available from all over the world right now. It is vital that we reach as many people as we can."

"I was out of the country myself for much of the time that Amanda was in the hospital and going through these challenges," MacKenzie, said, fudging the dates of her time in Europe to cover any ignorance she showed of the situation. "But Amanda told me so much by email and on the phone. I can't tell you how excited she was to visit your overseas clinic. She was so impressed by the presentations she was shown, the pictures of your hospital, and by the donor she was matched with. It was a very exciting time for her."

Dr. Dutton nodded, smiling widely. "I'm so glad. We try to take very good care of our patients. It's important to us that they are treated in a clean, modern facility and that there is no extra stress brought on by facing the unknown. We want them to know what is going to happen along every step of the way so that they feel fully prepared."

"Yes," MacKenzie gave another regal nod, enjoying her role. "Would it be at all possible to have a tour of this facility? It would allow me to see how the money would be best put to use, and what the opportunities are for memorializing Amanda and her story."

"Of course. I would be happy to take you around myself."

Without further conversation, MacKenzie stood up. She held herself ramrod straight and waited for Dr. Dutton to stand and begin the tour. The director looked startled and uncertain for just a moment, but then moved immediately toward the door. She led MacKenzie out the door, and then they walked side by side for the tour. Dr. Dutton led her down a hallway filled with portraits of various doctors and donors who had set up the clinic or contributed to it in some big way.

All men, MacKenzie noted. The new director was a woman, but she was obviously working in a man's world. They could use some female faces on the walls.

Dr. Dutton led her through corridors to family meeting rooms, examination rooms, offices with computers and big screens, a library full of thick, heavy tomes, and eventually back to the boardroom where they had begun.

17

MacKenzie looked around the boardroom at various pictures of happy, healthy organ recipients with their stories on plaques, the gold- and platinum-level donors to the clinic, and a couple of abstract shapes that she assumed were supposed to be awards for all that the clinic was doing in the donation industry. She took a thin folder out of her attache and placed it on the table in front of her, closed, the contents out of sight. Dr. Dutton sat down, leaning toward her like they were friends gossiping over luncheon.

"What other information can I give you today, Ms. Kirsch? Do you have questions?"

"Of course." MacKenzie gave a curt nod. "I would like to see the curricula vitae of each of your directors, senior officers, and top surgeons. I would like to see your five- and ten-year business plans and hear about what projects and expansions you are considering and what kind of funding they will need. I would like to talk to some of your other donors," she nodded to the donors wall, "and also some of your organ recipients." She saw the concern in Dr. Dutton's eyes, and went on smoothly. "Of course, I understand that not every donor or organ recipient will want to talk to me. I'm sure you have some who would endorse your clinic and share their thoughts with me."

Dr. Dutton sat back, nodding, her lips pressed tightly together. "Of course. It will take me a little while to get that information together for you."

MacKenzie looked significantly at the promotional material on the walls.

Clearly, they already had lists of donors and of transplant recipients who were willing to brag up the clinic. And the curricula vitae and business plans should be things that were already prepared and on hand for donors and investors.

"Really. How much time will you need?" MacKenzie looked at her watch as if considering her busy schedule.

"Umm…" Dr. Dutton didn't like being put to the test. She obviously wanted to put MacKenzie off with vague promises and to have the time to discuss MacKenzie with her associates and get together a package that was tailored to her. She didn't like being rushed into anything, but MacKenzie had swept in and demanded her time and attention. She probably wanted to step back and take a breath and to consider MacKenzie's requests and promises at her leisure. But that wasn't going to get MacKenzie closer to finding out everything she could about the clinic. She wanted Dr. Dutton to feel rushed. She wanted her to be a little anxious and feel like she had to pull the materials together immediately or she might lose a big donation.

"I would like at least a few hours to make sure I have everything together in a presentable format and that the people whose names I give you have agreed to talk to you and have been given a heads-up that you may call them…"

MacKenzie shook her head. "That's not acceptable. Why don't you give me a copy of your usual investor package?"

Dr. Dutton nodded. "Of course. I can get that for your right away, and then I can get back to you on these other requests…"

"You really should have this information on hand for when donors have questions."

"Of course, and we do, but they are going through some changes right now, and I wouldn't want to give you a product that was half-baked or was going to change tomorrow. I'm sure you want the most reliable, up-to-date information, and for that I need to touch base with our staff and see where we are on it…"

MacKenzie looked at her watch again. "You can get the rest to me this afternoon?"

Dr. Dutton hesitated. Her eyes darted around the room, checking in at the donor wall and at the transplant recipient endorsements. Calculating how much time it would take to call people to warn them about the big donor who might be calling them. "Yes. Of course. That shouldn't be a problem. Where should I send this information? To the address we have on file for your sister?"

"No. Do *not* send it there," MacKenzie said firmly. "I do not live in my mother's home and it will not get to me if you send it there. You can send me an email with the information, and then send me the hard copy…" MacKenzie picked up her purse and found a pad of sticky notes to write her information on. Maybe she should have had business cards ready to give the woman. Her mother had cards, more calling cards than business cards, but MacKenzie had never seen the point in ordering any. She went to functions that she had been invited to, so the people there already knew who she was and how to reach her. Why do extra work?

She wrote slowly and deliberately to make sure that everything was legible so that Dr. Dutton wouldn't have any excuse for not getting her what she had asked for. And to increase the tension that Dr. Dutton was already feeling. She pulled off the sticky note and handed it to Dr. Dutton.

"I will get the investor package from you now, and then you'll have the rest to me this afternoon," she verified.

"Uh—yes, of course. I'll pull that together as quickly as I can. Let me just get our usual package…" She got up and hurried out the boardroom door, leaving MacKenzie sitting by herself again. She went over to the donor wall and took a couple of pictures to collect all of the names of the donors. She went along the transplant recipient wall, taking a picture of each of the transplant recipients with their plaques. It would be interesting to see what information she got from Dr. Dutton and how it correlated with what was on display.

MacKenzie left the clinic with the package that Dr. Dutton had provided her tucked into her file folder and attache. She saw the same brochure that had been in Amanda's files, but there was additional information that she hadn't seen before. The clinic's financials, Board of Directors' bios, and so on. Not quite what she had asked for, but it was a start and Dr. Dutton promised her that they would provide pretty much whatever she asked for. They obviously knew the reputation of the Kirsch family and had no doubt that if MacKenzie said that a donation was forthcoming, it would be provided, assuming she was satisfied with the information she received.

She went back to the hotel. She had taken Amanda's laptop computer with her on the flight in the hopes that she would find something interesting on the hard drive, but then she had done other things on the flight and before bed. If she could get an internet connection at the hotel's business center, she could conduct some of the research she needed to do without having to go home to her own computer. Mobile technology was a wonderful thing.

Once there, she started plugging the names of the various doctors, managers, and directors at the clinic into Google to see what background information she could find on them. Most of what she came across was promotional material put out by the clinic, but there were, at least, a few news articles that had obviously not been paid for by the Forsberg Clinic.

MacKenzie tapped her pen on the computer, thinking about it. What she really needed to do was to find out what kind of reputation they had in the medical community. For that, she might be able to bend Dr. Proctor's ear again, if he wasn't tired of her questions.

When she had exhausted her internet research strategies, she closed the browser and again started going through the files on Amanda's laptop. She clicked on the Pictures folder and saw a long list of automatically named photographs. Probably taken with Amanda's digital camera or phone and then imported so she could see them on her desktop to view them and rename them. But she had apparently never gotten around to renaming them. MacKenzie started opening them one at a time. There was probably a better way to look through them quickly, but she wasn't very computer savvy, and she had the time to browse. She assumed that Dr. Dutton's additional package of information wouldn't arrive until late afternoon or early evening, the very latest Dr. Dutton could get away with and still claim to have met the imposed deadline.

There were random pictures of family and friends at different events. A number of them were obviously taken from the hospital, and MacKenzie looked at the dates, knowing it was going to be the interval before Amanda's transplant. She had obviously been much more ill than she had ever let on to MacKenzie. A cloud of sadness settled over her as she looked through the pictures, full of smiles and encouragement. People who had visited her at the hospital, showing up with flowers, cookies, pizza, and whatever else they thought would help to cheer Amanda up. MacKenzie knew that much of the time, Amanda had the nurses take her gifts to other units, especially pediatric, to help cheer up the patients who didn't have anything. That was just the kind of person she was.

Then there were pictures of the interior of the airport, out the window of what was obviously a privately chartered plane, pictures of Lisa and Walter sleeping while Amanda sat up, too excited and jittery or feeling too ill to sleep. MacKenzie looked at the pictures of her sleeping parents, shaking her head. Why hadn't they told her? Why hadn't she been there? She could have been, would have been if they had only told her what was going on.

A few pictures of white beaches and blue water, just like in the brochure. Then the interior of a building. MacKenzie leaned closer to the screen to examine it. It was not the pristine hospital that was shown in the glossy brochure. She tried to analyze it. The rooms appeared to be built from boards that had been painted white, not any kind of drywall, wallboard, cinderblock, or even cement building that MacKenzie had ever seen. She thought that there was glass in the windows, but she couldn't be sure. Even if all of the windows were covered, it obviously was not up to the same standards as first world construction, and MacKenzie imagined that insects could move in and out pretty freely. It wasn't quite the spotlessly hygienic environment that Walter had implied when he said that there was no way that Amanda could have been bitten by a malaria-infected mosquito.

But it didn't appear to be the hospital. Just somewhere they had stayed while preparing for the surgery. Mattresses on single, low bed frames. At least they were not rush mats on a dirt floor. MacKenzie imagined that most of the population of the tropical island probably lived in hand-built shelters with few modern amenities.

Her parents looked reasonably happy in the pictures, and one or two had been taken by Lisa or Walter, because Amanda was in the picture as well, looking pale and anxious, but smiling brightly. Getting ready for her transplant. The time was creeping closer and, having been through one transplant before, Amanda had some idea of what to expect and how she was going to feel after it was done.

There were a couple of dark, difficult-to-make-out photos, and then more outdoor and airplane pictures, apparently on their way back to the United States.

MacKenzie went back to the dark photos. She double-clicked the first one to open it in a photo editor, and then clicked on the brightness slider to try to make it a little more clear.

She stared at the dark, grainy photo, trying to process what she saw.

18

Back in Vermont, Dr. Proctor Insisted that this time he would choose the place they were to meet and would pay for the dinner. It wasn't any sandwich shop this time. But in spite of the fact that Dr. Proctor had chosen dinner at one of the higher-class restaurants, he was heartily professional with MacKenzie and didn't act like he thought it was just an excuse to have a date with her. They sat at one of the tables in the center of the restaurant, not a booth in the corner, and he didn't lean toward her or use an intimate tone when he spoke to her. MacKenzie relaxed and stopped worrying that he was going to think that she had a crush on him and was just using her sister's death as an excuse to see him.

They chatted about safe, social topics for the first little while. MacKenzie didn't really expect anything else different. He inquired after Lisa and asked how MacKenzie was doing and actually pressed for an answer instead of just accepting a social, 'oh, I'm fine.'

"Nobody is fine after their sister dies, MacKenzie. Don't blow me off. Are you okay? Is there anything I can do to help you?"

"You already are. Or you're going to tonight. I don't know… I think I'm handling it okay. I don't want to be alone, because then I start thinking about her and crying, and I don't want to spend all my nights crying. Makes for a terrible headache when I get up."

He smiled gently, nodded his understanding.

"And then this stuff with the clinic and the transplant… I don't know. I suppose it might not be the healthiest pursuit. I want to know what happened and what went wrong and why everybody is being so hush-hush about it. I mean… they always did try to give Amanda her privacy and dignity, letting her decide what she wanted to tell people and what she didn't. Not like a lot of parents who think they can just broadcast everything they want to about someone without their say-so. So, on one hand I get it, but…"

"But this is different," Proctor suggested.

"Yes. It is. I read some of what Amanda wrote in her journal, and she wasn't the one who decided not to tell me anything. It wasn't her trying to keep me from worrying. It was Mom and Dad. Why? I don't think there is something inherently bad about going out of the country for a transplant, do you?"

Dr. Proctor tipped his head slightly, maybe considering what he thought about it and maybe a sort of a shrug. "That's not an easy question to answer."

"You think there is something wrong with going out of the country?"

"It isn't exactly ethical to work around the system, jumping ahead of people who have been waiting longer than you have, using money to get what you want. Transplants are very difficult for the working poor to afford as it is, so they're already out of the running. So, the wealthier individuals are the ones who are on the list. The ones who are very wealthy and savvy know that they can buy their way onto waiting lists all around the country, increasing their odds, especially if they research what areas don't have a lot of people waiting for transplants ahead of them. And then the ones who have the kind of wealth your family does…"

"More money than sense," MacKenzie contributed.

"Not necessarily," Proctor said with a chuckle. "Well, those who are extremely wealthy can afford to go to private clinics overseas. They pay a huge premium to get what they want. They jump ahead of everyone else who is waiting."

"But on the other hand, it means that they're not competing for the same organs. They're not jumping ahead of the other people who are waiting, they're jumping right out of the pool."

Dr. Proctor nodded. "True. But the next problem is, how ethical are the practices that are being used in those other countries? Are they paying poor people to donate what organs and tissues they can in order to have a better chance of survival? Here, you can't actually pay someone for their organs, but in other countries, they don't have the same bias against paying donors."

"But it's a free market… They'll pay what the market will support… and if it helps poor families to get somewhere in life, is that a bad thing? If it's a way for them to climb up out of the slums…"

He nodded. "There are many different ways of looking at it. Different people have different perspectives. But we shouldn't leave it up to the people who need the organs. Because they are not going to have the same ethical standards as someone who doesn't have skin in the game, so to speak."

MacKenzie nodded and had a sip of her wine.

"But we know that's not the case here anyway. The donor came from Germany. They didn't pay her, they just paid for her expenses to get there and her medical care for the procedure. She did it out of the goodness of her heart, because she wanted to give something back, to give people like Amanda a chance at life that they wouldn't have had otherwise."

"I'm sure that helped them in making the decision to proceed. I would expect your father to take some of those things into consideration… if he was able to look at the situation dispassionately."

MacKenzie sighed. She wasn't sure what to think on that point. Her father was known as a 'white hat' lobbyist, meaning that the people he represented and the causes that he lobbied for at the senate were charities and not-for-profits. He spoke out against the 'black hats,' who were working for the corporations, sometimes mega-corporations, and were perceived as only being in it for the money. Walter could say that he was working for the good guys and trying to make the world a better place. But she also knew him to be a shrewd man, one who didn't forget his own needs or those of his family.

He didn't forget himself in service. He always remembered himself. He was number one. And his family fell somewhere behind that; MacKenzie wasn't sure what order they came in, but he was a devoted family man. Knowing that Amanda needed a kidney, and that throwing some money at the problem would make it go away, would he really have considered the ethics of the situation? Or would he just have taken the opportunity when it came up?

***

"MacKenzie?" Dr. Proctor said, watching her carefully. She shook off her uncertainty and smiled.

"Yes, I'm sure you're right. Daddy wouldn't have pursued it if he thought it was unethical."

Dr. Proctor buttered a roll for himself. "But you are still determined to dig deeper and make sure that they… what? That the clinic was ethical? That they didn't put Amanda at any unnecessary risk?"

"Yeah, I guess. I just want… to understand why they did what they did, why they did it the way that they did. Did Amanda really need a new kidney right away? She could have survived on dialysis, couldn't she? She could have waited for a year or two until her name came up and they found a match for her? She didn't need to put herself at risk for picking up malaria or some other tropical disease."

"I'm not sure she could have," he admitted. "I spoke with your mother frequently about Amanda's care and any changes in her case, and there were concerns that she was not going to last for very long on dialysis. As much as we try to mimic what mother nature can do, we knew we were losing ground. The machine doesn't replace a functioning kidney. Not completely. And the longer she waited, the more likely it was that she would come up with another infection or disease. Not malaria, maybe, but influenza. A resistant staph infection. Something else unexpected."

"Poor Amanda. I wish she had talked to me about it. She must have felt so alone."

Proctor wisely said nothing about that. MacKenzie looked around for their waiter, wondering how much longer it would be before their main courses arrived. He caught her eye from the other side of the room and raised one finger to her in a familiar gesture that MacKenzie recognized as meaning that it would be there shortly. One minute. Or just one more order before yours. MacKenzie rubbed at a smudge on her fork.

"I have collected the names of the directors and surgeons at the Forsberg Clinic," she announced. "I was wondering if you could look at them… let me know if you recognize them or know anything about their reputations."

"I know a couple of names off the top of my head. As far as I know, there haven't been any rumors of anything untoward associated with the clinic. I would have warned your parents if I had been aware of anything."

MacKenzie thought about that. It was strange, in view of the ethical concerns he had already mentioned, that he hadn't warned them against pursuing a foreign transplant through the Forsberg Clinic.

"So you didn't have any problem with them doing a foreign transplant?"

"I understand how desperately they wanted her to get a new kidney. How important it was for them. Who am I to step in the way of the one real solution they could find? Who am I to say that I have more scruples than they do? I have been friends with your family for a long time. I couldn't tell them not to get a transplant."

MacKenzie nodded. That made sense. She hadn't come into the picture until after the transplant was done, and it was easy to judge them for what they had done. It would have been different if she had known ahead of time. She would undoubtedly have agreed that they should go ahead with the one option they had. She wouldn't have dared to tell them that some high-ranking official's ethical concerns were more important than Amanda's surgery and survival. The pie-in-the-sky arguments went out the window when faced with the actual choice. Go ahead and get the kidney that Amanda needed and let others ponder the ethics of the situation. If it was legal, then why not? It didn't have to follow the same rules as the United States regulators had put into place. There were plenty of laws that changed from country to country and even from state to state.

The waiter greeted them in a soft, respectful voice as he approached them with a couple of steaming plates. Amanda waited for him to put the chicken in front of her, and she and Dr. Proctor both unfolded their napkins and prepared to eat.

MacKenzie looked over at Dr. Proctor's rare steak, and had a moment of nausea. She saw Amanda under the knife, the surgeon's scalpel separating the raw flesh, carefully preparing to graft in the new kidney.

"Are you alright?" Dr. Proctor questioned in concern.

"Yes... I'm fine. I just..."

He followed her gaze down to his bloody steak. "Oh... I'm sorry, does this bother you? I can have them cook it more..."

"No, no." MacKenzie shook her head. "That's always the way that Daddy has it. He could never understand anyone preferring it any other way. It doesn't bother me. Or... usually it doesn't. It's probably just low blood sugar." She gave a little laugh. "I'll be fine after I've had something to eat."

He sliced into the steak, looking back up at her after, weighing whether she was telling him the truth or not. "At least it's not steak and kidney pie," he offered.

"Oh!" MacKenzie shook her head at the mental picture and gave an unsteady laugh. "I'm glad you didn't. I think that might just be a little bit too much."

19

D r. Proctor looked at the list of people MacKenzie handed to him. He gave a frown of concentration. He didn't say anything initially, and MacKenzie waited to see what he would say. After a minute, he looked up, shaking his head.

"I don't know most of these names," he said. "I know they're not local, but I did expect to see a few more names that I recognized. I know most of the big players in transplants, and I thought they would have some of them in advisory positions on the board…"

MacKenzie nodded. "Most of the surgeons seem to be from other countries. I don't think any of the doctors who actually do the transplants are from the US."

"I suppose that would put them in a conflicted position ethically. They can't very well claim to be following the regulations that the US regulators have laid down if they are going out of the country to perform transplants that they can't perform here. So, they would have to hire people from countries that had different regulations. Or emigrate from the US for good."

"Yeah. Now from what I understand, or what I've heard, there are not a lot of surgeons around the world who are trained in or experienced in organ transplants. It's a specialty and needs very rigorous training."

"Here in the US, yes. You wouldn't find a transplant surgeon practicing general medicine. They would only be doing transplants. Because there is a limited supply of organs for transplantation, there is a cap on the number of surgeons who can be performing transplants. So only the cream of the crop can actually get jobs as transplant surgeons."

"But in other parts of the world? You don't think they're as well-trained?"

"I'm sure they must be well-trained. I'm just not sure that they would be *quite* as well-trained or specialized. These are very complicated surgeries that can take many hours. It's delicate work, and if you miss connecting some duct or blood vessel, it could mean the patient's life. You want someone who does a lot of these and has perfected their technique. Not someone who dabbles or has only read about it in books or watched training videos."

"I'm having a hard time finding anything out about any of these doctors. I have their bios, but they are short on details. I've asked for detailed curricula vitae…" MacKenzie looked at her watch. "They should have been emailed to me yesterday, but I haven't seen them yet. I'm hoping that you can tell from those whether these guys are properly trained or not."

"To make that judgment, we would have to know that the information they provide is true. It may not be verifiable. We would have to rely on them being truthful on their faces… which is a poor way to judge someone's experience. You know how often resumes are padded with information that, at best is a stretch, and at worst is an outright lie."

"Do you have colleagues in other countries who would be able to look into it?"

Dr. Proctor scratched his chin. "Is that really going to give you the information you want to know? I'm not sure it would be worth our time to chase that information down. You could hire a private detective to look into their backgrounds. Someone who is trained to do this kind of thing and can get you the information you are looking for quickly. I don't think I can do it. I don't have the time to be wasting on a fruitless investigation."

MacKenzie was surprised by this. She had been working on the assumption that he would answer any of her questions and be completely onside with finding out the rest of the information she was searching for. So far, he had been willing to answer her calls in the middle of the night and to take time out of his day to talk to her. He hadn't made any complaint or told her mother that she needed to rein MacKenzie in.

But apparently there were limits to what he was willing to do.

"Oh. Okay."

"I'm sorry, MacKenzie." He put his fork down and touched her hand briefly. "I don't like to disappoint you. But you know this is a wild goose chase. You're looking to assign blame to someone… and if you want to pin it on the foreign donation and the Forsberg clinic, you have every right to do so. But I can't waste my time checking into people's backgrounds. Especially when these people don't even live in the US. Get an investigator who is experienced in international investigations. Maybe he'll be able to find something. But don't involve me in this."

"No, I'm sorry. You're right. I know your time is valuable, and you've already spent a lot of time with me answering my questions and giving me advice. You've been more than generous with your time."

"Are you sure? I feel bad about it, but I do need to be aware of how I spend my time. I need to enforce some boundaries. I love you and your family, and I want to help… but there's only so much that I can do."

"Of course. You're right. I'll look into it further myself, or hire someone to look at these guys." She hesitated. "I do think there is something to it, though. You may not think so, but… I just don't get a good feeling about it. I think that at least some of the information that the Forsberg Clinic is giving is false and misleading. I don't think that they're quite as professional as their front in New Jersey suggests."

Dr. Proctor looked thoughtful as he cut pieces off of his steak and ate. MacKenzie turned her attention back to her own food, realizing that she had barely even touched her chicken since it had been placed before her. It was beautifully plated and MacKenzie was sure that it was delicious, but she couldn't even taste it. Everything just seemed to turn to sand in her mouth.

20

MacKenzie knew the name of the big private investigation firm that her father sometimes hired to look into backgrounds and dig up information for his lobbying efforts. He never referred to it as 'dirt,' but MacKenzie suspected that was exactly what it was. Walter would fight the other lobbyists and politicians with whatever means he could, and that included smearing reputations.

Using Walter's name, she got past the phone gatekeeper and was put through immediately to the senior manager of investigations. She wasn't sure whether he was actually the top of the organization or whether it was just a title intended to inspire confidence. But it didn't really matter. She knew that they would do their best to track down the information she was looking for, and if a lower-level investigator were not able to get it, then her name would be enough to get them to transfer it to a more senior investigator. MacKenzie had rarely traded on her name before. She had used it to get into functions that she wanted to attend, but usually people were calling her with invitations for her to attend rather than her having to ask a favor. She had been pleased with the way that the Forsberg Clinic and Dr. Dutton had responded, and the investigations firm seemed to be eager to jump at her command as well.

"Lance," MacKenzie was quick to use Lance Reacher's name to establish a more personal relationship between them. "I'm so glad you were available to take my call. You know that Mountain Investigations is always my father's first choice when he has a problem."

"Of course," Lance agreed. "We've been very happy with our relationship with Mr. Kirsch, and I hope you will be as well. Is this regarding one of his efforts, or…"

"No. Nothing to do with Walter's work. This is… a very personal matter."

"Oh, I see," his voice immediately dropped to a more intimate level. He was probably thinking that she wanted the background of a boyfriend checked. "Well, why don't you tell me how we can help you today?"

MacKenzie explained to him about her desire to donate to the clinic that had helped her sister get the lifesaving organ transplant, even though it had only given her another year, but that she wanted to check out everyone associated with the clinic and the transplants they did first to make sure there wasn't any bad PR that was going to come back as a result.

"Yes, of course," Lance agreed. "That's very wise of you. Especially if you're considering a large donation. If you become known as a supporter of this clinic, you wouldn't want to be associated with anything unfavorable."

"Right. Now, most of these doctors are international, so my doctor friends here in the States aren't of much help to me. And I'm not finding very much on Google when I try to look them up."

"Don't waste your time on your own investigations. That's exactly what we're here for. And we have associated firms all over the world, so we can look them up locally. We have all of the resources in place so that you don't have to worry about doing the legwork yourself."

"Okay, good. I asked the clinic for curricula vitae, but the bios I got back are… They're just press packages. All of the stuff that sounds good and nothing about who they really are and their education or jobs over the years. Just the very high-level, pumped up stuff."

"They should have at least given you a proper resume. No worries. We'll be able to trace work history, see whether they've had any complaints filed against them in the past, any malpractice issues or ethical violations. Do you want to get into their personal lives as well, or just professional?"

MacKenzie considered. She hadn't thought about that. How much did she need? Just enough to show that they were competent surgeons and not GP's who were doing their first transplant surgeries? Or was she looking for any dirt?

"I think…" MacKenzie blew her breath through her teeth, anxious about giving the wrong answer. "I don't think I need anything personal, unless it relates to… financial matters. I don't care if a doctor is cheating on his wife. But if he's deep in gambling debt, he could be doing transplants that he's not qualified to just for a big pay-off."

She could hear Lance's computer keys tapping away. "Uh-huh. Makes sense," he agreed. "How about addictions? If the guy's a drunk or if he needs a line of coke to keep him awake during the surgery…"

"Uh, yeah. Better be on the lookout for that too."

"No problem."

"Good. Great. Thank you for looking into this for me. I'll email you the names and the bios that I have."

"Perfect. We'll get started on it right away."

MacKenzie hesitated, unsure what else to say to him. She hesitated to reveal that she was worried that the clinic itself might be a scam and have contributed to Amanda's death. She didn't have any proof of it yet—and wouldn't telling Lance they might have been responsible for Amanda's death be slanderous? It was probably best if she kept that to herself until she was sure. Besides, Lance might be talking to Walter about another investigation and happen to casually drop a bombshell. Walter would not be happy to hear that she thought there were issues with the clinic.

"Was there something else, Miss Kirsch?"

"No. No, that's it. Thanks. I'll send you this email. Get back to me once you've had a chance to check them out."

"Will do, Miss Kirsch. Thank you for your business."

MacKenzie hung up the phone thinking about her father and how she was going to tell Walter and Lisa that she knew more about the clinic than they had been willing to tell her.

The next step in MacKenzie's plan of attack was to talk to other people who had been to the island for transplant surgery. Dr. Dutton had sent her the list of people who had agreed to talk to her. She compared it to the photos she had taken of the pictures and plaques on the wall of the boardroom. Why would anyone who'd had a successful organ transplant with the clinic, as evidenced by their photo on the wall, refuse to talk to someone who wanted to make a donation to the clinic?

So rather than calling the people she'd been told to, MacKenzie wrote down the names of the transplant recipients who had apparently not given their consent to be contacted. They had allowed their photos and stories to be posted on the boardroom wall, so what was it they had to hide?

The first name on the list was a Magnus Benjamin Phelps. MacKenzie looked up his name in the White Pages directory and dialed his number. It rang a few times before it was answered by a woman with a Hispanic accent, who MacKenzie immediately assumed was a maid or other household servant.

"I'm looking for Mr. Phelps. Is he in?"

"No, Mr. Leslie Phelps is out of town at the moment. Would you like to talk to someone else? His wife or his personal secretary?"

"Oh, Not Leslie Phelps," MacKenzie corrected. "I was looking for Magnus…?"

There was silenced from the maid. MacKenzie looked again at her notes to make sure she had gotten the name right and hadn't crossed up two different records.

"Is Mr. Magnus Benjamin Phelps there?" she asked, once she was sure of her information. Maybe the other Mr. Phelps went by Benjamin rather than Magnus, tipping the maid off that she didn't actually know the man she was calling.

"Are you a personal friend?"

"Well, no," MacKenzie admitted. "He knew my sister, though." She didn't have any idea whether this was true. "They both had transplants done at the same clinic."

"Ah. Is your sister there? Are you with her?"

MacKenzie swallowed. She was going to have to get used to saying the words. People who hadn't heard of Amanda's passing were going to ask her how she was or were going to invite her to events.

"No… my sister passed away recently. I was hoping to be able to talk to Magnus about… his transplant experience."

"I'm so sorry… Mr. Magnus has also passed."

MacKenzie sat there with the phone to her ear, feeling numb. That was not what she had expected to hear. How stupid she had been. Why would someone who'd had a transplant through the Forsberg Clinic not be on the list Dr. Dutton had given her? Because they had since passed away. How stupid and clumsy she had been, assuming that a name missing from Dr. Dutton's list was something suspicious.

"Oh… I'm so sorry to hear that. I apologize for disturbing you."

"Would you like to talk to Mr. Magnus's mother?"

MacKenzie considered. The maid had made the offer without prompting, so Mrs. Phelps must be willing to talk to people about her son. She must have talked to others or the maid wouldn't have offered.

"I don't know. I don't want to upset her. Do you think it would be good for me to talk to her, or just to leave it alone?"

"Oh…" The woman drew the word out, thinking about it. "I don't think it bothers Mrs. Phelps to talk to people about Magnus. And with your sister having passed as well… I think she would like to talk to you. It's good to have someone who understands your grief."

MacKenzie upgraded her assumptions about the woman who had answered the phone. Maybe not a maid. Not even a house manager. Someone who knew Mrs. Phelps well, and had been with her long enough to understand her feelings and reactions. A personal secretary? Old nanny? Not the maid.

"I… well, yes, I guess if you think she'd be interested in talking to me, and it wouldn't upset her… you could ask her if she wanted to take my call. But please, there's no obligation. She's not expecting my call and I don't want to be a bother."

"Let me check with her."

MacKenzie was put on hold while the woman went to talk to Mrs. Phelps. When the phone was picked up again, she was expecting to hear the Hispanic accent once more, but the voice that answered was more cultured, with a recognizable Boston twang.

"Hello, this is Geraldine Phelps."

MacKenzie swallowed her anxiety and let her extensive social training take over, speaking the words without really thinking about them, while her brain struggled to catch up with the moment. "Mrs. Phelps, I'm so sorry to hear about your son, Magnus. Are you sure I'm not intruding?"

"Of course not," Mrs. Phelps said graciously. "I'm always happy to talk to anyone who will listen about Magnus. We're at that stage where people no longer want to mention him, in case it is upsetting, but I can't go on as if he didn't exist and I'm not missing him. I want to talk about him, but people feel too awkward about grief."

MacKenzie let out her breath, nodding. "Yes, that makes sense," she agreed. It was surprising how quickly one reached that stage. People had already said that they were sorry about Amanda, and then they didn't know how to treat her the next time they talked. Mention Amanda again? Avoid the topic? Pretend that life just went on as normal after a loved one's death? "I hope I didn't mislead you; I didn't actually know Magnus. He had a transplant through the same clinic as my sister, Amanda, and I saw Magnus's picture and story on the wall. I wanted to…" she decided she didn't want to give Mrs. Phelps the story about considering a donation to Forsberg. "I wanted to learn more about the transplants that Forsberg is doing. For personal reasons. So I thought I would call some of the transplant recipients. I didn't know that Magnus had passed away."

"You want to know about the transplant?" Mrs. Phelps sounded confused. "What about it?"

"My family has been very quiet about the surgery… to be honest, I didn't even know she'd had a second transplant. But when she recently got sick, I had reason to believe that she might have gotten sick as a result of going out of the country for a transplant."

"Why? How do you think it was related?"

"My sister contracted malaria. That's not something you get in the United States. Only through foreign travel to tropical climates. I think she must have been bitten by an infected mosquito when she was there for the transplant. Nobody knew she'd been bitten at the time, not until she got sick a couple of weeks ago."

"I see. But that doesn't mean that the clinic did something wrong."

"No. I'm not throwing any accusations around. I'm just trying to… I don't know… follow Amanda's footsteps over the last year. Look at what happened and understand why…"

"You couldn't have prevented her death," Mrs. Phelps said compassionately. "Don't take yourself down that pathway… you mustn't. Your family did everything they could to help Amanda, it was just what was supposed to happen."

MacKenzie shifted uncomfortably. *What was supposed to happen?* She wasn't a believer in God or fate. She didn't believe that there had been no other pathway for Amanda. If they had made different decisions, then the outcome would have been different. If they had left her in the United States, on dialysis, until a new kidney became available, then she would not have contracted malaria and she would not be dead. That was the way it played out in MacKenzie's head. There wasn't any greater power directing matters on earth, pointing the finger at Amanda and dictating that she must die.

"If she hadn't gone to the island, she would not have gotten malaria. What happened with your son? What did Magnus die from?"

"His body rejected the graft. He received a lobe of liver. He had profuse internal bleeding… it was very quick."

"I'm so sorry." On one hand, it must have been a big shock for Mrs. Phelps. But on the other hand, maybe a quick demise would have been easier than to watch Amanda struggling and falling back into that cycle of fevers over and over again. Fighting and seeming to get better, only to be struck down yet again. Then at the end, when her breathing became so strained. MacKenzie would never forget the panic in Amanda's eyes as they took her away to intensive care, struggling to get enough oxygen.

"It is one of the potential outcomes of the transplant. We thought… their success rates were so high. We understood that there were risks, of course, but they had given us such assurances, we didn't think it would happen. I wish we had weighed the risks more carefully. If I had known then… maybe we would have at least put off the transplant… until it became more urgent."

"But then he would have been weaker," MacKenzie pointed out. "He might not have been able to travel, or to survive the surgery."

"Yes. You're right, of course. We made the best decision we could based on the information we had at the time."

"Looking back now… you don't think they were lying about anything, do you? The cleanliness of the facility? The training of their surgeons? The risk calculations?"

"I have often wondered. But what good is second-guessing going to do? It won't bring Magnus or Amanda back. It won't change anything."

"But if they are operating in a way that is dangerous… lying to people… then shouldn't we raise the alarm? So that other people can avoid having the same thing happen to them?"

There was a long silence from Mrs. Phelps. "Do you know something?" she asked finally. "I don't have any evidence that they lied about anything."

"I don't have proof. Just… well, some things that are bothering me. And maybe it's nothing. I'm just being paranoid and trying to make sense of why my sister died. I can't answer that yet… which is why I'm trying to talk to others about their experiences. Trying to reassure myself… or to discover the truth."

"We went to the clinic in New Jersey. It was very professional, very clean. They had a lot of information for us. Everything seems completely above-board. I realize that some people might not think it is right for us to go out of the country to do what the regulators wouldn't allow here… but no one is complaining. The people who were waiting in the US are still waiting. We didn't take anything from them, except maybe to reduce the demand to make way for someone else to get an organ that Magnus would have taken otherwise. I don't see anything wrong with that."

"Did you go with him to the island?"

"No. You sound like a very young woman, so I assume your sister was quite young. My son was in his forties. He took his companion with him, not his mother. Did you go with Amanda?"

"My parents did. They didn't tell me what was happening."

"I'm sure they didn't want to bother you. It's very stressful. But you and I are in the same position, we are looking at something that happened overseas… we weren't there. We didn't see any wrongdoing."

"No… but… my sister took pictures."

21

The feeling of being wrung-out emotionally was becoming familiar to MacKenzie. She sincerely hoped that wasn't the way she could expect to feel for the rest of her life. Sooner or later, the stress and the grief had to lessen. Had to become more livable. People had family members die all the time. They didn't become walking zombies like MacKenzie felt she had. She wanted to go to bed and not have to think anymore. But she didn't want to be alone. She wanted company without having to be company. Everything she did seemed to take more energy than usual.

The phone rang and she ignored it. She wasn't prepared to deal with anybody else's needs. Not even a telemarketer's. She needed to just let her heart and her brain recover.

After the landline stopped ringing, her cellphone started up. MacKenzie looked at it, frowning. It wouldn't be her mother; Lisa was still resistant to calling the cell phone, feeling like it was an intrusion on MacKenzie's privacy. Cell phones were for emergencies, not conversations. Some of her friends did have both numbers, but calling each in sequence meant that it was urgent, and none of her friends had any urgent business with her.

Her father. She knew even before she picked up her cell phone and looked at the number that it was Walter. As much as she wanted to just rest and relax, she knew she needed to talk to him. With a knot in her stomach, she answered the call.

"Hi, Daddy."

"I want to know what you think you're doing!"

He was never so cross with her. MacKenzie gasped at his sharp answer, taking a physical step back as if that would distance her from his anger.

"Daddy? What's wrong? I don't understand."

"First, I hear from your mother that you have taken it upon yourself to take Amanda's private medical files from the house. Then I hear that you're showing up at the Forsberg clinic asking questions. I want to know what the hell you think you're doing."

"I'm… trying to satisfy myself about what happened to Amanda. I think her death could have been prevented, and I'm worried about the clinic continuing to operate, maybe putting additional lives in danger."

"That's ridiculous. What have you gotten into your head? The clinic saved her life. It isn't their fault that she got sick a year later. That's just one of those things. Cruel fate. It wasn't something that could have been prevented or foreseen."

"She wouldn't have gotten malaria if she hadn't gone to that island."

"She wouldn't have survived if she hadn't gotten the transplant."

"She would have for a while. Maybe long enough to get a transplant here, locally."

"You're wrong. You don't know, you didn't know how sick she was."

"No. And I don't understand why you kept it from me. Shouldn't I have known? I could have spent more time with Amanda. I could have been involved in the decision to get the transplant. Or not get the transplant. I would have liked to have known."

"That's what all of this is about. You want to punish us for not involving you in the decision. We didn't exclude you to make you feel bad, MacKenzie. None of us would have wanted you to feel bad. But we wanted as few moving parts as possible. No extra variables. No one else who could have given her a virus, or talked her out of the transplant, or made her more stressed because she was trying to pretend to be happy and healthy when she was not."

"Did you see the clinic?"

"Of course. We went on a tour of it before we went overseas."

"No, I meant on the island. Did you see the hospital there? The place they would actually be getting her surgery."

"We had the pictures. I can show you the brochures, but I'm sure you already saw all of that when you visited the New Jersey clinic. How could you go there without even talking to me about it first?"

"I didn't think I needed your permission to talk to them."

"Well you don't," he admitted, disgruntled. "Are you really considering giving them a donation in Amanda's memory?"

"I may," MacKenzie lied. "I want to know more about their operation before I make that decision."

"You don't need to know anything else. She had the transplant. It was successful. It has nothing to do with getting sick later."

"Except that she wouldn't have contracted malaria if she had stayed here."

"You keep saying that. But it's a fallacy. She would not have survived if she hadn't gotten a transplant. She could not get a transplant here. She couldn't get one anywhere else. This was our only option. And it gave her another year that she wouldn't have had. I still don't believe all this about malaria. I think the doctors here made a mistake. It was another parasite. Or a bacterial infection. It wasn't malaria."

"There was something wrong with the clinic on the island," MacKenzie said.

"Something wrong? What do you mean?"

"Amanda took pictures while she was there. I have pictures of the place you stayed in while you were there. It was no Hilton."

There was silence from Walter that stretched out uncomfortably. MacKenzie waited, knowing that he would defend them.

"It was no Hilton," Walter agreed, blustering. "But would you expect it to be? We weren't there for our own comfort. We were there so that Amanda could get her surgery. The hospital was different. It was a fully modern facility."

"I don't think it was."

"I saw the pictures. They had all of the amenities, all of the technology they needed to perform state-of-the-art surgery."

"You didn't go there."

"No. Patients were isolated. To prevent them from picking up viruses or infections while they were in such a susceptible state. Just by implementing that one control, they were able to reduce the risks of infection by thirty percent. Would you want to put Amanda's life at risk by insisting on being there with her? You would accept an increased risk of thirty percent? You'd risk her death just to be able to sit by her bed as she recovered?"

MacKenzie thought of the last few days of Amanda's life. The last few minutes. It was an immeasurable comfort that she had been able to be there with her sister to the end. She didn't know if she could have obeyed the stricture that she couldn't be with Amanda after the surgery. Even understanding that it put her life at risk, MacKenzie didn't know if she would have been able to stay away.

So maybe it was a good thing she hadn't been told about it. She would have insisted on staying with Amanda, putting her life at risk. She couldn't imagine having to make that choice.

"You two were close," Walter said, "and I understand you feeling betrayed that we didn't tell you what was going on at the time. But we were protecting Amanda's health. Giving her the best chance we could at surviving and recovering."

"I want you to see the pictures."

He hesitated. "Amanda never said anything about taking any pictures at the hospital. She was asleep most of the time she was there. They kept her unconscious in order to give her the best chance to heal and recover."

"She never said anything to you about the conditions there?"

"She said it was like a spa. That she felt like she was on vacation instead of being sick."

MacKenzie didn't know what to say to that. Had Amanda been afraid to tell him the truth? Was her brain scrambled by whatever they had put her on to keep her unconscious and she didn't even remember it? Anesthesia could do strange things to the memory. When she had downloaded the pictures from her phone, had she even looked at them? Or maybe just a few of them? Maybe she didn't bother trying to correct the ones that were too dark.

"What was in these pictures?" Walter demanded. "I think you must have misunderstood things. Maybe they are more pictures of where your mother and I stayed."

MacKenzie suppressed a shudder. "No. I don't think so. I think you should see them."

"Send them to me, then. They're digital?"

"I don't want to send them to you by email. When are you coming back to Burlington next?"

MacKenzie was more careful with the next transplant recipient on her list. She searched for any obituaries or other press first, to make sure that John Hopewell had not passed away since his transplant. She didn't want to bumble into another surviving family's life. There weren't any obvious signs that he had died, so she looked up his contact information and called his number, crossing her fingers and hoping for the best.

"Hello?" It was a man's voice. Not quite brusque, but definitely giving the impression of impatience. Better not be a telemarketer, or he would hang up when the first two words were out of her mouth.

"Mr. Hopewell? You don't know me, but my sister Amanda had a transplant through the Forsberg Clinic," she said quickly, hoping to catch his attention before he decided that she was too much of a bother and hung up. He didn't immediately hang up, so that was a good sign.

"Yes?" he asked eventually. "What's your name?"

"MacKenzie Kirsch. My sister was Amanda Kirsch."

"I never met her."

"Yeah, I didn't suppose you probably had. I just… was hoping to talk to some of the people who have had transplants done through Forsberg, get a feeling for what the company is all about."

"Why?"

MacKenzie shifted uncomfortably in her seat, glad that he wasn't there to see her discomfort. "It's sort of hard to explain. Amanda recently passed away."

"Oh," his voice dropped to an appropriately somber tone "I'm very sorry to hear that, Miss Kirsch."

"Thank you. The thing is, it looks like she died because of her transplant, and I just wanted to know… whether anyone else had experienced similar problems."

"How did you get my name?"

"Your picture and plaque in the Forsberg boardroom."

"I see. I should call and ask them to take it down."

"You weren't happy with their services, then? You'd rather not be associated with them?"

Hopewell made a clicking sound with his tongue. MacKenzie waited out his silence. Finally, he spoke again. "They did what they said they were going to do. I got a new kidney. But certain things about the experience were… unsettling. And I've had a number of health issues since my return. I don't know whether I picked something up at the clinic, or if I'm just more susceptible with the drugs I'm on."

"What kind of health issues?" MacKenzie asked eagerly.

"I don't feel particularly comfortable discussing this over the phone."

He was shutting her down. He didn't want to share the details with her. And why would he? She was a complete stranger to him.

"Perhaps we could meet face-to-face?" Hopewell suggested.

"Certainly," MacKenzie agreed immediately, relieved. "I would be happy to meet with you at your convenience. Is there a particular time that would work for you?"

"Where are you? Are you in New Jersey?"

"No. Vermont. But I can make it there if you like. It's just a plane ride away."

"Actually, Vermont is better. I'm in New Hampshire. How close are you to Manchester?"

"I can get there," MacKenzie said, not telling him how many hours she would have to drive to meet with him. He was doing her a favor by answering her questions. The least she could do was to go to his house to show her face and let him suss her out in person. "Is tomorrow good? What's your address?"

"I could do this evening, if it isn't a bother for you. We could have supper. A public place is always better for a first meeting with someone you don't know."

"Sure. I have a couple of things that I need to do first... would an eight-thirty dinner be too late?"

"That would be perfect. I'll make a reservation for us at the Hampshire House. You can find it?"

"No problem."

"I will see you then."

2 2

MacKenzie had to hurry to get herself ready for supper. It was a three-hour drive to get to Hopewell, so if she wanted to make it on time, she had to leave within half an hour. But she'd gotten herself dolled up for a date in less time than that. She needed a dress that she could sit in for a number of hours without it seeming rumpled, so she looked through her closet quickly to find a black cocktail dress that had done well for her on other occasions. She threw a toothbrush and a few other items in an overnight bag, figuring she wouldn't be making the three-hour drive back after supper concluded at ten-thirty or later. Then she hopped into her car and was on her way.

At first, she drove with the radio on, but after a while it began to bother her. She was trying to think through what she knew about the Forsberg Clinic, to marshal all of the arguments that what they were doing was unethical and crossed the line against the arguments that the service they were providing saved lives both abroad and domestic, and that if people were prepared to pay the rates that were being discussed, there shouldn't be any impediment to their seeking the services overseas and leaving US kidneys in the US for domestic transplant. Was the clinic operating in a gray area? That much seemed clear. But she wasn't sure how dark that gray was, and if they had crossed into black, harming the transplant recipients they were supposed to be saving. Or if the pictures were what they appeared to be.

She reached the Hampshire House in good time. She introduced herself to the maître d', and he escorted her to her table. John Hopewell was already there ahead of her. He jumped to his feet and gave a little bow as the maître d' pulled out MacKenzie's chair for her.

"Miss Kirsch. It was very gracious of you to join me like this. I know making a trip like this on a whim isn't easy, but I appreciate your willingness."

"Of course."

She studied him as she sat down. He was skinny and pale. While a young man, his hair appeared to be thinning. It was hard to tell in the dimly lit dining room, she thought that his skin seemed yellowish. She put him at perhaps twenty-five years of age, yet at a quick glance he easily looked forty.

They discussed the weather and the menu. Hopewell ordered wine and then wouldn't touch it himself. "I have to be careful," he said obliquely, not offering any real explanation. MacKenzie felt awkward drinking without him, so she barely touched the wine herself, and the bottle sat there, getting gradually warmer as the evening wore on.

"I was hoping that you could tell me some details about your transplant surgery," MacKenzie said after a while. "I have run into a few... irregularities in my review of the Forsberg Clinic and I wanted to know if what happened to Amanda was related to her surgery, if it could have been prevented if they had followed proper procedures... or if she could have survived if they had just waited here until a kidney became available. I'm just... trying to make sense of it all, I guess."

"Trying to make sense of something that doesn't make any sense," Hopewell said. "Good luck with trying to justify who gets sick and dies and who doesn't." He shook his head. "I remember thinking as a kid that if I made all of the right choices, everything would turn out wonderful. If I ate healthy, I would be healthy. If I studied and did my homework, I'd be at the top of my class. If I followed the right path in dating and my relationships, then I would get married, become a father, and be able to have it all. I was very pragmatic. Just do this subset of things, and your reward will be..."

MacKenzie smiled. It was a bit simplistic, but she recognized similar magical thinking in herself as a child, and even as an adult, believing that if she did the right things, then that, combined with a little luck, would lead to a happy and satisfying life.

"I guess I can understand that."

"But then I got sick. Very sick, and in a few months, I was diagnosed with kidney disease, and soon after that, any plans and expectations that I had... I found out that I was going to be sick for the rest of my life. That I didn't have any control over the matter, over my body deciding to be sick when I had been doing all of the right things. Some of the things we do might prevent some of the disease subsets—reduce your risk of cancer, diabetes, heart disease—but you can't do anything about kidney disease. It isn't one of those things you can avoid the risk factors for. And once you've got it, you've got it. You're like a ticking time bomb. You never know when your time is going to be up, but it isn't ever going to get better."

"No," MacKenzie said quietly. Even though it hadn't happened to her, she still felt the same way. She had felt the same way since Amanda had been diagnosed. They had all been traumatized by it, discovering suddenly that life was not something they could control, but that this disease could sneak into their lives without warning and ruin all of their plans. Amanda would never be free of kidney disease; it would always be hiding in the wings.

Until it took her.

Hopewell gave MacKenzie a little smile and patted her hand. He didn't try any useless words of comfort. Just patted her hand and gave a little grimace of understanding.

"I'm sorry," MacKenzie said. "That really sucks. I wish it hadn't happened to you."

"Thanks."

"When were you diagnosed?"

"I was a teenager. Was on dialysis for six years. My tissue type seems to be difficult to match." He gave a shrug. "They didn't know when it would be that they'd be able to find me a kidney. Things were starting to look pretty grim. I knew I couldn't stay on dialysis forever, and that my health was starting to fail. I needed to get a new kidney, and I needed one pretty quickly."

"Did you already know about the Forsberg Clinic, or did someone tell you about them?"

"I started making some inquiries. I figured there had to be other pathways to getting a transplant, even if they were…" Hopewell hesitated. "Even if they were not approved methods here in the States. There had to be a way for me to get the surgery."

"So then you found Forsberg."

"They were mentioned to me by a friend and I followed up. I checked them out, saw the success they were having. They said that they were sure they could find me even if I was a hard subtype to match. They were sure they could get me a transplant within a year." Hopewell blew out his breath. "Funny how a year can seem so long and so short at the same time."

MacKenzie nodded.

"It was a godsend. I knew that I probably wasn't going to survive more than a year without a transplant. The system here in the States couldn't promise anything. Just that they would keep looking and they'd let me know if a kidney fell into their laps that was a match that they could use. And who knows how many people were on the transplant list before me. There was no guarantee that if they got a kidney it would be for me, even though things were getting pretty dire."

MacKenzie nodded with interest, encouraging him to go on. She took a sip of her wine, though she still felt weird about drinking when he was not. But Hopewell seemed to take no notice of it.

"So, how could Forsberg find you a match? I mean, if they couldn't find one in the US system, how could this little private clinic find you one?"

"There wasn't ever really any question of it. They said that they had a lot of potential live donors in their system. It was all on the computer so that they could search for certain combinations. They had recruiters. I don't think that's something you're allowed to do in the US, but maybe in some other places around the world... they actually have people who are in charge of signing up people who may be interested in donating an organ or tissue to someone in need. They weren't just waiting until people died and entered the system. For a number of organs and tissues, they can use live donors now."

MacKenzie nodded. "I know. I was Amanda's donor the first time. Gave her one of my kidneys."

Hopewell gave her a smile. "Good for you. I didn't have any siblings; nobody close to me was a close match. They can sometimes do media appeals, asking people if they would get tested to see if they are a match. It works with little kids, because people feel so bad, they feel driven to jump in and give a child the gift of life. An adult like me, not so much. There was no point in trying to get more donors through any kind of commercial effort for me." He shook his head, grinning. MacKenzie thought he had a very nice smile. He could say that an appeal to the public would never produce the organ he needed, but he couldn't know that. MacKenzie could just imagine the line of women signing up to see if they could possibly be a tissue match for the handsome young man who had appeared in the news.

"So you went to Forsberg, and they told you what a wonderful program they have. They said they probably had something in the system that they could help you with, because they have all of these people signed up."

"Yeah. It was pretty amazing to walk into the place and have them saying yes, they could find me a kidney, and they could have the transplant done within a year, so I could get off of dialysis and get healthy again. It was a life-saver, literally. I would have done anything to get that kidney."

Anything? MacKenzie took a deep breath and let it out again.

"So you agreed to go with them, and they told you that they had found a match?"

"Yes. Almost immediately."

"Who did you deal with at the clinic?"

"A Dr. Dutton. Not the friendliest woman, but she seemed competent, and she was getting me what I wanted, so I wasn't really concerned about personalities."

"I met her when I showed up at the clinic and asked for a tour," MacKenzie said. "I don't know if there is actually anyone else operating out of the New Jersey center."

"Maybe not," Hopewell agreed. "It was always pretty quiet whenever I went over there."

MacKenzie thought about her tour through the clinic. It had been pretty quiet. She hadn't run into any other staff in the hallways or as they looked around the clinic. But it was just an administrative center. The actual surgeries were not done there. The surgeons listed in their pamphlets or on the list that Dr. Dutton had given her were from other countries. There were probably management meetings, directors' meetings, and others at that building at strategic times, but that didn't mean they had to keep any amount of staff there full time.

"Where was your donor from?"

"Germany."

"They must have done a lot of recruiting there. That's where Amanda's donor was from too."

Hopewell nodded. "I don't know how many countries it is legal to do that; I haven't really looked into any of the international transplant law. But I got the feeling that a lot of stuff ran through Germany and Iran."

"Did you get to meet her? I know in the US, they have this policy where they keep it a secret and won't tell you the identity of donors. But those are dead donors. I don't know if the same thing applies to living donors."

"I didn't meet her, but they gave me a profile. Details about her."

"Yeah. I saw Amanda's. I thought that was pretty cool."

"It helped me to know where the kidney came from. That it wasn't coming from some impoverished third-world country. That even though I was paying for her to be flown to the clinic, she was donating out of the goodness of her heart, not because she was getting paid off."

MacKenzie nodded. "Exactly. I know Amanda was glad to know who her kidney was coming from too."

"I'd like to meet Sarah Hartwell someday. I'd really like to be able to thank her. I know it isn't done, but I'd like to be able to."

MacKenzie stared at him. "Who?"

"Sarah Hartwell. The woman who donated my kidney."

MacKenzie stared at him, mouth open.

2 3

MacKenzie was reluctant, for once, to step onto the sidewalk that led to the front door of her family home. Her brain was muddled with all of the facts and she wasn't sure how to present them to her father. Walter was not going to be pleased. But she didn't know how he was going to react. Outraged at what was going on? Defensive? The Forsberg clinic had given Amanda another year. Her parents kept repeating that and saying that MacKenzie shouldn't look any further into the surgery. Was that because they suspected?

Were they blind to what was going on? John Hopewell had told her that the transplant recipient and his family were required to sign confidentiality agreements with respect to the clinic. He and the others were not allowed to talk about the details of the clinic's operations. MacKenzie knew that meant that Amanda and her parents had also signed the confidentiality and non-disclosure agreement. That would be one of the reasons they were being so secretive about what had happened overseas. They had said they wouldn't tell.

But MacKenzie was family, not a member of the public. That was different. And there had to be exceptions to confidentiality agreements. Cases where one was required by law to reveal what they knew, whether there was an agreement in place or not.

She entered the house and closed the door behind her. She just stood there in the hall, wondering where Walter would be. She tried his office, but he wasn't there, and the room gave the impression of not having been used in

127

a long time. It was just a front, to make MacKenzie and anyone else think that Walter was really living there, not in a separate residence.

MacKenzie followed her nose to the kitchen, where Walter had a row of bread slices arranged across the counter as he put together some sandwiches.

"Hi, Daddy."

"MacKenzie." He gave her a smile, but it was reserved. Like he was required to smile at her, but didn't really have anything to say to her. MacKenzie sat on one of the stools on the opposite side of the island from Walter.

"So," Walter said slowly, his voice full of disapproval. "Have you come to your senses and decided that it's time to let this nonsense go? You need to accept Amanda's death and move on. She wouldn't want you to be wasting all of your time trying to find out what happened. Whatever events led up to her death, you need to just accept it and go on with your own life."

"But what about the other people?"

He frowned at her, eyebrows drawing down. "What other people?"

"The other people who get transplants through that clinic."

"Just let them live their lives. Who are you to tell them what they can or can't do? It's ridiculous, MacKenzie. You need to just move on."

He slapped cold cuts onto the bread. MacKenzie watched him add some lettuce to each and then close them. She wasn't hungry. In fact, the sight and smell of the meat was making her nauseated.

"What if what they are doing is dangerous or illegal?"

"Organ transplant carries risks. But Amanda was well taken care of. They never put her at risk. And as far as legal goes…" he gave a shrug. "Laws change. You know that. I've made a career out of lobbying for change. And you can believe that I'm lobbying to get changes made to the transplant laws. It's ridiculous to have such barbaric laws in place putting limits on who can get an organ when they need one."

"You think it should just be free market?"

He considered. "Why not? What harm is there in allowing people to pay for what they need? It benefits the donor as well as the recipient, so why not?"

"I think you should look at these pictures *before* you eat."

He snorted. "You really think I have that weak of a stomach? I've seen plenty of transplant pictures. Even watched movies of transplant surgery. I know what it looks like."

"I don't think you know everything."

He just looked at her. MacKenzie put her attache on the counter in front of her and took out the envelope the pictures were in. They were brightened and blown up, so they were grainy, but they were clear enough to make out. Walter picked up one of the pictures and looked at it, frowning.

She wondered if he saw the same thing as she did at first. A family asleep in the same kind of knocked-together shelter as Lisa and Walter had stayed at during their stay. Bodies of varying sizes lying side by side on a bare concrete floor with a sheet pulled over them.

She remembered the dawning feeling of horror as she looked at them, gradually understanding that they were not sleeping, but dead. Corpses lined up on the floor with a sheet pulled over them to hide the gruesome sight. A few feet poked out the bottom of the sheet. Dark-skinned feet.

Walter looked over the picture at MacKenzie. "Where did you get these?"

"Amanda took them. They were on her computer. Between the pictures of the place you stayed and the flight home."

The crease between his eyebrows deepened. "I don't know what this is, but she never said anything to us."

MacKenzie nodded. "She didn't say anything to me either. I don't know how she could see this and not talk about it to anyone. Maybe the anesthesia made her forget what she had seen. Or maybe she felt so guilty that she didn't want to admit what was going on. Or maybe because she'd signed a confidentiality agreement, she didn't think she could."

"What do you think you're seeing here? You're making assumptions. We don't know what this is."

MacKenzie scowled at him. "These are corpses. These are the organ donors."

"You don't know that. It's a medical clinic. They could have died of anything. Typhoid. Influenza."

"It wasn't a medical clinic. It was a transplant hospital. They didn't do anything else there, did they?"

"How could we know? They could have a community medicine program as well. Something to compensate the islanders who let them build there. Modern medicine for development permission."

"Do you remember the donor profile for Amanda's donor? Sarah Hartwell from Germany?"

"Yes, of course."

"Last night I had dinner with a man who also received her donor profile for his transplant."

"Maybe… she donated other tissues."

"He received a kidney."

Walter opened his mouth to argue with MacKenzie, then closed his mouth. A single donor could make multiple tissue donations. But a living donor could not give two kidneys, one to Amanda and one to John.

"A simple paper mix-up," Walter said finally. "They accidentally gave the same profile to both of them. One of them should have received a different profile."

That's what MacKenzie had been trying to tell herself. But coupling the identical donor profiles with the pictures of the bodies weakened the argument.

"Daddy. These are not a paper mix-up," she tapped one of the photos of the bodies. "People are dying at this clinic."

"I'm sure there's a logical explanation. You're jumping to conclusions based on very limited information. We have dealt with the people at this clinic. We've met them face-to-face and talked to them. We've been there, on the island. Believe me, if they were killing natives to harvest their body parts, it would be discovered very quickly." He gave a chuckle. "People disappearing from a little place like this, it would be noticed."

"But this many people dying of influenza wouldn't be unusual?" MacKenzie countered, looking at the picture of the bodies again. She pointed to the floor a few feet away from the bodies, where black-looking liquid pooled. "And what is this?"

Walter squinted at it. He looked through the pictures slowly. "I don't know, MacKenzie, and neither do you. It could be oil. It could be anything. You can't look at those pictures and tell me you can be sure *what* liquid is pooled in the room."

"It's blood."

"You can't tell from a picture. Certainly not one with this kind of lighting and resolution. I understand you are concerned. I understand you want to find someone to blame for Amanda's death. You want an explanation." He held his hands palm-up in a pleading gesture. "So do we. But the answer is simple. She had kidney disease. We did everything we possibly could for her, but in the end, her body simply couldn't deal with it."

"I don't believe that. I know she had kidney disease, but she didn't die from that. She died from malaria."

"She died from ARDS."

"Which was caused by malaria. Which was caused by her going to this tropical island to get a transplant from an organization that is… is…" She struggled to find the words, "…is engaged in questionable practices. And I want some answers."

He shook his head impatiently. "You need to get your head out of the sand. You're making up stories to suit yourself. You're looking for someone else to blame."

"And this doesn't bother you." MacKenzie nodded at the pictures. "They showed you pictures of a big, modern, clean facility. One where, as you say, she couldn't possibly have been bitten by a mosquito and contracted malaria. And instead, you find out that she was being operated on in some dirty shack where they're piling bodies up like cordwood. That doesn't make you question everything else they told you? Everything they showed you, from the glossy brochure down to the handwritten donor profile was fake."

"Yes, it is concerning," he agreed. He stopped, looking at MacKenzie and waiting for her to take this in and be ready for the next thing he said. "But there is a bigger picture." He lowered his voice, as if they were out in public and someone might overhear his words to her. "I am lobbying for substantive changes to the organ transplant business. I can't have you running around, looking underneath rocks, stirring everything up. You need to leave it alone. Trust me, I will look into it, and I will deal with it if they have been lying to us. But do not mess this up for everyone else. People need this system. They need these reforms. Or more people will die."

MacKenzie stared at her father, floored. "You're willing to let them get away with this? With killing your daughter?"

"That's overstating. I said I would look into it. I will take care of it. But if you are going to start spouting off about how the system needs more regulation instead of less, you are going to be the cause of the deaths of hundreds, even thousands of people who could be saved with these reforms. We're not just talking about one life," he said fiercely. "There are thousands of people waiting for organ transplants who will die before they get it. And thousands more who can't even get onto the waiting list because they are too sick. Think about that for a minute. The regulators say they are too sick to get a transplant, the only thing that could make them better. But because they don't have enough organs to go around, they have to eliminate people somehow. So those who are too sick, they lose out. Along with a lot of other people they have found a way to exclude."

MacKenzie covered her eyes, trying to wrap her mind around his argument. "You think it's okay, what this clinic is doing."

He held up a finger. "I think that what this clinic *claims* to be doing is okay. Obviously, or I would not have taken Amanda there. What they are supposed to be doing is providing a way for us to get around all of the over-regulation of the industry to get that transplant. If they are doing something else…" he looked down at the photos and shook his head. "I never said that was okay."

MacKenzie didn't know where to go with that. Walter put together several sandwiches. He put a single one on a plate and pushed it in her direction and put a couple more on a plate for himself. He stood eating, saying nothing more, while MacKenzie stared at the sandwich, not hungry and not sure how to even talk to her father.

"Daddy…"

"You need to leave it alone, MacKenzie. You leave it to me."

24

She declined her father's invitation to stay at the family house for the night. She didn't want to be in the same house as he was. She needed to get away and be able to think things through. Somehow, she needed to clear her head and figure out what was going on.

She hadn't expected him to argue with her once he saw the pictures. She thought that he would have the same reaction to them as she did—that they were proof of nefarious goings-on at the Forsberg clinic. Proof that they were not just providing a workaround for people who were willing to pay more for a transplant. Those bodies lying on the floor haunted her. She tried to make out the relative sizes of each. Were they a family? Were the smaller ones children? Women?

It hadn't occurred to her that they could be anything but the organ donors. She had immediately jumped to that conclusion, as Walter had observed. He'd been right about that, at least. As far as she knew, Forsberg wasn't offering general medical services to the natives. They were only doing transplants. But she didn't *know* that. They could be. The dark pool of liquid, though, she was sure it was blood. And why would there be blood pooled in the room, except if that was where they were performing surgery? Walter couldn't be right about the people having died of influenza or some other virus. They wouldn't have been left in a surgical room if that were the case.

MacKenzie wasn't sure she wanted to go home. But she didn't want to have anyone over, either. It was getting to be tiresome to have to deal with anyone else. When she invited men over, they wanted to be entertained. They wanted her attention. They didn't want to just keep her company, watching TV or doing something undemanding. That was the problem with not having a steady boyfriend. She didn't have anyone she could just let down her hair with and kick back to enjoy a quiet evening. Everything had to be an event.

Christopher had not been too bad. But she'd enjoyed her time with John Hopewell more than Christopher. What did that say about her? She would rather have dinner with a sick man than a night with a virile man like Christopher Marsh? She'd never been a Florence Nightingale, attracted to men who needed to be cared for. She'd always thought that kind of woman weak.

For a while, she just took random turns.

The phone rang and MacKenzie picked it up as she drove. She didn't see the number before she flipped it open.

"Hello?"

"Is this MacKenzie?"

"Yeah."

"It's Lance."

It took MacKenzie a minute for MacKenzie to remember who Lance was. The private investigator at Mountain Investigations. The guy who was supposed to be looking up the principals on the clinic's board to see what he could find out about their backgrounds.

"Oh, hey Lance. Good to hear from you. What've you got?"

"It sounds like you're driving."

"Yeah, I am."

"Why don't we meet somewhere. I don't like giving reports over the phone, that much less so when the other party is driving. I don't want you having an accident, and you can't really absorb everything if your attention is on the road."

"Just go ahead, I'll get it. There isn't much traffic and I'm just… driving around aimlessly."

"Do you know where the Fox and Hound is?"

"Sure." It wasn't somewhere MacKenzie frequented, but it was a popular pub and she knew where it was. More the kind of place that would suit Walter, which was probably what made Lance suggest it. He had probably taken Walter there at some point.

"Fine. I'll meet you there," she agreed.

"I'll be there in about ten minutes. See you whenever you get there."

MacKenzie hung up the phone. She turned the car around and headed toward the pub. It took her about fifteen minutes. There were hardly any spaces left in the parking lot when she got there, and she drove up and down the aisles for a few minutes before finding one that she could squeeze her little car into, beside a jeep that was taking up more than its allotted space. She grabbed her purse and attache, climbed out, and locked the doors.

She had seen Lance before, but she didn't really know him and wasn't sure she would recognize his face. But he was watching for her.

"MacKenzie."

She startled at the voice in her ear, turning to him quickly.

"Sorry," Lance apologized, putting up his hands, "didn't mean to scare you. It's Lance."

He was taller than she, in his late thirties, blond, with broad shoulders but not a heavy build. A handsome face, but marred on one side by what MacKenzie thought were burn scars.

She let out her breath. "Of course. Nice to meet you, Lance. Well, officially, I mean."

He nodded and smiled and motioned for her to go with him to a table that he'd managed to corner despite the busyness of the place. "Here we go, have a seat."

MacKenzie looked around. "I had no idea that this was such a popular spot. I mean, I know that Daddy came here, but I always pictured it as a pretty quiet place."

Lance shook his head. "No, it's almost always full during regular hours. You want to get it quiet and you need to get a private booking."

"I don't imagine that comes cheap."

"No, it doesn't. But it's effective if you want somewhere private to meet away from offices and homes."

MacKenzie nodded. He was younger than she had expected him to be. She had expected him to be Walter's age. Much closer to MacKenzie in age than she ever would have thought. It was funny how differently she perceived people's ages as she got older.

He had some fine lines on his face, most of them pleasant and reaching upward rather than downward. Someone who smiled more than he scowled. Which was something she hadn't expected in a private detective. They saw the seamier side of life, didn't they? She would have expected him to be more grim.

"Drinks?" Lance offered.

"I'm going to be driving, so… no more than a glass."

He motioned for a waiter and got the attention of one of them immediately. The waiter hovered as they placed their drink orders, then moved away to give them some privacy once more.

"So, how has it been going?" MacKenzie asked. "The investigation, I mean. Was everything what we expected it to be?"

He cocked an eyebrow. "That depends on what you were expecting."

"I don't know… everybody well-respected. Not too perfect, but nothing scandalous… nobody charged with manslaughter for killing a patient on the table, or something like that."

Lance smiled. "Well, no one was charged with manslaughter. So you got that part right."

"Good." MacKenzie nodded. If Forsberg were hiring unscrupulous surgeons, people who weren't' properly trained or board certified, then she would have expected there to be some charges. Somebody who said that they should never have been practicing medicine in the first place. "No… malpractice or anything?"

"Well, malpractice is another story."

Their drinks were delivered, and each sipped theirs for a moment before going back to the conversation.

"They've been sued for malpractice?"

"Hard to find an eminent surgeon these days who hasn't been. Seems like a lot more of them have been than not. But I think a lot of that is just our litigious society. You didn't like the outcome of your elderly mother's surgery? Sue them. So that in itself really isn't a red flag. Unless someone has a larger number of malpractice suits than you would expect. Or has actually been convicted of malpractice or lost his license."

"And was there anyone like that?"

"Well, you're rushing ahead a little bit. Why don't you let me give you my report, and then if you have questions after that, you can let me know?"

MacKenzie shrugged and smiled. "Daddy was just getting after me for jumping to conclusions. I seem to be doing a lot of that."

Lance took another sip of his drink and put it to the side to make room for the file he placed on the table. "Okay. Let's go over the directors first. Most of them are domestic, so they weren't hard to find or to trace their careers and other details."

MacKenzie listened carefully while he gave her a brief summary of each of the directors. He had a written report on each director, so she didn't have to make notes, but just listened to what he had found. They were the kinds of men that she would have expected. High-powered doctors or businessmen with a history of political involvement.

"None of them have been convicted of anything that would be of concern," Lance said slowly. "But on the other hand, none of them exactly has clean hands, either. Some issues with the SEC, sanctions from the medical board… just warnings to stay on the right side of the law and not to play it fast and loose. The kind of things that high-powered investors get involved in when they decide to see just how far they can push the envelope."

MacKenzie nodded. Her father was, she suspected, in the same boat. He wasn't a criminal, and he was known in the lobbyist circles as a white hat, but that didn't stop him from playing the stock market or making a business investment in a less-savory company. She didn't know whether he had ever been officially investigated or sanctioned by any regulator, but she could remember hearing more than once over the years how he was dealing with one board or government agency or another as they tried to sort out his affairs and he tried to answer their questions without giving the game away. He strove to remain on the right side of the law, but that didn't mean he didn't have the occasional reach over to the dark side.

"Okay, that all sounds pretty much what I expected," she said, taking a stack of reports from him so that she could look at them more carefully later. She'd had a long day and while the wine was soothing, it wasn't exactly conducive to studying research reports. She squared the pages and set them in front of her. "And what about the rest of them? The woman who is running the clinic, the surgeons they have overseas…"

"We'll come back to Mildred Dutton. But let's go overseas and take a look at the doctors that they have operating the clinic."

MacKenzie remembered the lined-up bodies and the pool of blood. She had a steadying drink and nodded at him to go on.

"First of all… most of them don't exist."

MacKenzie had to think about that one. "They don't exist?"

"Yeah. I told you, we have partner firms all over the world, so we have the best local access to information. It isn't just that they don't show up when you search them on Google. It's far deeper than that. These men are ghosts. If they do exist, they're just your run-of-the-mill GP's or general surgeons. Not transplant experts."

"Could someone like that be performing transplants?"

"Quite possibly, yes. Just because a doctor doesn't have a reputation as a great surgeon, that doesn't mean that he hasn't taken the necessary training or had someone to show him the ropes so that he can do it on his own. But these are not men who would be operating as transplant surgeons if they were in the US. Not out in the open, anyway. They may be perfectly competent.

But they may also be hacks. They didn't really exist until they started working for the clinic."

MacKenzie shook her head. "I don't really know what that means."

"We're still investigating, so I can't tell you for sure what it means either. They may be doctors who have operated in other countries who changed their names or who we can't be sure of because they changed their practice area. When you have a John Smith operating in England as a gynecologist, and then later a John Smith operating in some tiny island as a transplant surgeon, how do you know whether it is the same one? We have to get access to social security numbers, birthdates, photos, something that will tie the two of them together. They might have been trained in their own country but never passed the boards. Or they may have been trained in a country that doesn't really regulate their medical profession. It all depends on how far you want us to look. How deep do you want us to go?"

MacKenzie nodded slowly. "For now... maybe we'd better back off a bit. Daddy is on a rampage about me screwing things up for him. If I told him about all of this... he might have an aneurysm. I didn't tell him that I was actually investigating them. He only knows that I looked at Amanda's files and went to the Forsberg Clinic in New Jersey. You didn't tell him about this, did you...?"

"You are my client in this matter, not your father. I wouldn't tell him without your permission."

"And you don't have any kind of conflict of interest in looking this kind of thing up? When he would be against it?"

"I'll let you know if I see a conflict. Right now, no. He hasn't retained us to investigate anything in connection with the clinic or the transplant industry."

"He might. He says it's something he's lobbying on right now, so he could come to you and ask you to look something up."

"We'll cross that bridge when we come to it."

"Yeah, just let me know... I don't want to get in Daddy's way, but I do want to know what happened to Amanda."

He sat back, studying her.

MacKenzie raised her brows. "What?"

"Why don't you tell me the backstory here?"

"What backstory?"

"When you retained me, you told me that you just wanted to look into this clinic before making a donation, to avoid tarnishing your reputation. But you're not surprised that some of the principals are... risk takers and that the doctors may not be trained to American standards. So tell me, what *did* happen to Amanda?"

MacKenzie had forgotten the ruse she had used in hiring him. Her cheeks warmed.

"Oh."

"You obviously suspect them of some wrongdoing. This isn't just a background check to make sure there are no red flags for publicity."

MacKenzie nodded slowly. "You're right. Amanda's death… may have been related to her transplant overseas at the Forsberg clinic."

"You think they made a mistake? Malpractice?"

"At first, I thought it was just a fluke, that she got malaria because she had her transplant done overseas instead of stateside. But there have been other issues… a lot of secrecy around the transplant, like it's something they wanted to hide… I came across some disturbing pictures on Amanda's computer… and it looks like all of their brochures and literature are lies. So, hearing this from you… it isn't that surprising. I think what's they're doing is… dangerous."

"Knowing your father and something about the transplant industry, I expect there is a lot of money involved here. And people trying to protect their money can be dangerous too. I don't think that the transplant recipients are the only ones who have reason to be concerned. If you are putting their livelihood in jeopardy, you could attract attention of the wrong sort."

MacKenzie gave a little laugh and shook her head. "That's a little melodramatic. I'm not doing anything to put anyone's livelihood in danger. I haven't tried to stop them from doing what they're doing, I'm just trying to find out… exactly what it is."

"One will lead to the other. Are you telling me that if you discover it is a criminal enterprise and Amanda died because they were unconcerned about the conditions the transplants were done in, you wouldn't blow the whistle on them and try to get them shut down? Put them in prison? I realize that I don't know you personally, but I know your father and I know the way he talks about you. You're not going to let this go."

MacKenzie rolled her eyes at that. She had not been a particularly rebellious child growing up, and she had never been a fighter, but Walter frequently made comments about her being a spitfire. She suspected he just wished that she was more like he was. Wishful thinking.

But she couldn't argue with what Lance said. It was true—if the Forsberg Clinic were responsible for Amanda's death, she wouldn't be able to back down and let it alone. She was already feeling anxious about the pictures of the transplant hospital and her father's reaction to her poking around. She couldn't ignore the way that those bodies had been lined up on the floor. Not if it meant what she thought it did. She wanted to do what her father said, but she couldn't just ignore those bodies, and Amanda's death. She needed to know more. She needed to know the truth.

Lance was watching her, as if he could read the thoughts running through her mind. MacKenzie shifted uncomfortably. She tapped the attache enclosing her papers and the photos.

"Does your firm do any kind of… photo analysis?"

"What kind of analysis? Forensic? There are some specialists we could engage. Gets pricey, though."

MacKenzie raised an eyebrow. "I'm not concerned about price."

He laughed. "I guess not," he agreed. "You have them with you?"

"I took them to show to Walter. He… didn't react the way I'd hoped." MacKenzie hesitated, then opened the attache and pulled them out. She placed them on the table in front of Lance.

25

Lance examined the top photo with a casual air, then his eyes narrowed, and he looked at it more closely. His eyes moved from one part of the photo to another. He looked at MacKenzie.

"Where did you get these?"

"They were on Amanda's computer. By the date codes, this is the hospital where she received her transplant."

"Hospital?" His laugh was a sharp bark. "This looks more like a slaughter-house. Tell me what you think you're looking at here."

MacKenzie looked down at the table, suddenly tongue-tied. She was getting the reaction from him that she had hoped to get from her father. She had wanted him to be outraged. To swear that he would find out what had happened to Amanda in that place and see that it didn't happen to anyone else ever again. But instead, his reaction had been to stop MacKenzie. To tell her to back off. Was it because he was concerned about her? Or about his own projects? She didn't want to think that money overrode his love for his daughters. She had always thought herself a cherished part of his life.

"Kenzie..."

She looked up from the table, into Lance's deep blue concerned eyes. Amanda was the only one who called her Kenzie. And Amanda was gone forever. He put his hand on her arm.

"Kenzie, look at me. I need you to stay with me here. You might think this is something you can keep quiet, but it isn't. The police should be noti-fied. The feds. Interpol. We're not talking about malpractice here. This... this is something you can't ignore. This isn't a little fraud or trying to work around regulation."

"Daddy said it could have been typhoid or influenza. They could be operating a public medical clinic, and there was an epidemic."

"Of course that's a possibility…" His eyes returned to the photo. "But with all of the blood… Maybe a hemorrhagic fever, but still… this just doesn't look right. If a first-world clinic was offering their services in a place like this, I would still expect to see beds, body bags, medical equipment. Not just… bodies lined up on the floor."

"In an epidemic, they might have run out of beds and body bags."

"And they still had your sister and others into the hospital to do transplant surgeries? With an epidemic like that raging? You wouldn't bring someone with a suppressed immune system into an epidemic."

MacKenzie lowered her eyes. "No," she admitted. "They made a big deal about how they avoided exposing the transplant patients to infections. Family members were not allowed to stay with them at the hospital. They were put up somewhere else and the transplant patients were taken to the hospital without them."

"What did Amanda tell you about the conditions there? Did she verify these?" He indicated the pictures again.

"She didn't talk to me about it at all. I found the pictures after she had died."

"If these were the conditions at the hospital where she got her transplant," Lance gazed at the boards nailed together haphazardly and the concrete floor, the bodies piled along the wall and covered with a sheet, and the pooled blood. "Why would she not tell you about it? Why wouldn't she tell your parents? They were there on the island with her. If she got there and discovered these kinds of conditions, wouldn't she just turn around and say that she wasn't going to go through with it?"

MacKenzie shook her head. "I don't know. I don't understand what happened. It's like they were all brainwashed. They didn't tell me what was going on at the time, said she was just going to have a surgery to improve her kidney function. And she didn't say anything when she came back. I thought… maybe the anesthesia made her forget this, and anything else she saw there. Maybe there was another hospital where she recovered, and everything looked like it should."

"If they had a real hospital, then what was this?"

"I don't know."

He pondered, looking down at the pictures. The crowds around them were noisy, everybody having a good time. It was a strange place to be discussing something so nightmarish.

"I think you should talk to the police about it."

"And say what? I found these pictures on my sister's computer. She saw something horrific but she never told me about them. I think it was the Forsberg Clinic's transplant hospital, but I don't know for sure. I think they were… organ donors, but I don't know, that's just a guess. It's all just wild speculation."

"Maybe you could find some of the other transplant patients. Talk to them about it. See if anyone else saw anything like this, knows where it might be."

"I've been trying. Some of them are just following the clinic's party line, so I haven't bothered to talk to them. The ones that Forsberg didn't tell me I could talk to, I'm trying to get in contact with."

He nodded. "Good idea."

"Some of them have died."

"Ouch. I suppose so."

MacKenzie remembered her dinner with John Hopewell in New Hampshire. "Everybody who was involved, both the transplant recipients and their families, signed confidentiality agreements. They're not supposed to talk about it with anyone."

Lance looked into her eyes. "But…?"

"I met with someone… he's having a lot of the same symptoms as my sister. His doctors keep telling him he's just susceptible to whatever viruses are going around. I told him that they should test him for malaria."

"What could he tell you about the hospital where he got the transplant?"

"I didn't show him the pictures. I just asked if it was like the pictures of the hospital in the brochure."

"And…?"

"He said 'more or less,' and wouldn't commit to anything. He said that there were things going on that disturbed him, but he also said that he was drugged up a lot of the time, and he didn't know how much of it was real, and how much was nightmares."

"So he's a dead end, unless he decides he's willing to tell you more."

MacKenzie shrugged. "I guess so, yeah."

Lance walked MacKenzie to her car, though she really had no concerns about running into any bad characters in the parking lot at night. It was a brightly-lit lot, there was lots of activity, and there were security guards patrolling it on and off throughout the night.

"We want to keep you safe," Lance said lightly. "If your father thought I let anything happen to you…"

But she didn't think he was really concerned about people lurking in the shadows either. He just wanted to walk with her.

They stopped at her car. "This is me," MacKenzie said, gesturing to it.

He looked at the sedate little compact. "You should have something with a little more… power."

"I'm just buzzing around town. It gets me from point A to point B."

"I just think you should have something more interesting. Something… sexier. Like you." He chuckled. "Did that sound as cheesy to you as it did to me?"

MacKenzie grinned. "Pretty much."

"Then I apologize." He started to say something else, then shook his head. "Okay, no more comments about the car. It's all going to come out sounding lame."

"What do *you* think I should be driving? What do you picture me in?"

"Maybe a little red convertible. Something fun and powerful. You have the money. You could splurge on something that made you feel good instead of something that just got you from point A to point B."

MacKenzie nodded, looking at it. "Not exactly practical for Vermont."

"Exactly my point."

MacKenzie laughed. She turned away from him to get in. His hand was on her arm, stopping her.

"Kenzie."

The way he said it made goosebumps stand up on her arms. She stopped, looking at him. "Yes?"

"Just be careful. These guys have a lot at risk. They'll want to protect their investment. Don't talk about it to anyone."

MacKenzie nodded. "Okay." She thought about all of the people she had already talked to and felt guilty. But she was sure he was overreacting. Nothing was going to happen to her.

26

MacKenzie's mind was whirling as she drove home and parked in the parking garage. Not just with the new information about the clinic, but also with Lance's apparent romantic interest. She was used to men being interested in her due to her social standing and family wealth. But she got the feeling that Lance was interested in more than that. He was concerned about her welfare, which was sweet. He definitely knew about her father and that he wouldn't be an easy man to get along with if he became aware MacKenzie was seeing the investigator. Lance was not their social class and Walter would not be impressed.

As intrigued as MacKenzie was by Lance's advances, her mind fell quickly back to thoughts of Amanda. Had the doctors who performed her surgery even been properly trained? Was she operated on in some slapped-together shack rather than the big, modern facility that the brochures showed? What had she been thinking the last year as she had kept her experiences a secret? Had she wanted to tell MacKenzie about it but been worried about the confidentiality agreement she had signed?

How many others had died like Magnus Phelps or were currently sick, fighting bizarre tropical diseases that their doctors didn't know to look for? If they'd only caught Amanda's malaria a little sooner, would it have been enough to save her? If John Hopewell had the same thing, would treatment spare him the same death as Amanda?

MacKenzie reached out to fit her key into the lock at the apartment door, but it swung open at her touch, not latched properly.

MacKenzie looked at it, bewildered, as her mind ran through possible scenarios. Had she not pulled it shut behind her? Had she already unlocked it, but been so distracted by her thoughts about Amanda that she had just forgotten it? Had the doorman come up to deliver something for her and forgotten to shut it? Or maybe he was still in there?

MacKenzie rested her hand on the doorknob. "Hello? Is there someone here?"

There was only stillness in response. No answering voice or movement.

"Hello?"

MacKenzie pushed the door open. There were no packages in her front entryway. She pushed the door shut behind her, but it didn't latch. She looked at it to see what had blocked it, and saw the splintered frame. The door had been kicked in, busted through the doorframe. MacKenzie's heart was pounding hard, her breath caught in her throat.

"Hello? Is there someone here?"

She was afraid to walk through the entryway of her apartment into the large front room to see if there were anyone still there. She forced herself to look anyway, like when she was a little kid afraid of monsters under the bed or in the closet. If she just looked, then she would know that there was nothing to worry about.

There was no sound. She walked through to the front room. Nobody there.

But someone had been.

MacKenzie backed away, back through her entryway and the door out to the elevator. She waited impatiently for the elevator to make it back up to her floor, heart pounding like a train engine. When it finally got there, she jumped in and stared at the floor buttons blankly for a moment, freezing up. It seemed like an eternity before she remembered that the L button was the one she wanted, and she pushed it. The elevator lurched, descending back to the main floor. No one else got on to interrupt its descent. When it stopped and the doors opened, she tripped over the space between the floor of the elevator and the floor of the lobby, stumbling unceremoniously into the big, echoing lobby.

"Miss Kirsch? Is something wrong?" Eddie, the night doorman, was quickly at her side, taking her arm to steady her and looking into her face with concern. MacKenzie held on to him, trying to steady herself and get the words out.

"Someone in my apartment," she gasped out. "Someone was there."

"There is someone in your apartment?" He escorted her over to the little grouping of chairs and couches to sit her down. "Who? An intruder?"

MacKenzie breathed heavily, nodding. "Not anymore—or I didn't go all the way in to check—door is broken. They…"

His eyes widened with alarm. "You just wait right here, Miss Kirsch. I'm just going to get security and the police."

He hurried over to the phone at the desk and placed a couple of quick calls. MacKenzie sat there, looking around at the lobby like she'd never seen it before in her life, trying to sort out what was happening. Eddie returned to her in a few minutes.

"Somebody is going to check on it right now, and the police are on their way. Are you okay? Can I get you anything? A drink?"

MacKenzie clutched her purse to her, feeling the need to hold on to something and to ensure that her property was safe. She couldn't believe that someone had broken into her apartment. Why would anyone target her? She had money, but so did everyone else who lived in the building. Was it just because her suite had been unoccupied? Had anyone else been targeted?

"Miss Kirsch? What can I do for you?"

"That's good, that's fine," MacKenzie babbled. "I don't know why…"

"The police will find out what happened. Don't you worry about that. I'm going to get you a coffee, would you like that? Or tea?"

"Tea," MacKenzie said faintly. She didn't want something that was going to keep her up all night. "Thank you."

Her mother would want her to remember her manners, even if her personal space had been violated. A lady always remembered her manners. MacKenzie looked around for her mother. She wasn't there. Should MacKenzie call her? Tell her what had happened? Lisa would be concerned. She would want to know.

But it could wait until after the police had come and could tell her something.

"You just rest here for a minute, and I'll get you something soothing," Eddie promised.

She was aware of people coming and going, walking by her with curious looks, Eddie pressing a cup of herbal tea into her hand and encouraging her to have a sip. It seemed like forever before a couple of police cars pulled up in front of the building and the officers made their way into the lobby.

"It's the top floor," Eddie told them. "Penthouse. A couple of security guards are up there to secure the scene, they said that no one is there anymore."

One of the police officers took charge, a big man with a florid red face. "You're sure that someone has broken into the apartment? This wasn't just…"

he glanced at MacKenzie, "a misunderstanding? Someone forgot to lock up or let themselves in with a key...?"

"No one has a key," MacKenzie protested. She followed Walter's advice to never give anyone a key to her apartment, no matter how good she felt about them. A policy that applied to everyone, so she didn't have to make a judgment call.

"The door was broken," Eddie advised, repeating what he'd heard from the security guards, since MacKenzie hadn't given him any such details. "It was definitely a break-in."

"We'll go take a look. Why don't you stay with her," the cop said to the one female officer who had come with them, "get her statement. Find out if we have any suspects."

The female cop nodded and sat down with MacKenzie while the others went up to have a look.

"You must be very upset about this," the cop said, moving as close as she could to MacKenzie without crowding her. "Why don't you tell me, from the beginning, what happened when you went up to your suite?"

MacKenzie rubbed her eyes. She wasn't sure why tears were leaking out the corners of her eyes. She was afraid they made her look weak or hysterical. She blinked, trying to clear her vision, and looked at the officer's name bar. Ferris.

"I just went up to my apartment... nothing different than usual... but when I got there, the door was open. Broken through the frame. I only went a few steps inside... but there was stuff scattered everywhere. Like someone had *tossed* my apartment." She shook her head in disbelief. "I don't understand it. Who would do something like that?"

Ferris nodded sympathetically. "It's hard to make sense of it all, isn't it? You poor girl. Is there someone we can call to sit with you? You want to have someone to keep you company?"

"No... I don't know... maybe later. What are they doing up there? Whoever it was, they've left."

"They're just investigating. Seeing what was done and gathering any evidence as to who might have done it. Don't you worry about that."

"I don't understand."

"No. It doesn't make much sense, does it? Have you had any problems before?"

"No. I've never had a break-in."

"Do you have any valuables in your apartment...? You must..."

"I don't know..." MacKenzie thought about the contents of her apartment. Yes, it was nicely decorated, and she had some jewelry and art that were worth a pretty price tag, but she would never have expected anyone to break in to steal them. What kind of person did that? "I have… I have nice things."

"Yes, I'm sure you must. Is there anything new? Or anything anyone has particularly admired lately?"

"No… I don't think so."

Ferris nodded. "It might have just been a crime of opportunity. This is a nice building, and it makes sense that the penthouse suite would contain valuables… it might not be anyone who actually knows you."

MacKenzie blinked. Someone who knew her. Would someone who knew her have done something like that? Broken into her apartment and messed things up?

"Someone I know?"

"Have you had any arguments lately? Anyone who might have resented or targeted you for some reason? Sometimes the silliest little things can set people off. Someone that you brushed off, or who thought you should have invited them up to your room? Or maybe an ex who was jealous over a new boyfriend…?"

At MacKenzie's blank stare, she amended. "Or girlfriend?"

The suggestion made MacKenzie laugh, breaking through some of the inertia she was feeling. "No, definitely boyfriend," she said.

Ferris held pencil poised over her notepad. "Was there anyone who you can think of who might have wanted to get back at you for something? Or who maybe admired your jewelry just a bit too much…?"

"No… I don't know. There was Liam Jackson… he was irritated when I wouldn't let him stay in my apartment alone. I had to go see my sister, who was in hospital sick, and he was kind of pouting about it."

She watched Ferris write the name down and immediately felt guilty. "But I'm sure he wouldn't do anything. Just because he wanted to have a long shower, that doesn't mean… he wouldn't have turned around and done something like that."

"You never know," Ferris gave a shrug. "At least it's a starting point. Anyone else?"

MacKenzie was reluctant to suggest any other names. "I… well… Roger… he was pretty mad about getting kicked out, I threatened to call the police… but I needed some sleep…"

"Roger…?"

MacKenzie rubbed her forehead. What if the names she disclosed to the police ended up in the paper or community gossip? The last thing she needed was a reputation as a tramp or tease, someone who invited men up to her apartment and then kicked them to the curb when she was done with them. Her mother already thought her behavior was scandalous, and she didn't know half of what MacKenzie did.

"What was Roger's last name?" Ferris prompted.

"Milford. But I'm sure it wouldn't be him. Neither one of them. They wouldn't have any reason to steal anything from me, they're both quite wealthy themselves..."

Ferris wrote it down anyway. "That doesn't rule out revenge, though. They might not have taken anything. It might have just been to scare you or get back at you for kicking them out."

MacKenzie shook her head. She really didn't want the police going after these prominent families. "Look, I really don't think that it could be either of them. It could cause me real problems if you go after them..."

"No one is going after anyone. We are just investigating. We'll be discreet."

"I don't know..."

"Is there anything else you can think of? Have you had any threats? Any strange phone calls or hang-ups?"

MacKenzie thought of Lance's warnings, which she hadn't previously connected to the break-in. What if it was someone who was connected with the clinic? What if they had gotten wind of her investigation? Suddenly dizzy with the possibilities, she picked up her cup and had another sip of the tea. They couldn't have found out about her investigation. She had been careful. Lance's firm would have been careful not to tip the clinic off. Dr. Dutton still believed that MacKenzie was interested in making a donation to the clinic.

"What is it?" Ferris asked.

"I don't know... I don't think..."

"We need to be aware of all of the possibilities. We can't investigate if you're holding back information."

"I know... I'm just... I don't think anyone could know..."

But Lance knew. Walter knew. The other donors she had contacted knew. The pool of people who knew about her suspicions of the clinic was getting broader, which made it more difficult to keep the clinic from finding out. Someone might have said something to Dr. Dutton or someone else at the clinic by accident, or might have intentionally given them a heads-up. And Lance had warned her they could retaliate.

27

As she sat with her hands over her face, trying to sort it out, the big cop in charge came back down to the lobby to talk to her.

"Everything is secure. We'd like you to come upstairs, if you're up to it. Have a look around and let us know what, if anything, is missing."

MacKenzie looked at Ferris, who nodded encouragingly.

"Yeah, okay. I'll do that," she agreed.

It was a minute before she could convince her legs that she really did want to stand and stagger back into the elevator. The big cop looked like he was ready to catch her if she didn't make it.

"How bad is it?" she asked on the way up. "Did he destroy anything? Leave anything disgusting behind…?"

"It's pretty superficial. I don't think there is anything irreparably damaged. And nothing that seems… personal."

MacKenzie wondered how he could tell, but she was somewhat reassured by his words. Maybe just a regular burglar, someone she didn't know. He had tossed the apartment, taken whatever was quick and easy to liquidate, or maybe he even got interrupted before he was able to take anything, and had just gotten away while he could.

They got off the elevator at the top, and the big cop looked at MacKenzie. "You okay? You ready for this?"

"Yes, I think so… if it really isn't too bad…"

He nodded and led her to the door. She felt like it was foreign territory, not her own apartment. She saw everything in disjointed pictures. Saw the broken doorframe again. Heard the police officers who were still in the apartment as they talked in low voices. She went into the front room once more and looked around at the mess. The cop—she looked sideways at him to read his name—Hunt—had primed her when he said it wasn't too bad, and she was able to look at it clinically to see if he was telling the truth.

Furniture had been tipped over and throw pillows tossed around, but she didn't see any broken glass or ripped-up upholstery. She looked around at the decorative touches, looking to see what had been stolen. The paintings had been torn from the walls and thrown around but were still there. Some vases and other bits of pottery and glass was scattered but seemed to be accounted for. She moved slowly into the room. The other policemen quieted and watched her for her reaction. MacKenzie nodded at them politely but didn't say anything. She looked around the kitchen and again found that a lot had been dumped and thrown around, but aside from a few broken dishes that were not priceless china, everything seemed to be intact.

MacKenzie swallowed and went into her bedroom. That was where she expected to see the worst. All of her jewelry gone, including the brooch her grandmother had left her, something dead in the bed or threats painted on the wall in dripping red paint. She'd seen too many horror movies. But it was much like the rest of the apartment, ransacked but not destroyed. In the walk-in closet, her jewelry box had been dumped on the floor, but picking through it, she couldn't immediately identify anything that had been broken. The brooch was still there, and she picked it up and held it in her hand, warming the gold.

Hunt was following her, but keeping his distance, giving her room to look around.

"I don't see anything missing," MacKenzie said. "Not yet."

"Take your time and look around. This guy must have come for something."

MacKenzie nodded and continued to look around. Many of her clothes had been torn down from the hangers, but they were not ripped to shreds or sprayed with paint. Her lingerie drawers seemed to be untouched. MacKenzie frowned at them, opening and closing them without touching anything. She looked over at Hunt. He shrugged.

"Like I said… didn't seem to be personal."

"But if it wasn't personal, then what?"

He raised an eyebrow and waited for her to figure it out. MacKenzie left the closet and looked around again. She went through the other rooms of the apartment, and still didn't see anything that felt personal. It all felt like a violation, and she felt her anger growing at whoever had done this to her, who had dared bust down her door and enter her apartment, putting his hands on all of her stuff.

Then she turned and looked at her desk. All of her usual random papers; invitations, bills to be paid, requests for donations. And her computer.

But not Amanda's laptop.

MacKenzie hurried over to the desk, but she already knew that the laptop was not there, or anywhere on the floor around the desk. The folders of the papers she had photocopied from Amanda's files were also missing. MacKenzie pushed papers around and looked in the drawers of the desk.

"What is it?" Hunt asked.

"My computer. My sister's computer, I mean. And her papers. It's all gone."

"Those are the only things missing?"

MacKenzie nodded. She was having trouble breathing. The burglar hadn't broken in to steal her valuables or to make a statement. He had come for the documentation on the clinic.

"Could you sister have come to get them while you were gone?"

"No. She died."

"Oh, I'm sorry, miss." He looked appropriately embarrassed. "I had no idea."

"Of course you didn't." MacKenzie took a deep breath, still trying to get enough air. "This is crazy."

"Can you think of any reason your sister's things would be stolen? Was there someone else in your family who would have wanted them?"

"No…" MacKenzie thought about her mother demanding the files back and her father getting so angry about her having taken them and looking into the clinic.

Hunt could see that she was thinking of someone. He tilted his head, waiting for her to say something. MacKenzie looked around her apartment. Could Walter have done that to her? Or hired someone to do it? But how would he know that she had kept photocopies of Amanda's files?

He knew one thing, and that was that she had Amanda's computer. She'd told him that. She'd shown him the pictures and told him where she got them. MacKenzie sank to her desk chair, knees too weak to support her.

"Oh, no."

"If you think you know who might have done this, you need to give us his name so that we can follow up," Hunt said seriously.

"No. I just felt a little faint. I think this is all catching up to me."

"It's a shock," Ferris said, hovering in the doorway watching. "It has to be very unsettling to come home to something like this. And worrying about getting it all cleaned up again…"

"I don't care about that," MacKenzie said. "I can have someone in. It's just all so… I can't believe someone would actually come in here and do this…"

"Especially someone you know," Hunt said.

"I don't think I know the person who did this… it must just have been a random thing."

"A random burglar would not have made off with your sister's things. He would have taken the jewelry. And maybe the laptop. But not papers."

"They're probably here somewhere," she looked around at the items scattered over the floor. "I'll find them when I start to clean up. Whoever it was… they probably got interrupted."

He glared at her. "I'm sure you want whoever did this to be found and punished, miss. For us to do that, you have to tell us what you know or have guessed."

"I will… if I figure anything out or have any suspicions, I'll let you know."

Hunt did not look happy about this. But MacKenzie couldn't tell him that it could have been her own father. She still held the brooch clasped in her hand. He might have been angry, but he hadn't been able to bring himself to actually destroy any of her possessions and hadn't taken any of the jewelry. What kind of burglar behaved that way?

2 8

It wasn't until the police were leaving that MacKenzie realized she didn't have anywhere to sleep that night. The manager had been roused from sleep by Eddie, and was hovering near her front door, rubbing his hands anxiously. He licked his lips and nodded to MacKenzie when he saw her.

"I'll have your door fixed tomorrow, Miss Kirsch. It will be done right away," he assured her.

MacKenzie turned and looked at the door again. She wasn't going to be able to shut and lock the door while she slept, and after having her suite violated by an intruder, there was no way she was going to sleep without a locked door to keep her safe for the night.

"Yes, that's great," she said faintly.

"You should arm the burglar alarm when you go out," he advised. "That way, we'll be warned if something like this happens again."

MacKenzie never used the burglar alarms unless she were going away for an extended length of time. Not when she was just going out for an hour or two. If she were going out of town and going to be away for a week. That was when she wanted to make sure that her apartment didn't get broken into while she was gone without anybody knowing about it. Having dealt with one break-in, she would be more careful in the future.

"Of course," she agreed with him. "I will."

"I don't mean you're responsible for what happened," he added hurriedly. "This wasn't your fault, of course. We'll be reviewing the lobby camera security footage to see who might have gotten in here that didn't belong. I don't know how anyone got past the elevator without clearance…"

"Okay."

Where was she going to stay for the night? MacKenzie's first through was to go home to Lisa and to sleep in her old bed, but what if Walter was staying there overnight as well? That would make it extremely awkward. She couldn't sleep under the same roof as Walter if he was the one who had burgled her apartment.

He'd only had a couple of hours between meeting with her and her getting back to her apartment. Could he really have arranged to have the deed done in that short a time slot? He didn't even know that she wouldn't be going straight home. She had been planning to go home. Even she hadn't known that there would be a couple of hours' delay while she met with Lance on the subject of his investigation. So maybe it wasn't her father. Maybe it had been someone else, and they just got lucky, hitting her apartment while she was out. It could have happened earlier in the day, while she was with Walter. Then he couldn't have been the one to order it, because he didn't know about the pictures yet.

"Miss Kirsch?"

MacKenzie focused on the little building manager again. He was still wringing his hands and looking at her worriedly. "Do you have somewhere safe to go tonight? Could we put you up at a hotel for the night?"

"Uh… actually, that would help. I was just trying to figure out what I was going to do."

"Yes, of course. Why don't you get an overnight bag together, and I will call the Harbor Club and book you a room. I will have a car take you over, you shouldn't be driving after dealing with all of this."

She was going to argue that she was just fine driving herself, but then decided to let it go. Why not let him take care of her? She was still feeling shaky and she didn't have anything to prove by pretending to be unaffected by the burglary. He was right, they should have stopped the intruder before he ever got to her apartment, and since it was their fault and they had to fix her door before it was safe for her to sleep there, they could take care of her needs for the night.

"Okay," she agreed. "I'll just pull a few things together."

And so, not much later, she was at the Harbor Club in a luxury suite, feeling comfortable and safe, though a little out of sorts. She was still fuming with anger whenever she thought about her intruder. She couldn't believe that anyone would do such a thing to her, kicking down her door and putting his hands all over her stuff. She hoped it wasn't really Walter or anyone that she knew. Just a random break-in.

But even as she soaked in a hot tub full of frothy bubbles, she knew that it hadn't just been a random thing. As Hunt had said, no random burglar would have taken the files about the clinic. Only someone who didn't want her to succeed in her investigations. They didn't want her to have anything to show the police. They wanted to send her a signal to stop poking her nose into things that were none of her business, unless she wanted to face retaliation.

She tossed and turned most of the night, so when the phone rang in the morning, it didn't wake her up, but instead provided an excuse for her to get up and stop pretending to herself that she was going to get any more sleep. She flipped open her cell phone without looking at the number. She was expecting a call from the police and from the building manager, so she wasn't surprised by an early-morning call.

"Hello?"

"MacKenzie. You're up."

It was Walter's voice. MacKenzie sighed.

"I'm up now," she agreed. "What is it?"

She was aware that her tone was sharp, but she'd had enough of his advice and, right or wrong, the anger over the break-in at her apartment immediately surged back at the sound of his voice.

Water cleared his throat uncomfortably. "I talked with your mother last night and she informed me that I was… err… being unfair to you. That I'm letting my emotions get the better of me."

That sounded just like Lisa.

"And what do *you* think?" MacKenzie asked.

"That your mother is usually right where you and I are concerned. And that means that I was in the wrong. I'm sorry."

She'd heard him say it before in haughty tones that meant he was anything but sorry, but this time it was different. His voice was low and embarrassed. A real apology. MacKenzie's anger subsided. She took a breath.

"Thank you, Daddy. Things have been pretty rough lately. I don't want to be fighting with you."

"You're right. I think we both have the same goal, and we can each be grown up about it and recognize that the other person's position has value. You aren't trying to derail my efforts and I can respect your concerns over the circumstances surrounding Amanda's transplant. Especially since you were kept out of the loop. That must be difficult for you to understand."

"I just don't want to be the kind of person who stands by when I see something going on that is wrong or puts other people in danger."

"And why should I be surprised, since that is the way you were brought up? Neither your mother nor I are known for standing by when there is a wrong to be righted."

MacKenzie smothered a laugh. Between her mother's charities and her father's lobbying, no one could accuse the Kirsches of not getting involved.

"So, are we okay?" Walter asked tentatively.

She again felt the weight of suspicion about the break-in at her apartment. Was he apologizing because he'd already gotten what he wanted? If he was the one who had broken into her suite or hired someone else to do it, then he could afford to make up with her, since he wouldn't be worried anymore about her investigating any further. Without the computer and Amanda's files, MacKenzie would have difficulty in pursuing the matter any further. She wouldn't have any evidence of wrongdoing by Forsberg.

"MacKenzie?" Walter prompted.

"Daddy… I have to go. I have some personal matters to take care of."

"Okay. Well… alright, then. I'm headed back to Montpelier before long. I'll give you a call when I'm back in town?"

"Sure."

"Good. You take care of your personal matters, and don't worry about the clinic. I'll look into any issues there through discreet channels."

She had to wonder whether that meant he would look into her concerns at all, or whether he would just brush them under the rug with her out of the way. She could hope that he meant he would contact Mountain Investigations to take a deeper look into the clinic's operations, but then would Lance tell him about her investigation and what they had already discovered?

"I'll see you when I get back, then, MacKenzie."

"Okay. Thanks, Daddy."

MacKenzie hung up the phone.

MacKenzie had said that she could just call someone in to clean her apartment up, but once she got word from the police that they had finished with it and from the building manager that her door had been repaired and it was now secure, she headed back over to pick it up herself. She found the idea of having someone else in the apartment to clean it up as uncomfortable as finding out that her space had been violated in the first place. She didn't want anyone else in there to see the mess.

As the police had pointed out, there wasn't a lot of damage. It had been made to look violent, but it almost seemed as if care had been taken to make sure that things weren't broken. Mostly, it was just a matter of righting the furniture, replacing the cushions and decorations, and sweeping or vacuuming any debris left behind. While it took a while, it wasn't that much worse than cleaning up after a party, something she'd had to do a few times before leaving home, when she didn't want her parents to discover what she'd been up to while they were away and couldn't call in a cleaning service. In fact, it was easier than cleaning up after a party in some respects. Nobody being sick in the bathroom—or out of it. No passed-out partiers to kick out in the morning. No spilled drinks or food.

She took the opportunity to cull her wardrobe before hanging everything up, deciding to donate a few outfits she wouldn't wear again to charity. She was just standing back to take a look around her bedroom to confirm that everything had been tidied up when her phone started to ring. It seemed like her whole life was ruled by a ringing phone lately. She hadn't been going out with friends or attending any of the functions she normally did, living a much more reclusive life than she was used to. But things had happened. Things had changed. In some ways, she had changed. Maybe forever.

MacKenzie shook off the ennui and picked up her wireless phone. "Hello?"

"Kenzie? It's Lance."

"Oh, hi, Lance." Had it just been the night before she had seen him? She was surprised he had anything else to report so soon. Or maybe he wasn't calling to report, but to see how she was. He'd seemed very interested in her the night before.

"Is everything okay?" Lance asked. "You sound… different."

"I'm fine. Well… as fine as you'd expect."

"Because you're still worrying about your sister's death, you mean?"

"That… and everything else." She didn't know whether to tell him everything or not. But it would be nice to have someone she could tell. Someone who would be understanding, but not jump to conclusions. Being an investigator, he wouldn't be shocked by the developments. "I had a break-in last night."

"A break-in? When?"

"When I was out with you, I guess. Sometime during the evening. I came back to a kicked-in door and my possessions all over the floor."

"You're kidding. Kenzie, I'm so sorry. Is there anything I can do?"

"I don't see what you could do. I've already cleaned up. The door is fixed. There really wasn't much damage, just… disruption."

"Was anything stolen?"

MacKenzie sighed. "Yes… Amanda's laptop and files."

"No."

"Yeah. So I guess I've stepped on some toes. Somebody wants to stop me from looking into the Forsberg clinic any further."

"It sounds like it," he admitted.

MacKenzie cocked her head at the tone of his voice. "What?"

"Hmm?" He made a questioning sound, not sure what she was asking.

"What was that? You sounded… like you just got something."

Lance cleared his throat. "I don't know. I called you today for a reason… not just to check up on you."

"What is it, then?"

"You remember how you asked about what I would do if you and your father hired us on conflicting matters?"

"Yes." MacKenzie dreaded what he was going to say next.

"Walter did call this morning."

"What did he want you to do?"

"I can't exactly tell you that, due to client confidentiality."

"If you had a conflict, then you couldn't hire him, and there is no confidentiality."

She could hear his smile in his voice. "Unfortunately, I do need to keep it confidential when someone asks us to look into a matter, even if they don't end up retaining us. Those initial inquiries can be… inflammatory."

"So what can you tell me about what my father called about? He told me that he was going to look into the clinic and to sort out whether there had been any wrongdoing. He said that I shouldn't push any further, because he was going to do it discreetly."

"That's not exactly what he wanted. In that case, I would probably just ask for a transferal of the file from you to him. Since it's on the same matter."

"So it was on something other than the clinic?"

"It was… a conflict for us," Lance said delicately.

"A conflict with my case?"

"I'm afraid… I can't be much more clear about it."

"So did you tell him that you couldn't?"

"Yes."

"I'll bet he was pretty ticked off about that."

"There are other investigative firms that could help him. We suggested a few other names."

"So you're calling to tell me that he's going to hire someone else."

"I have no idea what he's going to decide."

"He's going to hire someone else to work against me. Trying to cover up what the clinic is doing."

"I really can't say."

MacKenzie shook her head. "He called this morning to apologize," she said. "I really can't believe he would call me to try to smooth things over and say he was going to look into it, when he was really doing just the opposite. Unbelievable. Against his own daughter! When I'm trying to figure out what happened to Amanda! You would think he'd care about her, at least."

"I think he does, Kenzie. But you and he have slightly different agendas, and different ways of going about it. I think you have similar goals, but..."

"That's just what he said. That we both wanted the same thing. But that can't be. Not if he's trying to whitewash what happened to Amanda."

"I'm sorry I can't tell you more."

He really did sound regretful. MacKenzie didn't doubt his sincerity.

"Is there anything I can do?" Lance asked. "I know you said you already have everything cleared up... but anything? Do you want me to run a security check on your apartment? Review whatever measures are in place and see how we can improve things?"

"Uh... maybe. I hadn't really thought about it. The building manager just said to make sure I set my burglar alarm when I go out. I don't usually do it unless I'm going to be away for a long time."

"I would second that. Set it whenever you leave, even for a few minutes. And depending on what kind of system you have, I would set it while you're home, too, so that you're warned of any intruders, or attempted intrusions. Home invasion is a thing. People of your caliber get kidnapped and held for ransom. You really can't be too careful."

"No one is going to try to kidnap me."

"That's what they all say." He said it in a lighthearted way, but it still held an ominous ring. Of course no one ever thought they were going to get kidnapped. If they did, they would take precautions.

"Well... when you put it that way. Maybe you should come and take a look at my system. I really don't even know anything about how it works. I don't think I *can* arm it while I'm inside."

"It may have an 'occupied' mode. I'll take a look when I get there. Are you there now? Is it a good time?"

MacKenzie hesitated, looking around. Everything was cleaned up, and she was tired and thinking it was time to get something to eat. But she could order in. She acknowledged Lisa's voice in her head that she should have food in her fridge so that she could at least get herself a sandwich in a pinch. And she did have bread, for her morning toast, but she wasn't sure how much of it there was or if there was anything else that could be satisfactorily made into a sandwich. She shrugged to herself.

"Sure, if you want to come over now, that works for me. I'm about to order something to eat. You have any preferences?"

"You don't need to get me anything. I'll be there to work, not to eat."

"No reason you can't do both. I assume you have to eat just like the rest of us."

"Okay… well, then, I'm pretty easy. Whatever you like is fine with me."

"What if I like sushi?"

"Sushi is fine."

A lot of men would turn up their noses at sushi, so Lance passed the test. "Actually, I think I'll probably get Italian."

"I was practically born in Italy."

MacKenzie laughed. "Italian it is, then. Do you need the address?"

"I have it."

She couldn't remember giving it to him, but he was a private investigator, so she supposed he had plenty of databases at his disposal to find an address, even if it was unlisted.

"See you soon, then."

29

The afternoon with Lance was enjoyable and the time went by much more quickly than MacKenzie had expected. They had a fine Italian lunch and then she watched him for a while as he investigated the electronic panel for the security system on the wall and prowled around her apartment looking at the various sensors. He also examined the doorframe that the management had replaced, *tsk*-ing and shaking his head as he looked at it.

"What's wrong with it?" MacKenzie asked.

"Well, they've at least replaced the wood instead of just gluing and patching what was already broken, so that's one point in their favor. But this is no stronger than the original work and would be just as easy to kick in a second time. You really need a steel door frame. You have a solid-core door, which is good, but the door is no stronger than its weakest part, which in this case is the frame. A half-inch of wood is not going to stop any determined burglar who can just kick it or use a pry bar to force his way in."

"Will you talk to the building manager or arrange to have someone come in and replace it?"

Lance nodded absently. "Yes, of course."

He continued to putter around the apartment. MacKenzie got bored watching him and went to her computer to check for email and see what else was on her schedule that she should be calling to give her regrets on.

She was checking the gossip columns when he appeared to give her the news.

"Do you have a few minutes to go over this, Kenzie?"

MacKenzie pulled herself out of the news and looked at him, blinking.

"Yes. Of course. Let's go into the living room and you can show me what you've got."

He obligingly led the way. MacKenzie motioned to the couch, where they sat down side-by-side to look over his handwritten list.

"You don't have to do everything at once, of course, but these are the changes that I would recommend. I'll show you how to switch between occupied and unoccupied modes on the burglar alarm, and you can get used to doing that instead of just leaving it disarmed all the time. We'll get that doorframe replaced with something more secure. And here are some other recommendations…"

He went through various items, including a camera pointed at the elevator, a wide-view peep hole on her door, remote monitoring with a hardline directly to the security company, and a few other bits that MacKenzie quickly lost track of.

"Can I put you in charge of all of that?" she suggested. "You're the expert and can ensure that they are actually doing what you've suggested. I won't know how to check that they've actually done what they say they have."

"Sure. We can work out some times for me to be here to get things installed."

MacKenzie wondered whether she should give him a key to let himself in and out as he needed to. But when they were talking about security, was it a good idea for her to just give her key out to anyone? She had hired Lance, but he also had an association with her father. Could she trust him to be there by himself?

He *had* called her to let her know that her father had tried to hire them in a matter that conflicted with MacKenzie's investigation. He was on her side, not her father's.

"Just… uh… let me know when you need to be here, and we'll make arrangements," MacKenzie told him.

Lance nodded his agreement. "Now… let me acquaint you with your security system."

She was a little embarrassed to have him showing her how to use her own system, and that he knew its capabilities when she didn't, but he was the expert, so why shouldn't he?

⁂

Since MacKenzie knew that Lisa was always collecting items for one charity or another, she stopped by the house to get rid of the clothing she had decided she didn't need anymore. She knew that Walter had headed back to Montpelier, so she could avoid running into him again.

Lisa looked pleased to see MacKenzie. "I've hardly seen you since the funeral. And then with you and your father fighting, I didn't think you would come around to visit."

"He's gone home, hasn't he?"

"Yes. He's off. But I wasn't sure you'd come by…"

MacKenzie explained about the clothing donation and held up the box that she had filled.

"Oh, that's perfect." Lisa rarely gushed. She was usually pretty reserved with MacKenzie, reminding her of her responsibilities and what her parents expected of her. But maybe the recent loss of Amanda and the fight between Walter and MacKenzie had prompted a change. She didn't tell MacKenzie that she should have given more, or something different, or collected for a charity of her own choice, she just accepted it and put it to the side to be added to whatever else she had collected. "Do you have a few minutes to visit? I know you're probably getting ready for the gala tonight…"

MacKenzie realized that, distracted by her conversations with Lance, she hadn't remembered to call in her regrets.

"I don't think I'm really up to it tonight, Mother. I was going to call and cancel. I'll still send in a donation, but…"

"You haven't been to anything since Amanda passed. And tonight is special. It's the Kidney Foundation. You're a special guest not only because of Amanda, but also because you are an organ donor. People need to see you, to understand that they can do live donations and still live a full life."

MacKenzie wrinkled her nose. "I don't really want to go out to anything…"

"Please come to this one. We're to sit together. I'd really like to have one of my girls there." A tear glittered in Lisa's eye. MacKenzie rubbed her forehead.

"Mother…"

"I had hoped that Amanda would be able to go with me. But now that she's gone… I'd really like you to be there."

MacKenzie should have waited another day to deliver the clothes to Lisa. But maybe it was time for her to put in an appearance. Lisa was right, the Kidney Foundation was an important cause for both of them. Dear to their hearts after all that Amanda had been through. If any organization needed their fundraising efforts, it was them.

"Well… alright. I'll go. But I hadn't planned to, so I'm not ready." MacKenzie looked down at herself. Dusty and sweaty from cleaning up at her apartment. She needed a shower, makeup, a good dress, jewelry, and of course, her checkbook.

Lisa nodded briskly. "We'll save our visit for at the gala. You go home. I'll take care of these clothes, and you get yourself ready. I'll see you tonight."

"Okay." MacKenzie leaned forward to give her mother a quick kiss. "Love you, Mom. And… I'm sorry that Amanda couldn't be there tonight too."

Lisa nodded. "Thank you, MacKenzie. I love you too. Thank you for coming tonight."

When she got back to her apartment, MacKenzie nearly forgot to put her passcode into the security system. It was down to the last few seconds before she managed to tap it in correctly and stop the countdown. MacKenzie breathed out in relief. It was going to take a while before she was used to that routine. But she imagined that it would become second nature if she stuck to it. It was always hard to start a new habit.

Even though she knew that no one had been in her apartment because the alarm had been set, she still found herself taking a walk around on tiptoes to make sure that nothing was out of place. Everything seemed to be as she had left it, including the dirty dishes that she'd left out after the Italian lunch. So much for being grown up and responsible. At least she had put the leftovers into the fridge.

And she would eat them before they went bad this time. Probably.

She took one last look around the apartment for intruders, though she didn't go as far as to look under the bed for monsters. She stood in her bedroom looking down at the street far below as lights started to come on. Everything was as it should be. There was nothing for her to be concerned about.

MacKenzie got down to work to ready herself for the gala. She would be expected to look as polished as if she had stepped off the runway, even though she didn't have a team of artists doing her clothing and makeup for her. The fact that she was bereaved wouldn't give her any latitude with the crowd that would be at the gala.

Checking her watch and looking at her hair and makeup one last time, MacKenzie transferred everything she would need, including her checkbook, to a small clutch purse, put on her coat, and let the limo know she was on her way down. It pulled in front of the building just as MacKenzie stepped out of the elevator.

Eddie opened the door for her, smiling and nodding, and the limo driver opened the car door for her. MacKenzie slid in, careful not to mash her dress or catch her coat in the door. It would only take a few minutes to get to the ballroom.

There was a car pulled over down the block with its flashers on, and MacKenzie studied it for a moment, frowning. It wasn't usual to see cars pulled over there. But maybe he was having engine trouble. As she was watching, the little black car turned off its flashers and pulled out into traffic, sliding into the lane behind the limo a few cars back.

Not engine trouble, then.

MacKenzie turned her mind back to the gala. From what Lisa had said, MacKenzie suspected she might be called upon to say a few words to potential donors or to accept some honor on Amanda's behalf. She wanted to clear her mind and be prepared to say a few gracious words in either event. It wouldn't do to look like a deer caught in the headlights and have nothing prepared. There would be reporters there, maybe even TV news cameras, and she wanted to do the best for the Foundation, and Amanda and Lisa, that she could.

She closed her eyes and worked through a few words, polishing up what she would say if she were put on the spot. She'd been speaking at such things since she was a teenager, so it wasn't something new or scary, but she wanted to do it right.

The limo pulled up to the event center and MacKenzie waited for the driver to come around and open the door for her. She got out of the car without tripping or stumbling and nodded at him.

"I'll likely need a drive back around midnight."

He nodded. "I'll be here, miss."

MacKenzie walked up to the building and followed the signs and the music to join the gala.

30

I t was good to be sitting with Lisa. MacKenzie had been at too many events alone before Amanda's death, or in need of a date to drag along for appearance's sake. It wouldn't do to appear alone at too many events. People would start to make assumptions. MacKenzie remembered Amanda's dancing eyes as she teased MacKenzie about the necessity of bringing a date, mocking their mother's frequently repeated warnings.

She wished that she were there with Amanda instead of Lisa, but either way, she was happy to be with a family member instead of a date. She wanted to get to know some of the men in her circles better, but on the other hand, if she saw someone too many times or appeared to be getting too close, the rumors of marriage would immediately start. Couldn't a girl get to know a man without their nuptials immediately being announced?

Dr. Proctor was also at the table, along with a woman who might have been his date or an executive assistant or administrator from the hospital. Their relationship was not clear. There were four other people at their table, faces that MacKenzie was sure she had seen at other events, but couldn't be bothered to recall. Everybody smiled and nodded as if they were old friends, and MacKenzie was sure many of them were. It tended to be the same people attending the gala and other similar causes one year after another.

MacKenzie mostly listened to the chatter around her and nodded and smiled as required.

"How are you ladies getting along?" Dr. Proctor asked MacKenzie and

Lisa sympathetically, leaning toward them and putting his hand over Lisa's. "Such a tragedy, losing Amanda like that."

Lisa nodded and blinked at him, giving a strained smile. There was nothing worse than honest sympathy to trigger tears. MacKenzie could deal with all of the social platitudes that were offered about her sister, but one truly sincere and heartfelt condolence would reduce her to tears. Lisa was obviously having a difficult time holding it together.

"We're trying to look forward," MacKenzie said, a little too loudly. "Raising money for the Foundation and other good causes, trying to help others so that they can have all of the benefits that Amanda did. That's what Amanda would want us to do."

Lisa nodded in agreement. She withdrew her hand from Dr. Proctor and looked at MacKenzie, getting strength from her.

"Yes, MacKenzie is exactly right." Lisa looked around the table, involving everyone else in the conversation. "We all need to give generously to this cause. We need ways to treat kidney disease before it is too late and transplants are the only solution. And we need to learn why transplants succeed and why they fail, and what else we can do to improve the quality of life for those who have kidney disease. This is a malady that doesn't just affect those who are old or who have not lived a healthy lifestyle. It strikes children and teenagers and people who up until then were perfectly healthy. We need more research and we need better treatment options. Dialysis is a miracle in itself, but we can't stop there."

Around the table, everyone's heads bobbed up and down. It wouldn't be long before they would be reaching for their wallets. Which was exactly why they were at the table with Lisa and MacKenzie. If there was anyone who could squeeze blood from a stone, it was Lisa.

MacKenzie nodded at her mother and smiled encouragingly. They would focus on the donations, not on Amanda. Even though it was in Amanda's memory, there would be no tears at the gala.

Eventually, the evening wore down. The financial officer had whispered in MacKenzie's ear that the donations had been better than they had dared hope for, and MacKenzie hoped that a good deal of that was due to their efforts on Amanda's behalf. Amanda might not have been able to be there in person that night, but she was there in spirit, delighted at all they had done for her.

Lisa was looking tired and worn by the time the night was over, and MacKenzie saw her on her way home before leaving. Otherwise, who knew how long Lisa might stay there to help encourage the last few guests and help with the clean-up and take-down. She had done enough and needed to get her sleep.

MacKenzie had called for her driver to make sure he was ready, and when she got to the front of the center, she could see a couple of limos waiting to pick up guests from the gala. She walked up to one and bent down to speak to the driver and see which one was hers. Down the street, a car's blinkers went off, and an engine turned on, amplified by the still, crisp night air. MacKenzie looked in that direction for a moment, then back to the driver.

"Are you here for MacKenzie?" she inquired.

"Miss Kirsch? Wait one moment." He got hurriedly out of the car and opened the door for her. "I'm sorry. I should recognize you by sight."

"Oh, there's no reason you should. Thank you." MacKenzie slid into the seat and looked behind her at the car that was waiting to pull into traffic. Was it coincidence that another little black car had been sitting a short distance away when she got into her limo?

She sat in the middle of the seat. As they pulled out, she took a compact out of her purse. She held it up as if to check her makeup and squinted in the mirror at the lights and the shape inside the car behind them. It was too dark and the compact too small to make out any details. MacKenzie closed it and put it back into her purse. When she got back to her building, she took her time, making the driver stand there waiting for her to get out as she kept a lookout for the black car behind them. She made sure that Eddie was standing outside the building ready to hold the door for her. There was no chance of someone jumping out of another car and snatching her. Not between the driver and the doorman. She wouldn't be out of sight of either of them for even a second.

Taking one more look down the street at the car that pulled over and turned on its hazard lights, MacKenzie walked from her car to her apartment building and stepped in the door.

31

How was your evening, Miss Kirsch?" Eddie inquired pleasantly as he followed her in the door.

MacKenzie turned to him. "I think someone was following me."

He looked back toward the limo as it pulled away from the curb. "Someone was following you… at the event you went to tonight?"

"Someone was following the limo. When I left here and when I came back. There was a car waiting a block back both times, and then it pulled out and followed the limousine…"

They both watched out the window, waiting for the car to appear behind the limo. It didn't. MacKenzie let out her breath.

"They know I live here. There's no reason to follow me once I got back. Or they're still waiting out there somewhere. They wouldn't keep following the limo after it dropped me off."

"No," Eddie agreed slowly. "I guess it wouldn't. Do you want me to call the police?"

MacKenzie bit her lip, thinking about it. She was tired and she didn't really want more drama. She just wanted to finish her night at home in bed and not worry about intruders or ill-wishers. She had just spent the night raising money for an important charity. Why would someone target her when she was doing something good?

"I… don't think so. But if you would walk me up or get someone from security to walk me up. I'm just… nervous of something happening." She looked at the elevator. "It's silly, I suppose. You can see me get onto the elevator and it opens right at my door. But I want to be sure."

"Of course," he assured her. "We don't want anything else happening to you."

MacKenzie took a few deep breaths and tried to relax while he contacted the security guard patrolling the building. There was nothing to worry about. Lance had already made sure that her apartment was secure. Or it would be, once the doorframe was replaced with something stronger, and the other items that he advised her to fix. It wasn't like Eddie was going to let her into the elevator with some predator waiting in the car for her. Though someone could get in from another floor on her way up, if there were someone outside watching her to advise them of the timing.

MacKenzie looked back out through the doors but couldn't see anyone lurking in the shadows or peering in through the glass. But there were binoculars, night vision; she didn't know how they might be watching her.

Eddie hung up the phone.

"Bruce is going to check out your floor first, make sure there is no one waiting up there. Then he'll come down, and he'll ride up with you. Make sure you get in your door and are safe before he comes back down."

"Okay. Good. I know I'm being silly about this, but..."

"I don't think it's silly. Not when you already had a burglary." He raised his brows curiously. "I didn't hear... how much was stolen. Did you lose a lot?"

MacKenzie wasn't sure she should tell him any details. But she knew Eddie. He'd been a doorman at the building for several years. Since she had moved in there. He was always around, making sure that her needs were attended to, inquiring politely as she returned from evening fundraisers and other events.

"No valuables," she said. "They took my sister's computer and files."

His eyes widened. "You sister's? I thought she died. Er, passed away."

MacKenzie nodded. "Yes. She did. And someone broke in, apparently just to steal her things."

"That's weird. What kind of information was in there that they wanted to access?"

MacKenzie looked at him, frowning, as she thought about it. Up until then, she had only thought about it from the opposite viewpoint. What was in the files that someone wanted to keep quiet? What was in there that they didn't want MacKenzie to know or to follow up on? But what if it was something that someone else wanted to know? Was it possible that her father would take those papers and the computer so that he would have the information he needed to investigate the clinic?

But that didn't make any sense, because he already had access to Amanda's original files at the house, and he had tried to hire Lance to do something that conflicted with MacKenzie's investigation of the clinic, not that aligned with it.

It was just too much to think about when she was tired at the end of the day, her feelings so tender after thinking about and talking about Amanda all evening, all topped off with a few glasses of wine to get herself through the evening. She rubbed her temples and watched the elevator for Bruce.

In a couple more minutes, the security guard stepped out of the elevator. He nodded to Eddie and MacKenzie.

"Everything looks fine upstairs. Your door is still closed and locked. There's no one hanging around. I'll take the elevator up in freight mode so that no one can interrupt it with a call from another floor. Did you see anyone down here?"

He walked over to the front doors and peered out onto the street.

"I haven't seen anyone suspicious on foot," MacKenzie said. "But I'm sure someone was following my limo to the gala and back tonight."

Bruce nodded. He stared out the doors for a few minutes, making MacKenzie uncomfortable with the amount of time he was spending checking out the street. Eventually, he turned back around. "I don't see anyone else. But that doesn't mean that there isn't anyone out there. Let's get you upstairs."

He escorted MacKenzie to the elevator. He inserted his key into the panel and switched the elevator mode, then pressed the button for the penthouse suite. The door closed. MacKenzie held on to the rail as it lurched slightly. Maybe one glass of wine too many.

They were quiet as the elevator made its way to the top floor. Bruce didn't try to make small talk or to ask her about what gala she had been to.

The doors opened onto MacKenzie's floor, and Bruce indicated she should wait. He poked his head out to check the alcove and make sure for the second time that there was no one hanging around. Then he nodded and motioned her ahead. MacKenzie walked up to her door and unlocked it. It swung open silently. There was no indication of trouble. No sound from within. MacKenzie reached for the security alarm panel and punched in her code. Bruce waited outside the apartment.

"Do you want me to come in with you and have a look around? Make sure that everything is secure inside?"

When MacKenzie was little, she had known there weren't any monsters under the bed, but that didn't mean she wasn't afraid of them grabbing her ankles when she got up to the bathroom in the night. She swallowed and nodded to Bruce.

"I know there isn't anyone here, but…"

"You wait right here," he told her.

MacKenzie looked back at the elevator, but it was still locked into position where he had left it. No one else was going to be able to come up while she was waiting there. They would have to use the stairs, and the stairwell doors were locked on the inside.

Bruce went into the apartment. MacKenzie had left lights on, so he didn't have to turn on any more or stumble around the apartment in the dark. He took a couple of minutes to thoroughly check out the suite, and then returned to the door.

"Everything looks fine. There is no one here, and I don't see any sign that anyone has been here or has gotten into anything."

MacKenzie breathed a sigh of relief. "Thanks, Bruce. I really appreciate it. I know I'm being a scaredy-cat because of what happened, but…"

"You're being cautious. And you should be. You should report to the police that you think someone was following you tonight. If they were, they may not have gotten everything they wanted when they broke in. You could still be in danger of another break-in or an attack."

MacKenzie's stomach flip-flopped. Definitely too much wine. She took a steadying breath and held it for a few seconds, trying to convince herself that he was just overreacting. "I'll think about it. Thanks."

He nodded and left the apartment, pulling the door shut behind him. MacKenzie hit a button on the alarm panel and listened to the elevator doors close in the alcove outside the door.

32

Sleep did not come quickly. She wished that she had invited someone home with her, but on the other hand, the idea of having someone else in her apartment was repugnant. She didn't want anyone else there touching her things and moving things around, taking things that didn't belong to them. She knew it was ridiculous, because nobody she brought home was going to do that. It had been a break-in, not an invited date.

But she still couldn't bring herself to have anyone else there. Not for a while. Without anyone there to distract her or cuddle her as she went to sleep, it was a lot harder to find her way to dreamland. She was feeling a little nauseated after the gala, but hadn't had enough to drink to actually knock her out, and wasn't about to try. She would just end up hanging over the toilet, and that was an even less pleasant way to spend her night than tossing and turning and flipping through channels on the TV. She would have thought that with the number of channels being offered in her TV package that there would actually be something good on, but it seemed to be a hundred channels of drivel.

MacKenzie eventually fell asleep, but it still wasn't a sound sleep. She kept dreaming about intruders and danger and her father telling her to mind her own business and go back to school, and would wake up shaking and trying to remember what had really happened over the past weeks and what was real. She hated the restless dreams, but she wasn't rested enough to get up yet.

Finally, MacKenzie rolled out of bed and had a hot shower. It didn't really wake her up, nor was she able to go to sleep after, but she felt better being up than lying in bed and moving from dream to dream, so she eventually decided to stay up.

She turned on the TV, not wanting to check her computer for email or to go down to the lobby to pick up her newspaper. She just wanted to know what was going on in the world and to know that life continued without her. Her little worries were nothing, compared to what was going on in the world. There were wars and disasters and plenty of other things to be worried about. No one else was worrying about the transplant industry. No one really cared about it other than the people who were waiting for transplants, and they were such a small percentage of the population.

She watched a morning show. The hosts were perky and talked to each other in teasing, sarcastic, and snarky tones to keep the audience interested and engaged. There were serious stories mixed with cat antics and traffic fails and headlines from around the world. All separate and removed from MacKenzie's world.

The world was, in fact, going on without her. Maybe she just needed to get out of her own head and find something else to do. She had been concerned with nothing but Amanda's transplant and the events that had led up to it for weeks. But there had to be other things that were more important in her life. She still had family, and she hadn't been concentrating on those relationships. She had friends she hadn't talked to since Amanda had gotten ill. She had dates that needed to be called back before they started to wonder if she had fallen off the face of the earth. The Kidney Foundation fundraiser wasn't the only thing she was supposed to be attending and helping to raise money for. Maybe she needed to find some other causes. Something that was different from what her mother was interested in.

There was a banner across the bottom of the screen showing other stories that were in the news or coming up on the morning show. MacKenzie watched them, uninterested in the hosts' discussion of deep-fried Snickers bars. Even if she hadn't been reading it, the words that came up on the banner would probably have grabbed her attention.

Kirsch family makes memorial donation to the Forsberg Clinic.

If the world had been going on without MacKenzie, she was pretty sure that it stopped at that point. A donation to the Forsberg Clinic? She had talked to Dr. Dutton about making a donation, but she hadn't actually done so. Had the woman leaked something, hoping to pressure MacKenzie into actually making a donation to save face? It would have been a good strategy. But surely, she wouldn't have done that. Had someone else at the clinic misunderstood that MacKenzie was merely looking into making a donation?

The words scrolled off the screen and were replaced by a line about a spelling bee. Won by a homeschooler, imagine that. MacKenzie waited for the words about the donation to come back up on the screen again. Like the next time they might be different. Maybe there would be a better description, or a correction. Someone in the prompt room had just managed to get the details wrong, mixing up two stories or having a stroke and typing out random words.

But the words were the same.

Kirsch family makes memorial donation to the Forsberg Clinic.

Then the hosts of the show turned from a segue about breakfast foods and eating to prepare for the day to address the story about the donation to the clinic.

"Well-known lobbyist Walter Kirsch and his philanthropist wife, Lisa Cole Kirsch announced today that they are making a sizable donation to the Forsberg Clinic, an organ transplant clinic that specializes in overseas transplants for those who are unable to get them in the United States. The donation was made in memory of their recently-deceased daughter, Amanda Kirsch, who had succumbed to kidney disease. Amanda had two kidney transplants in her short lifetime, one of which was facilitated by the Forsberg Clinic. The family said that Amanda frequently spoke about how thankful she was for the Forsberg Clinic and the chance that they had given her to live a normal life after the failure of her first donated kidney. There will be a presentation...."

MacKenzie stared at the screen numbly. Was this how Walter looked into any potential wrongdoings by the clinic? By giving them money and good publicity?

The hosts chattered on about organ donation and the tragedy of kidney disease and the loss of someone as young as Amanda. They talked about the good that the Kirsch family did in spreading their wealth to various charities and social organizations, in working to lobby for important changes to the law, and so on. They had apparently been given plenty of talking points.

MacKenzie shut off the TV abruptly. She didn't need to hear any more drivel. She was sure she could pull up Walter's press release online, if he hadn't already sent it to her via email. Would he have an explanation for why he had made the donation, or just pretend that she would understand his reasoning for it? Would he assume that she wouldn't even hear about it and he could just maintain the fiction about how he was looking into the clinic's operations and would take care of things if there were any wrongdoing going on there?

MacKenzie ate her breakfast and got dressed in a fugue, unfocused and moving like a zombie. She decided what to do and her body obeyed, even though she hadn't thought through the steps and what she was going to do once she got there. She just knew that she had to go over and figure it out. She accepted that her father was sabotaging her efforts. That much was obvious. If it hadn't been apparent before, it certainly was now. He had arranged for her apartment to be broken into and had stolen all of Amanda's documents and her computer, so that MacKenzie couldn't investigate them any further. He had put a tail on her so that he would know where she was at all times.

He had called Mountain Investigations and had tried to get them to help him with a cover-up of the clinic's activities. When that had failed, maybe he had hired someone else. He had made a big donation to the Forsberg clinic and plastered it all over the news, so that everyone would see that he supported them and that there was nothing wrong with whatever it was they were up to. He was trying to normalize the idea of people going overseas to get transplants, like it was the most normal thing in the world. They would start a new kind of tourism. Transplant tourism. Pretty soon, everybody would be doing it. It would be as normal as going to Mexico to get your dental work done.

She pulled her purse strap up over her shoulder, grabbed her keys, and headed out the door. She remembered at the last moment to punch her code into the security system before she opened the front door to avoid setting it off. That would have been embarrassing. But she supposed she would probably set it off a few times before it became habitual. She would just have to deal with the inconvenience.

She rode the elevator down and deliberately did not check for any little black cars following her when she drove her car out of the parking garage onto the street. If her father were going to have her followed, then so be it. He was about to get a shock.

The drive to the Forsberg Clinic was a pleasant one; it was a beautiful day with mild winter temperatures and snow blanketing the ground in a clean new sheet. But MacKenzie didn't have eyes for it. She was an automaton, another part of her brain taking over the driving and other functions while she intentionally ignored the thoughts that were trying to break through, questioning her decision and the wisdom of what she was doing. She wasn't about to be dissuaded by logic or emotion. She'd made a decision and that was that.

She didn't bother to park in the parking lot of the clinic, but pulled in front of the doors, in the "loading zone only, no stopping" area beside the curb, and parked the car. What were they going to do? Ticket her? Tow her? How would that play out when it hit the media?

When MacKenzie walked into the reception area, the woman at the reception desk obviously recognized her. She jumped to her feet, all smiles, eyes wide in surprise.

"Oh, Miss Kirsch! It's so good to see you again. The clinic is just so pleased about the donation your family made…" She put out her hand to shake MacKenzie's, and then when MacKenzie reached out, she pulled back a little, suddenly uncertain whether she should be shaking hands with such a celebrity. MacKenzie ended up just grabbing her hand and giving it a little squeeze, in a sort of grandmotherly gesture.

"It's nice to see you again too," she agreed. "Is Dr. Dutton in?"

"Well, she is, but she's in a meeting right now. Did she know that you were coming over?"

MacKenzie shook her head. "No. I just came over on a whim. After seeing all the coverage this morning, I really had to be here to just talk to her again and to tell her how much I appreciate what the clinic is doing. I was just at the Kidney Foundation gala the other night, and I couldn't help thinking about how Amanda never would have gotten that kidney transplant if it weren't for the clinic, and who knows how much longer she would have had without it. I can wait until Dr. Dutton is free…?"

"Well, I don't know, she could be a while…" The receptionist was at a loss as to what to do. Should she interrupt the boss? Let the big donor sit and wait? Either way, she was going against her training.

"Maybe you could take her a note that I'm here," MacKenzie suggested. "Then she could decide for herself whether she can see me."

"Uh… sure. I could do that." The receptionist found a pad of yellow sticky notes on her desk and dashed off a note. She reconsidered, threw it away, and tried again. She went through four different drafts before she finally decided what she wanted to say and, holding it stuck to her index finger, disappeared down the hall to take it to Dr. Dutton.

MacKenzie drifted over to the receptionist's desk and looked down at the clutter of notes and documents she had spread out over the desk. She was obviously the only administrative person in the clinic, as MacKenzie had noticed in her tour, and she had documents that needed to be changed, phone logs, and notes stuck to everything. MacKenzie looked for her father's name. It was on the press releases, and there should be a check or some other memo about the donation.

MacKenzie wasn't sure what she was looking for. Maybe the day that he had called to tell them he was making the donation. Was it before or after he had talked to MacKenzie? Before or after the break-in and the apology? Not that it really mattered. How could it matter what day or time he had called? Either he had known that MacKenzie had suspicions about the clinic and had rushed to make a donation without knowing what her concerns had been, or he had waited until after he'd heard everything and seen the pictures, and then decided to smooth things over by making the donation that MacKenzie had suggested she was willing to make to the clinic.

The little receptionist hurried back down the hall toward MacKenzie. MacKenzie leaned on the desk, feigning that she was bored and tired of having to wait for the extended length of time it had taken the receptionist to run her note to Dr. Dutton and to return to the front. The receptionist made a little flurry with her hands, as if trying to contain MacKenzie's impatience.

"I'm so sorry to keep you waiting," she said. "Dr. Dutton says that she can be with you in just a few minutes. Could I get you a coffee while you're waiting? Tea? Water?"

MacKenzie looked around the reception area. It was comfortable enough if she was going to have to wait. Who knew how long it was going to be? She didn't think that the woman would want to keep her waiting. Not with the donation still so fresh in her mind. Maybe she was wondering why MacKenzie had not been there for the ceremony in which Walter and Lisa had handed over their check in Amanda's name. Maybe her parents had given some kind of excuse for her not being there. But for all the woman knew, MacKenzie had been kept out of the loop and now needed her ruffled feathers smoothed and settled. She wouldn't keep MacKenzie waiting for too long. Not unless she was in a meeting with another big donor, maybe someone spurred on by Walter's donation. Or maybe Walter himself. That would be ironic. MacKenzie had no idea what she would do if Walter was already at the clinic ahead of her. They would have to come up with some sort of act to make it look natural.

"Yes, I could do with a coffee," she agreed. She could always do with another coffee. She wasn't sure if she had even finished her first cup that morning. She had forced herself to eat before leaving, but she had no idea whether she had drained her cup or whether it was still sitting beside the coffee maker waiting for her. Her brain had just shut down. Now it was buzzing away, fully engaged, running through scenarios and trying to decide what she was going to say once Dr. Dutton came out. She had no script prepared, no plan in place.

"Certainly, I'll get you one," the receptionist said, looking relieved. "How do you take it?"

"Black is fine."

"Are you sure? We have real cream."

MacKenzie smiled at her for trying so hard. She was sure that the *real cream* worked for some of the donors. They would be impressed that the clinic went all-out to get the good stuff instead of just offering the powdered creamer that everyone else had in their kitchens.

"No, that's fine."

"Artificial sweeteners? Whatever you like?"

In a minute, she would be telling MacKenzie exactly what kind of beans they had, from what side of the mountain, and how they had been ground. MacKenzie shook her head.

"I'll just have black. Plain old black coffee. Thank you."

The little woman nodded and disappeared through another door to get MacKenzie's coffee. MacKenzie swept one more look over the contents of the desk, but she decided that what she wanted wasn't there. They weren't going to put anything incriminating on the front desk in the reception area of the clinic. What was she thinking?

She went over to one of the well-upholstered chairs and sat down, sinking into the cushions until she wasn't sure if she were going to be able to get back out of it again.

The receptionist took longer than MacKenzie had expected to just get a cup of coffee. She must have decided that whatever was sitting on the burner wasn't good enough for MacKenzie and had decided to brew a fresh pot instead. MacKenzie could smell it wafting through the air and her stomach growled in interest. Eventually, the woman returned, and handed MacKenzie a china cup of coffee with great ceremony.

"Here you go."

"Thank you." MacKenzie looked toward the hallway that led to the boardroom. She didn't think Dr. Dutton could wait much longer. She would be wondering what her big donor wanted, worrying that there was going to be a big bust-up. MacKenzie complaining that she hadn't been recognized, a withdrawal of funds, something devastating. It must be gnawing at Dr. Dutton as she tried to finish with her previous appointment.

Finally, she heard a door and voices as Dr. Dutton moved out of the boardroom and down the hall with someone else. Final, finishing-up noises as she closed the deal or reassured him about what was in store. Then they were coming out of the hallway and into view.

MacKenzie raised her eyebrows.

John Hopewell. He was shaking hands with Dr. Dutton and hadn't yet finished turning around. Hadn't yet seen MacKenzie sitting there. And Dr. Dutton had probably not told him who it was that she had to meet with after finishing up their meeting either.

What had Hopewell been there for? He had led MacKenzie to believe that he wasn't very happy with everything that had gone on overseas. He had his own doubts and concerns about the way that the transplant had played out. And he'd been plagued by symptoms similar to Amanda's since his return. MacKenzie wondered briefly whether they did have the same donor—a deceased donor, obviously—or whether they just gave everybody that same donor profile. The fictional face of the universal donor. But surely then someone would have noticed before then that everyone was getting organs from the same donor?

Eventually, John Hopewell finished the handshake and goodbye and turned around. He took two steps toward the door and then his eyes caught on MacKenzie. She watched him for his reaction, giving him a tentative smile. She wasn't sure how he would take seeing her there, or how she should take his presence. Were they on the same side? Opposite sides? She had hoped that her information that Amanda had contracted malaria during her transplant trip would help him and he would be able to regain his health with proper treatment.

But he obviously did not have warm feelings toward her for supplying that bit of information. Rather than looking grateful or greeting her warmly as someone who had helped him out in the past, he scowled at her, his face darkening with anger and distaste. If he could have punched her in the nose and gotten away with it, she was sure he would have. She had never seen such an expression of hate and disdain on someone's face. Certainly not aimed toward her.

"Uh… John….?" Even as she was saying it, he was turning away from her and continuing his egress. MacKenzie tried to get to her feet, but the soft cushions kept her from being able to jump up quickly and by the time she put her coffee down on the table and managed to rise, tugging down her skirt to make sure she didn't expose herself to the rest of the room, Hopewell was out the door, striding toward his car without a backward glance. MacKenzie blinked after him.

She knew there was no point in following him. Even if she managed to catch up with him, to keep him from getting into his car and to talk to her, she wasn't going to like what he had to say. She wasn't going to be able to convince him that whatever he was upset about wasn't true, that the clinic was still lying to him and feeding him a big story. She just let him walk away.

There was silence for a moment. Had either Dutton or the receptionist been able to see the look that Hopewell had given her? Or had they both been far enough behind them that they couldn't see anything?

"Miss Kirsch," Dr. Dutton said in a smooth voice. "It's so nice to see you again. How are you?"

MacKenzie took a deep breath, pasted a smile on her face, and turned back around. "Ah. Miss Dutton. It is good to see you again. I'm fine. And you?"

She watched Dutton struggle with whether to correct MacKenzie that it was Dr. Dutton, not Miss Dutton, but the moment passed, and Dr. Dutton just let it go. She could have tried a "Just Mildred, dear," and avoided the issue again, but she didn't. Apparently that kind of casual greeting wasn't used, even for a major donor like someone from the Kirsch family.

"What can we do for you today?" Dr. Dutton asked, her teeth bared in a smile that was more of a grimace.

"I was wondering… I wasn't able to get here when Walter and Lisa were by, so I didn't get to see the language that was going to be used for the memorial donation… I just feel a little left out of the loop, and I wonder if you could fill me in on the particulars."

That was a pretty good bluff. Dr. Dutton frowned, but nodded. "Yes, certainly, of course. I'm sure your parents could have given you a copy…"

"I haven't seen them," MacKenzie said. "This all ended up happening so quickly. I'm not sure what the hurry was, but…"

"Certainly, of course. Let me see… Why don't you come to the boardroom with me, and I'll just get everything together? You can see the whole package and how it will all work."

33

MacKenzie looked over the documents that had been signed between Walter Kirsch and the Forsberg Clinic. She recognized his signature, but couldn't make out the name of who had signed on behalf of the clinic, even though she knew the names of the directors. The signature was an illegible scribble. She paged through the details of the donation and the recognition that Walter had asked for.

She felt the tension across her forehead as she looked it over, trying to figure out what he was doing. He was giving the money for an expansion of the hospital. He wanted to name a wing after Amanda and there were details of the picture and plaque that he wanted posted about her. That all seemed pretty generic. It was a lot of money, but he gave more to other causes. Money would stretch further in a third world country where most labor could be bought at pennies a day instead of dollars an hour.

She didn't know how much it would cost to have materials shipped there, if they really used the expected standard of materials and didn't just clap together a shack like the place where Amanda had taken pictures. If they even bothered to build what they said they were going to. How hard would it be for them to send Walter a mock-up of the wing that they expected to build, to take a picture of a plaque on a wall somewhere, and provide other photographic proof that they had done as they had agreed?

But as she read further, she started to admire her father's wolf-like cunning. The terms of the donor agreement demanded that he be given a tour of the hospital both before and after the construction, and that he be allowed to bring a small group of donors there for a fundraiser to drum up further donations for the clinic, to be used as the clinic designated them. Everything was worded in such a way as to seem natural and boilerplate, but MacKenzie could see his thinking behind it.

He wouldn't actually transfer the funds to the Forsberg Clinic until after he'd had a pre-construction tour of the facility. That would put to rest the question of what conditions Amanda had been treated in and whether there really was a hospital or whether she had been operated on in some jungle shack that was full of flies and mosquitoes and bodies piled like cordwood. He would get a chance to see if there was a building that matched the photos that had been taken. He would meet some of the surgeons that did the transplants.

There was to be an organ donor display recognizing the donors who had given living or post-mortem donations to the transplant recipients. MacKenzie supposed that would give Walter and whoever his investigators were more names to look into, to see whether they really were using live donors and the materials given to both Amanda and John Hopewell on their donors had simply been a paper mix-up, or whether they were using post-mortem donations and trying to pass them off as live donations.

There were clauses about Walter auditing the financial records of the clinic. Other due diligence clauses that would allow him to look into other aspects of the operations of the clinic.

Her father was a wily one. Her fury at him gradually dissipated. He had taken what she had started with, a bluff that she wanted to give a donation in Amanda's name, and he had finagled it into a huge media event and had talked the clinic into signing an agreement that would force them to show their hand, at least in some of the matters they were concerned about.

Why hadn't he told her what he was doing? Why hadn't he given her a heads-up on the donation, even allowed her to appear with them at the media conference? She would have liked to have been part of it. But maybe he hadn't trusted her to be able to keep her cool or to keep a pleasant expression throughout it all. If she had shown her hand, it could have blown the whole deal for him. Lisa was an old pro at press conferences like that one. She didn't know whether Walter had told Lisa the real purpose for his donation to the clinic, or whether she thought it was to recognize what they had done for Amanda and to memorialize her name. Would Lisa have gone along with the deception?

Lisa had been able to keep up the fiction of Amanda's kidney surgery on the island, rather than disclosing the details to MacKenzie. She had kept from both of them the fact that she and Walter had been divorced for several years. She certainly had the ability to stay quiet and perpetuate a fraud.

"This all looks so great," MacKenzie told Dr. Dutton, when she made an appearance to see if MacKenzie had finished going through everything. "I'm amazed that you were able to pull everything together so quickly. When was Walter first in to hammer out the details?"

Dr. Dutton passed a hand over her furrowed brow. "It all came together very quickly," she said. "It's only been a couple of days. He had his lawyers draw up the papers and we only had twenty-four hours to go through things and counter anything. He's a very… persuasive man when he puts his mind to it, isn't he?"

MacKenzie laughed. "That he is," she agreed. "He's had lots of experience in talking people into things. He's the master."

"We are very appreciative of everything that you and your family are doing here. Allowing us to expand the hospital to serve more people, to allow us to increase the number of transplants that we are able to do… this will serve so many people. Save so many lives."

MacKenzie nodded. "Yes. It will make a big difference to a lot of people, won't it?"

She thought of Amanda, laboring to breathe in those last few hours, and of John Hopewell, thin and pale and battling recurring fevers.

Indeed, it could change the lives of many people.

MacKenzie had a copy of the agreement setting out the terms, and the descriptions of the plaque and memorial that had been arranged for Amanda. That was what she should want, as a donor who wanted her sister's life to be recognized. She really only wanted the agreement so she could think about it and maybe talk to Walter later, when everything had settled down and they were able to meet and discuss it confidentially. She knew that he didn't want her to investigate any further and, seeing that he was indeed taking a hand in investigating it, she decided the best course was just to let him follow the plan that he had mapped out.

She drove home feeling much calmer and more in control of herself than she had on the way to the clinic, giving Dr. Dutton a pleasant "Goodbye and thank you, Miss Dutton," to leave her fuming about the professional discourtesy. She went back home to her apartment, resolved to let Walter take the lead in investigating the clinic's claims and proving that their facility on the island actually existed and was in use.

She went to her computer and checked her email when she got home. She had neglected it for a few days and, although she didn't correspond with a lot of people through email, she did have a number of invitations to respond to, some sympathy notes, and some notes and queries about the donation her family was making to the clinic, mostly from reporters who wanted more filler or follow up to their stories.

But in between all of the formalities and expressions of sympathy, there were a couple of emails that made MacKenzie frown. She couldn't tell where they had come from, the email addresses nonsensical collections of letters and numbers. She figured that if she replied to them, the emails would just bounce back. They were just spam. Except she had to stop and wonder why any spammer would suddenly be sending her emails about organ transplants. Were the online spammers that sophisticated? That they would be able to track her interests and target her specifically? She didn't think that technology was quite to that Big Brother level yet.

But her family's name had been in the media in association with organ transplant, so maybe that had triggered more targeted spam. It was one thing to have to weed through incessant noise about male enhancements and women who wanted to make friends online with graphic pictures that she really did not want to see. It was another to have some anonymous source sending her links about the transplant industry.

She looked at the links, wondering whether she dared to click anything. Once she did, they would be sure to publish her email address as a legitimate one, increasing the amount of spam that MacKenzie received. They would likely lead to sites about women and their forbidden desires; then she would have to spend the rest of the day trying to wipe that muck from her brain.

MacKenzie opened the header of the first email, something that one of the guys she had dated a year earlier had taught her to do, to see if she could see where the email had originally come from. There wasn't as much hidden code as she usually saw in spoofed emails, and she couldn't see multiple email addresses and domains, just the one that the email purported to have come from. She looked at the link again. It appeared to be an international news site. It probably redirected. It probably didn't go to a news site after all.

MacKenzie opened a new browser window and typed the main URL in, in case it said it was going to one site but actually directed to another. She waited for the browser to redirect and take her to another site, but it did not. The graphics on the page slowly downloaded, grinding slowly away, until she could see the front page of the paper.

There was no way she could tell whether it was a legitimate paper or not, but it appeared to be. The international stories that appeared were ones that she had seen in the newspaper lately, not wild stories about celebrities or bizarre stories that were targeted to outrage or trigger curiosity. She looked at the link in the email again and typed the page name after the URL. She again waited for it to redirect to a new site, but it did not, starting to download the new page.

MacKenzie swallowed, her eyes moving over the story. She avoided the pictures, yet kept looking back at them, fascinated and horrified.

It was an investigative piece on organ donations in China. It was one of the countries with a higher transplant rate and much lower waiting list than the US. She had assumed that was because of the denser population, maybe because of some government inducement or social pressure to donate organs post-mortem for the good of society. Asian countries had a different outlook on societal good from that of Western countries. They were far more oriented to public good. So it made sense that there would be a lot more pressure for organ donation, both living and post-mortem.

But that was not what the article said. There had been rumors for some time, and the investigative journalists were starting to uncover evidence that the donations for many of the organ donations being performed in China were not coming from living donors, or at least, not the kind that were expected in Western countries. There were indications that they were coming from death-row inmates and political prisoners. There were stories, denied by the authorities, discounted by the public as urban legend and hysterical conspiracists looking for attention.

After all, everyone knew that WHO and the United Nations and anyone else who knew anything had spoken out to deny that there could be anything illegal or untoward going on in the organ transplant industry.

MacKenzie opened a new tab in her browser and typed in a search for illegal organ transplants and black-market organ trade. The headlines and snippets that popped up on her screen were the familiar, reassuring statements. Statements that there could be no illegal organ trade. That it was impossible for a criminal enterprise to be organized around organ transplants. That they wouldn't be able to find surgeons with the technical skill to perform such surgeries. That there was no way such practices could have any existence and it was all urban legend.

That was what MacKenzie had heard before. The legends that popped up in whispered stories or emails that a friend had heard from a reliable source about people waking up without their kidneys, bleeding out or shivering in a tub full of ice were so ridiculous that she was sure no one could really believe them. There was no evidence that any kind of illegal organ trade was going on, so how could there be? The thousands of surgeries that would be required for it to be a profitable enterprise could not possibly be hidden away. There would be some whisper of it in the news. Police would have active investigations, cases where they knew that illegal transplants had actually taken place, and she had heard nothing.

She switched back to the original article, worried about reading more, but galvanized against what she was going to read there. It was just a story that someone had made up, or a mistake had been made. Like MacKenzie looking at the bodies in Amanda's photos and assuming that they were organ donors, it was easy to jump to conclusions without knowing the facts.

But the more she read, the more concerned she felt and the more her stomach sank, feeling sicker and sicker. She took a few steadying breaths.

She read the account of a prison worker who talked about the political prisoners and death row inmates being removed from the prison at night under suspicious circumstances. They were not due to be released or transferred, but they were taken away to hospitals for treatment that they didn't need. There had been no medical diagnosis made, so why did they have medical transfer papers?

She read the account of a hospital worker who testified of corneal removals from patients who were not only still living, but not under sedation. The screams and butchery described were so gory as to be unbelievable. Bodies being taken to the incinerator while they were still bleeding freely.

Dead bodies don't bleed.

She clicked away from the screen and checked to see if she'd received any other email that she hadn't reviewed. Her mind just wouldn't accept and process what the investigative article claimed. How could any government look on their prisoners as mere providers of organs? And where were those organs going? Were they all being used for domestic Chinese transplants? Or were they being used for the international organ transplants? The articles that she had read clearly stated that there was no transportation of organs across borders.

That was why the donors that the Forsberg clinic had used had to fly to the island themselves. Amanda's live donor couldn't just have her kidney removed in Germany and then have it transported to a location hours away before it could be transplanted. They had to have the donors right there. The Chinese atrocities, if they really did exist, had to be confined to the borders of China. They were closer to the island than Germany was, but still, they couldn't have been transported that far, possibly held up in customs or some other queue. They had to have the donors and the recipients in the same place.

MacKenzie thought about the pictures.

A row of bodies under a sheet. All with dark-skinned feet. If Amanda's donor was from Germany, then she couldn't be one of those people. She would have been white. MacKenzie had seen the picture of her, a young blond woman. There was no one like that in the dark shack.

Her father had to be right. Those bodies that had been temporarily stored in the shack had to be the results of some other tragedy. An epidemic. Poverty. Starvation. They could not be part of the organ transplant trade. They didn't match the identities that the donors had been shown before flying overseas to have their transplants done.

MacKenzie turned back to the article and once more looked at the pictures and the descriptions, trying to maintain a neutral, skeptical eye. They could be the victims of a natural disaster. Of a war. Of a terrorist attack. There was nothing about them that said that they were transplant donors or political prisoners. Their bodies were anonymous. There were no pictures of their injuries, no sign of what had killed them. There was, in short, no proof that they were actually of what they said they were.

And major world organizations had said that such a thing was impossible.

3 4

Eventually, MacKenzie went to the other email from the unknown informant or spammer. Which was he? Someone who was trying to lead her astray or make her click on something that was going to take her down a rabbit hole, or someone who really wanted to inform her about what was going on in the transplant business? The first one was a news article that appeared to be legitimate, so she wondered whether the second would take her somewhere nasty, or whether it would be another article, as bad or worse than the first.

She didn't think she could face much more as far as shocking pictures and blood-soaked sheets went. She just couldn't deal with it, even knowing that it was probably just a scam. What reason would anyone have for making her think that China was doing illegal transplants, harvesting organs from unwilling donors? Was it meant to lead her away from the clinic or to them? Were they connected in some way with such a thing? Or was it to distract her from a possibly low-level concern—less sanitary conditions, some unrelated deaths, marginally unethical payments for organs—with unproven, hysterically pumped-up nonsense? Was it just a distraction? Or was it true?

She looked at the other link. Like the first, there was nothing in the URL to tell her what it might be about. It did look like it could be another news site. But legitimate or not? And what was it going to be about? Verification of the veracity of the first? Maybe they had a source who could prove what it was that was happening in China. But why did she need it to be verified? She couldn't do a thing about what the Chinese government did in the transplant industry.

As before, MacKenzie typed in the root URL before anything else. Rather than a news site, it was an electronic bulletin board. She glanced at the top list of categories, and it seemed to be mostly medical related, but covering a wide range of topics. The page that she had been pointed to was obviously going to be something about transplants. MacKenzie clicked on a couple of subcategories, drilling down deeper into discussions of disease, organ failure, and transplants. She could see that most of what was being posted was written by patients who needed or had received transplants, or by other voices in the community. Not medical professionals. Likewise, not by reporters or government personnel. Just people on the street, like she would talk to at a fundraising event. Like John Hopewell and Magnus Phelps and Amanda. She clicked on a few topics and read through them. There was stuff on kidney donation and transplant, both live donors and post-mortem donations, but she didn't see anything on transplant tourism or China. Everything seemed to be safe and straightforward. Discussions of procedures, upcoming transplants, recovery and, for some of them, rejections and relapses. It was sad to see how many transplants failed, and families were left like hers, with their loved one back on dialysis or dead.

She returned to her email and referenced it while she typed the rest of the URL into the location bar. She pressed enter and waited for it to resolve, either taking her to some unrelated site or into a thread that she was supposed to be interested in.

MacKenzie waited while the thread loaded, then started scrolling through it. Immediately, she was assailed with pictures of starving children. A cautionary tale of how poorly other countries were doing, she assumed. Stop worrying about the rich few getting transplants and start worrying about real problems that affected millions, like starvation and preventable disease. But the headings and the text around the pictures were not about poverty. Instead, they were discussions of children being kidnapped for organ transplants. MacKenzie quickly closed the tab, not wanting to read any more.

Her gaze was drawn to her attache, where the pictures from Amanda's computer still resided. She remembered the varying sizes of the bodies under the sheet. The ones that she had wondered whether they were women or children. She knew for a fact that children were not being kidnapped for organ harvesting. She had read statements to that effect, very strong ones, and she knew that it couldn't be the case. No one was stealing children for their organs. It was the stuff that nightmares were made of, which was why people were trying to use it to frighten each other, but it was not something that was actually going on. The organizations that were in the know said so.

She switched back over to her research. The articles that proved the transplant scare stories were just urban legend. She pulled a report from 1994 up on the screen and read a portion aloud to herself.

Since January 1987, rumors that children are being kidnapped so that they can be used as unwilling donors in organ transplants have been rampant in the world media. No government, international body, non-governmental organization, or investigative journalist has ever produced any credible evidence to substantiate this story, however. Instead, there is every reason to believe that the child organ trafficking rumor is a modern "urban legend," a false story that is commonly believed because it encapsulates, in story form, widespread anxieties about modern life.

Given the total lack of evidence for the child organ trafficking myth, its impossibility from a technical point of view, and the widespread, serious damage that it has already caused and is likely to cause in the future, the United States Information Agency respectfully requests that the U.N. Special Rapporteur give maximum attention and publicity to the information in this report, which demonstrates the groundlessness of reports of child organ trafficking and the impossibility of such practices occurring.

That was pretty clear. And that was the United States Information Agency and the United Nations. If they said that such a thing was just an urban legend, then she was satisfied that it was so. They had far more ability to investigate such a thing than she did. There was no child organ trafficking, and there never would be.

The atmosphere of MacKenzie's apartment was suddenly stifling. She needed to get out and to get some air. She couldn't stay there reading horrific things any longer. She needed to go out and do something to take her mind off of all of the rumors that something horrible was going on in the organ transplant trade. What she had thought was a simple case of escaping strict regulation and ending up having to deal with the consequences of that choice was now a simmering hotbed of rumors and crazy accusations and conspiracies.

She didn't want to deal with it or even to think of it.

She turned her computer off and picked up her bag. She picked up her cell phone and realized that the message indicator was flashing. She hit the voicemail button and dialed in her passcode and listened. It was Dr. Proctor. She wasn't sure when he had called her, but he said he was concerned about her and Lisa after seeing them at the gala and just wanted to make sure that everything was going okay. He left a somewhat rambling message, but MacKenzie decided she should call him back just to reassure him that everything was fine with Lisa.

She wasn't sure what she was going to say about herself. Maybe she could gloss over that part and just focus on her mother. Lisa was of Dr. Proctor's generation and he was probably more interested in her mental health than in MacKenzie's. That was why he had called MacKenzie, for the evaluation of someone who was closer to Lisa and could better judge how she was managing in the wake of her daughter's death.

MacKenzie rehearsed a few lines in her head before pushing the buttons to call Dr. Proctor back. She waited, thinking it was going to go to voicemail on his end, and then he picked up.

"Hello?" He sounded uncertain, as if he didn't know who it was. MacKenzie supposed he didn't recognize her number from just having called her once, and cell numbers didn't have any caller I.D. information associated with them.

"Dr. Proctor, it's MacKenzie."

"Oh, MacKenzie." His tone warmed. "I'm glad to hear from you. I know that the gala was a great success, and I see that your family has made a donation to the Forsberg clinic, like you mentioned they might. I just had a nagging feeling… the other day when you and I talked, and I told you that you should probably go to a private investigator if you wanted someone to look at the backgrounds of the doctors at the overseas Forsberg transplant hospital…"

"It's okay, Dr. Proctor. I understand that your time is precious, and you can't really be using it to search people halfway around the world. I did get someone who could help me in sorting them out, so you really don't have to worry."

"Oh? Who did you get?"

"I went through a private investigations firm, like you suggested."

"I see." There were a few seconds of silence and MacKenzie frowned, wondering if he actually disapproved of her going to a private investigator after he had said that was what she should do. Had it just been intended to be a brush-off and he didn't really expect that she would follow through like she had?

"It turns out that it's actually a lot harder to track international surgeons than you would think," MacKenzie told him. "You need all kinds of other information like birth dates and where they trained and social security numbers, that kind of thing. Because two doctors halfway around the world from each other can have the same name, or a doctor can change his name, or not show up as being credentialed in another country."

"I imagine so! As much as we say the world is getting smaller, it is still a challenge to track people across multiple countries or continents."

"Exactly. I'm glad that you didn't waste your time on it. Better that we leave that to the professionals."

She hoped that with that, his anxiety over brushing her off would evaporate and he would be able to be happy and go on.

"I guess your family has made that donation, so you must have been satisfied with what you found out. I just wonder if there was anything else that you were concerned about. Anything at all…?"

MacKenzie hesitated. Was he really interested in hearing more… really interested…?

"I don't know. I guess things are okay now," she said. Even to her own ears, it didn't sound very convincing.

"It sounds like there is still something. Do you want to share it? I worry about you, MacKenzie."

"I really shouldn't bother you. It has all been straightened out now. Like you said, we've made our donation to the clinic."

"But you still have doubts? I thought you had worked through all of that."

"I have. We have. It's just… well, there's one loose end."

She wouldn't tell him about the emails and the urban legends. But maybe she could show him the pictures. Maybe then he would understand why she had been so concerned. Like Walter, he might just explain them away. Maybe a doctor's explanation would be more satisfying than Walter's. Or maybe like Lance, he would suggest that she should follow up with someone on them. Not the police or FBI, but a medical organization. Some overseer that would do the work overseas and be able to provide an explanation. There had been some kind of outbreak, or accident, or tribal war. They would know because they would already be watching what was going on. They wouldn't be cut out of the loop and just guessing about everything like she was.

She took a deep breath, picking up her purse and her attaché. If she showed the pictures to one more person, would she get one more interpretation? Or would he side with one of the other explanations, throwing more weight on one side or the other?

"Yes, please tell me about it. What is this one loose end?" Dr. Proctor coaxed.

35

She had thought when she arrived at Dr. Proctor's office that she would find it bustling with activity. She hadn't realized that she had spent her afternoon on web research on illegal organ trafficking and by the time she got to his office it was already after hours. There was no receptionist or nurse at the desk outside his office, no patients waiting, and the corridors of that wing of the hospital were almost deserted. But Dr. Proctor had invited her to go see him, so she knew she would find him still in his office when she got there.

She tapped on the door that stood slightly ajar and pushed it open far enough to poke her head in to alert him of the fact that she was there, without intruding on him if he were in the middle of something.

"Dr. Proctor?"

"Ah, MacKenzie. Come in."

He gave her a big, welcoming smile and motioned for her to enter. MacKenzie opened the door the rest of the way and sat down in the chair that he indicated.

"So… all of this fuss over the clinic…" He gave her a small smile and a shrug. "I suppose that progress will always bring with it controversy, especially when we are talking about transplants. There seems to be more demand for organs all the time, but the ethics of providing more and more organs to meet the demand becomes problematic."

MacKenzie nodded in response. The ethics became problematic? She could show him how problematic they had become. It was no longer just a matter of whether they had ventured into a gray area.

"Why don't you tell me what it is you are still having problems with?"

"When I looked at Amanda's computer after she died… I found some pictures."

Dr. Proctor raised his brows. "Pictures?"

"She took them while she was away for her transplant. Or what I thought at the time was just an innovative new surgery."

He waited for more. MacKenzie looked around. It was so quiet in that part of the hospital. She had never felt quite so isolated there before. It was like being in a school playground after all of the children were gone. Sort of uncomfortable and spooky.

"There isn't anyone who can overhear us," Dr. Proctor said. "It's just you and me."

"I know. It's just… I don't quite know how to talk about this. I haven't had much success in talking about it with anyone else."

"People don't believe you?" he asked sympathetically.

"People don't *want to* believe me, I guess," she agreed. It was an uncomfortable truth, and who wanted to deal with uncomfortable truths?

"I'll believe you, MacKenzie."

MacKenzie wasn't sure he would. He hadn't been terribly open to the idea that there was anything unethical—or worse—going on at the clinic up until that point.

She took a deep breath and tried to calm the racing of her heart and the tight knot in her stomach.

"Well, here it is." She delved into her attache to pull one of the pictures out. She looked at it for a moment herself, as if to confirm that nothing had changed, and it still showed just what it had the last time she had looked at it. Every time she looked at it. But it was exactly the same picture that she had studied so many times before. Ingrained upon her memory. She handed it across the desk to Dr. Proctor.

He looked at it, and his eyes widened a little. MacKenzie waited for the explanation. "Oh, you see, these are from…"

"So…" He stared at the picture. "I was afraid of something like this." He shook his head. "From the time you first started asking questions, I feared that something like this could turn up."

MacKenzie nodded, waiting.

"Why don't you come around here, and I'll show you," he suggested. He opened his desk drawer to pull out a highlighter or marker.

MacKenzie got up and walked around the large desk to his side. Her attention was completely occupied by the picture Dr. Proctor laid down on the desk. What exactly was he going to show her that would change her perspective and put it in a new light?

"I always told Lisa and Walter you were a very smart girl. The reason you did not do as well as they hoped in school was because you were too bright. You were bored by it all. There wasn't enough to challenge you."

MacKenzie didn't know if that were true. She'd never been a star pupil. Not one of those who rose to the top and was always getting the highest marks. She'd done well, never struggling to pull off respectable grades, but she hadn't been passionate about her courses of study and did just what she needed to to maintain a good grade point average.

"You were always very quick to understand what was going on with Amanda's health. The medical words and the biology behind what we were seeing was always plain to you."

MacKenzie shrugged. "Biology was one of my favorite subjects in school. I enjoyed the dissections…"

He chuckled. "Exactly. Now, if you'll just get really close here…"

MacKenzie bent down, squinting at the photo. It didn't get any clearer being closer to it. The resolution and the lighting were too poor.

MacKenzie felt a prick against her belly and pulled back slightly, uncomfortable. She looked down and realized that Dr. Proctor had not pulled a highlighter out of his drawer, but a scalpel. He now held it against her, the sharp point just grazing her skin. She looked at him, her mind denying the reality of the situation, trying to come up with logical alternative explanations. A joke. A misinterpretation.

"I'm sure you remember the locations of the major arteries and organs in your abdomen," he said quietly. "An experienced surgeon like I am could map them in his sleep."

MacKenzie looked at the picture, hoping for some kind of revelation. He would point to it and indicate what had been done to the torsos of the victims in the photo. But they couldn't see the torsos, not through the sheet. There wasn't any marking or indentation on the sheet that showed what had been done to the people in that picture. Not that she could see, anyway.

"I told your parents that you would be upset about the fact that the kidney you donated to Amanda had failed. That they needed to keep you out of the loop about the second donation so that you wouldn't feel bad about it. It was more kind to just let you go on thinking that your kidney was keeping Amanda alive."

"Why would I feel bad? I know that transplants can fail. The body can reject the organ or it just stops functioning like it was supposed to."

"I said it because I didn't want you poking your nose into everything. I didn't want you picking up on anything that was going on that wasn't in the normal course. I couldn't be sure that you wouldn't twig to something if you were there."

"You kept me away," MacKenzie said.

She still wasn't understanding what he was saying. She was sure that she was misinterpreting his intent. He had always been good to Amanda and her family. He was a respected surgeon, one of the most prestigious in the hospital. She hadn't had enough sleep and she was reading something into his comments.

"Yes, I kept you away. And if Amanda had not contracted malaria…!"

"I wouldn't have known," MacKenzie agreed.

"They should have tested the donors," Dr. Proctor muttered. "That was sloppy. Some people contract malaria without ever showing the signs."

"She got malaria from the organ donor?" MacKenzie asked, not sure she understood the leap.

"Of course. What do you think happens when you transfer an infected organ from one person to another?"

"But the donor was from Germany. How did she get infected that quickly?"

But she knew the answer without Dr. Proctor telling her. Looking down at the bodies in the picture. No white skin on any of them. No blond German woman.

"Who were they?" she asked Dr. Proctor. Her brain was starting to warm up, starting to understand that she had to get out of there before he killed her. So it was partially because she wanted to know the truth and partially because she wanted to stall, to come up with a plan that would get her out of danger.

No one knew she was there. She hadn't told anyone where she was going. She hadn't called Lisa to say that she would come by for dinner after visiting Dr. Proctor. She hadn't asked Lance to investigate him. She hadn't written it into her planner. No one looking at her room would have any idea where she had planned to go when she had left.

"Why does it matter?" Dr. Proctor said. "They were the people who were providing the organs that we needed so desperately. The people who could save Amanda and so many others. That was the important part. To get the much-needed organs for the Americans who were willing to pay for them."

"Their lives mattered just as much as the Americans," MacKenzie argued. "All life is… is sacred."

"Sacred?" He gave a little laugh. "Since when have you taken to religion?"

"I don't mean in a religious way. I mean… doesn't all life have intrinsic value?"

"If you saw the way these people lived, the things that they had done, you wouldn't have thought so. These people were refuse. They were just the packages the needed organs were being transported in."

MacKenzie felt like throwing up right there on his desk. How could he view human beings like that? He was a doctor; he was supposed to respect life. How could he have changed so suddenly from the kindly doctor to someone who was only in it for the money? MacKenzie tried to pull away from him, away from the scalpel, but he gripped her arm and pressed the blade more firmly against her.

"You can't get sentimental," Dr. Proctor insisted. "No more than you felt sorry for the animals that you dissected in biology. They were a learning tool. You didn't even recycle their parts. You just opened them up, looked at them, and tossed them out. If there was nothing wrong with that, what is wrong with transplanting organs to save lives? Not just Amanda, but others too."

"John Hopewell?"

He looked at her, raising his eyebrows. "Yes, John Hopewell. You got further than I had thought."

"He has malaria too."

Dr. Proctor nodded slowly. "That's not a surprise."

"They had the same donor."

"Yes. One kidney each."

"And any others? What about others who have died already? How many people were infected with dirty organs?"

"They would have died without a transplant. So you can't judge the correctness of what was done by whether they lived or died. All of them would have died without transplants."

"Amanda could have lived longer. She died from malaria. She wouldn't have had that without the transplant. She could have lived on dialysis, waited for an organ here in the States. Followed the proper protocol."

He pressed the knife into her. "You're so sure of yourself. So sure that you're right and that everybody else is wrong. You've just been manipulated by the system. When they tell you there's only one way to do things, you assume that they're telling you the truth. But they're not. There's plenty of room to do things differently. We could be saving a lot more people, if they would just listen."

"So is this all your operation? Your name wasn't on anything at the Forsberg Clinic. I didn't think you worked in transplants."

"They couldn't have done it without me. There are a lot of people who you wouldn't think were involved, but an operation like this takes a lot of manpower, a lot of different moving parts."

"My father?"

Dr. Proctor tipped his head, looking up at MacKenzie questioningly. "What about your father?"

"How long has he been involved with the clinic? How deeply? Has he been giving them money right from the start?"

"You need a lot of money to build a hospital and fund a business. Yes, he needed to put capital into it. But he wasn't the only one. There are a lot of funding sources. And the money required to fly these donors in from all around the world." He said it in a sarcastic tone. There was no one flying around the world. There were no donors from Germany or Iran. Wherever they were coming from, it was not around the world. They were islanders, or Chinese prisoners, or kidnapped children. A charter plane flying a couple of hours, not a whole day away.

MacKenzie closed her eyes, trying for a moment to push all of the emotion away, to keep it compartmentalized. She couldn't have it slowing her down and muddying her thinking at that critical moment. All of the grief and horror and disgust had to go away somewhere else. She stared down at the photo on Dr. Proctor's desk, but let her peripheral vision pick up the rest of his desk, trying to work out a strategy.

"What about this?" she asked, pointing to something in the dark corner of the photo, and then pulling her hand back so that Dr. Proctor could see it.

"What?"

She only needed him to look for a minute. She only wanted the momentary distraction, a shifting of his attention away from the scalpel he held against her body.

With the hand that had been pointing at the photo, and then drawn away, MacKenzie grabbed a rectangular paperweight of cut black marble with a commemorative plaque mounted on it and smashed it as hard as she could into Dr. Proctor's forehead.

She pulled his knife hand away from her body, aware that the blade had sunk deeper when she had hit him, rather than him pulling away so he could hold his head and protect his face. She tried to writhe away from the hand that had an iron grip on her arm, but it was harder than it should have been. He wasn't a frail old man. He was still in his prime and his hands had been strengthened by hours of surgery. She wrenched and twisted her arm, fighting wildly to get away before he managed to bring the scalpel back around to do further damage, hoping to capitalize on the blow to his face and the blood starting to drip down his forehead. She managed to wrench free and ran for the door, but he was right behind her, trying to trip her up, swinging the scalpel, and shouting at her.

MacKenzie got out the office door, into the office of the administrative assistant who acted as the gatekeeper and made for the next door. Her way was blocked.

Her brain was on fast forward, barely able to take in what she saw. A man blocked her exit.

Lance Reacher.

Was he the one who had been following her? Sending her email? He could have bugged her apartment under the guise of boosting security. She had no clue how he was involved in the racket.

Lance put out his hand to grab her and MacKenzie danced back.

"Kenzie. It's okay. What's—?"

He moved into the room and was distracted by Dr. Proctor's presence. As soon as his eyes darted to the side, MacKenzie slipped out the door behind him.

She heard an angry shout from Dr. Proctor, then a crash. She looked back but was unable to see what was going on inside the office. She had been home free. She could just run and leave it all behind. But she couldn't. Not if Lance could possibly be on her side. If there were even a chance of it, she couldn't run away and leave him there tangling with Dr. Proctor.

MacKenzie hesitated, then went back to the door and peeked in, worried that when she did so, she would be back in the line of fire. Both of them would grab her, and Dr. Proctor would be able to finish the job he had started. But she saw Lance holding Dr. Proctor off, refusing to let him get close to the door that MacKenzie had escaped through.

"Don't you have a gun?" she screeched.

Lance didn't look away from Dr. Proctor to see what MacKenzie was doing back again.

"Of course not," he said. "This isn't TV. I'm an investigator, not a cop. Get out of here. Call for help."

"I'll call. I have a cell phone."

"Go somewhere safe, then call."

MacKenzie ignored the instruction, digging into the handbag still slung across her body. She pulled out the phone.

"Give it up!" she shouted at Dr. Proctor. "You can't get away with this. You don't want to hurt anyone."

"Your belief that I can't get past an unarmed man is charming," Dr. Proctor said, advancing on Lance, who picked up a heavy binder and threw it at him. "But terribly misplaced. With a scalpel in my hands… I am the angel of life or death."

"Lance, be careful," MacKenzie warned. The phone rang through to the cell company's emergency operator, and then at her instruction, on to the city's emergency operator. MacKenzie described their location and answered the question about whether there were any weapons on the scene in the affirmative. She squeezed the phone tightly in her hand, wishing that she had chosen to pack a gun instead of just a cell phone. A cell phone might be fine for most emergencies she encountered, but not for a standoff with an armed assailant.

Dr. Proctor jumped forward and managed to get Lance's arm, making him jump and jerk back. He tried to grab Dr. Proctor before the surgeon could get another chance to bring the knife in. Dr. Proctor kept it low, aimed toward Lance's belly, rather than the overhand "Psycho" stabbing position.

"Careful," MacKenzie moaned.

Lance threw a stapler at Dr. Proctor, but the surgeon's reflexes were quick, and he batted it to the side. He suddenly jumped into Lance and, with his weight throwing Lance off balance and the knife still in his skilled hands, he managed to get a quick thrust into Lance's body.

MacKenzie screamed. She threw herself into the fray, even while her primitive brain warned her it was an exceptionally stupid move, but with the two of them both fighting off Dr. Proctor, the surgeon decided it was time to cut bait and ran for it.

MacKenzie didn't have any desire to chase after him. She turned to Lance. "Let me see. Move your hands." She pushed his hands back when he tried to stop her.

"I'm fine," Lance protested.

"No, you're not." Blood was flowing at an alarming rate. "Get down. Now. Lie down so I can put pressure on it."

She forced Lance onto his back and pressed both hands over the gash, using her weight to provide the pressure. But she couldn't seem to slow it.

"We're in a hospital," she said aloud to herself. "How do I get trauma doctors fast?"

She looked around the office, swearing. "Come on, Kenzie, think!" she ordered herself.

She took a chance on removing pressure for a moment, jumped across the room to pull the fire alarm switch, and grabbed the desk phone, throwing it on the floor beside Lance. She resumed the pressure with one hand and started hitting buttons on the phone. She needed someone, she didn't care whether it was security or the morgue, just as long as they could understand where she was and send help.

There was a tinny voice coming from the receiver. MacKenzie snatched it up. "Emergency in Dr. Proctor's office," she barked. "A stabbing. Send a trauma team now!"

"The fire alarm has been activated in that section," a calm male voice told her. "You need to evacuate the area."

"I pulled the fire alarm. Send paramedics. Emergency room doctors. Something. Right now!"

"The wing is being evacuated," he repeated.

"No! No, don't evacuate it, send help! I pulled it because I need help!"

"Ma'am, we have a protocol to be followed—"

MacKenzie shrieked. "Send help!"

"It's okay," Lance said. "Calm down, Kenzie. It's going to be okay."

She looked down at him. Lance's face was getting gray, but he smiled at her as if totally relaxed. "They always seem like they take too long," he said. "It seems like everyone is moving in slow motion. But they'll get here."

"How did you know? How did you get here?"

"Followed the followers." He grinned. "We knew that your father wanted you investigated, whether he was the one who had your apartment broken into or not. He had to go to another firm, so we watched to see who was watching you, and then we watched them…"

"Where are they?"

"They didn't come in. Must just be reporting on your whereabouts. But I didn't like the idea of you being in here alone, not knowing where you were or who you were talking to, so I came in…"

MacKenzie swore. She kept pressing on the knife wound, but Lance's clothes were soaked through. Dr. Proctor knew where every artery was in the human body. He had been fighting wildly, but he knew the human body like other people knew the bus routes or highway system.

"Stick with me, Lance," she urged. She could feel his body quivering under her touch and she didn't like his pallor. He licked his lips and tried to smile again, but his eyes kept sliding to the side and he couldn't seem to stay focused on her.

"It's fine," he assured her in a whisper.

"It's not fine. Where is my help? Where are they?"

Lance closed his eyes, not answering.

"Come on, Lance. Don't do that. Don't go to sleep." She nudged him, trying to keep him aware.

MacKenzie swore again. The fire alarm was still clanging loudly, getting on her nerves. She could feel Lance's resistance draining away, the tautness of his muscles relaxing.

"No, no, no…"

Finally, there were voices approaching. MacKenzie, kneeling over Lance's still body, shouted to hurry them along.

"Over here! Please help, now!"

They stopped talking and the footsteps increased in speed. In a moment, there were a couple of paramedics and a doctor, peering into the office to see if it was safe to enter.

"He's bleeding so fast," MacKenzie told them. "Come here, please. Help."

They were quick and sober, pushing in to examine Lance and to treat him, speaking to each other in quick mutters, calling for additional backup and equipment, saying nothing to MacKenzie. She moved back and sat on the floor, her back leaning against the secretarial desk, and watched them with warm tears running down her cheeks.

37

The next thing she knew, she was waking up in bed. MacKenzie lay there for a few minutes before opening her eyes, analyzing what she could remember and trying to decide how much of it had been a dream. Surely the part about Dr. Proctor being a villain could not be true. There was never a nicer guy. He'd always been very kind and attentive toward MacKenzie and her family.

Maybe the whole thing was a dream, all the way back to Amanda having malaria. Could there be anything more ridiculous? Amanda with malaria? Like she'd been serving in the war in India?

Eventually, MacKenzie had to open her eyes. She looked around for Amanda. She was in hospital, and that meant that Amanda must be there. Amanda was always the patient. The only time MacKenzie had ever been a patient had been when she had given Amanda her kidney. And she certainly couldn't do that again.

But there was no sign of Amanda. There was only Lisa, sitting in one of the visitor chairs beside the bed, just as she always sat next to Amanda's, when she was a patient there. MacKenzie blinked and tried to get Lisa's attention. Her mother appeared to be asleep sitting up.

"Mother," she whispered. She wanted to talk louder, but her voice was apparently not quite up to the job yet. "Mother. Lisa."

Lisa startled and her head came up, looking immediately for her daughter. She focused in on MacKenzie.

"Oh, MacKenzie. You're awake. That's very good."

"Why am I here?" MacKenzie asked. She was a little shaky and woozy, but wasn't quite sure why they would have put her in a hospital bed. She could have just weathered the flu at home in her own bed. Either in her apartment or at Lisa's house in her old room.

"You have a small injury," Lisa said. "I'm still trying to understand what happened. Something to do with Dr. Proctor…?"

"That was real?"

"Yes."

"Ooh…" MacKenzie shook her head. "I can't believe it. Really?"

"Tell me what happened."

"He was… he was the one who told you not to tell me about Amanda's transplant."

Lisa looked surprised. "Yes, that's right."

"They were harvesting organs. Not from live donors who had consented. But from people who… there is a black market for organ transplants… people who get kidnapped, children, death row inmates…"

Lisa's eyes widened. "No. That's just urban legend."

"No, it's not. It's happening. There are people being killed for their organs. For transplants like Amanda had. It's the truth."

"No, dear. No."

"That's how she ended up with malaria. Not because she got bitten by a mosquito. Because the person whose kidney she got had malaria. She was infected by the kidney."

Lisa frowned. She was still shaking her head, but she didn't protest verbally.

"Amanda took pictures while she was over there. Pictures of the bodies. They were on her computer."

"She would have told me that," Lisa insisted, eyes getting even wider.

"If she remembered. Maybe the anesthesia or the malaria fever mixed her up or made her forget it. But they were still on her computer."

"No there wasn't anything like that. I looked at her computer."

"You didn't look deep enough."

"You'll have to show me." Lisa's voice had a bit of an edge to it.

MacKenzie closed her eyes. "I can't. I don't have it anymore. Daddy had it stolen from my apartment."

"Walter wouldn't do that."

"You know how upset he was when I took the files."

MacKenzie met Lisa's eyes and Lisa looked away.

"I made photocopies, and he took those too. He didn't need them for filing taxes. He wanted to make sure that no one else saw them so that no one else would know what was going on."

Lisa frowned and didn't say anything. MacKenzie tried to twist to turn over and look at Lisa more easily and gasped at the pain that flared in her stomach. She clapped a hand over the spot, which was a bad idea and made her cry out.

"What is it, should I get the doctor?" Lisa started half out of her chair.

"No. No, it's fine." MacKenzie kept her hand over her stomach and probed it gently with her fingers. She could feel the bandage under her hospital gown. She remembered Dr. Proctor holding the scalpel to her stomach and threatening to cut her. He had cut her when she had hit him over the head, but it had been uncontrolled, not an intentional slash. She hadn't even noticed that she was hurt during all that had followed.

"Did they get Dr. Proctor?" she asked. "Did they arrest him and put him in jail for what he did?"

"They were looking for him. I haven't heard what happened. The police said they would come back and talk to you when you were ready."

MacKenzie let out her breath. "I'm not ready to talk to anyone yet. Except you. What about… What about Lance, is he okay?"

Lisa looked at MacKenzie, her mouth a long, thin line. Her eyes seemed very tired and shadowed. "MacKenzie, I don't even know who that young man was. How was he involved in all of this? You knew him? He was a friend of yours?"

"He was a private investigator. I hired him to do some background checks for me, and then he helped me with my apartment after it got broken into. And then… I guess he was following to make sure that I was okay after Daddy… tried to hire him."

"Hire him for what?"

"You'd have to ask Lance the details. He said that Daddy wanted… to know what I was doing. He had someone following me. He wanted to know who I was talking to, probably, make sure I wasn't going to cause any trouble for him, because of his lobbying."

Lisa didn't say anything. MacKenzie swallowed hard. She closed her eyes.

"Mom?"

"Yes, MacKenzie?"

"Lance? Is he okay?"

Her eyes were closed, and still she could sense Lisa shaking her head.

"Tell me he's not dead."

"The doctor said that the stab wound he sustained… it cut the aorta."

MacKenzie swore softly. "Why would he do that? I tried to stop it. I put pressure on it. I called for help. And the blood was just everywhere."

"They said you couldn't have done anything else. He bled out too fast."

MacKenzie was able to check herself out of the hospital pretty quickly. Her wound was only minor, unlike Lance's. She'd lost blood, but they'd given her a unit or two to top her off, and once everything was stitched up, she was ready to go. Her mother wanted her kept at the hospital for a few more days, but there was really no need. It was just a way to keep an eye on MacKenzie and make sure she was okay.

Her father was a problem. MacKenzie could only hold him off for so long. And the man was used to having his own way. Sooner or later, he was going to get it. So eventually, MacKenzie had to agree to meet with him, even though she was sure she was not going to like what he had to say.

Rather than picking out a coffee shop or somewhere that Walter would normally hammer out a deal or make his threats and demands, MacKenzie suggested a walk. It had probably been years since he'd strolled anywhere, and he seemed awkward and uncertain for once. MacKenzie was glad to have him off balance.

"I know you probably think I betrayed you with the donation to the Forsberg Clinic." He didn't sound apologetic, but he did sound uncertain.

MacKenzie lengthened her stride to keep up with him better. She disliked how much longer his legs were than hers and how it made her scurry to keep up. Long legs were one thing in a boyfriend, but quite another when she was trying to have a conversation. She tried to keep her voice light and matter-of-fact.

"Actually, I went to the clinic after the announcement and I got myself a copy of the agreement."

He looked at her, surprised. "You did what?"

"I wanted to know what was going on, so I snooped."

"Which is just what I told you not to do."

She nodded. "I know."

"And what did you think?" he asked grudgingly.

"I think you got an engraved invitation to go snooping on the island to see if you can figure out where Amanda took her pictures."

"It won't be there anymore."

"What? Why not?"

"It was just a little slapped-together shack. They could knock that down in a day. If they think that they're compromised, they'll get rid of all the evidence. It had a concrete pad floor, and that will be harder to get rid of, but they can just build something else over top. I'll go back there, and I'll look around the hospital and see where she was treated, and where they propose to put the new wing. And I'll look around the grounds, anywhere she might have gone on her own. But I won't find anything. I won't see what Amanda saw. They'll be far more careful after all of this."

"Are you going to go ahead then and give them the donation and build a new wing?"

"I'm studying their financials and their management policies. They might need someone with my skill set on the board."

MacKenzie looked at him, opening her mouth to object.

"And if they appoint me to the board, I can promise you there will be no… non-consenting donors."

"You think that's something the board of directors know about and can control?"

"It will be."

"And you'll keep working on changing the transplant laws."

"The current laws are stifling. Far too few transplants are being done here in comparison to more progressive countries in the world. I'm not saying we let them have a free-for-all. But things could be improved."

MacKenzie sighed and they walked in silence.

"What are your plans?" Walter asked.

MacKenzie took a quick look at him. "My plans? Why would my plans change?"

He didn't answer at first, letting the silence build up between them.

"Okay, I have been thinking about the future," MacKenzie admitted.

Walter nodded and waited.

"Dr. Proctor said a few times that he thought I should continue my education… in medicine. He said he thought I had a talent with it. And I always like biology and medical stuff at school."

"He told me a few times I should encourage your interest. But I happen to know… if I pushed you too hard in one direction, you'd just push back. Do you want to go into medicine?"

MacKenzie nodded slowly. "I kind of do. Maybe not a doctor at a hospital or clinic, but maybe… something in research. Or maybe pathology. This whole thing finding out about Amanda's transplant… it was kind of cool. The non-threatening parts. Figuring out that she had malaria. Finding out about the transplant industry and what people are dealing with. Yeah, I enjoyed that part. The research and digging up clues as to what had happened."

"It will mean a lot more education. You never were big on school."

"I know," MacKenzie agreed. "But mostly because I was so bored. If it's something that really interests me… that wouldn't be so bad."

38

One year earlier…

A manda pushed open the door and walked into the outbuilding. Her toes curled when she stepped onto the concrete floor, cold on her bare feet. She walked through the building, looking around, her eyes searching in the dark, trying to make sense of everything.

She had heard people there earlier. She had seen doctors going in and out of the building. It didn't make sense, doctors using such a dismal, dark little building when they had a big, modern hospital available. She supposed it was some kind of garage or tool shed. But what tools would the doctors need that wouldn't be stored in the hospital? She hadn't seen a lot of cars driving around. She didn't think there were more than a handful of them on the island, just enough to transport patients and their families between the various buildings. The air strip to the housing settlement to the hospital and back.

It was still too warm in the shed. It was too warm everywhere she went, and she knew part of it was her fever. When the fever finally broke, maybe she would feel comfortable again but, until it did, she was going to be hot and cold and uncomfortable. That's how it always was.

She pushed open another door. Nothing seemed to be locked. It was just what it appeared to be, an empty warehouse, something left over that had been built before the hospital. Fallen into disuse.

Amanda looked around. The stench was terrible. What was it? Rats? some other kind of vermin? It definitely smelled like something had been caged there. Defecation and urine and the odor of sweat and bodies. Some wild animals, and the natives who took care of them. Amanda covered her nose with the back of her hand, trying to control her gag reflex. She walked through the room to the other side. The floor under her feet was sticky, and she didn't look down, didn't want to know what she was walking through. She'd clean off her feet when she got back to the hospital.

When she got into the next room, she stopped, startled. She realized she had walked into somebody's sleeping chamber. Was the warehouse used, then, to house servants? People who worked at the hospital or kept the grounds? She thought they would have their own huts on the island, like the one that Walter and Lisa were being housed in.

She was about to walk out, and then realized that the people were not sleeping. They were still as statues. Maybe they were statues, waxworks or something that the hospital was going to use for an information display.

The sheet pulled over them covered up their faces and their bodies. There were a few feet sticking out the bottoms of the sheets. Amanda pulled out her phone and took a couple of pictures. It was probably too dark for anything to show up when she uploaded them to the computer.

She got closer, peering at the statues. Why were they being stored in the warehouse? It couldn't be because it was cooler there. The hospital was better air-conditioned than the shed.

She got close enough to be sure that she had been right the first time, and the figures lying there were not statues, but people. But they still were not moving, not even the small movements of someone deep in sleep, the rise and fall of their chests, the whisper of breathing.

They were bodies.

Corpses lying all in a line and covered up so no one would have to look at them.

Amanda looked around in panic. Flies buzzed in the air and she felt nauseated. It was just the fever. The fever was making her hot and nauseated and she was probably hallucinating too. She wasn't really seeing anything there, she was back in the hospital in her own bed, fast asleep.

She tucked her mini flip phone into her bra. Kenzie was always laughing about her shoving things into her bra, but Amanda was so often in hospital robes with no pockets, that she'd had to find some solution. So she insisted on a bra under the robe. If she had to take it off for some physical examination or test, she would, but most of her doctors wanted to examine her kidneys, not her boobs, and they didn't care if she felt more comfortable wearing a bra under the hospital johnnies.

Amanda started to retrace her steps. She shouldn't have left the hospital. She shouldn't have left her room. She should have just stayed in her bed where she was told to, and then she wouldn't be having this hallucination about horrific things in the shed.

She left the building and walked back along the well-worn pathway toward the hospital. She tried to reason that the shed was just where they stored dead bodies. Like a morgue. Except that it obviously didn't keep them cool. She couldn't come up with an explanation for why they would transfer the bodies there, but obviously they did. She hoped that none of them were organ recipients she had met at the clinic's social events. She had been introduced to a few people who would be getting transplants around the same time as she would. Hopefully, none of them had ended up out there, in the shed.

"Here she is!"

A couple of men hurried toward her. They had on white lab coats and were coming toward her from the hospital.

"Amanda. What are you doing out here? You are supposed to stay in your room."

"I wanted to… get some fresh air." Amanda couldn't think of a better reason. She wasn't sure why she had come there in the first place.

"Come back to your room. You shouldn't be wandering. You could pull out your stitches."

She allowed them to take her by the arm and lead her back to her room. She was getting tired and wanted to lie down. She wanted to stop the nightmares and wake up again. The hospital would be cooler, and soon her fever would break and she'd be able to think straight again. In a few days, she'd be able to see her family again and go back to the States. Then everything would go back to normal.

EPILOGUE

Kenzie was focused on the forms in front of her, making sure she got everything down the way that Dr. Wiltshire would want it. She was still learning the ropes and didn't want the medical examiner to be disappointed with her work. She heard the man's footsteps coming down the hallway and blocked him out, trying to finish before she allowed him to interrupt her.

"Hang on. Just let me finish this part up, before I lose my train of thought."

He was quiet while he waited. He didn't interrupt, insisting that his request was more important than her form. He didn't pace around and sigh loudly or fidget. Eventually, she filled out the last space and looked up at him raising an eyebrow in inquiry.

He was a small man. Not quite as short as she, but below average height, with a slim build. He had dark hair, buzzed very short. His eyes looked slightly hollow, as if he'd been sick recently.

"You must be Kenzie," he said.

"I don't know if I must be," Kenzie said in good humor, "but I am. Kenzie Kirsch. And you are?"

"Zachary Goldman. From Goldman Investigations."

She was surprised. "A private investigator?" She looked him over more carefully, comparing him to the ten-year-old memory of Lance Reacher. Physically, there was little similarity between them. But Kenzie thought she could see that same acceptance and compassion that she'd felt from Lance all those years before. Like he'd had a few hard knocks of his own along the way and would understand about hers. He didn't give off the same aura as some of the chauvinistic cops who came down to her basement desk blustering and expecting to be treated like they were something special.

"Yes."

"And what can I do for you today, Mr. Private Investigator?"

"Zachary."

"Zachary," Kenzie repeated, smiling. "What can I do for you?"

"I need to order a copy of a medical examiner's report. Declan Bond."

"Bond." Kenzie remembered the case. Who could forget the poor little fellow? Especially when he'd been the son of a celebrity. "That's the boy? The drowning victim?"

"That's the one."

She shook her head, studying him. "Why do you need that one? It's closed. A determination was made that it was an accident."

"I know. The family would like someone else to look at it. Just to set their minds at ease."

"You're not going to find anything. It's an open-and-shut case."

"That's fine. They just want someone to take a look. It's not a reflection on the medical examiner. You know how families are. They need to be able to move on. They're not quite ready to let it go yet. One last attempt to understand…"

Kenzie remembered how she had searched for meaning in Amanda's case. She'd needed something else. Some kind of explanation for why Amanda had had to die.

"Okay, then… there's a form…" She went through her drawers to find him the right one. He didn't argue that he didn't want to fill out his own forms or thought they were somehow beneath him. He just started working on it.

She went on with her own administrative tasks while he filled it out. There were always plenty of forms to be filled and filing to be done. It took him longer than she expected to fill out the form, which most of the cops she dealt with barely scribbled a few details into. He put the pen away and put the form down beside her, allowing her to finish what she was working on. Kenzie finished hers and picked it up. She was surprised at his neat printing.

"You have nice printing!" She laughed at herself. "No reason why you shouldn't," she said quickly. "It's just that the majority of the forms that get submitted here are… well, to say they were chicken scratch would be insulting to chickens."

Zachary chuckled. "That's the difference between a cop and a private investigator."

"Neat handwriting?"

"Yeah. Cops have to fill out so many forms, they don't care. You can just call them if you need something clarified. Me… I know if I don't fill it out right, it's just going to go in the circular file." He nodded in the direction of the garbage.

"I wouldn't throw it out," Kenzie objected.

"If you couldn't read it? What else would you do?"

"I would at least try to call you."

Zachary pointed. "That's why I printed my phone number so neatly."

Kenzie smiled and nodded. "It's very clear," she approved. She gave him an appraising look, sensing that maybe there was some chemistry going on between them. Maybe he had printed his phone number so clearly for *another* reason.

"You'll call me?" Zachary asked.

"I'll let you know when it's ready to be picked up."

Zachary nodded. He hesitated for a minute before turning to leave. He smiled one last time, and then left. Kenzie suspected it wasn't the last time she was going to hear from Zachary Goldman.

Read more about Kenzie Kirsch and Zachary Goldman in *She Wore Mourning*, book #1 of Zachary Goldman Mysteries by P.D. Workman and in *Doctored Death*, book #2 in the Kenzie Kirsch Medical Thriller series

Previews of both books follow!

BACKGROUND NOTE

The 1994 report that Kenzie read stating without reservation that child organ trafficking is an urban legend was:

The child organ trafficking rumor: a modern 'urban legend', A report submitted to the United Nations Special Rapporteur on the sale of children, child prostitution, and child pornography by the United States Information Agency, December 1994, by Todd Leventhal, United States Information Agency Washington, D.C.

Since January 1987, rumors that children are being kidnapped so that they can be used as unwilling donors in organ transplants have been rampant in the world media. No government, international body, non-governmental organization, or investigative journalist has ever produced any credible evidence to substantiate this story, however. Instead, there is every reason to believe that the child organ trafficking rumor is a modern "urban legend," a false story that is commonly believed because it encapsulates, in story form, widespread anxieties about modern life.

Given the total lack of evidence for the child organ trafficking myth, its impossibility from a technical point of view, and the widespread, serious damage that it has already caused and is likely to cause in the future, the United States Information Agency respectfully requests that the U.N. Special Rapporteur give maximum attention and publicity to the information in this report, which demonstrates the groundlessness of reports of child organ trafficking and the impossibility of such practices occurring.

By 2016, black market organ trafficking, including child organ trafficking, was an accepted reality. Here is the abstract:

Child organ trafficking: global reality and inadequate international response. Bagheri. Med Health Care Philos. 2016 Jun;19(2):239-46. doi: 10.1007/s11019-015-9671-4.

In organ transplantation, the demand for human organs has grown far faster than the supply of organs. This has opened the door for illegal organ trade and trafficking including from children. Organized crime groups and individual organ brokers exploit the situation and, as a result, black markets are becoming more numerous and organized organ trafficking is expanding worldwide. While underprivileged and vulnerable men and women in developing countries are a major source of trafficked organs, and may themselves be trafficked for the purpose of illegal organ removal and trade, children are at especial risk of exploitation. With the confirmed cases of children being trafficked for their organs, child organ trafficking, which [was] once called a "modern urban legend", is a sad reality in today's world. By presenting a global picture of child organ trafficking, this paper emphasizes that child organ trafficking is no longer a myth but a reality which has to be addressed. It argues that the international efforts against organ trafficking and trafficking in human beings for organ removal have failed to address child organ trafficking adequately. This chapter suggests that more orchestrated international collaboration as well as development of preventive measure and legally binding documents are needed to fight child organ trafficking and to support its victims.

KEYWORDS:

Child organ trafficking; Organ trafficking; Organ transplantation; Trafficking of human being for organ removal; Transplant tourism

DOCTORED DEATH

A KENZIE KIRSCH MEDICAL THRILLER #2

1

W ill awoke in a dark room. He couldn't remember where he was. He wasn't sure what had woken him up, but something was wrong. Something was definitely wrong. He sat up and looked around, straining his eyes in the darkness. His breathing was irregular and he had a difficult time swallowing. Was he sick? He must be sick. It looked something like a hospital room.

He needed to talk to someone and find out what was going on. He slid his feet out from under the covers and put them on the floor. It was carpeted rather than tiled like a hospital room normally was.

He realized as he slid out of the warm spot he'd occupied on the bed that he was wet.

Something was definitely wrong. A grown man didn't wet the bed.

His legs were wobbly and weak. He held on to the bed as he tried to push himself upright. The room lurched around him. He couldn't find his balance.

He needed to get help. Someone outside the room could help him. If he could just make it to the door and out into the hallway.

He felt for the wall to steady himself. He kept banging his legs against furniture as he made his way around the room. A couple of times, he fell to his knees and it was a struggle to get back up again. Eventually, he decided it was easier to crawl along the floor than it was to walk.

If he just knew where he was going.

He banged his head against something hard. It sent his brain spinning. Blackness gathered closer in to him. A warm trickle ran down his temple. As he lay on the carpet, giving in to the hopelessness of the situation, a line of light appeared across the room. It was too bright, making him squint. The line grew into an elongated rectangle. A partially open doorway?

Will was relieved. Someone was there. Someone had come to check on him and they would tell him what was wrong and help him back to bed where he could rest his head.

But it wasn't a nurse that came in to see to him. He felt a cold nose and warm snout against his hand and arm. A dog. It moved to his face and sniffed and breathed its warm breath on him, investigating his face, licking him in greeting and cleaning away the blood.

He murmured words to it. He didn't know the animal's name, but it brought him comfort to have another living being there with him. He wasn't alone.

The dog barked a couple of times. That would bring help. Then it lay down alongside him. It was warm and soft.

Will closed his eyes and breathed out.

2

Kenzie was awakened by the insistent beeping of her clock. She reached over to turn it off, forcing her eyes open. Friday. And she had the weekend off, provided nothing untoward happened that required her at the Medical Examiner's Office. One more day. Saturday she could sleep in. She sat up, hoping that would help to wake her enough to get her day going. She ran her fingers through her wildly curly dark hair to push it away from her face.

She felt the bed beside her to see if Zachary were there, but she knew he wouldn't be. It would have been more than rare for him to still be in bed when she woke up. It had only happened once or twice in the months Zachary had been sleeping there. After the assault, it had been different. His sleep patterns had become completely erratic and he was frequently unable to get out of bed or to keep from falling asleep where he sat on the couch or in front of the computer. But he was back to his normal routine, and that meant that he was up before she was. Sometimes hours before.

Kenzie pushed herself to her feet and staggered to the ensuite bathroom. She went to the bathroom and then started the shower. She rubbed her hands over her face and looked at herself in the mirror while she waited for the water to warm up. A cold shower might wake her up faster, but she preferred her creature comforts; she wasn't getting in until it started to steam.

After a quick shower, Kenzie tidied her spiraling hair into some order, put on her makeup, including the red lipstick that would have to be reapplied after breakfast. But she loved the way it looked, so she put it on anyway. She pulled on her usual work uniform. A blouse and slacks topped with a short blazer. Comfortable shoes, since she would be on her feet much of the day. Then she left the bedroom and went down the hall to the living room and kitchen area to see how her partner was.

"Morning, Zachary."

He didn't look up from his computer.

Kenzie hadn't picked Zachary Goldman for his looks. He was a small, slender man with close-cropped black hair. He had been feeling pretty good over the summer, but she thought he might be losing weight again. His cheeks, which had filled in since his last depressive cycle, looked a little thin and his eye sockets hollow. He hadn't shaved yet and might not. He frequently kept a scruffy three days' growth of beard. It made him look like a homeless man. Intentionally so. People looked away from him, discounted him, which made his surveillance jobs much easier.

The reason Kenzie was with him was because he was kind and cared about people and he made her laugh. He was also one of the few people she could discuss her job at the Medical Examiner's Office with. He was interested in the medical mysteries she helped to solve, not disgusted by them.

There weren't a lot of people she could look at autopsy photos with over dinner.

"Zachary." Kenzie leaned over his shoulder and gave him a peck on the cheek.

He gave a small start and looked at her. He smiled. "Oh, you're up." He stretched and massaged his neck. "I didn't hear you."

"Up and dressed and ready for breakfast," she pointed out, in case the private investigator didn't notice these clues. "Are you ready for something to eat?"

He stood. "Sorry, I didn't hear you in the shower or I would have put some coffee on."

"It won't take long." Kenzie picked up a couple of mugs from the side table, one empty and one half-full of lukewarm or cold coffee. Zachary was pretty good about keeping them away from his computer to prevent any accidental spills. Not so great at remembering to pick them up again later.

She carried them into the kitchen and, after dumping the one in the sink, put them into the dishwasher. She started the coffee maker and put a couple of pieces of bread into the toaster.

Zachary went to the fridge and got out the margarine and marmalade for her. They moved around each other, used to the flow of the morning routine. Kenzie put a granola bar in front of Zachary's chair. His meds made eating in the morning difficult, but he could usually manage one of the chocolate chip granola bars, and the doctor said that anything he could get down was better than nothing.

They both sat down once the coffee was finished brewing and the toast popped.

"How did you sleep?" Kenzie asked. She couldn't remember him getting up.

Zachary had a sip of the hot coffee and started to unwrap the granola bar. "Not the best night. Restless. But I got a few hours in."

"Good. I didn't hear you up."

He nodded. "I tried to be quiet. Don't like you to be tired at work."

"I know. But if you need me..."

He gave her a smile. The one he always gave when he was comparing her reaction to how his ex-wife Bridget would have treated him. Criticizing him from disturbing her beauty rest instead of inviting him to wake her up if he needed her. The bemused smile that said he wasn't sure he deserved to be treated so kindly.

Zachary broke off a corner of the granola bar and put it in his mouth. "Think you'll be busy today?"

"Things have been quiet lately. I just don't know if that means they are going to continue to be quiet or we are building up to something big."

"Hopefully quiet. But not too quiet. Enough that you won't be bored. But no mass murders."

"Exactly," Kenzie agreed, taking a couple of bites of her marmalade toast. "I don't think there's any need to worry about me getting bored. People aren't going to stop dying."

3

Kenzie arrived at the Medical Examiner's Office and went immediately to work, checking over any calls that had come in during the night and making sure that any remains which had been brought in while the night crew was on had been properly logged in and had all the necessary reports attached. She glanced over her email inbox and took a quick peek at Dr. Wiltshire's as well to make sure there was nothing hot that needed to be dealt with right away.

After squaring away those systems, she took a quick walk through the suite of rooms that comprised the Medical Examiner's Office, making sure that nothing was out of place. Dr. Wiltshire liked his desk left just-so. He didn't like to come in to find sticky notes or pink phone messages all over it, attempts by the police or other city employees to end-run the proper procedures and get their case in front of him next or ask questions outside of the proper protocol.

While there were proper procedures for everything, people were lazy and didn't always follow them. She and Dr. Wiltshire didn't want to end up with remains or tests not correctly logged in, or the opposite, disappearing without having been properly logged out. Dr. Wiltshire had seen it happen in other ME offices, and he ran a tight ship.

All of her housekeeping complete, Kenzie returned to her desk and started to sort incoming emails, responding where necessary, filing and printing lab reports that had come in, and forwarding messages to Dr. Wiltshire or other employees.

Dr. Wiltshire arrived, Starbucks cup in one hand and briefcase in the other. "Morning, Kenzie."

"Good morning, doctor. I've opened files for a couple of new arrivals. The John Doe that the police consulted you on last night. He's already in storage waiting for you. And we had a call from Champlain House. One of their residents was found deceased this morning. A Willis Cartwright. He is on his way in."

"Good. Any concerns?"

"No, I don't think so. Just an unattended death. He was in good health up until a couple of days ago. They had started running some tests but hadn't made any determination yet. He was eighty-seven."

Dr. Wiltshire nodded and sipped his travel cup of coffee. "I'll look at him after the John Doe, then. That is more pressing, since the police are hoping for an ID."

"Okay. The file is on your desk. I filled in what I could on the intake."

Since Dr. Wiltshire had attended the scene of death during the night, Kenzie didn't know all the details. He would need to fill in what he had observed and make sure that all police and witness statements were present and accounted for.

Kenzie hoped she would be able to scrub in for at least part of the post-mortems. While much of her job at the ME's office was administrative, she was a fully qualified doctor and was trying to get enough experience to someday be a Medical Examiner herself.

There was a lot of paperwork to manage. Far from heralding the arrival of the paperless office, email had only served to amplify the amount of paper that flowed through the ME's office. There was a never-ending supply of lab reports, police reports, interoffice correspondence, and research that piled up on each file, in addition to what Dr. Wiltshire dictated during the post-mortem or filled out on his computer as he evaluated each case.

But Kenzie managed to get it under control in time to assist on the post-mortem of Willis Cartwright, the man from the seniors' independent living center.

Dr. Wiltshire had done the preliminaries and was gowned up. Kenzie picked up the file and added the report she had received from the nursing home concerning Cartwright's health and death. She summarized aloud to Dr. Wiltshire before donning the last of her protective gear.

"Mr. Willis Cartwright, age eighty-seven, was discovered dead in his room this morning at Champlain House. He was on the floor. He has a laceration on his head. They believe that he got up in the night, disoriented, and hit his head before passing out. The body was cold and there were no signs of life. Dr. Archibald was on site and declared him."

"Medications at the time of his death?"

"Blood pressure... NSAID... antidepressant."

"What was the blood pressure prescription?"

Kenzie summarized it for him. Dr. Wiltshire nodded. "You said this morning that his health had taken a downturn the last few days?"

"Staff had noticed an increase in confusion and emotional lability. He was having more problems than usual with getting around. Wasn't eating much at mealtimes. They thought maybe he was fighting a virus. It didn't appear to be anything serious."

"What was his mental acuity before this?"

Kenzie scanned the report from the nursing home for details. "He was in the independent living quarters. No significant cognitive issues." She turned the page. "They have a living skills sheet that they fill out to indicate what level of help the resident needs with each task. He is at the independent end for all of them, able to feed and wash himself, change his clothes. Needed some assistance with shaving. Had his pills pre-portioned for him."

Wiltshire nodded. "Anything else?"

"Not offhand. We can review it in more detail later, but it seems like this was unexpected. Other than his age being a factor."

"Well, let's see what we can find."

Kenzie put on her mask, face shield, and gloves and approached the table. Dr. Wiltshire pulled the cover down to Mr. Cartwright's navel.

"George washed the body earlier. He noted that the deceased had urinated, probably perimortem, since the clothing was not wet in the same areas as show lividity."

Kenzie translated this in her head to tell Zachary later if he asked for details on the autopsy. The urine had flowed to one area of Cartwright's clothing due to gravity. But the blood in his body had been pulled to another location by gravity after death. It was a good catch by George, showing that Cartwright wasn't just wet because his sphincters had released on death.

She and Dr. Wiltshire both examined the body closely, looking for anything notable. Kenzie pulled a magnifying lens over the wound on his temple. Since the blood had been washed off, it seemed to be an unremarkable wound, like a toddler might get from running into the table. A bandage or a kiss and he'd be on his way to exploring again. But that wasn't the case for Cartwright. His adventures had been permanently curtailed.

"Small laceration," she announced to Dr. Wiltshire and the digital recorder. She described it as thoroughly as she could as to size, shape, location, and color. She explored the wound, but it did not appear to be deep. It would have bled a good amount, being a scalp wound, but she would be surprised if it were the cause of death. She pressed the wound gently, feeling the skull underneath. "There is swelling under the laceration, but not a lot. I can't feel any fractures in the skull. Do we have x-rays?"

Dr. Wiltshire hit a button on the floor with his foot to bring the imaging up on the large view-screen, tapping it several times to get to the photo they wanted. Kenzie walked closer to the screen.

"I don't see any skull fractures."

"I concur."

They continued their examination of the body. When they were finished with the front and sides, they rolled him onto his stomach to examine his back. The lividity had been on his right side. Kenzie didn't see any blood settled into the back of the body. He had, possibly, curled up in a fetal position on the floor after hitting his head. He had not been lying on his back.

Dr. Wiltshire had removed the drape. He frowned and pointed to Cartwright's backside. "Looks like diaper rash," he said. "I thought the documents from the home indicated he was continent."

"Yes. They did." Kenzie walked over to the desk where she had left the file. She didn't touch it, but looked instead at the inventory sheet that George had filled out, which had not yet been inserted into the file. She ran her eyes down the list of clothing items. "Pajamas and briefs. No diaper."

Wiltshire frowned, thinking about that. He made an official note of it on the recording and they continued with their examination of the body.

When they turned him back over, Kenzie examined his hands and trimmed his nails, looking for any dirt or foreign substances. Cartwright's nails were well-manicured and clean. He didn't have any injuries on his hands. Dr. Wiltshire examined the man's lower half and replaced the drape folded across Cartwright's middle before calling Kenzie over to look at the man's legs. His shins and knees were considerably bruised. Several cuts looked relatively recent.

"What do you make of that?" Kenzie asked.

"I would say he's been walking into things."

"That supports the theory that he was disoriented. Maybe he walked into something in the dark?"

"A few of these might be from last night, but not all of them." Dr. Wiltshire pointed at the edges of some of the other bruises and examined the healing cuts. "I would say... they go back about a week? What do you think?"

Kenzie looked at the bruises. Some of them had fading edges, colors changing from blue and gray to green and yellow. She thought about her own experience with bruises and nodded. "Some people heal faster than others, but for a man of his age, I wouldn't expect him to heal that much in a couple of days. We can compare them to the reference texts."

Wiltshire nodded. "Let's take some pictures. You can compare them later. I'm pretty confident in my timeline."

In other words, Kenzie needed to educate herself, but Dr. Wiltshire had been on the job long enough to know his bruises. Kenzie nodded. They took a few pictures with a camera on an articulating arm that hung down from the ceiling. Wiltshire reviewed the images before moving on to make sure they were what he needed.

Once the gross examination of the body was complete, it was time to open him up. If the cause of death had been obvious, perhaps if the wound on his temple had been more serious, they might not have gone any farther. But so far, they had not come across anything that clearly indicated Cartwright's cause of death.

4

Kenzie took one more walk around the lab to make sure that everything was tidied up and put away. That would make it an easier start the next day. She wouldn't be on. There wouldn't be anyone there in the evening unless they had call-outs. If there were remains to be brought in, one of the staff would be on call to go in and deal with it. Anything that could wait for Kenzie's return on Monday would wait. Hopefully, it would be a quiet weekend.

Once she was sure that everything was taken care of, Kenzie grabbed her purse from her locked desk drawer and headed out to her car. She waved to the night guard.

"Good night, Dr. Kirsch," he called out to her. "Have a nice weekend."

"I plan to! You too!"

He would be working through the weekend, so he wasn't exactly going to be enjoying his leisure. Kenzie was glad for the protected parking garage under the building. She didn't have to leave her baby out on the street all day. The little red convertible would attract too much attention and she didn't want anyone trying to boost it because it looked like an easy target. A guarded parking garage under the police building was about as safe as it could get in town.

There were a couple of lights on in the house when she got home, so she anticipated that Zachary was home, not out on surveillance. Which was good; she didn't like him doing night jobs. Daytime surveillance didn't bother her, but knowing that he was out after dark watching some adulterer or corporate spy always made her anxious. She found it hard to go to sleep on nights he was out. But he didn't do a lot of night surveillance. When he didn't have a big case going on, he was doing skip tracing, insurance fraud, and many other small projects that provided him with a steady income. The adultery and corporate espionage jobs were still there, but most of them could be handled during the day. At night, people went home to their wives or their televisions and relaxed.

Kenzie pulled her car into the garage and pressed her clicker to shut the big door. She walked through the house door into the back mudroom, then into the kitchen.

"Hey, Kenzie," Zachary noticed her immediately. "How was your day?"

"Pretty good." Kenzie stretched and arched her back. The table had been set to the right height for Dr. Wiltshire, but he was a little taller than she was, and her upper back and shoulders were feeling the strain by the time they finished the post. "Glad to be home. All weekend. You have time off too, right?"

Zachary was looking down at his phone and didn't acknowledge the question. Kenzie waited for him to look back up. "This weekend?" Kenzie prompted, when he eventually looked back at her.

"Do I have time?" Zachary asked, filling in the question with what he figured he'd missed. "Yes. I took time off. We're good."

"Great. It will be nice to have some real time together."

Zachary nodded. It was something that Dr. B—Zachary's therapist, who was also running their couples therapy—had been pushing them to do. Make more time to spend together. Not just the frayed edges at the end of the day when they both happened to be home at the same time. Some real quality time to visit, go to a movie, visit friends, or whatever other arrangements they felt like making. And, of course, she was right. Kenzie had been a workaholic throughout school, focused on her goal, and she was dedicated to Dr. Wiltshire and the office. Since Zachary had moved in with Kenzie—he did still have his own apartment in case one of them needed some space—they had fallen into the bad habit of assuming they would have time to do things together, with both of them filling up their time with work, chores, errands, meals, and sleep, until there wasn't anything left for quality couple's time or dates.

"Why don't you go get changed?" Zachary suggested. "I'll... set the table. Did you want to cook tonight, or do you want to order in?"

Kenzie considered. "I have one of those deluxe frozen pizzas from the grocery store. Why don't we have that?"

"Okay. Do you want me to put it in?"

"No. You can get it out, but don't put it in the oven yet."

Zachary nodded absently, looking back down at his phone. Kenzie went to her room to change. She dumped her purse on her writing desk and changed out of her work clothes into some comfy loungewear for the evening. She was pretty sure that Zachary wasn't going to put the pizza in the oven, but he hadn't really acknowledged what she had said. She knew from his past attempts that he was perfectly capable of putting the pizza into the oven with the plastic wrap on. Or forgetting to set the temperature or the timer.

It wasn't that he was helpless, but cooking, even just heating up meals, was not his forte. The poor executive skills and distractibility that came with his ADHD and PTSD meant that completing multiple steps in a particular order and keeping track of several things at once was a challenge. He would have to be completely focused, and he just wasn't interested enough in meals for it to keep his focus. He would be thinking about whatever cases he was working on, or their relationship, or his family, or Bridget, or some other random thought that flitted through his brain, and the dinner and all the remaining steps it would take to complete the meal would be forgotten.

When she returned to the living room, Zachary was still looking at his phone and had not bothered to get the pizza out of the freezer. Which was fine with Kenzie. Better that than trying to figure out how to get melting plastic wrap off the pizza before it was too late. She set the oven temperature, put the unwrapped pizza in, and set a timer. She had learned not to judge Zachary by how easy a task was for her to complete. And in the same way, he could run circles around her in private investigation, remembering camera f-stops, and out-of-the-box thinking. And he was sensitive and quickly attuned to others' emotions, when Kenzie might chatter with someone for half an hour without realizing that they were upset about something.

Zachary slid his phone into his pants pocket and entered the kitchen to pull out plates and set the table.

"Are you talking to someone?" Kenzie asked. "What's up with the phone?"

"Oh. Sorry, were you talking to me? I was just…" Zachary made a motion to his pocket. "Rhys."

Kenzie nodded and smiled. Rhys Salter was a teen Zachary had met on an earlier case and had remained friends with. He was Black and selectively mute. While he enjoyed messaging with Zachary sometimes, it could be hard to interpret his GIF messages or other pictures or brief words. He didn't just text sentences like Kenzie would, mirroring what she would have said aloud. His use of language was not linear and writing more than a word or two was a challenge. Zachary's intense focus on the phone at intervals made sense if he were trying to interpret Rhys's messages.

"Oh, I see. How is he?"

"Good, I think. It's been rough, but I think he's at school most days now. Hopefully keeping up with his classes."

Witnessing someone getting shot had set Rhys back significantly, bringing back to him the day when his beloved grandfather had been shot. He'd missed a lot of school but was getting settled back into the routine.

Zachary set the plates on the table, then stared at them blankly for a moment before moving to get glasses and cutlery. He filled a pitcher with water and put it in the center of the table. He looked at the settings, then at Kenzie. "Am I forgetting anything?"

"Looks good to me. Grab the napkin holder; I have a feeling the pizza is going to be messy."

He did so, setting the napkins on the table next to the pitcher. "Do you want anything else?"

"No." Kenzie knew she should probably cut up some fresh fruit and vegetables to go with the pizza, but it was the weekend, and she just wanted to chill, not to have to eat right. "You want to put something on TV?"

"After dinner," Zachary said firmly. "Dr. B said to focus on each other over meals. Not to be distracted by TV or other entertainment or devices."

Kenzie nodded. "All right. Good for you. Because you know I totally would have gone for eating in front of the TV today."

He looked pleased with the compliment. He glanced over at the stove. "How much longer until it's ready?"

The timer was counting down right in front of him. "Fifteen minutes. You want to clean up and get changed?"

His face flushed, maybe realizing that he'd been working all day in clothes that he'd probably been wearing most of the week. Fine, if he were pretending to be a homeless person to stay under the radar. Not so good if he wanted to get close to his girlfriend during and after supper. He pinched his shirt between his fingers and brought it up to his nose. "Sorry. Yeah. I'll throw these in the laundry."

Kenzie watched him hurry off to the bathroom for a quick shower and change. He wouldn't have time to shave off his stubble, but he could at least be clean and fresh in that length of time. While she waited for him, she would check her phone and review any personal emails she had received during the afternoon and maybe be able to check her social network accounts as well. At least one of them.

Zachary was back just after the timer sounded, his hair still damp, looking and smelling much better. He smiled at Kenzie and gave her a quick hug and kiss before she had a chance to cut the pizza into slices. She kissed him back, then squirmed away, knife in hand. "If you don't want to get cut, Romeo, you'd better back up and let me get my dinner. I'm starving."

Zachary grinned and sat down at the table to give her space to use the long blade to quickly cut the pizza into wedges. Kenzie put the sliced pizza on the table and grabbed a couple of slices to start out with. Zachary looked for the smallest slice and put it onto his plate. Kenzie took a bite of her first wedge.

"Did you eat any lunch?"

Zachary frowned and considered. He toyed with the slice for a moment. "I'm pretty sure I took a break."

"And ate?"

He pursed his lips. "Maybe."

"That's not good enough. Your body needs more than a granola bar and a slice of pizza in a day."

"I know. And I'm pretty sure I did." He looked at the platter of pizza that remained. "I'll have a second piece."

"You'd better."

He nodded and had a bite of pizza. Kenzie had another bite and swallowed. "Old guy we did a post on today, his nursing home said that his appetite hasn't been too good the last couple of days. And he had nothing in his stomach. *Nothing.*"

"You don't think they were starving him, do you?" Zachary's mind immediately jumped to elder neglect.

"No, I don't think so. They have a pretty good record. We get residents from there now and then, and we haven't seen any starvation cases."

Zachary nodded. "So what killed him?"

"We're not there yet. Have some slides to look at tomorrow, tests to be run at various labs. Nothing obvious, but the home said that he hadn't been well the last few days, and we did notice a couple of anomalies during that time. Not eating, bruises, just little things. Maybe he had a virus and just wasn't strong enough to fight it off. Although," she shrugged, "he seemed like he was in pretty good shape before it hit."

"Maybe a change to his meds?"

"Nope. He wasn't on a lot of different prescriptions. What he was on, he'd been on for a while. No changes that the home could point to in the last week or so. Just that he took poorly."

Zachary nodded thoughtfully. He took another small bite of the pizza and chewed slowly. He was only going to be half done his first slice in the time it took Kenzie to wolf down two.

"Other than that... We had a John Doe overnight. Dr. Wiltshire did that post by himself; I'll have to read his report when it comes back from transcription tomorrow. Monday, I mean."

"Where was he found? Was he mugged? No ID?"

"Homeless, I think. Found in an alley. No ID. Probably alcohol or drug overdose, or some secondary effect of drinking."

"Nobody knew him? It's not that big of a town. I'd think that anyone else out there, on the street, they'd know him. Or someone at the shelter. He must have gone there in the winter, at least."

That was one thing about Vermont that couldn't be said about warmer climes like Florida and California. The homeless didn't survive through the winter without help. Someone in the shelter or another service company would have run into him at some time or another. They would be able to give the John Doe a name, even if it were only a first name or a street name. They didn't have the flourishing homeless problem that the warmer states dealt with.

"The police will do a canvass. I'm sure they'll find something."

"Yeah. They're bound to. So that's it? Just two today?"

"That's enough. We still have other work to do too. It isn't just doing two posts and then going home because there's nothing else to do."

5

Kenzie and Zachary had fallen asleep in each other's arms. Kenzie awoke as Zachary's breathing got louder and he started squirming around and pushing her away from him.

He pushed his covers back, huffing hard as if they were restricting his ability to breathe. He murmured something over and over again but, like with most of his dream talk, she couldn't make out his words. She nudged his shoulder gently.

"Zachary. Zach, wake up."

He squirmed away from her touch, then flailed suddenly as if he were falling and jumped, all his muscles activating, holding himself as stiff as a board.

"Zachary. It's okay. Wake up."

He let his breath out and, at first, his muscles started to relax; then he began to whip his head back and forth, looking for an escape.

"You're safe," Kenzie told him. She reached over and fumbled for the switch on the lamp. She managed to click it on, and squeezed her eyes shut tightly at the sudden dazzling light. Zachary sat bolt upright.

"What was that?"

"It's okay. Just a dream."

Zachary looked around, but Kenzie wasn't sure whether he was truly awake.

"Zach. Are you awake?"

He rubbed his eyes and peered around. He didn't wear glasses, but he squinted as if everything around him was blurred. "We have to get them out," he told her. "We have to get them all out."

Kenzie knew which dream he was having. She blew her breath out slowly and kept her voice calm and soothing. "It's just a dream, Zachary. Everyone is okay. Everyone got out."

He cocked his head for a moment, unsure, trying to process her words. "They're all in there. They can't get out by themselves. They can't walk."

That was a new spin. When Zachary's house had gone up in flames when he was ten years old, his siblings had all been old enough to walk. They hadn't been strong enough to break the windows, but they had been able to walk. The firefighters had been able to rescue them, while Zachary remained trapped in the living room full of smoke and flames, sure that he and his entire family were all going to die. *Who couldn't walk?*

"Everyone is fine," Kenzie repeated. "Everyone got out."

Then his eyes finally focused on her. He looked at her, then at the lamp and at the room around him in confusion.

"You're safe," Kenzie said. "Everyone is fine. It was just a dream."

"Oh." He blinked. "A dream... I dreamt... the nursing home was on fire."

Kenzie raised her brows. "The nursing home? Because I was talking to you about Champlain House at supper today?"

"I don't know. I guess so."

Sometimes their conversations or worries about a case worked their way into Zachary's nightmares. It wasn't predictable, so there was no way to avoid it. They both enjoyed discussing crime and solving forensic clues, so they weren't likely to stop discussing anything that might trigger him.

Zachary ran his fingers through his stubbly hair. He rubbed his eyes with his palms. Kenzie reached over for the lamp.

"Okay now? Shall I turn this off?"

"Yeah. I'm fine."

Kenzie turned the light back off and then cuddled up to Zachary, hoping that he would be able to get back to sleep if they didn't spend too much time talking and focusing on the disturbing dream.

Zachary's dream had Kenzie thinking about the nursing home in the morning while she luxuriated under a hot shower. They had not found anything in the Cartwright case to make her think that they were not taking care of their residents properly and following all the rules and regulations they were bound by. If nothing showed up on the slides and lab tests that they had sent out, Dr. Wiltshire was inclined to write it off as simply heart failure. Possibly due to a virus. Even the most innocuous virus could be dangerous to someone who was old or had an otherwise compromised immune system.

All the paperwork that had come from Champlain House had been in order. It would have made her feel better if he had been discovered sooner, and not lain on the floor for half the night, but it wasn't a case where they were required to check on him every fifteen minutes. Until recently, he had not had any issues and therefore didn't have a bed alarm to alert the staff if he got up in the night. He'd been independent and that meant that they left him alone unless he pressed his call button for help.

There hadn't been any red flags. On the contrary, the facility had provided all the paper they were expected to and more. Willis Cartwright wasn't the first resident from Champlain House to make it to the morgue, and he wouldn't be the last. Being a senior care center, there would always be deaths at the home. Many of them would qualify as deaths that had occurred while in the care of a doctor and wouldn't even go through the Medical Examiner's Office.

While Zachary's dream had made Kenzie consider whether there were any issues at Champlain House, she didn't think that it was portentous. There wasn't going to be a fire at the nursing home. She knew exactly why Zachary dreamed about fire. There was no mystery in that.

6

Much of Saturday had been spent running errands and doing chores around the house. Things that got pushed to the wayside when Kenzie was working without breaks in her schedule. And while Zachary was pretty good about sharing her space and keeping his possessions to limited areas, there was still more cleaning and other chores to do with another person living in the house. Especially if he spent most of his time working from there rather than going back to his own apartment or out in the field.

"We should visit Lorne and Pat Sunday," Kenzie suggested to Zachary after turning off the vacuum cleaner. "We have the time; we should take advantage of it."

Zachary's eyes brightened. Lorne Peterson had been his foster father for a few weeks when he had first been put into foster care, and he was the only parent Zachary had kept in contact with. When Lorne had later separated from his wife and begun a relationship with Patrick Parker, it had been quite scandalous from what Kenzie could tell. But more than twenty years later, the two men were still living together and, for the most part, society accepted their partnership. For a lot of years, they had been Zachary's only family.

"I'm sure they'd be delighted," Zachary agreed. "I'll give them a call." He stopped and looked at her, something else in his expression that Kenzie couldn't read. "Unless..."

"What?" Maybe Lorne and Pat already had other plans Zachary was aware of.

"I just thought... I don't know when the last time you saw your parents was. Do you want to see one of them?"

Kenzie shook her head. "Not really."

"I don't want to keep you from your family."

"You're not. I talk to my mom on the phone and email her, but I really don't need a face-to-face visit. She's always so busy with all her causes. She would just try to get me involved in whatever she's working on right now. 'I'd love to see you, MacKenzie; you can help me to sort the clothes donated for the Kidney Foundation. And bring that young man of yours along to the Cancer Society fundraiser...'" Kenzie rolled her eyes. "Trust me, it's better to keep your distance."

"You're always so accommodating about seeing Lorne and Pat or one of my siblings, but we don't see your family. What about your dad?"

Kenzie groaned and shook her head. "No. Trust me. He's not your kind of person. I love spending time with Lorne or one of your sibs, but seeing my dad is not a holiday."

"Neither is Joss," Zachary pointed out.

Kenzie chuckled.

The first two siblings Zachary had been reunited with decades after the fire were Tyrrell and Heather, and they were both friendly and easy people to like. Kenzie enjoyed being with them and hearing their stories about when they had all been children, before the fire. Joss, on the other hand, was hard and acidic. She was challenging to get along with and kept everyone at a distance.

"Well... okay. But my answer is still no. I'd rather see Lorne and Pat than either of my parents."

Someday, she knew, she was going to have to introduce Zachary to her parents. They would all be gracious about it, but Kenzie didn't want to deal with her parents' questions about Zachary's suitability and stability. And she didn't want to have to explain her family dynamics to Zachary. She didn't really understand them herself. Their family was broken. Maybe not as badly as Zachary's, but Kenzie also didn't think there was any chance it could be put back together again. Amanda was gone. Her parents, while still friends, were divorced. And Kenzie had had as little to do with them as possible since uncovering the secrets they had been keeping about Amanda's last transplant.

Zachary nodded his understanding. He understood dysfunctional families. As far as Kenzie knew, he never had tried to find his biological parents. Neither had his siblings. And the two youngest siblings still hadn't made contact with Zachary.

"I'll call Mr. Peterson then, and make sure they're going to be around," Zachary agreed.

One of the few points of contention between Kenzie and Zachary was whose turn it was to drive when they went to visit Lorne and Pat. Zachary enjoyed highway driving. It was one of the few activities that tamed his hyperactive brain and anxiety and allowed him to just chill out and be in the zone. But he also drove much too fast for Kenzie's comfort.

With her little red convertible, she should have been the speed demon. But she wasn't. She occasionally allowed her baby to creep up over the posted speed limit by a few miles an hour, but she stayed within reasonable limits. Enough that she had never been cited for speeding and had only been pulled over once. The officer had been easy to charm and had let her off with a warning. Kenzie hadn't been pulled over since. Zachary didn't usually get caught, but he liked to fly. Kenzie was always sure he was going to get into an accident, but he seemed totally in control when he drove. Like a fighter pilot.

"You drove last time," Kenzie reminded him. "You said that I could drive the next trip."

Zachary looked for an argument. With Vermont's climate, he often pulled the 'weather' card, insisting that it was too cold to drive a convertible that distance. But the weather had been nice, and Kenzie's baby would enjoy getting out on the highway instead of being cramped up in city streets all day.

"You just had bodywork done," Zachary tried. "Out on the highway, if someone hits a bit of gravel..."

"I'm not afraid of a few dings and scratches. Most of them will buff right out."

"A windshield chip won't."

"I'm driving," Kenzie said firmly. She looked him in the eye.

Zachary shrugged and looked down, conceding as she knew he would. "Fine. You're right; I think it is your turn."

"It is," Kenzie asserted.

There was less leg room in the convertible than in Zachary's car, but neither of them had particularly long legs, so that wasn't an issue. Zachary settled himself in the passenger seat as Kenzie sat down and turned the key, bringing the engine roaring to life. She ignored his restlessness when they got out to the highway. He wanted to be at the wheel. Once or twice before, he had even proposed that they go in separate cars, just in case they needed to return home at different times. They both knew very well that convenience had nothing to do with it; he just wanted to drive. And once he had an idea in his head, it was hard to let it go.

"How did they sound?" Kenzie asked, trying to distract him. "Everything going good?"

"Sounds like it. Mr. Peterson—Lorne—said that they were going to try reducing Pat's antidepressants. See if he still needs them, or if a lower dose will work just as well."

"That's good. That sounds positive."

"Yeah. They wouldn't be doing that if they had any concerns. I think his depression was mostly situational. Losing a friend like that. Jose, and then Dimitri. Finding out that it was someone that he knew. That was tough on him."

"I can see why," Kenzie agreed. All things considered, Pat had fared pretty well. It was a lot to deal with all at once, and if he were able to keep stable at a lower dose or even without antidepressants, that was good news. Kenzie knew that both Lorne and Zachary had been concerned about him.

Zachary stared out the window now, his restlessness stilled, but, Kenzie worried, maybe now obsessing over his involvement in Jose's case and the dark paths it had led him down. Pat might have recovered from his loss, but Zachary hadn't been able to make as much headway against his demons. What had happened to him at the hands of the sadistic killer would be with him for a long time. Kenzie didn't know all the details, but she knew that those memories would always be in the shadows whenever she touched him.

"You okay?"

"Yeah. Fine."

Zachary took a few more minutes to pull his attention from the scenery racing past the window. He looked down at his phone and busied himself with checking his email or social networks.

"Anything exciting?" Kenzie prompted.

"No." Zachary tapped his screen. "Looks like your John Doe made it to the local news."

"Oh? What does it say?"

"Just that they are trying to identify him. They have a picture."

"It's too bad there wasn't anything identifiable on the body. Tattoos or implants. Something traceable."

"You think he was homeless?" Zachary stared down at his screen.

"That was what the police speculated."

Zachary made reverse pinching movements, zooming in on areas of the photograph. "He doesn't look homeless."

"You and I both know that you don't have to look homeless to be homeless."

"No. But he's... very clean and well-groomed."

"Well, we do that before we take a picture. Wash him, try to make him as presentable and lifelike as possible. It makes it easier for people to identify him."

Zachary still wasn't convinced. "You did his hair?"

"I wasn't involved. It must have been yesterday. But yes, we'd comb hair. Add a bit of makeup. Try to make him look natural."

"But you don't cut the hair."

"No. We don't change his look. You change someone's hairstyle, and it changes the shape of their face. We want to keep everything the same."

"His hair is shaped. Like a barber does. Not just cut one length."

Kenzie glanced sideways at Zachary. "He might have had a friend or family member do it. Or a freebie at one of those expo events, when they get service providers together."

"How about his teeth?"

"They were in good shape. But maybe he hasn't been homeless for long."

"Or maybe he's not homeless."

Kenzie shrugged. "Maybe," she agreed. "I can take another look tomorrow."

"Look at everything. How old his clothes are, what brands they are. His shoes especially. Teeth, nails, hair. Not just where he was found or how dirty his clothes were."

"Makes sense. If you're right, maybe the police are talking to the wrong people."

7

Kenzie could see Zachary straightening up and becoming more engaged as they approached Lorne and Pat's home. He slid his phone away and put his hand on the armrest of the door, waiting for Kenzie to take the last few turns. There weren't very many people in Zachary's life that were so important to him. When Zachary got attached to someone, he got really attached.

Zachary was out of the door as soon as Kenzie pulled to a stop in front of the house. He held himself back then, waiting for her to get her seatbelt unlatched and pick up her purse. Always the gentleman, walking her up to the house instead of leaving her behind while he ran to the door, no matter how eager he was.

"I'm coming. Just give me a second."

Zachary nodded politely. They walked up to the house together. Zachary rang the bell, then, after a moment's hesitation, opened the door and let himself in. Lorne didn't greet them at the door as usual, so Zachary looked around the corner into the living room for him.

Lorne was sitting in his usual chair, but his foot resting on the footrest in front of him was encased in a cast.

"What's this? What happened?" Zachary asked, leaning over to give him a hug of greeting. His brows drew down and there was a deep crease between them.

"It's nothing. I'm fine. Just a little mishap," Lorne assured him.

"Nothing? They don't put casts on nothing. What did you break?"

"I broke a couple of metatarsals. They said a few weeks in a cast and it will heal up fine. Tell him, Kenzie."

Kenzie wasn't a podiatrist or orthopedist, but she had her MD. She nodded her agreement. "If it's just a hairline or a clean break, it will heal in no time. What did you do to it?"

"I just dropped something on it. It wasn't anything."

"I told you those Polish sausages would kill you," Pat called from the kitchen. "Now you've been warned!"

"Sausages?" Zachary repeated, a smile replacing his worried frown.

"A package of frozen sausages, yes," Lorne admitted, shaking his head ruefully. "They jumped out of the freezer at me, and I didn't get out of the way fast enough."

"I hope we're eating them tonight."

Lorne looked surprised. "Do you like Polish sausages?" They were always looking for special foods that would tempt Zachary to eat more despite his poor appetite. If one of Zachary's favorite foods was sausages, Kenzie was sure that Pat and Lorne would both know it already.

"I don't know." Zachary shrugged. "But it seems a fitting punishment for them breaking your foot."

Lorne laughed. Pat poked his head in through the doorway to the kitchen. "I think so too! In fact, they are on the menu tonight. I'm making a stew."

"Whatever it is, it sure smells good," Kenzie told him. The hearty, spicy aroma filled the house, so thick she could practically taste it. "I can't wait."

"Good. I've just got a few more veggies to chop, and then I can let it simmer and join you for a visit."

Zachary and Kenzie sat down. Zachary looked at Lorne's cast and shook his head again. "Why didn't you tell me you broke it? When did this happen?"

"Just like you tell me any time you run into trouble?" Lorne teased. "It was just last night. After you and I talked. Or I would have mentioned it when you called."

"Hmm. Maybe." Zachary wasn't convinced.

"I would have, because I knew you were coming and would give me a hard time if I didn't tell you ahead of time."

Lorne leaned back in his chair. His face was round and cheerful. If the broken bone were bothering him at all, he didn't give any sign of it. His fringe of hair was gradually turning white, but he still moved like a young man. Other than when he was trying to avoid ferocious Polish sausages, apparently.

"I left some pictures in my office. You want to go get them?" Lorne suggested.

Zachary nodded. He retrieved Lorne's latest photographic creations and the two of them put their heads together, discussing perspectives and composition and the various settings on the camera. One thing that Lorne had shared with Zachary was his love of photography. He had given Zachary his first camera when he was living with the Petersons and they had developed pictures together in Lorne's darkroom over the years. Even at the height of digital photography, the two of them still used analog cameras and developed their own pictures when they could. Zachary used digital cameras for his work, but analog for his art.

Pat joined them in a few minutes. He rolled his eyes at Kenzie as he sat down. "Just nod and pretend you understand."

Kenzie laughed. "Yep."

"So, how have things been with you?"

Kenzie settled into the conversation, sharing what she could with Pat. That was mostly personal stuff because, unlike Zachary, Pat and Lorne were not interested in the nitty-gritty of forensic pathology. So Kenzie said only that things were going well at work and left it at that.

8

They went home feeling full and contented. Zachary was more relaxed than usual, all talked out, his eyes fixed on the highway as it spooled out before them. Kenzie listened to the music on the radio and left him to his thoughts. She valued any time he wasn't visibly depressed or anxious. One reason she liked going to visit Lorne and Pat—besides their company and good food—was that Zachary was usually relaxed and happy after a visit.

Once home, they vegged in front of the TV, but both knew Kenzie needed to get to sleep to be up for her work without being cranky or tired on the job, so they headed to bed.

"It was a nice weekend," Kenzie said as they cuddled.

"It was," Zachary agreed. "Good to take time off and just do some things together. Dr. Boyle was right."

"I'm sure she'll be glad to hear it." Kenzie rubbed Zachary's back, feeling for the tension he carried in his shoulders and neck, gently prodding and massaging, trying to get him nice and relaxed so he would sleep.

"You had a good time too?" he asked in a worried tone.

"Yeah. I did. It was great."

He didn't say anything in response. Kenzie kneaded his shoulders, making him flinch when she hit a tender spot.

"What is it?" Kenzie asked.

"Nothing. I just worry about you going back to work. That it's stressful."

"Well... sometimes it's stressful, yes. But I don't really mind. I knew when

I went into medicine that it was going to be a high-stress job. But at least where I am, I'm not working in the emergency room or in a kids' cancer ward. I can't really harm my patients."

"I'm sure they're dying to see you again."

Kenzie groaned. She could feel Zachary laughing.

"You don't need to worry, though. I enjoy my job. And Dr. Wiltshire is good about letting me get my hands into things so that I can move up the ladder and someday maybe have a morgue of my own."

"Just what every little girl dreams of."

Kenzie chuckled and molded her body against Zachary's back, holding him firmly. "I'll admit it isn't how I saw my life path when I was a little girl. I guess I thought I'd grow up to be like my mother. A socialite, staying at home with a couple of kids, going to all the important fundraisers and events. But that never particularly excited me."

Zachary nodded. "Doesn't sound like you."

"No. She and I are... well, we're pretty different. I'm not saying that she's not doing something important. She is involved in a lot of very worthy causes. But it's not what I want to do. I like the challenge of medicine. I was one of the few girls who was excited about dissecting frogs in school. To actually see all an animal's insides. In person, not just a diagram in a textbook. To me, that was really interesting."

Zachary didn't respond with what his own experiences in life sciences at school had been like. No anecdotes about dissecting frogs and putting the kidneys down the shirt of the cute girl at the next lab bench. Nothing about being too sensitive to participate, or whether he had even been given the opportunity. Much of his time as a teen had been spent in institutional care, and Kenzie supposed they didn't like to put scalpels in the hands of kids with poor impulse control and behavioral problems.

"Everybody likes different things," Kenzie said drowsily, feeling herself starting to slip toward sleep. "The Medical Examiner's Office really is where I want to be."

Zachary said something in response, but Kenzie didn't catch what it was and couldn't remember in the morning.

Despite her assertions of the night before, Kenzie did feel a little stressed as she got ready for work Monday morning. Not because she didn't like it, just because she knew how busy Mondays could be, catching up with emails and requests that had come in over the weekend, knowing there was likely a backlog of bodies that would take the rest of the week to catch up on. There wasn't enough action to justify hiring more workers, which meant that sometimes they were overwhelmed when there was a spate of deaths.

But bodies kept, more or less, and they always caught up again eventually. Dr. Wiltshire was a good boss and Kenzie didn't dread going into work. It was just a Monday thing.

When she made it out to the kitchen for breakfast, Zachary already had everything prepared. The coffee was hot. Her toast had been buttered and was awaiting marmalade. The jar was just in front of Kenzie's plate. And there were a couple of articles that Zachary had printed off from his computer and left on the table for her, their John Doe's face prominent.

"I thought you might like to see those so you're up to speed by the time you get in," Zachary said. "And you were going to take a closer look at the body and his clothes to see if you think he really is homeless."

"I haven't forgotten." Kenzie sat down and began slathering marmalade on her toast. She skimmed through the articles, which were pretty generic, with just a few tidbits of information the reporters had managed to get ahold of. Tidbits that Kenzie already knew. She looked at John Doe's picture in the article. It was small, so she couldn't see all the details that Zachary had been looking at the day before, but she could see where he was coming from. Doe's hair did appear to have been shaped by a professional. His teeth didn't show in the picture, but he didn't have the shrunken cheeks that many of the homeless did, not just because they didn't eat enough, but because their teeth had rotted away due to poor oral hygiene or drug addiction. Doe's skin was relatively smooth and his pores small, even though he did have a five o'clock shadow.

But his whiskers were not long. It might have been just that, five o'clock shadow because it had been late in the day when he had died. Not because he had been on the streets and had failed to shave for several days or weeks.

"I'll look into it when I have a chance," Kenzie promised. She took a few more bites of her toast. "You look like you're having a pretty good morning. Sleep well?"

"Yeah, pretty good."

"Good. How's the calendar look this week?" Kenzie laid her phone down on the table and brought up her calendar app to look at their schedules for the week. Zachary had given her access to his electronic calendar so that she could look at both at the same time and they could adjust if there were any conflicts, which there rarely were. "Couples therapy Wednesday."

Zachary nodded. "And ice cream."

That had been Kenzie's suggestion. A reward for both of them for doing something difficult, especially when they couldn't always see progress from one appointment to the next. Like any kind of therapy or personal development, there were leaps forward and falls back. The falls could be discouraging.

"And ice cream, of course," Kenzie agreed with enthusiasm. Zachary gave a little smile and nod.

9

Kenzie did her preliminary walk-through of the office, ensuring that everything was in order for Dr. Wiltshire's arrival. She didn't have a chance to get through the email, but she hadn't seen any top priority flags, so what was there would wait until she had an opportunity to go through it. Several bodies had been checked in during the weekend. Apparently, people didn't stop dying just because Kenzie took a couple of days off. Dr. Wiltshire had performed one post on Sunday, but the rest had been left. Kenzie familiarized herself with the check-in sheets, and then returned to her public-facing workstation to process any requests for records or lab reports.

Dr. Wiltshire arrived with his Starbucks coffee as usual. He also had a wrapped muffin, which he placed on Kenzie's desk. She'd never asked him to buy her any baking on his Starbucks run. But every so often, he brought something anyway. Kenzie had noticed a pattern after a while. The days that he brought her treats were generally the days he anticipated to be busy or stressful. She didn't know if he even realized himself that was what he was doing. He brought her a treat to show his appreciation for her being there and being a diligent employee. Still, apparently the times his mind turned most to his appreciation were those days when he knew he would be putting her through the wringer.

So Kenzie was forewarned by the chocolate chocolate chip muffin. She smiled and greeted Dr. Wiltshire just like any other day.

"Good morning, doctor. How was your weekend?"

"Not bad, Kenzie. Nothing too urgent over the weekend, so I got a bit of a break. Played some golf yesterday."

"I didn't know you're a golfer."

"I'm really not," he confided. "But it was a nice day and I sensed that my wife wanted me out of the house. So... golf."

Kenzie smiled and nodded. Dr. Wiltshire rarely talked about his wife. She wasn't actually sure whether there was a Mrs. Wiltshire, or whether the doctor just invented her for his stories. There was no picture of a wife or children on his desk or anywhere in his office.

"I'm glad you had a good rest. We've got a few new bodies to be scheduled."

"Let's sit down in my office. I think this is going to take a little longer than usual today."

And it had. Kenzie intended to just give him a straight briefing on each of the remains that had been checked in, but he also wanted to know what doctors or police officers were on each of the cases and to evaluate what urgency would be assigned to each of their new guests. Kenzie made suggestions on each of the cases and they set up a schedule. Kenzie stacked the intake sheets in order and promised to add the lineup to Dr. Wiltshire's calendar so that he could stay on top of it.

"And if anyone calls to find out where their case is in the pile, you can speak to them with authority," he advised Kenzie. "No need to guess or pass it back to me. Let them know how many cases there are ahead of them and promise we'll get to it as soon as we are able."

"Sure," Kenzie agreed. Of course, everyone would want their case to be first on the list, but that wasn't the way it worked. Potential homicides needed to lead the pack. And the cases where there were religious practices to be adhered to if possible. They would make an effort to process any cases that had to be interred within a certain length of time when they needed to be.

On returning to her desk, Kenzie found a couple of law enforcement officers waiting for her. She gave them the appropriate request forms to be filled out and started going methodically through her email inbox. Of course, there were a lot of requests to be processed and reports to be printed, reviewed, and filed. She had glanced at the email subjects on her phone a couple of times over the weekend to make sure she was not missing anything important, so she knew she could just start at the top and work her way down through the various emails.

She nodded when the law enforcement officers left their requests in her inbox, promising that she would get to them as soon as she could. Her laser printer was humming away, spitting out a constant stream of reports as she added them to the queue.

Kenzie opened one of the imaging files and was startled by what she saw. She looked up at the name of the patient again, just to make sure she had gotten it right, then sent it to the printer. She would have to wait for everything ahead of it to finish printing first, but Dr. Wiltshire would want to see it as soon as possible.

10

Kenzie knocked on the door as she entered the surgical suite. Dr. Wiltshire looked up from his work, surprised to see her there.

"Kenzie. What's up?"

Kenzie took a moment to finish suiting up so that she wouldn't contaminate any evidence and took her printouts over to Dr. Wiltshire. "Sorry, I thought you would want to see this right away."

Wiltshire looked curious as he waited for Kenzie to tell him what she had.

"These are the brain slides for Willis Cartwright."

He looked at her for a moment, thinking back. "From the nursing home."

Kenzie nodded. "Right."

"There was no bleed at the site of the blow to the head. Everything appeared to be normal. A little shrinkage attributable to old age, but gross examination seemed to be unremarkable."

Kenzie stood beside him and showed him the image from the first slide.

Wiltshire's brows shot up. Kenzie saw his eyes do the same thing as she had initially done. Double-check the name of the patient at the top of the page.

"But Mr. Cartwright hadn't shown any overt symptoms."

"No."

"Well... those are clearly amyloid plaques and tau tangles."

Kenzie nodded her agreement and flipped to the next page. She held a couple of images side by side for Dr. Wiltshire. He chewed his lip and nodded.

"Well, there have been cases of amyloid plaques being found in the brains of people who showed no symptoms of Alzheimer's disease before death."

"I've heard of that. And I guess... that's what we've got here. But does that mean that he did or did not have Alzheimer's disease?"

"We'll need to discuss it in more detail with his doctor and the nursing staff. He may have shown mild symptoms. But if he didn't have any..." He shook his head as he mused over the problem. "I'm reluctant to say that a patient had Alzheimer's disease if he showed no signs of dementia."

"Even with the size and number of these plaques and tangles?"

"If you brought me this brain with no other information, I would say that it is a patient who had advanced Alzheimer's disease. But we have to realize that what we know about the human body is really just a freckle on the backside of science. We don't know more than we do know."

"So then... it's just an anomaly?"

"If you add up all of the anomalies in Alzheimer's disease—or any disease—eventually you will have a new pattern. We may be able to use cases like this to find a way to protect people against the ravages of the disease. We may find something in this man's biology that could be used as a vaccine in the future. He appears to be resistant, in some way, to the progression of the disease. *If* we have the correct information from the nursing home and his family. And *if* this isn't a case of a sample being mislabeled or saved to the wrong file. We need to explore all of the possibilities before declaring this to be a case of a man being immune to the effects of amyloid plaques spreading throughout his brain."

Kenzie had her work cut out for her. She retrieved the slides from the Cartwright case and checked the label on the box in her own writing, as well as the individual bar codes on the slides. She put the slides under a microscope to view them directly. After adjusting the focus, she saw the same results as shown on the processed images.

That was pretty clear.

Just to be sure, Kenzie retrieved Cartwright's remains. She made another examination of the brain, which did not show the deterioration she would expect in a case of advanced Alzheimer's disease. She prepared additional slides of the brain tissue and took them directly to the microscope. There could be no doubt that Cartwright's brain was full of the amyloid plaques and tau tangles normally associated with Alzheimer's disease.

11

Kenzie didn't usually do any fieldwork, so it was exciting to go to Champlain House to follow up on the Willis Cartwright case. She pictured herself as a private investigator like Zachary, going out to interview subjects and ferret out the truth. She was experienced in the lab work and in understanding and interpreting test results. Actually going out and talking to people about a case was something that she hadn't done in... well, since Amanda had died. She had succeeded in digging up the truth in that case, or as much of it as she could, but there had been serious and long-lasting consequences that she preferred not to think about.

She told herself that wasn't her fault. But it was going to take a lot of convincing, because she didn't believe it, even after all the intervening years.

She pushed thoughts of that long-past case aside and pulled into the parking lot of Champlain House. She managed to find a parking space marked for visitors and pulled in. If there weren't any free visitor slots, she would have taken one of the reserved places. She was, after all, there on official Medical Examiner business. But it was probably better not to get people's backs up the instant she arrived.

There was still a chill in the air as she got out of the car. She had hoped that it would warm up more during the day, but she suspected it wasn't going to get much warmer. It was early afternoon, the sun already on its descent. She loved fall in Vermont, with all its gorgeous riot of colors, but she was sorry to see the summer go.

The reception area of Champlain House was quiet and comfortable. Dark wood, well-upholstered furniture that didn't look like it got a lot of use, the ringer on the phone at the reception desk set to a low murmur so that it didn't echo all the way through the room. The older woman at the desk, maybe a nurse but maybe just an administrative clerk, gave her a warm smile as she approached.

"Good afternoon. How can I help you today?" Her eyes went quickly over Kenzie, evaluating her. She knew that Kenzie was not a regular visitor for one of the residents.

"My name is Kenzie Kirsch. I'm from the Medical Examiner's Office."

"Oh. And what can we do for you?"

"I would like to talk to anyone regularly involved in the care of Willis Cartwright."

"I see..." The woman, the name Delores imprinted on her name badge, didn't make a move toward the phone or computer keyboard. "Can I ask if there's something wrong?"

"I'm just following up on a death."

"I don't remember ever having a personal visit from the Medical Examiner's Office before."

Kenzie didn't want to say that it was out of the ordinary, which might make people defensive. But she wasn't about to say that it was commonly done either, which Delores would know was a lie if she had worked there for very long. There were deaths at Champlain House regularly, like there would be at any other nursing home, and they would know that most did not require an in-person visit from the ME.

"There were a few things in this case that we wanted to be sure of," she said vaguely. "So if I could talk to nurses, doctor, housekeeping...?"

"You don't have an appointment..."

"No. And I think Mr. Cartwright's family would probably like to hold his funeral sooner rather than later. Shall I tell them that you're holding up the ME's report?"

Delores didn't like that idea. She wrinkled her nose. "I don't know who you'll want to talk to. He was in our independent living center, so he didn't have dedicated nurses assigned to him. There was staff around if he needed assistance, but he was pretty self-sufficient."

Kenzie hadn't anticipated that Delores would know any details. She leaned forward on the counter, giving Delores a grateful smile. "That was what the report we received said. You knew Mr. Cartwright well?"

"I don't know about well, but... yes. Certainly. He was around and I knew him by name to say hello or have a conversation. He wasn't one of the troublemakers, you know, just a very pleasant old gentleman."

"And had he been having any trouble recently? The report we received said that they had started running some tests, because his behavior had changed."

"Changed? No, I don't know if I would say that," Delores shook her head. "He was having some trouble... but everybody does now and then. He might have had a bit of a bug. We were all very surprised to hear that he had passed away. He didn't seem sick."

Kenzie nodded. "What kinds of things was he having trouble with?"

"I don't know." Delores looked to each side as if she were afraid someone might overhear her gossiping. But there was no one else around. The lobby area was quiet and empty. "I'm not a nurse. Don't have the stomach for it. He'd... had some dizzy spells. Seemed disoriented. He forgot names or would start to say something and then forget where he was going with it." She shrugged. "We all do those things sometimes. It doesn't mean anything."

"But it was enough that his doctor had ordered some tests to be run."

Delores looked reluctant, but nodded. "Maybe he saw something that I didn't. He would have been privy to Mr. Cartwright's private medical information. I only saw him casually, and I didn't see much change from one day to the next."

"So I should talk to his doctor for sure. And that would be doctor...?"

"Dr. Able." Delores sighed, like she had been trying to protect him, but the cat was out of the bag now. "I suppose so."

"Is he in today or will I need to set up an appointment with him?"

Delores looked at the watch on her wrist with a pretty silver-chain strap. "He will be doing rounds this afternoon. I can't promise you that he'll have any time to talk to you, but he is around."

"Great. And if I could talk to any of the nursing and housekeeping staff that has contact with him."

"People need to do the work that they're here for. They don't really have the time to be dealing with inquiries." Delores shrugged as if Kenzie were being unreasonable.

"If I need longer than a few minutes, then I'll set up an appointment for them to come into my office. But I'm sure they'd rather talk to me here than to have to set something up separately. And, of course, the Cartwright family wants to be able to proceed with their arrangements in a reasonable time period. We don't want to keep putting this off. Eventually, they will get upset and start making waves. Maybe even go to the media about how Champlain House is holding things up and wondering if you're trying to hide something."

"We are not trying to hide anything!" Delores's face grew red. "We're a very good nursing home; we do a lot of good for the community. I won't have you throwing around aspersions."

"I didn't say I was going to cause you any problems. I said that eventually, the family is going to get upset that the investigation hasn't been completed and the remains are being held up. I don't think either of us wants to be in that situation."

12

Delores gave Kenzie a long, hard glare before finally breaking down. Of course, she didn't want the facility to garner any negative media attention just because she was being a diligent gatekeeper.

"I will let Dr. Able know that you are here. But don't be surprised if he reports back to the ME's office about how... overzealous you are being here."

Kenzie nodded and took a couple of steps back to allow Delores a semblance of privacy while she called the doctor. Delores's job was to help the family and friends who came to see their patients and keep any media or unwanted attention out. They didn't want people poking around and implying that they were not providing the best care possible. Anyone in the industry had to be aware of other facilities that had been exposed for substandard care. It was enough to scare even the best facilities. Walk in and find one patient complaining about falling down on the way to the bathroom, or the bad food, or saying that the staff was stealing from them, and it could be blown up into a three-ring circus.

But they were still answerable to their regulators and law enforcement. They couldn't just brush off an inquiry from the Medical Examiner.

"Dr. Able is just finishing up his rounds now," Delores said. "He will be fifteen or twenty minutes, and then he will see you in his office."

"Thank you," Kenzie acknowledged. Rather than asking whether she could talk to the other staff in the meantime, she chose one of the comfortable-looking pieces of furniture and sat down to wait, pulling out her phone to check her email. Things would go much better if the doctor were satisfied with Kenzie's professionalism and reasons for showing up at Champlain House. He could smooth the way for her to talk to the rest of the staff. Or he could make a big stink with the ME's office and try to get her pushed out.

There were a few emails in her work inbox that she could handle with a brief reply or file into one of her action folders. But most of it was stuff that she had to print out or would take a longer time to handle. Kenzie switched over to her personal email instead. There were a few emails from friends, mostly girlfriends that she liked to go out to eat with. There were a few emails from online acquaintances or men she had previously gone out with or who had tracked her down through one of her dating app profiles. She just deleted them. She had closed her profiles since getting more serious with Zachary, but that didn't stop people from tracking her down.

Zachary had sent her an email with a query about a couple of prescription medications and what they might be for. He could search them on the internet just as easily, but he liked to refer medical questions to her since it was an interest they shared. Kenzie would have more insight on why someone would be taking a certain combination of drugs. The internet might tell him the possibilities for each individual one, but two or three together gave a better picture of what condition the subject might be dealing with. Kenzie glanced over the names. He had inverted a couple of letters, but it was still obvious what he had intended. She clicked reply and thumbed out a quick answer.

Viagra and blood pressure. Is this a cheating spouse?

It was email rather than an instant messenger, so she wasn't expecting an immediate reply, but either he was already in his email or he had an alert set up for her reply.

Looks like it, unless he's selling them on the street.

Kenzie thought it unlikely that they had a very high street value. It looked like someone was taking his extracurricular activities somewhere else.

"Miss Kirsch?"

Kenzie looked up at the man standing a few feet away from her. She hadn't even heard his approach. She glanced down at his shoes. Rather than the black dress shoes that she often saw doctors in, he was wearing white sneakers, like the nurses wore for long days on their feet.

"Yes." Kenzie stood and reached out her hand to him. "Are you Dr. Able?"

If he weren't, it was better to mistake a nurse for a doctor than vice versa.

"At your service." He smiled, "Ready, willing, and Able."

Kenzie laughed. She wondered how many times he had used that line. The nurses probably all rolled their eyes when they heard it. "It's very nice to meet you. Thank you for agreeing to see me; I know it isn't easy to make time for unexpected visitors."

"No, but if they were all as pretty as you, I would make the time." He smiled charmingly.

He'd hit a home run in the looks department. Several inches taller than Kenzie or Zachary, dark wavy hair, piercing blue eyes, and a ruggedly handsome face and strong jaw. He was undoubtedly used to women falling victim to his charms. Looks *and* money and prestige.

"And it's Dr. Kirsch," Kenzie said. "With the Medical Examiner's Office."

His smile wavered. He released her hand and gave a more professional nod. "Of course. I'm sorry."

"I'd like to ask you a few questions about Willis Cartwright, if I could. You were his regular physician?"

"Willie was in pretty good shape." Able gestured in the direction they were to go and escorted Kenzie into one of the long, brightly-lit corridors. "He didn't need a lot of my attention."

"But you must have still seen him fairly regularly. Was he on any medications?"

"Just blood pressure," Able said proudly, as if it were due to his own excellent care of Cartwright. "Maybe the occasional painkiller for his joints or something to help the digestion along, but those are pretty common in old age. Not much anyone can do about that."

"Wow. Good for him. He must have really taken care of himself."

"Ex-army, from what I understand. That type likes to stay in shape. Very well-disciplined. Got his exercise, watched what he ate."

Kenzie nodded. "Yeah. I've seen a few. But then in the last few days before his death...?"

They entered Dr. Able's office. He sat down behind his large, dark desk and Kenzie sat in one of the visitor chairs, sitting forward on the edge of it so that she was closer to him.

"Yes. I thought he might be fighting a virus. Certainly not anything dangerous. I was as surprised as anyone when we found him down in his room."

"He'd had a fall?"

"Yes. I feel bad that it happened. We are very careful with our patients' health. If he'd been someone who regularly had falls or was out of his bed in the night, we would have had either a bed alarm or a fall alarm or both. But as it was, they did not know that he'd gotten out of bed and fallen in the night. We're very sorry that happened. But as we told his family, we could not have foreseen that would happen. He wasn't a habitual wanderer."

"He had experienced a couple of falls, though, hadn't he?"

Able considered for a moment before nodding. "Yes, minor. He wasn't hurt."

"And he had several bruises on his shins or knees that would suggest he'd been walking into things."

He shook his head. "I wasn't aware of that. Elderly people often bruise very easily. They might have been caused by very minor bumps. Hitting a knee when he sat down at the table, for example. Not even enough that he would remember it later. He didn't have any complaints about walking into things, bruises, or hurting himself."

"And the staff didn't know anything about them?"

"Not that I am aware."

"Speaking of what he could remember..."

Able looked at her steadily. Kenzie looked for any sign that he was keeping secrets. She couldn't see anything that would suggest deception. "Yes?"

"Mr. Cartwright had been displaying some memory problems? Dementia?"

"No, I certainly wouldn't go that far. He'd had a couple of episodes just in the week before he died when he had experienced some disorientation or confusion. But it wasn't that notable. I wouldn't classify it as dementia."

"But you were looking into it."

"Certainly. Even if we thought it was only being tired or a simple mistake, we were still following up to make sure that it wasn't the development of something more serious. I had set up some blood tests, brain imaging, cardiac just in case. So many systems can affect the brain... I thought it was simply being short on sleep or fighting a UTI, but was following up just to be sure."

Kenzie nodded. She made a few notes on her phone just to make sure she wouldn't forget anything when she returned to the office to write up a report on her findings at Champlain House.

"And nothing showed up in those tests?"

"No."

"And up until his last few days, no problems at all. You felt he was in good shape."

"I figured he would live to be a hundred, honestly. Or older. He wasn't even ready for managed care yet. He was here for the convenience of having professionals around, someone else making his meals, having a community of people of his age to do things with. It wasn't because he could no longer manage on his own. I'm sure he could have. Up until... the end."

"I'm sure you're wondering why I'm here."

He gazed at her. "It did occur to me."

"Mr. Cartwright's brain showed signs of advanced Alzheimer's disease."

13

D r. Able's brows shot up. He leaned forward over his desk, staring at Kenzie. "What?"

Kenzie had brought several of the images with her. She assumed that working with seniors, Dr. Able would have at least a working knowledge of Alzheimer's disease and its markers. She took a couple of pictures out of her slim briefcase and slid them across the desk to him.

He looked them over, frowning, and shook his head. "I think the samples must have gotten mixed up at your lab."

"That was our first thought too. But I prepared slides and examined them myself today. There is no doubt that the man in our morgue under the name of Willis Cartwright had extensive AD markers in his brain tissue."

"But that just can't be. That much damage… it takes years to develop and he would have shown signs."

"There are cases of Rapidly Developing Alzheimer's disease."

"Rapidly Developing, yes. But overnight? No. This man," Able pointed at the images. "He wouldn't be able to function in our independent living center. I know the effects of Alzheimer's disease, Dr. Kirsch, and I can assure you that Willie did not have it."

"You don't think that the symptoms you saw the last few days might have been signs of Alzheimer's disease?"

"And he just got it last week?" Able's voice dripped with sarcasm. "He started showing symptoms last week and then was dead? Rapidly Developing AD takes weeks to months, not days, to kill."

Kenzie nodded slowly. The symptoms, then, were probably just what Able had initially thought. Cartwright fighting a virus. Something that might have been completely innocuous to someone else but had caused damage to his brain or heart that had resulted in his death. Nothing to do with the amyloid plaques.

"Let's say it's not AD," Kenzie said, following this train of thought. "Let's say it's something different. When did he start showing changes in behavior?"

"As I said, it was only a few days before he died. He had a couple of falls. Nothing serious. He would get dizzy or disoriented. Forgot people's names or the conversation you had just had with him. But that's all. It could have been vertigo from an ear infection."

"Yes. Except that we didn't find any sign of infection in his body. In fact, he was in pretty good shape, considering his age."

"And the fact that he was dead."

"And the fact that he was dead," Kenzie acknowledged. "He seemed to be strong and healthy. Other than the bruises, the blow to his head, and the brain pathology." She considered, trying to think of whether there was anything else she should ask Able about. "Oh. Can you tell me if he was continent?"

"Yes. Certainly. No issues there."

"And he didn't have much appetite the final few days."

Able shrugged. "Like a man with a virus. We weren't particularly worried about it. Like you said, he was apparently in good health and we figured he would rally and be feeling better again in no time."

"Yes, that's understandable. You had no way of knowing that there was anything wrong. We still aren't sure what it was that killed him."

"Not the fall? The blow to his head? That's what I was worried about."

"No. There was no hematoma. No clot. No concussion. Just a laceration."

"Well, thank you for that. I appreciate knowing that it wasn't the fall that killed him. Or the fact that it wasn't discovered until the morning."

"I wonder if I could talk to any of the nursing or housekeeping staff who are around today who are familiar with Mr. Cartwright? I won't take up a lot of their time, but it will be faster to deal with this and get Mr. Cartwright's remains back to his family than if we have to go back and forth making appointments."

"I don't see how they're going to help you. I've already told you everything we know."

"I need to do a full investigation. If I can't find out anything else... that's fine. That will be the end of it."

He rolled his eyes, but nodded. "I'll take you to his unit, and you can discuss it with the staff. But please be... discreet. I don't want you upsetting the other residents. And I don't want there to be rumors that there is something strange or ominous about Willie's death. Sometimes people do die unexpectedly. Sometimes we can't find a reason or an explanation."

14

Kenzie was escorted to the living unit where Mr. Cartwright had been housed. It was not locked or alarmed in any way. It was a pleasant, homey atmosphere. Clean, bright, open. They saw other residents coming and going as they pleased without any need for checkout. People took walks up and down the halls, dropped in on each other, played games, or watched TV in the common room they passed. Dr. Able took Kenzie to the nurse at the desk and introduced her, explaining in a low voice what Kenzie was there for.

"Mr. Cartwright?" Nurse Summers asked with a sad smile. "What a lovely gentleman he was. I was very sorry to see him go. It was a bit of a shock."

Kenzie nodded. "That's what I understood." She smiled and nodded at Dr. Able. "Thank you for your help."

He looked at her for a moment, then shrugged and left, heading back toward his office. Kenzie didn't want him hovering while she asked questions. She didn't need him monitoring her or feeding lines to the nurse to make sure she said the right thing.

Kenzie sighed. "I understand Mr. Cartwright went downhill pretty quickly?"

"Downhill? Who told you he went downhill? That's not what Dr. Able told you," Summers said accusingly, looking in the direction Dr. Able had gone.

"Not in so many words, no. But I understand he was forgetting things, disoriented, had lost his appetite... and then, of course, there was his sudden death. I'm pretty sure that all of that together counts as going downhill."

"You make it sound a lot worse than it was. Everybody forgets names now and then. It doesn't mean there is anything wrong. And his falling down and disorientation...? He was probably just fighting a virus. It happens. I fully expected that in a few days, he would be over it and would be right back to normal. His old self."

"So you don't think there was anything wrong."

"Not seriously, no. Now... I don't know what that means for his cause of death... but sometimes I think patients do just choose their own time."

"Do you mean suicide? Assisted death?"

"No!" Summer's voice climbed louder, and a few people stopped what they were doing and looked at her. She looked embarrassed and lowered her chin, looking down at the top of her desk at nothing in particular. She spoke more quietly, in an excessively reasonable tone. "I don't mean that he took something to cause his death or planned it out in any way. Just that sometimes, we have residents who... they know their time or they pick their time. They just decide that's when they are going to stop living... and they do."

Kenzie had heard this kind of thing before and thought it was a little suspect. She did not want to find out that they had an angel of death at the nursing home who was selectively ending its residents' lives, but that was the first thing that came to her mind. Not a supernatural reason. Someone who, with a vial of insulin or some other medication, was deliberately putting an end to the lives of those she chose.

Of course there were cases where the cause of death could not be determined, where they had to list it as 'sudden cardiac death' or 'natural causes incidental to age' or some other phrasing to satisfy the law. They couldn't always determine the exact cause of death. But that didn't mean that those people were simply choosing to die. She didn't believe that.

"I see," she told Summers, nodding wisely. It wouldn't do her any good to argue the point. She wanted to be able to continue with her investigation, not to get kicked out. "And those symptoms that Mr. Cartwright was having prior to his death, those were..."

"They were nothing, really. Just some minor changes that didn't mean anything. They happen as people get older. Knees start to wear out. Balance goes. People lose their appetites. It's all part of aging."

"Yes, I see. Do you think I could see his room?"

"It's already been cleaned out," Summers said doubtfully. "His personal effects have been turned over to his family. I don't think that there is anything in there that would help you. We've just refreshed it for the next resident. We have a waiting list, you know. We'll have someone else in there within a week."

"That's wonderful. I've always heard great things about Champlain House. It's quite the jewel for our little town."

"Yes," Summers nodded vigorously. "Nothing like the warehouses you see in the big city sometimes. I've worked places like that, and believe me, it is nothing like working at the House. We really are a close-knit family here. We care about our residents and we take exceptional care of them."

As long as that didn't involve a service to help them out the door at the end of their lives.

"I would still like to see his room and to talk to any of the staff who knew him. Just so I can wrap this up and say that I have pursued all appropriate avenues."

Nurse Summers still seemed reluctant, but she shrugged her broad shoulders. "I don't see any reason why not, if you want to waste your time."

Kenzie smiled her agreement. Summers pushed herself up out of her chair and walked around the counter to Kenzie. "It's just down here. Follow me."

She led Kenzie down the hall. Many of the doors had pictures or flowery wreaths on them, as well as the nameplates. Sometimes crayon pictures drawn by grandchildren or great-grandchildren, with scrawled expressions of love slapped onto them.

They arrived at a blank door. No decoration or personal effects. No nameplate. Nurse Summers paused for a moment, perhaps quelling the impulse to knock on the door to announce herself before going in. Maybe a gesture of respect, a second to acknowledge that the former occupant had moved on. A moment of grief. Then she turned the handle and pushed the door open smoothly. She reached for the light switch and turned it on, even though the room was still well-lit from the sunlight outside. The windows were large, giving the little room an airy feel despite how small it was.

But the room was cold and sterile. There was a bed, neatly made in white sheets and a light mint-green cotton blanket. The flooring was a low-pile carpet rather than the hard tile seen in a hospital. There was a small dresser, a TV, and a closet empty of all but a couple of folding chairs to be used when the occupant had visitors. There were, as Nurse Summers had explained, no personal items left over from Willie Cartwright's stay there.

Summers sighed and looked around, resting her hands on her hips. "This is it. Like I said... He was over there," she pointed at the carpet, halfway between the bed and the door. "Curled up on the floor with Lola. The blood on his face was dry. He was cool to the touch."

Kenzie frowned at this new revelation. "Lola?"

Summers gave a chuckle. "Not another of the residents, I assure you. Lola is a service dog. Emotional support. Makes a big difference to the residents here. Sitting and petting a dog is a very soothing, relaxing activity. Lowers blood pressure. We don't need to give out as many painkillers. She does wonders in seeking out the patients who need her the most and giving them attention."

"Oh, isn't that nice? Where is Lola now?"

"One of the staff took her over to the non-ambulatory unit." Summers looked at her watch. One of those fancy ones that counted steps. "She'll probably be back here in about fifteen minutes. I'll introduce you."

"It's nice that they can have an animal here. A lot of them probably had to give up pets before they could move in. And Lola stays here overnight?"

"Yes. She has a bed behind the desk, but more often than not, she goes and finds a patient to keep company."

Kenzie made a mental note to double-check Cartwright for any parasitic infections. Some, like toxoplasmosis, could be difficult to find if you were not looking for them. And toxo could, Kenzie knew, cause behavioral changes. Though she didn't think it could cause amyloid plaques.

"How long had Mr. Cartwright been a resident here?"

"Oh... I'm thinking it's about three years now? Not a newcomer. But not the longest, either. We have a few here who have been around for ten years or more."

"In this unit?"

"One of them. Mrs. Moses has been here for... twelve, I think."

"Wow. I guess she must like it here!"

Summers nodded and looked around. "Do you need to see anything else here?"

"What else was in the room when Mr. Cartwright died? Do you know what he hit his head on?"

"There were a few other things... a chair. There was an IV stand, because he hadn't been eating and we needed to make sure he stayed hydrated. We think that he hit his head on the corner of the dresser." Summers indicated the corner in question. "But otherwise... well, you know, he just had personal effects. Some pictures and medals on the wall. His clothing in the dresser. Maybe a book and some writing materials. He didn't have a lot of possessions. You really can't, in a room like this. It's hard for people when they come from a house crammed full of personal possessions to move into a room like this, where you have to fit everything you own into a little dresser." She looked again at the piece of furniture. "But Willie always had everything ship-shape in here. He wasn't one of those hoarders. Some residents, we have to clean their rooms out whenever they are not in there, because they'll just grab everything they can. Plastic forks. Presents from family. Books from the library. They feel like they have to have *things*. More things all the time."

"Someone said Mr. Cartwright had been in the army."

"Yes, that's right. He had medals up on the wall. And the way that he held himself, straight as a ruler, you knew he was military."

"Did he ever talk about what he had been through in the army? Had he ever been gassed? Attacked with a chemical or biological weapon?"

"No, he didn't talk about it. Not much."

"Sometimes the army experimented on the soldiers too. Giving them drugs or food or other experiences to see if it would improve their ability to fight."

"Oh, I don't think they ever did that to Willie. He never talked about anything like that. He was very loyal to the army."

15

Kenzie had to admit that there wasn't anything in the bedroom that would help her. She and Summers exited, and Summers pulled the door shut behind her. Kenzie thought she detected a slight relaxing of her shoulders, a sigh of relief. She didn't like being in that room, empty and bare of all decoration.

Kenzie nodded to a woman in a smock who was putting used linens and towels into a large wheeled bin. "Did she know Cartwright?"

Summers fumbled, not sure what to say. "I—I suppose so," she admitted. "But the housekeeping staff doesn't really have anything to do with the residents. They generally clean when the residents are out of the room, at meals, or participating in activities. They don't visit with them."

"I'd like to talk to her anyway."

Summers shrugged, looking baffled at the request. "Of course. If you think it will help."

Kenzie walked over to the little Hispanic woman and introduced herself. The woman's eyes immediately got big and round. "I am legal," she protested. "I have papers."

Her name tag said Maria.

"I'm not looking for papers, Maria. I just wanted to ask you about one of the men who lived here. One of the men who died."

"I just take care of the rooms. No medicine. I don't treat anyone."

"I understand." Kenzie nodded.

The woman still shook her head in protest. "I not have anything to do with Mr. Cartwright."

"Did you clean his room?"

"Yes."

"When he was alive? You worked here and cleaned his room sometimes?"

"Yes."

"That's all I want to talk to you about. I don't think that you did anything wrong. I just wanted to ask a few questions about his room. About whether you noticed anything strange the last week or two."

"Strange. How?" The woman cocked her head, mystified.

"I wonder if anything had changed. If you saw him do or say anything that was different than before. Or if he had anything in his room that he didn't before. Or if there was anything... anything at all that was different than last week."

"His bedsheets?"

"Yes... was there anything different about his bedsheets?"

"Well, he not wet the bed before. But at the end, he sick, then yes."

"He wet the bed the last week? And he never had before?"

She nodded her agreement.

"One time? More than one time?"

Maria thought about this, then held up three fingers. "Three times."

"Three times. And he never had before." Kenzie thought about the rash Dr. Wiltshire had noticed. "What about... was it ever dirty?" Kenzie wrinkled her nose to convey her meaning to Maria while trying to think of the Spanish word for feces.

Maria started to shake her head. Then she put her hand to her mouth. "Not the bed. But when I pick up his laundry, his pants... he had tried to wash them. In the sink, maybe. They were wet, and he did not get it all out."

"And he didn't wear diapers. Did anyone else know about this?"

Maria shook her head.

"You didn't tell anyone?"

"I thought... it is only once. He is an old man. Wait and see if it happens again."

Kenzie nodded. Two more symptoms to add to the last week of Cartwright's life. Both urinary and bowel incontinence. Symptoms of Alzheimer's disease, or something else?

16

Kenzie figured she had about worn out her welcome at Champlain House, having talked to everybody that she could. Others were not on shift, of course, but Kenzie figured the chances that they would have anything more to say than Kenzie had already heard was pretty low. She was getting pretty much the same information from everyone. Surprise that Mr. Cartwright had passed away, only minor concerns in the week before he died, certainly nothing that could have contributed to his death, other than the dizziness. Most thought that the cause of death had been the blow to his head. And Kenzie would have thought the same, except she had seen the state of Cartwright's brain. No bleeding in the brain due to the fall. Instead, tissue clogged with plaques and tau tangles. A very different picture from what they had expected.

She was just going up to the nursing station to thank Nurse Summers for her cooperation and that of the staff when Lola got back.

Kenzie had completely forgotten about the dog. She looked up to see a nurse with a shaggy mane of blond hair coming down the hall with a large, mostly brown German shepherd. Kenzie's mind went blank for a moment, thinking that the dog must belong to one of the patients, and then she remembered what she had already been told about Lola.

Lola had been curled up with Cartwright the night he died. She had apparently discovered him on the floor after his fall and had kept him company until after he had passed. Maybe they should have gotten a collie rather than a German shepherd. On TV, Lassie always went to get help and bring them back to anyone who was injured. If the dog had attracted attention instead of just curling up to go to sleep with the fallen man, would it have made any difference?

Kenzie smiled. She couldn't help but be attracted to the big dog walking down the hall toward her, mouth open in a broad doggy smile. "This must be Lola."

The nurse didn't know who Kenzie was, but smiled in return. "Yes, this is Lola." They walked up to her.

Kenzie immediately stooped down to offer her hand to the dog. "She's friendly?"

"Oh yes. She loves meeting new people," the nurse assured her. Her name tag said Ellie.

Lola proved Ellie's point, smelling Kenzie and then thrusting her snout and head under her hand to encourage Kenzie to pet her and scratch her ears.

"Oh, you are, aren't you? What a sweet girl," Kenzie cooed to the dog. "I'll bet everybody loves having you around here."

Ellie nodded. "She's very popular. Even people who are usually afraid of dogs don't usually have a problem with her; she's so well-behaved. She doesn't jump up or bark. She's just very quiet and friendly. She'll sit with someone for hours if she thinks they need it."

"She must be very patient."

"Yes. And intuitive. Dogs can tell things, you know, that we can't sense."

"I've heard of dogs that can sense low blood sugar or when someone is going to have a seizure."

Ellie joined Kenzie in scratching Lola's ears. Her tail waved back and forth in long, sweeping arcs, and she panted her appreciation.

"Yes. It's amazing what they can do. Lola hasn't even been trained as an emotional support animal; it just comes to her naturally. She always wants to take care of people. I think we're all her puppies here." Ellie grinned.

"Have you had her for long?"

"No, not long. The other units enjoy visits from her too. Even in the dementia unit, she's very good at soothing agitated patients, getting them to settle down."

Kenzie considered that. "Does she spend a lot of time with dementia patients?"

"A lot? No. We try to take her over there a couple times a week, maybe. She enjoys it, but she belongs here."

"You wouldn't say that she is more attracted to the dementia patients? That she is eager to spend more time with them?"

"No," Ellie shook her head slowly. She looked at Kenzie, her brows drawing down. She glanced around her. "Are you visiting someone today? I don't think we have met before."

"I'm doing some interviews. My name is Kenzie Kirsch, from the Medical Examiner's Office. I am following up with some questions on Willis Cartwright."

"Oh, poor Willie. I was very sad to see him go. He was such a nice man."

"Did Lola spend a lot of time with him?"

Ellie stared into the distance as she considered the question. Then she shook her head. "A lot? No, I wouldn't say a lot. They liked each other's company, but Lola didn't spend a lot more time with him than with anyone else."

"I remember something in the reports I received about Lola being with Mr. Cartwright when he died," Kenzie lied. It hadn't made it to the official reports; it had just been mentioned by Nurse Summers. But Kenzie didn't see any problem with fudging the source of her intel.

"I don't know if she was with him when he died," Ellie hedged. "But she was in there in the morning when he was found."

"You don't think she was with him when he died?"

"Well, no, I just don't know for sure. Maybe she was, or maybe she went in afterward. None of us knows exactly when he died. But she was in there in the morning when he was found. I guess... she wanted to keep him warm. She knew something was wrong."

"Has she done that before?"

"What do you mean?"

"You've had other deaths here. That's natural with a nursing home. People are not here because they are healthy and starting out on some new venture in their lives. They come here because they are getting older or have health problems. They are approaching the end of their lives."

"Well, yes. Of course that's true."

"I'm just wondering if there's any pattern. Has she shown any particular attention to someone who was dying or had just died before this?"

Ellie pushed a hank of blond hair back from her face. "I told you she doesn't have any special training. She wouldn't know someone was sick or dying."

"I just wondered if there was a pattern. Like you said, sometimes they can sense these things."

"No." Ellie looked away. "I don't know. I can't think if she's spent any more time than usual with someone who has been sick lately. I mean... everyone around here gets sick sometimes, even if they are in good shape like Mr. Cartwright."

"Have you had many deaths in this unit lately?"

"No more than usual. It is a nursing home. Usually, they are moved out of this unit as their health declines, so they don't die here."

Kenzie thought back to the cases they'd had come through the Medical Examiner's Office recently. There hadn't been any major influx. Most of the people who died at the nursing home were under a doctor's care at the time, so their deaths did not need to be investigated. She would have to go through the files to track down the last few deaths. Just to make sure there weren't any connections.

"Well, it's been very nice to meet Lola." Kenzie bent down and scratched the dog's ears vigorously, looking into her eyes. "She is a very nice girl."

17

It had been a long day, and Kenzie was late getting home. She dropped off her files and notes at the ME's office before finally getting on her way. The night guards were on and the sky was dark. She hadn't intended to let the job keep her so late, but there wasn't much she could do about it.

She couldn't face the idea of having to cook a meal after the rest of the day, so she stopped off at a fast food place on the way home. It would probably have been healthier to go out to the all-you-can-eat buffet, which boasted a pretty good salad bar, but she couldn't bring herself to go out and deal with people around her. She was a social person, but sometimes even she needed to get away from everybody at the end of the day.

Except for Zachary, of course. He was going to be waiting for her at the house, assuming he was back from whatever work he had been doing, and he would want to know all about her case and why it had run so late.

She started scripting it in her head, justifying why she had been so late and hadn't bothered to call him.

After all, they were both grown adults, and neither was required to account to the other for every minute.

Then why did she feel like she had to justify it?

She thought about the couples sessions they'd had with Dr. Boyle and tried to put her finger on the problem. She was making assumptions about how Zachary would handle her being late, which wasn't fair to him. He hadn't been calling her, demanding to know why she'd been silent all day or when she was going to get in. He wasn't usually the type of person who jumped all over her for a variation in her schedule. So why was she feeling so defensive?

Maybe just because she was tired and hungry and hadn't yet sorted out her thoughts about the Cartwright case.

When she got to the house, the outside light was on, but she didn't see any lights on inside. It would be very strange for Zachary to be sitting in the dark if he were home.

Kenzie entered through the garage door and put the bag of food down on the table. The aroma of fried food had been filling the car and she was famished. She took a quick look around and turned on lights, which confirmed her impression. Zachary wasn't around. She pulled out her phone and dialed him while trying to open the food bag one-handedly. Not so easy with the way it was stapled shut.

The phone rang many times and she was preparing to hang up, not wanting to talk to his voicemail. There was a click and then Zachary's voice, sounding very far away.

"Hello?"

"It's Kenzie. I just got home. I've got food."

"Oh, good. You must have been busy today."

Kenzie strained to hear him. "Where are you? Are you on surveillance?"

"Just doing a little job. I was going to swing by my apartment on the way home... you should go ahead and eat without me."

"Really? I thought we were going to always try to be home and eat dinner together."

"When we can," Zachary agreed. "But you were working late and I've got this thing. I should have said something, I guess... I didn't know you were going to pick something up."

"It's not going to keep. Everything will just get soggy."

There was no answer. Kenzie tried to picture Zachary. Where was he? In his car? He was right, of course. He had no way of knowing she would pick up food for him. If it was anyone's fault that the food would go to waste, it was hers.

"How long will you be?"

"Uh... maybe an hour. Don't wait for me. I'm really not hungry anyway."

"You need to eat. You've been losing weight lately."

"Maybe a little. I'll try to have something when I get home."

"You are coming back here?" Kenzie asked.

There was a brief pause before Zachary answered. "Yes... I was planning to. That's okay?" Even though his voice was faint, she could hear the anxiety kick up another notch.

"Yes, of course. I want you to come back here. You said you were going back to your apartment and I just wanted to make sure you were still planning to come back after."

He blew out his breath noisily. "Yeah. About an hour, I think. I'll be there."

"Okay. See you then."

Kenzie waited to see if Zachary would hang up first, and when he didn't, she ended the call. Now he was going to be worrying half the night that she hadn't actually wanted him to come home, that she'd been hoping he was staying at his own apartment. Because... she didn't know what he would imagine. Because she was bored with him or angry at him? Because she wanted to see someone else? She was sure he could come up with a dozen scenarios to feed his fears that she didn't actually want to be with him anymore.

She sat down at the table to unpack the burgers. She had lost her appetite. Zachary not being home and her worry that something was going on with him had thrown her off. Though she'd asked, he hadn't verified whether he was on surveillance or doing something else. Usually, if he were going to be away when she got home, he gave her a heads-up and told her what was going on. But this time, he hadn't. He might have called her to tell her during the day and she had been too busy to answer. And she hadn't checked her email since she'd been waiting at Champlain House for Dr. Able.

Kenzie forced herself to eat anyway, checking her social networks and her email and glancing over the day's news to see if the world was ending yet. It wasn't like she needed to worry about keeping up her weight like Zachary did, but if she were going to be in a reasonable mood when he eventually got home, she needed to eat.

<hr>

It was closer to two hours before Zachary returned. Kenzie was not happy about the delay. She was tired from her day and ready to head to bed, and he wasn't even home. Maybe she should have just told him to stay at his apartment so she could spend the evening how she wanted to and get a good solid sleep without being awakened by his nightmares.

But she immediately regretted the thought. She didn't like to think of him lying in his bed alone, fighting his demons. She wanted him to feel safe and to be comforted when he awoke from a nightmare.

"It's late," she said, keeping her tone neutral. "Were you working this whole time?"

He rubbed his forehead as if trying to erase the worry lines. "Yeah. Some work and some errands. When you work for yourself, there isn't anyone else to pass stuff off to."

Although he had been using his sister Heather as a consultant for some work, teaching her how to do skip tracing and some other basic detective work.

Zachary didn't have any shopping bags or boxes to indicate that he'd picked anything up. He could have been dropping something off, or he might have left whatever it was at his own apartment, but she thought his behavior seemed a little off.

That thought led her to segue to Cartwright's behavioral changes before he had died. Not because they were anything like Zachary's behaviors or she thought that he was going to drop dead. Just because she wondered how significant the changes had been and what they had meant.

Zachary joined Kenzie on the couch and put his arm around her tentatively. He pulled her close and kissed her cheek gently.

"It sounds like you had a long day. Dr. Wiltshire kept you? Was there an accident...?"

Other days when there had been a sudden influx of bodies from a traffic accident or some other tragedy, Kenzie and Dr. Wiltshire had stayed after hours to get a chunk of the work done without disrupting their usual workflow.

"No." Kenzie snuggled into him and closed her eyes, letting her body relax. "I was actually out doing detective work."

"Really?" Zachary was immediately interested. "What were you doing? If you can talk about it."

"Interviewing subjects at a care facility to get more information about the deceased. It's an interesting case and we need more information to sort it out."

"Isn't that usually the job of the police?"

"Yes and no. It isn't because we think it was a homicide; we're just trying to get background on his behavior and health before he died. Trying to solve all of the clues to put together the puzzle."

"Can you tell me anything about the case? Why is it hard to determine what happened, if you think it was natural causes?"

"Because the guy's brain pathology doesn't match what we were told about his behavior before his death."

"He was behaving erratically, but there wasn't any indication in the brain?" Zachary asked. Then he shook his head. "No… someone's behavior can change without being able to see any difference in the brain. But the opposite…" He looked at her, eyes sparkling in that way that they only did when he had an intriguing puzzle to solve. "You saw changes in the brain that should have affected his behavior."

Kenzie nodded, impressed that he had figured that out from the little she had said. "You nailed it. I thought you were tired!"

He smiled proudly, though he immediately tried to wipe it away. Always trying to keep his emotions hidden from the world. Kenzie pulled his head down toward her to kiss him. "There's nothing wrong with showing that you're proud of yourself."

He looked away from her. "No one likes a show-off."

She kissed him again. "I do. We both like solving mysteries, so why can't you show that you're happy about figuring my riddle out so quickly?"

He shrugged, but allowed another smile to cross his face again fleetingly. "So how did it go at the care center? Were you able to find anything out?"

"Some interesting stuff came up. I'm going to need to write up a report for Dr. Wiltshire tomorrow and… to see what I really got, I guess. Think it all through and see where it leads me. I know a few more tests that I'll want to run, and we might need to do some research, because what we're seeing doesn't really make sense."

"You ruled out human error?"

"Yeah. I made new slides and looked at them myself this morning. There's no mistaking the brain pathology. But his behavior was normal, right up until a few days before his death, and even then, he only had mild symptoms. Symptoms that could have had other explanations."

"So was it this brain disease that killed him?"

"I don't know. Anything is possible. But if he was somehow resistant to the disease until the final stages… it could be significant. It could point the way for future medical study. Maybe a treatment or vaccination."

18

"What about you?" Kenzie turned the conversation back around to Zachary. "What case were you working on so late?"

"A few different things." His answer was uninformative.

"Did you make any progress on your adulterous husband?"

His brows went up, surprised.

"You sent me a question on his prescriptions," Kenzie reminded him.

"Oh, yeah. I forgot about that. Well... I never know whether a client will be happy to have it confirmed that a lover is fooling around on the side or devastated that they were right. Or both. It's never easy news to break."

"I can imagine. But if she knows what prescriptions were in his medicine cabinet, then she probably already has a pretty good idea."

"I don't think she really has much doubt. She just wants proof that she can see with her own eyes."

Kenzie grimaced. "I don't think I would want to see for myself. What does she want? Pictures of him with another woman? In the act?"

"I don't do pictures 'in the act.' Too dangerous and inflammatory. Pictures of him with another partner, going into a hotel or out at a restaurant or somewhere romantic. But if someone actually wants intimate photographs or videos, they'll have to find someone else. I'm not giving someone ammunition for blackmail or a manslaughter defense."

Kenzie nodded, impressed with the thought that he had put into the policy. "I don't think I would want to gather that kind of evidence, personally. Talk about awkward. And how do you get it without getting caught?"

She pictured Zachary peering in a bedroom window with his camera to get a picture or masquerading as a waiter bringing them champagne and sneaking off a picture of the two culprits.

"Well, a hidden camera would be the best option. Remote operated or motion-triggered. But like I say, I don't do that."

"Good. You've gotten yourself into enough dangerous situations without that one to add to the list."

"I don't intentionally get into trouble."

"I hope not," Kenzie agreed. She knew that he was too impulsive and that he tended to jump in to help other people without thinking through the possible consequences to himself. All part of his ADHD. She stretched and nestled herself into his shoulder again. "Do you want to watch something before bed? I'm beat, but I could unwind for a bit longer."

"Sure." Zachary looked at the blank TV screen for a moment before looking for the remote, which was on his side of the couch. He stretched to reach it, then handed it to Kenzie.

"What do you want to watch?"

"Anything is fine. Whatever you want."

He looked over at his computer. He probably wanted to work while they watched, but that would be a bad idea. He would get caught up in work and not pay any attention to the show or to her, and when it was time to go to bed, he would be all wound up and would not be able to settle in to sleep for even the few hours that his brain would allow.

"Time for a break," Kenzie told him. "Some 'us' time."

He nodded and dragged his gaze back to the TV screen. He tilted his head to rest it against hers while she turned on the TV and browsed through the guide for something that would be acceptable to them both, eventually settling on a classic mystery show. How weird was it that they both worked in crime, yet that was what they watched to unwind together? Not a sitcom or soap or something to escape into, but more crime-solving TV. And some of it was pretty bad, if she were to admit the truth. Not even close to the way things played out in real life. And maybe that was why they liked it.

They watched for a few minutes. Kenzie thought that Zachary seemed distracted, but he didn't say anything and she didn't want to force him to reveal his thoughts if he wasn't ready to or it was nothing to do with her.

"Did you have anything to eat?"

"Uh..." Zachary's eyes were distant.

"Zachary. Food. You need food to keep your body running and to fuel your brain."

"I know."

"But you didn't eat anything tonight?"

"I might have picked something up."

"If you can't remember it, then you probably didn't."

"Well. Maybe not."

"Your burger is still on the table. Do you want that? We can zap it in the microwave for a couple of minutes. And there are fries."

He wrinkled his nose. "No."

"Are you nauseated or just not hungry?"

"Just not hungry."

"What about ice cream?"

He tilted his head slightly, a sign that he was considering it. She could often tempt him with ice cream when nothing else would work.

"I'll make you a sundae," Kenzie offered. "No—a banana split."

"You're just doing that to make me eat fruit."

"Whatever it takes."

He chuckled.

"So is that a yes?"

He shrugged and didn't say no, so Kenzie got up. "Let me know what happens," she said, indicating the TV. Though, of course, she knew how it was going to end. The plot was not complicated.

When she returned with his bowl of ice cream a couple of minutes later, Zachary was sitting with his head tipped back and his eyes closed. He startled at her touch and looked surprised by the banana split. He took it from her without comment and just poked at it with his spoon.

"Is everything okay?" Kenzie asked.

"Yeah."

"You're acting like you have something on your mind. Do you want to talk about it?"

"No. No, it's nothing. I'm fine."

"You remember what Dr. B said about 'it's fine'?"

He looked as if it took a great effort to drag his attention from the mound of ice cream to Kenzie's face. She waited, not feeding him any lines. If she asked a question or told him what she thought was the problem, he would just accept her suggestion and not process his own feelings.

"I'm just... thinking about this case. And about... Bridget."

Kenzie's anger flared at the mention of Zachary's ex-wife. She hated that Bridget still had a hold over Zachary. That so much of his emotional real estate was invested in her.

It was vital for Kenzie to react to this revelation without judgment, but what she really wanted to do was to tell him to *get over it*. Bridget was out of his life. She had kicked him out physically and emotionally. She was strong and independent. She had a new partner and was pregnant with his baby. Twins, in fact. Bridget had moved on in her life and it was time for Zachary to do the same.

"What about Bridget?" she asked evenly. She had asked him to tell her his true feelings, not to just brush them off as something that didn't matter. If she really cared about his feelings, then she had to accept them for what they were and let him express himself.

"I'm just... I don't know. I'm worried about her. About how she's feeling. About the babies. If everything is going to be okay."

In fact, they knew that everything was not going to be okay. Both Bridget and the babies had some serious medical issues. Which made it that much harder for Zachary to move on. Leaving Bridget behind when she was healthy and happy with her own life was one thing. But letting her go to deal with her own problems, or to get help from Gordon, her parents, or the community, was unbearable. He had been obsessed with Bridget since he'd met her, and Kenzie expecting him to be able to let go of that obsession was unreasonable. He was doing his best in both individual and couples therapy, but leaving that part of his life behind was not something that would happen overnight. Or even in a year. The wins were incremental, so small that they were sometimes almost impossible to see.

She thought about Zachary's faraway voice when he had answered the phone that night. The number of rings it had taken to get through to him. How he hadn't answered her when she had asked him where he was. Was he stalking Bridget? Sitting in his car staring at her house because there was no other way for him to be part of her life?

"You're worried about her," Kenzie repeated back, hoping he would go on and analyze his own thoughts and feelings to get himself out of the rut.

"Yeah. I know, I shouldn't be thinking about her. She's not part of my life."

"You can't stop yourself from thinking about something. But you can try to think about something else. To distract yourself from Bridget and think about the things that you have more control over. The things that make you happy."

"Yes." He looked down at his ice cream and deliberately pushed his spoon down into the mound of ice cream, bananas, chocolate sauce, and whipped cream. He took a bite. "Being here with you. The way things are going in my life. Our future."

Kenzie nodded.

Zachary took another large bite of the ice cream. He wouldn't be able to keep it up. Even at the best of times, he wouldn't finish a whole bowl. A few more bites and he would be done.

"You should have some too," Zachary held the bowl toward her. "Didn't you bring a spoon for yourself? I can't eat all of this."

"Eat what you can." Kenzie rubbed Zachary's back, trying to help him relax. "Bridget and Gordon have their own life. They have their own trials and they need to work through them on their own."

"Yeah. Just like everyone else."

Zachary stared off into space, eyes cloudy. Gone. Kenzie could fight to get his attention back and to work through what was bothering him, but she didn't have the energy and she didn't want to hear anything else about Bridget. She pretended that they were both engaged in the mystery show on TV and let it go.

19

Kenzie spent as much time as she could the next day going over her notes and thoughts that she had gathered at Champlain House the previous day, trying to put it together in a way that made sense. It was frustrating to see the pieces that did not seem to fit together correctly. Were they missing something, or did they not have the medical knowledge necessary to understand Cartwright's death?

In the afternoon when she had a bit more time, she began to go through the computer database and filing system to pull out the deaths that they had dealt with from the nursing home in the past weeks. Most of the nursing home deaths were considered attended deaths and therefore did not go through the ME's office. Kenzie was surprised when she started to compile the cases that they had dealt with to see how many there actually were.

Had there been an increase in deaths at Champlain House? Or were the numbers normal and she just hadn't realized how many there were before? To know for sure, she would have to go back through the database to previous years to see if there had been a change in the number or types of cases that had come through the office.

Kenzie started a simple table, trying to filter out all the noise. There was too much information on the files and she needed to distill it down to a few key points to look for commonalities. Beginning with name and cause of death.

There were no homicides. They were all either accidents or natural causes. They were old people living in a nursing home, not gang bangers or street kids. But writing down the causes of death didn't seem to produce any patterns.

Falls, strokes, dementia, respiratory issues. They were all very common in that population. There wasn't any connecting thread. No indication that the majority of them had contracted the virus that the staff thought Mr. Cartwright might have had. No spate of Alzheimer's disease or another type of dementia. She had hoped to be able to spot the pattern immediately.

She started adding in sex and age and pre-existing conditions. There wasn't a field in the database that would allow extensive discussion of their symptoms in the days or weeks immediately preceding their deaths, so she would have to go to the files for those.

Dr. Wiltshire walked out of his office suite to Kenzie's desk. He looked over the notes she was making. "What are you working on?"

"Previous deaths from Chaplain House. Looking for any patterns."

"Ah. Finding anything?"

Kenzie sighed and pushed it away from her. "No. Nothing obvious. That doesn't mean there isn't anything, but I haven't spotted it yet."

"What is your hypothesis?"

"I don't have one particular working theory right now. I'm kind of pursuing several different directions. First, we have the Alzheimer's disease or the non-Alzheimer's protein deposits. Alzheimer's itself can cause death when it becomes so advanced. He did have some minor symptoms the week or so before his death. Some of which his doctor was not aware of."

"Oh? What additional information did you find?"

"They didn't know about his continence issues. They knew he'd had a few falls, but weren't aware of the bruises on his legs that indicate he'd been walking into things. I'm not sure yet what else, but he was managing to mask some of his symptoms. I think there was more dementia than was indicated in the doctor's report."

"But still not enough to account for death due to Alzheimer's disease."

"No." Kenzie pressed her lips together and thought about the possibilities. "Then there is the possibility that someone caused his death."

"Murder?"

"Angel of death, maybe? I don't know. Just something I thought of while I was there. Patients don't usually die in the independent living unit. They usually get transferred to another unit when their health declines. The dementia unit or advanced care. It's possible that someone has decided to spare residents from having to go through that and 'save' them before their condition gets serious enough for them to be transferred."

"Possible. Method?"

"I was looking for a pattern in the previous deaths, but I don't see one. Something like insulin would be quick, but difficult to detect. Since we would have to test for it within forty-eight hours and it isn't something we normally look for. But these last few patients," Kenzie looked at her notes. "They've had a wide variety of symptoms. Nothing that I could blame on a single poison or method."

"One of the problems with nursing home killings is separating out the natural deaths from the unnatural deaths. Nurses can be pretty good at hiding their methods, and you can't tell when you start which ones are related. Very difficult to establish a pattern. That's why most of them aren't discovered until they confess or are caught in the act."

"Great. So if it is an angel of death, good luck on figuring it out. I have another possibility, it's a bit of a long shot."

"Uh-huh?"

"There is a dog in the unit. She visits other units as well. Not a trained dog, just for emotional support. Likes to sit and get petted by the residents. Maybe seeks out the ones who are sad or declining. She was with Mr. Cartwright when his body was discovered."

"With him?"

"Curled up with his body, apparently."

Dr. Wiltshire squinted off into the distance like he was looking into the sun. "They should have included that detail in their report. And you think the dog might have had something to do with his death?"

"It's possible. I'm wondering about parasites. Even toxoplasmosis. That can get into the brain and affect behavior."

"Do dogs even get toxoplasmosis?"

Kenzie had looked it up that morning, curious. She had known that people could get it from cats but didn't know about other animals. "They can. If they eat something that is infected. They don't normally pass it on to humans like cats do. But if it was the right environment, close contact with an infected animal by someone with a compromised immune system. Maybe someone who was already fighting another infection. It is theoretically possible."

"Or if they roll in infected dirt and then a resident pets them," Dr. Wiltshire suggested. "They get the parasite on their hands and then touch mouth or nose, or the particles become airborne and are breathed in. It's a possibility. Check the slides for any sign of toxoplasmosis. We can run blood and fecal tests." He gave a nod. "Those are all viable routes... Alzheimer's disease would explain the amyloid plaques, but the brain pathology might just be an anomaly that has nothing to do with his death."

Kenzie nodded her agreement. It was a puzzling case. It would be easy to just write it off as 'natural death' or 'unknown causes,' but they liked to have reasons. It wasn't very satisfying to say they didn't know why someone had died. It didn't provide the same closure to family members. And if they were dealing with a case of a nurse or someone else at the care center putting residents out of their misery, then shrugging off an unexplained death could lead to the deaths of others.

20

Kenzie sighed and put her project aside to work on the other things that were burning on her task list. She couldn't afford to spend so much time on just one case. People didn't stop dying just because she was still trying to figure out a previous case. She didn't have to wait for Dr. Wiltshire to tell her that. She would look at the Cartwright file again when she was fresh and the additional lab tests that they had requested had come in. It would be easier to sort things out if they had a bit more data. And if she were fresh, she might just have an insight or two that would help the case along. Until then, there was plenty else to be done.

Kenzie went to her inbox and started to print the various reports she had flagged earlier in the day.

She came across Dr. Wiltshire's transcribed postmortem for the John Doe and remembered her discussion with Zachary over the weekend. She opened the report and browsed through it. At least there was no mystery about the cause of death on that case. Kenzie took it with her to give to Dr. Wiltshire, but before going to his office, stopped to have a look at the personal belongings that had been carefully labeled and put to the side for the man's next of kin, if one were ever found. Kenzie opened the paper bag to look at the items, but did not take anything out. She frowned and thought about what Zachary had said, then went to talk to Dr. Wiltshire.

Kenzie poked her head in the door. Dr. Wiltshire was sitting at his desk, one elbow on the table, with his hand over his eyes, unmoving. It was late and he should probably have packed it in a couple of hours before.

"Can I interrupt you for a minute?" Kenzie asked tentatively.

He dropped his hand from his eyes, startled. "Kenzie. Are you still here?"

"Just finishing up a couple of things."

"We should both close up and head home. Get a good sleep tonight."

"Yeah. I just wanted to ask you about the John Doe." Kenzie entered Dr. Wiltshire's office and put the transcribed report on his desk in front of him.

"Of course. Sorry you couldn't be a part of this one, but it was pretty straightforward. Not much to learn from this one."

Kenzie nodded. She'd seen the blood alcohol results. There couldn't be much doubt about what had killed the man. The only question was how he had gotten so much alcohol down his throat before succumbing. "The thing is... I'm wondering if he was actually homeless."

"Well..." Wiltshire pushed up his glasses. "He was found in an alley. He was dead drunk—quite literally. Clothes soaked. Dirty. Unshaven. All of that says homeless to me."

"His clothes... I was just looking at them. They're not exactly what you would expect from a homeless guy."

"Oh? Why? Too expensive?"

"Well, not really high-end. But... trendy."

"And you don't think that a homeless man could be wearing something trendy? They get clothing donations. Whatever people clear out of their closets. He might have just had an eye for that style. Even homeless people can have good taste—or trendy taste—in clothes."

"Yeah. But looking at them, they're not stained or worn. Dirty from lying in the alley and having alcohol spilled all over them. Maybe got jumped or was rolled after he passed out."

Wiltshire frowned and tented his fingers, thinking about it. "Possible, I suppose," he admitted.

"His teeth were in good shape."

Wiltshire nodded. "If he was homeless, it was probably a recent development. He'd had good dental care. Fillings, no missing teeth, no gum disease."

"And his beard growth... doesn't look that extensive or unkempt in the pictures."

"With the way the young people grow beards these days, who can say? It was short by some of today's standards."

"Not tangled and dirty?"

"Dirty... not like some I've seen. Not full of food remains or bugs."

Kenzie shuddered at the thought.

Wiltshire smiled. "You wouldn't believe some of the things I've found living in unkempt beards."

"Ugh. Not before dinner." Kenzie had a strong stomach, but the suggestion made her nauseated. "We might want to suggest that the police broaden their search to professionals working in the area he was found, then. Maybe canvass some of the nearby office buildings. I'm sure they've already asked around at the nearby bars, but maybe if they say they are looking for a... businessman rather than a homeless guy, they would have better luck."

"I'll pass that along."

Kenzie nodded, relieved. "Sounds good. I think I'll lock up, then. You're heading out soon too?"

"I am. And Kenzie," he stopped her as she was ducking back out the door. Kenzie paused and looked back. "That was a good catch. Good thinking."

"Actually... I can't take the credit on that one," Kenzie reminded him. "Zachary saw his picture in the news and said he didn't think the man was actually homeless. Going by his haircut."

"Your Zachary has got quite the eye."

Wiltshire hesitated, but Kenzie could tell he wanted to say something else to her. She lifted her brows, waiting.

"How is he doing? How are... the two of you?"

Kenzie's cheeks burned. They didn't talk much about their personal lives while at the office. Wiltshire had known when she and Zachary had broken up. It had been impossible for her to hide her emotions. He had seen reports on Zachary's kidnapping in the news before that. And he knew, of course, that they were now back together.

"We're good. Uh... closer than ever, actually." Wiltshire had only ever seen the two of them together once, and Kenzie had been furious with Zachary at the time, so she probably hadn't made a great impression on Wiltshire about the strength of their relationship. Kenzie pressed her hand against her warm cheeks. "As far as how he's doing... he suffers a lot from depression, and I think... he's on a downhill right now."

"I'm sorry to hear it. Does he see someone? Is he on antidepressants?"

"Yes to both. A number of medications. We have a therapy session tomorrow afternoon. That's why I need to take off early tomorrow."

"Right. I had just assumed..." He trailed off and didn't complete the thought. "Well, hopefully, his doctor will be able to get him straightened out."

"I don't know. He has a lot of trouble before Christmas. I know that this is only October, but I can see he's already headed that way."

"Seasonal Affective Disorder?"

"No. Trauma. Once he gets past Christmas, he's a lot better. But as we approach it... it's not easy. I have to keep a close eye on him."

At least this year, they were really living in the same house, so it would be easier to keep track of Zachary and not worry that he might overdose on all his meds some night when he was in his apartment alone.

"I see. Well... do let me know if you need anything. I will help any way I can."

"Thanks. I'll see you tomorrow."

Wiltshire nodded and took off his glasses to rub the bridge of his nose. "See you then."

21

Kenzie was awakened by the ringing of her phone. Immediately alarmed and disoriented, she grabbed for it on her side table, knocking over a water glass and who knew what else from the surface. At least the water glass was empty. She continued to feel for the phone, then saw the glow of the screen on the floor and picked it up. She tried to keep her voice down so that she wouldn't wake Zachary up and swiped the screen to answer.

"Hello?"

"Good morning, Mackenzie," a pleasant, cultured voice replied.

Kenzie slumped back into her pillows. She squinted at the bedside clock, trying to get a good view of the time. "Mother... it's six o'clock in the morning."

"Yes, dear. I wanted to catch you before work."

"Well, you did."

There was a beat in which Lisa analyzed her voice. "Did I wake you up?"

"Yes."

"Oh. I assumed that you would have to be up to get to work in time."

"No. I'm not usually up by six. Is there something wrong, Mom? Is everything okay?"

"Yes, I'm well. Everything is fine."

"And Dad? He didn't have a heart attack or something?"

"No..." Lisa's voice was uncertain. "Has he been having heart trouble?"

"Not that I know of. But I can't figure out why else you would be calling me first thing in the morning. I have a phone with me all day. You can reach me any time. Why did you need to reach me so early?"

She realized that her voice was raised and looked over at the other side of the bed to make sure she hadn't disturbed Zachary. His space was empty. He was up before six. That wasn't unusual for him. She rarely beat him out of bed.

"It isn't because it's an emergency," Lisa explained. "Just because I wanted to be sure to get ahold of you. And I don't like to talk to you when you're at work. You're doing an important job and I don't know how your boss would feel about you taking personal calls while you were on the job."

"He knows I have a life. You can call me at work if you need to. If you don't want to get me at work, then call in the evening when I'm usually home. I'm usually out of there by five or six."

"Yes, but I have my events. Dinner onward, I am usually out. And when I get home, I want to get straight to bed because—"

"Because you're up so early. But couldn't you take a break from one of your events or call me some night when you are free?" Kenzie shook her head. She switched her phone to her other hand and rubbed her eyes. "It doesn't matter. I'm awake now and I won't be going back to sleep. So what did you want to talk to me about?"

"It would be nice just to visit with you sometime, without an agenda."

"Yes, it would," Kenzie agreed pointedly.

There was silence from her mother for a few seconds. Then Lisa went on as if the barb hadn't reached home. "There is a fundraiser in Burlington that I was wondering if you would like to attend with me. Of course, you could bring Zachary along, if you like."

She had asked to meet Zachary more than once. But Kenzie didn't think putting him into an emotionally stressful situation was the best idea.

"We're really not into fundraisers." Kenzie looked toward the living room where Zachary would be working, as if she could see him through the walls. "And he's not in the best of health right now. I don't think he would want to go."

"I would really like it if you could be there. It's only one night. Maybe he could stay home and you could just go with me. It would be really nice to see you again."

"I don't know if I'll be free. Or if I want to go to Burlington. Why do you want me to go?"

She knew that her mother usually found another escort to go with her, Kenzie's father or a widowed man or one of her society ladies. She had given up on taking Kenzie to all the premier events when she had gone into medical school. Kenzie had been justifiably too busy for a lot of social engagements.

"It's a kidney research fundraiser," Lisa explained, her voice taking on a pained tone. "It would be really nice if you could put in an appearance."

Kenzie took a deep breath and let it out, trying not to let the guilt in. If she caved in to her mother one time, it would be that much harder to maintain boundaries later. Lisa would be calling her for everything.

But she didn't want to forget Amanda or to pretend that her death didn't matter.

Kenzie's sister had died from complications of her last kidney transplant. Many of the fundraisers and events that Lisa went to were centered on kidney research, supporting survivors, making changes to regulations to make it easier and cheaper to get a transplant, or other kidney-adjacent issues. When she had been alive, Amanda had gone with Lisa to a lot of those events. When her health would allow it. She had been Lisa's very own poster child for any kidney disease or transplant issues.

Kenzie just wasn't the same. She had been an observer, not a victim of kidney failure. She had done all that she could to help Amanda but, in the end, there was nothing any of them could do to keep her alive. Kenzie had put everything she could into keeping Amanda alive, including one of her own kidneys. That had given her little sister a few more years of life without being tied to a machine. But eventually, Kenzie's transplanted kidney had failed too, and they'd been forced to consider other options.

It was after Amanda's death that Kenzie had decided to go into medicine. It had never been with the goal of doing kidney research or designing a new artificial kidney, or any of those things that Lisa had thought Kenzie should pursue. But Amanda was always there, a shadow in the back of Kenzie's mind, reminding her that no one was immortal.

"I really don't want to go to another one of those things," Kenzie told Lisa, aware of the whine that was entering her voice. "But why don't you email me the details and I'll see whether I can be there or not."

"It's on the twenty-fourth," Lisa said promptly. "Burlington. I'll send you the address. It's a masquerade. Because of Halloween, you know. Unmasking kidney disease and all that. It is a very big deal. A lot of the elite will be there. The governor and other government officials, all of the heads of the different foundations, families representing those who have been lost, and so on."

And current sufferers. White-faced waifs on display to make everyone feel bad if they didn't pull out their pocketbooks and give until it hurt. Or e-transfer donations on their phones.

"I'll check my calendar later, when I'm up. But I think I might have something else going on that night."

"You could make time if you wanted to," Lisa reproached.

They both knew it was true.

But Kenzie's way of dealing with Amanda's loss had always been very different from her mother's.

22

Kenzie wandered out to the living room, yawning, rubbing her eyes, and generally feeling like a zombie. Zachary looked up from his computer and assessed.

"Is everything okay? I heard you talking. Sounded like you were on the phone."

"Yeah, I was." Kenzie covered a big yawn. She looked down at the phone still in her hand. Still too early for her to be up, but if she tried to sleep longer, she would be even more tired and wouldn't be able to get ready in time for work. Best to get some caffeine into her system, have a nice shower, and get moving. The more she moved around, the better she would feel. "It isn't even light out."

"Sun is coming up soon. Is everything okay?"

"Yeah."

"Work call?"

"No. My mother. But it's okay. No one is dying."

"Oh. Okay."

"I'm glad she didn't wake you up."

Zachary smiled slightly. They both knew what he was thinking. Lisa would have to call pretty early to wake Zachary. Some nights he didn't sleep at all. He went to bed and cuddled with Kenzie until she was asleep or close to it, and then he would get back up without disturbing her and get back to work. Or maybe he would watch a late-night movie to relax. But she would

307

know when she woke up at one or two in the morning and reached for him and found an empty bed, that he was having a sleepless night.

"Do you want me to make you coffee?" Zachary asked. "Are you going to shower?"

"I need coffee before shower today, or I'll fall asleep in there."

Zachary nodded and moved to stand up, but Kenzie motioned him down again. "No, no. I'll get it. You stay put. We'll have breakfast together after I get out."

Kenzie was still feeling irritable and out of sorts when she arrived at the kitchen table. Zachary had laid out her usual breakfast, but she wasn't feeling like marmalade with toast. She wanted something more decadent. Comfort food. But her stomach was queasy and definitely did not want anything sweet or rich. She could feel for Zachary, trying to eat something every morning when he was nauseated due to his meds. She sat down and looked at the buttered toast, thoroughly disgruntled.

"So, what did your mom want?" Zachary asked. "If it's okay and you don't mind me asking."

"I don't really want to talk about it. Another one of her fundraising events. She's always trying to get me to go to them with her."

"Maybe you should..." Zachary started hesitantly. He toyed with the wrapper on his granola bar, not yet opening it. Maybe he was hoping she wouldn't notice and he could get away with not having any breakfast. She really wanted to help him keep his weight up. He'd looked so gaunt and ill the previous year, after the depression and not sleeping for days. Not to mention hunting down a vigilante killer who had turned on him. She was hoping things would be better for him this year, but if he was already going downhill in October, what kind of shape was he going to be in by Christmas?

It might be one of those times when he had to check into the hospital to get through it. She needed to be prepared for the possibility. And not as a last resort.

"I'm not going," Kenzie said firmly. "I have no interest in going to a fundraiser on my mother's arm. I did enough of that when I was younger. It brings back too many memories—*you* should get that."

He nodded, biting his lip.

She had only recently told him about Amanda. Until then, she had professed to be an only child. But the past came knocking at her door too many times and she had needed to talk to someone about what she was going through. That was what being a couple was all about, according to Dr. Boyle. A safe place where they could talk about their feelings and support each other.

"My mother thinks I should go to honor Amanda and show that I care about what happened to her. But it's just too painful. Like if you went to fundraising for... a program to help rehabilitate abusive parents. It's a good cause, yeah. And it would have been great if someone had been able to get your parents straightened out before everything that happened to you. But would you go to something like that?"

Zachary shook his head, his eyes dark pools of pain. Kenzie felt guilty making him feel that way, but she had to express to him how abhorrent the idea of having to go to such an event was.

"Do you want something else on your toast?" Zachary asked, looking down at the untouched triangles of buttered toast. Kenzie picked one up and nibbled on the corner.

"I don't know what I want. I just feel really... unsettled today. I really don't want anything."

Zachary got up from the table without a word. He hadn't touched his granola bar either. Maybe he figured if she could skip breakfast because of how anxious she felt, then he could too. He went silently to the cupboards, grabbing a few random items and eventually putting them into an insulated lunch bag she had bought for when he went on long surveillance gigs.

He handed it to her. Kenzie opened the lunch bag and looked inside. Zachary had given her an assortment of the snack foods she kept on hand mostly for him, trying to tempt him into eating healthy snacks during the day to keep his weight up and get the vitamins he needed. An applesauce cup. A yogurt drink. A box of raisins and a package of nuts. A cheese string. Kenzie chuckled at the odd assortment and looked at him.

"If you can't eat now, you'll get hungry later in the day," Zachary pointed out. "I don't know what you have in the vending machine at work, but it didn't look too appetizing last time I was down there. This way... when you start feeling like you can eat something... you can see what you feel like. Just grab something to eat at your desk when you're ready."

Kenzie smiled. "Thanks. That's really sweet. I'll need a spoon too."

"Oh, right." He opened the drawer beside the fridge and selected a spoon for her. "Sorry."

"Don't apologize. It was a great idea. And there are probably plastic spoons at the coffee station at work."

"No point in clogging up the landfills."

Kenzie rolled down the top of her lunch bag. "Do you want my toast?"

Zachary glanced at it and shook his head. There weren't very many foods he could manage first thing in the morning. Later in the day, he had an iron stomach. He just didn't eat enough. But first thing in the morning, even a strong smell could send him racing for the bathroom.

Kenzie looked at the time on her phone, then swiped over to review her task list and calendar.

"Oh. Don't forget about couples therapy today."

Zachary sighed and nodded. "I'll be there."

***

It had been a busy night and there was a lot for Kenzie to process on intake in the morning. She made sure that everything was accounted for and all the appropriate forms had been filled out, feeling clumsy and forgetful as she went from one room to another, making sure that everything was in order for Dr. Wiltshire's arrival. It wasn't like she was *that* short on sleep. But the combination of the early hour plus a request from her mother and then not eating was enough to put her into a fog. She kept getting things wrong, then criticizing herself for making such stupid mistakes, which made her feel all that much worse about herself and her abilities. Did she really think that she could be a medical examiner herself one day? Running her own office? When she couldn't even keep up with her job handling mostly administrative work? What if she'd been a surgeon trying to operate in that state? She'd end up cutting an artery or leaving a sponge inside of someone for sure.

She looked at the time and wondered where Dr. Wiltshire was. He didn't have a set time when he was always there, but it wasn't usually so late. Kenzie could hear the phone ringing out at her desk and hurried to answer it, banging her shin against a desk drawer she had left open.

She muttered a few curses under her breath and reached for the phone, but the ringing stopped and the lights and display went back off again. She'd missed it.

Kenzie closed the drawer and sat down. It was bound to start ringing again. She brought her digital notepad up on her computer screen and looked at the phone, waiting for it to ring again. It didn't. Kenzie went back to her inbox and started processing mail, printing off reports and filing things in the electronic system. There were a few emails to forward to Dr. Wiltshire for his response, stuff that Kenzie wasn't experienced or senior enough to deal with herself. And that she certainly wasn't qualified to handle them on such a harried day.

Her stomach started to rumble. Kenzie was glad for the snacks that

Zachary had packed for her. She dipped into the bag and decided to start with the raisins. If her stomach didn't like them, they were small but would still give her a concentrated sugar boost. They helped to quell her growly stomach, and Kenzie went to the coffee station for another cup. She told herself that she was short on sleep, so the extra caffeine would help her to get through the day without any significant foul-ups.

She looked at the time again as she walked back to her desk and nearly collided with Dr. Wiltshire, moving quickly toward her. Kenzie splashed the coffee but managed to stop in time to avoid drenching both of them with scalding coffee.

"Whoa. Sorry, I didn't see you," she apologized. "Everything okay? I was expecting you earlier."

Dr. Wiltshire grunted. "Got an early call. Didn't you get the message?"

Kenzie looked at her phone but didn't have any voicemails or texts from him. "Uh... no."

"On the other phone. I wanted the Cartwright file on my desk. The family is getting anxious and making phone calls to people who can make our lives very uncomfortable."

"Oh. Sorry. I'll get it for you. And there were some additional test results in the email this morning. I'll get it all assembled."

"Yeah. Great. Next time pick up your messages."

"Yes, sir."

He continued on to his office at a brisk pace. Kenzie moved more slowly to her own desk. She didn't want to spill any more of the hot coffee or risk making any further mistakes by being in too much of a hurry and forgetting or misfiling something. If Dr. Wiltshire was getting harassed by higher-ups, Kenzie couldn't afford to make any mistakes. He would want everything possible in front of him on his desk so that he could come up with required details in an instant. No matter how hard Wiltshire pushed, she needed to take her time and get everything assembled properly.

Eventually, she was confident that she had caught all the required reports and materials, and she took the file in to Dr. Wiltshire. He looked at the folder impatiently. "Are your memos in there too?"

"My memos?"

"What you were working on yesterday. The previous deaths, your hypotheses..."

"Uh..." Kenzie swallowed, hating to look stupid in front of her boss. "No. Sorry, I didn't know you would want them, so I haven't written everything up. I just have rough notes..."

"Well, give me what you've got then."

"Okay. I'll just be a minute."

Kenzie hurried back to her desk. There was no time to rewrite or type anything. Her notes and diagrams were a mess, never intended for anyone's eyes but her own. She knew that she should be flattered that Wiltshire had asked for them. She hadn't expected her half-baked ideas to be of any interest to him. Especially if he was getting pressure from higher up the food chain.

As long as he wasn't looking for someone else to blame. "My assistant is holding things up on a wild goose chase about a parasite or serial killer. Your guess is as good as mine as to which..."

But he wouldn't do that. He'd always been professional with her, honest and upfront, and he never dressed her down even when she probably deserved it. He treated her like she was already the Assistant Medical Examiner that she wanted to be.

23

Kenzie ended up having to take a late lunch, the morning too hectic for her to leave her desk for long, and she did have to use the evil vending machine that Zachary had referred to, choosing a sad-looking sandwich that she thought might be turkey, and a small carton of milk. Neither was particularly appetizing, but she was famished despite her stock of snacks and had to get back to her desk quickly. There had been an unusual number of request forms to see to that morning.

The phone was ringing when Kenzie got back to her desk and she barked her shins for a second time, even though this time the drawer wasn't open. She saw before she picked it up that it was an internal call from Dr. Wiltshire.

"Hello?"

"Kenzie, could you join me on a call?"

Kenzie froze, not sure what to do. "Uh... you want me to three-way someone for you, or...?"

"Come into my office. We'll take the call on the speakerphone."

"Okay. I'll be right there. I just have to get someone to watch the desk."

There were a few people that Kenzie could call upon when she couldn't be at her desk. She didn't like to unless she was assisting in an autopsy. Everyone else had enough work to do without taking her responsibilities too. But she couldn't just leave her station unmanned while she joined Dr. Wiltshire on whatever the call was. She called on Julie, a college student who bounced between departments as she was needed, to see if she could leave her duties in the forensic accounting department to help out.

"Thank you!" Julie breathed. "I needed a break from filing. You wouldn't believe the amount of paper this department produces. Paperless office? Remember that concept? Somebody got it backward. We aren't going to be paper-free until we're dead."

"Uh, have you seen my department?" Kenzie teased. "I'm sorry, but being dead just means more paperwork. Only the stiff is lucky enough not to have to fill it out himself."

Julie giggled. "I'll be right down."

"Thanks. I appreciate it."

It was closer to fifteen minutes before Julie showed up at Kenzie's desk. During that time, Kenzie was on pins and needles, worried that Dr. Wiltshire was going to call her again or to show up in person to find out why she hadn't yet made it to his office for what was obviously a very important call.

As long as that wasn't code for him firing her. But she didn't think she had done anything to warrant firing or even a reprimand. She had just missed a voicemail message. And she normally picked up voicemail several times a day. It was more efficient than stopping what she was doing every time she was notified that she had a message.

She hurried to Wiltshire's office, stomach full of butterflies, a pen and notepad in hand to be able to take down notes as required.

"Ah, there you are." Dr. Wiltshire looked up from his work and pushed his glasses up his nose. He looked at his watch. "That call should be coming through any time. Nothing to worry about," he assured her with a grimace. "Just the governor's office checking up on the investigation." He rolled his eyes. "The governor. Like he has any say over how I run my morgue. Why would anyone go to him to move a medical examiner along?"

Kenzie blinked, surprised. "Yeah. That's kind of weird."

"People will use whatever kind of political pressure they can reach. If they have a friend in the governor's office..." Wiltshire waved his hand like he was performing a magic spell. "You call the governor's office."

"I guess so." Kenzie was thinking of her father. A lobbyist often stationed at the statehouse, Walter Kirsch spent all day pressing the flesh and putting political pressure in the right places. Using personal relationships to get what he wanted was his bread and butter, and he was very good at it.

She sat down in the guest chair in front of his desk and put her notepad down on the desk. Luckily, Wiltshire kept a pretty tidy desk—which Kenzie helped to keep clean—so they were not crowded. Otherwise, she would have had to balance her notebook on her lap.

Dr. Wiltshire kept working on something on his computer while they waited. Kenzie looked around the room and looked at her phone a few times to try to appear occupied. Eventually, the phone began to ring. Dr. Wiltshire checked the screen, then answered it on speakerphone.

"Dr. Wiltshire, Medical Examiner."

"Doctor," a resonant voice boomed from the speaker. "Commissioner Toby Fletcher here. I'm glad I was able to get you. I hope I'm not taking you away from anything important?"

"Well, if your intention is to move the Cartwright investigation forward, then it might be best not to interrupt the process."

The man on the other end of the line chuckled. "I understand you've already completed the autopsy, so I'm not sure what else you would have to do. The body should be able to be released at this point, shouldn't it?"

"Just because we have done a postmortem, that doesn't mean that our investigation is complete or that we can release the body. There may still be some other tests that need to be done before we can make a determination. It isn't like you see on TV, you know, where I have a wall of computers that spit out the answer to every question I might have or test I need to perform. Things take time, and as our investigation proceeds, the data we find may require additional tests that weren't considered necessary in the beginning."

"Sounds like a lot of hot air to me. When will the body be released?"

"I have my assistant, Dr. Kenzie Kirsch, with me, and we can go over some of the preliminary investigations we have done. I think you will see that we have been actively pursuing the case and have several viable avenues of investigation we need to follow before making a determination."

"Who?"

Kenzie would have sunk down into the floor if she could have. She was a nobody. Of course, this politician from the Capitol didn't have any idea who she was. And he didn't care, either. The buck stopped at Dr. Wiltshire. He was the authority in the case; the responsibility all landed on him.

"Dr. Mackenzie Kirsch," Wiltshire repeated slowly and clearly.

"Kirsch. Any relation to Walter Kirsch?" Fletcher inquired.

Dr. Wiltshire looked at Kenzie, waiting for her answer. Kenzie's stomach muscles tightened and she found her breathing constricted. Her mouth was dry, but she hadn't brought a bottle of water in with her. She licked her lips, feeling like the silence was drawing out much too long. Fletcher would think she was an idiot.

"Walter is my father," she confirmed finally.

"Your father?" Fletcher laughed and swore jovially. "I probably bounced you on my knee when you were a little girl. Walter and I go way back. And how is Lisa these days? The two of them seem to get along pretty well for a divorced couple. Better than I get on with my ex-wives!"

"Yes, Lisa is fine. She's planning to be over your way for some masquerade fundraiser later this month."

"No kidding? I'll have to make sure I go to that one. So, Walter's little girl made it to the Medical Examiner's Office. Good for you! Do you have any other siblings? I remember Lisa and Walter lost one years ago."

"That was Amanda. Yes. So it's just me now."

"Ah, that's too bad. But at least you get all of mom and dad's attention, right?"

Kenzie rolled her eyes and didn't have an answer to this. She would much rather have had to split her time with a sibling. She would rather Amanda was still alive and demanding much of her parents' attention. She had never been jealous of the time Walter and Lisa had spent with Amanda.

"Can we focus on this case?" Wiltshire suggested, rescuing Kenzie. "As I'm sure you know, we're quite busy here, so we should get to the matter at hand."

"Of course," Fletcher agreed. "So what's going on with this Cartwright fellow? He was old. He was in a nursing home. You basically just certify that it was natural causes, right?"

"I'm sure it was," Wiltshire assured him. "But natural causes is the *manner* of death. And we also need to determine the *cause* of death. What it was that actually killed him."

"He was old. It was old age. His heart gave out. It wasn't exactly unexpected, was it?"

"Are you a doctor now?" Wiltshire challenged.

"You know I'm not saying that," Fletcher protested. "I'm just saying, there's no real mystery about it, is there? Nursing home death, it should be pretty quick to certify."

"In most cases, it is," Wiltshire agreed. "But there is not a clear cause of death in this case, and we're investigating it further. Sometimes when you open someone up... you find something unexpected. And you have to deal with that before you can move forward. Decide whether it is relevant, whether you have all the information you need about the circumstances leading up to death, and all that sort of thing. There are several complications in this case that have forced us to take a little longer with it than we normally would. That's just the nature of the job."

"Unexpected? Like what?"

Dr. Wiltshire sighed. He leaned forward, toward the phone. "You're not a medical professional, so I really don't know if it is helpful to discuss all of the details..."

But he'd had a pretty good idea from the start that Fletcher or whoever called from the governor's office was going to want details. That was why he had asked for Kenzie's notes and for her presence on the call.

"I have to have something to report to the governor."

"As you probably were told, Mr. Cartwright had a scalp laceration where he had fallen and hit his head. It was minor and didn't appear to have anything to do with his death. But we didn't find anything on the gross examination of the body that would indicate cause of death, and when we proceeded with the postmortem, his heart and lungs appeared to be in pretty good condition. The nursing home had reported that he had been in good health and I agree that appears to be the case."

"So maybe it *was* the conk on the head."

"That was our thinking as well. But when we examined the wound, there was no indication that it was serious. We did open up his skull to see if there was a bleed or swelling of the brain that might have resulted in his death. Closed head injuries don't have outward indications."

"And...?"

"That's where the unexpected part comes in. We did not find any sign of a bleed, concussion, or stroke. We had slides prepared of the brain tissue as a routine measure, and that's where we did find something surprising. Mr. Cartwright had extensive protein deposits in his brain tissue that would be expected to cause him problems."

"Protein deposits. What does that mean? What kind of problems?"

"He had amyloid plaques, which are a key indicator of Alzheimer's disease."

"Ah. Well, like I said, he was old."

Kenzie wished he wouldn't keep saying that. Eighty-seven was elderly, that was true, but if Fletcher was one of Walter's contemporaries, then he wasn't that much younger than Cartwright himself. He was likely in his seventies.

"He was getting on in years," Wiltshire agreed. "And Alzheimer's disease would not be unusual. Except that he didn't have dementia symptoms. He was supervised, but he was in the independent living section of the nursing home. He was able to look after himself and only had minimal support from the staff."

"They must not have noticed."

"That's one reason I had Kenzie out to the nursing home yesterday. To see if there was any possibility that the nursing home had missed symptoms or been negligent in their care of Mr. Cartwright. Maybe Kenzie could tell you a little bit about what she found there."

He nodded for Kenzie to step in. Kenzie swallowed and nodded back and tried to gather her thoughts.

"The unit he was in is not equipped to handle someone with serious needs like advanced dementia. If his care was too difficult, then they would have transferred him to one of the other units, based on his symptoms and the kind of care that he needed." Kenzie cleared her throat. "He did have some new symptoms cropping up in the week before he died. Issues with forgetting or disorientation. He had at least a couple of falls. He wasn't eating. But all of that could just have been the temporary effects of a virus, too. They were starting to run some tests, but didn't think it was serious enough to worry about. They figured it would just run its course and he would be fine again."

"Viruses can be pretty dangerous to the elderly."

"They can. But he didn't have a lot of viral symptoms like you would expect. No vomiting or difficulty breathing. No rash. Just those very vague symptoms that people sometimes get before the actual virus symptoms show up."

"But say it was the flu or something like that. His body is fighting the virus and he's just having bothersome symptoms. Maybe he doesn't even realize he's feeling sick because it's causing tiredness and confusion. Then it really hits in the night. He spends a few hours throwing up, but doesn't think he needs any help from the staff. Doesn't realize that he's gotten dehydrated, and..."

Kenzie looked at Dr. Wiltshire.

"Something like that is certainly possible," Dr. Wiltshire agreed. "But it still doesn't explain the signs of Alzheimer's disease in his brain. With everything that we know, he should have had advanced dementia symptoms. The question becomes, did he not have symptoms? Did he have them and they weren't recognized? Is there something other than Alzheimer's disease that caused these plaques?"

"But if it's the flu that killed him, then you don't need to worry about the plaques," Fletcher said reasonably. "You just focus on what *did* kill him. Any other... anomalies... well, they don't really matter, do they?"

"We haven't established that he had a stomach bug. We've sent in swabs for virology. He didn't have vomit on his clothing. There wasn't anything in his stomach, but the staff said he hadn't been eating. He didn't have an inflamed throat."

"It could be a virus," Fletcher said petulantly.

"Yes, it could. But a virus doesn't cause amyloid plaques."

Kenzie made a couple of notes on her notepad to follow up on. Fletcher was pushy, but hopefully, he was starting to get a better picture of what they were doing. And as Dr. Wiltshire had said, the governor's office didn't really have any say in how quickly he completed an autopsy. They could put on all the pressure they liked, that wasn't going to move anything forward.

"So what else causes amyloid plaques?" Fletcher asked.

"We'll do some more research into that. But it is a hallmark of Alzheimer's disease. I have heard of amyloid plaques sometimes showing up with Creutzfeldt-Jakob Disease."

"Mad cow?" Fletcher demanded. "Are you telling me that Cartwright might have had mad cow disease?" He swore.

"No," Dr. Wiltshire hurried to head Fletcher off before he could drop the phone and go tell everyone he knew that Cartwright had died of mad cow disease. "There are several kinds of Creutzfeldt-Jakob Disease. It can be inherited, sporadic, or it can be transmitted by eating contaminated meat. But we don't know anything about whether Mr. Cartwright had any form of CJD. So don't go spreading that around."

"Can't you test for it? You are going to test for it, aren't you?"

"We'll test," Dr. Wiltshire assured him quickly. "Of course. And if he had CJD, that doesn't mean that there is any problem with our food chain. Remember that it can lie dormant for years, even decades. Who knows when he might have been exposed if, in fact, he was? There are other prion diseases as well. Some of them are very rare and I would have to look up the symptoms to even know what to look for."

"If he had mad cow, what would that look like?" Fletcher demanded. "I mean, I know it's not like rabies, he's not running around trying to bite people or afraid of water. But what would his symptoms be?"

"Dementia," Dr. Wiltshire admitted. "Very much like Alzheimer's disease. The two can be easily mistaken for each other without testing. CJD is generally faster than Alzheimer's disease. It can take someone within a year of onset of symptoms."

"So it could be that."

"He wasn't showing any symptoms until just before his death," Wiltshire reminded him. "CJD is fast, but not that fast."

"Variant CJD is even faster," Kenzie said thoughtfully, careful not to refer to it as mad cow disease. Even though variant CJD was, in fact, the disease dubbed mad cow. "But still. Not a week. Sometimes as fast as six to eight weeks."

Dr. Wiltshire nodded, but his expression was disapproving. He didn't want Kenzie getting Fletcher wound up about the possibility of vCJD in the food chain. Kenzie looked down at her notebook, writing a few more details. She'd never heard of a case of vCJD that had taken someone that fast. But it was something to consider.

"We need to be thinking about how this is going to play out in the media," Fletcher said. "If this is a case of mad cow disease—"

"It isn't. If we find it is CJD, we can talk about the impact then, but right now, nobody is saying that it is Creutzfeldt-Jakob, and we are not going to start talking about it to the public. We are just investigating the death of a man who may have died of old age, a viral or bacterial infection, or Alzheimer's disease. All routine illnesses that everyone is familiar with. No one in my office is talking about CJD or releasing anything to the public. When we know what killed him, then we'll issue a report. Until then, no one talks about it."

"I'll need to take this to the governor," Fletcher said, still not calming down. He was acting as if he were in crisis mode already, trying to deal with an epidemic or another threat to public safety before anyone had any idea what they were dealing with.

The man needed to cut down on the caffeine.

24

After they were finally able to end the call with Fletcher, hopefully having deterred him going off like a cannon to the governor and telling him that there was an outbreak of mad cow disease, Kenzie stayed with Dr. Wiltshire for another half hour or more, going over the various points for each of them to follow up on while they tried to sort out the case. More swabs and samples to be taken and sent off for testing for bacterial, viral, or prion diseases. Research to get started on. Dr. Wiltshire had a few doctors to follow up with whose specialty areas would give them a better feel for what they might be looking at than Dr. Wiltshire or Kenzie had.

And there were other cases that they couldn't let drop off the radar either. The John Doe had not yet been identified. They would wait for a while, hoping to release him to his family rather than the city for a pauper's burial. And there was the new case that Dr. Wiltshire had been called out to that morning. Kenzie had done the intake forms, and they would need to get to the postmortem as soon as they could to keep bodies moving through the system. They couldn't let one case block everything up.

Kenzie left Dr. Wiltshire's office, rubbing her forehead and temples. She wasn't sure whether the headache that was starting was from tension, or lack of sleep, or lack of food. Maybe a combination of all three. It had been a long, intense day. She hadn't expected to be pulled into Wiltshire's office for so long. Poor Julie had been pressed into service for much longer than they had expected and was probably bored silly. And Kenzie had a lot of jobs to do that she would have to let slide until the next day. There was no way that she was staying any later with the headache that was starting to settle in.

"Sorry to be so long," Kenzie apologized. "I thought it would only be a few minutes." She looked at the time again, even though she had already done so at the end of the conversation with Dr. Wiltshire. "I'm so sorry. I should have told you to just go home if it got to be past closing time. You really didn't need to stay."

"It's okay," Julie looked up from the conversation or game she was involved in on her phone and gave Kenzie a warm smile. "Really. I didn't have anywhere else I needed to be. And I can claim overtime. Pay off my school bills faster."

"Then I did you a favor," Kenzie teased. But she knew it wasn't true, and she shouldn't have left Julie there to her own devices for so long. "Did everything go okay? Any problems?"

She had only been down the hall; Julie could have fetched her if something had really blown up while they were busy.

"No." Julie pushed herself back from the desk, sighing and stretching. "The only one was your boyfriend."

"My boyfriend? Zachary?" Kenzie's mind spun into high gear, forgetting about her headache and fatigue. "What happened? Is everything okay?"

"Yeah. Sorry, I didn't mean to make you think that anything had happened to him." Julie held her hands up in a calming gesture. "No, just that he called." She grimaced. "A few times."

Kenzie swore under her breath. She moved in beside Julie to get out her purse and lunch bag and to gather up the rest of her papers to put securely away for the next day. "Did he say what was wrong?"

Julie said he was fine, so he hadn't done something stupid like overdose on his meds or slit his wrists. But he knew better than to call her multiple times. He could call her once, and if she didn't answer, just leave a message and wait for her to call him back. Sooner or later, she would. He knew that her job was important and that sometimes it had to come before their relationship. Dinners and dates could be put off. Death and high-powered politicians could not.

"He said that the two of you had an appointment. He wanted to know if you were on your way." Julie shrugged, looking apologetic. "He wanted me to interrupt you, but I knew you and Dr. Wiltshire were on a conference call. He called back a few times. He wasn't screaming or rude or anything... but I could tell... he was pretty ticked off. Sorry," she said again.

"No, no, you did the right thing." It wouldn't have been good for Julie to interrupt the conference call. Not unless Zachary were in the hospital or there were some other dire news.

But she knew what she had missed.

Their couples therapy. The appointment she had reminded him of just that morning.

25

Kenzie would have kicked herself all the way home if her feet weren't already occupied with the pedals of the little red convertible. She had hurried past the security guard without their usual friendly conversation, focused solely on getting home and dealing with Zachary.

She couldn't believe she had missed the appointment. It was on her calendar. She knew about it. Dr. Wiltshire knew about it. She had reminded Zachary and she had always been there for him any time before then that he needed her. Other than when they were broken up. He had been so distant and remote then, angry at her for a conversation she'd had with Pat and Lorne without his knowledge. His anger over her talking behind his back had made him furious and had set their relationship back so far she had been afraid that it was unsalvageable.

And now she had screwed up again.

But that was the way relationships were. Sometimes, one person or the other fell short of expectations. No one was perfect. The important thing for them was to keep talking. She would tell him how sorry she was. Explain how Dr. Wiltshire had called her into the phone call without prior warning. He knew her job was important to her. He wouldn't hold that against her.

That was what she kept telling herself all the way home.

Kenzie was relieved to see lights on when she reached the house. At least he hadn't abandoned her and returned to his own apartment in his anger. There was still a chance for her to apologize and explain.

She entered from the garage and took a quick look around the kitchen. Had he eaten? Had he been drinking?

But the kitchen was clean, looking pretty much how she had left it that morning, as if he hadn't even been in there. If he had eaten, he had remembered to put all his dirty dishes into the dishwasher, which would be rare. Normally even if he remembered, he would still neglect one bowl or mug, either thinking he would use it again later or just getting distracted by something else.

"Zachary?" she called, not just wanting him to know she was home, which he had probably figured out when the garage door opener had ground into action, but because she wanted him to know that her first thought was of him and connecting with him.

There was no answer. Kenzie went from the kitchen into the living room, where he was sitting in front of his computer with headphones on. Kenzie glanced at the screen to see what he was doing. She didn't want to walk in on some conference session with a client. The moving image on the screen appeared to be a surveillance video. Maybe one he had taken, or maybe one taken from a camera at a business or someone's doorbell camera. Cameras were so omnipresent in their lives.

Kenzie took a few steps to the side, trying to get into Zachary's peripheral vision so that she wouldn't startle him. His eyes flicked to the side and he didn't jump. He pressed a key on the computer and lowered the headphones.

"Hi."

"Zachary, I'm so sorry I missed our session. I was tied up in a meeting with Dr. Wiltshire. I couldn't even call. We had a big phone call with the governor's office."

"Okay." He put the headphones back on.

"Zachary!" Kenzie touched his arm to regain his attention. He glanced at her again, then continued to watch the video. "Zachary. Come on." She tapped him several times. Zachary took a breath and lowered his headphones again.

"Yes?"

"We should talk. Don't just block me out."

"You were busy. I heard you. Now I have work to do." He indicated the computer screen.

"I know you're angry. You're probably hurt. Pretty upset with me."

He blinked and said nothing.

"Did you go ahead and have a single session with Dr. B?"

"Yes. Didn't want to waste the money. I have enough crap to deal with that there was plenty to cover all by myself."

"Did you talk about me?"

Zachary pointed to his computer screen again. "I should work on this."

"Did you at least tell *her* your feelings about me missing?" Maybe if he'd had a chance to vent already and to work through his emotions with Dr. Boyle, he was okay and didn't need to talk it through with her. If it were already settled without her apology and explanation, then insisting on going over it again could be more harmful to their relationship than helpful. If he'd already gone through it with an impartial third party, maybe that was for the best.

"I told her you were in a meeting. That's what the intern said."

"Yes. I was. I just... I don't want you to think that our couples therapy isn't important to me. It is, okay? This was just a one-time thing. I'll go in tomorrow and I'll talk to Dr. Wiltshire about it and explain that I can't stay if we have something scheduled. I can't go into a meeting right before an appointment."

"Sounds good." He looked at Kenzie, his aspect totally flat. He held the headphones ready, eyes drifting back to his computer screen. "Did you need anything else?"

"Have you eaten?"

"I'm not hungry." He put the headphones back on, blocking out any further discussion or argument. He pressed play on the video on his screen and watched it intently.

"I'll order something in. I don't have the energy to make anything today," Kenzie said. Maybe the headphones blocked her out completely, but she suspected they did not.

Kenzie went back to the kitchen to get herself a drink and decide what kind of takeout to order.

26

Kenzie didn't know how long Zachary was going to give her the silent treatment. She couldn't complain, since she was the one who had wronged him, and he did answer her when she spoke to him. Or at least, when she made him take off his headphones so that he could no longer pretend not to be able to hear her. She couldn't complain about him not sharing his feelings with her. He gave every indication that he had forgiven her and it was no big deal.

Except that she knew it was a big deal for him.

After being abandoned by his parents and kicked to the curb by his ex-wife, he didn't need any more rejection. He didn't need anyone telling him that he wasn't important, through their words or actions.

He wouldn't tell her how much it hurt. Maybe he would bottle it up, or maybe he had already talked to Dr. Boyle about it, in which case he had already been reminded how damaging it was for him to just stuff his emotions. He knew that for him and Kenzie to have a good relationship, they needed to talk about things.

But he wasn't going to talk. He would stay remote and resist any of her efforts to get in.

When the pizza arrived, Kenzie put a slice on a plate for Zachary and took it to him. She put it on the side table within his reach. Zachary glanced at it and took his headphones off again. "I'm not hungry."

"I know you said that, but you still need to eat. Even if you're upset."

He put the headphones back over his ears and continued watching his videos. He didn't touch the pizza. Kenzie sat down on the couch close by with a couple of slices for herself. "Did I tell you that we think you're right about the John Doe not being a homeless guy?" Kenzie asked, as if Zachary weren't wearing his headphones and doing his best to block her out for the evening. "I had a look at his clothes, and you're right. Trendy brands. Nothing with stains or ground-in dirt, just the oil and dirt from where he was found in the alley."

He didn't say anything.

"And his teeth. They were in very good shape. You don't see homeless guys with that kind of work. Not usually, anyway. Even if he was only recently homeless, you would still expect to see some gum disease. Signs that he hadn't been taking care of himself."

He still didn't look at her or give any sign he was listening.

"I could use another set of eyes on these nursing home deaths..."

Zachary's eyes darted to her for an instant and then were carefully turned away again as if it had never happened.

Kenzie sighed. She picked up the TV remote to find something to watch and ate her pizza in silence.

27

The rest of the evening was pretty much like that. Zachary going through video after video of surveillance. Or maybe watching the same one over and over again, Kenzie really couldn't be sure. She watched a little TV, but she was tired and ready to hit the hay. She put away the leftover pizza. At least Zachary would eat cold pizza for lunch if he remembered it was there or saw it when he opened the fridge.

She paused in the living room, looking at him. "I'm heading to bed. You going to come in?"

He turned his head slightly toward her, but he didn't meet her eyes. "I'll be in in a while."

"Okay." Kenzie hesitated for a moment. She had so many things to say to him. She wanted their relationship to be a good one and not be thrown off the rails whenever she made a mistake. Zachary got to make mistakes, to be impulsive and distracted, so why couldn't Kenzie forget something and make a mistake now and then?

She didn't want to go to bed alone. She didn't want to go to sleep with him angry at her. But he needed time to work things out for himself. She couldn't force him to see things her way.

Kenzie was quite sure the next morning that Zachary had not gone to bed any time during the night. His side of the bed was far too neat to have been slept in, even if he'd pulled the sheets straight upon rising.

She got up and found him in the kitchen, looking at his phone while he waited for the coffee to brew.

"Hey. How are you?" She forced herself to act as if everything were perfectly normal between them, walking up to him for a morning hug and kiss as usual.

Zachary remained stiff, but he gave her a squeeze and a peck on the cheek in return. "Fine."

"Did you get any sleep?" She studied his face. He hadn't shaved, which helped to hide the hollowness of his cheeks from her. But she could still see bags under his eyes. Of course, he almost always had bags under his eyes; it didn't mean that he had worked all night. His eyes were not bloodshot. So maybe he had stretched out on the couch once she was in bed.

"A bit."

"Good. You know you have to take care of your body for good physical and mental health."

"So they tell me."

She gave him another hug and a quick smooch on the lips, trying to draw him out. But he remained remote.

"I'm going to have a shower. Then we can have breakfast together."

"I'm eating now." He indicated a granola bar wrapper on the counter.

"That's good... then you can sit with me while I eat. You don't have to go out anywhere this early, do you?"

Zachary looked down at his phone to check the time and tried to come up with a lie about why he had to go out so he could avoid having breakfast with her.

"See you in a few minutes, then," Kenzie said breezily.

Breakfast was awkward, but Zachary did sit with Kenzie and made agreeable noises about having some pizza for lunch if he was at home when the hour rolled around. He had things to do that would take him away from the house. Unspecified things. She couldn't tell whether he was keeping client confidentiality or blocking her out.

She would allow him the rest of the workday to sulk, but she expected to see a change when she got home again. She wasn't going to put up with him sulking around for another evening. It would be time to either talk about things or move on. The choice was his. But she wasn't going to walk around on eggshells for weeks this time.

She gave him another hug and kiss in farewell and headed into work.

There was plenty to catch up on from the day before, and Kenzie also wanted to get some research done. She needed to make sure she understood everything she could about amyloid plaques. Anything that the scientific world knew about how they were formed, how they caused damage to the brain and loss of function, and what they might indicate other than Alzheimer's disease or CJD. They couldn't be the first ones who had run into that situation.

But first, there were new intakes to be done, email to process, reports to be printed, Dr. Wiltshire's desk to tidy, and taking care of anything else that had happened during the night. In a bigger city, they might have a fully functioning night shift as well as the day shift but, as it was, they operated with only a skeleton staff to keep an eye on things at night. The staff being one person, usually rotating in from other departments. And that meant that sometimes things didn't get done the way Dr. Wiltshire liked.

Eventually, Kenzie felt like she could take a few minutes to start on her education about amyloid plaques and differential diagnoses for Alzheimer's disease. Unfortunately, it was noon. And who knew what the afternoon would bring. She already had a list of things that she would need to take care of. So, it was another sandwich from the lone vending machine, eating over her computer while reading through medical studies and articles.

There were several theories about amyloid plaques. Everything from their being another prion disease like CJD, to being produced in response to attack by a virus or bacterial infection. It wasn't necessarily as Kenzie had imagined, just a metabolic error or something that built up as people aged. While it was the most common cause of dementia, they didn't affect everyone, like wrinkles or muscle degeneration.

One takeaway from her study was that tau tangles correlated better with how advanced the dementia was than amyloid plaques. But Cartwright's slides had shown extensive tangles, which suggested he should have had advanced dementia.

Another study suggested that amyloid plaques were not a problem until they started to appear in the synapses between neurons. Plaques inside the neurons apparently did not cause the communications problems that a build-up between the neurons did. All of that made sense to Kenzie. If the impulses between cells were obstructed by protein deposits, the cells could not pass messages along.

But once again, Cartwright's results defied the study. He had extensive plaques in the synapses. By every measurement and predictor Kenzie could find, he should have been disabled by the amount of damage in his brain. It would not be surprising for someone to die from such extensive damage. What was surprising was that he had not experienced any symptoms until a few days before his death.

Kenzie took notes and tried to come up with a hypothesis that made sense. Several of their theories so far had been disproved by the laboratory tests. She couldn't predict when they would get the bacterial and virology swab screens back to give them a better idea of whether they were looking for an infectious agent.

Dr. Wiltshire was at her desk just before Kenzie could finish her sandwich and clear away the work she was doing. "Oh, sorry, didn't realize you were on your lunch break."

"No, it's okay. I didn't really take a break. But I thought I'd better have something to eat." She wondered whether Zachary had or would actually have a slice of pizza as she had suggested. He hadn't called or texted her all morning. That wasn't particularly unusual, especially if he were engaged with a case, but she had hoped that she would hear something from him, just so she could stop being so anxious about whether he were okay.

"Good thinking." Dr. Wiltshire's eyes lingered on the few bites of her sandwich that were left. She hadn't seen him go to the vending machine or out for lunch. Had he brought his own lunch in, or was he, like Zachary, inclined to just work straight through the day without a thought of something to eat? She didn't know how Zachary could do it.

"I thought you would want to know that our John Doe has been identified," Dr. Wiltshire offered, his eyes returning to Kenzie's face. "Thanks to your insight on the fact that he might not actually be homeless and we should broaden our search to businesses in the area, not just services for the indigent."

"Oh, that's good news! Who is he?"

"He was a businessman living near the site where he was found. He lived alone, so he hadn't been reported missing. The police are contacting his next of kin, so we may get transportation instructions today or tomorrow."

"They didn't want anything else for their investigation?"

"Who, the police?" Dr. Wiltshire shook his head. "No, why?"

"I just thought that since he was killed by alcohol overdose and was found in a back alley... it's a little more suspicious if he wasn't actually a homeless man. If he was an alcoholic on the streets, it's not hard to believe. But a businessman going home from work at the end of the day..." She shook her head. "I would think they would want to investigate that a little more."

"And they probably are. But they haven't asked for anything else from our end. We've already collected all the evidence and established cause of death. Manner of death is accidental, unless I get other information."

"Yeah." Kenzie scratched the back of her head, thinking about it. Alcohol toxicity was almost always accidental. Unless they had some kind of evidence showing that the alcohol had been forced down his throat, which they did not. His teeth had not been broken, as they might have been if a bottle were forced into his mouth. There were no bruises or defensive injuries to indicate that he had fought off an attack. "I guess so. I'm just surprised that it was someone white-collar."

"The rich can still be closet alcoholics and can overdose if they consume too much too fast."

"Yeah. But he wouldn't be drinking at work, would he? They would catch on if he was drinking that much on the job."

"Maybe he went out for drinks with the boys after work. Hit a bar or two. Everyone heads for home, only he doesn't make it. Maybe he continued drinking after they went home."

"But then wouldn't they wonder what had happened to him if he didn't show up at the office the next day?"

"We don't know that they didn't. They may have called him to see if he was okay, but not reported it to the police or to the boss at work because they didn't want to get him in trouble. They might say that he was sick, or that they don't know what happened to him, to cover for him."

Kenzie nodded. "Yeah. I guess that makes sense."

It wouldn't be the same with her friends. If one of them thought that she had drunk too much the night before and she had dropped out of sight, they would undoubtedly do more than just call her and cover for her. But it was different for women. They were more vulnerable. Her friends wouldn't even have left her at a bar or let her walk home by herself if they thought she might have had a bit much to drink. But with men, it was different. They wanted to show their crew how invulnerable they were. How they could drink massive quantities without being affected. Walk alone at night as if it were nothing.

She remembered how Zachary had been jumped after leaving a bar when on an investigation. He had been badly beaten by a gang of skinheads. Men were not invulnerable, even if they thought they were. Zachary and John Doe could both attest to that.

"What was his name?"

Dr. Wiltshire looked down at his hand, where he held a sticky note. "Jeremy Salk. We can update our records."

Kenzie nodded and typed it into her notepad. "I'll do that."

<h1 style="text-align:center">28</h1>

D r. Wiltshire looked down at Kenzie's notes. "You've been working on the plaques?"

Kenzie nodded. "There was a lot to do today, so I haven't spent a lot of time yet. But it's interesting stuff. We never really covered the theories in school, just that Alzheimer's disease was caused by these amyloid plaques, and if you saw amyloid plaques, it was Alzheimer's disease."

"But things are rarely that simple in medicine."

"No, I guess not. There is the whole question of why people get these plaques. I thought that it was just a function of aging. Some processes in the body slowed down, and these plaques started to accumulate. But that's not necessarily the case."

He nodded. He glanced around him. There was nowhere to sit down around Kenzie's desk. People stood there to make inquiries or fill out forms, and then they left. They didn't stay to chat.

"Let's grab the boardroom," Dr. Wiltshire suggested. "You can still see if someone comes in."

Kenzie nodded and picked up her notes. She would hear if her phone rang. No need to call Julie in this time.

They sat at the table and Dr. Wiltshire got comfortable. "So, what can you tell me?"

"I don't know how much of the theory you know…"

"Pretend I know nothing. I'm a layman. You're explaining it to Zachary."

"Okay." That helped Kenzie to relax and feel less anxious about it. She didn't want to be lecturing her boss, either assuming he was ignorant or that he knew something he didn't. The permission to treat him like a layperson meant that she didn't have to worry about offending him.

"One of the most compelling theories is that amyloid plaques are actually a defense mechanism. Like fever. We see it as a symptom, something that must be treated to make the person well again. But when we artificially lower a fever, we are not letting the body use its own defenses. We should let it run its course, unless it is too high and endangers them."

"Right. So amyloid plaques could be a defense against what?"

"There are several bacteria implicated and possible viral involvement as well. For example, we know that people suffering from dental infections are at a much higher risk for Alzheimer's disease. There is a significant risk of bacteria making its way from the teeth to the brain and causing real damage. A brain infection puts the person's life at risk."

"So the plaques may be a way to prevent bacteria from entering the brain, or they might interfere with the bacterial growth or be a sort of scar tissue caused by bacterial damage."

Kenzie gave a nod. "We don't know why or how, but we know that people who have amyloid plaques are able to fight infections for longer. They are somehow protective and slow down the disease process."

Wiltshire nodded. "What bacteria appear to be involved?"

Kenzie gave him the specifics. She paused. "Also, there is the possibility that they protect against some viruses as well. In particular, herpesviruses."

He considered. "Which herpesviruses?"

"Human Herpesvirus 1, 6A, and 7. That we know of."

Dr. Wiltshire shook his head. "Which, all together, are endemic to what percentage of the population? Ninety percent?"

"I haven't been able to come up with a number for all three together. But yes... it is endemic. But not in *brain tissue*. Usually, our immune systems are effective in keeping herpesviruses out of the Central Nervous System. The percentage of the population with herpesvirus in the *brain* is much lower."

"So if the plaques were caused by a virus, the serology is not going to tell us what we need to know. We don't need to know what viruses were in the blood; we need to run PCR on the brain tissue and CNS fluid."

Kenzie nodded. "But this is all theory, and we could still be looking at two separate issues—what caused the plaques, which may be benign, and what caused his death. He could still have died from a virus or bacterial infection, and the plaques have nothing to do with it." Kenzie had her doubts about that, but it was a possibility. The literature confirmed that some people with amyloid plaques did not seem to have any AD symptoms.

"Of course," Dr. Wiltshire agreed. "We'll pursue both avenues and, hopefully... come to a conclusion in the end."

29

Despite how busy Kenzie was, she watched the clock, and when five o'clock rolled around, she put away her active projects and began the night shut-down procedure. Before the clock struck six, she was pulling into the garage and went into the house.

"You home?" she called out as she walked in the door.

She could hear Zachary moving around in the living room. He poked his head into the kitchen, looking at her and rubbing the bridge of his nose. He looked tired and drawn. He had probably not crashed on the couch during the day like he should have.

"Yeah, I'm here. You're home early."

"Well, I'm home on time. For once. After how crazy it has been this week, I decided I'm not spending any longer at the office today. Unless there's an emergency, I'll put in my time tomorrow and take the weekend off." Considering the fact that she frequently put in at least one weekend shift, that was significant. She hoped it signaled to Zachary that he was an important part of her life too. That she was willing to make the time for him.

"Sounds nice," he said noncommittally. No inflection. No suggestion of something they should do together, since they would have the time. She hadn't asked whether he had any surveillance he would need to be away for or if he wanted to drive out to see one of his siblings.

"Did you have any plans?" she asked tentatively.

"I don't know. I'll need to look at my calendar." He didn't pull out his phone to look and she knew he was just putting her off.

"We could do something nice. Go out to Old Joe's. A movie. Something we haven't done for a while."

He nodded.

Kenzie sighed. "What do you want for supper?"

"Nothing. Whatever you like is fine."

"I'm not sure I'm even going to make anything." Kenzie kicked off her shoes and hung up her jacket on the hook on the mudroom wall.

"You don't have to. Do you want me to order in?"

"Not if you're not eating."

Even though Zachary was giving her something of a cold shoulder, she could see his consternation over this statement. He knew that she got concerned when he didn't eat, so it was something he could fall back on if he were angry and wanted to let her know it in a passive-aggressive way. He hadn't exactly said that he wouldn't eat supper, but he had implied it. On the other hand, he would be very upset if Kenzie didn't eat because of him. Ordering in was one way that he nurtured her and showed that he could be a partner in their relationship, but if she didn't accept his offering and intentionally went hungry because of him, he would obsess over it for days.

Kenzie went to the bedroom to put down her bag and change into something comfortable. It might still be early in the evening, but she was going to pamper herself with a nice cozy set of jammies.

When she finished and left the bedroom, Zachary was standing there in the hallway, looking as though she had caught him red-handed at something. He looked back the way he had come, then ahead to the bathroom, and didn't know what to say. He had clearly wanted to continue their conversation but didn't know whether to follow her or give her some space.

Kenzie raised her brows. "Yes?"

He just motioned to the bathroom and hurried past her. He shut the bathroom door and turned on the tap. Kenzie waited for a moment, then went back out to the living room. Zachary had learned a lot of different coping mechanisms in foster care, not all of them functional. She turned on the TV while she waited for him to sort himself out and decide to talk to her. He could keep pretending that he wasn't upset with her, tiptoe around and act like everything was normal, and be increasingly anxious because of it. Or he could just get it off his chest and they might be able to enjoy the upcoming weekend.

30

Unfortunately, it was doomed to be a tense and awkward evening of avoiding speaking to each other unless absolutely necessary and pretending that everything was fine when they did speak. Kenzie eventually broke down and heated up the leftover pizza, which they both had some of.

"How was your day?" Kenzie asked as she nibbled at her slice. "Work good?"

"Yeah. How about you? Make any progress on that case? The... nursing home case?"

"Not really. We're waiting for a bunch of testing back. I did some research for it today, but I'm not sure how it will turn out. We may be seeing a problem where there really isn't one."

Zachary nodded. He lifted his slice and smelled it, but didn't eat. She waited for more questions, but there didn't appear to be any forthcoming.

"We identified that John Doe. You were right; he wasn't homeless. He was just... in the wrong place at the wrong time. With the state of his body and clothes, the police assumed that he was homeless and that's what they told us. They happened to be wrong, and we were operating under a false bias."

He nodded again and looked away from her, into the living room where he had a line of sight to the front window. He always sat in the same kitchen chair. In the beginning, she thought it was just habit. Zachary had a definite preference for sameness and rituals. But she had started to see that maybe it wasn't just habit, but the need to be able to see as much of his surroundings as possible. To know if a stranger were lurking around the house, a car parked on the street that shouldn't be there, any sign of emergency vehicles or other possible dangers. The kitchen only had a small window and a door into the mudroom and garage. The window faced a neighbor's house. While it helped to brighten the room during the day, it wasn't much of a view. Only the big living room window afforded him a good view of the street.

"We were both pretty impressed that you could guess that he wasn't homeless just from his hair," Kenzie offered.

"Not just his hair. The way he was groomed. His skin. A lot of little things."

"I guess that's what makes you such a great private investigator. Being able to see all of those little things and draw conclusions from them."

Zachary shrugged off the compliment. He took his first bite of the pizza. Kenzie was nearly finished eating her first slice.

"Nothing interesting for you today?" she prodded. "Talk to Heather or anyone?"

"Talked to Heather," he admitted. He had introduced his big sister to PI work, and she quite enjoyed the work she was able to do for him from her computer and phone. She didn't do fieldwork like surveillance or accident reconstruction, or going to people's houses or places of business to talk to them. The home-based work was enough for her.

"How is she?"

"Good."

"It was really a good idea to get her involved with your work. You needed someone to help out with those jobs to free up your time. And it's been really good for Heather and her self-esteem."

"Uh-huh."

Kenzie ate her second slice of pizza without any further attempt at conversation and put her plate in the dishwasher. She walked away from the kitchen without excusing herself or saying another word to Zachary. A few minutes later, she could hear him putting his plate into the dishwasher as well. There wasn't really enough in the dishwasher to run it, but she heard him start it anyway. Hopefully, he had remembered to put detergent in the dispenser.

***

Kenzie shut herself in the bedroom and worked from her laptop and her tablet on the bed, catching up on some correspondence with friends, paying bills, and writing dutiful emails to her parents. She downloaded a book and read for a while, but couldn't focus on the story, her mind on Zachary and work. The puzzle of what had killed Willis Cartwright festered. Would they end up just writing it off as natural causes? Age? It wasn't a great solution, but she wondered if they would be left with any other option.

She started to think, after a while, that she should call Dr. Boyle. Of course, she should call during the day when Dr. B would be at her office. But she would probably have appointments booked most of the day, and Kenzie would have a hard time finding private time during her own workday. She didn't want to be discussing ultra-personal matters while sitting at her public-facing desk. For most of the day, she was alone, but she could be approached by the police or a member of the public for a request at any time. That meant that she had to be careful what she said and did there.

Dr. B had told Zachary and Kenzie to call her at home if they needed to. Kenzie didn't like to do that unless it were an emergency. But she was worried about Zachary. Not about his immediate safety, but she did worry that if she let him go downhill now, in October, then there wouldn't be anything she or anyone else could do when he hit the really black time in the week or two before Christmas. Maybe there wasn't anything any of them could do anyway, but she had hoped that if she kept track of his moods and was there to give advice and help him along, that he would do better this time. They could have a quiet December and give Zachary plenty of time and control over his own surroundings, and with her help, he could get through it more easily.

Maybe that was naive of her. She'd seen him the previous Christmas and really understood for the first time that it wasn't just December blues, but a real crisis point.

The other question, besides whether Dr. B would want to get a call from Kenzie during the evening when it wasn't an emergency, was how Zachary would feel about her calling Dr. B.

Kenzie had made mistakes in that area before, talking to outside parties instead of directly to Zachary. But he wasn't talking to her. Any time she asked him how he was, she got a one-word answer. She'd tried to engage him in various other conversational topics, but had failed.

Eventually, Kenzie gave in. She would call. She would see what Dr. Boyle thought. And if necessary, she would go back to Zachary to ask for his permission. Dr. Boyle was Kenzie's therapist too, after all. Maybe just for the couples stuff, but they did have a professional relationship.

The phone rang a few times and then was answered by Dr. Boyle's quiet, cultured voice. "Hello?"

"Dr. Boyle. Hi, it's Kenzie Kirsch. I don't like to disturb you at home. Are you busy? Is there a time I could talk to you tomorrow?"

"I have a few minutes now. What can I help you with?"

Kenzie took a couple of deep breaths, trying to prepare herself. "Well... I guess you know I missed couples therapy this week."

"I did notice," Dr. Boyle said dryly.

Kenzie gave a weak laugh. "Yeah. I guess you probably did. How was Zachary? Was he okay?"

"You should ask him that."

"I did. He says everything is fine. He says he understands that sometimes I have to work late unexpectedly and that I was called into a meeting with my boss and couldn't call him to let him know what was going on. But... I know he's still upset. He won't talk to me about it. I'm not sure what to do. I don't want to just let it go until he's ready to talk about it. That's what I did the last time, and it was weeks before he was ready..."

"I would suggest that you continue to let him know that you will talk to him about it, that you're prepared to hear his feelings. But know that he isn't necessarily going to be open to sharing those feelings right now. It was a bit of a shock for him when you didn't show up."

"And in the meantime, when he won't talk to me? Do I pretend that everything is fine? Act like it's all normal? Because things are pretty tense around here. I don't know how to deal with him. He's blocking me out."

"He might need a bit more time. It was just yesterday."

Kenzie let out her breath. Was it even possible that it had only been a day ago? It seemed like ages already. Every minute that she sat with Zachary, or separate from him, it felt like there was a war going on between them. A silent war, but a war nonetheless. And she didn't know how to win it. Or if she needed to win it. She wanted things to go back to normal. Like the blissful night when she had invited Zachary back, and they had lain in each other's arms for hours. It had seemed like everything had been healed between them and nothing else could ever open that rift again. And now she'd done it. It was as easy as forgetting an appointment she'd promised to attend with him.

"There isn't anything I could do to help him get through it faster? I'm worried about him. About his depression. It's already getting worse and Christmas is more than two months away. What if I can't reach him before that?"

"That's two months away," Dr. Boyle assured her. "A lot can happen in that length of time. If you've apologized for what happened and he's accepted it, I think you just need to wait patiently. He has a lot of emotions to work through."

And it would take longer than a day. Kenzie knew how he was still stuck on forgiving his mother for abandoning him and his siblings to the foster care system. She had demanded that they be taken away because she didn't want to deal with them anymore. That was a decades-old hurt.

And he was still dealing with his feelings for Bridget when she had kicked him out of the house and divorced him. That one festered not just because of Zachary's feelings, but because of the things that Bridget had done since, using him, being verbally and emotionally abusive, if not physically abusive. Kenzie had seen Bridget slap Zachary once, and she was pretty sure that wasn't the only time it had happened. The recent revelations about Bridget's unborn twins and her own challenges had not helped Zachary to put the past behind him.

So why did she think that he should be able to recover in a day after they'd had a major disconnect? Especially when his feelings with her were bound to be wrapped up with his feelings toward his mother and Bridget?

"How do I wait? I want things to go back to normal. Not to feel like I have to tiptoe around here and avoid doing anything that will make him feel worse? I keep trying to talk—just about normal stuff, not the relationship and my screw-up—and he just won't engage."

"Do you want me to talk to him?"

Kenzie considered. She wasn't sure whether that would be helpful or harmful. She'd talked herself into calling Dr. Boyle, telling herself it was the right thing to do, but was talking to Dr. B or asking her to intervene a betrayal of their relationship? Kenzie didn't want to do that again.

"No. I don't think I should put this on you. I think that if he feels like I went to you and asked you to straighten him out..." Kenzie shook her head to herself. "That's just going to make things worse. It's going to break our trust again."

"Okay. Then all I can say is that you're doing the right thing, letting him know it's okay to share his feelings and then trying to live a normal life while you wait for him to process it. It isn't going to be a smooth, easy path. There might be a few blow-ups along the way. But you're going to need to give him time. More time than you think it should take."

"All right." Kenzie sighed. "That's what I'll do, then. At least... at least I know what he's upset about this time. Before, when I didn't know why he had suddenly withdrawn... all I could think was that something had happened and he didn't care anymore. He didn't want me around and just didn't know how to say it. When Lorne told me... it was a relief to at least know what it was we were fighting about."

"Good luck. You have his schedule, so you know when his next therapy session is. Expect some fireworks that day. And then the next week we'll have another couples session. And hopefully, Zachary will be okay with that, and you will be able to be there. Make an effort to be around when you say you will, to keep all appointments, even if they seem like small, unimportant things. He can get through this. If you both work at it."

"I will. Thanks."

31

After hanging up with Dr. B, Kenzie just lay in bed for a while, sometimes with her eyes closed and sometimes staring up at the ceiling. She tried to put herself into Zachary's place. To imagine what was going on inside his head and how it was affecting him. Eventually, she forced herself to roll out of bed, put her devices away, and go out to the living room to talk to him one more time.

Zachary's head twitched toward her for an instant when she entered the room, so she knew that despite the fact he pretended to be occupied with his computer, he wasn't so hyperfocused on his work that he didn't see her.

"Hi," Kenzie said and sat down on the couch. Near where he was seated at his computer, but not too close. His eyes went to her, then to the empty space between them. He turned back to his laptop.

"Zachary."

"Uh-huh?" He deliberately made his voice sound far away.

"I called Dr. Boyle. I wanted to make sure you knew. So you don't think I'm talking to people behind your back."

His eyes turned to her, dark and intense. Already looking hurt and betrayed. "What?"

"I wanted to know her thoughts on what I can do. I know I screwed up. I just wanted to know if there was anything she thought I should be doing to... let you know that I'm sorry and that I care about how you feel. To let you know that you can talk to me about it. When you're ready."

He looked away again, tapping a key on his computer as if he were still engaged with what was on his screen.

"Great. You didn't need to do that. What did she say?"

"Just to carry on. Give you time to process. However much you need."

Zachary nodded.

"And I'm doing that. I didn't come out here to push you to talk or to feel differently than you do. Just to let you know that I'm working on myself. And that I talked to Dr. B. I'm not trying to hide anything or to push you."

There was a long period of silence. It might have only been a few seconds, but it felt like forever. After a long time, Zachary nodded and said, "Okay."

***

Kenzie didn't know how long it would take before things were normal again between them, but she felt like at least they had made a step. She had made sure that he wasn't going to be taken by surprise by her call to Dr. Boyle and that he knew she was just going to continue to be patient and wait. As much as she was able to do that. What she would really like to do some days was just to smack him and tell him to grow up and get over it. But the fact was, he really *was* still that ten-year-old he'd been when his mother had abandoned him. And he was still the damaged kid he had been in foster care when his behavior had been too much for the Petersons to handle and he had spent much of his time in institutional care. And he was still the man he'd been with Bridget, beginning their life together, happy as two lovebirds should be, and then devastated when her love for him had soured and she had kicked him out. He was still all those people and stuck in all those relationships.

But in an improvement over the night before, he agreed to go to bed with her. His body was too stiff and his movements conscious and forced, but he was at least trying to go through the motions, just as Kenzie was.

After the restless night before and a couple of very long workdays, Kenzie couldn't stay awake even if she was worried about their relationship. After a few minutes, her body relaxed and she drifted off to dreamland.

But it wasn't to be the peaceful, regenerating sleep that she hoped for. She was jolted out of sleep by Zachary a few hours later. Not having nightmares, but shaking her shoulder gently. Kenzie tried to open her eyes, rubbing one with her fist.

"What? What's wrong? Did you have a dream?" Kenzie croaked.

"Your phone."

"What?" Kenzie forced herself to sit up and look for it. It flashed and vibrated on the bedside table. "Oh... dang!"

Her phone was set to Do Not Disturb after ten, and the only people who were allowed through were Zachary and Dr. Wiltshire. And her parents, of course. Kenzie couldn't shake off the memory of late-night and early-morning calls when Amanda had been alive. Gut-wrenching calls when no one knew if Amanda was going to make it through the night. Kenzie wouldn't leave her mother to her own devices if Walter had a heart attack, or vice versa. She would be there when her parents needed her, no matter what their relationship was like.

Kenzie fumbled her phone and scooped it up. She squinted at the bright screen. Not one of her parents. Dr. Wiltshire. Kenzie swiped and put it up to her ear. "Hello? Dr. Wiltshire?"

"Sorry to call you in the middle of the night, Kenzie."

"No. It's okay. What is it?"

"There has been another death at Champlain House. I'm going to attend this time. Do you want to come along?"

"Oh. Yes." Kenzie pulled off the blankets. "Are you going right now?"

"I'll be on my way shortly. You don't have to come if you don't want to. But you've been very involved in the Cartwright case and I thought you might..."

"Yes, definitely." Kenzie slid out of bed and went to her closet, squinting into it by the light of her phone to pick out a shirt and pants for the visit to the nursing home. "I will be there as soon as I can be. Do you know what we are looking at yet?"

"No, not yet. They did not sound concerned. They don't, I think, view it as suspicious."

"Okay. I'll see you there."

Kenzie hung up the phone and started to dress.

"Where are you going?" Zachary asked.

"Champlain House. It's just down by the river. Not far."

"I can drive you."

"And then you'd have to just sit in the car in the dark and cold waiting for me. You don't need to do that. Just go back to sleep."

"You know *that's* not going to happen," he said with a hint of a laugh. "And I'm not exactly a stranger to sitting in a dark, cold car. If I take you, then I'll know that you're safe and not worry about you."

"I can drive myself. I'm awake. You may as well get what rest you can."

She could feel him watching her in the dark. "If you tell me not to go, I won't. But if you don't mind... let me drive you."

Kenzie was irritated and pleased in equal measures. He wasn't acting remote and angry. And he wasn't acting needy. He communicated his feelings, gave Kenzie a choice, and then waited. Just like they'd been taught in couple's therapy.

"You'd really rather sit in the car than stay here?"

"Yes."

"And you know that afterward, we'll have to come back here so I can get my car for work? I don't want you to have to pick me up at the end of the day too. That's a lot of extra driving around when I'm just going in to... observe."

"I know. I'd rather go."

Kenzie sighed. "Okay, then. I suppose I should be grateful to have you along and give me time to wake up." She knew that Zachary didn't need time to wake up. Even in the middle of the night, his usual state of affairs was hypervigilant, not drowsy. He had woken up to the vibration of her phone, hadn't he? While she was yawning and rubbing her eyes, he sat on the bed like he had just come in to watch her sleep rather than needing any sleep himself.

He sprang up off the bed and was fully dressed before Kenzie, despite her head start. He slid out of the room as silently as a ghost, not waiting for her. Kenzie finished dressing, went to the bathroom, gathered her bag and her phone, and made her way out to the living room.

"If you can wait thirty seconds, I've got coffee on," Zachary told her, looking at the time on his phone.

Kenzie didn't want to wait, but thirty seconds for coffee beat going out immediately with nothing to fortify herself. She breathed out, trying to catch her breath and slow her heart, which was thumping rapidly with excitement. "Okay. Thanks. That was thoughtful."

"Dr. Wiltshire can take you for donuts in the morning."

Kenzie chuckled. He probably would, at that. They wouldn't be taking time to go back home and follow their usual morning routines. Another reason it was probably a good idea to go with Zachary. Then he wouldn't feel like he had been abandoned by her the whole day.

"I'll get the car warmed up." Zachary pulled on a jacket, turned off the burglar alarm, and went out the front door to his car parked at the curb in front of the house. His breath was frosty in the air, reminding Kenzie that she'd better get her coat as well. She put on her jacket and shoes while she waited for the coffee machine to finish filling the large carafe, then used it to fill the two travel mugs waiting on the counter. Try to get Zachary to make a simple lunch while he was distracted by something else, and he would forget a major component. But when he was focused on a mission like getting Kenzie safely to the nursing home, it was a totally different story. He was as prepared as a boy scout. Or a drill sergeant.

Kenzie grabbed the two mugs and her bag, re-armed the burglar alarm, and left the house.

32

Zachary drove up to where the official Medical Examiner's van was parked to drop Kenzie off at the correct doors. The night was quiet and still. It wasn't like crime scenes that Kenzie had seen on TV. Not bustling with action, police walking in and out, crime scene techs dusting every surface for fingerprints or scouring the property for other evidence. No bystanders or media calling out questions, wanting to know what had happened.

Instead, it was quiet and peaceful. Like the hospital room of someone who was gravely ill or a funeral home. Everyone spoke in hushed voices, moved slowly, and showed deference and respect. When Kenzie entered through the side door, she was met by a security guard who clearly knew who she was and escorted her to the room where the body and Dr. Wiltshire awaited her.

Dr. Wiltshire talked to one of the nursing staff in a low voice, both of them nodding and looking grave, but not worried. Dr. Wiltshire nodded to Kenzie as she entered the room. There were no police there, no one saying that she needed to put on booties and coveralls to avoid contaminating the scene.

"This is my assistant," Dr. Wiltshire introduced her. "Dr. Kenzie Kirsch. Kenzie, Nurse Sheila Cook. We have here," Dr. Wiltshire indicated the bed, "Mr. Stanley Sexton, age seventy-two. Nurse Cook...?"

"He pressed his call button," Nurse Cook explained. "When Jason—Munro—came to see what he needed, Mr. Sexton was unable to speak. He made some noises, but it wasn't clear whether he was coherent and unable to speak or whether he was unaware of his surroundings and making random noises or the kinds of sounds someone makes when they are asleep. Jason attempted to communicate with him, and when he was unable to get a coherent response, he returned to the nursing station to get someone else to help. By the time he and I got back to the room, Mr. Sexton had passed."

Kenzie looked at Dr. Wiltshire to see if there were anything else. It sounded pretty straightforward. Maybe a stroke. They would know better when they examined him. She and Dr. Wiltshire approached the bed together. Kenzie didn't touch anything, looking the bed and nearby surfaces over for anything that didn't sit right. It all looked straightforward. No blood or other fluids. No strange smells. No indication that Mr. Sexton had been trying to get out of the bed. The call button was within reach.

Kenzie heard the click of claws on the hallway floor and turned to see Lola coming in. She approached Kenzie and nuzzled her hand. Kenzie petted her for a minute. "This is Lola," she told Dr. Wiltshire. "I met her last time I was over."

"Hello, Lola," Dr. Wiltshire said solemnly before continuing with the investigation. He put his fingers over Mr. Sexton's pulse and waited for a moment. He checked the man's pupils for reactivity to light. Kenzie certainly couldn't see any signs of life. "Dr. Kirsch, would you verify lack of pulse?" Dr. Wiltshire said formally.

Kenzie moved in to obey, wondering why he would want her to verify his findings. When she touched Mr. Sexton's arm, she was surprised and almost jerked her hand back away. His skin was cool to the touch, waxen under her fingertips. She looked at Dr. Wiltshire. Sexton had been dead for longer than the half hour it had taken them to get to the scene.

"Better do a liver temp," Kenzie said in a near-whisper.

He nodded his agreement.

Kenzie looked around the small room again. If the staff had lied or misled them about one thing, chances were, there were other things. And it was probably their only chance to spot anything out of place or any evidence that needed to be preserved.

Lola whined. Looking at how Sexton was positioned on the bed and the sheets pressed down on one side, Kenzie turned to look at Nurse Cook. "Was the dog in here with him?"

"Well..." Cook looked awkwardly from Kenzie to Dr. Wiltshire and back again. "Yes, Lola was in here earlier."

"Sleeping on the bed with him?"

She nodded. "I didn't see any harm in it. Mr. Sexton had been agitated earlier, and Lola helped to settle him down so that he could go to sleep. She's very good with the residents."

Dr. Wiltshire raised his eyebrows at Kenzie and nodded, a signal that she had done well. Kenzie scratched Lola's ears. She examined the dog covertly for any sign of illness. Her eyes and conjunctivas were clear. Her nose, when she shoved her snout into Kenzie's hand for more love, was wet and cool. Kenzie didn't smell anything foul. Lola wasn't limping or favoring any part of her body that Kenzie could see. Her fur was well-brushed and shone. Nothing that Kenzie could see that would give her any reason to believe that Lola was sick with any illness that she might have passed on to the residents at Champlain House. Of course, she could be a carrier of numerous pathogens without ever showing any symptoms.

"What time was it when Mr. Sexton hit the call button?" she asked Cook.

"I'm not sure. Not long ago."

Kenzie waited for further explanation. Nothing was forthcoming. She looked at Dr. Wiltshire, then back at Nurse Cook. "Don't you have a system that registers what time a call button is pushed?"

"Uh, we do," Cook admitted. She waited for more questions, then looked uncomfortable. "I suppose I can check, if you really need me to."

"That would be most helpful," Dr. Wiltshire agreed.

Nurse Cook didn't move to do so.

"If you could do that now," Dr. Wiltshire suggested.

"Well... I suppose." She eventually gave a shrug and left the room.

Dr. Wiltshire looked at Kenzie. "The timelines may be a lot broader than they would like us to think. Things don't move quickly in a place like this. Even at a hospital, it may be an hour before someone answers a call, if it is a busy time or the patient had been bothering them with trivial things."

"And he was 'agitated' earlier. They might have waited, hoping he'd go back to sleep on his own, rather than having to deal with him."

"Would you mind making note of the ambient temperature...?"

Kenzie went to Dr. Wiltshire's medical bag and found the electronic thermometer. She turned it on and waited. The room was warm, as she had previously noted. Mr. Sexton's body temperature would not fall very quickly in that environment. She opened her notebook and wrote down the date and place, Stanley Sexton's name, the ambient temperature, and a couple of other notes they would want to include when they did up their site report.

Kenzie looked at the doorway. She had expected Nurse Cook to be back with the information about the time that Sexton had pushed the call button. But so far, there was no sign of her. Had she been unable to find the information? Trying to cover it up? Maybe she had just been sidetracked by another patient or a task that only she could take care of. Dr. Wiltshire pulled off Mr. Sexton's bedding to examine him in situ. Kenzie looked him over, but nothing jumped out at her as being wrong. He was dressed in light pajamas and had been covered by a sheet and a single thin blanket. Kenzie would have been too warm to sleep there with even just the blanket.

There were no significant marks or bruises on Sexton's face or neck. Dr. Wiltshire pulled up his shirt to inspect his torso, then let it fall back into place. Kenzie moved closer. She indicated the mark on Sexton's arm.

"He's had an IV recently."

Wiltshire nodded his agreement. There was an IV pole nearby, though no bags hung on it.

"If there is any possibility that this is an angel of death," Kenzie murmured, looking toward the door to make sure that Nurse Cook didn't walk in on the conversation unexpectedly, "then we should take the opportunity to check for insulin tonight. Before it's had a chance to break down."

"Yes. Good thinking. And screen for any other popular drugs used in mercy killings."

Kenzie nodded. "Yeah." She thought about one of Zachary's previous cases. They had thought at first that it might be an assisted death or mercy killing, but it had turned out that just the opposite was true. The perpetrator had wanted the victim to experience as much pain as possible before her death. People's motives could be very complex.

Nurse Cook returned to the room with a young man, also a nurse. Kenzie took a couple of steps toward him to confirm that he was, in fact, Jason Munro, the one who had discovered Sexton in distress and had gone for help. He looked extremely uncomfortable. He glanced back at the door as if measuring whether he had the time to run for it. But how far would he get if he ran? Champlain House undoubtedly had his address and would have cops there waiting for him to explain himself. He shifted his feet back and forth and looked at Nurse Cook but didn't meet her eyes.

Nurse Cook's face was stiff, her lips pressed together in a long, thin, downward curving line and her eyes hard and unwavering.

"This is Nurse Jason," she said unnecessarily. "He would like to revise his story." She turned her stony eyes on him and waited.

Jason gulped. He was still eyeing the door and trying to decide how to get out of the fix he was in.

Dr. Wiltshire tried to meet Jason's eyes, giving him an encouraging smile. "Jason? I'm glad you were so quick to come forward so that we can find out the truth of the situation here. It's essential that we get the real story about what happened tonight, even if you are embarrassed about it or think that we will be upset. I assure you that it will be nothing compared to what would happen if you continue to obfuscate the truth."

Jason gave a mute nod.

"Did Mr. Sexton press the call button tonight?" Dr. Wiltshire prompted, hoping to get the ball rolling.

Jason shook his head. "No. That isn't the way it happened."

"Ah. Why don't you tell me, then, how it did happen?"

"He didn't press the call button. It was Lola. She was barking."

"And you came in here to see what the matter was or to take her away or quiet her down?"

"Not at first." He swallowed and looked at Nurse Cook.

"I see. To begin with, you let it go, hoping that she would quiet down on her own."

"Yeah. I mean, yes, sir. Sometimes she barks. She sees a squirrel outside, or she wants to play. Or, I don't know, she just likes to hear the sound of her own voice."

"It's not the first night that you've heard her bark."

"No. Sir."

"How long did you wait before going to see what she was barking about?"

Jason's eyes rolled up toward the ceiling, thinking about it.

"Tell them the truth," Nurse Cook warned.

Jason shrugged with one shoulder. "I don't really know. That's the truth. I was trying to ignore her. I didn't look at the time; I just tried to block her out."

"Wasn't her barking bothering anyone else?"

"No. No one had woken up. The other staff... they're used to hearing her bark now and then. And she wasn't barking constantly. Just one or two barks every now and then."

"Go on."

"When I went in and looked to see what she was barking about, that's when I found Mr. Sexton dead." He stared at a spot on the rug in front of him.

"He was already dead when you went in there," Dr. Wiltshire stated.

"Yes."

"He wasn't incoherent, trying to communicate something to you."

"No. Well—no."

Kenzie pursed her lips, wondering what else he was trying to hide. They didn't yet have the full story. He was still trying to hold something back. Dr. Wiltshire recognized this as well.

"He was dead," he said slowly. He raised his brows at Nurse Cook. "He has been dead for some time."

She rubbed her head, tense fingers showing that she was just barely keeping herself in check. If they weren't there, she suspected Cook would have flown at the young man, berating him at least, if not giving him a few sharp thwacks with a ruler or whatever else she might have handy.

"How long?"

"We will have to determine that. It would be good if we had a witness who could narrow the time frame."

"I don't know," Jason admitted. "I hadn't been in there all night."

"Not at all?" Kenzie asked in surprise. She was sure that protocol must suggest checking in on each patient at least a couple of times a night. Then again, they were in the independent care unit. Maybe the residents were allowed to just sleep all night without any observation.

"I checked in on him after he went down to sleep," Jason said. "He'd been shouting at everyone, angry about something that didn't make any sense. Kept saying that he was right and trying to sell us bears. Don't ask me. He was... delusional. I don't know if he was seeing things or just having trouble finding the right words. Sometimes, dementia patients, they mislabel things, and if you can't figure out what they meant to say, they just get more upset because you can't understand them."

"Did Mr. Sexton have dementia?" Dr. Wiltshire beat Kenzie to the question.

Jason said "yes" at the same time as Nurse Cook said "no." Everybody stood there, looking at each other. Nurse Cook gave Jason a warning look and spoke.

"Mr. Sexton was not diagnosed with dementia. But he had shown some behavioral changes over the last couple of weeks. That is not uncommon. I don't know if he would have eventually been diagnosed with dementia or not. And clearly, we will never know now."

"So..." Dr. Wiltshire addressed his words to Jason. "Where did this story about Mr. Sexton trying to say something but being incoherent come from? Was that pure invention?"

"No," Jason said defensively. "That really happened. I said I checked in on him. He was quiet and Lola was on the bed with him. But he wasn't asleep. His eyes were open and he was making noises. Like... animal noises. Not words."

"Was he moving around? Restless?"

"No. Just laying there, rigid, his hands kind of, up here." Jason demonstrated a posture with both hands raised to chest level, fingers forming stiff claws.

"And did you ask for help?"

"No." Jason was looking at the floor again, avoiding Nurse Cook's wrath. "I just let him be. Figured... at least he was being quiet, and I didn't want to have to deal with more swearing and paranoid crap."

"You should have talked to another nurse if you weren't sure what to do," Nurse Cook said. "You should have called the doctor to find out whether to call for an ambulance or if there was some medication he needed. You don't just leave a distressed patient alone in his bed."

And even though he had known that Lola was in with Sexton, a patient in a clearly altered state of consciousness, he had still not looked in on him when Lola began to bark.

33

Kenzie had been so caught up in the on-site visit with Dr. Wiltshire that she had completely forgotten Zachary was outside in the car waiting for her. She felt guilty about it, but he had been the one to insist upon the arrangements. And it had been nice to have someone drive her over while she woke up and not to have to worry about being out by herself when it was dark out. It wasn't like Zachary was the big tough gun-toting private eye they liked to portray on TV. He had a lot of issues and imperfections, and in a situation where they faced mortal danger, she wasn't sure she would rate his skills over hers. It was just nice not to have to drive and walk through the dark parking lot alone, feeling exposed and vulnerable.

As she walked behind Dr. Wiltshire and Carlos transporting the body on a gurney to the van, Kenzie tapped the icon with Zachary's face in her phone app.

He answered almost immediately. "Hey. How's it going?"

"Good. We're just getting ready to transport, so I'll be out in a minute."

"Great. I'll drive up."

She heard his engine start through the phone and saw his headlights come on across the parking lot. She walked around the van. "That's Zachary. He's going to take me home, then I'll grab my car and come in."

Dr. Wiltshire pushed up his glasses. "If you like, you can take a break. Have a nap. Come in a little late."

"No. I'd like to help with the initial prep. I don't usually get to be involved in all stages."

"All right. You should have told me you were going to have Zachary bring you in. You could drive back to the office with me, and I could drop you at home after work."

"No, it's okay. It was his idea; he wanted to come with me, even though it meant him sitting in the car and extra gas." Kenzie shrugged. "Just being a gentleman, I guess."

"He is a fine fellow." Wiltshire slapped Carlos on the back, indicating that they were done, and he walked around to the passenger door.

Kenzie walked over to Zachary's car and got in. It was cold outside, but there was a toasty pocket of air inside the vehicle, already heated to just the right temperature. Kenzie leaned over to kiss Zachary on the cheek. She buckled herself in and settled down into the seat and her coat, enjoying the warmth.

"Were you bored to death?"

"If I was, at least the Medical Examiner would be close by," he joked.

Kenzie smiled, happy to see him making a joke, even if it was just a minor one. It was much more natural than the tense silence between them for the last couple of days. "Yes, and I could always assist."

"You wouldn't be allowed to, would you?" he asked. "If you knew the deceased, you would have to... recuse yourself or whatever."

"I don't think there's any policy that says I would have to. It's not like a policeman investigating someone he knows. It would probably be best practice, but not a requirement."

"Well then, I feel much better knowing that."

He pulled out of the nursing home parking lot and drove back toward the house in silence.

Kenzie watched the road in front of them, but what she was thinking of in the darkness wasn't just the trip home, nor Sexton's postmortem. It was her fear that someday it *would* be Zachary on a slab. And, of course, she would not be involved with his postmortem. No matter how many autopsy photos she and Zachary had looked at together over some meal, there was no way she would be able to handle his like it was just routine.

One of her worries before they had been living together was that one day, she would return to his apartment to discover his suicide. Every time she went back, she had a little twinge of pain and tightness across her chest as she held her breath and opened the door. Especially on those blacker days. There had been one time...

"Kenzie?"

Kenzie looked over at Zachary, suddenly aware that he had said something, but she had been too lost in her own dark thoughts to hear him. She had to stop doing that. She was a happy, upbeat person. She didn't want to change into someone who was always worrying and having morbid thoughts.

"Sorry? I guess I was thinking about the case."

"I shouldn't interrupt you. I was just wondering if you wanted to get something to eat. When we get home, or a drive-through or coffee shop on the way?"

"No. I'm not hungry yet. I'll get something at the office. Like you say, Dr. Wiltshire will probably bring in some donuts or pastries. Bad for me, but..."

"When you get up that early, you burn off extra calories. So really, you need them," he offered.

Kenzie nodded. "Yeah. Exactly." She smiled

He didn't say anything for a few beats. His expression was still serious, his jokes delivered deadpan. He glanced over at her, saw her watching him.

"Are you okay?" he asked.

"Yeah, fine. Why?"

"Nothing. Just wondered if you were okay."

"Sure." She didn't tell him the direction of her morbid thoughts. Dwelling on his potential suicide was not the way to help keep him from sliding farther into depression. Let him think that she had just been occupied with thoughts of the new case.

"How was he? Or she?" Zachary asked, with a jerk of his head back the way they had come. "Your... new client."

"Well, pretty dead. Certainly not feeling any pain."

"I just mean... you didn't say what kind of death it was. It wasn't anything violent? Something that upset you?"

"No. Nursing homes see a lot of deaths. It's only natural. This one was in the independent living unit, so he wasn't wasting away sick with something. And nothing violent. Just died in his own bed."

"Natural causes?"

"That will be for Dr. Wiltshire to determine."

"But, I mean, it *looked* like natural causes?"

"Yes. And I'm sure it was. But we'll need to check out all the possibilities, just like with any other unattended death."

Zachary nodded, not turning back to her as he drove. In a few more minutes, he was pulling into the parking space in front of Kenzie's house. They both got out of the car.

"Do you need anything from the house?" Zachary inquired.

"No, I have everything I need for the day. Just got to grab my baby." Kenzie indicated the garage.

"Okay." Zachary stood there as if uncertain what to say or do next. Kenzie covered the few feet between them and gave him a hug.

"Thanks for looking after me. I'll be fine the rest of the day. Just the usual stuff at the office. So you don't worry about it."

"Nothing to worry about," Zachary agreed with a shrug. As if he were the calmest, coolest guy ever. But of course he would find something to worry about. He always did.

Kenzie used her key fob to open the big garage door. She hopped into her car and smiled as the engine roared into life. It made her feel warm all over. She really did love that little car. It wasn't very often anymore that she thought about Lance Reacher, the private investigator she had known before Zachary. He had suggested that Kenzie really needed something flashier than the boring little compact she had driven then. Who cared about maintenance costs? Gas mileage? Foreign parts? Those were not the things she was thinking about when she got behind the wheel. What she was thinking of was how she loved the power of the car, the silky red paint job, and, in the summer, driving with the top down. She would pay what she had to. She had a trust fund if her salary at the Medical Examiner's Office didn't support it.

She backed the car out. Zachary was still standing on the sidewalk, watching for her departure. Kenzie waved at Zachary as she left him behind.

On her way there, Kenzie's phone buzzed in her bag, but she ignored it. There weren't likely to be any emergencies in the few minutes it would take her to get to work. If it were Dr. Wiltshire, he could wait until she arrived. If Zachary had some last-minute concern, she could call or text him to reassure him once she was at her destination. For a few minutes, she was just going to relax.

Kenzie turned the radio up to drown out any additional buzzes from her phone.

When she arrived at the office and pulled into her reserved parking space, she pulled her bag into her lap and dug the phone out. She looked at the screen, expecting to see Dr. Wiltshire's number or Zachary's. Instead, there was a long list of missed calls, some of them Zachary's and some of them her security company or a blocked number. Kenzie knew immediately what had happened.

She swore under her breath.

She couldn't very well call the blocked number back. She tried Zachary first to try to calm him down.

There was no answer on his phone.

Kenzie hung up when it rolled over to voicemail. She dialed her security company and identified herself.

"Ah, Miss Kirsch," the male phone operator greeted after getting her passphrase and other confirmations of her identity. "Thank you for calling back. We've had a call out to your home. Everything is fine. The police and our representative are on the scene, and as far as we can tell, nothing has been harmed or stolen. But there is a male subject who claims that he lives there, and..."

"Yes. Yes, Zachary lives there. He's not a burglar. I armed the system when we left early this morning, and he must have forgotten to disarm it when he got back."

"That can happen," the man admitted. "Everybody has false alarms sometimes. There is a warning period after the system has been triggered to allow you to turn off the alarm before the police are alerted. Does your friend have the code to arm and disarm the system?"

"Yes. I haven't been able to talk to him yet. I don't know whether he panicked and forgot the code or if he just didn't notice that he'd triggered it in the first place. I'm really sorry about this."

"I'm very glad that nothing was stolen or damaged. Your system has been silenced and reset. We will have our representative confirm to the police on the scene that your friend is authorized to be there and can be left in the home...?"

"Yes, please. I'm really sorry. It won't happen again."

Although chances were, it would happen again. Kenzie had set off the alarm more than once herself; Zachary was bound to trigger it again too.

"Listen, can I add Zachary as someone authorized to talk to you to have the system reset? If anything goes wrong and he's around instead of me, he should be able to deal with it."

"We can do that, of course," he agreed politely. "I will need his full name and particulars, and we will need to set up a passphrase for him. It shouldn't take more than a few minutes."

There was a beep in her ear. Kenzie pulled the phone away from her ear to peer at the screen. There was a call incoming from Zachary.

"I'll have to call you back with that information. I need to take another call now." She hung up on the man without waiting for an answer, taking Zachary's call. "Zachary. I'm sorry. Are you okay?"

"Yes. I'm fine." He was terse, his voice clipped but toneless. Definitely upset.

"The security company will be calling to give the police the all-clear and then you can go back inside the house."

"They already have. Which is why I'm no longer in handcuffs."

The phone operator must have sent out a text or some other remote notification to his man on the scene while still on the phone with Kenzie.

"They put you in handcuffs? Zachary, I'm sorry. I never thought they would do that. I didn't even think to remind you about the alarm when we got home."

"I should have remembered. Or at least noticed that it was beeping," Zachary said with disgust. "I didn't have a clue there was a problem until the alarm started whooping full-force. If anyone in the neighborhood wasn't yet awake at six..."

"These things happen," she said, echoing what the security guy had said to her. "I've set it off before too. I'm going to get you added as a person authorized to give them the all-clear and have the system reset, okay? So that if it happens again, they'll talk to you instead of just having the police arrest you."

"That would be nice," he acknowledged, voice still tight.

"I should have thought to do it before. I don't know why I didn't."

In fact, she had thought about it, but had disregarded the need. She hadn't anticipated that Zachary would set it off when she wasn't around or that the police would react the way they had even after Zachary explained that he lived there. It was one more thing that she had thought would be better if she could just keep it under her own control.

"I am sorry," she repeated to Zachary.

"Not your fault. Well, you'll be wanting to get to work now, so I'll leave you to it..."

"You're okay?"

"I'm fine."

"Okay. We'll talk later. Have a good day..."

34

Kenzie had made notes of the things that needed to be followed up on immediately with Sexton's postmortem, calculating the rate at which he would have lost heat in the ambient temperature of the room in the nursing home and drawing blood to check for insulin. She browsed through a number of internet articles on angel of death killings and wrote down a few medications favored by nurses and doctors who killed. If Jason or one of the other nurses had had something to do with Mr. Sexton's death other than ignoring his medical needs, she wanted to know right away. They did not want to be guessing about it months later or exhuming his body to look for something else.

They proceeded to the gross examination of the body, looking for any other bruises, puncture wounds, or anything else indicating what the conditions had been like at Champlain House. Like Cartwright's body, the gross examination was unremarkable. He had a few minor bruises like everyone got —especially people who were over eighty and tended to bruise more easily as a result.

"Hypotheses?" Wiltshire asked as he began the Y incision.

"Nurse Jason's description sounds like a stroke or a seizure. So I'm inclined to think something neurological. Of course... it could be whatever it was that Cartwright died of. They were both in the same unit, dying within days of each other, both with similar early symptoms of dementia before their deaths."

"Right," Wiltshire agreed with a nod. "Anything else?"

"Angel of death killing. Or some drug self-administered. I still find it interesting that the dog was in each of the men's rooms at the time of their death or shortly thereafter. Why? Did they call her? Did she sense something? Did something she did trigger their deaths? I haven't had any luck identifying a parasite or other condition that might have come from the dog."

"What could a dog have that would give them neurological symptoms and such a quick death?"

"I don't know... rabies? But the dog wasn't acting like it has rabies. They are supposed to be violent and aggressive."

"There have been cases where the animal has not shown signs of aggression, but has been unusually friendly. It really doesn't matter which, as long as their saliva transfers the virus from one host to the next."

"Do you think these men had rabies?"

"I doubt it. But they were showing signs of dementia, maybe delusion. The nursing staff noticed that Mr. Cartwright wasn't eating or drinking and had an IV for Mr. Sexton. Problems with drinking and swallowing are red flags for rabies."

Kenzie remembered petting and scratching the dog and letting it lick her hand. She tried to remember whether she had washed right away. Whether she had any cuts on her hands that would have allowed a virus to get into her bloodstream. She shuddered at the thought. But Wiltshire had said no, he didn't think the men had died from rabies.

Kenzie watched as Wiltshire proceeded to examine and weigh each organ. If he saw anything unusual or educational, he would point it out to Kenzie, having her examine it and asking questions to help direct her to the right answers.

The heart and lung tissue were not quite as healthy-looking as Mr. Cartwright's had been, but they still looked pretty good. They didn't find anything to show that a clot had traveled to the heart or lungs. The big vessels feeding into Sexton's heart were partially occluded with fatty deposits, but they didn't find anything to show that one of these had been the cause of his death.

In due time, Dr. Wiltshire moved from the torso to the brain. He gave Kenzie a brief nod. Now they would see whether there were any other similarities in pathology between the two latest nursing home patients.

Kenzie drew closer to watch the careful removal of the top portion of Sexton's skull to expose the brain. She and Dr. Wiltshire both bent close to examine the surface of the brain for signs of intracranial bleeding or any other obvious signs.

"This one was in his bed," Wiltshire said aloud, "so no fall or bump on the head to confuse the issue."

Kenzie nodded her agreement. Both of them moved around the table, making what observations they could.

"Some age-related shrinkage," Kenzie observed.

"Yes. But not drastic changes like you might see with Alzheimer's disease."

Kenzie nodded. She was eager to get some samples of the brain tissue to see if it showed the same amyloid plaques as Cartwright's did. But she didn't say so. She let Dr. Wiltshire continue to direct the postmortem, going through it one step at a time, unhurried, careful not to miss anything or to jump to any conclusions.

Finally, he nodded to Kenzie. "Okay. Let's get some slides, swabs, blood and CNS samples, anything that might help point us to an answer. If this is some brain disease that we have not yet recognized, we need to get it pinned down. Is it something known or unknown? Or are we chasing after something that is not there?"

He and Kenzie worked together to gather all the samples that they could conceivably need to run.

"Can I...?" Kenzie started, indicating the microscope.

Dr. Wiltshire nodded. "Of course. Please."

Kenzie hurried over to the bench to prepare the slides and secure them to the stage of the microscope. She took a deep breath and looked through the eyepiece. It took a few moments to focus on the cells. Kenzie let out her breath in a whoosh.

"It's almost identical. Extensive amyloid plaques and tangles."

Dr. Wiltshire approached and Kenzie moved to the side to allow him to look through the eyepiece to study the sample.

"Identical," he repeated. "What are we missing here? This is not the dementia unit. These are not Alzheimer's patients. These men did not come from the same background or experience. Why would they both have plaques with no noticeable Alzheimer's disease until a few days before death?"

"It could be a coincidence."

She could tell Dr. Wiltshire did not like the idea. "Granted. But we need to look for other explanations first."

"Something in their environment? Or it's some genetic thing and they are actually related?"

"Could be old Vermont families. Intermarriages over generations. There are genes known to be associated with Alzheimer's disease, but none of them are great predictors. Environmental... sounds more likely. But what in the environment could have caused this pathology? There are possible links to DDT and other toxins, but this is not an area with high levels of pollutants in the air."

"And that's Alzheimer's disease, not non-Alzheimer's amyloid plaques."

He squinted at her. "Is that what we're calling it?"

"Tentatively." Kenzie shrugged, embarrassed. She wasn't trying to name a new disease or condition, just to label the signs that they were trying to understand. It wasn't like she was writing a paper on it. Thought it might be a good idea to, once they had a better handle on what they were seeing.

"Ideas? What could be in the environment to cause the development of these plaques?"

"Do you think that they developed rapidly or slowly?" Kenzie ventured. It was something that she had been puzzling over. These were old men. The plaques could have been developing for years. Or they might have developed very quickly, like the symptoms the men had experienced before death. Was the rapid development of dementia symptoms followed by death symptomatic of how quickly the amyloid plaques were growing?

"Difficult to form any hypothesis on the limited information that we have," Dr. Wiltshire mused. "Are these the only two patients with these signs? It seems unlikely that we would find the only two men and that they would die so close together in time and space. How many of the physician-attended deaths during the last few weeks have had similar pathology? How many deaths that we may have put down to accident or natural causes and never knew they had amyloid plaques because we didn't examine the brain? If it is developing slowly, then why did these two men die within a week of each other? Coincidence?"

"Maybe. But I think it must be rapidly developing. And if it is..." Kenzie didn't like the conclusion this led her to. "Then everyone in that nursing home is potentially at risk. Whatever toxin or pathogen they were exposed to, everyone else in that building could also have been exposed to."

35

The very early morning made it a much longer day than Kenzie had anticipated. She was definitely lagging by the afternoon. Returning from a meeting in another part of the building, Dr. Wiltshire saw Kenzie yawning as he walked past. She smothered the yawn the best she could.

"About time for another coffee," she confessed.

"Or about time to go home. Get Julie to cover the desk for the rest of the afternoon. We can afford for you to go home. Have a nap and then enjoy the evening instead of turning into a zombie. I'm sure Zachary will be much happier if you aren't spending your entire evening trying not to fall asleep."

"I have things I should be working on."

"One of the benefits of working in the morgue is that you don't have to worry about your patients taking a turn for the worse when you are gone. You're better off catching up tomorrow when you are fresh than making mistakes because you are too tired today. You've put in your hours. So go home."

Kenzie tried not to yawn again. Just thinking about being tired was making her exhausted. And she still needed to drive home. It wasn't a long way, but she didn't want to be falling asleep at the wheel.

She sighed. "All right," she agreed. "When you're right, you're right."

She and Zachary had a more normal evening together, after Kenzie had taken a couple of hours to catch up on her sleep. She thought about Zachary doing night surveillance and how he often functioned on only a couple of hours of sleep on a regular basis. She didn't know how he did it. Kenzie had always needed her sleep to function properly. Even in medical school, she hadn't been able to pull all-nighters to study. And residency had been brutal.

Once up and bright-eyed once more, Kenzie was happy to find that she and Zachary were able to talk casually without the same level of tension that had underlaid their conversations since she had missed the couples session. There was still emotion there. She could feel it and she thought a couple of times that Zachary was close to bringing it up, but then he would look away from her again and not say anything, pretending all was normal.

They went to bed in good time even though Kenzie wasn't sure she would be able to get to sleep after her afternoon nap. She was yawning again, and if she didn't want to get thrown off her usual sleep schedule, it was important to stick to her usual bedtime and rising times.

And as it turned out, falling asleep again did not end up being a problem.

Morning was a different story. Kenzie awoke early and tossed and turned restlessly, trying to get back to sleep, unwilling to get up again so early. But her body had decided that she'd had enough sleep. Or maybe it had decided it liked getting up early the day before. She wasn't able to sleep as late as usual.

Lisa would have been shocked to see her out of bed so early in the morning. Zachary seemed slightly surprised and she saw his eyes slide to the clock to verify that she was up early, rather than his having lost track of time.

"You ready to be up already?" he asked. "Or are you sick?"

"No, I'm fine. Just couldn't sleep any more. I'll hit the shower and then we can have an early breakfast?" Kenzie's stomach was already growling. It didn't realize that she was still supposed to be asleep.

"Uh... sure." Zachary wasn't excited about breakfast, but he never was. They both enjoyed the morning ritual, seeing each other and spending a little time together before Kenzie left for the Medical Examiner's Office. But morning and food didn't go together in Zachary's world.

"You don't have to eat yet—though you probably should so that you don't forget—but I'm already hungry."

"Sure. Of course. I'll get everything ready."

When Kenzie was out of the shower and dressed, and walked into the kitchen, she saw that it was one of Zachary's distracted days. That was probably her own fault, throwing him off their usual schedule.

The coffee machine had been run. Luckily, he had remembered to put a mug under the spout, but it still sat on the counter when normally Zachary put it on the table. There was toast sitting in the toaster instead of buttered and on the table. Nothing else was ready. Kenzie busied herself with buttering her toast and putting everything on the table. Then she went back to Zachary's computer station in the living room.

"Ready to take a break?"

"Uh, yeah..." Zachary looked up from what he was reading. At least she didn't have to shake him to physically pull him from his focused state. Zachary sat back and rubbed his fingers over his eyes. "There's a story in here. I think it's to do with your case yesterday."

Kenzie looked at his computer screen. It was a news site, and the story he indicated included a large picture of Lola, with the headline "Comforting the Dying" and a caption below the picture with something about a hero dog.

Kenzie swore. "I can't believe it! Who called the media? It must have been someone at Champlain House. Can I see?"

She could have searched it up on her own phone or computer, of course, but with it being right there on Zachary's screen, she didn't even consider that. Zachary scrolled down and moved to the side so that she could read it and take over the trackpad. Kenzie read quickly through the article. It was mostly fluff, of course, but it had clearly been one of the nurses who had called the news outlet. A nurse, Camille Jackson, was quoted extensively, though there were brief comments from other staff as well.

"I can't believe she called the news," Kenzie muttered again. She pulled out her phone and dialed Dr. Wiltshire. She waited impatiently, and he answered after three rings.

"Kenzie. How are you doing this morning?" His voice was cautious, probably wondering if she were calling in sick or saying that she couldn't be there for some other reason related to her early morning the day before.

"I'm fine. I'll be in today," she told him to immediately assuage any concerns he had about her not being available. "I don't know if you've had a chance to see it yet, but there is a news story on the Sexton death."

"What? What does it say?"

"It's a story about the dog. How she senses who is going to die and spends extra time with them to comfort them."

Wiltshire swore. "Why didn't anyone say anything like that yesterday when we were there?"

"I don't know. I asked when I was there about Cartwright. Apparently, she was with Cartwright when they found him. I asked Nurse Ellie if Lola had spent more time with other residents who were sick or dying. She said no. Which is completely contradicted by this article. It makes a big thing of her knowing who needs her and spending time with them."

"We're going to need to go back to the possibility that the dog has something to do with their deaths. You checked for parasites?"

"I ran through some slides myself and sent others to the lab. Haven't heard anything back yet, but I couldn't see anything of concern. What about something else... what if she laid on them and hampered their breathing? Or smothered them somehow?"

"It sounds from Nurse Jason's story that Sexton was in trouble before the dog went in there. They said that he'd been showing signs of dementia or behavioral changes for a couple of weeks. He was angry, paranoid, and delusional the evening before his death. When Jason checked in on him, he was already in some kind of seizure or altered state. I don't think the dog laid on them or blocked their breathing."

"Can we get in there and get swabs from the dog? Do you think they would let us? Or get a vet to get what we need, including blood and stool samples?"

"They may object. I'll give the boys upstairs a call and see if they can get a subpoena. I think that with an article saying that the dog has been with multiple patients who have died, we would look negligent if we didn't."

"Yeah. And we're going to need to re-interview Nurse Ellie. And Jason. And whoever else over there will confirm or refute these allegations."

"Leave that to the police. They are the ones trained in interrogation. It's our job to point them in the right direction, not to do the questioning ourselves. And I think we need to know this dog's history. Where she came from, what her background is. I doubt if she's been there since she was a puppy or they would have said so. Probably some rescue!"

Kenzie could practically hear Dr. Wiltshire rolling his eyes. "Yes. Knowing something about where she came from might help us to track down any pathogens."

She and Dr. Wiltshire exchanged a few more remarks, and then Kenzie hung up. They could—and would—continue the conversation later when she arrived at the office.

"Not good news, I guess," Zachary commented.

"No. Well, even though I say that, it could still be helpful. Having the information that was 'leaked' in this article might just help us to figure out cause of death in a couple of cases."

He watched her eat, not yet tackling his own breakfast. "Are you going into work today?"

"Yes. Why?"

"It's Saturday. Didn't know whether you were on or not."

"Oh, yeah." The day of the week had completely gotten away from Kenzie. She wasn't scheduled to be on, but she had just finished telling Dr. Wiltshire that she would be in, and she didn't feel like calling him back to say she'd gotten her days mixed up. So it looked like she was going in. "Just for a while. Maybe not the whole day."

36

Kenzie didn't look at the ringing phone before picking it up. She was intent on what she was reading on the screen and, while she would stop reading once she was actually on the phone, she wouldn't break her focus until she absolutely had to.

"Medical Examiner's Office. Kenzie speaking," she rattled off, reading the next couple of lines on the screen.

"Mackenzie. You sound a million miles away."

Kenzie's attention snapped to the call immediately. Even though she knew the voice, she still looked at the LCD screen to confirm the number that was calling her. Walter Kirsch.

"Hi, Dad. I wasn't expecting to hear from you. Everything okay?"

"Of course. Right as rain. How are you doing?"

"Pretty good." Kenzie leaned back in her chair, closing her eyes, and thought about what to tell him. it had been a few weeks since they had talked. He was always interested in little tidbits of her life, but his attention didn't last long. And he almost always wanted something from her when he called her instead of waiting for her to call him. "Job is good. Zachary and I are..." she faltered, then recovered. He didn't actually want to know the details. It didn't matter whether she told him the whole truth or not. "Zachary and I are good. I heard from Mother the other day."

"Oh, did you? Glad you're keeping in touch." There was a pause as he considered his approach to her. "I can't believe it's already so late in the year.

Seems like just a couple of weeks ago, we were heading into spring. Now it's long gone."

"Yes. Fall now and getting colder." Weather? They were going to discuss the weather? "Before you know it, it will be Christmas." Her heart gave an extra little thump. She wanted it to be Christmas already, to know that Zachary was past his worst days, but she dreaded the fact that she had to get through all of the days before Christmas as Zachary sank deeper and deeper into himself.

"Christmas was always one of my favorite times of the year," Walter boomed cheerfully. "You remember what the house would look like? All of the decorating Lisa did? It would look so good... I was afraid to touch anything. Like just stepping into the house might break some fairy spell. It was so stunning."

"*Was?*" Kenzie was surprised to hear him use the past tense. "Doesn't she still decorate?"

"Not like that, no. Maybe a wreath and a tree, but... just sedate and understated. Nothing like what she did when you girls were young."

It hurt Kenzie to think that her mother, who was always so excited about Christmas, had left that tradition behind. Kenzie remembered those magical fairyland decorations. It was like stepping into a dream or a scene in a movie. Otherworldly. But the little girls were gone. Amanda had passed away years ago, and Kenzie wasn't sure when the last time was that she had gone home for Christmas. It never appealed to her. With her parents divorced and Amanda gone, it didn't feel like she had a family anymore. It was just a house. Lisa always invited her, but Kenzie still found a reason not to go. She didn't even realize that Lisa had given up on decorating without them both there.

"That's too bad. I didn't know that. Is she... okay? Does she get sad at Christmas?"

"Of course. She's a mother. She can't get through Christmas without thinking about her family and the way things used to be. It's not your fault, Mackenzie. You're a grown woman with your own life and starting your own family. We fully expected you to. That's the way things work. Maybe one day you'll have children, and you can visit Grandma for Christmas, and she'll make the house just like she used to for you girls."

"I don't know." Kenzie didn't really see herself as the motherly type, even though she had loved and doted on and helped to raise Amanda, who had been several years younger than Kenzie. And maybe that was it. Perhaps she was afraid of getting that attached to another person and then having them die. Having them disappear from her life forever, with no hope of reunion.

She knew Zachary would like children. He confessed that he had always been more baby hungry than Bridget, who was now pregnant and expecting twins. He loved his younger siblings. Being one of the older children, he had helped to raise them. He had more parenting experience than Kenzie, and she knew he would love to have a big family of his own. But she had a career, one she didn't want to give up to have babies.

"I should probably get off the phone," she told Walter. "Things are pretty busy here today and I have a lot to do if I'm going to get home in good time tonight."

"What's got you so busy?"

"People are dying to see us," Kenzie quipped.

Walter chuckled, even though it was a line she had probably used on him a dozen times. Had they actually talked a dozen times since she had started there?

"I guess they are," Walter agreed. "Don't tell me you've had a crime spree there. Some serial killer? I understand that boyfriend of yours might be helpful there."

Kenzie had never talked to him about the serial killer case that Zachary had solved. Or about the effect it had had on his life. While it had been essential to get the man off the street and protect the community he had been preying on, the negative impact on Zachary had been significant. A year later, it was still affecting him and the relationship between him and Kenzie. The way that Walter talked about it, in a laughing, teasing manner, didn't match up with the way it had impacted Zachary's and Kenzie's lives.

"Yeah. That was a really bad thing, Dad. Not something we joke about."

He didn't say anything for a moment, taken aback by her serious tone.

"Oh. Of course it was. I didn't mean to offend you. So what's going on? Do you have more going on than usual right now? Stacking them like cordwood in the refrigerator?"

Kenzie nearly hung up on him. She didn't need the images his words brought back to mind. Even years later, she was still affected by what she had seen in the pictures taken during Amanda's overseas surgery. Images she could never wipe from her mind. She didn't usually think about them or connect them with the work they did in the morgue. They were two different worlds.

"We have had a few new bodies in. More than usual." She hoped that her clipped tone would dissuade him from asking any further details. "We have a couple of... very puzzling deaths to deal with."

"I haven't heard anything in the news. Nothing... violent, I hope?"

"No. Just strange. We need some more data before we can make a call. And speaking of which, it looks like I just got some samples back," Kenzie lied. "I have to go now. Take care, Dad. And say hi to Mother if you see her before I do."

She kept talking right over his protests and pressed down the hang-up switch, holding it there for a few minutes to ensure that the call was dropped before releasing it and putting the phone receiver down.

37

"Just got a call from the police," Dr. Wiltshire announced as he walked toward Kenzie's desk at a quick clip. "We've got another body I need to check out. Violent death, from the sounds of it. You've got quite a bit on the go here...?" He looked over the piles of papers and files on her desk.

Kenzie looked around at them, sighing. "Yeah. I'd like to say that this can all wait and come along with you, but I think I'd better keep trudging away here. Do you need me?"

"I'll be fine with Carlos to help transport the body. I'll send you pictures," he said in a teasing voice.

"Oh, will you? Please?" Kenzie laughed. "What happened? Do you know?"

"I don't. Not yet. Dead body in a motel room, but it doesn't sound like it was just a heart attack. Police wouldn't want to light a fire under me for that. It would be 'whenever you can' for a routine death like that. Not 'grab your bag, Doc, and get your butt over here. You'd better see this.'"

Kenzie nodded. "Sounds serious. I hope it isn't too bad."

"Well, that's the thing about our patients... they aren't going to complain about how we treat them. They're past caring about how they look. There isn't much that would shock me anymore."

"I guess not. Well, good luck."

At least if it was a violent death, it wouldn't be so hard to figure out the cause.

Dr. Wiltshire gave a nod and headed out.

There was no one from the public around, so after he had left, Kenzie pulled out her mobile radio unit and turned it on to listen to the chatter back and forth between the police and the Medical Examiner and anyone else being dispatched to the crime scene. Although they didn't say much over the radios, it sounded like Dr. Wiltshire was right and it was a violent death.

While she worked through her emails and reviewing reports as they came in, she kept an ear on the radio and what was happening. She heard Dr. Wiltshire arrive at the scene and begin issuing instructions. "I don't want anyone in there who doesn't have to be," he snapped. "And no one walks in without full gear. There is biological matter all over this place. Techs are on their way?"

Kenzie had heard this confirmed just a few seconds earlier on the radio and had no doubt that Dr. Wiltshire had heard it too.

"They'll be here soon, Doc," the dispatcher acknowledged. "Are you able to confirm death without damaging any evidence?"

Dr. Wiltshire grunted. "Looks like half a dozen people have already been traipsing through the blood. One more isn't going to make much of a difference."

Kenzie felt sorry for him. He hated it when people didn't follow proper protocols. Even though he wasn't a detective and didn't "own" the scene, he was still pretty possessive about any location where there were bodies. He was a stickler about every piece of biological matter getting back to the Medical Examiner's Office for processing. It sounded like that was going to be a challenge.

But of course, the motel manager or maid who had discovered the body would have walked in without realizing they were trampling through evidence. When they called the police, the officers who initially arrived at the scene would also have to walk through to confirm the victim's death. That was at least three people in and out. Hopefully, the officers would secure the scene and not let anyone else in until a representative from the Medical Examiner's Office had arrived. Still, if they were a bit green or not as well-trained as they should be, they might let other law enforcement officers in to look things over. It could end up being a three-ring circus, with half a dozen different shoe prints to be eliminated as well as Dr. Wiltshire's own.

There was a lot of routine calling back and forth to confirm orders and arrival times. Kenzie heard Dr. Wiltshire come back on over the radio. "Confirmed death of the subject. As if anyone needed me to confirm that someone with his head beaten in so severely is actually dead."

Kenzie heard one of the detectives in the background before Dr. Wiltshire released the button on his radio. "Is that cause of death?"

"You need a doctor to tell you that?" Dr. Wiltshire growled back.

Dr. Wiltshire would have to let Kenzie know the details of what had gone on at the crime scene, but she could fill most of it in herself. She set up several bins in the autopsy room for the various bags and samples to be collected when Carlos and Dr. Wiltshire returned. It would be less stressful for them if everything were ready upon their return.

She tried not to imagine what the inside of the motel room might look like. Or what the subject would look like when his remains were brought to the morgue. She could maintain her medical detachment. Pretend to herself that it was no more than a picture or a movie prop. Or one of the models or cadavers she had dealt with when she was in medical school. People who had died in their sleep. People who had wanted their bodies to be used for education when they were gone.

Those bodies were a lot easier to deal with than an eight-year-old who had fallen into the rain-swollen river or a teenage dope addict. Or so many more of the tragic things that they saw from one day to another. The nursing home deaths were, by comparison, clean and peaceful, and any lingering questions could be brushed away gently in the end. There was no one responsible for their deaths. No one she needed to help the police to catch so that the streets would be safe again.

38

Kenzie had been right to prepare herself for her first view of the dead body. Dr. Wiltshire and Carlos brought the anonymous-looking body bag in through the delivery doors and took it straight to the morgue.

"I'm going to need bins and labels," Dr. Wiltshire advised. "And a ton of swabs and tubes. I'm going to want to get started right away—"

"Already done," Kenzie advised him briskly. "Let me know if you need something you don't see."

"Thanks, Kenzie. That's great."

"I'm free to help if you need some assistance."

Dr. Wiltshire looked at Carlos. Although he was technically available to help out, he preferred to stick to transportation and helping to move bodies when they needed another hand. He could hand Dr. Wiltshire equipment, bag evidence, and put things into the right bins for the right labs, he was already looking pretty green and Kenzie doubted if he would last.

"Yes, that would be helpful. Carlos, you can help me with the transfer to the table, and then go have a coffee."

Carlos helped Dr. Wiltshire to heft the body in its bag from the gurney to the slab, then gave a nod. "Call me if you need me. I'll be close by."

But not too close, Kenzie knew. He wasn't a full-time employee and would clock in and out as needed. It wasn't like they had enough bodies rolling in to keep him occupied with transporting them full time. Like Julie, he had contracts with several other departments as well.

Dr. Wiltshire, eager though he was to get started, waited until Carlos was out of the room before beginning to unzip the body bag. Though undoubtedly Carlos must have helped him to get the body into it in the first place.

"You heard enough to be forewarned?" Dr. Wiltshire asked, his eyes on the task at hand and not on Kenzie.

"It sounds like he took quite a beating to the face. And there was a lot of spatter."

"Yes," Dr. Wiltshire confirmed.

Kenzie waited while he opened up the outer bag and then the inner one. She had prepared herself the best she could, thinking about her job as an observer and investigator. Steeling her stomach. Putting on her "clinical" hat to observe the body dispassionately. It was going to be difficult. He would look bad. But it wasn't a family member or a friend. It was a stranger. And whatever had happened to him, he was past feeling now.

Not that she would have been able to recognize if it were a family member. The damage done to the face had wiped out any hope of making an identification by either facial recognition or dental records. They would have to employ another method. Kenzie looked down at the hands. She could start on fingerprints once Dr. Wiltshire had swabbed down the hands.

But when she looked at them, it became apparent that wasn't going to help them either. The man had been tortured before he was killed. Burns that had destroyed any fingerprints as well.

"How was he checked into the motel?" Kenzie asked. "Did he have any ID on him?"

"Police will be following up on that end of it. But... no, I gather any wallet or electronics that he had on him were stolen. It doesn't look like robbery gone wrong, but... who am I to say? The police will get back to us on anything they think might help to identify him."

"It's going to be hard. Maybe just checking his general description against missing person reports."

"That's a start. Maybe they could hire your Zachary to find out his identity."

"Yeah, I don't think that's going to happen."

Zachary had a good relationship with Campbell, and, of course, with Mario Bowman, but many of the other law enforcement officers were not on nearly as cordial terms with him. Zachary was careful to communicate to the police whenever he was involved in a case that they had been or were investigating. He always passed on information he found if it were pertinent to the investigation. But still, many cops just didn't like PI's around out of general principles, and it didn't matter how careful he was not to get in their way.

Dr. Wiltshire began by removing the clothing still on the body. Kenzie helped in silence, removing or cutting away each article of clothing and inspecting them for what trace evidence might need to be processed. Hair, fiber, bloodstains or other biological materials. They laid each item out individually, assigned them evidence numbers, and read the inventory aloud for the autopsy transcription.

The victim was male, white, with dark hair and brown eyes, and was of medium height and build. He had a sizable port wine birthmark on the outer side of one thigh. Wiltshire took all his measurements and carefully logged them.

"What would be your age estimate?" he drilled Kenzie.

She looked over the body. Good muscle mass. A bit of a belly, but not enough that it would be noticed when he was dressed. No age spots or wrinkles in the neck or places an older man was likely to get wrinkles—all in all, relatively young.

"Maybe thirty," she said, "I don't think as old as thirty-five."

He nodded. They would do other tests to try to determine age, but the visual inspection was important. They inspected the body thoroughly for any trace, then carefully washed the body.

"Body is unremarkable," Dr. Wiltshire said. "I don't see any injuries or signs of disease on the torso or extremities. Everything seems to be confined to the face and hands."

Kenzie frowned, thinking about that. Wiltshire raised an eyebrow. "You have a thought?"

"He wasn't beaten up?" She touched his ribcage, looking for any perimortem bruising or sign of broken ribs. "It seems to me that if you're going to burn someone's fingers and beat their face in with a baseball bat—or whatever he was beaten with— that there would probably be a struggle. He must have been restrained either manually or mechanically. There are no defensive wounds, no sign that he took any blows to the body to subdue him."

Wiltshire nodded. "True. He must have been restrained."

They both examined his wrists, ignoring the burned flesh of his hands. Kenzie shook her head. "Some faint bruising, but I don't think there are ligature marks. Maybe it will darken in a few hours and we'll be able to see how he was held down."

"We'll do a tox screen too. He might have been given something to sedate him."

"And *then* torture him? Wouldn't you get your information from him before sedating him instead of trying to rouse him enough to get a coherent answer after?" Kenzie shook her head, trying to sort it out. "And if they sedated or restrained him, then why destroy his face like that? That's rage. Don't you think?"

"Maybe, maybe not. You may be jumping to conclusions too quickly."

"You have another theory?"

"I do," he agreed, but didn't tell her what it was.

Kenzie sighed and they continued.

"Let's get x-rays," Dr. Wiltshire said. "I want to see the damage to the skull and to confirm that there are no other broken bones before we start on the head."

39

Kenzie looked at the clock on the wall. She knew it was going to be late. Dr. Wiltshire hadn't headed out to pick the body up until the afternoon, and they had been processing it for a couple of hours.

He saw her look at the clock and glanced at the face himself. "Why don't you head home? I can finish up here."

"I should stay until it's done. And help you to move him to cold storage."

Wiltshire shrugged. "You need to take time for yourself and your family when you can get it. I've been handling dead bodies for years; this one won't be hard to wrangle. Go home. Get a good rest. Take Sunday off. We'll send out samples for processing Monday morning."

"You're sure?"

"I'm sure, Kenzie. I won't be here much longer. We can't send samples out for testing until Monday. You're not going to miss anything earth-shattering."

"Well... okay. Are you hungry? Do you want me to grab you something from the machine?"

"No. I'll hit a restaurant after I'm done. Those sandwiches are atrocious. Somebody should be autopsying *them* to see what they died of."

Kenzie grinned. "They are pretty bad," she agreed.

"Get on your way. I'll see you Monday morning."

"Shoot me an email if you have anything particular you want to be done when I get here."

"I will."

Kenzie cleared away her files and got ready to go. She would pick up food on the away home so she didn't have to make anything. But then she remembered that Zachary hadn't eaten what she bought the last time she had done that. She hadn't checked with him first, which was the sensible thing to do. She didn't like to call him when she was late getting home, because it just emphasized the fact that she was away from him rather than being home. If she just went straight home without talking to him, then his first contact with her was when she was home, which was what they both wanted. It just felt kinder for some reason. No extra anxiety as he waited, wondering if something had happened to her on the way.

But that wouldn't solve the supper problem. Kenzie picked up her phone and hit the icon with Zachary's picture on it as she walked to her car.

"Kenzie."

"Hi. I know I'm late. I'm on my way now. I was going to stop to pick up some takeout on the way home. What do you feel like?"

"Uh... whatever you want to get is fine."

"But what do you feel like? Chinese? Burgers?"

"Either one."

"Pizza?"

"Sure."

"You're not being helpful. So you're going to eat whatever I bring home?"

He didn't answer at first, then finally agreed. "Yeah. A bit."

"You need to eat more than a bit. You should talk to your doctor about your lack of appetite. Maybe there's something else he can—"

"I've already tried everything else, Kenz."

She knew that he had been through a lot of different protocols, from the time that he'd been just ten years old. He probably had tried pretty much everything on the market. And switching meds was not just a simple change from taking pill A each day to taking pill B. Many of the drugs, he would have to wean off. Get a baseline. Maybe have to have hospital supervision because of the danger of suicide. Then start on the new medication. Wait for weeks for it to reach full efficacy. Then determine whether the benefits outweighed the adverse side effects. Adjust, wait, adjust again, wait some more. It could take months to get him stabilized again. If they could.

"Yeah, I know," she sighed. "Well, I'll grab something, then, and I'll be home soon."

"Do you want me to order in, so you don't have to stop somewhere? You can just come straight home."

"Faster if I stop for something. And then we don't have to pay delivery fees. Unless... you need me home sooner. It should only take ten minutes."

"I'm fine. Ten minutes isn't going to make any difference."

"Okay. See you soon, then."

Kenzie felt like Chinese, and Zachary usually ate a good amount of that, so she picked up their favorite dishes. That took more than ten minutes like getting a burger or pizza would, but she thought the benefits were worth it. She texted Zachary while she was waiting so that he wouldn't be worried.

They had a nice meal. Things seemed to be mostly back to normal, though there were a few times when the conversation became stilted and she wondered whether it was because he was distracted or that he was thinking about her failure to show up for their couples therapy and whether he could trust her. Which wasn't really fair, since there were plenty of times when he had forgotten about things she had asked him to do. And she had always forgiven him. Eventually.

Zachary put on an old movie, but Kenzie had a feeling that neither of them was paying close attention to it. Zachary had his computer in his lap, and it looked like work, rather than checking his personal email or social networks, which was what Kenzie was doing on her phone. She just needed to make sure she hadn't missed anything, and then she would turn her phone screen off and put it away so she could focus on the movie and Zachary. He was busy anyway.

Skimming through her unread email messages, Kenzie saw that there was one from her father. She clicked it and checked the time. It had been sent after she had talked to him. Probably this was the hit, the real reason he had called her. She read through the message and snorted.

Zachary looked at her, eyebrows up, mouth quirked into a half-smile. "What was that?"

"Is everybody in Vermont going to this masquerade ball?"

He looked blank. "Uh... my guess would be no. What masquerade ball?"

"There's a fundraiser thing. I guess all the bigwigs are going to be at it. The one my mom called to ask about?"

"Oh yeah. You're not going to go?"

"Not if I can help it. I don't like these things. They're just a lot of posturing and hot air. I'd rather write a check than to have to shake every-one's hands and listen to them prattling on about their concerns."

"And who else?"

"What?"

"You said everyone in Vermont. So I assume there's at least one other person you know who is going and wants you to go too."

"Yeah. My dad."

"Also because it is for kidney research?"

Kenzie considered that. Her dad was, of course, interested in raising money for kidney research. But he was more interested in changing the political landscape, making changes to transplant legislation, and making high-power political contacts. If he wanted her to be at the ball, he wanted to show her off or make introductions for some reason.

"He doesn't say," she told Zachary.

"Maybe he's just going to support your mom."

"I don't think so. They are still good friends, but he doesn't do things just to support other people. Not since Amanda died, anyway."

Zachary slowly closed the lid of his laptop. "Things changed after that?"

"I don't know if things changed, or if the way I saw him did. Or maybe he was so shattered when she died that he decided he wasn't getting emotionally involved again. But after that... he was a lot more distant. It's not surprising that he was more distant from me, because of the difference in our foundational beliefs... he and I had a falling out. But I've seen it with others too. He doesn't get together with my mom like he used to, and when he does, it's more like a chore. He's not... open to her like he used to be. Even when they first got divorced, it wasn't because they fought or didn't love each other anymore. They were just on different trajectories. Interested in pursuing different things. At least, that's what they told me. But maybe it was all a bunch of crap."

"And it must have affected you pretty deeply."

"Their divorce?" Kenzie didn't offer that she hadn't even known about it when they got a divorce. They were already leading very separate lives. All that had been left was the division of their property.

"No, I mean when your sister died. It must have been pretty horrible for you."

"It was." Kenzie snuggled into Zachary's side and he put his arm around her. "It totally changed my life. Her dying and... everything that happened around that. That's when I decided I was going back to school. To go into medicine."

He nodded as if it were perfectly normal for her to decide to become a doctor after losing her sister to kidney disease. But he didn't know all the details. And there was the fact that she had gone in with a focus on death and forensic investigation rather than living patients. That wasn't normal. Plenty of people went into medicine to save the people who represented the loved ones they had lost. Not so many went into it to track down killers, whether human or pathogen.

40

Monday morning, Kenzie went through all the work that Dr. Wiltshire had done on the body from the motel, noting the samples he had taken, the tests he wanted to be performed, and any other questions or concerns that he wanted to follow up on. She played back the recording of the postmortem, jumping to the point when she had left, and then listening to the items he had dictated, and not the silence in between. It wasn't quite the same as finishing the autopsy with him, but it was pretty close.

She applied labels and sent the various packages out to the labs where they would be processed. While it would have been nice to be a part of one of the big cities where they could do a lot more of the processing in-house, that wouldn't have afforded her the same opportunities as working for Dr. Wiltshire, where she could learn at his feet and get hands-on experience. As a tech or receptionist for a big medical examiner's office, she wouldn't have been able to do those things.

Dr. Wiltshire was later than usual getting into the office. Which might have had something to do with the fact that he was still catching up on sleep. Or he might have had an early meeting he hadn't mentioned to her.

She was well into her desk work when Dr. Wiltshire arrived. He nodded and greeted her cordially, as usual. "Feeling better today?"

"Bright-eyed and bushy-tailed," Kenzie told him. "It was good to just take yesterday off."

"Glad to hear it. You needed a break. And you've started in on our new guest?"

Kenzie nodded and summarized what had been sent out and the status of his dictation.

"I was thinking about how we're going to identify him," she confessed. "No face or teeth. No fingerprints. No tattoos, though he does have a large birthmark that might help. We can't just rely on missing person reports. We don't even know where he is from. He was checked into a motel; he could be from another city or state, even another country. And unless someone is looking for him *here*, we don't have a lot of leads on identifying him."

"The police are doing what they can. We've ordered DNA and we can hope that it triggers a match in the offender database."

"I was reading about this forensic artist out in Montana..."

"Given the state of his skull, I'm not sure we could ever reconstruct a face for our latest John Doe."

"She doesn't use bone structure. She uses DNA."

Dr. Wiltshire had been looking toward his office. He turned back to look at Kenzie, frowning. "She uses DNA to do what?"

"To do forensic DNA phenotyping. Using the genes to construct a picture of the victim. They do it for unknown suspects too. In this case, we'll at least be able to tell her hair and skin tone without her going from the DNA."

"That can't be very accurate."

"She does some great work. I've been looking at their website. Hang on, let me show you some of the pictures." Kenzie quickly typed the URL for EvPro into her browser and brought the site up again. "Look at this... here are some examples of the pictures she generated and the actual subject."

There were various samples, ranging from the criminals they had caught to the victims they had identified and blind tests for demonstration purposes. Dr. Wiltshire lowered his glasses and looked at the screen as she showed him the comparisons.

"Obviously, they are only going to put the best matches on their website, but these *are* remarkable."

"Some of them, she generated several pictures, you can see the others if you click..." Kenzie demonstrated, fanning out a stack of pictures on the screen so that Dr. Wiltshire could see the portfolio of faces that the artist had created, with varying ages, weights, and hair or facial hair styles.

"Amazing. I had no idea that our DNA science was to the point that we could do this."

"The website says that they are the only company that has established protocols for epigenetic data as well as genetic data. So they can more accurately predict age, diet, and other background factors that help to produce a better representation."

"That can't be established science."

"Not established, no. Cutting edge. Experimental, maybe. But they seem to be able to produce a really good product." Kenzie raised her eyebrows in a question. "What do you think?"

"There is probably a pretty hefty sticker price."

"Well, there is, but it's not that much more than we would pay for other tests. And if it will allow us to identify a subject that we wouldn't otherwise be able to..."

"It would have to go up the chain for approval. Why don't you find out what you can? Talk to this artist. Find out what the options are, how long it would take, what their match rate is like. Something that we can present to the detectives in charge of the case to show that it's a reasonable expense. Then if they want to pursue it with their sergeant..."

Kenzie nodded. It would take time to work its way up the chain of command to either get a yes or a no. It would be best to get started on it right away before the case went cold. "Sure. I'll find out more. They'll have brochures and presentations too, I'm sure."

"New technology is always a hard sell. Don't be disappointed if you don't get it in this case. We'll probably have to present it as a possibility on several different cases before they decide it's well enough established that they'll risk it."

Kenzie nodded. While she wanted to see if forensic DNA phenotyping would work, and this was a perfect case to try it out on, she would have to be patient. Sometimes it seemed like the cops she worked with were back in the dark ages as far as the technology was concerned.

Dr. Wiltshire went on to his office to start on his day's work, and Kenzie clicked through screens to find the contact information for EvPro. There wasn't anything about their artist on the website, so she would have to go through the main switchboard. Kenzie called the company and explained to the young woman who answered the phone what she was looking for.

"That would be Micah Miller," the receptionist told her politely. "I'll put you through. If she doesn't answer, please leave a message. She doesn't like to be interrupted, but she will return calls."

Kenzie waited while the phone rang through. Maybe she wasn't going to get to talk to the artist after all. Until she wasn't busy, whenever that was.

The phone rang several times and there was a click. Preparing a message in her head, Kenzie was surprised to hear a live voice rather than a voicemail greeting.

"Micah here."

"Oh. Micah. Hi. I asked the receptionist who does the forensic DNA phenotyping in your company, and she put me through to you."

"Yes," Micah agreed briskly. "That's me. Are you familiar with what forensic DNA phenotyping is?"

"I'm a doctor, and I read through the information on your website. So I get the basics."

"Great. What's your name and email address?"

"Uh..." Kenzie was surprised at the request. She faltered for a moment before giving Micah Miller the details.

"I'll send you an intake package," Micah promised. "What evidence do you have? Blood?"

"Whatever you need. I work with the Medical Examiner's Office."

"Fresh body? Not a cold case?"

"Yes."

"Okay. That sounds good. I'll need as much background on the subject as you can give me. Even stuff that seems irrelevant. Every little bit can help me to generate a better picture for you."

"I will. It's just... I don't know yet whether we'll have the approval to use you. I wanted to ask some questions about the cost, time turnaround, match rate, things like that. So I can present a case."

Micah let out an impatient breath. "You'll find all of that in the intake package."

"Okay... can I ask if you're the artist, the person who actually does the pictures?"

"The computer generates an initial composite, which I then alter based on different possibilities for hairstyles, dress, that kind of thing. And then I render them with colored pencils so that they look more lifelike."

"Are you the only one in the company who does it?"

She could hear Micah typing in the background and wondered if she had already lost interest in the conversation and was moving on with something else while she tried to get Kenzie off the phone.

"Why do you want to know?" Micah asked.

"Well... just curiosity. I was looking at the pictures on the company's website, and I wondered whether you do all of them or whether you have a pool of artists."

More keyboard tapping. Kenzie closed her eyes and rubbed the back of her neck, waiting for Micah's response.

"The reason my name and information are no longer on the website is that I have been targeted in the past," Micah said. "I don't want to be the bulls-eye for everyone my pictures helped to put behind bars."

"Oh. I never even thought of that."

"I see your name on the medical register in Vermont and listed as a staff member at the Medical Examiner's Office."

She'd looked that up pretty quickly. "Yeah. I'm not a stalker, I promise," Kenzie laughed.

"That's exactly what you would say if you were."

"But you can see from my credentials that I am not."

"I can see that you've assumed the identity of someone at the Medical Examiner's Office, anyway. I'll call you back."

Kenzie looked down at her phone and saw that Micah had disconnected. She shook her head at Micah's abrupt manner and looked at her screen to determine her next task for the day. A few seconds later, the main line started ringing. Kenzie looked at it, but it wasn't the caller ID for EvPro in Montana.

"Medical Examiner's Office, Kenzie speaking."

"Yes, I'd like to speak to Dr. Wiltshire."

Kenzie raised her brows at the familiar voice. "Hello, Micah."

"Hi. So I guess you are who you say you are."

"I am," Kenzie agreed. "Do you still want to speak to Dr. Wiltshire?"

"I don't think there's any need to bother him."

"What number are you calling me from?" Kenzie asked curiously. "That's not even a Montana area code, is it?"

"With cell phone plans now, you don't need to live in the area that your phone number is in. I got an out-of-state number to make it more difficult for people to identify me. For cases like this when someone is asking too many questions."

She really was paranoid.

"I'm sorry for asking too many questions. I was just very interested in what it is that you do. All those pictures on the website... if all of them are yours, you have certainly been involved in a lot of cases, and your phenotypes are very lifelike. I can see how helpful they would be in narrowing down suspects and identifying victims."

"Thanks. I'm sorry for being so suspicious, but... they broke into my house, attacked me, kidnapped me, put me in the hospital. I can never let my guard down."

Kenzie blew out her breath in a whistle. She knew a little bit about what kind of effect an experience like that could have on a person. Zachary had not been the same person since his kidnapping. He tried, but he wasn't the same. Someone could argue that he should have been tougher because of the traumas he'd been through as a juvenile and not have been so affected by it. But it had brought to light a lot of bad stuff he'd previously been able to bury.

"I'm sorry you've had to go through all of that."

"Thanks. I am the only artist with the company. All the phenotyping that you see for the past three-plus years is mine. I'm a forensic scientist as well. One of the lucky few who can combine both art and science in my job."

"You do an amazing job of it. I'm very impressed."

"Tell me about your case," Micah suggested, sounding more relaxed and willing to talk with her.

"We have a victim who needs to be identified. Checked into a motel using a pseudonym, no ID or credit card. Severe injuries to the face, so we can't identify him by facial recognition or dental match. Tortured before he was killed, no recoverable fingerprints."

"A good case for phenotyping. You can give me a lot of the features; I only have to do the facial structure."

"I guess so, yeah."

"You can tell me hairstyle and color, age, height and weight, skin tone, how he dressed. Normally I don't have those details and have to get them from the genome or epigenome, or to hypothesize based on where the body was found, cultural background, that kind of thing."

"Right. We do know all of that already."

"In fact, you might be able to get an ID even though you don't have his face. Once a missing person report shows up."

"I figure from the fact that he was staying in a motel that he might be from out of town or even farther afield. So we might not ever see a missing person report, even if one is filed."

"Well... I've sent you the introduction and intake file, so have a look through there, show it to your guys, and if you get approval to go ahead, fill it all out and send me some blood."

"I'll do that. Thanks for your time, Dr. Miller."

"Micah. You're welcome. Look forward to working with you if the expense is approved."

Again, Micah hung up without an actual goodbye. Kenzie shook her head, bemused, and checked her email inbox for the package.

41

Things were pretty quiet the rest of the week. Kenzie caught back up on her pending projects, and nothing untoward happened at work or at home. It was Zachary's week for individual therapy, so she didn't have to be there. She felt like she was on top of everything.

"Did you put a rush on the virology for Mr. Cartwright?"

Kenzie looked up from her work. Dr. Wiltshire stood in front of her desk, looking down at his tablet, puzzled.

"No..." Kenzie frowned, shaking her head. "Did you want me to? I didn't think there was any need to expedite it... I know they're pushing you to make a finding, but I didn't know you wanted it rushed."

"No, I didn't. I'm just surprised to see results back already. The lab is always backed up. Someone must have put a flag on it for some reason, because I never see results back this quickly unless it's a high-profile case with a rush on it and feds standing around with their hands out."

Kenzie chuckled at the mental picture. "So was there anything interesting? Is it all of the virology, or only the blood?"

"I don't even see the bloodwork. Just the later test for the brain tissue."

Kenzie straightened, bracing herself for whatever the tests showed. Helpful or another dead end? She laced her fingers together, waiting. "Well...?"

Dr. Wiltshire grinned. He was clearly enjoying drawing it out, making Kenzie wait for the punch line.

394

"Well, let's see here…" He tapped his screen. "I'm always all thumbs operating this thing…"

Which Kenzie knew wasn't true. He needed a hand getting something straightened out every now and then, but he was actually pretty good at it most of the time. He was just teasing her.

"Why don't you give it to me?" she suggested, putting her hand out. "I'm sure I could figure it out."

He laughed. His eyes started scanning back and forth and he read through the results of the report he had opened. Kenzie was quiet, waiting.

"Remarkably clean, considering his age and the fact that he's dead. The blood-brain barrier did what it was supposed to, keeping invaders out of the brain."

"So, nothing?"

"There was one virus in the brain tissue. An active infection, from what they could tell."

"Great!" Kenzie felt like punching the air in celebration. "Maybe that's our answer. Was it one of the herpesviruses?"

"Yes and no."

"How is it yes and no? Either it's a herpesvirus or it's another virus family."

"It is a herpesvirus. But not one of the ones that you suggested. Human Herpesvirus 4."

"HHV-4," Kenzie said slowly. She tried to remember if she had read anything in the studies she had looked at about HHV-4 having anything to do with amyloid plaque production. But she didn't remember seeing it in any of the medical journals. So had they made a new discovery, or were they on the wrong track? "That's Epstein Barr Virus, isn't it? The one that causes mono?"

Dr. Wiltshire, still looking at the report, nodded. "Apparently, that isn't the full story, though."

"Was there another pathogen?" Sometimes it took several viruses together to take down a person's immune system. And that's how viruses mutated, one virus borrowing a sequence from another virus present in the same host. Recombining to form something that hadn't been seen before, something that no one had an immunity to.

"No, not that they have mentioned, but they asked me to call them after reviewing the report to discuss further details."

"If there were further details to be discussed, then why didn't they put them into the report?"

"That, Dr. Kirsch, is an excellent question."

Of course, it figured that the lab tech that had done the virology was not available to talk to them. Dr. Wiltshire and Kenzie both tried several methods to get ahold of him, but neither of them was having any success. The receptionist wouldn't explain why he wasn't available, and Kenzie wondered if he had left on vacation or called in sick since writing his report.

"We'll just have to wait," Dr. Wiltshire said. "We weren't expecting to have these results today anyway, so if we have to wait a day or two to find out what he wanted to discuss, then we're no further behind."

"I know, but it must have been something important if he wanted you to call him back."

"Can't be helped. If it was important, maybe he'll have left a message for one of his coworkers to call us. Until then, we'll just have to do a bit of our own research and hypothesize about whether this had anything to do with Mr. Cartwright's amyloid plaques or his death. Or both."

"It must have something to do with it. If he had an active infection when he died."

"That's a leap in logic. If you have the flu and I shoot you through the heart, it isn't the flu that killed you."

"Well, no, but in this case, when we can't find anything else..."

"You're assuming a connection that we can't just assume. It might have something to do with the cause of death, but it might not."

"Okay. I'll do a bit more research. But I've got other files to work on too."

Kenzie's phone chimed once, and she checked the screen for the notification. An email from Zachary. He didn't often email or text her during the day, so she opened her phone to have a quick read and make sure nothing was wrong.

The subject line 'you were right' didn't tell her anything other than that he had finally noticed the obvious. She opened the email.

Everyone and his dog is going to the masquerade ball

There was a snippet from a news article with a picture of Lola the dog. Kenzie tapped the link. The news article appeared in her browser.

It was a puff piece about how the hero dog, Lola, had been invited to attend the premier social event of the fall, along with the likes of... there was a list of minor local celebs who had RSVP'd that they would be in attendance.

It went on to describe the various charities that funds were being raised for, the prevalence of kidney disease and prominent people who had died from it, and so on. Kenzie closed the news article.

Her email back to Zachary was short.

Oh, brother

Kenzie's desk phone rang. She looked over at it to see that Dr. Wiltshire was calling and picked it up immediately.

"Hello?"

"Kenzie, can you join me in the boardroom? They've finally got their ducks in a row at the lab, and it isn't the tech who will be talking to us; it is the Executive Director. And some of his staff."

"What's going on?"

"I don't know yet. But I think we're about to find out."

"I'll see you in a minute."

The boardroom was closer to her desk than to his, so she beat him there. They both put down their notepads and pens. Dr. Wiltshire had a printed copy of the lab's report. He checked his notes and, putting the phone on the table into speaker mode, dialed the lab and gave his name. In a few minutes, they could hear the background hum of voices as they were transferred into a meeting room at the lab.

Dr. Wiltshire introduced himself formally and added Kenzie's name. Then the Executive Director, a Pascal Savage, gave his name and position and the names of a few of the techs or assistants who were there to back him up.

"Dr. Wiltshire, we'd like to know a little more about the patient whose samples you sent us," Savage explained. "These results were very unusual, and we need to track the source of the infection if we can."

"I know we don't usually look for HHV-4 in the brain," Dr. Wiltshire agreed. "What exactly are you looking for? This was an old man; maybe his immune system was compromised. I think that while we don't expect to see it crossing the blood-brain barrier, it's not unheard of."

It was like they were both feeling each other out, trying to figure out how much the other already knew. Both trying to keep their own information private.

"This wasn't a normal HHV-4 virus," Savage said reluctantly.

"What does that mean?"

"It was a variant we haven't seen before."

43

D r. Wiltshire leaned forward, putting his elbows on the table.

"A variant?"

"We have been analyzing it. It isn't like any version of HHV-4 we've seen before. We're concerned that if this infection is in the wild, and you're seeing people die from it, we could end up with an epidemic on our hands. No one will be immune to it. We don't know what its spread might be since this is the first time that we've seen it. This victim, you say he was an elderly man? What kind of a situation was he living in? Was he a farmer or a veterinarian?"

"A farmer. No. He's living in a nursing home. He's been there for several years, right Kenzie? He wasn't a new resident."

"No. He'd been there for a few years. As far as I know, he didn't go out anywhere. We can ask the nursing home whether he went anywhere or had any visitors that he might have caught this virus from."

"Could it have been dormant?" Dr. Wiltshire suggested. "Something that he picked up years ago before he moved to the nursing home?"

"I think if this was an old virus, we would have seen it before," Savage countered. "We've been looking through databases and other media, and we can't find any suggestion of it having been seen before."

"Maybe *really* old?" Kenzie suggested, "from when he was a kid or a young man? We don't know what exposures he might have had that far back. There wouldn't be any records showing you the genome of this virus. Some herpesviruses go into dormancy and then pop up again years later when the patient is stressed or there is some other activating trigger. Maybe triggered by the presence of another herpesvirus. Did you find anything in the serum sample we sent previously?"

"Was there a serum sample for this patient?" Savage addressed his own people, but no one seemed to have an answer.

"We sent it earlier," Kenzie explained. "Before the brain tissue. But it has the same patient number on it."

There was some back and forth among the lab folk before Savage broke in again. "It looks like it hasn't been processed yet if we did receive it."

"I can send another sample if you think it got lost."

"I'll have someone get back to you to either let you know that we've got it or that we need you to send a second sample. Blood is more backed up than brains at the moment."

"What?" Kenzie asked blankly. Then she realized he meant that it was taking longer for the lab to process blood samples, probably because they received a lot more of them. That was why the brain had been processed first. "Oh, I got it. Sorry."

"Nothing to apologize for," Savage said. "I'm sorry we don't have the serum results on hand yet. That would have been helpful."

"We had another patient with similar symptoms to this one," Dr. Wiltshire told Savage and his people. "From the same nursing home unit. They died a couple of days apart."

"You need to send me his samples as well. To be processed as soon as possible." Savage swore. "If this is highly contagious... you know how endemic herpesviruses are..."

Dr. Wiltshire looked at Kenzie.

"His brain samples have already been sent in," Kenzie confirmed. "I'll send you the patient number."

"That would be helpful. We'll get right on it."

"There have been other deaths at that nursing home recently. But there always are. It's a nursing home. That said, it was the independent living unit, so we didn't expect to see as many deaths there."

"How many deaths?"

"We had a few through here—more than I had thought. But even more were just handled by the nursing home as doctor-attended deaths and didn't come through our office. I'm not even sure where to start."

"With the samples we have," Dr. Wiltshire said with a shrug. "We'll need to assemble any samples from nursing home patients in the last... let's start with three months. We can send the tissue samples in for testing. Do you want blood samples too?" Dr. Wiltshire directed this question to the speak-erphone.

"Yes. I think it's important to see how many people were infected and what percentage of those had the virus in their brains. Does this virus migrate to the brain? Do we only see it when it reaches a certain level in the body? Only in the immunosuppressed? We need to start gathering data."

Kenzie jotted a few notes down on her pad of paper, thinking through everything that had been said during the phone conversation.

"Dr. Savage... you're obviously very concerned that this could spread. Is it just because it is a variant you haven't seen before and you don't know how infectious the new variant is? Because it may be associated with our patient's death?"

The background noises on the speakerphone ceased as if everyone in the room at the lab had gone still. No more shuffling papers or whispered conversations. Kenzie looked at Dr. Wiltshire, and they both waited for Dr. Savage's answer.

"I am most concerned," Savage said slowly, "because it would appear that this virus was engineered in a laboratory."

44

Kenzie and Dr. Wiltshire looked at each other.

"What makes you think it was engineered in a lab?" Dr. Wiltshire asked. "Or rather, how can you tell it was engineered in a lab?"

"This is highly confidential," Savage warned. "Is there anyone else within earshot? I need your promise that this will not be written down or communicated to anyone else."

"We are alone," Wiltshire said, with a glance at the open boardroom door. Kenzie got up and shut it. "And of course, you have my word that I will not communicate any confidential information outside of this office."

There was silence as Savage apparently considered this wording. Then he spoke. "There is a protein sequence in the RNA of this virus that constitutes... a signature, if you will. In the same way as you can recognize an artist by his brushstrokes or a computer programmer by specific subroutines that he reuses from one program to the next, we can tell that these proteins were edited in a lab. They are a different sequence than you would find in any virus in nature."

"Can you trace them back to a specific lab or scientist, then?" Dr. Wiltshire asked.

"We're working on that. Experimental material does get transferred from one lab or project to another, so there's a bit of detective work to do... lab A passed it on to lab B and C for subsequent studies, lab B passed it on to E, and C to F... It's going to take some time, especially if the transfer wasn't well-documented or a sample was mislabeled or mixed up. If, for instance, they were supposed to send out a non-engineered virus and sent out the engineered one instead."

Kenzie reached to write something down on her notepad. Dr. Wiltshire caught her eye and shook his head. Savage had asked them not to write down anything about the virus being engineered.

"The next question is how did our patient contract the virus?" Dr. Wiltshire said. "Did he take part in an experimental program? Or is it in the wild? Has it mutated from the form that the lab developed?"

"All good questions," Savage agreed. "We are concerned that it may be in the wild. Were you aware of your patient taking part in any medical testing?"

"Not that we know of. It wouldn't be normal course to be testing a virus on seniors unless they are targeting a disease that would normally only be found in seniors."

"Like Alzheimer's disease?" Kenzie asked him softly, her face turned away from the phone so they wouldn't pick up her question. Dr. Wiltshire's eyes widened as he considered the possibility.

"What makes you think it is in the wild?" Kenzie asked. "Do you have anything to back it up? Have you seen it somewhere else?"

"We are working on identifying the origins of this virus. The sequencing suggests that the HHV-4 has recombined with at least one other virus to form a new variant. Of course, it is possible that it was recombined in a laboratory setting, but usually, a lab wants to maintain more control than recombining two viruses would allow. They splice specific gene sequences rather than the larger chunks that we are seeing. What happens when two viruses recombine is too unpredictable."

"So it has mutated, and now you don't know what properties it has."

"Yes," Savage agreed, his voice suddenly lower and gravelly like he'd been up all night talking. As he probably had. "Your case confirms that it is contagious. How contagious it is, we don't yet know. Epstein Barr is usually transmitted through saliva. That's why mono is called the kissing disease. Did it contribute to the death of your patient? If it did..."

"There may be an outbreak at the nursing home and they don't even know it yet. And it could be fatal."

"We have no idea how many people may have it already. A nursing home is a perfect environment to spread an infectious agent. Lots of vulnerable people close together on a daily basis. Outside visitors, doctors, nurses, cleaning staff, volunteers, lots of ways for viruses to get into—and out of—

the nursing home. Kids with runny noses visiting grandma...” Savage made a noise of disgust. “You couldn't engineer a much better environment for spreading a novel virus.”

45

Kenzie's head was whirling after they hung up the phone. She and Dr. Wiltshire just sat there for a while, saying nothing, considering everything they had heard. Dr. Wiltshire wrote a number of notes on his pad of paper. Kenzie didn't interrupt him, not wanting to break his concentration. Eventually, he put his pen down and looked at her.

"I don't know what to think," Kenzie said. "This is incredible."

"We have a list of things to do, including sending them Mr. Sexton's ID number so that they can test his samples next, and pulling samples for any other cases from the nursing home that we have handled in the last three months. That is going to take a while. I have some other calls and research I would like to do while you get started on that."

"What about talking to the nursing home?"

Dr. Wiltshire's lips pressed together tightly as he considered this. "We don't want to start a panic. But we have to be responsible and prevent harm wherever possible. It's too early to recommend a quarantine. Not until we have more data. For all we know, Mr. Cartwright did take part in a medical experiment and it is not contagious at all. One dead man with this novel HHV-4 does not constitute an outbreak."

"But that's not what the lab thinks."

"And since they are the ones who discovered it and have the expertise, it falls on them to inform the Vermont Center for Disease Control and to make recommendations on quarantines or other measures to be taken."

Kenzie scribbled on her notepad. Not words, just shapes and scribbles, trying to get her mind around all of the issues. "What if we told the nursing home that there is a particularly virulent strain of the flu around and that might be what killed Cartwright and Sexton?"

"That's not exactly honest. It would be a breach of ethics."

"But so would *not* telling them."

"We might be able to get away with slightly different wording... a virus that we are trying to identify. Something that they should take extra measures to avoid transmission from one patient to another. Hand-washing, staff wearing masks, and so on."

"And you don't think that will cause panic or spread to the news media?"

Dr. Wiltshire shook his head, not liking the question. They were in trouble either way. They couldn't ignore the potential for an outbreak, but they didn't want to cause unnecessary panic. No matter how careful they were in their wording of a warning to the nursing home, the staff there could over-react or underreact.

"We need more data," Dr. Wiltshire said finally. "We don't know what we're looking at or what the danger is until we have more. We can't make an informed decision without the facts. Then we can make a careful, informed decision. If the lab hasn't already issued a warning. And they may do that once they know enough. It really is their responsibility. Or that of the lab that released the virus. It isn't the place of the Medical Examiner's Office to give warnings about contagions."

Kenzie nodded slowly. "Okay. But if it turns out there is an outbreak of this new, engineered virus... we can't ignore it."

"We won't."

Kenzie stood up and picked up her notepad. "There's one thing that the lab didn't say, and we didn't ask."

Dr. Wiltshire nodded his agreement. "*Why* was this virus created? Was it part of a study to prevent disease or part of a bioterrorism program?"

Kenzie walked back to her desk, a knot in her stomach. She knew why they hadn't asked the question.

46

At the end of the day, there was nothing to do but wait. Kenzie had sent the information and samples that Savage and his team needed to the lab. Dr. Wiltshire was making his phone calls and doing research, but she didn't know who he was consulting with or exactly what he wanted to know about the virus.

So it was a waiting game. Wait for the lab to process all the samples and then get back to them about whether they were positive for the virus as well. Sit through the weekend wondering whether more people would end up dead because of the length of time the testing process would take.

Kenzie felt like a zombie throughout supper, her brain in a completely different place from her body. She tried to talk with Zachary as if everything were normal. She couldn't tell him that they might have an outbreak of a genetically engineered virus. She had been told not to tell anyone about it, and telling him wouldn't do her any good anyway. It would just mean that he was worrying about it as well as she was. And Zachary could take worry to a whole new level.

Kenzie made spaghetti and then pushed it around on her plate, not feeling up to eating. If that was how Zachary felt every day, she could certainly sympathize with him. Especially with being told every day by her and by his doctors that he had to eat more. Looking at the food that she should have enjoyed just made her feel slightly sick. And how could anyone enjoy spaghetti if they were already feeling nauseated?

Zachary looked up from his own plate, which was still just as full as hers. "Are you okay?"

"I'm fine. Well, maybe feeling a little under the weather. But okay, really. Not contagious." She grimaced about letting the word "contagious" slip. *Thanks, Freud.* She needed to be more careful.

"You don't have to eat if you're not feeling well," Zachary pointed out. Unlike him. He did have to eat whether he felt sick or not. She had the option of waiting until she felt better.

But she had a feeling she wasn't going to be able to shake the knot of dread in her stomach until they had the results of the tests. And until she was sure that they had everything under control. And how long was that going to be? A few days? Weeks? What if the virus was more widespread than they had feared? There was nothing to say that there weren't other people dying of the virus, in other facilities, in other jurisdictions. Just because their lab had picked up the RNA signature on the virus, that didn't mean that all labs would.

Why had Dr. Savage sequenced the RNA? Had he known that there was something to be found? Was it strange enough to find HHV-4 in the brain that they wanted to find out more about it and why it was there? Or had he seen other cases already that he wasn't telling them about? Maybe he hadn't been surprised by the results at all. Maybe they had just been watching for more cases in the wild. Maybe he was gradually gathering the data that he would need to present his findings to the authorities and make a case for them to take action and lock down the nursing home—and wherever else the virus had shown up.

"Kenz? Do you want to lie down? I can clean up here. Take care of that for you." Zachary nodded to her plate.

"Sorry... I'm only half here. I'm not very good company today."

"It's okay. Understandable if you aren't well. Why don't you go have a nap? You might still be overtired from when you had to get up early the other day. It can take a while to recover from a lost night's sleep."

"I'd rather put something on TV and distract myself from—" Kenzie barely caught herself in time, "—from my stomach. If I have something else to focus on..."

He nodded. "Yeah. Sure."

He stood up and reached his hand toward her. It wasn't like she needed help up. But she accepted it anyway. Zachary put his arm around her and kissed her cheek lightly. He escorted her out to the living room and turned on the TV. He picked up one of the throw blankets that they mostly used during the winter and draped it over her, fussing like a mother hen. "What do you want to watch?"

"Here, give it to me." Kenzie held her hand out for the remote control. Zachary hesitated, then put it into her hand.

She was certainly capable of paging through the menus and finding something to watch. She didn't know what she wanted to watch, but she would find something. Zachary watched her for a moment, then moved out of the way and went back to the kitchen to clean up.

"You still have to eat," Kenzie reminded him.

Zachary stopped and looked at Kenzie through the doorway, his face disappointed. Kenzie shook her head firmly.

"Don't forget who you're talking to. You don't get out of eating just because I'm not up to it."

He leaned against the doorframe, rolling his eyes.

"You pretend that you don't like me making you eat, but I think you really enjoy it," Kenzie said. He liked to be mothered. After losing his own mother so young and then losing Bridget, who he thought would be there for him forever, why wouldn't he want that? Someone to take care of him. Kenzie didn't exactly see herself as a nurturer, but she had been a good big sister and mini-mother to Amanda, and she did care about Zachary and wanted to help him.

"What if I eat later?" Zachary negotiated.

"When?"

"I don't know." He looked at the clock on the microwave behind him. "Maybe... in a couple of hours."

Kenzie couldn't see any good reason to make him eat at a specific time. Other than the possibility of getting more calories in him before the day was over. "On one condition. You have a granola bar or other snack now, and then have your spaghetti—or another meal, but not just a snack—in a couple of hours."

Zachary considered this for a moment, then nodded. He went into the kitchen and rattled and banged dishes until everything was cleared away and the dirty dishes were in the dishwasher. He joined her in the living room with a granola bar, which he brandished dramatically to make sure she knew he was keeping his end of the bargain.

"Don't get crumbs on the couch."

He pulled his computer table over. His laptop was put away, so the table was clear, and he ate over it carefully, brushing all the crumbs carefully into his hand when he was done. He was clean and tidy when he was paying attention. But she had seen how he could get when he was distracted or severely depressed.

He brushed his hands off into the kitchen sink, ran water over his fingers for a few seconds, and dried them on a dishtowel. He returned to sit with Kenzie on the couch, cuddling up close to her and trailing his fingers through her hair as they watched the movie.

47

Although Kenzie had the whole weekend off, they didn't visit Lorne and Pat again. They wouldn't normally make the trip again so soon unless there was something to be concerned about. Like when Zachary had been investigating the disappearance of Pat's friend. When he'd been there to meet his siblings or Pat's family. Or even if Pat needed some help painting the house or Lorne with cataloging photos on the computer. They were family. Zachary tried to keep in close touch with him, so he tried to at least call most weeks. Lorne was almost a pro at video calls now.

"How are things with you and Kenzie?" Kenzie could hear Lorne's cheerful voice over the speaker even though she was in her home office on the computer.

"We're pretty good," Zachary told him. "Kenzie's fighting some kind of stomach bug, but other than that, we're fine."

"There are some things going around right now," Lorne agreed. "Of course, they never declare it an epidemic until it's practically over, but everybody else knows what's going on."

Which was exactly what Kenzie was worried would happen with the novel HHV-4 virus. No matter how much effort they put into tracking infections, the authorities wouldn't consider it a threat until far too late. Either when it was already on the decline, or when it had put too many people into the hospital and morgue to deny it any longer.

"I might be fighting something too," she heard Lorne say a few minutes later, distracting her from her mail. "I've been so exhausted lately. Just want to sleep all day. And it isn't like I've been doing a lot of extra. If this is what getting old feels like, I think I'm going to opt out!"

"I don't think that's actually an option," Zachary said, chuckling. "If you're tired, then make sure you get enough sleep. That's what your body needs."

"Like you do?"

"Do what I say, not what I do. I try to sleep. It isn't by choice that I don't."

"I know," Lorne agreed warmly. "You have plenty of challenges. But you'll get through it."

"I'm not actually going to get over it, though. Ever." Zachary's voice was low. Confiding. Kenzie stopped typing and listened intently. Maybe it wasn't right for her to be listening in on Zachary's conversation without his inviting her. But he could have put on earphones or gone somewhere private to talk. Or asked Kenzie to shut her office door.

"Zach, I don't think you realize how far you've come over the years," Lorne responded. "You're not the ten-year-old boy who came to us all of those years ago. You've grown up and become a successful business owner. You're in a committed relationship. You've been reunited with three of your siblings. Those are things that... back when you were a teenager, you would have told me were impossible. Things that you would never be able to achieve."

"But I'm still... *broken*," Zachary protested. "You remember how much trouble I had sleeping when I lived with you. I had to have meds to even get a few hours of sleep. And I still have those issues now. And I will for the rest of my life!" At the end of his words, there was a blankness that Kenzie mentally filled in, hearing what he didn't say. *However long that is.*

She moved to get up. To go talk to Zachary and reassure him that things would get better. Maybe not one hundred percent. Maybe he would never act or feel like everyone around him. But the cyclical depression he was experiencing now would recede after Christmas. Of course he knew that. He'd been through it many times before.

"You're depressed," Lorne acknowledged. "And you do need to make sure you get enough sleep. Are you taking a sleep aid? At this time of year, you need to be especially careful to get enough sleep."

"I don't like to take them," Zachary said stubbornly.

"I know that. But sometimes they are necessary. For your mental health. For your physical health. Have you talked to your doctor?"

"I already know what he would say. That it's okay to take them occasionally." Lorne started to reply, but Zachary spoke over him. "But I know it wouldn't be occasionally. It would be every night. Because I know I can only get a few hours of sleep without them. The more I take them, the more I would rely on them and not on my own abilities."

"Okay." Lorne's voice was calm and reassuring, even though Zachary's had risen in both volume and tone. "So what do you want to do? How are you feeling right now—and don't just tell me 'fine.'"

"I'm f—" Zachary cut himself off, swearing under his breath. She could hear him take a few deep breaths, and when he spoke again, his voice was flat and even. Shutting off his emotions. Pulling away from himself and his feelings. "I know it's that time of year and the depression is setting in. I go through this every year. It's only temporary. I know that in my head. But I don't believe it. And my body is telling me this will never end."

"Does Kenzie know how you're feeling?"

"Of course." Zachary's words were clipped. "She sees me every day."

"Have you talked to her about it?"

"Sort of. Sometimes."

"Are you suicidal? Do you need to go to the hospital?" Lorne had learned to ask, not to hint around. Not to use careful euphemisms, but just to put it out in the open. If someone were having appendicitis or a stroke, they wouldn't be expected to speak of it in veiled terms. Zachary's mental health had to be treated the same way. Matter-of-factly. Not as if it were a dirty secret that had to be hidden away.

"No." There were several long seconds of silence. "Not yet."

"Okay. You make sure that you tell someone if you start having suicidal thoughts."

"I have *thoughts,*" Zachary clarified. "But no plan."

"Talk to Kenzie. She can help you to be safe. And talk to your therapist about it. What about your meds?"

"I don't want to do a med review. I can't switch meds right now. I wouldn't be covered properly by... then."

By Christmas. He could barely even stand to say the word.

"Right. Talk to both of them. Make sure they know exactly what you're thinking and feeling. And if it changes."

"Yeah."

"And you know that you can come here any time. Any time, Zachary. If you need to be with someone and Kenzie is at work. If you just need to vent or go for a walk together. Or binge on ice cream. Come. You're family. We're here for you."

Zachary cleared his throat a few times. Kenzie stayed where she was, knowing that she couldn't go out there now and interrupt, telling him that she had heard the entire conversation and putting her two bits in. Lorne had said what needed to be said, and Zachary needed to know that there were other people in his support network. Plenty of people who were willing to step in and help if he just gave the word.

He sniffled. Kenzie listened for Lorne's voice, hoping that Zachary hadn't disconnected the call when it got too emotional for him.

"Thanks," Zachary said eventually, his voice shaky. "Thank you. For everything."

"Of course. And I mean it. Those aren't just words."

"I know."

There were a few minutes of quiet while Zachary pulled himself together again. "How's Pat?"

"I told you we're both good. Pat is already into Christmas preparations. Decorations and baking to put in the freezer and all kinds of plans."

"Are you having his family over again this year?"

"I think they want us to go there. But it won't be until Christmas Day, probably in the evening. You'll be starting to feel better then."

Zachary didn't say anything.

"You know you will," Lorne said. "It's the same every year. You know that once you get past Christmas Eve, you'll start to feel better."

"I don't know."

"Then just trust me. I've seen it before. Even the worst years, you've been better after the anniversary."

"Okay."

"Come by any time. Including Christmas Eve. And if you are up to visits on Christmas Day, you can go with us to see Pat's family. They'd love to see you again."

"I don't know if I made that great an impression the first time."

"You solved a case. How is that not impressive?"

"But I bombed out on dinner. I was rude."

"They understood you were working on something important. Gretta and Suzanne ask after you all the time. They don't have any hard feelings toward you."

"You're sure?"

Kenzie knew that both Pat and Lorne had repeated this several times in the months since Zachary had met Pat's mother and sister for the first time. His anxious brain wouldn't accept their reassurances that it was just fine. But hopefully, with enough repetition, he would eventually stop worrying about it.

And move on to something else.
Kenzie grimaced and went back to her computer work.

48

The weekend seemed interminably long. Kenzie didn't tell Zachary that she was anxious rather than physically sick, so he continued his ministrations. Promising to get whatever food she decided her stomach could handle. Making sure she slept in and didn't stay up too late at night. Just generally cosseting her and treating her like an invalid for the rest of the weekend.

Kenzie thought of Bridget and what it would be like to have a cancer diagnosis and Zachary hovering over her every day, sure she was going to break. While she could never approve of how Bridget had kicked Zachary out of her life when she got sick, she could understand not wanting him to smother her.

It was a relief to get back to the office. She did her usual Monday-morning sweep of all the rooms and surfaces in their suite. Making sure that everything was properly logged and recorded.

What she really wanted to do was to check the office email for any reports from the virology lab on the additional testing for HHV-4. But she promised herself that she wouldn't look at the report until she reached the point in her schedule that she usually checked the email. During her time at the Medical Examiner's Office, she had learned that if email was the first thing she looked at in the morning, her day was far less productive. She ended up taking much longer processing it, and it was likely to take all morning instead of Kenzie being able to zip through it in half an hour or an hour. She would reward herself for dealing with the weekend full of anxiety and not breaking down and telling Zachary what was going on by checking to see if the results were in.

Eventually, she sat down at her desk and opened her email. "Come on," she coaxed. "Be there. If this testing was so important, you should have stayed there all weekend to do the processing and sequencing. Show me what you found."

***

Dr. Wiltshire arrived at the office at his usual time. Kenzie guessed that, he didn't want to jinx the results by being too impatient to get them either. Though she knew it was magical thinking, her brain was convinced that if she just did things the way she did every workday, they would find the test results in email as hoped for.

Dr. Wiltshire looked at Kenzie, an awkward approach that said he was as afraid to ask for the test results as she had been to look for them.

"They came in," she told him quickly, reaching out with the printed copy of the report.

Dr. Wiltshire didn't pretend not to know what she was talking about. He took the stapled report from her. "Did you look?"

Kenzie nodded. "I couldn't really not look when I was printing them... I hope you don't mind."

"Summarize."

"Five more cases, including Mr. Sexton."

"Five." He rubbed the bridge of his nose under his glasses. "Over what period?"

"Going back six weeks. Before that, nothing from the samples we sent."

"So we didn't miss a whole bunch of cases. That's helpful, at least."

Kenzie nodded.

"And any mention of how they are doing at the lab? Tracing it to the source of the contagion?"

"No, no word on that. I guess they didn't think we needed to know."

"Not necessarily," Dr. Wiltshire said with a forced smile and a slight shake of his head. "I'm sure it is long, tedious work. And not just a search that can be done on the computer. They'll have to do a lot of interviews to figure out each transfer point. And any labs or scientists that didn't follow proper protocol and might have been an infection point aren't going to want to talk to anyone. Not without a subpoena or some kind of order from public health."

"But we can't afford for it to take a long time. People are dying."

"So far, it doesn't appear to be widespread. Champlain House is currently the only known outbreak."

"As far as we know. But most doctors are not going to do a test for HHV-4 or to collect brain samples when a patient comes in complaining of memory issues or vertigo," Kenzie snapped back.

"No. You're absolutely right. No one is going to know what to look for until it is announced. But an announcement cannot be made based on what we have so far. We're going to need to find out any commonalities of the six victims. If they were all in the same part of the unit, all played poker together, or had something else in common. We don't know yet how the infection is spread. Person to person contact. Surface contact. Large droplet. Aerosol. Epstein Barr is typically spread through saliva. But the new variant could be different. We need to get a better idea of whether those patients all knew each other and were in close contact with each other. Or whether... I don't know... it's in the heating ducts or the shower heads. Or on the doorknobs."

"Okay... I'll give them a call and see if I can get anywhere."

"Good. And I will call and see if I can get any more information from Dr. Pascal Savage."

49

Kenzie hadn't gotten advice from Dr. Wiltshire as to how to go about talking to the staff of Champlain House without letting the cat out of the bag about the possibility of an outbreak. Exactly how was she supposed to gather information on those six particular residents without the staff wondering what was going on? It had to be clear that Kenzie was not just being nosy and using her position with the Medical Examiner's Office to ask idle questions.

She tried to play down the six deaths and any connections between them as much as possible.

"We're doing an audit of a random selection of cases we have received from Champlain House over the past few weeks," she told Nurse Summers. "Just to make sure that everything has been handled correctly by the Medical Examiner's Office. We have to perform self-checks to ensure thoroughness and consistency of results."

"This seems like make-work," Summers objected. "I and my staff are very busy. We don't have the time to be answering a bunch of unimportant inquiries. We have quite enough work to do without your office adding their own requirements into the mix. I don't think there's any legal requirement for us to answer your questions when they aren't even connected to a case."

"They are connected to a case. We have six different cases that we are examining. I realize it's an inconvenience. It is for me too. Believe me, I don't want to be wasting my time and adding extra busywork into my schedule either."

"Yet here you are," Summers said acidly, "taking up my time on the phone."

"Would you prefer that I come there in person? It would probably be a good idea if I do anyway. Then I can talk to everyone who is in and see the various rooms and common areas in the unit." She thought about the various potential points of infection.

"No, I don't need anyone poking around here, either."

"I will probably need to do a quick walkthrough, at the very least. But I'll start with the phone interview. The more information you can give me, the quicker it will all be over."

"Now is not a good time."

"What time would you like me to call you back?" Kenzie tried to pin her down. "What time are you off? Maybe that would work better."

"No, I'm not spending my off-time dealing with this."

"Whatever time you prefer, just let me know..."

"How about never?"

"Nurse Summers," Kenzie let some of her frustration and impatience into her voice and formed the words very precisely. "If you are impeding a legitimate investigation by the Medical Examiner's Office..."

"What? You're going to throw me in jail?"

Kenzie had no idea what the penalties might be for something like that. She strongly suspected that the penalties for refusing to talk to an ME's office were not very harsh. "Do you really want to find out?"

Nurse Summers sighed. "Fine. What exactly is it you want to know?"

"I have a list of patients here. The first thing I am going to need are the room numbers for each."

"The room numbers?"

"Where their living quarters were?" Could a nurse really be that dense?

"Fine."

Kenzie ran through the list of six, and on each patient page, noted the room they had slept in. "Great, that's very helpful. And now, I don't know what the options are for food. Does everyone eat meals together in a common room? In their own room? Are they allowed to bring in outside food?"

"A combination. Most of the residents in our room take meals together in the common room. They like to socialize. Some residents prefer to take meals in their rooms, or have occasional outside meals brought in by family or friends. But that is less common."

"I have the same six patient names and would like to know where they took their meals."

Nurse Summers listed a few off before stopping to ask, "And who else? I didn't catch them all the first time."

Kenzie mentioned the additional names. She wrote the responses on each of the sheets of paper. As Summers had said, most preferred to take their meals in the common room, but a couple took some or most of their meals in their rooms. There wasn't an obvious pattern. But from what Kenzie could interpret from the nurse's answers, everybody went to the common room to eat at least sometimes.

"Extra-curricular," Kenzie announced next. "Did these patients play games together? Visit with each other? Keep to themselves?"

"With each other?" Nurse Summers tapped her nail impatiently on the phone. "No, they weren't all a secret club, if that's what you mean. They might play a game together now and then, but not regularly."

"What kind of games do you have? How are they sanitized?"

"How are they sanitized?"

"Disinfected. Are they wiped down after the residents use them?"

"No. Of course not. That would be a lot of extra work for the staff, and I'm not sure you could wipe down cards or puzzles. I don't understand what you are looking for. Do you think one of these patients had Hep B or staph? The residents are responsible for their own hygiene. We haven't had any lock-downs due to infections in this unit. Not even flu or pneumonia."

"That's a great record. Please don't take these questions as a criticism of your practices; that's not my intention. I'm just trying to learn what I can about these patients we have selected and how thoroughly their deaths were investigated."

"It sounds more like you want to check on our practices than yours."

"Let's move on to contact with staff. I know that this is the independent living unit, so they do not require significant nursing care, but they must still have some contact with the nursing staff and housekeeping."

"Of course."

"Can we go over each patient and the extent of the care they had from the nursing staff? None of them were assigned any particular nurse, is that right?"

"No. All of the nurses are available to deal with residents as needed. Some might need a bit of help with showering, or need someone to give them their pills so they don't get mixed up, that kind of thing."

"Can you go through each of these patients and tell me what kind of assistance they needed?"

"I don't know if this is appropriate for me to be talking to you about under the privacy laws."

"They are dead and this is part of our investigation into their deaths. You are not required to get any consents to communicate information to the Medical Examiner's Office."

"So you say."

Kenzie waited. Nurse Summers sighed in exasperation and began to list each of the patients to describe what care they needed or may have had with the nursing staff before their deaths.

"Is that everyone?"

"You haven't mentioned Mr. Sexton yet."

Summers summarized Sexton's information briefly.

"That's great. Now, what about contact with the housekeeping staff?"

"The residents don't have any contact with the housekeeping staff."

"Housekeeping enters their rooms to clean, don't they?"

"Not while they're there. If they are in their rooms, they are asked to go for a walk until housekeeping is done."

"And they pick up their laundry. And what else? I assume they wear gloves to avoid contamination with soiled clothing?"

"I don't know. I suppose so."

"Do they change their gloves between rooms? What is the protocol for handling soiled items?"

"I don't know what their practices are. That is all dictated by administration, not nursing. Of course they will protect themselves from contaminants."

"And are the residents' laundry items all kept separate from each other, or all washed together?"

"They are kept separate, just like washing at a laundromat or at your house. They are removed from the resident's room in a marked laundry basket and returned to them washed and folded in the same basket."

"And is the basket sanitized?"

"I don't know. You would have to talk to housekeeping about that part."

Kenzie looked for other areas she might have missed. "And they disinfect all high-touch surfaces in the residents' rooms?"

"I assume so."

"How often?"

"Residents' rooms are cleaned once a week unless there is a specific problem requiring the housekeeping staff's attention."

"Do residents visit each other in their rooms? Or only in the common areas?"

"They are allowed to visit with each other privately. We don't supervise interpersonal socialization unless there are known to be problems."

"Like what?"

"What do you mean?"

"What kinds of problems?"

"Just like anyone else, residents don't always get along together. Some of them, they have disagreements or don't like each other. As much as we try to provide a good environment, we can't make everyone like each other."

"Are we talking about arguments or physical altercations?"

"Most of them are too old for a physical fight... but we have had a few of them." Nurse Summers blew out her breath. "Some men... you would think their testosterone would be low enough by the time they get here that we wouldn't have fights. But there you are."

"And have you had any problems with any of the patients on my list? With physical altercations?"

"Well... I feel like I'm telling tales out of school. You know what they say about not speaking ill of the dead..."

"We're not making any judgments about them. Just talking about how they got along together, what the interactions between the patients were like."

"You really need to know this for your report? What does this have to do with how your office investigated these deaths?"

"Well, I know I was the one who came and talked to you about Mr. Cartwright. But I never thought to ask whether he had been in any fights with other residents there. Now that we're having this conversation, I can see that's an area that should be addressed in the future."

"I suppose so," Nurse Summers agreed grudgingly. "But your Mr. Cartwright wasn't in any fights during the week before his death, so I don't think that was a contributing factor."

"Not in the week before his death? So he was one of the patients that did sometimes get into fights?"

"He had, in the past, been involved in the occasional argument that got physical. Old military man, you know, they have been conditioned to react physically to what they perceive as a threat."

Kenzie jotted down this note on her page for Willie Cartwright. "Does that mean that he had PTSD?"

"PTSD? No, men his age were never diagnosed with PTSD. But I can tell you... if he perceived a threat, he would react."

"Physically. By attacking someone."

"By defending himself. Yes."

"And the other patients that we picked out? Any of them have any physical altercations in the past?"

"I don't think so. Margaret Ashbury, that nice old English lady, she was a spitter. Cross her and see where it got you! A big loogie straight to the eye, if you didn't watch out."

Kenzie made a note of this too. They knew the virus was likely to be spread through saliva. "That's great. Thank you for all the details. Anything else that you can think of with any of the other residents we talked about that I should know about? Health problems? Psychiatric or neurological symptoms, negative interactions with other residents?"

"No. I mean, they all had health problems. They were old. They needed to be in assisted living. But most of them were in pretty good physical condition. Until they died."

Kenzie rolled her eyes. "Maybe we can just quickly run through each of them and you can let me know if they had any diagnosed issues or if there was anything that you noticed that you think should have been diagnosed."

"Is this the last question?" Summers asked in a long-suffering tone.

"I think so. Unless it triggers another thought."

"Well, let's hope it doesn't." Summers ran through each patient briefly to discuss any conditions that they might have had before they died. There were many issues with blood pressure, weight, diabetes, and other issues for being a relatively healthy lot. Kenzie scribbled them all down quickly so that she wouldn't have to ask again.

"Now, if that's everything, I would like to get back to my actual work."

"Of course. If you could just email me a floor plan of the unit so I can see where each of the rooms was in the unit. That would be very helpful. Aside from that... I guess I'll let you know if anything else occurs to me. And I'll probably stop by in the next day or two to touch base briefly with the other nursing staff and housekeeping. Just to make sure that we haven't missed anything."

"You have been very thorough," Nurse Summers said, and Kenzie didn't think it was meant as a compliment.

50

Kenzie was logging in test results received via email and was surprised to see one that had come from a lab she was unfamiliar with. She opened it to scan through the information and was also unfamiliar with the doctor's name. She looked to the patient name, pretty sure by now that it had been forwarded to the wrong Medical Examiner's Office. She started to type a reply to the email to let them know of the error when the pieces began to fall into place.

Lola Canine was, of course, not one of the bodies that they had dealt with, but she was certainly part of their ongoing investigation into the deaths of Cartwright, Sexton, and now four other subjects. Lola the dog, from the care center. She didn't recognize the doctor or lab names immediately because they were veterinary rather than those she usually dealt with. She deleted her reply and paged down into the report to see what they had discovered.

She didn't even remember tapping Dr. Wiltshire's name into the phone keypad, but she had the phone to her ear and was waiting for him to answer.

"Kenzie?"

"Dr. Wiltshire... I just got in a report from the veterinary lab on Lola, the dog at Champlain House."

"Oh. Anything interesting in the results?"

"Well, yes... it says that she is positive for HHV-4, as well as a couple of other viruses."

She heard Dr. Wiltshire put something down with a clack. Maybe his coffee mug or his fountain pen. "She's positive? You're sure? For HHV-4?"

"Yes. That's what the serology shows. I didn't even know that dogs could get HHV-4. I mean, it is *Human* Herpesvirus 4. Can dogs get it?"

"Apparently, they can in this case. I would have to look at the research to see if it is common. I'm afraid I'm not up on my canid virology."

"Maybe it's just this novel variant. I'm really surprised. Once we identified the possible culprit as HHV-4, I assumed that the dog was out as the source of the infection." Kenzie shook her head at herself for not looking into it further.

"Did you find anything out about her history?"

"There was a bit of back and forth. I guess she was a friend of a friend's dog or something like that, they couldn't take care of her, she needed somewhere stable to live, Nurse Ellie who took her couldn't have dogs in her building... blah, blah, blah, so Lola ended up being the mascot of the independent living center."

"You're going to need details. We still don't know how *Lola* got HHV-4. She might have contracted it *from* one of the patients rather than giving it to them. Most viruses don't jump between families of the animal kingdom. We still need to find out where the virus came from, if it came from some laboratory, so that we know what has been done with it, its transmission pathways, and what the mortality rate is."

"Right." Kenzie jotted down notes on her computer scratchpad. "I will start getting names and addresses and see if we can find any association with a lab."

"I will call Champlain House and advise them that the dog is to be isolated from patients. And whoever is caring for her should be extra careful about contact. Wear gloves and mask, frequent hand-washing, keep feces away from anyone else and don't dispose of them in the general garbages."

"Okay. I'll forward this email to you in case there is anything else in it that is important. It doesn't look like they did any PCR, so I should probably get them to send samples over to Dr. Savage so his lab can map them. See if they are the same variant."

"Definitely. He's going to want to run his own tests and factor it into their investigation tracking the virus."

"Can I ask a really ignorant question?"

"Fire away," Dr. Wiltshire invited, a smile in his voice.

"Exactly how does a virus escape a lab? I mean... how shoddy do their isolation protocols have to be if they are accidentally letting it out into the wild?"

"It happens. Each time, if we can identify how it got out, we can add to our knowledge of how to properly keep them isolated even when doing testing. But take a look at history—there have been several cases where plague has escaped labs to contaminate and sometimes kill unsuspecting people."

"Plague? Really?"

"Don't quote me, but I believe there have been three accidental releases since the seventies. Labs worldwide are still running tests on the plague virus to unlock its secrets, whether it is to develop new defenses against virulent plagues, bioterrorism research, whatever. And unfortunately... it would seem that even the most careful lab can make mistakes. None of them are bullet-proof. Sometimes it is wastewater, sometimes a ventilation shaft that wasn't properly sealed from the rest of the building. Suddenly you've got someone in the same building dropping from the plague, probably after infecting members of their own family. There have been some fatalities and some recoveries. It isn't something we ever want to see in the wild again."

"But something like HHV-4 is so endemic to the population... so many people already have it in their systems... how could we track it and control one variant? You can't isolate everybody positive for HHV-4. That is half the population in North America. And we don't have a test for just this variant, so it would just be... trying to sequence every positive HHV-4 result... it would be impossible."

"If there is an outbreak, scientists will have to come up with a rapid test for it and treat it pretty quickly."

51

Kenzie double-checked the address that she had been given and looked at the doors of the buildings, trying to sort out which she was looking for. Ellie, the nurse who had taken Lola in, told her that it wasn't an apartment building, but there were living quarters over several businesses. The numbers on the buildings were difficult to make out from the street, so she pulled into the parking lot and found an empty stall. She walked along, checking all the numbers. It was a few buildings down from where she had thought it would be.

She opened one of the glass doors and was able to walk up the stairs, but the door at the top of the stairs was locked. Kenzie rattled the doorknob, knocked, and tried the phone number that Ellie had given her. No luck. Kenzie went back down the stairs and tried a couple of the ground-floor businesses, asking if they knew any of those who lived in the building, or if there were a building manager around.

Receptionists flashed smiles but shook their heads. *No, can't help you, would there be anything else?*

Eventually, she had to give up. She would keep trying to call. Sooner or later, Lola's former owner had to answer.

Kenzie was sitting in her car looking at the GPS map and trying to decide whether to run over to Champlain House to have a face-to-face chat with

Nurse Ellie and look at the unit with new eyes, or whether it was just too late in the day and she should get something to eat and tackle the matter again the next day when she was fresh.

Though she was worried about the virus spreading, they didn't yet have confirmation that it was even the same virus as Lola had. Dr. Wiltshire had called the nursing home to isolate Lola, so there wouldn't be any more opportunities for infection on their end.

Her stomach was growling loudly just thinking about the possibility of getting food, so she broke down and admitted to herself that she wasn't going to be any good getting anything else done on the case. She needed to go home, eat, and spend some time with her boyfriend. She didn't like to leave Zachary isolated for too long. He could go out and do things with other people at any time, of course, but he tried to be there for supper. And when he was depressed, he didn't want to leave the house or reach out to others, even if it would help him feel better about himself.

Kenzie picked up her phone and tapped Zachary's avatar. Of course, he would tell her he didn't care what kind of cuisine she bought, but she wanted to ask him anyway. Show him that respect. Show him she cared about his opinion, even if it were just on something unimportant.

"Kenzie?" Zachary sounded out of breath; his voice unusually intense.

"Hi. Are you okay? Did you have to run for the phone?"

"There's someone here."

"What? Who is there?"

A client? Someone he was entertaining? One of his siblings? And why was he out of breath and sounding so strange?

"I don't know who it is. Someone has been parked in front of the house for... at least half an hour now. I don't know who it is. An older man. Dark car. Lexus."

"Someone is parked in front of the house? One of the neighbors?"

"No. I don't know who it is. He's been sitting out there. He's in his car. Waiting."

"You think he has the house under surveillance?"

"Yes."

Who would be watching her? Kenzie had lived a pretty quiet life since she had gone back to school. She hadn't gone out with anyone but Zachary in the last year. So it wasn't an ex-boyfriend. She hadn't exactly been out painting the town red every night when she was younger, but she had been out a lot more, interested in a lot of different men without being able to commit to one. She could understand if someone held that against her. But that had been a long time ago.

It didn't make sense that it was anything to do with work. It wasn't like she was investigating live people. She helped out with the forensics when she could, but it wasn't like she was the one putting people behind bars.

Her mind flashed back to Micah. *They came to my house. They assaulted me. They kidnapped me.* The true horror of Micah's words hadn't really sunk in before.

They had gone to her house.

And now someone had come to Kenzie's.

A chill ran down her spine, raising goosebumps on her neck and arms.

"I don't know who it is," Kenzie told Zachary. "Are you sure he is watching the house? He's not there for the neighbors... or a delivery man or something like that?"

"If he was a delivery man, he wouldn't still be sitting there half an hour later."

"But if it was someone who was surveilling the house, he wouldn't be so obvious, would he? I mean, just sitting out there in his car? People are bound to notice."

"People are blind to their surroundings," Zachary dismissed. He'd been on enough surveillance jobs to know the truth of that situation. On TV, people noticed someone sitting in a car on the street for ten minutes. But in real life? There wasn't much reason for people to watch the street and pay attention to whether vehicles were occupied. "He doesn't exactly blend in, but I haven't noticed anyone else paying him any attention. People out walking their dogs or coming and going to their houses... they just walk on by."

"Well... does he have a camera or anything? Is he filming? What would he want from me? I don't exactly live an interesting life."

"Do you want me to go out there and ask him who he is?"

"No, don't do that." Kenzie was immediately protective of Zachary. He didn't carry a gun. He wasn't one of those macho hard-boiled detectives like on TV. He was a small man without a weapon and she'd seen him hurt before. She didn't want him walking into a dangerous situation. Especially if it were because of her.

Then again, maybe it *wasn't* because of her. Perhaps it was something to do with Zachary's private investigation business. Surely there must be people who were not happy with him for proving that they were stepping out on their spouses, committing insurance fraud, or stealing from their employers. There might even be friends or lovers of the men he had put in prison out to get revenge.

Or the human trafficking ring he had managed to rescue a couple of teenagers from. They might have thought that the kids were dead, as they were supposed to, or they might have somehow figured out it was a con. Luke could have decided to go back to them and spilled the beans.

"It could be dangerous to go out there and confront him," Kenzie told him firmly. "I don't want you to do that. If you think it's someone who shouldn't be there, why don't you call the police, have them check it out?"

"I don't want to do that if it's someone who has a legitimate reason to be there."

"Well, you're the private detective. You figure it out. But don't go out there and expose yourself to someone who could be dangerous."

"Nothing is going to happen," Zachary said, chuckling slightly at her naïveté. "Don't confuse what you see on TV with real life. Everyone isn't walking around with guns, trying to get the jump on everyone else."

"You're the one who brought up guns. And since you don't have one, I don't want you walking into someone who might. If he's just sitting in his car, he's not doing any harm. Just watch and see what happens."

He breathed in her ear for a few seconds, considering. Still out of breath because his anxiety was pumping up his heart rate.

"Are you coming home?"

"Yes. I won't be long. I was just trying to decide what to pick up on the way home."

"You could come straight home. There's stuff in the freezer."

Kenzie mentally reviewed what was in the freezer. Mostly burritos and stuff she didn't really want for supper. She weighed her own cravings against the fact that Zachary was obviously anxious and wanted her to be home as soon as she could be. He might not be having a meltdown yet, but she didn't want to send him into a full-blown anxiety attack because she was taking longer to get home than he thought she should and he thought something had happened to her.

"Okay, fine. I'll heat up something in the freezer. You'll hang in there until I get home? Don't do anything stupid like running out there to confront this guy?"

"No, I won't."

"You're not going to change your mind?" She knew how impulsive he was. And something might occur to him that seemed like a good reason to go charging out there by himself. She wanted him to promise he would stay inside.

"You'll drive straight into the garage, right?" Zachary checked, more worried about Kenzie than about himself. "Don't open the garage door until you're right in front of it, and then shut it right away, so no one can slip in. Then come in through the house, so you're not exposed."

"Okay. I will. I'm coming from across town, so it's going to be a few minutes longer than you expect. Okay? Don't panic when I'm not home right away. I'm not at the ME's Office."

"All right." Another quick, anxious breath. "See you soon."

52

Kenzie knew that it probably wasn't the best idea, but she approached from the direction that would require her to drive the street in front of the house to catch a glimpse of the stranger surveilling her house.

Even though she had told Zachary that the watcher might be dangerous, it was hard to make herself believe that. There had to be a good reason for someone to be sitting in front of her house. And the chances that he would have a gun? Zero to none. Kenzie had rarely met anyone but police who carried guns. That she knew of.

She saw the car that Zachary had referred to immediately and took a look at the driver as she drove past. She did what she had promised and went straight into the garage and shut the door. She went into the house, where Zachary hesitated between running to meet her and keeping an eye on the car through the front window.

"Hey, it's okay," she told him. "Everything is fine."

"He's still out there. Did you see him?"

"I saw him. It's okay. It's nothing to worry about."

"I should have called the police. I shouldn't have waited until you got home. What if he—" Zachary broke off, looking out the window, his anxiety rising. "He's getting out of the car!"

"Calm down. Nothing bad is going to happen. I know who it is."

"You know?" Zachary had been walking back over to the window to get a better look at the stranger, and froze where he was. "You know him?"

Kenzie nodded. "I do. And you don't need to worry. It isn't anyone who wants to hurt me. Or you."

"You know who it is. Someone from work?"

"No."

Kenzie walked to the front door and flipped on the switch for the outside light, as dusk was beginning to fall. She tapped in the burglar alarm code for the front door and opened it as the man walked up the sidewalk. Kenzie reached out and gave him a hug, which was returned. It felt good to be held, to be in his arms again. Even though neither of them was demonstrative, she had missed that.

She turned back toward Zachary, jerked her head for him to join her. "Zachary, this is my dad."

Zachary looked stunned. He looked at Kenzie as if he wasn't sure if she were telling the truth. She had not invited him over to her mother's house or to any family events. She had preferred to keep her parents and Zachary separate and not to have to deal with both of those worlds at the same time. It wasn't because she was ashamed of Zachary—or ashamed of her parents, for that matter. She just didn't want to mix those two worlds and have to deal with them both simultaneously.

But, as she should have expected would happen sooner or later, her father had broken down that wall all by himself. As far as Walter Kirsch was concerned, there were no walls. Only doors to be opened, one way or another. He would knock, phone, pound on the door, ring the doorbell, find a key, or pick the lock, but one way or another, he would get through every locked door that was placed in front of him.

"Dad, this is my boyfriend, Zachary Goldman. Zachary, Walter Kirsch."

Kenzie sighed, realizing she couldn't just leave her father standing on the doorstep, so she stepped to the side to let him in. Walter had been at the house once or twice before. Not very often, and always, as he had this time, just showing up when he decided he needed to see Kenzie about something. She hadn't invited him into her sanctum.

Once they were all in the living room, Walter held his hand out toward Zachary, extending it in greeting. Zachary took it hesitantly.

"Nice to meet you, Zachary," Walter greeted pleasantly. Then silence hung in the air when he should have said, "Kenzie has told me a lot about you."

Because, of course, Kenzie had told him as little as possible. Her personal life was none of his business.

"You too, sir," Zachary responded. Again the awkward pause, because Kenzie hadn't told him much about her father either.

The two men continued to shake hands for another second or two, and Kenzie hoped that her father wasn't squeezing the life out of Zachary's hand in a show of male dominance. Eventually, the two dropped the grip and shifted away from each other slightly.

"Dad." Kenzie wasn't going to wait for him to work his way through the entire spiel this time. "What's up? Why are you here?"

Walter took his time, sitting down on the couch and pinching the sharp crease in his pants. Kenzie didn't want to sit down with him and be forced to exchange pleasantries. She stayed on her feet. She needed to make supper. And to figure out how to get Walter out of there as quickly as possible.

"I can't just stop in to see my little girl?" Walter asked, smiling at her.

"Zachary said you've been sitting in front of the house for an hour. You're making him think you're a stalker. What's going on?"

Walter chuckled. He looked Zachary over, evaluating him. Kenzie didn't like the smirk on his face, the suggestion that he was somehow more superior because he had made Zachary worry. That he was superior because Zachary was clearly smaller and more fragile than he was. She hated him looking down on her partner that way.

"No need to worry," Walter assured them. "I just wanted a chance to talk to Kenzie. I was in the area, so I thought I would stop by. I didn't want to bother you at work. So I thought I would hang out here while I did a little work in the car and catch you after work."

"A lot of nights, I don't get home until late. You could have been out there for hours."

"Oh, I would have called you if it looked like you weren't going to get back in good time. I had plenty I could do while I was waiting."

Of course he did. He was always schmoozing with someone, pressing his agenda and trying to negotiate for whatever bill he happened to be lobbying for at that particular time. All he needed was his phone and his golden tongue.

"So what did you want?"

"Do I have to want something to come and see my own daughter? It used to be that people were happy to see their parents, to take a little time out of their day to visit."

"You could have called me. No need to make this trip."

"I could have. But I wanted to see you face to face. It's important to see your children every now and then."

Except now, he only had one child, and Kenzie couldn't help blaming him partially for Amanda's loss. Of course, nothing would have saved Amanda. They might have been able to get a few more months for her. But not years. However lucky they had been in keeping her alive, she wouldn't still be alive now. Not with another kidney. Not with five new kidneys. She had just been too fragile.

"It's nice to see you too," she said through her teeth. And she waited. She had already asked what he wanted. Sooner or later, he was going to have to come out with it.

"I wondered if you had decided to go to the masquerade ball."

"The masquerade ball? No. I don't know why you and Mother are so intent on me going. I know it is for kidney research, but I'm not interested in going out to these events. I contribute in other ways. Balls have never been my thing."

"You could have a great time there. You could bring Zachary. You could wear matching costumes. Some couples' thing. Dance, enjoy some good food, just be seen there. So people know that the Kirsch family is still there, representing."

"Considering that you and Mother are going to be there, I hardly see why I would need to."

"I'd like you to be there. I'd like to show you off. We don't see each other often enough, honey. You need to get out of that morgue more often. See life instead of death."

"I do get out. I do plenty of things other than just attend autopsies all day. You really have no idea what my job is like. Or what my life with Zachary is like. Don't judge."

Kenzie's face warmed a little as she protested. Because she knew that the truth was, she did spend too much time at the morgue. And she didn't get out very often. With Zachary at home, she didn't even do very much with her girl friends. She couldn't remember the last girls' night out. Maybe sometime when he was out on surveillance, she should give them a call. She didn't want to completely abandon her outside life. She didn't want to get so wrapped up in her work at the ME's office and with Zachary that she didn't have her own life anymore.

She wasn't obsessed with death. Even working with dead bodies, she was really focused on life. What had happened before the person had died. How it could be avoided in the future. By investigating death, they really examined life.

"I'm not judging. I'm saying I would like to see more of you. Is that bad?"

"No, of course not."

They both just looked at each other for a few minutes, studying each other's faces, looking for the familiar tells.

"I was talking to the governor just the other day," Walter said casually, as if there were a natural segue to this topic.

Kenzie's stomach clenched. *The governor?* Walter had his high-powered friends. Everyone who was anyone knew who Walter Kirsch was. And Kenzie had a feeling that her father's conversation with the governor had not been a casual mention of his daughter over drinks.

"You just happened to be talking to the governor?" Kenzie demanded. "And my name just happened to come up?"

"My family is important to me. Of course you came up."

"And what were you discussing?"

Kenzie knew precisely where it was going, and she wasn't going to give him the chance to approach the subject softly. She wanted it up-front. No couching everything in politically correct language. No hints or opacity. Walter frowned. He liked to play the part of the gentleman, who would never say anything to offend anyone, and always knew exactly how to approach every topic.

"Honey..."

"The governor wants Dr. Wiltshire to issue a death certificate on Willie Cartwright," Kenzie said. "Are you telling me that's why you're here? To interfere with the proper investigation of the Medical Examiner?"

"Of course not. I just wondered how it was going. The governor has his concerns about the way it is being handled."

"Why? Doesn't Willis Cartwright's family want to know the truth?"

"The family already knows the truth. Willie Cartwright was an old man. Old men die. Eventually, things just wear out."

"Well, nothing wore out. He had a virus. And we're trying to find out more information about this virus and where he got it and how it developed and led to his death. That takes time. You may think from watching TV that every lab test can be done on the equipment in the autopsy room and that there is never any doubt about any of the results, but that's fantasy. That's not the way things actually work. Tests take weeks, even months to come back. Sure, the families would like everything to be resolved in a day or two, but that's not the way it goes in real life."

"Even if you're waiting for tests back, haven't you already done everything you need to? At least release the body to them."

"If we're not sure that we have all the samples collected and tests ordered that we need, we are entitled to hold the body for longer. It doesn't do us much good if we release the body and then decide later that we need a sample from another part of the brain, or need another liver sample from a different lobe, or find out that we didn't get something else that we needed. By then, it's too late."

"We're just not sure why you're acting like this is such a problematic case. He's an old man who died in a nursing home. It isn't like it was someone in the prime of their life who just dropped dead over his bowl of Cheerios. It isn't like you have some plague that has to be quashed. It's an old man who died in the night."

It was a mistake for him to refer to a plague. Because that's just what Kenzie and Dr. Wiltshire were worried about. If the HHV-4 variant was fatal, they needed to find out how often and trace it back to its source and everyone else who might have caught it. Screen them all for who was positive for the virus and get them quarantined. Watch them for developing symptoms. Keep track of their vital signs so that they would be immediately warned if someone started to deteriorate rapidly.

"You don't know what's going on," she told her father icily. "And neither does the governor. And he doesn't have the authority to tell the Medical Examiner's Office what to do in an investigation."

"No one is telling anyone what to do," Walter said reasonably. "We just don't understand what is going on here. Have you discovered something? If so, you need to report it. Let him know what's going on."

"No, we don't. We have our own reporting lines. As we figure things out, we will report it to the proper authorities." She met her father's eyes. "Not the governor."

Walter shrugged, but she knew from his face that she'd hit her mark. He might act as if her words didn't have any effect on him and he was only casually interested in the matter, but she had seen him in enough negotiations to know the tiny tells. She had spent the years since Amanda had died learning his face and everything she could read from his expression.

Zachary shifted. He had remained quiet during the discussion. It was, after all, something that concerned only Kenzie and her father. But he spoke now, his eyes also fastened on Walter's face, reading him. "You wouldn't let anything happen to Kenzie, would you?"

Walter looked startled at this. He laughed and shook his head, but his face was not amused. "No, I would never let anything happen to her. What are you talking about?"

"The governor has a lot of power. Not just politically. There have been rumors that he has been involved with some... unsavory people. If you thought he was going to take any action against Kenzie, you would tell us, wouldn't you?"

Kenzie looked at Zachary in amazement.

Walter reached over and took Kenzie's hand in his. "Of course. Kenzie is my only living child. I wouldn't let anyone put her in danger." He turned his eyes to hers. "You believe that, don't you honey?"

"Yes," Kenzie agreed faintly.

"Now would not be a good time for rumors of some new virus or disease," Walter said slowly and softly. "Full-scale panic would reverse many of the gains that have been made. There is an election coming up, and the last thing we need is for people to be worried that the government cannot protect them."

"What have you heard?" Kenzie demanded. How could he know about the HHV-4? Kenzie and Dr. Wiltshire had kept it carefully under wraps, just as Dr. Savage had requested. There were more people in the lab who were in the know than in the Medical Examiner's Office, so the leak must have come from there. But who would be talking to the governor about it? Especially before the tests on Mr. Cartwright's tissues had even been completed.

The governor had been pushing back against their investigation even before they knew about the HHV-4 variant.

53

Walter looked at Kenzie, considering her question. "What have I heard? I hear a lot of things. I talk to a lot of people and I have a pretty good picture of what things are being discussed at the Capitol."

"Why are you talking about an outbreak? An outbreak of what?" Kenzie did her best to bluff, speaking in a tone that implied she didn't have a clue about any outbreak and how it might be related to Willis Cartwright.

"It's a benign virus," Walter said. "You'll get everyone all stirred up over something that isn't even a danger. People carry around these viruses their whole life without being impacted by them. They don't even have symptoms. Maybe sometimes they get stressed out and one of them gets activated, you get a cold sore on your lip or run a mild fever. You get a sore throat. Is that worth getting everybody in a panic about?"

He didn't say he was talking about herpesviruses, but his words testified that he was. Herpesviruses were notorious for hiding out, inactivated, for years. Until stress set in and then the sufferer started to have symptoms. Usually mild, but occasionally... there could be fatal complications. Not usually the brain pathology that they had seen, but liver failure or other serious complications.

"I don't know what you're talking about," Kenzie said with a shake of her head.

"You can't lie to me, Kenzie." He let go of her hand and rubbed his temples. "I know you are loyal to your job and have to respect the confiden-

440

tiality of the office and of the families of the deceased. And even if you didn't," his eyes were sad, "you wouldn't tell me about it. You think we're on opposite sides, but we're not. I just want what's best for you. And for the state."

"The governor, you mean. You want him to be re-elected."

"No. It's never been about the individuals. You know me and what I do. It's the people I care about. All the people who depend on me to help protect their rights and keep the government and large corporations accountable. That's what I care about. Not the money. Not the governor. All of the people who could be affected."

"You think this is nothing. Just the sniffles."

He nodded. "More or less."

"You don't think it is the cause of death for Willie Cartwright or anyone else."

"No. I don't. If it was that bad, you would be hearing about it before bodies started hitting the morgue. Yes, Mr. Cartwright may have had it when he died, but that doesn't mean he died as a result of it. After all of this, what goes down on his death certificate will likely be natural causes. And if it did have something to do with his death... then it's because he was an old man with a compromised immune system."

Kenzie sighed. So far, she didn't have anything to suggest that he was wrong. They hadn't had time to figure out the way the virus worked and whether it contributed to Cartwright's death or not. And if it had, then, as Walter said, he was an old man and that was not unexpected. Seniors died from influenza too. Thousands every year.

"You've said your piece," she said finally. "I'm not in authority at the Medical Examiner's Office anyway. Even if I wanted to push Cartwright's certificate through, it isn't my job."

"You do have some influence, though," Walter suggested, his eyes glittering. With Walter Kirsch, it was always about influence.

"No. I'm just an assistant. I'm there to answer phones and to learn."

After Kenzie saw Walter to the door, she returned to the living room to talk to Zachary. He watched the man get into his car and drive away before he turned back to Kenzie.

"So, that was your dad," he said lightly.

"Yeah. I'll bet you were really impressed."

He shrugged. "Better than mine. Trust me, you wouldn't like him either."

"I don't dislike my dad," Kenzie hurried to clarify. "But I don't trust him. His moral compass... well, you can probably tell, it isn't the same as mine."

Zachary nodded understandingly. He lifted each seat cushion on the couch and swept his hand underneath through all the cracks and crevices. Kenzie watched him put them back down and then shake out each of the throw blankets and decorative pillows. He arranged them again neatly.

This was new behavior. Paranoia? OCD? Probably something that should be reported to Zachary's medical team.

Zachary looked at her sideways. "Bugs."

"What?" Kenzie shook her head. He was concerned about bugs crawling around under the seat cushions?

He finished tidying the couch and went on to check the underside of the side table, then walked out to the front door, scanning the walls and running his fingers around the doorframe molding and picture frames.

"They want to keep an eye on you. You're his window into the Medical Examiner's Office. He knew he wasn't going to make any difference by coming here to talk to you. Would he ever be able to talk you into altering records at the office? Would you be able to talk Dr. Wiltshire into changing his mind on a cause of death determination, even if you wanted him to?"

"Well, no. It would be pretty rare. You got him to reopen a couple of cases. But that's pretty rare."

"Exactly. So he came here because they want to keep an eye on you. Or an ear."

Zachary returned to the living room and opened the soft-sided briefcase that housed his mobile office. He pushed things around until he found what he was looking for, then turned on a device he held in the palm of his hand and extended the antenna on it. Kenzie watched as he began to sweep it back and forth in slow arcs around where Walter had been sitting. As he turned to talk to Kenzie, the device gave a squawk. He started to pass it over her like a security wand at an airport. It squawked a couple more times. Zachary nodded to Kenzie's purse.

"In there, I think. Can I look?"

Kenzie handed it to him. She had come straight into the house and into the visit with her father upon returning home from work. Her purse had been sitting beside the couch while they had been talking. Certainly within reach of the man, but she hadn't seen him touch it.

Zachary removed the contents of Kenzie's bag a few items at a time, passing the bug-finder over them and then reaching back in. When the purse was empty, he felt around the pockets and lining, and eventually came up with a small, round, black device with a pin at one end to make sure it would stay where it was placed and not be jostled around too much by Kenzie putting things into or taking them out of her bag.

Kenzie was stunned. She knew that her father had crossed the line more than once in the past. He always claimed to be on the side of the angels and things had always turned out okay in the end. But bugging his own daughter's handbag?

"He knows that you take it into work," Zachary said. "He didn't just want to hear the conversations between you and me. That wouldn't be very enlightening. He wanted to hear what was going on at the office."

He ran the antenna around Kenzie once more and it didn't squawk. He walked to the front door and back, moving the electronic device slowly until he was sure that there wasn't another bug in the front hall, then returned. He shut it off, pushed the antenna back in, and stowed it back in his bag.

Kenzie sat in the living room as Zachary went about in the kitchen, getting something together for dinner. Kenzie just stared at Zachary's bag. She couldn't believe that her own father would betray her like that. The only reason he had shown up at her house was to be able to put a bug on her? A bug that she would then take with her back to work so that he and the governor and whoever else was putting pressure on Dr. Wiltshire could listen to their conversations. It was unbelievable.

When she had been a little girl, she always saw Walter as a sort of knight in shining armor. The way that he and Lisa described the work they did—how he helped to protect people from big companies that wanted to take their money and big government that wanted to take away their rights—he had seemed larger than life to Kenzie. He was her protector and the protector of everyone else in the state. Kenzie grew up and adjusted to a more mature world view. And then Amanda had died and she had seen him as something else. Someone willing to bend and break a few rules to get what he wanted. He would put his ethics behind him if they prevented him from protecting his family or getting his own way. He had excused his behavior, saying that it had been for Amanda, just as he would justify his conduct in this case, saying that it was for the greater good, but it wasn't.

But she wasn't sure Walter was a bad guy, either. He did what he did out of love and passion and a sense of fair dealing. He really did believe in the causes that he lobbied for. And if he occasionally went a little overboard, out of passion, did that make him a bad person?

But he had tried to use her. To spy on her. She couldn't deny what she had seen. She didn't know how he had managed to slip the bug into her purse without either of them realizing it, but was grateful that Zachary had seen through his mask and had taken the time to check.

"Do you want some dinner?" Zachary asked tentatively, framed in the kitchen doorway.

"Yeah... I need to eat, but I don't know what I want..."

"I heated up some of those frozen burritos. I know it's not a great supper, but..."

"That's just fine," Kenzie said. She forced herself to get up off the couch, even though her body felt so heavy and slow that she could barely move it. She wanted to go to bed. To shut off.

But her feet moved in the direction she pointed them and she walked into the kitchen and sat down in her chair. Zachary had managed to heat a couple of burritos without filling the kitchen with smoke and had even melted cheese over top of hers.

"I thought you couldn't cook," Kenzie teased, giving him a weak smile. "You've been holding out on me."

"I was focused." Zachary smiled, his neck starting to get red. "I knew you needed me to get something ready, so I had a mission and I stuck to it."

"You did good." Kenzie knew how hard that was for him, even if it seemed like a simple thing for her. "Thank you."

Zachary sat down, then bounced back out of his chair to get the carton of milk out of the fridge for Kenzie. "Unless you want something stronger..."

Kenzie thought about it. She wouldn't mind a bit of chemical help to get relaxed. But she shook her head. Zachary always said that he didn't mind her drinking when he couldn't, but she always felt a bit awkward about it anyway. And she needed a clear head to think things through, even though her brain was trying to shut her down.

Zachary poured milk in her glass and sat down again, looking around the table to see if there was anything else he had forgotten. He apparently decided there was not and cut off a bite of his burrito.

"Do you think you're safe?" he asked in a neutral tone.

Kenzie looked at him, shocked. "Am I safe? Of course I am. Why wouldn't I be?"

"If he's working with the governor... there has to be some big money involved. And big guns. When people like that start putting you under surveillance... well, they're probably willing to go farther, if they have to."

"Yeah, like what?" Kenzie laughed, shaking her head. "This isn't a TV thriller. I can't even believe he would plant a bug on me. The only other person who has ever done anything like that was... well... you."

She could remember how angry she had been when she had a mechanic put her car up on a lift to check for any foreign objects, and they had discovered a tracker mounted on the inside of her rear bumper. It was before she and Zachary were serious, and had been such an invasion of her privacy that she had immediately stopped talking to him.

The red flush rose from Zachary's neck to his cheeks and ears. "Uh... yeah. That was stupid, and I'm really sorry about all of the crap I put you through..."

"I understand that you were anxious and that you wanted to protect the people you were close to. But it really was over the line."

"I know." It had been almost two years ago now. They had alluded to it once or twice since getting back together, and Zachary always apologized and looked embarrassed by his own behavior. "But since we changed my meds around, and I started seeing Dr. B regularly... it's been better. I haven't done that—anything like that—since then."

Kenzie didn't actually think that he had. She kept a pretty close eye on his mental state and how he acted around her, and she watched for any signs that he was trying to hide things from her or cover up his activities. Of course, there were many hours in the day when she couldn't monitor what he was doing. He could be having an affair and bugging everything she owned. The bug in her purse could have been his, rather than Walter's. Except then he wouldn't have had a reason to find it there and show it to her.

"What did you do with the bug?"

"I drowned it."

Kenzie looked over at the kitchen sink, filled with water, and grinned. "Well, I guess we don't need to worry about anyone overhearing this conversation, then."

"No. It's just you and me."

"Unless he or someone else has bugged another area of the house."

"No." Zachary's voice was confident. "No other bugs."

"How could you know that? Someone else might have left something here another time. Or I might be bugging you to keep track of you during the day."

He shook his head.

He was so sure about it that Kenzie was unnerved. "How could you possibly know that?"

"Because I check."

"You check?" Kenzie repeated. She thought about the bug detector in his bag. Right there where it was close at hand. How paranoid was he? Did he actually think that she might be bugging him?

"Not every day," Zachary assured her, as if *that* might be considered over the top. "But... every few."

"You sweep this house for bugs every few days."

"Yes."

"Why?"

He blinked at her, as if only realizing now that this might not be considered normal behavior. "To... keep you safe. To protect your privacy. Make sure that no one is watching or listening to us when we're here. After that business with that cartel, especially... it wouldn't be a good idea to assume that they believed what they were told and weren't checking up on us. On me. I don't want any harm to come to you because of what I do. It's just like you having a burglar alarm. An extra layer of protection."

"Well... I appreciate it. But I would have liked to know about it before. I think that's the kind of thing you might want to tell me about."

"Oh." Zachary took another bite of his burrito and chewed, thinking about that. "I just figured... you wouldn't want to know. You'd feel better not having to think about it."

"No, I think I want to know if you think that there are bad guys after you. Or me."

"Hmm." He stared down at his plate, not at her.

"What?"

"I think... are you sure?"

"Am I sure I want to know? Yes, I am."

He scratched the back of his neck. "I think... you should consider... who your father is working with, and what their stakes are."

"Really?"

He didn't say anything. Kenzie poked at her burrito. She cut a few pieces off and worried them rather than putting them into her mouth. Her stomach was roiling. Probably best not to add a bunch of beans to that fermenting mess.

"You think I'm in danger?"

She didn't want to discount his expert opinion. Yes, he was anxious, even paranoid at times. He had PTSD and the least trigger could set him off. She was sure that just having her father parking at the curb for that hour had wound his brain up into overdrive, which might explain why he was so concerned for her welfare. But he'd been right about the bug. And he'd dealt with unsavory characters and criminals who wanted him out of the way before. And Kenzie herself had learned before that just because someone seemed kindly and safe, that didn't mean that they were. She'd been fooled in the past. That was one reason she wanted him to tell her suspicions, even if she did think that they might just be imagination. She needed to know what to watch for.

"Maybe. It's possible. Or, he may want to keep an eye on you to make sure you're *not* in any danger. But that would still mean that you might be in danger from others."

"Yeah. I guess either way... I should take extra precautions."

Zachary blew out a breath, nodding. His shoulders dipped down. He'd been holding himself tense. It was a relief for him that she had seen his point and would consider what she needed to do to protect herself.

"Maybe I could help out for a few days, just to make sure everything is okay."

"Like what?"

"Drive you to work. Or follow and make sure no one is watching you. Maybe put a tracker in your car and in your bag. So I know where you are if there is any trouble."

"Oh, so we're back to trackers now, are we?"

He shrugged. "Only if you said yes. Not covertly."

"I'll think about it."

"And... can I help with this case that you're working on? I know you've been worried about it."

"You do?" Kenzie looked across the table at Zachary. "How do you know that?"

"I can see it. That you're worried. That you're getting stressed about work and trying to figure out what's going on."

"Well, yeah. I am."

"Can I help? Is there any way? I know you can't tell me anything confidential, but if there is something you need. Something I could help with. I'd really like to."

"No, there isn't anything you can do," Kenzie said immediately, discounting the idea.

"Well... think about it. You know I rely on your medical knowledge when I'm trying to sort out a case with medical involvement. Think about whether there are things that my expertise could help with. Skip tracing. Surveillance. Background research."

"I'll think about it," Kenzie agreed. "But I don't think there is anything you can do."

55

Kenzie was trying to read a book sitting in bed to quiet her mind and Zachary, sitting with her, was looking through email or messages on his phone. "You know," Kenzie ventured, "There might be one thing you could do to help me out. With our investigation at work, I mean."

Zachary lowered his phone immediately. "Sure. What do you need?"

"I need to track someone down. I've been trying to call her or get into her building, but I haven't had any luck. It would probably take you an hour, and you'd not only know if she still lives there, but also most of her life story."

Zachary smiled. "Not all of that, but I can probably track her down for you. What do you know?"

Kenzie outlined the details she had on Francine Mudd, the woman who had owned Lola before the dog ended up being given to the nurses at Champlain House. Zachary tapped details into his phone, nodding.

"How long since she's lived at this address, do you know?"

"I don't think it could be long. Maybe a few weeks or months. It was recent."

"I should be able to track her down."

"That would really help. We need to talk to her about something. Related to the case."

Zachary didn't ask what it was. He was very good at not asking her about things that might be confidential. He didn't usually ask her directly about the cases the Medical Examiner's Office was working on, though sometimes he heard things through other channels. Kenzie shared interesting tidbits when she thought it would be okay. Non-identifying things so she wouldn't be breaching anyone's privacy. She didn't actually have any live clients.

"You're careful at work, right?" Zachary asked after finishing his phone notes and setting the phone onto the nightstand on his side of the bed.

"Careful about what?" Kenzie asked. "I'm not sure what you're talking about."

"Just... your dad was talking about viruses and whether they could kill anyone... I don't want you to do anything that might be dangerous. I can't do anything to protect you from microscopic invaders."

"Oh, that." Kenzie nodded. "Well, he was really talking out of school. It isn't anything that I can discuss."

"That's okay. I don't expect you to. I just hope... you're taking precautions. I don't know. Wearing a mask and gloves. Whatever else doctors are required to do to avoid viruses spreading. Sealing them off or showers or whatever."

"Of course. We are very careful." But Kenzie was mindful of what Dr. Wiltshire had said about viruses escaping from labs. It happened, even when scientists thought they were taking all the proper steps to keep them isolated. The morgue was not sealed from the rest of the building. Not normally. They could take measures if they thought that a case might involve biohazards, but they usually didn't wear hermetically sealed suits or set up air locks between the autopsy room and the outside world.

"Good."

Kenzie put her book down. Even if she wanted to, she knew she wasn't going to be reading anything else. Her eyes just kept going over the same information.

"Let's see if we can get some sleep."

Zachary turned off the light on his side of the bed and waited for Kenzie to turn off her light and cuddle up to him.

***

Kenzie wondered from Dr. Wiltshire's face the next day if something had happened overnight. A child's death or one of those other heartbreaking cases that made everybody depressed as they handled the body and other evidence. Trying to look past the tragedy of a life cut short and just focus on the evidence.

"Morning, doctor."

"Kenzie... I need you to prep Mr. Cartwright's body for transport. The funeral home will be picking him up later today."

"Oh." Kenzie was surprised. "Have you made a ruling on cause of death, then?"

"We're still waiting for a few tests to come back, so no, I'm not ready... But we've collected everything we need to, and his family is waiting to hold a funeral." He shrugged. "I think that we need to move on to other cases; we've got a few that need to be cleared out. I've been spending too much time on this possible outbreak. There's really no reason to think that this virus is any worse than typical HHV-4. Mankind has been dealing with Epstein Barr for hundreds, possibly thousands of years."

"Okay." Kenzie didn't want to argue with him about it. Maybe if he released Cartwright's body, the political pressure would go away and she wouldn't have to worry about her father or anyone else who might feel like making trouble. "Any... special precautions to be taken? Do you want me to say something to the funeral home about the possibility of contaminants?"

"HHV-4 is not known to be dangerous," Dr. Wiltshire said flatly. "You can tell them he is positive and they should take appropriate action. Wear gloves and a mask, avoid any physical contact with fluids. They would do all of that anyway, but if you remind them... then we've done our duty."

"Is everything okay, Dr. Wiltshire?"

"Yes, of course, Kenzie. Everything is just fine. Take care of that for me, won't you?"

"Sure."

He went on to his office. Kenzie did as she had promised, going into the morgue and preparing Cartwright's remains for pick-up.

Kenzie's phone rang just before noon. Kenzie considered ignoring it, claiming that she was already on her lunch break and wandering down to the vending machine to see if anything edible had been stocked.

Then she saw who it was. Zachary.

"Hey, Zach. How's it going?" She tried to sound as relaxed and unstressed as possible for his sake.

"Good. I have contact information for you for Francine Mudd."

"Already?" Kenzie smiled. "You don't know how much I appreciate that."

Zachary carefully dictated to her the information he had gathered, which was, as Kenzie had expected, a little more than just her phone number and address. The reason she was no longer at the old address was that it had been her boyfriend's apartment, and they had since broken up. She was now back to living on her own—in a dog-free building, Kenzie assumed—and usually worked evenings as a waitress or hostess.

"Perfect. That's really helpful."

"Are you going to talk to her today?"

"Yes, if I can," Kenzie agreed.

Zachary was silent in response. Kenzie tried to figure out if she were supposed to have given him a different answer.

"Okay," Zachary said eventually. "I'll see you later, then."

"See you tonight," Kenzie agreed.

Kenzie decided that sooner was better than later, and if she were to go out, she could avoid eating something from the vending machine. She could stop and get some good takeout, or even just a grocery store salad, and save herself from the questionable sandwiches and other items in the vending machine.

So she headed out right away. She would talk to Francine Mudd and see what information she could offer and still be able to get back to the Medical Examiner's Office to get a few more things done and shut down for the day.

It would probably have been wise to call ahead, but Kenzie didn't want to give Francine an opportunity to offer any excuse for not being able to talk. So she found the woman's apartment and knocked on the door. She hadn't even had to get Francine to let her in through the double set of doors in the vestibule downstairs. A delivery man had been let in ahead of Kenzie. She caught the door and continued as if she belonged there. No one stopped her.

She rapped sharply on the door, intending for it to sound brisk and businesslike. It was a couple of minutes before a woman arrived at the door. Kenzie looked her over, frowning.

"Are you Francine Mudd?"

"Yes. And you are...?"

Kenzie had expected the woman to say that she was Francine's mother. She had imagined Francine to be a college student, someone just trying to make it on her own for the first time. Living in cheap apartments. Getting a dog and then not being able to take care of it. Breaking up with her boyfriend. Working as a waitress. All those things had predisposed her to think of Francine Mudd as a young woman, not the middle-aged woman who stood in front of her.

"Oh. Sorry. My name is Kenzie Kirsch. I'm with the Medical Examiner's Office."

"Has someone died?"

"No. Well, yes, people have died, but not someone directly connected with you."

"Oh, good. You scared me for a minute; I thought that maybe…"

"I'm sorry. I should be more careful. I'm actually here about Lola."

"Lola?"

"A dog you used to own."

"Oh. That Lola. Well, she isn't dead, is she? And if she was, it wouldn't be handled through your office."

"No. We're looking into a death that occurred at the senior center where Lola is living. I was asked to look into Lola's background as part of our survey of the environment."

"Why would you need to know about Lola?"

"Well, she was with him when he died. It's just routine, ma'am. Do you think I could come in? We could sit down and work through these questions and then I'll be on my way."

"I suppose." Francine opened her door the rest of the way to allow Kenzie in. She led Kenzie to a clean, neat, bright sitting room done in a sort of grandmotherly style. Old furniture with light upholstery or accents, needlework hung on the walls, and smelling faintly of roses or another perfume.

"This is very nice."

"It's comfortable," Francine said, looking around to evaluate it. She acted as if it weren't actually her place, but just somewhere she had landed for the day.

"So tell me about Lola. Did you get her when she was a puppy?"

"No. She belonged to a friend of the family. He passed away, and everyone thought I should take Lola. She wasn't left specifically to me. But no one else could take her. I was living somewhere that allowed dogs at the time, and Jay said he didn't mind, so I took her in. She's not a young dog. She's… mature."

Kenzie nodded encouragingly. "And your family friend? What did he die of?"

"I don't know. I think it was maybe a stroke. Something quick. By the time anyone found him, it was too late. He had a bad heart, you know. He'd always said that. Had this surgery a few years ago to replace faulty valves. He said he was doing better. But then…" Francine trailed off.

"Yes. I'm sorry to hear that. What was his name?"

"Do you need that? It seems to me that you don't need to document the dog's entire life to do... whatever this is. An investigation into a death. You said someone at the nursing home died, right?"

"Yes. This is just background information, but I do need to know who owned her before you did."

"I can't imagine why," Francine muttered. But she was on the move, walking over to a side table with a tiny drawer in it, from which she removed an address book. "Eugene Hopewell. No current address or phone number," she added tartly.

Kenzie smiled. She liked Francine. "Thank you. Much appreciated. And when Lola was with you... was she ever sick?"

"Sick? No, I don't think so. Dogs eat things and throw up sometimes... or eat things and get the runs... or they roll in something or get sprayed by a skunk. But nothing, really, she was a nice dog to have around. Friendly. Never bit anyone even if they deserved it."

"No viruses or infections that you knew of."

"No."

"And where did Eugene live, when he was still alive? Was he in a nursing home? Or in an apartment building or a house...?"

"He lived on his own. In a little bungalow."

"Where was that, do you know? Do you have the address?"

Francine looked down at her address book and gave the address to Kenzie. Kenzie wrote it down along with his name.

"That's really helpful. And when you had Lola, you lived here?" Kenzie looked around at the small apartment.

"No. I was with my boyfriend at the time. Lived at his place. I told you that."

"Oh, of course. And that was at..." Kenzie looked through her notes and read off the address that she had previously visited in hopes of meeting Lola's owner.

"Yes, that's right. Is that everything?"

"Almost done. Does your boyfriend still live there? If I wanted to see the place that Lola lived, do you think he would talk to me? Maybe you could call him and let him know that I'm not some crank?"

"As far as I know, you could be. I'm not really in touch with him anymore. It was a mutual break, but... we didn't stay friends. As far as I know, he is still in the same place, but he could have moved. He wouldn't have bothered to tell me, and we don't have mutual friends."

"Do you have his phone number?"

Francine flipped the pages in her address book to refresh her memory. Kenzie could see that his information had been struck through. But Francine was still able to read it and nodded after she recited the phone number. "Yes, that's his number," she confirmed.

"I really appreciate you taking the time. Thank you so much."

"You're welcome." Francine stood up. "I hope you find everything you're looking for."

As Kenzie left Francine's apartment, her phone buzzed. She looked down at it to see if she had received a text message and saw a calendar reminder that she was supposed to be at couples therapy with Zachary. She swore and double-checked the time. She had completely forgotten that they had an appointment. And Zachary had, she thought, carefully avoided mentioning it or reminding her, maybe testing to see if she would show up this time without any pressure from his end. But it was a thirty-minute warning reminder, which meant she still had time to get there.

She climbed into the car and headed toward Dr. Boyle's office. On the way, she hit her Bluetooth button and called Dr. Wiltshire.

"Kenzie."

"Hi. Uh—I forgot that today is my early day so I can get to therapy with Zachary. I'm sorry. I've left a bunch of stuff up in the air there that I planned to get back to after I talked to Lola's owner."

"I should have remembered this was your usual day."

"Well, so should I," Kenzie said in embarrassment. "If you'll just leave everything where it is, I'll pop back over after I'm done the session and finish up. Is that okay?"

"I can just put your files away and you can pick it up again tomorrow."

"I know, but I really do need to get some of it done today. It's not very good planning on my part."

"We all forget things sometimes. Things have been a little disrupted lately. I'm sure that your files can wait until tomorrow."

"I still prefer to come back in. So just leave them; I'll get them put away tonight."

"Okay," Dr. Wiltshire agreed with a chuckle. "I won't touch anything."

Kenzie checked the time after she parked. It was still ten minutes until the appointment with Dr. Boyle, so she didn't need to rush in, looking all disheveled and apologizing for having forgotten about the appointment. As far as anyone other than Dr. Wiltshire knew, she had remembered all along that she had an appointment. She was a responsible adult. Missing one session didn't make her irresponsible. Just a busy person who sometimes got caught up in things.

She locked the car and walked into Dr. Boyle's waiting room calmly. Zachary was sitting in one of the chairs, elbows on knees, face cradled in his hands. He looked up when he heard Kenzie enter and a smile blossomed on his face.

"Kenzie!"

"Hi." Kenzie made a show of checking the time. "I'm not late, am I?"

"No. Still five minutes to. I'm just... glad you made it."

"Of course. I know I missed the last session, but that's not going to be a regular occurrence. It was just one mistake."

He nodded agreeably. "Of course. You don't forget things like that."

Kenzie let out a breath. No. Of course not. She wouldn't just get busy with something else and forget all about their appointment. Again.

When the session was over, Kenzie was tired and emotionally wrung out, but she had promised Dr. Wiltshire that she would be back to the office, so she explained to Zachary that she needed to spend another hour or two there and then would be home.

"We can have our ice cream today after supper if that's okay with you?"

They had instituted a reward of ice cream following couples therapy to reward themselves for going and doing something that was difficult for both of them. A reward that had been Kenzie's idea. Although Zachary seemed to have taken to it without any difficulty.

"Oh." Zachary looked disappointed, lowering his eyes and fiddling with his key as they prepared to get into their separate vehicles. "Yeah, that would be fine."

"Sorry, I don't mean to screw up the routine. But I really do need to spend some more time at the office today, make sure everything is in order."

"Yeah, of course. Work is important."

"That doesn't mean it's more important than you or our relationship. It just means I need to spend a bit more time there before we can relax."

He nodded.

"I made it here," Kenzie pointed out. "I didn't just work through. That wouldn't have been fair to you, and I've made a commitment to go to these sessions. I'm glad we're doing them."

"Yeah. Well, I'll see you later, then. After work."

Kenzie nodded and suppressed the impulse to apologize to him again. She had explained. He had accepted. She needed to just move on. She would see him again once she was done, and then she could give him her full attention.

The morgue was as silent as... well... a morgue. Kenzie worked through the files she had left on her desk, checked quickly through her email to see what else was awaiting her attention, and decided to tidy up and get on her way. She stowed away the files she hadn't worked on yet and took the ones she had completed into Dr. Wiltshire's office for his review and approval the next day.

His office was in disarray. Dr. Wiltshire was usually pretty tidy, so Kenzie was surprised to see papers on his desk, books and ornaments out of place on his shelf, and his computer screen turned at a different angle from usual, as if he had been displaying it to someone else in the office with him. And maybe he had. She didn't remember him setting up any appointments for the afternoon, but since she hadn't remembered her own appointment, she couldn't rely on her memory.

She spent a few minutes straightening everything back to the way Dr. Wiltshire liked them and looked through the papers and files on his desk. It was going to take longer than she had expected to get out of the office and home. Still, she would rather know she was going back to an environment where everything was tidy and sorted for her and Dr. Wiltshire's arrival than to think about how much work she was going to have to do as soon as she got there in the morning to put things shipshape.

It took half an hour to get his desk put back to rights. Kenzie sighed and turned off his light, then moved on to the autopsy room and cold storage to make sure that if any new remains had been signed in, all the paperwork was in order and she was aware of who their most recent guests were.

As she opened the door, she heard the clatter of sample jars. The sudden, unexpected noise made her jump. Apparently, she wasn't as alone as she had thought.

"Hello?" Kenzie called out, walking into the autopsy room. "Who's here?"

Something was wrong. Surgical tools had been knocked to the floor and not picked back up. There was no body on the table, but there were evidence bins on the counter. Kenzie hadn't left them there, and Dr. Wiltshire would not leave them there when he went home. Only while he was in the process of conducting an autopsy.

"Doctor?"

There was no answer, but there was more banging and movement from the evidence room and the cold storage. Who was there? The night shift could be bringing in some remains, but she hadn't seen or heard anything while she was at her computer to indicate another body being brought in. No texts or messages, nothing in her email. Something could have happened while she was working in Dr. Wiltshire's office, but if a call-out had just been made, they wouldn't be bringing the remains in already.

"Carlos?"

Something was wrong. The space didn't feel right. It didn't smell right, like someone had walked through it carrying their lunch or cut flowers and had left their imprint on the air behind. Kenzie walked across autopsy and opened the door to the cold storage room.

A black shape hurtled toward her and they collided. Strong hands grasped her wrist and shoulder and threw her to the floor. Kenzie tried to catch herself with her hands, but it happened too quickly and she landed on her shoulders and the back of her head, a blow that sent yellow lightning racing through her brain.

"Hey!" Kenzie protested. She tried to get up, but the figure that had hit her was receding, hurrying away from her now. There were shouts, but she couldn't sort out the words. "Stop! Hey!" She couldn't seem to come up with anything more coherent than that. Her knees were wobbly and getting to her feet did not seem possible. If she had a chair, maybe she could use that to get herself up. She felt around herself, disoriented, not sure what might be within reach. Could she reach the counter to pull herself up?

Her fingers encountered a twisted plastic cord, and when Kenzie pulled on it, something came clattering down on her head. A phone. Kenzie tried to orient the phone in the proper position and to focus on it. How many times had she used it to call out to someone in the building? She wasn't sure which end was up, couldn't bring her eyes into focus on the numbers on the buttons. She pushed several buttons in a row, trying to remember where the zero and the nine were on the keypad. There was a tiny voice from the receiver. Kenzie held it up to her ear.

"Trouble in autopsy," she managed to get out a halfway coherent sentence. "Help. Now."

57

Kenzie was still sitting on the floor, but was upright, with the cabinets behind her back, while she applied ice to the back of her head and tried to sound normal and unflustered as she spoke to Detective Cameron, who crouched beside her.

"Did you get a good look at their faces?" Cameron asked. "Was it anyone you recognized?"

"No. I didn't see anything. Heard noises. Called out. Went to see what was going on. But the one I saw—it was just a shape; I have no idea... no idea who it was or what he looked like."

"That's okay. Perfectly understandable. But this is a secure building. You can't get in without identification, without going through security checkpoints."

"I don't know. Don't know what happened, how they got here. When they got here." Kenzie continued to shake her head, even though it was making her a bit giddy. "I was working late..."

"Were they here when you got in?"

"Maybe. I don't know. Everything was quiet... I decided to close up and go home. Went to Dr. Wiltshire's office. It was a mess."

"Dr. Wiltshire's office had been tossed?"

Kenzie thought about that. It had been disorderly, but not like on TV when there were slash marks in all the upholstery where they had searched for hidden evidence. But Dr. Wiltshire had never left his room in disarray like that before.

"Files and papers that should have been put away were out. Things had been moved on his shelves... things he wouldn't normally even touch during the day. You know, medical texts, ornaments. He might take out one text at a time and then put it away when he was done, but with so much being available online now, there wasn't really even much need for him to look something up on paper."

"Did you call anyone when you saw it had been left in a mess?"

"No. I didn't think... that there was an intruder. I just thought that he'd been... upset or in a state when he left. Something upset him, or he got a call-out. I don't know. He seemed worried this morning, and I just thought... it was a continuation."

"So what did you do?"

Kenzie raised her brows and looked Cameron in the eye. "I tidied up."

He laughed.

Kenzie couldn't say she was sure what there was to laugh about, but she was glad he saw the humor in the situation.

"Of course."

"That's my job."

"You're medical staff, not cleaners." It was half a statement, half a question.

"Yes... but I'm his admin as well. So it's normal for me to file stuff at the end of the day. Make sure that everything has been checked in or out correctly. Just generally... make sure everyone keeps their rooms clean."

Cameron nodded, still smiling. Kenzie shifted the ice pack to find a colder spot. The lump on the back of her head was beginning to throb. She winced and waited for it to settle down again.

"So what did you do after cleaning up the doctor's office?"

"I went to check things out in storage and check-in, make sure all of the tests that were supposed to go out had gone, see if we got any other remains while I was gone, that kind of thing."

"While you were gone?"

"I was out. I had a... personal medical appointment."

"Would anyone have known that?"

"Well... a few people, I guess. Julie covers my desk sometimes, so she knows that some Wednesday afternoons, I have an appointment. Dr. Wiltshire knew; I talked to him on the phone earlier to confirm that. Uh... I don't know. Anyone who works closely with the office probably knows that I am away some Wednesday afternoons."

"What time do you usually get back from that appointment?"

"Usually, I don't. I just go home from the doctor's office. But today, I had some other things I needed to clear up before I could go home."

"So normally, at this time, the suite would have been empty."

"Yes."

"And people know that."

"I guess. Not a lot, but yeah... people do know."

It would make sense that if someone wanted to mess with things at the Medical Examiner's Office, they would pick a time when Kenzie wasn't supposed to be there. When it should have been empty and silent.

Kenzie shifted the ice pack again. "Did they get anything? Take anything away?"

"You'll need to check against your inventory. Things have been rifled. Broken. I don't know if anything has been taken."

"I'd better look." Kenzie moved to stand up.

"Are you sure you should be getting up?" Cameron held out his hand as if to grab her or to steady her. "You should sit until you're sure..."

Kenzie leaned against the counter and waited for the head rush to subside. He was probably right. She should wait for a while longer until she was absolutely sure she was okay and that she was steady on her feet. But once the blobs of color stopped flashing before her eyes, she looked around, scanning to see what was out on the counter and what might be missing from the bins.

She had a growing feeling of dread as she looked at the labels on the sample bottles. The glass was cold against her hands.

"We should probably put these things back in the fridge."

"Can you tell what's missing?" Cameron asked. "Is there anything?"

"Yeah." Kenzie shook her head. "All of the Cartwright samples. And Sexton's." She rubbed her forehead. "Uh... the John Doe. Or former John Doe. And the new one, no identity yet."

"That's a lot of samples."

"It's most of our latest cases. What's left... these are mostly older samples that we needed to retest for something."

"Are all of those cases related?"

"No. Just because they are recent." She didn't tell him that Cartwright and Sexton might be related. "Most of them... I think we still have the remains, so we'll be able to get new samples." Kenzie looked toward the cold room. "Do you know if they... took any bodies?"

"If you could have a look; I don't know your cataloging system and don't want to screw anything up."

"Yeah. I'll see."

"Kenzie! Kenzie, are you all right?" Dr. Wiltshire hurried into the room. It was a tight space for two people, a long, narrow room with a counter, designed for one person to work at a time. Dr. Wiltshire squeezed himself in anyway and took Kenzie by the shoulder. "Are you okay? What happened? There was a break in?"

"Yes. I don't know who it was," Kenzie told him. "Or how they got in."

"We'll leave that to the police to sort out. I just want to make sure you are okay."

"Just a bump." Kenzie indicated her head. "Nothing serious. They took samples. We have to make sure they didn't take the bodies too."

"Who would do that?"

"I don't know. I don't understand it..." Kenzie's thoughts were still so scattered from the attack that she couldn't come up with an explanation. "I don't understand why anyone would want to break into the morgue."

"I'll check the inventory. Don't you worry about it." Dr. Wiltshire turned to Detective Cameron. "Has someone looked at her? Checked to see if she has a concussion? Sometimes these things are more serious than they look at first."

"There were a couple of paramedics here. They cleared her. Said she could go to the hospital if she wanted to, but everything looked fine."

Dr. Wiltshire squeezed Kenzie's shoulder again, looking worriedly into her eyes.

Kenzie was reminded of her father holding her hand to comfort her at the same time as he was putting a listening bug in her purse. Was Dr. Wiltshire just acting? Pretending to be concerned and searching her face to see if she had any suspicions?

But that didn't make sense. He had known that she was coming back. He was the one person who had known that she would return to spend a couple more hours clearing files. If he had arranged a break-in, he would have known to make it later at night.

"They were in your office too," Kenzie told Dr. Wiltshire. "You should look to see if anything is missing. I didn't realize... I thought you had just left stuff out. I cleaned up and didn't even know that someone else had been in the room. I should have realized."

His face paled. "In my office? What are they looking for?"

"I think... anything to do with Willis Cartwright. The samples that were taken from here were all taken since his intake. Somebody outside the office wouldn't know how the numbering system worked. It looks like they just went by the dates on the samples."

"But Cartwright..."

He didn't have to say it. Kenzie could see exactly where he was going. "We released Cartwright today," she finished for him.

"Yes." He swore and hit the heel of his hand to his forehead. "I should have known! I should *not* have released him!"

"He'll just be at the funeral home. Even if they have started the embalming, we can still get some samples. And everything that has been done so far is on the computer, all documented."

Cameron looked back and forth between Kenzie and Dr. Wiltshire. "What's going on? You think this Cartwright was the target of the break-in? What is he, mob?"

"No." Kenzie shook her head. "An old man who died at a nursing home."

Cameron's nostrils flared. "Why would anyone be interested in him?"

Kenzie looked at Dr. Wiltshire. He shook his head. "We'll tell you when we're in a more secure location."

Cameron looked around at the various law enforcement officers who were moving around the suite. "I don't think you can get much more secure than this."

"It will have to wait," Dr. Wiltshire said firmly. "Kenzie... can you call the funeral home? Confirm that we need a hold put on the body. I'll check in with the lab and let them know there has been a breach. They'll want to increase their security as well. If this is about the pathogen, they may be the next target."

58

Kenzie walked slowly out to her desk to sit on her own chair and be surrounded by her familiar things while she made the call. She didn't want to search for the phone number on her phone while leaning against the counter in a place where she had just been attacked, trying to keep her balance on shaking legs while her head whirled with disconnected thoughts and vertigo.

She sat for a few minutes, just trying to regain her equilibrium. Then she pulled up her electronic contact list and checked to see which funeral home had picked up Mr. Cartwright's remains.

After talking to the funeral home, she tried to call Dr. Wiltshire, but his phone rang through to voicemail. He was probably on the phone with the lab. Or talking to one of the cops there. He would either call her or come find her when he was ready. She opened her email to work through a few other chores while waiting for him to free himself. She should call Zachary and let him know that she would be later than expected. Except she didn't know yet how long she would be and she didn't want him freaking out over her having been assaulted in the midst of the robbery. She wasn't badly hurt. When she could see him face to face, she would tell him about it, when the evidence that she was okay would be right in front of his eyes.

She logged in to her email, but the system kept asking for her password and then not accepting it. She had a strong suspicion there was a problem with the server, which she couldn't fix. The tech guys would have to fix it in the morning. Kenzie probably wasn't the only one locked out.

She tried to get into the file system and ran into the same problem. Definitely the server, then. There would be a lot of people screaming by the time the techies got it sorted out. Kenzie didn't know if the problem was localized to their own space on the server or whether it would affect all the law enforcement in the building. She hoped the techies got a good sleep, because they would need to use all their brain cells in the morning.

So she played solitaire on her phone until Dr. Wiltshire made his way out to her desk.

"Oh, there you are. How are you managing?"

"Fine. I should head home soon. I don't want Zachary worrying, especially if word of this leaks out before I can get there."

"Yes. You should be able to be on your way in a few minutes. I'm hoping that you talked to the funeral home and they agreed to hold the body until we can get more samples?"

"I got the funeral home—"

"Good. That's a relief!"

"There is a problem, though."

"They wouldn't argue with the Medical Examiner's request to hold the body, would they?"

"It's too late. He's already been cremated."

Dr. Wiltshire's face looked long and drawn, worse than Kenzie had ever seen him on his worst days. He shook his head, looking at her with eyes as hollow as Zachary's.

"What is it?" Kenzie asked. "The lab still has samples there. And we have all of the imaging and test results in our file system."

"I talked to the lab." Dr. Wiltshire shook his head. "Kenzie... they were broken into as well. A security guard is in serious condition. All of their physical samples are gone."

It was no coincidence, then. It wasn't a coincidence that the body had been cremated and all the samples burgled the same day. That left them only the electronic files and the print copies that were in Dr. Wiltshire's office. Kenzie looked at her computer. She wanted to reassure Dr. Wiltshire that not all was lost. They still had access to everything they needed in the file system. Only she couldn't log in. There was a computer glitch that wouldn't be solved until the morning, at least.

"We still have our files."

"When you cleaned up my office, did you see any of the Cartwright reports?"

"No. They would be in your..." Kenzie trailed off as Dr. Wiltshire shook his head.

"Everything couldn't be gone," Kenzie insisted. "There's no way anyone could wipe everything out. What about back-ups? Offsite storage?"

"The lab is going to check theirs. I'm going to give tech support a call tonight to have them look at the system." Dr. Wiltshire nodded to Kenzie's computer. He had apparently tried to log in as well and come to the same conclusion as Kenzie. "If they can't get it up and running... I'll ask them to restore what they can from backup. Assuming that hasn't been destroyed too."

They just looked at each other, unwilling to believe that any third party could have had the audacity to do what had apparently been done. A brute force attack on the Medical Examiner's Office, both physically and electronically. Wiping out everything they had on the Cartwright case.

"What did the lab say about their backups?" Kenzie asked tentatively.

"Savage is quite sure that they have everything saved to several physical and cloud drives. He says that everything is backed up multiple times in multiple places. They've been working hard to map out the virus's genome, figuring out where each piece of RNA originated. He said this may slow them down for a day, but they'll have everything up and running soon. Even without the physical evidence, they still have the raw genome data."

Kenzie walked slowly out to the parking garage. She was feeling more unsteady than she would like to admit, though the lump on her head wasn't throbbing anymore. She still didn't know what to think of everything that had happened. It seemed absurd, like something that would happen in a Jason Bourne movie on TV, not in real life. Fantastical and far-fetched.

"Dr. Kirsch."

"Hi." Kenzie gave the guard a nod and kept walking.

"Dr. Kirsch, wait."

Kenzie waited. She supposed that they had higher security protocols in place than usual after what had happened. They would want to make sure that everything was buttoned down and no one else could walk out with evidence. She turned to Frank, the guard, expecting him to demand to see her security card or to wand her with the metal detector. He got closer to her, what felt like uncomfortably close, but maybe that we just because of what Kenzie had been through that evening. She didn't want anyone getting too close to her.

"I have a message for you."

Kenzie blinked. "A message?" She frowned, thinking about her father and now the men who had attacked her and stolen evidence from the office. Now someone wanted to warn her off? Someone else?

"Your... friend. He said that you should call him."

"What friend?"

"That private investigator." The guard pulled a business card out of his shirt pocket. One of Zachary's. "Him."

Kenzie pulled her phone out to look at it. Zachary hadn't sent her any messages or tried to reach her, even though it was getting late enough that she had been expecting to hear from him. Was her phone dead? In airplane mode? Had they messed with her stupid phone too?

"He said he didn't want to worry you," Frank explained. "He said that if you knew..." He went slowly, trying to get it right. "If you knew *he* knew what had happened to you, then you would be worried about him, so no one was to tell you until you were out."

Kenzie gave a weak laugh. Just like she had avoided calling Zachary because she didn't want him to be worrying about her. He had known what was going on but had let her think that he didn't.

"How did he know?"

"He's a private investigator." Frank shrugged. "Don't ask me where he gets his information."

"So I'm supposed to call him?"

"Yeah. Before you get into your car."

Kenzie case a nervous glance toward her baby. "Why?" she asked tentatively, "What's happened to my car?"

"Nothing, nothing," he held up his hands for her to stop. "Your car is here, safe and sound. But he didn't want you driving."

"Of course." Kenzie tapped Zachary's picture on her phone and waited for him to pick up. Usually, she had to wait for a few rings, and sometimes he didn't even hear her call and she had to try him several times before he was able to pull himself from what he was doing to realize she was trying to get him.

But this time, it was only one ring. "Kenzie?"

"Hey. I'm done. And Frank says I'm supposed to call you."

"Uh, yeah." Zachary gave an uncomfortable, coughing laugh. "I hope you don't mind. I didn't think you should drive."

"I'm fine. And it's not far."

"I'm parked on the street. Just come out, I'll drive you home. I'll drop you in the morning, and Frank will make sure your baby is fine tonight."

"You don't need to do that."

"I'm already here."

Kenzie stood there, stymied. It wasn't really that she even wanted to drive, just that she had planned to, and she was finding it remarkably difficult to change directions. She was usually a flexible person who could weigh all the solutions and pick the one that worked best at the moment, even if it weren't her original plan. But apparently, when she was traumatized and had been hit over the head, it wasn't so easy. Maybe that gave her some insight into Zachary or others she knew who could be very rigid about their plans or routines and had difficulty changing direction when another avenue opened up.

"Where are you?"

"In front of the building. I would have parked at the back entrance, but I didn't want you walking into the alley where it is dark. Nice and bright out front."

"Yeah. That's probably a good idea."

Kenzie waved to Frank and changed directions, exiting out the front of the building instead. There were more guards there, and since she usually entered and left via the parking garage, they didn't know her as well as Frank. Her ID was checked several times. The guard who appeared to be most senior knew who she was.

"You were injured, Dr. Kirsch?"

"Just a bump on the head," Kenzie explained, slightly embarrassed. "He knocked me down."

"You're not driving home, are you? Do you need a cab? You should have taken the ambulance to the hospital..."

"It isn't that bad—just a bump. And my boyfriend is picking me up. He didn't want me driving either, apparently."

"Where is he?"

Kenzie indicated the front doors.

"I'll walk you out," he told her.

"You don't need to do that. I'm quite able to walk out on my own."

"I'll walk you to your ride," he insisted.

"Fine." Kenzie let him walk her out of the building. She pointed to Zachary's white compact and the guard walked her slowly down the stairs, watching for any sign that she was unsteady and might need him to swoop in and catch her.

Kenzie made it to the car without mishap. Zachary didn't get out of the car to consult with the guard, as Kenzie had been afraid he would. He just leaned over and kissed her on the cheek after she got in. "How are you? Is everything okay?"

Kenzie pulled her car door shut and waved at the guard.

"Yes. Everyone is overreacting. I just got knocked down. Bumped my head, and not even hard. The paramedics were not concerned. No concussion."

"Good." Zachary waited while Kenzie fumbled with her seatbelt. Eventually she managed to get the metal tongue into the buckle and snap it into place. Then he pulled out and drove toward her house without any further argument about her physical condition.

59

When they got home, Kenzie noted that Zachary disarmed the burglar alarm after unlocking the door.

"I didn't think I'd be long, but I figured... we don't need any unexpected guests around here."

"No," Kenzie agreed. "I don't have a clue how they got into the office. We have security. They shouldn't have been able to."

"I think it must have been through the ambulance bay."

That made sense. There were guards at all the public entrances, but for the loading dock, you had to be let in from inside or have the special clicker to get in, so there were no guards checking IDs. But that meant that they'd somehow gotten ahold of someone's clicker or they had fooled the system into thinking they had one. Forcing the door would have set off alarms.

"You're probably right," she agreed.

Zachary steered Kenzie to the table to sit down. He hadn't prepared anything for dinner and Kenzie didn't have the energy to make anything. They would have to order in.

But as she watched Zachary, he placed two bowls on the table, followed by the ice cream. A couple of half-pint containers with their current favorite flavors. He put glasses in front of each place setting and pulled an unopened bottle of wine out of the fridge.

"Ice cream and wine? Is this dinner?" Kenzie demanded. "A bit... bohemian, don't you think?"

He poured her a glass of wine and got a cola out of the fridge for himself. He poured it into his glass. "I don't know what that means."

"Oh... well, sort of free-spirited and nonconformist."

"Ah." He waited for his drink to stop fizzing and then topped it off. "Then yes. Tonight, we are being bohemian."

Kenzie picked up her glass and had a sip before even dishing up her ice cream. She closed her eyes and tried to relax, letting the stress of the day go.

"Thank you for this. And for picking me up." She opened her eyes and looked at him. "How are you not having a meltdown about this?"

"You need me." He shrugged, studying her closely. "I'm worried, but the most important thing is for me to be there for you. That makes me... stronger. When the problem is just in my head, it's easier to get overwhelmed by my own thoughts and feelings. When it's an actual crisis, someone needs my help... It's different."

She remembered how he had been with Madison, Luke, and Rhys when they'd had people shooting at them and several medical crises on their hands. Zachary had been focused and planned things out. He hadn't freaked out and panicked. The same was true of when Lorne and Pat were in danger or when he had been looking for a bug that Walter might have planted. He was a different person when he was protecting someone else. He didn't disappear into himself. He had laser focus.

She tipped her glass toward him, toasting him. "Good job."

Zachary smiled. He scooped a curl of tangerine ice cream into his bowl. "You want chocolate?"

"Yes. As if you need to ask."

He scooped a couple of balls of double chocolate fudge swirl into Kenzie's bowl. Kenzie picked up her spoon and had a couple of bites of cold deliciousness.

Best supper ever.

While Kenzie couldn't tell Zachary any confidential details about the cases she was working on, she could tell him what she knew about the break-in and what she had or had not seen. She told him about the theft of the recent samples, files from Dr. Wiltshire's office, and the possible hacking of their computer systems.

"I can see how they could break in through the loading dock," Zachary said. "There is a weakness in security there. You don't generally have people trying to break into the morgue. It's not an area that's targeted. But the computer systems..." He thought about that and shook his head. "You've got good security. I think... you would need a pretty heavy-duty hacker to break into that."

"I would hope so. I always thought we had all the firewalls and encryption and everything to protect the Medical Examiner's Office and the police systems. It's kind of scary to think that someone could break into it." Kenzie took another sip of her wine. "Everything should be backed up, unless they've somehow been able to break into that too. I think it is at another location, with some security company."

"It should be."

"Yeah. Well, we've all seen system fails before. Usually on the human end." She breathed out heavily. "They broke into the lab too, and I guess... they had injuries over there. At least one of their security guards in critical condition at the hospital." Kenzie rubbed the bump on the back of her head.

"You're lucky that all you had was a bump. If he'd decided to pull a gun on you or to make sure that you couldn't follow or identify him... You're always telling *me* to be careful. Who would have guessed that you would be in danger in the Medical Examiner's Office?"

"Not me. I thought I had a pretty safe job. I haven't even heard of anything like this happening before. People don't... people just don't break into a Medical Examiner's Office like that. Even on TV."

"The way that this was coordinated, it couldn't all have been perpetrated by just one person. This is a group acting in concert. And a pretty powerful group. You need money and influence to pull something like this off." Zachary ticked points off on his fingers. "Break in at your office, taking both samples and files, break in at the lab around the same time, with more violence, breaching your server and the lab's server. The kind of person you hire to do a smash and grab is not the same kind of person as you hire to hack sophisticated computer systems. Even if one person hacked both systems, that is still at least three teams coordinated to act at once."

"And with the body being cremated today... I mean, that just doesn't happen. The funeral home doesn't usually cremate a body the same day that they pick it up. And I had the feeling..." Kenzie trailed off, not sure how much she should say. She was only speculating, and she might be building the situation up to be worse than it was. She didn't need to make it worse. It was bad enough without her blowing it up.

But Zachary leaned forward, his eyes searching her face. "What? What is it?"

"I got the feeling... I know Dr. Wiltshire wasn't really ready to release the body yet. I know he was being pressured by the governor's office. And then my dad trying to talk me into influencing him. He talked about the governor too. And then Dr. Wiltshire just decided to release the body when he hadn't yet made a determination. Just the timing of it... do you think he was threatened or coerced somehow?"

"If you think he was, then you're probably right. You know him. You know how he usually works. If this was unusual, and he was under that much pressure.... then you're probably right."

"What are we going to do?"

"Do you have other avenues of investigation you can pursue while you wait to see what can be recovered from the lab and the computer backups?"

"No... not really."

"What about the woman that you were looking for? Have you talked to her?"

Kenzie thought about Francine Mudd. It seemed like a long time ago. "Yeah. I talked to her today. But I would still like to talk to her ex-boyfriend as well. It's his place that the dog lived at before. I can't go back any farther to the previous owner, because he passed away. But I should probably at least take a look at the place Lola lived at before the nursing home, see if there is any obvious source of infection. If we've got a zoonotic virus—a virus that can be passed from animal to human—then it is possible that the dog got it from another human in the first place. That could be Francine's boyfriend."

"Why don't we see if we can track him down tomorrow, then?"

"We?" Kenzie repeated with a smile.

"I could help you with that. I've already done half of the work, tracking Francine down. I have most of the background I need to start with."

"Well... since it's probably going to take at least a day before they've been able to restore whatever information they can from the backups, I guess we might as well. You don't have anything else you have to do tomorrow?"

"Nothing I can't reschedule. I've got a pretty good relationship with the head boss of Goldman Investigations."

60

Kenzie had a restless night. Even after a couple of glasses of wine, her mind was still whirling as she tried to make sense of what had happened and tried to predict how things would unfold over the next few days. And the bump on the back of her head hurt. It wasn't bad, but it reminded her every time she moved. She couldn't lie on her back comfortably. Not that she was usually a back sleeper, but knowing that she couldn't made her hyperaware of her position and she couldn't get comfortable on her stomach or sides either.

She jumped at every sound in the house, even though the house's night noises were familiar to her. Zachary stayed with her for a couple of hours, but then she was aware that he was gone, and every time she awoke, she listened for him, trying to discern where he was in the house and what he was doing. He was quiet, either working on his computer or sleeping on the couch where he wouldn't be disturbed by her tossing and turning.

She fell into a restless sleep full of dreams early in the morning, just as she gave up on being able to get any sleep before it was time to get up.

Kenzie shut off her alarm when it buzzed and went back to sleep. Dr. Wiltshire wouldn't be expecting her in with all that had happened, and they probably wouldn't be able to do any work until at least the afternoon, maybe the next day. She slept for another hour and a half and then got up, feeling sore all over and still exhausted, but she was too restless to sleep anymore. She wandered out to say good morning to Zachary before her shower.

"Hey, hon'." Kenzie covered a big yawn.

"You look like you could use some more sleep."

Kenzie rubbed her sticky eyes and looked at him. "Well, to be honest, so do you."

"I slept okay."

Of course, his "slept okay" was different from the average person's. He regularly survived on less sleep than a hyperactive squirrel.

"You still want to go looking for Francine's ex today?" Kenzie asked.

"Yeah. I've done some background. Shouldn't be too hard to find him. He is at the same address as you checked already."

"Doesn't help much if he doesn't answer the door."

"We can still scout around. You said you want to see if there are any obvious sources of infection nearby. We can do that, and hopefully be able to raise Jeremy by phone, find out what time he will be home... meet him somewhere so you can ask your questions."

Kenzie nodded. She ran her fingers through her hair, which felt coarse and sticky. "Okay. I'm going to have a long shower. Then something to eat, and then we can go."

Zachary nodded his agreement and went back to his work.

"Jeremy?"

Zachary was going through the cryptic-looking notes in his notepad when Kenzie got out of the shower and walked into the living room, towel-drying her hair, another towel wrapped around her torso.

After a moment, Zachary looked up. "What?"

"You said Jeremy, we would try to get a hold of Jeremy."

He nodded. "Right. Francine's ex."

"She said her boyfriend was Jay."

"Nickname. Full name Jeremy..." Zachary flipped through the pages of his notepad to find it. "Jeremy Salk."

The name sounded familiar to Kenzie, so it must be right. "Oh, okay. I'm going to get ready now. Have you eaten breakfast?"

He opened his mouth to answer and Kenzie shook her head. "Of course you haven't. Why don't you brew some coffee and pop a couple of pieces of bread in the toaster? You can tell me what we know about this Jeremy, and then we'll go over to his building. If he's got a nine-to-five job, he's still going to be working, so it's sort of a waste of time, but it isn't like I have a lot else to do right now, until the office is back up and running."

She had emailed Dr. Wiltshire before getting into the shower, and he had confirmed what she had already suspected. That he wasn't expecting her in and they couldn't work until the police had cleared the area and the techs had the computers working properly.

Zachary nodded and Kenzie went back into the bedroom to dress and make herself look presentable. She suspected that Zachary was too involved in what he was doing to get the coffee and toast started, but she wasn't in a hurry, so it didn't matter. For once, they could have a long, relaxed breakfast if they wanted to.

Kenzie was feeling somewhat more like herself when they reached the building she had previously visited in trying to reach Jeremy Salk. She looked around, unsure why she thought she would be able to find anything significant by just looking at the building. But Zachary's eyes were bright and alert, looking around for anything that was out of place.

"Were you able to get into the building?" he asked.

"No, everything was locked up. I mean, the glass doors are unlocked, but there is a hall door at the top of the stairs, and that's locked."

"Did you try to get anyone to buzz you in?"

"No... I just tried reaching Jeremy. Or rather, Francine. But I couldn't get her."

Zachary nodded. He pulled out his phone and placed a call. To Jeremy's number, she assumed. He walked toward the glass doors that she had previously used. Kenzie followed him in. There was a panel near the door, but it wasn't quite like the electronic directories Kenzie usually saw at apartment buildings. Only four buttons, and none of them were properly labeled. Some numbers and names had been struck through, but Kenzie couldn't make out who the current residents were or which apartment Jeremy lived in.

Zachary pressed each of the buttons, a long press on each of them.

One of the residents answered over the speaker. A woman's voice, mature. Slightly suspicious or irritated.

"Yes?"

"I have a delivery for Jeremy Salk."

"Then ring his doorbell."

"I have, but he's not answering. He's not answering his phone, either. I can't stand around here all day. Can you buzz me up and I'll just leave it outside his door?"

Kenzie had no idea what Zachary was planning to do if the woman said yes and then wanted to know where the package they were supposedly delivering was. Maybe it was a ploy he had used other times in other cases, but she would think that he would at least want to carry a generic parcel around and put it down in front of the door if someone let him in.

"No, you can't leave it outside his door."

"Can I leave it with you? Would you give it to him?"

A deep sigh. "*Who* are you?"

"Delivery."

"Come up."

There was no buzz. There was no vestibule to go through like there was at Francine's building. They both climbed the stairs and tried the door at the top, and this time there was no resistance. It was unlocked and they were able to let themselves through. Kenzie looked down the corridor and saw a woman looking out one of the doorways. She was an older woman, brunette turning gray, jowls starting to sag, wire-rim glasses, and a knotted housecoat.

"You're not a deliveryman," she said accusingly.

Zachary handed her one of his cards. "Private Investigator." He looked at the door down the hall from her. "Do you know what time Jeremy gets off work? He isn't answering his phone."

"What would you be investigating him for?" She shook her head. "And he doesn't go by Jeremy, he goes by—"

"Jay. Yes, I know. I'm not investigating him. I have some questions that he might be able to answer about a consumer transaction."

Her brows lowered. "What?"

Kenzie wasn't sure what that was supposed to mean either. Did he mean the sale of the dog? Except that it hadn't been a sale, it had just been Francine taking the dog when its previous owner had died.

"Do you know what time he gets off work?"

"I don't think he's even in town."

Zachary looked at Kenzie and then back at the woman.

"You think he's out of town? Did he tell you that?"

"He hasn't been around for... at least a week. More. Maybe two."

"Oh." Kenzie was disappointed. "Do you know if he's having his mail forwarded somewhere else? Or where he might have gone? Was it a vacation?"

"I don't know. Why would he tell me? We're not close. He's just a neighbor."

"Is there someone else we can talk to? Maybe he is friends with someone else in the building?" Zachary looked at the other doors in the hallway. "Or is there a building manager who would be in charge of sorting mail that might know something?"

"You can call the building man," the woman shook her head. "But he isn't going to be able to tell you anything."

"How do you know that?"

"Because he was asking the other day if I knew anything about where Jay was. He missed paying his rent."

"So he's just disappeared. No one has any idea whether something is wrong or whether he's just gone on vacation."

She shrugged. "What could be wrong?"

"He could be sick, hurt, who knows?"

"He could be dead," Kenzie pointed out. Since that was her wheelhouse. Then she had a sudden feeling of vertigo. *He could be dead?*

Jeremy Salk.

Zachary held Kenzie's arm to keep her from falling over. "Kenz? What is it?"

Jeremy Salk.

"I thought that name sounded familiar."

"Yeah." She could see him nodding even though she couldn't focus on anything in the present. "Because that's the name of Francine's ex-boyfriend."

"Francine? Oh, I remember her," the old lady said approvingly.

"No," Kenzie said, shaking her head slightly. "Because that's the identify of our John Doe."

61

Kenzie was leaning against the wall for support. Zachary held on to her to steady her, but he wasn't following her train of thought. "What?"

"The one who was in the news. You remember? You looked at his picture and said that he wasn't homeless. And you were right. Once they stopped looking for him in the homeless shelters and community, they were able to identify him. And his name was Jeremy Salk."

Zachary looked at her, then looked at the woman in the doorway. "How long has he been gone?"

She was tentative, uncertain in the face of this news. "Maybe two weeks."

Zachary looked back at Kenzie. "If it's been two weeks and he's been identified, then why doesn't anyone here know? There should have been someone to get his personal effects. Clean the apartment out. And inform the landlord that he's passed."

"No. Next of kin is out of state. They have to make arrangements to travel here, get his things, arrange for the body to be cremated and shipped, all of that. It will be up to them to clear out the apartment and let the landlord know."

"So Jeremy Salk is dead." Zachary considered this. "What did he die of?"

"Alcohol poisoning." Kenzie swallowed and gave a little bit of a head shake. "Not a virus or unexpected death."

"Alcohol poisoning?" the neighbor demanded. "Jay? He wasn't a big

481

drinker. Every now and then, he'd have a beer, but I don't think he ever had much more than that. How would someone like that get alcohol poisoning?"

"I don't know. But that's definitely what he died from," Kenzie told her firmly.

"How would you know that?"

"Because I'm with the Medical Examiner's Office."

The woman looked a little taken aback by this. She looked at Kenzie and Zachary, then shrugged her thin shoulders. "Well, if you don't have anything to deliver, and now you don't have anyone to talk to, then I assume you'll be leaving now." She shut the door firmly.

"Yeah," Kenzie said. "I guess I am. Leaving. Now."

"Just take a minute," Zachary said. "You're very pale. Are you sure your head isn't bothering you?"

"No. Just a bit. I'm fine. It was just a bit of a surprise to realize that the man we are looking for is... the man we were trying to identify."

"Quite the coincidence."

"Yeah. I guess it is. That's very weird."

Kenzie peeled herself away from the wall. "I'm okay. And we don't have any reason to stay here now."

Zachary walked beside her, watching her for any sign she was dizzy or faint. They reached the stairs that led down to the main level and he paused, considering.

"You're sure you're okay. Not going to get dizzy on the stairs?"

"I'm fine. Quit treating me like I'm made of glass."

He nodded and started down the stairs. Kenzie stayed close behind him, watching his feet go down the steps one at a time, keeping pace with him easily. She had a feeling that he was going more slowly than usual to make sure she didn't have to hurry to catch up. They reached the bottom and headed toward the car.

"So, we can't get into the apartment," Zachary said, reminding Kenzie of why they were there in the first place. "But we can at least have a look around the building, the neighborhood, see if we can find anything that might suggest how Lola got the infection in the first place."

Kenzie sat against the hood of the car, nodding. She was a little bit unsteady despite all her protests and didn't want him to see that her legs were shaking. She looked at the businesses on the main floor of the building again. They were not the kinds of places a person would go to eat or shop. Instead, they were light industrial offices, most of them with names she had never heard of before. Places that took care of things behind the scenes and were not usually in customer-facing positions. She went through the names in her head, parsing them and trying to predict what each of them was. She had gone into some of them the last time she was in the area trying to find Francine. She didn't much feel like going to each of them now to see if they had known the late Jay Salk.

Virutek Labs.

Kenzie blinked at the name and studied the shape of the logo. She'd never heard of Virutek Labs before. As far as she knew, it was not a medical lab that drew blood or did ultrasounds or other work for living patients. And likewise, not one of the labs that she dealt with as a representative of the Medical Examiner's Office.

"There's a lab," she said quietly to Zachary. Like they might overhear and all run for cover. Like they might slip out of her grip as Jay Salk just had.

"Do you know them?" Zachary asked.

"No."

"So they probably don't have anything to do with Salk."

"No," Kenzie agreed, pushing herself away from the car and walking toward it.

The V in Virutek appeared to be a double-helix strand of DNA separating into two single strands at the vertex. DNA? Or a double strand of RNA? Or were they using single-strand RNA viruses to modify DNA? Did the logo tell a story, or was it just designed by someone who had no idea what the difference was?

Zachary followed a step or two behind Kenzie, letting her take the lead this time. He was good at finagling his way into a locked building and talking to neighbors. She was good at talking to medical people.

Kenzie pushed her way through the glass door with frosted lettering. There was a small, sterile-looking reception area, where there really wasn't anywhere to sit down. A larger brushed-aluminum copy of the logo was the focal point on the wall to their right. To the side were several pictures in a grid and a plaque with a corporate name on it. The counter was polished white resin and the woman sitting at the computer looked at Kenzie as if she must be lost.

"May I help you?"

"Can you tell me what this company does, please?"

"I beg your pardon?"

"What does Virutek do? It looks from your logo like maybe you're a medical research lab?"

"Yes."

"Does Virutek mean 'virus technology'?"

The woman's penciled eyebrows rose. "It sounds like you already know all of the answers. Who are you, again?"

"Did Jeremy Salk work here?"

"Jeremy Salk?" She shook her head. "No, there hasn't been anyone by that name here."

"Jay, I mean. Jay Salk."

"Still no."

"He lives in this building. In the apartments down that end..." Kenzie motioned.

"No one from Virutek lives in the building. I'm sorry. You must have been misdirected."

"No, I'm just checking. I need to talk to one of your researchers. Is there someone who could spare a few minutes to talk to me?"

"About what?"

"About what experiments they are doing. Whether they are doing anything with HHV-4."

The woman gave her a puzzled look, frowning and shaking her head. "And who are you? Why are you asking these questions?"

"I'm with the Medical Examiner's Office. My name is Dr. Kenzie Kirsch."

"The Medical Examiner's Office."

"Yes. We've had a number of cases lately that have had lab-engineered HHV-4 infections."

The woman blinked. She started to stand, then sat and reached for her phone, but couldn't seem to complete the action. "We don't do human studies," she said flatly.

"That doesn't mean you haven't had a virus escape. If you are doing any work with HHV-4, you'd better get me in to talk to someone ASAP." Kenzie was already standing against the counter, but she leaned over it toward the woman, deliberately getting into the woman's personal space.

The receptionist looked at her for another minute longer, her eyes wide, then seemed to overcome her inertia. She tapped a few buttons into the keypad. It didn't look like 9-1-1 from where Kenzie stood. But it could still be internal security. She waited for an answer.

"Dr. Ducros?" she asked, her voice high with anxiety that hopefully, Dr. Ducros could hear clearly. "There is a woman here from the Medical Examiner's Office demanding to speak to someone about your studies."

"Dr. Kenzie Kirsch," Kenzie repeated. Not some woman. She was a doctor and she was there to get answers.

A few more words were exchanged between Dr. Ducros and the receptionist, with Ducros apparently doing most of the talking and the woman giving one- or two-word answers, keeping the content of the discussion from Kenzie.

"Dr. Ducros will be out to get you in a moment," the woman eventually said as she pressed a button to hang up. Her eyes strayed toward Zachary, wondering who he was and why he was there, but Kenzie didn't fill him in on any details.

It was sort of awkward that Zachary was there when she was trying to do her job. But on the other hand, it didn't hurt to have someone backing her up and acting as a witness to what she discovered. He was staying quiet, not interfering or trying to give her any advice.

A man entered behind them and looked startled to find someone else in the small reception area. He smiled and raised his eyebrows questioningly. He had a sweet, woodsy-smelling cologne or aftershave on, and it quickly filled the small, warm area.

"Oh, Mr. Fisk," the receptionist smiled and nodded at him. "We are expecting you." She shot a look at Kenzie as if to point out that people didn't just barge in at Virutek. They made appointments. "I'll just make sure everything is ready."

She turned away from them for privacy and spoke quietly into her headset.

"Aaron Fisk," the man introduced himself, holding his hand out to Kenzie.

"Dr. Kenzie Kirsch."

"A pleasure to meet you. Are you here for the..." he indicated the receptionist and trailed off.

"Oh, no. We have some other business."

"Oh...?" he leaned forward, head cocked slightly, waiting for more.

"What company did you say you are with?" Kenzie asked.

He smiled pleasantly. The receptionist took off her headset and stood. "I'll just take you in." She led him to a door on the left and swiped her card to unlock it. Aaron Fisk nodded at Kenzie and Zachary and followed his escort.

Kenzie had thought that Dr. Ducros might play power games and keep her waiting before coming out. And if he did, she was prepared to take the discussion to the next level. But he entered the reception area from behind a door behind the reception desk that blended in with the rest of the wall. Kenzie wouldn't have known it was there if she hadn't seen it open. He was younger than Kenzie would have expected, wearing a long white lab coat. He had round, black-rimmed glasses and smudged shadows under his eyes like he regularly worked too late or worried too much.

"Uh, Dr. Kirsch, is it?"

"Yes."

"Come with me, if you would."

He frowned when Zachary followed, but didn't try to stop him. Neither did Kenzie. It might not be Zachary's area of expertise, but as she was swept into the lab behind the door, she was glad she wasn't there alone.

62

Ducros led Kenzie to a small meeting room, and they sat down. The walls of the room were glass with some frosted striping that afforded little privacy. The table was shiny white, as was pretty much everything else she could see. Miles of shining white counters covered with experiments that might take months or years to complete. Or which might quickly discover the cure to some disease they currently had no purchase on. Kenzie recognized much of the equipment, but of course, she couldn't tell what they were working on.

"Now, explain to me..." Ducros said slowly. "You are from the Medical Examiner's Office, and you came here because..."

"This is where my investigation led me," Kenzie said honestly. "We have come across a number of deaths that have all had one thing in common. A lab-engineered HHV-4 virus."

"That doesn't make any sense. How would that lead you back here?"

"Is that what you are working on? Some experiment with a modified HHV-4?"

"That may be one of the things we are working on," he said carefully. "But I don't see how that could have anything to do with your deaths or how you would trace it to this lab."

"It would appear that your virus has escaped into the wild."

"Impossible. No."

"It isn't impossible. Do you know how common escapes are from laboratories that should have had all the best isolation features known to the scientific world? Look at plague just as an example. There have been three escapes from supposedly sealed laboratories." Kenzie looked around her. "I don't see a lot of isolation protocols being used here, actually. None of you are in biohazard suits. I see samples in open containers. I don't know what kind of ventilation system you have, but you realize that if there is even one vent that isn't properly isolated, you could be venting your virus into this building."

"It isn't possible. No. We are very careful. There have not been any escapes."

"You wouldn't know until we connect up the deaths with this lab. And then... it's too late to keep arguing."

"If you had the proof, we wouldn't just be sitting here. You would have... a subpoena or a court order. You'd have the CDC behind you. But I don't see anyone but this..." He looked Zachary over, trying to classify him. "This assistant with you."

"Oh, we'll be calling in the troops. You can bet on that." Kenzie stopped talking and waited for that to sink in. "Now is the time to talk about what you are doing and to mitigate any damage before any accusations can be made."

"It seems like you're already making them."

"I can come back here with the Medical Examiner and the CDC if that's what you want."

He considered that and shook his head, lips pressed tightly together. "Why are you here, then?"

"I'm investigating."

"What do you want to know?"

"First of all, confirmation that you are working with a variant of HHV-4."

"We are doing several different studies here. One of them might be HHV-4."

"What are you doing with it? How have you changed it?"

"That's proprietary."

"What are you trying to do with it?"

"Really, we do have the right to trade secrets. Considering the fact that we are not doing any human studies, I don't see how you think this could have infected any of your... patients."

"A man in this building has died. With lab-engineered HHV-4 in his brain." Of course, that might be a stretch. Kenzie didn't have evidence that Jay Salk had HHV-4 in his brain like the four victims from the nursing center. Not yet. And they couldn't even prove that it was cause of death for those whose brain tissue did test positive. It certainly wasn't Salk's cause of death, as she was implying.

"That…" Ducros shook his head. "That really doesn't make sense."

"Somehow, it got out. Has anyone in the lab been sick? Or died?"

"No. Of course not. Colds, maybe, certainly nothing that we have been studying here."

"You haven't had anyone who has shown… unusual symptoms?"

Ducros raised his hands palms-up. "I don't know what you're talking about."

"A number of the victims we have seen were showing signs of dementia before they died. Not far in advance, just a few days before death. You haven't had anyone who is… I don't know… being forgetful, erratic… incontinent?"

Salk gave a sharp bark of a laugh. "What?"

"Have you had anyone who has been behaving strangely lately? Altered personality. Unable to find the right words when describing something. Emotionally labile."

Ducros sat back abruptly. He looked at Kenzie, his face a blank mask.

As if that weren't a big tell.

Kenzie watched him, waiting for him to think it through and tell her what he was thinking. Now he was worried. Maybe he was starting to see that Kenzie could be telling the truth. It might not be some fantastic tale.

"We had one employee who was feeling a lot of stress. He was… advised to take a vacation. He hasn't shown up at the lab again since."

"So he's missing?"

"He's not missing. He was told to take some time off and he did. It certainly would have been better if he had arranged his schedule with us first, but…" Ducros shrugged. "Scientists can be a funny bunch. We don't always have the best social skills. You tell him to take a break, he takes a break, and then wonders what you're going on about when you complain that he didn't make the proper arrangements. No one is missing. No."

"Where did he go? Does anyone know?"

"No."

"And you don't know when he's coming back."

"No. But he will."

"What was going on with him? You said he was stressed? How was that manifesting?"

"He was very anxious. Accusing others of stealing his equipment or changing his results. He had a couple of blow-ups, getting angry over noth-ing. Everybody kind of had enough of him, so he was asked to… please take some time off."

Kenzie nodded. It was a possible fit. But of course, it could just be a scientist getting stressed out and having a bit of a breakdown because he needed a rest. What were the chances that he was at home, dead in his bed? Or in the street? Another John Doe in her morgue?

"What's this guy's name? And description?"

Ducros frowned, looking at her. "Why?"

"I think someone should make sure that nothing has happened to him. If you haven't heard from him, it may just be that he's taken some time off like he was told to. But it could also be because something happened to him. He could be in the hospital. Or at home, sick, in need of assistance. Or he could be..." Kenzie trailed off and didn't finish her sentence.

Ducros didn't like the question. Kenzie could see his indecision. Did he give a description of his missing employee, hoping that nothing had happened to him? Or hold it back? If something had happened and he withheld information, could he be held responsible? It wasn't like Kenzie was a cop.

"He's... late twenties, I think. Medium height, slim. Brown hair. Too long, but not in a ponytail. Pretty average."

Kenzie thought through the bodies that she had in the morgue or had seen recently. "What's his name?"

Ducros hesitated.

"Really," Kenzie said. "I need to know."

"Abernathy. Joe."

Not the name of anyone who had been through the Medical Examiner's Office recently. Kenzie would have remembered that name. She let out a breath of relief. Maybe he was just taking some mental health time.

Unless it was another John Doe. She was a little paranoid about that, seeing as how Jay Salk had ended up being in the morgue as a John Doe. It was pretty much impossible that the same could be true of Abernathy. The only current resident who was unidentified was the DB from the motel. And Abernathy was local. There wouldn't have been any reason for him to be in a motel.

"Did Abernathy know Jay Salk, who lives in this building?"

It was a stretch, of course. How would the two men, who were probably decades apart and with totally different lifestyles, know each other? Just living and working in the same building wouldn't do it. The apartments were completely separated from the lab. Although they might have shared ventilation.

"No, Abernathy wasn't friends with any of those people."

"Do you know any of them? Did they ever have reason to come in here to make an inquiry? Maybe you run into each other at a convenience store close by?”

“Sometimes you run into people you recognize. But that doesn’t make you friends or mean that you’re close enough to each other to pass a virus on to someone.” He shook his head. “A virus that is only transmitted through *bodily fluids*, not through the air.”

“Which people from this building have you seen outside or other places?”

“I don’t know. People come and go. I don’t remember faces very well, couldn’t tell you what someone’s face looked like if my life depended on it.” He paused. “There was that woman with the dog.”

Kenzie drew in her next breath with difficulty. She tried to continue the conversation without any change in her expression. Not to give away that she was about to fall apart completely. “What woman with a dog?”

“I don’t know if she even lives here anymore. I don’t think I have seen her for a while. Older woman. Had a dog, very friendly. The dog, I mean. The woman was friendly enough too, but the dog always wanted attention. Everybody’s best friend.”

“Was the dog’s name Lola?” Kenzie asked, her voice breaking slightly.

Ducros considered. “Yeah, that might be right...”

“So you would see them outside the building or around the neighborhood somewhere, and you would pet the dog?”

“Sure.” He shrugged, not seeing how this could be a problem. “Friendly dog. Why not?”

“Because you’re working with viruses and not following a proper isolation protocol. It could be clinging to your clothes, your hands, your face. And the dog comes, and you pet her, and maybe transfer it to her fur. Or she licks you.” Kenzie felt a certain amount of revulsion at the thought. She had never been one of those people who was okay with dogs licking people. Especially on the face, even the mouth.

What better way to spread a virus?

“We always use gloves and a mask when handling the virus,” Ducros said uncomfortably. “So there is no chance that someone was contaminated when they left here.”

“You don’t know that. You hope so, but you don’t know that.”

He shook his head in disagreement but didn’t say anything.

“I think you need to call this Abernathy. Let him know you’re concerned about his mental health and just checking in. If you can’t get through to him, then you should at least notify the police. Do you have a next of kin?”

“I don’t think so. He lived by himself, didn’t have anyone in the area.”

"Maybe you could... give him a call now. I'd feel a lot better about it if I knew he was okay."

Ducros rolled his eyes. He tapped away on his cellphone, looking for the number, then tapped it and waited. After waiting a few seconds, he shook his head at Kenzie. "It just goes to voicemail."

"Right away? Or is it no answer and then to voicemail?"

"Right away. He's probably still ticked off with us and doesn't want to talk. So he's rejecting it when he sees my number."

Or something had happened to him. "Leave a message, tell him that you need him to call back or you will be in touch with the police to do a welfare check."

"Seriously?" Ducros made a face. "You deal with your employees how you think is best and leave me to deal with mine."

Kenzie shook her head, irritated. "So tell me... what were you doing with this HHV-4 virus? What were you hoping to achieve? And what kind of results have you had?"

"We are only in the beginning stages of development. It is solely in vitro at the moment. No live hosts, human or animal. We have been... editing it. Hoping that we will be able to use it to insert certain information into human cells, which will allow them to combat disease from the inside out."

"Which cells?"

"Neurons. We are hoping to be able to reverse the course of brain cell degeneration in Parkinson's Disease and a number of others. The same principles apply. If we can cure one, we open the door to curing the rest."

"Huntington's Disease?" Zachary suggested.

Ducros looked at him in surprise, as if he had forgotten that Zachary was even in the room. "Possibly."

"So you have engineered these viruses to cross the blood-brain barrier," Kenzie said.

"Well, they have to get into the brain to do their work."

"What are they supposed to do once they get in there?"

"We are still working through the processes. It's not like programming a computer, you know. We have a lot of theories right now. Putting them into practice will be a different story." Ducros looked at Kenzie. "When we start testing out different scenarios, it will be on genetically altered mice, not humans. There is no way we are ready for human studies."

"You may have unintentionally started human studies already. And the results are not looking good."

63

When they eventually made their way out of Virutek, Zachary looked at Kenzie. "So, you found the source of your virus."

"It looks that way. I can't believe they are working with viruses without proper isolation protocols in place. If they have an employee with this virus and he's out there spreading it around..." She put her hands out in a pleading gesture. "Even if Abernathy doesn't have dementia from the virus, any of the employees could be carrying it. The whole place needs to be shut down until they can be tested and cleared."

"Do you think... do they have the ability to shut this down now? It hasn't spread too far 'into the wild'?"

They got into the car. Kenzie immediately started rifling through her purse. Zachary started the car and watched her, clearly ready to drive wherever she wanted to go next, but waiting to make sure she wasn't going to be disrupted by the movement of the car. Kenzie held up a finger to make him wait.

"Are you looking for your phone?" Zachary suggested.

Kenzie was already holding it in her other hand. Not that she hadn't ever caught herself looking for her phone when she was already holding it.

"No, just for..." Kenzie found the small bottle and pounced on it. She squirted a generous amount of alcohol-based gel cleanser into her palm, then passed it to Zachary. "It may not be one hundred percent effective, but it's better than nothing."

Zachary took the bottle and followed Kenzie's example, working the gel around his hands, between his fingers, into his fingertips around the nails. Kenzie put the bottle back into her purse. Hopefully, that would keep the heebie-jeebies at bay. Her skin had been crawling ever since she had realized how lax the protocols were at Virutek.

"And now... I'd better talk to Dr. Wiltshire. I'd go to the office to meet him, but he probably isn't even there."

"So do you want to go somewhere? Or just sit here for a few minutes?"

"I think we'd better go to the nursing home." Kenzie thought about Lola wandering around to meet all the patients. Licking their hands or faces. They had asked the nurse at Champlain House to keep her isolated away from the patients until they had things sorted out, but they would have to be more aggressive than that. Lola should be in quarantine in a lab somewhere while they ran tests on her.

Zachary nodded and pulled out. Kenzie tapped Dr. Wiltshire's cell number on her phone screen and put the phone to her ear.

Kenzie didn't even waste time on greetings. As soon as she heard the click that told her Dr. Wiltshire had picked up, she started talking.

"Doctor, I think I found the source of the viral infection. Lola and her previous owner lived in a building that leases space to both residential and commercial businesses. There is a lab on the main floor called Virutek. They are working with viruses, including HHV-4, which they have modified to make it easier to penetrate the blood-brain barrier."

"Virutek." Dr. Wiltshire said the name slowly, so Kenzie knew he was writing it down. "And you've talked to them?"

"Yes. I was in the lab, and believe me, I wish I wasn't. I've disinfected my hands, but..." She trailed off. "Anyway. They are handling the virus with mask and gloves and believe that the only way for it to be transferred is via bodily fluids. The guy we talked to said that the ventilation is sealed off from the rest of the building, but who knows if that is true? Or how well-sealed it is? He was familiar with Lola, remembers running into her outside or around the neighborhood. That she was very friendly, liked contact with people. I assume that includes licking people who pet her. If not, at least licking her own fur, which people then touch..."

"So you think the dog picked it up through contact with someone at Virutek or through the shared ventilation."

"Yeah."

"And it sounds like it could be the right form of the virus. But we'll need to check with Dr. Savage. His team will need to compare the virus obtained from Cartwright and the others to whatever virus strains Virutek started with and has developed. They'll be able to tell if it has the same origin."

"You'll have to see if you can get Virutek to cooperate on providing samples of their work product. I have a feeling... it's not going to be that easy."

"It never is," Wiltshire sighed. "But this is good work, Kenzie. Well done."

"Thank you. That's not everything, though."

"What else?" he asked cautiously.

"You remember that I said Lola's former owner used to live there?"

"Of course."

"Well, the owner's boyfriend stayed there when she moved out. And he is —or was—Jeremy Salk."

"Jeremy Salk." Dr. Wiltshire took a moment to place the name, but was faster than Kenzie had been. "The John Doe? Alcohol poisoning?"

"Yes."

"Well, that's... bizarrely coincidental."

"If we didn't have such a clear cause of death, I would wonder if he died from the virus."

"We didn't test him for it. We had no idea that there was any connection to the nursing home deaths. I suppose we can go back and test the samples now." Dr. Wiltshire stopped speaking abruptly.

Kenzie tried to finish his thought process. "Were those among the samples stolen or destroyed?"

"Yes. They were."

Kenzie swore. "I thought that they just didn't know which samples were Cartwright's. But what if all the samples they took were from victims who were positive for the virus? What if the cover-up is... much bigger than we thought?"

"How would anyone know that Jeremy Salk was positive for the virus? Or had at least been exposed to the virus?"

"There's no way, is there? That is... *we* don't have any evidence that he had contracted it. Maybe someone else did. If he was acting strangely, and someone recognized the symptoms as those that this virus causes..."

"No," Dr. Wiltshire said firmly. "That would mean that they had seen enough other cases to recognize the symptoms as a pattern. And for that... there would have to be a lot more cases."

"There were others at the nursing home. Maybe there were other outbreaks that we don't know about. Another pocket somewhere in the city that they could trace back to Virutek. And we only went back three months at the nursing home. How long has this virus been spreading? It could be longer."

"This is all wild speculation." Dr. Wiltshire's tone told Kenzie he wasn't going to allow it to go any farther. And she knew he was right to pull her back. It was too easy to get wrapped up in conspiracy theories and to see proof of it wherever you looked. "Any outbreaks would have been identified by the authorities. We have nothing to suggest that there were any. Salk's death was alcohol poisoning. We don't have any evidence to the contrary. We don't know if he contracted the virus or not."

"It's a pretty wild coincidence that he died at the same time that the rest of this stuff was going on."

"This life is full of coincidences. It is our nature to see patterns and connections, even where there are not any. You're aware of that through your studies of medicine. Similar theories and medicines being developed around the world from each other, with no apparent connection between them. Constellations of symptoms that are similar between diseases with different causes. Scientific advancements that started out as mistakes. There is not necessarily a connection."

"Will you see whether Salk's body is still available or whether he was cremated?"

By his hesitation, Kenzie knew what he was going to say. "I don't have any reason to do that. The Medical Examiner cannot just make demands willy-nilly. He needs to have reasons and follow the evidence."

"You need to be able to get the evidence."

"We already pushed our luck on the Cartwright case. If I am seen as wasting taxpayer money and investigating conspiracy theories, I'll lose my job."

Kenzie sighed. "Okay. And... there's more."

"Something worth looking into? Or more theories?"

"Do you buy into the theory that the engineered virus was probably contracted by Lola from Virutek?"

"I am willing to consider it as a possibility. To check into it farther."

"When I asked about any employees who might be showing symptoms of dementia, Dr. Ducros identified one employee who had been showing increased emotional lability, anxiety, and paranoia."

"What did you advise him?"

"The man is currently missing."

"He's been reported missing?"

"No. He stopped showing up at work. I asked Dr. Ducros to call him, and he didn't answer."

"Did they report him missing?"

"No, they figured he just took some time off. I suggested they at least call for a welfare check, but he declined. I don't think he's going to. They said he lives alone and they don't know of any family in the area, but he wasn't convinced."

"Maybe that's one action we could take without raising any red flags. What's his name? Do you have a phone number or address?"

"Just the name. Joe Abernathy."

"Phone number is in my notebook," Zachary said.

Kenzie looked at him. "What? How did you get his phone number?"

"I watched him dial it."

Kenzie reached into Zachary's pocket and withdrew his notebook. She hadn't even seen him write it down.

"Who is there with you, Kenzie?" Dr. Wiltshire asked.

"Zachary. He came along to be my driver and to see if we could get into the building. I guess he watched Dr. Ducros dial the number and took it down." Flipping through the notebook, Kenzie found the phone number and read it to Dr. Wiltshire.

"Okay. I'll get the police to do a welfare check."

"And what about calling in the CDC to look into Virutek and whether they have accidentally released this virus into the wild?"

But she knew what Dr. Wiltshire's answer would be before he gave it. "Not enough evidence, Kenzie. We need actual proof before we can call the authorities in."

"There's a lot of evidence."

"There's not enough. They won't listen and I'll end up with egg on my face. I don't want to be branded a conspiracy theorist by the CDC. I want them to listen when we have something."

64

They were at Champlain House, but Kenzie wasn't yet ready to go in. She needed to talk to Dr. Savage first and run her theory past him. He was the one who had all the data about the virus. He was the one who would be able to trace where it had come from, who was already working on tracing where it had come from.

"I'll just be a minute," she told Zachary.

He gave her a wry smile. "Take however long you want. It doesn't make any difference to me."

It was, after all, her case, not his.

Kenzie nodded, a bit embarrassed, and scrolled through her contacts to find Dr. Savage. Hopefully, he wouldn't be too busy to talk with her. He could be sitting around because all his data had been corrupted and he was waiting for it to be restored. Or he could be deeply involved in the restoration of the data and not want to take the time to deal with someone who really didn't know as much as she thought she did.

There were a few rings, and then the call was answered.

"Savage."

"Doctor, it's Kenzie Kirsch. I don't know if you remember me—"

"Of course I do, Dr. Kirsch. How are things going over at your office today? And how are you feeling?"

"I'm out in the field today, since there were still police in the Medical Examiner's Office and our server hadn't been sorted out yet. And I'm feeling okay, thanks. Just a little tender. Nothing but a bump on the head, but you'd be amazed at how many times during the day you rest the back of your head against something..." In fact, Kenzie was leaning slightly forward in the car, keeping her head off the headrest.

"I was certainly sorry to hear about your trouble. And I gather you heard about ours."

Kenzie shook her head. "It sounds like it was much worse. You had guards injured? Someone in the hospital?"

"Critical condition," Savage agreed. "Who would ever have thought that this type of... thuggery would happen in our offices?"

"Not me."

"So, what can I do for you today?"

"You may not have your data restored yet, so I don't know if this will be something that you can act on right away...?"

"We have restored almost full functionality at this point. One thing I have always been very cognizant of is the need to make multiple backups at different locations. And the ability to remotely access at least one of those backups without any specialized software, equipment, or tech support."

"Wow. That shows great foresight."

"You only have to lose critical data once to have the point driven home. I'm no smarter than anyone else."

"So I may have found the source of the escaped virus. I thought I would run it by you, give you what we know, and maybe you would be able to go farther with it."

"Really? That's great detective work. I'm afraid that the tedious process I have been going to was likely to take at least another week to trace it, unless I was lucky."

"We traced the dog that we think is the source of the virus being spread at the nursing home. Before the nurse who has her now owned her, she lived in an apartment above a virus laboratory."

Savage blew out his breath with a triumphant "ha!"

"No kidding. What is the name of the lab?"

"It's Virutek." Kenzie started to spell it out for him.

"I'm familiar with them. They are on my list of labs to talk to. Have you talked to anyone over there?"

"A Dr. Ducros."

"And I expect he told you that it is impossible that the virus escaped from his lab."

"Yes. But I walked through a part of the lab... and they had no containment protocols. Gloves and mask. Maybe a sealed ventilation system. That's it."

Dr. Savage snorted. "Unbelievable. And where exactly *does* their air system vent? Into the alley outside the building, I'll wager."

Kenzie hadn't thought about that. Even if there was no shared ventilation between the apartments and the lab, what were they doing with the exhaust air? Were they scrubbing it? Was it even possible to make sure that it was virus-free before venting it outside?

"Dr. Ducros remembered the dog. Volunteered it when I asked him who he would recognize from the neighborhood. He said she was very friendly, liked people. They would see her when she was out for walks or around the neighborhood."

"And all it takes is a small transfer of saliva..."

"Yeah."

"Do you have access to this dog?"

"Yes, I'm just going to go talk to the nurse at Champlain House. I didn't know whether to tell her to take the dog to you, or some facility where she can be isolated...?"

"We do have animals in isolation cubes here, so if you can get her here or we can pick her up, we can make sure that she's safe. Or that everyone else is safe. And we have decontamination here for you if you need it. Best to handle her with as much protective gear as you can, just to be safe, and we can help ensure that you're clean of the virus once you get here. Start you on an antiviral protocol as well. You've already been in contact with the virus in your morgue, so you should consider the antiviral protocol even if you aren't in contact with the dog."

"Yeah. So this Virutek place, you agree that they are probably the contamination point?"

"Yes, you're probably right, but we'll need to test to be sure. I was actually expecting it to be a place that does live animal trials, not just in vitro."

"But if it came from a dog, does that explain any anomalies?"

"One of the large viral segments that the virus gained from recombining with another virus is porcine. So I was expecting pigs to be involved."

"Pigs?" Kenzie echoed. She tried to think of any way that pigs entered into the equation. She hadn't seen anyone walking a potbellied pig around the lab. There hadn't been any meat-packers close by. If there had been any kind of live pig farm nearby, they would have been able to smell them. Kenzie had only been around pigs a few times, but they always had that distinctive smell. Maybe one of the scientists in the lab had a pet pig? "What kind of sources would you look for?"

"Like I said, I expected a live animal trial to be involved somehow. That's why Virutek is way down my list. I know that they got an early version of the engineered virus for use in their studies, but they are not supposed to be doing any live trials. So I didn't think the source would be them."

"Anywhere else?"

"One of the people who was in contact with the dog might have already been in poor health. While humans do not generally get porcine viruses, it is still possible, especially if their immune system is compromised. In that case, someone in your dog's circle might have picked up a porcine virus... somewhere."

"But the victims at the nursing home all live there. There wouldn't be a lot of opportunities for transmission of a porcine virus."

"Maybe from a visitor or a nurse. It's impossible to say. We see strange things happening with viruses. They are rather unpredictable."

Kenzie thought through what she knew about Lola and her history. Where had she picked up a pig virus? "Could she have picked it up from food? Being fed pig scraps?"

"They would have to be uncooked, of course, and most people know that pork carries nasty parasites and would not give it to their pets raw. I wouldn't say it is impossible. But it seems unlikely. Viruses don't generally live long without a live host."

What other way could Lola have been exposed to someone or some creature with a porcine virus? Maybe one of her doggy friends at a dog park? Another animal that had been sick, like a squirrel?

What about...?

Kenzie's heart dropped to her stomach. She didn't even want to think of other possibilities. That was one area of medicine she wanted nothing to do with.

"Dr. Savage... what about a xenotransplant?"

65

"A transplant of another species?" Kenzie could hear the surprise in Savage's tone as he considered the possibility. "There are very few cases where xenotransplants are successful. Pigs are certainly high on the list for xenotransplants since their organs are largely compatible with humans and develop to full size within months rather than years. Pig hearts, lungs, kidneys... but they don't generally last for more than a few weeks."

"Except in a case where it is a tissue transplant rather than an organ transplant," Kenzie amended. "People sometimes get porcine heart valves instead of artificial valves. Particularly if they are old, so the heart valves may outlast them and not need to be replaced."

As much as Kenzie disliked the field of transplantation, she knew her stuff.

"Yes. It's possible that someone at the nursing home has porcine valves," Savage agreed. "They are supposed to be disinfected in an antiviral solution before transplant to avoid just that problem. And as you can imagine... not everyone remembers, or there could be confusion over who on the team is supposed to do that step. Or just plain sloppiness. Third world transplants are notorious for transferring diseases along with the transplanted tissue or organ."

"So I've heard," Kenzie agreed tonelessly. Zachary gave her a sympathetic look and squeezed her knee gently. "My point is, the dog's previous *previous* owner, before she lived above the Virutek lab, died of heart issues. The woman who got Lola from him said that he'd had surgery a few years earlier to replace his valves."

"Indeed." Savage's voice was impressed. "Dr. Kirsch... I think you've nailed the source. That explains both the genetic tag of the lab-manipulated HHV-4 and the large porcine segment."

"Virutek was designing a virus that they hoped to use to cure brain degeneration like Parkinson's," Kenzie told him. "It has been designed to go through the blood-brain barrier. What effect would the pig virus have on the brain of a human?"

"We have no way of knowing. Except to say... you have already seen some symptoms repeated across several victims. Those symptoms are probably not just coincidental."

"You mean the protein deposits and dementia?"

"That is what I fear."

"Yeah. Me too."

They were both silent for a moment. It was Savage who broke it.

"If you will get me the dog, I will see if I can do some magic and talk Virutek into giving me a sample of their re-engineered HHV-4."

"Do you think they will agree? They seem pretty possessive about it."

"That's why I said it will take some magic. We will see."

Kenzie sat in the car after hanging up with Dr. Savage, thinking it all through. The pieces were gradually coming together and, while she didn't like the picture, she was happy to be making progress. If they figured out enough details, maybe they could stop the virus's spread before it became an epidemic. She hated to think of all the people whose lives could be lost if they didn't manage to stop the novel virus.

"Are you okay?" Zachary asked.

"Yes. Just... it's a little overwhelming. Finding out these details while everyone else in the world still has no idea of what's going on. Even though we can see the virus spreading, causing deaths, the situation potentially getting worse and worse... but no one else knows."

Zachary nodded. "Imagine what the world looks like to a paranoid schizophrenic."

Kenzie raised her eyebrows, thinking about it. Seeing conspiracies and connections everywhere and having no one believe them. Even if they weren't yet satisfied that there was enough evidence, Dr. Wiltshire and Dr. Savage at least didn't think she was crazy. Just that they needed to gather more information before they could take any action. "Sheesh. Can you imagine? What a horrible world it would be for them."

"Very scary."

"Very," Kenzie agreed.

She dug around in her purse again. She really needed to organize it a bit better so that she could lay her hands on what she wanted to quickly. Zachary was quiet this time, not asking her what she wanted. Kenzie pulled out a plastic zip bag with gloves and a mask inside it.

"You keep those in your purse?" Zachary asked.

"You never know what you're going to run into. Stopping to give someone first aid beside the road... best to be prepared. I should have put them on before going into Virutek. I had no idea what we were walking into over there."

"I'm sure we will be fine."

"Probably. I hope so." Kenzie put on the mask and gloves. She touched the door handle. "Do you mind staying in the car? I probably should try to maintain some level of confidentiality here. I should be pretty quick in and out." She looked into the back seat. "Do you think we have enough room for a large dog kennel back there?"

Zachary looked. "Well... I can lay down the seats. That gives a bit more cargo space. But it really depends on the size of the kennel."

"Okay. Put them down. I will try to be quick."

"Take the time you need to. We don't want to mess anything up because we are rushing."

"True. Thanks."

Kenzie left him there and went into the nursing home. The receptionist didn't seem to remember or recognize her, so Kenzie showed her identification and gave her name. "I'm going in," she said, without asking for permission. Act as if being the Medical Examiner's assistant gave her the right to just march in there, and no one would stop her.

And she was right. The receptionist looked flustered but didn't try to stop her or run after her or call security. Kenzie went to the nursing station in the independent living unit. She took a quick glance around.

"Where would I find Nurse Ellie?" she asked briskly.

It was not Nurse Summers at the desk, and Kenzie hoped that if she again confidently demonstrated her authority, it would not be questioned. It was a break, Nurse Summers not being there, because Kenzie had a feeling she would have objected to what was about to happen.

"Nurse Ellie? She's not here."

"Where is she? And where is Lola?"

"They're not here."

Kenzie focused on the nurse's name badge. Camille Jackson. "Nurse Jackson. Please tell me where she is. I understand she wasn't able to keep Lola at her apartment, so are they out for a walk? Visiting one of the other units? Where would they have gone?"

Nurse Jackson's face folded into a scowl. "Just who do you think you are? You can't come marching in here and demand to know details of where everyone is. How is it any of your business?"

"I am with the Medical Examiner's Office, and that dog was supposed to be under quarantine. Where has Nurse Ellie taken her?"

"Oh, you're the one who's been making all of the trouble? The one everyone keeps talking about? You don't have the right to know where Nurse Ellie and her dog are. You can't interfere in their freedoms as citizens."

Lola was a citizen? Kenzie suppressed the urge to laugh at the statement.

"Nurse Jackson, please. I'm not here to make trouble. I'm here to help to protect your patients. That dog is carrying a dangerous virus and needs to be examined. You don't want her killing off any other patients, do you?"

"The dog doesn't kill patients. She helps them. She can sense when they are sick and dying, and she helps to make their last moments more peaceful."

"I'm sure she does."

"You and your kind can't come around here and do whatever you like. That dog is not yours! She is smarter than you will ever be. She knows what's going on, and she wouldn't let you near her. Neither will I!"

Kenzie shifted uncomfortably. The conversation had rapidly gone to a bad place. Nurse Jackson was not just being obstructive and provoking, but she sounded paranoid. Kenzie tried to remember what she and Zachary had just talked about. How scary the world would be to a person who had paranoia.

"I'm sorry if I scared you," Kenzie said soothingly. "I didn't mean to do that. I'm not here to do anything to hurt Ellie or Lola. They will both be very safe with me. I'm a doctor, you know, and we promise to do no harm."

"You're not a doctor. You're with the coroner's office."

"Yes. I am an assistant to the Medical Examiner. I am a doctor. Do you want me to show you my credentials?"

Nurse Jackson drew back suddenly when Kenzie reached into her purse for her wallet, cringing as if Kenzie had pointed a loaded gun at her. "Stop! No!"

Kenzie glanced around herself. Others were watching, puzzled and concerned. Kenzie looked at Nurse Jackson, cowering back as if Kenzie had threatened her. When Kenzie saw Nurse Summers coming down the hall at a quick clip, she was actually glad.

"What is going on here?" Summers demanded, looking at Nurse Camille Jackson and Kenzie with a scowl.

"I was just asking Nurse Jackson about where Lola and Ellie are," Kenzie said. "I'm sorry, I think she has misunderstood me..."

Nurse Summers looked at Nurse Jackson. "What's the matter?"

Nurse Jackson slapped her hand down on the counter with a loud crack. "That's enough! No one is going to touch me!"

Summers's eyes were wide. She glanced uncertainly at Kenzie as if she might have the explanation for Nurse Jackson's behavior.

"How long has she been like this?" Kenzie asked.

"Like this?"

"Confused, paranoid, emotionally labile."

"I... don't know." Summers shook her head. "There's got to be something wrong. This is not... she's never behaved this way before."

"I think... she's got it."

"Got what?"

"The virus that Lola is carrying."

Kenzie wanted to say, "The virus that killed Mr. Cartwright," but she didn't want to cause panic. That would probably be enough to send Nurse Jackson right over the edge if she hadn't already crossed it.

"The virus?" Summers repeated.

"Yes. That's why we called and gave instructions that the dog was to be isolated and anybody who had anything to do with her should be gloved and masked." Kenzie motioned to her own face. "Because we don't want anyone else catching this."

"What virus are you talking about?"

Kenzie didn't have the time to walk Nurse Summers through it. "A novel variant HHV-4 virus that causes dementia." She looked at Nurse Jackson. "Dementia that appears to develop very, very quickly."

Nurse Summers swore. She looked at Nurse Jackson as if trying to convince herself that it was true. Then she looked at her watch. She looked back at Kenzie, her mouth opening wide.

"What?" Kenzie demanded.

"The dog... there was a big write-up about her in the news. She was a celebrity."

"Yes."

"Well... she was invited to the Halloween Masquerade Ball."

Kenzie remembered the article that Zachary had sent her.

It took a few more seconds for everything to click into place. The ball. The one her mother and father were going to. That they had begged her to go to. All the people who would be there. Politicians, celebrities, the wealthiest and most influential people in the state. All jammed together in one room, with a friendly, hero dog carrying a deadly virus.

Kenzie swore. It wasn't under her breath and she didn't stop swearing. She just kept swearing over and over, like a mantra, as she hurried away, leaving Summers to deal somehow with Nurse Jackson. Kenzie swore all the way back to the car, one final time as she sat down in the passenger seat and pulled her door closed.

Zachary looked at her. "She... wasn't there?" he guessed.

Kenzie swore again. "Okay. I'm stopping now."

And then she swore again.

66

"**S**he's gone to the ball."

Zachary's head tipped slightly to the side as he tried to understand what she was saying. "Who has gone to what ball?"

"Lola. The dog. And her owner. You remember you saw the article...? They have gone to the masquerade ball. The big fundraiser that my dad and mom were trying to get me to go to. That place is going to be packed, and Lola will be the star of the show. Do you know how many people are going to want to pet her or shake a paw? Or how many will let her lick their faces? Especially for a well-placed photo in the big magazines?"

"Oh." Zachary repeated Kenzie's swear.

"Exactly," Kenzie agreed.

"What do you want to do?"

"Go to my office."

"Your office?"

He had clearly been expecting other directions from her. Such as to go to the ball so they could get Lola before she infected everybody of importance in Vermont.

"Yes. As quickly as we can safely get there. And not get pulled over for speeding."

Zachary was happy to comply. He pressed the gas pedal down and focused on the road ahead.

Kenzie called Dr. Wiltshire again. "We have a problem."

"Kenzie." The sigh that carried down the line let Kenzie know that her call was not cause for celebration. "What problem? What do you mean?"

"I went to Champlain House to get Lola."

"To get Lola?"

"Dr. Savage said that they could properly isolate her while they ran tests to find out if she carries the virus. So I went to pick her up."

"Okay."

"She's not there. They did not isolate her as we instructed them. Instead, they have sent her to the big masquerade ball to meet all the celebrities."

There was silence from Dr. Wiltshire. He didn't swear. But Kenzie knew he wanted to.

"Not only that, but when I got there, one of the nurses freaked out. She wasn't making any sense. She was making accusations, acting paranoid. Inappropriate emotions. Confusion."

"She's got it."

"Yeah. So it isn't just old, sick people who can get it. And it progresses *very* fast. Everyone kept telling us that the victims had only had symptoms the last few days, and we thought that they had just missed the earlier symptoms. But maybe... it actually does progress that rapidly. That once it gets a foothold, there are only a few days until it is fatal."

"What did you do about this nurse?"

"I called you. I am going to the masquerade. I get that the CDC won't act that fast, and I'm going to go get that dog out of there before she infects half the state. I'll leave dealing with the nurse to you. Her name is Camille Jackson. Nurse Summers is there if you want to give her a call. She might have already called for an ambulance."

"Where are you now?"

"Heading back to the office to get geared up. Then we're going to Burlington."

"Okay." Dr. Wiltshire didn't say anything for a minute. "I have news for you too."

His tone of voice indicated that it wasn't good news. Kenzie wasn't sure she could take any more bad news. Maybe she should hang up and pretend that they had been disconnected accidentally. Her phone had died, so she couldn't talk to him until later, when they had dealt with the dog and everything was okay. But she couldn't do that.

"What did you find out?"

"The police did a welfare check on Joe Abernathy. When they couldn't raise him on the phone, they tracked down his address and sent someone over there."

Kenzie had a growing sense of unease, her chest and stomach muscles tightening. She was suddenly nauseated. When was the last time she had eaten? Was she going to be sick?

"Tell me he's not dead." She pictured them finding Joe Abernathy in his bed, dead from the virus. His body lying there, putrefying while Ducros waited for his eventual return to the office.

"He is dead," Dr. Wiltshire agreed.

Kenzie let out her breath and held one hand to her forehead, as if by doing so, she could keep her brain from exploding.

"He was a competitive swimmer a few years ago," Dr. Wiltshire said, seeming to go off on a tangent. What could being a competitive swimmer have to do with his death from the virus?

"Oh. Was he?"

"So there were pictures of him in his home, dressed in swimming trunks."

"Uh-huh?"

"He had a large port wine birthmark along the outside of his right thigh."

Kenzie swore under her breath. Zachary glanced over at her, one eyebrow cocked, wondering what she was upset about.

"He is our other John Doe. The one from the motel room."

"Yes."

Kenzie's head whirled. "Why would he be checked into a motel? He had a house or apartment in town, right? So why would he check into a motel?"

"According to the manager the police talked with, his behavior was erratic. He was grumpy, didn't want anyone to talk to him. Had requested a room that was farthest from the motel office. Insisted that there couldn't be anyone in the room next to his. Yelled at passersby for spying on him."

"So he had the virus."

Of course he had the virus. She knew from the start that was why he had been so paranoid and moody when he was at Virutek. Not because of the stress of his job. Not because he needed a vacation. But because he had the virus.

"He was paranoid about people being after him, so he left his house," she offered, not waiting for Wiltshire's confirmation. "He thought that by going somewhere else, he could escape... whoever he thought was after him."

"Whoever he *thought* was after him?" Dr. Wiltshire repeated.

And then the full implication of that statement hit Kenzie. Abernathy hadn't just been paranoid. He hadn't, as she had imagined, died in his own bed after the virus had clogged up his brain with tangles of proteins. He had been tortured. His face was beaten in. So that not only could he not tell anyone what was going on at Virutek, he couldn't even be identified.

"Do you think Dr. Ducros is involved?" Kenzie asked. "He is the one who should have asked for a welfare check. If someone silenced Abernathy, isn't it most likely someone at Virutek?"

"It's... worth considering. The police will be looking into it. They'll look into Virutek and anyone else who might have threatened Abernathy. Because *his* death was clearly not accidental or natural causes."

67

Zachary pulled up to the building. It might have been quicker to go in the back way, but Kenzie didn't have a clicker for the ambulance bay door and her electronic pass card for the parking garage was in her car, not Zachary's. So he pulled into the loading zone in front of the building.

"Do you want me to come in?"

"You'd better stay here to make sure we don't get ticketed or towed. That would really put a crimp into our plans. I'll get everything we need. I know where it all is, so it really wouldn't be any faster for you to come in than it is for me to just grab everything myself."

"Okay. Is there still security around down there?"

"I don't know. Dr. Wiltshire didn't say."

"If there isn't... maybe you should get someone to escort you down. Just to make sure that you're safe."

"There isn't going to be anyone there after what happened yesterday. They already got everything they needed. And the police have been there and still could be. Someone would have to be stupid to go back there."

"Don't discount it. And they didn't get everything."

"What do you mean?"

"It sounded like you said this body that has been identified as being Abernathy is still in your morgue."

Kenzie stilled and thought about that. "Well... yes. We didn't know until now that he was part of this."

"But you can bet that they do."

"Who is *they*?"

"Ducros. Or the person or people who killed Abernathy."

"How do you know it was homicide?"

Zachary shrugged. He could read her, even if he hadn't been able to hear everything that Dr. Wiltshire had said to her on the phone. She had to be pretty careful if she wanted to keep him from seeing what she was thinking and feeling. He'd cultivated his ability to read people not just as a private investigator, but also as a child in the foster system, having to evaluate strangers every time he was transferred to a new home or school. To get a feel for who was safe and who was a threat. To read all the hidden undercurrents that ran through a family.

He was very good at what he did.

Kenzie put her hand over Zachary's, still resting on the gear shift after putting the car into park. "I'll make sure someone walks me down."

"Good."

Kenzie got out and entered the building. After being admitted through the security checkpoint, she told the guard that she was hoping someone could escort her downstairs just to make sure everything was safe and secure. "I'm not going to be there long; I just need to pick some things up. But I'm kind of nervous after the break in. I was attacked, you know..."

He looked sympathetic. "We've got a guard down there already. He's stationed outside of the Medical Examiner's Office, but you show him your ID and he'll go in with you. I'll call ahead."

"Thanks. I appreciate it. I suppose... it's going to be a while before I feel safe down there alone."

"Well, usually there are other people around. No one today because of all of the problems."

"Yeah. That's true. I probably won't be staying late, though. Until I feel like all of this is behind us."

"We have beefed up security. You can no longer get in through the loading dock without showing your identification to the camera first. So we know exactly who is there. No more clickers."

"That's good." And anyone coming in through the front had to go through the security checkpoint. "How about the parking garage?"

"We have a guard down there like we always have. And someone doing a regular walk around to look for anything suspicious."

"Good. Thanks."

Kenzie did as he had instructed and met another guard when she got down to the office. He checked Kenzie's identification and walked her in.

"I've been here all day, and there hasn't been anyone else in," he assured her. "And they've changed the ambulance bay protocol."

"Yeah, he was telling me upstairs."

"Let me go ahead of you."

Usually, a man would stay back a step to allow Kenzie in ahead of him. But he did the opposite this time, motioning for her to stay back. He unlocked the door and walked in with his hand on his firearm, looking around alertly for anything that was out of place.

"Looks all clear, doctor."

"I'm going to need some gear from the supply room."

He led the way, again opening the door first and peering around to make sure that everything was safe. "Clear."

Kenzie went into the room and started to pick up everything she needed. The guard watched her for a moment and then withdrew into the autopsy room. Ten minutes later, Kenzie was headed back up the elevator to Zachary's car.

They didn't discuss what they were going to do in detail. Their main goal was obvious, to get Lola out of the ball, away from where she could contaminate people. Put her in the car and get her over to Savage's lab to be properly isolated until they were finished running all the tests they needed to. Kenzie didn't anticipate that it would be difficult to get into the ball. Her mother and father had both been begging her to attend. All she had to do was drop their names. Even though she hadn't responded that she would go, there were always last-minute cancellations or appearances at such an event.

"We don't have a kennel for the dog," Zachary pointed out.

"No. But if we can talk Ellie into it, she must have a kennel in her car. She had to transport Lola there somehow."

"But some people just let their pets roam free in the car."

"If that's what she did, then that's what we'll have to do. And she must be used to riding. So she shouldn't get all wild because she's not kenneled."

"Unless she has doggy dementia. Why hasn't she been affected by the virus?"

"That happens sometimes. The same virus can cause a bunch of problems in one animal family, and yet have practically no effect in another. So this one causes dementia and possibly death for humans... but dogs seem to just be carriers. If you can judge from just one case, which is pretty presumptuous."

"Or maybe she's just like... what's that expression? Typhoid Mary?"

Kenzie nodded. "Yes. She wasn't affected by the typhoid pathogen that she carried, but she passed it on to dozens of other people. Because she wasn't sick, she didn't believe them when they told her that she could make other people sick."

"So what if Lola has been to a dog park and passed it on to a bunch of other dogs?"

Kenzie shook her head. "Don't make any more suggestions, okay? I'm pretty freaked out about this already."

"Okay. Sorry."

"It's okay. There's nothing wrong with suggesting it, but I'm going to shut down the conversation anyway. I just don't want to talk about it."

He nodded. He stared at the road ahead, and she wondered whether she had upset him. But Dr. Boyle had encouraged them both to share their feelings to be fair to each other. Hiding their emotions was bad for the relationship. If Zachary were bothered by her asking him not to discuss it any further, he would get over it.

It didn't take too long to get to Burlington. Nothing in Vermont was too far and Zachary tended to have a lead foot out on the highway. He usually tried to curb it when he was with her, but Kenzie had made it clear that they were in a hurry. She wanted to limit Lola's exposure to all the other guests as much as possible. She didn't think she would be able to get there before the event was in full swing, but she would sure try.

They pulled up to the conference center. Kenzie got out and separated the gear into two piles. She suited up, showing Zachary how to get into the protective coveralls, and to put on the gloves and the helmet-like face mask with integrated breathing apparatus.

"Aren't you worried about what people are going to think when we walk in there?" Zachary asked. "Your father's warning about not panicking people...?"

Kenzie smiled. "This is a costume ball. Aren't these great costumes?"

Zachary's eyebrows went up as he struggled to get everything properly fastened. "I pictured... big ball gowns and those little decorative eye masks on a stick."

"I'm sure we'll see that too," Kenzie agreed. "And tuxedos. Vampires. But other people will have plain old Halloween costumes too. Not everybody goes for the highbrow masquerade stuff."

"Then I guess we'll fit right in."

Kenzie finished fastening her mask and checked her breathing. Then she helped Zachary with his.

"How does that feel? Good?"

Zachary nodded, testing his movement and range of vision and taking a few experimental breaths. "Yeah, it's okay."

"No claustrophobia?"

"No."

"All right. Let's go in. Follow me."

They walked together, drawing some looks and pointing fingers, but pretty much everyone was getting the same as everyone checked out each other's outfits. As Kenzie had predicted, there was a full range of costumes, from superheroes to French ballgowns. Kenzie stopped at the check-in counter.

"Do you have your invitation?" the elderly woman at the desk asked, peering at Kenzie through glasses on a chain and then looking down at her list.

"No, I didn't get a printed invitation. My name is Dr. Kenzie Kirsch. My parents are Walter Kirsch and Lisa Cole Kirsch. I'm sure you have us all on your list."

The woman checked it slowly, flipping through pages. She nodded when she reached the K's. "Walter and Lisa, yes. I see them here."

"I don't know if there is space at their table or not. We can sit somewhere else if not."

The woman had to check. She stood up to discuss the matter with one of the event planners circulating behind the check-in counter. Kenzie sighed and rolled her eyes at Zachary. It was difficult to see facial expression behind the face shields, so she tipped her head to the side slightly and shrugged dramatically. "I'm sure they'll sort it out."

Zachary's posture was less confident. He shrugged his shoulders slightly. "If not, you can show them your ME identification."

"I'm not sure that would gain me admittance anywhere."

The man the name-checker had whispered to approached the counter, smiling a cultured smile at Kenzie. "Miss Kirsch?"

"That's Dr. Kirsch," Kenzie corrected sharply. She rarely corrected people on her title, but the circumstances warranted it. She wanted to put the man off-balance, if he weren't already.

"I'm sorry, Dr. Kirsch. I don't have your response on our official list...?"

"No. I didn't expect to be able to be here today. But things were fluid, and I found myself available. It's such a good cause. I'm sure you know that my younger sister died of kidney disease. Our family is very passionate about raising awareness for kidney research. And funds, of course. I was told the governor would be here tonight?"

He looked startled by this. "Uh, yes, certainly. We're hoping that he will be available."

"It will be great to talk to him again. Are my parents here?" Kenzie mimed looking at her watch. If she had been wearing one, it would have been under her coveralls, but the gesture was just to nudge him forward. "They're always very prompt, so I'm sure they made it ahead of me. I cut it a little closer than I meant to. You know how doctors' schedules are."

"Yes." The man looked toward the dining room. "They are just going to make sure there is room at the table for you... and your guest?"

"Yes. Zachary is here as my plus one. He's looking forward to meeting the governor."

"I will go check on that seating. Feel free to mingle for a few minutes while we arrange everything."

Kenzie nodded politely. She looked back at Zachary, and they broke away from the check-in counter, walking into the ballroom without any problems from security.

"We're in," Kenzie told him with a smile.

"I can see that. Well done."

"I've attended enough of these things. I know how they work. As long as you have money and know the right people, you can get in anywhere, no matter how exclusive the invitation list was or how late you are in responding. They don't care about pushing extra chairs up to the table. They want your money."

"So, will you make a donation tonight?"

Kenzie was a little surprised by the suggestion. They were only there for one reason, and that was to get Lola. But Zachary did have a point. She had made out that she would make a donation, and her family name was well-known. And kidney research was important. "If I don't get a chance tonight, I'll mail them a check."

68

They looked around the ballroom at the chattering crowds. The helmet of the protective gear limited their range of vision. Kenzie found it necessary to turn her whole body, rather than just her head. Zachary was doing the same. They were both scanning for Lola or the nurse. Kenzie didn't know if the nurse was costumed or would be recognizable. The dog, however, would be a dead giveaway.

"Mackenzie!"

She turned right into her mother, dressed like some fairy godmother out of a Disney movie, with a pretty blue eye mask obscuring part of her face.

Kenzie's mouth dropped open. Even though she had known that her parents would be there, she had not expected to run into them. She was so focused on getting Lola and getting her away from the crowds that she had tunnel vision, everything else forgotten.

"Mother! Hello."

Kenzie stooped slightly to hug Lisa gently around the shoulders and blow air kisses past her cheeks. Was that really necessary when she was wearing a biohazard suit?

"Why didn't you tell me you were coming?" Lisa gushed. "It's so good to see you. I'm so glad that you came."

"I didn't think I would be able to. It was all very last-minute. And there is someone here that I need to see... I don't know how long I will be able to stay."

"Nonsense, of course you must stay. There are people I need to introduce you to."

"Another time. I really do need to find someone."

"And this..." Lisa turned to Zachary. "Is this your young man? Is this Zachary?"

"Hi, Mrs. Kirsch," Zachary said politely, his voice muffled behind the protective gear. "It's so nice to meet you."

Lisa peered at him. She lifted her eye mask so that he could see her face and peered into the depths of the protective suit. "You need to take that off so I can see your face!"

"Not now, Mom," Kenzie insisted. "You know we're not supposed to remove our masks until the end of the festivities."

"Well, you won't be able to eat with those on!"

"We have a plan," Kenzie promised.

She spotted a cluster of people at the end of the ballroom, laughing, bending over, surrounding something of interest that was closer to the ground. Kenzie recognized the clustering behavior. It had to be Lola. One dog at an event where one didn't usually see any pets, Lola would be sure to garner lots of attention. Everyone would want to pet her. Especially since she had been labeled a hero.

"Over here, I think," she told Zachary, steering him in the right direction.

Zachary walked beside her at a quick clip, nodding his head as he saw the crowd around the dog too. "That has to be it. Your mom seems nice."

"Oh, she is. Being nice was never an issue. She's very gracious. I'm sure you'll like her. But another day. When we're not trying to save the world."

"Is your dad here too, then? Did they come together or would they have been separate? Each coming from their own direction?"

"Separate. Unless Dad is staying over at the house."

Kenzie pushed past a few people who didn't move out of the way fast enough. "Excuse me. I'm sorry. Sorry."

Zachary stayed close behind her, not letting the crowd close back in around him. The guy could use his elbows when he had to. Kenzie broke through into an open space where she caught a glimpse of Lola and her adoring crowd for a moment. She swore under her breath at how close people were to her, how they reached out to pet her or to let her smell and lick their hands. All of them just begging to contract the virus and head quickly into dementia and an early grave. Kenzie put on an extra burst of speed.

"Ellie. Nurse Ellie, we need to talk to you."

A few people looked over at her curiously, but most didn't hear her over the conversations going on. Kenzie stepped firmly forward, pushing waiting fans aside.

"Ellie! Hey!"

The nurse was dressed... like a nurse. She had on a nursing smock as well as an old-style nurse's cap, just in case anyone wasn't sure what she was supposed to be. She had on a white Zorro-style eye mask.

"Yeah?"

"Dr. Kirsch from the Medical Examiner's Office. Do you remember me?"

"Well... yes, I guess so. You came and talked to everybody that one day. I didn't expect to see you *here?*" Her tone was questioning.

"Move back, please," Kenzie said in a raised voice, speaking above the hum of voices. "Everyone, please step back from the dog."

"What's going on?" Ellie asked.

Others around them were grumbling and complaining, not eager to move out of the way and lose their chance of saying hello to the hero dog.

"You were told that this dog was to be in isolation."

"Lola got an invitation to attend the masquerade ball. From the governor himself. You don't turn down an invitation like that."

"You do if you are infected and don't want to make everyone in the place sick!" Kenzie raised her voice still more, making sure that everyone around her understood. "This dog was quarantined for a reason. The governor does not have the right to override the Medical Examiner's directions."

There were a few whispers and laughs from the crowd, thinking that Kenzie was putting on a show. Acting in character.

"I don't know what you're even talking about." Ellie shook her head. "What is all this? You don't have any jurisdiction here."

"I have been authorized to pick this dog up." Kenzie didn't know how that would play when she was in another city, but she wasn't going to take the time to find out. "I'm to put her into isolation until they've had a chance to run all of the necessary tests on her and to ensure she is no longer a danger to *everyone around her.*"

People were starting to back off a little. Beginning to realize that maybe it wasn't just a joke or an act. There really was something going on.

"You can't just come barging in here and take Lola away from me. She's my dog."

"Do you know that her previous owner is dead in my morgue? And that her owner before that is dead? Do you think you won't catch this virus too?"

Ellie shook her head. "What are you talking about? Dead? Francine isn't dead."

"No, but Jay is. Francine's ex. And they lived in an apartment over the lab. The lab that engineered this virus and was stupid enough to let it into the wild. Do you understand me? This virus is killing people at Champlain House. People like Willie Cartwright and Stanley Sexton. And others over the past few months. Nurse Jackson is showing symptoms. You couldn't see what was happening right in front of your own eyes. Lola doesn't sense which people are going to die and give them comfort. She gave her favorite patients the virus that killed them!"

Ellie's mouth hung open. She was no longer protesting, her face draining of color.

"How stupid is it to take a dog to a ball with hundreds of vulnerable people when you've been told by a medical authority to keep her isolated?" Kenzie demanded. All conversation around them had now ceased. The room was silent and hanging on her every word. People were scurrying away from Lola now. Backing up, spreading out in a wave around her as each consecutive ripple moved farther.

"Mackenzie!"

She should have known that her father would be there to interfere. As soon as he realized she was causing trouble, of course he would be there at her side to gently pull her away and see that she quieted down.

He was dressed as a cowboy. White hat, of course, declaring his status as one of the "good guy" lobbyists acting to protect the people.

"Dad. You need to stay out of this."

"Mackenzie, what's going on here? What are you shouting about?"

"I'm here to do a job, Dad. This is work. So butt out."

"What are you talking about." He looked baffled. "What about work?"

"This dog is infected with a deadly virus. She was supposed to be quarantined. Instead, she's exposing all these people, including you, to a nasty virus that could cause your death within days."

People continued to flee, leaving the ballroom altogether. Pretty soon, they would be alone—Kenzie, Zachary, Ellie, and Lola. And Walter, who was undeterred.

"You don't want to make a scene here," he said reasonably. "Couldn't this wait until tomorrow? What's the difference now, really?"

"I don't want hundreds of people's blood on my hands. That's the difference."

He seemed stymied for a moment. He looked around him, trying to find someone in the crowd that had dispersed, leaving the rest of them an island in the room.

Someone was striding toward them now, wearing a Phantom of the

Opera mask, black cape, and white gloves. One of the event planners, no doubt, getting ready to throw them out.

"Walter. What's going on here?"

"Some misunderstanding," Walter assured him. "I'm just talking to my daughter. I'll get it straightened out."

"No, you will not," Kenzie said firmly. "I'm taking this dog." She reached for the leash and pulled it out of Ellie's hand. Ellie was confused enough by this point, worried enough that what Kenzie said could really be true that she allowed it to be pulled out of her hand. Lola whined and looked back and forth at them, wondering what was going on. But she was a happy dog, a friendly dog, and she would go with Kenzie if that was who was holding her leash.

"You can't do that," the man snarled. He stepped forward abruptly and shoved Kenzie. It took Kenzie off guard and she nearly fell over, as she had during the break-in. But she managed to catch herself and Zachary reached out and steadied her. He stepped between them, trying to keep the Phantom from touching Kenzie again.

"Stay out of this," Zachary warned. "She's here on official business."

"Official business? There is no official business," the Phantom asserted. "She's not a real doctor. She assists in the morgue. That's not a *real* doctor. You don't have live patients. You aren't a doctor any more than this dog is." He reached out for the leash.

Kenzie jerked it back. The three of them danced around, the man trying to grab the leash away from Kenzie. Zachary pushed the Phantom back once, and the other man swung, hitting Zachary somewhere in the side of the head. Kenzie wasn't sure whether he connected with an ear or the face shield or another part of the apparatus. It wasn't good for the isolation suit, though. They weren't made for roughhousing.

"This dog is contagious," she told the Phantom forcefully, hoping to get through to him. "If you contract this virus, it could kill you. Why do you think I'm in this protective gear?"

"You're just making this up. I don't know who sent you, but this is completely ridiculous. The dog is safe. She's perfectly safe. If she had this virus, she would be dead months ago."

He had admitted there was a virus and that he knew something about its incubation period. Something about his voice was familiar. Kenzie tried to see his face under the mask, to reconstruct the part that was covered so that she could recognize him. "Who are you? I don't understand why you would interfere with a case like this. Do you want to get sick? Do you want everyone here to get sick?"

"That's not the way viruses work. Even with the most virulent virus, it isn't a hundred percent. It isn't ever *everybody*. Someone will always survive even direct exposure. What is more important? A few people dying, or being able to cure terrible diseases like Parkinson's and Alzheimer's that thousands die of every year?"

Kenzie glanced over at her father. Was this who had been whispering in his ear? Was Walter of the same opinion? That it was okay if a few people died from the virus, as long as the Virutek studies were allowed to go on?

They wanted to keep it all quiet, hush it all up so that they didn't have a virus outbreak to distract everyone from the upcoming election. The governor was bringing in all the goodwill he could with the masquerade ball, schmoozing and making people feel like they were making a difference and that he was helping to advance medicine and the well-being of his population.

The announcement of an outbreak would ruin that illusion.

"Mackenzie," Walter said quietly. "I think this has gone far enough. You've made a scene. There's going to be talk. I don't know if this event can be salvaged. Why don't you just quietly take the dog and go? We'll smooth things over here."

"No!" the Phantom shouted. "She's ruining everything. That dog is the best thing that happened to this ball! Do you know how many more people responded when we started to publicize that he would be here?"

"*She*," Ellie corrected, looking angry. Like maybe she'd already had to correct people on the dog's gender half a dozen times.

"They're here," Walter pointed out. "But after this scene, they're not going to want their pictures with the dog. They'll leave if it stays. So let Mackenzie just take it."

"*Her*."

They both looked at Ellie in irritation.

Kenzie tugged on Lola's leash and took a step back. If both Walter and Ellie were no longer fighting it, Kenzie could get out of there. She could get Lola to the lab and properly quarantined and stop the spread from dog to humans. There was still the human-to-human spread to be concerned with, but Typhoid Mary had to be stopped.

The Phantom grabbed Kenzie's arm and held on tightly. Zachary moved in. He was no ninja, but he didn't quail before the bigger man. The first thing he did was grab the edge of the Phantom mask and pull it away, snapping the elastic.

69

Kenzie swallowed. She stared at the face, trying to sort out all the conflicting images crowding into her brain. His iron grip on her arm and the smell of his body and his aftershave sent her hurtling back to the attack in the morgue. This was the man who had attacked her there. She hadn't seen his face during the attack, but she recognized that smell, the shape of his body, and his hands on her.

But before her stood Aaron Fisk, the pleasant man from the lobby when she had visited Virutek. He had seemed so cultured. A great addition to any board of directors. Maybe a family guy, sort of like her dad.

Like Walter.

The two of them clearly knew each other. So who was Aaron Fisk? Why did he care about Lola? About the Virutek studies? Why had he been at Virutek earlier?

Kenzie tried to jerk her arm out of his grip. Zachary gave Fisk a shove back, but didn't manage to dislodge him. Zachary drove a hand toward Fisk's face, fingers bent into claws, going straight for the eyes, and that did cause a reaction. Fisk stepped back, flinching out of the way and releasing Kenzie.

Kenzie's relief at being released lasted for just a split-second. Her shoulders dipped and she looked down at Lola for an instant, regrouping, ready to make a dash for the door.

Then Fisk was on Zachary—hitting him, Kenzie thought, until she saw the blossom of red on the protective coveralls. She registered the fact that Fisk was armed and had attacked Zachary with some kind of weapon. Then

Walter went hurtling into the fray, his white hat flying off. There were shrieks from the other side of the ballroom where partygoers were crowded in the doorways watching from a safe distance away. Kenzie reached out a hand toward Zachary.

"Are you okay? Let me see."

He covered his side and shook his head. "Just a graze. Your dad—he's going to get hurt!"

Kenzie forced her attention away from Zachary and the blood on his suit to her father and Fisk, rolling around on the floor, both trying to get control of the knife in Fisk's grip. "Dad! Be careful!"

She didn't know what to do. If she joined in the struggle, she might be hurt or make things more dangerous for Walter. She looked around for some kind of weapon, but there was just open space intended for visiting and the dancing that would come after dinner and the fundraising pitches.

"Dad!"

And then, as quickly as it had begun, the struggle was over and they were both still. Kenzie looked at the two men on the floor in horror, unable to take it all in.

Walter rolled over, off of Fisk. Fisk didn't move. His white shirt was also turning red. Kenzie looked once more at her father to make sure that he wasn't hurt. She didn't see any sign of injury. But Fisk's condition was grave.

Kenzie put her gloved hand directly over the wound and pressed hard. At least she was protected by her gear from any blood-borne disease. She leaned close to Fisk's face, watching for the rise and fall of his chest, listening for his breath.

"I had to protect you," Walter said breathlessly.

"Put your hand here," Kenzie ordered, gesturing to the wound. "Press down. Zachary, are you okay?" She looked over her shoulder to him.

"Fine," he said. He was still on his feet, not looking any worse.

"Call 9-1-1."

He nodded and looked for his phone, zipped away into one of the pockets of the coveralls. Kenzie adjusted Fisk's head and neck and started chest compressions.

"I don't know what happened," Walter said. "I've never seen him like that. So... unreasonable. I don't understand. He's tough and hard-nosed, but this was... animal-like..."

Kenzie continued the chest compressions, feeling breathless herself. "This virus... it changes people. It causes rapid dementia. Personality changes, confusion, emotional lability..."

"But... like this?"

If Fisk had somehow contracted the virus, then Kenzie's chest compressions were probably less than useless. A stab wound in the belly. No pulse or respiration. That was bad enough. The chances of bringing someone back from that with just chest compressions were extremely remote. Add in the virus, and his brain was probably so clogged with proteins that he would have been dead within hours anyway.

But Kenzie continued the compressions. She had committed to the rescue; she had to continue until Fisk was declared dead.

70

Kenzie realized suddenly that she had another patient, one who might benefit from her attention, unlike Fisk. She looked around for Zachary as she continued compressions.

"Zachary? Are you okay?"

He was slightly out of her line of sight due to the limited field of vision of the face shield. He moved closer, where she could see him. His hand was still pressed to his side.

"I'm fine," he assured her.

Kenzie remembered another private investigator, years before, and the stab wound that he had sustained. She remembered the blood pumping out under her hands as she screamed for help. Was history repeating itself?

But what she could see of Zachary's face through the shield was still a healthy color. As healthy as Zachary's face ever was. Pale, but not blue or gray. He seemed to be steady on his feet, not weak or staggering.

"You're sure you're okay?"

"Yes. It burns, but that means it's just a surface wound. It's not bleeding much."

Lola nosed at Fisk, whining. Kenzie didn't know what to do about the dog. She would still have to take Lola into the lab for quarantine. After she was done there. Despite the little bit of wrestling, her suit still seemed to be intact, so she was protected from the virus.

The integrity of Zachary's suit, on the other hand, had been compromised. He was now exposed to Lola and the virus. The risk wasn't significant because he was still breathing clean air and had his gloves on, but the wound in his side did offer another entry point for the virus.

"You need to stay back from Lola," she told him. "I don't want you to be exposed."

"Okay."

The chest compressions seemed to go on forever. But eventually, an ambulance arrived. The paramedics were shown through to the ballroom. Everyone else stayed back, mindful of Kenzie's raving that Lola was a deadly contamination risk. But apparently, no one told the paramedics of the danger and they approached without any concern.

"I don't think there's anything you can do for him, but I have been keeping up compressions," Kenzie told the first paramedic to kneel down at her side. "And you need to treat this patient as a biohazard. He may have a virus that has caused several deaths recently."

He looked at her in disbelief. "Is this some kind of joke? Because of the costume?"

Kenzie shook her head. "No. I'm wearing the biohazard gear because of the virus. It's not a costume. I came to take the dog," she nodded toward Lola, "to put her into quarantine, because she is carrying the virus and has spread it to a number of people already. We need to get her into isolation."

"I can't do anything about that."

"I don't expect you to. I have a place to take her to. But you need to treat this patient very carefully, even if he's dead."

The paramedic already had gloves on in preparation for examining the patient. He put on a second layer of gloves and motioned to his partner to do the same. He opened up his case and pushed things around to find a face mask, which he put on.

"Could you look at Zachary?" Kenzie motioned to the other paramedic. "He was stabbed, but he says it's not bad."

The second paramedic approached Zachary to attend to him. The first knelt over Fisk, feeling for a pulse. As Kenzie had expected, there was no sign of a pulse.

"Keep up the compressions until I tell you to stop."

Kenzie nodded. "I will."

"Let's have a look at the wound." The medic motioned for Walter to give him access to the stab wound. Walter lifted his hand and moved out of the way. The paramedic poked around, pulling Fisk's shirt back to have a look. Walter stood and looked down at his hand.

"Uh, Mackenzie...?"

Kenzie looked at Walter staring down at his bloody hands, her stomach tightening in a knot. She wanted to swear, but kept it to herself. "Go straight to the nearest restroom and wash up. Don't touch your face. Keep the water on a low stream. You don't want it splashing back in your face or aerosolizing any contaminants. Warm water, soap, wash for two minutes, making sure you get in between your fingers, under your nails, everywhere. Okay?"

"Okay. You don't think...?"

"No, unless you have open wounds on your hands, your skin should protect you. It can be spread through bodily fluids, but you shouldn't be able to absorb it that quickly with the natural barriers that skin provides." And once she had a chance to talk to Savage, they would work out what antiviral protocol to give the people who had been exposed to the virus. Zachary, her father, the other residents and staff at the nursing home. Anyone who had petted Lola. The Virutek people. The list was not going to be short.

Walter nodded and walked toward the nearest restrooms. Kenzie was happy to see that he was walking, not running in a panic. The chances that he would follow her instructions to the letter were much greater if he stayed calm.

"There's no point in continuing the compressions," the paramedic advised. "There's not going to be anything we can do for this patient, and if there really is a biohazard here, we need to focus on containment rather than pursue extreme measures. Exactly who are you and how do you know about this virus?"

Kenzie sat back, relaxing her shoulders and massaging her arms. "Dr. Kenzie Kirsch with the... I'm from the Medical Examiner's Office in Roxboro. We've had some deaths that may or may not be related to a novel HHV-4 virus that escaped a lab. The lab virus is designed to cross the blood-brain barrier and we've seen cases of very rapidly progressing dementia, leading to death within a few days."

"Good grief. Where is the CDC on this?"

"We're still in the evidence-gathering stage. We don't have enough for them."

The paramedic looked around at the ballroom, Lola, and all the people peering in at the doors. He swore. "I'm not doing anything without bringing in the infectious disease experts. Let's lock this down."

Kenzie let the paramedic make the calls their protocol dictated. She went over to Zachary and the other paramedic. "Is he okay? Really?"

"Should get stitched up, but it's clean and didn't go in deep," the paramedic said. "If he'll let me access it properly, I can bandage it up temporarily, and they can suture it at the hospital."

Zachary blocked the paramedic, and Kenzie realized the man wanted to cut the suit or for Zachary to take it off. Kenzie was with Zachary on that note. "No, he needs to keep the suit on, for whatever protection it will still give him. We need to get the dog into quarantine."

"The dog isn't leaving here, and neither is anyone else," the first paramedic said firmly. "When I say lockdown, I mean lockdown! Until we have someone with authority clear the site, no one is going anywhere. I'm not going to be responsible for releasing any carriers."

Kenzie looked at Lola, then back at Zachary. "Well... I guess we're here for a while. Do you mind if we find a place to sit down? My legs are shaking."

Zachary nodded, looking happy to comply. "Yeah, I think we could all use a few minutes, after all this..." He nodded toward Fisk's body.

"I can't believe it."

Walter was walking back from the restroom. He gave Kenzie a weak smile. "All okay now. Washed off the first two layers of skin. And it looks like you're finished." He glanced over at his friend's form. "Or Aaron is, anyway."

"Yeah. I'm sorry, Dad. There wasn't anything I could do."

"Of course not. I had to protect you..."

"We were talking about finding a place to sit down. I don't suppose they're going to want us in the dining room or around anyone else now."

"There are bound to be private rooms available. Let me find out."

Walter strode toward the crowd watching through the doorways. People backed away, giving him space to pass, definitely nervous about the talk of a contagious virus. Walter was back a minute later with one of the venue staff. "Mackenzie, Zachary, come this way."

The two of them followed, and the employee led them to a private room where they could meet. Kenzie looked at the engraved plaque next to the door. *The Champlain Room.*

It started and ended with Champlain.

Kenzie sat down in one of the soft, comfortable leather chairs arranged around the heavy boardroom table. Zachary fell into one next to her. He gave a sigh. Kenzie was sure he was just as glad to get off his feet as she was. Probably more so, since he was injured. He didn't want to show her any weakness, but she knew he must be shaking worse than she was. All the adrenaline from the day, peaking at the point that they were attacked. Walter sat in one of the chairs on the opposite side of the table. He leaned forward, examining them, looking eager to begin a long list of questions. And Kenzie wasn't up for more questions. She needed an answer.

"How do you know—did you know—Aaron Fisk?"

Walter looked surprised that she had beat him to the punch. "I've known him for many years. He's a lobbyist."

"I thought he was some kind of scientist. We saw him at a laboratory."

"No." Walter shook his head. "But he does a lot of lobbying on behalf of medical corporations. Big pharma. We've been on opposite sides of the table more often than on the same side."

"So what was he doing there? And what was he doing here?"

"Medical studies have to be funded. You know anything about the funding that this laboratory receives?"

"No." Kenzie wished that she could take her suit off so that she could scratch an itch. But she didn't want to take any chances. It was safer, for the moment, for her and Zachary to remain in the biohazard suits. "I never thought to ask. I guess I just saw them as a little independent lab studying whatever it was that interested them."

"Not really the way it works. Studies need to be funded."

"There was a sign on the wall at Virutek," Zachary said. "A plaque that had a name like Something Gesundheit GmbH. That's like a German corporation, right?"

"That's right," Walter agreed. "AFG, maybe? They're very big. Or it could have been a smaller one. Aaron hired out to a lot of those companies. He had a reputation for succeeding when others had only run up against roadblocks. A troubleshooter."

A troubleshooter. Someone who was prepared to go above and beyond to clear the way for a big corporation. For a nice chunk of money, Kenzie assumed.

"He was the one who broke into the Medical Examiner's Office," she told them. "The one who knocked me down."

"Are you sure? I thought you didn't see who it was!" Walter demanded.

Kenzie hesitated before answering. She was pretty sure she hadn't told him that. So who had he gotten it from?

"Not to describe him, no. But he was the same size and shape. And he has a certain scent. His deodorant or aftershave. It's distinctive. I recognized it when he grabbed me."

"I don't know if something like that would hold up in court," Walter observed skeptically.

"It's not going to court. He's dead."

"Well, yes," Walter agreed uncomfortably.

"If he's the troubleshooter," Zachary said slowly, "the one who pushes things through and makes them work, the one who broke into the office, then the police might want to look into the possibility he was involved in Abernathy's death."

Kenzie frowned. "You don't think that he was killed by someone unrelated to Virutek? It could have just been a mugging..."

"In his motel room. Where he was hiding out."

"Well... maybe. That's only a guess."

"Fisk is clearly not someone who is opposed to violence. To solving things with force instead of negotiation. Not above breaking the law."

Kenzie looked at Walter for his opinion. Her father gave a reluctant shrug. "He was known for being... kind of a cowboy." Walter brushed his fingers over his own hat, which he had retrieved at some point. "Getting things done his own way. If you can make some headway... these difficult cases can bring in a lot of cash."

"Wow. But all of that... killing Abernathy, breaking into the ME's office and stealing evidence... that would mean that he knew there was a problem. He knew the virus had escaped from the lab and was helping to cover it up."

"Yes," Walter agreed. "I suppose it does."

"And it means that he should have known to wear protective gear. If he knew the virus was out there, that maybe Abernathy had it, that the samples he stole from the morgue might be infected, he should have worn something to protect himself."

"You can't exactly walk into a motel room wearing something like this without attracting attention." Zachary indicated their protective gear.

"Not to this extent, but he could have a least put on gloves and a mask. The blood splatter in that motel room was... extensive. He basically aerosolized the blood. He was breathing it in. Right along with the virus."

71

They had been isolated, been put through decontamination procedures, had extensive medical examinations, and Zachary's knife cut had been stitched up. Kenzie lifted Zachary's shirt and checked out the sutures, touching the wound lightly to reassure herself that the injury was minor and she wasn't going to lose him as she had Lance.

Zachary gave a shiver and hugged her to him, giving her a comforting squeeze. "It's all over. Everything is going to be okay."

"I hope so. But what if the CDC doesn't find the same things as we did? What if they think the virus doesn't have anything to do with the dementia and deaths? I mean... my whole career could be down the crapper if they come back and say that I acted without reasonable proof that there was a danger."

"You were acting under Dr. Wiltshire. So... it would be his career down the crapper."

"And mine too."

He held her more loosely so that their bodies were just lightly touching. "What would you tell me?"

Kenzie thought about it. "To stop worrying about what's going to happen. Quit catastrophizing it."

Zachary nodded and rested his head against hers. "I'm glad that you're okay. That you and your dad didn't get hurt."

"And I'm sorry that you got hurt. But glad it wasn't serious. Now you just have a cool scar to show your buddies and say 'yeah, I got this protecting my girlfriend from a maniac with a knife.'"

Zachary grinned. "That *is* pretty cool."

"Everybody's going to want one." She looked around. "I can't believe that the CDC went all-out. Dr. Wiltshire said that we would need more proof before they would do anything."

He gave a shrug. "Well, if you can't get proof, get publicity."

One of the staffers came into the hospital room that Kenzie and Zachary had been assigned to. She was wearing a protective suit similar to the ones that they had worn to the ball. She handed them each a bag of their personal possessions. Anything that they had been able to properly disinfect.

They each sat down on one of the hospital beds. Kenzie turned her bag around to survey the contents inside. Zachary immediately delved into his to retrieve his phone. Kenzie preferred not to look at her phone yet. There would be calls from her mother and father, from Dr. Wiltshire, and who knew how many others. She wasn't ready to deal with it yet.

She looked over at Zachary to say something to him, but the remark fled her lips. He was scrolling through a screen, looking worried.

"What's up?" Kenzie asked.

He passed the phone across to her. Kenzie took it, unsure what she was going to see. A worrisome message from Rhys? Bad news about Bridget or her babies? Another break-in at the lab or at the house?

She saw a column of texts from Lorne Peterson, asking for one of them to call him as soon as possible. But specifically asking not for Zachary, but for Kenzie. Lorne probably didn't have Kenzie's number handy, as he always talked to Zachary.

Rather than pulling her own phone out, Kenzie just tapped Lorne's name and 'Call.' The phone started to ring through. Kenzie put it on speaker so that she and Zachary could both hear and talk.

"Hello? Zachary?"

"We're both here, Lorne," Kenzie said. "Is everything okay?"

"Well... I'm sure it's all right, but I wanted to talk to you, Kenzie, to see what you thought. Seeing as you're a doctor..."

So something was wrong. They hadn't just seen Zachary on the news or heard that he'd been injured. "What is it?"

"Pat's been fighting this bug," Lorne said. "The same one I had. Or that's what we figured, anyway. He was dragging around tired all the time, kind of cranky and depressed. You know how a sick toddler behaves!" Lorne tried to joke, but the concern in his voice was clear.

"Is it his meds?" Zachary asked. "Have they adjusted the dosages lately?"

"No. I don't think it's anything to do with his meds. But... he fell down today—said that he just tripped—and he's asked the same questions several times... I know it's nothing, but I'm worried. He doesn't have any of the symptoms for a stroke; I looked them up on the computer..."

Kenzie's eyes met Zachary's. Zachary swore.

"I'm sure it's nothing," Lorne said apologetically.

"Actually... it might be," Kenzie admitted. "Lorne... I was exposed to a virus before I came down to visit you guys last. And I might have passed it on to Pat."

"Then it isn't anything to worry about. If you've already had it."

"I didn't get any symptoms. But sometimes, people are just carriers or are asymptomatic. This is... a brand new virus, and we don't know yet how it might behave"

"So what should I do? Rest and fluids? Like the flu?"

"You need to get him to the hospital right away. I'm going to call someone so they will be expecting him when you arrive. Go to the emergency room doors, but wait there and don't get out of the car. They'll come to get him. They'll be wearing protective clothing, like HAZMAT suits. Don't open the doors to anyone who isn't wearing protective gear."

"Kenzie?" Lorne's voice shook. He had been worried when he called, now he was clearly frightened. "Is it that serious? Is it the plague?"

"It's not the plague. It's something new. It has... it has caused some deaths. I'll convince the doctors to treat it aggressively. I'll get them to treat all of us, you too. The earlier we catch it, the better our chances."

"Do you and Zachary have it too?"

"Neither of us has been showing any symptoms. But we're already in isolation because we were exposed. We'll just have to take it up a level and not wait to see if we test positive for it. If I passed it on to Pat, then I have it for sure. Maybe Zachary too. Maybe you."

Lorne swore, worried. Kenzie had never heard him swear before. "Pat? Pat, you need to get ready to go. Come on. Pull on a jacket and your shoes. We have to go to the hospital."

They could hear Pat grumbling in the background, obviously not wanting to take the trip.

"I talked to Kenzie, and we have to go. Get ready." Lorne spoke back into the phone. "I'll let you know when we're there."

"Okay. Remember what I said and only open the doors for someone with proper protection. I'm going to light a fire under someone now."

72

Neither of them could look at the other. Zachary took his phone back after Kenzie hung up, but he didn't look at it like he normally would, diving into his email or messaging apps to see what else he had missed. He just held it in his hand, looking blankly in front of him.

Kenzie hit the emergency call button, which brought a couple of nurses hustling into the room within seconds, unlike in a regular hospital ward where they usually didn't show up for a while.

"The emergency button is not for—"

"This is an emergency. We just got word that a family member is showing symptoms," Kenzie snapped. "That means I am a carrier, because I'm the only vector between him and the outbreak. And if he's showing symptoms already, he needs aggressive treatment or he might not survive."

The nurse looked at Kenzie for a moment, then nodded. "I'll get the doctor."

The two of them retreated.

The beds were close together. Kenzie reached and took Zachary's hands, holding them out in front of her, the two of them sitting facing each other with their clasped hands in the center.

"It's going to be okay, Zachary. We caught it before the symptoms got too bad, and we'll throw everything at it that we can. He's going to recover. It's going to be okay."

"If anything happens to them..." Zachary's voice was rough. "They are... the only family I had for years. I can't lose them."

"It's going to be okay."

73

From the chair beside his bed, Kenzie watched Zachary sleep. His chest rose and fell in a steady rhythm.

He slept so little when he was well that she'd rarely had the opportunity to watch him sleep. Or she hadn't taken the opportunity when she'd had it.

He looked younger. The lines on his face and bags under his eyes were less pronounced. She could imagine what he had looked like as a little boy. She'd seen a few pictures that Lorne had taken over the years, but she'd had a hard time reconciling the young Zachary's face with the one she knew, all angular and frequently unshaven, a man who had been through a lot in his life that no one should ever have to.

He stirred and opened his eyes. He lay there for a moment, eyes glazed and unseeing before he focused on her face and smiled.

"Kenz."

"Hey, Zach. How are you feeling?"

"Ugh."

That was pretty much how he felt all the time, and Kenzie was glad they were nearly at the end of the treatment protocol and they would be able to get back to their lives soon.

"Do you think you could eat something?"

"I'll try."

Kenzie raised the head of the bed. Any time he was awake, they tried to get him to eat. Zachary was already thin and nauseated from his depression and medications, and the side effects of the Acyclovir and the chemo drugs that they were using to fight the virus off made it hard to keep anything down. They didn't want him to lose more weight.

Kenzie reached for the snacks on the bedside counter. "Jell-O?"

"Yeah."

She tore the sealed top off a new Jell-O cup and handed it to him with a spoon. He took a couple of bites and closed his eyes. Kenzie nudged him. "Hey. Stay awake. Have some more."

He focused on the gelatin again and had another bite.

"Heard from Lorne today," Kenzie said. "He's back home."

Zachary's lips twitched. "He is? That's good. He didn't get any symptoms?"

"Nope. And he handled the protocol like a champ. No trouble."

"We'll be done soon."

"Yep," Kenzie agreed. "And then back to work. Dr. Wiltshire says that he's tired of me lazing around on vacation when everyone else in the office tested negative and is hard at work. And your family has all been calling. Heather says she's running out of work and needs you to send some more files her way."

"Yeah." Zachary nodded. "Be good to be home again."

Kenzie didn't tell him that she'd already finished her protocol. Zachary's viral load had been much higher, so he was on higher doses and had not yet completely cleared the virus, though they figured he would be done in another day or two.

"Let's see if we can get Lorne on the tablet," Kenzie suggested. Zachary's eyelids were starting to droop, but she knew that if he could talk to Lorne, he would make an effort to stay awake longer.

"Yeah, okay."

Kenzie pulled the wheeled table across Zachary's lap and set the tablet on it, propped at an angle. She tapped the buttons on the screen until a call started to ring through to Lorne Peterson's account, and then they both watched to see if he would answer.

After a few rings, Lorne's round face fringed with white hair appeared on the screen as he bent down to answer the call. He smiled tiredly, happy to see his former foster son, and sat down.

"Zachary! How are you managing?"

"Good," Zachary proclaimed, though he obviously wasn't well. "Going to be done here soon. Then I can go home and get back to work."

"You might need to take it easy for the first little while," Lorne warned. "I thought I would be back to normal when I finished, but I can still barely walk from one room to another without getting out of breath."

Kenzie made sympathetic noises. The chemical cocktail that they had been on had left her tired too. A couple of days off it and she was starting to feel more normal, but not quite ready to go back to her usual routine yet.

"And it's so quiet around here," Lorne said.

Zachary's head was starting to nod. Kenzie nudged him and tried to keep him awake for a few minutes longer. Another bite or two of Jell-O to keep up his strength.

Pat's head appeared over Lorne's shoulder. "The reason it's so quiet around here is that whenever I put on the music, you say your head hurts and you want a nap, old man," he teased.

Lorne turned his head to smile at his partner. Pat put his hand on Lorne's shoulder, and Lorne put his hand over it and gave it a squeeze.

"Well, that might be true," Lorne admitted. "Don't ask me how he's so full of energy and bouncing around here when he was the one who had symptoms," he complained. "Weren't so bouncy a couple of weeks ago, were you?"

"It's those green drinks," Pat said. "If you want me to whip you up some wheatgrass shots..."

"No!" Lorne made a face. "You don't need to go to all of that bother. I'll just lie down for a nap when we're done talking. If you'll keep your music down."

Zachary's head sank into his pillow and Kenzie couldn't shake him awake again. She took the Jell-O cup and spoon out of his hands.

"I guess that's it," Kenzie said softly to Lorne and Pat on the tablet. "We'll call again tomorrow. Take care of yourselves."

"We will," they both agreed.

"Look after that boy," Lorne said.

"Sure will." Kenzie gave a little wave to the camera and ended the call. She rested her head on Zachary's pillow, just touching her forehead to his head. "Sweet dreams, Zachary."

DOSED TO DEATH

A KENZIE KIRSCH MEDICAL THRILLER #3

1

H ow's it going?" Kenzie asked Zachary, poking her head into the bedroom to see whether he had finished packing.

Zachary was sitting on the bed looking at his duffel bag. It didn't look as if he had made much progress since the last time she had seen him. She cocked her head to the side.

"Tired?" she asked sympathetically.

Zachary raised his head to look at her. His face was painfully thin, eyes dark hollows. He attempted to hide how sunken his cheeks were with the dark stubble, but she could still tell. The antiviral protocol that the two of them had been through had been much harder on him. Kenzie was feeling pretty much her old self. She just tired a little faster than usual. But Zachary had already been sinking into his annual depression and didn't sleep or eat well, so it had really taken its toll on him.

But better thin and tired than dead.

"I just don't know if I can do this," Zachary said.

Kenzie had already taken care of everything else. The only thing left for Zachary to do was to pick out the clothes he wanted to wear for the holiday and throw anything else he wanted to take along into the bag. Once they were at the resort, he could rest and sleep as much as he needed to. They had a cabin to retreat to that was separate from anyone else, so they didn't have to worry about thin walls or people being aware of their comings and goings. They would have both the privacy they needed and socialization activities to boost their spirits.

Rather than criticizing him or telling him to just focus and get it done, Kenzie entered the bedroom to see if there were anything she could do to help.

"Do you know what you want to wear?"

He looked at his flat bag listlessly. "No."

"Does that mean you don't care? Can I just pick some stuff out for you?"

Zachary rubbed the back of his neck. "Yeah. Sure."

Kenzie went through Zachary's drawers and his side of the closet to pick out a few outfits, folded them neatly, and set the piles into his bag. "There. What else? Do you have your meds?"

"Yes."

Kenzie opened the toiletries case to see what was in it. Comb, toothbrush, razor, and a few bottles of pills. She checked the names on the sides of each, and didn't think he had everything he needed. She left the bedroom and went down the hall to the main bathroom, which was the one that Zachary usually used, leaving the ensuite bathroom to Kenzie. She opened up the medicine cabinet and looked through the remaining pill bottles, picking out a couple more that Zachary probably couldn't go without for a week. She grabbed his deodorant and toothpaste and glanced over his toiletries for anything else he might need that the resort wouldn't have on hand.

She returned to the bathroom and added the items she had picked out to his toiletries bag. Zachary watched her and didn't comment.

"What else are you taking? Your computer and phone? Anything else?"

"Computer," Zachary echoed.

"It's in the living room? Let's go grab it and you can tell me if there is anything else you need."

She picked up the duffel bag. Zachary took a few extra seconds to consider this, then pushed himself to his feet. He took the bag from her as they walked to the doorway, and Kenzie let him. She didn't know whether he was being chivalrous or just didn't want someone else touching his stuff, but it didn't matter. It was good he was taking some part in the preparations, however small.

In the living room, he put his bag down on the couch and picked up his laptop computer, which was sitting closed on his mobile desk, and put it into his soft-sided briefcase beside the couch. He picked up the cord, unplugged it from the wall, and carefully coiled it up to add to his gear. Kenzie stayed back and watched him gather the peripherals he wanted. An external drive and mouse. A couple of notepads. He stood there looking at his desk, again grinding to a stop.

"Is that it?" Kenzie prompted.

"I don't know if I can do this," Zachary said again.

"Do what?" Kenzie had assumed that he meant he couldn't do the packing on his own, but since he was now packed, she wasn't sure what he meant.

"Just... this whole thing. Going to this place. Being around other people. Leaving my business behind when I've already been neglecting it because of this virus protocol..."

"You wouldn't be able to do it if you were here anyway. You still need more time to recover. Just because you're out of the hospital, that doesn't mean that you are one hundred percent better. What about after your car accident? You couldn't go right back to work a couple of weeks after that, could you?"

"No. But that was different. I had a lot of rehab to do... I couldn't physically do the work."

"And how is that different from now? You're not being weak or lazy. You're recovering from a virus and treatment protocol that could have killed you. Just like that car accident. Your clients will understand that you can't service them right now. They will wait, or go to another private investigator, or Heather will help them out with what they need. And when you're feeling better, you can get back to it."

"Heather can't do everything. She's not trained. She doesn't do field work."

"I know. I said that they could go to another PI if they need to. If they just need backgrounds or skip tracing or other computer stuff, Heather can do that."

He scratched his head. "Yeah."

"You can't work like this. And if you're out of town, people will get that. Everyone takes a vacation now and then. It's not healthy to work all the time. Most jobs will wait a couple more weeks, until you're ready."

"I thought this vacation was only a week."

"Yes, the vacation is only a week. But I don't think that's going to be enough time for you to recover enough to work cases again."

"I can do some. Maybe not everything, but I can start doing some work, can't I?"

"I'm not the one dictating it. That will depend on your body."

Zachary started to sit down on the couch. Kenzie stepped forward and picked up the duffel bag. "Don't get comfortable. Let's get the car loaded up."

He took the bag away from her firmly, then bent down and picked up the laptop bag as well. "Which car are we taking?"

It was always a fight to see who got to drive. Zachary enjoyed driving, especially on the highway, where he was able to zone out and let go of his usual anxieties. Kenzie loved getting out in her baby, a sporty red convertible. But she had decided they would take Zachary's nondescript white compact instead. It was better in the fall weather in Vermont, which was supposed to be taking a turn for the worse in the next few days. And she wanted to give Zachary that time to drive, to get out of himself and be in the zone for a while. It would help him as much as any vacation. She also preferred not to have her baby sitting outside unprotected when they were at the resort. It was safer in her garage.

"Yours. But you have to watch the speed limit."

Which meant that he'd better not go more than ten miles or so above the speed limit. Zachary preferred to drive way too fast for Kenzie's comfort. At least, when they weren't racing against time to stop a viral outbreak.

Zachary brightened a little at this news. He hefted his bags higher and headed to the front door. Kenzie grabbed the food bags from the kitchen and her suitcase from the hall and followed him out to his car.

Zachary had the trunk open and carefully stowed his bags, then took Kenzie's from her and fit them in.

"You aren't taking a computer?" he noted.

"I'm on vacation. I've got my phone and tablet for simple emails or looking things up, I've got some books I intend to read, and I'm going to participate in some of the group activities and spend time with you. No work."

He considered this. "They *do* have Wi-Fi, right?"

"Yes, they have Wi-Fi. I don't know how fast their internet service is, being up in the mountains like they are, but there is internet. And you could always hotspot to your phone."

"Maybe I should have bought some extra data..."

"You can do that later if you need to. You don't have to be home to do that. Now, is there anything else? Last chance."

Zachary gazed back at the house, but his eyes were far away. She didn't know what he was seeing or remembering. "Yeah. I'm fine. Got everything."

2

Kenzie kept an eye on Zachary as he drove out of the city and settled into highway driving. He gradually became more relaxed, the lines in his face softening and his hands loosening on the steering wheel. Kenzie gave him a while to enjoy the drive before trying to start a conversation.

"Now are you happy to get out of town?"

Zachary nodded. "Yeah. You're right. Some time away from work will be a good thing, even if I have already been off for a couple of weeks. There's money in the bank and I don't think I would be able to do much in the shape that I'm in right now."

"I think you'll feel a lot better once you've been able to relax for a while. Lorne says this resort is really nice."

"Did Pat take him there?"

Kenzie grinned. Patrick Parker had previously taken his partner, Lorne Peterson, to a day spa as a Christmas gift. While Lorne had said that he enjoyed it, it really wasn't his type of thing. Pat was far more concerned about healthy living and taking care of his body. Lorne was more of a pizza and beer guy. Zachary was clearly trying to set his expectations of the resort based on which of the men had first suggested it.

"No. It's run by an old friend of Lorne's."

Zachary nodded, understanding it was more of an indulgence than a health spa. Somewhere he wouldn't be expected to be fit or to eat clean.

"Sounds nice... Do you think..." Zachary trailed off.

Kenzie gave him some time to rethink his question and tell her what he wanted to know, but he fell silent and didn't finish the question.

"Do I think what?"

"It's just stupid."

"It's not really fair, deciding you know my answer without asking the question. How do you know what I'm going to say?"

"I don't. I just decided it was a stupid question and I don't want to ask it."

"Ask me anyway."

Zachary pulled out to pass a few cars. Kenzie watched the speedometer to make sure that it settled back into place once he pulled back into the right-hand lane.

"Okay. But it is stupid. I was just wondering if we could *not* tell people what I do for a living. People find out I'm a private investigator, and suddenly they're telling me their whole life story and asking my opinion about cheating spouses and Poirot and Monk and if I could help them find a long-lost family member..."

Kenzie laughed and nodded. "Like when people find out I'm a doctor and want to know what I think of their mole or if there really are untraceable poisons."

Zachary smiled. "Exactly like that."

"Well, I'm game. What do we want to tell people we do instead?"

"I can be unemployed. Then no one will ask me any questions requiring my expertise in any other area."

"Okay. Then I'd better be something that makes money. But something really boring. How about... an accountant. Hmm... not just an accountant..."

"How about an IRS agent?" Zachary suggested. "No one will ask you for your opinion on any creative accounting if they think you might turn around and audit them."

Kenzie nodded, pleased. "Great! I'm an IRS agent. An auditor. If anyone starts a conversation, I don't want to be a part of, I'll just start asking them questions about their income and whether they have ever been the subject of a detailed audit."

Zachary chuckled. "You are evil."

"It was your idea. I'm putting the blame on you."

3

Despite the fact that Zachary enjoyed driving, Kenzie suspected that driving the whole way would be too much for him. He was blinking a lot and his forehead was lined with concentration.

"Are you getting tired? I think maybe we should switch drivers."

Zachary blinked and used the heel of one hand to wipe his eyes. "I'm okay."

"I know you're used to long hours on surveillance, but there's no reason we can't divide up the driving. I'd like to do at least part of it."

"I'm not tired, though."

"Then say that you're tired so that your girlfriend can get a chance at the wheel," she urged, appealing to his caring nature. There was no need for him to admit that he didn't have the strength to do the whole trip on his own. Not when she really wanted to drive partway herself.

Zachary blinked slowly a couple more times, and Kenzie caught an infinitesimal head bob. If he waited much longer, he was going to be asleep at the wheel.

"Zachary. Pull over here. My turn."

He glanced at her, then sighed and pulled to the shoulder. The highway was quiet, so they didn't have to worry about the traffic whizzing by them as they got out. Kenzie made sure that Zachary had shifted into park, then got out. They crossed paths as they circled the car, and Kenzie gave Zachary a quick kiss. "Thank you."

He nodded, ears getting a bit red, then went around to the passenger side. Kenzie pulled back into the lane, and within five minutes Zachary was fast asleep, his head against the door.

"Not tired, my foot!" Kenzie said softly and shook her head.

She let herself relax. As much as she loved Zachary, it was stressful trying to look after him while he was sick. She was constantly trying to monitor his depression to make sure that he wasn't a danger to himself. Being human, she couldn't help but feel more down when he was depressed and didn't want to talk or to do things with her. She wanted to lift him up, but it was a struggle not to be pulled down instead.

A vacation would help. Getting him away from work to somewhere he was allowed to relax rather than moping around about not being able to do his job. They hadn't ever taken a holiday together. She hoped to be able to get his physical and mental health on track before December, so it would be easier to get him through to Christmas, when his anxiety and depression would start to return to their normal levels.

And it wouldn't hurt Kenzie, either. She had been through the same antiviral protocol as Zachary and, although it had been easier on her system, she still found herself tiring more easily than usual, dealing with brain fog, and just being generally out of sorts. She wanted to be one hundred percent when she went back to her job at the Medical Examiner's Office. Or at least, as close as she could get to it.

4

Zachary started to move around as they were making their way up a winding mountain road. At first, Kenzie thought he was awake, but he started to moan and mutter under his breath, and she realized that he was dreaming. He must have been really tired to not only be able to sleep in the car, which she had never seen him do, but to actually be in a deep enough sleep to dream while he was there.

He moved his head back and forth. Kenzie said his name a few times to try to rouse him gently, before the dreams turned into nightmares. She should have known it was already too late.

"Zachary. Zach. Wake up." She shook his arm. Then she put her hand back on the wheel. She didn't want to risk an accident because she was trying to wake him up.

He grunted and made a gesture of pushing something away in his sleep, but there was nothing there for him to push away.

"No. No," Zachary insisted.

"Zachary. It's okay. You can wake up."

"No!"

Kenzie tried shaking him once more when she was on a straight portion of the road. He startled suddenly and went rigid, hands out protectively in front of him. It would have been funny if Kenzie didn't know how terrifying his dreams could be.

"It's okay," she told him. "Just a dream. You're safe."

Zachary blinked a few times and looked at her. He looked around him, looked out the window, looked at the interior of the car. Maybe wondering why she was driving instead of him.

He blew his breath out in a puff and took a few deep breaths to try to calm himself. He rubbed his eyes and relaxed back into his seat.

"I fell asleep."

"Yeah. Have a look at the scenery, this is gorgeous."

He looked out the window again. "It is," he agreed.

The Vermont autumn was spectacular. She knew Zachary didn't like snow and Christmas card scenes, but the beautiful reds and oranges of the leaves were stunning. As a photographer, he had to appreciate them.

"Did you bring a camera with you? You might want to take some pictures while we're out here."

"I have my phone. Other gear is in my bag in the trunk."

"Good. I hadn't even thought about you being able to do photography while we're up here. That will be a nice break, won't it?"

Though she had seen a little of his artistic photography, he was mostly confined to surveillance photos while he was working. He hadn't had much time to do any hobby shooting lately. That was one thing they could plan to do together. Kenzie wouldn't mind going for some scenic walks, both at the resort and when they got back home. It would be a nice way to unwind together.

"Yeah," Zachary agreed. He sat up and watched out the window with more interest. "Are we getting close?"

"I think we're about ten or fifteen minutes out."

Kenzie was glad they were at the end of the road trip. It had seemed like an easy drive when she had mapped it out, but she hadn't been taking their lack of energy into account. Zachary was wiped out, and Kenzie was nearly as bad, yawning and fighting a fatigue headache.

"What were you dreaming about?" she asked, trying to keep a conversation going, which would help to keep her awake and alert.

Zachary didn't answer right away. He kept looking out the window, acting as if he hadn't heard her. Eventually, he glanced over at her and, seeing she was still waiting for an answer from him, shrugged.

"I dunno. Just something."

Not his usual nightmare, then, of the house fire he had been trapped in as a ten-year-old. The last straw that had broken his family up. Zachary was the only one injured in the fire. A fire that he had accidentally set with Christmas candles and decorations. Which explained why he still hated Christmas even now, decades later. It had been traumatic and a defining point in his life. He could never leave it behind, even when he slept.

"You don't remember what it was?"

Another shrug. And another evasive answer. "Not really."

Kenzie was silent, thinking it over. She had been wondering lately how often he dreamed about Bridget, his ex-wife, and the twins she was expecting. He had told her about a few dreams, mostly when he had first found out that she was pregnant. After that, he had stopped talking about it. But the babies would arrive any day now, and it had to be on his mind. Another reason Kenzie wanted to get Zachary out of town and focused on something else. He didn't need to be worrying about his ex and her babies on top of everything else.

And she suspected that he had been doing more than just worrying about Bridget, a suspicion that gave her a sinking, heavy feeling in her gut every time she considered it. He had previously monitored Bridget's comings and goings, putting a GPS tracker on her car so that he would know where she was at all times. He had managed to shake himself free from that compulsion, under threat of stalking charges, by a med change and returning to therapy.

But Kenzie feared that he was back up to his old tricks. When he wasn't home when she expected him or when he was vague about where he had been or what he had been doing, she couldn't help wondering.

5

There was a sign pointing right for The Lodge, the resort they were booked at. Kenzie slowed and looked for the turnoff, eventually finding a narrow gravel road that led into the trees. She slowed some more and turned onto it. As they bounced and crunched through the gravel, Kenzie was glad that they were in Zachary's car instead of hers. She hadn't even thought of gravel roads and what they could do to her paint job. And as she thought about it, there were probably other dangers too. Not just birds leaving evidence of their presence, but the possibility of goats or horses licking or munching it. Or stray shotgun pellets slicing holes through the panels. Tractors and machinery rolling right over it as if it weren't even there.

Of course, none of that was going to happen. But she was glad she didn't have to worry about it.

Kenzie hoped that no one would come down the road in the other direction. She wasn't sure there was space for two cars to pass each other. Especially if one of them were a truck or jeep, or some kind of farm machinery.

They made it to the end of the road without incident. Kenzie looked around at the painted fences, the pretty farmhouse, and the cottages nestled down the hill among the trees.

"Well, this is it."

Zachary opened his door and stepped out of the car. He looked around. "This is it?"

"Yes. You don't need to sound so disappointed."

"No... I'm not. I just thought... I don't know. I pictured a hotel, a town, stores, and maybe a lake..."

"There is a lake. But it's a resort, it's away from other settlements so that people can come here to regenerate without all of the interruptions of city life. Just... nice and quiet. Relaxing."

Kenzie got out of the car. Zachary started to pace restlessly. Kenzie had told him all about the Lodge, but little of it appeared to have actually stuck. Or he had heard the words but not understood that she was being literal about how isolated they would be. It was a retreat. Somewhere for them to just be themselves and not have to worry about work. Or exes having babies. Or viruses.

"Try to relax," she advised. "You're going to love it."

"It's fine," Zachary said quickly. But it was clearly going to take some time for him to adjust to the place. "We should... find out where our room is."

"Yes," Kenzie agreed. "Let's go into the main office and find out."

She gestured to the farmhouse. Zachary looked around, checking to see if there were, perhaps, a more obvious office, more modern or hotel-ish. But there wasn't. They walked up to the house together. Kenzie knocked on the door and entered.

It was quaint. Charming. It was not a city hotel. Zachary looked around, and looked back at Kenzie.

"Isn't it great?" she enthused. "You should take some pictures. I bet there are lots of good subjects here."

A man came out of one of the back rooms to greet them.

He was an older gentleman, well past retirement age. Probably the original owner of the farmhouse. Or maybe the son of the original owner. He smiled at them pleasantly but, having done so, his mouth fell back into a creased, unhappy-looking state. He had a head of gray hair and was thin, though not as thin as Zachary.

"Welcome to the Lodge," he told them in a gravelly voice that attested to many years of cigarettes or scotch. Or both. "I hope you will enjoy your stay with us."

Kenzie nodded. She stepped forward and put her hand out toward him. "It's nice to be here. You have a lovely place. I'm Kenzie, and this is Zachary. I guess we should get checked in and find out where our cabin is...?"

He returned the handshake, but it wasn't really a grip and a shake. He just barely touched her and then let go. One of those men who didn't think ladies should shake hands or take the initiative, she supposed.

"Stuart Dewey," he said shortly. "Why don't you come over here to our registration table," he invited. "I have your reservation here already, printed out, you just need to sign it. Fill in your license plate number. I think that's everything. We already have your credit card on file."

Kenzie nodded and followed him to a small writing table. He showed her the printouts, which were identical to the ones Kenzie had printed out for herself, and had her sign a form.

"There's no smoking in the rooms. If you want to smoke, you have to do it in a safe area. Not out in the woods with all of the dry leaves. There is a sort of a compound behind the groups of cabins. You can smoke there, if you are so inclined."

"We don't smoke," Kenzie assured him.

"Good. Darn place is as try as tinder this year. Whole thing could go up in a blaze."

Kenzie's gaze immediately went to Zachary. He had been hanging back, letting her handle everything, and hadn't moved from the space he had occupied since stepping in the door. His hands went out blindly to steady himself against the wall. Kenzie could see sweat on his face, and his skin turned a shocking white.

"Excuse me. Just a sec," Kenzie told Dewey.

She went over to Zachary and took him by the hand. "Come sit down. You're all right. Tell me five things you can see," she suggested, beginning an anchoring exercise.

Zachary's legs moved automatically when she tugged him over to an inviting couch. But his mind was far away.

"Five things, Zachary," Kenzie said, keeping her voice slow and reassuring.

He collapsed into the sofa. "The... books," he said faintly, looking at the bookshelves that lined one wall, filled with Readers' Digest Condensed Books. "The light. The... windows."

"That's three things. Give me a couple more."

Zachary's head turned. His face relaxed slightly. "The stairs. Something green."

The "something green" was some sort of macramé wall hanging. Kenzie wasn't any more sure than Zachary what it was supposed to be.

"Five things you hear?"

"Your voice. Mine."

"I think that's cheating. What else?" Kenzie strained her ears to listen and identify sounds around them.

"Outside... voices. Horses." Zachary thought about it. "Birds."

His color was starting to return as he pulled himself out of the flashback. "Good. How are you feeling?"

He put his hand over his heart, which was pounding hard and fast. Kenzie had her fingers over his pulse and was paying attention to the pace.

"Out of breath."

"Yeah. But you can breathe freely. And it will be back to normal soon."

"Okay."

Kenzie released his wrist, rubbed his shoulder for a few seconds, then went back to the registration table.

"What's wrong with him?" Dewey asked, a little too loudly. Zachary would be able to hear him clearly.

"Nothing is wrong with him. He had a bad experience with a fire. It's best not to talk about it."

The man eyed Zachary for a moment, then turned his attention back to the registration process. "License plate here. Initial here and here. There is a damage deposit of five hundred dollars. You get that back if everything is clean and undamaged at the end of your stay here. If the room smells of smoke or you have... remodeled... you lose your deposit on top of the rental fee. Understood?"

Kenzie nodded and initialed the spots he indicated. "Zachary, what's your license plate number?"

He recited it for her, his voice steady. Kenzie wrote it into the space provided.

"There is dinner at the house every day at six," Dewey advised. "There are no restaurants within an hour's drive. Every Thursday in November is Thanksgiving dinner. It's all included in the package you paid for."

Kenzie nodded.

"Here is a brochure setting out the various events that will be taking place over the next week," he handed her a flyer printed on an inkjet printer. "We have bonfires," a covert glance at Zachary, "Don't suppose you'll be going to those. Hayrides. Fireworks. Live entertainment at nine."

"It sounds like it's going to be great. I'm really looking forward to it."

He nodded dourly. "If you go walking, stick to the trails. They will bring you back here. If you get turned around, just keep taking right turns. There are wild animals. Most of them are not out during the daylight. I'd advise you to stay out of the woods at night. They're more afraid of you than you are of them, but don't be stupid and try to feed them or get your picture taken with them."

"I don't plan to!"

"No one ever plans to get mauled," he snapped. "But people are still all-fired eager to get themselves et. The Lodge isn't liable if one of you goes off into the forest molesting the wildlife."

Kenzie tried to keep a serious expression, nodding her agreement. "No sir. We'll be careful."

"Good. Welcome again to the Lodge. I'll see you at supper." He handed her a key with a large plastic square with the number five on it. "Out the door, down the hill, and to the right. You can't miss it."

"Thank you."

Kenzie went over to where Zachary was still sitting on the sofa. The owner disappeared back into a back room. Kenzie thought he was probably going to the kitchen. She looked down at Zachary.

"Good to go?"

"Yeah." Zachary stood up. He stayed still for a moment, getting his legs back. Then they walked together toward the door.

6

He didn't say anything at first. When they left the house, he took one look back over his shoulder. He raised an eyebrow at Kenzie.

"Molesting the animals?"

Kenzie snickered. "Bothering them. Trying to get too close. Throwing sticks at them or trying to get them to eat out of your hand."

"Why would anyone want to do that?"

"Some people see wildlife and lose their minds. They want to show everyone back home how brave they are, or how cute the animals are. So they do something stupid."

"If I ever get the idea of taking a selfie with a bear, please just shoot me and get it over with."

Kenzie grinned. She looked around. The road continued down to the individual cabins, so they didn't have to walk their luggage all the way there.

"You'd better be careful what you say. You are the one with problems with impulse control."

Zachary nodded, letting out a low chuckle. It sounded forced, but she was glad that he was at least trying to enjoy himself.

"Still. I've never had an impulse to cuddle with a wild animal."

"That's good. I don't want to wake up one morning and find out that you've wandered off with Yogi."

They got back into the car, Kenzie in the driver's seat, and she coasted down to the parking pad in front of cabin five.

"Well, here we are. Let's take the bags in."

She popped the trunk and they each took out the bags they had put into the trunk back at the house and carried them to the cabin. Kenzie put hers down to unlock the door and push it open. Zachary grabbed her bags as well as his own and stepped in.

Kenzie took a look around. She had looked at all the pictures on the website, so she had a good idea of what to expect. The cabin felt larger than it had looked in the picture. Not a cramped little place like her great-grandparents might have built with ventilation cracks between the logs, but a spacious, well-sealed modern building. She flipped the switch beside the door and the lights went on. Not that they needed them in the middle of the day, but it was nice to know that they worked.

"Electricity," Zachary observed. "I was worried for a few minutes."

"They have all the amenities. Electricity. Indoor plumbing." Kenzie grinned at him. "Including a hot tub."

He considered this thoughtfully. "Would that be a hot tub big enough for two people?"

"I believe it seats eight."

Zachary nodded slowly, smiling. "We'll have to test it out."

"I agree."

He looked around again. "Heated. Forced air."

"Yes." No need for them to light a fire in the fireplace. They would be comfy cozy without the need for an open flame.

Zachary wandered farther into the cabin. The living room and kitchen were together in the right side of the cabin. He went through a hallway to the left to check out the other rooms. Kenzie followed.

There were three bedrooms. Lots of space for them to spread out. They wouldn't be right on top of each other for a week. Zachary picked one of the bedrooms and put their clothing down. He took the bags of food back out to the kitchen.

"You brought a lot of food with you. He said that they have dinner every night in the main house."

"I know. And there is a continental breakfast, and sandwiches and cold cuts for lunch. But I wanted to make sure that you had familiar food that you like. I know how hard it is for you to eat when your meds make you nauseated."

She had packed chocolate chip granola bars, one of the only things he could get down in the morning. And the various other snack foods that he subsisted on when they didn't have meals together. She didn't want him to have any excuse for not eating. The vacation was to fatten him up, not to let him waste away any more.

"Thanks," Zachary said, sounding surprised, like he was amazed that she would have considered such a thing.

"We take care of each other," Kenzie said simply.

It wasn't just her looking after Zachary when he ran into problems. He helped her too, when she was working late, when she had run into trouble at work and needed help with a case.

When he had jumped in between her and a crazed killer at the masquerade ball. He'd only needed a few stitches, but it could have been much worse.

7

They were both tired from the packing and the drive, so they ended up napping most of the afternoon. Kenzie was up before Zachary, which, if he weren't recovering from his treatment, would have been remarkable. Even just sleeping during the day was unusual for him, despite how little he slept at night.

Kenzie got up slowly, careful not to wake him up. She got out one of her paperbacks and curled up to read it on the couch. Zachary was up in another hour, rubbing his eyes sleepily.

"How are you doing?" Kenzie asked. "Good nap?"

"I'm sorry. I didn't mean to sleep the whole afternoon."

"You're still recovering. Don't worry about it. We're here to rest."

"Rest, yes, but not to sleep the whole vacation away."

"You won't. I slept a lot of the time too. You weren't the only one. Are you getting hungry?"

Zachary shrugged. "I could eat something."

For him, that was about as good as it got. He usually said he didn't want anything, so Kenzie took it as a good sign.

"Great. They'll be serving dinner at the farmhouse pretty soon. Do you want to go up and meet the other guests and have dinner together?"

Zachary hesitated, then nodded. "Yeah, sure. That sounds good."

"You sure?"

"You don't want to stay in the cabin all day, do you? And you'll want a good dinner."

"Yes, but we don't have to rush into it. If you want to just have dinner ourselves tonight, we can do that. I brought plenty of food."

"No. Let's go have dinner with the others."

Kenzie smiled. She was looking forward to meeting the other vacationers. It felt like going to camp as a kid. She'd never gone to any that were real wilderness experiences. Lisa, her mother, had only selected camps with modern facilities. But Kenzie had enjoyed being closer to nature, making new friends, and trying new things. It was always an exciting time. Maybe that was why she had been drawn to the Lodge.

"Great. Give me a few minutes to freshen up, and then we'll head up and join the others. They have cocktails before dinner, so we can meet everyone and mix a little."

Zachary's eyes followed her as she got up and headed back to the bedroom. "I guess... I should change and shave."

She stopped in front of him and laid her hand over one whiskery cheek. "If you have the energy. If not, there's no dress code. You can go looking like a mountain man, I don't think anyone will object."

He put his hand over hers for a few seconds, his fingers warm and his touch light. "I'm not sure this rises to the level of mountain man, but it could use a trim."

"Okay. I'll see you in a few minutes."

Kenzie changed into a blouse and slacks. She didn't want to be over-dressed. She would see how everyone else was dressed before going to dinner in a dress. She applied fresh red lipstick and touched up her makeup in front of the mirror in the bedroom. She could hear Zachary's razor buzzing in the bathroom.

They met back in the living room. Zachary had managed a trim, and she supposed he had probably run a comb through his close-cropped dark hair, though it was impossible to tell. Which was exactly why he kept it that short. Kenzie touched her own spiraling dark curls. Her hair looked pretty good for having slept on it half the afternoon. Zachary hadn't changed his clothes. Shaving had probably used up most of his available energy.

"Looks good," Kenzie approved. "Let's go meet the other campers."

They walked up to the main house together, Kenzie's hand through Zachary's arm. The sky was dark and the stars out, shining brightly overhead.

"Wow. It's beautiful," Kenzie breathed.

Zachary raised his head and looked up at the stars. "You never see them like that in the city. I've seen photographs, but this is... amazing."

"How do you take pictures of stars? Do you need special equipment? Because you're taking pictures in the dark?"

Zachary went into a detailed explanation of what he would need to do to capture the brilliance of the stars, what equipment he would use and what camera settings. Kenzie didn't pay much attention to the details, just listened to his voice, relaxed and passionate about his hobby. By the time he was done, they were to the door of the farmhouse.

A young woman was walking up at the same time, and Zachary opened and held the door for her and Kenzie. The other woman barely acknowledged his existence. She was blond and, Kenzie had to admit, absolutely gorgeous. She probably had all kinds of men running to open the door for her with regularity. Zachary's eyes lingered on her as she walked away from him. Kenzie wondered whether he was thinking of Bridget, also blond and beautiful.

But he didn't watch her for long. He took Kenzie's hand again and walked with her into the main living room area where the guests were gathering for drinks.

It was an intimate group, not too noisy and overwhelming. It was a relaxed, peaceful atmosphere rather than a party with music blasting. The blonde went directly to the drinks at the side table and she poured herself a glass of wine before looking around at the other vacationers.

"Do you want something?" Zachary asked.

"A glass of wine would be nice."

He let go of her and went to the sideboard to pour her one. She watched him pour a glass of ginger ale for himself.

He returned with her wine.

"Thank you." Kenzie looked around, smiling at the others. One man smiled back and approached them, reaching out his hand to shake with them. He had round apple cheeks that made him look very young despite his beard, which Kenzie thought was an obvious attempt to look mature.

His grip was firm. "Redd Flagg."

Kenzie blinked and looked at Zachary to see whether he had heard the same thing as she had. He looked just as bemused as she felt.

"What?" Kenzie asked.

"My name. I'm Redd Flagg. That's two D's, two G's."

"Oh, well that's unique. I'm Kenzie, and this is Zachary." Using their first names only would help to preserve their anonymity.

"Nice to meet you! It's a pen name, actually. I'm a thriller writer."

Kenzie nodded and smiled pleasantly. It sounded like a good name for a thriller author, but was not one that she recognized. "Would I have read anything that you've written?"

"Not unless you're a time traveler. Right now I'm... in the drafting stage."

"I see. Just starting out."

"I decided to go on my own little writer's retreat. Just me and my computer, in a room, until I get my manuscript written."

"Wow, sounds intense."

"How is it coming along?" Zachary asked politely.

"Well... not as much progress as I would hope. But I'm getting words down on the page. That's the main thing."

"You can't do much without them," Kenzie agreed. She looked around the room. "So is this everyone?"

"Uh," Redd looked around. "Yeah, most of us. Do you recognize her?" He nodded toward the blonde who had entered the house with them.

"No. Should I?"

He nodded vigorously. "Brittany. Brittany 'the Bombshell' Blake. You've heard of her, right?"

Kenzie recognized the name of the celebrity, but didn't know what she was actually famous for. An actress, probably, but backwoods Vermont was a strange place to find a famous actress. If she were a Hollywood starlet, shouldn't she be living on the west coast and holidaying in a spa? "I know the name," she said, "but I have to confess... I don't keep up with a lot of pop culture."

"She's a really big thing. Has her own website and this following that call themselves The Bambas."

Kenzie wasn't much more enlightened. But she supposed she could go search the Bombshell up on the internet any time she pleased.

"Interesting. What's she doing here?"

"Getting away from the paparazzi is my guess. Trying to stay under cover. We'll see how long that lasts. All it takes is one person posting where she is, and we'll be surrounded by The Bambas."

"Well, I hope that doesn't happen."

"Don't we all," Redd agreed, but his tone and expression suggested otherwise. Kenzie guessed that nothing would thrill him more than to be able to be caught in the middle of a media frenzy.

"Who are the lovebirds?" Zachary asked, looking at a young couple cuddling and occasionally smooching on the couch, in danger of spilling their drinks during their amorous activities.

"The newlyweds," Redd advised, rolling his eyes. "Mr. and Mrs. Andy Collins. And no, I don't know her first name at all. She's just Mrs. Andy Collins, she is so smitten with him."

Kenzie chuckled and felt about a hundred years old. She had dated a lot of guys before Zachary, but had she ever been so cow-eyed and dumbstruck over any of them? Not even secret crushes. She'd been out to have her fun, but didn't think she'd ever been quite that silly.

"We have another bachelor," Redd continued, indicating a dark-haired man with a smile Kenzie instinctively distrusted.

Seeing that they were looking at him, the man approached them. He raised his eyebrows and didn't offer to shake hands. "Jack Fowler. And you are our newest arrivals."

"Kenzie and Zachary," Redd introduced them. "Just filling them in on everyone's details."

"So you've already met our writer in residence," Jack said sardonically, managing to make it sound like a writer was the most ridiculous career ever. "Be careful or he'll write you into his story."

"It's a *thriller*," Redd pointed out. "Lots of military and spy types. Not..."

Kenzie suppressed a smile. If he only knew some of the cases that they had been involved in! Redd was just the sort of person they wanted to keep from knowing their actual jobs.

"I'm a forensic accountant for the IRS," Kenzie said, making it sound as boring as possible. "And Zachary is..." she trailed off.

"Between jobs," he contributed.

Redd shrugged at Jack and rolled his eyes as if Kenzie and Zach couldn't see him. "You see?"

"You think spies would actually tell you that they are spies?" Jack challenged. "You think you would be able to tell just by looking at them? Kenzie and Zachary are exactly the type of ordinary, boring people that a spy would be masquerading as."

8

Redd looked speculatively at Kenzie and Zachary and shook his head. "I don't think so," he dismissed.

Kenzie waited until Redd looked away, then smiled at Zachary, enjoying their shared secret and how wrong Redd was.

Stuart Dewey, the gray-haired owner, entered the room and called for everyone's attention. "Dinner is served. If everyone could adjourn to the dining room, we will partake."

Everyone started to move toward the dining room, some faster and some slower. Zachary was looking back at something behind him when Kenzie caught sight of the set table, and her heart dropped to her stomach. She moved quickly to Dewey's side.

"We need to get the candles off of the table," she told him urgently. Her mind spun as she looked for an explanation. "You realize they're against fire codes, don't you? Like you said, it's been dry as tinder this year. One accident and everything could go up in smoke."

He looked at her. "I've been running this facility since you were learning your ABC's. I think I know the rules."

"Can we please get them out of here? They're not safe."

"They're perfectly safe. We've had them on the table for decades of dinners."

"Please." Kenzie put her hand on his arm. "You saw earlier... Zachary has a fear of fire. Can you please dispense with them while we're here?"

He rolled his watery blue eyes, raising his brows. "Your boyfriend is afraid of candles."

"His house burned down in a fire started by candles when he was ten. Please, have some compassion."

"Seems like he's had long enough to get over it."

"Some things you never get over. It's still really traumatic for him. Can we please?" Kenzie looked back at Zachary. He had seen the candles as well by now, and was standing back in the living room, face pale and sweaty. He was doing pretty well to be able to hold it together, when a bad flashback could send him crashing to the floor, curled up with his arms over his face. The same position he had assumed as a boy, trying to keep the smoke and flames away from his eyes and to make a pocket of breathable air.

Dewey relented. "Fine," he said gruffly. "We'll take the candles off the table."

Kenzie helped to blow them out and remove them from the table. She tried to do it unobtrusively, but her actions were out of the ordinary, so people were watching and wondering what was going on.

"Just need to get these out of the way," Kenzie said lightly, not trying to explain to the rest of the observers, though some of them had undoubtedly heard Kenzie's words to Dewey and were looking back at Zachary speculatively.

When they were all cleared away, Kenzie went back to where Zachary stood. "All clear. Can you do this? Or do you want to go back to the cabin?"

He swallowed, Adam's apple straining. "I'll be fine," he assured her. They walked together back over to the dining room table and found seats. There was another woman Kenzie hadn't noticed before. She had apparently joined them while Kenzie was taking care of the candles.

She was a slim black woman with an afro. She had the effect of studied calm, moving slowly and deliberately and watching everyone around her carefully. She seemed serene, but at the same time, watchful. Kenzie ended up sitting down next to her.

"Hi. We haven't met. I'm Kenzie and this is Zachary."

"Raven." The woman nodded at Kenzie and looked past her to Zachary. "Everything okay?"

"Fine," Zachary said tersely. "Thanks for asking."

"You... had an accident? Your house burned down?"

"We really don't like to talk about it," Kenzie said, raising her voice so that everyone would hear. "Okay? It's not something that's easy to talk about."

Raven paid no attention to Kenzie's protest. "Did you get burned?" she asked curiously.

Zachary was already breathing heavily. Had he brought any of his anxiety pills with him? Kenzie figured they were going to end up going back to the cabin before dinner was even underway.

But he pushed up his sleeve in response, showing off one of the worst scars from the fire. Despite the skin grafts, it was still a deep, ugly scar. Everyone stared at it, some openly and some covertly, pretending that they had no idea what was going on across the table from them. Zachary gave Raven a good look, then pushed his sleeve back down again.

"Kenzie's right," he said in a flat, unemotional tone, "I don't like to talk about it."

Raven nodded and turned her attention to her plate and to a fork that apparently needed polishing. They all waited, but no one else posed any questions about the fire.

Dewey extended a welcome to the newest guests, who had already become the center of attention, and Kenzie and Zachary quietly accepted the good wishes of the other guests.

"We will have one more guest arriving tomorrow," Dewey informed them. "Or at least, I assume he will get here tomorrow. Then that's it for the rest of the week. This will be our group."

Kenzie looked around at the others. It was a nice sized group. Most of them seemed friendly enough. She wasn't sure how big the staff for the lodge was, but she was pretty sure that Dewey was not doing everything himself. Not if they were having "Thanksgiving" dinner every Thursday. There had to at least be a Mrs. Dewey or a cook.

As she considered this, two women came in, bussing the dishes to the table. An older, white-haired woman who might very well be Dewey's wife. And a slender, Slavic-looking blond of around twenty-five who gave everyone big smiles as she helped with the table.

It was a roast beef and potatoes dinner, with several sides of vegetables available. A nice hearty meal for people who had been hiking, horseback riding, or doing whatever other activities the Lodge offered. Kenzie was careful not to take too much. She could always have a snack later in the evening if she wanted to, but if she stuffed herself, she would be uncomfortable all night. And she knew she needed to watch her portions to keep her figure, especially when she spent most of her workday sitting at a desk.

Zachary's servings were scanter than hers, but even so, she doubted he would eat everything he had taken.

"Is that all you're going to have?" Jack questioned, staring at Zachary's plate as if fascinated. "That wouldn't feed a bird. It's no wonder you look like you do."

Everyone else was shocked into silence. But they looked at Zachary to see what his answer would be.

"I just finished a round of chemo," Zachary said, "In case that means anything to you."

"Oh." Jack rubbed his upper lip, thinking about it. "Okay then. I guess that makes sense."

It was the truth; Zachary had been on chemo drugs as well as antivirals. They hadn't known for sure what would get rid of the virus, but from what they knew of its deadly effects, they knew they had to throw everything on it that they could without killing the patients in the process. There was no room for error. So Kenzie and Zachary had both been on the chemo protocol.

Kenzie took a couple of bites of the roast beef and gravy, making appreciative noises. "And who is the cook? This is wonderful."

"That would be Mrs. Hubbard," Dewey said, making a gesture to the older woman. "She has been cooking here for quite a number of years now. She does a very satisfactory job."

The compliment fell a little short. Kenzie nodded politely and repeated her praise. If that was the kind of gratitude that Mrs. Hubbard got from Dewey after quite a number of years, it was a wonder she had stayed.

"My late wife hired her," Dewey muttered, mostly to himself, "She was always good with the staff."

"Your late wife?" Brittany the Bombshell chimed in. "That means that she died? That's so sad. How long ago?"

Everyone's eyes turned back to Dewey.

"Couple of years now," Dewey said, looking down at his feet. "An eternity."

9

They learned a little more about each of the guests and what kind of behavior to expect from them over the next hour, and then Kenzie begged off, noting that Zachary was nearly falling asleep in his plate and had long since reached his limit as far as food went.

"There's a bonfire later," Jack offered. "Maybe we'll see you there."

Kenzie stared at him. "I don't think so," she said pointedly.

He laughed. "Oh yeah. Forgot about your *problem*," he said to Zachary.

Zachary paid no mind. They walked down to their cabin arm in arm. Kenzie didn't make any comment about the stars this time. The weather had cooled and there was a bite in the air. Kenzie cuddled closer to Zachary. They kept their heads down against the wind and hurried to the cabin.

"Whew!" Kenzie removed her coat and hung it on a peg next to the door. "I'm not sure anyone will want to be out there tonight, bonfire or not."

"Maybe they won't light one." Zachary removed his jacket as well. He rubbed his arms briskly. "Nice inside. I'm happy to just stay in."

"Me too. That was a bit of an ordeal... sorry about the candles and everything."

"Sorry?" his tone was surprised. "For what? You took care of it."

"Well... yeah. But I'm sorry they were there in the first place. Maybe I should have asked about candles when I was booking the holiday. I never even thought about it."

"Why would you? Most places use those little lights now. Live candles are dangerous." He choked up a bit over the word. "People reaching across them, around them, they could..."

He was sweating again. Kenzie rubbed his back and ushered him over to the couch.

"Everything is fine. Disaster averted. And he won't put them out the rest of the week, so you don't need to worry about it. How are you feeling, do you need another nap?"

"I slept most of the afternoon. I shouldn't sleep more now. I'll just stay awake... until I can't anymore, I guess."

"You don't have to push yourself. Whenever you want to sleep is fine."

Zachary shook his head. "No... you remember how bad my sleep got messed up before. I have to be careful, I don't want to end up sleeping during the day and laying awake nights."

"I don't think you need to worry about that. Your body is still trying to heal, and you need to sleep when it tells you to."

"I'm going to stay up for a while." His voice was determined.

"Okay. Great. Shall we put on a movie? Or did you want to test out the hot tub...?"

Zachary considered this offer. "Do we... have time for both?"

"I don't see why not. We don't have to be anywhere in the morning. Which do you want to do first?"

Kenzie supposed that Zachary would have ended up asleep on the couch while they watched the movie no matter which order they picked. The hot tub was great for soothing muscle aches from the drive and holding herself tense during the dinner. And for a little couples time together, just enjoying each other's company without any expectations.

Zachary had been dealing with intimacy problems ever since his kidnapping a year before and, while they had been going to couples therapy regularly and working on communication, they were not yet back to where they had been before the kidnapping. But Zachary had made a lot of progress, dissociating far less and enjoying intimate moments more.

One day, they would be back to where they had been. Kenzie was glad to be past the days when she couldn't even touch him without his flinching or pulling away.

She watched him sleep on the couch beside her, head tilted all the way back in what looked like an uncomfortable position, snoring slightly. She wasn't sure what movie they ended up watching or what it was about. She just enjoyed sitting there with him, watching him sleep.

Kenzie awoke to a thumping noise and was disoriented at first, thinking that someone was knocking on the door. Or maybe the window. She turned her head and tried to pry her eyes open.

"Who is it?" she asked Zachary. "Can you get that?"

He moved beside her, sliding his feet out of the bed and walking over to the window. He looked out, shading his eyes against the bright morning light. They had slept late.

"It's a helicopter. What would a helicopter be doing out here?"

"Really?" Kenzie squinted at him. "Are you sure I'm not just dreaming?"

"Looks pretty real to me."

"Mmm." Kenzie rolled over, turning her back to the window and the intrusive sunshine. "Come back to bed."

Zachary stood at the window for another minute. "No, I think I'm going to get up now. You go ahead and sleep as much as you need to."

"If I still need more sleep, then you need more sleep."

Zachary didn't argue. He just walked quietly out of the room, leaving her to sleep alone. Kenzie tried to get back into the comfortable, drowsy space that she had been in, but it was no use. Now that she'd been awakened, she couldn't get back to sleep. She got up and wandered out to the living room, where Zachary had pulled out his computer and was staring at the screen.

"You'd better not be working," she warned.

"Just checking email."

"Work email?"

"Uh... no."

Clearly, he was. "Do you want to hit the hot tub again this morning?"

Zachary grimaced. "My stomach is pretty rocky this morning. I think I'd better not. I might get seasick."

"Seasick? Really?"

He shrugged. "I can't help it. The water sloshing around..." He looked a little green just thinking about it.

"Okay, okay." Kenzie held up her hands. "No morning hot tub for you, then. As for me, I am going to have a soak for a few minutes. Then we can have breakfast."

He was studying her face intently. "Do you mind? Is it okay?"

"My morning would not be enhanced by you throwing up on me in the hot tub. So no. I would rather you refrained."

He let out his breath in a little laugh. "Okay, good."

"Did I just dream the part about the helicopter, or was there really one there before we woke up?"

"Yeah, there was. Some guy in a pinstripe suit and dark glasses. Like he's the president traveling incognito or something."

"Maybe it is."

"No. Not the president. But somebody... wealthy. Someone who thinks he's important and wants to make a statement."

"Why would someone like that stay here? It isn't exactly an expensive resort. I mean, I paid enough for it, but it's not a millionaires' retreat."

"Maybe he wants to meet up with someone else. Brittany Blake, maybe."

Kenzie nodded. "Yeah, that would make sense, I guess. Do you know anything about her? Brittany Blake? I know the name, but I really don't know anything about her."

Zachary moved his hands up and down like a scale. Maybe he knew something, maybe he didn't. "She's one of those famous YouTubers. But I don't really know what she does that is so special. I don't think she actually *does* anything."

Kenzie shook her head. "I guess if you look like her, you don't need to."

"I'd rather be with someone like you. Real. *And* beautiful," he said quickly, in case she took his words the wrong way. He gazed at her. "And real."

Kenzie gave Zachary a kiss, even though she hadn't yet brushed her teeth. "You're sweet. Thanks."

She went off to have her solitary soak in the hot tub.

10

After what was not exactly a short soak in the hot tub, Kenzie dressed and made herself presentable. She looked at the time on her phone and joined Zachary again in the living room.

"Do you want to eat here or up at the house? The continental breakfast should still be on."

"I'll stay here, I think. But if you want to go up to the house..."

"I can eat here with you."

"They might have something good. Fresh fruit and pastries. Stuff that you don't usually get."

"There's a reason I don't get fresh pastries..."

"But this is a holiday. Calories you eat on holidays don't count, do they?"

Kenzie laughed. "No. Okay, if I'm going to go up to the house you have to tell me something to grab for you. Just humor me and pretend that you're going to eat something other than a chocolate chip granola bar."

Zachary shook his head. "Okay... a muffin."

"I'll get you a muffin. What kind do you like?"

"Anything. It doesn't really matter."

"Pick something."

He gave her a mischievous smile. "A chocolate chip muffin."

"Perfect. If they have chocolate chip muffins, I'll bring you one back. That's my mission."

Kenzie gave him a kiss before heading up the hill to the farmhouse again.

There were not as many people around for breakfast as there had been for dinner. Or maybe it was just because they came at different times, spread out more. As Kenzie browsed over the offerings, she could hear raised voices in the back of the house. A woman's voice that might have been Mrs. Hubbard's, and a man's voice that she didn't recognize. Certainly not Stuart Dewey's voice. Someone much younger.

Kenzie raised her eyebrows at Raven, who was sitting at the table eating a muffin and looking at something on her phone. Raven looked back at her phone without reacting. Kenzie picked out some fresh fruit and a small danish for herself. And there were muffins, including a chocolate chip one, for Zachary. Kenzie put it in a napkin and sat down at the table.

"How is everyone this morning?" she asked pleasantly.

Raven glanced at her again, and again didn't have any answer. Redd Flagg, the author, was sitting down at the other end of the table. "As well as can be expected, considering how we were all wakened up early this morning," he grumbled.

"How you were wakened up?"

"By that darn helicopter. You didn't hear it?"

"Oh, yes, I did. I just figured I slept in later than the rest of you. Later than I would normally sleep."

"It's vacation. No one wants to wake up at nine o'clock. Why do you think they serve breakfast until eleven?"

"So did you get an early start on your book this morning?" Kenzie asked. She didn't hear her answer, distracted by a man who came striding from the back of the house to the front, looking as if he were ready to shoot someone.

"I guess I shouldn't expect good service in a backwoods little rat hole like this," he snapped, to no one in particular. "I suppose Mama's home cooking means that Mama cooks whatever she pleases, and there's no way to get what you want."

Kenzie glanced toward the kitchen, then back to the man, who was obviously the "millionaire" that Zachary had seen getting off of the helicopter.

"I don't think we've been introduced," she told him frostily. If he was going to act like they were friends, or in all of this together, then he could at least have the courtesy to drop his name first.

He stopped short and looked at Kenzie in astonishment. "I am Vance Stiller," he said, so haughty it was clear that she should have known him on sight. Or she should at least know who Vance Stiller was on hearing his name. But she didn't. She had no idea.

"Nice to meet you," she drawled. Though, of course, it was anything but nice. If that was the way Vance Stiller treated the people around him, then she was glad that Mrs. Hubbard had turned down whatever outrageous requests he'd made. "I take it you're the last guest for this week."

"I wouldn't know anything about that. I just arrived this morning and I don't have the lay of the land yet. And you are?"

"Kenzie."

Kenzie didn't dare give her full name in case he happened to know her or one of her parents. Their names were fairly well-known in Vermont. Though she didn't know if Stiller was a Vermonter or just vacationing there.

Raven looked at Stiller and decided that he wasn't asking her for any of her details, so she went back to whatever she was reading on her phone.

"So that was your helicopter this morning," Redd piped up. "It was a little noisy first thing in the morning, don't you think?"

"I wasn't aware that there were any rules about noise way out here in the boonies. I certainly wasn't going to waste my time driving in." He tapped his wrist. "Time is money, you know."

"Oh, time is money," Redd repeated mockingly. "I'm so glad that you told us. So why would you come vacation somewhere like this, if you don't like it and don't like to waste your time? Wouldn't you be better off in New York? Wall Street? Why would you want to be here?"

Stiller waved this comment away as if he were wiping something off of a whiteboard. "I can work anywhere. Even here. My computer and internet access, and I can make money wherever I am."

He waited for one of them to ask what it was he did. No one obliged him. Stiller looked over the various foods available for breakfast and shook his head with disgust. "I don't know what you call this, but it's not breakfast where I came from. The brochure said that there was a professional cook on staff. This stuff isn't even cooked in-house. It's obviously store-bought."

"Mrs. Hubbard is a great cook," Redd objected. "You should have tasted the dinner last night. Or any night. All of the dinners I've had here have been fantastic. But maybe they wouldn't meet your standards."

"Probably not," Stiller agreed.

The door opened, and the newlyweds arrived. So intertwined that they had to go through the door together, bumping into the frame and laughing giddily at each other. Kenzie rolled her eyes. But she kept in mind that she didn't want to seem just as dismissive and supercilious as Stiller, so she gave them a warm smile, even if she did look past them rather than into their moonstruck expressions.

"Good morning."

"Good morning," they chorused together.

And then, "Isn't it a beautiful day?" asked Mrs. Andy Collins.

"A little brisk," Stiller pointed out.

"You should have felt it last night." Redd gave a mock shiver. "That wind coming down the mountain... brrr."

"We stayed warm," Mrs. Andy Collins declared, looking into the adoring face of her husband.

"I'm sure you did," Raven muttered, just loud enough for Kenzie to hear. Kenzie gave her a small smile.

Kenzie was not enjoying the barbs and attitudes being thrown around, so she made short work of her pastry and fruit, and picked up the napkin-wrapped muffin to take back down to Zachary.

"Hey, how is Zachary?" Redd asked. "Was he okay after last night? Seemed like he isn't in the best shape."

"He was pretty tired last night, but good this morning. He has good days and bad days, and last night with the candles and everything..." She shrugged. "It was difficult, but he's tough. He'll be okay."

"He was really in a fire when he was a kid? That was a pretty nasty scar."

"Yes. And not his only scar. It's understandable that he doesn't like fires, even candles. *Especially* candles."

"So don't expect the two of you down at the bonfire."

"No."

11

Kenzie presented Zachary with his chocolate chip muffin at the cabin. He looked at it, surprised. "I didn't think you'd actually find one."

"Well, there you are. Do you think you can eat it?"

The muffin wasn't one of those greasy jumbo muffins that sold at some of the coffee shops, but a small, denser product more suited to breakfast than dessert. Zachary smelled it, and then broke off a small piece to nibble on.

"Not on the couch. You'll get crumbs everywhere, and I'm sure Dewey will not be happy if we attract mice."

Zachary sighed and got up. But he was pretty good about using plates and not eating over his computer. He'd been sitting long enough, it was probably time for him to get up and move around anyway. He found a plate in one of the kitchen cupboards and sat down at the table.

"It's good," he assured Kenzie. "But I'm not sure how much I can eat."

"Well, give it a try. It would be nice if there was more than one thing that you could tolerate for breakfast. A little variety is nice."

"How were things up there? Everyone happy and well-rested this morning?"

"If I didn't know better, I would suspect that you could hear the yelling down here. No, actually, things were pretty tense."

Zachary nodded as if unsurprised by this news. "Some strong personalities in that group. I figured this new guy would probably stir things up a bit."

"Well, stir he did. He and Mrs. Hubbard were arguing about something.

I guess he thinks he should be able to order whatever he wants, not eat whatever she makes."

"He should probably have picked a different resort if he wants that kind of treatment." Zachary grinned.

"If you're right about him being here to see Brittany Blake, then he might not have had much choice in the matter."

Zachary hadn't been up to taking a walk in the woods or doing any of the other activities that were available, so they had stayed in the cabin. Kenzie had been keeping an eye on her phone, so she had expected the car that drove up to the cabin midway through the afternoon. Zachary, on the other hand, private investigator though he was, had apparently not figured out what she had planned.

"Looks like we have company," Kenzie told him as the car drove up and parked behind Zachary's car.

Zachary turned his head to gaze out the window. "Who is that?" He stood up and looked more closely. "That looks like...?"

Kenzie was grinning away, but he wasn't looking at her.

"It's Tyrrell!" he said, stunned, and hurried to the cabin door to let his younger brother in. "T! What are you doing here?"

His mouth dropped open when he saw the two children getting out of the car. "Are these your kids?"

Tyrrell nodded, smiling fit to burst. He gave Zachary a tight hug. "I've got them for a few days. They've got professional development days or something. When Kenzie asked if I could come up while you were here..."

Zachary turned and looked at Kenzie, it finally dawning on him that she had to have set this all up.

"You did this?"

"Sure. I didn't know at the time he'd have the kids. That was an extra bonus."

Tyrrell motioned for the kids to join him at the door. They hung back a little, looking nervous about meeting a new person.

"This is Zachary, my big brother. I told you about him. Come say hi."

As they got closer, Tyrrell put his arm around the girl, the older of the two, and brought her forward, cuddling her against him reassuringly. "This is Alisha."

Alisha looked about ten years old. She had dark hair like her father and uncle and pretty hazel eyes and delicate features that probably came from her mother. Tyrrell's blue eyes shone in pride as he showed her off to Zachary. He looked back over his shoulder at the younger child. "Come on, Mason. Come meet your Uncle Zachary."

The boy came reluctantly forward. Tyrrell positioned the boy in front of him, putting his other hand on Mason's shoulder. "And this is my son, Mason."

"Nice to meet both of you," Zachary said breathlessly.

Mason's eyes were dark and darted back and forth, examining Zachary, the interior of the cabin, and Kenzie. He twisted away from his father and stepped into the cabin.

"Wipe your feet," Tyrrell told him, trying but failing to hold him back.

Mason stomped on the doormat and continued into the cabin. He looked at Kenzie. "Who are you?"

Kenzie guessed he was probably eight or so. She smiled at him. "I'm... your Uncle Zachary's girlfriend. My name is Kenzie."

"Kenzie? I've never heard that name before."

"You've heard me talk about her," Tyrrell reminded.

"No," Mason said with certainty, shaking his head.

"Come in," Zachary encouraged, motioning for his brother and niece to come in out of the doorway. His eyes shone in a way they hadn't in weeks. Not since sometime before Halloween.

Tyrrell and Alisha settled onto the couch, Alisha still cuddling close to her father and looking nervous of the strangers. Mason wandered around the room, looking at and touching everything.

"Come sit down," Tyrrell told him, but didn't do anything when Mason ignored him.

"It's so great to see you," Zachary told Tyrrell. "It's been too long."

"Yeah, well it's pretty hard to visit you when you're in quarantine. How are you doing? You're feeling better?"

"I'm good. Just tired, mostly. They said I'll recover quickly."

"And that's because of this virus? It must have been pretty bad."

"It's because of the treatment. I never had any symptoms. But my viral load was pretty high."

"And they couldn't just wait and see if you actually got sick?"

Zachary shook his head and looked at Kenzie for her explanation.

"There isn't a lot that we know about this virus," Kenzie said, "but we know that it is fatal within a few days of getting symptoms. They couldn't wait to see whether he developed symptoms; that might have been too late."

Tyrrell shook his head. "No, couldn't chance that."

"Is this a zombie virus?" Mason demanded, turning to Zachary and fixing him with an intent stare. "There's a virus that turns you into a zombie, you know."

"That's pretend, Mason," Tyrrell told him. "That's just in games and on TV. There isn't really a zombie virus."

"There is," Mason insisted. "Bobby told me so. It's real."

"There is no such thing as zombies. Bobby is just having fun with you. Trying to scare you."

"I'm not scared of zombies."

"You should be," Alisha told him. "It would be really scary to see a real live zombie. Or to be one."

"I'd like to be one," Mason blustered. "Because they can kill people, but it's really hard to kill them. So you would be safe. You could do whatever you wanted to."

"You wouldn't want anything," Alisha told him. "Zombies don't have brains, stupid."

"They do too!" Mason insisted, his voice rising in pitch. "Daddy, tell Alisha—"

"Zombies are not real," Tyrrell told him again, rolling his eyes and shaking his head at Zachary.

"But if they were real. They would have brains, right? People can't walk without brains."

"They're not real. Now that's enough, okay? Zachary didn't have a zombie virus. He had a virus that makes you sick. But they gave him medicine, and now he's okay."

"So he didn't turn into a zombie," Mason agreed.

"No," Tyrrell sighed. "He didn't."

Mason looked at Zachary again. "You *look* like a zombie."

Kenzie cracked up. "I don't know if I can disagree with that," she laughed. "You are looking pretty rough still. But he's getting better, Mason. He'll get better and start to look less like a zombie." She chuckled, enjoying Tyrrell's look of discomfort over his son's comments. Zachary didn't seem to be offended by the comment that he looked like the walking dead. He'd seen himself in the mirror.

12

How long can you stay?" Zachary asked, looking at the time on his phone. "There are some activities the kids might be interested in. A hayride or a hike? Or we could find something else that's more interesting for them than just sitting around listening to the grownups talk."

Tyrrell looked at Kenzie and raised his brows. "Actually, I'm told that you have a spare bedroom we could use for a day or two."

Zachary's mouth dropped open again. He turned and looked at Kenzie. "Really? You told them they could stay over?"

"I didn't think you would mind."

"No, I don't mind. That's great!" Zachary looked at Tyrrell. "I haven't slept over with family since... it happened."

"Well, I was there at Lorne and Pat's overnight last year," Tyrrell reminded him. "We sat through last Christmas Eve together. Didn't sleep, but I was there overnight."

"That's right. You did." It had been their reunion. The first time Zachary had seen anyone from his family in decades. Zachary was at his lowest point on the worst day of the year, and Tyrrell had been there to save him from being sucked into himself. "Wow. This is great. So, do the kids want to do a hayride?"

Tyrrell looked at the children. "Well?"

Alisha snuggled into Tyrrell. "If Daddy's coming."

Mason darted around the room, making airplane noises. "I could go all by myself. I'm braver than Alisha."

"We could all go," Kenzie said. "If you're up to it?" She looked at Zachary.

"Yeah." He nodded. "That would be really fun, right?"

Kenzie smiled at his question. "Have you ever been on a hayride?"

"No."

She could see how he might never have had the chance to participate in something like that as a child and youth in foster care, and frequently in a supervised facility. It was completely outside his realm of experience.

"Well, why don't we do it? Everyone bundle up, because there's a bite in the air and it will feel a lot colder when you've been sitting outside for a while. Hats and gloves for everyone. Winter coats, not just hoodies."

Alisha and the men didn't complain and went about gathering their gear together. Kenzie noticed Zachary lingering over his electronics bag, eventually pulling out a camera to take with him. Mason didn't object to the idea of a hayride, but he zoomed around the room, making noise and darting here and there, ignoring his father's instructions to get ready.

Eventually, ready to go himself, Tyrrell managed to grab Mason by the arm and to wrestle him into a coat and hat. He couldn't manage to get gloves onto Mason's hands without his cooperation, but stuffed them into the large pockets of his coat so that they would be available when Mason decided he was getting cold.

"Everybody should be gathering at the barn," Kenzie said, checking the time again. "Our timing should be perfect."

"Are there animals in the barn?" Alisha asked.

"I haven't been down there myself, but yes, there would have to be. They need horses to pull the wagon."

"Anything else?"

"I don't know. We'll have to see when we get there."

"Are there any baby animals?"

"Probably not. Animals usually have their babies in the springtime."

Alisha nodded understandingly. Kenzie locked up the cabin and they traipsed down the hill to the big barn, where some of the other guests were standing around, waiting.

A man that Kenzie hadn't seen before was getting the horses ready for the trip. He was big and broad. Husky. With a full beard that he seemed to be scowling behind. It made sense that they would have someone younger and hardier to do the hayrides. Kenzie didn't imagine that Stuart Dewey would want to get behind the wheel. Or rather, the reins.

He ignored the guests while he got everything ready, then straightened up and looked around at them. "Is this everyone?"

Kenzie shrugged, and everyone else's reactions were pretty much the same. They didn't know whether anyone else was planning to come or not.

"I am Harold Burknall," the man introduced himself. "I am the handyman around here and do a lot of the outside maintenance and activities. Everyone needs to follow the rules and do as I say, or you will not be coming to any other activities. Is that understood?"

He looked in particular at Mason, who was jumping around excitedly, looking at the horses and the farm equipment and everything else in the barn.

"Mason will follow the rules," Tyrrell said, trying to grab his son and bring him under control. "Won't you, Mason?"

"Are we going on a horse?" Mason asked, his voice falsetto. "I want to go on a horse."

"We're going to get into the wagon behind the horses," Tyrrell explained to him. "They're going to pull us around. That will be fun, won't it?"

"Can I touch the horses?"

Tyrrell looked at Burknall. "Is it okay?"

"He has to stop jumping around. Horses don't like people making sudden moves. If he wants to touch them, he has to do what I say."

Mason stopped jumping and looked at him.

"Come here." Burknall beckoned to him.

Mason looked back at his father, then advanced toward the big man, taking small, slow steps.

"That's right," Burknall approved. "Just like that. Nice and slow. You don't want to scare them." He put his hand on Mason's shoulder when he was close enough, and guided him toward the horses' heads. He patiently walked Mason through letting the horses smell him and get used to him before allowing Mason to touch them.

Kenzie was surprised. She would have written Burknall off as being crusty and impatient, but he was kind and spoke in a way that made Mason listen to him intently. Eventually, Mason was stroking the heads of the big animals. They nickered at him and sniffed at his pockets, looking for food.

Kenzie heard a series of clicks and turned her head to see Zachary taking pictures. His expression was just as intent as Mason's. Mason looked back to smile at his father. "Look at me, Dad! I'm patting them."

"You're doing a great job," Tyrrell told him. "Really good listening."

"All right." Burknall raised his voice again to address the group. "You can all get into the wagon and get yourselves settled. There's no smoking of any kind. Keep any lighters or matches in your pockets. No yelling or intentionally spooking the horses. All arms and legs stay inside the wagon, and you don't get out without talking to me." He patted Mason's shoulder. "Do you want to sit up front with me?"

"Yes! Can I, Dad?"

Tyrrell hesitated. "Are you sure it's okay? He's not going to be in the way?"

"He'll be better sitting up front with me than in the wagon."

Tyrrell nodded his agreement. "Okay, then. Mace, you need to do what Mr. Burknall tells you to, okay? Just like a teacher at school."

Mason nodded eagerly. "Yes. I will."

"Okay, good. Alisha and I will be in the wagon if you need anything."

There were a few minutes of jockeying and everybody getting into position, finding a seat on the bales of hay and getting comfortable. There were blankets, and Kenzie put one down on a hay bale, and then when she and Zachary were sitting on top of it, wrapped it up around them and snuggled. It was cozy. Zachary's arm tightened around her, and he smiled when she looked into his face.

"This is good?" Kenzie asked.

"It's good," Zachary agreed. He rubbed her back, and looked over at his brother and niece. "It's perfect."

13

Kenzie had been on a couple of hayrides when she was younger. Usually in the early autumn when it was warmer, sunny days with lots of other kids, joking around and doing all the things that Burknall had warned against. The trips were usually short, barely enough time to break out illicit drinks. And maybe that was why. The supervisors knew teenagers just a little too well to give them that much latitude.

By contrast, the hayride at the Lodge was cold and long. She was glad for the blankets and Zachary's shared body warmth. Tyrrell wrapped his blanket around Alisha, comfy in his lap instead of on the poky hay bales, and she peeked out to watch the passing scenery.

After a few minutes out, Mason climbed down from the driver's seat to get his gloves from Tyrrell. When Kenzie looked at him later, back with Burknall, Mason had the reins in his hand and was looking as pleased as punch. The horses probably knew their way through the hayride loop without any guidance, but Mason took his job very seriously. When they all got off the wagon at the end of the ride, Mason appeared to have grown about two inches.

"Daddy, Daddy, did you see me driving?" he demanded. "I drove the horses! You won't even let me drive the car, but Mr. Burknall let me drive the horses."

"That was pretty cool," Tyrrell said. "You did a really good job."

"I did everything he said."

"I'm going to tell your mom when I talk to her. She'll be very proud of you too."

Mason looked disappointed by this. "I want to tell her!"

"Okay. You tell her all about it, and then I'll tell her later, after you, what a great job you did driving and listening. Okay?"

Mason nodded seriously.

It took them all some time to get out of the barn. Mason wanted to help let the horses out of the traces and to help care for them and feed them. Eventually, Tyrrell managed to talk him into returning to the cabin, only on promise that Mason could return to see them and Mr. Burknall the next day.

All the way back to the cabin, Mason told them the minutiae of everything he had seen and done during the wagon ride.

"Need a nap?" Kenzie asked Zachary when they got back indoors and were rubbing their hands and arms, trying to warm up again more quickly.

"Well..." He was looking tired and worn, but clearly didn't want to miss out on any time with his brother and the children.

"It's okay to take a break. They'll be here all night and for the next few days."

"Yeah. I should take a few minutes."

"Okay. Off you go then, and we'll try to keep the noise down to a dull roar."

"Maybe I should just stay up..."

Kenzie shooed him with her hands. "Go, go! You need to get your sleep. You'll crash and make yourself sick. We're here for recovery, not to make you worse."

At her insistence, he finally nodded and went back to their bedroom, after extracting a promise from Kenzie that she would wake him up after he'd had a decent amount of time for a nap. She was not to let him sleep the whole evening away; he still wanted time with his family.

Hopefully, he would be able to sleep with other people in the cabin.

"Maybe we should put on a movie for the kids," Kenzie suggested to Tyrrell. "That will probably help keep things quiet until the others get here."

With the kids entertained, Kenzie pulled out her phone and started running through her task lists and plans, filling Tyrrell in on any details he did not know. Together, they would do what they could to ensure that the evening ran smoothly.

Kenzie turned on the outside light and peered out the window for any sign of their additional guests. There was a set of headlights just coming down the road as she watched. It was too dark out to recognize the vehicle until it was right in front of the cabin. Lorne and Pat pulled in beside Zachary's car. Kenzie opened the door to wave to them and waited there while they pulled bags and boxes out of the car to bring inside with them.

She leaned in to give Lorne a kiss on the cheek in greeting as he hobbled to the door on his cast. "Zachary is sleeping, but he'll want to be up soon. Don't worry about any noise."

"Good to see you, Kenzie." He paused beside her. "How are you feeling?"

"I'm doing pretty well. Nearly back to normal. Zachary's going to take longer, but now that he's done his protocol, it's just a matter of making sure he gets enough sleep and calories."

"We'll see what magic we can work there," Pat said, leaning close so that Kenzie could give him a kiss as well. He indicated the box he was carrying with a nod. "This will get him back on his feet."

It took several trips back and forth to the car before they had brought in everything they needed, then Pat set to work on their final preparations. Kenzie and Tyrrell helped with whatever they could, while Lorne sat down with his leg elevated and watched the movie with the children.

It wasn't long before Kenzie's sharp ears picked up the sound of the bedroom door opening. She turned around and watched Zachary walk into the living room, rubbing his eyes.

"You didn't let me sleep too late, did you?" he asked.

Then he did a double-take when he saw Lorne sitting there with the kids.

"Mr. Peterson? What are you doing here?"

It was cute how he still called his old foster father by his last name. Lorne always told him to use his first name, and Zachary tried, but when he wasn't consciously trying to call him Lorne, he always slipped back into the old habit.

"We came for dinner," Lorne said, as if that should have been obvious.

"Dinner?" Zachary looked into the kitchen area and saw Kenzie and Tyrrell working with Pat. "We're having dinner here?"

"We don't need to go up to the farmhouse every night," Kenzie pointed out. "There's a stove here. We can cook whatever we need to."

"And we're... and everyone is..." Zachary's eyes glinted with tears, and he laughed. "I can't even talk!"

"We thought we'd have an early Thanksgiving dinner," Pat told him. "Kenzie told us all about the planned vacation, and it sort of... all came together. We need a break too. Kenzie booked a three-bedroom, so there's room for all of us for one night."

"One night?"

"We're not going to stay the whole week. Just thought we'd drop in on you for a day or two. We were listening to the forecast on the way up, and it isn't good. Probably best if we hit the trail by late tomorrow, if we don't want to get caught in a storm."

Zachary's gaze shifted to Tyrrell. Tyrrell anticipated the question and raised his hand in a "halt" gesture. "We're still planning on staying a few days," he promised. "If we end up getting snowed in and have to spend an extra day or two here, it won't hurt our feelings. Will it, kids?"

They were watching the movie and not paying him any attention.

"You don't mind if you miss a few days of school, do you?" Tyrrell directed at them.

It was Mason who looked up first. "Miss school?" He grinned. "Mommy would kill you."

Everyone laughed.

"I don't think she would literally kill me," Tyrrell protested. "If we were snowed in and *couldn't* get back. That's not our fault."

Alisha shook her head. "Mommy won't be happy."

"Well, we'll see what happens. Just because there is a storm coming in, that doesn't mean the highway will be impassable. It could blow in, dump some snow, and then be gone again. I've just watched too many movies about getting snowed in at mountain resorts."

"When are we eating?" Mason asked with a hint of a whine. "I'm getting really hungry."

"We'll eat when it's ready. You be patient and polite."

"It won't be long," Pat promised. "Everything is precooked, I'm just warming up here. I didn't think we wanted to spend hours cooking the bird once we got here."

"It smells good," Zachary declared, sniffing the air. "Is it turkey?"

"It sure is. Turkey, my famous cornbread stuffing, glazed yams..."

"Mashed potatoes?"

"Mashed potatoes," Pat confirmed, smiling.

"You know what a good cook Pat is," Zachary said to Kenzie, "but until you've had his turkey dinner..."

Kenzie wondered how many turkey dinners Zachary had partaken of with his old foster father and his partner. And how many he had missed because he had been too sick or in the hospital when the special day rolled around.

"I can't wait. It smells fabulous."

"I'm a vegetarian," Alisha piped up.

Tyrrell looked across the room at her, raising his eyebrows. "That's news to me,"

"I am. Mom said she told you."

Tyrrell's brow wrinkled as he considered this. "Well, maybe she forgot to mention that."

"There will be plenty to eat other than turkey," Pat assured Alisha. "Do you still drink milk?"

Alisha nodded. "Mom said I have to. And I don't like that soy stuff."

"Well then, you can have everything except the turkey and gravy. And I didn't even cook the stuffing in the bird, so that's safe for you. Sound good?"

Alisha gave him a broad smile.

"Good," Pat repeated.

Tyrrell looked at Alisha. "So when did this happen? And why? You've never mentioned being interested in vegetarianism before."

Alisha shrugged. "I don't want to eat animals." She shot a look at Mason, who was making faces. "Would you want to eat those horses you were making friends with and driving today? In some countries, they would eat them. You wouldn't like that, would you?"

"People don't eat horses."

"Sometimes! And what about all the other animals? Chickens and pigs are really smart. Smarter than a dog!"

Mason rolled his eyes and shook his head at his sister's ridiculousness. Tyrrell didn't reprimand him.

"Well, that's fine," Tyrrell told Alisha, "but next time can you tell me? In case Mom forgets?"

"She was supposed to tell you."

"I know. I get that. But you can tell me too."

She looked down at her hands for a few seconds, then nodded. "Okay."

"You don't have to be afraid to tell me. I'm not going to get mad."

There was a heavy silence among the three of them. Kenzie turned back to the salad she was making, feeling like she was intruding on the little family. There were clearly a lot of things not being said between them. Alisha didn't immediately jump in and say that she knew her dad wouldn't get mad at her. The silence suggested otherwise. Tyrrell had mentioned, the previous Christmas, that he was a recovering alcoholic. Kenzie had thought at the time that he had probably been an alcoholic in his late teens or early twenties, and then had woken up to what he was doing to himself and sobered up. But maybe it had been much more recent than that. Recent enough that the kids could remember and were still worried that he might go into a rage over something like finding out that his daughter was a vegetarian.

"Do you need any help?" Zachary asked Pat, breaking the silence.

"I think we have as many cooks as this kitchen can handle," Pat said. "Why don't you get washed up? We'll have food on the table in a few minutes."

14

U nlike the dinner the previous night, there was no need to worry about things like candles. Pat knew Zachary's triggers as well as anyone, and would never have put candles out when he knew Zachary was around, much less light them.

The movie ended and Tyrrell turned off the TV to the children's moans and complaints.

"You don't have time to watch anything else. We're eating soon."

"We can eat and watch TV at the same time," Mason contributed helpfully.

"Not today, you can't. We're all eating together at the table today. Mr. Peterson and Mr. Parker have made this wonderful meal for us, and we're going to enjoy it all sitting together visiting."

"I had very little to do with it," Lorne objected. "It's all Pat."

"Well, Mr. Parker, then. I want you guys to be on your best behavior for dinner, okay? Remember your manners? No goofing off."

They gave their grudging agreements. Zachary had finished taking his dinnertime meds and washing up, so the children were sent to make themselves presentable, and by the time they were finished squabbling over the sink and had returned to the table, Pat was just setting out the finishing touches.

As they started to pass the dishes around Mason picked up his table knife and started jousting with Alisha, waving it back and forth to clink against her raised fork and jabbing it toward her.

"Mason!" Tyrrell shouted.

Mason jumped and dropped the knife with a clatter.

"What did I tell you about good manners?"

Tears welled up in Mason's eyes and started to race down his cheeks. "I was just playing!"

"No. No playing at the table. You know better than that. Does your mother let you sword fight at the table?"

Mason sniffled and shook his head. "No."

"Then you're not allowed to do it here either. Just behave yourself!"

"I'm trying!"

"Try harder," Tyrrell insisted.

Mason stared down at his plate, silent tears still flowing down his cheeks. Tyrrell spooned some of the various dishes onto Mason's plate as they went around, since Mason was making no move to serve himself.

Kenzie felt sorry for the little guy. As far as she could guess, without making any kind of clinical examination or doing any testing for hidden disabilities, he was at the upper end of the hyperactivity scale. He was clearly bright and observant, but also impulsive and constantly on the move. Even as he sat there, trying to be well-behaved for his father, he was swinging his legs back and forth and twisting his hands together in his lap. Trying harder wasn't going to help him to overcome ADHD or whatever other disabilities he might have. Medication might help settle him down a little but, as Zachary had observed in the past, there wasn't anything that worked reliably for impulse control.

Everyone was quiet for a few minutes while they dished up. Tyrrell's neck was flushed red with embarrassment over either his son's behavior or his own reaction to it. As they began to eat, they all made an effort at conversation, and gradually things returned to normal.

"This is just fantastic," Kenzie told Pat. "You've really outdone yourself. When we started to plan, I thought that maybe we could have sandwiches together. Nothing like this!"

"It's what I do," Pat said with a modest shrug. "I love to cook for people."

"And people love it when you cook for them," Kenzie declared. Everything was delectable, and she regretted that unlike Zachary, she didn't need the extra calories. She tried to eat slowly and savor every bite.

15

Zachary sat down with Lorne after supper to look at some photography he had brought with him, which inevitably led to the discussion of cameras and camera settings that could go on all night.

Getting the children to bed was not an easy affair, especially as far as Mason was concerned. Alisha was cooperative, though she got out of bed and made too many special requests and delays, but Mason was a little fireball who seemed to get more hyper the more tired he got, and Tyrrell looked exhausted by the time he finally managed to get both kids down to sleep.

"You wouldn't believe how much energy that kid has," he sighed. "I wish I had half as much as he does. Actually, I wish he had half as much too. We have a bedtime routine when they're visiting me, but being somewhere else, somewhere unfamiliar with such exciting things going on, everything just falls apart."

"Routine is everything at this age," Lorne agreed. "With a lot of the kids that we had, it wasn't worth it to do anything during the evening if it took away from the usual rituals. Change one thing, and you end up with kids who can't settle until they are literally falling asleep on their feet." He put his foot up, scratching around the top of the cast and grimacing. "With some of them, they were so hypervigilant that if you changed one thing, they would go right off the rails."

He looked over at Zachary. Zachary scratched the back of his neck. "I'm sure you're not talking about me," he said uncomfortably.

Everyone laughed. Zachary had a strong relationship with his foster father as an adult. As a child, he'd only been in their foster home for a few weeks. Zachary's own hyperactivity and other issues had been too much for them to handle. Too much for most families to handle.

"Even with night meds, you were always a tough one to get down for the night."

"I remember. I couldn't shut my brain off. Couldn't stop worrying about things. About what was going to happen. About... a fire or something happening to one of the other kids. About school and getting left back because I couldn't understand the work. Or having to go back to Bonnie Brown or go to juvie. My brain would just never settle down."

Zachary didn't usually talk about his anxieties or problems sleeping. Even in therapy, it was hard to get him to be open about what was going on inside his head. Maybe talking about his childhood gave her a little window into what it was like in there. She could picture his brain as a racing engine. Racing, racing, racing, and never slowing or stopping.

"Have you considered meds for Mason?" Lorne asked Tyrrell.

"His mom is talking to the school. They want to put him on something to make it easier on the teachers. I think we're both a little worried that it will change him. He's such a bright, inquisitive kid. I don't want them to squash that curiosity, that little spark. I remember what it was like, some of the stuff they put me on when I was his age. It didn't make me feel better. It did help my focus a bit. But I always felt like... I was swimming through wet cement."

"They've got some better options now," Zachary offered. "But even if it works without side effects, it's hard feeling like... you're defective and need to be medicated to even look like... neurotypicals."

Tyrrell nodded. "I'm just glad I grew out of that."

When they all got up in the morning, the storm was all over the news on Kenzie's phone apps. Weather warnings had been issued and they knew they could be looking at a big dump of snow. Though Lorne and Pat had been planning to stay most of the day and only head home in the evening, satellite maps showed the storm moving in much more quickly than expected, maps that were verified by the strong wind that swept in through the door whenever they opened it.

Pat had packaged up all of the leftovers of the turkey dinner and left them in the fridge for Zachary and Kenzie to use in the upcoming week if they didn't feel like going up to the farmhouse for dinner. It was nice to have something so good on hand. Better than the prepackaged stuff that Kenzie had brought with her. Pat packed up the rest of his dishes and ingredients to take back with them.

They all exchanged regretful goodbyes at the door, but they didn't hang around with the door open to watch Pat and Lorne leave. Zachary watched through the window and waved as they pulled out.

"Should we go up to the house for some breakfast?" Kenzie suggested. "You know now that they have muffins, and you were able to eat one of them yesterday. We can put in an appearance, see how the rest of the vacationers are doing."

"I think I'll stay down here. You go ahead, if you want to." His expression was frozen and his tone flat. Definitely feeling the absence of their guests.

"I think it would be good for you to come. You don't want to just mope around here feeling bad for yourself."

"Tyrrell and the kids are here. I'm not by myself."

"I know. I just think... it might help to get out of yourself a bit. See the other cabins."

Zachary sighed heavily. "Is it that important to you?"

Kenzie nodded. "Yes. Come on up with me."

Dr. Boyle had suggested that if they knew something was important to the other person, they should act on it, even if it wasn't something that they felt like doing themselves. Couples did things for one another. Made concessions. Joined them in their activities even when they didn't share all of the other's interests. It would help bring them closer together.

"Okay." Zachary said simply. He looked at Tyrrell. "Do you guys want to come up?"

"If you don't mind, I think we'll keep a low profile. I don't know how, uh… how many fragile, expensive items they might have around the place…"

Zachary looked at Mason, eating cheese strings and apple slices in front of the TV, and nodded. Maybe remembering all of the things he had broken when he was Mason's age.

He began to put on his coat and other winter gear without further objection.

16

It was a chilly walk up to the farmhouse, but the wind had died down, so it wasn't too brutal. Kenzie supposed they could have driven the car up, but Tyrrell was parked behind Zachary's car, and the exercise was good for them.

They didn't have much conversation on the way up. Kenzie sensed that Zachary was disappointed in Lorne and Pat leaving so early and was brooding over it. Having them come to share dinner with them had been a good idea. It had really helped to cheer Zachary up. But it would have been better if they had been able to stay longer.

Zachary quickened his pace slightly to reach the door of the house before Kenzie, and he opened it for her, standing back to give her room to enter. Kenzie smiled at him and went in. They shucked off the winter coats and gear and hung them up on the hooks provided. It looked like most of the other guests were there ahead of them. Kenzie couldn't help noticing the luxurious suede jacket hung next to hers. Brittany Blake's, she supposed.

They proceeded to the dining room. Zachary nodded briefly at the others already gathered there and went to the muffin dish, looking them over and picking out another of the chocolate chip muffins for his breakfast. Kenzie grabbed herself a plate and was choosing from the various offerings that had been laid out. Similar, but not identical to what had been there the day before.

"Where is Mr. Dewey?" an aggrieved voice demanded. "This really is not acceptable. I spoke to the cook yesterday and let her know my requirements."

Vance Stiller, of course. Still thinking that he could order whatever he wanted rather than choosing from what was on offer.

"I haven't seen him this morning," Redd Flagg offered. "You could ask someone on the staff."

"He's the host, why isn't he here? He should be making sure that everything goes smoothly."

"He usually does. Must be something else going on this morning. Maybe something is going on down at the barn that needed his attention. A place like this has to be maintained."

"He should have a man to take care of that. What about the one who drove for the hayride yesterday? Didn't he say that he was the handyman? He's the one that should be looking after any of the outdoor stuff. People like this just don't know how to prioritize and delegate."

"You're pretty vocal when you don't even know what's holding him up," Jack observed. "Why don't you give the guy a break? Those of us who have been here longer than you know that he's very conscientious."

"I can only judge by what I see, and he's clearly not here."

There were some more murmurs of disapproval. Kenzie couldn't tell for sure whether they were in support of Vance, disapproving of the service, or whether they objected to his casting aspersions on their host.

Kenzie was inclined to agree with Vance just a little. Their host didn't seem to be quite as pleasant and diligent as she would have expected from a place like the Lodge, which made its living off of customer service. But the man was tired, running a resort when he should have been retired. The loss of his wife had been fairly recent, and he probably didn't find it easy to run the Lodge without her. When they had run it together for decades, it would be difficult for him to pick up all of her responsibilities on top of his own.

Kenzie made her choices as to her breakfast plate and sat down at the table with Zachary and his muffin.

"What do you think?" she murmured. "You think Mr. Dewey is off dealing with other Lodge business?"

Zachary shrugged, picking at the muffin. "Could be things that have to be done before the storm blows in. He might have been here earlier. It looks like everything has been taken care of. No reason he has to stay here the whole time breakfast is available. Didn't you say it's out until eleven? He's not going to spend all morning hovering over the guests." He put a chocolate chip in his mouth. "Not with the storm coming."

Kenzie nodded her agreement. All good points.

The young woman who had helped to serve dinner, Samantha, checked on the coffee carafe and made sure that nothing else needed to be refreshed.

She tried unsuccessfully to avoid Vance Stiller. He put himself in front of her and wouldn't let her pass.

"So where is Dewey? Did you talk to him? Tell him I want to see him?"

Samantha tried to get around Dewey gracefully. "I haven't seen him this morning."

"Well, what about the rest of the staff? What about the cook?"

"No, Mrs. Hubbard says that she hasn't seen him either. I'm sorry. I'm sure he'll be back... sometime. You can tell him then if you have complaints. In the meantime..." She motioned to the sideboard laden with food. "There is coffee if you want it."

"Where is he?"

"I don't know."

"Don't you have any way of reaching him? A cell phone? Walkie-talkie? You're telling me that he just takes off, and you have no way of letting him know if there is an emergency?"

"He's not answering his phone. Coverage can be spotty up here sometimes. With the storm coming in, the cloud cover might be blocking the signal."

"So you have no way of reaching him. What if there were a medical emergency?"

"The staff have first aid training. We could call the county for help. But... this is not an emergency." She raised an eyebrow at him.

"I demand to see him."

"Vance," Brittany Blake, who was prodding a few berries with her spoon, sounded as if she'd had enough. "You're being a pain. Get a coffee and sit down."

He looked at her, color rising to his face. Apparently, he was not accustomed to being spoken to like that. He was used to deference, even when he was being unreasonable. Brittany held his gaze, waiting. Eventually, Vance stalked over to the coffee carafe and put a mug under the spout.

"It's probably not even fresh," he complained. He sniffed the air as the coffee dribbled into his cup. "They don't grind their own beans, I'll tell you that. Cheap grocery store ground coffee."

"Sit down and drink it," Brittany told him.

Vance obeyed. Everyone was watching him, and he definitely did not appreciate being spoken to that way in front of the whole room. He sipped the coffee, grimaced dramatically, and set it down in front of him.

"I thought you were here to relax," Brittany said. "So why are you so uptight?"

"This isn't exactly relaxing."

"If you're going to act like a pain, then no. If you focus on enjoying the atmosphere and what they have to offer, you could let your hair down and not be so tense."

He grunted and had another sip of coffee. Maybe he just needed his caffeine fix for the day.

"You can talk to Mr. Dewey at supper or some other time today when he's not busy with other stuff. But you treat him like you would treat another business owner instead of your servant."

"I don't treat people that way."

She raised an eyebrow at him and didn't comment.

Suddenly, there was a siren-like wail that raised the hair on the back of Kenzie's neck. She and Zachary were instantly on their feet. Everybody else seemed to be frozen where they were.

"Upstairs," Zachary said.

The two of them were halfway up the stairs before anyone else in the dining room could say anything.

Kenzie and Zachary rushed to the top of the stairs just as everyone in the dining room started to talk, asking each other questions and looking up as if they might be able to see through the walls. The cries were coming from one of the bedrooms. Kenzie made it through the doorway just ahead of Zachary.

Mrs. Hubbard stood over the bed, her hands over her mouth, crying out again.

"It's Stuart. He's... I thought he was out at the barn... but then, Mr. Burknall said he wasn't, and I came up here to make sure that he wasn't sick, and..."

They could see that there was no immediate danger. No one was being attacked. Kenzie moved forward, shifting immediately into her professional persona. "Stay back, please, and let me have a look."

Mrs. Hubbard took a couple of steps back to make room for her, and Kenzie approached the bed and pulled back the blanket. Mr. Stuart Dewey was pale and stiff, clearly dead for some hours. Kenzie went through the motions anyway, checking for a pulse, pulling back an eyelid, testing for how advanced rigor was. She could hear the others approaching, coming up the stairs to see what was going on.

"Zachary, keep them out of here. Shut the door. Mrs. Hubbard, is there a doctor who comes out here? Maybe an ambulance or medical examiner?"

"I don't know!" Mrs. Hubbard wiped at her eyes. "Nothing like this has ever happened before."

"Do you have 9-1-1 service?"

"No. Not up here. You have to call the police department directly. I... I don't have the number. Maybe Mr. Dewey does."

Kenzie took a glance around the room. She didn't see a personal address book or a cell phone. "Does he have an office where he keeps a phone book or a Rolodex?"

Dewey was old school. He wouldn't have it on a computer or electronic device.

"There is... his wife's writing desk. Down the hall."

"Go check there."

Kenzie looked around for any other relevant details in the room, noting Mr. Dewey's position, the glass of water on the nightstand, a couple of pill bottles. There was no sign that anything had been disturbed. The body looked natural, with no blood or sign of violence. Pictures, personal effects, some that were probably his wife's.

Zachary finished dealing with the other guests and returned to the bedroom. "That Vance Stiller is a pain in the neck," he observed, shaking his head. "Thinks the rules don't apply to him. He can demand or buy whatever he wants. He doesn't understand the meaning of the word no." He got closer to the bed, but not close enough to make Kenzie anxious that he might disturb the scene. "How does he look?"

Kenzie shrugged. "Can't tell much from just looking at him. Looks natural. Heart attack, maybe."

"No one stabbed him in his sleep?"

"No." Kenzie lifted the blanket to visualize his back, but still couldn't see signs of anything untoward. "Nothing suspicious about the scene. He was an old man. Not happy with life. Missing his wife. Sometimes people are just ready."

Zachary nodded.

"Can you find me a phone number for the police or county medical examiner?" Kenzie asked.

Zachary pulled out his phone and started tapping. "I wonder about a next of kin. If there is some family member that we need to call. Someone will have to make decisions about the Lodge and what to do with it."

Kenzie nodded. She had been wondering what impact this would have on everyone's holidays. Was the Lodge set up to just keep running, even though the guiding hand had passed away? Or would they all have to pack up and go home? She didn't want to have to drive through what the weather bureau was saying would be the storm of the century.

Zachary found a phone number and read it out to her. Kenzie pulled out her own phone and tapped it in.

The answer came quickly. "County Police Services. Darleen Star, Officer of the Day."

"Officer Star, my name is Dr. Kenzie Kirsch. I'm staying at the Dewey Lodge, and there has been a death. I wasn't sure who to notify to take care of things."

"A death? What kind of death? Was there an accident?"

"It looks like a natural death. He didn't wake up in the morning. Maybe a heart attack."

"All the way up at the Lodge," Star murmured to someone in the background. "Doctor, what is your area of expertise? Are you a medical doctor?"

"Yes. I'm a pathologist; I assist in the Medical Examiner's Office in Roxboro."

"Well, aren't we lucky," Star laughed. "Sounds like you're the right person to have on hand. You have verified death?"

"Yes... he's definitely dead."

"We're going to have trouble getting anyone up to you in the next little while. We are overstretched right now battening down the hatches for the storm. It's going to be a doozy, if you haven't been watching the news."

"Yeah. We're aware of it."

"We will get someone up to you as soon as possible to take care of arrangements. In the meantime... if you could do what you can to secure the scene?"

Kenzie looked around to see how she was going to manage that. She couldn't exactly stand guard on it until the authorities arrived. Who knew when that would be? Probably not in the next few hours. Mrs. Hubbard returned, shaking her head at her failed mission to find a phone number for Kenzie.

"Mrs. Hubbard, does that door lock?"

"Well... yes; of course it does."

"Who has keys to it?"

"Mr. Dewey. The maid, Samantha. I really don't know if there are any other copies."

"Okay. We need to lock up until the police can send someone up here. It might be a while. Go get Samantha's key. Do you know where Mr. Dewey keeps his?"

"His keys should all be on the ring in his pocket." Mrs. Hubbard looked around and nodded to the clothes discarded on the floor. "Probably in his pants."

Kenzie bent down and picked the pants up. They were weighty and jingled, so she inserted two fingers and pulled out a key ring with a large number of keys on it. "I guess it's on here somewhere. Along with keys to every other lock on the property."

Mrs. Hubbard nodded solemnly.

"Okay. Get Samantha's. Please."

Kenzie waited until Mrs. Hubbard left again. She looked at Zachary. "If they can't get up before the storm rolls in, and it doesn't sound like they will, then it might be a few days before everything has cleared up enough for them to get here."

"Are you worried about decomposition?"

"I don't normally have to worry about it. We have refrigerated drawers. I haven't ever had to preserve a body without them."

"You could open the window."

Kenzie looked at the window and considered. It was the obvious solution. It would definitely be cold enough. Probably too cold, since she didn't actually want to freeze the body. But she would take freezing over the evidence breaking down before the authorities could reach them. And no one wanted the whole house smelling like decomp.

"Uh, yeah, I guess that will have to do." Kenzie sighed, at loose ends. "I don't have my liver probe with me, so I can't take a reading to determine approximate time of death."

"You didn't bring your liver probe on vacation?" Zachary teased.

"What was I thinking when I packed?"

"I could see if they have a thermometer we can use. Maybe one in the kitchen like you use for turkeys?"

"I think they might be a bit freaked out if I poke it into Mr. Dewey, and it won't be calibrated properly. It's meant for much higher temperatures. I guess... I'll need to make a determination based on rigor mortis and external temperature. Can you see if someone has one of those digital ear or forehead thermometers? And I'll need the current room temperature as accurately as possible. I'll write down all of my observations and the County Medical Examiner can make a determination based on that."

"I'm sure that will be fine. It isn't like we're trying to figure out who had an opportunity to murder him. He died sometime between going to sleep last night and when he would normally rise this morning. The staff should be able to give you the outside parameters."

Kenzie nodded. Zachary departed to find a thermometer. Kenzie pulled out her phone, tapped the notepad app, and started making observations. Rigor appeared to be complete, so Dewey had probably been dead for a minimum of three to six hours. Kenzie took a number of pictures of Mr. Dewey and the scene. Mrs. Hubbard gasped in shock when she returned.

"What are you doing?" she demanded, aghast.

It took Kenzie a minute to realize what Mrs. Hubbard was so upset about. Most people didn't go around taking pictures of dead bodies. Mrs. Hubbard probably thought she was ghoulish or maybe that she would post them to social media for everyone to see.

"No, no, it's okay." she assured the cook. "I'm just trying to get a record of everything for the authorities. They'll take their own pictures when they get here, but we don't know how long that will be, and I want a record in case anything changes between now and then."

She was careful not to mention that she wasn't sure how much Mr. Dewey might decompose before then. That might just do Mrs. Hubbard in.

Mrs. Hubbard sniffed. "I don't know about all of this," she said, shaking her head. "Mr. Dewey wouldn't like it. Guests in his room taking pictures. Acting like they own the place."

"I don't mean to upset you, Mrs. Hubbard. I'm just trying to make sure that everything is done the right way. You wouldn't want the police accusing us of wrongdoing, would you?"

"No! Heavens, no. I wouldn't have anything to do with such... behavior."

"Of course not," Kenzie agreed. "So this is for your protection. I can show them that nothing has been touched or moved. You won't have to defend yourself against accusations that someone was in here and... moved the body or went through Mr. Dewey's possessions. If anything of value were to disappear, you would want me to be able to show them that it didn't happen on our watch, wouldn't you?" She said it in a confidential tone.

Mrs. Hubbard drew a little closer, nodding. But then her eyes dropped to Mr. Dewey's corpse, and she looked away again, trying to keep control of her emotions. She dabbed at the corner of her eye with a handkerchief. "I just... don't understand it. Poor Mr. Dewey. I didn't even know he was sick."

Kenzie leaned closer to read the labels on the pill bottles on the night-stand. "It looks like he had high blood pressure and depression."

"Yes," Mrs. Hubbard wept some more, pressing the handkerchief to her eyes. "Yes, but he was in good health. He never expected to go now..."

"Well, he's with Mrs. Dewey now, isn't he?" Kenzie comforted. Not that she believed in heaven or loved ones awaiting the newly departed. But it gave comfort to many people.

"Yes," Mrs. Hubbard agreed, with more sniffling. She looked at the picture on his dresser, a much younger Stuart Dewey with a woman of about his age. And a son, a dark-haired older teen or young adult standing between them. Possibly a son. "He loved her very much. He hasn't been the same since she passed."

"Yeah. It's a mercy that he didn't have to suffer through a protracted illness and now he can be with his wife."

Mrs. Hubbard nodded. Zachary returned. He hovered just inside the door frame, looking at Mrs. Hubbard. "Did you find that key, ma'am?"

"Yes, of course I did," the older woman snapped. "I'm not incompetent. There's no need to 'ma'am' me."

"Uh..." Zachary looked startled at her response. "I was only trying to be polite."

"I don't need your kind of polite. Looking down your nose at me."

"No. Nothing like that," he protested. "You've been very professional while we've been here. Trying to get through this..." Zachary motioned toward Mr. Dewey's body. "I can't imagine what it must be like for you. You have been with the family for a long time."

Mrs. Hubbard's shoulders relaxed. She nodded. "Yes... they've been my family for the last ten years. Longer than that, I mean, but since I've been on my own, all of my own family dead and gone." Her eyes misted again. "We were both alone, Mr. Dewey and I." She dug into her pocket and produced the key. She handed it to Kenzie, giving Zachary a look that told him she didn't trust him with it.

"Thank you so much," Kenzie said. "We'll just finish up in here, and then we'll lock it. No one else will be able to disturb things in here until the authorities arrive."

18

Mrs. Hubbard left them again. Zachary stepped forward and handed Kenzie the ear thermometer he had found.

Another man might have disparaged Mrs. Hubbard after she left, calling her an old bat for the way she had reacted to his polite inquiry. But Zachary wasn't that kind of guy. He shook his head. "Poor woman."

"Yes. And depending on what the arrangements are for the Lodge, she might be out of work now. I'd hate to be looking for a new job at her age."

"Yeah. Maybe she already has enough to retire on. She might just have stayed on with the family because of her attachment to them."

"I doubt it. Working class women like her... She probably lives paycheck to paycheck. She has room and board, so her expenses probably are not too much, but even things like medication can be expensive at her age without some kind of plan."

Kenzie took a temperature reading of Mr. Dewey's body and recorded it.

"Thermostat downstairs is set at 72 degrees," Zachary advised. "This room is a few degrees cooler."

Kenzie tried taking the room temperature with the ear thermometer, but it gave an error. Not what it was designed to do. Kenzie added the information they had to the notes.

"Do you need to do anything else?" Zachary asked.

If she were in the morgue, Kenzie would have at least performed a gross examination of the body, checking for needle marks, bruises, or any other signs. But she couldn't see Mrs. Hubbard allowing them to strip Mr. Dewey down, even if they did tell her Kenzie's actual profession. And more than ever, Kenzie wanted to keep that a secret. If she let on now that she was a pathologist, there would be no end to the questions and speculation. It would be like being a performing monkey.

"I suppose that's it," she sighed. She went to the window and released the catch. She was glad to note that there were screens in the windows, so they wouldn't allow the snow in, unless the wind were blowing directly against that side of the house. On sliding the windows open, they were immediately assaulted by the chilly air.

Zachary walked out of the room ahead of Kenzie and waited. Kenzie pulled the door shut behind her and locked it with the key. She continued to stand there, looking at the door.

"What else?" Zachary asked.

"I'm just thinking of police tape."

"We don't have any. And I'm not sure it would do any good. Everyone knows that this is where the body is, and I think they will stay away."

"Maybe. But I would still like to have a bit more certainty. Where did Mrs. Hubbard say that the writing desk is?"

Zachary pointed down the hall.

"Would you see if there is some masking tape and a pen?"

Zachary didn't demand an explanation, he just went ahead and tracked down the items she needed. Kenzie tore strips off the roll and taped them flat along the door jamb and the door, sliding her fingers over them to press them down firmly. She scribbled her initials over each one.

"I don't think it would be easy for someone to get all of those off without breaking any of them."

"Looks good," Zachary confirmed.

"I suppose now we need to go explain to everyone else... and to tell them why they should listen to us when we're just a lowly accountant and..."

"Unemployed bum," Zachary provided.

"I'm sure you're not a bum. You're recovering from cancer. You're just temporarily out of work."

Zachary grinned.

<hr>

Everyone immediately wanted to know all the details of what had happened. Kenzie did her best to be vague and yet impart to them that no one could or would be allowed to go into Mr. Dewey's bedroom until the authorities had cleared it.

"This is outrageous," Vance Stiller objected. "I've never seen such a shoddily-run inn before—"

"I'm sure Mr. Dewey didn't plan to die," Kenzie told him, her voice heavy with sarcasm. "I suppose you already have your death date picked out?"

"I'm certainly not going to die like that—" Stiller gestured toward the room.

"In your sleep? No, I don't imagine so. Someone will shoot you or stab you in the back."

Jack laughed, making no effort to cover up his enjoyment of Kenzie's response like the rest of them were trying to do. Everyone seemed to be at the farmhouse now, having heard about what was going on and wanting to get more details, maybe even get to see the dead body themselves.

"Not that any of that matters right now," Kenzie said. "The main thing is the police said we were to lock up the room and stay out of there. No one is allowed to go in. I think everyone is here, so you all understand, right? I don't think there's even any reason for anyone to go up the stairs. It was only the Deweys' living quarters up there? No common areas?" Kenzie looked at Mrs. Hubbard, Samantha, and Burknall.

"No common areas," Samantha repeated. "But there are supplies up there. I need to get my cleaning things, and it's my responsibility to keep it all clean, up there and down here."

"Well, you don't need to do Mr. Dewey's room," Mrs. Hubbard told Samantha. "That is out of bounds."

"It's probably best if you don't do any of the upstairs," Kenzie said. "Just leave everything as it is, in case the police want to look at any of the other rooms too. Mrs. Hubbard can go with you while you gather your cleaning things, and you can keep them in the kitchen or somewhere else on the main floor."

Mrs. Hubbard nodded her agreement to this.

"And no one else needs to go up there," Kenzie repeated. "We all need to do what the police said."

"How do we know that you even talked to the police?" Vance asked, making a face at Kenzie. He did not like to be told what to do by a woman, that was clear. It was one thing when Brittany, who Kenzie assumed was his girlfriend, told him what to do. It was quite another to have to listen to some random guest who thought she had the right to be giving him instructions.

"If you want to, you can look up the phone number and call yourself," Kenzie said crisply. She assumed that Vance would not. Hoped that he wouldn't, because she didn't want Officer Star to give away Kenzie's actual profession. "Then you can confirm that I called and they told me to secure the scene for them. They are overworked right now because of the storm, but if you want to bother them with your questions about whether you *really* have to stay out of the dead man's room..."

Vance shifted. "I'm not saying I would break into his room. I'm just saying I think it is a bit much to tell us that the entire upstairs is off limits to use, just because you want to act like a big shot and boss everyone around."

"There is not anything for you in the upstairs anyway," Mrs. Hubbard insisted.

"How do I know that? What if I need something that is up there? What if the main floor bathroom is occupied and I need to use the facilities upstairs? There are dozens of reasons I might need to go up the stairs."

"No, there are not," Mrs. Hubbard insisted. "No guests ever go up there. Only Mr. Dewey."

"And the maid," Vance reminded her, looking at Samantha.

"And she will only go up to get her equipment, and then she will stay downstairs. You do not need the cleaning equipment. *You* are not going to clean anything, are you?"

Mrs. Hubbard darted at glance over at Kenzie, proud of herself for standing up to the rich man or checking to see if Kenzie approved of her response. Kenzie nodded and smiled.

Kenzie's stomach rumbled. She put her hand over it and looked around. She had forgotten all about breakfast, but her body clearly had not. She needed to eat, and then they could go back down to their cabin where she didn't have to deal with know-it-alls and the tension that permeated the house with the news of Dewey's death.

"I need breakfast. I suggest that we all eat so that Mrs. Hubbard can get things cleaned up. Do you have everything you need for the next few days, Mrs. Hubbard? I mean... with the storm coming in, we might not be able to get out for a supply run for a few days."

"We always have plenty in storage here. I can make do."

Several heads turned back toward Kenzie. They had been relaxing and getting ready to go their separate directions, but Kenzie's words had stopped them.

"What do you mean, we won't be able to get out?" Raven asked.

"Haven't you been watching the news?" Brittany demanded. "There's a big storm coming in."

19

S o?" Raven didn't seem to be able to comprehend this. "So there's going to be a big storm. Why wouldn't we be able to get out of here? There are roads all the way here, we can just drive out any time we want."

"No!" Brittany laughed. "Haven't you ever, like, been out of the city before? If we get snowed in here, the cars won't be able to get to the highway. And if they do get to the highway, it isn't going to be plowed for a few days. We are isolated here. That's why everyone chose the Lodge, isn't it? Because you wanted to be by yourself, away from all the stress of civilization? Well, here you are. If we get a huge dump of snow like they're predicting, it might be a week before we are able to get out."

Guests looked back and forth at one another. Redd Flagg shrugged. "Well, it's a good thing I don't have anywhere I'm supposed to be. I guess anyone who does had better get in their car and get away now while they still can."

Kenzie wanted to protest that everyone should stay there until the investigation into Mr. Dewey's death was complete, but of course that was silly. Police said that on TV, not in real life. Everyone could leave if they wanted to. And if they did want to, it was best to get on their way as soon as they could, otherwise they would get stranded.

Jack looked at his watch. "When is it supposed to hit? I only need to throw my crap into a bag, and then I'm out of here."

"It's supposed to be here within a couple of hours," Kenzie said, checking the time on her phone. "I would hit the road as soon as you can. It might already be too late. If you get into the teeth of the storm and it's too bad, turn around and come back here. There isn't anywhere else to get help anywhere close by."

Jack swore under his breath and agreed.

The newlyweds spoke to each other in whispers, and Kenzie thought that they were also going to see if they could beat the storm. So much for the honeymoon.

Kenzie sat down at the table with her breakfast. She was glad she didn't have to rush to get away from the Lodge. She didn't want to pack in a hurry or throw everything into the car and try to get down the mountain at a breakneck pace in order to beat the storm. It was much better to sit back and wait it out. They had everything they needed. She nodded toward Zachary's muffin, barely touched.

"Are you going to eat?"

Zachary sat next to her, perched on the edge of his seat, looking as if he were ready to jump to his feet at any moment. Though he had acted calm and focused during the moment of crisis, he was now too wound up and hypervigilant to relax. He didn't even touch the muffin, looking from one guest to the other as they sat down to eat or left in their various directions. Mrs. Hubbard returned to her kitchen and Samantha followed her. Burknall grabbed a couple of danishes and went outside, headed back to the barn or wherever he lived on the grounds. He probably had a small cabin of his own, either with the guest cottages or somewhere else on the property.

It was difficult to eat slowly and enjoy herself with Zachary looking like a jack-in-the-box ready to pop, but Kenzie tried not to let him rush her. When she was finished and picked up her plate to put in the tub Mrs. Hubbard had left for the dirty dishes, Zachary sighed audibly. Kenzie didn't say anything to him about it as they moved to the clothing hung by the door and got their winter gear back on. Then they were out the door and into a very cold wind.

"Sheesh!" Kenzie wrapped her arms around herself. "It wasn't like this when we came up. I should have driven."

"Then you would have to warm the car up."

"But at least it would be out of the wind. Have you ever felt it so cold?"

He was hunched against the wind and she wasn't sure whether he shrugged at her question or just ignored it. They both hustled down the hill much more quickly than they had climbed up it. It was practically a race to the door, and they both burst into the cabin at the same time, laughing a little in breathless relief.

It wasn't until then that Kenzie even remembered about Tyrrell and the kids being there. All thought of them had been driven out of her mind when she had run up the stairs at Mrs. Hubbard's shrieks.

"Oh, Tyrrell!"

From the look on Zachary's face, he too had forgotten about his brother being there.

Tyrrell looked at the two of them, bemused. "What? Did you run all the way here?"

"Pretty much," Kenzie agreed. "It is *cold* out there!"

"As cold as a witch's behind," Zachary said, reminding Kenzie of the fire chief who had been in charge of the rescue from the wreck Zachary and Kenzie were in on New Year's Eve a couple of years earlier. Zachary hadn't been able to remember much about the accident that had nearly taken both of their lives, but he remembered the fire chief's colorful expression.

Mason giggled loudly and Alisha covered her mouth, primly shocked and entertained. Tyrrell rolled his eyes. "How many more times do you think I'm going to hear that expression on this trip?"

"Well, maybe a few," Zachary admitted, grinning.

"It must have been a good breakfast up there, you took quite a while. Did you bring anything back with you?"

"Well..." Kenzie sat down near Tyrrell. "No. But we have some news."

20

"Do you think we should stay here or try to get home?" Tyrrell asked, after hearing about the developments up at the farmhouse.

Kenzie looked at the time, though she didn't need to. She already knew it was too late to leave. It had probably been too late when they had discussed it at the farmhouse. With the wind that had already blown in, she wasn't sure they were going to be able to get anywhere before running into the snow.

"I think we'd better batten down the hatches here. I don't think we have much hope of getting home. I'd rather not be battling the blizzard."

Tyrrell nodded. "Okay, good. And you think... it's safe?"

"Safe? I think it's safer here than out there. We have everything we need here."

"I mean... you don't think that Dewey died of anything that might be contagious, or that someone..." Tyrrell cleared his throat and glanced at the children. "Helped him along?"

"No!" Kenzie laughed. "I think he just passed away in his sleep. Heart failure, probably. Even if he was in relatively good health, it's not unheard of, especially for someone who has recently lost a loved one. When they open him up—"

Tyrrell cleared his throat again. Kenzie was not used to having children around when discussing medical examiner stuff.

"You said that it's been a couple of years since he lost his wife, though," Tyrrell countered.

"Yes, but that's really not long. And he was on medications for depression and high blood pressure."

Tyrrell shrugged and nodded. "Okay. If you're comfortable with that."

"I don't think you have anything to be worried about. This is not a TV murder mystery. Just a natural death."

"I just wondered, with all of the stuff you had to do to determine time of death and preserve the scene. It sounds like you thought it might be something else."

"No. Those are things we do all the time. There may not be any evidence to protect in this case, but if someone else discovered a bo— discovered that someone had passed and our ME's office had to attend, I would want them to do everything they could to preserve the scene just as it was too. It's just best practices."

Tyrrell nodded slowly. "Okay, then. Is there anything that we should be doing to prepare for the storm?"

<hr>

There wasn't much that they could do to prepare. It wasn't like a hurricane, where they boarded up the windows to prevent them from breaking. The cabins were meant to be used year-round, so they were weathertight and had forced air heating already. There was a fireplace if they needed it, but of course they weren't likely to use it with Zachary's issues. The Lodge had a handyman on site, and he hadn't said that he needed anyone to help with arrangements to be made up at the main house. They had plenty of food on hand. Entertainment by way of the TV and the other devices they all had. They would be able to get through the storm easily enough.

The wind picked up until it was howling around the little house and, despite Kenzie's assurances that the house was well-sealed and weatherproof, she could still feel the wind through the cracks around some of the windows. They didn't have any way to seal them better, so everyone donned extra clothing. The furnace hummed and the fan blew warm air throughout the cabin. The snow started to come down outside, blown at a sharp angle by the brisk winds, until they couldn't even see the cars in the driveway or the shape of the next cabin over.

The kids stared out the window oohing and ahhing to start with, but quickly grew bored of watching the snow fall and went back to the TV.

Until the power went out.

Alisha gave a little shriek of surprise. Mason went barreling across the room to his father, nearly knocking him over when they collided. Tyrrell didn't scold Mason, but put his arms around him and held him close.

"It's okay, bud. It's just the power. Sometimes a storm like this makes it blink off. You've seen the power go out before."

Mason held on to his father fiercely. "Turn it back on," he insisted. "Go find the box thing and flip the switches."

"I don't think it's the breaker box." Tyrrell shuffled over to the window with Mason glued to him. "You see, there aren't any other lights on. It isn't just our cabin. It's probably everything in the resort and for miles around."

"You said it blinks." Mason blinked his eyes several times. "It's not blinking. It's not going back on."

"I can see that. But you're okay, Mason. Daddy's here. We just need to find something else to do until it comes back on."

"Like what?"

"Like... see if we can find some board games. It would be fun to play some games, wouldn't it?"

"In the dark?" Mason challenged.

"It's not that dark. It's still daytime; it's just a little bit dark because of the storm. We can still see well enough to play a game, can't we?"

"I saw some games," Alisha offered. She went into the bedroom that Lorne and Pat had used overnight, and pulled a stack of boxes from the closet. "Look. There's lots of them."

Kenzie hadn't even thought about the power going out. That was going to throw a wrench into things. The storm would last for a few hours, and then, hopefully, someone from the County would be able to get out and fix whatever lines had gone down. In the meantime, there was no electricity to blow the heated air through the house, to keep the food cold in the refrigerator, to heat the food, or to light the house.

She looked over at Zachary.

He avoided her eyes.

While Tyrrell and the children chose a game and started to set up the pieces, Zachary started to pace. At first, it looked like he was just making sure that everything in the cabin was in order, but after the first couple of circuits around the rooms, it was obvious that he was just moving to try to keep his anxiety under control.

Mason had run straight to his daddy for comfort. Although he was a grown man, part of Zachary was still just a little boy. A little boy who had been trapped, terrified, in a house fire and was now thinking through the same things as Kenzie was. That they would need some alternate source of heat and light by nightfall. The power out wasn't just a blink, as Tyrrell had suggested, but could quite possibly be out for a day or more.

And the thought of having to light a fire in the fireplace or candles to see by was terrifying to him.

Kenzie approached him. She held out her arms and, after a moment of hesitation, he stepped into them, and they held each other tightly.

"Are you okay?"

Zachary cleared his throat. "Sure. I'm fine."

"What does Dr. B. say about sharing your feelings? Is saying you're fine sharing your feelings?"

He swallowed, his Adam's apple prominent in his thin neck. "No. But with the kids..." he said in a hoarse whisper, looking over at them. "I don't want to scare them or make them think there's anything to worry about."

"Okay, that's fair." Kenzie rubbed Zachary's back. His muscles were as hard as rock, knotted up in tension. "Then let's just say not fine. Do you want to call her?"

Zachary looked at Kenzie blankly.

"Do you want to call Dr. Boyle? Tell her about what's going on and see if she has some suggestions that might help."

Zachary considered this, then nodded stiffly. "Yeah." He glanced over at the children. "I'll call from the bedroom."

Kenzie released him from her hold. "Okay. Just shout if you need me."

Tyrrell watched Zachary's departure. "Is he okay?"

"This might end up being pretty rough if the power doesn't come back on. He's going to talk to his therapist."

"He brought his pills with him, right?"

"Yeah. That will help, but I'm hoping that having a meltdown and medicating to the eyeballs are not the only two choices if we have to use that." Kenzie nodded to the fireplace.

21

It wasn't long before Zachary was back. He didn't look much calmer, and Kenzie didn't think that he'd had enough time for a good chat with the therapist.

"You couldn't get her?"

Zachary held up his phone. "Just for a couple of minutes. Bad connection. And then it cut out." He peered out the window at the flurry of snow blowing almost straight across and the dark clouds overhead blocking out most of the sunlight, even thought it was early afternoon.

"Did you try to get her back?"

Zachary looked at her. Like he might not have tried again? Of course he had tried her again. Knowing Zachary, he'd probably tried again a dozen times.

Kenzie sighed. "I'm sorry. Did she have any suggestions in the two minutes you managed to talk?"

"Keep my distance. Positive self-talk. Meditating or saying a mantra." He ran his fingers through his short, stubbly hair. "Apparently, exposure therapy is really good for anxiety."

A choked laugh escaped Kenzie's throat. "Yeah. In this nice, controlled environment."

"At least you're a doctor. If I have a heart attack, you could give me CPR, right?"

Kenzie was momentarily distracted by his mention of a heart attack. Was there something that Stuart Dewey had been extra anxious or stressed by?

Could an outside factor or situation have triggered his heart attack, if that was what had killed him?

She went over to Zachary and gave him a quick hug. "We'll get you through this. One step at a time. You can have some control over when we switch to... alternative heat or light sources."

She wanted to say that the decision was his alone, but decided she couldn't put it all on him. He might decide he'd rather freeze than light a fire. Or he might feel pressured to make the decision for everyone else's comfort as if his own didn't matter. It was better if they all decided together.

Tyrrell had played with the kids until they were too bored to attend to it anymore. Kenzie made some sandwiches with some of the leftover turkey, and everyone had eaten a quiet supper together. It was too dark to see much after that, so their options were limited to going to bed, a game that could be played in the dark, such as hide and seek or murder, or lighting some candles or the fire.

There was a knock at the door. It sounded more like a mule kick than a knock, making them all startle or shriek. The sudden noise breaking the silence of the cabin was alarming. It was a minute before Kenzie could steel herself to go to the door. Who would be out and about when the weather was still so nasty? They had watched the snow piling up outside. It was getting pretty deep and would not be easy to slog through. She wondered whether anyone had made it out before the storm hit. Were the newlyweds getting home now? Getting tucked into a warm, cozy bed?

Kenzie opened the door, holding it tightly to keep it from banging open with the wind. A large shape shouldered its way into the room, putting down heavy equipment with a clang. Kenzie jumped back, unable to tell who it was or why he was nearly dropping the hardware on her feet. She pushed the door shut behind him.

Burknall unwrapped the scarf around his face and pulled down his face mask to speak. Kenzie felt a little better being able to see who it was.

"Space heater," Burknall declared, giving the big piece of machinery a kick. "Could see that you folks didn't have your fireplace lit." He gave Zachary a look.

"Oh." Kenzie felt a sudden, warm rush of gratitude toward the big, curt man. "Thank you so much!"

He grunted, took a moment to stomp most of the snow off of his big boots, then lugged the heater over to the fireplace. "We'll vent it up the chimney. That will help keep fumes from building in the room."

"Thank you."

She watched him get the heater set up, attaching a tube that led to what she assumed was a propane tank. She moved in closer to him. "You have to light a burner, though...?"

He glanced at her. "Just a pilot light, like the furnace. It's got an auto-igniter." He tightened up the connections and pressed a button in a few times. "There. Just like that." He stripped off his gloves and held his hands in front of it to feel the warmth from the heater. "Got all kinds of safety features. Tip over protection, oximeter. It will stop if there are any problems."

"That was very thoughtful," Zachary spoke up, his voice hoarse. "I really appreciate it."

"Don't let the kids play near it," Burknall said, ignoring the thanks. "It does get hot enough to burn you if you touch it." He dug through several large pockets, looking for something, then pulled out a long, flat box, which he tossed on the floor. "Don't use those all tonight. I don't have any more."

Kenzie picked up the box and opened it. It was filled with long plastic cylinders filled with chemicals.

Glow sticks.

"You run into any trouble, I'm in the barn and Mrs. Hubbard is in the main house. Phone lines are down as well as power, so we are cut off from the outside." Burknall stood and looked out the window. He gestured to the last piece of equipment that he had left by the door. "Camp stove. If you need to heat something up. The dining room up top is still providing meals, but if you want to take your meals here..." He shrugged.

Kenzie assumed that the Lodge would be lit with candles, so it was probably a good idea for them to eat on their own.

Burknall went on. "Strange things going on tonight. I suggest you stay in your cabin." He went back to the door and started to gear up to go outside again.

"What does that mean?" Kenzie asked, confused. "Strange things going on tonight? You mean something about the weather?"

"No. People. Acting squirrelly. That little Raven tore up one side of me and down the other, said that she saw me stealing from her cabin. The newly-weds—they didn't make it more than a mile or two down the main road— they are..." he paused, considering his words. "They go from arguing and acting like they're going to kill each other to flying as high as kites, if you know what I mean."

"You think they took something?"

"Oh, they took something, all right. And who knows what they'll do before they come back down. You can never predict. Keep your door locked. Don't let anyone in."

With that, he pulled his scarf around his head, pulled on his gloves, and departed.

Kenzie locked and latched the door before turning to face the others.

It was dark, so she couldn't see their expressions, just the shadows across their faces. Zachary looking even more skeletal than usual, though she was sure that he would be feeling a lot more relaxed knowing that they weren't going to have to light a fire.

"Well, that was nice of Mr. Burknall, wasn't it?" Kenzie said cheerfully. She walked closer to them and handed a glow stick to each of the children. "You know how to use these, right?"

"I like Mr. Burknall," Mason declared. He took the glow stick and began to snap it down the length. He shook it vigorously and it started to shine. They actually threw a good amount of light. The room immediately felt warmer and more cheerful.

"He comes across as an old grouch," Kenzie said, "but he really is very thoughtful, isn't he?"

"He let me drive the horses," Mason reminded her.

"Yes, he did. Let's sit closer to the fireplace and warm up. Now that we can see, we can play another game or read a book."

"But no TV," Mason said sadly, as if missing a departed friend.

Kenzie smiled at him. "No. No TV."

22

Kenzie noticed that the kids started to act ready for bed much earlier than they had the night before. Maybe because there were no devices to keep them entertained. They had all shut off their phones, tablets, and games to conserve batteries until they used them again or the power came back on. Zachary had a couple of battery packs that he used for charging devices when he was out on surveillance for a long time, and they held those in reserve. With no TV or internet access, once the children grew tired of playing board games or reading books, they were ready for sleep.

It probably helped that it wasn't the first day in a strange place and that there hadn't been a big dinner with more strangers, as there had been the night before. Mason put up a little bit of a fight over going to sleep, but it was nothing compared to the difficulty Tyrrell had with him the night before. Tyrrell stayed up for a bit longer, enjoying a chance to talk with the grown-ups, and then he headed off to bed as well.

Kenzie put the glow sticks into the snow out the back door, as freezing them was supposed to preserve the glow, and she turned the heater down to a lower holding temperature for the night. They all had plenty of blankets and each other to help keep them warm for bed.

Zachary moved around the bedroom slowly, seeming reluctant to settle in for bed. There wasn't really anything to do to get ready for bed. No staying up catching up on social networks or working on his computer.

"Do you want something to read?" Kenzie suggested. "I could help you find something you like. There's a pretty good selection on the shelves here."

"No." Zachary shrugged. "I've never really been able to read for pleasure."

"Maybe now, with no other distractions...?"

He shook his head vigorously. "There are plenty of distractions here."

"There are?" Kenzie thought that without the electronics, he would, like the children, be bored. He would go to bed earlier than usual because there was nothing else to do.

"Yeah." Zachary looked out the window, putting his face close to the glass and cupping his hands around his eyes to see better. After a minute he withdrew, apparently not seeing anything of concern. "Mr. Dewey dying. The snowstorm. The power and phones being out. Worrying about how long it will be and whether we'll run out of fuel for the heater. People acting squirrelly."

"But we're in here, safe and sound. We have heat and light for now. Everything is good."

"For now. But it won't last forever."

"You're worrying about things that you don't need to worry about yet."

"I thought I would get a head start."

Kenzie smiled at this. "Really, though. Dr. B. has talked to us about catastrophizing. Thinking that the worst possible things are going to happen and blowing everything up out of proportion. The snow is slowing. By tomorrow it will probably be stopped. The plows will clear the highway and Mr. Burknall will clear the Lodge's roads. The power will be fixed and the cell phones won't be blocked by the clouds. It's only temporary, and by this time tomorrow, you'll probably be wondering what you were so worried about."

"I've never wondered why I was so worried."

"Maybe you should worry about that," Kenzie said flippantly. "That's not normal." Then she held up her hand. "Forget I said that. Don't worry about not wondering why you were worried..."

Zachary sat down on the edge of the bed. "What do you think Burknall was talking about with weird things going on? It's normal for people to be stressed at a time like this. Was he just overreacting or being dramatic? Like telling ghost stories?"

"I don't know. I get the feeling that he doesn't joke around a lot. But sometimes really serious people still have a good sense of humor, they are just understated or keep it to themselves. He might think that it would... make things more entertaining for us."

"Yeah. You don't think there's anything to be concerned about?"

"I think that everything is under control. We're safe in the cabin, so it doesn't really matter what everybody else is doing. And I'm sure that with this storm, everyone else is going to stay inside too. Who would want to be out wandering in weather like this?"

"And the newlyweds? He said they were high as kites?"

"They might just be tipsy. Or giddy with the stress. Some people get like that, just a little hysterical and out of control. Or they might have taken anxiety meds. Sometimes those can make people a little loopy."

"It could be something else. Illegal drugs. Something that could make them dangerous to us. Bath salts or PCP…"

"They didn't strike me as the type of people to experiment with that sort of thing. I think that Mr. Burknall was probably just overstating. Raven was extra stressed, so she took it out on him by getting angry and accusing. The newlyweds are feeling jittery, and they argued and were a bit silly. You know how it is when people are stressed."

Zachary rubbed his jaw. Kenzie could hear his fingers rasping across the whiskers in the dark, and it set her teeth on edge.

"Maybe we should have stayed at home. Maybe coming here was a bad idea," Zachary said

"Well, it was my idea, so if it was bad, then I'm the one who should be beating myself up about it, not you. Let's get into bed."

"I'm too restless."

"Just try. Once you're in bed, maybe your body will decide it is safe to relax and sleep."

Zachary began to undress, not arguing with her logic. It was something she had said before, and while it never really seemed to work that way for Zachary, she persisted. She was convinced, despite the evidence and everything she knew about anxiety disorders, that he could relax if he just did normal, relaxing things, and focused on clearing his mind instead of worrying over everything.

She had her delusions too.

Kenzie took off her day clothes and pulled on some soft flannel pajamas. Not sexy, maybe, but they were warm and comfy, which was exactly what she needed on a night when they were snowbound. She slid in under the covers, with several more blankets on hand if she got cold in the night. Zachary climbed in. He put his arms around her and explored her curves under the pajamas.

"This is cozy."

Kenzie snuggled up to him. "It is." She put her arms around his bare back. "I should get you some too. They're very fashionable," she teased.

He jerked suddenly, turning to look at the window. Kenzie waited, watching his dark shape against the slight glow from the window.

"What is it?"

"I heard a noise."

Kenzie breathed slowly, regulating her response. "I didn't hear anything. What did it sound like?"

"It sounded like someone is out there."

He got back out of bed and looked out the window again. He stood there for a long time.

"Don't see anything?" Kenzie surmised.

"No." He finally turned back around and returned to the bed.

"Did you take something for anxiety tonight?" she asked. Normally she didn't prompt him about his meds. He was a big boy and knew what was best for his body and mind. But she was afraid that his anxiety was getting the better of him and he would never be able to settle down for the night without an aid.

"No."

"Have you thought about it? You are still recovering from your treatment; your body needs the rest."

"Not tonight." He turned his head and looked toward the window again.

Kenzie cuddled, trying to get comfortable and to distract him from his hypervigilance. But he turned away from her, lying on his other side so he could watch the window. Kenzie spooned against his back and breathed slowly, drawing her breath out long to see whether he would unconsciously match her slower rhythm and allow himself to relax. He had been still for a long time, and she was wondering if he were drifting off when he sat up abruptly and slid his feet back out of bed again. Kenzie stifled a groan and rolled onto her back. She watched him check the window once more and then moved toward the open bedroom door.

"What is it? Do you need something?"

"Just checking the doors."

Kenzie knew she had already checked the doors before going to bed, and so had Zachary. The house was very quiet, and she heard him checking not only the front and back doors of the cabin, but also going quietly into each room. To check the windows, she assumed. They were all properly latched, and probably frozen shut as well. Which might actually be a problem for Zachary, if he started to worry about how they would all get out of the house if the heater started a fire. But the children were in the room with Tyrrell, not sleeping on their own, so if there were a fire, Tyrrell would know to break a window rather than trying to get it unstuck. He'd been trapped in his bedroom the night of the fire when Zachary was ten and Tyrrell was just four. The firefighters had needed to break the window from the outside to get him out.

She continued to listen, but despite herself was almost asleep again by the time Zachary returned.

"Everything okay?" Kenzie murmured.

Zachary got back into bed again. The third time now? Kenzie was losing track. "There are people out. I can hear them walking back and forth." His body was tense, and his muscles did not relax when she rubbed his back, shoulders, and neck.

"It's okay if there are people out," Kenzie told him calmly. There was no point in telling him that there were not people out. He had already decided that there were. "We are safe in here. No one else can get in. We're snug as a couple of bugs in a rug."

"Five bugs," he corrected immediately, taking his brother and family into account.

"Snug as five bugs in a rug," Kenzie agreed sleepily. "Don't worry about what anyone else is doing."

"Uh-huh."

Kenzie closed her eyes. Maybe Zachary wasn't going to get any sleep, but she was. She was warm and cozy in the bed and it had been a busy day.

23

Kenzie was awakened by a loud crash. She jolted awake, and her first thought was that the noise had been caused by Mason, or Mason and Alisha together. Jumping off of the bed or playing Jenga or getting into something they were not supposed to. She tried to hold back her anger and get reoriented to time and space. She reached out for Zachary but, as she expected, he was not beside her. If he had gotten any sleep, he had risen before her, which was his usual practice.

Kenzie rubbed her eyes and looked around. The room was light, so the sun was up and was forcing its way down through the clouds. Maybe they would have some cell reception. She climbed out of bed. There was a braided rug beside the bed, but when she stepped off of it, her feet hit icy wood floor that made her want to get right back into bed. She forced herself to keep going. Zachary had probably not thought to turn the heater back up, and she would have to do it herself.

She walked out to the living room and looked around. She had expected to see the children, but they weren't there. Maybe they had gone out and it was the door slamming behind them that had woken her up?

Zachary was sitting in one of the easy chairs, facing the main window, very still.

"Was there a noise?" Kenzie asked. "Something woke me up."

"The door."

"Did the kids go out?"

"No. Someone at the door."

Kenzie looked pointedly at Zachary sitting there like a statue. "Why didn't you answer it, then?"

He didn't respond. Kenzie rubbed her arms. Her toes were going numb on the cold floor.

"Can you at least turn the heater up?"

She hated the anticipation of opening the cabin door and letting all of the cold air in. Her skin was covered with goosebumps already. It was cold as a witch's behind out there.

Kenzie reached the door and put her hand on the latch.

"Burknall said not to let anyone in," Zachary reminded her.

"That was last night. When he thought weird things were going on. But everyone will be asleep now. Anybody with any sense is still in bed."

With that, she flipped the latch and unlocked the door. She didn't even have time to turn the door handle when the door flew open, pushed by someone outside. Kenzie stepped back to avoid getting hit, her anger rising the second time in two minutes. Or the third time, counting her irritation at Zachary for not turning up the heat or answering the door himself.

Redd Flagg stepped into the room, and he shut the door quickly, blocking out the cold air. He swore and slapped his hands against his arms. He was wearing leather gloves that didn't even look as if they were lined and an autumn jacket. What was wrong with men who couldn't dress themselves properly for the weather?

"Is it ever cold out there!" Redd declared.

"Yes, it is. What are you doing up already? I thought writers sleep in."

"Something has happened."

Kenzie had been looking at Zachary to see whether he were going to turn up the heater. Her head snapped back around to look at Redd.

"What?"

"Cabin four. I don't know what's going on; I can't get a coherent answer out of anyone. Did you hear or see anything last night?"

"No. I mean, I didn't. Zachary said he could hear people going back and forth. What time? Mr. Burknall said that... people were acting strangely last night. I assume it was just the stress, but..."

"I don't know what it is, but you should probably get dressed. There's not even anyone in charge now, with Mr. Dewey dead. I don't know who is supposed to take charge. One of the help? That doesn't seem right."

And from what Kenzie had seen of the three of them, none of them was particularly suited to leadership. Burknall seemed the best bet, but he was brusque and more likely to tackle a job alone than to lead anyone else.

"Okay, I'm going to get dressed."

Redd nodded, looking relieved. Zachary followed Kenzie to the bedroom. He was already dressed. Of course he hadn't been sitting around in the cabin in his skivvies. Even if he had been distracted, he was bound to notice sooner or later he was cold and put some clothes on.

"What do you think it is?" Kenzie asked. "Could you tell what was going on from what you heard last night?"

"No. It was all pretty confusing."

"You said you heard footsteps. People walking."

"Yes. You would think that in the middle of cold weather like this, people would stay indoors. But they were back and forth all night."

"Who was?"

"I don't know."

"I imagine people were probably uncomfortable. Hyped up. Maybe Burknall had to build a couple of fires or take care of frozen pipes or flooding. Or just calm people down."

Zachary nodded, making no suggestions.

Kenzie changed as quickly as she could, both so that she didn't have to deal with the cold air on her skin and so that she could get out and see what was going on. Redd was right. Someone would have to take charge until Dewey's replacement got there. And it was better for everyone if that someone were not Vance Stiller.

Zachary left the bedroom. When Kenzie finished and headed back to the living room, he was just coming out of Tyrrell's bedroom. "Just letting him know that we were going out," he explained.

"Oh, are you coming too?"

Zachary looked taken aback. "If there's trouble, I'm not letting you go on your own."

Was there trouble? Or was Redd just being overly dramatic, as she'd suggested Burknall was the night before? Kenzie's brain was coming up with random ideas of what could have happened to upset Redd so much. And why Burknall had been so worried about the lovebirds the night before.

Kenzie and Zachary put on their boots, coats, and the rest of their winter gear in silence. It wasn't far to the next cabin. The newlyweds'. Kenzie joined the little cluster of people around the door.

"What's going on?"

Raven just shook her head. Only her eyes were showing through her ski mask, and to Kenzie they looked abnormally wide, her pupils dilated way too much in the morning sun. Mrs. Hubbard was there, and shushed Kenzie as though she had been talking too loudly in a library. Kenzie was about to protest, then realized that the others were trying to hear what was going on behind the closed door. She cocked her head and waited, ears pricked to hear whatever she could. Two male voices. Mr. Andy Collins, of course, and she thought that the other was the curt, abrupt cadences of Mr. Burknall. Certainly not Vance Stiller's. She hadn't paid much attention to Jack and the way that he spoke, but it sounded too low and measured to be the younger man.

The door opened and Burknall stood there, looking at them all, caught eavesdropping. Kenzie refused to be embarrassed by the fact. Of course she had been trying to overhear them and figure out what was going on. Anyone would have. Everyone was.

"We have a missing person," Burknall said briefly.

Kenzie looked around at the group around her, but she already knew who it had to be. She hadn't heard a female voice behind the door. "Mrs. Collins?"

Burknall nodded.

"Oh dear." Kenzie looked around. Trails had been trampled up and down the front of the cottages, and there were several inroads going between them to the back yards which bordered on the woods. There had been too many people back and forth to simply follow Mrs. Collins's footprints away from the cabin. And Zachary had said that people had been coming and going all night. How long had it been since Mrs. Collins had disappeared? With the temperature so low, she wouldn't last very long outside. "Are you sure she's not up at the house? If they had a fight, then maybe she just went somewhere else to cool down. *Calm* down, I mean. She might have fallen asleep on a chair or something and doesn't even know anyone is looking for her."

Mrs. Hubbard and Samantha looked at each other. "I didn't see her at the house," Mrs. Hubbard said, "but the door was left unlocked all night. She could have come and be asleep in one of the spare rooms…"

"I'll go look," Samantha said immediately.

A bundle of furs that had to be Brittany spun in a circle, looking all around. "Where could she have gone if she didn't go to the house? Where else is there to go? She didn't come to my cabin. Raven?"

"No, not mine either," Raven provided.

Zachary looked down at the trails trampled through the snow. "We'd better check out each trail that has been broken. Even if only one person has walked through a certain place. We should divide into teams of two so that no one else can get lost."

Kenzie had a sneaking suspicion that the suggestion to go in pairs was not just so that people didn't get lost in the snow. The whole world outside seemed to be white, but she didn't think anyone would go far enough afield to get lost.

Zachary didn't want anyone to be alone where they could do mischief.

Kenzie's stomach clenched.

Something had happened. Mrs. Andy Collins had not just gone out for a morning constitutional.

24

Zachary and Kenzie helped organize the search. Of course they paired themselves up.

"Where do you think we should look?" Kenzie asked.

Zachary gazed around, looking at the trails that had been trampled into the snow. It was surprising how many people had been walking around since the snow had fallen. Or even while it was still falling, as she could see that some footprints had been partially filled in after they were made. She had assumed that everyone would be bundled up cozy and warm in their cabins, like she and Zachary and Tyrrell's family had been. She had written off Zachary's claim that he could hear people walking around outside as paranoia. Hearing things because he was anxious.

But clearly, people *had* been wandering about when they should have been in bed.

Zachary pointed toward their own cabin. "Let's circle around ours and see if there are any trails branching off from there."

Had he heard anything else the night before? Voices? Snatches of conversation? She didn't ask in front of the others. There would be opportunities for private conversation later.

Kenzie started walking along the trampled trail that led behind their cabin. Zachary followed close behind her. She liked that he didn't act all macho and insist on going in front of her. He didn't think that she was weak or less able to handle whatever they encountered than he was.

Directly behind the cabin, almost leading from their back door, was a trail leading back toward the woods. Kenzie wasn't surprised that Zachary had been right about that. He said he had been up all night listening to them. He would know that they had been behind the house, then fading off into the distance.

"Into the woods?" Kenzie asked.

"Yes," Zachary said gruffly.

Kenzie took the branching pathway and led the search into the woods.

The snow wasn't as thick on the ground under the trees. There were bare patches where there was thicker foliage overhead catching the snow. But the trail was still easy to see. Kenzie stopped and studied it. The snow wasn't trampled down as much as it was around the cabins. She could see the distinct treads as people had gone into the woods and returned. Three different treads, she thought. If they'd had a tech team there, they could have taken casts of the shoe prints.

Kenzie took out her phone and powered it up.

"You won't be able to get a signal in here," Zachary said.

"I don't need a signal."

Kenzie waited for the phone to boot up, then took off her glove to unlock it with her fingerprint and tap the buttons. It was too cold to go without gloves for long, but she would have to put up with it for a few minutes. She crouched down and took pictures of the various footprints. They didn't come out very well.

"Try more of an angle and turn on the flash," Zachary suggested. "That will cast shadows that will show the print better."

Kenzie obeyed, and got a few shots that were reasonably good. She put her own foot next to one of the prints to use as the scale for the picture. One of the distinct treads was smaller than hers. The other two were bigger. Two men and a woman?

"Okay." Kenzie put her phone back in her pocket and put her gloves back on, then tucked her hands under her armpits to warm them up faster. She continued along the trail, the dread growing in her belly.

They didn't speculate about what they were going to find, if they were to find anything. A missing woman in a snowstorm? Kenzie hoped that Mrs. Hubbard found her sleeping in the main house, unaware that people were concerned about her.

The trail didn't take them far. A few twists and turns through the woods. Not as far as they had gone on their hayride. Kenzie could see a shape in the snow ahead, and picked up her pace, hoping she wouldn't find what she did.

Mrs. Andy Collins lay crumpled in the snow. There were footprints around her. Someone had been there, knew where she was and what had happened to her, but hadn't told them so. More than one set of footprints. Kenzie tried to avoid them as she got closer to the fallen woman to examine her.

She had on a coat over her nightgown; boots, but no gloves or hat. The coat had not been buttoned up, maybe just thrown on as she tried to make her escape from whatever had caused her to leave her cabin the night before.

Freezings were a tricky thing. The heart slowed and the mammalian cold response could kick in, preserving life at a level undetectable to medical professionals. A person wasn't dead until they were warm and dead, as the aphorism went. Mrs. Andy Collins would have to be brought inside and warmed slowly to see whether she could be revived.

But even as Kenzie stooped to check for a pulse and evaluate the newly-wed's condition, she saw the blood on the front of Mrs. Collins's nightgown. Kenzie stripped off her glove and felt for a pulse anyway. Ice crystals crunched under the rubbery skin. No detectable pulse.

In the cold, that didn't mean that she was dead.

But the stab wounds down the front of the woman's torso told her that there was nothing that could be done for the woman, who was almost as pale as the snow in which she lay. Kenzie's anatomy classes, the dissections she had done, and the autopsies she had attended told her that Mrs. Andy Collins had sustained at least one stab wound directly to the heart. And no mammalian cold response would save her from that.

"Nothing?" Zachary asked, as Kenzie stepped back.

"No sign of life. She's been here a few hours, or there wouldn't be ice crystals forming. She's been stabbed multiple times." Kenzie surveyed the holes in the victim's nightgown, each with a blot of blood around it, some of them spread out and merging. "By my count, about nine times." Kenzie paused. She took out her phone again, took off her gloves to operate it, and turned on the video recording. She took a long shot, then zoomed in on the injuries, dictating her observations again for the record. She panned over the footprints that went all around the body. None of the footprints continued into the woods; they stopped at the body and returned again along the same path they had come on. Except for the set of footprints which didn't return.

Kenzie dictated the time and date and her and Zachary's names. She needed to record everything for the medical examiner who would eventually get the case. Make sure that he had all the details he would need. The police would also need the footprint evidence to interpret the story it told.

"What do we do?" Zachary asked, his voice low, almost reverent.

"The practice should always be to leave the body *in situ* until the medical examiner can get there, and to preserve as much of the scene and forensic evidence as possible. But we don't know how long it will be until someone can get up here, and we can't leave the body subject to predation." Kenzie pondered what to do next. "I think that we should get a couple of blankets. Wrap the body and create a sling to carry her in. Take her up to the house where her body can be preserved. Like Mr. Dewey's."

"Is there any connection between what happened to Mr. Dewey and... Mrs. Collins?"

"The two deaths couldn't be more different. I don't see any connection between the two except that they were proximate in time and place."

Zachary didn't say anything to disagree, but Kenzie knew that he did. He was looking for the connections, analyzing everything he knew about both deaths. He was a trained investigator. He wouldn't be satisfied until he had the answers.

Maybe there was no connection between the two deaths. But maybe there was. Could it really be a coincidence that both people had now died at the Lodge?

25

They made their way back to the cabins. Zachary stopped at the edge of the woods.

"I'll wait here. I want to make sure that no one else touches the evidence while you're getting help."

"Yeah. Good idea. I'll be as quick as I can."

She hurried on and returned to cabin four, where the others were starting to gather again. Apparently, none of the trails had led very far away.

"No luck," Redd Flagg called to Kenzie as she got closer. "No one has seen her."

Kenzie drew up closer to them. "We found her," she said, her tone somber, letting them know that it was not happy news.

"You found her?" Raven repeated. "But... she's okay, isn't she? Where is she?"

Kenzie shook her head. "No. She's not okay. I need a couple of blankets, and someone to help me to... transport her up to the house."

Andy Collins came out of the cabin, his face white. "What is it? Do you have news? Did you find her?"

Kenzie looked down at Andy's hands, but he was wearing winter gloves. "You should wait in your cabin. You don't need to see this."

"What does that mean?" he asked in a confrontational tone, then repeated it, voice breaking, "What does that mean?"

"It means you should go inside," Kenzie told him firmly.

"I want to know what you mean by that!"

Kenzie looked around the group for help. Burknall would be of the most assistance to her, she thought. Jack? Redd? She chose the author. "Redd, could you go in with him? Look after him until we get everything taken care of?"

"I don't really know what to do."

"Just keep him company. Listen. Don't... don't ask him a lot of questions, try to just keep him calm and in one place."

Redd's eyes widened a little in surprise. Kenzie couldn't see the rest of his face because it was obscured by a scarf. Redd nodded his head and took Andy by the arm, turning him in a circle back into the cabin.

Kenzie waited until the door was shut before saying anything. She then nodded to Burknall. "I could use some help. I'm used to moving—uh, things," she caught herself before revealing that she had occasion to move dead bodies with regularity. "But I need a way to get her up the hill to the main house. We can wrap her in blanket and then use another blanket as a sling-style stretcher between two of us. It's a fair distance up the hill, carrying a weight like that."

"I have a snowmobile with a freight sled. Will that work?"

Kenzie raised her hands palms-up, uncertain. "I've never seen one, so I can't picture how big it would be. It sounds as if it might work."

"I can fit a deer carcass on it."

"Well then... that would be perfect."

Burknall nodded and, without another word, walked back toward the barn. He was a man of few words, but intuitive and efficient.

Raven moaned and covered her eyes. "Why did she do it? Why didn't she come see me? I told her about the monsters."

Kenzie looked at her uncertainly. "The monsters?"

"I told her. I told her they were out last night. I saw them out the window. Shadows in the trees. They were waiting. Watching us and waiting..."

"What did these monsters look like?"

"I don't know." Raven dropped her hands from her face and peered around. "Are they still out? I thought they would go away when the sun came up. I told her about the monsters. I told her."

"Are you feeling okay, Raven? Have you taken something? Some pills?" Burknall had said that he thought that the newlyweds had taken something the night before, and Raven was acting as if she were hallucinating. It could just be the shock, but hallucinating or having paranoid delusions were not typical reactions to emotional shock.

"I'm not on anything! Just my meds. I don't do anything illegal!"

"Okay. I believe you. Have you had a fever? Achy joints?"

"Maybe. I don't know. It's so cold out."

"Yes, it is," Kenzie agreed. She put her hands under her armpits again to try to keep them warm. Her gloves were good for casual winter use, but they were not good for working outside for any length of time in sub-zero temperatures. Kenzie looked over the faces of the others. Vance Stiller was still not in evidence. Was he just sleeping in? Or had something happened to him too? Maybe he didn't care that something had happened to one of their number. He didn't think he was one of them. He thought he was better than everyone else. He probably had some sort of morning routine that could not be broken under any circumstances. Winter storms and sudden deaths were no exception. "Brittany, do you think you could take Raven inside and make sure she is okay? Maybe something to eat...? I don't think she should be on her own, but staying out here in the cold isn't helping anything."

Brittany's eyes slanted up, seeming pleased to have been given an assignment. "Of course! Come on, sweetie. Let's get you inside and warmed up."

That left Kenzie with Jack Fowler, Samantha the maid, who had returned from the house after a fruitless search for the missing woman, and Mrs. Hubbard, her bare face red with the cold. Kenzie shifted uncomfortably. She didn't want to answer a lot of questions about what kind of shape Mrs. Andy Collins's body had been in, and she thought Jack was just the type of character who would ask.

"I'm going to go back and meet up with Zachary. When Mr. Burknall comes back, just have him follow this trail into the woods. That's where we will be."

Zachary and Kenzie trekked back to the place where they had left Mrs. Collins's body. Zachary looked around carefully. "No one came by here while I was watching."

Kenzie also scanned the snow for any new footprints or any other disturbances. "I don't see anything. I think we can rest assured that nothing has been touched in the time we've been gone."

He nodded. "Good."

"Burknall should be here any minute, I doubt it will take long for him to get his sled hooked up to the snowmobile and to get here."

Zachary nodded. They both stood in silence, watchful. It wasn't as windy as it had been the day before, and while snow was still falling, Kenzie could hear animals in the woods around them. A chickadee. Rustling in the leaves and bushes. Maybe a rabbit out foraging for something to eat. And deer. Burknall had said that there were deer. As long as the wind wasn't too strong, Kenzie imagined the deer would go out to search for food. They were used to the snow. It felt as if they were all alone in the world, isolated from the rest of civilization. Kenzie would not have guessed, if she had been dropped there, that there were people only a few minutes' walk away.

In a few minutes, the silence was broken by the sounds of Burknall's snowmobile. He came alongside the trail, skiing in the fresh snow beside the footprints rather than over them. He climbed off the snowmobile and walked over to have a look at Mrs. Collins without a word. He looked her over, observing the bloodied nightgown. He shook his head.

"It's a crying shame."

"It is," Kenzie agreed. "I have no idea what happened last night. If she and her husband got into a fight, or if someone else came upon her here. Or even chased her. The police will have to analyze the footprints, compare them against everyone's boots to see who else was here. I can't believe that something like this could happen just a few yards away from our cabin. It's frightening."

Burknall went to his sled and pulled a couple of blankets off. He stretched them over the undisturbed ground near Mrs. Collins, one on top of the other, then approached her to pick her up.

"Let me help," Kenzie told him. "It's always easier to move a body with two people."

She took the woman's ankles and let Burknall handle her shoulders. That gave him more weight, but he was bigger than Kenzie was and had better upper body strength. They lifted her carefully from the ground and laid her down on the blankets. Kenzie wrapped her up like a taco with the top blanket. The woman's limbs were in rigor or frozen, so she wasn't a long, thin package like a body bag, but closer to a ball shape.

Then they used the corners of the bottom blanket to lift her and carry her over to the sled. There was plenty of room. They folded the outer blanket loosely over her, disguising her shape a little more, and Burknall pulled several straps over her to secure the cargo. They certainly didn't want her flying off the sled as they went up the hill.

"Thank you," Kenzie said. "This is really helpful."

He gazed at her, his eyes unwavering. "Who are you really?"

"What do you mean?"

"You're not an accountant."

Kenzie opened her mouth to protest, but he shook his head, looking grim. "You might be able to fool the others. But probably not for long. Who are you really? Are you police?"

"No," Kenzie sighed. "I work with the medical examiner in Roxboro."

Burknall nodded. "That makes more sense."

"You don't think a forensic accountant would have that much experience in moving bodies?" Zachary asked wryly.

Mentioning that might have been a mistake.

"That and other things," Burknall agreed. Kenzie thought she detected a twinkle in his serious eyes.

Kenzie shrugged, embarrassed. But it wasn't surprising that she would be caught out in a situation where there had been an unexpected death. How many other people would be used to dealing with such a situation? And what was the point in continuing to hide her identity? She was no longer worried about people asking her unwelcome questions. Now that there had been a homicide, it was probably best that everyone know who she was and that she had special expertise in the unusual situation.

"Things have changed," she admitted. "We thought we would both be able to take a vacation from our jobs and avoid talking shop the whole time we were here. But now…"

Burknall looked at Zachary, his brows raised. "And what about you? Just some stiff she brought along from the office?"

Zachary chuckled. "Not quite. A stiff from home. I'm a private investigator. But I don't know if anyone needs to know that yet."

"People have already been speculating."

"They have?" Zachary's voice went up a few notes. "What have they said?"

"Hit man. Leg breaker. On the run for something or other."

"They think he's a criminal?" Kenzie asked, amused. She looked Zachary over. He did have a certain grim look to him. Like he was prepared to do whatever was necessary.

Zachary nodded, accepting their suspicions. He looked back down at the body on the sled. "We'd better get her up to the house. Then Kenzie can examine the body more closely."

"You want to ride on the sled?" Burknall asked. There was still plenty of room around the corpse. But Zachary shook his head and Kenzie was inclined to agree. It might be more work to walk up the hill, but it seemed disrespectful to ride with the body.

"No, we'll join you up there. Just wait when you get there, I'll help transfer the body again."

"I can do it myself," Burknall offered. "She's not that big. Where do you want her?"

"One of the upstairs rooms. She doesn't need to be in with Mr. Dewey, but we'll preserve the body the same way. Leave a window open to keep her cold and prevent decomposition until the medical examiner or other authorities can get here to transport her."

"I'll take her upstairs."

Kenzie wasn't too sure about that. "It's more awkward to handle a dead body than you might think. Especially a frozen one. And if you drop her, something might break."

"I'm not going to drop her. I move deer carcasses. I can handle a small woman."

"I'd still prefer that you wait."

He shrugged and climbed aboard the snowmobile. He raised a hand in farewell, turned the snowmobile in a wide circle away from the pathway, and then returned over the ski tracks he had already made.

Kenzie looked over the ground where Mrs. Collins had lain, looking for any evidence that they needed to preserve. She didn't find the murder weapon or letters written in the snow to identify the name of the woman's killer. There wasn't anything that provided any more clues than the footprints in the snow that they had already observed.

Kenzie opened up her phone again and made a brief recording of the ground where the body had lain. Then they turned around and walked out of the woods, past their cabin, and up the hill to the farmhouse.

26

At the top of the hill, Kenzie saw Burknall's snowmobile pulled to the side of the driveway, but there was no bundle of blankets on the sled behind it. Burknall had ignored her suggestion and had taken the body into the house by himself. A spurt of anger and irritation shot through Kenzie. Just like a man to think that he knew better just because she was a woman. He should have listened to her as an expert in the field.

But she didn't have the time or energy to waste being angry with him. It was what it was. She wouldn't win that battle anyway.

She and Zachary entered the house without a word. Kenzie stood there for a moment, just letting the heat soak into her. They'd been outside for a long time. She didn't think she had been outdoors in weather like that for long since she was a child, building snow forts and snowmen. She'd come a long way from childhood battles and snow angels. She remembered playing with Amanda...

Kenzie quickly shut these thoughts off. She would not think about Amanda and the times they had shared together. Times that were gone and lost forever. She wasn't ever going to make snow angels with Amanda again, and there was no point in pining over it. Kenzie began to take off the winter gear with deliberation. It would be nice to get some circulation back into her fingers.

They hung up their coats and pried off their boots and headed upstairs to where Burknall had placed the deceased on the bed in a spare bedroom.

Kenzie was glad to see that she was still wrapped in the blankets. Burknall had not pulled them open to examine Mrs. Collins's body.

"Thank you." Kenzie tried to treat him with the same professionalism as she would have one of the workers in her office who had helped to prep a body for Dr. Wiltshire. "Zachary, would you shut the door, please?"

Zachary put his hand on the door and looked at Burknall. Burknall didn't move. "Do I have to leave?"

"It would probably be best," Kenzie said. "This is my job. You don't need to see this."

"I really don't know you two or anything about you. Maybe I should observe so that I can be a witness to the fact that no one tampered with or destroyed evidence."

Kenzie looked at him steadily, but he didn't back down. Finally, she nodded. It was true, she and Zachary really couldn't alibi each other. Anything either of them said would be suspect. Burknall, an unrelated third party, would be a better witness if called on to verify what procedure had been followed.

"Do you know where the thermometer we used for Mr. Dewey is?" Kenzie asked Zachary.

"I put it back where it came from. Let me go see."

He walked out of the room, shutting the door behind him to keep unwelcome guests from just wandering in. Kenzie pulled back each of the corners of the outer blankets, and then unwrapped the taco folds she had made, exposing the woman's body to view.

The blood and the holes in her nightgown seemed even more pitiful in the light filtering into the room through the windows. How could anyone have done that to her? How could anyone have any excuse for killing this woman, a lovestruck newlywed on a snowy honeymoon? Especially—Kenzie hated to even consider the thought—her new husband. Had they had a fight? Had he done this to her because he was high? Delusional? Or had it been something even more base? Jealousy or a life insurance policy? Who would do such a thing to a defenseless young woman?

Kenzie examined each of the stab holes more carefully, pulling the nightgown this way and that to see the size and shape of the wound and the skin around it. She took another video with her phone, getting in several close-ups. With Burknall there observing, she didn't dare undress the body. That would be for the proper authorities to do. And Kenzie was not the proper authority in this case.

When would they have cell coverage again? Kenzie looked for any signal bars on the display of the phone, but there was still a little "no service" notation there instead. Zachary returned with the thermometer. Kenzie tried taking the body's temperature. The numbers on the thermometer counted down, and then 999 and ERR alternated on the LCD screen. A fever thermometer was not calibrated to read temperatures that low. Kenzie sighed. "That didn't work. I'll have to go with other signs I can see and feel, then."

Neither of the men said anything as she repeated the exercise of searching for a pulse, pulling back an eyelid and shining the phone's flashlight LED into her eye, and feeling the stiffness of the limbs and the ice crystals formed underneath the rubbery skin.

"You think the stab wounds killed her or the cold?" Burknall asked.

"The stab wounds."

"There is a lot of blood."

Kenzie shook her head. "No, there really isn't. There's some, but not a significant amount. And the flow differs between the earlier stab wounds and the later ones."

"Because the blood pressure dropped as she bled out?" Zachary suggested.

"No. Because the heart was no longer pumping. It's only seepage. Postmortem blood loss."

Kenzie examined Mrs. Collins's hands, which were cut. "Defensive wounds on the hands. She fought off her attacker before she was stabbed."

"So she saw it coming."

"Yes. She knew what was happening. It didn't take her off guard."

Kenzie continued her examination, but there wasn't much else to find. She would leave any trace to the medical examiner whose job it was. Looking for hair, skin under Mrs. Collins's nails, testing the blood to ensure that it was all hers and there hadn't been a contribution from the killer. Eventually, Kenzie sighed and wrapped the blanket back around the body loosely.

"That's about all I can do here."

"What's next?" Zachary asked.

"Nothing. Go back to our cabin."

"We have to find out who did this, though."

"It's really not our jobs. Leave it to the police to investigate. We don't want to mess anything up."

"Who knows when the police will get here. In the meantime, there is a killer at the resort."

Kenzie held Zachary's gaze as she turned her phone off and slid it back away. "It's not our job. Our job is to keep ourselves and your family safe. If we go bumbling around getting involved in something like this, you don't know what could happen. I don't want to be in this guy's crosshairs."

After opening the window to keep the room cold, they moved out of the room in a group. Kenzie still had the house keys and locked the bedroom door. Zachary had already retrieved the masking tape, and she sealed the room and initialed the tape as she had with Mr. Dewey's room.

"You think whoever did this has motive to kill anyone else?" Zachary asked. "You don't think it was just... passion or being high?"

In other words, he too figured Mr. Andy Collins was the most likely suspect. Women were killed by their husbands. It was an unfortunate fact. There were rare occasions where it was a stranger, but in the majority of cases, it was an intimate partner. And Zachary was right, Collins would not have a motive to kill anyone else. But Kenzie wasn't sure that meant it was a good idea to confront him with their suspicions. Cornered, he might do whatever was necessary to preserve himself.

"It might have been. But that doesn't necessarily make it safe for us to investigate. I think we should just stay out of it. In a couple of days, the police will be here, and they can handle it."

They went back downstairs, each thinking their own melancholy thoughts. Kenzie could hear Mrs. Hubbard in the kitchen and went to talk to her, to make sure she knew about the body in the second room upstairs and that she shouldn't open that door either. As if she wouldn't be able to figure that out herself by the tape sealing it and Kenzie's initials on the tape.

Mrs. Hubbard was sitting at a small table in the kitchen, her face buried in her hands, supported by elbows on the table. She was sobbing.

"Mrs. Hubbard... it's okay. I know this is really hard on you, but everything is going to be okay," Kenzie told her lamely.

"Gladys," Mrs. Hubbard sobbed.

"What?"

"Call me Gladys." Mrs. Hubbard sniffled and drew in a long breath, then let it out in a controlled stream. Her body shuddered. Kenzie rubbed her shoulder and neck.

"Gladys. I'm sorry. It will be okay."

"I don't know how. I don't know what's going to happen to me or to the Lodge. And we've never had such a thing happen to a guest before. Once we had a heart attack, but he survived, and the ambulance took him to the hospital. He was back two days later to get his things. Said they put a stent in, and he was good to go."

"It must be shocking to you, I know. But we have to make the best of what we've got."

"What we've got? I've got nothing. I've got decades of employment at a place where there is no one to give me a reference. I am an old woman and I have to find another job. I don't want to still be working at this age, let alone looking for a job."

"I know. But we'll get it sorted out." The words were empty platitudes, but Kenzie had to try to cheer the woman up.

Gladys Hubbard just continued to cry, sobbing as if her heart were breaking.

27

It was difficult to separate herself from the crying woman in the kitchen but, eventually, Kenzie managed to get away, although she felt guilty for leaving Mrs. Hubbard alone with no one to comfort her. Burknall looked into the kitchen at her, but he didn't go in to talk to her. Whether it was because he didn't know how to deal with a woman crying—something that was a challenge for most men—or because of something else, Kenzie didn't know. They seemed to know each other well, but he was still not inclined to go to Mrs. Hubbard's aid.

Kenzie was reluctant to get her snow gear on again and brave the elements. But if they wanted to go back to the cabin, they needed to dress and walk down the hill again.

"I could give you a lift," Burknall offered, noticing Kenzie's slow movements.

"Maybe that would be a good idea," Kenzie admitted.

They got dressed and went back out into the frigid air. Kenzie shivered, even though most of her skin was covered. Burknall gestured to the sled. He pulled a strap tightly across it. "Sit down and hold on to that. I'll go slowly."

Zachary and Kenzie climbed on board. Burknall did as he had promised, and there was no trouble staying on the sled. He stopped in front of their cabin.

"Thank you," Kenzie called to him.

He nodded and gave a brief salute, then sped off down toward the barn. Kenzie intended to go straight back inside. Her work on the case was done, as she had told Zachary. The best thing for them to do now was to stay well out of the way and leave the rest for the trained law enforcement officers to deal with.

But as she reached for the doorknob, the door to cabin number four opened, and Redd stood on the threshold.

"Are you coming in? What are we supposed to do now?"

Kenzie looked at him in consternation. She had asked him to stay with Collins. But for how long? Until the police got there? Was he just supposed to leave Collins and go back to his own cabin? Or was he supposed to stay there keeping an eye on things? Kenzie wasn't usually involved in that side of the homicide business. Bodies were her thing. Dead ones.

"Uh..."

Brilliant.

Kenzie looked at Zachary. His eyes were bright. He was an investigator. He was often involved, privately, in cases that law enforcement had investigated. He came in and reviewed the evidence, re-interviewed suspects and witnesses, brought in his out-of-the-box thinking to come up with new theories of the crime. He was a good investigator, dogged and determined.

"Uh... I guess maybe we'd better have a talk with him. Just to reassure him that everything will be handled when the police get here," Kenzie suggested.

Zachary nodded his agreement.

Kenzie swore under her breath. She really did not want to talk to Andy Collins. She did not want to be facing a man who might be a murderer. Pretending that she didn't suspect him, or that everything would be okay, as she had told Gladys Hubbard.

Kenzie let out a long sigh, and she and Zachary walked over to the door of cabin four. Redd stepped back and let them in, looking relieved.

Collins's cabin was similar to theirs, but not identical. Kenzie got the feeling that they had been built at different times and that an effort had been made to make each cabin unique rather than cookie-cutters.

Kenzie had made an effort to keep their cabin tidy, which wasn't easy with other people there, especially a couple of bored children who didn't like to clean up after themselves, and the usual differences between what Kenzie considered acceptable and what Zachary did. Their big dinner had been cleaned up and Kenzie had tried to stay on top of the random dishes produced by meals and snacks of five people throughout the day. The inside of Collins's cabin, however, looked like a hurricane had hit.

There were dirty dishes piled in the sink and on the counter, clothing strewn on the floor, and the furniture all seemed to have been bumped out of position, looking disrupted from their proper groupings. A kitchen table had been tipped over and not set upright again. There were not, to Kenzie's relief, any blood spatter or handprints on the walls. Mrs. Collins had, most likely, been killed where they had found her body. Despite the mess around them, it didn't look as though the attack had begun in the cabin and then carried on outside as Mrs. Andy Collins fled her murderous husband.

Collins was sitting on the couch. When Kenzie entered, he looked around the cabin, as if he were unsure what he was supposed to be doing. Kenzie was equally unsure. What was her role? Just to break the news to him about his wife? It couldn't very well wait until the police managed to make it through the storm. He had to be told something. And she would have to observe his reactions, to be sure she could tell the police every nuance when they eventually began their investigation. Kenzie looked at Zachary for reassurance. He was the one who was used to dealing with members of the public, whether clients who had lost loved ones or suspected cheating husbands, or whether suspects themselves.

Zachary smiled reassuringly and nodded. He motioned to the seating around Collins. "Let's all sit down."

Redd hovered nearby. Not wanting to participate in the discussion, but wanting to observe it. Kenzie and Zachary sat down. Zachary pulled an oblong silver box out of his pocket, pressed a button with his thumb, and laid it on the occasional table beside him in a practiced, casual movement. A digital recorder. Good idea. Collins didn't seem to notice.

"Mr. Collins," Kenzie began. It sounded too formal. He would know it was a death notification. "Andy. How are you doing?"

"I don't know. I don't understand what's going on. I'm so worried about Brooke. When I woke up this morning and she wasn't here. And the cabin looking like this..." He looked around himself. Kenzie allowed her eyes to travel over the disarray. Books and throw pillows on the floor. Ornaments that should have been on the shelves and side tables tipped over or on the floor. What should have been a tidy, homey cabin looked instead as if a burglar had ransacked it.

"What happened last night?"

"I don't know." Andy shook his head and rubbed his eyes. He looked haggard, as if he had only managed to get a couple of hours of sleep the night before. Which was probably true.

There were people coming and going all night.

"What do you remember?" Kenzie prompted. They had to have somewhere to start, She couldn't just tell him baldly that they had found the body of his wife, brutally stabbed to death.

"Nothing. We must have had dinner up at the house," Collins looked over to Redd for confirmation of this fact, and Redd nodded his agreement. "But I can't remember that, or anything afterward. That doesn't make any sense. Why wouldn't I remember?"

"How much did you have to drink?" Kenzie scanned the detritus around them for empties. They must have had a significant amount for so much disruption and for him to have a memory blackout.

"It couldn't have been very much. We had packed everything to go home. But then... we only got a few miles down the mountain before we ran into the storm. We knew that we weren't going to be able to make it through, so we came back here. Like you said. Thought we would have to stay another night or two... better that way... at least we knew we would get home in safety. If we tried to make it through that storm, there's no way. We got back here for dinner..."

"How much did he have at dinner?" Kenzie asked Redd.

"Not a lot that I noticed. A glass of wine or two. Maybe one before the meal and one with."

Collins nodded. "We're not big drinkers."

"And then you came down here to your cabin and...?" Kenzie waited for Collins to fill in the rest.

He just looked at her blankly. "I told you; I don't remember. I can't remember anything from last night."

"Mr. Burknall said that the two of you were fighting. Did you have an argument?"

Collins looked at everything scattered on the floor. "We never fight."

"You must have had one last night. You don't remember what it was about?"

"No. That doesn't make any sense."

And Burknall had suggested that they were high. "What about drugs? Medications? Maybe you took something for anxiety because of the storm?"

"No. I don't have anything like that." His eyes flicked toward the bedroom.

"Nothing?"

"Well... maybe Brooke had something in her bag. To help her to relax. But I don't know. I didn't take anything."

Kenzie was pretty sure that it was a lie. So what had he taken? Something had made him forget what had happened. And someone had killed Brooke Collins. The most likely suspect had to be her husband.

"Did you find her?" Collins asked, begging for a happy ending. "What did she say? I don't know what happened last night, but whatever it was, we can talk about it. Neither of us was in the best mood. We can go back, start over, whatever it was we had a fight about. What did she say?"

"How do you know that neither of you was in the best mood if you can't remember what happened?" Zachary asked.

Collins made a motion to take in the state of the cabin around him. "All of this... Brooke not coming back last night... things must have been pretty bad, right? We were both grumpy when we had to turn around to come back. Pretty tense. I need to apologize. To tell her that it doesn't matter. We can't let one night derail everything."

Collins looked from Zachary to Kenzie.

"Please."

28

ndy..." Kenzie was not practiced in delivering such news, but she dealt with people who had recently found out about the deaths of loved ones. She knew the right pitch of her voice, the language around death and loss. "I'm so sorry to have to tell you this. But we found your wife. We found... Brooke's body."

"Her body," Collins repeated blankly. "But she's okay, right? I mean... she has to be. Tell me she's okay."

"I'm afraid... she didn't make it. She's dead."

"How could that be true?" Andy Collins's voice rose angrily.

Wasn't that the first step? Denial? Anger? Kenzie couldn't remember what all the stages of grief were supposed to be. She could remember, though, when her sister Amanda had died. How hard it had been to accept that they hadn't been able to save her, even when they had known that she might not survive. She had faced the specter of death so many times and escaped it. It didn't seem possible that Amanda had finally succumbed.

"Brooke was just here," Collins insisted. "She was just here last night. We just got married. Nothing could happen to her!" He covered his eyes with his palms, fingers digging into his hair.

Redd was pale too, his eyes wide with shock. He surely must have suspected something, or he would not have been concerned enough to rouse Kenzie and Zachary to have them help with the trouble. And he had probably watched them take the snowmobile up to the house with something on the sled and return without it.

"I'm so sorry, Andy," Kenzie told him. "I really am. Are you sure you can't remember anything from last night?"

"No!" He shook his head. "I don't know what happened. It's all just... blank."

"Did she..." Redd licked his lips. "Was it the cold? Hypothermia?"

He had to ask that, didn't he? He couldn't let Collins just get to that point on his own. Couldn't let him have a little bit of peace before realizing that his bride hadn't just wandered off and died in her sleep or succumbed to the cold. He had to know the reason.

"No," Kenzie said shortly. "Something happened to her."

Collins removed his hands from his eyes and looked at her. "What happened? What do you mean?"

Kenzie looked away from him, looking out the window. She was getting deeper and deeper into something that she was really not qualified to investigate. She wasn't a cop. She didn't interview suspects.

"I think maybe we should leave that to the police."

"The police? What do the police have to do with this? It was an accident."

Kenzie raised her eyebrows. She wasn't sure how he could decide that it was an accident if he claimed not to remember what had happened.

"No, it wasn't an accident."

"Of course it was," Redd said. "Wandering off in the middle of the night like that. It doesn't really matter what she died of, it was obviously an accident. She didn't go out there intending to get killed."

"What do *you* remember?" Zachary asked. "You were out last night, weren't you?"

"No. Well, yes. But that was... I was just checking on the weather. And I did hear a bit of the commotion. I just wondered... A person can't help what they overhear. I wasn't eavesdropping. It wasn't as if I was listening with my ear pressed to the door."

Collins looked at Redd. "What's that supposed to mean?"

"The two of you were pretty loud," Redd said defensively.

"Loud?" Collins's face flushed. "We're not loud enough for the neighbors..."

"You were arguing," Redd explained. He made a gesture to indicate the room. "Look around you. What do you think happened here? You were yelling at each other, throwing things around." He shook his head. "I've never seen anything like it."

"You were here?" Collins asked. "In our house?"

Redd shifted uncomfortably. "I knocked. You guys were... I thought maybe someone had broken in. Attacked you. Or you were trying to chase out a burglar. A wild animal. I don't know." He shook his head. "Weird stuff was going on. I thought I saw something outside... I thought... I don't know what."

"You saw what outside? You were in here? How did you get in?"

"You left the door unlocked. I just... you know... opened it to see if everything was okay. I knocked, but you didn't hear me, with all the noise you were making. So I just opened the door to have a look. It was unlocked," he repeated.

Collins looked at the front door as if he might be able to prove Redd wrong. Kenzie remembered Burknall telling them to lock their door. Had he seen Redd go into the Collins's cabin uninvited?

"So what happened?" Zachary asked. "We're trying to figure it out. You're the one who seems to know something, so why don't you tell us what it was you saw or know?"

Redd paced back and forth and ran his fingers through his hair. He tried to compose an answer, but obviously he wouldn't be able to come up with something that would suit everyone. Collins, at least, would be embarrassed. A woman was dead. Redd had already admitted to walking into the cabin through an unlocked door, knowing that he hadn't been invited in. He was guilty of that much, if nothing more.

"I just wanted to see what was going on, see whether anyone needed my help," he repeated. "They were being really loud. Yelling and throwing things around. So I opened the door; I thought there might be an intruder."

"And...?" Zachary prompted.

"There wasn't anyone else there, just the two of them, screaming at each other. Pushing, throwing things, acting like... wild. I don't know. You don't see people behaving like that. Grown adults. A married couple. After all of the mooning around, making out, ignoring everyone else and pretending to be in love..."

"We *are* in love," Collins insisted.

"They were behaving like wild animals," Redd repeated, not meeting Collins's eyes.

"Okay," Kenzie said, trying to keep her voice calm and nonjudgmental. Neither one of them needed to hear how she felt about their behavior the night before. Or her suspicions. "So you saw that they were fighting. Did you know what it was about? Did you stay and talk, or leave again? What happened next?"

"I just kind of stuck my head in the door, and I saw what was happening. I thought maybe it was an act. They were pretending, or doing it for a video, or role playing. I don't know. But they seemed to be really... both of them really angry, like none of it was put on."

"And..."

"And I left. I couldn't do anything about it. I couldn't stop them, could I? I didn't want to get in the middle of something and end up getting hurt, or maybe someone else getting hurt because... I made things worse." He gave a sort of a shudder, standing still in one place.

Kenzie saw the motion mirrored by Zachary, sitting on the other side. It was very small, and if she weren't so attuned to his emotional state all the time, she would probably never have noticed. But what Redd had said had caused an emotional reaction in Zachary. Kenzie closed her eyes briefly, and she could see Zachary, a little boy, peeking around a doorway at his parents in a drunken fight. He had told her that they used to fight. Not just yelling and arguments, but hitting and shoving each other and throwing things. Probably leaving the house in much the same state that the Collins's cabin was in now. He knew the feeling that Redd was talking about. Knowing that if he made a sound, if he put himself into the middle of the fight, he would get hurt or make it worse for one of his parents.

"So you left," Kenzie said. "You thought that was the best thing to do."

Redd nodded. "Yeah. I'm sorry I didn't know how else to handle it. You can't get into the middle of something like that. One person can't stop it. Sometimes... several people together can't stop it."

"Did you go to get help?"

"I saw Mr. Burknall. He was coming out of Raven's cabin. She must have had trouble getting a fire going or something. He was all over this place, trying to make sure everyone was comfortable last night. He was probably up half the night."

And so were several others, apparently.

"And you tried to get him to help?"

"Kind of... I told him that something was going on... that I thought they needed help."

And then ran the other direction and hid behind his own door.

"I'll talk to him later about what he did," Kenzie said. "But I know he said that the two of you were... acting strangely," Kenzie addressed this to Collins, who was looking bewildered by Redd's description. "Later, when he came over to our cabin."

"It was a spooky night," Redd said. "All of that wind and snow. The whole world looked different. And then it was suddenly quiet, the wind gone, like we were in the eye of a hurricane. Everything was... too still. And there were things..." Redd scratched his arms and shook his head, looking small and afraid. "I don't know what. It doesn't make much sense when I look back at it now. But last night, when it was all going on... I could see things."

"What kind of things?" Kenzie asked.

"I don't know. Shapes in the dark. Shadows. Maybe they were animals. But with weird shadows."

Kenzie had to shake her head at that one. She had no idea what it was Redd had seen. But it didn't seem to be anything to do with Andy and Brooke Collins.

"And that's the last that you saw of Brooke last night?"

Redd paced to the window to look out. "No."

29

You saw her after that? Doing what?"

"She and Andy were outside. I guess... I don't know if the argument spilled outside, or she wanted to go to one of the other cabins
to get away from him. But she ran out. And he ran out, and they were still
talking, arguing, going back and forth, around the cabins..."

Creating at least part of the trampled-down snow trails outside. Like a
bizarre game of fox and geese, a tag game she used to play in the snow at
school.

"Did you see either of them... hurt each other?"

"Just chasing around. Arguing."

"I don't remember any of this," Collins insisted. "It doesn't make any
sense."

"No." Redd lifted his hands up helplessly. "It didn't."

"So did they eventually go back inside?" Zachary asked.

"I don't know. They were all over the place, I had a hard time keeping
track. And I was trying to watch the other shapes. Worried that the storm
would come again when we had passed through the eye. If I went out there, I
might get stuck in the blizzard or caught by one of the monsters. So I didn't...
I didn't go back outside again. And I don't know... what happened eventually,
if they both went back inside."

But of course, they knew that she hadn't gone back inside. Or if she had,
initially, then she had soon left again. Going off into the woods. Being
stabbed to death and dying out there of a stab to the heart.

"None of this makes any sense," Collins said. "We love each other. I would never do anything to hurt Brooke. She must have gone off and... did she trip and fall? Or maybe a wild animal...?"

"No." Kenzie decided she would have to be up-front about it. She couldn't very well keep the truth from Andy Collins. They were going to keep asking questions and guessing and making up bizarre excuses and explanations until it was all out in the open. The police might have made a different choice in their interrogations, but the police weren't there. And who knew how long it would be before they were. "Andy, I'm sorry to have to tell you, but your wife was stabbed."

"Stabbed." He looked at her with wide eyes. "What do you mean, stabbed?"

"With a knife or another blade-like instrument. In the chest. Somebody intended to kill her. And they succeeded."

"Who would do something like that? What kind of monster could even consider..." Collins shook his head in disbelief.

His choice of the word monster echoed what Redd had just said about being afraid of being caught by a monster outside. What the heck had been going on the night before? Weird stuff, Burknall and Redd had both said. But something must have triggered it. Some animal shape or noise? A person with a mask? Brittany in her furs?

What could Redd have mistaken for a monster? Or what had he taken to trick his brain into thinking that he had seen one? Collins claimed that he and Brooke had not taken anything, but she was pretty sure he was lying. Had they shared with Redd? Or had he taken something on his own? Or just had too much to drink and his writer's fertile imagination had taken over? How much of what he had seen in the night had been real and how much had been imaginary or a nightmare when he had nodded off to sleep?

"I don't know who it was," Kenzie said. She slid her chair an inch or two closer and leaned toward him. "I wanted to make sure that you don't have any injuries. I thought maybe if the two of you had fought off an intruder, like Redd suggested, or if you were both attacked in the woods... maybe you hit your head and you don't remember."

"No. I don't have any injuries," Collins said doubtfully. He ran his hands over his head, searching for a goose egg. He patted his body lightly. His chest in case, like his wife, someone had stabbed him and he had somehow failed to notice. He didn't appear to have sustained any injuries in his fight with Brooke or in the aftermath of that fight.

"Maybe I could take a closer look?" Kenzie offered. "I have some training in first aid." No need to tell him that she was actually a doctor. He would probably be more comfortable if he thought she was a nurse or had just taken a corporate first aid class. She stood up and approached him.

As soon as Collins nodded, Kenzie looked at Zachary to make sure that he had seen the man consent, and then moved in. She touched his head lightly. "I'm just going to make sure there are no bumps or bruising."

She took longer than he had to examine his scalp to make sure he didn't have any sign of a head wound. There wasn't anything. There was a scratch down one cheek that she hadn't noticed from farther away. A scratch that could have come from a stray tree branch on the trail. Or his wife's fingernail.

"One scratch here," Kenzie murmured, hopefully loud enough that Zachary's recorder would pick it up, "high on your left cheek. Let's see your hands."

He offered them to her palms-up. Kenzie checked for any cuts on his palm that might indicate he had been the one to stab Brooke, his hand slipping off the handle and running down the blade. She turned them over, checking the knuckles for bruising or split skin. "No marks on your hands."

She didn't lift up his shirt or make any examination of his torso. "And you don't have any injuries anywhere else? Any tender spots that I should check?"

"No." He moved experimentally, feeling his range of motion. "Sore muscles, that's all. As if I had worked out or slept on an uncomfortable bed."

Or the couch or the floor where he had eventually collapsed.

Or maybe he was sore from a physical altercation with his wife.

30

I can't understand what happened," Collins said. He dropped his head into his hands and held it as if it were throbbing. Depending on what he had partaken of the night before, he might have a pretty nasty hangover. Maybe things would get clearer when he was feeling better. But for the time being, she didn't think she was going to be able to get anything more out of him. The previous evening did appear to be one huge blank for him. There was no indication that he remembered anything that had happened after dinner, however bizarre it all seemed. "It doesn't make any sense. I can't believe that Brooke is dead. How could she be dead? Are you sure?"

"Yes, I'm sure."

As difficult as it was to call a death in the freezing temperatures Brooke's body had been exposed to, Kenzie knew that she wasn't going to revive when her body thawed out. Not with a stab wound through the heart. Kenzie gave Collins a smile that was as sympathetic as possible. "I'm so sorry. I think... you probably shouldn't be alone. Someone should stay with you."

She looked at Redd, who immediately understood. Redd looked at Zachary. "Maybe you could stay with him? I've already been with him... I should probably get breakfast. Get to work. I am here on a writing retreat, not just to relax."

As if anyone would relax sitting with the man whose wife had just been murdered.

"I need to stay with Kenzie," Zachary said. "Make sure nothing happens to her."

"She can just go back to her cabin. Or she can stay here with you. You can both stay here," he said brightly. "That would be better, wouldn't it?"

"We need to go find Vance Stiller," Zachary explained.

Kenzie's heart sank. She didn't want to deal with the man again. No matter what kind of mood he was in or what had happened the night before. She didn't want to ever speak to the insufferable man again. Especially not when she was feeling so tired and raw from everything that had already happened that morning.

"We need to," Zachary repeated softly, reading Kenzie's expression.

"I know."

"Sorry."

"Why do you need to go find Vance Stiller?" Redd demanded. "I can do that."

"We need to do it. But before we go..." Zachary looked at Kenzie, raising one eyebrow.

Kenzie was uncertain what he was trying to impart to her, what he expected her to say. She shook her head slightly. *What?*

"We should probably make sure that you're not hurt either," Zachary explained. "With everything that happened last night, all of that disruption and the weird stuff that happened. You could have gotten hurt too."

"I didn't hit my head," Redd insisted. "And I didn't fall asleep and dream this whole thing up, I'm telling you that."

"No, of course not," Kenzie agreed. "And Zachary's right. With all of that weird stuff, you'll want to know that you're okay."

He seemed far less certain of this than Collins, but when Kenzie approached him, he gave a shrug and let her take his hands, examine both sides and his forearms, and then his face. "No marks," Kenzie said for the recorder. "Face and hands are fine." She ran her hands over Redd's head, fingers light, alert for anything that was not as it should be. He was very warm. Did he have a fever? That might account for the claim he had seen monsters the night before. And it might account for anything he had seen of Andy and Brooke Collins, too. His was the only eyewitness testimony they had so far, but that might be tainted if he had a fever.

"Maybe a bit warm. Are you feeling okay?"

Redd felt his own forehead as if this might help him to answer the question. "I don't know. I feel strange, but I don't think I'm sick. I haven't been throwing up or anything. I don't have those usual 'flu-like symptoms' they're always talking about." He gave a small laugh. "Why is it so many diseases start with flu-like symptoms?"

"I don't know," Kenzie said, shaking her head. "It's a mystery, isn't it? Do you hurt anywhere else? Do you have sore muscles or joints?"

"No, all pretty much the same as usual. A little writer's elbow, maybe," he said, rubbing the back of his right elbow. "But that comes with the territory."

"Really." Kenzie knew that repetitive stress injuries for workers who used computers all day tended to be in the wrists and shoulders. But who knew what kind of posture he used at the computer? Maybe he did have writer's elbow.

"Okay, we better be going then," she told Zachary. "Let's see if Mr. Stiller is in his cabin."

Zachary nodded. He picked up the recorder and slid it into his shirt pocket without turning off the recording. They both went to the door and started putting on their warm-weather gear again. Kenzie was not excited about going out into the cold again. She had just started to thaw out.

"Do you know which cabin is Stiller's?" she asked Zachary.

"Farthest one back, I believe. He needs his privacy."

"Yeah, acting like he's better than any of the rest of us," Redd sneered. "That guy has got to be the biggest—"

"I agree," Kenzie headed him off. "And I don't usually say that about people. You know, a person can be wealthy and powerful without acting like a giant butthead. People like him give wealth and fame a bad name. I've met plenty of people who were very gracious and humble about a lot more fame and fortune than he probably has."

"He's got an inferiority complex," Redd agreed. "The ones like him always do. It doesn't matter how much they get what they want, they're always afraid that everyone else is better than they are. Or that someone else is better than they are. And they have to trample everyone down to prove it."

Kenzie nodded. "You're probably right about that." She lowered her voice and leaned closer to him. "Thank you so much for helping out with Andy. I just don't think he should be alone right now. You're being a really good friend. A really good human being."

Redd smiled, straightening to stand a little taller. "Of course. How could I leave him alone after something like that?"

Kenzie nodded. "Yeah. But thanks."

She turned back toward the door and, in doing so, tripped over the two pairs of boots standing to the side on the doormat. She set them back up carefully after a glance at the soles. Both were very similar to each other, maybe even the same brand and model, in slightly different sizes. Both similar to the treads of one of the pairs of the boots that had walked the same path as Brook Collins on her way to her death.

They went back out into the cold. Kenzie walked as quickly as she could to the farthest cabin away. They were all within easy walking distance. In the summer. In the cold temperatures, it was brutal. Kenzie held her hand up in front of her mouth and nose to keep them a little warmer, tucked her chin in, and hunched into the wind, looking down at the snow trail she was following. She had to look up every now and then to correct her course, but in a few minutes, they were outside of Stiller's door. Zachary raised his hand and knocked on it hard. The knock was muffled by his glove. They waited for a minute to see if Stiller had heard. When there was no response, Zachary took the glove off and knocked on the door as loudly as he could. He shook his smarting knuckles out and they waited again.

31

D o you think… he went out?" Kenzie suggested. "Maybe he went up to the farmhouse while we were talking to Collins?"

"No, I haven't seen him all morning. He didn't walk by the cabin while we were talking."

Kenzie didn't know how he had been able to keep an eye on what was going on outside and keep up with the conversation and everyone's faces and body language inside of the cabin at the same time. She felt exhausted from trying to read everyone's faces for any tells as she conducted the questioning.

"Then maybe… he could be in Brittany's cabin? If the two of them are together…?"

"Why would they rent separate cabins if he was planning to stay with her?"

"Maybe so that he had a place of his own to work. Or they might not have planned to spend the night together, but he fell asleep while they were at her place, so she just let him sleep there."

"It's possible," Zachary admitted. "He wouldn't have had to walk past our cabin to get to Brittany's."

"Maybe we should knock on her door?"

Zachary tried the doorknob. It didn't turn under his grasp. "Okay, we'll check hers. But if he isn't there…"

"We'll come back. I still have Mr. Dewey's keys."

"Yeah, okay." Zachary led Kenzie to one of the other cabins. She knew he was a private investigator, but it still amazed her how he knew which cabins were whose when it had never been discussed. When they had all introduced themselves at the dinner that first night, they hadn't introduced themselves by cabin number. Zachary had just paid attention. Kenzie had been so wrapped up in her own plans that she hardly even noticed who was next door to them.

Zachary knocked on the door. This time, there was an answer. Brittany opened the door and looked at them. "What is it? It's cold out there."

"Can we come in, then?"

She looked as if she would tell them no, but then took a couple of steps back and let Zachary and Kenzie in. She didn't indicate that they should make themselves at home. "What is it?" she asked, crossing her arms in front of her and rubbing her arms to warm them up.

"We were looking for Vance," Kenzie explained, assuming Brittany would probably be a bit warmer toward another woman. "There's no answer at his cabin, and we thought that maybe..."

"Why would he be here?" Brittany asked.

"I just got the feeling that... you two knew each other. Isn't that why you were both here?"

Brittany shrugged. "Maybe."

"But he's not around?"

"Not here. He's got his own cabin, that's probably where he is."

"Does he sleep late? I assumed he would be the type who was up before dawn to get a head start on making money."

"Yeah, he's usually an early riser," she admitted. "But he was up late last night, so maybe he decided to sleep in for once."

"Was everything okay last night? I mean... with the storm...? And the two of you didn't see anything unusual?"

"Unusual? Like Mrs. Andy Collins wandering off in the middle of the night? No. Why would we have seen anything? They wouldn't have to go by our cabins to get to the house. Maybe the barn, but why would they go to the barn? No hayrides in the middle of the night."

"Maybe there was something they needed. Help with a fire or finding candles when the power went out. I think Mr. Burknall was at the barn all night."

"I didn't see them," Brittany said, making a wiping-away gesture with her hand. Not something she was concerned about or wanted to talk about anymore. "There were a lot of strange sounds last night. Heard voices and howling. Maybe owls. They can be very creepy at night. Or wolves. Even a mountain lion. They make this screaming noise..."

Kenzie was a little surprised. She had pictured Brittany as the quintessential city girl. Someone who wouldn't know anything about mountain lion screams or owls that sounded like ghosts.

"You're right, yeah. So you heard a lot of noise. But you didn't think it was human."

"Animals can make sounds that you think are human. I just figured they were animal noises."

"Did you see Mrs. Collins at all last night? Were you at dinner at the house?"

"Yes, of course I was. You guys have guests, so maybe you don't want to socialize with us, but the rest of us... part of the reason we come here is to have a little fun. Do a little socializing outside of our circles, with people that we wouldn't have a chance to meet otherwise. People who aren't all starstruck and who have interests that extend beyond getting a celebrity's picture or autograph."

Kenzie nodded understandingly, even though that was never something she'd had to contend with. While people sometimes knew her by her parents' reputation and her family wealth, she hadn't had to worry about celebrity status and people always wanting something from her. She'd been able to be her own person, though she was expected to put in appearances.

"So after the dinner... did you all stay up at the house visiting, or...? I don't imagine there was a bonfire last night."

"Too windy and wet for a bonfire. Unless you want to soak the whole thing in gasoline." Brittany gave a short laugh. "No... we talked for a while, but everyone was feeling kind of restless and hemmed in by the weather. We wanted to get back to our cabins before it got so bad that we couldn't see them or get through the snow drifts."

"So you came back here. You and Vance?"

"No." Brittany gave Kenzie a hard, cold look. Then she finally thawed a little. "I went to his cabin. For a little while. I didn't spend the night. I wanted to be back in my own space. Everything just seemed... *off* last night. I thought it would be romantic to be caught in the storm. Power out, a fire and candlelight, cuddling under a blanket on the couch... talking half the night..." She shook her head. "But it wasn't like that. With the wind, and the noises... it just all seemed so wild and disjointed, and we were both out of sorts and couldn't agree on anything. Ugh. I hate it when you just can't... connect with someone."

Kenzie nodded.

"So after a while, I just said I wanted to come back here to get some sleep. It took me a long time to get settled in, but eventually I did get to sleep, and I didn't wake up until my alarm went this morning."

Kenzie must have shown her surprise that Brittany would set a wake-up alarm when she was on vacation. Brittany chuckled.

"I still vlog when I'm on vacation or traveling. I generally do it first thing in the morning so that it is done and I can work on other things the rest of the day. It's my job, so I am professional about it. I didn't turn my alarm off last night because I didn't think about it. Not having any power or internet capabilities today, I mean. So my alarm still went off. I did a recording anyway, and I'll post it when we have internet again. People will think it is exciting that I shared my blackout experience with them."

"And then you noticed that something was going on outside?" Kenzie suggested.

"Yeah, lots of voices. They carry when it's cold like this. So I put on my coat and went out to see what was happening."

"And you haven't seen Vance yet this morning?"

"No. I figured he's still in bed. He's usually an early riser too, but we were both pretty wrecked last night, so maybe he decided to sleep it off."

"Do you... want to check on him? I'm just worried with everything that has happened here that something could be wrong. It's possible that he's not just sleeping. He could be sick or need assistance."

Brittany looked uncertain of this. Her lips pursed and she considered, studying Kenzie and then Zachary. Apparently, she decided they weren't just paparazzi out to get a good shot of Vance. She nodded.

"I'll see if he's okay. That means that I'm going in there, not you."

Kenzie would have to be satisfied with that. "If there is anything wrong... I have some medical training."

"So do I." Brittany gave Kenzie a challenging stare. Kenzie had no idea what Brittany did in the real world before she had become famous. Or what she did now that she was. The woman was obviously intelligent. She could be a doctor, nurse, or first responder. Or maybe just someone who took first aid and felt qualified to make an evaluation when she went in.

Or it could be a lie and she had no training, and just didn't want anyone else near her boyfriend.

Her gaze held steady. Kenzie didn't know whether she was telling the truth or was a very good liar.

32

G reat," Kenzie said, forcing a smile. "I really appreciate your being willing to do that. We just want to make sure that Vance is safe and well. It's important for us to take care of each other, when we're isolated like this. There isn't anyone else he can rely on, no matter how much money he has."

"Yeah, well, money doesn't make people any more inclined to help you. It just means you pay a premium price for it."

Brittany sighed and reached past Kenzie to grab her coat from the peg by the door. She slipped her arms through the thick fur sleeves and pulled it around her. She pulled the hood over her head, almost obscuring her face. She drew leather gloves out of her pocket and pulled them on. Then she opened the door, letting in the frigid air once more, and they all stepped back out into the cold.

Even though they moved quickly, Kenzie was already feeling the cold by the time Brittany put her key in the lock. Her toes were numb. She hadn't had enough time inside Brittany's cabin to get thawed out.

Brittany knocked on the door a few times. Much more quietly than Zachary had. Then she turned the key and opened the door. She gave Kenzie and Zachary a look that clearly said they were to stay outside, not even standing just inside the door to get warmed up.

Kenzie wrapped her arms around herself and tucked her hands under her armpits. She stomped her feet, trying to get the blood circulating again, but they stayed numb. They were going to hurt when they started to warm up again.

"Vance?" They could hear Brittany calling him before she shut the door all the way.

"Do you think he's okay?" Zachary asked.

"Yes... probably. It sounds like he's maybe just sleeping off whatever they had to drink or any recreational substances that they enjoyed last night. I have to say, everyone certainly seems to have gone a bit overboard last night. Do you think it's just the idea that they were isolated? They wanted to escape their troubles with a little chemical assistance?"

"Maybe. It could have triggered a lot of fears... claustrophobia, being out of control, fear of death... maybe the kind of people who come here to escape are more likely to escape through others means as well."

"Yeah." It seemed strange, though, that she and Zachary would be the only ones to break that mold. They had booked the Lodge to get away from the stress in their lives, but neither of them was inclined to take drugs to escape.

They waited, stamping their feet and trying to stay warm. Kenzie started to relax. If Brittany had found Vance badly injured or dead, she would have come back for help. But since she hadn't, that hopefully meant that all was well. It still seemed like forever before Brittany came to the door again.

"He's fine," she said curtly.

"Can we come in and talk to him?"

"He doesn't need you. You can go back to your own cabin and warm up."

"I'd like to be able to see that he's okay," Kenzie said. "Forgive me for being so untrusting, but with everything else that has happened around here and two people dead, I think it is important for me to check. And we need to know if he saw or heard anything to do with Brooke Collins's death."

Brittany rolled her eyes. She blew out her breath and eventually nodded, gesturing them in. Once more, they were forced to stand just inside the door, not invited in to get comfortable. But at least it was warmer. Kenzie kept shifting her feet, trying to get the blood circulating again.

Vance was in his kitchen, heating what Kenzie supposed was instant coffee in a pot over a camp stove. Zachary tensed at the sight of the flame and watched it intently.

"Mr. Stiller," Kenzie said. "I'm glad to see you're okay. I just wanted to ask you about what you remember from last night. We're trying to get a picture of people's movements and to see if anyone saw Brooke Collins during the night."

He tapped on the side of the pot, as if that might encourage it to heat up faster. He was probably desperate for his caffeine fix. "Which one is that? The maid?"

"The newlywed," Kenzie told him crisply. He could at least have paid enough attention to his fellow vacationers to know who was who.

"Oh, her." He shook his head, rolling his eyes. "Not like she had anything to do with anyone but her husband. I don't think she even looked at anyone else. The rest of us might just as well not have been there."

Kenzie might have said the same thing about him. But apparently, he had noticed her behavior, even if he hadn't remembered her name. Even Kenzie hadn't known that her first name was Brooke until after she died. But Kenzie had known she was Mrs. Andy Collins.

"Did you see her?"

Stiller rubbed his temples. "I have no recollection of last night. I haven't the foggiest idea. I don't even know how I slept for so long. I never do that. But I feel like..." he squinted at her, his head obviously painful. "I don't know if it's the flu or what. I feel like I could sleep for another full day. Or two. I can barely focus."

"Would you mind if I have a look at you? If you have a fever or other symptoms..."

"Why would I want an accountant to examine me?"

He had, at least, remembered that much.

"I'm actually not an accountant. That was sort of a... misdirection." Kenzie smiled apologetically at Brittany as well. "I'm actually a doctor."

Stiller studied her balefully. "Sure you are."

"We're just supposed to take your word for that?" Brittany demanded. "After you have apparently lied to us already?"

"I'm sorry about that. We never foresaw that we could get into a situation like this where it could be important." Kenzie shrugged. "I just wanted to avoid getting asked to look at everyone's weird moles or hearing all of their other medical complaints."

"Then why would you want to know now?" Stiller asked.

Which was a good question.

He apparently decided that the coffee was warm enough. He wasn't going to wait any longer for his caffeine fix. He took it off the burner and poured it into a mug. He turned off the cook stove and Zachary relaxed visibly.

"I'm concerned by the deaths that we've experience already. Especially Brooke Collins's death. Mr. Dewey's looks like natural causes, but Brooke's... was not."

"What do you mean? Because she went outside and got hypothermia?

That's natural enough. If she's stupid enough to go outside in the middle of a storm like this and to stay out until she's in trouble..."

"It was not hypothermia."

"I'm sure it contributed," Stiller argued.

"No. I don't think it did," Kenzie told him firmly.

He took a sip of the coffee and grimaced, either because it was still too cold, or just due to the fact that it was instant. Assuming it was instant.

"What was it, then?"

"Do you remember seeing her last night? If you think that she was outside and got hypothermia, then you must remember something."

He glanced over at Brittany. "Just something someone said."

"It wasn't hypothermia. It wasn't because she was outside."

"What happened then? A fall? I don't have a clue what everyone was doing outside. We weren't. We were inside where it was nice and warm and safe."

But it hadn't been particularly safe in the Collins cabin. Things had actually been rather dangerous.

"How do you know that you were inside when everyone else was outside?" Kenzie asked. He was clearly remembering some details. Or at least, some impressions.

"Why do you keep asking questions instead of answering them?" he shot back. He stared at her fiercely, challenging her to face him and discuss what exactly was happening.

Kenzie relented. "Brooke Collins was stabbed to death. She was murdered."

Vance's mouth fell open. Kenzie looked from him to Brittany, waiting for the woman's reaction. Brittany looked impassive. Maybe she had already guessed that part. Or maybe she didn't care.

"Murdered," Vance repeated, stunned. "Who killed her? Her husband?"

"We don't know yet." Kenzie looked at Zachary, gauging how much they should tell Vance. The fact that he had immediately assumed that it was Andy Collins who had killed his wife was telling. Zachary gave Kenzie a slight frown, indicating she shouldn't tell him too much. "No one saw what happened, and we are trying to find out where everyone was last night... even if you only saw her for a few minutes. It could be helpful."

"What would help is if I could remember anything at all about yesterday," Vance said, pressing the knuckles of his left hand into his forehead. "But the whole thing is a blank."

Kenzie frowned. It was the same line as Andy Collins had given, though he only said he couldn't remember anything since supper. Had they both had too much to drink? Or had one particular choice of drink produced an amnesiac effect? She had assumed it was something that Andy and Brooke had taken together, to enhance their evening, but where was Vance in that equation? Unless they had bought something from him or sold it to him. She couldn't see them all just sharing illicit drugs out of friendship and goodwill. They didn't seem to have anything in common and Vance in particular was not the friendly type. He got Kenzie's hackles up every time they spoke.

"Did you take anything that might have contributed to this loss of memory? Have you ever experienced anything like this before?"

"I'm not the type to take recreational drugs," he said stiffly, which was exactly what Kenzie would have expected him to say, whether it were true or not. "I may occasionally have a drink or two for social occasions, but I do not drink to excess. I feel like... like I'm coming down with something. Or maybe I got food poisoning. I got roofied once in college; some stupid fraternity prank, and that felt very similar." He shook his head. "It's not a natural feeling."

Roofied. Food poisoning. There was one commonality among the other guests, and that was that they had all eaten the evening meal together. Kenzie turned this over in her mind.

What could have caused the symptoms that they had been encountering? Unusual anger, high, amnesia. There were many possibilities. Many substances, taken to excess, could cause one or all of those symptoms.

"Roofied," she repeated, looking at Zachary and Brittany. "That makes some sense. And if that's the case..." she looked back at Vance. "I wonder if we could get a sample... for later testing, when the police get here. It may be a few days, and we would want to preserve any evidence until then. If you took something or were given something, it will be gone from your system in a few hours or days."

"A sample? Like what?" He frowned. "You may be a doctor, but I still haven't seen any proof of your qualifications. I'm not letting any random person stab me with a needle."

"No... I was thinking more along the lines of... a urine sample."

"You want my pee."

Kenzie's face heated. She should have been professional enough for it not to embarrass her, but the circumstances were bizarre. She wasn't in a hospital or clinic setting. She was in some guy's cabin, trapped by the snow, asking for his pee. And what was she going to do with it? She needed a container. And then to keep it somewhere secure and cold. Somewhere cold wasn't a problem, but somewhere secure might be.

"If you've been roofied, you would want to know about it, wouldn't you? You would want to catch the person who did it."

He considered this, but didn't immediately say yes or no. Kenzie could understand that it would be a difficult thing for a man to admit to. Men were not the ones who were supposed to be targeted by such drugs. If a man were drugged, then of course that didn't make him weak or helpless, but it might make him feel that way. Society didn't give him a script to follow.

Stiller looked at Brittany, and at first Kenzie thought that he was seeking her opinion about whether he should try to find the culprit or not. But the look lasted, and Kenzie finally twigged onto the fact that *she* had been his date. She had been the one who was close to his drinks and who had gone back to his cabin with her. If someone had had clear access to his food and drink, it had been her. Kenzie looked at Brittany, weighing the possibility.

Brittany flushed red. She shook her head. "You think I would do a thing like that? Why? I can get whatever I want. From you or any other man. I have no reason to drug anyone." She wrinkled her nose. "Certainly not you."

Stiller chuckled rather than being offended by her declaration. He motioned her closer to him.

"You don't," he agreed. "Certainly not me."

Brittany held back at first, trying to maintain the same level of disdain, but she failed. She walked up to Stiller and he put one arm around her to snuggle her up close against his side, and then he nuzzled her cheek and kissed her.

"No need at all."

Kenzie looked away, waiting for the two of them to come back down to earth. Zachary caught her eye and raised an eyebrow at her. She just shrugged and shook her head. It certainly didn't look like there were any problems between Stiller and Brittany.

But that still left the question open. If someone had drugged Stiller, then who? And why? And had they drugged everyone at the dinner?

33

Eventually, Stiller and Brittany returned to the conversation. Brittany had a mischievous sparkle in her eye that hadn't been there before. Stiller was looking a little wider awake, but he still had a certain lethargy in his movements, and he didn't answer questions as quickly as Kenzie expected him to. As if he had to think them through and compose his answer carefully, which she hadn't seen him do before.

"So where does that leave us?" Stiller asked. "You can't think that I had anything to do with Mrs. Collins's death. Why would I? I didn't have any motive. And I have my own issues. Obviously, I can't swear that I never saw her. I could have had an hour-long in-depth conversation with her, but I haven't a clue. I can't tell you anything about last night or yesterday. Maybe she told me she was afraid her husband was out to kill her for her life insurance policy. But we'll never know now. If someone roofied me, if that's what happened, then they wiped that all out."

"Where we are now is, I want you to be tested when the police get here. And that means giving a sample now, before it all metabolizes."

"When do I have to decide?"

"Some drugs are out of your system pretty quickly. I would do it right away, to ensure the best results."

"I don't know. I don't think that's something I want to do. I have a reputation to maintain. People like me don't go around getting roofied. It just doesn't happen."

"And what if a video showed up of you doing something that you don't

677

remember? Something worse than being targeted by another person. What if you did something or said something or hurt someone when you were under the influence? Under the influence of a drug that you didn't take voluntarily?"

Again, he looked to Brittany before answering.

"I think... that I'm better off keeping quiet. No one has any internet access here. If something comes to light... then I can work the story. But that will probably never happen. This was just... a weird night. Nothing criminal happened."

"Something criminal did happen," Zachary pointed out. "A woman was killed. And you were possibly drugged. Maybe others were too. Maybe to cover for the perpetrator of the murder. Maybe for some other reason. If you're being set up..."

"I didn't have anything to do with any of that."

"You don't remember."

"I don't remember," Stiller agreed, an edge to his voice. "And no one is going to convince me otherwise. So, no. You're not getting any piss or any other bodily fluids from me. And you're not getting any more cooperation. I'm done. I'm going back to bed."

"Sorry to have bothered you," Kenzie said. She stepped forward, off of the welcome mat. Onto the wood floor and across to the kitchen where Stiller and Brittany stood, separate from each other, just as they always were. A different class from everyone else. Lone wolves. Kenzie offered her hand to Stiller in a show of good sportsmanship and peace. He looked at her for a moment, then finally reached out his hand and shook hers. A firm shake, just a little bit harder than it needed to be. Showing her the edge. That he had the upper hand. Kenzie smiled and released, withdrawing from him. "We'll see you around."

She stumbled over his boots at the door and set them upright again. They didn't look like a match for either of the treads she had seen, but they might not be his only pair of boots.

She and Zachary left the cabin, back out into the biting cold. They had seen almost everyone, and Kenzie hoped that meant that she could go back home. There was still Jack. They had talked to him earlier, but had not had a personal interview with him. Did they need to? And did they need to conduct interviews with the staff? Or could they leave all of that for the police to review? They had talked to the most likely suspect. They had done their best to preserve all of the evidence. They had made sure that Vance was okay and hadn't been another victim of violence. If he had been drugged, he wasn't going to allow them to test him. By the time the police got there, then whatever was in his system, if anything, would be gone.

Surely that meant that now she could go home and just relax for a bit. Warm her bones and have a little nap to regenerate.

"No marks on his hand?" Zachary asked as they walked back toward the cabin, the wind at their backs now.

"No marks on his hand," Kenzie agreed. "I'm pretty sure that he's right-handed, and there were not any blade marks or defensive wounds on his hand or wrist."

"So he isn't the culprit."

Kenzie nodded. She thought about it as they walked back to their cabin. "Or else whoever stabbed her was wearing gloves."

Zachary considered this. "Not just any gloves. Something pretty tough. Leather. Work gloves. Not just wool mittens."

"Yeah. And maybe the gloves have knife marks on them."

They both glanced around as if they might find a pair of leather gloves lying right there at their feet, as if it were a TV police drama and the clues would show up at exactly the right time.

"Might have burned them," Zachary said. "Or tossed them out in the woods. Or in the pond."

"The pond is frozen."

"Not the pond, then. Maybe buried under the bonfire wood. Or sliced into little bits and flushed."

"Maybe. Or maybe they didn't realize the gloves are cut. If they didn't get cut all the way through, maybe they don't even know."

"Maybe. Maybe we'll still be able to find them."

"Do you think Stiller was drugged?"

They reached the door to their own cabin. Zachary slowly twisted the knob to open the door. "Yes. I think he was."

"Yeah. Me too."

***

The kids were setting up games on the floor in front of the fireplace where it was warmest. They seemed resigned to loss of their electronic devices and the fact they would have to entertain themselves. People said that kids didn't know how to entertain themselves anymore, but Kenzie saw that they were quickly adapting. They had been at a loss the day before when plunged into the dark ages, but they seemed engaged now, discussing new games, rules, and possibilities. If it warmed up a little, they could kick the kids outside to play in the snow awhile. Make snowballs and snow angels and forts to defend themselves.

It was amazing how quickly she could forget about the real horrors that had happened not that far from their own back door. Would it even be safe for the kids to go outside to play? Would it be safe for the adults? How long would they have to stay inside before the police would arrive and take over the investigation?

"You guys have been a while," Tyrrell remarked. "I thought you would be back before now. I take it you found the missing lover?" He munched on a sandwich. Peanut butter, by the smell of it.

"Actually, we did find her," Kenzie admitted. "But..." A glance at the kids to make sure they were not listening too closely. "Things were not good."

Tyrrell's eyebrows went up. He looked at Zachary, seeking out the older brother whom he could communicate with more naturally than Kenzie, seeing whether he had interpreted her words and manner correctly or whether he had jumped to the wrong conclusion. "What?"

Kenzie began to divest herself of her outdoor gear. She wasn't going to go out there again for a very long time. Maybe not until spring. She was cold to her bones.

"Yeah," Zachary agreed, nodding, confirming that Tyrrell had understood correctly. "About as badly as possible."

"Oh, no. That's terrible. What are we going to do? Is someone going to get the police?"

Mason looked up from his game, alert to the mention of police.

"We can't get anybody right now," Zachary said. "The roads are not passable. We'll have to wait until the highway is plowed and Mr. Burknall clears the roads here. And that might be a few days. It's not snowing right now, but this storm is supposed to last at least another day, maybe more."

"Why do we need to call the police, Daddy?" Mason piped up. "They can come even if they can't drive on the roads. They could come in a helicopter."

Stiller had come in a helicopter. But the weather conditions had been far more favorable. "When the clouds clear and the winds die down," she agreed. "They can't get a helicopter here in this kind of weather. But you don't need to be worried. Everything is just fine."

Mason looked at Kenzie and immediately discounted her opinion. She could read it in his face. Which meant that there was something to be worried about and they needed the police to come.

"What are you talking about?" Alisha took longer to realize that there was another conversation going on around her. One that she should pay attention to because it impacted her daddy and maybe others too. "What's wrong?"

"We have to call the police," Mason told her. "Where's your phone, Daddy? Why don't you call?"

"You know that we don't have any electricity right now," Tyrrell said. "I can't charge my phone. And I can't make a call without a signal. We'll have to wait until the storm is past."

"You have to try," Mason insisted. "Maybe if you hold it up high." He held his hands up in the air, looking up at them. "Sometimes if you go up high, you can make it work."

"Yes. Sometimes. But today I need to stay in the cabin and just wait. When the storm passes, then we should be able to make phone calls again."

"There's no storm right now."

"It's not blizzarding like it was. But there is still lots of cloud cover and trying right now would just run down my battery."

"Use the internet then," Mason directed. "Or send them a text."

"I know all the things to do. But I can't do them without a cell signal or a charged battery."

"A text doesn't take any battery. And Mommy says there is no charge for them because they are so small." Mason looked at Tyrrell with all the superior knowledge of an eight-year-old born into the technology age. Silly adults didn't always know how things should be done. But kids did.

Tyrrell looked pained. He pulled his phone out of his shirt pocket. "You can use it for five minutes," he said. "You show me how I can get ahold of the police."

Mason took it from him. Kenzie watched him hold down the power button to boot it up. She wouldn't have given in. She would have told him that it simply wasn't possible. He was wrong and simply didn't understand the situation. But Tyrrell didn't want the argument. He didn't want to be harassed about it. So he had given in.

Mason tinkered with the phone for a few minutes. He tapped the screen angrily.

"Daddy, there are *no bars,* and the text says, 'not sent.'"

"Yes. I know. That's because there is no signal."

"But there has to be a signal." Mason held the phone up over his head. He went into the kitchen and stood on a chair and held it over his head. He stepped onto the table and held it as high as he could reach. Zachary went over to the table and put his arms out. Mason looked at him for a moment and then allowed Zachary to pick him up and put him on his shoulders. Zachary wasn't tall, but Mason could almost touch the ceiling with the phone as he strained to get it higher. "We need to go outside. I could climb a tree."

"You can't climb a tree in weather like this," Tyrrell told him. "It's cold and icy. Very dangerous."

"You climb it then."

"No. Not me either. I'll fall on my a— on my backside. Maybe I'll break it. You want me to break my backside?"

Mason giggled. He finally gave up on being able to reach anyone by phone. He reached toward his father with the phone. Zachary walked over so that Mason could hand it to him. Mason kicked his feet as if Zachary were a horse that needed a good kick to get going. He bent down to speak in Zachary's ear.

"There's no signal."

"No," Zachary agreed.

34

It took a long time for Kenzie to get warmed up again. She sat as close to the heater as she dared and toasted her feet. She warmed her hands, rubbing them together. She rubbed her toes. She wrapped a blanket around herself and stayed under it until she was sweating. It was not going to be easy to get her back out there. She was done. Enough investigating. She would wait until the police got there. They would relay everything they knew to the police and let them sort it out.

Zachary had a granola bar without prompting and made Kenzie toast. He didn't actually toast it, but he put bread and marmalade on a slice of bread and served it to her sitting in front of the heater. He sat at the table watching her.

As the kids went back to their games and argued noisily with one another, Kenzie and Zachary gradually imparted all the details to Tyrrell. He kept shaking his head in disbelief.

"What is going on in this place?" he asked. "This is all so bizarre. Like reading a murder mystery by Agatha Christie. Everyone being picked off one by one, you know?"

"They're not," Kenzie said firmly. "Mr. Dewey died of natural causes. There has only been one homicide." Kenzie glanced at the children and then went on. "The most likely suspect is the husband. He didn't have any marks on his hands, but maybe he was wearing gloves and didn't get any cuts. They had an argument, things got out of hand, and..." She shrugged. "The same thing happens in the city. Believe me. I know."

"Of course it does," Tyrrell agreed. "But how do you know that's what happened here? It sounds like everybody was hopped up on drugs."

"It does," Kenzie admitted. "I wonder about what they ate at the dinner last night. Maybe there was something in it... some mold or fungus that is hallucinogenic."

"I doubt it was anything like that," Zachary disagreed. "For all of them to have symptoms, they all had to be dosed. If it were just a few spores of some mushroom, then one person, maybe two would get enough to have an... experience. But for all of them to be acting strangely? There had to be enough to dose everyone. Or maybe it was in all the drinks." He closed his eyes, thinking about it.

"How could it be in all of the drinks?" Kenzie challenged. "No one could know what everyone was going to drink and put it into all of the drinks being served. What about the person who decides that they just want a glass of water? From a pitcher or straight from the tap?"

"It could have been dissolved into each of the glasses," he suggested. "Dissolved and then the water evaporated, so that the drug was already in each of the glasses. It would mix with whatever was poured into them."

"And just what do you suggest it was? And why would anyone do such a thing? I think it must have been an accident. What about carbon monoxide? There could be a problem with the furnace at the farmhouse. Everyone got dosed with carbon monoxide. Just enough to affect their moods and thinking, not enough to cause physical symptoms like vomiting or passing out."

"Maybe. A gas would explain a lot. That would be easy for someone to release in a room, without anyone noticing or tasting anything."

"I didn't mean intentionally. I meant a faulty furnace."

"I know. I'm just thinking."

"But there's no reason to do something like that. Was this just... a prank? Like when Stiller was roofied in college? Someone just thought that it would be funny to contaminate everyone here, to see whether they did anything funny? Saw flying pink elephants?"

"I've never hallucinated flying pink elephants," Zachary said, cocking his head and looking at Kenzie.

"That was just an example."

"But why do they show things like that on TV? Funny, silly, safe things? They make hallucinating look like... a fun party game. When it's nothing like that. At least... I've never had any hallucinations like that."

"Uh... how many times have you hallucinated?" Kenzie asked. She wasn't sure she wanted to know the answer. Things had been bad for Zachary as a teen and a young man, and she would be the first to admit that she didn't know what kinds of things he had gotten into during that time. He could have been into all kinds of illegal drugs and activities.

"I don't know," Zachary shook his head. "More than I can count."

"Oh...?"

He laughed at her expression. "Reactions to meds. Fevers. Stuff they had me on when I was recovering from my burns. Meds that they aren't supposed to prescribe together." He shrugged. "It isn't like I wanted to hallucinate. Like I said... I never saw flying pink elephants. Some of it was innocuous. But usually... it was pretty scary."

Kenzie chuckled along with him, relieved. She wouldn't judge him if he had experimented with drugs when he was a kid. Lots of people did, and he'd certainly had a crappy enough life to have wanted to escape from it however he could. But she was happy that he hadn't been taking hallucinogens intentionally. Some of those could really mess up a person's brain, and Zachary had a hard enough time without doing that kind of damage.

"Well, maybe you've got a point there. Maybe it was someone who bought into the TV image of hallucinogens. That it's just a fun time, silly and harmless. Maybe it was just someone who wanted to spice up the dinner hour."

"Jack?" Zachary suggested.

Kenzie shrugged one shoulder, tilting her head to the side as she considered. "Maybe. He's the kind of guy I would expect to stir the pot. To want to see what would happen if he tried something like that."

"But we have no evidence."

"What we really need to do is to find whatever they were given. If Jack or someone else put something into the food, then there must be a pill bottle or something around as evidence."

"Yes." Zachary didn't say anything for a while and Kenzie thought that the conversation was over. Then he tapped his fingers on his knees, restless, and leaned forward to talk to her. "You're absolutely sure that Mr. Dewey's death didn't have anything to do with this?"

"How could it? He died the day before."

"I don't know. If someone is intentionally poisoning the guests with some hallucinogen, then why couldn't they have poisoned him the day before?"

"But... that would imply that they wanted to kill everyone else," Tyrrell objected. "If you poison one person, and they die, then if you poison half a dozen other people... you do it knowing that they could all die."

Kenzie was inclined to agree. But Zachary shrugged.

"Some people wouldn't care about that. Or it could be someone who knew that he had a heart condition and that it wouldn't do the same kind of harm to someone who didn't."

Kenzie shook her head slowly. "I don't know, Zachary. It doesn't seem likely. Like Tyrrell said, it isn't exactly logical."

"In my experience, people who intentionally hurt and kill other people aren't logical. They don't think the same way as you do. My question is *could* it be the same substance? Could the same thing kill Dewey and cause the others to have a bad trip?"

"Yes," Kenzie admitted. "There are a number of substances that could cause both heart problems and hallucinations."

Zachary sat back, looking satisfied.

"But I still don't think that's what happened," Kenzie warned.

"It's your job to be skeptical. You can't advance any theory on a death unless there's some evidence to back it up. I don't need evidence or proof to speculate."

Kenzie looked at Tyrrell, who shrugged. "He's got a point," he pointed out. "You guys are coming at it from two different backgrounds."

Zachary got up and started to pace. "I do think we should go to dinner tonight."

35

W hat?" Kenzie was floored. "Why would we go to dinner if you think that everyone was poisoned there and whoever did it has not been caught? What's to stop them from doing it again?"

"Well, I wouldn't suggest eating anything you didn't watch being prepared. But I think we should see if we can get everyone to buy in on a search of the cabins for any medications that might have been used to do this. And the knife, for that matter."

Kenzie blinked, thinking about it. "If someone did this intentionally, why would they agree to a search of their cabins? Why would anyone agree to a search?"

"Because if the majority agree, they would look guilty for arguing against it. Whoever did it... they probably didn't come out here with the intention of poisoning everyone. They probably have a legitimate reason for having whatever it is, whether it's medical or recreational. They can say that someone else got into it. We can't prove who actually had access to it."

"Then what's the point in doing a search?"

"To secure the poison. To make sure that they can't do it again tomorrow. The police can sort it all out when they get here, but that doesn't mean we have to be sitting ducks."

"I doubt whether everyone will go to dinner tonight. They'll probably all be too spooked."

"I don't think everyone else realizes that they were all poisoned. Stiller and Collins can't remember what happened. The others just know that Andy

Collins and Brooke had a fight and Brooke ended up getting killed. They don't all have the big picture, that they all had symptoms. I think they'll still want to get together to find out more about what happened to Brooke, or at least to gossip about it if they can't get any facts."

"He's probably right," Tyrrell agreed. "Whenever something bad or shocking happens, people want to talk about it. They are isolated and can't even post about it on social media. The only social group is the rest of the vacationers. Maybe Collins will want to stay home and won't go to dinner, but the rest probably will. With us, we've got our own little group here," Tyrrell made a motion that took in Kenzie and Zachary and the children. "But most of the others are on their own. They won't want to be totally isolated for days."

Kenzie didn't relish the idea of trying to convince a group of vacationers to let other people search their belongings. It was, as Tyrrell had said, like being stuck in the middle of an Agatha Christie novel. Except the sleuths in those mysteries always seemed to be in charge and to know exactly what they were doing. Kenzie didn't have any authority and didn't even want to be involved in the whole mess.

"But we're not all going to go up for dinner, right?" Kenzie looked at the children. "I don't think... probably just Zachary and I..."

Tyrrell nodded. "Yeah. I don't want my kids anywhere near this psycho."

They spent most of the day resting and staying warm. Napping, playing with the kids, grazing on their snacks and leftovers. Tyrrell and Zachary had moved the perishable leftovers from the fridge to a snowbank outside, hoping that there were sealed well enough that the animals would not smell them and get into them. The little cook stove worked well for heating up small amounts of the leftovers at a time, though Zachary disappeared every time it was in use. Kenzie thought it was progress that he wasn't having a meltdown over it, just moving to where he couldn't see the flame.

They talked about the strange night once or twice more, puzzling over some of the details. But they didn't come to any conclusions. They didn't have enough clues to point them in the right direction, and too many suspects. Too many, and not enough, because while pretty much everybody had opportunity, no one really had a motive to kill Brooke. Aside from Andy, who might have regretted his decision to marry her or have been after her life insurance. No one else had any reason to kill her. It was probably just the unfortunate effect of whatever hallucinogen they must have been exposed to.

As the dinner hour approached, Kenzie changed her clothes, tried to finger-comb her hair into some order, and gave up on applying makeup by the green light of a glow-stick. She was just going to do more harm than good, and who cared whether she had made herself up for a dinner that was going to be held in near darkness?

They grabbed a few glow sticks for the dinner, hoping they'd be able to prevail upon the others to forgo candles, put on their heavy winter gear, and trudged up to the farmhouse at the top of the road.

It had started snowing again. It wasn't blowing like the night before, but big, fluffy flakes floated gently to the ground, and Kenzie suspected it would pile up pretty quickly. How long was it going to take them to dig out? When the weather system eventually passed over, would the rescue be immediate? Or would it take several more days for them to plow the highway? What other jobs would take precedence over the road? If there were power and phone lines down, people trapped in various farms throughout the county, and possible medical emergencies to deal with, how far down the list would the Lodge be?

When they reached the house and let themselves in at the front door, Kenzie glanced over at Zachary. He began removing his coat and other gear, a grim expression on his face. He was probably wondering exactly the same thing. How much longer?

Inside, the mood was a bit giddy, even celebratory. Not the kind of gathering one would expect when two people of their company had died. But death was like that sometimes. People had to escape the grief and pain however they could, often with inappropriate jokes, comedic movies, or loud carousing. There was a reason they had a term for gallows humor.

"Kenzie! You decided to join us today!" Raven gave Kenzie a dazzling smile, as if they were best friends, and leaned close to buss both cheeks. "How was your day?"

"Well, I'm glad we have the kids around to help keep us entertained. When you're trying to keep someone else engaged, it doesn't leave much time to be bored."

"You should have brought them up! I would have liked to meet them. They're your niece and nephew?"

Raven had seen them on the hayride. She hadn't seemed very interested in them at that point. But that was then. They lived in a whole different world now.

"Zachary's. Tyrrell is his brother."

"And remind me their names?"

"Mason and Alisha."

"What great names. They seem like fun kids."

Kenzie nodded. "Like I said, it's nice to have someone else to worry about. And they keep the atmosphere light."

"Zachary, good to see you again." Raven shook his hand, touching his elbow with her other hand as if they were old friends and she was extending her sympathies to him. "How are you holding up? I wondered, with the power being out and you having to deal with F-I-R-E."

"You don't need to spell it. Mr. Burknall brought us a propane-fueled heater, so we don't have to have a fire. And we have these." Zachary showed off a couple of the glow sticks. "To replace candles. Hopefully, no one here will mind so much..."

"What a great idea. I didn't even know there *was* a propane heater."

Zachary shrugged. Why would she? Burknall had known, and he'd known what to do about it.

They were welcomed into the small circle of vacationers. Because they were bored? Because Kenzie and Zachary were fresh meat? Kenzie excused herself from the gathering.

"I just wanted to see how Mrs. Hubbard is doing. I'll be back in a few minutes."

She felt awkward going back to the kitchen, where she hadn't been invited and probably wasn't welcome. But she had a job to do, and she'd just have to bluff her way through as if she belonged there.

"Knock knock," she called out as she walked through the archway into the kitchen. There was no door to knock on to announce herself, and she didn't want to sneak up on Mrs. Hubbard and give *her* a heart attack.

The older woman startled anyway. She turned around and looked at Kenzie. "Oh. Hello, dear. Can I get you something?"

"Oh, no. I'm not back here to make any special requests. I just wanted to see how you are doing. I know it hit you pretty hard, losing Mr. Dewey like that."

"I don't want you to think that there was anything between us," Mrs. Hubbard started. "It wasn't like that."

"I didn't think it was. You've worked with him for years. Of course you would be upset and shocked by the whole thing."

Mrs. Hubbard nodded. "Yes, that's right. You don't know what it's like. Even if we weren't that close, it's still like losing a family member."

"I'm sure it is. I guess maybe you heard from Mr. Burknall that I'm not actually an accountant..."

Mrs. Hubbard gave her a sideways look, then nodded. "That's what he said."

"I work at the medical examiner's office. So I know what it's like, how shocking it can be to lose someone."

"Yes." Mrs. Hubbard gave each of the pots on the stove a stir.

Kenzie stepped closer to have a look, surprised to see the stove in use. Mrs. Hubbard smiled.

"It's propane. This isn't the first time we've had a snowstorm."

"I guess not! I didn't even think about it until now. I guess I pictured you working on a little camp cook stove like we have been."

"Not for a big meal like this. Wouldn't be practical. We can pretty much carry on here like usual, power or not."

"That's great." Kenzie smiled and hovered, trying to think of a way to segue into the subject she wanted to bring up.

Mrs. Hubbard eyed her, then hummed as she moved around the kitchen.

"Umm... I wondered if you get lonely in here, working all by yourself all day," Kenzie offered.

"No, I don't mind working by myself. And I'm never alone for long. The staff come and go. Samantha is in here and helps with the serving. Sometimes she gives me a hand if there are a lot of dishes to assemble. Mr. Dewey, he was always in and out, checking on things, testing new dishes, just shooting the breeze." She looked pensive. "He was lonely after Mrs. Dewey passed. It was hard for him. They'd been together for so long, he wasn't used to doing it all on his own. And even if he had all of the help that he needed, there was still... he still missed her. And he was too old to start up with someone new. Maybe folks do remarry when they're old these days, but Mr. Dewey wasn't part of the social scene. There aren't many people to visit with up in these parts. We're pretty isolated. He always liked it, before. Anyway..." Mrs. Hubbard tapped a spoon on the edge of one pot to shake the sauce off and set it to the side. "He was around a good deal. And Mr. Burknall, he is the same. He'd be up at the house to talk to Mr. Dewey, and he'd drop in to say hello and see what was cooking. You might think this is a lonely place, but it isn't."

As if proving her point, Samantha appeared in the doorway. "Natives are getting restless. Can I give you a hand with anything else?"

"No, we're done. Just the serving now."

"What about guests?" Kenzie asked.

"What about guests?"

"Do *they* ever stop in? Or are they banned from the kitchen?"

"Oh, nobody is ever banned," Mrs. Hubbard shook her head. She and Samantha started to get out serving bowls and to transfer the contents from the pots on the stove and some plastic storage bowls in the fridge. "Guests don't have the run of the place, but they're welcome to stop in and say hello, see what's going on. People are often very interested in all of the work that goes into running this place." She smiled. "Some of the women are so used to doing all of the cooking at home that they don't know what to do with themselves after a day of vacationing. They're in here, looking for some way to help out."

"And everyone who is here now? Have any of them been into the kitchen?"

Mrs. Hubbard shrugged. "Yes. Of course. I can't think of who has been in and out, but some of them have been around to talk or see how the sausage is made, so to speak."

"You must have a lot of patience, to put up with all of that coming and going. I thought you would be lonely, but maybe it's the opposite. Maybe you wouldn't mind having some time to yourself for a while."

She smiled pleasantly. "It's been a good job. I don't know what I'm going to do if they decide to shut the Lodge down. I don't know where I'll go."

Kenzie nodded and excused herself, returning to the others before they could start to wonder what was taking her so long. Mrs. Hubbard certainly wouldn't have any motive to want Mr. Dewey out of the way, seeing how it had put her job at risk. It wouldn't be easy for her to find something else if she found herself out of a job now.

She returned to the dining room to find everyone assembling around the table. She found that she and Zachary didn't need to part with their last few glow sticks, as the table was lit by an LED lantern. Mr. Burknall seemed satisfied with the arrangements and left via the kitchen, presumably getting his own dinner on the way out.

Kenzie and Zachary followed the plan they had worked out that afternoon in their cabin, dishing up the meal as if they were going to eat with the other guests, so that they would fit in and not make anyone feel uncomfortable. But then they would broach the rather uncomfortable topic of searching everyone's cabins.

36

Jack was eyeing Kenzie as she dished up her food and passed the serving bowls around the table. She tried to ignore his looks, but she could feel him watching her even when she turned away from him.

"I assume everyone has heard the latest news about our lady accountant," Jack said, looking around the table to make his announcement.

Well, that was one way to break the ice.

"What about her?" Raven asked.

"That she's not an accountant at all. She's been pulling the wool over everyone's eyes. Pretending to be one thing when she is actually another."

Raven raised her brows, looking bored with his dramatics. She clearly recognized his need for attention and would not play into his hands. She continued to dish up the meal.

"She is a doctor," Jack announced. Trying to get her attention back. He looked around the table self-importantly. "Not just a doctor, but a medical examiner."

There was a crash as Samantha put a bowl down too hard, rattling all of the silverware and china on the table. Kenzie laid her palms on the table, trying to stop the vibrations.

"Sorry," Samantha apologized. "It's the lighting. I missed the edge of the table."

Or had it been something else? Kenzie watched her, interested in her reaction. She, at least, had not heard the gossip about Kenzie's real profession.

693

After everyone stopped reacting to Jack's announcement, Kenzie corrected him.

"I am not a medical examiner. Not yet. I assist in the medical examiner's office."

Jack sat back in his seat, smirking. "You're certainly no accountant."

"No, I think anyone who looked at my check book would agree about that," Kenzie said. Though she was really no slouch in the financial department. "As I said to Mr. Burknall... I was just hoping to avoid having to look at everyone's weird moles or to discuss other medical issues and diagnoses." She shrugged. "I'm sure that anyone who has a doctor in the family has heard it all before. A doctor is never off duty. Everyone is always looking for special advice."

The guests looked at one another, sorting out who had known this fact before Jack's announcement and who had not. Looking around the table, Kenzie was glad that both Andy Collins and Redd Flagg had made it to the dinner. Even Vance Stiller, who had sounded as if he would be in bed the rest of the day, had managed to make it to the farmhouse for the dinner. Probably because he didn't want to have to scrounge his own. She doubted he had brought a bunch of snacks or ready-to-eat meals for himself.

"So you can tell how Mr. Dewey died. And... you know... Mrs. Collins," Raven said, with a sympathetic nod to Andy Collins, acknowledging his loss and apologizing for bringing her death up.

"I only know a limited amount," Kenzie said. "I obviously can't do a full autopsy here at the Lodge, and it wouldn't be my place to do so. All I've done is make observations and to preserve the bodies the best I can for the authorities when they are able to make it here. Just like we told everyone already."

"But you didn't say that you knew all that stuff before. That you are trained."

"No. I didn't. But we decided to share it now, because I think it is important for everyone to know." Kenzie smiled at Jack to show that she had been planning on sharing that news at dinner anyway. Stealing his thunder. He didn't smile back.

"Why does it make any difference now?" Stiller demanded. "Like you say, you're not doing an autopsy. You're not here as a medical examiner." He made a face when he looked at her, maybe remembering how she had told him she was a doctor earlier in the day, offering to examine him and suggesting that he preserve a sample of his urine for testing. The fact that she was the kind of doctor who worked on dead people did not make him well-disposed toward her. Kenzie had encountered that reaction before. As if she were some kind of vampire or zombie and her touch was unclean. Despite the fact that she nearly scrubbed her skin off every time she had been assisting in autopsy.

"Well... I have been thinking about... what happened here last night. And I have some concerns."

They just looked at her blankly.

"Several of you have talked about hallucinating or not being able to remember what happened last night. Or about others being aggressive."

Looks were exchanged, but no one jumped in to either confirm this observation or to deny it.

"And I wonder whether there was something in the food or drinks last night. Something that caused those symptoms."

Raven stopped with her fork raised, ready to take a bite. The others reacted in various ways, some of them stopping and putting down their cutlery, and others continuing to eat as if they didn't have any concerns about the food.

"What do you mean? Who would put something in the food?" Jack asked. He smirked. He gave a bit of a muffled chuckle before stifling it. Kenzie wondered whether he was intentionally giving off signals to make her think him more suspicious, or if he could possibly be stupid enough to gloat over the thought of what he or someone else had done. She decided to assume that he was not stupid at all, but just trying to get her riled up. That made it easier to stay calm and collected.

The others at the table were thinking about the question. Who would have put something in the food? And why? Had their symptoms been caused by a foreign substance, or was Kenzie just being paranoid? She was a medical doctor, or so she now claimed.

"What makes you think that someone put something in the food?" Redd asked.

"Because you all had symptoms, one way or the other. Hallucinating. Seeing monsters or thinking you could see or hear something weird and out of place. Noises in the night. People fighting who wouldn't normally fight with each other." Kenzie didn't look at Andy Collins, but let everyone draw their own conclusions. "And those of you who can't remember what happened since dinner last night. Or even for all day yesterday. You all agree that weird things were going on last night, and that you didn't feel well or feel like yourself this morning."

There was silence around the table. No one was eating any longer. Kenzie saw that Mrs. Hubbard and Samantha were hovering in the doorway, listening and not serving or preparing anything else.

"And then there was what happened to Mrs. Collins," Kenzie said gently.

"You have to admit that her death was not something that could have been expected or predicted. A healthy young woman. No one expected her to die. No one would have expected her to run out into the snow in the middle of the night. And no one would have expected her to be attacked and killed in the woods. None of that is normal. And if you have been paying any attention to the media, you know that certain drugs can cause hallucinations and violent behavior. They can make people do things that they would normally not have done."

"We aren't exactly in New York," Jack Fowler sneered. "Exactly where do you think someone got these drugs? There isn't a drug dealer on the corner as you drive in. We're out in the middle of nowhere."

"People may have brought medications or recreational drugs with them. Maybe never planning for them to end up in the meal, but... it is a possibility."

"No one *accidentally* put drugs into the food," Jack pointed out. "If this really happened, then it was intentional. You're telling us that someone intentionally put drugs in our food that could have killed someone. That maybe *did* result in someone getting killed."

Kenzie nodded. She had hoped to gloss over that point. To say that the food had been tainted without dwelling on the fact that someone had intentionally poisoned it. Because then the guests would be looking at each other exactly the way that they were now, with suspicion and disbelief. It was almost too bizarre for anyone to believe. They would rather categorize it as something that was too bizarre to have happened than to protect themselves further.

"What I would like to do," she said slowly, "is to check each of the cabins, and of course the house and the outbuildings, and to gather up any medications or other substances that could be used that way. And by doing that... prevent it from happening again."

"You're saying that one of us is a killer," Brittany said baldly. "You think that someone killed Mrs. Collins, and that whoever did that might do it again."

"Someone *did* kill Mrs. Collins," Kenzie said. "I don't know whether it was premeditated or if it was just the result of someone being high on whatever substance might have been administered to the food. But whether it was intentional or not, I don't want it to happen again." Kenzie looked around the table at the food still on everybody's plates. No one was eating any longer.

"Why should you be the one to do this search?" Redd asked. "What makes you more qualified to do it than, say, me?"

"The fact that I am a doctor means that I'll have a better idea whether any particular medication could lead to hallucinations and some of the rest of the stuff that went on last night."

"And you're going to do this by yourself? You could frame anyone you wanted to. You could be the one who poisoned everyone, and you just want to shift the blame to someone else."

"Actually. If you think about you, you'll remember that we were not at the house yesterday. Not at any time. We had no opportunity to poison the food. We were never in the house, let alone the kitchen."

"Could have snuck in," Redd said petulantly.

"I think if we had been here, someone would have seen us."

No one jumped in to say that they had seen either Kenzie or Zachary at the house the day before. Everyone was quiet.

"You can talk to Mrs. Hubbard. She can confirm that we were never in the kitchen or anywhere near it."

Heads turned toward the kitchen, where Mrs. Hubbard and Samantha were listening. Mrs. Hubbard shook her head. "No, they were never around." Her eyes went around the table to the rest of them. Mentally checking off who she had seen at the house the day before and who had stopped into her kitchen for a chat or to smell or taste the dishes on the stove? Thinking about just who'd had the opportunity to tamper with the food?

"Well, if anyone might have poisoned us all at dinner last night, you know who the most likely suspect is," Vance Stiller announced, fixing his gaze on Mrs. Hubbard. "There's only one person who has unlimited access to the food."

"I did no such thing," Mrs. Hubbard snapped. "After all these years, why would I decide to poison my guests now? You think I'm crazy? What happens to my job if I do that?"

"The same thing that happens to you if Mr. Dewey dies," Jack said. "You lose your job. Is it any coincidence that right after he dies, this happens? Maybe he knew she was a poisoner and he's the only thing that kept her from murdering everyone before."

It was a ridiculous accusation. Jack looked away, as if it had sounded false even to his own ears.

But of course Mrs. Hubbard had to be a suspect. Anyone who had access to the food had to be a suspect and she was the one with the most access. Anyone else would have had to get past her.

37

I don't think that any of us have all the information that we need to make any accusations," Kenzie pointed out. "The fact is, practically anyone here could have tampered with the food at some time yesterday. But what's done is done, and the police will have to do what they can to sort it out. My concern is to prevent anything from happening again. We don't want anything to happen to anyone else here."

Raven reached for her drink, then pulled back her hand and just stared at her glass. If the alcohol had been poisoned, they had already had their cocktails. Was it possible that every bottle had been tainted? Or every glass, as Zachary had suggested to Kenzie earlier? Kenzie thought it more likely that the toxin had been put in the food.

"So you want to conduct this search on all the cabins," Jack said. He spread his hands wide. "Well then, have at it. Why not?" He looked challengingly around the table, daring anyone to argue with him.

"I don't want anyone going through my things," Redd objected.

Stiller nodded. "Absolutely not. I'm not having anyone pawing through my possessions either. I have some very... high-end articles. I don't want anyone near my things."

There were murmurs of agreement around the table.

"So," Zachary spoke up, "you're good with either being poisoned again or not eating here for the duration. Until the plows get through and the police can begin an investigation." He shrugged. "Okay."

"Why not let people bring their own medications here?" Redd suggested.

"Anyone who has anything can declare it, and Kenzie can say whether it could have caused these hallucinations, and if it could, we flush them."

"What an idiot," Andy Collins said flatly, voicing what pretty much everyone around the table was already thinking. "You think that whoever intentionally poisoned everyone else is just going to bring forward the poison because we ask him to? Or *her*? And *flushing* everything to get rid of the evidence? Just what do you have in your cabin that you're so worried about them finding?"

Redd's eyes darted around the room, landed on Kenzie briefly, and flitted away again. "Look..."

"Of course you have to search the cabins," Collins said. "Start with mine. Whenever you want. Go ahead and look through all of my stuff and all of my wife's things. Because I want to know who did this. I want to prove to everyone here that I did not kill my wife. I know that's what you're all thinking, so there's no point in looking so shocked. Go ahead. Search my cabin."

Kenzie nodded. That was two down. She looked around the table, waiting for other volunteers.

"You can search mine," Brittany agreed. "I've got nothing to hide."

Kenzie looked at Jack Fowler, waiting for his offer. When he didn't say anything, she moved on to Raven. Raven rolled her eyes and laughed. "Well, you're going to find a whole pharmacy of pills in my cabin. I'll admit that straight out. I've got pills to put me to sleep and pills to wake me up. And for just about anything else you can think of. Could any of them cause hallucinations?" She shrugged. "I have no doubt. So go ahead and look, and confiscate whatever you think is dangerous. As long as you'll dispense them to me whenever I need them." She laughed, bringing out several smiles around the table.

Eventually, everyone agreed. The naysayers were outweighed by those who had already agreed, and peer pressure did its thing. Eventually, they got everyone's consent.

The prevailing opinion was that Kenzie and Zachary would need to be accompanied by someone else to ensure that they were not planting evidence, and that their cabin would need to be searched as well. After some discussion, Raven was nominated to accompany them.

Kenzie tried not to think about the long night before them. Even if they only took fifteen to twenty minutes on each cabin and building, it would be hours before they were finished. It was already dark. People were hungry and grumpy, afraid to eat anything that had been prepared, no matter how much Mrs. Hubbard tried to convince them all that it was safe. How could she possibly know that, when she didn't know how the food or drinks had been tainted the day before?

"You must have canned food in the pantry," Zachary suggested to Mrs. Hubbard.

"Yes. Of course. All kinds."

"How about everybody gets a can of something that doesn't have to be prepared, and everyone opens their own can and eats it without anyone else touching it?"

"Yes!" Raven said with relief. "I'm starving, but as good as this smells, I can't eat it. Not now. There is no way someone could get poison into a sealed can, right?"

Kenzie couldn't think of a way, unless they had a canning machine of their own, and that would be rather elaborate. No one else offered any objections to this plan, and Mrs. Hubbard took everyone's orders for what food they wanted brought from the pantry.

"Kenzie and I have already eaten," Zachary said, "so I think we should get started on the search while the rest of you have your dinner. The sooner we get done, the sooner you can be back in your own cabins."

Raven was given a can of peaches and after opening it, dipped her spoon in. She drank off some of the juice so it wouldn't spill, and was ready to go with Kenzie and Zachary to supervise their search.

38

"W ho do you want to start with?" Kenzie asked.

Zachary didn't need to stop and think about it. "Redd," he said immediately. "Big old Redd Flagg."

Kenzie laughed. "What do you suppose made him pick that as his pen name? And what do you think his real name is? Is it something that we would recognize, or that no one has ever heard of?"

"Probably five syllables and Polish or Russian."

Kenzie nodded. "That would make sense."

The three of them hurried to Redd's cabin as quickly as they could. It took Kenzie a few minutes to find the right key on Mr. Dewey's key chain. Zachary was watching her, trying not to look impatient. He could probably have picked the lock in half the time it took her to find the right key. But maybe not with thick winter gloves on.

The cabin was much warmer than the weather outside, but the fire that had been burning in the fireplace had died down to embers. Zachary looked at it, swallowed, and looked around the cabin to analyze the space that they would have to search.

Raven took off her gloves, but didn't remove the rest of her gear. She just stood on the welcome mat slurping her canned peaches.

Kenzie looked at her. "When I was little, I used to try to swallow sliced peaches whole, pretending that I was in one of those goldfish swallowing contests. Is that weird, or what?"

701

Raven laughed. "Doesn't that take all the enjoyment out of it? You would hardly even taste them."

"I guess not. But little-kid me thought that it was pretty fun."

Raven shook her head. "That's hilarious."

"Let's start in the bedroom and bathroom and work our way outward," Zachary said. "If he has anything, it's most likely to be close at hand."

Kenzie agreed and, armed with flashlights from the farmhouse, they started with Redd's bedroom, searching through his suitcase and night table first, then quickly checking the rest of the bedroom and the bathroom. He had a number of over-the-counter medications in the bathroom, nothing too surprising. Mostly headache or stomach ailment remedies. He had some alcohol in his bedroom. Not surprising for a writer, Kenzie supposed. If one were to believe all of the TV tropes about struggling writers. "Write drunk, edit sober," Hemingway had said.

Zachary returned to the bedroom after the bathroom search and looked around, frowning.

"I thought we were going to work our way out," Kenzie reminded him. "Shouldn't we check the living room and kitchen now?"

"Yes," Zachary agreed. He looked around the bedroom once more as if he had lost something. Then he followed Kenzie out to the living room. It didn't seem like Redd had touched anything there. It was all the furnishings that the Deweys or their decorators had picked out. Zachary pulled a few books off of the shelf and looked behind the rows of books, but there was nothing hidden there. Likewise, the kitchen didn't appear to have been touched. Redd was taking all of his meals at the farmhouse. There weren't even dirty dishes in the sink.

Kenzie figured they were finished with Redd Flagg's cabin. Zachary, however, went back to the bedroom. Kenzie followed him.

"What are you looking for? We should get on to the next cabin or we're going to be all night."

"Something isn't right."

Zachary took a quick look at the night table that they had already searched. He moved things around in the suitcase and pointed out a tear in the lining to Kenzie.

"Okay. Why does that matter? Is there something in there?"

He shook his head. "No. But I think there was. What was he trying to hide?"

"Maybe it was just torn. Something snagged on it."

"No. It's one of those things... people think they're being clever, not realizing that it's what everyone else is doing and that customs or the police or whoever he is trying to hide things from are going to see it immediately."

"Drugs, you think? He's smuggling something?"

"It's not very big. So whatever it is, he's not muling for someone else. It's just for personal use. Unless it is something really high-priced, like diamonds."

"Somehow, I don't see Redd smuggling diamonds."

"No. Me neither."

Raven stood in the door of the bedroom, watching them but not offering any comment. Zachary started to go through the room more carefully, checking under the mattress, inside the lamp shade, and feeling the backs of the drawers. He pulled a small screwdriver from his pocket and unscrewed the plates over the light switch and the electrical outlets.

"Ah-ha."

Kenzie watched him pull a small baggie out of one of the electrical outlet holes.

"What is it?"

Zachary held the baggie close to his eyes, examining it. Then he took it over to Kenzie and offered it to her for her opinion. Kenzie looked at the gray-brown dust. It was difficult to tell what organic substance had been crushed into powder, but she had an idea. She opened the top of the bag and passed it under her nose. She didn't inhale, but just let the scent waft up into her nose. It had a musty, earthy smell. She zipped the bag closed again.

"I would guess mushrooms."

"Ah." Zachary nodded. "So, we found our first hallucinogen. You think this is what was used?"

Kenzie hesitated, looking at the baggie. "I'm not familiar with the dosing. If I had internet access, I could look it up to be sure, but I don't think this is enough to affect everyone like they were last night. This is a pretty small amount, so unless he has a larger stash somewhere else... I think this is just enough for personal use. One dose or several microdoses."

They looked around the room. Zachary went back to the electrical outlets and unscrewed the rest of the cover plates. There were no more baggies.

"Looks like that's it."

"Okay." Kenzie put the baggie into her pocket.

"You're going to take it?" Raven asked. "Even though it isn't enough to poison everyone?"

"We said that we would take anything that could be used to poison everyone. This could be combined with something else. And we want to treat everyone the same way, not to show any special consideration."

Raven didn't argue the point. They got their outdoor clothing back on and exited Redd's cabin.

He was waiting outside the door, pacing back and forth. The snow was all trampled down; he had been there for a while. He looked at Kenzie and Zachary, shoulders tense and hunched up inside his coat.

"All done?" he asked, attempting to mask his anxiety and look casual.

"All done," Kenzie agreed.

He looked relieved and moved toward his door.

"We did find your mushrooms," Kenzie advised. "They'll be locked up with everything else."

"What?"

"Your mushrooms."

He shook his head, a crease appearing between his eyebrows. "I didn't have any mushrooms. Where were they?"

"No one would leave them there and forget about them," Zachary said. "Don't assume we're stupid."

Redd considered this and changed his approach. "Okay. Yes. But they were just for... they help me to open my mind, make it easier to write. I have friends who have had a lot of success with—"

"You can save it," Kenzie said. "I know all of the arguments. When you take something like this," she patted her pocket, "you have no idea how much of the active ingredient you are getting from one dose to the next, you could end up on a really bad trip when you think you're taking a safe dose. You can't tell."

"If you're experienced or have someone who is experienced to help you—"

"You still can't control it," Kenzie asserted.

Redd's eyes flicked to the side, over Kenzie's shoulder to the dark woods behind her. She automatically looked behind her to see what he was looking at, then looked back at Redd's face. His pupils were widely dilated.

"You're hallucinating right now!" she accused.

"I didn't take anything," Redd insisted. "I haven't had anything in two days. I swear it."

"Right." Kenzie shook her head in disbelief. "After all that went on last night, I can't believe you would still want to take hallucinogens."

"I didn't. You're right, after last night... I wouldn't take anything. And I didn't. Is it possible that whatever I got is still affecting me...?"

Kenzie didn't believe a word he had said. He'd probably been high ever since they had arrived. His talkativeness... who knew what he was like when he wasn't on something?

"We're doing you a favor by taking this away, then. You wouldn't want a repeat of last night."

He looked for an argument to this, but gave up, shrugging and shaking his head at the same time. "Can I go back in my cabin?"

"Yes. And if I were you... I'd stay put for the night. Sleep this off."

He didn't say anything to that, just opened his door and disappeared into his cabin.

39

"Collins's cabin next," Zachary suggested.

They walked past their own cabin. Kenzie suspected that Raven would want to search their cabin as well, but that hadn't been discussed, so they would just leave it and see whether she pressed the matter later.

Somehow, Zachary had ended up with Dewey's key ring in his hand, and he was faster at figuring out which was the proper key for the cabin. He pushed the door open, and they all went in.

It looked pretty much as it had that morning. It didn't look like Redd or Andy Collins had made any attempt at cleaning it up. Raven looked around at the disorder with wide eyes.

"Wow. They really did have a knock-down blow-out fight, didn't they?"

Kenzie nodded. She was relieved, once again, that there were no blood spatters. Brooke had, at least, not been attacked there. Kenzie had not been to many crime scenes. Most of her exposure to dead bodies had been confined to the morgue. Dr. Wiltshire had only taken her out to crime scenes a couple of times, and they had not been horrific bloody scenes. He was pretty good about preparing her for each new procedure and experience, and Kenzie knew they would work their way up through the least disturbing scenes first, until she was gradually prepared for the worse ones.

"Okay. I guess we'll need to go through all of this," Kenzie said, looking at the litter of objects on the floor.

Zachary shrugged. "I doubt there's anything there. Let's check the most likely places first."

So they again started with the bathroom and bedroom. Unlike Redd, Mr. and Mrs. Collins had not bothered to hide their stash. There were small packets of white powder on the nightstand beside the bed.

"I would guess that's not sugar," Kenzie said.

"I would guess not," Zachary agreed.

"I don't have a field test kit. And despite what you see on TV, I'm not going to taste the stuff. We'll just confiscate and let the police sort that out later. I assume it's coke."

"More than likely," Zachary agreed.

Kenzie shook her head. "Why do people have to do things like this? They're newlyweds, they're supposed to be on this wonderful natural high just from being with each other. Why would they feel the need to... add chemical enhancements?"

Raven, standing in the bedroom doorway, tilted her head slightly. "I take it you haven't ever tried it?"

"Well..." Kenzie couldn't help feeling a little embarrassed. But she had never been tempted in college or society life to try a little coke to see what all of the fuss was about. She had never felt the need for it. "No, I haven't."

"If you haven't tried it, then you can't really knock it, can you? What does a coffee drinker say to someone who's never tried it? You drink coffee?"

"Sure. Yes."

"How do you explain to someone how that first cup of coffee in the morning makes you feel? The smell of it percolating? Wrapping your hands around a warm mug and taking your first sip. And the clarity and energy boost that you get when it kicks in? You can describe it all you like, but if it's not an experience they have shared, then they really aren't going to understand it like a fellow coffee drinker does."

"No. I guess not."

"Well... the same with coke or other drugs. If you've never tried it, you can't understand the feeling you get. The way it can enhance other experiences."

Kenzie put the packets into her pocket, considering. "But on the other hand, it could lead to what happened last night. Instead of the high you're looking for, you could react violently to the coke or whatever else it is adulterated with. You could end up having a psychotic break or hurting someone you love." Kenzie looked at the bed, where Andy and Brooke had slept in wedded bliss and to which Brooke would never again return. Two had become one, and not by merging with each other.

"You can't predict," Raven said. "But that's life. You never know what effect your actions are going to have."

"You can have a pretty good idea."

"Maybe. Maybe more for some people than for others. But you could also... get hit by a bus. Be poisoned by someone. Die in a snowstorm." Raven gazed out the window into the blackness outside. "You can make all of the right, sensible choices, and die just like the person who took all of the risks."

She was right, of course, but Kenzie had to believe that most people who lived safely did not die violently, and those who took risks were more likely to lose their lives. It didn't hold true for every person, that was true, but overall.

"Let's see what else we have here," Kenzie sighed. She looked through the pill bottles beside the bed and in the bathroom, trying to identify each one and how dangerous it would be if used as a weapon. "This is really tough," she told Zachary. "I'm so used to being able to look medications up. Remembering what everything is for and what all of the side effects are... I don't have as much of the information stored in my head as I would like to think."

"Just do your best. If you're not sure, assume it's dangerous. A lot of them say stuff like 'keep away from children' or 'contains enough to seriously harm a child.' Or the maximum dose is really low."

"Right," Kenzie agreed.

There was a noise outside, and Kenzie and Zachary both turned toward the window at the same time. Kenzie rolled her eyes at her own reaction, but nonetheless... how could she not be concerned about the possibility of someone lurking outside the cabins? It could be an animal or someone going about their own business. But they had to consider the threat real. Two people were already dead, and one of them by violence.

"There are three of us," Zachary said in a low voice. "That makes us less vulnerable than one person off on their own. We should be fine."

"*Should* be," Kenzie agreed. "But that doesn't mean that we will be."

Raven's words echoed in her head. *You can make all the right, sensible choices, and die just like the person who took all the risks.*

Just because they were trying to keep themselves and everyone else safe, it didn't mean that they would succeed. And someone out there might be ready to take a big risk to prevent Kenzie and Zachary from uncovering his—or her—secret.

Zachary walked closer to the window and looked out at an angle, pressed close to the wall.

"You see anyone?" Kenzie asked.

"No. Might just have been an animal. Or the wind. Everyone should be staying up at the house until their cabins are cleared."

They should be. But Redd had been hanging around outside his waiting for them to finish, and Collins was probably out there now, waiting for them to be done with his cabin. And he had a lot more to lose, if he had killed Brooke. No one else really had a motive to kill her, so unless someone had been so off their head that they thought she was a threat, it didn't make sense that it had been anyone else.

"Is it Collins?"

"I don't know," Zachary asserted, his voice taking on an edge. "Can't see anything clearly through the frost on the window, the dark, the glare of our flashlights, the snow outside... You might as well ask me to use my x-ray vision to see through the solid wall."

"Okay." Kenzie was a little hurt by his sharp retort. He hadn't said all of that the first time; how was she to know?

Zachary let his breath out slowly. "Let's keep going. I want to be out of here. I don't like this cabin."

Was it really any different from any of the others? Kenzie too felt more anxious being there. Maybe it was just because Brooke had lived there and her presence still clung to the place. Her clothing and empty suitcase were a reminder that her life had been cut short very suddenly. And all of the stuff that had been thrown around in the living room made it feel like a war zone. Someplace unsafe.

Their search of the living room was cursory. The kitchen hadn't been used much. There was nothing in the fridge and only a few dirty dishes in the sink. "Okay. Let's get out of here."

40

ollins was waiting for them, but he was waiting farther from the cabin than Redd had. He didn't want to talk to them. So they didn't bother to tell him that they had taken his coke. He would figure that out pretty quickly.

The next closest cabin was Raven's. Kenzie approached it awkwardly. They should probably have gotten someone else to supervise them while searching Raven's cabin. She shouldn't be allowed to be in the cabin while they were searching it, just like the others hadn't been allowed to be in there until they were finished. But there was still an issue if Kenzie and Zachary searched it alone, the accusation that they had planted something.

Raven produced her own key and unlocked the door. She pushed it open and stepped back to let them in first. Kenzie and Zachary entered and looked around. Once they had again shed their outerwear, Zachary reached into his pocket and pulled out his digital recorder. Showing it to them both, he pressed the record button, announced the date and time and who was there, and slid it back into his shirt pocket. There would be one unbiased record, at least.

"Do you want to wait for us outside?" Kenzie asked.

Raven shook her head. "I'm not standing around outside. You're taking at least half an hour to forty-five minutes to check each cabin. I'll be a Popsicle in that time."

"We should stay together then, so that... everyone knows what everyone else is doing."

Raven rolled her eyes. "I trust you."

Kenzie didn't know what to say to that. It wouldn't exactly be friendly to tell Raven that they didn't trust her. But it was the truth.

"I'm going to get the fire going," Raven said. "I know you don't like fires, but it's cold in here and I want to get it warming up."

Kenzie looked at Raven, then at Zachary. Zachary was, Kenzie thought, getting more accustomed to the fact that fires had to be lit while the power was out. He was starting to get desensitized, but that didn't mean he wanted to be in the same room as a fire or would be able to watch her.

"Why don't you get started on the bedroom, then?" Kenzie suggested. "You can see whether there is anything in there, and I'll keep Raven company for a few minutes. Once the fire is going, we'll join you."

Zachary nodded. He swallowed, looked as if he were going to say something, then walked out of the room without another word.

Raven watched him go. "He really does have a problem with fire, doesn't he?"

Kenzie was getting tired of everybody's interest in this fact. They had told everyone that it was a problem. They had said why. Zachary had shown off one of his scars. Wasn't it time for them to all just get over it?

"He was trapped in a house fire when he was ten," Kenzie informed Raven yet again. "He couldn't get out. He was burned. It would be a big deal for you, too."

"I know... but for so long. I mean, there were things that happened to me when I was a kid... but I got over them. You have to go on with life. Spending your whole life being afraid of something like that... it seems like such a waste."

Raven gathered her fire-building materials together, setting lightweight materials over the glowing embers, topped with larger sticks and logs. In a few minutes, she had a roaring fire going. Kenzie looked for another way for Zachary to get out of the house. Whether he went out the front or the back, he was going to have to go past the fireplace. Was that why Raven had built it so large? Just to see how Zachary handled it? To see if she could send him into a panic attack?

"Pull the screen over it and let's go join Zachary," she told Raven.

Raven looked at her for a moment, as if she weren't sure whether she was going to do it or not, then she pulled the screen over the fireplace to keep embers from flying out and got up. She and Kenzie went to the bedroom.

Raven hadn't been kidding when she had said that her cabin was a virtual pharmacy. Zachary gestured to the side table where he had staged everything he had found. There had to be a dozen bottles, a combination of prescription and over-the-counter aids. Kenzie started looking through them. She had half-expected to find heavy-duty prescriptions that would indicate that Raven was under treatment for cancer, an immune disease, or some other big issue that they were trying to suppress or cure with a wide range of experimental treatments.

But they were mostly psychotropic. Meds for depression, anxiety, mood control, sleep, along with a variety of painkillers and stomach ailments. Raven had said that bad things had happened to her as a kid and she had gotten over them. Kenzie suspected that she hadn't actually gotten over anything. She was just medicating heavily enough that they didn't bother her as much anymore. If she stopped treatment, those demons would come galloping back full-force. Kenzie started separating out the drugs that she knew could have hallucinations and mood changes as side effects, which was the majority of them. Raven watched her, eyes shut partway, acting as if she didn't care what Kenzie left and what she took away. If it had been Kenzie, she would definitely have been panicking over someone taking half of her "pharmacy" away. She had promised to dispense whatever the guests needed as they needed it, but Raven was pretty trusting to just take them at their word.

"A lot of these could be a problem," Kenzie said, unnecessarily, she was sure.

Raven shrugged. "So does that mean you think I'm a killer? I'm the poisoner?"

"I didn't say that. I'm just saying that many of these could be a problem if they got mixed in with people's food."

"Accidentally," Raven said sardonically.

"Well... okay, I know it isn't something that happened accidentally. I actually don't know what to say about that."

"I didn't poison anyone."

"Okay."

"You believe me? Just because I said it?"

"It isn't my place to figure out whether you did it or not. Just to prevent anyone else from getting hurt."

"This isn't going to stop anyone from getting hurt."

"What do you mean?"

"I mean... it will just necessitate whoever it is changing their method. If they actually want to kill someone else. Maybe they don't want to. Maybe it was just a joke. But if they actually want to kill someone else in the group... anyone else, some random target... then they'll have to find another method. A different kind of poison. A gun. Knocking them over the head with a fireplace poker and leaving them to freeze to death outside." She smiled sweetly. "I've read Agatha Christie, you know. There are lots of ways to kill someone who gets in between you and what you want."

Kenzie looked at Zachary and didn't say anything. She tried to pick up all the pill bottles, then realized she wouldn't be able to carry them or shove them all into her pockets, even with the large pockets of her outdoor coat.

"Do you have a bag I could put these in?"

Raven went over to her suitcase and pulled out a large zip-top plastic bag. Probably what she had transported the pill bottles in in the first place. Kenzie filled it up with the pill bottles. She looked at Zachary. "Is that it? Anything else?"

"I haven't checked the bathroom yet."

Kenzie sighed. She headed toward the bathroom. "Do you have anything else in there?"

Raven shrugged. "I don't know what else you'll want to take."

Kenzie entered the room and found more pill bottles on the counter around the sink. As well as the pills, she also found eye drops.

"Seriously?" Raven asked. "I have contacts. I can't wear them without my drops."

"You should have artificial tears. This particular kind of eye drops can be very dangerous if taken internally. Squirt a bottle full of these into someone's food, and there would be serious problems."

Raven shrugged. "Why would I waste the stuff in someone's food?"

Kenzie worked in silence, gathering up the rest of the potentially dangerous items and putting them into the bulging bag. "What else have you got around?"

"Booze in the liquor cabinet. Some of it mine, some not. I don't know what else. If there is rat poison in the kitchen, it's not mine."

Kenzie walked down the hall back out to the living room. The fire was crackling away, throwing waves of heat into the room. Kenzie appreciated being nice and toasty, but was still worried about how Zachary would handle it. She stood in front of the fireplace to help screen Zachary from it, and looked back.

He proceeded down the hallway slowly, sweat glistening on his face that wasn't just from the warmth of the fire.

"Anchor," Kenzie suggested. "Five things you see?"

He looked at Raven and clearly didn't want to do the exercise in front of her. He pushed himself onward, the sweat gathering at his temples and dripping down his face. He walked past Kenzie without looking at her or stopping for a kiss as he often did when they passed each other in the hall.

"You're doing good," Kenzie encouraged.

He said nothing, putting on a burst of speed and going into the kitchen, where he started opening and shutting cupboards loudly. Kenzie looked around for the liquor cabinet and started going through it. She wasn't sure why she was bothering. Liquor in abundance could be found at the farmhouse. She didn't think that was what had caused everyone's symptoms. There could be something that was more likely to cause hallucinations. Absinthe was supposed to. But she didn't find any in the cabinet, and she didn't find any other pills or substances wedged in with the bottles. She put them back away and closed the liquor cabinet.

While Zachary continued to check the kitchen, Kenzie looked for any other hiding places in the living room. Behind books or cushions, in the boots at the door. She didn't find anything else unexpected. Raven hadn't expected her cabin to be searched, and she hadn't made any effort to hide any of the many medications that could have been used to poison anyone. Kenzie suspected that if Raven had wanted to kill someone with poison, she would have done it easily. She was certainly the best equipped out of all of the cabins they had searched so far.

Kenzie realized that there was no more noise coming from the kitchen, and looked around the corner to make sure Zachary was okay. His face was still shiny with sweat and, having apparently finished his search, he was frozen, staring off into space. Kenzie went to the door and pulled her coat on, then took Zachary's from its peg. She went into the kitchen and touched his arm.

"Come on. Here's your coat. Get it on and then we can get out of here."

He didn't move, didn't look at her. Kenzie pulled one sleeve on over his hand, and he automatically went through the motions of pulling it on the rest of the way and putting his other hand back to feel for the other sleeve. Kenzie helped him to get it on, then put her hand behind his back and guided him to the door. She put on her boots and indicated Zachary's to him.

"Boots. Let's get your boots on, then we'll go."

He didn't move. His eyes were glazed, far away from the cabin. Stuck in a flashback to the fire, unable to break free from it. Kenzie opened the door, letting in a gust of frigid air. Zachary put his arm up in front of his face to fend it off, blinking and grimacing. He coughed, his intakes of breath between the deep coughs sounding strangled. Kenzie kicked one of the boots over onto his toes.

"Get those on."

Zachary looked down, and with fumbling fingers was able to get them set upright again and put his feet into them. Raven took her coat from the peg beside the door, groaning.

"Just when I get it nice and warm, you have to do that. Come on, everyone out so it can warm up again. I want it to be nice and warm when I get back."

They still had several more cabins and the outbuildings to search. Kenzie's head hurt. She wasn't sure how long they could keep going. They would need rest and sleep. Zachary especially would be wiped out after a flashback. He always was.

41

Zachary was still coughing and wheezing in the cold air outside, nearly doubling over with the wrenching coughs.

"Are you okay?" Kenzie asked, bending over and trying to get close enough to see and hear if he responded to her. "Do you need an inhaler? What's going on?"

As far as she knew, he didn't have asthma and didn't use an inhaler, but sometimes people hid things from each other. Especially things that made them look weak. Kenzie already knew many of Zachary's weaknesses and perhaps he had tried to keep at least one thing a secret.

Zachary shook his head. "The smoke," he croaked, dragging the cold outside air into his lungs in loud wheezes.

"There's no smoke. It's okay. Try to slow down. Look around. You're not there. You're safe. There is no smoke."

Though, of course, the tang of woodsmoke filled the air as everyone used their fireplaces to keep their cabins warm. But it wasn't enough to impede Zachary's breathing. She knew he was still caught in the past, a ten-year-old rescued from a burning house. She knew about the burns he had suffered. And the most dangerous thing about a house fire was not the burns, but smoke inhalation. Tyrrell had said that he and the other kids had suffered from smoke inhalation, and they had been away from the fire, behind closed doors. Zachary had been right in the middle of it. When they had pulled him out of the house, they would have put an oxygen mask over his face to help him breathe.

With one arm around his shoulders to keep him in place, Kenzie brought Zachary's scarf up to his mouth and nose to help to warm the air that he was pulling in. He would end up with inflamed and congested lungs if he kept breathing the frigid air so deeply. With the scarf over his mouth and nose, she cupped her hand loosely around them, imitating the shape of an oxygen mask.

"You're safe. You feel that? You can breathe. Nice warm, filtered air. Slow down and feel it. Just try to breathe normally. You're safe. You're out of the house. Just take a few minutes to breathe."

Raven was stomping her feet, impatient for them to go into the next cabin. But Kenzie didn't feel bad for making her wait. It was Raven's own fault that Zachary was dealing with a flashback. She had, Kenzie was sure, fully intended to trigger Zachary's anxiety with the fire. She wanted to know just how far it would tip him over the edge. So Raven was going to have to wait until he was ready to go on, and she could get nice and chilly while she waited.

Zachary's breathing started to slow down, the coughs and choked gasps smoothing out. Kenzie kept her hand over the scarf to keep it in place. He needed the warm air, not air that was so cold it would freeze the moist lining of his lungs. His body started to relax under her other arm, shoulders releasing, neck and back straightening a little as he looked around, locating himself in space, getting reoriented.

"Where...?"

"We're just outside Raven's cabin. We're finished with hers."

"And we should get on to Jack's," Raven encouraged, arms wrapped around herself, stamping her feet to keep the circulation going.

Zachary looked around, studying Raven's face for a moment, then looking around slowly to cement all the landmarks in his mind. Pulling himself out of the past and remembering where he was and what he was supposed to be doing. He took long, slow breaths. He touched Kenzie's hand over his mouth, then gently nudged it away, continuing to breathe slowly and evenly. He held the scarf against his mouth and nose himself.

"Okay. I'm okay."

"Are you ready to go on?"

Zachary looked at Jack's cabin, then turned and looked longingly back at their own cabin. "I need... a break."

"If we take time out now, this is going to take all night. I'm not sure how we're going to get done as it is." Kenzie rubbed her head, pounding from lack of sleep.

"Maybe it's too much, tonight."

"But we need to check the cabins before people can go home and go to bed. To make sure that everyone is safe. If we don't, whoever did this can just go back to their cabins and hide the poison and we'll never find it."

"I need a break," Zachary insisted. "You... keep going. I'll send Tyrrell, he can help for a while."

Kenzie didn't like it. She wanted to work with Zachary. He was the trained investigator. He was the one who had cultivated his ability to observe and remember tiny details. To know in his gut when something was wrong, and be able to look until he found it. Tyrrell... he would be an extra witness and a deterrent from any attack, but that was all. He didn't have the same skills.

But people had limits, and apparently Zachary had reached his. She knew he would push through if he could. He often pushed himself too far, so if he was saying that he was done, she needed to listen. She didn't want him curled up in a ball on his bed for the rest of the time they were at the Lodge.

"Okay, send Tyrrell over." She tried to keep the frustration out of her voice. "I'm going to get started."

Zachary opened his mouth to argue about her starting on her own, then closed it. He turned away from her and went back to their cabin.

Kenzie motioned toward Jack's cabin. "Let's go," she told Raven.

She managed to find the key before her fingers froze, and opened the door.

Kenzie wasn't sure what she had been expecting from Jack Fowler. He had given her the creeps since the first day. She supposed she had expected to see squalor, maybe a shrine or a pinboard with lengths of red yarn connecting various newspaper articles, like they always had on TV when the police finally got to the serial killer's private lair.

But there was no sign that he had been plotting the murder of anyone in the group at the Lodge. No pictures or newspaper articles pinned up, taped to the wall, or hanging from the ceiling. Kenzie had thought maybe he would have a bunch of candid shots of Brittany showing that he had stalked her there.

The living room was neat and cozy. There was a paperback book lying on the couch. Not some serial killer horror book, but a thick tome by a Russian author. One of those ones that Kenzie always thought she should get around to reading one day, but didn't have the inclination to actually begin.

There was no clutter. No beer cans on the floor. No duffel bag of suspicious objects.

Kenzie walked through to the bedroom, and again looked around in something akin to wonder. Jack was not just a neat man. The room was obsessively neat. At first glance, the room was empty. Like an unoccupied hotel room. No personal effects, no suitcase out or clothes draped over a chair as she had seen in the other cabins. Nothing on the night table. No vacation sloth.

Kenzie checked the closet, wondering if Jack were even staying in that cabin at all. Maybe she had walked into a vacant cabin. Or he was registered there but was staying with one of the other guests. Maybe Raven herself. Or Samantha, the maid. Or even Vance Stiller—Kenzie couldn't make assumptions.

There was an empty suitcase in the closet, and a few items of clothing neatly hung from the rod. The suitcase was entirely empty. Jack wasn't living out of it. He hadn't taken out just the items he needed right away and left the rest stowed there for when he would need them another day. It was spotless, as if she were looking at it in a luggage store. Kenzie went through the pockets of the clothing that was hung in the closet, but she already knew they would be empty. He would empty everything out of his suitcase and then leave something in his pockets when he hung his clothes up? Not likely. The creases in the clothing were crisp. Not like they had been mashed into a suitcase, but as if he had taken the time to iron them before hanging them up.

"This guy is something else," Raven murmured.

Kenzie nodded. "I've never seen anything like it."

She went to the dresser and opened the drawers. They slid smoothly out and, as she had expected, his underwear and other non-hangable clothes were neatly folded and stacked. In the top drawer were a few other sundries, all laid out in the sections of a collapsible organizer tray.

No medications. Those would be in the nightstand or the bathroom. She closed the drawers, making sure they were all pushed in all the way, the fronts perfectly flush. She didn't want Jack to feel like she had tossed the place. Everything that he had taken such care to put in its place should be left just as she had found it.

She opened the drawer of the nightstand. It was empty. Kenzie looked at it for a minute, frowning. She had expected pill bottles, probably something to help Jack to calm his obsessive brain in order to be able to sleep at night. Or at least a bottle of Tylenol. Maybe reading glasses, chargers for his watch and phone, a few other things that he would want close to his bed. Earplugs and an eye mask to shut out world.

She closed the drawer, again making sure that it was shut tightly.

"Nothing?" Raven asked.

"No. Nothing." Kenzie went on to the bathroom. There was a small toiletries kit on the counter. Kenzie opened it to find Jack's brush, comb, razor, and toothbrush, along with anything else he needed to get himself ready for the day. But again, no medications. Not so much as an aspirin, vitamin, or sleeping pill. Kenzie looked at the bottles of shampoo, conditioner, and soap. They all appeared to be exactly what they were labeled. "I've never seen someone as neat as this."

Raven shook her head. "The sign of a sick mind for sure," she joked. "Why would someone like this even come out here? I mean... nature is messy. And having someone else do all of the cooking for you, the cleaning being done in a substandard way... You would think someone like this would want to stay in his own house and never leave it."

Kenzie nodded her agreement. "Yeah. And I would never have guessed that's the kind of person he is. He seems very... casual. Undisciplined. I never would have thought it was just a mask."

Thinking about Raven's comment about the cleaning, Kenzie checked under the bathroom sink for cleaning products and found some travel-size bottles of bleach and cleansers. She went out to the kitchen and found the same.

"Are you going to take those?" Raven asked.

Kenzie shook her head. "I don't think it was anything like this. They might be toxic, but this isn't what was put in the food. Besides, you would know. You would taste it. It would smell strongly. And it would burn."

"So you're not going to take it? Even though it could be poisonous?"

"No. You don't think you would smell this if he put it in your food?"

Kenzie held one of the bottles, still screwed shut, under Raven's nose. Raven reared back, nostrils flaring. She shook her head.

"No. I guess not."

Kenzie did one more sweep of the cabin and didn't find anything else worthy of note. She and Raven got their coats back on again and stepped out of the cabin.

42

Tyrrell was coming the opposite direction and nearly collided with Kenzie.

"Oh! Sorry, Kenzie." He looked over her shoulder. "Are you already finished?"

"Not much to see in this one. We can go to the next cabin, which I guess is... Brittany's."

They were all quiet as Kenzie sorted through the keys to find the one for Brittany's cabin. Kenzie wondered what it would be like. She had been totally wrong about Jack. Maybe she had misjudged Brittany as well. She hadn't taken much in when she had gone there looking for Vance Stiller. She had only stood inside the door and hadn't been able to see the rest of the cabin. She didn't remember it being untidy, like the Collins's cabin, or extra neat, like Jack's. Somewhere in between. Like she would expect from someone on vacation.

She managed to find the right key and twisted it in the lock. They went inside and took off their boots and other winter gear. Kenzie looked around, assessing the cabin. It was a larger one, like the one she had rented. More than just a single bedroom. And that meant it was going to take longer to search.

She wasn't lingering and doing a detailed search anymore. There was too much to be done. Her stomach felt tight and heavy at the idea of having to search the barn and outbuildings too. How could she be expected to do that on her own, at night, in the freezing cold, when she was already bone tired?

For the time being, she had to focus on the guest cabins. Even the residences of the staff would probably have to wait until the next day. It would be easier when it was light out and she'd had a few hours of sleep.

It wasn't likely to be the staff anyway, was it? If they'd had murderous feelings toward guests, they wouldn't have lasted there as long as they had. They would have been fired for having a bad attitude or would have already poisoned someone and been arrested. The Lodge couldn't have a history of poisonings, or it would never have lasted.

Kenzie started with the bedrooms, as before. The first room was not being used as a bedroom. The furniture had all been pushed to one end of the room, with the mattress leaning up against the wall, to make room for a small seating area surrounded by lights and camera equipment. A recording studio for Brittany's vlog. Kenzie took a quick look around, but there were no pills, food, or chemicals there. Just expensive-looking electronic equipment.

They went to the next bedroom. Half of it had been set up with an exercise mat and various elastic bands and other lightweight exercise equipment. Brittany's computer equipment had been set up at a writing desk on the other side of the room. Kenzie couldn't identify all of the electrical components. It was a more sophisticated system than she would have been able to deal with. Brittany was clearly experienced in taking her show on the road and setting things up in a way that allowed her to work efficiently and maintain her lifestyle.

The last bedroom was Brittany's sleeping room. Her clothes were unpacked, the nightstand full of miscellany, and the bed hadn't been made. Kenzie went to the nightstand and looked through the pill bottles there. Nothing but Tylenol and an herbal sleep aid. Nothing in the drawers. Nothing illegal.

"You can take another look through here," she told Tyrrell. "Just make sure I haven't missed anything."

"Okay." Tyrrell looked a little lost, but he nodded and looked around.

Kenzie stepped into the bathroom, where there appeared to have been an explosion of cosmetics, jewelry, and other feminine detritus. Kenzie smiled and started looking through it for pill bottles. She fished a few out from the mess and pocketed only one of them. The cabin was a fascinating behind-the-scenes insight into the celebrity. Kenzie didn't know a lot about Brittany, but the general perception of such successes was often that they were totally lazy and had hit it big for doing nothing. It was pretty obvious from Brittany's set-up that she was a professional who worked hard to achieve the success that she had. Still setting her alarm to get up early and record a session, even while she was supposed to be on vacation.

Kenzie looked around for anything else she might have missed, then went on to do a cursory review of the living room and kitchen.

Brittany had a number of prepackaged snack foods in her kitchen. Unlike the others, she was not completely reliant on the meals up at the farmhouse. They were mainly portioned diet foods. Like Brittany's exercise mat, they were a testament to the fact that she had to work at maintaining her image. She had to watch what she ate and make sure that she exercised if she were to keep her audience. The Bambas wouldn't be very forgiving if she ballooned up three sizes.

Tyrrell joined Kenzie. Raven was standing at the door, not even putting on a show of supervising Kenzie. After having watched Kenzie search all of the other cabins, Raven had probably concluded that she was not out to frame anyone by planting drugs. Like Kenzie, she probably really wanted to get back to her own cabin and get to sleep. It wasn't as though she had volunteered for the job in the first place. She had been nominated by all the others.

"Nothing?" Raven asked.

Kenzie held up the one pill bottle she had taken. "Just this. Pretty clean." She cocked her head at Raven. "I thought you would be really interested in seeing how a famous vlogger like Brittany lived. Not your thing?"

Raven rolled her eyes and shook her head. "No. Why would it be? I get that she has a big audience, but I'm not one of her fans. I have better things to do with my life than just to watch some inane monologue about how Brittany the Bombshell lives her life every day."

"I've never met someone like her before."

"How do you know? She's not that different from anyone else."

"Well, I mean... I've met people who were wealthy or famous before. But not that much of an icon. Or doing whatever it is she does." Kenzie motioned to the room full of recording equipment. "I just thought it was interesting."

"Not very."

Kenzie nodded. "Okay." She turned to Tyrrell. "Anything?"

"No, I didn't see anything else. I'm not exactly sure what I'm looking for. You already saw the pill bottles beside the bed, right?"

"Yes. Nothing I'm concerned about there."

"I wasn't sure about the herbs." He shrugged. "You can never tell what the side effects might be. Or even if it's the same thing in the capsules as it says on the bottle. I saw this one study where they tested a bunch of herbal supplements, and a lot of them were just grass clippings."

Raven snorted. "Wouldn't that serve them right?"

"Serve who right for what?" Kenzie asked curiously. "Someone who is trying an herbal remedy for their health isn't that different from someone who is taking a medication. Sometimes they work. A lot of the medications we use now originally started as folk remedies. Scientists distilled down the active ingredients, and..."

"People who take all of that homeopathic junk are always so virtuous about it. Like they don't take drugs, because that would be wrong or it would mean there was something wrong with them. But if they can cure their problems with herbs, that's different, that's just living in harmony with nature or some stupid thing. I hate people who get all high and mighty and say you should be able to solve any illness without medications."

Kenzie nodded, understanding. "Yeah, I see what you mean. I wouldn't want to put up with that either. If you need a medication, there's nothing wrong with that."

"That's right. And people who think that everyone should just 'go natural' or whatever they want to call it, they should think again. They should have to go through everything that the person they're criticizing goes through. Seriously. Maybe then they would stop being so superior."

"Sorry that you went through that."

Raven looked at Kenzie for a minute, then nodded. "Yeah. Fine."

Kenzie didn't know what Raven had been through, but from the looks of the pharmacy that had been in her room, life hadn't been very easy for her. Kenzie looked at Tyrrell.

"How was Zachary?"

"You probably know that better than I do. All I know is how he looked when he got back, and that he said he was done. He needed a break, but he wanted me to keep an eye on things in case you needed a hand. Make sure that nothing happened to you." Tyrrell spread his hands apart. "I'm not exactly a fighter. I don't carry and I'm no karate expert. So if push comes to shove..." He grinned, his cheeks getting a little pinker. "Well, pushing and shoving I can manage. But if it's something serious... I'm not much of an asset."

"I think it's just the safety in numbers that he's concerned about," Kenzie said. "Three of us, one of whoever else might be out there. It isn't like anything is going to happen. Everyone is supposed to stay up at the farmhouse until we finish with their cabins."

Kenzie finished getting on her winter gear and opened the door. Brittany was stamping her feet in the snow, waiting for them.

"You're getting faster," she commented.

"We're tired," Kenzie admitted. "And most of these cabins are the same design, so we already know where everything is going to be."

She didn't tell Brittany that they were not checking electrical outlets or light switches for hidden contraband. If they were that thorough with every house, they would never get to bed.

"Well, glad you're done." Brittany covered a yawn. "That means that I can get to bed."

"Have a good sleep."

"Oh, I plan to. I'll be up bright and early tomorrow."

"Are you going to shut off your alarm tonight, or still get up at the usual time?"

"Well, I'll probably still get up the same time as usual. I like to be able to get my routine done early, even if I can't upload everything right now. I just feel better if I can get my workout and video and everything else done."

"Have a good sleep. I guess we'll see you sometime tomorrow."

Brittany raised her face to look up into the dark sky. There were no stars out overhead. Thick clouds still covered the area, blocking out any light from the moon and the stars. Snowflakes still drifted down in thick flakes, gathering on the trees and drifting around the ground. "When will it finish, do you think? Tomorrow?"

"I don't see any sign of it clearing yet. I don't know. I hope it's soon, so that we can get some reception and hand this investigation off to the police."

"Not much of a vacation for you either, is it?"

"I guess not. But I did plan for it to be. I fully intended to have a nice relaxing holiday."

Brittany laughed and entered her cabin. "See you tomorrow."

She shut the door and Kenzie heard her slide the bolt to secure it.

Funny, Brittany had said that she had medical training, but she hadn't shown any curiosity about what Kenzie might have found so far. Had that just been a line? If she did have medical training, what area was it in? Was she laughing at Kenzie's attempts to sort out what had happened at the Lodge? Or was she just as confused about the situation as everyone else?

•

43

───────

Vance."

Kenzie looked at the next cabin. She had already seen inside once, but like with Brittany's cabin, only from the front door. She didn't know what kind of a person he was behind closed doors. What secrets or indulgences he might have. She had not found anything in any of the other cabins that pointed the finger at one particular suspect. Several people had substances or medications that could have caused hallucinations, if used in fairly large amounts, but Kenzie didn't know how they tasted or how much would have been needed to cause the effects that they had seen.

And had the perp intended to get the results that he or she had? Was it just about making people hallucinate and lose control? To make them forget what they had done? Or was it intended to hurt someone? To cause an overdose death? As much as she kept telling everyone that Mr. Dewey's death was just a natural death and was completely unrelated, she couldn't help but wonder. Had he been given the same drug, and it had caused a fatal heart attack? Or had he been given something else? Was he the test case and the poisoner had been disappointed that everyone else hadn't died?

If everyone was supposed to die, then who was the poisoner? Was it Mrs. Hubbard, who no longer had a job or cared what happened to her? Was it attempted murder or murder-suicide? Could it had been Burknall? Maybe he wanted to steal valuables from the wealthy guests and disappear into the wilderness, never to be heard of again.

Kenzie found the key for Vance Stiller's cabin. She pushed the door open and took a deep breath, steeling herself for one more search. Just one more, and she could be done for the night. She couldn't go on and do the searches of the staff's quarters. That would have to wait until the next day. If one of them were the poisoner, then it would give them a chance to get rid of the poison. Kenzie admitted that. But the point was to keep everyone safe.

If the poisoner got rid of the poison, then they didn't have to worry about being dosed again. And they could all eat canned foods again the next day if there were any concerns. Everyone could keep eating canned food that they themselves had opened until the police got there and everyone else could get out and go home. Maybe the poisoner would never be found, but she was so tired, she just didn't care. She wanted to finish with the search and go to bed. Whose idea had it been to search everyone's cabins, anyway? She didn't feel like they were any further ahead than they had started.

Vance's cabin looked the same as it had when they had seen it earlier. Other than the fact that it was dark. Kenzie played her light around the interior, and headed for the bedroom, as they had with every other cabin.

And like with Jack's cabin, she couldn't help being a little surprised that the bedroom looked as ordinary as any other bedroom in a cabin or hotel. Nothing to indicate the dark workings of Vance's mind. Nothing to indicate that he was a selfish jerk who didn't care about anyone else. No way to tell whether he was a psychopath and a poisoner, taking this vacation just to give him an opportunity to kill his girlfriend, or one of the other guests, or everybody there.

He probably was a psychopath. A lot of people like him were. Wealthy, famous, ready to push everyone out of his way in his climb to the top. That was how some people succeeded; they didn't have the moral compunctions that others did. Some people were worried about how everyone else would feel, about who they stepped on on their way to the top. A psychopath didn't have all of those things to worry about. They had a goal, and as long as they reached the brass ring, it was all good.

There was nothing in Vance's room that suggested he was out to poison or hurt anyone. His computer sat on the bed, where he had probably reviewed his emails when he was finally awake enough to focus on them. Kenzie wondered if he were feeling back to one hundred percent, or whether he were still under the weather. He hadn't said one way or the other. There was a safe in the bedroom closet. One that took a key, not a combination. It was hefty, but small enough for one person to carry. Kenzie wondered whether she should ask Stiller to open it for her. She suspected the results of such a query would not be favorable.

There was a glass on the nightstand. Water or alcohol? Kenzie picked it up and sniffed it. She couldn't detect anything. Probably water. She opened the nightstand drawer and found several pill bottles. She picked up the prescription bottles first. Diabetes, blood pressure, a statin. Vance was not in particularly good shape. He was still a relatively young man, but his lifestyle was catching up to him already. Too many rich foods, too much stress, not enough exercise. She picked up the non-prescription bottles. A painkiller. A sleep aid. Vitamins. An herbal remedy for men's health issues.

Kenzie made a quick search through the rest of the room, the dresser, the closet, the writing desk. She looked through the books on the shelves but couldn't see anything that appeared to have been touched recently. Everything was lined up flush and there was a light sprinkling of dust along the front of the shelf in front of the books. Kenzie checked the next room down the hall. Like Kenzie and Brittany, he had rented a multi-bedroom cabin. But there wasn't anything in the next bedroom. No sign that anyone had used it, or that Stiller himself had used it for any other purpose as Brittany had. Everything was still and untouched. Maybe he had expected someone to join him later. Or maybe he'd just wanted to rent the most expensive cottage there so that he wouldn't be shown up by Brittany or anyone else. Kenzie checked the other rooms and ended up in the bathroom, which was quite a bit larger than the one in Kenzie's cabin, with both a shower and a hot tub, his and hers sinks, and a sauna. Not bad for a little cabin in the woods.

She looked through Stiller's toiletries bag, which was not organized as neatly as Jack's had been. Kenzie pricked her finger on something and pulled her hand out quickly, sucking on the tip of her finger. She looked back into the bag and carefully moved the contents around to see what she had poked herself on.

There was a razor blade in the case. Not in a protective plastic case or even a folded paper. Just loose, a straight edge, bound to cut someone who put her fingers into the bag unaware. Kenzie carefully pincered it out, grasping the back instead of the sharpened side, and put it onto the edge of the counter. Had he used it for something and then forgotten it was there? Kenzie bent down and studied the rusty edge, glad she was up to date on her tetanus shots.

"What's up?" Tyrrell asked, poking his head into the room. He had finished with his search of the living room and kitchen.

"This," Kenzie said, pointing to the edge of the blade. "I don't think it's rust."

44

Tyrrell frowned and leaned forward, getting his eyes close to the razor blade and staring at it steadily. "Well, it could be... but I don't think it is. It looks more like blood." He switched his attention to Kenzie, her finger in her mouth again. "Did you cut yourself on it?"

"Well... poked myself. Nothing serious."

"But if this is blood, it isn't yours. It isn't fresh."

Kenzie nodded slowly. "No, it's not," she agreed.

They both stared at it. Raven was in the hallway, and she too came to see what they were looking at. She didn't need to look as closely as Kenzie and Tyrrell to see it for what it was. She drew her breath in sharply.

"Is that...?" She shook her head, eyes wide. "That's not the murder weapon, is it?" She continued to shake her head. "He couldn't have killed Mrs. Collins with that."

"No. It's not consistent with the blade that killed Mrs. Collins. This is not the murder weapon. But it is... somewhat concerning."

"Especially since you just cut your finger on it," Tyrrell pointed out. As if Kenzie wasn't already thinking that. "Can you get AIDS from dried blood? Or does it have to be fresh?"

Kenzie stared down at the little rectangular blade. It looked so harmless, and yet wickedly sharp. "I don't think that a virus could survive like that for long. I'm pretty sure it has to be fresh blood or bodily fluids. I don't think it's anything to worry about."

"Then what...?" Raven asked. "He cut himself shaving? Why isn't the blade actually in a razor?"

That was a very good question. Kenzie thought about Mr. Vance Stiller, revising her opinions of him. A psychopath? Someone who didn't feel anything? No. She thought not. If she were right about Stiller, then despite his mask of apparent indifference, he actually felt things very keenly.

"I don't think he cut himself shaving," Kenzie said. "But I think he cut himself."

Raven frowned. She looked at Kenzie and shook her head. "Men don't do that."

"Men can cut too. It's not solely limited to teenage girls."

"No," Tyrrell said, "I've known of a couple of guys who cut. Usually in the name of body modification, but you still know... you just know with some of them, exactly what's going on."

"Why would Vance Stiller cut?" Raven asked. "That doesn't make any sense. The man has more money than he has a right to. He can buy anything he wants. Do anything he wants. So why would he cut? What reason would he have to do that?"

"It isn't about having money. It's about pain. And feeling." Kenzie shook her head slightly. She had misjudged Stiller too. She would never have guessed that he was troubled by anything. But how likely was it that the man would have gotten through life without the same trials as anyone else? Maybe more. Maybe he pushed so hard because of what had happened to him in the past. Or maybe a privileged upbringing had actually put him in harm's way, raised by nannies or other servants, not by parents who kept a close eye on his well-being. Whatever had happened, the man she had thought was just a jerk, rude because he figured having more money than anyone else gave him the right to be rude, was not as indifferent as she had believed.

She remembered the way that he had looked at Brittany, wondering whether there was any possibility she had been the one to roofie him. Wondering whether she had taken advantage of him, drugging him to get whatever it was she wanted. It was just for a few seconds, a moment in time, but for a moment he had been naked, his emotions visible for everyone to see.

Kenzie looked down at the razor blade. What to do with it? Put it back in his bag and pretend they hadn't seen it? Throw it out or take it with her so that he couldn't use it to cut himself more after she had gone? She didn't want him getting an infection from using a dirty blade. He might have more razor blades around, but at least he would have to open a fresh one and maybe not poison his system with whatever bacteria clung to the old one just thrown carelessly in his toiletries bag.

She eventually decided that she couldn't leave it there. Maybe he would think he had just lost it. Maybe he would guess that she had taken it. But she couldn't leave it as if she hadn't seen it. She was a doctor, and it was her job to try to protect people from further harm. Maybe she would take him aside quietly and give him some resources for those who self-harmed. Maybe no one had ever reached out to him that way before and he didn't know where to go.

"Can you grab me a piece of paper or cardboard?" Kenzie asked Tyrrell. "Maybe in the writing desk?"

"I doubt he writes anything longhand."

"No, but the writing desk is stocked by the Lodge, so there should be some kind of writing paper in there. It doesn't matter what it is. I just don't want to put this in my pocket without wrapping it first."

"You're taking it with you?" Raven demanded.

"I think I have to. I don't want him getting an infection."

Raven rolled her eyes and shook her head. "He probably uses a lighter to sterilize it."

"Maybe. But I can't assume he's following any safety measures. So... I'm taking it with me."

Tyrrell went back to the bedroom to see if he could find a piece of paper for Kenzie. He returned a minute later with a sturdy sheet of writing paper. Kenzie folded the blade up in it before putting it in her pocket.

"Okay. What did you find in the kitchen and living room? Anything I need to see?"

Tyrrell shook his head. "No. Not really. Alcohol, but Raven said you don't care about that. Some notebooks and stuff. No more pill bottles." He shrugged. "No bloody knives."

Kenzie shuddered. She was glad that she hadn't found any bloody knives in any of the cabins. Coming across the blood-encrusted razor was bad enough, even though she had known immediately that it could not have been the blade that had killed Brooke Collins.

"Okay. Let's call it a night. I really can't do any more tonight."

Tyrrell nodded. They donned their winter gear and Kenzie let out a deep sigh. "That took a lot more out of me than I expected it to. We should have started in the early afternoon. I never even thought... how dark it would be after dinner. That's not the time to start a search like this."

They left the cabin, heading back toward their own. Kenzie saw Stiller walking down a pathway created by a truck or piece of machinery that had been driven down the farm road. She raised a hand to wave at him, but he didn't wave back. Like she, he was probably tired. And he probably didn't want to talk to anyone else. Especially someone who had just gone through all of his personal stuff. He needed distance.

Kenzie expected Raven to turn off to her cabin, but she didn't. She kept walking with Kenzie and Tyrrell to their cabin door. Kenzie raised her brows. "You don't need to come all the way with us. You must be tired too."

"There's still one more cabin to be searched."

Kenzie looked at her blankly for a minute before realizing that Raven meant theirs. "Oh... yeah, I guess so. Do you want to get someone else to search it with you...?" Kenzie was awkward. Of course, the others would want to be sure that they were not the ones who had poisoned the meal. On one hand, they shouldn't be suspects because they hadn't been up to the house and hadn't taken part in the meal. But on the other hand—they hadn't partaken. They had not been affected like everyone else had. Maybe because one of them had been the perpetrator. Maybe Raven would want to have Brittany with her.

"I don't need anyone else. I can do it myself," she asserted.

Kenzie let everyone in. She was happy to be taking her coat and gear off for the final time. Putting it on and taking it off half a dozen times left her feeling sweaty and clammy. She was too warm as soon as she put it on, and as soon as her sweaty skin was exposed to the cool air of the room or outside, she was immediately shivery and uncomfortable.

She hung her coat and took Tyrrell's gear from him to hang up as well. Zachary had left his coat flung to the side even though the pegs were right there within reach. Kenzie picked it up and hung it on an empty peg.

She felt like she had been away from home all day. It had only been since supper, but that felt like a long, long time ago. And by the looks of the living room, the children had been bored. The game boxes had been pushed to the side, but there were still cards and game pieces and spinners left here and there. Like maybe they had been making up a game of their own, bored with playing the same games over and over again. The room was a little cool. Warmer than the cabins that had been left with their fires burned down to embers. Cooler than Raven's cabin with its blazing fire.

Kenzie still couldn't believe that she had lit such a large fire with Zachary in the cabin, knowing how it would affect him. She must have realized how much it would bother him, if he couldn't even stand to have a candle burning at the table when he ate. For someone who appeared to have as many mental health issues as she did, Raven was pretty ruthless.

45

I 'm going to check on Zachary."

Raven looked at her, frowning. "You should stay out here while I do the search."

Kenzie was irritated by the suggestion, but knew that Raven was right. They had told the others that they needed to stay out of their cabins until the searches were complete. She wouldn't have wanted one of them hovering over her while she completed the search, or to worry about them going into another room and hiding or taking something before Kenzie had had a chance to find it. It had been awkward to search Raven's cabin while she was there.

"Come in with me," she told Raven. "Then you'll know I didn't touch anything. After I make sure Zachary is okay, I'll wait in the hallway so I'm out of your way. We've got Tyrrell's kids, too. It's not the easiest, having to search around everyone here."

"There are too many of you," Raven agreed. "I'd rather you were out here. Both of you."

Kenzie looked around. Maybe Raven figured that if they had anything toxic, they wouldn't have left it out where the kids were playing. Or around the food in the kitchen. Logically, the least likely place for a poison to be stored was out in the front rooms of the cabin where everyone congregated and where people might see it if they came to the door. In all of the cabins they'd searched, medications and possible poisons had been in the bedroom and bathroom.

"Okay," she agreed. "Tyrrell and I will stay out here. But can I please check on Zachary first? If he's up to it, he can come out here too, where he won't be in your way while you are searching."

Raven rolled her eyes. "Fine. Go ahead."

Kenzie walked back to their bedroom. Raven followed her and stood in the doorway to keep an eye on her. While Kenzie chafed at the idea that she or Zachary would do anything to hurt any of the other guests—they didn't even have any motive—she knew that she needed to be okay with Raven doing what she had to in order to protect herself and the other guests. Zachary and Kenzie had to be watched like anyone else. Their cabin had to be searched like any other cabin.

Kenzie tried to block out the distraction of Raven being there and to act just like she would if she and Zachary were alone. Zachary was curled up in a lump under the blankets of the bed, pulled up right over his head. Kenzie sat on the edge of the bed in the dark room and tugged the top blanket back to expose his face. She didn't turn on her flashlight, not wanting to shine it in Zachary's eyes, but that meant that all she could see was his shape by the slight glow of the window.

"Zachary. Hey, how are you doing?"

"Not yet," he mumbled. "Just need a break."

"I don't need you to search any more cabins. We're done for the night. I just want to know how you're doing."

He groaned and didn't answer.

"Can you come out to the living room so that Raven can search this room?"

"No."

"Come on. It's warm there, and you can visit with me and Tyrrell. It will only be a few minutes, and then you can go back to bed if you want."

"Don't want to get up."

"I know. But it will only be for a few minutes. You don't want to be in here while she's searching, and she wants us out of the way."

And it would give her a better opportunity to evaluate Zachary and whether she needed to be concerned about his mental state.

"Don't want to." Zachary attempted to drag the blanket up over his head again. Kenzie pulled the blankets away from his body instead. He would be more likely to get out of the bed if she made him uncomfortable. If he couldn't snuggle under the blankets there, and it was warmer near the heater in the living room, he would be more likely to go with her without her having to insist or drag him by force.

"Bridget..." Zachary protested.

Kenzie's breath caught in her throat. *Bridget?* After the length of time he had been separated from Bridget, it should not have been her name that had come to his lips. Kenzie pulled the blankets back harder, frustrated and angry.

"Not Bridget," she told him tightly. "Kenzie. And you are getting out of bed and coming with me. So quit being such a—" She caught herself before she could say something really damaging. As much as she wanted to retaliate for the hurt he had caused her, she didn't want to *be* Bridget. She hated the way that Bridget treated Zachary, for the anger and disdain that she had for the man she had once been married to and had claimed to love.

Kenzie could be kind and understanding of Zachary's limitations and challenges no matter how frustrating they were. She had not entered into the relationship with the intent to change or cure him. She had known how difficult his behavior could be and had vowed not to turn into Bridget.

"Come on," Kenzie told Zachary, her voice neutral. "We need you to come to the living room." She swiveled his legs around to the edge of the bed and pushed his feet to the floor, bringing him up into a sitting position. Zachary was still fully dressed. He held his fingers against his temples, moaning. "I know you just want to go back to sleep, and you can soon. Just come out and let Tyrrell know that you're okay. It won't take long for Raven to search the room."

She put her hand under his arm and behind his back to encourage him to get up. He rose unsteadily to his feet and she stabilized him. He didn't lean his full weight on her, but shuffled and was wobbly as she walked him out of the bedroom, past Raven, and down the hall to where Tyrrell waited. A blanket had been left on the couch, so Kenzie encouraged Zachary to sit down, then pulled the blanket over him. He hunched over, holding it against his face but not pulling it over his head.

"Hey, bro. How are you doing?" Tyrrell asked.

"Fine." Of course he wasn't fine, and if he had told Kenzie that, she would have reminded him that "fine" was not an acceptable answer when she really wanted feedback on how he was doing.

"You need anything? I could get you a drink—of water—or if you need one of your pills...?" Tyrrell suggested.

Kenzie didn't like to ask Zachary. It was better if he decided what he needed and asked her for it.

"No." Zachary rubbed his eyes. "Sorry... just... tired." He directed it at Kenzie rather than Tyrrell. An apology for resisting getting out of bed or for calling her Bridget?

How many times had Bridget berated him and forced him to get out of his protective shell to go to a party or event with her? How many times had she told him that his feelings didn't matter, only his attendance at her side?

"I wouldn't normally force you to get up," she explained, "These are special circumstances."

"I know."

Kenzie thought that rubbing Zachary's back might be a good idea and help him relax, but he was sitting just a little bit apart from her and might not want to be touched. "I don't think she'll take too long."

Zachary leaned with his elbows on his knees and his hands covering his eyes, as Kenzie might if she had a migraine. Kenzie listened for Raven's movements. She didn't know how thorough Raven would be, since this was the only cabin she was searching. She would want to be thorough enough that she could tell the others she was sure Kenzie and Zachary weren't hiding anything. The time ticked past slowly. Kenzie was glad for the gentle heat of the propane heater. Grateful to Burknall for making sure they had a way to stay warm without having to light a fire. Despite Dr. B's statement that exposure was the best way for Zachary to desensitize himself from his anxieties, Kenzie wouldn't have wanted to try several days with him in a cabin with a fire blazing in the fireplace. That might be a bit much, if his reaction to Raven's fire was any indication.

Eventually, Raven came out of the bedroom. She had her hands full with both prescription pill bottles and over-the-counter and herbal remedies. She shook her head. "He's got as many as I do."

"Yeah." Kenzie shrugged. "But there aren't very many pills there. Not enough to poison a group of people."

"Not now. I don't know how many he started out with. And maybe if a few of them were mixed together...?"

Kenzie raised her hands in a surrender. "Probably not, honestly. But you would have to take my word for it."

"Yeah," Raven agreed. "And I'm not inclined to do that."

Zachary pulled his face up from his hands and studied her. "You suspect me?"

"It doesn't matter if I do or not. If one of the others does, and I didn't check carefully and take all of the precautions, then they're going to blame me."

"But you don't."

"Seeing how sick you are?" Raven looked down at the pile of bottles in her hands. "You got trouble, dude."

Zachary didn't argue the point.

"Are you finished?" Kenzie asked. She knew Raven wasn't and wanted to move the proceedings along. There was no point in their chatting about what she had found. They all knew what Raven had found and what all of the medications meant. As Raven had said, Zachary had his troubles. If someone were looking for a man with mental health issues for a scapegoat, Zachary was an easy target. There was no evidence that he had done anything to poison the other guests up at the farmhouse. In fact, they had all agreed that no one had even seen him at the house. But that wasn't proof.

"No. This is just the bedroom." Raven shook her head. "Do you have a bag I can put these in?"

Kenzie tracked down a zip-top bag, similar to the one they had put all Raven's medications into. If the quantity of pills were any indication of guilt, then Raven was just as much a suspect as Zachary. And she *had* been up at the house.

Raven sealed the top of the bag and kept it with her while she went back to check the room that Lorne and Pat had vacated, and then the one that the children were sleeping in. No one told her that she shouldn't be checking the children's room. Kenzie knew from her time talking to law enforcement officers that criminals were not above hiding contraband in their babies' diapers or carriers. There wasn't anything hidden in the children's room, but Raven had to check anyway, before she could confirm to the others that she had been thorough. Then, finally, Raven moved on to the bathroom and took her time going through their toiletries and the additional pill bottles she found there.

Eventually, she came out. "Okay. I'm done in there, if you want to go back to bed."

Zachary stayed where he was. Kenzie was a little relieved that he didn't go straight back to bed. Maybe since he'd been forced to wake up, he was more himself.

Raven looked around the living room, but mostly just moved around the kids' messes and didn't find any contraband. Then she checked the kitchen and took a long time going through the food. She opened the fridge and frowned. "Nothing in here?"

"No electricity. It's not cooling anymore," Kenzie pointed out. "We put the food outside. I'll show you."

She took Raven to the back door, opened it, and showed her where she would find the leftovers from Pat's Thanksgiving dinner feast.

"It's no wonder you guys didn't come up for the dinner," Raven commented.

"No. We had plenty here."

"Why did you have so much? Was that planned?"

"Well... in a way, yes. You can see Zachary needs to put on some weight, so we're always looking for ways to tempt him to eat more. I didn't know how much of the food provided by the Lodge he would eat, so I needed to make sure we had enough to eat without it. And our friends who visited—not Tyrrell, but Lorne and Pat, who were here the first night—they made the big dinner. Pat loves to cook, and it was a surprise for Zachary." Kenzie closed her eyes briefly. She was tired. She felt as though she had been awake for a week. All of her plans for the vacation had been turned upside-down. She had planned everything so carefully, but that was the way things went in life. She could never plan everything and have it all work out. Life was too messy. "It was nice, but they had to leave early the next morning to beat the storm. I'm glad they did, but... it would have been nice to have had them for longer like we were expecting."

Raven shrugged as if it didn't matter. But Kenzie knew that these points would all be brought up with the rest of the guests. Zachary had a lot of medications on hand, many of which, Raven would know from experience, were psychoactive drugs. They had brought lots of their own food and had not planned to eat all their meals at the farmhouse as the others had. It wasn't proof of anything, but in the face of the lack of evidence pointing to anyone else, it looked at least mildly suspicious.

"How are we going to secure everything we found?" Raven asked. "All of the stuff that you took from the other cabins, and this stuff?" She indicated the bag of Zachary's medications.

"I'll need you to leave a single dose of Zachary's night and morning pills here. Then tomorrow, we can get a second dose."

"Same with me," Raven agreed.

"Right. I guess you'll need yours too. And the rest... we need to secure them in a way that no one else can get into them."

"And that you can't by yourself," Raven pointed out.

"Right..."

They were all quiet, considering possibilities. They could take them up to the farmhouse and lock them in one of the rooms, but a single key would open the door. Who were they to trust it to? Kenzie? Raven? One of the house staff? None of them could be beyond suspicion.

46

I t was Zachary who worked out the method of securing all of the pills. Kenzie had counted him out, assuming he was too tired to be coming up with a solution.

They imposed on Stiller to borrow his safe. It was just large enough to hold everything they had confiscated from the cabins and a few of Stiller's possessions which he insisted be locked up. Hopefully, there wouldn't be much more to take from the staff or the outbuildings the next day, or they were going to have to come up with an alternate solution. They placed the safe in the trunk of Zachary's car. The keys to the car were given to Raven, as was Dewey's key to Raven's cabin.

Kenzie ticked off the safeguards in her head. Raven was the only one who could get into her cabin, so the only one who could get into Zachary's car. Vance Stiller had the only key to the safe. The other guests would not know where the pills were stowed, but even if they did, they would have to break into either Raven's cabin or Zachary's car to be able to get at the safe, and into Stiller's cabin to get the key to the safe. With three levels of security, the pills were out of play. Everyone would be safe from any further tampering with the food, which had been Kenzie's initial goal.

Of course, there were still the staff quarters and outbuildings to be searched the next day. But they could be reasonably sure that the food would be safe. The vacationers could either eat food from the cans of food in the pantry, or they could watch Mrs. Hubbard cook. Maybe she wouldn't like

739

being watched, but they were talking about something that might be life and death, not just someone having privacy and her own space.

Kenzie's head hurt. She and Zachary needed to go to bed. In the daytime, when they were all fresh and feeling better, they could decide if there were a better way to secure the medications. And maybe the snow would stop and there was a chance that the police might make their way out to the Lodge to take care of Mr. Dewey.

But that was wishful thinking.

Raven left. Kenzie shut the door behind her and was relieved to finally be alone with Zachary. And Tyrrell.

Kenzie gave a long sigh. "Got your night meds here," she offered Zachary.

He didn't always take everything. In fact, he rarely did, but she had grabbed a dose of everything he might need, because once they were locked up, it would be impossible to access them until morning. Zachary put his hand out, and Kenzie transferred the pills to him. He stared down at the capsules in his hand.

"You remember that first day they prescribed me meds?" he asked Tyrrell. "I was so embarrassed that I had to take all of those pills. And I wasn't used to taking pills, I couldn't swallow them."

Tyrrell shook his head, frowning. "No. Was that while we were at home? I don't remember any of us having meds then."

But he had only been four years old at the time of the fire, so maybe he had forgotten about it.

"Oh." Zachary continued to stare at the pills in his hand. "Maybe not. I guess it was at Petersons'. I forgot you weren't there."

Tyrrell glanced over at Kenzie. It wasn't like Zachary to forget any details about where he had been or the fact that he hadn't seen any of his siblings after the fire. He had not gone into foster care with any of them, but had been kept separate the entire time he as in foster care. He hadn't been reunited with any of them until Tyrrell had sought him out a year earlier.

Kenzie shook her head and shrugged. It wasn't usual for Zachary, but after his big flashback due to Raven's fire, she couldn't be surprised by any lapses. He was probably still struggling to keep his head in the present. He needed rest. A good night's sleep would help him to reset. Tyrrell seemed to sense this. It would not be a night where he and Zachary sat up together talking and reminiscing.

"You going to be okay, bro?" he asked in a cheery tone, slapping Zachary on the shoulder.

"Yeah, I'm fine," Zachary assured him.

"Okay. You take care of Kenzie. I'll see you in the morning." Tyrrell made a face. "I'll try to keep the kids quiet so you guys can sleep in if you need to, but I'm warning you ahead of time, that's kind of like trying to stop a stampede of wild horses..."

Zachary gave a small smile. "If I'm still asleep by then, I don't want to be."

"You need to get what you can. It's been a brutal day."

Zachary shrugged. Tyrrell gave him a brotherly hug goodnight, clapping him briskly on the back. He went to the second bedroom to join the children in dreamland.

Zachary picked through the pills in his hand and gave several of them back to Kenzie. She bit her lip when she saw that he wasn't taking a sleep aid or anti-anxiety pill. It would probably have been better for him to take both. But it was up to him to decide what was best. Maybe he was tired enough from his flashback and the day's events that he would just fall back asleep once they lay down.

"Okay? You want some water?"

"Yeah."

Kenzie went to the kitchen and cracked a water bottle open for him. He tended to get a dry mouth from some of the meds. He swallowed the pills he had chosen with a few gulps of water, then rose unsteadily to his feet, keeping the blanket wrapped around him like a robe and taking it and the water bottle with him to the bedroom. He didn't follow his usual bedtime routine and brush his teeth, but headed directly to bed. Kenzie left him to get settled in and performed her own evening ablutions, running a cold washcloth over her face and brushing her teeth. It had been a very long, difficult day, and she thought she was doing well to not skip brushing her teeth as Zachary had.

She went quietly into the bedroom. Not tip-toeing, exactly, but being quiet to avoid waking Zachary if he were already asleep. He didn't move. Kenzie slid in under the blankets and lay down behind him, wrapping her arms around him to cuddle. He didn't make any movement or snuggle into her. Already fast asleep. That was good, he certainly needed all the sleep he could get.

Kenzie started to drift herself, her brain winding down and the sleepiness welling up like a tide until she was nearly asleep.

"Who do you think it was?" Zachary asked quietly. Maybe not addressing her, but just the quiet, dark room, or maybe his own subconscious. "Who would do a thing like that?"

Kenzie didn't answer.

47

The herd of elephants that were Zachary's niece and nephew awakened them in the morning as it began to get light outside. Kenzie shifted and groaned. Her muscles were cramped, as if she had been holding herself tense all night, even in her sleep. She felt Zachary move beside her. It was so rare he was still in bed when she awoke, she was startled. She put her arm around him and moved in close to kiss his cheek.

"Hey, handsome. Good morning."

Zachary grunted. He didn't kiss her back, but one arm wound around her and he squeezed her against him, then released her, and he just lay with her, their bodies lined up with each other.

"Feeling better this morning?" Kenzie asked. She rubbed his back, making him purr in appreciation.

"Bit better."

"A bit?" Kenzie propped herself up slightly on her elbow. "You're still feeling the aftereffects?"

He nodded and rubbed his eyes, not looking at her, lids still lightly closed.

"Maybe you should take a Xanax today."

"No. Be fine."

It was harder than usual not to give him her advice. She might be a medical professional, but she wasn't his doctor, and he was far more qualified to know what his body and brain needed at any time than she was. But Kenzie wanted to be in control of something. To gradually gather the lost threads in her life and to bring them back into order. She took a few deep breaths, letting them out slowly.

"You sound anxious too," Zachary observed.

"Yeah. I guess I am. I don't like the uncertainty. Feeling like I'm supposed to stop this runaway train, but not being able to do it. I want my own lab and computer and law enforcement officers investigating and telling me what's going on. All the things I normally have. This... chaos is really unsettling."

There was a shriek, and the bedroom door burst open, and two little cannon balls landed on the bed, nearly sending Kenzie straight up to the ceiling.

"Whoa! Take it easy," she protested, reaching for the two troublemakers and trying to corral them.

"Alisha! Mason! You're supposed to be leaving Zachary and Kenzie alone!" Tyrrell shouted from across the cabin. Probably in the kitchen, preparing their breakfasts.

Kenzie tried to get control of them so she could send them back to their father with a stern word. But beside her, she heard a strange, unexpected noise. Zachary chuckling. He managed to catch the smaller whirlwind and pinned him to the bed, tickling Mason and making him shriek with laughter for his father to come rescue him. Tyrrell didn't. Alisha dove in to try to stop Zachary and pull Mason away, but Zachary managed to get her too, somehow holding on to both children and causing fits of giggles as they tried to escape. Kenzie blinked and shook her head at the sight.

Zachary, often so grim, drowning in his depression lately and still suffering from the previous evening's flashback, laughed as he tickled and wrestled with the two children. Kenzie's heart filled with affection at the sight of him happy and enjoying himself with his niece and nephew. Her eyes filled too, and she swiped at them, not wanting Zachary to see her tearing up.

Eventually, the three of them collapsed on the bed, all exhausted by the game and breathing heavily. Tyrrell stuck his head in the door.

"Is anyone listening to me?"

Zachary shook his head. "No. No one."

"It's time for breakfast. Come on. I made you food. I am your provider; you need to eat the food I bring home to you."

"You didn't bring any food," Alisha declared. "Kenzie did."

"Still, I'm the one who assembled it into some semblance of a meal. You're supposed to show me your immense gratitude."

"Thank you, Daddy," Mason said sweetly, not moving. "Can you bring it here?"

"This is not breakfast in bed! You need to come to the kitchen and eat there. What would Kenzie say if you got crumbs in the bed?"

"She'd say, 'you got crumbs in the bed,'" Mason informed him.

Kenzie couldn't help laughing at his deadpan response.

"Don't encourage him!" Tyrrell protested. "Come on, everyone out of bed."

"But I don't want to get out of bed!" Kenzie protested.

"If you guys are going to encourage them to be wild, you have to get up too."

"But I didn't. That was Zachary."

Tyrrell brandished a wooden spoon at Zachary. "Zachary, is this true?"

Zachary chuckled again. Kenzie shut her eyes and basked in the sound. That was why she had arranged for their vacation. That was why she had planned for Loren and Pat to be there. Why she had invited Tyrrell to join them. To surround Zachary with family and hope that it helped to turn him around. Even if it only helped to lift the depression for a day or two, he needed the break so desperately. The antiviral regimen had taken away everything extra he had in him. He needed to regain some of the ground he had lost.

"Everyone up," Tyrrell repeated. "Kenzie, Zachary..."

Kenzie opened her eyes and sat up. She held the blankets against her body. "I need some privacy to get dressed."

"Come on, kids," Tyrrell ordered. "You heard her."

Neither one moved. Zachary sat up and started to log-roll them, until he'd pushed them both off the bed. Alisha and Mason giggled and, tickling each other, eventually crawled out of the room.

"You've got five minutes," Tyrrell told Kenzie, and shut the bedroom door. "If you're lucky!"

48

It took Kenzie longer than five minutes to dress and make herself presentable, but Tyrrell managed to keep the kids away from the bedroom until she was finished. She and Zachary wandered out, stretching and yawning without covering their mouths, to join Tyrrell and the children at the table.

Tyrrell had managed to toast a few slices of bread on the camp stove. Kenzie helped herself to one and put it on her plate. The marmalade and jams were out, and she helped herself to her usual morning marmalade.

"I don't like that kind with peel in it," Mason observed. "It's gross."

"A lot of kids don't like marmalade," Kenzie told him. "They are more sensitive to bitter flavors, so they sometimes don't like things that taste good to adults."

"It is bitter," Alisha agreed, wrinkling her nose.

Zachary stood near the kitchen sink and downed several pills, the morning meds that they had kept back from the stash that was locked away. Kenzie looked toward the front window of the cabin. She couldn't see the car from where she sat. Zachary's quick eyes caught her glance, and he stepped forward. "What is it?"

"Nothing. Just wanted to make sure that the car is still there, safe and sound."

Mason looked at the window. "Where else would it be? It's stuck in the snow."

"Yes, it is," Kenzie agreed.

Zachary went over to the window to look out. He rubbed at condensation and frost on the inside of the window and peered through the small patch he had cleared. "Yep. Still there." He leaned closer to the window, and Kenzie saw his body language transform from relaxed and happy to anxious.

"What?" she asked.

Zachary walked to the door. He pulled his coat off the peg and slid into it as he put his feet into his boots.

"Zachary?"

"I can't see very well through the window."

But Kenzie knew it was more than that. There was no reason for him to be so concerned that he just couldn't see the car well. She tried to decide whether to get up and see what was wrong or to pretend that everything was okay and just eat her breakfast. Her concern won out, and she went to the window as Zachary darted through the door and slammed it shut behind him.

He went to the driver's side door. Kenzie pressed her nose against the window glass and saw, as he had, a dark place on the car's window, where all the others were white with frost and snow. As she watched, Zachary opened the car door. The door that was supposed to be locked with the key Raven had kept, shut away safe in her cabin. And Kenzie could see that the dark spot wasn't a place where the glass had been cleared of frost and snow for someone to look inside, but a hole where the glass had been broken.

Zachary reached into the car to hit a button below the dash. The trunk popped up a couple of inches. It didn't go all the way up like usual because of the weight of the snow holding it down. Zachary went around to the back of the car and brushed the snow off the trunk with his arm. The hatch opened the rest of the way. Kenzie held her breath. *And the safe?*

Zachary reached down with both hands and retrieved it. Using his elbow to shut the trunk, he retraced his steps, kicked the car door shut, and hurried to the front door of the cabin. Kenzie left her place at the window to open the door for him. Zachary hurried in, snowflakes flying from his coat. He put the safe down on the floor with a thud.

"What's that?" Mason demanded.

"Is it okay?" Kenzie asked, looking down at it. "It's still locked?"

Zachary stared down at the heavy metal box. He shook his head grimly.

"What?" Kenzie looked at it, trying to process what she was seeing. Vance Stiller was the only one with a key. But they had tried to ensure he couldn't open it either, putting it in the locked car, with the car key in Raven's locked cabin.

But the place where there used to be a keyhole, there was now a large, round hole. Kenzie looked at Zachary for an explanation, feeling her eyes go wide, unable to believe what she was seeing.

"They drilled it," Zachary said. He looked back toward the door and the car. "Someone broke into the car and drilled the lock while we were sleeping."

Kenzie bent down and swung the door open, her stomach queasy. It was empty. The items that Stiller had insisted had to remain locked in the safe were gone, as well as all of the medications and other items that Kenzie and Zachary had gathered in their search of the cabins the night before. Kenzie sat on the floor, unable to believe it. She looked back at Zachary.

"But no one knew. The only people who knew how we had secured everything were you and me, Raven, and Vance." Which one of them had broken into the car? Raven? Would Vance have drilled his own safe? That didn't make any sense.

"Anyone could have been watching us out their windows. We put a safe in the trunk of the car. They knew we wanted to protect something. It had to be something valuable or something dangerous. Or both."

Who had the contents now? Burknall had access to all the tools he would need. Not that he needed anything other than a rock to smash the door and a drill for the lock of the safe. Presumably everything in the barn wasn't locked down, and any guest could have walked over there and taken what they needed, then returned it or thrown it into a snowbank.

"I can't believe it," Kenzie moaned. "After all that work last night." She held her arms over her stomach, feeling sick.

"But why?" Zachary mused. "Why would anyone take the contents? They can't be out to poison everyone again. They know that there are enough canned goods in the pantry to keep everyone safely fed until the police get here."

"No..." Kenzie agreed. "You're right. It would have to be..." She rubbed her forehead, thinking. The headache of the night before was returning. Everything from the night before was returning, as if they had gone back in time. All they had done had turned out to be a waste of time. The searches, Zachary's flashback, Kenzie's headache and exhaustion. "I suppose... because the police will be able to identify the toxin once they get here. That would have to be it, wouldn't it? Whatever it is, it doesn't metabolize fast enough, and it might still be in their systems when the police get here. In Brooke's system, at least. Then they'll know what the poison was, and they'll know whose prescription or... recreational aid it was."

"But you know what came from each cabin. If they tell you what the toxin was, you can tell them whose it was."

"Well, more or less. Sometimes more than one person had the same thing. You and Raven had a lot of similar medications. More than one person had the same sleeping pills or tranquilizers."

"But the culprit doesn't know that. The only person who knows what you know is... you."

"Oh, this is crazy." Kenzie ran her fingers through her hair, tugging at it, trying to get her brain to engage. She couldn't sort it out quickly enough for her satisfaction. "Maybe it was just someone after Stiller's valuables. He had documents and written records in there. We don't know what was in the zip-up deposit case in there. Silver or gold or currency. Bearer bonds. Do they even make bearer bonds anymore?"

Zachary shook his head. "We have to protect *you*. Your knowledge of pharmaceuticals could solve this case. Either now, when you figure out which drug was used, or when the police run their tests and tell you what it was."

49

Kenzie was too stressed and nauseated to eat her breakfast. She could empathize with Zachary. She couldn't imagine even being able to stomach one of the granola bars. There were some applesauce cups in with the other snack foods that she had brought, and she thought she might be able to tolerate one later, but not right away.

"What are we going to do?" she asked as they sat down at the table again, though Kenzie knew she would not touch her toast.

"We have to be careful," Zachary said slowly, thinking things through. "I think we'd better stay here as much as we can. I don't want something to happen to you if whoever broke into the safe realizes that you know what was in there and can still implicate them. Any time we leave the cabin, it puts you at risk, so we can't do that."

Kenzie hadn't been too worried about being stranded until then. Yes, they were snowed in, but they had a warm, safe place to stay and, sooner or later, the snow would stop, and the authorities would get there.

But knowing that she couldn't leave the cabin made her feel claustrophobic. She hadn't wanted to leave. She'd just wanted to stay there and relax and have a good visit with Tyrrell and Zachary. Cocoon and play with the kids and make some camp meals. An adventure that would be over in a few days. Something that they would look back on with fond memories in the future.

That vision had already been eroding away as people died and she had to consider the fact that there was a killer in their midst. But she'd still been able to hold on to it.

But if she *had* to stay inside, that was different.

Being afraid and being forced to barricade herself against the rest of the guests was different. And she didn't like it.

"We have to keep you safe," Zachary said, watching her face, reading her expression.

"I get it... but I feel like you're overreacting. I don't like the idea of being forced to stay inside."

"You didn't want to go out in the freezing cold, did you? It isn't like we were going to be out there making snowmen."

"No. I'm tired of the cold. I had to go outside and inside so many times last night, going from cold to warm to cold again, I don't want to have to go out. But I want to *be able* to."

Zachary nodded sympathetically.

"Can we go outside and make a snowman?" Mason demanded.

Tyrrell looked at Zachary, who shook his head slowly. "I don't think it's a good idea. I think the kids are safe, but... I wouldn't want anything to happen."

"We want to make a snowman," Mason insisted. "Daddy, you come outside with us."

"Zachary doesn't think it's a good idea, Mason."

"He doesn't know," Mason said scornfully. "He just doesn't want to make a snowman."

"No, he wants to keep everyone safe. You don't know what things might be dangerous outside."

"Yes, I do! I'll wear a hat and everything. Even the one with the mask!"

Kenzie had gathered from previous conversations that Mason was very sensitive about having something touch his face and was resistant to having to wear a ski mask even with the weather being so cold. They had been lucky that up until that point the children had been happy to stay inside and play games there. The weather outside had been so inhospitable, they hadn't even asked to go out. But now that Zachary had mentioned snowmen...

Zachary rolled his eyes, realizing that he'd made a mistake they would all regret for the next few days.

"Sorry."

Tyrrell shrugged. He looked at his watch. "Maybe if it warms up a bit later, we can take a few minutes and build a snowman in the back. But we can't be out for long, and if Uncle Zachary or I say that you can't go out, then you can't. We're the grownups, and we have to make the decisions about when it is safe or not."

"It's safe," Mason insisted. "We'll wear gloves and hats."

"I know you will. Because you know how to take care of yourself in cold weather, don't you? But there are other things going on too. Zachary and I have to make sure that there isn't anyone around who might bother you. You have to listen to us."

Mason clearly didn't approve of this course of action. "We can go out later, right? In the afternoon. When it's warmer."

"Maybe. It will depend."

Mason rolled his eyes, oozing attitude. Kenzie had to grin despite herself. She was worried about the missing medications and the possible danger, if Zachary was right. But Mason's attitude was so classic, so over-the-top dramatic, she couldn't help being amused.

"Why don't you guys find something to play with now," Tyrrell told them. "And I'm going to have some jobs for you to do later on. We all need to help in keeping the cabin clean and tidy, right?"

"We didn't make a mess," Alisha said, looking around the kitchen and what she could see of the living room.

"There's a lot of stuff out right now. The grownups don't want to be stepping on spinners or playing pieces."

"Then you should watch where you're going," Mason advised.

"And you can help me to make the beds and put the clothes away," Tyrrell said, ignoring the smart comment. "And we need to think about what we want for lunch. Do you want to help to cook something on the camp stove?"

Mason looked at the camp stove set up on the counter. "Yeah, I want to cook something!"

"Good. Think about what you want to cook. Remember, we can't go to the store, so we have to make do with what we have. It's like a cooking challenge."

"What do we have?"

"You can look in the cupboards. And we still have some leftovers from when Lorne and Pat were here. Turkey, potatoes, stuff like that. We just have to thaw it out."

Mason got down from the table and went to work, looking through the cupboards and whispering to Alisha about the possibilities. Apparently, their special lunch was to be a secret from the adults.

"How much can you remember about what you found in each cabin?" Zachary asked Kenzie.

"Well... I was getting pretty tired. I don't remember all the specifics."

"Maybe you can write down what you remember and fill in more as you can."

"Do you think that will help us to figure out who took the contents of the safe?"

"I hope so. We need to compile all of the information we can, see whether we can figure it out." He nibbled at his granola bar. "And if you have to testify in court, it's better if you have something written down the day after, rather than relying on your memory months later, when you might have been influenced by the questions and revelations in between."

Kenzie nodded. All of that made sense. She and Dr. Wiltshire always wrote everything down and dictated notes as they worked for exactly that reason. Notes written at the time were far more reliable than memories which could change and fade over time.

"Okay... I guess I'll do that now. There's paper in the writing desk?"

Mason looked up from his discussion with Alisha. "There's paper in the desk," he confirmed. "Alisha and me were using it to write down scores and rules."

"Thanks, Mason." Hopefully, they hadn't used it all. There was sure to be more writing paper in the other cabins, but she didn't relish going to one of the others to say that she needed paper to write down the notes about who might be guilty of what. Zachary was already making her feel a bit creeped out over the idea that someone might want to silence her to make sure that she couldn't tell what she knew. Was that the reason Zachary wanted her to write down everything she knew? So that if something happened to her, they would still have a record of what she had discovered?

Kenzie stood up from the table and looked through the writing desk. There was, thankfully, a good supply of stationery and pens. She grabbed a sheaf of paper and sat down on the couch, where she could wrap a blanket around herself and get comfortable while she racked her brain, trying to remember all the details of what she had discovered the night before.

50

The morning was quiet. Kenzie had expected Raven and others to come knocking on the door to ask about the contents of the safe and the fact that there was a hole in their driver's side window. Someone was bound to be wondering if they had figured out who the poisoner was. And the staff would know that their quarters had not been searched and had to be wondering if she were coming to do them next or if she had found something that made it unnecessary.

Everyone would have questions, and Kenzie anticipated trying to turn them all away at the door to keep herself safe from any potential attack.

But it was all quiet. If anyone was wondering what had happened to their car or the safe, they didn't let on. Even Vance Stiller didn't come over, and he would have been concerned about what happened to his valuable papers and articles if he realized that the safe had been compromised.

For the first little while, Kenzie worked on her lists, keeping a separate sheet of paper for each cabin and adding to each one as she remembered more details. She talked it through with Zachary, and he contributed what he remembered and any little things that he thought might help her to remember what pills she had found in each cabin. In the end, Kenzie had a pretty good list. She thought it was generally representative of what had been found in each cabin, though she didn't remember all of what had been in Raven's pharmacy, or the exact details, brands, or dosages of most of the medications.

How valuable would the list be if she ever had to testify in court about the various pills and substances they had found? Kenzie wasn't sure. She supposed it all depended on what the authorities decided Brooke and Mr. Dewey had died from. If Kenzie could point the finger at who had been in possession of that substance... it wouldn't quite be a lock, but it might help.

She was drowsy after spending a couple of hours concentrating on the lists, with all of the activity that was going on inside the cabin. While they hadn't been disturbed by a bunch of questions from the other guests, the children were bored and restless, alternately whining about having nothing to do and getting too wild doing it. Kenzie rubbed her temples. She still had some over-the-counter painkillers. Maybe if she took a couple of pills and had a short nap, she would feel better. She would catch up on her sleep from the night before and feel more like herself.

"Stay there; what can I get you?" Zachary offered, seeing her prepare to stand up.

"Just a Tylenol."

"Sure. One or two?" He got up and stepped toward the bathroom.

"Two," Kenzie decided.

As Zachary disappeared into the bathroom, Kenzie made a sudden realization. Her heart sank into her stomach, filling her with a feeling of dread and causing bile to rise in her throat.

She tried to keep her face impassive so that Zachary wouldn't read anything in it when he returned with the pills.

They had taken all of Zachary's and Raven's pills and put them into the safe so that they couldn't be used to cause further harm. Psychoactive medications that could not be stopped cold turkey.

She didn't know how Raven would react to the sudden withdrawal of her medications, but Zachary would destabilize within a day or two, and they might not be able to get him back on track even if they restarted the regimen as soon as they were able. The chemicals had to remain at a consistent level in his system if they were going to do their job. Disrupt that, and there was going to be trouble.

Both Raven and Zachary might respond as the others had to a new toxin being introduced into their bodies—with hallucinations, mood swings, and irritable, unpredictable behavior.

And then there were the guests who were taking medications for blood pressure, cholesterol, and other ailments. They wouldn't go into immediate withdrawal. Probably, they would be okay until they could get back onto the medications that had been seized. But it was also possible that they wouldn't. That the process had already begun and without their daily meds, they could be looking at heart attacks, strokes, seizures, and all kinds of other issues.

Zachary returned from the bathroom and handed Kenzie a couple of white Tylenol capsules and a glass of water. Kenzie swallowed them down without comment.

"Do you want to go lie down?" Zachary asked. "You probably didn't get enough sleep last night."

"You're probably right. But... I hate to bow out on the two of you."

Zachary looked over at his brother, who looked quite relaxed, sitting with a glass of Tang in one hand, watching the children play. "I think everyone is fine. Things have been quiet. Why don't both of us go stretch out for a while...?"

Nothing could possibly sound better than lying down in a warm, soft bed and cuddling with Zachary until she fell asleep. "That sounds like heaven."

Zachary's eyes crinkled at the corners. "Come on, then. Let's get you into bed."

"Lock your door," Tyrrell warned, "if you want any privacy."

It wasn't the kids who woke Kenzie and Zachary up an hour or two later, it was Tyrrell. He pounded hard on the door to wake them up, and Zachary was on his feet and to the door before Kenzie could even wake up enough to know what was going on. Zachary quickly unlocked the door and pulled it open.

"T? What is it? What's wrong?"

Tyrrell's face was white as a sheet. "Mason. He went outside. Just for a minute. He's not there. I don't know where he went. I called him, but he didn't answer me—"

"Is Alisha with him?" Zachary shouldered his way past Tyrrell into the hallway. Rubbing her eyes, Kenzie forced herself out of the bed to follow.

"Alisha is here. She said she doesn't know where he would go. She was going to go out with him, make a snowman in the back where no one could see that they were out, but when she got out there, he wasn't there."

Kenzie followed the two men out to the living room. Alisha was there, tears running down her red face.

"I don't know where he is!" she wailed.

Kenzie hugged her around the shoulders. "It's okay. No one is blaming you. Do you know where he might have gone? Was there something he said he wanted to do?"

"Just building a snowman. He wanted to build a really big snowman. And then he wanted to make lunch. We planned it all out."

"What did he want to make for lunch? Was there something he was missing?" Zachary suggested.

"I don't know. We were going to make it with just what we have here. Like Daddy said." Alisha sniffled. "Just like Daddy said to do."

"It's okay, Alisha," Tyrrell assured her, though it was clear he was struggling to stay calm. "We just need to find him. You know how your brother is. He gets distracted. He wandered off to do something and forgot to let anyone know first. That's all. It's happened a million times before."

Alisha nodded. She sniffled again and hiccupped. "I know, but this time, it was dangerous. You said it was dangerous and he's gone, and what if something happens to him like that lady?"

Kenzie hadn't realized that the kids had heard about Brooke's death. She had thought that they had refrained from talking about it in front of them. But one of them had said too much, or the kids had been hanging around with their ears open when the adults thought they were out of the way.

"Alisha, it's okay. We want to protect you guys, but no one is out to hurt you. Nothing is going to happen to Mason. He'll be okay."

It wasn't like it had been with Brooke. People had been hallucinating. They had been fighting. It was just an accident, someone overreacting to an argument or a vision. Striking out at a nightmare. But it wasn't like that now. It had been more than twenty-four hours since they had been exposed to the toxin, whatever it was, and no one posed a danger to the children. The biggest danger was Mason himself. That he would wander off and end up too far from the Lodge or fall into a pond and catch hypothermia. It was the environment they had to worry about, not the other guests.

But Kenzie didn't immediately suggest that they raise a search party to go looking for him.

"We need to think clearly," she said. "Not to rush into this. Think about Mason. What he was interested in. What he might do if he wandered away. He was distracted or he remembered something that he wanted to do and didn't think it would take that long. He just did something without thinking. What was it?"

Zachary already had his coat on. He looked at Kenzie, then around at the others. If there was anyone who could put himself into Mason's shoes, it was Zachary. He had been a kid like Mason. Always in trouble because of the way his brain was wired. Too distracted, too quick to make the wrong choice. Hyperactive. He could get himself into trouble much faster than it would take them to figure out what he had done.

"Check the back," he told Tyrrell. "That's where he was supposed to be, so that's where you should start."

"I already checked the back—"

"Look for footprints. Check the perimeter, his footprints have to lead off somewhere, unless he was snatched. And then someone else's footprints will give them away."

"Where are you going?" Kenzie demanded as Zachary reached for the doorknob of the front door.

"I've got a few places to check out. You guys be methodical," he told her and Tyrrell firmly. "I'll be impulsive."

Kenzie nearly laughed. Zachary was out the door and slammed it shut behind him. Tyrrell went to the back door as instructed. He put his boots back on.

"You stay here with Kenzie, Alisha. I don't want you wandering around too. We need someone to be here in case Mason comes back, and I need you to look after Kenzie. She can't be out here searching, understand?"

Alisha looked at Kenzie, baffled. "What?"

"Just do what I say. You stay here with Kenzie. The two of you need to stay inside. Don't let anyone else in. Keep the doors locked."

He left out the back. Alisha and Kenzie looked at each other. It was clear that Alisha didn't understand why her father had told her to take care of Kenzie and not let anyone into the cabin. But Kenzie did. Zachary had said that the poisoner might target her. He or she would see Kenzie as a threat because of her knowledge and might try to remove her from the equation.

Now Kenzie was stuck in the cabin by herself, except for Alisha. Someone could have taken Mason just to get the men away from the cabin. It might all be a ruse to get Kenzie alone or to persuade her to leave the cabin to join in the search.

"Okay," Kenzie said calmly. "Let's lock the doors."

Alisha nodded solemnly. She reached out to the back door and locked the handle and then the bolt. She looked out the window of the kitchen, watching her father as he walked around the yard, looking down at the markings in the snow. Kenzie and Alisha couldn't see much from inside. Kenzie hoped he would be able to find Mason's trail and find him quickly. Kenzie went to the front door and did the same there. She looked out the living room window, but couldn't see Zachary. He was already out of sight. She wondered where he had gone. Where would she have gone to look for Mason?

One of them would find him. She was counting on it.

51

I don't know what else to do," Alisha told Kenzie.

And what could they do? If they weren't allowed to leave the cabin, there wasn't much they could do. Even if they had an idea, even if Alisha suddenly realized where her brother had taken off to, they wouldn't be able to call Zachary or Tyrrell and let them know. They had no bars. The storm was still blocking out any cell signal.

"Well... why don't we sit down and play a game?" Kenzie suggested. "I know it won't help them find him any faster, but it will help us to distract ourselves so that we don't worry as much."

Alisha put her hands on her hips. "I don't want to not worry!"

"Well... okay. What do you want to do about it, then?"

Alisha looked around, trying to find an answer. "We'll clean up," she said finally. "Daddy told us that we needed to clean up. So we'll do that, and when we get done... he'll be back. And he'll have Mason with him."

"Okay," Kenzie agreed. She was willing to buy into Alisha's magical thinking. They would clean. And when they were done, Mason would be back.

They picked up game pieces and matched them to the appropriate boxes, then stacked the boxes back in the closet where they had been stored. They picked up various wadded-up and torn papers and threw them out. There were dishes from breakfast that had not been cleaned, so they washed them and put them away. Kenzie looked around again. There had to be some way for them to occupy themselves. There was always more work to do.

There was a knock at the door. Her heart in her throat, Kenzie looked out the front window. She had known that it wasn't Zachary's knock, but she'd been hoping that it might be Tyrrell's. Burknall stood there, looking back at her through the window, waiting for her to let him in.

What if he were the culprit? He had tools, he'd lived at the lodge for a long time, he was clearly smart and able to think things through. What if he'd been the one who had decided they didn't need any more guests at the Lodge? Or that if he got rid of his boss that he'd be able to get some sort of benefit. Did the Lodge go to Dewey's next of kin? Did it get divided among the staff? Did he leave something to his loyal workers to make their lives more comfortable? Kenzie stood there, not opening the door.

Burknall knocked again, insistently. "Kenzie!" he shouted through the door.

Kenzie finally went to the door and unlocked it. She opened it a couple of inches.

"What is it?"

"You need to come out to the barn."

Kenzie shook her head. "I'm supposed to stay here."

Burknall was looking down. He could see the safe on the floor by her feet. He probably knew that it was empty. Maybe he was the one who had emptied it.

"Come on. You want the kid, don't you?"

Kenzie frowned. "Mason? Of course. Is he in the barn?"

Burknall rolled his eyes. "Where else would he be?"

He sounded so genuinely irritated, Kenzie didn't doubt him. She reached for her boots and her coat. Alisha grabbed at Kenzie's coat as she tried to put it on.

"Kenzie, no!"

"I'll just be a minute. I'll go get Mason, and I'll be right back."

"Daddy said no. He said to stay here."

"Well, he didn't know that anyone else would find Mason while they were gone. You want me to bring Mason home, don't you? You want him to be home safe."

"Yes..." Alisha drew her answer out, looking unconvinced.

"You can lock the door behind me, right? And only open it for one of us?"

"Yes. But I don't want to be here by myself."

"It will only be a few minutes. I'll be right back."

Kenzie finished pulling her winter gear on. She promised once more to be right back, then left the cabin.

"Come on," Burknall told her, and strode toward the barn.

His stride was much longer than Kenzie's, and he broke through the snow that wasn't yet trampled down much more easily than Kenzie did. She wasn't used to getting around the grounds, especially with all of the drifted snow, and she kept taking the wrong paths, tripping and stepping into holes and off the sidewalk into the gutter, neither of which she could see in the snow. She wanted to ask Burknall to slow down and wait for her, but she didn't want to look like a helpless woman either. She was as competent as the next man.

By the time Burknall reached the barn, Kenzie was well behind. She could see her destination, but she was no longer within calling distance.

"Come on," she muttered to herself. "City slicker here. Give me a bit of a break."

But he didn't. He was into the barn and out of Kenzie's sight.

The last couple of minutes it took Kenzie to struggle through the uneven snow into the barn were worse. She could no longer see Burknall and reassure herself that she was doing the right thing. All that she could think of was that she had done the wrong thing. The opposite to what Zachary and Tyrrell would have told her to do.

What if Burknall were the poisoner? What if he were just trying to lure her to where he could dispose of her out of sight of all the other cabins? No one would know what had happened to her. Alisha was the only one who even knew that Burknall had come to the door and that Kenzie had gone with him. She was the only one who knew that Kenzie had gone to the structure. After dealing with Kenzie, Burknall could go back and take care of the last witness.

But Kenzie couldn't think of a reason he would go through all of that. She couldn't think of any motive he had to poison them all or to kill Brooke. It just didn't line up.

She entered through the big doors of the barn and looked around. It was warmer in the barn than it was outside, despite the big doors being open. There was some sort of furnace or heater running to keep it warm. That, and the warm animals helping to heat it with their body heat. The big horses that Mason had been so proud of making friends with and of driving during the hayride.

"Mason? Are you in here?" Looking around, Kenzie couldn't see Burknall, which made her even more anxious. Why wasn't he standing there waiting for her? He had said that he would take her to Mason. Why the disappearing act?

"Kenzie?" A small voice called back.

"Hey. Where are you?" Kenzie looked around, trying to pinpoint the sound.

"I'm up here."

Kenzie looked up and kept raising her gaze higher until they reached the top of the hay loft, where she could see Mason looking tentatively down at her over the edge.

"What are you doing all the way up there?"

"I was climbing." Mason's voice was thready and uncertain. Had he figured out how much trouble he was in for taking off? Where was Zachary? Kenzie figured the barn would be the first place Zachary would have looked for him.

"Is your Uncle Zachary up there with you?"

"No." She could see Mason's head shake. "It's just me..."

"Why don't you come down now. You still want to help make lunch, don't you? Alisha said that the two of you had it all planned out. You don't want her making it all herself, do you?"

"No! It was my idea. She has to do what I say!"

"Come on down, then. Let's go back to the cabin and make lunch."

"Me and Alisha. Not you."

"Okay." Kenzie waited for him to decide to come down from his high perch. Had he imagined climbing Mount Everest to get there? He was several stories high. Kenzie tried to avoid thinking of what would happen if he slipped and fell. Unfortunately, she knew way too much about those kinds of accidents. The kind of tragic case that made them all shake their heads and say how they would never have let that happen. The parents must have been crazy to let the kids get away with climbing so high or taking part in other risky behavior.

Yet when it happened, there really wasn't anyone to blame. Parents did blame themselves, and so did the public, but Kenzie knew that if there was any way they could take back what had happened, they would. They would give up anything to have the child back safe and sound.

Mason's head disappeared, which meant that he had backed up and was on his way to picking his way down, climbing back over the mounds of hay and the ladders or ropes or whatever else he had used to climb to the pinnacle. She waited, trying not to be impatient with him. If he thought that he was going to get punished for his little adventure, he would be far less likely to come down and go back to the cabin with her. She needed to act as though it were nothing.

"Kenzie?"

She tried to follow Mason's voice, but she could only hear him, not to see him. "Yes?"

"Are you my auntie?"

Why would he be concerned about such a thing while climbing down from the loft? Kenzie rolled her eyes and tried to keep her voice relaxed and soothing.

"If you want to call me auntie, you can. Zachary is your uncle. We're not married, but we're together, and I don't think anyone minds."

"Auntie Kenzie." Mason tried it out to see how it sounded and felt.

"Yes?"

Mason giggled. "I wasn't calling you."

"Did you see Zachary? He was looking for you."

"Yes," Mason admitted. "I saw him."

"Did you talk to him? Did he find you?"

"Well... no..."

"You hid from him?"

"Well... not exactly."

"We'd better let him know that you're found. Do you know where he went after he looked here?"

"Yes. Into the woods."

Kenzie's throat felt tight. "Into the woods? Why would he go there? Did you go into the woods?"

"Yes. That's where the knife is," Mason said quietly.

52

Kenzie walked to the back of the barn, craning her neck to see up into the loft where Mason should be. "What knife, honey?"

"I found... I was going to build a snowman. I was looking for sticks. You need sticks for the arms, and rocks or something for the eyes and mouth."

"And a carrot for the nose," Kenzie said lightly.

"Yeah. I was looking for sticks, but I found the knife."

"Where are you, Mason?" Kenzie called softly.

"I'm here!" Mason jumped down from somewhere above Kenzie, tumbling into a pile of loose hay. Kenzie was so startled that she let out a shriek.

Mason laughed. "Auntie Kenzie!"

"Mason!"

He laughed again.

"We'd better go back to the cabin now," Kenzie said.

"I want to stay here with Mr. Burknall."

"Where is Mr. Burknall?" Kenzie asked. "He brought me over here, and then... he disappeared."

"He didn't disappear. He just went to check on the animals. There are lots of animals, and he has to take care of them all."

"So where is he?"

Mason shrugged. He waved in a random direction. "Maybe looking after the pigs."

764

"There are pigs?"

Mason nodded. "There are lots of animals. I always thought that pigs were little. Like in that book about the spider. And Templeton the rat."

"*Charlotte's Web?*"

"Yeah. The pig in that was just really little. But Mr. Burknall's pigs are big."

"Okay." Kenzie's mind went to the stories she'd heard of pigs and how good they were at disposing of dismembered bodies. Something she didn't want to be thinking of and certainly didn't want to talk to Mason about. "We need to get back to the cabin. Unless... maybe you should show me where you found the knife, on the way back. Did you tell Zachary where it was?"

"No."

"You just hid from him."

Mason looked down at his feet. "Yeah."

"You should have told him."

Mason nodded.

"You should have come out from hiding and told him where to find the knife. That was important."

"I'm sorry."

"Okay."

"Do you want me to show you where it is?"

Kenzie hesitated. She knew she should get back to the cabin. That was where Tyrrell and Zachary would go when they failed to find Mason. And that's where Alisha was waiting, all by herself, where Kenzie had abandoned her. She shouldn't have left the little girl there alone, but when Burknall had come calling, it was the only thing she could think to do.

"Yes. You'd better show me."

Mason led Kenzie out the back door of the barn, through a couple of muddy, trampled paddocks, into the woods that the cabins backed onto. Whoever had killed Brooke had probably thrown the knife away, hoping no one else would find it.

Mason looked around as they walked into the woods, his head swiveling back and forth. Kenzie hoped that he knew where the knife was and could find the cabin again. The last thing they needed was to get lost in the woods. Everything looked alike to Kenzie. She didn't know how he would be able to navigate through it.

"Do you remember where it is?" she asked.

"Yeah."

"Okay." She let him lead the way.

Mason looked down at the snow as he tromped through the trees. "That's where Zachary went." He pointed at a footprint.

Kenzie looked down at the zigzag pattern in the footprint. It looked about the right size, but she hadn't noticed the tread on the bottom of Zachary's boots. If Mason said it was one of Zachary's footprints, he was probably right.

"But he went the wrong way," Mason said after a minute, looking at the footprints as they diverged to the left.

"Maybe he saw something. Or someone."

"Maybe," Mason said doubtfully. "But I think everyone is in their cabins."

"Not everyone!"

Mason chuckled, nodding. He rubbed his face, red with the cold. "Was Daddy mad?"

"No, not mad... but he was worried about you when he didn't know where you went. You weren't supposed to go off on your own."

"Yeah... I forgot. Kind of."

"And kind of wanted to go off even though you weren't supposed to."

Mason looked at her sideways and didn't answer. After a couple of minutes, he motioned to the underbrush. "Over here. I thought it would be a good place to get sticks."

Kenzie bent down and looked where he pointed. She could see a long, thin-bladed knife. A kitchen knife of some sort, not something that was intended to be used as a weapon. She could not see any blood on the blade, but it might have been wiped off. The police would send it to the lab to see if they could find microscopic amounts of blood.

"Did you touch it?" she asked Mason.

He shook his head. Kenzie continued to look at him. After a minute, he dropped his eyes.

"Yes, but I put it right back where it was."

Kenzie hadn't brought her phone with her to take any pictures. She hadn't even thought about it when Burknall had knocked on her door. Kenzie looked around.

"Are we close to the cabin now? I'm turned around."

"It's just over there." Mason pointed. He smiled proudly. "Mommy says I have very good visio-sp..." He struggled to remember and form the word.

"Visual-spatial memory?" Kenzie suggested.

He grinned. "Yes!"

"I bet you hardly ever get lost."

"Nope. I can always find my way home. Daddy plays this game, where he asks us how to get home when we're out in the car. I always know how to get home. Alisha doesn't. Sometimes she does, but not always."

"You're very lucky. That's a great skill to have. If we can go back to the cabin, then I can get my phone to take some pictures, and a bag or something to put the knife into, so we don't destroy any evidence. That would be a big help to me."

"Okay. This way."

Kenzie followed her small guide to the back door of the cabin. They knocked and called out to Alisha.

It was a few minutes before Alisha finally opened the door, cracking it open and peering out at them. Mason pushed on the door. "Let us in, Alisha!"

Alisha finally stepped back from the door and let Mason open it the rest of the way.

"Where were you, Mason?" she demanded, as Mason bent over to pull off his boots. Her face was still red and visibly tear-streaked. "Daddy was really scared."

Mason tried to put on a brave face. "I was just over at the barn. I didn't do anything wrong."

"You weren't supposed to go anywhere. You were supposed to stay in the yard."

"But I just went to the barn. Dad should know that I would go to the barn."

"You hid from the people looking for you," Kenzie reminded him. "So you knew it was wrong and you tried to keep anyone from finding you."

"I didn't hide from you."

Kenzie admitted this was true. "No. You were good about telling me where you were and coming down. But you shouldn't have hidden from Zachary and your dad. You should have stayed in the yard like you were supposed to. Someone out there... could have wanted to hurt you."

"I can run really fast," Mason protested. "If anyone tried, I would run away."

Kenzie made sure that the back door was shut and locked. "If I was you, I wouldn't give your daddy those excuses when he comes back."

Mason bit his lip, looking away from her. Kenzie wondered again about Tyrrell's past relationship with his family. He seemed stable now, a loving father, patient with the children most of the time, but what had he been like when he had been married? When he had been drinking? Was Mason afraid of him because of the way he had been before he sobered up? Or was it just the natural reaction of a child to a parent who was in authority, knowing that he was going to be in trouble for having broken the rules? The fact that he had come down for Kenzie and not for Tyrrell or Zachary suggested that he was more comfortable with women than with men, which was natural for most children.

"Let's see if we can see them outside. I want to get back to that... spot... to take pictures."

Mason nodded wisely, looking at Alisha and not telling her about the knife.

"And maybe you and Alisha can make that lunch, once your dad is here to supervise."

"We're going to make—"

"Alisha!" Mason shouted her down. "You're not allowed to tell! It's a surprise!"

Alisha closed her mouth and didn't give it away. Mason glared at her fiercely to make sure she didn't think about opening her mouth about it again.

"What about Uncle Zachary?" Alisha asked. "If he comes back, we can cook, right?"

"Well... I think you'd better wait for your daddy."

"Zachary doesn't like to cook," Mason said with authority.

"He doesn't mind cooking. But it is hard for him. And with that camp stove... he doesn't like it. He'd rather use an electric stove, when we have the power back again."

"He was in a fire when he was little," Alisha offered, surprising Kenzie. She hadn't known that the children were aware of this.

"Yes, that's right."

"Like Daddy. But he got burned. Daddy's not scared of fires, but he didn't get burned."

Kenzie nodded. "Different people are afraid of different things. Fire makes Uncle Zachary very nervous. He might be worried about you getting burned, even if you were being careful and safe."

Alisha and Mason both nodded understandingly.

Kenzie opened the front door, looking around for either of the men.

53

Kenzie spotted Tyrrell coming out of the trees on the other side of the road. She waved at him.

"Tyrrell! Tyrrell! Hey!"

He looked up and saw her. His face was still a frozen white mask. Worried and angry and trying not to let it all out.

"He's here," Kenzie shouted at him. "Mason is back."

Tyrrell looked at her for a minute as if unable to process what she had said, then headed toward her at a quick clip.

"He's back?" Tyrrell demanded. "Mason came back?"

"He's here," Kenzie confirmed, nodding in an exaggerated way to make sure he could see it. "Come on back."

Tyrrell made his way across the snowy road to the cabin. "Where was he? I'm going to tan that boy's hide!"

"He was at the barn. But he's back and he's safe."

"I checked the barn."

Kenzie nodded and didn't reveal that Mason had hidden from them. "He's kind of worried about being in trouble, so..."

"He should be," Tyrrell agreed.

"I'm just saying that maybe..."

"Don't try to tell me how to parent. He knows he's not supposed to take off like that."

Kenzie stepped back to let Tyrrell in, then shut the door against the cold.

"He's hoping that he and Alisha can make lunch now," Kenzie said, hoping that would distract Tyrrell from a focus on punishing Mason. "They've got something all planned out. I'm going to go up to the farmhouse, see if Zachary is up there. He'll be relieved to know that Mason is safe."

"I should go up there," Tyrrell suggested. "He didn't want you to be out on your own."

"I'll be okay going that far. I'll be visible the whole time. And there will be people up at the house. I won't be alone."

She didn't mention that she and Mason had just been off in the woods alone. She would have to find a way to tell Zachary about that without upsetting him too, which might not actually be possible. She was all right. Nothing had happened to her. Like Mason, she hoped to avoid censure by pointing out that the outcome had been good. Nothing had happened, therefore she hadn't been in danger, therefore she hadn't made a bad choice by leaving the cabin when she had been warned not to.

"I'll just be a few minutes," she told Tyrrell. "Why don't you get the kids started on lunch, and then Zachary and I will be back in time to eat it?"

***

Kenzie climbed the hill to the farmhouse, thinking about Mason. She hoped that Tyrrell wouldn't be too hard on him. He had disobeyed and walked into a situation where he could have been hurt—both into the woods where Brooke's killer had disposed of the knife, and up into the barn loft where he could have fallen—and she could understand why Tyrrell was upset about that. But Mason hadn't intended any harm and hadn't been hurt, so it had worked out okay in the end.

She knew that Zachary had dealt with parents who were abusive when he had broken the rules or been distracted due to his ADHD. Both his and Tyrrell's biological parents and foster families that he had lived with. She could see how parenting a kid like Mason, who couldn't conform to the rules, could become a power struggle, with a parent trying to force his compliance. And a power struggle could quickly lead to being too harsh physically or emotionally.

Even trying to get Zachary to stick to a short set of rules for their relationship and the upkeep of the household frequently failed. He was an adult and he was willing to do whatever it took to keep their relationship on the tracks, but the way that his brain was wired, all of the good intentions in the world did not result in his being able to stick to the program. He would forget to tell her about something. Abandon a job right in the middle. Forget how she had told him something was to be done a hundred times before. Not because he didn't care what she had to say, but because he frequently didn't have the executive skills to follow through. And that was something he couldn't control, no matter how he tried to focus or to remember the simple steps she had given him.

She sighed. Maybe Mason would grow out of the worst of his symptoms. Scatterbrained or willful children could still become adults with good jobs and family relationships. It was impossible to tell how their brains would mature and how their interests might lead to success. Despite all his challenges, Zachary was still a good investigator, photographer, and partner. He nurtured a number of friendships and professional relationships, and he was very close to his siblings.

She reached the house and paused for a moment for a breath. "Okay."

She knocked briskly on the front door and entered. It was not yet time for lunch to be served, but Raven was sitting reading a book, a glass of wine at her side, and Jack was fiddling with the blinds, presumably trying to get them at the right angle to take the best advantage of the sun, weak though it was through the clouds. Kenzie smiled.

"Hey. Is Zachary up here?"

They both looked at her as if surprised to see her there. Eventually, Raven replied. "He was. Check the kitchen; see whether he's with Mrs. Hubbard, I guess."

Kenzie nodded. "Thanks." She paused, hesitating. "Is Mrs. Hubbard still making meals? Even though...?"

"Do you really think that we believe she was trying to poison us?" Jack asked. "Or that someone else here was? It's pretty ridiculous, when you get right down to it. Doesn't make any sense. So a couple of people had a bit too much to drink one night." He shrugged. "That doesn't mean that we were all being given some mythical hallucinogen."

Kenzie blinked in surprise. They had all been more or less onboard the night before. But she supposed that after a good night's sleep, they had shaken off their anxiety and decided that skipping meals or making their own until the police got there was unsustainable. If it were impossible to avoid a danger, people eventually accepted it, even if it were something that would previously have seemed untenable. The other guests had to eat, so they had to accept it in spite of any warnings.

"You don't even like to take over-the-counter medications," she pointed out to Jack.

Maybe it was a mistake to use something she had learned about him during the search the night before as an argument against him. Her mother would certainly have frowned on it.

Jack narrowed his eyes at her. "What does that have to do with anything?"

"You already confiscated everyone's medications," Raven said. "So even if someone was trying to harm us, they can't now. So it's safe to eat here."

Kenzie closed her mouth and kept her lips pasted together. It would not help her to argue with either of them. Pointing out that Mrs. Hubbard's possessions and the kitchen had not been searched would just make both of them antagonistic toward her.

5 4

Kenzie shook her head and went to the kitchen. She knocked on the door frame as she entered, trying to give Mrs. Hubbard notice that she was there and not to just walk into her domain as if she had the right to be there.

"Good morning, Mrs. Hubbard."

Mrs. Hubbard turned. She raised her brows at Kenzie and didn't look pleased to see her there. Kenzie figured she had probably already made enough of a disruption for the cook. Telling people that the food was poisoned was not exactly likely to endear her.

"Sorry to bother you. I was just looking for Zachary. Is he around?"

Mrs. Hubbard nodded, turning back to her stove. "He went downstairs to make sure that boy didn't end up down there somehow."

Kenzie walked over to the stairs and looked down. She didn't think that the farmhouse had a full basement. Probably just a dugout for some preserves or wine to be stored where they would be cool and out of the sun.

"Zachary?"

"Kenzie?" Zachary appeared at the bottom of the stairs, twisting his neck for a good look at her. "What are you doing here?"

"We found Mason. I wanted to let you know."

"You found him!" Zachary began to climb the steep, creaking stairs. He kept one hand on the wooden stair rail, the other hovering an inch from the wall next to him, as if the whole thing might collapse and he needed to be ready to catch himself or to hold it up. "Where was he?"

Kenzie waited for him to get to the top of the stairs. She touched his arm, but he didn't move closer to embrace her or give her a kiss.

"He was in the barn, up in the loft. Way up the top. Mr. Burknall found him and came to the cabin to let me know."

"I checked the barn."

"I know. So did Tyrrell. But he hid from you. He didn't want to get caught or to be in trouble."

Zachary rolled his eyes. "Well, I'm sure that helped."

Kenzie smiled. "Not so much. I didn't stick around for the fireworks, but Tyrrell was pretty steamed when he got back to the cabin."

"T won't be happy."

"No. I hope he's not too hard on Mason, but..."

"He'll be okay," Zachary assured her. "Kids are tough."

"Yeah. But I don't want him to have to be tough. I want Tyrrell to be..." Kenzie searched for the right word and shook her head. "To be easy on him."

"Well, I guess we found him," Zachary told Mrs. Hubbard, though of course she'd heard the conversation and already knew that for herself. "So we can all stand down. Are you expecting everyone up for lunch and supper?"

"I expect so," Mrs. Hubbard agreed. "Other than you folks."

"Yeah. We still have plenty at the cabin to eat. I wouldn't want it to go to waste."

Kenzie caught Zachary watching Mrs. Hubbard very carefully for her reaction. Did he suspect her? Think that she had been the one to put something into the food? She was the one with the best access, but Kenzie could not think of a reason the woman would have to hurt anyone. She was sure that Mrs. Hubbard was not the kind of person who would do something like that out of pure mischief.

Though Kenzie's searches of the night before had shown her that her assumptions and judgments of others were not always right. She had been very wrong in some of her conclusions.

"If you get tired of it, you know you can always come here," Mrs. Hubbard told him. "It's our Thanksgiving night. Turkey, potatoes, a couple of salads..."

Zachary's expression did not change. "You're a very good cook. I'm sure it will be delicious."

Mrs. Hubbard nodded her agreement.

"I'll see you tomorrow, then," Zachary said pleasantly. "Maybe the weather will have cleared by then and we'll actually get some company."

Mrs. Hubbard's eyes rolled up toward the ceiling. "I certainly hope so. Mr. Dewey and the young lady will not improve with age."

Kenzie grimaced. At least she didn't have to work in the house, in the company of a couple of corpses. She wasn't sure how she would feel living under those conditions.

But then she realized that she did work under exactly those conditions, and it had never bothered her. But then, that was what she had signed up for. She didn't suddenly just find herself in the middle of a situation where she was required to put up with bodies being stored in her workplace.

Zachary nodded to the back door. "Let's go out this way," he invited.

"I... my coat and things are at the front door."

"Oh." He paused to consider her. "I guess they are. Why don't you grab them and come out this way, then?"

"I'll just go out that door. I can walk around the house and meet you out back, if you like."

Zachary nodded. "Yeah. Do that."

Kenzie wasn't sure why he wanted to go out the back instead of the front. Clearly that was where he had taken off his outerwear, but he could have grabbed it and gone out of the front with Kenzie, where it was a clear shot down the road to the cabin.

"Okay, see you in a minute."

Zachary exited the kitchen through the other door, which Kenzie assumed led to some kind of mudroom or porch. She said a quick goodbye to Mrs. Hubbard, which wasn't returned, and she returned to the front door to get her winter gear. Andy Collins and Vance Stiller had joined Raven and Jack in the living room. No one seemed particularly interested in or happy to see Kenzie. She supposed she had made enemies of all of them by going through their private belongings. It wasn't nice to have someone pawing through your personal, private things, even if you didn't have anything that was really secret to hide. People just didn't like it. Raven's search of Kenzie's things the night before had seemed like the ultimate imposition. She hadn't been worried about Raven learning her deepest, darkest secrets, but she hadn't felt good about having someone go through all their things.

"Couldn't find him?" Raven asked.

"Oh, I did. He just went out the back door."

"I saw that kid of yours messing around by the barn," Vance Stiller commented, fixing his gaze on Kenzie. "You should keep him in the house if he isn't being supervised."

"He's not my kid. But thank you for keeping an eye on him. We found him and he's back at the cabin now. He wasn't supposed to take off like that."

"Kids." Stiller shook his head. He looked like the thought of having kids around, of starting a family himself, was repulsive. *Why would anyone want to have children?* "This isn't really the kind of place to bring them."

"Actually, they provide a lot of family activities," Kenzie pointed out, as she slid her hands into the sleeves of her coat. "Hayrides, bonfires, board games, hot chocolate. When it isn't so cold and snowy, there are other activities for them too. It's a family resort."

"Shouldn't be," Stiller said unapologetically. "A place like this should be adults only. So that we can enjoy it properly without worrying about children and what they might say or do."

"Hear, hear," Jack chimed in. "I'm all for adults-only."

Kenzie just shook her head. She wasn't sure why they were trying to get her goat about it, but they weren't going to draw her into an argument.

"Enjoy dinner. I'll see you later," she told them blandly. She pulled on her gloves and let herself out.

There were no fences or guard dogs to get past outside; it was an easy walk around the house from the front door to the back where Zachary was waiting. He nodded as if confirming something to himself.

"What's up?" Kenzie asked.

"Nothing. I just wanted to come this way." Zachary motioned to the woods. "We can cut through this way."

"I thought you wanted to avoid me being killed by someone."

He raised his brows. "I do."

"Then shouldn't I stay where people can see me, instead of tromping off through the lonely woods?"

"No one comes through here. They all go up on the road."

Kenzie thought about the knife in the bushes. "Not everyone. Someone killed Brooke in the woods."

"Well... yes. But that's not going to happen to you. You're not alone, and you're not high on some illegal or prescription drug."

Kenzie remembered Raven's conversation with her the night before. A person could make all the right decisions, all the low-risk choices, and still end up killed. She and Zachary could only control their choices, not what happened as a consequence. Or just as a random happening. Sometimes a person's decisions had nothing to do with how things unfolded.

Kenzie let Zachary lead the way. Like Mason, he had better visual-spatial memory than Kenzie did, and his better sense of direction meant that he could get her back to the cabin way before she could sort it out herself.

"Mason and Alisha are making lunch," she informed Zachary.

"Uh-oh."

Kenzie smiled. "I just hope it's edible."

"At least with it being winter, you don't need to worry about him putting poisonous berries into it."

"Yikes! You're right. He's only allowed to choose from the food that we have. So we should be safe."

"That's one of the reasons I came up here." Zachary explained. "In case he went looking for more ingredients."

Mason going to the house for more ingredients was something that hadn't even occurred to Kenzie. And she had known that Mason and Alisha were putting their heads together to come up with something they could make for the adults for lunch.

"Well, probably a good thing that they didn't, since we still don't know where the toxin came from."

Zachary nodded. "Down in the basement, there were a lot of preserved plants and herbs. I don't know what they all were."

"Jars of fruits and vegetables?" Kenzie asked, since that was what she had pictured when she thought about the small basement room.

"Some," Zachary said. "But also lots of herbs tied into bunches." He made a movement, trying to sketch it out with his hands. "Like flower bouquets without any flowers. Tied together and hung to dry. I don't know what they all were. Some kinds of herbs and spices for her cooking, right?"

"Herbs," Kenzie repeated thoughtfully.

Zachary's brows went up as he considered her response.

"Does that surprise you?"

"No... But it does make me wonder what she might have down there."

55

D o you want to go back and look?" Zachary asked, turning back toward the house and gesturing.

"No... I want to get back to the cabin and get warmed up. Before the kids are finished whatever they are making. So that we don't have to eat whatever it is cold."

Kenzie could just imagine some of the bizarre combinations the kids might come up with together. And they wouldn't be better once they had cooled.

Zachary chuckled under his breath.

"But I do wonder what she has," Kenzie said. "I would say we should go back after and see... but I'm not even sure how I would know what I was looking at. I might be able to identify poison ivy, but I'm afraid that my plant identification abilities don't go much farther than that."

"Do you think there is anything we need to worry about?"

"I don't know. And without the internet, I can't even look them up. I would just have to take her word for it that everything she said was true."

They walked in silence for a few minutes, their gloved hands shoved into the oversized pockets of their jackets.

"Oh," Kenzie remembered one of the reasons she had wanted to get Zachary right away instead of waiting for him to return to the cabin on his own once he'd run out of places to look for Mason. "Mason found a knife."

Zachary stopped walking. Kenzie halted to continue the conversation.

"A knife?"

"Well, *the* knife, I guess. A long kitchen knife. The murder weapon, I'm guessing."

"Did it have blood on it?"

"Not that I could see. But hopefully some microscopic traces."

"Where?"

"Under a bush. He was looking for sticks to use for his snowman."

"Well, that was lucky."

"I haven't told anyone or retrieved it yet. But I grabbed my phone and a bag from the cabin to preserve any evidence."

"We should go get it before whoever hid it decides to retrieve it again. If he remembers where he put it."

"It is sort of back behind our cabin." Kenzie looked around. "We're pretty close, right?"

Zachary nodded. He raised an eyebrow. "Do *you* remember where it is?"

"Uh... I sort of do. But Mason and I were coming from the barn, not back this way, so it's a little different. I don't know whether I'll recognize the exact place..."

"And you didn't happen to mark that particular bush in some way...?"

"No." Kenzie's face warmed. "It isn't like I had an evidence kit with me, you know."

"Clearly not. Do you remember what kind of a bush it was? What it looked like?"

"I don't know my bushes any better than my poisonous plants. It was about... this high..." Kenzie raised her hand above the ground, trying to convey the approximate size of the bush to him.

Zachary looked around.

"You walked close to it before," Kenzie told him. "You were coming back from the barn, and you turned off to the left, instead of back toward the cabin, which was to the right."

Zachary thought about that. "How do you know that?"

"Mason pointed out your footprints. He said they were yours."

Zachary looked down at his boots. He made a print and stepped to the side to study it. Kenzie saw the same zigzag pattern that Mason had pointed out. She looked around the ground for more footprints.

"Okay..."

"Let's try this way." Zachary pointed. "If I was coming back from the barn, then this should be the approximate path I took..."

They walked slowly, watching for more zig-zag footprints. It took a while, but eventually, Zachary spotted his previous path. "Here. This is the way I went..."

"When Mason and I came back from the barn to the cabin, we turned away from your footprints, and he found the bush and showed it to me..." Kenzie looked around. Everything looked the same. She couldn't figure out where the elusive bush was. She looked under all the nearby bushes for the knife. It had to be close by. She could feel Zachary's tension. He was trying to follow her instructions and knew that they must be close to the spot where the knife was hidden.

Kenzie's stomach started to growl. She covered it with her hand and laughed. "I don't know whether I should be hungry... who knows what they are cooking up..."

"Well, you like all the food that we brought, don't you? So it doesn't matter what they make."

"Except kids mix weird things together. I don't want ketchup on granola bars or anything bizarre like that."

Zachary made a face. "I don't want ketchup on granola bars either," he agreed. "That might put me off of breakfast foods forever."

They kept looking for the bush.

"Here!" Zachary called finally. "Over here."

Kenzie hurried over to him. Zachary pointed. "Your footprints and Mason's."

She sighed with relief. "Perfect. This will lead us right to the bush."

She let Zachary go first, leading the expedition. She had already seen the knife. He would be the better tracker. Kenzie didn't pay much attention where they were going until she saw the cabin in front of her. "Uh... this is too close. We missed it. It's back farther."

Zachary reversed and walked alongside the footprints. He stopped a couple of times. It felt like they had been following the trail for too long. Kenzie shook her head, puzzled. "Something isn't right."

"These *are* your footprints."

"I know, but..." Kenzie looked around and saw the barn. "It wasn't all the way back here. It was in the woods. You couldn't see the barn *or* the cabin." She was getting hungry and frustrated. It didn't make sense that they had lost the knife. They were in the right place. They couldn't both be that blind.

Zachary looked at her for a minute, then followed the trail back again, toward the cabin. He moved slowly, carefully. "Here?" he asked finally, pointing to a bush.

"Yes! That's it!" Kenzie agreed. She got closer, pointing to the base of the bush. "Right... there..." The words faded away. Kenzie looked at Zachary, then down again. "This can't be right."

"Are you sure this is the bush?"

"No... I think it is. They all look the same to me. But it looks like the right one."

Zachary looked around at some of the other shrubbery. He pointed down at the footprints. "You can see that this is where you and Mason stopped. Did you stop to look at more than one thing? Maybe there was a bird or an animal...?"

"No. The only time we stopped was to look at the knife. I didn't want to pick it up, because I didn't have my phone or a bag to put the knife in. I didn't want to destroy any evidence."

"Did you bring your phone with you this time?"

"Yes, but..." Kenzie shook her head. "We need to find the knife."

"It isn't here."

"I know, so we need to find it..."

"No," Zachary said firmly. "Someone has picked it up. It isn't here anymore."

Understanding dawned on Kenzie. "Oh, no."

Zachary nodded. "Yeah. I'm sorry, but... we took too long."

Kenzie looked down at the bottom of the bush. "There isn't any point in taking pictures of nothing."

"There still may be something here that helps." Zachary pointed at the footprints in the snow. "The police may be able to sort out who has been by here. Not just you and Mason. Whoever left the knife there and whoever picked it up. Not necessarily the same person, but more than likely."

Kenzie nodded. She patted her pockets to find her phone, then removed her glove in order to unlock it and launch the camera. "I can't believe someone came here while I was up to the house to get you. What are the chances that they would come right at that time and take the knife?"

"They might have been watching."

Kenzie tried to suppress a shudder. If they had been close enough to see her and Mason leave the knife and go on, or to see Kenzie go up the hill to the farmhouse, then she should have seen them. She should have known that someone was watching the house and she should have done a better job at protecting herself and the little boy. She had put him in danger and hadn't even known it. They had walked right by a murderer. Or at least, they had walked by the person who had retrieved the knife. If that hadn't been the killer, then who else could it have been? Would anyone else have picked up the knife if they had seen it? They would all want to preserve the evidence, wouldn't they? To prove that it was someone else who had killed Brooke. Nobody would want to hide the identity of the killer.

At least, she hoped not.

Kenzie took several pictures of the leaves under the bush, of the footprints. She took close-ups and shots from farther out, hoping to capture all the evidence the police would need.

"Who do you think it was?" Kenzie asked Zachary. She put her phone in her pocket and slid her fingers back into the nice warm fleecy interior of her gloves. "You think that the person who retrieved the knife is the person who killed Brooke?"

"Probably. I don't know. We'll have to see whether anyone says anything about it. They might have just been trying to do the right thing, like you. To gather evidence for when the police get here."

Kenzie nodded. She really hoped that was all it was. She felt very exposed, standing out there with Zachary, taking pictures of the bush. She hated to think of the unknown shadow watching her and Mason when they had walked through the first time. She was lucky that whoever it was had waited to see if she would pick up the knife or not. And she was probably lucky that she hadn't picked up the knife. If she had, and whoever had killed Brooke had wanted to keep it a secret, then she might not have made it back to her cabin at all.

She shuddered.

"You're cold," Zachary observed. "We've been out here long enough. Let's get back to the cabin and have a hot meal."

Kenzie just hoped it was edible.

<h1 style="text-align:center">56</h1>

It wasn't far to the cabin, but Kenzie was feeling tired and wrung out, as if she had a run a marathon instead of just walking around in the snow. She had walked more than she had expected to, to the barn, back to the cabin, up to the farmhouse, back to the barn again, and back to the cabin. But still, that couldn't add up to very much if one were just counting miles.

The back door was locked, so Zachary knocked and called out a few times before Tyrrell came to the door and opened it.

"You're back! I was afraid you had gotten lost."

"Goldmans don't get lost," Zachary said lightly.

"Yeah!" Mason agreed, jumping down from a chair and running over to give Zachary's legs a hug. "Goldmans don't get lost!" He grinned up at his uncle. "That's because we have excellent visio..."

"Visual-spatial memory," Kenzie contributed.

"Yeah!" Mason agreed. "We have that, right?"

"We do," Zachary agreed. "So... how are we in cooking skills?"

Mason considered this seriously. "We made pasta."

"Pasta is good," Zachary said agreeably.

"It has pieces of turkey in it. And a tomato sauce. Daddy says it tastes really good."

"Well, we should all have some, then. You know, Kenzie's stomach was growling so loud, I kept thinking that we were being stalked by a wild animal!"

Alisha giggled loudly. "You did not!"

"You should have heard it," Zachary said dramatically. He looked around, acting out how frightened he had been. "Every time we went around a corner, I was sure that it was coming..."

Kenzie put her hand over her stomach. "It growled once! And that's just because I didn't have any breakfast."

"You should always have breakfast," Mason told her, his voice taking on a lecturing tone. "It's the most important meal of the day."

"Yeah, Kenzie," Zachary teased.

Kenzie glared at him.

Alisha put bowls and spoons on the table for them, and Tyrrell supervised Mason handling the hot pot and bringing it over. Kenzie and Zachary sat down. Mason placed the pot on the table with a large serving spoon. "Do you want me to dish it up?"

"I'll get my own." Zachary reached for the spoon.

He dished up more than he would normally eat. Kenzie wondered whether he had worked up an appetite from walking outside, or whether he was taking more so that Mason wouldn't think that Zachary didn't trust his cooking. When he had dished up, Kenzie took the pot. She leaned over it and sniffed the savory steam.

"Mmm, it smells really good, Mason. What made you think of this?"

"We just looked in the cupboards to see what we had," Mason said with a shrug. He had a wide grin at her compliment. "I make pasta with Mommy sometimes. It's not hard. And we had turkey. Usually, we put ground beef in it, but I thought turkey would be okay. Sometimes we make other kinds of pasta with chicken or turkey."

"Sure," Kenzie agreed with a nod.

"We have dessert too," Alisha piped up, hovering over them. "So don't eat too much!"

"Ooh, dessert," Zachary murmured. "I'll have to leave some room. I might have taken a bit too much."

This gave him an excuse for not being able to eat all the pasta that he had taken. Not a bad plan.

Kenzie watched Tyrrell and Mason. Whatever discussion had taken place after Kenzie had left didn't seem to have resulted in any tension between them. Maybe Tyrrell had only given Mason a lecture on leaving when he wasn't supposed to, hugged him and said how worried he had been, and then moved on to lunch preparations. Kenzie hadn't been gone for long enough for much more to have taken place.

If Mason were under house arrest or facing some other punishment, he didn't seem to be upset about it. Alisha had washed her tear-streaked face and seemed to be back to her usual cheerful self.

Kenzie took her first bite of the pasta. The children had managed to cook it properly without letting it get too mushy. It wasn't underdone or overdone. The pasta sauce was a bottled sauce that Kenzie had brought with her, but she thought they might have added something to it. The turkey lent it a nice heartiness. She might actually try adding turkey to pasta at home.

"This is really good. You did a great job!"

Both children beamed, happy with her reaction. Kenzie dug in, her body ready for a larger meal after skipping breakfast. Zachary took only a few bites. He praised Mason and Alisha, but they could see how little he was eating and obviously doubted his assurances that he enjoyed it.

Zachary got up, muttering something that Kenzie couldn't make out, and started to wander around the kitchen. She didn't realize at first that he was pacing; she thought he was looking for something. She ate a little more and tried to get him to return to the table. At least for their dessert.

"What's up?" she asked. "You're thinking about something."

"Trying to figure it out... who took that knife and what they did with it. And all of the pills that you searched out and collected... where are they? I was hoping that when I looked around this morning, I would find them. Disposed of in a ditch or shoved into a pile of snow. Because... no one is going to want to deal with them, are they? They won't try to poison anyone." Zachary shook his head. "Did anyone actually put any of them into the food to start with? Or were we wrong?"

Kenzie looked at the kids, wishing that Zachary wouldn't say so much around them. But he didn't follow her glance and didn't stop talking about it.

"A lot of drugs can have the kinds of effects that we saw or heard about."

"But *did* they?" Zachary demanded. "How much would be needed to make everyone suffer the effects? And they wouldn't be able to taste them? For them all to be affected, Kenzie. Does that make sense?"

"What are you suggesting, then? That we were just being paranoid? That everyone was just... feeling their oats that day? It was a full moon? What about the amnesia? Both Vance Stiller and Andy Collins had pretty significant memory blocks."

"Maybe they drank too much? They're both drinkers, right? But we don't know how much they usually drink. If they went overboard or if they started out dehydrated?"

Kenzie tried to follow Zachary's reasoning. "So... you don't want to think that it was an intentional poisoning. It was just... a series of coincidences, and we made it out to be something that it wasn't?"

"We misjudged."

"I did, you mean. It was all my idea from the start, not yours."

"We both thought it," Zachary said firmly. "Everyone except us had... weird experiences that night. But what if it was just... mass hysteria? One person setting another off? Like kids telling ghost stories. Like the Salem witch trials. A couple of people had too much to drink, maybe Redd was into his mushrooms, and between them... they managed to influence everyone, to make them see and hear things that weren't there. But in reality... it was just..."

"A couple having a fight that ended in disaster."

"It happens." He grimaced at her. "It happens a lot."

Kenzie knew that was true. She was the one who worked in the medical examiner's office. She knew very well how easy it was for a domestic dispute to turn bloody. And fatal.

"It could be," she admitted.

Zachary continued to wander around. Kenzie rubbed her forehead and thought about what he had said. Had they gone way overboard in their theory that someone had poisoned the food? Had she been that far off base? If so, then why had someone broken into the safe and stolen the drugs? Just like the knife under the bush? Someone was cleaning up, trying to sanitize the area and get rid of any evidence. They would say that Dewey's death had been by natural causes, and Brooke's was just a tragic accident. A newlywed's argument gone bad. Would there be any evidence to the contrary?

Had Kenzie just let her imagination get the better of her? Was she prone to flights of fancy without Dr. Wiltshire there to bring her down to earth?

It was true that they didn't have much in the way of evidence. There would be more once the authorities had a chance to examine Mr. Dewey's and Brooke Collins's bodies. The medical examiner for the county would be able to find a hallucinogen, if he knew what to look for.

"Are you done?" Alisha asked. "Are you ready for dessert?"

Kenzie brought herself back to the present. The children were watching, hovering nearby, eager to serve them the next course.

"Yes," Kenzie agreed, pushing her dish away. "I had a lot, but I left a little bit of room..."

"It was really good, right?" Mason asked.

"Yes, it was. I'm going to make some at home sometime. It's a really good use of the turkey and other ingredients that you have on hand. I was afraid you guys were going to come up with something really weird. I used to do experiments in the kitchen when I was little, mixing potions and coming up with some really bizarre—and totally inedible—stuff."

Alisha giggled. "Really?"

"Really. Like... mixing chocolate milk and orange soda and... brown sugar and cinnamon." Kenzie made a face. "It was not something you would have wanted to drink."

"Eww!" Both children broke into giggles, making little shrieks to express how disgusting it was and then laughing until they were out of breath.

Kenzie shook her head. "Okay, you'd better tell me what you've made for dessert, before you bust a gut."

Mason wiped at his eyes, wet from tears of laughter. "Can you really do that?" he asked seriously. "Bust a gut?"

"No. It's just an expression."

"You can break a rib laughing," Zachary contributed, walking back to the table. "Or get a nosebleed. Or... if you're drinking milk, it could come out your nose."

"Or if you're mixing together chocolate milk and orange soda," Alisha gasped. "And cinnamon!"

"Don't spray that through your nose," Kenzie said. "Trust me."

That sent them into more gales of laughter. Tyrrell moved into the kitchen, interceding. "You guys are a terrible influence!" he scolded Zachary and Kenzie. "These two are going to be in hysterics before long. Dessert!" he told Mason and Alisha sternly. "No more nonsense!"

The children's faces fell, and they went to the counter to get the dessert ready. They tried to pout and stay serious, but Kenzie could see them still exchanging looks with each other, trying to keep their expressions serious.

"We have peaches and yogurt," Alisha said, bringing over bowls of each and a couple of small dessert bowls for Kenzie and Zachary to dish up their individual desserts.

"Are we supposed to choose one or the other?" Zachary asked mischievously. "Or mix them both together?"

Alisha giggled. But she glanced at Tyrrell and quickly stifled it. "You're *supposed* to mix them. And you can sprinkle granola on top. If you like granola." She supplied a small dish of clumps of granola that had once been formed into bars.

Kenzie and Zachary dished up their desserts with solemn expressions. Once they had tasted a couple of bites, Tyrrell shooed the children away, telling them that they could play for a while and work out their silliness.

He shot a glance toward his brother that told Kenzie without a doubt that he had picked up enough of their conversation to not be happy about the way they were talking around his children. Kenzie imagined him trying to explain to his ex-wife why the children were suddenly obsessed with the idea of their food being poisoned or were talking about dead bodies at their vacation resort. She grimaced and took another bite of her peaches and yogurt.

57

The children were in the living room, playing, already arguing over what they were going to play and what the rules would be. If they had been disturbed by overhearing any of Zachary's and Kenzie's discussion over lunch, it didn't seem as if it were bothering them anymore. Kids were like that. Flexible. Able to switch from something worrisome to something safer in a few minutes.

Most kids, that is.

Kids who hadn't been traumatized as Zachary had been as a child. Children who didn't have OCD or other obsessive conditions that forced them to relive the conversations over and over again.

"The Salem witch trials," Kenzie said in a low voice.

Zachary raised his brows. He took a bite of the peach and yogurt concoction.

"You said that it was all mass hysteria," Kenzie said.

He looked at her. "Wasn't it? You're not contending that it was actual magic, are you?"

"No, that's not what I meant." Kenzie smiled and shook her head. "I'm not arguing for actual magic and witchcraft. There might have been some traditional herbal healing that was identified as witchcraft, I'll admit to that. It's easy to attribute malice to things that you don't understand. But I don't think it was just mass hysteria, either. That might be part of it. And the same kind of pressure to inform on your neighbors as you might have dealt with in the anti-communist era or in Nazi Germany. But it was more than that."

"What, then?"

"They think that part of it might have been ergot."

Zachary shook his head. He blinked at her, trying to make sense of it. Clearly not a theory he had heard before. "What is ergot?"

"It's a disease that rye and other grains can get. And if people eat the infected grain, then they can experience hallucinations and other odd behaviors. So some of the 'hysteria' surrounding the trials might have had to do with people having hallucinations about things that other people were doing, or hallucinations about performing magic themselves."

"Ergot. I've never heard of it before. So... is it one of those diseases that doesn't exist anymore? Like the plague?"

"It still exists, but with the commercialization of grains and regulations on care and handling, it rarely affects anyone anymore. Maybe a farmer who grows rye for himself and doesn't know what to watch for. But it doesn't generally enter the market."

"Could they have it here? Could something that Mrs. Hubbard cooked with have been contaminated with this disease? She makes bread, buns, all of that kind of thing. Whatever they need, she makes from scratch."

Kenzie thought about it while slurping down a few more bites of peaches and yogurt. It was a nice, sweet treat. Not chocolate ice cream, but something nice to have when they were separated from most of her usual comfort foods. The kids had really risen to the challenge and had produced a very nice lunch.

"I don't think they could have it here, but of course anything is possible. I would think that if Mrs. Hubbard had any diseased rye, she would recognize it and not cook with it. But if a neighbor had it and ground it up..." Kenzie shrugged. "It could be something shared between households in these parts. A farmer's market or a barter group."

"How would we find out?"

"We're just going to have to wait until the authorities can get here. They can check Brooke's body for ergot and any other toxins that we think she might have been exposed to. We can't test everyone else, but *her* metabolism stopped while she still had it in her system. Unless it's got a really short half-life, it will still be present in the body."

"But there's nothing we can do until then?"

"Just talk to Mrs. Hubbard. Ask her where she gets her flour. If she's ever heard of anyone having this in the area. But I don't know how forthcoming she will be. Not if she thinks that we suspect her of wrongdoing. It's one thing to say that someone came into her kitchen and put something into the food without her realizing it. It's another thing to say that she did it herself, either through negligence or intentionally."

Zachary nodded slowly. He stirred his peaches and yogurt around, then licked off the spoon. Sometimes he ate at a maddeningly slow speed. Like a kid who took three hours to eat Brussels sprouts, hoping that Mom and Dad would give up and not make him eat them all.

"Mushrooms, ergot, what else?"

"What else what?"

"What other plants can cause hallucinations? We were looking for drugs. Something that would have to have been intentionally added to the food to have this effect. What if it were something that was in the food by accident? Something that... Mrs. Hubbard thought was something different. There are mix-ups sometimes. Berries, wild parsnips, herbs that someone thought were one thing, but they were actually another. You hear about people being poisoned by accident because something was misidentified. So what might have caused these other symptoms? Psychedelic mushrooms and moldy rye. Anything else?"

"It's not really my area."

"But it is. How would you find out if someone ate something poisonous by accident if they came to your morgue? It happens, so there must be some kind of protocol to figure it out."

"Okay, yes," Kenzie agreed. "Of course there is. We talk to the people who were around the deceased last, find out what they were doing and if they showed any signs or symptoms. Actually, the police usually do that, but sometimes the ME's office has follow up questions. We take stomach contents and try to identify what their last meal consisted of. If it seems suspicious or poisoning is suspected, then we will take a longer time doing that. Not just observing what is in the stomach contents, but testing the various ingredients. And we do tox screens. The most basic ones just check for drugs someone is likely to overdose on, but if there is something specific we are looking for, a particular plant or drug, then we can test for those."

"But you can't do any of that here."

"The only thing I can do here is to talk to people and look for signs and symptoms of what they might have eaten. And people are not being really cooperative right now. I think everyone is tired of the questions and just wants to pretend that nothing happened. It was just... a nightmare or a drunk. Nothing more than that."

"And you don't know what other plants could cause these symptoms?"

"Which symptoms? I know a few, but I'd have to look most of them up in a database. I at least need internet access so I can look them up."

"And we can't." Zachary sighed. "Oh, well. Hopefully, it won't be very long until the weather clears up and the authorities can get here. I know we won't be first priority, but they know we already have a body here. Even if it were just natural causes, the ME is still going to want a look while it is still as fresh as possible. In three days, a body is already starting to decompose."

"Luckily, ours is in cold storage. I'm glad we ended up here in the winter rather than the summer. But yeah. They don't know that and... hopefully they're eager to get here before it decomposes too much."

Zachary went back to stirring his fruit around. Kenzie worked through the symptoms in her head. She kept starting a list and then getting distracted, so she tried to work it through out loud. "Hallucinations or delusions. Amnesia. Anger, irritability, oppositional behavior. Maybe heart attack."

Zachary's eyes sparked. He was eager to work it out with Kenzie. They both enjoyed it when they could work on a case together, bouncing ideas off each other and seeing what they could come up with. Kenzie providing the medical knowledge and Zachary making suggestions based on his observations of human behavior.

"What about fever?" he suggested. "You thought that Redd might have a fever."

"Yes... a fever can cause hallucinations, but what caused the fever? It could be a virus."

"And we know that viruses can cause a lot of other neurological symptoms as well."

"Yes," Kenzie acknowledged, and rolled her eyes. "They certainly can. And you and I would be less likely to catch a virus, staying down here away from the rest of the crowd and having just gone through an antiviral protocol."

"What else could fever be caused by? Is a virus the only possibility?"

"Bacterial infection. There are definitely drugs that can raise your core temperature as well. Ecstasy is one of them."

"Did you find any of that when we searched the cabins?"

"No, but that doesn't mean that no one had any before I did the search. Or had it on their person, since we didn't search everyone to see what they were carrying."

Zachary nodded. "What else?"

"Redd had dilated pupils as well. Very wide."

"Not pinpoint like with opioids."

"No. Opioids are out. If everyone were exposed to the same thing as Redd. His pupils were definitely dilated."

"Anything else?"

"They seemed drunk. More than they should have been for having a drink or two with dinner."

"They might have started drinking earlier, or have had more than you thought."

"Or it made them act drunk."

Zachary nodded, conceding. "So what does that tell you? Anything?"

"Death. Drunken. Delirium. Dilated pupils." Kenzie blinked, trying to put it all together.

"You sound like... you know."

"The ten D's," Kenzie said. There was something tickling the back of her brain, but she couldn't bring it to the fore. Why did they have to have no internet access? With a few searches, she could have looked up the ten D's. She could have reminded herself what the others were, so she could see whether they fit. And they would tell her, if they all fit, what the toxin was. "This is maddening! I can't think of it."

"This is something you learned in medical school?" Zachary suggested. "What class?"

Kenzie tried to picture it. Which professor or doctor had listed them? Was it a class? A case she had attended to on rounds? The emergency room? Something that had come up in the medical examiner's office? She pressed her fingertips to her forehead, trying to remember.

"Yes, but I can't remember. It's just on the tip of my tongue, but I can't remember it."

"There were ten D's? What else could there have been? What other symptoms start with D?"

"There are too many of them to count. I have to remember what those ten were. Or what they indicated. It was... it was a toxin, I'm sure of that. Not a genetic disorder. Nothing congenital."

Zachary was quiet, watching her. But despite the fact that he was respecting her process and giving her the time to think it through, Kenzie was irritated by his focused interest. It was too much pressure.

"Are you done with that?" She indicated his dessert bowl. "If you are, then get rid of it. Don't keep *playing* with it."

Zachary stood up. He picked up the bowl and took it with him to the sink. Of course he was hurt. He was trying to help, and she had snapped at him for something that wasn't even the issue. Kenzie would make it up to him later. She would thank him for being quiet and leaving her to just think about it. She would thank him for getting up and washing his dish without making a big deal of it. Once she had sorted the symptoms out and knew what it was they were looking for.

Tyrrell had heated a pot of water for washing dishes. Kenzie tried to ignore Zachary as he scraped his dessert bowl and his main course into the garbage, then splashed around in the sink, cleaning them up. He returned to the table and didn't say anything to Kenzie about whether she had solved the puzzle yet. He indicated her dinner bowl. "You're done with that one?"

Kenzie nudged it toward him. She looked down at her dessert bowl, but wasn't really interested in the fruit and yogurt anymore. The kids were both in the other room, so they wouldn't see whether she finished it off or not. She took one more bite, and then pushed that bowl to Zachary as well.

"Thanks."

He nodded and took them both away without a word.

Kenzie leaned her head back until she was staring up at the ceiling.

She was a trained medical professional. She had seen the group of symptoms that had been described to her. It might have been rare, but that wasn't any excuse for not remembering the details. Doctors had to be able to consume and retain vast quantities of information. She had been too lazy, relying on her ability to perform searches to find out what she needed to instead of on retaining the new information that she learned. She couldn't stop learning. Just because she was in the Medical Examiner's Office now, that didn't mean that she could just coast. There was far more that she could be learning from each and every case that went through their autopsy.

Zachary finished the dish-washing and didn't return to the table to check up on her and see whether she had figured out the information she was trying to remember yet. He knew, of course, that she would tell him when she remembered. It wouldn't be a secret. She wouldn't hold back to surprise him later when he least expected it. It wasn't some kind of game or power play.

They both knew that however safe they felt there in the cabin, their lives could depend on it.

5 8

I t sounded melodramatic, but it really wasn't, was it?

She needed to know what it was that the guests were being poisoned with, if anything. It could be the difference between someone living or dying. Not only that, but if someone had intentionally poisoned the food or drinks, then they were not going to want Kenzie to figure it out. They would already be looking for a way to take her out. To remove Kenzie and her knowledge from the equation.

And she had seen the knife. Maybe that wasn't a key piece of evidence. She hadn't been able to see what fingerprints were on it, of course. Seeing the knife itself hadn't told her anything about who it was that had stabbed Brooke. It was just a knife. She hadn't even been able to prove that it was the knife that had killed Brooke, though she was sure it was. Why else would someone have thrown it away behind the cabins? People didn't just randomly throw knives away in the bush.

It was a matter of life and death. Kenzie's, and maybe others' as well. She couldn't afford to treat it like a case she was only remotely interested in. People could die if she didn't figure it out. Like on a medical mystery TV show—the doctors always kept looking until they found out exactly what the patient's problem was. It didn't matter how rare the disease or syndrome was or how expensive the testing or treatment were. It didn't matter how long it would have taken doctors in real life to figure out what the problem was. A TV show doctor would figure it out.

And that was what Kenzie had to do too.

She got up from the table. Sitting there wasn't bringing her any inspiration. She needed to move around, to think through what they knew again. Maybe make a written list this time. Like she had written down the drugs that she had found in each of the cabins. She should probably look at that again to see whether she could add anything to it. She might remember one or two more medications.

Not that it mattered. Not if, like Zachary suggested, it wasn't even someone's medication that had been used to poison the guests. Something that occurred naturally or had been added in. A berry? Belladonna? Wild parsnips? Something that Mrs. Hubbard had foraged and saved, thinking it was a harmless substance. It wasn't her fault. People made mistakes.

Tyrrell looked at Kenzie as she wandered through the living room. He too gave her the space she needed. Maybe he didn't know what they had been talking about and he was just tired or enjoying watching the children. But he didn't interrogate her and ask her if she had figured out what the ten D's were yet, or what they signified.

She would write down all of the D symptoms she could think of. Then she would pick out the ones that fit together. And once she had the list of ten, she would remember what it was that they were looking for. And they would be one step closer to figuring out the answer.

It wasn't just mass hysteria. She was convinced of it. The constellation of symptoms was too familiar.

Kenzie finished going over her written lists and pushed them to the side, sighing loudly. Zachary was playing with the kids on the floor and looked up at her.

"Maybe you need to distract your mind. Sometimes, when you're trying to remember something, the best thing to do is to not think about it. Distract yourself with something else, and then it suddenly pops into your head."

"I don't think that's going to happen here."

Zachary shrugged. "Well, you've written everything down, so it isn't like you're going to lose something if you put it out of your mind. Why don't you play a game with us. Distract yourself and see what happens." He looked toward the window, which was starting to get dark. "It doesn't make any difference whether you remember tonight or tomorrow. I don't think anything is going to happen tonight."

But the fact was, something had happened every night since they had arrived there. Deaths, the theft of the drugs from the safe, something had happened ever time the sun had gone down. But she'd better keep it to herself. She didn't want to upset the kids and give them nightmares.

Maybe the weather would break, and they would be able to get help the next day.

The doors were locked and, unlike in many of the houses in the city, they were not hollow core doors, but heavy, thick, hardwood doors with bolts that sank into thick log walls. Practically impenetrable. Or so she hoped.

They were safe for the night. Help would not arrive until at least the next day. She might as well put her worries aside and do something that the kids would enjoy.

"Okay, what? What do you guys want to do?"

"Play *Clue*?" Alisha suggested.

Kenzie laughed. *Clue*. When they were trying to figure out a real murder. That would be distracting, all right.

But at least there were no poisons or toxic plants in *Clue*. It was all manual murder weapons. Knife, gun, rope, candlestick. No one could leave a poison in one room and then leave, so that their crime was not discovered until much later.

Kenzie shook her head, but she agreed. "Okay, *Clue*. You guys get it out. I want to be Mrs. Peacock."

"I like Professor Plum," Alisha said. "I like purple."

"You can't be Professor Plum," Mason objected. "You have to be one of the girls."

"Girls can be professors."

Mason looked skeptical. He pulled the box out of the pile and started going through the cards. He showed Alisha the one for Professor Plum. "He's not a girl. He's a man. You have to be one of the girls."

"No I don't. And that doesn't mean that Professor Plum has to be a man. They just had to make him a man or a woman when they drew the card. He can be anyone you want. If I want him to be a woman professor, he can be." Alisha looked at Kenzie, appealing to her. "A lady can be a professor, right?"

"Of course," Kenzie agreed. "I'm a female doctor. I had lots of professors at school who were women."

"In this game, he's a man," Mason grumbled.

"He can be a woman," Alisha asserted. "And that's who I'm going to be. What color do you want, Mason?"

Mason made a face. "Mr. Green."

"Okay. Mr. Green. Who do you want to be, Uncle Zachary?"

"Colonel Mustard."

"He's the yellow one," Mason declared, setting the figure on his square. He sounded the word out. "Col-o-nel. Why do you say it *kernel*?"

Zachary shook his head. "That's how it is pronounced. I don't know why."

Mason accepted this. "Daddy, you have to be White or Scarlet, because Alisha took Professor Plum." He lowered his eyebrows at Alisha. "See? You should let Daddy take Professor Plum. You can be one of the girls."

"It's okay, Mason," Tyrrell told him. "I'll be... Miss Scarlet."

Mason giggled.

Tyrrell tried out a falsetto voice. "Is this how Miss Scarlet talks?"

Mason guffawed loudly. He pushed Alisha over.

"Hey!" Alisha objected.

"You still sound like a girl. You have to make a voice like a man."

"No. I'm a lady professor, not a man professor, so I don't have to use a deep voice."

Alisha continued to set up the board game. Mason sighed and sorted through the cards to select out the murderer, weapon, and room.

<hr>

"Kenzie?" Zachary touched Kenzie on the shoulder to get her attention. "Kenz, it's your turn."

Kenzie blinked and looked at Zachary. She looked at the game board and the clue sheet in her hand. She had completely lost track of the last few moves, when she should have been marking down each of the clues she gathered as the other players passed cards back and forth.

"Are you okay?" Zachary asked. He looked at the window. "What time is it? Do you want to go to bed? I know you didn't get very much sleep last night."

"No."

He waited. "You don't want to go to bed, or you aren't okay?"

Kenzie looked away from him. Zachary was sitting on the floor in front of the bookshelves. As with the other cabins, the books in the shelves covered a wide range of genres and topics, hopefully providing something of interest to everyone who stayed there. There was genre fiction and non-fiction, topics ranging from food to gardening in Vermont and history of the area. All kinds of things.

"Umm, I pass," she told the other players. She moved toward Zachary, who hid his cards and clue sheet.

Mason and Alisha protested that Kenzie couldn't pass on her turn. She had to roll the dice and make a guess if she could.

"Someone else roll for me," Kenzie said. "I'm going... over there," she pointed to one of the rooms the farthest away from her playing piece. "I need to find out about the Ballroom."

She, of course, had the Ballroom in her hand, but hopefully they didn't know that. Kenzie kept going. Not directly to Zachary, but to the books behind him. *Gardening in Vermont. Traditional Vermont Cookery. Wildcrafting and Backwoods Forage. Early Virginia History.*

59

Kenzie started to pull books off the shelves. The children protested that they were still playing the game, but Kenzie ignored them. "Someone else can take my turn. Zachary, can you play my cards?"

"That's not fair!" Mason insisted. "Then he knows all your cards too and he will win!"

Kenzie ignored the protest. They could sort it out without her. Her attention was needed elsewhere. Zachary picked up Kenzie's cards and dealt them around the table. "Now everyone has more. Let's keep going. Kenzie can't play right now."

"Why can't she?" Mason continued to whine.

Kenzie opened up the gardening book and started to leaf through it.

As she had told Zachary earlier, she could identify poison ivy, but that was about the extent of her plant identification skills. Other than the obvious. Daisies and strawberries and things that everyone grew in their gardens. But all of the different types of plants and flowers and berries and herbs... there were just too many for her to make any headway on them. She had too many other things she was trying to learn and retain as a doctor. She slowed down and started really looking at the plants and skimming through the side-bars, looking for any warnings about plants that were toxic or could cause people health problems if they were susceptible. Some of the warnings were just lore, and others had actual medical warnings on them. She stopped halfway through and picked up the cooking and wildcrafting books. She didn't know a lot about wildcrafting, but knew that the general idea was using plants that grew wild in your environment for food or other purposes. Medicine, fuel, decoration, soap making. Whatever people could think of to do with them.

She couldn't read all the books simultaneously, but she was sure going to try. She looked over the pages for keywords, skipping from one book to the other, turning each of the pages and checking again. She wanted to absorb all the information at the same time. It seemed ridiculous that people were only able to read one document at a time, when a computer could have easily searched all the books at the same time and come up with the hits for her. Old school was so slow!

Zachary continued to play the game with the children, but she could see him watching her out of the corner of his eye. Kenzie continued to leaf through the books, impatient to find something that would help. Maybe, as Zachary said, it had all been a mistake. Mrs. Hubbard had gathered some plants she thought were safe, and they were not. She had no way of knowing that they could have caused the hallucinogenic effects or that they could lead to death. She would never have intentionally killed her employer, something that might force her into an early retirement.

Kenzie turned the page in the gardening book and found that the next chapter was "A Poison Garden." Kenzie stopped and stared at the page. Would someone actually plant a garden they knew contained poisonous plants? Certainly not someone with children or animals who might get into the plants. The introductory paragraphs in the chapter referred to a garden in England that was famous for the number of poisonous plants that it contained, and how it was becoming the new trend among gardeners in the US.

There were, of course, plenty of warnings about fencing the garden and keeping it secure from children and pets. No warnings about making sure you didn't have any budding serial killers in the area. Kenzie slowly turned the pages, studying the leaves, flowers, and fruits shown on each panel and reading through the descriptions of the effect of each poison. Some of them were extremely toxic in small amounts, and Kenzie couldn't imagine growing them intentionally, knowing what heartbreak they could cause. What if your fence wasn't high enough? Or a neighbor unknowingly let a child into the garden to retrieve a lost ball or to look at the pretty flowers or berries? It would be horrifying to discover that you had made a mistake and someone had suffered or died because of it.

Kenzie stopped at one panel, reading the symptoms over again carefully. She looked at the heading. *Datura stramonium.*

"Datura," she said aloud.

"What's that?" Zachary's head turned toward her.

Kenzie scanned the common names of the plant with the purple, trumpet-shaped flowers.

"*Datura stramonium.* Jimson weed."

"What is that?"

"It's... a plant that grows all over North America." Kenzie read through the description of the areas and type of soil the plant grew in. "It is part of the same family as deadly nightshade and tobacco. Many of our popular vegetables come from that family, but it has some toxic members as well as the edibles."

"And do you think... that someone used it by accident?"

Zachary abandoned the *Clue* game, apparently not even hearing the protests of the children as he turned his back on them, completely focused on Kenzie.

"An accident... I don't know. It sounds as though it is fairly well-known. Some people smoke it for its hallucinogenic properties, but it is very toxic. Easy to overdose and kill yourself."

"Do you think it grows around here?"

Kenzie showed him the cover of the book. *Gardening in Vermont.*

"Okay, so I would guess that it does." Zachary considered. "Does it cover all the symptoms?"

"Yes. And I remember hearing about it in rounds. The doctor talking about how you don't see a lot of it, but you have to be able to recognize it. The ten D's. Dry mouth, dry hot skin, delirium, delusions, death, I don't remember all of them. I'll have to look them up when we get internet access again. This article doesn't list them all as D's, but it's all in there..." Kenzie's eyes were focused beyond her, thinking about it.

"We should go up and talk to Mrs. Hubbard."

Kenzie looked at the window. It was very dark outside. She didn't want to be wandering around so late. "We should wait until tomorrow."

Zachary followed her gaze. He shifted restlessly. "I don't think it's that late yet. She won't be in bed. We could talk to her tonight."

"Not at night. With everything else that has happened... I don't want to be out there after dark."

"We could get Burknall to take us up there. He would be a good guard, make sure that nothing happened."

"As long as he isn't the poisoner. He has access to the kitchen. He visits with Mrs. Hubbard. He could slip something into the food." Kenzie looked down at the book. "It doesn't take very much Jimson weed to cause an overdose. You can't tell how much of the active compound is in the leaves. Or the seeds. It's very concentrated."

"But why would he do that? This is his livelihood."

"Why would anyone do it? It doesn't make any sense to me. Maybe it's just... someone who likes to cause excitement. Or to see other people suffer. There are plenty of sadists out there. Of all people, you know that."

"We could sort this out tonight. Figure out what's been going on and who did it."

Kenzie shook her head emphatically. "We're not going to rush into this. We can't afford to be impulsive."

Zachary turned his face away from her. Of course he recognized that impulsivity had been his downfall in other cases, leading to him or someone else getting hurt. They needed to take it slowly. To be sure of each step so that they didn't run into a dangerous situation or start throwing around accusations that someone would be desperate to stop.

But who?

"It could be any of them," Kenzie said. "They were all here the night Brooke was killed. They were all up at the house and would have had access to the food and drink."

"This was planned," Zachary suggested. "If it was one of the guests, then they must have brought the Jimson weed with them. Because there's nothing growing right now."

He was right, of course. Everything was buried under layers of snow. The gardens, the ditches, the woods, anywhere Datura might have grown was covered.

"Mrs. Hudson could have some in the basement, where you said she had dried herbs hanging."

"Because she thought it was something else? Or did she know it was Jimson weed?"

Kenzie thought about how broken up Mrs. Hudson had been over Mr. Dewey's death. She was sure that emotion had not been fake. Mrs. Hudson really was sorry that Mr. Dewey had died, and the effect that losing her employer would have on her. That hadn't seemed fake.

"I really can't see her using it knowingly. Maybe she thought it was something else. The book says that sometimes people mistake it for tobacco."

"She doesn't strike me as a smoker."

"No. But maybe she used them in some poultice. They do that, don't they? A poultice for bruises or to draw out poisons?"

Zachary shrugged and indicated the books with his chin. "You're the one with the medical training and the reference material. Maybe there's something in there about uses."

Kenzie nodded, flipping a few more pages. "We'll go up to the house tomorrow. See if we can find anything out from Mrs. Hudson."

"I suppose."

"And if it's not her... then someone must have planned this whole thing and brought it with them."

It wasn't a very pleasant thought.

6 0

Kenzie felt bad about the *Clue* game starting with all five of them, but ending with just the kids and Tyrrell. But Tyrrell waved off her apologies, and they did eventually finish the game, with Mason crowing about how he had figured it all out. Nothing to do with the extra cards that he had received from Kenzie's and Zachary's hands.

"You guys are trying to figure out what really happened," Tyrrell said, careful not to mention murder or killing in front of the kids. "That's important. We're just playing a game. It didn't mess anything up. We still finished."

"Well, I am sorry," Kenzie said to Alisha. Mason was bouncing around the room like a pinball, jumping and yelping and not looking as if he were getting ready for sleep. "Maybe I can read to you guys before bed? Would that be good?"

Alisha looked doubtfully at the big texts Kenzie had spread out on the floor.

"Not these ones," Kenzie said quickly. "Something more interesting. Did you guys find some books that you like?" Kenzie looked at the bookshelf, which seemed to have a bit of something for everyone.

"Well, there was one about animals," Alisha said. "I know maybe it's a little young, but it was interesting."

"That sounds good. Once you guys get settled for bed, I'll come in and read a chapter or two for you, okay?"

Alisha looked at Mason with raised eyebrows and sighed the long-suffering sigh of the big sister of a hyperactive boy. "Sure."

It took Tyrrell some time to get Mason corralled and started on his bedtime routine. Kenzie had hoped that without screens to wind him up, he would have a fairly quiet night. He seemed to have been doing better at sleeping since the power went out. But he kept bouncing around and thinking of one more thing he had to do before bed, and by the time Kenzie's story time came around, Tyrrell was having a hard time keeping his voice even. He told Mason firmly to get into bed and stay there, but he seemed to be fighting a losing battle.

"What day is it?" Mason demanded. "When are we going home? I want to see Mommy again. And to play with my games. My *real* games."

"It's Thursday," Tyrrell told him. "And we'll go home when we can. Right now we can't get anywhere on the highway. We need to stay here until it stops snowing and the plows come and clear the snow."

"But it's a school day! And I haven't talked to Mommy at all. She said to call every night before I go to bed, and I haven't called her." He shook his head, brow knitted in worry.

"Mommy knows that there was a storm coming in. She'll understand that you didn't call because you couldn't. I'll let her know, when we can get through again. Okay? I'll let her know that it wasn't because you forgot, but just because you weren't able to get through."

Mason nodded. "I really want to go home now."

"We will when we can. But you've had a good time here, haven't you? We've played lots of games, and cooked on a cook stove, and you got to go outside for a while today. Even if you didn't build a snowman."

"Can I build a snowman tomorrow?"

"We'll see. You need to be supervised so that you can't just wander off again. That was really scary. You can't do things like that."

"I was okay. And I came home."

"I know you did, and I was really glad that you were safe. I don't want to worry like that, so you need to be more careful of your decisions."

Mason considered this, but didn't say that he would. Kenzie wondered what was going on in his head. Did he understand that his impulsivity wasn't something that he could control, even if the adults in his life told him he needed to? Did he understand that it was part of a disorder? Or did he think that he did things that were dangerous and that his parents told him not to because he was a bad kid? Did he avoid promising to stay close to home and make his snowman because he knew that he'd never be able to keep his promise, or did he not promise to obey because he didn't want to and didn't think that Tyrrell's rules were fair?

"Can Kenzie read to us now?" Alisha asked.

Tyrrell nodded. He kissed each of the kids on the forehead. "You guys lay down quietly and let Kenzie read. I don't want to hear another peep from you. You stay in bed, as still as you can, until you fall asleep."

Alisha nodded obediently, and Kenzie imagined she would do just that. Mason was already looking away from his father, eyeing the window rattling in the storm. Kenzie hoped it was the last hurrah of the weather system, and that, like a tantruming child, all would be peaceful and forgotten in the morning.

Kenzie had found it difficult to settle down and go to sleep. Not because she wasn't tired. She was exhausted. But she kept trying to puzzle through everything they knew about the poison and the other people stuck at the Lodge. Was it a guest with a grudge? One of the staff? Someone who was just out to do some mischief? She kept thinking of their personalities, their faces, and the things she had discovered when she searched their cabins. A lot could be learned about a person by how they lived or the possessions they decided to take with them on a holiday.

Look at Kenzie and Zachary. Kenzie had been concerned about having comfortable clothing, the toiletries she needed, and food she knew Zachary would eat even if he were nauseated. Zachary had been unable to pack his clothing and the other things that he would need, feeling too overwhelmed by the idea of going away. But he had picked up his bag of electronics and detection equipment. Kenzie had not brought anything work-related with her. Some of the guests brought with them all of the comforts of home or everything they needed for work—thinking of Brittany in particular—and others had brought little, expecting to be entertained and provided for by the staff at the Lodge. Some had a lot of medications like Zachary, others had almost nothing.

She didn't know as much as she would like to about their backgrounds. She didn't even know Redd Flagg's real name. And despite Brittany's fame, Kenzie hadn't really figured out what it was she was famous for. If Kenzie had been an Agatha Christie detective, she would have gathered a lot more information about everyone's backgrounds and how they were related to each other. They would all be bound to be related by different connections. People who had served in the war together, estranged family, employers, nannies— the Grande Dame always had lot of interesting ways to connect different people and their pasts together.

Zachary sat on the edge of the bed for a while, but couldn't seem to settle in. Normally, he could at least lie down with her for a while to cuddle, even if he didn't go to sleep right away. Or if he only went to sleep for a few hours and then was up again. Kenzie listened to him breathing for a while. Too uneven and too quick.

"Hey. Are you okay?" she ventured.

Zachary startled and turned toward her slightly. "Yeah," he whispered back. "I'm fine."

Fine. Which meant that he wasn't.

"What's wrong?"

He rubbed his hands down the pants of his thighs, drying his palms or smoothing his pants. He normally didn't wear pajamas, but the cabin bedroom got cold even with the heater running in the other room, so he was wearing some light gray sweatpants.

"No meds," Zachary said eventually. "I'm feeling a little... anxious."

Kenzie rubbed her eyes. She was going to suggest that it would be okay for him to take one of his anti-anxiety pills when she suddenly realized. When he said no meds, he meant no meds. Raven had confiscated everything and put it into the safe. Whoever had broken into the safe had taken the meds, hiding or disposing of them, and leaving people like Zachary and Raven who depended on them to get through the day with nothing. They had both kept a dose of night meds and of morning meds, and had expected to be able to have more dispensed the next day as they needed them. But the day had come and gone, and they were left with nothing.

Kenzie sat up, swearing as the realization hit. She pushed off the cozy blankets and rubbed Zachary's back and shoulders. "I didn't even think about that. I'm so sorry! What can I do?"

"Nothing. I'm just going to have to... take a med holiday. I've done that before. No big deal."

But she knew it was a big deal. It was always a big deal. And several of the meds he was on were not supposed to be discontinued cold turkey. He was supposed to cut down on them under a doctor's supervision, not just to stop taking them. She rubbed his neck, trying to loosen the knots of the muscles he was holding so tightly.

"What about... what other things would help? Dr. B. has given you relaxation exercises before. Meditation, progressive relaxation...? How about that?"

"I've been trying to relax."

"With her exercises?"

His head ticked to the side. Not quite a nod or a head-shake. Sort of a diagonal. Which Kenzie interpreted as *I tried.*

"How about... a soak in the hot tub." Kenzie suggested it before thinking it through, then laughed at herself. "Except with no heat, it is more like one of those polar bear dips. Sorry. What about exercise? Or a drink?"

"Yeah." A definite nod this time. Zachary usually avoided alcohol because of the contraindications with several of his meds. But if he had no way to take the meds, there was no reason he couldn't have a drink or two to help him to relax.

"Yeah? Why don't we both have a drink? Go relax by the heater and toast our feet for a while." Kenzie's feet were cold, even with the blankets and socks on. It wasn't quite like staring into a crackling fire, but the heater would keep them cozy and warm. Burknall had replaced the propane tank before bedding down for the night. Always thinking about his guests and their needs. Kenzie shook her head over thinking that he was too gruff and bad-tempered the first day there. No matter how crusty his exterior was, he was just the right man for the job of keeping things up and making sure the guests were comfortable and happy.

Zachary nodded his head. "That sounds really good."

"Okay, come on. Quickly, because I don't want my feet to freeze between here and there."

She grabbed Zachary by the hand and they skittered like a couple of squirrels over the cold floors to the rug in front of the fireplace where it was nice and toasty. Kenzie threw cushions and blankets on the floor so they could make a nest for themselves, and Zachary went over to the liquor cabinet.

Kenzie wrapped herself up, getting comfortable.

"What do you want?" Zachary asked, shining a pen light into the cabinet.

"I'm not really picky. I'll have a glass of whatever is in there."

She heard bottles clinking and liquid sloshing.

"Kenz?"

Kenzie looked over at him, detecting worry in his voice. "What is it?"

"Did you have something already? I mean, since we got here?"

"No." It was sort of a strange question. Kenzie propped herself up on her elbow, looking over at him. The pen light cast just enough light for her to see the outline of his face. "Why?"

"Because... I looked when we got here. Just to see what there was. And... more than one of the bottles are lower than they were when we got here."

"Really? Are you sure?"

Zachary fingered the bottles. "If I didn't have any, and you didn't have any..." He turned his head toward the bedroom where Tyrrell slept with the children.

Tyrrell. Recovering alcoholic. Snowbound and in close quarters with the children, stressed out trying to handle a wild eight-year-old twenty-four hours a day. One who had disappeared completely for a while.

Kenzie shook her head. "Tyrrell? You don't think so, do you? He wouldn't."

"I don't know. I don't think so, but... it must be pretty stressful."

"Yeah. I was just thinking that."

"Raven was here. She might have had a drink."

"Yeah. For sure. She was drinking like everyone else when we were up at the house together," Kenzie agreed. "And what about Pat and Lorne? They might have had something while they were here."

"Mr. Peterson doesn't really drink very much," Zachary said doubtfully. "Just on special occasions, a glass now and then."

"And it was a special occasion. It was Thanksgiving with his family. There isn't a *lot* missing, is there?"

Zachary considered. "No," he said finally. "Not a lot. Maybe a couple of drinks each, Raven, and Pat, and Lorne. Maybe." The bottles clinked again.

"Well, there's no point in worrying about it tonight. Pour us each a drink, and we'll see if we can relax for a bit."

Drinking wasn't really going to help relax him if he was worried that his alcoholic brother was hitting the bottle again. But maybe the suggestion that the others had helped themselves to moderate portions would help. He could deny that Tyrrell had had anything to drink, at least for a while, until they had to confront him about it.

Zachary didn't say anything. He poured a couple of glasses and brought one over to Kenzie. She sipped hers. A red wine. Something pleasant. She was no connoisseur. Didn't have a clue what the vintage was. But it went down easily.

"Come cuddle with me." She held up a blanket for Zachary to slide under. "I'll see if there's any way I can help you to relax..."

Zachary got comfortable next to her, but she could still feel his tension. Kenzie had another sip of her wine and set it to the side. She couldn't see much in the dark and was afraid she was going to knock it over if they moved too much.

"I can't see you."

Zachary took his pen light out of his pocket again and turned it on. He pointed it at his face, at hers, and then eventually set it on the couch behind them so that it shone toward them and shed its dim glow on both of their faces. The battery wouldn't last long if they left it on, but Kenzie wanted to be able to see Zachary's face. She needed to be able to see his eyes and read any changes in mood.

"Much better."

61

Kenzie leaned over to kiss Zachary gently.

He was distracted to begin with. Thinking about Tyrrell and the liquor cabinet. Thinking about having to go the next night and maybe a couple more days without any chemical assistance. Thinking about what had gone on up at the house and their agreement to see whether they could make any headway on it again in the morning. But after a few minutes of kissing and teasing, he started to focus on her, his body losing some of the tension and his face smoothing over. He still looked cadaverous in the strange lighting from the pen light, but the deeper ridges disappeared.

"This is what we needed," Kenzie told him. "Some time just to get away and get to know each other again."

"Mmm-hm."

Kenzie smiled, feeling the planes of her face against his shifting in the darkness. "We haven't had much time alone."

He broke away from her for a moment to speak. "You're the one who invited other people along."

"Well... I suppose I did. I didn't expect us to get stranded together. I thought a day or two with everybody, and then some alone time for you and me..."

"Uh-huh." He kissed her again. She could feel his fingers exploring under the blanket. Tentative, but interested. His body hadn't released all the tension, but she could work on that. She pulled him closer and just held him for a few minutes, glad for their shared warmth and the blankets and heater, but mostly for his eagerness. For a long time, they had been dealing with his dissociation during intimate moments, and with meds that, while they took the edge off of his worst anxieties and compulsions, also reduced his drive. The combination of the two was brutal, but couples therapy was helping, and they were finding more moments together without Zachary dissociating or withdrawing.

Kenzie tried to focus one hundred percent of her attention on him, pushing all the other concerns and worries away, for just a few minutes.

"Do you mind if I turn the light off?"

Kenzie shifted, opening her eyes a bare slit to remind herself where she was. In the cabin with Zachary. Enjoying some couples time in front of the heater. She was glad that Tyrrell had eventually been able to get Mason to sleep for the night.

"Yes," she whispered back to Zachary. "Go ahead."

He switched off the pen light and put it back down. Neither of them had made any move to get dressed again, so Zachary didn't have a pocket to put it into. Kenzie was barely even awake. She ran her fingertips along Zachary's arm. "Nice."

"It was," he agreed.

Maybe there was something to be said for a med holiday, or at least a reduction. If Zachary could make do with less medication, maybe they could have a drink together and some other recreation more often.

"You feeling better?"

He shifted, snuggling her body closer to his. Not that they could get much closer. His muscles were much more relaxed than they had been. "Yeah. better."

"We'll have to add it to your relaxation tools."

He chuckled, his breath giving her goosebumps for a moment. Kenzie rubbed her arms and laughed. She felt like everything that had happened on the holiday had been leading up to this. It had all turned out better than she had expected.

She closed her eyes again, breathing in the smell of Zachary's body against hers.

When she awoke again, everything was wrong. Zachary was moving around frantically, muttering and sobbing, searching through the blankets for something. Kenzie reached out her hand to him and tried to quiet him.

"It's just a dream, Zach. It's okay."

"No, no, no! It's not a dream. Look! Look for yourself!"

Kenzie tried again to press him down and calm him. "You had a dream. It's okay. Let's cuddle some more." She rubbed her eyes. "Do you want to go back to the bed? Maybe you'd be able to settle down better there."

"No!" He said it firmly, almost angrily. "You're the one who needs to wake up." He shook her arm roughly. "Look!"

Kenzie blinked and rubbed her eyes again. She squinted at him, trying to see what it was she wanted him to look at. Sometimes his dreams were very real and it would be several minutes after waking up before he was able to get his head out of the dream and realize where he was. Being at the cabin had probably disoriented him. Waking up in a living room instead of a bedroom might have been a trigger for a dream or a bad feeling.

Zachary pulled on a shirt. He tossed clothing at Kenzie, and she tried to feel its shape and sort out what part of her body to put it on. "Zachary?"

"Look!" He tugged on her arm, trying to get her to her feet. Kenzie tried to keep one of the blankets wrapped around her. He positioned her in front of the living room window, looking out, up toward the farmhouse on the hill.

It was lit up. Kenzie closed her eyes and opened them again. Why would it be lit up? It was too late for dinner. Everybody had finished and gone back to their cabins.

Was the power back on? Was that what Zachary was so excited about? If it were, they could finally call for help. See when the county was going to send someone to check on them and take the bodies back to the county medical examiner's office.

Kenzie realized with growing horror that it wasn't electric lights that had lit up the farmhouse.

It was a fire.

Kenzie swore. A fire. And not just the flicker of candlelight in the windows.

Blazing light in nearly every window that was visible from the cabin.

62

Zachary had his boots on. He kicked his way through the cushions and blankets scattered on the floor and strode to Tyrrell's room.

"T!" he shouted, voice already hoarse, "T! There's a fire! T, you have to get up! There's a fire!"

It wasn't just a flashback. It wasn't just a nightmare. It was the worst possible thing for Zachary to face. A house fire. Trying to save his brother and the children from the fire. It didn't matter that it was actually up the hill at the big house. For Zachary, it was right there; he was living through it all over again.

She could hear Tyrrell's voice through the door. Tired, trying to reassure Zachary that everything was all right. Trying, as Kenzie had, to convince him it was just a dream and he should go back to sleep.

"Tyrrell," Kenzie shouted, taking a few steps toward the door as she tried to sort out her clothes and pull them on. "Tyrrell, there *is* a fire. Get up."

"Kenzie?"

In a few moments, Tyrrell was at the bedroom door, opening it slowly, breathing hard. Probably confronting his own memories of the fire. He and the other children had been trapped in their rooms, unable to get out because of the heat and smoke, trapped and terrified until the firefighters had gotten there, broken the windows, and rescued them.

"Kenzie, what's going on?"

"It's up at the farmhouse. A big fire. You need to stay awake, reassure the kids if they wake up. Make sure that... if it spreads to the woods, you get out of the house."

She could barely make out his face in the moonlight that made its way in through the windows. Three dark holes. Two eye sockets and a mouth open in horror. Kenzie squeeze his arm.

"It's okay. You're safe here for now. It's all right."

Tyrrell's head turned to look at Zachary. "Zachy?"

Zachary sniffled. "I have to go. Take care of the others."

He turned away, heading for the front door of the cabin. Kenzie hurried after him. "Zachary? What are you doing? Where are you going?"

He already had his boots and coat on. He pulled a hat on over his head and patted his pockets for the gloves. "We have to get help."

Kenzie shook her head, not understanding. "There's no way to reach anyone. There's nowhere to go for help."

He opened the door and stepped out. Kenzie hurriedly pushed her feet into her boots and pulled on her coat. She raced after him. He moved the opposite direction from the farmhouse, yelling and banging on doors. "Get up! Get up! We need help! Come out!"

Flashlights and candles went on, people came to their doors, bleary-eyed and confused. Kenzie pointed to the farmhouse. She didn't know what to do. It was in full blaze. There was no fire department. No way to reach any help. Zachary ran down to the barn, leaving Kenzie behind. He would get Burknall. Burknall would have some idea what to do. Maybe he had a pump in there. Something that would help them get water onto the blaze.

Kenzie turned around and led the group up the hill.

"What are we going to do?" Brittany demanded, running to catch up with Kenzie. She had her coat pulled on over a thin white nightgown.

"I don't know. Make sure there's no one inside."

"What happened?" Redd was trying to get his gloves on. Kenzie didn't even know whether she had hers. She felt her pockets, but couldn't find the flaps to open them.

"We don't know. Zachary saw it first. He went to the barn." Kenzie looked back, over her shoulder. She couldn't see Zachary or Burknall. "Maybe Mr. Burknall has a hose. Or a well. I don't know. I don't know how anything works up here."

"An ember must have fallen out of the fireplace," Redd suggested. "Or a candle got knocked over."

"Maybe a chimney fire," Brittany said, breathing hard as they climbed the hill

"Maybe." Kenzie shrugged. Did it really matter how the fire had started?

There was a fire, and that was what they had to deal with. Make sure that no one was in danger. Mrs. Hubbard and Samantha both slept in the house, didn't they? They must have been woken up by the fire. The smoke detectors would have awakened them. They could still operate on battery power, even if the main power were out.

If they hadn't woken up... Kenzie wasn't sure what she was going to do. She could see fire in every window. Not just the main floor, but upstairs too. If anyone was still in there...

She ignored the other questions, from both the others and her own brain, as they hurried toward the fire. Nothing mattered except making sure that no one was caught inside the blaze and that it didn't spread to the woods.

It felt like a dream, climbing and climbing and climbing the hill and never getting to the top. But finally, they were there, and Kenzie stood staring at the house, trying to comprehend what was going on. There was no one in front of it, standing clear and watching it burn. Did that mean that they were inside?

"I'm going around back," Kenzie told Brittany, though she didn't know why she felt the need to tell anyone what she was doing. Brittany wasn't her boss. She wasn't someone that Kenzie had to report to.

Brittany nodded. Kenzie hurried around the side. She was yards away from the house and could feel the heat of the flames. It was like walking into a sauna. A dry sauna, obviously, not a steam bath. Kenzie hurried around the side, trying to see into the windows. Hoping to see something other than just flames inside. Some sign of people, or that the whole house wasn't going to burn to the ground. They would be able to save something. To salvage the structure or their valuables. She couldn't believe that the whole thing would burn like that.

Behind the house were three shadows, three silhouettes against the light of the fire. Three people, safe. Kenzie hurried toward them.

"Mrs. Hubbard? Is everyone okay? Everyone got out?"

As she got close, she could see it was Mrs. Hubbard, Samantha, and Jack. Their faces were a little sooty from smoke, but they seemed unharmed. They weren't even coughing from smoke inhalation. Kenzie took Mrs. Hubbard's hand, wanting to reassure herself that the woman was safe and sound. She was a medical professional, but not one who often treated living patients. Her hand went automatically to Mrs. Hubbard's pulse. Fast as a train engine, but hammering away nice and strong and even. Mrs. Hubbard had the constitution of an ox. She would live to be a hundred. Kenzie looked at Samantha and Jack. They both seemed fine as well.

"How did you get here so fast?" Kenzie asked Jack.

"I was up to the bathroom. Saw a reflection in the window, and when I looked out... I could see a fire in one of the windows. Thought I must be seeing things. That it was just the fireplace. But... I had to go see." He blew out his breath in a puff of white vapor. "I got up here in enough time to make sure that everyone got out."

"There's no one else in there, right?" Kenzie asked Mrs. Hubbard and Samantha. "It was just the two of you?"

"Mr. Burknall sleeps down at the barn," Samantha said, her voice a little breathless. "In case anyone needs anything."

"So it was just the two of you."

Samantha nodded.

"We should tell the others. They're out around front." Kenzie looked behind her at the dark woods. She mentally gauged the distance from the house to the woods. Far enough that there was no danger of an ember or flame reaching any of the trees? She wasn't so sure.

"Jack... you want to stay back here to make sure it doesn't spread into the woods? I need to talk to the others... then maybe we need to set up a perimeter, or get Mr. Burknall to help us make a firebreak... I don't know."

"With all of this snow?" Jack gestured around. "I don't think we need to worry about the fire spreading."

"It could, though. Mr. Dewey said it was a fire hazard. The cold dries everything out... even though it's snowy, the air and the trees are so dry..." She couldn't help thinking about Zachary, as a little boy, watching the dry branches of their Christmas tree going up in flames. She shuddered, and it wasn't because of the cold. "Just wait here, I'll talk to the others."

Kenzie returned to the front of the house. The others were spreading out, some of them starting to check around the sides of the house as well, moving toward the back.

"Everyone is out," she announced. "Mrs. Hubbard and Samantha, they're both okay."

Raven looked up at the burning building, pulling her coat tight around her. "It's so... primal. I don't know."

"It's scary," Kenzie agreed.

"Is there no way to get outside help?" a man demanded.

Kenzie turned her head to see who the query came from, but she knew before she saw that it was Vance Stiller.

He had pulled out his phone and was looking at the useless brick. He looked at the house, then down the hill at the barn. "Doesn't anybody have... a short-wave radio? A sat phone? There should be some way to reach help in the event of an emergency!"

"If there was, don't you think we would have done it in the last few days?" Kenzie asked, irritated.

"But that was just..." Stiller waved his hand. "Nonsense and speculation. This is serious. This could spread to the forest, to the other buildings on the property. It could decimate the business."

"Yes, it could," Kenzie agreed. She didn't make any comment on the fact that he thought the murder of one of the guests and possibly his own poisoning as nonsense and speculation.

Kenzie heard the growl of an engine starting and looked around. At first, she couldn't see anything, but eventually, she could see a large, dark shape coming into view down by the barn. Her spirits lifted. It was Burknall, coming to the rescue. Always competent, he knew exactly what to do.

The shape lumbered toward them. Kenzie squinted, trying to make out the shape in the darkness. As it drew closer, the light of the fire illuminated a John Deere tractor with some kind of digger attachment. Kenzie's heart fell again. She was hoping for a fire truck pumper, or something similar. She knew it was probably ridiculous to think that a resort might have their own fire engine, but maybe something used to spray chemicals on crops or on fields they needed cleared of weeds? There must be a need for such things.

The heat of the fire swelled up behind Kenzie. She turned to look at the house and saw that the flames were no longer just behind the windows, but had eaten their way through the roof and were reaching up to the sky. She murmured a curse under her breath. Without a fire hose, they had no hope of being able to save the house.

There had probably been no hope by the time Zachary had woken her up. Mrs. Hubbard and Samantha were lucky to have gotten out of the building unharmed. They were lucky that Jack had been up and around and had noticed the flames.

The tractor emitted several loud beeps, and Kenzie and the others decided to get out of Burknall's way. He rolled up to the house, engine growling loudly, and circled around it, moving toward the back of the house. Kenzie followed at a distance to see what he would do. More horn honks to get Mrs. Hubbard, Samantha, and Jack out of the way. Then Burknall started to dig a trench across the back yard between the house and the trees. Dark clumps of dirt were piled up on the snow.

"What is he doing?" Raven demanded, watching from a few feet away from Kenzie.

"It's a firebreak. To try to keep the fire from spreading into the trees. If there isn't any fuel between the house and the trees for the fire to burn, it can't spread. As long as no embers from the fire float up over into the trees..."

"Why isn't he trying to put the fire out?"

"He probably can't do anything about it at this point. Even if the fire department was here, it would take several trucks to get this under control."

"So he's just going to let it burn?" Raven sounded outraged at the idea.

"Yes. If there's no way to put it out, then the best thing to do is to keep it confined and let it burn itself out."

Kenzie wondered if there were anything that the fire department—if there were one that served the outlying areas—would do if they had been called. There were no fire hydrants to hook their hoses up to. Maybe they would have been able to put an intake hose into a stream somewhere. But if there were one, it would have been frozen over. She supposed all they would be able to do was to watch it burn, like the rest of them were doing.

She turned away from the tractor and moved back to the front of the house where she could see down to the cabins and barn. A figure was making its way up the hill. Hunched over, moving slowly as if in pain. With his bulky coat on and slow, pained movements, Kenzie barely recognized Zachary. She walked down the hill to meet him part way.

"Zachary. How are you? Are you okay?"

He didn't answer, but kept moving toward her. Eventually, he was close enough to touch. She couldn't see his eyes in the darkness.

"Zachary." She reached out and took his arm. "Hey. Are you with me?"

"Yeah." His voice was hoarse. From calling out to everyone else to warn them of the fire? From crying? From dragging the cold, smoky air into his lungs as he tried to get enough oxygen, lost in flashbacks? "I'm here."

She pulled him close and put her arm around him. "This must be awful for you. I'm so sorry. Do you want to go back to the cabin? You don't need to go up there."

"No." He looked up toward the house, then put his head down again, marching forward like he was walking into a strong wind. "I want to go up."

Kenzie didn't argue with him. He knew what was best for him. His fear of fire was something that had plagued him for decades. If he was ready to face it now, she wouldn't get in his way.

63

This time... everyone else can see it."

Zachary and Kenzie stood arm in arm, watching the flames consume the farmhouse. Zachary's voice was still hoarse. She could feel how tense his body was, feel his limbs quivering from standing in such close proximity to the fire.

"You can see it," Zachary said.

"Yes," Kenzie agreed. "We can all see it." She gave him a squeeze. "Is this what it was like, watching your house burn?"

He shook his head. "No... when they got me out... I couldn't really see anything. Too many people around me. An oxygen mask on my face... people talking about me, cutting my clothes off." He clutched his coat against him, as if trying to convince himself that he was fully dressed and no one was going to cut his clothes off this time. Kenzie thought about what she knew of the fire. It had been Christmas Eve. It would have been cold outside. Snow on the ground. Being taken from the heat of the fire to the chill of the winter air outside and having the clothes cut away from his body so they could treat him, he must have been freezing. At least, the skin that wasn't burned. Maybe the cold air had helped to soothe his burns and to stop further damage.

When he had first told her about being rescued by the firefighters, she had imagined him standing outside, safe like he was now. Upset, even devastated by the fire, but walking away under his own power. It wasn't until later that she learned about the hospital stay, debriding, skin grafts, and rehabilitation he had gone through before going to the Petersons, his first foster family.

"You're safe here," Kenzie assured him. "You're not burned, and neither is anyone else."

"Everyone got out?" His voice was a little choked as he asked the question.

"Yes. Everything is fine. Jack woke up before you did and he got up here in time to make sure that Mrs. Hubbard and Samantha got out of the house."

Zachary nodded.

"And Mr. Burknall is digging a trench around the house, to keep it from spreading. Everyone will be okay. Everyone is safe."

He nodded again. He pressed his face into her knit hat and the wild, curly hair that puffed out all around the bottom edge of it. He breathed in, his mouth close to her ear and neck and making her shiver, goosebumps running down her neck. But she didn't pull away from him. He needed her there, calm and giving him strength to face the fire. To see his memories clearly and process them instead of running away from them as he had for years.

"Everyone got out," Zachary repeated. "Everyone got out."

A couple of the guests went back to their cabins when it became clear that the rest of the Lodge was safe. Kenzie couldn't imagine how they could go back to sleep. And maybe they didn't, but just wanted to be away from the cold and the smoke and the other guests huddling together and speculating on what had happened.

She had a pretty good idea that Zachary would not be going back to bed. No hope of that. Even on a normal night when he was awakened by a dream or a noise outside, he wouldn't go back to sleep. No chance he would be able to after dealing with a fire.

"What do you think happened?" Kenzie asked Burknall, when he had finished trenching around the house and parked his tractor. "A gas line? Propane leak?"

He stared at the house. The fire was beginning to settle down instead of getting bigger. Starting to burn itself out. But it would still be a long time before it was completely extinguished and the ruins cool enough to examine.

"We've had propane appliances for decades," he said, giving his head a shake. "There wasn't anything wrong with them. They were perfectly safe. Same with the boiler. It was inspected regularly, never had any problems. Fireplaces, same thing, we got the chimneys cleaned and kept everything in perfect condition."

"So you don't know what could have caused the fire," Kenzie said.

"What about candles?" Zachary asked.

Burknall looked at him, brows drawn down. "We only use candles if someone is in the room to keep an eye on them. And never sleeping with a candle lit. Mrs. Hubbard knows that. Samantha too. She didn't even like candles. That's why we had the glow-sticks."

"Something started it," Zachary observed.

Burknall nodded his agreement. "Something."

There was something more in his expression. Something that he was not saying. Maybe he had suspicions, but he wasn't sharing them. Kenzie watched the burning house. All of that history. The families that had grown up in there. Mr. Dewey's pictures and all the reminders of the wife he had lost.

It wasn't until that point that Kenzie thought about Mr. Dewey.

And Brooke.

It wasn't just Mr. Dewey's memories that had been burned up, but his remains as well. Maybe they wouldn't be completely destroyed, but all of Kenzie's efforts to preserve the scene and the trace evidence was for naught.

They couldn't even test Brooke's body now to see whether it had been Jimson weed that had caused all of the trouble that night. Brooke's remains were probably damaged past any hopes of retrieving evidence of toxins. Kenzie turned her gaze toward Zachary to see if he had twigged on to this as well. He was probably light-years ahead of her in sorting out the implications. He had wanted to go up to the house before they went to bed, hoping that Mrs. Hubbard could help them or that there would be some evidence of the use of Jimson weed. But it was too late. Now, Mrs. Hubbard was the only possible avenue. If she knew anything.

Zachary gazed back at Kenzie. He rubbed away a smudge on her face. He gave a little grimace, confirming that he understood they had just lost all of that evidence. Everything they had, other than what Kenzie had managed to record on her phone or Zachary's digital recorder. They had no remains, no scene or trace, no weapon, and no pills. Everything was gone. Kenzie held on to Zachary, for her support this time rather than his. She felt sick at the thought of all they had lost.

"At least everyone was okay," she said weakly.

Zachary nodded, holding her tight. "Yeah."

Kenzie took a few deep breaths. She looked around at those who remained, watching the destruction. She let go of Zachary and walked slowly over to Mrs. Hubbard, who was looking tired and worn, dark circles around her eyes.

"Mrs. Hubbard, would you like to come back to our cabin? We have a spare room. You could go to sleep or just have some time to yourself."

Mrs. Hubbard smiled at her. "That's very sweet of you, my dear. That would... I think that would be very nice."

Kenzie took her arm. "Why don't we walk down, then?"

The sky was starting to grow light. A column of smoke was still going up from the farmhouse.

Zachary followed, saying nothing. Mrs. Hubbard clutched Kenzie's arm, holding tightly as if she were afraid she might fall. Or maybe just as if everything else had slipped out of her grasp and she didn't want to be left alone and anchorless. Kenzie didn't say anything. What was there to say?

"I can't believe it," the older woman said after a few minutes, as they made their way slowly down to the cabin. "I can't believe that everything I own has just gone up in smoke. All of the memories. Everything I ever owned. What am I supposed to do now? I don't have a job, a place to stay, even a spare shirt to my name. I got out of there with my life, but I don't have anything. Even my purse." She shook her head. "My ID, my bank cards. How am I going to survive?"

Kenzie looked over at Zachary, walking a few feet away from them, giving them some privacy. "Zachary might be able to help you out there. He actually lost everything he had in a fire just a little while ago. His wallet and ID too. I know it was really hard to get things replaced, but he can tell you what to do. Where to start."

Mrs. Hubbard looked at Zachary. "Really? I thought that the fire you guys were talking about happened when you were a little boy. I didn't realize that it was recent..."

"Well..." Zachary cleared his throat. "There were two fires."

"Two of them." Mrs. Hubbard looked overwhelmed by this thought, like it was too much to grasp.

"Yeah. There was one when I was ten. An accident. That's when I was injured." Zachary indicated one of the scars visible on his neck. "And... I lost everything then. My whole family too. Then... two years ago, there was another fire, in my apartment. Arson. And like Kenzie said, my wallet and everything was burned up. I had to start from scratch. Lived with a friend while I was trying to get my ID reissued and to get access to my bank accounts and everything. I didn't use any cloud storage, so I didn't have my passwords to any of the online stuff. Had to get people who could verify my identity to the government." Zachary rolled his eyes. "It's arduous... but it's possible. I can help you to sort it out."

"Oh, you're a godsend. Thank you. I don't know what I would do without you."

"Someone else would help you," he assured her. "There are a lot of helpful people in the world." He looked at Kenzie, smiling a little. "People who you wouldn't think had any reason to help you out... step up and become the best friends you ever had."

Kenzie's cheeks warmed. She blamed it on the fire, even though they were getting farther away from it. They reached the cabin and Zachary dug out his key to let them in.

"Whatever you need, just ask. In the next little while... you're going to learn how to ask for things. Even if you're a person who has never had to depend on anyone before. But we'll help out however we can."

They stepped into the warm, welcoming space of the cabin. Mrs. Hubbard took off her coat and smoothed back her hair. She was, of course, in her night clothes, a matched set top and bottom of warm-looking purple velour with flowers embroidered on the left breast and hip. "I guess... the first thing is sleep. You would think that I would be too worried to sleep, but... I'm exhausted."

"Your brain doesn't want to deal with all the trauma," Zachary told her, nodding. "Go ahead and get some sleep while you can. You can worry about other things later."

"I'll show you where," Kenzie offered, and took Mrs. Hubbard down the hall to the room that Lorne and Pat had stayed in. The sheets hadn't been changed, but Kenzie had no way to remedy that with the power out. Mrs. Hubbard didn't appear to notice or to care.

"Thank you for this, Kenzie. You're so thoughtful."

"You're welcome. I'm glad you accepted. Just lie down and rest, get as much sleep as you can. The kids might be a bit noisy when they get up, but we'll do our best to keep them to a dull roar."

Mrs. Hubbard smiled. "Oh, that's fine. I don't mind children's voices."

Maybe not when they were well-behaved children talking and playing in the distance. She might revise her position if she ended up with Mason jumping on top of her, or with both of them screaming at each other, wrestling, or fighting over a book. Kenzie helped Mrs. Hubbard into the bed and pulled the covers over her. After another murmured good night, she left, pulling the door behind her.

64

Good plan," Zachary told Kenzie when she returned to the living room.
Kenzie raised her brows in query. "What do you mean?"

"Keeping Mrs. Hubbard close. Where we can talk to her and keep anyone else from getting access to her."

"Well... she might know something. And if she does... I wouldn't want her to be the next casualty."

"Her and you. We don't know how much you know that could catch the culprits either. They could come after you next, try to burn this cabin down." Zachary's eyes darted around the interior of the cabin. He turned to look out the window. It was getting brighter outside. Kenzie didn't see anyone nearby, hanging around the house.

"I don't really know anything. Nothing that can be proven, anyway."

"I think...we might know enough to figure it out."

Kenzie frowned. "What do you mean?"

"I get this feeling sometimes... when I know that I'm getting close to solving a case. When I get this feeling that I have all of the pieces to the puzzle, if I can just put them together the right way. I guess subconsciously, my brain knows I have what I need. But it can be really frustrating, if I feel like I'm at the end of a case and nothing has come together."

Kenzie sat down on the couch. Zachary sat beside her. His fingers tapped the arm of the couch, his knee, the back of the couch behind her, fidgeting and restless, his brain trying to unlock the clues he believed they had.

There was the sound of a door opening, and Kenzie leaned forward to look down the hall and see what Mrs. Hubbard needed.

It wasn't her, but Tyrrell. He blinked and rubbed his eyes. He didn't look like he'd gotten much sleep. Kenzie had told him to keep an eye on the fire to make sure that he moved the kids if it happened to move along the treeline and endanger the cabin. So he'd probably been awake until he had seen Mr. Burknall dig the trench around the house and the fire start to burn down again.

"I thought I heard voices." Tyrrell looked out the window, studying the house up the hill, then sat down in one of the easy chairs. "Everything is okay? Under control?"

Zachary nodded.

Tyrrell stared at him, studying his face closely. "And you, bro?" He cocked his head slightly. "I expected you to be... bad."

Zachary took a deep breath and let it out. "My therapist... she's talked about exposure therapy before. How if you let your brain get past the panic stage, then it will even back out, and you'll start to adjust to... whatever the trigger is."

"Yeah? And you think that this," Tyrrell made a motion toward the farmhouse, "got you past that stage?"

"I've always avoided it before." Zachary still didn't name his fear of fire. "Even... thinking about it. If I ever started thinking back to what happened, or was around candles or some other trigger, I would go straight to panic. Try to shut down my response, but if I couldn't, I'd go right into flashbacks and not be able to deal with it."

"But this time it wasn't a candle," Kenzie said slowly. "It was a house fire. With other people in danger, and your family close by. And you couldn't tell yourself that it was just a flashback."

"I had to... deal with it. To keep everyone safe, I *had* to..."

"Well, I'm sure you'll have a lot of unpacking to do with Dr. B. But she's going to be very proud of you."

Zachary smiled. That shy, little-boy smile that sometimes broke through his carefully-masked emotions when he was proud of himself. He had been criticized and humiliated by so many people in his past that he rarely allowed himself to take any pride in his accomplishments. He looked down, closing his eyes and trying to compose his expression. But the hint of a smile lingered in the corners of his mouth.

"You helped to keep everyone safe," Kenzie told him. "It was really scary for all of us too, but you were strong."

He ducked his head, partly a nod of acknowledgment, and partly hiding his face, hiding behind the mask.

"So what's going to happen next?" Tyrrell asked. "I mean... are we even allowed to be here anymore? If there's no one managing the place, then...?"

"We're still paid-up guests," Kenzie pointed out. "We still have the staff taking care of things, even if they don't have a... home base anymore." She looked at Zachary. "And then there's the food. Everything that they had stored up at the house, and their cooking facilities... they won't exactly be able to feed the guests three meals a day anymore."

"We have some food here... and there are still farm animals and their feed. It won't exactly be a feast, but there is enough to get by on, until the roads are clear. Maybe today or tomorrow the plows will be able to get through." Zachary twisted to look out the window at the iron gray sky. "If people have seen the smoke from the fire... someone will have to investigate. We'll be a priority now."

"If anyone saw the smoke. There's no guarantee."

"I think the chances are pretty good. Close neighbors might have been able to see the flames too."

"Maybe the staff can gather some roots and berries," Tyrrell contributed.

Zachary and Kenzie both looked at him. Tyrrell shrugged.

"Well, you left that wildcrafting book out. I had to stay awake, so I looked through it."

Kenzie smiled and nodded. "I don't think I'm going to eat plants anyone else has gathered," she told him. "After what happened..."

Tyrrell shook his head. "What?"

"The way that everyone was hallucinating and having other symptoms. I think they were dosed with Jimson weed."

"Jimson weed?"

"You can look it up in the book. It's pretty dangerous stuff."

Tyrrell nodded. "I'll say!"

Kenzie heard the emphasis in his voice. She tilted her head, looking at him. "You'll say? You sound like... you've seen the effects before?"

Tyrrell nodded. He looked from Kenzie to Zachary and made a movement that was meant to be casual, but looked jerky and self-conscious.

"When I was drinking... you know, as a kid... I would try anything." He rolled his eyes. "I mean *anything*. If you told me I could get high on Corn Flakes, I would have eaten a whole box. Huffing fumes, drinking vanilla or mouthwash, hand sanitizer, I would do it all on a dare. Not even on a dare, just on the suggestion that it might get me to a 'higher level of consciousness.'"

"You didn't!" Kenzie said in horror.

"Yeah, you bet. Anything I could get my hands on. Including Jimson weed. Locoweed. Some kid at a party... I don't know, like... a hillbilly. He said it was the best high ever. As long as you didn't kill yourself."

Zachary swore under his breath. "I can't believe you tried it. And...?"

Tyrrell shrugged. "I don't remember. Every now and then, I get a little fleeting recollection of it... like deja vu. Remembering the feeling of being outside myself, flying, seeing... weird, weird stuff happening. Knowing that I was hallucinating, but not caring. I felt... I liked it. Most people who try the stuff remember it as being a good high, if they survive. But it's so dangerous. It's just... do you take it again, knowing you might die the next time? The hillbilly died, and I didn't look for another source. Seemed like it would just be asking for trouble."

"Thank goodness for that." Kenzie gave a laugh of disbelief. "I feel like I should smack you just for trying it."

Tyrrell chuckled. "Yeah, you probably should. Wasn't the brightest thing I ever did. I promise I won't do it again."

"No, don't," Zachary agreed vehemently.

The hillbilly died. Tyrrell had been lucky that hadn't been him.

Tyrrell was clearly embarrassed, maybe wishing that he hadn't told them the story. He rubbed his jaw, blinking and looking up at the ceiling, trying to think of something else to say that would distract Zachary's and Kenzie's attention from his youthful stupidity.

"It's not like I cornered the market on stupid," he reminded Zachary. "Not like I'm the only one who ever did anything that endangered my life."

Zachary nodded solemnly at this. He had tried to end his own life several times in the past. Kenzie hoped against hope that he never would again, and knew that she always needed to keep an eye on him and to be aware of his mental state. She couldn't let her guard down just because of a good day or an achievement. She knew from experience that a big step forward was often followed by an even larger slide back.

"What do you think we know?" she asked Zachary, changing the subject back to what they had been discussing before Tyrrell had shown up. "You said that you think we know enough to figure out what happened. So... like what?"

Zachary scratched his stubbly chin. Tyrrell looked relieved to have the conversation topic move away from his stupid teenage exploits. Kenzie watched him for a moment longer, thinking about the liquor cabinet, before turning her attention back to Zachary to see what they could piece together.

"Well. I guess first is that you know what all of the other guests were given," Zachary said. "We followed a false trail to begin with, thinking that it was a pill or some other chemical. Rather than something like Jimson weed, that someone could gather from practically anywhere in the state."

"Right." Kenzie nodded. "The symptoms, the ten D's, all point to Jimson weed."

"The ten D's?" Tyrrell repeated.

"Delusions, dry mouth, dry hot skin, delirium, death..." Kenzie trailed off. "I can't remember them all right now, but they fit. If it's not Jimson weed, it's something very close. Some other *datura* species, probably."

"Okay."

"And..." Kenzie turned back to Zachary. "It's wintertime. So whoever it was couldn't have gathered it anywhere in the state. It's under a blanket of snow. They would have had to gather it before they came here. They had to have some kind of premeditation. Planning."

"Maybe it was just for personal use," Tyrrell suggested.

"But like you say, it's very dangerous. There are better ways to get high more safely. Just buy some weed before coming out here. Or like Redd Flagg, bring some mushrooms."

The two men both nodded, agreeing.

"So it was planned and intentional," Kenzie asserted.

65

P retty much had to be," Zachary agreed.

They were all quiet, thinking about that for a few minutes.

"Then it would have to be someone on the staff," Tyrrell said eventually. "Wouldn't it? Who else would know everyone would be staying here?"

"Well... not necessarily," Kenzie disagreed. "I would assume that they were only targeting one person, even though everyone got dosed. Wouldn't you?"

"Probably," Zachary agreed, the word slow and thoughtful.

"And if you were only targeting one person, then you only have to know that one person will be here. You don't have to know any of the other guests or staff."

"I suppose," Tyrrell said.

"Everyone was poisoned to hide who the actual target was," Kenzie speculated. "If just Vance Stiller was poisoned, then we would know that it was someone who knew he would be here and had a motive for wanting to kill him."

"But no one was killed," Zachary said, holding up his hand to stop her from interrupting. "Not by the Jimson weed. Dewey died the day before. And Brooke didn't die from the Jimson weed. She died from being stabbed."

"That could have been planned. Maybe the Jimson weed was to cover up the fact that she was killed on purpose. Make everyone think it was just an accident due to hallucinations."

"Okay." Zachary nodded and remained focused on the point. "Let's take a minute and say that's what happened. It's a simple, clear-cut situation. So who would want to kill Brooke?"

"The husband is always the first suspect," Tyrrell offered. "That's what they say on TV."

"Right," Kenzie agreed. "And I've seen that, working in the ME's office. Lots of spousal killings. Pretty common, though usually it is in a fight, a crime of passion, not pre-planned."

"Motive?" Zachary queried. "Jealousy? Insurance?"

"If it was Andy Collins, then I'd go with insurance," Tyrrell said. "That, or she had a lot of money or an asset he wanted. He marries her, she changes her will to make him her beneficiary, and then he kills her. It looks like an accident, someone off their head on a hallucinogen. Case closed, and he gets the money."

It was a neat package. But Kenzie wasn't sure it was the right answer.

"Then why burn down the farmhouse? What's the motive for that?"

"It was an accident," Tyrrell suggested. "Unrelated. Someone knocked over a lantern."

"Burknall says not," Kenzie said. "They've been without power plenty of times before. They're used to using propane and the fireplaces and candles. It's all normal for them and they haven't had any accidents before."

"That doesn't prevent one from happening," Tyrrell argued. "Or... how about one of the guests goes up to the house. They want a midnight snack. They light a candle or a lantern, but they're not used to using them and they put the candle under a towel rack. Or knock over a lantern. Or light a fire in the fireplace and forget to close the screen to keep embers from flying out."

Kenzie looked at Zachary. His eyes were closed. She took his hand. "You okay, Zachary?"

She felt his pulse. It was pounding away, twice as fast as it should have been. But there was no panic in his expression. His breathing remained even.

"I'm fine."

She wouldn't normally accept that answer from him, but he probably didn't want a big emotional discussion in front of Tyrrell, and she didn't want to be distracted from the topic of the fire at the farmhouse. So far, Zachary was holding it together. She would have to accept that he would be able to manage the discussion of how the fire might have started.

"Any of those are possible," Kenzie admitted. "But do we think that it was just a coincidence? There just *happened* to be a fire that destroyed all of the physical evidence we still had?"

Tyrrell shrugged, thinking about it. "Probably not."

"I don't think so either. So if it were just straightforward, Andy killing Brooke for her money, then why burn down the house? What evidence were they getting rid of?"

Zachary started to tick possibilities off on his fingers. "Any drugs or toxins in Brooke's body. Any other marks on her—bruises, needle marks, fingerprints. Pregnancy. Trace evidence. The same with Mr. Dewey. You didn't think that his death was related, but what if it was?" He spoke rapidly. "It could have been to hide anything in the rooms that we put them in or in the rest of the house. The cooking dishes. What ingredient was contaminated. If there was Jimson weed stored in the cellar with the other herbs. Papers belonging to Mr. Dewey or someone else in the house. Identification. Fingerprints—both marks left behind and the fingerprints of Mr. Dewey and Brooke themselves. Were they really who they said they were?" He considered. "Did I miss anything?"

"Pictures," Kenzie said slowly. "Dewey had one beside his bed of him and his wife and a young man that I assume was their son. There could be other pictures that show some relationship to a guest or someone else at the Lodge."

"Blackmail," Tyrrell said, sounding excited. "Could have been blackmail pictures too. Poison pen letters. Tax fraud."

There were so many possibilities, Kenzie started to see the hopelessness of their ever being able to figure out what evidence might have been destroyed that they had no way of knowing even existed.

"And what if Brooke wasn't the intended victim?" Zachary proffered. "What if she were an accidental casualty?"

"Well... if it wasn't intentional murder, then what was it?" Kenzie asked. "Did they mean to kill someone who didn't die? Or did they not mean to kill anybody?"

"Or was Mr. Dewey the intended victim?"

"But he wasn't—" Kenzie stopped herself. They were brainstorming. Every possibility had to be explored. What if Mr. Dewey's death had not been accidental? What if someone had meant to kill him, and the Jimson weed poisoning the next night had just been to muddy the waters or keep everyone off-balance? Or to give the killer a chance to eliminate evidence at the house while everyone was flying high? Maybe they hadn't been able to destroy whatever evidence they wanted to and they had resorted instead to burning the house down?

"Okay," she said instead. "Why kill Mr. Dewey? He's the one who owned the Lodge, so the first obvious motivation was to acquire the Lodge. Who would have inherited it from him?"

"The son?" Zachary suggested.

"Maybe... I haven't heard anyone mention him, so I don't know if he was still around, or if he had died or been disinherited. If the Lodge didn't go to a son, then who?"

"If it went to one of the staff, then any of them might be the culprit," Tyrrell said.

"Yes... I don't think it could be Mrs. Hubbard. She's pretty broken up about having lost everything," Kenzie pointed out.

"It could be an act," he argued

"I don't think it is."

Tyrrell shook his head. "That Burknall is kind of creepy. He could get anywhere, do anything he wanted to."

He did have opportunity, Kenzie had to admit that.

Kenzie looked at Zachary. They didn't seem to be any closer to figuring it out.

"Who else knew someone who was going to be here?" Zachary asked, bringing the conversation back around.

"Well... Vance Stiller and Brittany seem to be a thing. So they must have planned to be here together."

"Could one of them have poisoned the other? In hopes that they would overdose or have an adverse reaction? Or be able to get the other alone and they just happened to fail at that part?"

"Vance had cardiovascular disease. I certainly wouldn't recommend someone like that take Jimson weed."

"It could have killed him?" Zachary asked.

"It could have killed anyone. But someone with heart disease? He would definitely be more susceptible than someone who was healthy."

"Like Brittany."

"Brittany takes pretty good care of herself," Kenzie said, remembering the exercise equipment. "So... a lot less likely than Stiller to die, if they were both poisoned. if she were the poisoner, then she could avoid eating whatever was contaminated and eliminate the possibility of overdosing herself."

"What reason would Brittany have to kill Stiller?" Zachary asked.

Kenzie couldn't come up with anything. The two seemed to like each other and to be a good match. They weren't married, but it was possible that Stiller could still have left something to Brittany in his will. "Stiller seems like he got a pretty good dose. He couldn't remember anything that happened the day before, and slept pretty heavily all that night and the next day. That's typical of Jimson weed. Brittany, on the other hand, didn't really act like she'd been dosed at all."

"So that's a possibility," Zachary said.

"But without a motive...?"

"We don't know," Tyrrell said. "Maybe he had done something to someone in her family in the past and she was out for revenge. Or he insulted her, or thought her business and fame was a sham. We don't know what went on between them."

66

There were voices outside the cabin. Kenzie turned her head and looked out the window. It was getting brighter outside, the sun up over the horizon. Raven and Jack were walking by, returning from the site of the fire up the hill. Kenzie studied their body language as they approached their cabins. She had wondered before if there were a previous relationship between Raven and Jack. They had not said so, but they seemed very familiar with each other and to have a sort of rapport between them. Sometimes, people just clicked the first time they met, but they acted like people who had shared something before they had come to the Lodge. It didn't feel like a first meeting to Kenzie.

But she could be wrong.

Raven's voice was raised as they walked near the cabin. Not just a typical talking voice. Maybe she had been affected by all of the excitement. Maybe, like with Zachary, the fire triggered some emotional reaction in her and she was agitated by it. But she seemed angry.

"What's going on with them?" Tyrrell asked.

"I don't know." Kenzie leaned closer to the window, trying to pick up their words. "Arguing about something, I think."

Watching their faces and straining for their words, Kenzie thought Raven said, "What were you doing up there?"

She frowned at Zachary. "What was he doing up there?" she repeated. She shook her head in confusion. "He went up to the house when he saw the fire. To make sure that everyone got out safely."

Zachary raised an eyebrow. "Is that what he told you?"

"Well... yes. It is. He said he got up to go to the bathroom, and he saw the fire, so he went up to make sure that Mrs. Hubbard and Samantha got out okay. And a good thing he did. It would be awful if we had lost someone in the fire. A third death, or a third and fourth, that would have been terrible."

"How did he get up there so quickly?"

"He saw the flames when he got up in the night," Kenzie repeated. "Just by luck. He was the first one to see them, so he was the first one to the house."

"And he didn't wake up anyone else? Try to get help? He just decided to run up to a burning house and try to rescue everyone himself?"

"Yes." Kenzie couldn't help the way that her voice curled up at the end of the sentence to make it sound like a question. She couldn't understand what Zachary was getting at. That was exactly what had happened.

Zachary shook his head. "No way. He was already up there. There's no way that he saw the flames and got up there before Mrs. Hubbard and Samantha woke up to the smoke alarms."

"You can't know that."

"The smoke alarms would have sounded long before the flames were visible through the windows."

"But if it started in one room and then spread, he might have seen the flames in the kitchen before they spread to the rest of the house."

"I'm with Raven on this one. What was he up at the house for?" Zachary looked out the window at them, having a heated discussion just a few feet from the cabin.

"Why would he lie? Maybe he went up for a midnight snack. Or a night cap."

"Or to see someone."

Kenzie looked at Jack. His face was red. From the heat of the fire? The cold air? The exertion? Or something else? Was he embarrassed or angry about Raven's questions?

"You think he was up there to see Samantha...?"

"It's possible."

"I suppose... but she never seemed that interested in him."

"She wouldn't have to be. Attraction doesn't always flow in both directions."

"Well, if we're eliminating coincidences... then what are the chances that he went up to the house to visit Samantha and there just happened to be a fire when he got there?"

Zachary nodded his approval of the question. "Maybe because it was no coincidence."

"Jack didn't start that fire!"

Kenzie and Zachary both startled and looked over at Mrs. Hubbard, who was standing in the hallway looking at them, her eyes blazing.

Zachary stood up quickly. He faced Mrs. Hubbard, his body language wary. "How do you know that?"

"He wouldn't do something like that. When I got downstairs, he was trying to put out the fire!"

"How?"

"He was... I don't know. He was trying to push all of the stuff that was on fire to the side, away from the furniture..."

Zachary looked at Kenzie. Using a fire extinguisher or trying to beat it out would have made sense, but trying to push burning debris to where it wouldn't spread didn't sound quite right. Kenzie saw Jack in her mind's eye, hunched over the burning materials, whirling around when Mrs. Hubbard came up on him from behind. Stammering out an explanation that he was trying to stop the fire from spreading. And then getting them all out of the house.

"He was a hero!" Mrs. Hubbard insisted. "He *didn't* light that fire! He'd never do something like that."

"Do you... *know* Jack, Mrs. Hubbard?" Kenzie asked tentatively.

"Jack is..." Mrs. Hubbard shook her head impatiently. "You don't understand! He was trying to put the fire out."

She moved to the door and jerked it open.

"Jack! Jack, come here!"

Jack turned from his discussion with Raven and looked at Mrs. Hubbard. It took him a moment to overcome his consternation at seeing her there. "What?"

"You need to tell them."

He walked slowly toward Mrs. Hubbard. He cast one worried glance over at Raven, then looked back at Mrs. Hubbard.

"You need to tell them who you are," Mrs. Hubbard insisted.

Jack hesitated, stopping just outside the door. He looked back at Raven, then at Mrs. Hubbard. He sighed. "Maybe you'd better come in too," he suggested.

Raven scowled. "What's going on? You can't just walk out on me."

"I'm not. I'm asking you to come in with me. If we're going to have this discussion... it may as well be all together."

"What discussion? I was talking to you, not to... anyone else." Raven shook her head in irritation.

"Please, Raven..."

Raven sighed loudly, then followed Jack, and the two of them entered the cabin. Mrs. Hubbard shut the door. She had eyes only for Jack, not even glancing at Raven.

"You have to tell them," she insisted.

Jack pulled off his hat and gloves and unzipped his jacket. He didn't take off his boots or his coat. He was clearly not staying. Raven pried off her boots and went directly to the liquor cabinet and poured herself a drink without asking anyone else. She glared at Jack.

"So what is all of this about?"

Jack looked at her, then at Zachary and everyone else, waiting for him to say something. He rubbed a hand across his eyes as if he just wanted to go back to sleep, and not to explain anything.

"I am Stuart Dewey's son."

There was dead silence. Kenzie tried to reconcile this to what she knew. She remembered the picture beside Dewey's bed, the picture with his wife and son. A blond boy. Fair, not dark like Jack. Their faces had not been the same, and it wasn't just a matter of hair color. He was also, Kenzie thought, younger than the boy in that picture. Too young to be claiming Dewey as his father.

"I don't think you are..."

"Not that one," Jack shook his head. "And... not by his wife." He looked at Mrs. Hubbard. "Someone else."

That explained his not having the same last name. Or there being any pictures of him around the house.

"You're Dewey's son," Zachary repeated. "Are you... his only issue?"

"His heir?" Jack asked. He shrugged his shoulders and spread his hands apart. "I haven't seen his will. But... I could be. Or I could contest it, if he's left me out of it. As far as I know, I was his only living child."

"Why are you here? And did he know who you were?"

"He knew. Didn't want to talk to me, but he knew who I was. Not that any of that matters anymore." He shook his head. "It's not like I'm going to get to know him now."

"You hadn't ever met him before?"

"Met him? Didn't even know he was my father. Not until recently."

"And you were staying here... to meet him?"

"No. Maybe. I wanted to see the place. Where... my roots were. Whether it meant anything to me."

If he had set fire to the place, Kenzie assumed that the answer to that question was no.

"That's why we're here?" Raven demanded. She slugged back a swallow of her whiskey. "Because the old man was your father?"

"Yes."

"I thought..."

It was clear what she had thought. Even if she didn't say it in front of Zachary and Kenzie, they understood. She had thought that he had invited her there on a romantic getaway.

But that still didn't explain why Jack had gone up to the house. If he knew his father was dead, what was the point in going to the house? To search for his will or some other documents? To break into that bedroom and get a good look at his deceased father?

Or to burn it all to the ground?

"I thought that you went up there to see—"

"Raven." He shook his head, trying to silence her.

"I won't shut up! Why should I? I haven't done anything wrong." Full of righteous indignation, she turned to Kenzie, her closest ally in the room. "He stole my things!"

Jack opened his mouth to protest.

"Where did they go if you didn't take them?" Raven demanded. "Clothes don't just go walking off by themselves. You were the *only one* with access to my cabin."

Jack shook his head. "Raven..."

"I couldn't understand why you would take them. Then you were up *there*. Going to *her*! So I knew you had taken them. To give to another woman as some sort of sick gift."

Jack continued to shake his head. "You don't know what you're talking about. Raven, please..."

But it was too late to stop her. A picture was already beginning to form in Kenzie's head. Why would Jack take Raven's clothing? Especially if they were lovers. He didn't need any kind of trophy.

Why had the house been burned down?

What would Jack have done with Raven's clothes? It wasn't, as Raven thought, to take them as a gift for his new love interest. And he hadn't been trying to stop the fire from spreading when Mrs. Hubbard had come upon him.

He'd been trying to destroy the evidence. Raven's bloody clothing.

67

Kenzie looked at Jack. He was still shaking his head at Raven as if he could put the words back in her mouth. He pressed his hand to his forehead, focused, trying to think his way out of this one. Too many people knew. Now it wasn't just him. Zachary, Kenzie, Tyrrell, Mrs. Burton. He couldn't silence all of them. He needed to change his approach.

"Look..."

"Was Raven the one who killed Brooke Collins?" Kenzie asked, her voice flat. She wasn't making an accusation. She didn't want them getting all emotional and overwrought. If Raven had killed Brooke in a hallucinatory or agitated state because she had been poisoned with Jimson weed, then she wouldn't necessarily be guilty. If she hadn't voluntarily taken Jimson weed, but it had been administered to her without her knowledge, she couldn't be held responsible for what had followed.

Jack just looked at her, pain in his eyes. He didn't say anything to Raven to explain or defend his actions.

If he had knowingly destroyed evidence, then Jack was guilty of something. And if he had been the one to put Jimson weed into the food, then *he* might be responsible for Brooke's death to some degree. And what about Mr. Dewey? Had he killed Dewey when the man refused to acknowledge him or have a relationship with him? He could have burned Raven's clothes in his own fireplace. He'd wanted to destroy more than that.

"What are you talking about?" Raven asked.

"You don't remember everything that happened that night," Kenzie suggested. "One of the problems with Jimson weed is that it causes memory blanks. Episodes of amnesia that can cover hours or days. Sometime that night, you went out and met up with Brooke Collins in the woods. And when you went back to your cabin, or to Jack's cabin, you were covered with her blood."

Raven's eyes widened. She looked at Jack, no longer accusatory. "No."

"Jack?" Kenzie pressed.

Jack nodded, not looking at her. "Soaked with blood. And cold as ice, out there without any coat or warm clothes on. You'd just put my boots on. I... helped to warm you up. I tried to wash them, but they didn't come clean. And all of those TV shows, they say that you can never get all of the blood out."

"So you burned them. Along with the rest of the evidence. Brooke's body. Anything that might point to what Raven had done. Or what you had done."

"*I* didn't do anything," Jack shot back. "None of this had anything to do with me."

"The Jimson weed was yours. That makes you guilty of Brooke's death, even if it was Raven who had killed her."

"No! Jimson weed? I don't even know what that is. You're crazy. I don't know what happened that night. What she did," Jack looked at Raven, "but it was nothing to do with me. She has..." His eyes moved back and forth between Zachary and Kenzie, trying to identify which of them would be the most sympathetic. "She has problems. Medical problems. Something set her off. Andy and Brooke fighting. I don't know. But something happened."

Raven's whole face was a scowl. "You think I had a psychotic break that night? I didn't. I would know."

"Do you remember what happened? Do you remember coming back covered in blood? What happened before that?"

She shook her head.

"Then you had a break," he insisted.

"It wasn't just Raven," Kenzie said. "Others had hallucinations, strange behaviors, fights," she reminded him. "That's why we searched everyone's cabins."

"But you didn't find anything."

"Are you the one who stole the medications too?" Kenzie challenged. "You know, other people need those. Just like Raven needs hers."

Jack looked at Raven and didn't admit to it. But Kenzie had a pretty good idea he was the one who had drilled the safe. He had been worried about making sure that Raven got her meds. Or he'd wanted something else in there. Maybe he'd needed a tranquilizer in order to stay calm and function, knowing that his girlfriend was the one who had killed Brooke. And he'd lost his father, too. Had *that* been a coincidence? An accident?

If they weren't accepting coincidences, then why had Dewey died? Had Jack intentionally killed him? Had they had an argument? Had Jack tested out the Jimson weed on him, and then given it to everyone else to cover up what he had done?

"How did you know who Jack was?" Kenzie asked Mrs. Hubbard. "Had Mr. Dewey told you about him? Did he know that Jack was coming?"

"We knew who Jack was." Mrs. Hubbard didn't explain how they knew. "We knew he was here to confront—to talk to Mr. Dewey."

"Who is included in the 'we'? How many people knew that he was coming?"

Mrs. Hubbard shrugged. "I don't see how any of it matters," she declared. "It was just me, and Harold, and Mr. Dewey."

"Harold?" Kenzie repeated stupidly.

"Mr. Burknall."

"Oh. Sure. So it was only the three of you who knew who he really was? That he wasn't here to vacation, but to see Mr. Dewey and to *talk* to him."

"It was a vacation," Jack said. "I wanted to bring Raven here, see what she thought about it. Relax and enjoy the atmosphere. The planned events. Meals. It was a nice retreat. I don't take a lot of vacations."

He looked at Raven, smiling at her, trying to get something from her other than the scowl she was displaying. She probably was not pleased that the romantic getaway he had planned had actually had the ulterior motive of seeing his biological father and scoping out the landscape. And that he had poisoned her and everyone else. *What kind of a psychopath did that?*

"I didn't poison anyone," Jack growled, reading Kenzie's expression.

"The evidence suggests that you did."

"What evidence? You never found anything on me or in my cabin. The only thing I'm 'guilty' of is trying to protect Raven from prosecution. I knew no one would understand. I had to take it upon myself." Jack shook his head. "I would think *you* would understand that."

What would Kenzie have done if she thought that Zachary had done something that put him in danger of being prosecuted? What if he came home with his shirt soaked with blood? How would she handle it? She would like to think that she would do the right thing, but what was the right thing? Turn him in or protect him?

She had an obligation, working in the medical examiner's office, to the truth. But did that apply to every circumstance? Or only to official evidence that came to her through her job?

She hadn't hesitated when Zachary had come to her with Madison and Noah, when Noah had been shot and Zachary wouldn't take him to the emergency room in case they put a dirty cop on to him. So she had already been tested in that arena. She knew that if Zachary came to her with something possibly unethical, she would still help him to cover for it. How could she fault Jack for doing the same?

"I can't condone the destruction of evidence," she told Jack anyway, "It would have been better if you had left it to the police to sort out. If Raven did something in an altered state... they would investigate it. Figure out how to deal with it."

"And decide to put her away for life. Come on. You know it."

Kenzie shrugged. She put her face in her hands and rubbed her eyes and her temples. "I just want... to understand what went on here. If you weren't the one who poisoned everyone with Jimson weed, then who did?"

Jack folded his arms across his chest, staring at her sullenly.

"Two truths and a lie," Zachary said.

Kenzie looked at him. "What?"

"You know, it's that game where you try to figure out which statement that someone made was a lie."

Kenzie nodded. "Sure. I know that."

"It isn't coming together because we have taken as true something that was a lie. What do we believe that isn't actually true?"

Kenzie sighed. They couldn't keep going back over everything again and again. She had already accepted everything Zachary had suggested. That there were no coincidences. That Dewey's death was somehow related.

They knew more now, with a better understanding of Jack's and Raven's roles in the events, but they still didn't have the whole picture. They needed the police to investigate it and to sort it out.

"I don't know, Zachary. What do we believe that is a lie?"

"The night that we searched the cabins. What did we accept as true?"

Kenzie closed her eyes and thought it through. "That no one could have spiked the food with their pills. That the mushrooms were Redd's. That each of the medications we found belonged to the person whose cabin it was. That we found everything that was hidden." That one clearly wasn't true, if Jack had been in possession of Raven's bloody clothes at that point. Where had he hidden them in his neat-as-a-pin cabin? Maybe outside under the snow? In the barn or one of the other outbuildings? Until he decided he couldn't hide them any longer and they needed to be destroyed.

She sighed.

"That everyone was telling the truth about their own symptoms," Zachary added. "Hallucinations, fights, amnesia, that all of that was true."

"And it wasn't?" Kenzie asked. Her eyes snapped open.

Zachary shrugged. "Maybe... maybe not. What does your training tell you?"

"What did we observe?" Kenzie mused. "The argument and people coming and going, you saw that."

Zachary nodded.

"Redd having hallucinations. He was still hallucinating the next day. I could see him... the way his eyes would move to follow something that wasn't there. Dilated pupils. Jimson weed is known for causing hallucinations for days, even weeks sometimes."

"Raven had dilated pupils too," Zachary said, giving Raven a nod. "I remember noticing that."

Kenzie thought back, nodding. "Yes. She did."

"Andy Collins said that he couldn't remember. That's another of the symptoms of Jimson weed, so—"

"But we can only take his word for that. It may be true, but he could just be covering up."

"And Stiller too," Kenzie said. "He said it felt like when he'd been roofied in college."

Zachary scratched his jaw. "That seems... like something a man of his standing wouldn't usually admit to."

"No, but it's one of the things that made me realize they'd all been given something. Not just him, but all of them."

"Did he eat or drink more than the others? Does the amnesia mean that he was given more?"

"I don't think there's a correlation. Some people get one symptom, some another."

"And if someone knew the symptoms, that would be an easy one to fake. A lot easier than dilated pupils."

"Vance Stiller." Kenzie thought about him. "Why is he even here? It doesn't seem like the type of place that a high roller like him would vacation. Brittany is known for being 'one of the people,' so I can see it in her case. But Stiller? The man came here in a helicopter."

Jack looked from Kenzie to Zachary. "He wasn't here for a vacation."

"Well, to see Brittany," Kenzie clarified. "I guess maybe she picked the venue."

Jack shook his head. "No. He wasn't here for any of that. He told Brittany about the place and she decided to come too, but *she* followed *him*, not the other way around."

"How do you know that?"

"Because he was talking with Dewey about buying the place, came to try to talk him into it, get the lay of the land."

"Buying it?" That seemed even more unlikely than his choosing to vacation there. Why would he want to buy a place like that, so far out of his comfort zone? He was a city boy, high finance, a tech guy. Not the kind of person who enjoyed camping in a cabin. And he'd been vocal about it. Why would he buy a place like that if he didn't even like it?

Jack nodded. He motioned to Mrs. Hubbard. "Tell them. He was trying to talk Dewey into selling it to him."

Mrs. Hubbard shrugged. "Mr. Dewey said he would never sell. Especially not to a man like Mr. Vance."

Kenzie nodded slowly. Her eyes found Zachary's. "There was no way he would sell to a man like Stiller. But maybe his estate or his heir would."

They both looked at Jack.

"Was that the plan?" Kenzie asked him. "Mr. Dewey wouldn't sell to him, Vance decided to go to the next in line. You."

"I never talked to him before I came here. And like I told you, I have no idea if Dewey left me anything. You'd have to check his will."

"But you could contest it if he didn't. Make a claim on his estate as his sole living relative."

"Maybe. If I wanted something from him."

"A place like this would bring in a lot of coin," Zachary said, motioning around them. "Medical care can be expensive. Specialized therapy." He was looking at Raven. "For someone who didn't grow up with a lot of money, it would be a windfall."

"I hadn't made a decision," Jack said, keeping his arms folded in front of his chest, giving off a stubborn, belligerent air. "There was no reason to rush into anything."

"Did Stiller give you an offer? Suggest a price?"

"No."

Watching his eyes, Kenzie didn't believe it for a minute. They had been in negotiations, without Jack even knowing if he would inherit the Lodge, or a portion of it.

"And Stiller could bring down the price," Zachary said. "If it turned out the Lodge wasn't as valuable as you thought initially... if things didn't go well and it got a bad reputation..."

"If there was a death or two," Kenzie filled in, as the pieces clicked into place, finally making sense. "People going crazy there. A rumor that it was bad luck or cursed. A series of tragedies."

"*He* did this?" Jack demanded. "Vance Stiller poisoned us? Caused—" he looked at Raven, "—caused Brooke to get killed? Endangered all of our lives with his poison to get a better price on the deal?"

"Maybe," Zachary said cautiously. "It's speculation right now. But it fits the facts. He could pretend that he had been affected by the Jimson weed. Throw anyone who was suspicious off of the trail. Use anything that happened here as leverage to lower the selling price of the Lodge. And you played right into his hand, burning the farmhouse down."

68

Jack opened the door and bolted. Raven hurried to get her boots back on and follow him. "Jack! Jack, wait!"

"We'd better stop him," Zachary warned.

Kenzie got her boots on and grabbed her coat. She was out the door right after Zachary, leaving Mrs. Hubbard and Tyrrell in the dust. Jack was already pounding on Vance Stiller's cabin door, making threats, demanding that he show his face. If Stiller had any sense, he would know to keep as quiet as possible.

He didn't answer the door. Zachary and Kenzie caught up with Jack. "We need to let the police take care of this," Kenzie told him. "Another day or two, and they'll be here..."

"And by the time they can get here, he's going to be on a helicopter away from here, and I'm never going to be able to get close to him again. This is it. It all comes down to this." Jack hammered on the door, calling Vance names, trying to needle him sharply enough for him to lose control and come out of the cabin to fight Jack.

But Stiller didn't come out. The cabin was quiet. No movement that Kenzie could detect. She turned toward Brittany's cabin. Close enough to see what was going on. Maybe Brittany would know whether her boyfriend were there or if he had somehow bolted, escaping without their realizing it. She wouldn't put it past the guy.

As she turned and looked at the other cabin, she heard a noise. The soft click of a door latch between Jack's assaults on the door. The front door hadn't moved, so it had to be the back. Kenzie stepped to the side, trying to see into the back yard to see whether Brittany were making her escape. She saw Stiller, head down, moving slowly and quietly so as not to attract any attention.

Jack turned toward Kenzie. Following her gaze, he caught sight of Stiller. "Vance! Hold it right there! You're not going anywhere!"

Vance turned around to see Jack. In doing so, he revealed the fact that Brittany was with him. At first, Kenzie thought that he just had his arm around her. A gesture of protectiveness and possession. But Brittany's face was white, and it only took Kenzie a fraction of a second to realize that she was Stiller's hostage.

"Just stay back," Stiller warned. "There's no need to get all hot under the collar..."

"No need?" Jack shouted, drawing closer. "You poison us? Cause someone's death? Ruin people's lives? And there's nothing to get hot about?"

Stiller took a few steps back, trying to keep distance between himself and Jack. His arm was tight around Brittany's neck and he held a knife in his hand. Was it the knife that had killed Brooke? Kenzie wasn't sure if it was the same one, but it looked wickedly sharp and deadly. Brooke's body had been a bloody mess. Knife wounds were not pretty. A slash across Brittany's throat would cause her death within minutes. She would bleed out right there in the snow, with no chance of their saving her. Not without a trauma team on hand and a surgeon to sew her up before she bled out.

"Vance..." Kenzie tried to keep a calm, professional tone. Something that would make him feel validated. Make him feel like someone was listening to him. "I don't think we need to do this, do you? You don't want to hurt Brittany."

She could see Brittany swallow, trying to pull her throat back from the knife as she did so. "Vance," she whispered hoarsely. "Honey..."

But Vance had trained himself to be a shark. To ruthlessly go after what he wanted. No matter what personal pain it brought him. However much grief and regret it might cause him later, it would not stop him from proceeding.

For a moment, Kenzie could hear nothing but the rushing of blood in her ears. Then she looked around, puzzled by a noise outside her head. It was like the crash of an ocean. Waves of sound swallowing them up. She tried to separate them out, but they all rushed together. People shouting. Snowmobiles. Heavy equipment. A hundred voices all crying out at once. Kenzie looked around, trying to understand what it was and where it was coming from.

There was a dark flood coming down the hill. Kenzie's brain couldn't break the surge of movement into its component parts, dazzled by the sun coming out from behind a cloud and hitting the bright white snow. Overwhelmed by all the images flowing together, as if the flood were made up of a thousand moving parts.

As the flood engulfed them, Kenzie saw people on snowmobiles, some of them standing or waving shovels. Followed by ranks of tractors, everything from little Bobcats to heavy-duty plows. All coming in from the highway, down the hill, and into the middle of the stand-off.

Stiller seemed as stunned as any of them. He didn't have his sunglasses on, and a beam of sunlight suddenly broke through the clouds, causing tears to run down his face. He swiveled his head, trying to see or make sense of all the moving, shifting shapes.

There were shouts of "He's got Brittany!" and "The bombshell" and "Go Bambas!"

A hostage situation should be carefully controlled, managed by a skilled negotiator who was trained in de-escalating situations and ensuring a positive outcome. Everything should be kept quiet and calm, and nothing should be done to startle the hostage-taker.

The fence between the front yard and the back was no obstacle. Snow machines went airborne over it and, shrieking like pigs being slaughtered, the riders mobbed Stiller and Brittany, parting them with overwhelming force. Kenzie tried to get to Brittany, visions of a severed carotid filling her brain. She shoved the people in the crowd aside, insisting that she be allowed to see Brittany to give her medical care.

"I'm a doctor! Get out of the way! Let me see!"

She managed to bully her way through them, over the broken remains of the fence pounded into the snow, until she reached Brittany, stretched out on the ground.

"Let me see!" Kenzie insisted, jerking and pulling on coats and sweaters that got in front of her. "Brittany! Brittany!"

Brittany held up her hands, laughing. "It's okay, Kenzie. I'm okay! I'm fine!"

Kenzie shoved more people away. She stared at Brittany. Her throat was unmarked, though there were several tears in her coat. Kenzie held out her hand to Brittany and helped her to her feet.

"Is Vance okay?" Brittany asked, looking around.

Kenzie searched the crowd for him, but couldn't see him and wasn't sure she wanted to. "What just happened here?"

"The Bambas!" someone shouted close to her ear.

Kenzie winced. "What?"

"My fans," Brittany said, her laugh soft. "It looks like... they found me."

"How? How did they find you and how did they get here?"

"We hadn't heard anything from the Bombshell in, like, three days!" one of the men nearby blasted Kenzie. "So it was like, everybody was looking for her! And no one knew where she was. We had to follow the trail here, but there was literally no way to get here through the snow. We called out for every dang snow removal vehicle in the state, and we made our own way here!"

Kenzie blinked, trying to take it all in. "Your fans plowed the highway," she said to Brittany.

"Looks like it. And not a moment too soon!" Brittany laughed.

"I thought... I thought Stiller was going to kill you!"

Brittany forced a banal smile, keeping all the anxiety out of her face. Two minutes before, she had been as white as a sheet, begging for her life, and now she was doing her best to show that nothing had fazed her. She looked around her, again looking for some sign of Stiller, then shook her head.

"I'm not sure... what happened to him. But I guess... everything is okay now."

Kenzie heard sirens whoop and looked up the hill to see fire trucks and police cars turning in from the highway. "A little late for them now."

"We saw the smoke!" another of the fans shouted. Kenzie didn't know whether everybody just sounded loud after the isolation of the past few days, or if all Brittany's fans were just natural yellers. "We were afraid that something might have happened to Brittany!"

She nodded. "Well... we're glad that you got here when you did."

It was some time before Kenzie managed to make it back to the cabin. Zachary caught her arm as she pushed her way through the crowd of Bambas.

"Kenz! Are you okay?"

"Yeah. I'm honestly not sure what just happened, but I'm fine. You?"

She managed to focus on his face and saw that he had a black eye.

"Oh. We should put some ice on that. Grab a handful of snow."

They holed up in the cabin and watched as the police gradually got the fans moved out of the area. Kenzie saw a white tent go up in the yard and knew that there was only one reason for the scene to be processed that way. Somewhere under the awning was Stiller's beaten and trampled body. She was glad that it wasn't her investigation, that she didn't have to be part of that particular crime scene and to view Stiller's remains. To be an effective pathologist, she needed emotional distance, and she didn't have it in this case.

Before long, the police would be making their way to her cabin and would want to know all about everything that had happened. They weren't going to be happy with the destruction of the evidence in the fire.

Soon, there would be a lot of questions for her and the others. And she wasn't sure she had many answers for them.

69

Kenzie helped Tyrrell and Zachary load up Tyrrell's car and get the kids ready to go. They were all eager to get out of there, Mason chattering on about how he was going to see his mom again and about all the things that he would tell her.

Kenzie smiled at Tyrrell sympathetically. "I guess your ex will have a lot of questions on just what happened here this week."

Tyrrell nodded and rolled his eyes. "Uh, yeah. She is definitely going to have some words about putting them in this situation."

"It isn't as though you could have done anything to prevent it. You did everything you could to keep the kids out of the way, and they didn't actually *see* anything."

"Thank goodness! Oh, would I be in some deep trouble then. But... maybe I should have headed out when I knew the storm was coming in. I knew that we might get stranded for a couple of days, but I didn't think there was any harm in it. Even with the power and communications out, the kids were still safe and had food and everything they needed."

"Maybe even a good thing for them," Kenzie contributed. "No screens. Just books and games and finding ways to entertain themselves."

"It didn't actually go too badly, other than when Mace took off and hid in the barn."

"And he didn't fall or get hurt in there. I'm sure it's not the first time he's wandered off."

Tyrrell chuckled. "By no means. But my ex still thinks that we should be able to prevent it. If we're just vigilant enough."

Kenzie shook her head. It would take a bit more than just vigilance to keep track of everything Mason did. An ankle monitor and a body cam, for a start. Maybe one of those perimeter collars that you put on dogs to keep them from crossing the property line.

"Well, good luck."

"Thanks." Tyrrell turned back toward the car to get the children settled and to make sure they hadn't forgotten anything.

"And Tyrrell...?"

He turned back around and looked at her.

"Is everything okay with you...?" She knew that Zachary had brought up the alcohol cabinet with Tyrrell, but the younger man had denied falling off the wagon. It would have been understandable under the circumstances, but he said he'd never touched a drop.

Tyrrell nodded. "Sure, I'm fine. You take good care of this brother of mine." He grabbed Zachary, who was headed back to Kenzie's side, and gave him a fierce hug. "You did really good, bro. Really good. Take care."

Zachary slapped him on the back. "I will, T. You too."

"Let me know how you're doing. I know that this is... a tough time of year." Tyrrell looked at him for a moment, meeting his eyes. "For me, too."

"Yeah. Will you have the kids this year?" In keeping with his usual practice, Zachary didn't say "for Christmas," but it was understood.

"I'm supposed to. It's my turn."

Zachary swallowed and nodded. Kenzie knew that he wanted to say something like "We'll have to get together" or to suggest an activity they might like to do with the children. But he had a mental wall where Christmas was concerned. He could not plan anything until after Christmas Eve was past.

Tyrrell gave Zachary an understanding pat on the back and climbed into the car.

"I'll give you a call."

70

Kenzie finished tidying up Dr. Wiltshire's office and putting everything else back to rights, which had taken quite a bit of work after all the time she'd been away. Between the antiviral protocol and her last-minute vacation, she'd been away for several weeks, and none of it had been planned, so Dr. Wiltshire and the part-time staff that he could get in had run things the best they could while she was gone. And, she was happy to see, they badly needed her to get things straightened out again. They had managed to get along without her, but it was clear that they had struggled and that several of the department protocols had fallen by the wayside as they tried to make do without her.

They needed her. And that was a good feeling.

She had gotten there early to make sure she would have a lot of time before Dr. Wiltshire got there. She wasn't a morning person, but it had been worth it to get up extra early for one day.

She was back at her desk when Dr. Wiltshire got there, just starting to go through the accumulated email in her inbox to sort out the priorities and get started on printing and filing.

"Kenzie!" His greeting was more enthusiastic than usual. "Look at you! You don't know how much I have missed seeing your smiling face when I get in each morning."

"Well, from the state of the office, I can understand why."

"We did our best to keep things running while you were gone," he said, scratching his head, "but we have clearly come to rely on you for nearly everything around here."

He had a tray and a box from the donut shop down the street. He put them on the ledge of Kenzie's desk, and carefully removed a cup of coffee from the tray.

"For you."

"Thank you!"

"And there are donuts..." He opened the box and held it tilted for her to pick out her choice of pastries.

"Oh, I shouldn't..." But Kenzie knew that she would take one, and so did he. She'd already burned up all the calories from her marmalade toast that morning, running back and forth getting things tidied up. She was ready for something decadent after hospital food and camping food. It seemed like a long time since their Thanksgiving dinner with Lorne and Pat. Though the real Thanksgiving Day was still coming up.

"So, how was your vacation?" Dr. Wiltshire asked. "Nice and relaxing?"

"Well... it didn't turn out quite the way that I expected."

"Oh? I suppose they never do happen quite the way that we plan, do they?"

Kenzie shook her head. "No. I guess that would be asking too much."

"You'll have to tell me all about it. But right now, I should check to see what's on my desk. And I think you have a few things waiting for you in your inbox."

Kenzie nodded. "Yes... it would appear that I do."

GENTLE ANGEL

A KENZIE KIRSCH MEDICAL THRILLER #4

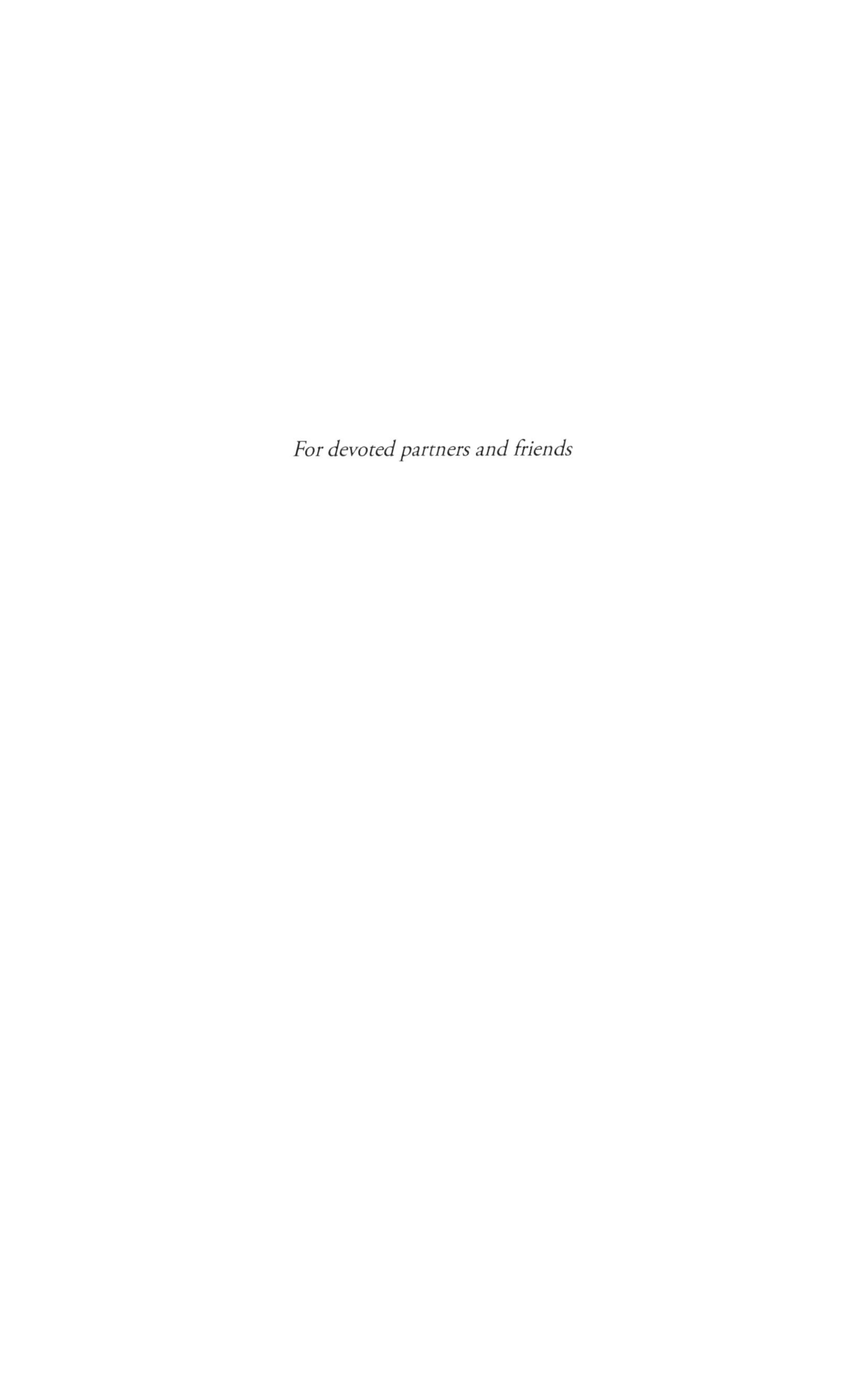

For devoted partners and friends

1

I t felt good to be back in the morgue.

It might sound strange, but after their stressful vacation in a mountain resort, Kenzie and Zachary were both glad to be home and back into the usual daily routines—Zachary running his private investigations business and Kenzie returning to the Medical Examiner's Office where none of the bodies she dealt with were people that she had known personally. Most people considered the work of a medical examiner to be gross and depressing, but Kenzie was fascinated with the work of uncovering what the deceased had died of and found it life-affirming rather than discouraging.

Dr. Wiltshire and the part-time staff had let a number of things slide while she had been gone. She had been prevented from coming to work first due to a virus she had contracted and the antiviral protocol to kill it, and then on a short holiday that was supposed to be a chance for her and Zachary to recover their health and rest before getting back to work. It hadn't exactly turned out that way.

There were a lot of requests and reports to be processed in Kenzie's physical in box as well as in her email queue.

A couple of bodies had been transported from the hospital, and Kenzie reviewed the intake forms to find out the details and make sure that everything had been filled out correctly. She opened new files for each of them and checked the bodies themselves to make sure that the names and numbers matched the forms that the hospital had sent with them. Always better to catch any clerical errors early. Families tended not to like it when bodies got mixed up.

She was back at her desk printing reports when Dr. Wiltshire got in. The idea of the ME's office being paperless was a joke. They went through reams of paper.

"Morning, Kenzie," Dr. Wiltshire greeted.

"Morning, Doctor. Got a couple of intakes from the hospital today."

He nodded and took a sip of his coffee. "Anything of note?"

"One from a single-vehicle car accident. And one a request from a doctor."

Neither was particularly out of the ordinary. A doctor-attended death did not automatically go to the Medical Examiner's Office, but if the attending physician had any doubts about the cause of death or deemed it suspicious in some way, he could request that the medical examiner perform an autopsy.

"What is the doctor's name?"

Kenzie hadn't made note of it, so she brought the form up on her computer to check. "A Dr. Philemon?"

"Philemon…" Dr. Wiltshire pondered this for a moment. He frowned. "He's in geriatrics, isn't he?"

Kenzie went to the Vermont Health Network website and searched Dr. Philemon in the directory. "Yes, looks like that's his specialty. Does some general practice as well."

Dr. Wiltshire nodded. "Okay. I'll look at them today. How is your workload?"

"Still trying to get caught up. Lots of printing and filing to be done."

"Yeah… we might have let that slide a little."

"A little," Kenzie agreed. She wasn't sure anyone had done any filing during the weeks she had been gone. And since no filing had been done, she couldn't be sure what reports had been printed already. She had to keep going back and forth between the computer and the piles of printouts and the files to try to make sure everything was accounted for and that they could put their hands on what they needed immediately. It wasn't any good if there were lab results floating around that hadn't been reviewed or if they were holding on to bodies that should be moved on to funeral homes because they hadn't been cleared yet.

"Sorry about that. But we didn't want to mess up your system…"

Kenzie laughed and shook her head. "Good excuse!"

He smiled and took another sip of his coffee. "Well, we had to come up with something to explain this mess."

Maybe they could have put some of the time that had gone into thinking up an excuse into actually getting the work done.

"I'll do what I can to get it all whipped into shape… but I'll be ready for a break from the paper this afternoon, if you don't mind me scrubbing in on one of the autopsies."

"Sounds good. I'll be sure to start early enough that you can get through it and still get back to Zachary in good time."

Dr. Wiltshire knew Zachary from a couple of previous cases that he had been involved with. And he knew a little bit about the challenges that Zachary faced.

Only someone who lived with Zachary or was close to him could know the real extent of his difficulties, but Kenzie appreciated Dr. Wiltshire thinking about her and her home situation in setting his schedule for the day. Despite the amount of work she had to do, Kenzie didn't want to be there too late. She would get caught up over time. Being able to spend time with Zachary and keep an eye on his health was important too.

———

Kenzie was a little disappointed that the autopsy she was able to scrub in on was Dr. Philemon's patient rather than the accident victim. The accident victim would have been more interesting. She suspected that a geriatric patient who had died at the hospital wasn't going to be a particularly intriguing case. Although she couldn't make that judgment. They had recently autopsied a nursing home patient whose death had turned out to be anything but routine.

George had already prepped the remains for them, gathering any forensic evidence and washing the body off. The old man's body lay on the table with a drape over it, awaiting their investigation. Dr. Wiltshire tapped the button on the floor with his foot to start recording, and dictated the patient's name and file number, the date and time, and his and Kenzie's names. He began as usual, making note of the patient's height and weight and his appearance on gross examination. Nothing remarkable. He didn't look any different from any other geriatric patient who had passed away in his sleep.

They checked for any cuts, bruises, or needle marks, as well as making notes of livor mortis. Time of death had been noted by Dr. Philemon, and Kenzie didn't see anything that would indicate that the timing was off.

"Bruising to the chest and ribs," Dr. Wiltshire commented. "Let's get some films and have a look."

He and Kenzie donned the appropriate radiation shields and took several x-rays of the body. The images were processed and ready for their review immediately. Dr. Wiltshire called them up on the screen.

"Some inflammation and fractures," he commented. "What does that look like to you, Dr. Kirsch?"

Kenzie was the student, and Dr. Wiltshire preferred the Socratic model of leading her with questions rather than lecturing. Kenzie had seen the victim's injury pattern in textbooks and didn't have a problem coming up with the answer.

"Looks like CPR was performed."

"Would you perform CPR on an elderly patient like this?"

Kenzie looked at him. "Probably not. He's very frail and what would be gained by reviving him? Even if he could be revived with CPR, chances are he would have brain damage or his quality of life would not be good. Not with broken ribs at his age. I'm surprised there was not a DNR."

"There might have been. If it's not properly recorded and flagged, they might proceed with CPR anyway. Although with a patient of this age," he shook his head, "I'm not sure why."

"I don't remember there being anything on the records we got from the hospital about CPR being performed. They should have noted it."

"Unless this was from a previous incident. If he had a cardiac event earlier, we might not have all the relevant records. We'll need to follow up on whether there was a DNR or a previous incident that required resuscitation."

Kenzie nodded her agreement. She couldn't stop and make a note in the middle of the autopsy, but it would be on the transcript she got back from the recording. She moved the magnifier over the deceased man's arm and examined the IV catheter and tube.

"See something?" Dr. Wiltshire asked.

"No. I just wondered whether I would be able to tell whether anything was injected into the IV."

"Doubtful," Dr. Wiltshire shook his head. "Sometimes there is trace evidence. Crystals, bubbles, things like that. But if it was meant to be injected, adrenaline or some other lifesaving measure, then no. It would just mix with the IV fluid and not leave any visible traces."

Kenzie examined the tubing for another minute, but couldn't see anything unusual.

"Okay. What's next?"

2

I t was a little later than Kenzie would have liked when she got home, but considering how late she had worked other days, it wasn't really bad. She hadn't had to eat a sandwich from the vending machine, but she was more than ready for her supper. She pulled her baby—a cherry red convertible—into her garage and walked in through the kitchen door. Zachary was sitting on the couch with his computer table in front of him, but he looked up when she opened the door, not so focused on his work that he failed to notice her.

"Home, sweet home," Kenzie declared.

Zachary smiled. "How was it today?"

"Still getting caught up. But Dr. Wiltshire understands that I can't get through three weeks of backlog in a couple of days, so I'm not going to kill myself trying."

"That would sort of defeat the purpose. Then you'd never get out of the morgue."

"Well, I would eventually, but it would be on a gurney."

Zachary chuckled. He pushed his table away from him and stretched. "Do you want me to order something?"

"I'm too hungry to wait for delivery." Kenzie put down her bag and opened the freezer door to see what supplies they had. Even a pizza would take half an hour to heat, and she wasn't in the mood for frozen burritos. She closed the freezer and opened the fridge but, as she had expected, there wasn't much to eat there. Some fruit, a salad that she'd made with perfectly good intentions but then not even touched. Some leftovers from Sunday that she should probably throw out. Kenzie sighed.

"You could have a snack while we wait for delivery," Zachary suggested.

"Well… maybe." Kenzie considered the fruit. She could have an apple with some cheese while she waited for something better to be delivered. That would hold her over and help to keep her calm and relaxed to visit with Zachary but wouldn't take the amount of effort that actually coming up with something and preparing dinner herself would.

Her mother would despair over the lack of culinary and homemaking skills her daughter possessed. But then, Lisa Cole Kirsch had employed a cook for most of Kenzie's childhood. Granted, she'd had a sick child to take care of, which was far more important than making sandwiches. Or mini quiches.

Kenzie removed an apple from the crisper drawer. She decided she didn't have the energy to get out the cheese and cut herself a couple of slices. She sat down on the couch with Zachary.

"Go ahead and order us something."

He nodded and picked up his phone. "What do you want?"

"I don't really care. As long as it isn't something that I have to make." Kenzie bit into her apple. It had been a long time since lunch. While Zachary poked through his phone and decided what to order in, she picked up the remote control and listened to the news headlines as the local news began. As she had come to expect, there wasn't much in the way of good, uplifting news. Negative headlines garnered more attention. When they switched to a story about Brittany "the Bombshell" Blake and her recent close-encounter with a possible killer, Kenzie quickly turned it off.

She turned her attention to Zachary. "So, tell me about your day today." Kenzie mentally reviewed what she remembered of his schedule for the day. "You got in to see Dr. Boyle for therapy today?"

Zachary nodded. He suppressed a smile, looking down at his hands. "It was good. I caught her up on… some of the stuff that happened while we were on vacation."

"I guess you kind of left her hanging before, when we lost cell coverage."

"Yeah. So she's been wondering how everything turned out, but I guess since she didn't get any reports that I'd had a breakdown and was in hospital somewhere, she figured that everything was okay."

"Well, I hope you told her that you did more than just *okay*. For you to be able to deal with the fire at the Lodge was huge." Kenzie smiled at him encouragingly. "I hope you really bragged it up."

His pale face was turning pink. He smiled again, nodding, but not raising his dark eyes to look into hers. It was nice to see him smile, especially as they approached Christmas, the worst time of year for his depression. He ran a hand over his short, stubbly hair.

"She was impressed. She said that she knew I could do it."

"I guess it's pretty amazing what we can do if we have to," Kenzie said. "We think we know what our limits are, but then something comes that pushes us out of our comfort zone… and we don't know until we face it if we can handle it."

"I told her…" Zachary licked dry lips, speaking hesitantly, as if worried how she might react, "that I'm worried… that nothing has changed. That the next time I remember the fire again… the flashbacks will be just as bad. That I won't have progressed at all."

Kenzie wanted to jump in and reassure him that of course he had made huge progress, and he wouldn't fall right back to where he was before. But psychology was not her area and, even if it were, she knew better than to counsel someone so close to her. She was too close to Zachary to have an unbiased opinion. "So… what did Dr. B say about that?"

Zachary picked at a thread in his jeans. "She said that… I'll probably still have some anxiety around it, but now that I know I can get through it, that she doesn't think it will be that bad. She's done exposure therapy with patients before, helping them to get over phobias or anxieties." He shrugged. "I don't know. I guess… we'll find out."

"We could go to a restaurant with candles or a fireplace. See how you feel."

Zachary shook his head immediately. "No way."

"Are you sure? You don't want to take some time to think about it?"

Zachary started to protest again, then looked at her and realized that she was teasing him. He ran his hand through his dark hair again, chuckling. But it was forced. Kenzie might have pushed it a bit far.

"Sorry," she apologized. "I'm a little punchy. Long day."

He laughed again. "No, it's fine. Sometimes… I don't realize when you're joking."

"I shouldn't do that. I'm glad things went well with Dr. B. And if you didn't brag enough about how well you handled the situation out there, I'll tell her at our next couples session too. Because what you did out there was… remarkable. It really was."

"It's not such a big thing for anyone else."

"You were the one who took charge. That would be impressive by itself. Add in the fact that even a candle flame is usually enough to break you down, and that you faced a blazing house fire…?" Kenzie shook her head. "I can see I'm going to have to brag you up more. If that's how you told her about it."

He looked away from her, but not fast enough that she didn't see his smile of pleasure over her insistence that he deserved praise for having faced his biggest fear.

Kenzie had nibbled away most of her apple. She looked down at the core. "How long before dinner is here?"

He checked his phone screen. "Fifteen minutes."

"Okay. I'm going to go get changed. I'm not wearing grown-up clothes for the rest of the day."

She disposed of her apple core and went to her bedroom to change into a pair of comfortable pajamas. It wasn't so much that she hated her work clothes or that they were uncomfortable. She just needed a transition from "work Kenzie" to "home relaxing Kenzie." She would put away any worries from the office and just focus on herself and Zachary for the evening.

She had hoped, with the holiday to the mountains, that she would be able to boost his mood and help him to get to a better place before December. He had already been sliding into depression in October, before the two of them had to endure the antivirus protocol, and his physical decline during the treatment had been much worse than hers. Maybe because she kept herself in good condition, eating and sleeping well, and he had difficulty with both. His viral load had ended up being much higher than hers, even though he had contracted it from Kenzie. And that meant that they had also hit him a lot harder with the drugs they hoped would wipe out the virus before it could affect him as it had the nursing home victims.

The holiday had not gone as expected, but she didn't think he had lost more weight at the Lodge, and he had returned knowing that he had handled one of the things he had feared the most in life. If he could beat his fear of fire, maybe he could beat the depression and some of the other challenges as well. She hoped so.

"Food's here," Zachary called out.

"I'll be right there."

3

Kenzie took her first couple of bites of the Thai curry and relaxed, moaning to express her pleasure.

"This is so good. Great choice, Zach."

He had taken a little of the rice and Thai curry himself, and a piece of naan bread, which he dipped into the curry. "It's pretty good," he agreed. He took a bite or two of the bread. "So how was your day today? You said you didn't get caught up. So does that mean you're stuck with just filing and administrative stuff right now?"

"No. I scrubbed in on one of the autopsies this afternoon."

"Anything interesting?"

"The only interesting thing so far is that it was a doctor-attended death, but the doctor wanted us to look into it."

"Oh. Does that mean he thinks it is a suspicious death?"

"Maybe. He doesn't have to give us his reasons. In fact, it's better if he doesn't bias us in one direction or another. It may just be that he didn't foresee it and wants to be sure of what it was that killed him. So he can be more aware of it next time if there is something they should have caught. Or it might be that he thought there was a problem with the treatment, or even foul play."

"And did you find anything in the autopsy?"

"Not yet. Other than the fact that he was given CPR when it probably wasn't advisable. And wasn't recorded on his chart."

"Why wasn't it advisable? Is there a case where... CPR does more harm than good?"

"In a way, yeah. CPR is an extreme measure, and not often successful, even in a hospital setting where the patient had a cardiac event under supervision. If he does survive resuscitation, then you may be looking at brain damage, broken bones, a lot of pain, and he probably has another heart attack within the week and dies anyway. When you're looking at an elderly patient without a good prognosis... it's better to just let nature take its course. Sometimes."

Zachary nodded seriously as he stirred his soup and then took a bite. He blew on his next spoonful to cool it off. "That makes sense. And that was the only thing you found?"

"So far. We've sent out samples for testing. Asked for some tox screens. If the doctor thinks that there might have been an error made in his treatment, then we need to look for anything that might have caused his death. What was he given? Was it the wrong amount or wrong concentration? Did someone give him the wrong thing? Misread the doctor's instructions? Decide to help him on his way? There are a lot of possibilities. And of course, you only find what you're looking for, and I don't know if we've asked for all the right tests. Hopefully... something will show up, or we'll think of something else that needs to be run before we release the remains."

"Well, I hope something shows up."

"You hope he was poisoned, or that the medical staff made a mistake?" Kenzie asked with a grin.

"Well... I don't know. It isn't as if I have a particular preference. I just hope that you figure it out. Give his family some closure. Reassure his doctor. Whatever else needs to happen."

"Yeah." Kenzie had a drink and some more curry. "So how about you? All I've heard about is your session with Dr. Boyle."

Zachary stared off into space, thinking about it. Kenzie knew how a day could go by and leave her wondering what she had even accomplished, so she assumed he was confronted by the same thing. A full day of work, but what had he actually done?

"I don't know," Zachary said finally. "Worked on a bunch of small files. Getting caught up on the backlog, like you. I talked to Heather and we went over the files that she worked on while I was... unavailable. I'm glad that I had someone to take some of those things off my plate."

Heather was Zachary's older sister, whom he had just been reunited with recently. Prior to meeting with Zachary, she had never held a job. But after helping her with her own case, Zachary had offered to train her on some of the computer work that he did for clients, such as skip tracing and running backgrounds. She was very good on the computer and took to it immediately. She loved having something productive to do and took whatever Zachary threw at her.

"It's pretty amazing how the two of you have just clicked, and she's been able to work on that with you."

Zachary nodded. "Goldman Investigations… I never thought there would be any other Goldman than me. Now there's Heather too."

He looked pensive. Thinking of the two younger siblings that he had not yet been reunited with? Wishing that Tyrrell or Joss were also interested in the private investigations business? Or just thinking about the years that they had all lost together, being separated from each other when Zachary was ten and they were sent to various different foster homes?

"It's pretty cool," Kenzie said. "You can never predict what could happen."

Maybe that would help him to think positively about the future. Good things that could happen in the future, instead of the bad things that he envisioned and dreaded.

"Got anything interesting on your plate?" she asked, when he didn't say anything.

Zachary looked down at his dinner plate blankly for a second, before realizing she was speaking figuratively. "Oh… well, hard to say. I'm still catching up on emails and seeing what people need. And what I'm willing to take on."

That seemed to be the end of their shop talk for the day. There was only so much they could squeeze out of a discussion of their jobs. Especially when they were both just getting back into the swing of things.

"You want to put on a movie tonight?" Kenzie suggested. "Or do something productive like going out shopping?" She looked at the fridge. "We don't have a lot in the house right now."

"We probably should."

But he didn't sound any more enthralled about the idea than Kenzie felt.

4

Kenzie was starting to imagine that she might see the bottom of her in basket soon. Or at least, that it would only be as full as it normally was on a weekday. She didn't want to get too excited, but maybe she was getting caught up.

She looked through the lab reports that she had printed off for Michaels, the hospital patient that she had assisted with the autopsy on. She hole-punched them at the top and slid them onto the brads on the file as she read through the results.

Her heart started to beat fast as she looked at it. She walked with the file to Dr. Wiltshire's office.

He was sitting at his desk, but he was talking on the phone. It didn't seem to be a very animated discussion, but she didn't want to interrupt him in the middle of a call. He looked up, saw her in the doorway, and motioned for her to enter.

Kenzie walked in hesitantly. She couldn't tell him what was going on without interrupting the call. He motioned for the file, maybe thinking that she just needed him to sign off on a report. Kenzie folded the pages up so that the relevant results were showing and slid it across his desk to him.

Dr. Wiltshire looked down at the page and scanned it quickly. He straightened up.

"Larry, I'm going to have to call you back," he told the party on the other end of the phone and, without further discussion, set the phone down in the cradle. He looked up at Kenzie, head cocked to the side slightly.

For a moment, they just looked at each other.

"Kenzie, would you get me Dr. Philemon's phone number, please?"

Kenzie leaned forward to snag the file from him and leafed through the pages pinned to the other side of the folder. "Here it is." She read it out to him; then, after he had dialed the phone, gave the file back to him, open to the lab results. She waited while Dr. Wiltshire waited for an answer. She knew she should probably leave. Dr. Wiltshire didn't need her standing there over him while he informed the doctor of the results. But she wanted to hear the call. At least the beginning of it. At least Dr. Wiltshire's half of the conversation.

She was afraid it was going to go through to voicemail but, eventually, Dr. Wiltshire's call was answered by a real person.

"I'm looking for Dr. Philemon, if he is available," Dr. Wiltshire informed the other doctor's assistant or phone service.

There was a pause. Kenzie couldn't hear the other party's reply.

"It's rather urgent," Dr. Wiltshire advised. "This is the Medical Examiner's Office. If there's any way you could get a message to him…"

They both waited. Eventually, Dr. Wiltshire nodded at Kenzie, indicating that he would be put through to Dr. Philemon. He motioned Kenzie to the guest chair on her side of the desk.

"Have a seat for a moment."

He hit the speaker button on the phone, and they sat listening to cool jazz for a few minutes before the call was picked up.

"Dr. Philemon," the voice on the other end answered brusquely. He sounded younger than Kenzie had pictured him. She had imagined that a geriatric doctor with his own private practice would be elderly, white-haired, able to easily relate to the patients he treated. But he sounded as though he were in his twenties, thirties at the latest.

"Yes, this is Dr. Wiltshire, Medical Examiner. I have my assistant, Dr. Kirsch with me."

"Hello, doctors." A slight hesitation. "Does this mean that you found something of note in your autopsy?"

"In fact, we did," Dr. Wiltshire agreed. "Your patient's potassium levels were off the charts."

"Hyperkalemia." Dr. Philemon considered this for a minute. "So… could it have been kidney failure, or was something administered to him?"

"Given the concentration, I'm afraid that this wasn't a natural death," Dr. Wiltshire advised. "He must have been given potassium chloride in his IV line."

"And I never prescribed it. Harry was in good health. Not perfect, obviously, or he would not have been in the hospital. But I figured he still had some good years left in him."

"He was in the hospital for treatment of kidney stones?"

"Yes, with an attendant infection. We figured the stones would pass on their own. Decided to do a few days of IV antibiotics and see how things went from there."

"So you weren't expecting him to die on you."

"No. Of course, you could lose a geriatric patient at any time. That's the nature of the practice. But I thought... well, I was surprised. Obviously. Or I would not have sent him to you."

"Do you have... suspicions of who might have administered potassium chloride?"

"Well... no. And yes. I mean, there isn't anyone who I would suggest would do something like this... but on the other hand, we know... this kind of thing happens. Someone decides to play God..."

"Yes."

"I'll have to go over the records of the staff... see if I can narrow it down. Who was on the floor when he coded. If anyone has any previous suspicions. I just don't know."

"You're not aware of any other suspicious deaths?"

"We've... lost other patients. But as I say, I specialize in geriatrics, and that's the nature of things. I will... also review any recent unexpected deaths."

"You'll want to look at expected deaths too. Sometimes someone... just wants to hurry things on a little."

"Yes. Of course."

"If there is a pattern, we will need to get the FBI involved."

Dr. Philemon groaned. "I've never been a part of an investigation before. Is that... what's it going to be like? They're not going to suspect me, are they?"

"If you're the one reporting the deaths, then you will at least be lower on the list of suspects. But yes, they're going to want to ask you a lot of questions about where you were when each of the patients died, what medications you prescribed, whether you felt that the staff followed your instructions to the letter... they'll have a lot of questions. As long as you are open and honest, you don't have anything to worry about."

"But are people going to think that I did something even if they determine it was someone else? Or if they can't figure out who it is? Are people always going to think that I had something to do with it and they just couldn't prove it?"

Dr. Wiltshire didn't answer right away. He looked at Kenzie and raised his brows. They both knew what the answer was. Dr. Philemon himself knew the answer, or he wouldn't have voiced it in the first place.

"There will always be people who believe that you were involved and got away with something," Dr. Wiltshire admitted. "But you can't let that keep you from reporting it to the proper authorities. If there is a killer on your staff, then we need to catch him before he can cause any more harm."

"Yes. Of course. I wouldn't hesitate to report it. I'm just… I am just establishing my practice. Something like this… a blot against my name before I'm even established…"

"People have dealt with worse," Dr. Wiltshire assured him. "I can't tell you what's going to happen, but it will be stressful and you'll probably ask yourself why you even became a doctor in the first place. But hang in there. Wait until it has all concluded before you make any decisions about what to do with your practice."

"Yeah. You're right. Just because I have this one patient… that doesn't mean that it's happened to anyone else. It could just be one case. An accident."

"I will not be certifying this as an accidental death."

"No, I didn't mean that, of course. I'm just saying… maybe someone administered the wrong medication. That it was unintentional. Still a case of a poisonous substance being given to him, but… maybe they didn't plan to kill him."

Dr. Wiltshire decided to go on and not to debate the details with him. "We noticed that CPR had been administered."

"CPR. No."

"The patient has inflamed and broken ribs. It looks very much like CPR injuries."

"I didn't. No one attempted CPR while I was there. If they did… I should have been informed. It should have been charted."

"Yes. It should have been."

"I will have to talk to my staff. Make sure that I have the full story."

"I would suggest that you speak with each person independently, without allowing them to talk to each other in the meantime."

"You don't think that they would try to cover for…" Dr. Philemon sighed. "Maybe they would."

"If someone attempted resuscitation by CPR and didn't chart it, then they are already trying to cover something up. Take that together with the patient's potassium levels, and I think you need to be concerned about what's going on in your unit. There needs to be an investigation, even if you can't identify any other suspicious deaths."

Dr. Philemon groaned. Kenzie felt for him. A young doctor, trying to get his practice established, trying to develop his reputation, and suddenly he had to investigate his own staff to see whether one of them were killing patients. It was a doctor's worst nightmare.

"Let me know what you find," Dr. Wiltshire said. "I will be waiting to hear from you. And if you think this goes farther than one patient, then get the FBI involved sooner rather than later."

"Okay. Thank you for your advice, Dr. Wiltshire. I appreciate it."

They disconnected. Dr. Wiltshire shook his head and slid the file across the desk to Kenzie again. "Run a copy of everything in there for the FBI. Or scan it or save copies in an electronic folder, whatever your process is. They're going to want it yesterday."

"The FBI?" Kenzie asked, surprised that he wasn't waiting for Dr. Philemon's findings.

"Yes. I've been here before, and I can tell you that things will move very quickly once Dr. Philemon identifies even one other death that he has questions about. I want to be ready to hand over everything we have within minutes of receiving a call from the FBI."

"You think they'll react that quickly?" Kenzie had always found that law enforcement moved much more slowly than she expected after watching a lifetime of cop shows on TV. Fictional police departments and FBI agents always acted on even the smallest suspicions immediately and, of course, solved the case within an hour. In real life, closing the net on the criminals could take weeks or even years.

"With an established pattern like an Angel of Death killer, they'll react. They'll want to start interviewing suspects and narrowing their focus very quickly. It can take a long time to build a case," he admitted, "but they'll do whatever they can to ensure that he or she cannot keep killing patients."

"Okay. I'll get a copy made right away."

"Of course, if we're lucky, they'll get a confession. Often, that's the only way to get one of these killers. They don't leave a lot of evidence behind, and some of them are very adept at pulling off multiple killings without getting caught. Just think of all the people who die in the hospital or under a doctor's care and never come through this office. People who are sick or dying... make ideal targets."

Kenzie thought back to a case that Zachary had investigated, the death of Robin Salter. Everyone had put it down to either her cancer or the cancer treatment protocol. No one but Bridget and Zachary had thought that it could be anything else. But they had been right. Killing someone who was already dying was much too easy.

5

Home with Zachary the next night, Kenzie ventured to broach a topic that had been on her mind. Zachary seemed to be in a good place mentally since their return from their holiday and his session with Dr. B, so she hoped that he would be open to discussion. They had finished dinner and were just relaxing together, starting their weekend with some focused couples time. Cuddling on the couch, but with the TV off and other devices put away. He rubbed her shoulder as she leaned against him.

"So, I wanted to talk to you about something..." Kenzie started.

She could feel him stiffen immediately, not even knowing what it was she wanted to talk about. She didn't usually start a conversation that way, so of course he was wary. Maybe he thought it was the beginning of a breakup speech, or the suggestion that he should go back to spending more time at his apartment and not consider her house his home base.

"It's not anything bad," she assured him. "I just know that it's hard for you to talk about."

That didn't help to relax him. "Okay..."

"I want to talk a little bit about Christmas."

She could almost feel the wall go up between them. Zachary may have been forced to confront the specter of the house fire that he'd been trapped in as a child, but his anxieties about Christmas had not gone down with it. The Christmas Eve disaster had had serious, long-term consequences.

"I can't really... talk about that."

"I'm not asking you to do anything, or to plan a Christmas party. I want to talk about what things I can do to celebrate Christmas that we can enjoy together. Things that won't trigger you."

She was quiet while he considered this. They did have some experience in learning how to build their relationship without triggering Zachary's defenses. After his encounter with a sadistic serial killer, Kenzie had barely been able to touch him without his dissociating and withdrawing from any intimacy mentally and emotionally even while still going through the motions physically. But with Dr. Boyle's help, they had been able to gradually build on touches and actions that he could tolerate, until they were almost back to where they had been before the kidnapping.

"What were you thinking?" Zachary asked finally. "I can't do… candles or trees with lights."

Considering that the house fire had started with candles igniting the Christmas tree, that was perfectly understandable, and Kenzie had already taken it into account when thinking about things that they might be able to do.

"Well, I had some thoughts around treats. Cut-out sugar or shortbread cookies, Mandarin oranges, hot chocolate…"

She ventured a look at Zachary's face. She didn't want the conversation to be too intense or confrontational, which was one reason she had waited until they were side-by-side. If Zachary didn't have to look her in the eyes and read her face as they spoke, it would be easier for him.

He looked relieved at the food suggestions. He nodded. "Sure. I like all of those." He breathed out, sighing slightly. "It's not like… we ever had those things at home."

Kenzie didn't know very much about the way his family had celebrated Christmas. She knew that his parents had fought on Christmas Eve over the tree and decorations. A knock-down blow-out fight that had ended with none of it getting done. So ten-year-old Zachary got up in the night to set it all up himself, including lighting the special Christmas candles. Kenzie knew that they had been poor, without money to spend on presents for the children. Or, apparently, any special Christmas treats.

She smiled, pleased that the first item on her list had been approved without any resistance. "Great. I'll have to be careful how many shortbread cookies I eat. Those things are basically just butter and sugar. But they'll be good to boost your calorie intake."

Zachary grinned at that. Kenzie usually tried to make sure that he ate as healthy a diet as possible, which was difficult when she was trying to tempt him to eat more. Since his meds caused nausea in the morning and reduced his appetite overall, concessions had to be made for higher-calorie foods when she could get something into him. He apparently wasn't too disap-pointed at the prospect of more cookies in his diet.

"How about decorations? I know some things are out of the question." No need to mention candles or trees specifically again. "But there must be some things that wouldn't bother you that would still be festive. Are there decorations some of your foster homes or care centers had that didn't bother you? Or something that Lorne and Pat do?"

"Most of the stuff they did at Bonnie Brown didn't bother me too much," Zachary said slowly. "But it was a concrete building. Not... a wood frame house. So I didn't have to worry so much about... you know."

Fire. And even having faced his fear at the Lodge, he was still concerned about thoughts of fire triggering flashbacks as they always had.

"What kind of decorations did they have that you think would be okay?"

"They had... lights on the walls. High up by the ceiling where kids couldn't reach them. The little twinkle lights. They don't get hot. And they were concrete walls." He gave a little shrug.

"So how would you feel about some little lights here? On the walls?"

Zachary nodded. "Okay."

"You think that would be okay?"

"Yeah."

"And what about the little twinkle lights in jars. The ones that flicker." She didn't call them candles. "Are they okay if you know that they're not real?"

She could feel the tension re-enter his body. They'd been able to go to restaurants that used small twinkle lights or LEDs instead of candles on the tables, but apparently having them at home might be too much.

"I don't know."

"It's okay to say no. I don't have my heart set on it. This is a discussion about what you are comfortable with."

"Then... I guess, no."

Kenzie nodded. "That's okay. I don't want you to have to deal with an environment that makes you feel uncomfortable and on edge. That's why I'm asking."

He still seemed uncomfortable with having told her no. Kenzie consid-ered whether to continue or leave it at that. She had a couple of answers; she could always add more later when he'd had a chance to relax and think about it some more.

"Are there other decorations that wouldn't make you feel anxious? I was thinking about things like a snow globe, some Christmassy fridge magnets, maybe a wreath on the door."

Zachary rubbed his hands on his jeans. Sweaty palms were a sign that she might be overloading him with too much at once.

"A snow globe sounds good," he said. "It's filled with water and it's not a… hazard."

"Yeah. It's kind of the opposite of a fire hazard," Kenzie agreed.

"So that's okay. Fridge magnets?"

"They have them around. Seasonal symbols and shapes. Snow scenes. Ceramic or metal or plastic."

Zachary nodded. "Okay."

He didn't say anything else. Kenzie guessed that was an answer in itself as far as the wreath went. Still too similar to a Christmas tree. No branches that could catch fire, even if there were only the remotest chance that such a thing could happen. She slid one arm behind Zachary and gave him a squeeze.

"Thank you. I know it's not easy for you to discuss. If you have more thoughts, or if we put something up and you change your mind about it, just let me know. It's an experiment, and if it makes you too uncomfortable or depressed, we'll change things."

"Okay." He put his arm around her too and kissed her on the cheek. "That's really nice. When I was with Br—" he cut himself off and turned his face away from her, realizing what he'd been about to say.

"When you were with Bridget," Kenzie finished for him. "What was it like around Christmas? Did she want lots of traditional decorations?"

Bridget was Zachary's ex-wife. Kenzie didn't bar Zachary from bringing her up, but acknowledged to herself that it provoked an emotional reaction whenever he did. When they had first met, Kenzie had been amused by Bridget. Bridget said that she didn't want anything to do with Zachary, to the extent that he wasn't even supposed to go to any of her favorite stores or restaurants where she might bump into him, and yet she didn't seem to be able to let go of him and her emotional reactions to him were dramatically over-the-top. She was clearly still attached to him.

And Zachary was still in love with her, despite the way that she abused him and had kicked him to the curb when she had been diagnosed with cancer. The cancer was now in remission. Bridget's venom toward Zachary had only grown, and Kenzie no longer thought it was funny. Their recent discovery that she was suffering from Huntington's Disease tempered Kenzie's feelings toward her a little, but she hadn't been able to overcome her gut reaction to Zachary's continued obsession with her. It wasn't a choice on Zachary's part. He couldn't help the fact that his obsessive thoughts constantly returned to her. But he knew how Kenzie felt and tried not to bring her up.

Zachary shrugged, looking down. "Yeah. She had a professional decorator and everything. I did my best to… stay out of the rooms that were decorated."

And she probably hadn't appreciated that response.

"She didn't know, in the beginning, how big of a deal it was. She thought I was sulking."

"But she must have figured it out eventually. I mean… I did."

"She always thought it was something I should be able to control."

Kenzie sighed. "Well, this year you don't have to worry about it. We're going to work together. If there's a problem, we're just going to be open in our communication about it, right? Just like we've been doing in couples therapy."

"Right," Zachary agreed.

But his voice wasn't strong. It would take an effort on Kenzie's part to watch for his reactions and ask questions to help him sort out and verbalize his feelings.

6

Even though it was the weekend, Kenzie went into the office for a few hours on Saturday. Zachary said that he had some outside assignments to take care of and she figured she could get caught up on some more of her sorting and filing while he completed them. It would make it that much less stressful returning to the office on Monday.

Sunday, they were both home, spending some couples time together. Kenzie talking to her parents on the phone. Zachary visiting with Lorne Peterson, an old foster father, and Lorne's partner, Patrick Parker, on video conference. Kenzie's parents were divorced, though they were still friendly with each other, so she spoke with them separately. Lisa spoke of her Christmas parties and other functions, and Walter was trying to get a bill pushed through the Legislature before they closed for the Christmas break. Both were focused very much on their own personal projects and, as long as Kenzie was well and safe following her anti-viral protocol and failed holiday, they weren't particularly interested in her work.

"I barely got a chance to meet your Zachary at the masquerade ball," Lisa commented. "We must get together for Christmas so that we can get to know each other."

Kenzie winced. She didn't really want them getting to know each other. She preferred to keep her parents and her boyfriend separate for as long as possible. Lisa and Walter were not Zachary's kind of people. They wouldn't understand him and would just brush off his feelings and challenges as unimportant.

"We won't be able to do anything before Christmas," Kenzie said firmly. "Maybe after. We could do New Year's maybe. Something in January when you're not busy."

Lisa was never *not* busy, and Kenzie hoped that the proposed get-together would be forgotten with her busy social calendar.

"You can't do anything before Christmas? Surely your schedule isn't that crammed."

"Sorry. We can't manage anything before then. You know… Daddy said that you don't really celebrate Christmas anymore. Not the way that you used to when we were young."

"Well…" Lisa's voice was hesitant. "No, of course not. The way you celebrate when your children are young is very different from the way it is when you're an empty-nester. There isn't really any reason for me to decorate like I used to. There's no one to do it *for*."

Kenzie felt the weight of guilt in her stomach. After Amanda's death, it was Kenzie's duty to make her mother feel useful and part of the family, like she wasn't alone. She should have carried that legacy, but she had failed. And no doubt Lisa wanted grandchildren. Maybe if there were, she would decorate the house again, just like in the old days. But Kenzie didn't have children and wasn't convinced that she wanted any. Or that she and Zachary had the time and emotional resources to raise them properly.

Zachary wanted children. He'd helped to raise his brothers and sisters until the family had been broken up, and there had been other children at the various other foster homes where he had lived. Bridget hadn't wanted to have children with him, but was due to have twins with Zachary's replacement, Gordon Drake, sometime soon. It had been a real blow for Zachary to find out that she was pregnant.

"Well… maybe when we come after Christmas, you can have a few decorations up." They wouldn't bother Zachary so much after Christmas. Kenzie remembered all the fairy lights and garlands when she was a little girl. The house had been transformed into a magical world.

"There isn't any reason to have the house decorated *after* Christmas," Lisa pointed out.

"There's no magic about the date. You could decorate and leave them up a few days after Christmas."

Lisa sighed. "Maybe you could find some time in your busy schedule to come before then."

Kenzie rolled her eyes, glad that they were on the phone and not on video, so she could indulge in the small rebellion. "I'll see what we can do," she promised.

But she knew there was no way they would be visiting Lisa before Christmas.

<hr />

Monday rolled around and Kenzie was ready to get back to work. She enjoyed her time at home with Zachary, but his anxiety and depression did take their toll over time. He was doing well, considering that they were moving into December, but she still needed a break from his dark cloud when she could get it.

When Dr. Wiltshire strolled in with his cup of coffee and his briefcase, Kenzie held out a file for him. "More from Dr. Philemon," she offered.

Dr. Wiltshire put his coffee cup down on the counter of Kenzie's reception desk and took it from her. "What has he found?"

"He's been going back over cases covering the past year, documenting the unexpected deaths and resuscitations. There's a fairly extensive list."

"Did any of them come through this office?"

"No. Mr. Michaels was the first." Kenzie paused. "I expect that some of these others probably registered on his subconscious, until he got to the point where he became suspicious of something, even if he couldn't put his finger on why."

"Is that what he said?"

Kenzie shook her head. "Not in so many words, no. He's been pretty… stingy in what he has offered. Probably thinking about his professional liability insurance."

"Oh, I think I can guarantee that he's thinking of his insurance," Dr. Wiltshire agreed with a grin. He took a slug of coffee from his grande cup. "He'll be very careful of everything he says between now and whenever this is all over."

Kenzie suspected he was right.

"So what happens with this list?" she asked. "Do any of these patients get exhumed? All of them?"

"We won't be rushing into anything. He'll need to start compiling what staff members were involved with each case. Who the assigned doctors and nurses were. Who was on the floor when they died. If there is a pattern in time of day, symptoms, cause of death. See if there is any surveillance footage of the patients or wards. Start installing surveillance cameras in the patient rooms. All of those things. Medical professionals who kill are very hard to catch. They are really good at covering their tracks."

They had been lucky to find Robin Salter's killer. If it had turned out to have been caused by an insulin overdose, they might never have been able to catch the culprit. It was only by luck—or Zachary's careful investigation and out-of-the-box thinking—that had enabled them to catch her. And if the killer hadn't panicked and run, maybe they would never have been able to gather enough evidence to prove it.

"So there's nothing for us to do at this point?" Kenzie asked.

"Just for me to issue my findings. I've already advised our friends upstairs." Dr. Wiltshire rolled his eyes upward to indicate the police department that was housed above them. "They have opened their investigation and are just waiting for my official report. With Dr. Philemon identifying other possible suspicious deaths, they will get the FBI involved. It will be up to them to make the decisions on any exhumation or other follow-up."

7

Kenzie arrived home to an empty house. She called out to Zachary, but knew before she did that he wasn't home. There was just a different quality to the house when he was home. She could sense it as soon as she walked in the door. And it wasn't because he sometimes let the homeless garb he wore for surveillance get a little too ripe. It just didn't feel as much like home if he weren't there.

She checked to see whether he had left her a note on the fridge or sent her a text that she had not noticed. There was nothing to indicate where he had gone.

Kenzie took a deep breath in and let it out slowly. There was no reason to panic just because he wasn't there when she got home. He was a grown man and was allowed to come and go as he pleased without reporting his movements to her. He could be off on a job, running errands, meeting with Heather, or having supper with a friend.

Though he rarely had supper with a friend and always informed her when he wasn't going to be home to eat with her. They had agreed that dinner was couples time, when they would spend the time together catching up with each other, unless there was an emergency that required them to be somewhere else.

Zachary had been doing well since they got home. She wasn't that worried about him. He might have simply gone back to his own apartment to get something he needed or spend some time in his man cave. Everyone needed their own space now and then.

It wasn't necessarily a sign that something was wrong. If he'd been more depressed, she would have noticed it. He wasn't one of those people who was a clown or covered up his pain with fake cheer. When he was suffering, it was obvious. To those closest to him, at least.

Kenzie pulled out her phone and dialed his number. It rang several times, becoming obvious that he wasn't going to pick it up. He was busy with something that couldn't be interrupted. She waited for his voicemail to pick up, trying to compose a message in her head that didn't sound like she was nagging or excessively worried.

Eventually, his businesslike voice answered, announcing that she had reached Goldman Investigations and asking her to leave a message.

"Just me," Kenzie said, keeping her voice light. "Wondering whether you will be home for supper or if I should go ahead without you. Let me know your plans. Okay, talk to you soon."

She hung up and considered the message. Too much? She didn't think so. Once he finished whatever he was working on or the meeting that he was in, he would call her back and let her know where he was or what he was doing.

But of course it wasn't instantaneous. He didn't text her back to say that he was in a meeting and would get back to her. He didn't return the call right away. She changed and put her things away, then went back to the kitchen to consider the situation. She was hungry, so she couldn't wait all night for his reply. Have a snack and hold dinner until he answered? Assume he wasn't coming and go ahead with supper? Make enough for both of them so that he would have something available when he eventually returned?

"Zachary, where are you?" she grumbled.

He had suggested not long ago that she let him put a tracker on her car so that he could be aware of where she was in case anything untoward happened. She hadn't thought about needing to track him in return. There were phone apps, she knew. Maybe they should exchange location tracking on their phones so that she would at least know what part of town he was in.

Of course, being a private investigator, client confidentiality was an issue, and he probably wouldn't want her tracking him any more than she wanted him tracking her. While she had friends who shared locations between spouses, it felt like an invasion of privacy to Kenzie and just reminded her of the fact that Zachary had once before tracked her movements without her permission. It was before they knew each other well and had nearly ended the relationship. She had been furious. Justifiably.

Kenzie took out her phone again and looked at it, just in case she had missed a call or message from him. She knew she hadn't and a glance at her screen confirmed this.

She started pulling ingredients out of the fridge to make herself a sandwich.

Kenzie was reading through a news feed on her phone when it started to ring. First she jumped. Then she was glad that Zachary was getting back to her and reached out to swipe the call. But it wasn't Zachary's name and picture on the screen. It was a number unfamiliar to her.

She considered letting it go to voicemail on the assumption that it was a telemarketer. But she didn't know where Zachary was or what he was doing, and it was possible that his phone had run out of juice and he'd borrowed someone else's to call her.

She accepted the call anyway and put the phone up to her ear. "Hello?"

"Is this—uh—Kenzie?" a cultured male voice inquired.

"Yes. Who is calling?"

She waited for the sales patter, even though he didn't sound like any telemarketer she had heard before.

"My name is Gordon. I was wondering… if you happen to know where Zachary is?"

Kenzie frowned? Gordon? She knew that was the name of Bridget's new partner, a man that Zachary had done a couple of jobs with before. But he wouldn't be calling Kenzie if he had something to ask Zachary for. He would be calling Zachary directly. It must be another Gordon.

"He's not here at the moment," she told him crisply. "Can I give him a message for you?"

"This is… awkward. You don't know me, Kenzie. But Zachary has mentioned you before. I thought that I saw him a few minutes ago. But when I called him, he didn't answer."

"He may be busy right now. He hasn't returned my last call either."

But it was a relief if Gordon had seen him. At least that meant that Zachary was alive and well, whatever he was doing.

"The thing is, he shouldn't be here."

Kenzie swore under her breath. It *was* Bridget's Gordon. Zachary wasn't supposed to be there because he wasn't supposed to get anywhere near Bridget's house. There was no protection order outstanding, but Bridget had said more than once that she would take one out if he continued to stalk her.

And for two years, that had not been a problem. Zachary had recommitted himself to therapy, his doctor had changed his prescriptions, and he had been able to stay away from her.

At least, as far as Kenzie knew.

She had suspected recently, before going on their vacation, that he might be following her again. If he were, it was Gordon's own fault for involving Zachary in their problems. Gordon should have known enough to leave Zachary out of it and to hire another private investigator for any investigative work to do with Bridget.

"Where is he?" Kenzie asked finally, closing her eyes.

"If it was him—and I can't swear that it was, but it looked very much like his car and the driver bore a striking resemblance to Zachary—then he's at our home. Bridget's home. He can't be here. He knows that."

"Yes. I know." Kenzie rubbed one hand over her face, trying to keep her rising anger, disappointment, and dread in check as she considered the situation. "What do you want me to do, Gordon?"

"I don't know. I was hoping that if you called him, you could get him to go home. But if he isn't answering your calls… well, I really would rather not involve the police, Kenzie."

"I appreciate that."

She didn't want Zachary to spend the night in a jail cell. For a normal person, a night in a cell might be a deterrent from stalking Bridget. But for Zachary? He couldn't help the obsession. Maybe his meds needed to be adjusted again. One of the unfortunate things about psychoactive drugs was that they could just stop working one day, and then the doctors had to scramble to find something else that would work. She'd noticed a few issues creeping in since their holiday. She had tried to ignore them, to deny what she herself was seeing.

"Gordon… what's your address? I could drive over there, see whether I can see him."

"Certainly." He gave her the address, and Kenzie scribbled it down on a flyer on the kitchen table.

"Thanks. I'll come have a look around. Where did you see the car?"

He described the place where he had seen the car parked. Kenzie jotted down it down as he spoke.

"All right. Be by soon. Is this number your cell phone?"

"Yes…?"

"So I can text you back."

"Yes. Of course."

"Okay. I'll let you know what I find."

He said a polite goodbye and hung up. Kenzie looked down at the address she had written, shaking her head. "Zachary, what are you up to now?" she demanded aloud.

She looked at her phone again, in case Zachary had texted her while she'd been on with Gordon, but there were still no notifications.

Kenzie drove up and down the streets, looking carefully at the parked cars, and was initially relieved not to find Zachary's car where Gordon had described it. He must have just seen someone else and mistaken them for Zachary. But she kept looking, just in case. Zachary had, after all, not returned her call. He had to be somewhere, and if he were somewhere outside Bridget's house, then it was much better for him if Kenzie found him than Bridget or the police.

It was getting dark. She had almost circled all sides of Bridget's house—which was more of a mansion and would probably have fit six of Kenzie's house inside—when she spotted a white compact of the same make as Zachary's.

"Don't be Zachary," Kenzie said under her breath.

But on the other hand, she hoped that it was, because she didn't want to be left wondering where he was after driving all the way over to look for him. The longer he was away without returning her call, the more she worried something had happened to him. She didn't only have to worry about self-harm. He drove like a demon and could have been in an accident. Some adulterous husband he was tracking might have shot him. A hundred different things.

As she approached the car, she could see that it was Zachary's license plate. She sighed and pulled to the curb a couple of spaces ahead of him. She got out of her car and walked up to his window. He was sitting in the driver's seat, a pair of binoculars to his eyes, which prevented him from noticing her approach. Kenzie rapped on the window with a couple of knuckles.

Zachary jolted and lowered the binoculars abruptly to look at her, face white and frozen.

At first, his face showed relief. She wasn't a cop there to demand what he was doing, or Gordon or Bridget herself. Kenzie was a safe person.

But then she saw him swallow hard as he considered the situation. Kenzie discovering him stalking Bridget was not a good thing. He knew she would be furious about it. And there was the question of how she had known to look for him there.

Kenzie motioned for Zachary to roll down the window, and he did.

"Uh. Kenzie." He licked his lips. "I was just…"

She glared at him, wondering what excuse he was actually going to come up with. But he looked away from her and didn't finish the sentence.

"It's time to go home," Kenzie told him in a calm, even tone. "You've missed dinner."

Zachary touched his phone, mounted on the dashboard, and the screen came on with the time in big, bright letters. "I… didn't know that it was so late."

"It's dark out," Kenzie pointed out.

"Yeah… I guess it is."

He was the private investigator. He was the one who was supposed to notice subtle clues like that.

"I called you."

He could see the missed call list on his screen and nodded. Kenzie could also see Gordon's name on that list. Zachary darted a glance at her and pressed the button on the screen to dismiss the notifications. He reached for the key in the ignition.

"I'm so sorry… let's go home. I didn't mean to be so late."

Kenzie didn't tell him how she had known where to find him or the fact that she knew it was Bridget's house. He had probably guessed that already, but if they started that discussion out on the street, it could get emotional, and she didn't want him to take off instead of going back to the house. She wanted to know that he was home safe.

"Yes. Let's go home."

He turned the key to start his engine. Kenzie walked back to her car. She let him pull out first, and followed him all the way back to the house.

8

She waited on the street until Zachary got out of his car and walked up the sidewalk to the house. Then she drove around to the garage and let herself in that way.

Zachary stood there, his eyes darting around, knowing that he was in trouble and looking for some kind of escape. She could picture him as a little boy or a young teen, having impulsively gotten himself into a fight or another bad situation and knowing that he was going to be punished for it.

"Do you want something to eat?" Kenzie asked, going to the fridge.

"No. I'm not hungry."

His stomach was probably roiling worse than hers. Kenzie opened the freezer and took out a pint of ice cream. She grabbed a spoon from the drawer and pushed it shut. She sat down at the table. "You sure?"

He nodded and sat down in his usual chair. The one that allowed him to see through the front window. He licked his lips nervously, waiting for Kenzie to begin. Kenzie took a bite of her Chocolate Fudge Explosion and let out a long breath.

"I was worried."

"Yeah." Zachary ran his hand over his hair. "Sorry."

"You didn't answer or call me back. You didn't leave me a note or text or anything. I didn't know what to think. Someone could have shot you on a surveillance job."

"They'd have to see me first," Zachary said wryly.

"I saw you before you saw me."

"Well…" He gulped. "Yeah."

"And Gordon saw you."

Zachary scratched his ear and grimaced. "He did. I thought so. I moved after that, but…"

"You should have come home instead of finding another spot to park."

"Yeah."

"How long has this been going on? How long have you been watching her again?"

"This was the first time—"

"No it wasn't. Don't try to sell me that."

Zachary looked down at the table. He sat there thinking about it while Kenzie ate her ice cream. He was licking his lips a lot and Kenzie knew his mouth was dry. Not just because he was in trouble and trying to get out of it, but also because it was one of the side effects of his meds. And he had probably not had anything to drink while on surveillance. She knew he rationed liquids while on surveillance to avoid other inconveniences. She got up and poured a glass of water from the pitcher in the fridge. She sat back down and slid it across the table to him.

Zachary chugged a few swallows. He held one mouthful in his mouth for a few seconds and then swallowed it. He licked his lips again

"You may as well tell the truth," Kenzie said. "I already know you're watching her. It doesn't matter how long or short it has been, we both already know that you need help. So let's get it all out on the table."

"Not a long time."

Kenzie considered that. She thought about what she knew for sure. The worries that she'd had and how his daily patterns had changed.

"Since before the virus," she offered.

Zachary considered, then nodded. "But not much. Just… a little before that."

"Since your investigation for Gordon?"

He shook his head. "No. Not that long. But… I think… that was a problem."

Of course it was. He'd been able to get his behavior under control. He'd been managing it for almost two years. And then Gordon came to him, asking him to find out whether Bridget had a lover on the side. Zachary was supposed to surveil her for a few days and then just stop again? Gordon had no concept of how hard it had been for him to stop in the first place. Most people had no idea what it was like to fight the kind of compulsions that Zachary had.

"Have you talked to Dr. B. about this?"

He considered for a moment before shaking his head. "No."

"You know that this is the kind of thing that she's there for. When you have a problem that you need help with, that's why she's there."

"I was just… embarrassed. I didn't want to tell her… I thought I could manage it myself."

Kenzie checked the time on her phone. "I think you should call her."

Zachary shifted. "I'll talk to her on Wednesday."

"Wednesday is couples therapy this week. I think you need to talk to her about this individually first. We could change Wednesday to an individual day, but I've already arranged to take time off for it. And maybe there are things we should discuss together, after you've had a chance to talk to her about it alone."

"I don't want to call her at home."

"At least call to see if you can get on her schedule tomorrow, then."

"Her schedule is fully booked with her regular sessions…"

"You don't know that. She might have a cancellation. Or fit you in at the end of the day. Or else talk to her tonight. She said that we could call her at home. You don't want to have to wait two days to bring it up with her. You'll be a wreck."

He still didn't like the idea. Kenzie stood up. She put her bowl in the dishwasher.

"Go use the bedroom. For privacy. Call her. I'll put on the TV and give you some space."

Looking like he'd been given a death sentence, Zachary got up and shuffled to the bedroom. Kenzie heard him shut the door. She turned on the TV and turned up the volume so that she wouldn't be able to overhear any of the conversation.

9

An FBI agent had been assigned to the Michaels case. Dr. Wiltshire was in the office ahead of Kenzie, having received an early call from Agent Josie Menendez. They were already in Dr. Wiltshire's office deep in conversation when Kenzie arrived, but Dr. Wiltshire had left a message for Kenzie to advise her of the developments and to ask her to join them when she arrived.

All thoughts of Zachary and his difficulties were swept from Kenzie's mind as she copied the electronic files she had prepared onto a USB drive, grabbed herself a cup of coffee from the break room, and hurried to Dr. Wiltshire's office. She knocked on the door and entered without waiting for an invitation. He had already asked her to come into the meeting.

"Ah, Dr. Kirsch," Dr. Wiltshire greeted, nodding to acknowledge her. "Thank you for coming. Agent Menendez, this is Dr. Kenzie Kirsch, my assistant, who also scrubbed in on Mr. Michaels's autopsy."

"Josie," Agent Menendez said, standing up and reaching out to shake Kenzie's hand.

"Kenzie." She shook Menendez's hand and then handed her the USB drive. "Our files on the case."

Menendez, a tall slim woman with Hispanic features, smiled broadly and put it into her pocket. "Talk about service. Thank you very much."

"Kenzie is familiar with all the details of the case," Dr. Wiltshire said. "Feel free to ask her any questions if I'm not around. Or even if I am." He smiled. "It's no secret that Kenzie is actually the one running this office."

895

Kenzie grinned, her face warming. She didn't have the experience or expertise that Dr. Wiltshire did, but she did try to keep things running efficiently for him. It was nice to be recognized, even if it was hyperbole.

"Glad to meet you," Menendez acknowledged with a nod. "I'm sure I'll have plenty of questions for you. I don't have a medical background, but I pick things up pretty quickly. I will be meeting with Dr. Philemon this afternoon. It may take me a few days to get fully up to speed…"

"But these things don't move as quickly as they do on TV," Dr. Wiltshire filled in.

"Unfortunately, no. It can take months to sort out who had access to all the victims. Even figuring out who the victims are may be tricky. We often don't know more than one or two of them for sure. Then we find out when we catch the killer that they have twenty-seven on their list." Menendez rolled her eyes and shook her head. "Unfortunately, this kind of killer can operate for years without any suspicions being raised. And if there are suspicions…" She shrugged expressively. "They just move to another office or another state and start over."

"What about references?" Kenzie asked, sitting down in the other guest chair at Dr. Wiltshire's desk. "How do they get another job if there have been suspicions?"

"Medical staff are in high demand. References can be faked. Or if the staff member is terminated under some kind of agreement, the former employees may be unable to say anything about their suspicions under a nondisclosure clause. Remember that if you don't have proof… well, you don't want to get sued for slander. So the employer agrees to keep it to himself if the employee will leave quietly."

"But… doesn't that just put other patients at risk? Perpetuate the problem?"

"It does. But as long as they are not *your* patients…"

Kenzie shook her head. "Well, luckily my patients are already dead, so I won't ever have to deal with that scenario."

Dr. Wiltshire laughed appreciatively. "We've never had a patient lodge a complaint," he agreed. "All five-star reviews on Yelp."

They all chuckled.

The meeting with Menendez took a lot longer than Kenzie had expected, considering they really didn't have anything to tell her other than what she had already been informed of. And everything was in the files that Kenzie had given her. But of course Menendez hadn't yet read the files, and she didn't have the medical background to interpret everything when she did. She needed it all explained in layman's terms to be sure she had all the facts she needed to pursue the case.

She felt a little sorry for Dr. Philemon, who was bound to have to deal with an even more intense session with Menendez. He would have to go through all the patients he had identified as unexpected or possibly suspicious deaths and to describe what had happened in each. With the number of patients on the list, it might take him several days. Kenzie didn't envy either of them.

Kenzie escorted Menendez out of the suite of offices and sat down at her reception desk. "Just let me know if you need anything from me," she repeated once more. "I'll do whatever I can to help."

"You're just trying to avoid having to do more work," Menendez joked. "By avoiding getting any more patients through here."

"People are dying to get in," Kenzie agreed, repeating their well-worn joke. "But honestly, we're never going to stop the flow. There will always be more work to do here. But I'd rather not have to worry about a serial killer."

"And as far as we know, most of the victims, if any of the people on Dr. Philemon's list are victims of the same killer, didn't even come through this office."

"No. If they were doctor-attended deaths, then we don't get involved unless the doctor believes there's a reason for us to."

Menendez nodded and shook Kenzie's hand once more. "Thanks for your cooperation. I'll be giving you a call."

Kenzie nodded and said another goodbye, then Menendez walked down to the elevator and took it back upstairs.

Kenzie looked over the last few items to arrive in her email inbox, and then decided to give Zachary a call.

He answered on the second ring. Not deeply focused on a job. Maybe trying to make up for having missed her call when he'd been watching Bridget's house.

"Kenzie?"

"Hey, Zachary. I just wanted to check in and see how you were doing. Taking a short break between jobs, here."

"Oh. I'm okay. How is your morning going?"

"Been busy. Interesting. I'll have to tell you about it later." She wouldn't give him any identifying details, but he would be interested to hear of the involvement of the FBI in one of her cases. That was definitely not in the normal course.

"I'm looking forward to it," he said with interest.

"How about your morning? Anything interesting going on over at Goldman Investigations?" Kenzie didn't want to ask him straight out whether he'd stuck to his work or whether he had been over to watch for Bridget again. She wasn't his parent or his therapist. She didn't want to get stuck in the role of supervising his activities or making him report to her. She didn't want to back him into a corner and put him in the position of either having to admit his faults or to lie to cover them up.

"Nothing big. A new insurance file that I'm doing some preliminary work on. Injury claim."

Which meant that he would have legitimate surveillance to do, watching to see if the purported victim were only pretending to be disabled by an injury while continuing other demanding physical activities when he thought that no one was looking.

"Those are always interesting. Think it's legitimate?"

"The accident is. I've looked through the pictures of the vehicles, and it was a serious accident. Whether the victim has long-term disabling injuries... well, that's what they're paying me to find out."

They had been meeting with Agent Menendez in the boardroom and had, Kenzie thought, answered all her questions, until the FBI agent came up with one more request.

"I'm wondering whether we could borrow Kenzie for a day."

"Borrow her? For what?"

"I'd like to get her thoughts on the hospital geriatric unit. As it is before they find out there is an FBI investigation. Another doctor going in there, just checking up on some things, I think that would be a lot more natural than FBI agents showing up and asking questions."

"Well..." Dr. Wiltshire thought about this. "Yes, I can see that. And Kenzie has done some good work investigating in the field before. But it's not really her job. This case has been passed on to the FBI for your investigation. We've done everything we can on our end with the one body that we have."

"I know. It would be a favor, like I said. It could be a follow up to your autopsy. Before you issue your opinion. Then it isn't like we sent her in as our agent."

"Except that you are."

"But not *really*." Menendez grimaced. "I'm not going to give her questions to ask or any specific instructions. You can give her your instructions on anything you would like to know that would help to further your understanding of what happened to Mr. Michaels. I just... would like someone with a medical background to have some familiarity with the unit, the staff, how things work over there..."

"Don't you have any medical personnel employed by your office? No one with a medical background who could look around?"

"Not without revealing that it was part of an FBI investigation. We have strict protocols for dealing with hospitals and situations like this. I can't really send someone in undercover. To act as a patient or a visiting doctor. It's just not feasible. But Kenzie is here. Or you, but..."

"If I went in, I would attract too much attention," Dr. Wiltshire finished. "People would know there was something going on just as much as they would if you sent an agent in. They would immediately want to know why I was investigating a death they thought to be natural."

"They're going to wonder that anyway, but at least with Kenzie, she's younger, less threatening. Less of a..." Menendez looked for the right word.

"I'm just an underling?" Kenzie suggested. "A gofer? Nobody will think that I'm anyone important? I can just do routine follow-up without anyone thinking anything of it?"

"We want someone who is unobtrusive and nonthreatening," Menendez agreed, not using any of Kenzie's words. "From what I've seen of you and your work, I think that you would be able to provide me with a lot of insight, without attracting attention to yourself."

Kenzie thought of the investigating she had done at the Champlain House care center previously. It had been interesting work. She liked pretending to herself that she was a private investigator like Zachary, wondering what he would do in her circumstances, what questions he would ask to elicit the information he needed. What he would see that she wouldn't. She looked at Dr. Wiltshire to see whether he were inclined to grant Menendez's request. He raised an eyebrow at her, a query as to whether it was something she was interested in doing. If it wasn't, he could just shut Menendez down, and Kenzie wouldn't have to find an excuse.

"I don't mind," she told him, "if you can do without me for a day."

"Well, that's not exactly easy, but I suppose if I have to," he grumbled good-naturedly.

"Wednesday is my early day anyway. I could spend some time at the hospital in the morning and do my appointment in the afternoon, and not actually miss a full day's work."

Dr. Wiltshire nodded. "That sounds reasonable," he agreed. "I'll see if I can get Julie in to help with the phones and public inquiries."

"Great." Menendez gave a big smile. "That is very helpful, Kenzie. Thank you."

Kenzie nodded. "Sure. It sounds like an interesting assignment."

"I'll walk out with you," Menendez offered, following Kenzie from Dr. Wiltshire's office. Kenzie walked with her, thinking about the unit at the hospital and what she should look for while she was there.

"What exactly do you want me to find out?"

"You have good instincts. Just follow your nose... see whether there is anything that raises your suspicions. We will be getting as many records as we can for these cases that Dr. Philemon has identified, trying to track which medical staff were present when. But sometimes there are things you see on the ground that you would not know by just reading files and tables. You don't need to worry about interrogating anyone, because we'll still follow up with a tour of the facilities and speaking to the subjects afterward. I'm just looking for... what someone is going to see when people are not on their guard, like they are when they know there is an FBI investigation under way."

That wasn't particularly helpful. But Kenzie didn't want to get too bogged down in the details anyway. She couldn't go in there with crib notes and a series of questions to ask everyone. It was best if she were just free to follow her own instincts, as Menendez suggested.

"Okay, I can do that."

"So, what do you have Wednesday afternoons?" Menendez asked.

Kenzie glanced at her, surprised by the question. It wasn't any of the agent's business what she was doing on Wednesday after she was finished at the hospital.

"I have... a private medical appointment."

"Oh. I see. Anything to worry about? I hope you're okay...?"

"I'm fine," Kenzie said tersely. "Like I said... it's private."

"Of course, of course," Menendez said, and then proceeded to dig some more. "I'm just hoping it isn't chemo or dialysis or something like that. That would really suck."

"Uh-huh."

"I'm guessing it's not just a dentist appointment, or you'd just say that…"

Kenzie shook her head and didn't answer. The woman was persistent, Kenzie would say that for her. Agent Menendez was probably used to getting what she was after.

10

Kenzie took a walk through the geriatric unit. It looked pretty much like any other hospital unit that she had visited or worked in. The patients were all older, of course, but that was true of many hospital units. As people got older, things broke down.

It was quiet. The nurses talked to each other in low tones, and there weren't many loud visitors disrupting the whole unit. There was an occasional yell from a man partway down the left side of the ward. Kenzie wasn't sure whether he were in pain or perhaps had dementia. No one else seemed to be paying much attention to him, so she assumed that it had been going on for some time and everybody was tuning him out for the sake of their own sanity.

After having a look around, she approached the nurse at the nursing station in the middle of the ward.

"Hi. I'm Dr. Kenzie Kirsch. I think Dr. Philemon told you that I would be coming?"

"Yes, he did mention something," the heavyset nurse agreed. Her name tag read Geraldine Pierce.

"I guess… were you on duty the day that Mr. Michaels passed?"

Pierce looked her over with a gaze that matched her name. She raised an eyebrow. "I imagine Dr. Philemon has probably already told you that."

"Well, no. He didn't give me any particulars."

"I don't see why the Medical Examiner has any interest in Mr. Michaels's death. He was an old man. He was sick. There's no reason for the medical examiner's office to involve itself in his death."

So Dr. Philemon had not apprised her of the fact that he was the one who had requested Mr. Michaels's case be reviewed. Did that mean that she was a suspect, or just that Dr. Philemon was playing his cards close to the chest and wasn't giving anyone any information on his suspicions or what the Medical Examiner's Office had turned up so far?

"There are cases that the Medical Examiner's Office has a duty to review," Kenzie said, keeping it as vague as possible. "I take it that as far as you knew, everything was routine with Mr. Michaels's care and his passing?"

"Like I said, he was sick," Pierce repeated, her voice firm.

Kenzie nodded. "He was in for treatment of kidney stones?"

"Well, it was more complex than that," Pierce waffled.

"Oh, yes?"

"Well there are laws," she said. "I can't give you any private details about Mr. Michaels's medical condition or care."

"Actually, since he's dead and it's the Medical Examiner's Office making inquiries, those privacy laws are not in play. We don't need a subpoena for information."

Pierce looked as if she doubted that.

"So, how long was he here?" Kenzie inquired pleasantly, looking away. It was always a good policy to start with easy questions and then work her way to the more complex or controversial ones. It was harder for a person to stop answering once they started. The brain liked to continue down the same path on which it started.

"He had been here for a week or so." Pierce hesitated, then tapped the query into the computer at her desk and looked at the result. "Six days. He was admitted through emergency."

"He was in quite a bit of pain?"

"Yes. In case you don't know, kidney stones are one of the most painful medical conditions. Similar to childbirth." Pierce's eyes went over Kenzie, assessing her. "But I take it you haven't been through that either."

"No. I haven't." Kenzie's anger flared, but she kept her voice even and pleasant. She didn't appreciate being judged by the nurse, even if she were correct in assessing that Kenzie's hips had not widened during pregnancy and delivery.

Nurse Pierce shrugged as if to say that Kenzie couldn't understand that kind of pain if she hadn't been through it.

"He was on painkillers, then? Narcotic?"

"Of course. It would be medical malpractice not to give the man some kind of painkiller when he was suffering with kidney stones. But he didn't have a reaction to the medication. He just…" She shrugged. "His heart went. It's a lot for an elderly man to go through."

"It is," Kenzie agreed, gritting her teeth as she smiled.

"He wasn't given too much, either," Pierce insisted. "We are very careful here. You can check our records."

"I haven't heard otherwise," Kenzie assured her. "You seem to be under the impression that I'm here to find fault with your nursing. I'm not."

"Why else would you be here?"

"Because it's my job to review the circumstances surrounding the death of one of our patients." Kenzie continued to smile pleasantly, as if she were perfectly comfortable having to face the big, obstinate woman.

"I suppose your boss is too good to come here himself. So he sends a…" Nurse Pierce looked at her and didn't say whatever word she had been considering. "One of his staff instead. How long have you even been with the office? You don't look old enough to be out of medical school."

"I'm flattered. I've been with Dr. Wiltshire for a couple of years now. But I'm sure you've seen a lot of doctors who look younger than me. Some of the doctors graduating now… I swear they don't look a day over eighteen."

Pierce nodded, smiling and showing her teeth. An attempt at looking good-humored even if she weren't really amused by Kenzie's comment.

"Yes, that's true. Some of the baby faces we get through here now! And their training…" She shook her head. "You have to wonder if they are even qualified to take a pulse, let alone to perform surgery or some of the other medical procedures that they are expected to."

Kenzie chuckled, nodding. "I remember when I first had to start treating real patients. I was terrified. I didn't feel like I was competent to do anything. Especially telling the nurses what to do, when half of them had twenty years of experience to my… zero."

"Well, you wouldn't guess it by hearing any of them. They seem to be just fine ordering the nursing staff around as if we were their personal slaves. It's shocking. The *privilege* these young doctors seem to have, right out of the womb. If I had ever talked that way to my elders…"

"It's a different world. Helicopter mothers. Millennials. Phones that can do everything but write prescriptions themselves."

"But all of the technology in the world is no substitute for good old-fashioned know-how. You wouldn't believe some of the young doctors we get through here who make prescriptions based on what they read on their phones." Nurse Pierce shook her head. "No experience, and they're taking their advice from Google."

"You have to keep them in hand. I'll bet you have to do a lot of hand-holding and explaining things to them."

"You'd be right." Nurse Pierce changed direction suddenly. "I don't want you getting the wrong idea about Dr. Philemon, though. He's one of the good ones."

"Not a snot-nosed brat?"

"No. He studies. You can tell. And he's always asking the more experienced staff about their experience and thoughts. Very respectful, recognizes that he doesn't know everything and that some of us might have picked up a few tricks along the way." She nodded approvingly.

"I'm so glad to hear that. I've only spoken to him on the phone so far, but he seemed very… genuine and down to earth. And like he knew what he was talking about. He's not right out of medical school."

"No. Older than you. Although you are…" Pierce hesitated, looking at Kenzie. "You didn't go straight into medicine, am I right?"

"Yes. You're right. I have a few wasted years there where I was trying to figure out what to do with myself. So I'm a bit older than some of the doctors that I came up with."

"And Dr. Phil—that's what we call him, you know. It's a little funny—Dr. Phil is older than you. In his thirties. He's still young compared to those of us with some experience. But he's always respectful. Willing to admit when he is wrong or if he doesn't know the answer to something. A different kind of doctor than a lot of those that we breed now, if you know what I mean."

"He seemed very competent," Kenzie agreed. She shifted her feet, trying to figure out the best way to shift the direction of the interview. "Sorry, I think I got a little sidetracked. Mr. Michaels. He was here for a couple of weeks. In a lot of pain. On antibiotics?"

"Yes. He had an infection and he wasn't doing very well. We had switched to an IV antibiotic and were hoping it would make the difference. But some of the infections that we treat here, it takes a few different antibiotics before we find the one that will work."

"Antibiotic misuse," Kenzie agreed. "It leads to resistant bacteria."

"Doesn't seem like it matters how many times you tell someone that they have to finish their full prescription. They stop once they're feeling better. Then it comes back, stronger, and we have to give them something stronger to even touch it. They say that between that and the antibiotics used in the meat industry, that before long we're going to end up right back where we were a couple of hundred years ago, without any effective antibiotics. Can you imagine? Do you know the number of people who used to die from what we now consider treatable infections? Babies and children. Women in childbirth. And patients like these?" She made a circular motion to include the rooms around them in the geriatric unit. "Older people whose immune systems have taken a beating? Life expectancies were so much shorter. One infection… and that could be the end of grandma and grandpa. Living to be one hundred used to be a big thing, almost no one ever achieved or even thought of being able to achieve such a thing."

"I hope we never see the day when antibiotics are completely ineffective."

"You just watch. We're on our way there now."

Kenzie shook her head grimly. "I hope not. Did Mr. Michaels show any improvement? With his infection? The kidney stones? Were they going to do surgery for the kidney stones?"

"He'd been through one round of ultrasound treatment. You know, trying to break them up in a non-invasive procedure. That didn't work, so they were looking at doing a basket retrieval next."

"Minimally invasive. Were there any concerns about that? Suggestions that it might be too much for him?"

"No. He was in generally good health. Infections and kidney stones are treatable. He didn't have any major problems. Heart or respiratory. Cancer. Nothing like that. He would have handled the treatment just fine."

"If he had survived."

Pierce nodded. "We couldn't have predicted that. Sometimes… there are other conditions that the doctors don't know about. Symptoms that the patient doesn't report or things that he isn't even aware of. I guess… maybe he did have heart problems. Or maybe it was an embolism or a stroke." She shrugged her big, round shoulders. "I don't know what you found."

And Kenzie wasn't about to tell her. Nurse Pierce, like all the rest of the staff on the unit, was a suspect. If Pierce had been the one to administer potassium chloride, then she already knew Michaels's cause of death. She might have been fishing to see whether the Medical Examiner's Office had found anything yet. Kenzie hoped that she didn't give anything away in her facial expression or body language.

"I would like to talk to some of the rest of the staff while I'm here. I assume that everyone else on duty here was employed when Mr. Michaels passed?"

"Yes," Pierce said slowly, as if looking for some other answer. "We haven't hired anyone new since then. But not everyone who is on now was on at the time that he died."

"No, I understand that. I'm just interested in talking to people, getting a feel for the unit. It seems like a very warm, peaceful place."

Pierce was apparently mollified by the compliment. She nodded vigorously. "Of course, it's never good to have to go to the hospital, but we try to make everyone's stays here just as pleasant as we can. If you can't be home, we want them to be at home here." She gave Kenzie a sugary smile.

"Yes," Kenzie agreed, and turned away so that she didn't have to look at the sickly sweet expression.

11

Despite what she said, Kenzie was not overly impressed by the unit. Like many hospitals, it was a combination of both the antiseptically clean and years of neglect. The floors and walls were stained. Furniture in the family visiting areas looked worn but was not ripped up or obviously mended. The TVs in the visiting rooms were old.

Everything in the rooms looked as Kenzie expected it to. Not too many surfaces to be wiped down. Clean white beds and patients with terrycloth robes wrapped around their thin bodies and hospital johnnies. Quietly murmured conversations beside the beds of sick and dying loved ones.

"Can I help you?" A young nurse asked as she came out of one of the patient rooms, immediately identifying Kenzie as someone who didn't belong. "Are you looking for someone?"

"I'm Dr. Kenzie Kirsch. From the Medical Examiner's Office." Kenzie didn't offer her hand this time. Who knew what procedure the nurse had just finished with and how well she attended to her hygiene afterward. "I've just been talking to Nurse Pierce, and I'm taking a look around and meeting the staff who are on today." Kenzie looked at the nurse's name badge. "Nurse Loudwell."

She nodded. "Mostly they just call me Nurse Cherrie around here. It's nice to meet you. So… you didn't need anything?"

"Just having a walk around. Have you been here long?"

A crease appeared between Nurse Cherrie's brows. "Do you mean today, or how long I've been working in this unit?"

"I meant how long you've been working here."

"Well, I'm not, actually. I fill in some days when they are short. I need the extra hours, and it seems like some units never have enough staff. So I'm on call if they need anyone to fill in here. If someone is sick or has to pick up their kids from school." She shrugged with one shoulder.

"Ah, well that's good of you. So… were you on when Mr. Michaels was here? He was here for a couple of weeks."

"Oh sure, I remember him. Nice old guy. He, uh, passed, didn't he?"

"Yes, he did. He was friendly with you? You enjoyed working with him?"

"Sure. I mean, he was in a lot of pain. The kidney stone patients always are. It can make them kind of crabby, but he was always careful of what he said. Didn't snap back or complain too much. But you could tell… poor guy. What was it, do you know? Sometimes stones can cause internal damage. Blockages or perforations."

"No, I don't think it was the kidney stones."

"Oh. Well, that's good. Not something that they could have prevented, then. I think Dr. Philemon is a pretty good doctor. Young, you know, so some of the oldsters around here don't trust him, but I think he did a good job."

"I don't think it was anything caused by negligence. I think Mr. Michaels received the care that he needed."

"Ah, that's good." Nurse Cherrie nodded. "Glad to hear it." She cocked her head slightly, not sure how to properly disengage from the conversation. "Well… good luck then, on whatever it is you're doing here."

Kenzie didn't offer a more full explanation. Nurse Cherrie nodded once more, then went her own way, looking back one last time to try to figure out why Kenzie was there.

Kenzie couldn't say exactly what she was looking for herself. Someone like Cherrie would look good for an Angel of Death killing. A nurse who regularly subbed in the unit when she was needed could easily be overlooked when Dr. Philemon or the FBI started making lists of suspects. She might not appear on the staff lists. She might not have even been on duty the day that Michaels had died, but could still have come and gone without attracting any suspicion. People were used to seeing her and wouldn't think anything of it or remember later that she had been there.

She continued her tour of the ward. As she passed one door, she could hear a man moaning within. She stopped and listened for a moment. He didn't call out or talk to anyone else, but kept moaning to himself. Kenzie hesitated for a moment, then entered. The bed nearest the door was empty. The moaning man lay in the second bed.

"Hey, are you okay?" Kenzie asked softly.

His eyes flew open, startled by her presence. He moaned again, his watery blue eyes unfocused. "It hurts," he complained.

Kenzie looked at the pump hooked up to the IV tube in his arm. But it would appear from the screen of the pump that he had already hit his maximum dosage of painkillers.

"Do you want me to get a nurse?"

"They won't come," he said. "Who are you? Aren't you a nurse?"

He continued to moan as Kenzie answered. "I was just walking by and heard you. I can try to get someone for you if you like."

"They just tell me to stop calling them," he explained. He gave a sharp cry as if he'd been hit with a stabbing pain instead of the pain that had been making him moan.

Kenzie couldn't help remembering the nephrology unit Amanda had been in before she had died. The nurses there were all friendly and pleasant. They all knew Amanda and Lisa by name, and some of them learned Kenzie's name too. But they did tend to get irritated with multiple calls over the same issues. They promised to page the doctors, who were never on duty when they were needed. They promised to pass messages along. And they got irritable and reminded them that there was nothing else they could do about Amanda's sickness and pain. They did their best to take care of her but, in the end, there was nothing else that they could do. When Amanda's breathing had gotten too bad, she had been whisked away. And that was the last they had seen of her before the end.

Kenzie realized that she had closed her eyes with the remembered pain of it all. It had been awful, losing her little sister like that. Seeing her mother's acute pain and grief over the loss. Her father's emptiness and anger that the laws had not given them all the tools they needed to save Amanda. He had done everything he could for her, including skirting legal and moral issues and, in the end, that was what had killed her.

She realized that she was holding the patient's hand. It was thin and fragile in her grasp. He gave her a tiny squeeze, staring up into her face, seeming confused and lost, like a little child instead of an old man.

"Is it... kidney failure? Stones?" Kenzie gazed at him, feeling his pain and her own merging together in her chest.

"Cancer," the man said. "It's eating away at my insides. I can feel it, burning holes through everything." He moaned and pressed his other hand to his mouth. "A drink. I need a drink, please."

Kenzie looked at the side table, where there was a small cup of ice chips. She used the plastic spoon to take one out and place it in the man's mouth.

He sucked it, making smacking sounds, and closed his eyes again, moaning and sliding into the pain.

Kenzie didn't stick around to find out whether he had known Mr. Michaels. She tiptoed out of the room, doing her best not to disturb the man any further.

There were cheerful voices down the hall. They seemed to intrude on the ward, like they didn't belong there. Didn't the speakers know that people were sick and dying? They should be quiet, like at a library, not allowing their happy, raised voices to disrupt people's peaceful moments. But despite the feeling that the voices didn't belong, Kenzie found herself walking toward them, curious as to whom they belonged.

She found a couple of volunteers talking to the nursing staff.

Candy stripers, they sometimes called hospital volunteers whose job it was to make things easier for the patients and to bring a little joy and relief into the dreary hospital setting. One of the volunteers had a thin leather satchel or briefcase over her arm. The other had a dog in harness.

Kenzie eyed the dog. She was still leery of dogs around patients after her experience with the virus. She wasn't about to pet the dog or allow it to lick her, that was for sure. She sidled closer to the group of people, to listen in on the conversation without forcing herself into their little circle.

"Blue is excited to be here," the young woman with the dog said. "Where do you think we should start? Who could use a cuddle today?"

"Why don't you try Mr. Damon in room 32," one of the nurses suggested. "He's been feeling lonely lately. No one comes to visit him, and he's an old grouch if you try to engage with him and cheer him up. I'll bet Blue is just what he needs."

The candy striper nodded cheerfully and led Blue toward room 32.

"And…" the nurse looked at the other volunteer. "What are you doing today?"

The woman with the satchel was a little older, but still had that "glow" of a volunteer who knew she was there to make someone's day. She smiled and indicated her bag. "I'm writing letters for people. There are lots of people around here who can't use computers or phones to reach their loved ones, and letters are a great way for them to connect."

The nurse nodded. "And it keeps them busy, gives them something to think about other than how miserable they are feeling."

Kenzie thought about the patient she had just left. She didn't think that dictating a letter would be possible for him. He would need something quite a bit more powerful to get his mind off his pain. Like maybe a higher dose of narcotics. The man was dying of cancer; they could afford to give him a little more relief. If it shortened his life by a day or two, that didn't matter. He would at least have better quality of life for those last few days.

"Try Mrs. Brown in 35. She'll chatter your ear off. It will give her a way to direct her energy."

"Sounds good," the volunteer agreed cheerfully.

Kenzie watched her walk off to visit with the patients. She turned back to Nurse Stevens, a male nurse who had taken Nurse Pierce's place at the nursing station at least temporarily.

"Do you get a lot of volunteers in this unit?"

"A good number," Stevens agreed, looking Kenzie up and down. "Pediatrics probably gets the most, but geriatrics is right up there. People recognize that a lot of them don't have anyone else and could really use the lift."

"That's great. Really nice to see it. How are they vetted?"

Stevens blinked several times. "I'm not involved in that part of the program. You would have to ask someone in administration."

"Are records kept? Of who is here when?"

"Of course. They all check in and out." He leaned on the reception desk. "Why all the questions?"

"I'm with the ME's office. Just looking into a couple of things."

"Why?" His tone was somewhat confrontational.

"Because when we investigate a death, sometimes there are questions that need to be asked outside the morgue. Circumstances surrounding the death. Who might have been around. The events leading up to the death."

"What death? Who are you talking about?"

Kenzie didn't like the confrontational attitude, but there was no point in avoiding his questions. He just had to ask Nurse Pierce or someone else Kenzie had talked to and he would hear the whole story.

"Mr. Michaels."

"Michaels. Our Mr. Michaels? Why would you be investigating that death?"

"That really isn't any of your business. There are certain deaths that we are required to investigate, and Mr. Michaels is one of them. We expect cooperation from the staff."

"Who's not cooperating? I don't like strangers showing up in my ward asking questions. I'm sure you wouldn't be too happy about anyone who showed up at your office and started asking nosy questions about your job either."

"No, I probably wouldn't," Kenzie agreed.

He looked surprised at her response. Whatever barb had been on his tongue to deploy next was checked. He closed his mouth and looked at her.

"But I still need to investigate the case that's been assigned to me," Kenzie said. "Even if you don't like it. Even if I don't like it."

"Why Mr. Michaels?"

"Like I said, it was assigned to me. You take care of the people and duties that you're assigned to, right?"

He nodded his agreement. "Of course. Wouldn't do me much good to avoid it."

"No point in getting fired," Kenzie agreed. "You're here as a nurse, so you nurse the people you are assigned to."

"Yeah."

"Were you on the floor the day Mr. Michaels passed?"

"No. I was off that day."

Kenzie nodded. If he were lying, the records that the hospital passed on to Menendez would tell them so. But she suspected he was telling the truth. And if so, then he was not a suspect in Mr. Michaels's death.

"Do you have the records for the volunteers? Do you know whether either of those two was on the day that Mr. Michaels passed?"

"Why does that matter? Why would you care if a couple of volunteers were around the day he died?"

Kenzie didn't answer. She just waited for his answer. Stevens glared at her for a few seconds longer, then broke eye contact and went around the desk to the computer.

"It isn't like volunteers are involved in patient treatment," he pointed out. "As you see… they take a service dog in, or write letters, or read books. They are not involved in the actual patient care."

But that didn't mean that one of them could not have injected something into Mr. Michaels's IV. They didn't even have to be able to find a vein to administer poison. Anyone could stick a needle through the IV port and inject potassium chloride, even if they were squeamish.

"Were there any volunteers on the day that he died?"

Stevens tapped a query into the computer and moused around a bit before he was able to find the report or filter that he was looking for. He looked at the data displayed on his screen.

"Roda, the one doing the letter writing, she was around," he said finally. "But I still don't see what that has to do with anything."

"Do you keep records of who she worked with that day?"

"No, just that she was here."

"I'll maybe talk to her, then."

Stevens shook his head. "That's ridiculous."

12

Kenzie followed in the direction that Roda had gone, looking into each room until she saw the young woman sitting at Mrs. Brown's bedside. Kenzie hesitated. She probably shouldn't interrupt the letter-writing process.

Mrs. Brown saw her in the doorway and said something, and Roda turned around to see who was there.

"Hi."

Kenzie walked into the room. "Oh, hello. I'm sorry, I didn't mean to interrupt you."

Looking down at the pen and paper on Roda's lap, Kenzie saw that she hadn't yet started on a letter. Maybe she wouldn't even get that far. It could just be a way to get people to start talking, and the planned letter would never even get written. Like getting someone to talk about herself by offering to write her memoirs.

"Did you need something?" Roda asked, her brows drawing down.

"Well, I was just hoping to talk to you for a few minutes. We can set up a time later, since you're busy right now…"

Roda looked at Mrs. Brown, who seemed unperturbed by the interruption. The old woman smiled at Kenzie, unusually white dentures gleaming from her wizened face. "Oh, that's okay, dear. I don't mind an extra visitor anytime."

Kenzie smiled back at her. "How are you doing, Mrs. Brown? I hope you're not in too much discomfort."

"The worst thing is the boredom. I'm used to being able to get around to visit all my friends. I'm a volunteer, you know, I help to take care of old people."

Kenzie was a little startled by this assertion. Mrs. Brown laughed merrily.

"I know, you think that I'm old, but I get around pretty well. There are a lot of people a lot worse off than I am. I take people meals, sit and visit with them, help to do a few things around the house. Tidying up, washing dishes, making sure their pills are all sorted into containers. I have my whole route…" She sighed. "But here I am, sidelined by a little infection."

"I'm sure you'll be able to get home soon," Roda said. "You're a lot more perky than you were the last time I was by."

"Yes… that nice young doctor said he wants to keep me for another day or two, and then he'll let me go home. In the meantime…" She folded her hands over her chest, giving the appearance of someone trying to appear peaceful and serene. "I try to behave myself and not bother the nurses too much."

Kenzie laughed at her contrite expression. "Well, I'm sorry that you have to stay here so long. I'm glad that you're getting better, though."

"Hospitals are a necessary evil, I suppose," Mrs. Brown said. "Though I would have preferred to just take antibiotics at home."

Roda shook her head at this. "You were far too sick to stay at home. You needed IV antibiotics, and you couldn't take those at home."

"Sometimes you can," Mrs. Brown told her. "They put the IV in and give you a little pump in a belt bag. Gladys had one a few months ago, and she could go wherever she wanted to."

"But you were too sick. You needed to stay in bed, and Dr. Philemon knows very well that you won't stay in bed if you have any say in it."

Mrs. Brown nodded and laughed.

Kenzie drew over a chair and sat down so that she wouldn't be towering over Mrs. Brown. An intimate discussion group. Maybe having Mrs. Brown there would actually make Kenzie's questions seem less intrusive.

"You like Dr. Philemon?"

"He's a nice young man," Mrs. Brown agreed.

Kenzie looked at Roda to extend the question to her. She shrugged, seeming surprised at the question.

"Yes, he's a good doctor. I don't really work with the doctors, I just interface with the patients…"

"I've only talked to him on the phone," Kenzie offered, "but he seemed like a nice man. And very professional. Like he knows what he's talking about as a doctor. Sometimes you get the feeling that a doctor is just not quite up to speed. But not him."

She waited to see whether they would agree with her or not.

"Oh, yes," Mrs. Brown agreed. "He listens to me. So many doctors, if you're a woman or if you're over sixty, they think you don't know what you're talking about. I've lived in this body for eighty years! I know when something is not right."

"I've always thought he was a good doctor," Roda contributed. "I mean... I'm not a patient, so I can't really say, but he seems like he knows what he's talking about."

"Yeah. One of his patients here was Mr. Michaels...?"

"Harry," the older woman said immediately. "He was a nice man. I was pretty sick when I got here, but I have met him before."

"I saw him." Roda brushed her fingers over the paper mounted on the clipboard in her lap. "He was here for a couple of weeks. But he was too sick for me to do anything with him."

"He was in a lot of pain?"

She nodded. "Yeah. Poor guy."

"Were you here when he died?"

"Such a tragic thing." Mrs. Brown shook her head, her eyes going shiny.

"I was here..." Roda seemed uncomfortable with the question. "Not like I was in the room or anything, but I heard the code, saw the nurses rushing in."

"Dr. Philemon wasn't here when it happened?"

"No. He wasn't around. It was just the nurses, an intern..." Roda trailed off uncertainly. "I don't really know how many people were in there to help him."

"Did they do CPR? Use the defibrillator?"

"I wasn't in the room," Roda repeated. "I don't know what they did. They worked on him for a while. But not at *long* time."

"It never seems much like they show it on TV," Mrs. Brown said. "They like to make it all very dramatic on TV. Bringing the person back from the dead. But in the hospital... well, especially here, where it's just old folks... it isn't like that. There isn't any panic, you know. They do what they can, and then it's over."

Kenzie nodded. "You probably wouldn't want them taking heroic measures." Then she felt awkward saying such a thing to Mrs. Brown. The implication that older people didn't have as much to live for or that their lives were not as valuable made her squirm. Mrs. Brown was full of life. Someone who might live for another twenty years, helping out her less-vigorous friends. "What I mean is, you might not want to be kept alive on a ventilator, or risk having a bunch of ribs broken, that kind of thing."

"Oh, I know dear." Mrs. Brown patted Kenzie's hand. "You have to decide just how much you want them to do. What kind of quality of life you would have afterward. I wouldn't want to be a vegetable. I don't want to be a burden on other people or spend the rest of my life hooked up to a machine. My kids are grown and I've arranged with Shirley that she would take my cats. Everything is in order when it's my time. But it's not my time yet."

Kenzie laughed and smiled at her. "I'm glad it's not. You seem as though you still have a lot to give to the world."

"Thank you! That's a very nice way of putting it."

Kenzie looked back at Roda, trying to figure out how to squeeze any more information out of her. She hadn't been in the room when Michaels had died, so she didn't have much information to give Kenzie. Merely being on the unit didn't make her a suspect. Unless she'd been on the unit when a lot of the other people had died. Kenzie couldn't really see her sneaking into patients' rooms and poisoning them, then sneaking back out again before she was discovered. These Angel of Death killers usually liked to be in on the action, not waiting in another room for the end. But it was possible that Roda still had information she didn't know might be important.

"Which nurses were here when Mr. Michaels died? Which ones were helping him, I mean? That must have been very upsetting for them."

"Well, I guess if they're working here, they have to get used to the fact that some of their patients will die," Roda said slowly. She looked at Mrs. Brown. "I mean... you can't know just by how old someone is, of course, but..."

"We're obviously closer to our expiry dates," Mrs. Brown contributed, making them all laugh awkwardly.

"Yeah, I guess. I think they have to... develop a thick skin. Not let themselves get too close to people."

"Was Nurse Pierce on that day?" Kenzie prompted, hoping to get some names.

Roda thought about it. "Yes, I think she was one of the nurses who responded. And... Nurse Crawford... the new nurse with the blond, curly hair... and I don't know the names of the interns; it seems as if they come and go so quickly."

Kenzie tried to imprint these names on her memory. She didn't want to take out her phone to make note of it immediately. That would probably shut Roda up. "Did he have any family? Mr. Michaels?"

"I don't have any idea," Roda shook her head. "I've never seen anyone visiting him."

"He had a son," Mrs. Brown advised. "He lives out on the coast. I don't think he made it in for a visit before Logan passed. No one knew… it was unexpected. He didn't have any way of knowing that his father was going to die during this hospital stay. He's been here before. But this time… it was a surprise for everyone, I think."

13

Before leaving the office for the day, Kenzie wrote down notes of her visit to the hospital for Agent Menendez, replaying her memories of her visit on Tuesday and consulting the few notes that she'd jotted down once she had left the unit. It was important to get down her impressions before they started to fade. Not just to give Menendez a clear picture of the people she had spoken with at the hospital, but also in case she ever had to testify in court about any of it. It was much better to be able to refer to notes made at the time than to be trying to recall things over the months or years without any memory aid.

She gave the memo a read-through before emailing it off to Menendez, then checked the time to make sure she wasn't running late for her couples therapy appointment with Dr. B and Zachary.

She wasn't looking forward to it.

Couples therapy wasn't her favorite time. That was one reason they had instituted the ice cream treat after each session. So that they'd be rewarded for going to sessions and it would be easier to go back. And she knew that it would be an even more difficult session than usual, with the revelation that Zachary had again been stalking Bridget.

Dr. Boyle welcomed Zachary and Kenzie into her office and they sat down in their usual places. Zachary was walking slowly and casting sideways glances at

Kenzie. Trying to assess her mood and how she would approach their couples session given the latest developments. Kenzie did her best to ignore the looks and to pretend that it was just a regular session, no different from any other.

"So…" Dr. B leaned back in her chair and steepled her fingers together. "How are you both today?"

"Good," Kenzie said, trying not to let it sound clipped or perfunctory. There was no "I'm fine" in Dr. Boyle's office when things were clearly not fine. Hopefully, the "good" would be acceptable and they would move on to Zachary, which was where the focus needed to be.

Dr. B looked at her and didn't say anything. Kenzie looked away, waiting for Zachary's answer.

"You already know how I am," Zachary said finally. "I… screwed up. I don't know what to do."

The therapist nodded her understanding. "How do you feel about it?"

"I know that I'm supposed to stay away from Bridget. And I want to. I just… needed to check on her. With the pregnancy, and the Huntington's, I've been worried. I had to see her to reassure myself that she was okay."

"So you were justified?"

Zachary shifted. He looked at Kenzie, but she didn't have anything to say. "No. I didn't say that. Just saying… what was in my head. I've been really concerned about her."

"But she has a partner taking care of her, doesn't she? She's not alone."

"I know. But Gordon works long hours. It's fine if she can call him if she's in trouble… but what if she can't? What if she can't get to the phone or dial his number? How would he know?"

"Doesn't she have an assistant?" Kenzie asked. "I thought they had someone coming in to help her?"

"Yes. But she's not there all the time that Gordon is gone. She comes in early, and then when she's done everything that Bridget needs help with, she leaves. So… Bridget is alone for the rest of the day."

"If she was in danger, then they would get her more help, don't you think? They have all kinds of money. It isn't like full-time help would be beyond their means. If Bridget wanted someone there full-time, they would have someone there full-time. Or if Gordon thought that's what she needed."

Zachary scratched the back of his neck. He didn't nod or acknowledge her comment. "What's going to happen when the babies are born? Are they going to have a full-time nanny? Bridget can't take care of them by herself."

"From what you said, I thought that Bridget was still in the early stages of Huntington's," Dr. B said. "So what makes you think that she won't be able to take care of them?"

"Bridget doesn't even like children. She never wanted to have kids in the first place. She doesn't have any experience." Zachary shook his head. "Everything… her health, her mental state. She never even wanted to get pregnant."

"She used in vitro. So clearly, she wanted to get pregnant," Dr. Boyle reminded him. "What you mean is, she didn't want to get pregnant when you were with her."

"No. She didn't want my babies," Zachary muttered.

"And that hurt you. Do you think that might be part of why you are obsessed with her pregnancy?"

"Yes. Sure. I haven't been able to get it out of my head ever since I found out."

It was the first time Kenzie had heard him admit that.

"But I was doing good. I was still… staying away from her. Mostly." A glance in Kenzie's direction.

"What does 'mostly' mean?" Kenzie asked, using as neutral a tone as she was able.

"I still… ran into her once or twice. Saw her when she was out shopping or getting gas."

"Unintentionally?"

He nodded and licked his lips.

"Or maybe sometimes intentionally?" Kenzie suggested.

"No. Not on purpose. It wasn't like that."

Kenzie wasn't sure she believed him. She suspected that he had probably driven past her house, even if he hadn't stopped to watch her. Maybe shopped at some of her favorite stores just to see if he happened to see her. The first time they had run into Bridget at a restaurant and Bridget had blown up over it, Kenzie had assumed that it was Bridget's problem. In a town the size of Roxboro, you couldn't expect *never* to run into a person anywhere. And if they both shared similar tastes and had gotten used to dining certain places, then they were bound to run into each other occasionally.

But now, she wasn't so sure that Bridget had been completely wrong. Zachary had been tracking her. Had watched her house. And if he occasionally bumped into her around town, it wasn't beyond belief that he had engineered it that way.

But she let it go. Dr. B could call him out if she believed he was shading the truth. Zachary looked back at the therapist, licking his lips again.

"I was doing good before," he maintained. "I was staying away from her."

"And the pregnancy changed that?"

He shook his head. "Maybe a little," he admitted. "But…" He fiddled with the zipper on his jacket. "It was when Gordon hired me. That's when…" He trailed off and shrugged.

Dr. Boyle frowned. She looked at Kenzie to see whether this made sense to her. Apparently, this had never come up in Zachary's sessions with her previously.

An oversight on Zachary's part? Definitely not.

"Gordon hired Zachary to look into whether Bridget was seeing someone else," Kenzie explained. "And to look into the pregnancy."

"What does 'look into' mean?"

"Put her under surveillance," Zachary said in a low voice. He cleared his throat when his voice cracked. He looked down.

"Her current partner asked the man she accused of stalking her to follow her around?"

"Uh-huh."

"I thought this guy was supposed to be one of our brightest minds?"

Kenzie snorted. She couldn't help it. She tried to quell the impulse to laugh and make a big joke of it. Venting her feelings about Gordon would distract them from the real issues. "In some things, maybe."

Dr. Boyle let out a long sigh. "And surprise, surprise, returning to your addiction sent you tumbling off the wagon."

Zachary raised his eyes to study Dr. B's face, trying to read every detail of her expression.

"No, it doesn't get you off the hook," the therapist said. "Because no matter what triggered this behavior, we still have to deal with it. Don't we?"

Zachary nodded.

"Is this something you *want* to overcome?"

"Yes." Zachary's voice was nearly inaudible. But Kenzie was glad to hear his answer, even if it was quiet. She was afraid that Zachary got too much of a hit from feel-good neurotransmitters when he saw Bridget. That he wouldn't want to stop, even if he knew it could lead to Kenzie breaking up with him.

"Okay." Dr. B gave a brisk nod. "We need to look at the med cocktail, among other things. It was helping before. I wonder whether we need to change anything."

"Can't change anything right now," Zachary said. "I can't afford to… go on a med holiday right now."

"No. We don't want to take you off of anything before Christmas," Dr. Boyle agreed. It was the most dangerous time of the year for Zachary. The time of year when historically he had attempted suicide or self-harmed. "But we might increase dosages or try adding in something new."

"Nothing new," Zachary insisted. "If there are new side effects or if it interferes with something that I'm already on…"

The woman's lips pressed together as she considered this objection. "Are you taking everything as directed?"

Zachary nodded.

Dr. B's gaze shifted to Kenzie. Kenzie held her hands up.

"I don't supervise his meds. That's his responsibility. I know he takes morning and evening meds. I know he gets prescriptions refilled. I don't keep track of when he is taking each pill or when he is supposed to."

Dr. B nodded. "That's perfectly fine. I don't think we need to make it your responsibility. But I know that Zachary has decided to stop taking meds in the past." She looked back at Zachary and raised her brows.

"Yes," Zachary admitted. "It's my body and I know how they affect me. I only take ADHD meds when I need to. I only take anti-anxiety or sleep aids when I really have to. Not every day."

"And the anti-depressants?"

"Every day."

She nodded. "And you believe they are still working?"

"Yes."

"Are they helping with the compulsions or only the depression?"

Zachary was silent for a few moments, considering this. Kenzie wondered whether it was a question that she would have been able to answer if it were her. Was it possible for Zachary to slice and dice his brain activity that way? To see the cause and effect that each med had on each symptom?

"It was easier when I started taking them," he said. "Two years ago. I think they helped me to… put my need to monitor Bridget to the back of my mind. Until… I gave in and started doing it again for Gordon."

"Then maybe with some cognitive therapy, we can help get you back to that point."

He stared down at the carpet and shrugged. Kenzie could feel some resistance to whatever this would entail.

"But that's something that we can discuss in our individual sessions," Dr. B told him. "Now… we should focus on the relationship. I imagine that this has caused some issues between the two of you. Let's get started."

14

Kenzie felt raw leaving the therapist's office. She imagined that Zachary felt the same way, probably more so. While she knew it was probably a good thing for them to talk their feelings out in the controlled environment of the sessions with Dr. Boyle, she couldn't help wondering if it caused more trouble than it healed. She felt a lot more vulnerable and isolated from Zachary than she had going into the session. She had been angry with him over the breach of their trust and his continued obsession over another woman, but she'd been able to keep the extent of those feelings from him. She didn't see how sharing them helped either one of them.

They had come to the session in their own vehicles, so they had to drive home separately. But maybe the quiet of their own vehicles would give them each some time to recover before they tried to go on with the day together.

"Should we stop at the grocery store?" Zachary asked, as they walked out to their cars. "Or at the Fro Zone? We might not have enough ice cream for tonight." He was half joking, half serious.

"I think I definitely need a new flavor," Kenzie decided. Something with chocolate and caramel and marshmallows. Something even more decadent than her usual. "How about you?"

He considered, then nodded. "Maybe something with different flavors in it. A mixture."

Kenzie went for chocolate. Zachary tended to prefer fruit flavors or highly artificial flavors like bubble-gum or cotton candy. He didn't usually like ice creams with mixed flavors, like Neapolitan. But maybe he was

924

stressed enough that he wanted to go wild this time. A rainbow sorbet, maybe. In bright neon colors.

"Fro Zone?" Kenzie concluded. The grocery store had a good range of popular flavors, but it sounded like they were going to need to step it up a notch.

"Fro Zone," Zachary agreed.

"Okay. I'll meet you there."

They each returned to their own cars.

Wouldn't it be ironic if Zachary decided he had to drive by Bridget's on the way to the ice cream shop? After all the talk about her during the session, his obsessive thoughts about her were probably pinging around his head at light speed.

Kenzie decided to leave the parking lot first so that she wouldn't be tempted to follow Zachary, dogging him to make sure that he didn't take any detours.

But when she pulled up to the ice cream shop, he was already there ahead of her.

Kenzie awoke the next morning feeling slightly hung over. She hadn't had anything to drink, so she could only blame it on the ice cream and the emotional wringing-out that she had done during the therapy session. Zachary was, as usual, out of bed ahead of her and already hard at work on his computer in the living room. Only when she looked in on him, Zachary wasn't occupied with typing or reading what was on the screen of his computer, but was watching out the window.

"Hey, stranger," Kenzie greeted.

He turned and saw her watching him. "Oh. Hi. Did you have a good sleep?"

"Yeah. Not bad. I feel as though I could have used another three or four hours, but… work calls."

"Did you wake up a lot?"

"I don't think so. And I don't remember having any dreams. But… I feel like I had too much to drink."

"You didn't have anything," he said with surprise. "Did you?"

"No."

"Maybe you're dehydrated, then. They say that alcohol makes you feel so bad because it dehydrates you."

"You're right." Kenzie headed to the fridge. "Maybe that's it." It wasn't as if she'd made sure to have a properly balanced meal and enough water the evening before. She had been treating herself. Way too much sugar and chocolate and nothing good for her. She filled a tall glass with water from the filtering pitcher in the fridge and forced herself to drink half of it before heading to the shower. She left the rest on the table to drink before her coffee.

"How about you?" she asked Zachary. "I know I don't need to ask whether you slept well, but how are you this morning?"

"Okay." He swallowed. "Kenzie… I'm really sorry. About all of this. You don't need to be dealing with all of my crap, and Bridget and all…"

"You've apologized. I understand that it's… that you can't control what thoughts come into your mind, and that it's difficult not to give in and act on them. I'm trying not to be angry or judgmental about it. We've both got stuff to work on to make this relationship better."

"But it all starts with me. You wouldn't have all of this in a *normal* relationship."

"What's normal? All relationships have problems. They're all made up of two people with different outlooks and problems and ways of communicating. Look at the divorce rate. At the dating apps. I'm glad that we have Dr. Boyle to help us work through it all. That was a good suggestion."

His earlobes got a little bit red. He always did have problems taking a compliment. But this time he didn't push it away or put himself down. He just gave a short nod and looked down at his computer screen as if occupied.

"Okay," Kenzie said. "See you at breakfast."

Following her shower, Kenzie hadn't even sat down at the breakfast table when her phone started ringing. Looking down at the screen, Kenzie saw Menendez's number. She tried to decide whether she needed to answer it, or whether she could return the agent's call once she was at the Medical Examiner's Office.

What if there had been another death?

"Sorry," she told Zachary, walking back out of the kitchen and toward her bedroom where she could shut the door for privacy. "I just have to take this."

She swiped the screen and put the phone to her ear. "Agent Menendez?"

"Josie."

"Josie," Kenzie corrected. "Can I help you with something?"

"I have your memorandum of your conversations at the geriatric unit, and I wondered if we could go over it. Get your impressions and discuss possible directions to go with the investigation."

Kenzie paused in her walk to the bedroom, irritated. She had put all her impressions into the memo. That was the whole point of writing it. To memorialize what she had thought and felt about each of the people she had talked to, and about the unit in general. And Dr. Philemon.

"Yeah, I'm not at the office yet. Can I call you back in a while?"

"Oh, of course. I thought maybe we could get together for coffee or breakfast?"

"I'm just having mine now. Sorry. I'll call you back in an hour."

It would probably be longer than that, since she would want to sort things out when she got into the office, and wouldn't call Menendez back until everything was ship-shape for Dr. Wiltshire's arrival.

"Oh, okay," Menendez agreed, sounding disappointed. "I guess… we'll talk then."

Kenzie disconnected the call and turned around to rejoin Zachary for breakfast. He looked surprised. "That was a quick call. Usually when you say just a minute, it's a bit longer."

"I thought there might be some urgency, but there's not. I can call her when I get into the office."

"Good."

They worked together to get everything ready, then sat down and ate. Kenzie found it difficult to focus on Zachary, thinking about Menendez and why she had called so early. Was there something in Kenzie's report that had caught her attention? Something important? Or was Josie Menendez just lonely and looking for some company before jumping into her workday?

15

Her call with Menendez had been unremarkable, and the day's tasks routine, which helped Kenzie to relax and feel more like herself.

Kenzie had noticed that Zachary seemed restless and agitated most of that evening, but he said he was okay when she talked to him and didn't offer if there was something in particular that was bothering him. Dr. B had raised the dosage of his antidepressants after some discussion, and Kenzie wondered if it were causing negative side effects.

He went to bed with her as usual, but kept shifting around and couldn't find a comfortable position to cuddle with her. Kenzie was getting irritated that every time she got settled in, he moved again. She needed to get her sleep if she were going to be able to function at the morgue in the morning.

Eventually, he whispered an apology and got out of bed. He would go watch TV for a while and maybe fall asleep on the couch. That's what usually happened on those nights that he couldn't settle in. Though she didn't like it when they had to be separated at night, she was also relieved that he'd decided to get up. She really wanted to be able to get a few solid hours of sleep before she had to get up again. She never did well when she was short on sleep.

She thought that she had drifted off for a while, but when she was next aware and turned over to get comfortable, she thought she could hear something. It niggled away at her, and she couldn't get back to sleep again, despite how tired she was. She finally listened to the little voice in her head that kept telling her she needed to get up and make sure that everything was okay.

Sometimes there was a reason for those worrisome little thoughts. A door left unlocked or strange activities at a neighbor's house. Or maybe just a branch scraping on the side of the house in the wind, bothersome but not a worry.

She stepped into the living room and saw that Zachary was pacing up and down the room, into the kitchen and back. His movements seemed stiff and agitated.

"Zachary?"

He didn't look at her, but kept pacing, a fixed expression on his face. Grim. Lost in his troubled thoughts, whatever they were. Kenzie raised her voice.

"Zachary!"

He didn't see her until she stepped into his path as he paced back across the room. He stopped, startled, and stared at her for a minute before appearing to recognize her.

"Kenzie!" He looked around, trying to orient himself in time and space. He looked at the dark window, then back at her. "Are you okay?"

"I am. It looks like you're having trouble, though."

He shifted around, itching to be pacing again. Kenzie took a step back so that she wasn't in his way. He stayed put for the moment, opening and closing his hands.

"Can't sleep," he acknowledged.

"What's going on? Is it your meds? Were you having a flashback? How can I help?"

"Nothing you can do." He stepped from one foot to the other.

Kenzie looked at him, waiting for an explanation. Normally, she wouldn't push him to say what was bothering him. But that rule did not apply when he was so agitated during the night that he woke her up, whether it was with a nightmare or with pacing around the house looking like he was going to explode.

"It's just my brain. Won't quiet down. I can't… stop it from spinning."

"Do you think it is because of the dosage increase? Is it making you anxious?"

"No." He started to pace again, unable to keep still. "It's just… things. I can't get them out of my mind."

"What things?" She didn't want to bring up Bridget's name in case it were something else. She didn't want to introduce more restless thoughts if that weren't what he was already focused on.

Zachary cleared his throat a few times as he paced, as if he were trying to begin, but couldn't quite get the words moving. Kenzie was becoming more convinced that it was a problem with his prescriptions. She knew that he'd had reactions in the past. Some severe ones when he had first begun taking medications as a kid. It might be that he just didn't recognize what was going on.

"I'm worried about Bridget," he said finally. "Her and the babies."

Kenzie let out a long sigh. So the increased level of his antidepressants wasn't helping to control the obsessive thoughts. Not yet, but it could take weeks for them to see a change. "I'm sorry you've having problems with that. Is there anything that might help? You could try a meditation technique, or you could watch something on TV to distract yourself."

"She's in the hospital," Zachary said. He pulled out his phone and looked at the screen. "I don't know whether everything is okay."

Kenzie walked into the living room and sat down on the couch. She put her feet up beside her and pulled a blanket around her. She was so tired. But she couldn't go back to sleep while Zachary was in this state. She needed to help him to sort it out.

"How do you know she's in the hospital? Did Gordon tell you that?"

He slid the phone back into his pocket and shook his head. "No."

Kenzie's stomach clenched. Gordon hadn't told him. She highly doubted that Bridget would have told him. That meant that he knew some other way. By personal observation.

"How do you know, then?"

"She collapsed. She had to go to the hospital in an ambulance. I don't know what that means for her or the babies."

"How do you know she collapsed?" He hadn't remotely tracked her car to the hospital. That really left only one answer.

Zachary ran his hand through his hair, frowning. "I saw her."

"When? Tonight? Were you out just now, after bed?" If he had been taking off after she was asleep, that was new behavior. At least, she believed it was. It could have been going on for some time. How would she know the difference? She could check the security logs on her burglar alarm. See whether he had been deactivating the alarm to leave the house late at night. But she didn't want to be monitoring him. She didn't want to snoop through security alarm logs to see whether he were telling her the truth or not.

"Not tonight. Earlier. This afternoon." He swallowed hard and kept pacing, not looking at her. Probably not wanting to see any judgment in her eyes. "She was out in the garden. By herself. She just... she fell down and didn't get back up again." He chewed on his lip. Kenzie saw a fleck of blood. "I watched for her to get up again, and she didn't."

"So what happened?" Kenzie prompted. She could see him in her mind's eye, rushing into the garden, holding her head in his lap and trying to wake her. Calling 9-1-1.

"I called Gordon. He called for an ambulance." He met her eyes. "I didn't go into the yard. I just told him."

It must have been excruciating for him, but he had tried to follow the rules. Never to go onto her property, even though he knew she was in medical distress.

"So Gordon knows that you were watching her."

"Yes."

"And he didn't hire you again, did he? To keep an eye on things? You just did this on your own?"

He nodded. "I was just checking. Making sure that she was okay. I knew she would be alone."

"But you know you're not supposed to."

"Yes."

He resumed his pacing. Kenzie thought about the timeline. If Bridget had collapsed in her garden in the afternoon, then probably twelve hours had passed since then, with no word back from Gordon as to how she was doing. No wonder Zachary was so anxious.

"I would invite you to come sit and cuddle…" She patted the spot on the couch next to her.

"I can't sit," he said ruefully. She had known that he wouldn't be able to. She couldn't cuddle and comfort him. That wouldn't solve his problem.

"Did you message Gordon? Ask him to let you know how she was?"

"Yes."

And he still hadn't gotten back to Zachary. Gordon was usually considerate and tolerated Zachary's interest in Bridget as if he weren't threatened by it. She didn't think that he would hold back information maliciously, because he was angry with Zachary for spying on Bridget when he knew he wasn't supposed to. If Bridget had suffered a medical emergency, he would be grateful to Zachary for having seen it and for letting him know. He might not give out any details about Bridget's condition, but he would let Zachary know that all was well.

"It's been a long time if it was fainting spell," Kenzie said. "I would expect them to give her fluids and put her in a bed or send her home within a few hours. Maybe run some tests to make sure it wasn't anything serious. But it *isn't* a long timeline if she's gone into labor."

16

Zachary stopped walking at looked at Kenzie. "It isn't?" he asked hopefully.

"No. Labor and delivery can last for hours. Eighteen, twenty-four, thirty-six... It isn't as if she just skinned her knee and they put a bandage on it and send her on her way. If Gordon hasn't texted you back, he is probably in the delivery room with her, with his phone turned off. And that doesn't mean that there is anything wrong. It just takes a long time sometimes."

Zachary considered this. His eyes were far away. "I don't remember... with my mom... I don't remember it taking that long."

"Some women are faster. And subsequent deliveries are usually faster than a woman's first. You were the third child, right?"

He nodded.

"So you might not remember when Tyrrell was born. And the youngest children, her fifth and sixth, might have come quite quickly. And you probably didn't even know she was in labor for the first few hours. Having had a few, she might just keep working. Or maybe she just laid down for a while. But you wouldn't tell your six-year-old that you were in labor. Probably. Maybe 'Mommy is sick' or 'Mommy needs you to be quiet so she can have a nap.'"

Zachary scratched his chin, thinking about that. "She didn't talk like that," he informed her with a wry smile.

From what Zachary had told Kenzie about his mother, probably more along the lines of "Shut up, you little monster! Get out of the house or I'll tan your behind."

Kenzie sighed. She shifted, pulling the comfy, warm blanket close to her. "Anyway, regardless of how quickly your mother delivered, it's not unusual for a woman's first delivery to take twenty-four hours or longer."

He took a few steps into the kitchen, turned around, and returned to the spot he had been standing in. "So I shouldn't expect to hear anything yet."

"No. Probably not. Gordon not calling you isn't a sign that something went terribly wrong. Just that he had to turn off his phone while he was in the hospital, and she is probably in labor and delivery. And could be for another day."

Zachary let out a long sigh of relief. "Nothing is wrong," he said aloud, attempting to soothe himself and to make his brain believe what she was saying. "There's nothing wrong. She's just having the babies."

"She was getting close to her due date, wasn't she?"

"I don't know her exact due date," Zachary said, but he was nodding his head slightly. Maybe he didn't, but maybe he did. "But she was pretty big. And it's been…" He thought back. "She was in the hospital with morning sickness, back when I was in…"

Kenzie counted the months in her head. It sounded about right. "Twins are often a little premature. There isn't always space for them to grow to full term. They have probably given her steroids to develop their lungs, so that they'll have a better chance of being able to breathe on their own, even if they are a few weeks premature."

"So they'll be okay."

"It's impossible to predict anything with confidence. But we don't have any reason to believe that there is anything wrong with either Bridget or the babies."

"Other than…"

Kenzie nodded. "Other than Huntington's. It doesn't activate until later in life; the babies will have a perfectly normal childhood."

Zachary paced back and forth thinking about that. He didn't say out loud that it wouldn't be a normal life with their mother already suffering Huntington's symptoms, but Kenzie couldn't reassure him in that respect. It was better if she just didn't mention it.

"Does that help? Do you want to sit down and cuddle for a while or watch TV? If you know not to expect anything tonight, can you settle down?"

"I don't know."

He went to the fridge and poured himself a glass of water. At least he wasn't drinking coffee. She didn't understand how he could drink coffee at night and expect to be able to go to sleep. But he said it relaxed him, and she knew that a mild stimulant could help someone with ADHD rein in his restless thoughts.

Zachary drank one glass and poured another, then joined Kenzie on the couch. He bounced around for a bit, trying to calm down and find a comfortable position. Kenzie leaned toward him and tried rubbing his back and shoulders. She closed her eyes and lengthened out her breathing. If his breathing became entrained to the slow rhythm of hers, it might help him to slow down and relax.

"It's all okay," she assured him.

Elbows on his knees, Zachary put his face in his hands and rubbed the muscles around his eyes. He was undoubtedly exhausted. "I'm sorry about going over there again."

"Are you?" Kenzie asked. "I would think that you'd be happy you went over there, since you were able to get her help when she needed it. There was no one else with her and she couldn't exactly call for help herself when she was unconscious."

"Gordon said she had a fall alarm. It had already beeped him and he was trying to call her back to talk to her. So… he would have been calling emergency to help her anyway, even if I hadn't called."

Kenzie nodded and didn't say anything. He couldn't see her, with his hands over his face.

"I was glad I was there," he admitted. "But I'm sorry I… broke your trust."

"If you try your best, that should be good enough," Kenzie said neutrally. She preferred not to tell him how much it hurt that he had to keep going back to Bridget. They had already discussed it in therapy with Dr. B. and Zachary couldn't help that his brain kept going back there.

"It's never been good enough before."

Kenzie rubbed Zachary's back some more. She couldn't tell whether it was helping him at all. But at least he wasn't pulling away from her or telling her to stop.

In the morning, when they had both had some sleep, their emotions would not be so raw. Zachary was bound to be more depressed and Kenzie more annoyed and disappointed when they were tired. Tiredness amplified negative emotions. Her mother had always told her "Wait until morning. Everything always looks better in the morning."

But for her to feel better in the morning, she would have to have some sleep before then.

17

Dr. Wiltshire looked at Kenzie's face in the morning, then down at his large coffee. Maybe regretting the fact that he hadn't bought Kenzie a coffee that morning as well, as he sometimes did when he knew they were going to have a more than usually difficult day.

"Kenzie. Good morning. Are you… feeling all right?"

"If I look bad enough for you to notice, then you can assume I am not."

"Well, it's not that," he lied.

Kenzie shook her head. She had done her best to camouflage the bags under her eyes and the tired lines across her forehead and around her mouth. But there was too much to hide her state. It was still obvious to Dr. Wiltshire, who was not the most observant person she knew.

"Are you sick? You should have stayed home," he reprimanded gently.

"No, just tired. We didn't sleep very well last night." Kenzie grimaced at the *we*, which had slipped out inadvertently. She didn't mean to imply that it was Zachary's fault or suggest that they had been kept up by amorous activities. She felt that he needed an explanation. "We have friends who are expecting twins. She went into labor last night, and we were both a little too wound up to get much sleep."

"Oh, I see," Dr. Wiltshire gave her a big smile. "Well, congratulations on the imminent arrivals. Is everything going okay?"

"Don't know. That's one of the things that kept us awake. I'm sure that everything is fine, but phones have to be turned off in the hospital, and I

935

wouldn't expect him to be calling us during labor and delivery anyway. But you know how babies make you wait."

"Yes, they do," Dr. Wiltshire agreed. "Well, maybe if we don't have too much land on our desks today, you can sneak out early. Get in a nap and be refreshed for the evening."

"I'll try," Kenzie agreed. It sounded like a great idea. She didn't know whether she'd be able to leave early. But if she were too exhausted to work and made mistakes, that would be worse than cutting her hours short. Mistakes would cause a lot more trouble than being late on a deadline or taking an extra day to release a death certificate or a body.

But Dr. Wiltshire hadn't been there for an hour when he informed Kenzie that they were expecting two bodies in that afternoon. Both were exhumations of Dr. Philemon's former patients. The first two families that he had been able to talk into signing off on an exhumation so it didn't have to be ordered by the state's attorney. It would be a lot easier to keep it quiet and out of the media if they were able to do it privately.

It was fitting that both of them would come in when Kenzie felt like the walking dead herself.

Kenzie glanced at the caller ID and saw that it was Agent Menendez.

"Hi, Josie."

"Kenzie. I just wanted to call and make sure that you got my bodies."

"*Your* bodies?" Kenzie repeated.

"Darling and Scott. The ones that we got exhumation approvals on."

"I know who you mean… but they're not exactly *your* bodies," Kenzie pointed out. In fact, the FBI had no claim to them. They had been released by the families to the Medical Examiner's Office, not to the FBI. Dr. Wiltshire would report any findings to them, but the bodies themselves were the property of the families, on loan to the ME's Office.

"No, they're not mine!" Menendez agreed. "I didn't mean it literally. Just wanted to make sure that they had arrived."

"Yes. They are both here. Dr. Wiltshire and I will be looking them over this afternoon, preparing samples to be tested."

"I don't suppose you can tell anything by looking at them."

"They are well-preserved. We shouldn't have any problem finding poison. If they were poisoned and if the poison doesn't have a short half-life."

"But they'll be like Mr. Michaels. You found the potassium in his system."

"If it is the same poison, we'll find it. But there's no guarantee that the killer, if there is a serial killer, will use the same substance on every victim."

"That's the way it works, though. Serial killers use the same method each time. It's what makes them serial killers."

"No… I've been reading up on Angel of Death killers, and they often vary their methods. It isn't the method that makes them serial killers, it's the fact that they kill repeatedly."

"Those are exceptions. In all the well-known cases, the killer used the same method each time."

"People only recognized it as the work of a serial killer if they used the same method repeatedly. They couldn't identify a serial killer if they varied their methods. But Angel of Death killers sometimes confess to their crimes, and they have often varied their method from one victim to another to avoid detection."

"Hmm." Menendez sounded unconvinced. "All the cases that I've studied, the killer has used the same method."

"What about the Golden State Killer? DNA shows that he operated in various areas around California and used different methods at different times. They couldn't tie them all together until they could match the DNA."

"That's one exception."

"That is just one example. Anyway, if the killer uses potassium chloride in all cases, then we will be able to find it. If he or she used insulin sometimes, we won't find it. That's a popular method. And if they used smothering or an air embolism, we won't find those either. So it depends. We'll do our best to find any foreign substances or anything else that confirms that they didn't die of natural causes or of the illness that they were being treated for, but there's no guarantee. There isn't even a guarantee that any of these other cases *are* murder. If something like this had happened to a patient of mine… I'd be paranoid about any other death that seemed the least bit out of the ordinary or unexpected. Dr. Philemon put together a pretty extensive list. But that doesn't mean that all of them were victims of an Angel of Death killer. He's just looking back and worrying over these previous cases."

There was silence from Menendez for a few minutes. Kenzie was beginning to wonder whether she had insulted the woman or the connection had been broken.

"Josie?"

"We're counting on you and Dr. Wiltshire, Kenzie. We're counting on you to produce the evidence that this is a serial killing."

"To find evidence, you mean," Kenzie said. "If the evidence is there. It isn't like you want us to manufacture evidence."

Again, there was a lengthy silence. Kenzie was getting uncomfortable with the situation.

"You need to follow your professional requirements," Menendez said eventually. "And your conscience. We need to catch this person. We can't let her keep killing. Men and women are at risk. We need to track her down and prove what is happening before it is too late."

"Yes. And we will. If the evidence is there."

"Just think about it," Menendez cautioned. "Think about all of the vulnerable patients under Dr. Philemon's care before you go into autopsy. And then you find what we're looking for."

"I'll let you know the results as soon as we have them," Kenzie promised. She hung up the phone firmly. She sat looking at it, feeling like she needed to wash her hands.

"Was that Agent Menendez?" Dr. Wiltshire asked, coming from the suite of offices into Kenzie's reception area. Kenzie wondered how much he had overheard.

"Yeah. That was her. And I think she just told me to manufacture evidence that each of these patients was killed by the same person and in the same way as Mr. Michaels."

Dr. Wiltshire raised his brows. "Really." He took a deep breath and let it out. "I have been getting a vibe from her. I didn't want to believe that it was true, but…"

"So I'm not just imagining it or being dense, right? She did… want us to prove her theory. Whatever it takes."

"But we're not going to," Wiltshire said firmly. "We will follow the evidence."

Kenzie nodded her agreement. She was glad they were both on the same page. Of course Kenzie wanted to catch the serial killer, if there was one, just as much as Josie Menendez did. But she wasn't willing to go to any lengths to secure an arrest and conviction as Menendez seemed to be suggesting.

18

Kenzie was glad to get out of the autopsy and into the fresh, crisp December air when they were finished examining the bodies of the two potential victims and gathering samples. She drove from garage to garage, so it wasn't as if she were outside for a stroll, but it was still much nicer to be breathing the air in the underground parking and the air that filled her own garage when she raised the door than it was to be breathing the putrefying scents of the two bodies.

Zachary was sitting at the kitchen table. He didn't generally work at the kitchen table, and he certainly didn't eat there unless Kenzie cajoled him into it. His back was to the door. She touched him on the shoulder as she entered.

"Zach? Everything okay?"

Zachary breathed for a minute before answering. He didn't pull away from her, and she could feel the tension in his body as he sat there. Not relaxing and hanging out, that was for sure.

"Pretty rough day," he said finally.

"Yeah?" Kenzie rubbed his shoulder and slid her hand over to the back of his neck to rub it as well. "What's going on? Still worrying about Bridget?"

"She had the babies," Zachary offered. His voice was flat and without emotion. If she didn't know him better, she would assume that it didn't mean anything to him. That it was news he felt he should pass on to her, but not something that he was personally connected to. But Kenzie knew that he only spoke that way when he had pulled back from his feelings. When he was trying very hard to separate himself from the pain and to feel nothing at all.

She sat down at the table and put her purse down beside her. She didn't take off her coat or go to the fridge to get a bite to eat. Nothing that would distract her attention from him.

"You want to tell me about it? Is Bridget okay? The babies?" For once, she didn't feel the stab of jealousy when she talked to him about Bridget. She wasn't worried about whether Zachary was attracted to his ex more than he was to Kenzie. She needed to reach Zachary in the dark corner of himself that he had walled off. There was a real, physical pain in her chest as she gripped Zachary's arm and tried to give him some kind of comfort and relief from his distress.

"She's recovering well. Gordon said she was a champ."

Kenzie nodded and waited. Zachary swallowed. After sitting in stillness and silence for a few minutes, he reached into his pocket to pull out his phone. He thumbed it on and turned the screen to Kenzie so she could see the picture. Two tiny babies in an incubator. Both around four pounds, Kenzie guessed, both with respirator tubes affixed to their faces, wearing impossibly tiny diapers and hats.

"They both survived," Kenzie said, pointing out the good news. Despite all that modern medicine had to offer, people still lost infants in childbirth. Especially twins and preemies. Gordon had the money to get Bridget whatever medical treatment she needed, but he hadn't been able to prevent her falls while she was pregnant, her collapse in the garden—whatever that had been caused by—or the expanded form of the Huntington's disease gene that the twins had inherited. Money couldn't prevent medical problems.

Zachary nodded. He was looking down, his expression difficult for Kenzie to see or to interpret.

"Did he say what the doctor told them? About the babies' condition?"

"They are 'guardedly optimistic.'"

"Well, that's good. They aren't in critical condition. Even though they're on respirators now, that doesn't mean that they won't recover. They may just need support for a day or two until they are able to breathe on their own."

"They're so tiny."

"Yes. It would be better if they were bigger. But they are not micro-preemies. They have a good chance of survival. Maybe with no ill effects."

Kenzie squeezed Zachary's hand, trying to connect with him. To get some feedback that he understood and believed what she was telling him. He didn't squeeze back or look at her.

"They'll be in the hospital for a few days," Kenzie said. "But they will go home. When they are breathing on their own and are up to five pounds or so, Gordon and Bridget will be able to bring them home."

He said nothing.

"Is there another problem with them that you aren't telling me?" Kenzie asked.

He shook his head. "No. That's all I know. It was just a short message from Gordon, and I didn't think I should ask any more." He gave a shuddering sigh. "It's not my business. Not my family."

"No, you're right. You're doing really well, not pushing him for more. That must be hard."

He nodded his agreement. Kenzie could only imagine the struggle that must be going on in his brain. His brain told him that he needed to see her. It produced feel-good neurotransmitters when he did, reinforcing the message. Not engaging with Gordon or going to the hospital was the equivalent of a junkie in withdrawals refusing a fix rather than chasing it.

Zachary licked his lips and breathed in and out, his breath still shuddering and catching.

Kenzie gave his hand another squeeze. "Let me get you a drink of water."

She got up and went to the fridge to take out the water pitcher and pour him a glass. She opened the door of the fridge and reached for the pitcher, then froze in place.

What appeared to be every sharp kitchen knife she owned was piled on one of the refrigerator shelves.

19

Kenzie stood there for a moment, just staring at the glistening blades. Then she did what she had planned, pulling out the pitcher and pouring a tall glass of water for Zachary. She poured one for herself too. She put the pitcher back in the fridge and took both glasses back to the table. She sat down and positioned each of the glasses in easy reach.

Zachary picked his up and drained half of it in a few gulps.

"So… what's with the knives in the fridge?" Kenzie asked.

"It seemed like the safest place to put them."

"Why is that?"

"Because… I'm not hungry. So I wouldn't open the door and see them."

Kenzie looked at the empty butcher's blocks on the counter. Maybe there was something to be said for not displaying an array of knives in full view of a severely depressed person.

"You haven't said that you were having thoughts of self-harm."

He wiped his nose with the back of his hand, sniffling. "I… am."

"Okay. How bad is it?"

"I thought it was okay. Under control."

"But maybe not, now?"

"Maybe not."

"Have you had any sleep?"

"No."

"In how long?"

"I'm not sure. Maybe… three days."

"Maybe up to three, or maybe more than three?" Kenzie's heart was pounding, adrenaline coursing to every part of her body. Her partner was in danger. Yes, it was from himself, but he was still in danger. Just as if someone else were standing over him, threatening him with a knife.

"At least three," Zachary said after some consideration.

"Well, you know you're not supposed to let it go that long. Without sleep, your brain can't operate properly."

He mumbled something she couldn't hear.

"Do you want to take a pill and lie down?"

"It's too early."

"If you haven't slept in more than three days, then what time it is doesn't really matter. You should have said something."

He said nothing in response. Kenzie waited for a while in silence. Her instinct was to rush into things and to try to fix him. She would tell him all the things he was doing wrong if he wanted to maintain good mental health. Order him to sleep. Order him to take all the meds he'd been prescribed. And most of all, to put Bridget and her babies out of his mind. He needed to think of himself and his safety. He needed to think about how his actions affected Kenzie and the other people who loved him.

But she waited, letting all her impulses and criticisms flow through her until her brain was quiet enough to listen.

"What do you want to do?" she asked Zachary.

"Do you want me to call Dr. B?"

"If that's what you think you should do. Sure."

"Do you think she'll tell me to go to the hospital?"

"If you think you should go to the hospital, you don't need her to tell you that."

"Do you think I should?"

"I think that's your decision. If you think that you need to, you should. If you think you are going to harm yourself, then we should take action."

He rubbed a hand over his face. "You think I'll feel better if I can sleep?"

"I think you'll feel much better if you can get a good sleep. I don't know if that will be enough, but you can decide that yourself. Do you want to have a sleep and then see how you feel?"

He nodded.

Kenzie was relieved that he didn't say he needed to go to the hospital immediately. She knew he had checked himself in before, and she hoped that he wasn't to that point again. But if he were, then of course that was what she wanted him to do. A sleep was a good first step.

"Would you get me a pill?"

"Yes, sure. Just one? You're allowed to take two at a time, aren't you?"

"Yes… but I don't know whether I should. What if I don't wake up again when I should?"

"You should sleep as long as you can, not confine yourself to a certain time limit."

"But it could mess up my sleep schedule. My… rhythm thing."

"Circadian rhythm. Don't worry about that. We'll set up a schedule once you've had a nice long sleep. And we'll stick to it so that your sleep cycles are not thrown out of whack. I'll help, okay?"

"Okay."

"So can I get you two sleeping pills?"

"Yeah. I guess."

Kenzie left him at the table and went to the main bathroom to get his pills from the medicine cabinet. But when she opened it, the cabinet was nearly empty. None of his prescription pill bottles were there.

"Zachary?"

"Yeah?"

"Where did you put your pill bottles?" Maybe she should have checked the fridge.

"They're in your bathroom."

Zachary never used the ensuite bathroom attached to Kenzie's master bedroom. Unless he were sick and couldn't make it from the bed to the main bathroom. Kenzie went through her room and opened the door to the smaller bathroom, to find all the pill bottles in the sink.

They followed the practice of only getting small numbers of pills prescribed at a time, refilling them often, so that it would be harder for Zachary to overdose on an impulse. But it was a bit of a shock to see how many bottles there were. She needed to go through them and cull out the ones that Zachary wasn't taking anymore because they were older prescriptions or dosages. Or have Zachary do it when he felt up to it.

She sorted through the bottles for a few minutes before finding the prescribed sleep aids. She took out a couple of pills and then read the label and the warnings carefully. She also found his antidepressant and took one out. She took the three pills out to Zachary in the kitchen.

"I don't take the antidepressant again until nine," Zachary pointed out.

"Not usually, but you're going to be asleep at nine. And once you're asleep, I'm not going to wake you up. You need to get a good long rest to recover. So you're taking it now rather than having to skip a dose."

Zachary nodded. He knew that skipping even one dose of the antidepressant could cause him problems. He'd missed a dose while they were on vacation. It had taken a week to start feeling an improvement again, and she had counted them lucky. The destabilization could have lasted for a month or more, and they couldn't afford that so close to Christmas.

He drank down the three pills, draining his glass. He set it down. "I'd better use the john before falling asleep. Would you… get me another drink?"

"Sure."

She didn't want him opening the fridge and looking at the knives.

When Zachary returned from the bathroom, Kenzie looked him over, wondering if there were anything else she needed to worry about. He'd already moved the two biggest temptations out of sight, which showed that he was thinking and was aware that they might be too much of a temptation if he had to look at them. Was there anything else that she should put away? Anything that he might have on him that could be dangerous if she weren't in the same room with him?

She was glad that he wasn't a hard-boiled PI like those on the old movies. A firearm in the house would be a very bad idea.

"Do you want to cuddle on the bed or sit on the couch?"

"I'll try the bed."

She knew he must be very tired, but he didn't look much worse than usual. She was too used to the dark shadows under his eyes and the sunken cheeks he tried to camouflage with his growth of whiskers. They retired to the bedroom, Zachary taking his glass of water with him to put on the nightstand. He didn't bother undressing for bed. Maybe because he still felt it was too early to be going to sleep. Maybe because he couldn't summon the energy. He lay down on the bed, facing the window, his back to Kenzie's side of the bed. She lay behind him and rubbed his shoulders and back for a few minutes before putting her arms around him and snuggling up against his back.

"Everything is fine now," she told him. "You just need some sleep, and you'll feel better when you've had it. Everything will look better when you wake up again."

He shifted. "Will it?" His voice didn't sound confident or hopeful.

"Yes. Everything seems worse when you're tired, and you are exhausted. Your brain is too tired to deal with anything. It will seem more manageable after you've caught up on some sleep."

He didn't express his doubt about this, but Kenzie still knew he was thinking it. She snuggled up so that her face was next to his neck and cheek, and concentrated on long, deep breathing. It wasn't long before she was drifting off to sleep.

20

Kenzie knew she had been asleep for a couple of hours when her consciousness finally forced itself to the surface. She moved slowly and carefully, withdrawing from Zachary. She had fallen asleep with her arms around him, and her hand was asleep as a result. She listened to Zachary's even breaths in the dark room. Hopefully, he would sleep all the way through the night, maybe even into the next morning. If he hadn't slept for three or four days, he needed a lot of hours to be functional again.

She left the room quietly. She woke up her phone after returning to the kitchen and glanced through the notifications on the screen. She swiped a text from Gordon. It was brief, but telling.

How is Zachary?

Kenzie texted him back. *Sleeping now. Hope he didn't bother you too much. Any update on the girls?*

There was no answering text or "message read" notation. He was probably back inside the hospital, his phone dutifully turned off while he sat with Bridget or the babies.

She was relieved that the babies had been born. Hopefully, that would ease Zachary's anxiety about Bridget's health and help him to resist the impulse to follow her. If the babies didn't have any setbacks, they would be out of the hospital in a couple of weeks and he could stop worrying about them too. Kenzie wasn't sure why Zachary was so concerned for the babies. It wasn't just because they were Bridget's. Another man, pining after his ex-wife, would be put off by her pregnancy and not interested in her offspring by another man. But Zachary still seemed to be hanging on to the fantasy that he'd had when they were married of raising children with her. Maybe it was partially the being separated from his siblings when he was ten. He and the older girls had helped to care for and raise the younger children, so the loss of his younger siblings was akin to the loss of his own children. And he was still trying to recreate that bond with someone else.

Kenzie rifled through the fridge and pulled out random leftovers. She didn't have the energy to make anything. Even warming up a frozen dinner or ordering in felt like it would take too much energy. She could eat cold pasta and vegetables dipped in salad dressing. That would have to do for her supper. She sent out another text, this one to Dr. B.

Zachary in crisis. May need to be admitted.

The response from Dr. Boyle was swift. *You both know what to do. Don't wait too long.*

Sleeping now. Apparently hasn't slept last 3-4 days.

Good if he can sleep at home. Keep me apprised.

Kenzie texted back a thumbs-up, and considered whether there was anyone else she should call or message. Lorne Peterson, Zachary's old foster father and the closest thing to a loving parent that he had, would want to know of any developments. But he knew it was a bad time of year for Zachary and that he was going through a depressive cycle already. Unless Zachary were admitted to the hospital, there wasn't really anything new to tell him.

Tyrrell? The same applied to him. And Kenzie was a little leery of putting any extra burden on Zachary's younger brother. The Christmas season was difficult for him too. As he was a recovering alcoholic who may or may not have had a recent slip, Kenzie didn't want to push him.

She would let Heather know if Zachary slept through the next day. Since she worked with Zachary, she would expect to hear from him and would need to be informed in case there were deadlines to be met between them.

Kenzie was feeling better after having something to eat. It was several hours past when she normally ate supper, so her body had not been happy with her. Add to that the hours standing in the odoriferous autopsy, and it was no wonder she still had a headache despite her nap. Now she had the rest of the evening to entertain herself, since Zachary would not, she hoped, be getting up again before the next morning.

She had jinxed herself by thinking about having free time to do whatever she wanted to. Her phone rang and, looking down at the screen, Kenzie saw that it was not Gordon or one of Zachary's family members, but Agent

Menendez. Who of course wanted to know what they had found in the autopsies.

Kenzie drew in a deep breath and let it back out. She answered the call. "Josie. Hi."

"I was expecting a call from you, Kenzie!"

"Someone will get back to you in due time. We need to wait for the transcription of the autopsy audio and Dr. Wiltshire needs to draft his summary report. We were in autopsy most of the day."

"That doesn't keep you from giving me the unofficial news."

Kenzie sighed. "There isn't much to report. We have sent samples off to the labs for analysis and won't have the results for a few days. There wasn't anything remarkable about either of the bodies."

"That means that you can't tell whether they were poisoned until you get the lab results back."

"That's right."

"You said that sometimes Angel of Death killers use smothering or other methods."

"Yes."

"Did you find any indication of that? Smothering?"

"Smothering, unfortunately, does not leave many signs. I know that on TV, there is always petechial hemorrhaging, bruising around the mouth, and fibers in the throat or lungs. But in real life… you don't always see those signs. You might see nothing at all."

"Then how can you make a determination?"

"Like I said, a lot of times, you can't tie deaths to a serial killer until they confess. If they're careful… it might be impossible to figure that out without their confession."

"Well, considering we don't even have a suspect yet, much less a confession…" Menendez said irritably.

"I know. It's still early days. These things take time."

Menendez muttered. "I understand that. This isn't my first rodeo."

In which case, Kenzie couldn't see why she was so impatient and worked up. She had to understand that a case like that was solved over weeks and months, not days.

"We will let you know when we know something. Maybe there will be something in the lab tests. We just have to wait and see."

"My boss said that Dr. Wiltshire has a very good reputation."

"Yes, he does." Kenzie wasn't sure where Menendez was going with the comment.

"I just wonder whether he's really putting all of his effort into this case."

"Of course he is!" Kenzie was indignant. She couldn't believe the nerve of the FBI agent, suggesting that Dr. Wiltshire might be falling down on the job. He always did his best. They might have a very small office compared to the big cities, but Dr. Wiltshire was very professional and diligent in all his work.

"I would think that he would be able to keep me apprised of developments without me chasing him down. And that when he did an autopsy, he would be able to actually tell me what the person died from." Her voice, though light, was biting.

"Listen," Kenzie said. "It isn't my fault or Dr. Wiltshire's that you have unreasonable expectations. Maybe that is just because of your inexperience. But you need to back off and wait. We will let you know what we find out when we have had the time to do a full investigation. How are you doing on screening the hospital staff and the others in Dr. Philemon's practice?"

"No one with a criminal record or any significant complaints to the Medical Board. But there really isn't a place to report nurses, volunteers, or janitorial staff. I need access to all their personnel files, and there is no centralized place for that. I can look at Dr. Philemon's HR records, but they are sparse. Doctors aren't actually very good at screening and hiring and the administrative stuff. Some of them, we don't even know what their last job was, let alone who to contact about getting their previous records. Even why they were terminated or left."

"So you still have plenty to do," Kenzie pointed out.

"I'm fully aware of my job. I just need you to do yours."

"We are," Kenzie said tightly.

Mendendez's sigh carried over the phone lines. "I'm sorry. I don't mean to be so hard-nosed. But I'm getting a lot of pressure to show some progress on this case."

"It isn't our problem if your superiors have unreasonable expectations."

"I know. And I appreciate that you guys did both autopsies today, as soon as you could, when you probably had other work to do."

"Yeah. We were there late. And we do have families and personal responsibilities. We don't spend twenty-four hours at the office."

"Tell me about it," Menendez agreed with a laugh. "I don't know the last time I actually went out on a date…"

She left space at the end of her words, as if expecting Kenzie to chime in with her personal issues or talk of her social life.

"If that's everything," Kenzie said evenly, "I need some time to relax before bed."

"Dr. Wiltshire said that you were married to a private investigator? What's that like?"

"Not married. And really, I don't want to chat about it right now. Maybe we can share war stories some other time. But not tonight. I need some time and space tonight."

"Things not going well?" Menendez asked sympathetically. "I don't hear any TV in the background, so maybe he's off on surveillance somewhere? Leaves you alone a lot at night, does he?"

Kenzie shook her head in disbelief. "Talk to you later, Agent Menendez. I'll call you Monday if we know something."

She didn't wait for any further inquiries from Menendez, and quickly ended the call.

21

Kenzie considered her course of action. She didn't normally communicate with Dr. Wiltshire during her off time, but she thought the situation warranted it. She first planned to text him, but then decided that text would probably not communicate her tone, and she didn't want him to misunderstand her reasons for calling him. She thought through several scripts, and then called him.

"Dr. Wiltshire, I'm sorry to call you at home…"

"Kenzie. What can I do for you?" He sounded friendly, not irritated with her calling him on his personal time.

"I just wanted to give you a heads-up… Agent Menendez called me tonight and was pushing hard for the results of the autopsies. I told her that we wouldn't have the lab tests back yet for a few days, and that we hadn't found anything obvious on the examinations… she's making a lot of noise about us being unprofessional… I don't know. She's a very… eager investigator. She wants results, and she wants them now, even if that isn't the way that the real world works."

"Ah." She could almost see Dr. Wiltshire's familiar nod of understanding. "She has been a little troublesome. I suspect she is probably getting a lot of pressure from her superiors to make some headway on the case. Show that it is a serial killer or shut it down so they don't have to waste resources on it."

"Yeah, she said her superiors were pressuring her."

"Don't worry about it. Just handle it as you would any inquiry from the public. We will publish our report when we have satisfied ourselves as to the cause of death. Until then, it is in the works.”

“Okay. That's basically what I told her, but she's very… persistent.”

“I have noticed,” he agreed dryly.

Kenzie snickered. “Oh, and… don't share anything about my personal life. She keeps asking about medical appointments, how I spend my time, Zachary, all that. She's not my girl friend and I don't feel like sharing anything personal.”

“I haven't said anything.”

“She said that you told her I was married to a private investigator.”

“Hmm. I'm pretty sure I didn't say married. I might have mentioned Zachary in passing, talking about the Salter case. There are similarities between what happened with Robin Salter and an Angel of Death case. Two different sides of the same coin.”

“Well, she's picked up on it. Wants to know what he's doing tonight. If I'm alone. It's kind of creepy, to be honest.”

“Do you want me to talk to her superiors? Have them speak with her about maintaining professional distance?”

“Not yet. But if she keeps it up…”

“I'll be more aware of it. Sorry if I caused you any trouble.”

“No, it's okay. Normally it wouldn't be an issue. But she seems to… have some problems with boundaries.”

“Yes. Changing the subject, if we're done with this one…”

“Yeah, that's everything I wanted to say.”

“I'm wondering how Zachary is. You've seemed distracted lately. I know you were worrying about him before Halloween and said that Christmas was a bad time. Is everything okay…?”

Kenzie tried to think of what to say. She did not want her home life to interfere with her job. But she also didn't want to lie to Dr. Wiltshire or to say that everything was fine, only to call him on Monday to say that she needed to take a personal day because Zachary had been admitted to the hospital.

“Confidentially and as a friend,” Dr. Wiltshire said. “No notes on your personnel record. Your work is stellar, as always.”

“Well…” Kenzie blew out her breath. “A bit of a crisis this week. I told you that we had a sleepless night last night. It turns out that Zachary's had a few more than that, and he was in pretty bad shape tonight. He may need to be admitted to the hospital psych ward. I'm not sure yet. Going to see how he is over the weekend.”

“Oh, I'm sorry to hear that. Are you okay?”

"I've had a nap, so I'm good now. He fell asleep and will hopefully get a good number of hours in before he's up. Sometimes when he crashes, it could be ten or twelve hours, or more."

"And… are you safe? Some people can get violent when they are in a crisis."

"Oh, I'm fine. Nothing like that. I've never seen Zachary do anything more violent than to grab someone, and only when I was in danger. He's not a violent person."

"No weapons in the house?"

Kenzie thought about the knives in the fridge and gave a slight chuckle. "No."

"Okay. Sorry to be an old man fussing over it, but when you've seen as many bodies come through the office as I have…"

Kenzie had only been there for a couple of years, but she noticed how many of the deaths were related to domestic violence. She appreciated Dr. Wiltshire for being straightforward enough to ask and make sure she was safe.

"Thanks for caring. No, I'm only concerned about Zachary's safety, not my own. And hopefully… he'll be able to cope better once he has slept."

"Good. You let me know if there is anything I can do to help. Anything. And just give me a heads-up if you're going to need Monday off or come in late."

"I will."

"And I won't mention it to Agent Menendez!"

"Yeah. Just tell her I'm out in the field. That should get her nice and wound up!"

Dr. Wiltshire laughed. "Take care, Kenzie. Talk later."

Kenzie followed up her cold supper with a helping of ice cream. Maybe hot chocolate would have been more appropriate for a chilly December night, but she liked her ice cream, and there were a few flavors in the freezer to choose from. She really needed to finish one of them off to make room in the freezer for other things. So, putting an old movie on the TV, she curled up under one of the throw blankets on the couch and used Zachary's portable computer desk as a table for her treat.

She was awakened later by the buzzing of her phone. She hadn't even realized that she was still tired enough to drop off again, but she had clearly fallen asleep at some point during the movie. Maybe she should have gone back to bed with Zachary after eating dinner.

Kenzie rubbed a crick in her neck and focused on her phone. She touched the screen to wake it up, unsure whether it had been ringing a moment before or whether it was vibrating from other notifications. She saw a text from Gordon.

Baby 1 holding her own. Baby 2 fluid on lungs. Praying she'll make it through the night.

Kenzie's heart went out to Gordon and Bridget. As much as she disliked Zachary's ex-wife, she wouldn't wish a critically sick newborn on anyone.

So sorry, Kenzie texted back. *Will hope for the best.*

Thank you. Zachary ok?

Still sleeping. Will see what morning brings.

Two different vigils being kept through the night. Kenzie was glad their positions were not reversed. But she did worry about how Zachary would take it if he knew that one of the babies had taken a downturn. Or if they lost her in the night. He had been so concerned with Bridget's unborn children right from the start, behaving as though he were responsible for keeping them safe.

Kenzie didn't really believe in God or religion, but she couldn't help reaching out mentally to the universe, pleading that Baby 2 would pull through.

After checking her mail and making sure she hadn't missed any important calls, Kenzie changed for bed and crawled in beside Zachary. She pulled a light blanket over him, but didn't want to make him too hot, as he didn't normally wear much to bed. She didn't want to wake him up by causing him to overheat.

In the morning, when she awoke, the room was light, testifying to the fact that she had slept late. And Zachary was still there beside her.

She held her breath and listened for a moment to make sure that she could hear him breathing. His respirations were long and slow, a sign that he probably wouldn't wake for a while yet. She whispered a good morning and luxuriated for a while beside him, enjoying their closeness and the fact that she didn't have to hurry out to work or to run any errands. It was rare for her not to have a list of things to do. But for once, the thing that was at the top of her list was to ensure that Zachary slept for as long as possible and that he was okay when he got up.

She eventually got up and had her morning shower. She dusted, then cleaned the bathrooms, but did not run the vacuum cleaner, which she feared would wake Zachary. There were no further texts on her phone, so she didn't know how the two babies had fared through the night. As she cleaned, she thought about the autopsies, about Mr. Michaels, and about how an Angel of Death killer would think and feel and how they would operate.

If an Angel of Death killer was that hard to catch, then how were they going to catch him? Would it be the killer's signature? Tabulating who was on the floor with every death that they could connect to him? And what if he weren't a nurse, but was someone who wouldn't be tracked through the medical charts? A volunteer, janitor, security guard, or someone she hadn't even thought of? The water boy? A flower delivery person?

Who else could walk in and out of the unit without even being noticed? It was something she could bounce off of Zachary. He was good at hiding in plain sight. Using his homeless appearance so that people looked away in disgust or to avoid being asked for money. No eye contact, keep moving on… and five minutes later, they couldn't even tell you that he had been there, let alone describe him. That wouldn't work in a hospital, where a homeless man wandering around the floor would be obvious, but there had to be other people whose comings and goings were so ubiquitous that no one even saw them.

Kenzie heard movements from the bedroom and left what she was doing to check in on Zachary.

"Hey, sleepyhead. How are you feeling now?"

Zachary made a face. He wiped his eyes and scratched his head. "Like something curled up in my mouth and died there." He saw that his glass of water was still sitting on the side table and picked it up, gulping down the first few swallows, and then swishing it around his mouth to get rid of the taste. He drank down a few more swallows and put the nearly-empty glass down.

"Ugh." He groaned and scrubbed his eyes with his fists before looking for his phone. He pulled the charge cord off and looked at the time. Kenzie saw him look toward the window to see what time of day it was. He cleared his throat and tried his gravelly voice once more. "It's noon?"

"Yeah. I'm thinking about making some lunch. What do you want?"

"Nothing. Need to take my meds."

There were a couple that he was supposed to take on an empty stomach. And then another that he was supposed to take with food once the nausea from the first couple died down enough to force something down.

"Right. Let me get them for you."

Kenzie went back to the ensuite bathroom, where she had lined the bottles up along the wall instead of leaving them all in the sink as Zachary had done. She needed to be able to wash up and brush her teeth, after all. She located the two early-morning pills and took them to him. It was late to be taking them, of course, but it was the lesser of two evils. He had needed the sleep more than to be awakened to take them.

"What day is it?"

"Saturday. You got about sixteen hours."

Zachary shook his head. "I never sleep that much."

"No. You really needed it. Starving your body of sleep is just as bad as starving it of food. Worse. You can't function without it. Why didn't you take a pill sooner?"

"Couldn't last night. The night before," he amended, trying to keep his days straight. "Not when… what if Gordon had called?"

"Why would Gordon call? He doesn't need a private investigator to help deliver his babies. If the babies had been born during the night and he had wanted to let you know—since clearly you had been asking—then he could have sent you a text and you could read it in the morning."

"I was too wound up. I couldn't have slept even if I had taken something that night."

Which was probably true. Someone like Zachary who was really determined to stay awake would, even with a full dose of the sleep aid. It could be overcome by strength of will. Or obsessive thoughts.

"You said it had been at least three days. Maybe four. So you had other opportunities to take a sleeping pill and get caught up. If you don't sleep at all one night, you *need* to take a sleeping pill the next."

Zachary scratched at the seam on his jeans, saying nothing.

Kenzie had to remember that reason didn't win all arguments. Especially not when dealing with mental illness and disordered thinking. Zachary had probably had a reason for not taking a sleeping pill that first night that had seemed perfectly reasonable to him, even if it didn't make sense to her. Or to him when he was having a better day.

She opened her mouth to ask him how he was feeling, to try to get a general idea of whether he would need to be admitted to the hospital. Then she forced it closed again. The man had just woken up. He wouldn't know how he felt yet. He had just taken his meds and nothing had kicked in yet. He probably felt pretty groggy and like he was hung over. It was not the time to ask, however much she would like to plan her day or the rest of the weekend.

"It's Saturday?" Zachary repeated.

"Yes."

"I think I lost a day. I didn't sleep a whole day, did I?"

"No. About sixteen hours," she told him again.

Zachary looked down at his phone and started scrolling through notifications. "Have you heard anything…?"

"I talked to Gordon last night. One of the babies was having trouble. I haven't heard anything this morning."

Zachary's right hand moved to his chest and clenched into a fist, like he was squeezing his own heart. "You don't know if she's okay?"

"Not yet. Unless he texted you. He hasn't texted or called me. If he stayed up all night with the baby, he might be sleeping now, so I don't want to call. He'll get back to us when he's ready to tell us something." She shook her head. "You're lucky that he's so open to communicating with you about it. Most men would not be talking to their wives' exes."

Zachary nodded. "Gordon's a good guy. But I was probably… over the line asking him."

"Maybe. But at least you were asking instead of going over there. So that's good."

Zachary shrugged.

"Why don't you have a shower, see if that makes you feel a bit better? I'm going to make myself some lunch."

He nodded. Kenzie backed out of the room and gave him some space.

22

Kenzie thought by Sunday morning that Zachary was doing pretty well, and that she would be able to get through the weekend without needing to take any further action. He would settle back into a proper sleep schedule, the worries over Bridget and the babies would fade, and he would immerse himself back into his business.

The house was quiet, and he had slept two nights in a row. Saturday afternoon, Gordon had gotten back to them to advise that both babies were still alive and getting stronger, and that Bridget would soon be allowed to go home.

Kenzie was just lying in bed, checking through her email and social networks and trying to avoid reading anything about politics or thinking of anything to do with work and the Angel of Death killings. She could almost convince herself that there was no Angel of Death, it was just one medical mistake or accident.

There was a crash in the kitchen, and Kenzie was out of bed in an instant, her heart pounding. "Zachary?"

"No!"

She hurried into the kitchen. The knives that he had previously stashed in the fridge—Kenzie hadn't thought of a better place to put them yet—were scattered across the floor. The crash she'd heard had been Zachary sweeping them all out at once. She looked at him in fear, expecting to find him holding one of the knives threateningly to his throat or wrists, or even worse, covered

959

in blood. But he appeared to be unharmed, just standing there looking angry and aggrieved, his skin chalky white.

"Are you okay. Are you hurt?"

"I'm fine!"

"Okay. Do you want to sit down? What's going on? Sit. You look like you're going to pass out."

He looked at the kitchen chairs and shook his head. Kenzie motioned to the living room. "On the couch? Please, tell me what's going on."

"My *stupid* brain!"

"Yeah. Okay. I'm going to pick these up and put them somewhere. You didn't cut yourself?"

He shook his head. Kenzie looked him over once more but could not see any blood or even small cuts.

"Please sit down. You may not be big, but I don't want to move bodies around on my day off. Sit down so I know you're not going to pass out. You can think about if you want to talk to me. Or Dr. B. I think… you need to talk. So you should sort out who you want to talk to and what you want to say."

He stood there for a moment in silence, glaring at her, then finally turned and went into the living room. Kenzie took several deep breaths to calm herself. Her heart was pounding hard and fast. She felt like she had been attacked. But Zachary wasn't angry at her. It was his own recalcitrant brain and emotions that he was frustrated with.

She gathered the knives slowly and laid them out on the counter to make sure that they were all accounted for. The knives from the butcher block. The set of steak knives. A couple of paring knives from the drawer. Then she took them all into the garage and put them into one of the file boxes with her old financial and school papers. She settled the lid and went back into the house.

Zachary was in the living room but had not sat down on the couch.

"Okay," Kenzie said, in as calm a voice as she could muster. "You want to talk?"

"I can't."

"What do you want to do, then?"

He clenched his teeth, making the muscles and tendons in his neck stand out. "Will you drive me to the hospital?"

"Sure. You want to take anything with you?"

"No."

"What about your prescriptions?"

"Dr. B will email the list to the hospital. They wouldn't let me take mine anyway."

Possibly patients tried to smuggle in drugs that they weren't supposed to be taking and pass them off as legitimate prescriptions. Kenzie nodded her acceptance of this.

"I'd drive myself, but then I have to pay for parking," Zachary explained. "Long-term parking at the hospital…" He shook his head.

Kenzie waited for him to joke that it cost an arm and a leg, but Zachary didn't.

"You probably shouldn't be driving right now anyway. If you don't need to bring anything, then let's go."

He followed her to the garage and slid into the driver's seat in the convertible without a word. Kenzie waited for an explanation. What he was thinking or feeling. If there had been a particular trigger. If he thought he needed a med review or evaluation or a longer-term admission.

She had hoped that she'd be able to keep him out of the hospital until Christmas. She'd really thought that she'd be able to do it. That if she were just careful about what Christmas reminders he was exposed to and encouraged open, nonjudgmental communication, things wouldn't get too bad.

It wasn't fair. It just wasn't fair.

She felt like throwing a pile of knives on the floor herself. Something loud and dramatic to show how frustrated *she* was. But she couldn't indulge herself. She had to be the strong one, giving Zachary whatever support he needed.

She swore under her breath.

Loud enough that Zachary could hear it, but not loud enough that he knew he was *supposed* to hear it and respond in some way.

At the hospital, she stood back as Zachary spoke with one of the triage nurses in emergency, explaining that he needed to be admitted. Kenzie had seen or heard of cases where people were turned away from the emergency room with the explanation that their depression was not bad enough and that they should go home and talk to their regular professionals for evaluation or medication changes. But the triage nurse hooked Zachary up to a monitor and switched her gaze between him and the monitor as they talked, jotting down notes about his appearance, vital signs, and what he told her, and apparently was convinced that he did, in fact, need to talk to someone in psych about possible admission. She gave Zachary a bracelet and instructed him to sit in the waiting room. She watched Zachary walk up to Kenzie, and after meeting Kenzie's eyes, the nurse nodded and called the next person waiting in the triage line.

Emergency room waits were always long and tedious. At least, as a patient or friend accompanying a patient who wasn't bleeding out. For a doctor, emergency medicine moved forward at a frantic pace, with one priority interrupting another, and then dealing with angry parents who brought a child to the ER because he was throwing up and then couldn't understand why everyone else saw the doctor ahead of him.

Zachary, usually busy with his computer or phone, sat in a chair and watched the silent TV hanging on the wall or the other patients waiting to be helped. He didn't even have a book. But then, Zachary had never been one to read for pleasure. His dyslexia and ADHD made that too difficult. He read what he had to for work but never could understand the joy that other people got out of reading fiction or exploring new concepts.

She was going to suggest that he find a game to play on his phone or message Rhys or give Lorne a call. But if he didn't have his phone in his hands, there was probably a good reason for it. She wasn't even sure whether he had brought it with him, or if he had left it behind at the house. She'd never seen him separated from his phone before, but if something on his phone had been causing more depression or distress, then he was undoubtedly right to stay off of it.

They had been there for a couple of hours, not saying more than half a dozen words to each other, when Zachary finally spoke.

"One of the babies had a heart attack. Or whatever you call it when it happens to a baby. A cardiac event."

Kenzie looked at him. "And…?"

"They got it going again. He said they're both on monitors that will ring if… their hearts go too fast or slow or in the wrong rhythm." He looked at her eyes to confirm he got this right.

Kenzie nodded.

"How can they be talking about Bridget going home? Doesn't she need to stay here with them?"

"She'll probably come back during the day to be with them. Express milk to feed them until they're big enough and strong enough to nurse. She's not going to abandon them."

Zachary swallowed. He stared down at his hands, too overcome with emotion to discuss it any further.

"Mackenzie Kirsch!"

Kenzie looked up, startled. Her first thought was that her mother was at the hospital. Few people other than her parents, still called her by her proper name.

A woman in a nursing smock bustled toward her. A middle-aged woman, her hair still blonde rather than gray, substantial, but not really overweight. It was her smile that Kenzie remembered. A broad, toothy, pleasant smile, both friendly and motherly. It took Kenzie a few seconds to place her, her mind going rapidly through her mental database to find where the woman belonged in time and place.

"Nurse…" Kenzie fumbled, unable to remember the woman's name. She had been one of Amanda's nurses. One that they had seen a number of times over the years as Amanda was readmitted to the nephrology unit for various kidney issues. Kenzie stood up to greet her. The woman got close enough for Kenzie to read her name tag. "Nurse Debbie! I can't believe it's you! How many years has it been?" Kenzie gave her a hug and received a firm squeeze in return.

"Oh, I don't think we want to be counting the years!" Nurse Debbie laughed. "How are you? I heard you went into medicine."

Kenzie nodded. "I did. I'm an MD now. I'm with the Medical Examiner's Office."

"Amazing!" Debbie looked Mackenzie over, shaking her head. "Not that I'm surprised, of course. You always were very quick to understand the medical issues and to pick up on nuances. You have a very quick mind."

Kenzie smiled, her face getting warm. "Thank you. Uh, Nurse Debbie, this is Zachary Goldman." Kenzie felt a little awkward introducing them. Zachary was sitting with his face in his hands and was clearly not in a place to be excited about meeting anyone. "Zachary, Debbie was one of my sister Amanda's nurses. Always took very good care of her."

Zachary peeled his hands away from his eyes to look Nurse Debbie in the face, and gave a smile that was more of a grimace.

"That's great," he said, forcing the words out. "It's nice to meet you."

Kenzie gave Debbie an apologetic look. Nurse Debbie might deserve a more enthusiastic greeting, but she wasn't going to get it when Zachary was feeling so bad.

"Zachary Goldman," Nurse Debbie repeated. She lifted the clipboard that she was carrying and looked at it. "Actually, it is you I'm here to see."

Zachary stared at her, uncomprehending.

"I'm with the psychiatric unit," Debbie explained. "I'm here to talk with you. Do your intake and get you admitted. Okay?"

Zachary looked at Kenzie, frowning. Maybe wondering whether she had somehow engineered things so that her old friend would be the one to do his intake. Kenzie just shrugged. It wasn't any of her doing. The meeting was serendipitous.

"Debbie will take good care of you," she told Zachary. "She's a really good nurse."

He nodded and stood up. Nurse Debbie dutifully checked his bracelet and compared the name or ID number to that on her clipboard. She smiled. "Great, if you'll just come with me, then, we'll get you started."

"Do you want me to come with you?" Kenzie asked, unsure whether Zachary had been counting on her moral support or if the only thing he'd needed her for was to drive him to the hospital.

"I need to interview him alone," Nurse Debbie said. "Lots of privacy laws, you know."

And the fact that he would be asked whether he was in an abusive situation. He had to be alone when they asked him that, even if he consented to Kenzie joining them and hearing his private medical information. She might be able to join him later, but not until they'd had a chance to ask him questions about his circumstances without someone else there to hear his answers.

"Okay. Do you want me to stick around, Zachary?"

He shook his head. "You don't need to. It'll be... I'll be safe once I'm admitted. You don't need to worry about me."

"Of course I'll worry about you." Kenzie looked at the time on her phone. "I'll come back and see you tonight. If that's okay."

Zachary shrugged as if he didn't care.

"Do you want me to bring you anything? Pajamas? Something from home?"

"No."

"Okay." Kenzie leaned in to kiss him on the cheek and gave him a squeeze around the shoulders. "You take care. You're in good hands. I'll see you later."

Zachary nodded. "Thanks for bringing me."

"Of course." She kissed him once more, then nodded to Nurse Debbie. "Take care of him for me."

23

Kenzie was accustomed to spending time alone. Or at least, she had been before Zachary had started staying over. Now he was at her house almost all the time when she was home, only going back to his own apartment when she was gone during the day or running errands. He really didn't have to maintain his own place anymore, but supposed it was good for him to have something to fall back on just in case. Or just if he needed some mental space for a few hours.

But she'd gotten used to his being around the house and it felt empty whenever he wasn't there.

She didn't have to worry this time that he was off on surveillance that could turn bad, or that he might be following Bridget again. She knew where he was, and that the hospital was the safest place for him to be. They would keep a close eye on him and he wouldn't have access to anything he could cut himself with or meds that he could overdose on. She didn't have to be aware of his every move and mood. That meant that she could start on the backlog of chores and other things she always put off because she didn't have the time, either at work or spending time with Zachary most of her waking hours. Or too tired to start anything.

But she didn't. She didn't even look at the task list on her phone.

The first person she called was Lorne. He sighed, but wasn't surprised to hear that Zachary had admitted himself. He'd seen Zachary through a lot of difficult times. "It's not your fault, Kenzie," he comforted her. "I know it feels like a personal failure, but it isn't. Zach knows you're there for him. But he also knows from experience that when things get bad… he needs to be in a safe place, with a team behind him. You can't expect yourself to be his sole support."

"I know. And I'm not. He has you guys, and Dr. B and his other doctors, other friends here and his siblings now too. There are a lot of people who can be there and help out."

"Yes, but you can't keep a watch on him twenty-four hours a day. You can't remove everything that isn't safe from his environment or give him intensive therapy. Or make changes to his prescriptions. They'll take care of him and make sure that he's safe until he gets past the crisis."

"You think he'll be there until Christmas, then."

"More than likely. It won't just be a seventy-two-hour hold. He knows he needs to be there. It's voluntary. And he knows that he's not going to start feeling better until after the anniversary. It's possible that he'll end up with a doctor who tries to push him out before then. It's happened before. But if they try to release him to you before then, tell them you won't take responsibility for him."

"Okay." Kenzie was hesitant. What if Zachary was feeling better and agreed to coming back before Christmas? She couldn't tell him that he couldn't come home. If they managed to get him to a better place, it was possible, wasn't it?

"You can't, Kenzie," Lorne told her. "You remember how bad he was last year on Christmas Eve? He's not going to be ready to come home before Christmas."

"But we got him through it last year. He didn't have to be admitted."

"And if Tyrrell hadn't been there that night, do you think it would have been safe to leave him alone?"

"No. Of course not. But as long as we had someone to stay up with him…"

"Every night? You don't know when he's going to hit the lowest point, and if he seems to be okay and the person up with him falls asleep… it's just safer at the hospital, where they will check on him every fifteen minutes. Where it is more difficult for him to find a way to harm himself."

"I don't know how you have dealt with this for so many years."

"He is pretty good about recognizing when he reaches the point when he needs to go to the hospital. Of course we worry. All the time, but especially in December. But Zachary is a grown man and he's independent. We can't treat him like he's helpless. That would just make it worse."

Kenzie sighed. "I hate this."

"Of course you do. It's emotionally draining and mentally exhausting.

You need to build yourself up. Recognize what your needs are right now. He'll be home in a few weeks. Look forward to that. He will be back."

Kenzie called Tyrrell and Heather to give them the news as well. No one was that surprised. They had both heard an abbreviated account of Zachary's life and his many visits to the hospital and other treatment facilities. Heather admitted that she had sensed it coming.

"He hasn't been doing a lot of work. I don't know what he was spending his time on, because I would call and he wouldn't answer, or if he did answer he didn't say where he'd been. I've still been taking the small jobs, but he hadn't taken on much else new."

"He's been a little distracted by Bridget and her health," Kenzie kept it deliberately vague, not wanting to give away anything that Zachary or Bridget wouldn't want spread around.

There was a snort from Heather that sounded more like Joss, the oldest and most jaded of the siblings. "A little distracted, yeah."

So Heather had been aware of Zachary's activities or had at least suspected them.

"How is Bridget?" Heather asked.

"She's okay. Had the babies a couple of days ago, but they are struggling. I think that's what pushed Zachary over the edge today. They nearly lost one of them."

"Zachary always did love babies," Heather said, her voice tender. "That boy was hell on wheels, but put a baby in his arms, and he was the most attentive person ever."

Kenzie had seen how, when focused on an important project or protecting someone else, Zachary could hyperfocus. He was kind and compassionate, and she had seen how well he got along with teens and children.

"He's talked a little bit about it. It sounds like your mom might have had some pretty severe postpartum depression. She's lucky she had you older kids to look after the younger ones."

"Yeah, I guess that must have been the problem. I had some postpartum after my births, but... well, it wasn't anything like Mom's. She wouldn't be able to get out of bed. I seriously think she would have just died, if there weren't people feeding her and looking after her. And the babies. Mindy wouldn't have survived if it wasn't for Zachary. I'm sure of that."

"What was wrong with her?" Kenzie asked, fascinated to hear Heather's perspective.

"She was really hard to feed. She wouldn't take the bottle and Mom wouldn't nurse. Zachary would dip his finger in formula to get her sucking on it, and then slip the nipple in… he was the only one who could get her to eat anything. He'd skip school. Stay home with her until the truant officer started showing up, and then skip out of classes to run back home and take care of her. It was a good thing they didn't slap him in some detention center. I'm sure Mindy wouldn't have made it."

"That's amazing. He would only have been… how old, eight?"

"Yeah, that sounds about right. But he was so determined. Nothing was going to keep him from taking care of Mindy."

Kenzie's heart ached when she thought about everything his mother had put him through after a showing like that. How she had told him that he wasn't good for anything and she didn't want him anymore. All the abuse and challenges that he had gone through in foster care and at school because she had abandoned him. A little boy who cared so much about his family.

"I'll have to ask him about it," Kenzie said. "He's probably never even been told what a good job he did. What a difference he made."

"No," Heather agreed after a moment. "He got told off when he did something wrong, but if he was quiet and out of the way… no one would have ever said anything about it."

"Do you think we should let Joss know about him being in the hospital?" Kenzie asked. "I don't know her very well… whether she would want to know, or just not to be bothered."

"Who knows what makes Joss happy," Heather said, with a slight laugh in her voice. "I'll call her and let her know. You don't have to deal with her."

Kenzie thought about saying that Heather didn't really have to do that, Kenzie didn't mind calling Jocelyn. But it wasn't true. She was relieved that Heather had offered, because Kenzie would prefer not to have anything to do with Joss's sharp edges.

"Would you? That would be really great."

"Sure. Thanks for letting me know. I'll try to come in and visit him. If that's allowed."

"I'll give you a call once I know what the visitor situation is. I assume visitors will be restricted to the bare minimum to begin with, until they feel as though he is stable enough."

"Okay. Yeah. Let me know. I need to come in to do some Christmas shopping anyway, so I'll plan around it."

"Just don't plan on talking to him about your Christmas shopping."

There was a pause, Heather not answering right away. Not chuckling about it like Kenzie expected her to.

"Is it that bad?" Heather asked.

Kenzie realized that it had been less than a year since Zachary and Heather had been reunited. It seemed like a lot longer than that, with the two of them working so well together. Zachary had hit it off with both Tyrrell and Heather right away. But Heather hadn't been around the previous year, or for any of the previous Christmases, so she had no way of knowing how bad Zachary's depression was around Christmas, how even a discussion about Christmas or seeing all the Christmas lights or decorations around town could bring him down farther.

"Well… yes, it is. Christmas is a really bad memory for him, and as a kid he was almost always institutionalized around that time. Sometimes as an adult too, like now."

"It was terrible," Heather recalled. "I was really scared that we were going to die. And when the firemen got us out, Zachary was hurt, and I thought he would die. But I was older than him when it happened, and I guess I also have happy memories of Christmases with my own kids. Same with Tyrrell. Zachary was just… I wish he could understand that it's in the past. It was terrible, but… it was a long time ago now."

"He understands that logically," Kenzie said. "But his brain is… damaged in a way. He would like to stop being depressed. He'd like to be able to stop thinking about the fire and just enjoy Christmas. But his brain is convinced that anything to do with Christmas is dangerous. That the fire could happen again this year, just like it did decades ago. He's made some progress on the fire thing. But he didn't even tell his therapist about his problems with Christmas and why until this year, and that was with… a bit of encouragement from me. I was hoping that with better support this year he would do better, but…"

"It's not your fault," Heather pointed out, just as Lorne had.

Kenzie didn't think that she'd been blaming herself. She knew that Zachary had severe depression every year, and that it centered around Christmas Eve and the house fire when he'd been ten. That wasn't her fault. But maybe she was blaming herself a little bit for not being able to stop it. She was a medical professional and his partner, and she thought that with everything she knew about mental illness and how much she was willing to go all-out for Zachary, that she would be able to help him through it. That she would be sitting back at Christmas, satisfied that she'd been able to get him through it without a major depressive episode or the need for hospitalization.

Taking Zachary to the hospital had shattered the egotistical vision she'd had of herself. She wasn't a miracle worker. She didn't love and understand him enough to change his brain chemistry. And it was true, she did blame herself for not having what it took to do that.

How did that make her any better than Bridget, who had assumed when she married Zachary that she would be able to fix him? Bridget thought she could get rid of all the parts of Zachary that she didn't like and train him to be the husband she expected him to be.

Was that any different from Kenzie thinking she had what it took to heal him?

24

Kenzie sulked around the house for a while and ate a bowl of ice cream. If she were going to resort to treating any negative emotions with ice cream, she would have to start getting more exercise. She would put on fifty pounds before Christmas.

She tried watching TV. Tried reading. Eventually, she decided to talk to her mother.

Kenzie didn't usually go to her mother with her problems. She considered herself a big girl, an adult who could solve her problems by herself. She had decided what to do for her education and career and had gone out and done what she had to. No one had to coach her through that, and she had a trust fund so she didn't have to take out loans or go to her parents to ask them for money. She prided herself on her independence and in the fact that she didn't *worry* her mother.

Lisa had suffered enough with Amanda, worrying day and night about her daughter's health and what she needed. And Kenzie had vowed to herself that she would never cause her mother any anxiety. So she didn't go to her with problems or discuss the speed bumps in her grown-up life.

But maybe it was time to stop acting like a rebellious teen who didn't need anything from anyone and to give her parents a chance to be a part of her life again. Even if it were only in a small way.

Kenzie tapped her phone to dial through to her mother and listened to the phone ringing. Dread clutched at her guts, but she ignored it. Calling her mother did not mean that anything was wrong. Having a conversation with her was not a dangerous or stressful proposition. Lisa was always there, always happy to help with anything Kenzie asked for.

"Mackenzie," Lisa greeted, her voice a little over-loud. "It's good to hear from you! Is everything okay?"

"Sure. I just wanted to talk," Kenzie assured her breezily. Then she realized what she was doing. Calling her mother for comfort and then pretending that nothing was wrong. How much sense did that make? How was that going to help her. "Actually, Mother..." Kenzie spoke over Lisa to correct herself. "Actually, I'm having a crappy day, and everything is not all right."

"Oh." Lisa stopped short in her pleasantries. "What is it, honey? Did something happen?"

"Yeah. Zachary had to go into the hospital. He'll be okay, that's why he checked himself in, but I'm feeling really down about it and thinking I should have been able to do something for him. So I thought..." She trailed off.

"What is he in the hospital for? Was there an accident?"

"No. He has depression. And some things have been going on that are making it worse, and he had to check himself in because he's suicidal."

"Oh!" Lisa gasped. "Oh, no! I'm so sorry, honey."

"It sounds worse than it is. I mean, I knew that this might happen. And it's good that he recognized he was a danger to himself and asked to be admitted so that he can't self-harm. But it's also... a real disappointment. I feel responsible, even though I know that I'm not."

"Of course. If you're anything like me, you take it all personally. Everything that goes wrong in the family. A mother or wife should be able to manage it all. Even though you know it's not true, that doesn't stop you from feeling betrayed and guilty and responsible for letting something bad happen."

Kenzie's heart throbbed extra-hard. She put her hand over the spot where it pounded away in her chest. It felt full and warm and painful, but a little bit better because Lisa understood what she was talking about.

"Is there anything we can do?" Lisa asked.

"No. There isn't really anything that anyone can do. I mean, he has the doctors at the hospital and his usual medical team, and they help."

"And I'm sure it helps him to have you in his life too; it just doesn't mean you can change things like that."

"I don't feel like that right now, but you're right. At least I try to be understanding and don't usually lose my temper. Which is more than I can say for his ex."

"You were always so good with Amanda, even when she was tired and whiny, and nothing would soothe her."

Kenzie breathed in and out, thinking about Amanda. There had been good times and bad, of course. She preferred to remember the good times, but there were always times when Amanda was sick and nothing any of them did helped her to feel any better.

"Yeah. I guess that's where I developed some patience. I knew that she couldn't help it. Anyone would have been crabby, having to go through dialysis and everything else she had to deal with."

Lisa made a noise of agreement.

"Do you remember one of the nurses Amanda had in the kidney unit? Nurse Debbie?"

"Hmm. I'm not sure. What would I remember about her?"

"She was a big blond woman. Very cheerful. Jolly."

"Ohhh…" Lisa drew the word out, thinking about it, clearly remembering some impressions. "I do recall her… she was there for a long time. One of the regulars that knew Amanda because she'd been there so much."

"Yeah. And she was so good. She wasn't brusque and dismissive like some of them. She was always willing to help out, whether it was turning Amanda over or bringing her some ice chips…"

"Yes. That's right."

"Well, I ran into her at the hospital this morning!"

"You're kidding! How did that happen? Is she still in the same unit? I haven't seen her in years."

Lisa spent a lot of time on kidney causes, so she probably would have known if Nurse Debbie had still been in the nephrology unit. Even though Lisa was no longer required to be at the hospital, as she had been when Amanda was there sick, she still went back a lot, chatting with the administration and raising funds. Making sure they had all the latest equipment and treatments for the young people who, like Amanda, lived out much of their lives there.

"No. Actually, she's in psych. She was there for Zachary's intake."

"Well, isn't it a small world! You be sure to tell her hello for me."

"I will. I'm planning to go back in an hour or two. I haven't heard anything, but I should be able to see him and find out what the plan is for the next little while."

"They won't send him home, will they? When he's feeling so badly?"

"No. I don't think so. They'll have me to deal with if they try a stunt like that. He's there for a reason."

"What does he need? Can we send him a care package? Pajamas? Cookies? I don't know if that unit will allow me to send anything."

"He said he doesn't need anything. I offered to bring him things from home, and he said no. I'll find out more tonight about the rules for visitors and anything brought into the unit. They have to be very careful, in case it is something that could be used... for self-harm."

"Of course. But maybe a potted plant, with some flowers..."

Kenzie smiled. "I don't know how long it would last. Neither one of us has much of a green thumb."

"You let me know."

"I will."

"And what about Christmas? You don't want to be worrying about making Christmas plans while you need to look after him in the hospital. Why don't you plan to come here?"

"I can't plan anything like that."

"He'll be out by then, won't he?"

"No. Christmas is a very bad time for him... the anniversary of a family tragedy." Kenzie tried to put it into words that her mother would understand, without telling her too much of Zachary's story. "Hopefully they can stabilize him, but he won't really feel *better* until after Christmas."

"Oh." Lisa's voice was sympathetic. "You should have told me that before. Christmas can be such a difficult time for people. I understand the suicide rate is very high—" She cut herself off. "I don't need to tell you that. I just mean... I have friends who have a difficult time then too, because of loved ones they have lost. I remember years when Amanda was sick... when we didn't know if she would make it to Christmas. We even had it early one year..."

Kenzie remembered. She thought it was before she had turned eighteen and given Amanda one of her kidneys. The girl had been gravely ill, and the doctors had advised them to say their goodbyes and not wait. So they had opened their Christmas presents and had a little party. Amanda had fallen asleep, exhausted. And they had just sat around her and watched her breathe. Kenzie choked up thinking about it.

In the morning, Amanda had rallied, and they'd joked that she had just wanted to open her gifts early.

"Yeah, that's right. I remember."

Lisa was quiet for a moment.

"So we can't have anything before Christmas," Kenzie said. "He won't be out before then and discussing anything about Christmas will make him worse." She was thinking it through out loud, not having processed it yet previously. "But after Christmas, then it will be better."

When Kenzie arrived in the psych unit, she wasn't surprised to be met with some resistance. A doctor on Zachary's team shook his head adamantly.

"He is under observation right now. We need to get an accurate read on his baseline. Visitors right now would just disrupt that. After we've had a chance to evaluate him, then he will be able to have a limited number of visitors whom he will approve."

"I'm his girlfriend. I'm going to be on the list. And I'm a medical doctor."

"You will still disrupt our observations. So you may not see him today."

Kenzie shrugged. She wasn't going to argue it. She had only given herself a 50/50 chance of being able to get in.

"Has Dr. Boyle or anyone on his medical team been by? Do you have all of his prescription information and anything else you need from them?"

"Yes. They have been very responsive; we have everything, or else it is on the way. I gather this is not his first admission." His lips twisted in a slight sneer. As if Zachary could help being a repeat offender.

"If you've read through his history, then you must know that. This is a bad time of year for him."

"As it is for many. That's not unusual."

"But the amount that he reacts to Christmas stuff is. It isn't just that he gets more depressed because it's cold and dark. He has a history."

"Yes, Dr. Boyle mentioned that."

"Okay. You need to know that. This isn't just seasonal depression. It is a traumatic reaction."

The doctor nodded. "Thank you for your input, Miss Kirsch," he said in a dismissive tone.

"Dr. Kirsch," Kenzie reminded him. He didn't correct himself.

"Oh, are you Kenzie?" A nurse walking by turned toward Kenzie, smiling.

Kenzie raised her brows and tilted her head slightly. "Yes... I'm Kenzie."

"You're Zachary's girlfriend."

"Yes. Have you been in to see him? How is he doing?"

"Don't you worry about our Zachary." The woman patted Kenzie on the arm. "We know how to look after him."

The familiar way she spoke of him made Kenzie inquire further. "Do you... know Zachary? From before this?"

She nodded. "Of course. I've been here for six years." She gave Kenzie a broad smile. "He's had a few visits during that time."

"Oh. I guess so. Well, I'm glad there are people here who know him." Kenzie glanced at the doctor, who definitely didn't know Zachary. It was good there were nurses there who knew him from past admissions and would be looking out for him.

"And I understand that you know Nurse Debbie!"

Kenzie nodded. "Yes. Funny thing. I just ran into her when Zachary was admitted. I had no idea she was in this unit!"

"She's just new here. So *she* doesn't know Zachary, but she was telling us all about you."

Kenzie chuckled uncomfortably. "I don't know how much there is to tell. It's been a lot of years since I've seen her."

"Nurses don't forget as easily as you might think." The nurse gave her a wink. "We remember the patients and families that we have spent a lot of time with. She knew you as soon as she saw you in the waiting room."

"Well, yes, I guess she did." Kenzie didn't offer that she'd had to check Debbie's name tag. She patted the nurse's hand on her arm. "Is there anything Zachary needs? Anything I should bring for him?"

"No, he doesn't need anything. You just take care of yourself, and we'll take care of him. Someone will call you once he's able to have visitors. He'll be happy to see you."

Kenzie nodded. She wished that she could go in and see him and let him know that everything would be okay. When she thought about him being there all by himself overnight, fighting his demons and nightmares, her throat got tight and hot. She blinked rapidly, not wanting to cry in front of the nurse, and especially not in front of the doctor.

"Thanks. I'll be happy to see him too. Thank you… for looking after him."

25

Sunday night was rough on Kenzie, and she was glad to go to work in the morning to try to get her mind off things. Monday passed in a blur. Kenzie hoped she didn't screw up too many things in her distraction. Agent Menendez called several times to ask about tox results, but they didn't have anything in yet. Kenzie eventually stopped answering, letting the persistent calls go through to voicemail. Agent Menendez needed to learn a little restraint.

Monday night was also rough, but in the morning, she got a call from one of the nurses on the psych unit advising that she had been added to Zachary's visitor list and could see him that evening if she chose. So Kenzie went into work feeling a little more cheerful and relaxed. Instead of being distracted by the fact that she couldn't see Zachary, she was distracted by the fact that she would be able to. She shook her head at the irony of it and tried to focus on each job at hand. There would not be any multitasking, or she would end up putting reports in the fridge and samples in the outgoing mail.

"How are you this morning, Kenzie?" Dr. Wiltshire greeted.

"Better today, thanks. But I still wouldn't trust any calculations I do. Double check any of my work before it goes out. I'm trying to triple-check everything myself, but I could still miss something."

"Zachary doing any better?"

"I don't know if he is any better, but I'll be able to see him tonight. So I'm a lot happier about that. It's been months since I've gone two nights without him home… it's weird. You would think that I would adjust pretty quickly to being alone, since that's what I'm more used to. But... not so much."

"I'm sure it will give him a boost to see you too."

"I hope so. I'm all about making sure he gets whatever boosts I can give him!"

Dr. Wiltshire raised an eyebrow questioningly, making Kenzie laugh. It felt good to laugh. She slit the next envelope in the stack of mail and scanned it to see how to sort it. She dropped the piece of paper like it had burned her.

"What is it?" Dr. Wiltshire drew closer and peered over the edge of Kenzie's reception desk to see what it was.

STAY OUT OF THE HOSPITAL KENZIE KIRSCH. OR ELSE

Kenzie blinked, trying to make sense of the note, written in black Sharpie in large block letters. Stay out of the hospital? Her mind went immediately to Zachary, and whether someone didn't want her to visit him. But that didn't make any sense.

Dr. Wiltshire's forehead was creased with lines. "Stay out of the hospital. You don't suppose this is something to do with the Michaels case, do you?"

"Oh..." It suddenly made more sense. "Yes, I suppose it is. I must have upset someone with my questions in the geriatric unit last week."

He nodded.

"What do you suppose the 'or else' is?" Kenzie asked with a nervous laugh. It was like some melodramatic murder show on TV. Stuff like that didn't happen in real life. People didn't make threats. And they didn't say "or else."

"I don't know. I don't imagine you have anything to worry about, but you should probably call Agent Menendez and update her on the situation."

"Oh, great. I've been trying to avoid talking to her."

Dr. Wiltshire laughed. "Well, maybe if you have something to tell her, she won't be as annoying."

"Except I don't really have anything that will help the case. I mean, this... This isn't what she wants. She wants positive tox screens on the two exhumations, and I don't think we're going to get anything she can use."

"I have my doubts too," Dr. Wiltshire admitted. "I'm afraid that if those two deaths *are* somehow related to Mr. Michaels's death, the killer has changed his method enough that we cannot detect it months later."

"That's what I told Menendez. But of course... she doesn't want to hear that. She wants something we can trace and prove it's the same person."

"We might have to get more exhumations to find a pattern. And the more we do, the more likely it is that word will leak out. Then either people won't want to give us permission, or everyone will think that their loved one's death is related, and we'll be overwhelmed. And we'll start getting letters from every crackpot in the county." He looked down at the note on Kenzie's desk.

"Do you think this is just some crackpot?"

He shook his head slowly. "This is someone who knew you were asking questions at the hospital. That's not a member of the public, it's a very small group of people."

Kenzie's mind immediately went to Roda with her letter writing supplies. Kenzie hadn't seriously considered the possibility that one of the volunteers was involved. But here was someone who had not chosen to email her or to contact her on one of the social networks, but had written a letter and mailed it to her. Kenzie thought back to Roda in the hospital. Of course she had been holding a pen, not a Sharpie. But did that mean that there wasn't a Sharpie in her bag too? Or that she didn't have one at home that she could grab?

"Where was a volunteer at the hospital writing letters for the patients," she told Dr. Wiltshire.

"Well, that sounds like a possibility. Be sure to pass that on to Agent Menendez." He considered the letter on the desk. "What about the stamp? They could get DNA from it. It would take forever, I suppose, but it's a possibility."

Kenzie shook her head, laughing. "They're all self-stick these days, Doctor. I don't know when the last time was that I licked a stamp."

"Oh. Of course. And the same with the envelope flap, I suppose?"

Kenzie picked up the envelope and examined it. She nodded. "Yes. Not all of them are self-sealing, but this one is."

"Today's inventors just don't understand how valuable saliva is in solving a case," Dr. Wiltshire lamented, his eyes twinkling. "Or they never would have done that."

Kenzie forced a laugh. "Yeah. Investigators constantly need to upgrade their skills and look for answers in different places as they are sabotaged by inventors." She looked at the envelope, wondering if there were any other clues as to where it had come from. There was, of course, no return address. Little of the mail she got had visible postmarks on it anymore.

"I guess I shouldn't be touching this, in case it has fingerprints or other evidence on it."

She handled the envelope and the letter by the edges and slipped them into a page protector. She would, as Dr. Wiltshire said, have to give Agent Josie Menendez a call to pick up the letter and find out whether there were anything the FBI could find out from it. Maybe handwriting analysis or some kind of behavioral analysis based on the language that was used. But it was a pretty short note, not like the Unabomber Manifesto.

"Well..." Dr. Wiltshire took a deep breath and stepped back slightly from Kenzie's desk, giving her space. "Sorry about getting *that*. But I don't imagine you really have to worry about the 'or else.' It isn't like you're the investigator in this case anyway. You were only over there one day to preview the unit and pass your impressions on to Agent Menendez." He sighed. "I am glad to hear that you'll be able to visit Zachary tonight. Give him my best. I hope he's able to get turned back around quickly."

"Thanks."

Dr. Wiltshire nodded and left Kenzie alone, heading to his own office.

Most of the day's work was routine, and Kenzie didn't have to worry too much about fouling something up because she was distracted. Her brain knew what to do with the routine stuff and she didn't have to pay that much attention to it.

Midway through the afternoon, a review of her email inbox revealed that they'd received some of the lab results back on the Darling and Scott postmortems. She saved them to file and printed them off, reading from the screen as they printed. She grabbed the sheaf of papers and went to Dr. Wiltshire's office.

"Kenzie. What have you got for me?" Wiltshire asked genially.

"Tox results." Kenzie thrust them at him, eager to discuss the reports.

"I gather from your expression that they were not all negative."

"Nothing on Darling. But Scott..." Kenzie indicated the report that she had put on the top and flipped past the first couple of pages to the results as Dr. Wiltshire looked at it. "They detected the presence of succinylcholine."

"Sux."

Kenzie nodded. "Sucks for him," she agreed wryly.

Dr. Wiltshire rolled his eyes and shook his head. "And there was no reason for Sux to be present."

There were few reasons for a patient to be treated with the paralytic. It had not been used in any procedures that were recorded on Mr. Scott's chart.

"Nope."

"All right. We now have our second confirmed homicide. Give Agent Menendez a call."

"Do you want me to do it here?" Kenzie asked, motioning to Dr. Wiltshire's phone.

"Sure, you may as well. Then I can give my confirmation at the same time."

Kenzie turned the phone to face her and tapped in the number that she knew by heart from Agent Menendez's repeated calls to her.

"Agent Josie Menendez," the agent acknowledged on picking it up.

"Josie. Kenzie Kirsch here, with Dr. Wiltshire."

"I got your message regarding the letter you got," Menendez said, sounding a little annoyed. "I'll pick it up later, when I have the time. Or maybe tomorrow," she amended, probably looking at the clock and realizing that the office would be closed by the time she got around to it. "But I really don't think you're in any immediate danger."

"No, it's not that," Kenzie said. "You can pick that up whenever you want. Or I can have it sent over to you, if you prefer. But we got some of the tox reports in on the two exhumations."

"And you found something? Was it potassium chloride?"

"No. Something called succinylcholine. It's a paralytic. It—"

"I'm familiar with succinylcholine. It paralyzes all the muscles. Including breathing, right?"

Kenzie nodded, surprised that Menendez knew about it. But then, it had been used in a number of TV and thriller plots. And it had been used by Angel of Death killers in the past, which was why it was on Kenzie's list of drugs to test for. Menendez might have run into it in another case that she had reviewed as she investigated Dr. Philemon's list of deceased patients.

"Yes, that's right," Kenzie agreed, realizing that Menendez couldn't see her and was still waiting for her answer.

"So will Dr. Wiltshire change the cause and manner of death?" Menendez inquired. "Did you find it in both?"

"Only in Scott," Dr. Wiltshire advised. "And yes, I will be amending his manner of death to homicide. There was no reason for sux to be in his system based on the medical procedures he had been given. The only reason for it to be there was that someone wanted to kill him. Or to almost kill him and revive him. Sometimes these Angel of Death killers want to be in the spotlight for having saved someone's life."

"I have begun to compile a list of possible suspects," Menendez said. "Maybe tomorrow, we can get together and go through it so I can get your thoughts."

26

Kenzie pondered the developments on the Michaels case—or more correctly now, Dr. Philemon's serial killer case—as she drove to the hospital. Both to ponder whether there was anything they had missed and what their next steps should or would be, and also to think through her visit with Zachary. He wouldn't want a visit that was focused on his mental health or the Christmas season. It would be better to talk about something that would interest him and distract him from his own troubles and from Bridget and the babies.

The threat in the mail was disconcerting. It confirmed, just as much as the positive tox screen, that they were on the right track, that there was a serial killer on Dr. Philemon's team, and that the Angel of Death was aware of their investigation. Kenzie wished that the killer's attention had been focused on Agent Menendez and the FBI instead of her.

Maybe best not to tell Zachary that the serial killer was aware of her involvement in the case and where she worked. Zachary's own experience in disturbing a serial killer's work had been pretty traumatizing.

It took her a few minutes when she got to the psychiatric unit to get checked in. They had to check her name against the visitor list, which seemed to take much longer than it should, and then to confirm that Zachary was taking visitors, which Kenzie assumed meant both that he wanted to and that he wasn't isolated in an observation room, as he probably had been initially. Then she waited as an orderly was called to escort her to the common room where she would be able to visit with Zachary, even though Kenzie was sure that she could have just found it herself.

The orderly escorted her to a large open room that was mostly filled with chairs and tables that were probably used at mealtimes. Since it was not suppertime, most of them were clear, though there were a few puzzles and games out. No big poker games going on; everyone seemed to be doing their own thing. There was not much conversation. There was a TV and some upholstered furniture near the window at one end of the room, the TV volume turned down low so that anyone who wanted to hear would have to be sitting within a couple of feet of it.

Zachary was sitting at one of the tables waiting for her. Kenzie nodded her thanks to the orderly. "There he is. Thanks."

He nodded back and watched her approach Zachary. Kenzie smiled, forcing herself to look happier than she felt at seeing him there, looking fragile in the light hospital garb.

"Are we allowed to hug?" she inquired.

In response, he stood up and they embraced. Nothing that would embarrass anyone watching or make the staff worry that Kenzie was trying to pass some contraband on, just a quick but heartfelt hug to let him know how much she had missed him and how glad she was to see him again.

"Hi, Kenzie. Thanks for coming," he murmured.

"Of course. I've missed you. It's weird, the house being empty."

They both sat down.

"You're still there. And your stuff," Zachary pointed out

"I know, but it's not the same. Even though I was used to living alone, I don't like the way it feels when you're not around."

He looked down at the top of the table, nodding slightly. She thought she detected a slight reddening of his earlobes, a sign that he was pleased and embarrassed.

"I miss being there too."

"Well, you'll be back once you're feeling better," Kenzie said bracingly. It wasn't the end of the world that he was in the hospital for a bit. At least she knew that he would be feeling better and back home after Christmas. Back when they'd been in a car accident and his spine had been bruised, there had been a few scary days during which she didn't know whether he would recover fully. It had taken time and physiotherapy for him to get back on his feet. Now she couldn't even see the aftereffects.

She didn't know for sure how much to say about his mental health and his treatment plan. But she figured it was best to be up front, and if he didn't want to answer certain questions or told her to back off, then she would know.

"How are you feeling, being here? You feel… safer? Protected?"

Zachary's eyes wandered around the room. "Yeah. I don't have to worry about what I might do… they've got me doing more therapy, but I don't think they really understand… that I've been through all of this before. Talking about it isn't going to make that much difference."

"Well, I guess you have to give them leeway to figure it out. Doctors have a lot to learn. You know how it works for you, but they don't."

He nodded.

"I ran into a nurse who works in this unit. She said she's been here for a few years and that she knew you, because you have been here before. So there must be a few people that know more about your history, even if the doctor doesn't."

"Which nurse? That one that you knew that used to treat Amanda?"

"No, no. Not her. Someone who knew you from before. Oh… she was brunette, taller than me. Older. Said she'd been here for six years maybe?"

"Oh." Zachary nodded, a smile of recognition coming to his face. "Val."

"Val." Kenzie nodded. "So you know her from other admissions?"

"Yeah. She's good. It's nice to come here and see people you know. To have things that are… familiar. It makes it easier."

"That makes sense. It's a pretty drastic transition. Having familiar people and things around you would help."

"Not a lot changes, even if the people here do. And sometimes, I even know some of the patients. Because we've all been here before."

It wasn't a long-term facility. If Zachary had needed to stay there for a few months, or longer, he would have been transferred to one of the other facilities where those with mental health issues were able to stay longer-term. Kenzie was surprised that she knew some of the other patients, but she supposed there was no reason she should be. Mental health issues didn't just go away. The doctor would try to get the patients onto a medication cocktail that would provide long-term support, but you never knew when a medication would suddenly stop working, or the patient would stop taking it, or, like Zachary, there would be some other trigger that would push them past the point where they could handle things alone.

"Are they going to do anything else?" she asked Zachary. "Change around any meds or try some other therapy?"

"No. Don't want them to. Things have been okay… mostly. It's just… with the other stuff going on right now. The season and… you know."

Bridget and the babies. Kenzie wondered whether she should talk to

Zachary about them, or whether that would just make things worse. She decided she'd better let him bring it up on his own.

"Everybody sends their love. Lorne and your family. And Dr. Wiltshire says to get better soon."

Zachary rubbed his ear. "Dr. Wiltshire knows…?"

Kenzie nodded. "If you don't want me to tell anyone, let me know. I thought that you wanted to be open about it."

"Yeah, I do," he agreed. "I just didn't think about him knowing. You don't think that will cause you any problems, if he thinks you have trouble at home? Or if I am trying to get copies of documents or a case opened?"

"No," Kenzie shook her head. "Not at all. He's cool with it. He told me to take time off if I need it and said to let him know if there's anything he can do. If you need anything."

"And it won't affect his opinion of you?"

"No. And not of you, either. He's a doctor. He understands that mental illness isn't something that you can control and that it doesn't mean that you're weak or that you're not competent in your work." Kenzie met Zachary's eyes, trying to impress these words on him. "You are a strong person. Coming here isn't taking the easy way out. Acknowledging your problems openly isn't easy, is it?"

"No."

27

Kenzie nodded firmly and decided it was time to move on. She had resolved not to spend the whole time talking about depression. "You remember the case I was telling you about? That the FBI is in on?"

Zachary's eyes immediately brightened, interested in hearing more about it. "Yes. How's that going?"

"We had a couple of the doctor's previous patients exhumed. These are patients that he identified as possibly being suspicious, and the families gave permission for us to re-examine them."

"How long ago…? What kind of condition were they in?"

"Not bad, all things considered. Modern embalming procedures are pretty good. But they did still stink. You just can't get that smell out of your nose at the end of the day, it seems like it clings to everything."

Zachary nodded.

"I looked up as many other Angel of Death serial killers as I could to research their methods. Because people generally stick with what has worked before, right?"

"Yeah."

"So when we got the bodies, we did a bunch of tox screens, based on that research. Not just the usual illegal drug screens, but specialized testing for some of the drugs that we were hoping to find."

"And you found something? Was it more potassium?"

Kenzie held up her finger. "Not potassium."

"What, then?"

"Succinylcholine."

"I've heard of it. Don't know much about it."

"It's a paralytic. They use it in some surgical procedures. But you have to provide respiratory support because it also stops the patient's breathing."

"Ohhh."

"It paralyzes the person, but they stay awake and aware; they know what's going on until the end, when they can't get enough oxygen to stay conscious. Then the heart stops, and they're gone. It looks like a natural death, if you're not looking for it."

"It has to be injected?"

"Yes. But that's easy enough in a hospital setting. The people that an Angel of Death killer is taking out are usually already in bad shape. So they probably already have an IV."

"And even if they don't, they've probably had some kind of injection in the past few days. So another needle mark wouldn't be noticed, or you could go in through an existing location," he suggested.

"Yeah. There are definitely ways around it. And needle marks are easy to miss if they are well-hidden. Between the toes. In areas that are hairy. Spotting injection sites isn't always easy, like you might think."

"Did you find succin— this drug in both of them?"

"No, only in one. No clear cause of death in the other yet. We don't have all the testing back, so we might still be able to find something. But not yet."

"It could be insulin."

"Yes, in which case, we're not going to find anything. But we'll keep looking. And hopefully, we'll get a few more bodies for examination, and we can establish enough of a pattern to find out who was present for all of them."

"Will you be able to? Not everyone who is working in the ward gets on the chart, do they?"

"No. It makes it tricky. Especially if it was someone who was supposed to be off shift, or if it was someone who wasn't a medical professional at all, but who could come and go in the unit without looking suspicious."

"Janitors."

"Yup."

He rubbed his chin, thinking about it. "There must be other maintenance staff too. Plumbers and electrical. Builders. Security guards."

"Volunteers. Chaplains."

"Social workers."

Kenzie hadn't thought of that one. She made a mental note.

"Technicians—people who take blood, deliver test results, bring the food up to the ward."

"Hmm." Zachary closed his eyes, thinking about it. "I like people who bring the food up. Some drugs or poisons could be administered in food. Maybe not that one, but others."

"Yeah. Especially something like antifreeze. Easy to slip into drinks or put into Jell-O or yogurt." Antifreeze wasn't something that Kenzie had included in the tests that they had requested. "Huh. Hadn't thought about that."

Zachary gave a half-smile. "Always happy to help."

Kenzie caught the movement of a nurse walking toward her out the corner of her eye and turned to look. She saw that it was Debbie and stood up to greet her and to give her a friendly hug.

"Hey. Good to see you again."

"And how is my favorite patient?" Debbie asked Zachary cheerfully. "Don't you go telling anyone else I called you that," she added conspiratorially, "The other patients will be jealous!"

Zachary smiled, but Kenzie could see it wasn't genuine. He wasn't in the mood to be teased or treated like someone's eight-year-old nephew. Kenzie had always appreciated Nurse Debbie's good cheer when things had been so grim, but she could understand how it might grate on a person.

"Especially that old grouch, Kennedy," Nurse Debbie told him, leaning in a little. "If he thinks that I have a boyfriend in the ward, he's not going to make my life easy."

Zachary rolled his eyes and looked at Kenzie, hoping she would save him from the ebullient nurse.

"I don't think you're allowed to have even one boyfriend on the ward," Kenzie countered, trying to take Nurse Debbie's attention off of Zachary. "How are you? It's sure nice to have you here in the ward. I'm sure Zachary appreciates having you around, knowing what a professional you are."

"And I love having him here." Debbie gave Zachary a light tap on the shoulder. "He's one of my easiest patients. No whining from this one. Always polite and trying not to make any waves. A real gentleman."

Kenzie nodded. "How long have you been here? In this ward, I mean?"

"I'm pretty new! Just been here for a few weeks. I needed a change of pace. You know, you get tired of the same thing day after day. And there aren't as many diapers to change or vomit to clean up in psych!"

She must have been in pediatrics before.

"I would hope not," Kenzie agreed. "So you're enjoying it?"

"Certainly. What's not to like?" Nurse Debbie laughed, then leaned closer to Kenzie, taking the spotlight off of Zachary. "Well, of course there are challenges in every department. We do get our share of crazies in this ward. And I don't mean the depressives..." She flipped a hand in Zachary's direction. "The schizophrenics and psychotics who go off their meds. Kids with their brains fried by LSD. Transfers from the jail." She blew out her breath, making a noise of disgust. "We get our share of colorful characters, I'll tell you!"

"Yeah, I bet." Kenzie remembered a few characters she had met on her psych rotation. And not all of them had been patients. "Well, we shouldn't keep you. I'm sure you have a lot to do."

Nurse Debbie nodded her agreement and started to move away. "Yes, that's true. A nurse's work is never done. If it is, it must be time for another shift! Don't you worry." She slapped Zachary on the back. "We'll take care of Zachary while he's here. I can already tell he's a favorite."

Kenzie nodded politely and watched as Nurse Debbie moved away. She sat back down. "Sorry about that."

"She seems very nice," Zachary said, trying to excuse his reaction. "She's just very... intense. It's hard to handle all that extra emotion."

"I could see that. And I'm sorry because I think that because she knows me, she's giving you extra attention, which is uncomfortable for you."

"She's pretty much like that with everyone.; I don't know where she gets all that energy. All of the smiling and joking." Zachary shook his head. "It looks exhausting."

"She was always like that with us too, when Amanda was in hospital. Well... maybe not always, I can remember once or twice seeing her when she wasn't putting on as much of a front. When she didn't know anyone was looking and she seemed tired or upset about a patient or frustrated with a doctor. Like anyone does in unguarded moments."

"So she's actually human?"

"Apparently so. Or she was then, at least. She may have been replaced by an artificial life form since then. It seems just as likely."

"I'm sure it cheers people up. All her jokes and smiles and backslapping. Just... not me."

Kenzie was also starting to fade. Not because she'd done too much physically, but just because it was difficult being around Zachary when he was so depressed, and she had to watch everything she said. He sucked the energy out of her, and she found herself getting down when she didn't really have any reason to be.

"You look tired," Zachary said, reading her face. "You don't have to stay here all night. I'm okay."

"I'm glad to know that you're safe here. But you must be bored. There's not really much to do." Kenzie looked around. There weren't a lot of people just sitting staring off into space. Most were playing with cards or puzzles, visiting, or watching the TV. There were probably more in their rooms. Maybe reading books or writing letters. But there wasn't much excitement.

"I'll watch TV after you go. That's probably what I'd be doing at home anyway."

But he'd be doing work at his computer while he was doing it. Or he might not have been home at all, but off watching Bridget's house or following her around town. TV might not be that exciting of a pursuit, but he was safe, and they would help him until he was well enough to be home again.

"Okay. I guess so. But if you want me to bring anything. Something that I'm allowed to bring, I mean. Just let me know."

"I don't need anything right now."

"I know you're not into reading, but..."

"Yeah. That's okay. I'd rather watch TV."

"Who else is on your visitor list? Your family would like to visit you, but I didn't know what the situation is."

"Lorne is already on there. I'll get them to put Tyrrell and Heather..."

"Joss too. I don't know whether she'll come, but you'd better not include your other siblings and not her."

"Yeah. Okay." Zachary nodded. "I'll add her too. She probably won't want to come." He tapped his fingers on the table. "And Rhys. Would you let him and Vera know?"

Rhys wasn't family, but Zachary had taken the teenager in under his wing. They had both been through various institutionalizations and had to deal with being "broken" by past traumas. Rhys was mostly mute, but he was still able to communicate and had visited Zachary in the hospital before.

"Sure. I'll give Vera a call."

"Thanks."

"Anyone else?"

Zachary shook his head.

"Mario?" Kenzie suggested. Mario Bowman was one of the police officers that Zachary knew. While not all of them were tolerant of a private investigator, some of them had become friends over the years and the various cases that Zachary had investigated. Mario had allowed Zachary to sleep on his couch after he'd lost everything in the apartment fire. For several months. That kind of friend didn't come along very often.

But Zachary shook his head again. "No. I'm not ready for anyone else."

Kenzie nodded her understanding. "Okay. No problem." She blew out her breath, anxious about saying goodbye to him again. "Well, then…"

She stood up. Zachary recognized his cue and stood as well. The hug that Kenzie gave him this time was longer and tighter. She didn't want to overwhelm him with emotion, but she wanted to convey to him all those things that she couldn't say.

"Take care of yourself," she whispered against his neck, and gave him a kiss on the cheek. "Hang in there, okay? I'll be back tomorrow."

Zachary kissed Kenzie gently, then let her go, stepping back slightly to put space between them. He nodded. "See you tomorrow. Thanks for coming."

2 8

Kenzie needed a few minutes after she left the psych ward. She found a cluster of furniture in an alcove area, where families or friends might meet in small groups, and she sat down, breathing heavily in and out, trying to relax her body and keep her emotions under control. She kept repeating to herself that Zachary was safe where he was and would be home soon. She wasn't abandoning him by going back home.

She managed to get herself calmed down. She wiped her face and got up and walked down the hall to the elevators. She was planning to go straight back out to her car, but when she got into the elevator, she saw the departments and their floors listed on the back of the elevator and her eyes caught on the Maternity Ward and NICU. She could stop in and see whether she could find anything out about Bridget and Gordon and the twins while she was there. It would be an efficient use of her time.

So she pressed the floor number and got back out of the elevator a couple of floors down instead of going all the way to the parking garage.

NICU was generally off-limits to everyone but the parents, unless they brought someone else in with them, so she didn't attempt to get in and find out about the babies by herself. The nurses wouldn't give her any information, even if she held herself out as a doctor. She wasn't their doctor, so the privacy rules still applied.

She headed instead to the maternity unit, following the signs on the walls until she reached the nursing station for the unit. She ignored the desk and

992

started to walk around the cluster of rooms, peeking in the doorways for Bridget and Gordon.

She knew that they might have gone home. Zachary had been worried about Bridget being released before the babies. With the cost of health care, it wouldn't make much sense for Bridget to stay at the hospital as a patient if she didn't need to.

"Uh, miss…?" She heard a nurse calling after her but ignored the call and kept going. She could probably get most of the way around the unit before anyone actually caught up with her or stopped her to ask her business there.

Kenzie looked in the next doorway and saw a man she thought was Gordon sitting beside the bed. He was blocking Kenzie's view of the woman, so she couldn't be sure, but she stepped in anyway, hoping she didn't make a fool of herself. But would it be so awful to say that she thought they were someone else? She only had a view of the man's back, after all.

"Uh, hi?" Kenzie took a couple of steps into the room for a better view, and both faces turned toward her. It was Gordon and Bridget after all.

Bridget looked at Kenzie for a moment before her face went taut and Kenzie supposed Bridget recognized her from when she had been together with Zachary out in public. Gordon smiled politely.

"I'm Kenzie," she introduced herself. "Sorry, I know you weren't expecting me here. I don't mean to disturb you."

"Kenzie." Gordon gave her a welcoming smile. "You don't need to apologize. What a nice surprise."

Bridget didn't look nearly so welcoming. She looked at the doorway behind Kenzie, waiting. Kenzie realized she was looking for Zachary, expecting him to come in behind her.

"It's just me. I'm alone."

The nurse who had been calling after Kenzie walked up to the doorway to look in at her and seemed satisfied when she saw that Kenzie was engaged in a discussion with the couple, apparently an expected guest. She turned and walked back away. Kenzie bit her lip and smiled at Bridget, acting as though she'd been greeted with warmth as a friend.

"I was here, and when I realized how close I was to the maternity unit, I thought I would just stop in and see how everyone is."

Gordon stood up to retrieve another visitor chair and slid it beside his. "Come, sit, sit."

Kenzie sat down in the uncomfortable chair and smiled once more at Bridget, the muscles in her face feeling the strain.

Bridget was pale and didn't appear to have put on any weight with her pregnancy; not that showed in her face, anyway. She swept long, blond hair over one ear and looked at Kenzie accusingly.

"Bridget is recovering quite well," Gordon said, as if he didn't notice any of the awkwardness between them. "It was quite an ordeal, but they tell me women have been having babies for thousands of years and I just need to stay out of the way and let her do her job." Gordon smiled affectionately at Bridget. "She really was a trooper. I can't imagine any man I know going through such a thing."

"Then it's a good thing that they don't have to," Bridget said.

Gordon nodded his agreement. "I never have bought into the 'weaker sex' thing. The strongest people I know are all women."

Kenzie nodded politely. "I'm so glad everything went well. I can tell you; we have been quite concerned."

Gordon let out a sigh and nodded. "The girls have had a difficult time. But if they are anything like their mother, they will pull through."

"I heard something about a heart attack?" Kenzie ventured, being careful not to name Zachary or to indicate that this news had come to them from Gordon. She didn't want to say anything that might trigger a tirade from Bridget.

Gordon nodded. "Julia. They managed to revive her, and she's still holding her own. They can't tell us anything about brain damage or any other permanent effects at this point. Just that she's improving. We haven't had another incident, which is what they warned us about. That sometimes, they just aren't strong enough and even though they are revived the first time…" Gordon trailed off. "But it's been a couple of days, and it hasn't happened again, so maybe she's through the danger period."

"I'm sorry, that must have been terrifying." Kenzie made sure that she met both of their eyes, not just speaking to Gordon and ignoring Bridget because she was more difficult to deal with. Bridget was the mother; she should be a full part of the discussion as well.

"Tricia, though, is off the respirator now," Gordon told her, smiling at this. "And that is very good news. She has been breathing on her own for twenty-four hours. The next step is feeding. She has a tube right now, but if we can start getting some milk into her by mouth…"

"That's great. I'm glad to hear that they're improving."

"What are you doing here?" Bridget demanded. "Where is Zachary?"

Kenzie swallowed and looked at her, trying to decide whether Bridget were trying to start something, or if she actually wanted Zachary to be there. She did go through occasional periods when she wanted something from him or started to show concern for him, before her mood started swinging the other direction again and she was haranguing him for something.

"He's not with me," Kenzie said slowly.

"Why wouldn't he come with you?"

Kenzie felt her way through the conversation uncertainly. "This is a difficult time of year for him, and he's been quite concerned for you and the twins. It's been hard on him."

Bridget wasn't being put off. She stared at Kenzie, waiting for Kenzie to give a proper answer to her question.

"He's been admitted," Kenzie said finally. As she and Zachary had discussed earlier, it was not a secret. Not something that Zachary wanted to hide as though he were ashamed of it. "He's quite depressed right now and felt that it was best if he was here, where it's safe."

"Here?"

"In the psychiatric unit." Not in maternity, obviously. Kenzie waited for the explosion—Bridget demanding to know why Zachary just happened to be in the same hospital as she was at the same time as she was. Was it a coincidence that they had both ended up in the same place? Kenzie waited for the accusations that the only reason that Zachary had admitted himself was because he wanted to be close to Bridget. To spy on her.

But the medication that Bridget was on seemed to have smoothed out some of the paranoid and angry outbursts that she had displayed previously. Or maybe she was just too tired from the births.

"Always at Christmas," Bridget said, nodding. "I thought that it would be different. We both thought that it would be different when we were together. And he did manage to stay out of the hospital those years. But it was not fun. Trying to drag him out to functions that we needed to appear at when he just wanted to curl up on the bed in a darkened room. Getting home from them and fighting half the night. I didn't think he was trying hard enough."

But the first year that Kenzie had known Zachary, Bridget had gone to Zachary's apartment at Christmas to check on him and clear out his meds to make sure that he couldn't overdose, even though they had no longer been together. So at some point, she had realized just how severe Zachary's depression was and that it wasn't something he could control.

"So that's why he's here," Kenzie said. "And why I'm here. He didn't ask me to come see you, but I thought I would check in on you and then I can reassure him that you are all okay when he asks next time."

"Why does he care how I am? Or how the twins are? After everything that we went through, all the troubles, why would he care?"

Kenzie gave a little laugh. "If it was me, I'm pretty sure I would stay away as far as possible," she agreed. "If somebody didn't want me around and we'd had as rocky a relationship as the two of you have, I wouldn't even want to know that you were pregnant."

"No. It's none of his business."

"But you and I don't have to deal with having his brain. With all the trauma and mental illness and everything that goes along with his ADHD and learning disabilities. He doesn't really want to be obsessed with you."

Bridget pondered that, a crease between her eyebrows. Gordon shifted in his seat. "You are looking tired, my dear." He looked at the shiny gold watch on his wrist. "It's late. You know you can't neglect your health."

Bridget closed her eyes and held her hand over her eyes and forehead for a moment. "Yes. I am getting tired."

"Go to sleep." Gordon got up and leaned over her to give her a kiss. Kenzie stood and prepared to leave.

"Let me walk you out," Gordon offered.

Kenzie walked to the door and waited for him to finish his goodbye with Bridget, then he joined her, and they walked out of the unit together.

"Would you like to see them?" Gordon asked.

Kenzie didn't have to ask who. "Yes, of course I would!"

He smiled and walked her past the elevators again, toward the NICU. Kenzie remembered her internship in maternity, and visits to the nursery and NICU, looking at the tiny, miraculous infants. No matter whether she believed in God and heaven or not, she believed that every baby was a miracle.

As a child, she had been thrilled when Amanda had been born. She had held her hand over Lisa's stomach to feel the baby kick. She had not been present for the birth but had been introduced to baby Amanda soon after that, and she had been enthralled. Despite her youth, she had changed diapers, fed Amanda, and entertained her for hours on end.

But she didn't think she could ever have worked in the NICU. Not knowing that she could lose any of those tiny infants at any moment. It was amazing to walk around and look at them, to see what challenges they had survived, but she hadn't wanted to know the long-term outcomes. Too many of them would die.

Gordon led her to an incubator that held two babies. Kenzie was glad to see that they were being kept together. She had seen videos and news reports on twins who had languished when they were kept apart and had immediately improved when put back together again. They needed each other.

One baby had breathing support.

"Julia," Gordon murmured, indicating her. He reached in through the access port and stroked her little stomach and arm.

Kenzie looked at the baby's vital signs monitor. Her oxygen saturation was good.

"And Tricia," Gordon said, and switched to the access port on the other side to touch her as well. Tricia stirred, turning her head toward him slightly. "Hello, sweetheart," Gordon crooned to her. "This is Daddy. You're getting so strong, aren't you?"

They were both pink and small, but not as tiny as some of the neonates Kenzie had seen. They had good skin color and vitals, and she hoped they would both be able to pull through. For their own sakes, and for Bridget and Gordon. And for Zachary.

"He's been so worried about them," she told Gordon in a whisper, not wanting to disturb the twins or confuse them with another voice. "When he heard about Julia's incident… I don't know if that is what triggered his suicidal thoughts this weekend, but he was very upset by it."

"I probably shouldn't have told him."

"If he asks, then you're being kind to tell him. You don't have to tell him anything, but you've been very compassionate toward him."

"I figure if I don't tell him, he'll be here checking up on them himself," Gordon said with a smile. "The only hope of keeping them separated is to let him know what he asks."

Kenzie chuckled and nodded. "Yes, you're probably right," she agreed. None of them would be able to keep Zachary away from Bridget and the twins if he thought that they were in danger and that Gordon was keeping information from him.

Gordon leaned in toward the incubator, getting his face as close to the little girls as he could. "Did you know that he was there again, when Bridget collapsed?"

"He told me."

"He must have ESP where she is concerned. To be there at that exact time."

"I'm sure that wasn't the only time he was there. We are talking to his medical team, by the way. They are increasing his meds and therapy to try to keep him away from her. Hopefully once everyone is out of the hospital…"

Gordon nodded. "It isn't like he doesn't try. I've seen that."

Kenzie hesitated to say anything further, then decided to bite the bullet. "But you need to stay away from him, too. Quit hiring him. Don't ask him for his opinion on anything. Putting him on surveillance of Bridget…!"

Gordon grimaced. "Not my best idea, maybe. But I knew he would be like a dog with a bone. He wouldn't rest until he knew the truth."

"You sent him back over the edge. I don't think he would have gone back to stalking her, if it weren't for that."

Gordon shrugged. In the end, he had gotten what he had wanted. Zachary had chased down the information Gordon had needed, so it had all worked out in the end. It may have wreaked havoc on Zachary's life, but that wasn't really Gordon's problem.

"I won't hire him again," he conceded.

"Good. If he asks you about Bridget or the twins and you want to answer him, that's fine. But don't reach out to him."

He nodded.

But Kenzie wondered whether he would keep his promise.

29

I t had been a long day and Kenzie was ready to go home. She had done everything she could for Zachary, and she needed to take care of herself so that she could do her job and so that when Zachary eventually got out of the hospital, she would be ready for him, and not worn away to nothing because she had been so focused on taking care of him. He had people there to look after him. The hospital staff would see to his physical needs and do what they could to improve his mood.

She left Gordon in the NICU. He looked as if he would be there for a while. She couldn't imagine that he was staying with the twins overnight. He had a business to look after. Like Kenzie, he would need to leave care of the patients to the hospital staff and to take care of himself.

But she didn't think that taking care of himself had ever been a problem for Gordon. He didn't strike her as someone who was shy about going after what he wanted. Even though it was the first time she had met him face to face, she had known that about him for some time. It was obvious by the way that he treated Zachary.

As she walked toward the elevators, Kenzie was surprised to see another familiar face. She blinked at the young male nurse walking toward her and tried to remember where she had seen him before. Had he just been up at the psych unit? She didn't think that was it.

She smiled and nodded at him, then studied his name tag as he walked toward her, until she could focus on the name.

"Nurse Stevens," she greeted. "I didn't expect to see you here."

And then she remembered where she had seen him before. He had been one of the nurses on duty in the geriatric ward. He had been there the day she had been conducting her investigation into Mr. Michaels's death and who had been on the floor when he had died.

Stevens was looking at her in confusion. He had only seen her once, and probably couldn't place her either. Kenzie lifted her chin slightly, holding his gaze.

"Dr. Kenzie Kirsch," she reminded him. "With the ME's Office."

"Oh, yes. I'm sorry, I recognized your face, but I couldn't remember where we had met." He looked around, checking whether anyone was watching them or within earshot. "So… what brings you here? I didn't think the Medical Examiner made house calls."

"Well, we do attend the scene when there is a suspicious death," she reminded him. "Even at a hospital."

"Well… yes, I suppose so. But there can't be many of those. Especially… in the NICU."

"As it happens, I'm not here on business. I was visiting a patient. And stopped in to see someone else I know."

He nodded, and his eyes darted around. "Sure. Of course."

Kenzie waited for him to say what he was doing away from his unit. It wasn't as if he could claim to have forgotten where the cafeteria was. There wasn't much call for a geriatric nurse to be on a maternity floor.

"I'm just up here to see a friend too," Stevens said eventually.

"Oh? How is she doing?"

"Uh… fine. Really good." He started moving again, passing her in the hallway. "Have a nice day."

Kenzie turned her head and watched him go, wondering what he was really there for. Pretty lame to use the same excuse as she had. It could be true, of course, but then she would have expected more of an explanation of how mother and child were doing, rather than just a generic "fine."

She waited until he had turned the corner and was out of sight, and then tapped his name into her phone.

Agent Menendez was at the Medical Examiner's Office bright and early the next morning. Well, not particularly early, but she was there the next morning. She examined the threat that Kenzie had received and looked down at it without much apparent interest.

"How did you get it?" she asked. "Was it in the mail? Dropped off in person?"

"The envelope is in there too," Kenzie pointed out. "It came in the postal mail."

Menendez studied it through the plastic sleeve. "Stamp hasn't been canceled. You're sure someone didn't throw it into interoffice mail or bring it down and leave it here in person? Are you just assuming it was in the postal mail?"

"No." Kenzie was irritated that Menendez would think she didn't have the intelligence to know whether something had come in through the mail or other channels. "We have a locked mailbox. No one but USPS can put anything in there."

"You don't have a mail room that sorts and delivers your mail?"

"No. I get it out of the box myself. The police have a mailroom up there," Kenzie motioned overhead. "But that isn't shared with the Medical Examiner's Office. Our mail system is completely separate."

"So no interoffice mail, you're totally autonomous."

Kenzie nodded. "Our interoffice mail is me taking stuff down to Dr. Wiltshire's office. But most of the time, I wouldn't even do that. I'd just email him."

Menendez nodded. "Right. Makes sense."

"It came in through the mail. I know that for sure."

She nodded and slid it into her soft-sided briefcase. "Great. I'll take care of it. See whether trace can get anything from it."

"Thanks. I don't usually get threats!"

"I guess that would be a bit of a shock, then. FBI..." Menendez shrugged. "We get them all the time."

Kenzie raised an eyebrow. She wasn't surprised about that. Especially with Agent Menendez, who didn't have quite the social skills Kenzie would have expected from an FBI agent working in the field.

"And you've got my tox reports?" Menendez asked.

"I have *my* tox reports," Kenzie corrected. "Which I've made copies of for the FBI."

Menendez put out her hand, flicking her fingers in an impatient *give-it-to-me* gesture. Kenzie picked up the envelope of reports that she had printed out for Menendez earlier.

Menendez took it with a nod and slid it into her bag as well.

"You said that you were starting to put together a suspect list," Kenzie said, "and that you might want to go over it with us?"

"Is Dr. Wiltshire available?"

"Not at the moment. He's on a conference call, but he should be off soon."

Menendez gave her a look of exasperation, as if Kenzie and Dr. Wiltshire should have known at exactly what time she would come by and have made sure that no one would be occupied with anything else when she arrived.

Kenzie rolled her eyes.

"I guess I'll wait, then," Menendez said.

Kenzie sat back down in her chair and leaned back. "Something kind of funny happened at the hospital yesterday. I wondered what you would think of it…"

"What happened? What were you doing back at the hospital?" the agent frowned, studying Kenzie "Especially after receiving this note?"

"I was visiting a friend who is sick," Kenzie said evenly.

"A friend who is sick. This friend wouldn't happen to be in the geriatric unit, would they? I would think that you'd know well enough to stay out of the way once our investigation started."

"No, he isn't in the geriatric unit. I wasn't anywhere near there."

"Okay. But still. Why would you go after getting this note?"

"I don't think that note meant anything about me visiting a friend. It just meant not going to investigate anything. Not to keep asking questions about who was around the day that Michaels died."

"It doesn't say that. If someone happened to see you there, they could spread the word to our killer that you are still hanging around. It could cause you trouble."

Kenzie shifted uncomfortably. "I didn't imagine that I would run into anyone who was from the geriatric unit or who knew that I had been there. Usually, professionals stay pretty close to their units. They might go down to the cafeteria for something to eat, but they wouldn't have a reason to go traipsing to other parts of the hospital."

Menendez studied Kenzie for a moment, then gave a wide shrug. "Well then… what happened that was funny?"

Kenzie cleared her throat, not so sure that she wanted to tell Menendez about it now. Not right after she had said that it didn't make sense that someone who worked in another area of the hospital would show up somewhere else.

"I saw one of the nurses who I had seen in the geriatric unit when I was asking questions. I thought it was really strange to find him there."

Menendez glared at her. "Well, as you said, maybe he was just on his way to the cafeteria."

"Well… I know that he wasn't. It wasn't anywhere near the cafeteria. When I asked him about it, he said that he was there to see a friend."

"Maybe he was. People who work at the hospital can have friends. Friends who might invite them to come over for a visit if they happen to have a free moment."

"Yeah. It's possible. He just didn't sound to me as if he was telling the truth."

"Maybe he was, or maybe he wasn't. No way for us to know. What did you tell him that you were doing there?"

"Visiting a friend."

Menendez grunted her acknowledgment. "So why couldn't he be too? How far away from the geriatric unit were you?"

"I was in the NICU."

Menendez leaned in and didn't say anything.

"Neonatal Intensive Care Unit," Kenzie explained.

Again, there was no response from Menendez. She was not perky and friendly, unlike the other days she had been by. Maybe she'd been told by one of her superiors to shape up and start acting like a grown-up FBI officer.

"It's practically the other side of the hospital and up five floors," Kenzie explained. "It's not close. I had no reason to think that I might run into someone from the geriatric unit there."

"Well, there's no reason that a nurse couldn't go visit a friend in another unit. If you want to give me their name, I'll make sure he's on the list of people to investigate and see whether we can get any details of why he was there and who he was seeing."

"Stevens. A male nurse. I don't remember his first name."

"Stevens." Menendez nodded, appearing to thaw a little. "Yeah, I remember that name. He's already on the list."

"Good."

Menendez leaned on the edge of Kenzie's desk. "And who were you there to see?"

Kenzie could see that things were just going to continue to be more awkward if she tried to preserve her private life. Insisting that Menendez interrogate others about what they had been doing in another part of the hospital, and then refusing to explain her presence would not be taken well.

"I would like a little privacy," Kenzie said. "My life away from this office really isn't anyone else's business."

"You having an affair or something?"

"No." Kenzie's face warmed. She tried to ignore the blush and press forward. "I'm not having an affair. I was visiting Zachary. We live together.

It's just that this is very private information. Personal, private medical records," she said firmly.

"Who am I going to run around telling? Your boyfriend, Zachary." She lifted one eyebrow and stared at Kenzie.

"Yes. What?"

"Did Zachary recently have a baby?"

Kenzie had to laugh at the incongruity over her answer and what she had already told Menendez. "No—no, sorry. I was there to see Zachary. He's upstairs, in psychiatric. But a friend of ours—" Kenzie elected not to tell Menendez that she was Zachary's ex, "—just had twins, and they are in the NICU."

"So who were you there to see? Your boyfriend or these friends?"

"I had already been in to see Zachary. I was on my way out. Going home. Then I realized that maternity was right there, so I went in to say hello."

"And ran into this Nurse Stevens."

"Right. I ran into him on my way out of NICU; he was on his way in. And he didn't say who he was there to see or what had happened. Normally, if you go to visit someone with a baby in the NICU, you would talk about what happened—the baby was premature or they had to deliver early because of some medical problem—but he didn't. He just said he was there to visit a friend."

"Which could be perfectly correct."

"Of course," Kenzie agreed. "Absolutely. It was just disconcerting to see him there, especially after getting this threatening note. He didn't 'belong' there in my mind. But that doesn't mean he didn't. It could be completely innocent. The only problem is that he was one of the people who was around the day that Mr. Michaels died. And that doesn't mean he had anything to do with it."

Menendez nodded. "As long as we are agreed."

30

I t was a while before Dr. Wiltshire got off his conference call. Kenzie set Menendez up in the boardroom and got her a coffee, so that Kenzie could get back to work. She didn't want to sit around talking to Menendez, who seemed to think that Kenzie wanted to be her best friend and tell her all about her life.

"Kenzie, sorry to keep you waiting." Dr. Wiltshire looked toward the boardroom. "Everything okay?"

"Yes, just fine. She's been out of the way. Mostly."

"Why don't you freshen your coffee, and we'll see what she has to share."

Kenzie thought that sounded like a pretty good idea. She went to the kitchenette to get a refill, then joined Dr. Wiltshire in the boardroom where he was talking casually with Agent Menendez.

"Well, looks like we're finally all here," Menendez observed when Kenzie sat down at the table. "I've been away from the office longer than I should have been, so let's get started here."

Kenzie hadn't seen Menendez take any calls or have to make abject apologies to her bosses. Kenzie got the feeling that she was allowed pretty wide latitude to do whatever she wanted to do, not that she was only let out of the office for limited windows of time. Kenzie couldn't judge by TV shows, of course, but on the ones she had seen, they always spent a lot of time in the field and could pursue leads as they came up. They didn't just sit at their desks all day and make inquiries on their computers or phones.

Just like Zachary didn't do all his investigative work from home. He had to get out on site, talk to people, make contact in the real world.

Kenzie pulled her thoughts away from Zachary yet again as Menendez took a few items out of her briefcase. It was difficult to stay focused on the task at hand and not wonder how Zachary was doing. She just had to keep reminding herself that he was fine where he was. There was nothing to worry about.

Menendez leafed through several pages of notes, some computer generated and some handwritten.

"So, you were talking about Nurse Stevens, and he was one of the nurses that we had down as having been on the floor the day that Mr. Michaels died. He has not been in the unit for a long time, though, so if we are trying to reach all the way back on the list that Dr. Philemon provided, he could not be involved in the earlier ones."

"But we don't know whether any of those cases are actually related," Kenzie said. "It's all just speculation until we can prove that they were homicides."

"Right." Menendez nodded and took a sip of her own travel cup of coffee. "It's difficult to come up with a concrete list when we don't know which deaths were actually homicides and which were not. We don't know which ones we have to correlate schedules with, so it all becomes a little... amorphous."

Kenzie knew this to be true from previous cases. It was hard to correlate when you didn't know which deaths were representative. It all ended up being a hodgepodge of facts.

Menendez read off a few of the names on her list. Some of them, Kenzie recognized, like Nurse Pierce. Even Dr. Philemon had to be considered. Sometimes people wanted to be caught. They wanted to explain to someone how smart they were, show them how much they had gotten away with. Just because he had started the investigation himself, that didn't eliminate the young doctor from the list of suspects.

"And the people who were not medical professionals?" Kenzie asked. "There was a volunteer there, her name was Roda. I don't know who else might have been there the day Mr. Michaels died. There are a lot of administrative and support people who could have been around. Even if they don't normally interface with the patients, like a security guard or a plumber, they could still get around the ward and put something in an IV without being noticed."

"There's no way for us to track all those people. Not unless they have gotten themselves noticed enough for someone that we interview to bring them up. There's no way to know who might have walked in and out. But history says that it is likely to be a doctor or nurse, so that's really what we need to focus on."

Kenzie nodded slowly. It was frightening, when she thought about it, how many people could walk in and out of a place that you thought was secure, like a hospital. How someone who was dangerous could be lurking right under their noses and they wouldn't even know it. Any of the doctors and nurses she had talked to that day. The ones she had seen in the psychiatric unit when she had gone to visit Zachary. The ones she had seen in maternity and NICU. Any of those people could be deeply disturbed to the point that they were murdering patients, and if they were clever, they could kill dozens before they were caught.

Finding the one person who really was dangerous was like searching for a needle in a haystack. Or in a box full of needles.

"Can I see the list? Get a copy?" Kenzie asked.

"I only have one copy. And I shouldn't really let it out of my control."

So she wasn't likely to let Kenzie make a copy of it or write the names down herself. But just looking at the list might trigger something.

"Could I just see it then? Read through it?"

Menendez looked wary. Where was the girl who wanted to be Kenzie's best friend now?

"I can't really be of any help if I can't even see the list," Kenzie pointed out. "I helped you to compile that list. It isn't like it's a secret."

"I really shouldn't…" Menendez trailed off. She looked around her as if one of her bosses might have snuck into the boardroom without her noticing and be listening to see what she said.

She slid the papers across the table to Kenzie.

Kenzie picked them up and started to read through them. She had no doubt that Menendez had them organized in a particular way, but Kenzie couldn't make sense of it. It all seemed to be slapdash, cobbled together. But it wasn't like Kenzie's thoughts on the topic were any clearer than the FBI agent's.

Kenzie stopped as she read through the notes and put her index finger on one of the names. "Nurse Debbie. That's funny, I just met a nurse that I knew a long time ago when my sister was sick, and her name is Nurse Debbie. But she doesn't work in that unit. She's in the psychiatric unit."

Menendez frowned. "Really." She scratched the back of her neck. "That name was specifically suggested by one of the other nurses. She used to be in the geriatric unit, but isn't any longer."

"Well, I'm sure it couldn't be the same Nurse Debbie. It isn't exactly a rare name."

"You don't know her last name?"

Kenzie knew she had seen Nurse Debbie's name badge and tried to remember. She shook her head. "No. I don't remember. We always just called her Nurse Debbie."

Menendez picked up her phone. "Easy to find out." She tapped the screen for a moment, then put it to her ear.

Kenzie couldn't hear who answered it; the volume was low enough that she could only hear Agent Menendez's voice.

"Hi. Agent Josie Menendez here," the woman snapped out. "I just had some follow up questions to our conversation."

She listened for a moment.

"This will only take a few minutes," she said, overruling whatever objection the other party had. She ran through a few casual questions and comments before getting to the one she actually wanted to ask. "You mentioned a Nurse Debbie. You said she wasn't in the geriatric unit anymore. Where did she go? Is she still with the hospital?"

Kenzie held her breath in anticipation.

"In psych," Menendez confirmed, raising an eyebrow at Kenzie. "Thank you very much. I'll let you know if I need anything else." She tapped to close the call and looked at Kenzie. "The same."

"Nurse Debbie?" Kenzie gave a laugh of disbelief and shook her head. "There's no way it's *her*. I know her, Josie. I've known her for years. I've seen her in action, what a good nurse she is. My younger sister was in the hospital a lot. She had kidney failure. She spent a lot of time in the nephrology unit when Nurse Debbie was there, and the woman was a saint. Always cheerful. You know how many of these nurses drag around and complain about anything you ask them to do that makes them raise a finger. She was never like that. Always happy to help with whatever she could. Cheered everyone up. She was just amazing."

"Then why isn't she still doing that?"

"People burn out. If she went from nephrology to geriatrics, then she's probably tired of dealing with people who are slowly dying. So she gets transferred to psychiatric instead, where you aren't usually dealing with patients who are dying."

"Just people who are crazy," Menendez laughed.

"No. Not crazy. Mentally ill. Remember that Zachary is one of those people. He's not crazy, but he's depressed. He needs support. And Nurse Debbie is just the kind of person he needs." Kenzie pushed aside the memory of how uncomfortable Nurse Debbie had made Zachary. Most people in psych needed someone just like Nurse Debbie. Always cheerful and upbeat, trying to include everyone and to make them happy.

"You can't make a judgment based on whether you think she's a good nurse or not," Dr. Wiltshire pointed out. "Nurses who follow this pattern tend to be very competent and well-liked."

"Well, there's more to it than that," Kenzie said. "For one thing, how long has she been out of geriatric? I thought she's been in psych for a few weeks."

"Yes," Menendez agreed. "She did transfer units a little while ago."

"Then she couldn't have been involved in Michaels's death, and that's one of the two that we know was actually a homicide."

"She was still in the hospital. As you were saying this morning, there's nothing to stop nurses from going to visit someone in another unit."

Dr. Wiltshire looked at Kenzie, raising an eyebrow. Kenzie shrugged. "Yes, of course." She stared down at the notices. "But if she was an Angel of Death killer, then she wouldn't transfer to a unit where nobody dies. People might notice if there was a sudden rash of deaths in psych, people dropping dead from apparent heart attacks when there wasn't anything physically wrong with them."

"The body and the mind are intertwined," Dr. Wiltshire said. "People with severe psychiatric disorders are often unhealthy in other ways as well."

"I know. But don't you think it's true? If she wanted to watch people die, then why not go to oncology? Or stay in geriatrics?"

"She couldn't stay in geriatrics," Menendez said.

"Couldn't? Why not?"

"Because there were questions about her patients dying."

31

Kenzie stared at Agent Menendez. "I don't think that's very funny."

"It was one of those situations where no one could prove anything or even back it up with statistics, but your Nurse Debbie was one of those people who often ended up with patients who died."

"If you can't prove it statistically, then she didn't get any more than anyone else," Kenzie said flatly. "It's simple math."

"She's a suspect; she hasn't been arrested. Obviously, we don't have the evidence to back it up, or she wouldn't still be working at the hospital. And the same goes for her superiors. If they could prove that there was anything wrong, they would get rid of her, not let her stay at the hospital."

"Maybe they're the ones who figured it would be safer to put her in psychiatric," Dr. Wiltshire suggested. "Like you said, not many people dying there. So either they put a stop to deaths on her watch, or she decides to quit and go somewhere she can do what she wants to."

"Or they wanted to put her where she belongs," Menendez said. "Into the psych ward. Maybe they couldn't commit her, but they could transfer her there as a nurse."

Kenzie glared at Menendez. "I don't appreciate the psych ward jokes, Josie."

"You're being overly sensitive. Just because you have a boyfriend there. If you didn't, you would think it was funny."

"I'd appreciate it if you would stop."

"You make jokes about your work, don't you?" Menendez challenged. "Don't tell me you've never made inappropriate jokes about dead people."

Kenzie looked at Dr. Wiltshire and grimaced. They tried to keep the Medical Examiner's Office a solemn and respectful place, but they did enjoy their puns and gallows humor, when circumstances called for it. Sometimes the only way to deal with a horrific death was to find the humor in it.

"You see?" Menendez said smugly. "We all joke about things that are inappropriate. All this proper and politically correct stuff is just politics. We joke to relieve stress. If you don't take offense, it doesn't hurt you."

Kenzie tried to explain it in a way that was logical, but couldn't. "Okay, then I'm being oversensitive," she said. "I'm feeling pretty raw about it. You would too if you had to worry about a loved one committing suicide. I don't want to hear jokes making fun of people like Zachary who have serious problems to deal with, and who have no control over the problems they have."

Menendez shrugged. "All right. I'll try to temper it," she agreed. "But if I slip up…"

"I'll try to be more patient."

They both eyed each other, dissatisfied.

<hr>

Kenzie was thinking about the conversation as she drove to the hospital for another visit with Zachary. Why did she feel like it was okay for her and Dr. Wiltshire to make morbid jokes about their work, but not for Menendez to joke about Nurse Debbie taking a job in the psych ward?

For one thing, Menendez didn't work there herself. Maybe Kenzie would have felt as though it was okay for her to make crazy jokes if she worked there herself. But on the other hand… she didn't think so. Even if it was just a way to relieve stress, it was still disrespectful of people like Zachary who were struggling with mental illness, in a way that Kenzie's jokes were not. They didn't target the dead or treat them disrespectfully, they just made puns, mostly. It was something that she might have to watch, even if it were just so that she could explain to people like Menendez what the difference was.

The nurse at the front desk of the psychiatric unit recognized Kenzie this time, and nodded at her. "Nice to see you again. You're here to see Zachary, right?"

Kenzie smiled at her. "Right. How is he today?"

"I wouldn't want to say. You can't tell what's going on in people's heads. He's seemed pretty calm."

Kenzie took a step toward the common room, but the nurse held her hand up. "He has other visitors right now, and we try to limit numbers, not have too many people in to see one person at the same time."

"Oh. Who is with him?"

The petite nurse pushed a lock of hair away from her eyes and looked at the register or notes that she had in front of her. "Let's see, a Lorne Peterson and—"

"Patrick Parker," Kenzie finished. "We'll be quiet and not get him wound up. Three people isn't too many, is it? We're not going to be playing poker or starting any fights."

The woman smiled and shook her head. "Well… I suppose that will be okay. But we would appreciate it if you could coordinate, so that you don't get too many people here at the same time. Or overwhelm Zachary with too many visitors."

Kenzie nodded. "Sure, of course. We'll talk."

The nurse looked around for an orderly to escort Kenzie, but there was no one around. Kenzie made a motion. "I know where it is. I'll just go in."

"Well… yes, of course. I'm sure that would be okay."

Kenzie slipped past the desk and went to the common room where she had met with Zachary before. He was sitting at one of the tables with Lorne, a former foster father he'd kept in touch with over the years, and Lorne's partner, Pat, who fell somewhere between Lorne and Zachary in age. He and Lorne had been together for more than twenty years, since Zachary had been a teenager.

Zachary saw Kenzie as she arrived and stood up to greet her. Pat and Lorne turned around and were all smiles. Kenzie hugged and kissed Zachary first, then hugged each of the older men. "Nice to see you! I didn't think you'd be around until the weekend."

"We both had some time, so we thought we'd make the trip," Lorne said with a shrug. "See how this troublemaker was doing."

They all sat back down. Kenzie drew her chair close to Zachary's. As usual, he had picked a position that would allow him to see the rest of the room. No one could enter or approach without his seeing. Was it because of his training as a PI? Or learned behavior from being in situations where he had to be wary of abusers or bullies when he was growing up?

"How was the drive?" she asked the two men, keeping the focus from Zachary to begin with. She was sure he didn't want to be asked again how he was doing, to have to come up with an answer that would not upset any of his visitors. No one would expect him to say "fine," under the circumstances, but she didn't want to put him into the position where he had to talk about suicidal thoughts in front of all of them.

"Some ice and snow, but the highways have been cleared, so it wasn't too bad."

"Not like when we got snowed in at the Lodge!" Kenzie offered.

She and Zachary had been trapped for several days by a snowstorm that had blown in. An experience that Kenzie did not want to repeat.

"No. I'm glad we got out before the snow came in," Pat agreed. "I don't know how you guys managed without any electricity or cell coverage. Especially you," he told Zachary in a teasing tone. "The way you're attached to your phone."

"You should have seen Mason," Zachary said with a smile. Mason was Tyrrell's son, Zachary's nephew. "He'd never been without power or internet connectivity before. He kept telling Tyrrell to just call or message someone."

Kenzie laughed. "He was climbing up on the table, trying to get a signal on Tyrrell's phone. Couldn't understand how it was possible that there was no connection."

"How did he survive being snowbound?" Lorne asked. "He was so hyperactive while we were there…"

"It was a challenge," Zachary said.

Kenzie nodded and agreed. "He did get into some scrapes. But there were board games, and he and Alisha played quite a bit. He still got bored, but without any screens to entertain him, he was a little easier to get to bed."

"Maybe they'll get a chance to visit you," Pat suggested to Zachary. "The kids will be getting out of school for Christmas, and didn't Tyrrell say that he had them for the holiday this year?"

Zachary nodded. But he looked around at his surroundings, frowning. "I don't think he'll want to bring the kids here."

Kenzie glanced around. It wasn't the happiest place, but it didn't look any different from the rest of the hospital. No one was raving, threatening, or obviously delusional. Nothing that should be too traumatic to the kids.

"Why not?"

"I just don't think it's a good place for kids. He shouldn't bring them here."

"Do you want me to tell him that? Not to?"

Zachary hesitated. "Well… maybe. Yeah. But he won't be able to come then either. Because someone will have to watch the kids."

"I can look after them for a while. They know me."

"Where, at the house? Mason might make a mess."

"I can manage a little mess."

"Maybe you could take them somewhere else. One of those play places at the mall."

Kenzie rolled her eyes. "And what if Mason takes off and I lose him? I'd rather have him at home where I know he'll be safe."

"Well… yeah, I guess so. Maybe just tell Tyrrell that I can see them when I'm out. I don't want him to have to drag the kids here and then not be able to bring them in."

"It's up to you. You can decide who you want to see and who you don't. I'll just pass the message along."

"It isn't that I don't want to see him. Just that the kids…" Zachary looked around again. "It's not a good place for kids."

"It's not that different from Bonnie Brown, where you spent most of your Christmases as a kid," Lorne pointed out.

"But that was because I belonged there. They don't belong here," Zachary said stubbornly. He rarely talked about his time at Bonnie Brown, but Kenzie knew that the institution was a pretty grim place for kids like Zachary. Kids who were unable to keep a placement with a foster family due to behavioral issues or delinquency.

"Okay," Kenzie agreed. "I'll call Tyrrell and let him know."

"It's quiet right now. But it isn't always." His eyes were restless, moving back and forth at the other patients. "Sometimes patients get agitated. They can be loud and scary for little kids."

"You can get together with them after Christmas, like we had planned."

"Yeah." Zachary tapped the table in front of him, fidgeting.

Kenzie studied him covertly. He didn't look too bad, all things considered. The year before, when he had been able to stay out of the hospital before Christmas, he had looked pretty rough on Christmas Eve. And even the previous week, when he hadn't been sleeping, it had really showed physically. She suspected that the hospital was probably insisting that he take a sleeping pill at bedtime and forcing him to eat, two things that she couldn't do when he was at home. And maybe if they could keep him sleeping and eating properly, he would be able to avoid slipping further into depression.

32

She's coming over to talk to you again," Zachary said.

Kenzie followed his gaze and saw Nurse Debbie, who was, as Zachary said, heading with deliberation in their direction. Kenzie could feel Zachary tense beside her.

"Sorry," she said. "I know she annoys you."

"It wouldn't be so bad if she would keep her hands to herself."

Lorne raised his brows and turned his head to see who they were talking about.

Kenzie stood up to greet Nurse Debbie. If she could stop the woman's progress a few feet away from Zachary, then she wouldn't be able to pat him on the shoulder or the back as she tried to cheer him up.

"Debbie! Hi, so nice to see you again," Kenzie greeted, giving her a social hug and keeping her body between Nurse Debbie and Zachary. "How are you doing?"

"In the pink," Debbie declared with a big smile. "And how's my favorite patient tonight?" She took a half-step to the side to get around Kenzie, but Kenzie mirrored the movement, smiling and touching Nurse Debbie's arm warmly, as if she wanted to tell her something important.

"He's looking pretty good," Kenzie said. "You guys must be taking good care of him."

"Well, we do our best! And I know that Zachary isn't feeling himself, but at least he doesn't get crabby and grouch at the nurses the way that some of these people do."

Kenzie nodded in agreement. She knew that Zachary tried not to bring her down with his moods, but living with him, she couldn't help but be affected.

"It must be hard working with patients whose moods are all over the place," Kenzie observed. "And when it's chemical, there's not really anything you can do to cheer someone up and make them feel better. You know it's not personal, but it's hard not to take it personally."

"You hit the nail on the head," Nurse Debbie agreed. "I do my best to be in control of my own mood and not to take any of it personally." She shook her head. "But some of them do get under your skin!"

Kenzie dropped her hand from Nurse Debbie's arm. "Well, we should let you get back to work. I'm sure you have a lot to do."

Debbie didn't take the hint and withdraw. She leaned a little closer to Kenzie. "What are these rumors I hear about you," she asked, dropping her voice. "That you're working with the FBI on some serial killer case?"

Kenzie hesitated. She didn't want to make a big deal of it in front of Zachary and the others, who were all likely to get anxious at the idea of her trying to identify a serial killer. But she also wanted to hear what Nurse Debbie had to say about it and couldn't very well deny her own involvement in the case.

"Well…" she drew the word out and kept her voice low. "I can't really say anything about it, of course…"

"Oh, no," Debbie agreed, looking excited about it. "Of course not. And I won't breathe a word of it to anyone else."

"We're still establishing the facts. Of course, I'm not really involved with the FBI, but my services at the Medical Examiner's Office have involved me in it collaterally…"

"And they really think that there's a serial killer in the geriatric unit? Do *you* think so?"

"I can't say what the Medical Examiner is going to put on the death certificates. But…"

Debbie shook her head, grinning. "That's my old unit, did you know that? I worked with those people. I just can't see it. Everyone that I worked with is completely trustworthy. I just can't imagine how you could think that one of the staff would do something like that."

"You used to work there?" Kenzie repeated, feigning surprise.

"Yes! For several years! But it got to be too much for me, you know. People burn out. I needed to try something else. Get away from all the death and despair…"

"It must be very difficult to work there day in and day out," Kenzie agreed. She wondered whether Nurse Debbie were telling the truth that she trusted everyone she had worked with there completely. Did a person ever know their coworkers that well? Kenzie knew she would be looking askance at the people she worked with if there were any suggestion that one of them might be a killer.

"Yes. So… I came up here." Debbie smiled. "And I'm so glad that I did, or I would not have reconnected with you."

Kenzie smiled in return. All of Debbie's exuberance seemed a little too dramatic to be genuine. But she certainly didn't seem like the person they were looking for. Kenzie had seen her in action and knew first-hand how well she took care of her patients and cared for them and did what she could to make their lives easier.

But word was apparently getting around that Kenzie was involved in the serial killer investigation case. If Nurse Debbie had heard it when she wasn't even in that unit anymore, then Kenzie had no doubt that a lot of people must know. And that was going to make it all the harder to work out who had sent her the threatening letter.

After watching Nurse Debbie walk away, Kenzie sat back down beside Zachary again. He blew out his breath.

"Thank you."

Pat looked over his shoulder in the direction that Debbie had gone. "I get that she might be a little overbearing, but I think she's just trying to be friendly."

Zachary didn't answer at first. He rubbed the back of his neck, staring down at the top of the table. "Sometimes, that 'being nice' is a way of bullying people into doing what you want. Nurses are especially good at it, but there are others, too. Salespeople. Teachers and principals. Police, sometimes. It sounds like they're being nice, but they don't stop until they've talked you into doing what they want. And when they won't stop touching you, putting their hands on you to encourage you to do what they say…"

Pat's brow wrinkled as he thought about that. He shook his head slightly. "I've never thought about it that way. I just think… people are being nice and polite like society says they should. Sometimes they might push harder than you're comfortable with, but if you just say 'no'…"

"They don't listen to no. Have you ever listened to any of those training videos for marketing? *No is just another way to get to yes…*"

"Well, if they really won't listen when you say no, then that's wrong."

"Yeah."

Pat still looked as if he were having a hard time with this idea. He looked at Lorne, then back at Zachary, his head cocked slightly. "Do you feel like *I* act that way toward you?"

"You?" Zachary looked up from the table, eyes widening. "No!"

"Because I might be like that. Trying to cheer you up. To make you eat something. You say no to one thing, and I offer something else instead. Giving you... a pat of encouragement..." He shrugged. "If those things bother you...?"

"No, it's not the same," Zachary told him. But Kenzie had to admit, it was hard to see the dividing line between the two.

"No?"

Zachary chewed on his lip. "I know you do those things because you're... family. We have a relationship. You're not some stranger trying to twist my arm. You care, and you're looking for ways to help, not... trying to force me to do what *you* want."

"Yes," Pat agreed thoughtfully.

Lorne put his arm around Pat. "Zachary knows that we love him. No one forces him to come over to the house. And he knows when he comes over that you're going to make him something to eat and do your best to make sure that he's happy and comfortable when he's there."

"Yeah," Zachary agreed, nodding vigorously. "You trying to help me isn't the same as them—" Zachary nodded to indicate the direction Debbie had gone, "trying to make me behave the way they think I should." He paused, blinking and looking up toward the ceiling. "Even if you *said* exactly the same thing, it wouldn't *feel* the same."

"Hmm." There were a few minutes of silence. Then Pat said, "Can I ask you a favor?"

Zachary nodded.

"Since I can't feel what you're feeling, will you tell me if you feel like I'm pushing you or not respecting your boundaries? Tell me 'no' if it's a firm no, instead of 'I don't know' or 'maybe later'?"

Zachary grimaced. "I'll try," he agreed, dropping his eyes again. "It's hard. Dr. Boyle says that I need to be better about saying what I'm feeling to people I love. I'm better at deflecting and telling people what I think they want to hear."

"Well, if you try that, I'll try not to push you into things that you don't want to do."

33

Pat turned to Kenzie. He smiled brightly. "So… you're working on a serial killer case?" he asked in a light tone.

They all laughed. Kenzie glanced around to make sure that they were not disturbing anyone around them. A few glances swung in their direction at the laughter, but then everyone looked away again, going back to their own conversations or activities.

"Well… I'm not really working the case. The FBI is working the case. I am just involved because I was helping out with a few autopsies."

"Is this something I'm going to regret asking about?" Pat checked. "Is it gory or," he glanced at Zachary, "too close to home?"

"No, it isn't like that at all. It's what we tend to call an Angel of Death or Angel of Mercy killer. Usually a doctor or nurse or other medical practitioner who kills patients. On the surface, at least, to put them out of their misery. To send them to a better place, where their suffering is over."

"Oh, well, that's nice of them."

Kenzie smiled at his sarcasm. "Of course, whether that's really why they're doing it, or whether they have a morbid fascination with death and just pick the most vulnerable victims… that's for the psychologists to figure out. Or sometimes, they have a 'hero complex' and want everybody to see them as a wonderful, heroic caregiver. So they *almost* kill patients, and then bring them back from the brink. Or aren't able to, but they at least try. It's like a fireman who lights a fire and then comes back with his brigade to put it out."

"So this one that you're trying to catch, what do you think their motivation is?"

"I don't know. I'm not a psychologist, and we don't have enough data yet. So far, we have only been able to prove two of the cases in the series were homicides. We'll need more to prove that there is a serial killer, and then something distinctive or some connection between them to be able to find the killer." Kenzie shrugged. "This kind of killer can be very difficult to find. They might get away with it for years before they get caught. Some of the most prolific serial killers in history have been Angel of Death killers."

"But they're not dangerous to *you*," Lorne said. "As someone investigating the killings. They're only a danger to the patients they work with."

Kenzie thought about the note she had received. *Or else.*

It was probably best not to mention that detail.

"No. They're not usually dangerous at all to authorities. When they get caught, they usually confess. To everything. And..." Kenzie pointed a finger at him. "*I* am not investigating the killer. The FBI is. Even if, for some reason, they decided to focus on the Medical Examiner's Office, they would threaten the Medical Examiner, not me. I'm just a lowly worker bee. It's Dr. Wiltshire's name that will be on the death certificates."

"That's good," Lorne nodded. "We don't want to run afoul of a serial killer."

Pat looked down at his watch. "We should probably be getting on our way. We want to get home in good time."

"Yes. And we don't want to tire Zachary out."

They stood and began their goodbyes, giving hugs and murmuring encouraging things to Zachary, promising to come back and see him again.

"Let me walk you out," Kenzie offered.

Lorne shook his head. "He wants you to himself for a bit. We can find our way out."

Kenzie looked back at Zachary and saw his expression. Lorne was right; it did look as though he wanted to discuss something with her. But the wrinkles around his eyes told her that he was tired, so she shouldn't stay too much longer. She said goodbye to the two men, then sat down across the table from Zachary, where Pat had been. She took his hands in the middle of the table.

"Hey," she greeted, smiling.

"Hey."

"You look like you're doing good. Do they have you on anything new?"

"No. And it wouldn't make a difference this quickly if they did."

"You're sleeping better?"

"Yes."

"What's up?"

He looked away, uncomfortable.

"Come on," Kenzie encouraged. "I'm here. What did you want to talk about?"

"Well, it's nothing. Not about my treatment or about *us*."

"Are you worrying about your work? Heather's holding down the fort."

"No. I've been able to handle it before, when I didn't have her working with me. People are impatient, but when you are in the hospital, they just have to wait. If they can't wait, they go to somebody else."

"Okay." Kenzie waited.

"It's just… I never heard anything about the babies. If everything worked out. I don't feel like I should be asking you to talk to Gordon… but…"

"I saw him yesterday."

Zachary blinked, looking surprised. "You did?"

"Yes. After I left here, I saw the sign for maternity and thought I would pop in and say hello. Get caught up in case you wanted to know how everyone is."

Zachary chuckled. "Well… I didn't expect that. You know me too well."

"It's been obvious how concerned you've been about the babies ever since you found out that Bridget was pregnant. I didn't think that would stop just because you were in psych for a while."

"Maybe Dr. B would say that I should stay out of it. Am I just… feeding my obsessive needs if I ask? Will it make them worse?"

"You'd have to ask her. I don't know. You know yourself pretty well, though. What do you think?"

"I think…" Zachary pondered the question. "I think that if I get the information from you or Gordon… then I don't feel as compelled to go see Bridget and find out for myself."

"That's good enough for me. Is it good enough for you?"

"You shouldn't have to put up with this," Zachary said, his face getting pink. "Women don't want to hear all about their partners' exes all the time."

Kenzie remembered one of the men she had dated briefly who had done just that, talking about nothing else, all the way through their date, but the woman he had just broken up with and every single thing about her, until Kenzie thought she probably knew the woman better than she could know herself. What had his name been? Roger? Kenzie hadn't gone on a second date with him.

"No," she agreed. "But you don't talk about her most of the time. If you want to know how the babies are, then I can understand that. As long as that's not the only thing you talk about."

In fact, if he could obsess about the babies instead of Bridget, that was a little easier on Kenzie's ego. She would prefer that he was thinking about a couple of helpless infants than a woman that Kenzie could never be. She would never be able to live up to the image Zachary had built of Bridget in his imagination. *That* Bridget was not real and did not reflect the flaws of the real person.

Zachary finally nodded, satisfied that it wasn't a relationship-breaker for him to ask about the twins.

"Okay. What did he say?"

"The one who had the heart attack, her name is Julia. We may as well refer to them by name, instead of just 'the babies.' They are real people, not just a concept."

"Julia. And… she's okay? You said her name *is* Julia."

"Yes. They are both still fighting."

It was interesting that they used the verb *fighting* for life. A word that normally had negative connotations, that referred to violence. Yet in this context, it was positive.

"The other baby is Tricia. And she's off the respirator, breathing on her own."

Zachary's eyes brightened. "That's good."

"Yes, it's real progress. They can start feeding her by mouth, and that will help her to gain weight and develop more quickly. She'll get stronger."

"But the other—Julia—is still on the respirator."

"For the time being. And both are on lots of monitors to try to catch any problems before they become serious. Julia has not had any more heart problems. So maybe it was just a one-time thing, caused by a blood clot maybe."

"Thanks for checking on them. I really appreciate it." He pressed his lips together, and Kenzie had an inkling that he was trying to keep himself from asking how Bridget was. And if he didn't ask, she wouldn't bring her up.

"I actually got to see them," she told Zachary. "Julia and Tricia. They're in the same incubator, which is really good. It means they can touch each other and not be totally isolated. It's hard to balance a baby's need for the controlled environment of the incubator with their need for human contact. There are access ports, so that the parents can touch them without taking them out of the environment. And as they get bigger and stronger, they will get more opportunities to touch and hold them."

Zachary looked pleased at this. "That's good. Babies need to be held."

"When I talked to Heather, she told me about how you helped to take care of Mindy when she was born. You never told me about that."

Zachary looked uncertain for a moment, then smiled. "I haven't thought about that in a long time. It was so long ago."

"She said that you were the only one who could get Mindy to eat anything."

"Yeah. You kind of had to fool her into taking the bottle. It was tricky."

"If you hadn't gotten her to eat, she wouldn't have survived."

"Well… I guess they would have taken her to the hospital. And maybe social services would have taken her away if she was starving."

"It's possible, yes. But it can also take hardly any time at all for a baby to get dehydrated and die. Sometimes that happens before you realize there is a serious problem and can get them to the hospital. A parent thinks that they are just off their feed, maybe fighting a flu bug, and then they're dehydrated and it's too late to do anything for them."

"I'm glad that didn't happen to Mindy."

"Me too. You took good care of her."

Zachary smiled his shy, proud smile. He didn't get a lot of praise. Especially for things he had done as a child. His own mother had told him he was worthless and that she didn't want him. And from what she gathered from the little that Lorne and Zachary said about his years after the fire, he had been unmanageable and had probably never been praised for doing his best.

"And now… you look tired. Are you ready for bed?"

His eyes roved to the clock on the wall. It was much earlier than he ever went to bed at home, but the psych ward was probably very strict about his going to sleep, and with no electronics to occupy him, there was nothing to keep him up but his own thoughts.

"I'm not tired."

"You look tired, even if you don't feel it. And once you take a pill, that will help."

He nodded.

"All right. I'm going to leave you alone, then. You take care of yourself." Kenzie leaned forward and kissed him. Not on the cheek this time, but on the lips. "I miss you."

"You too. I'm sorry… that I have to be here."

"I'm sorry too, but I'm glad that you're safe."

34

<hr>

It was getting easier to sleep without Zachary there, though Kenzie still missed him and wondered how he was doing while he was away from her. It helped to know that he was sleeping better. Not having dark raccoon shadows around his eyes helped her to see his hospital stay as a positive thing, something that was helping him, even if they couldn't reverse the depression brought on by the upcoming anniversary. They were still doing what they could for him.

She woke up the next day feeling well-rested. That, combined with the assurance that he was okay without her, helped her to be able to focus on her own work. It would be nice not to have to do every job twice because she was so afraid of screwing things up due to her preoccupation and lack of restful sleep.

She used to leave her phone messages until later in her morning routine, but after running into trouble once for not picking up an early-morning message from Dr. Wiltshire, checking them was the first thing she did when she got into the office. She was glad that she had, because he had left one for her late at night or early in the morning.

"I have a suicide to attend early, Kenzie. So I won't be in until later, and we will be checking in the remains later today. If you could do some prep for me..."

She could hear him moving around as he dictated his instructions. Maybe dressing, or maybe already doing a scene review, with the police standing back respectfully while he talked into the phone.

Kenzie jotted down notes so that she wouldn't forget anything and got started. She wanted to have everything prepared by the time Dr. Wiltshire got there, whether it was sooner or later. After that was done, she went on with the rest of her routine.

Dr Wiltshire arrived at the office a little later than usual but, of course, she knew that his day had started quite a bit before hers. He stopped at her desk to offer her a Starbuck's coffee and Danish. Kenzie took them without objection.

"Going to be a tough one today?" she asked.

Usually when he brought her treats, it was because consciously or unconsciously, he recognized it was going to be a long or particularly stressful day. And those were often days when he came in with a body in the morning.

"Suicides are never pretty," Dr. Wiltshire sighed. "No matter how much TV movie dramas like to romanticize it, making it look as if the victim just slides peacefully into oblivion, that's not what it looks like. Physician attended end-of-life choice being the exception, of course. Anyone killing himself without assistance… just leaves behind a mess for everyone else to clean up and grieve over."

"What have we got?" Kenzie asked. She hoped it wasn't a young teenager. Those deaths always seemed to hit her the hardest.

"Ken Kennedy, fifty-nine, single and alone. Psych ward patient."

Kenzie tried to suppress her reaction to this news, but she couldn't hide it from Dr. Wiltshire. He nodded gravely.

"Gave me a turn when I heard I had a male suicide in the psych ward to attend. My first thought…"

Kenzie nodded. Of course he had thought of Zachary. Zachary, who had been admitted just a few days earlier for suicidal thoughts. She took a deep breath in and let it out slowly.

Zachary was fine. He had been okay when she had left him the night before, and she knew the name of the deceased that Dr. Wiltshire had brought in. It had not been Zachary.

Ken Kennedy. A man she had never met before. She would see him for the first and last time on the autopsy table. It was not personal. He was no different from any of the other remains she had worked with in the past.

"Will you be okay?" Dr. Wiltshire asked. "Do you want me to take this one myself?"

"No. I'll be fine. I'm pretty much caught up from my vacation—finally—so I can make time to assist. And I know that Mr. Kennedy is not Zachary. I will get through it."

"If you need to bow out at any point during the procedure, just go ahead. I understand completely."

Kenzie nodded. She took a bite of her Danish, girding up her loins.

The autopsy was scheduled for the afternoon. Kenzie looked at the time and decided that she had time to check the postal mail and get it sorted and then to have lunch. Then she would assist with the autopsy of Mr. Kennedy.

She stood at her desk as she slit open envelopes and quickly sorted them into the various piles, baskets, and workflows that she had organized. It usually took her no more than ten minutes, even when scanning hard copies into the system when necessarily. Most of the reports that came in print form, they had already received electronic copies of ahead of time, so they just went into the basket destined for the file cabinet.

She held the sharp letter opener in one hand as she sliced open an envelope, removed the contents, and then sliced open the next. But when she saw the piece of paper she pulled out of one of the envelopes, she accidentally stabbed herself in the hand with the letter opener.

She swore and dropped the letter opener, then grabbed a tissue and pressed it over the cut. It was an unusually sharp letter opener, not one with a safely-rounded tip, which would have been more difficult to get under the letter flaps. She swore again and looked down at the letter.

"Everything all right, Kenzie?" Julie asked.

Kenzie startled, not having realized that she was there. She had called Julie earlier to cover the phone and reception desk for her while she assisted in the autopsy. And Julie had arrived early so that Kenzie could sit down and have a quiet lunch instead of wolfing down a sandwich while she worked at her desk.

Kenzie picked up the corner of the paper, and hesitated about whether she should let Julie see it or not. Reluctantly, she turned it around to show to the younger woman.

Julie gasped and covered her mouth as her eyes scanned the letters block-printed with a marker. The same as the last one. Except the language in this one was quite a bit more explicit.

"Do you get a lot of those?" Julie asked, eyes big.

"No. I don't usually have to deal with threats." Kenzie sat down abruptly. Her legs were shaking like she had just climbed a hundred stairs.

"I'll get you a drink of water," Julie offered, and sped into the office suite to fetch a drink from the kitchenette.

In a few minutes, both Dr. Wiltshire and Julie were at her side, Julie handing her the water and encouraging her to drink and Dr. Wiltshire teasing the letter out from under Kenzie's hand to look at it.

"Another one!" he exclaimed, looking at it.

"There were more?" Julie asked.

"One other." Dr. Wiltshire looked at Kenzie. "I assume there was just one other."

She nodded. "Yeah. I'm not saving them up."

"Are you hurt?"

Kenzie looked at her left hand, at the bloody tissue wadded up over the wound, remembering what had happened. "It was an accident. Stabbed myself with the letter opener."

He prodded the tissue and looked underneath. "I don't think you need stitches. Just a bandage."

"I'll get one," Julie offered, and again headed to the kitchen, where the first aid box was stored.

Kenzie looked at the letter again, shaking her head. "I guess we should call Agent Menendez about this. Not that she seemed too excited to get the last one. I thought that at least they have some evidentiary value…"

"I haven't heard back whether there were any fingerprints on the last one. But yes, we should at least keep her up-to-date on what's going on. This one is… considerably worse than the last."

Kenzie nodded. Both the words used to address her and the threat were much more explicit this time. There could be no doubt that she had seriously disturbed someone with her questions in the geriatric ward. She looked at the envelope for a postmark to see when it had been mailed. It didn't make sense to her that the killer would be getting angrier when she hadn't had anything else to do with the investigation. At least, not on the public end. But it was possible that both letters had been mailed some days ago and were just arriving at her desk now.

This time, the envelope did have a postmark on it. It had only been mailed the previous day.

"Well, it's local," Dr. Wiltshire observed, also looking at the stamp.

"It would have to be. For someone to know that I was involved in the investigation personally, it would have to be someone at the hospital. Someone in the geriatric unit who saw me or talked to me."

"Right. You have a list of the people you talked to that day, right?"

"I already gave it to Agent Menendez."

"Good."

Julie returned with an assortment of bandages. Kenzie looked through them. She only needed one. It wasn't that big of a wound. Just deep. A good thing that, as someone who worked with needles regularly, she was up-to-date on her tetanus shots.

"You should use one of those flat, rectangular letter openers," Julie suggested. She took the bandage that Kenzie had selected from her and peeled off the wrapper and backing to apply it to Kenzie's palm. "They have a razor blade on the inside edge, so that you can't cut yourself on it. You just poke the little end under the flap and slide it along, with the cutter on the inside."

Kenzie nodded. "Yeah, I guess I might need to get something a little safer. I've never done that before. I thought I was better-coordinated."

"Anyone can have an accident," Dr. Wiltshire said, brushing it off. Kenzie was glad he wasn't making a big deal out of it. They both knew it was just a small cut, nothing life-threatening.

Kenzie smoothed down the edges of the bandage Julie had expertly applied. "I guess I'm ready for that autopsy now."

"Are you sure, Kenzie?" Dr. Wiltshire asked. "You don't have to scrub in on this one if you are having second thoughts. After all this, maybe you want to just stay out of it. This letter is reason enough to be upset; you don't need to pile on anything else."

"I'll be just fine." Kenzie glanced at Julie and didn't explain to her why Dr. Wiltshire thought that the autopsy might bother her. She was friendly with Julie, but she hadn't explained about Zachary's issues and Julie didn't know anything about his being in the hospital. "Let me just finish sorting the mail."

"I can do that," Julie offered.

"No. I know whether we have already received stuff through email or not. There's no point in processing reports a second time; they can just go straight to file."

Julie nodded. "Okay. Do you want me to open the envelopes? That would make it go faster."

Kenzie sighed. She didn't need to be babied. But she just nodded. "Fine, yes, go ahead and open them." Julie might as well do something useful and not just stand there watching Kenzie.

"I'll get autopsy prepped," Dr. Wiltshire said. "See you in a few minutes."

35

Kenzie was glad not to have Dr. Wiltshire hovering over her while she finished processing the mail with Julie. He seemed to sense that she didn't want a big thing made of either the letter or the autopsy that might make her think about Zachary. She appreciated that he didn't see the need to mother and fuss over her and would instead just go on with the autopsy. The more normal everything was, the easier it would be for her.

After finishing the mail, Kenzie took a quick minute in the restroom to gather herself and do some deep breathing. She would put the threatening letter out of her mind. She would put Zachary out of her mind. She was assisting with the autopsy of Mr. Kennedy. Not someone she knew. She could maintain professional distance and not get wrapped up in it emotionally. Dr. Wiltshire had not given her a heads-up that it was anything more bloody or gory than she was used to. Patients in the psychiatric unit didn't generally have access to guns or knives, so it was far more likely to be an overdose, strangulation, or head trauma. She could manage that.

Kenzie entered the autopsy and suited up. The clean surgical surfaces shone. Everything was neatly laid out in its proper place. A homicide detective was standing by to observe. Dr. Wiltshire had not yet begun with the body, but appeared to be ready to once Kenzie joined him. As she walked up to the table, he tapped the button on the floor that would start the recording, and announced Mr. Kennedy's name and file number, followed by his height, weight, and appearance. Kenzie concentrated on keeping her breathing regulated and settled into the usual routine of an autopsy.

Kenzie couldn't see any wounds when Dr. Wiltshire folded down the cover to reveal the top portion of the body. No bruising around the neck, so it would appear he had not hanged or strangled himself.

Mr. Kennedy, aged fifty-nine, single, no children. He was white. A little overweight, but not in bad shape. Kenzie suspected that when he wasn't in the psych ward he was in a physically demanding trade. His hands were rough and calloused. He was well-muscled under the layer of fat. Not cut like a bodybuilder, but someone who could hold his own in terms of physical labor.

He had a dark but grizzled beard. His hair was cropped short, but not buzz-cut like Zachary's. Easy care. His temples and body hair were also going gray.

"No obvious wounds or bruising," Dr. Wiltshire observed. "No tattoos or birthmarks. Let's examine Mr. Kennedy for any needle marks or smaller wounds."

The two of them spent some time with the magnifying lenses, checking carefully for needle marks. They didn't find any. Unlike the geriatric patients they had dealt with recently, he had not had an IV.

Kenzie thought fleetingly of her conversation with Nurse Debbie. *At least people don't die in the psych ward.* But of course they did. People died everywhere; there was no predicting where and when the end of the line would be. The psych patients were not dying of cancer or kidney failure, but suicide was a risk. Usually, it could be prevented while they were in the hospital, but if a patient were desperate enough, he could find a way.

Kenzie took a couple of deep breaths, trying to reset. She needed to stay focused on Mr. Kennedy and the examination of his body. Nothing else.

Dr. Wiltshire raised his eyes and checked on her, then looked back down at the remains and continued his examination.

"Indications at the scene were of drug overdose," he told her in a professional, detached tone. "Vomitus present. Indications of cyanosis." He picked up the hand closest to him and indicated the nails. Kenzie looked down at the hand on her side of the table to confirm the dusky blue-gray under the nails. He was slightly blue above the mouth as well. Cyanosis. Something that had kept him from getting enough oxygen. Possibly a medication that had slowed or stopped his heart, since there were no marks to indicate strangulation. There were other possibilities, but Dr. Wiltshire classified it as a potential drug overdose, and he was probably right.

They continued with their careful review of Kennedy's body and found no signs of recent violence. Kenzie noted scarring that showed he had been a cutter at some point, but he didn't have any recent self-inflicted cuts. The marks were all old.

When they had completed a full review of his body, top and bottom, front and back, Dr. Wiltshire indicated it was time to begin with the internal examination.

"Would you like to make the Y-incision, Dr. Kirsch?"

Kenzie was eager to do more than just gross examination, slides, and samples. She nodded and moved over to the instrument tray to begin. Dr. Wiltshire talked her through the process, even though Kenzie had previously practiced on medical school cadavers, and her lines were neat and straight. Dr. Wiltshire nodded his approval.

"It is my suspicion that Mr. Kennedy died of a drug overdose," Dr. Wiltshire said. "So…"

"Stomach contents first?" Kenzie suggested.

Dr. Wiltshire nodded. He didn't move in to take over on the procedure, so Kenzie proceeded carefully herself. Without any nicks or other mishaps, she removed the stomach and emptied the contents into a tray.

Examining and smelling stomach contents was not her favorite part of the job. But a close examination of Mr. Kennedy's stomach contents was not required. It appeared as if he had swallowed the entire contents of a couple of bottles of pills. The yellow tablets and blue tablets were partially dissolved, but still intact enough that there could be no doubt what they were.

"Well…" Kenzie made a gesture toward the pile of mushy, acid-covered pills. "There you go. We can take blood levels, but I think it's pretty obvious what we are going to find."

"Yes," Dr. Wiltshire agreed.

His eyes remained fastened on the stomach contents, and Kenzie wasn't sure why he wasn't moving on.

"How many pills would you say that is?" Dr. Wiltshire asked.

"I don't know. A lot. I was thinking it looked like a full bottle of each. A month's worth, maybe?"

Dr. Wiltshire nodded slowly. Kenzie knew he was looking for something more. For her to follow the question to a conclusion. It took a few seconds for her to get there.

Zachary's doctor wouldn't even give him a prescription for a full month's worth of any of his prescriptions at a time. She considered it too risky. When Zachary was feeling particularly tempted to put an end to his life, he had Kenzie dispense them. And in the psych ward, he would be given his meds on a schedule. He would never be given more than one dose at a time.

"Where did he get that many pills from in the psychiatric unit?"

"That's a good question."

"Maybe he broke into the dispensary?"

"That is a question we should ask. Certainly no one mentioned that early this morning when I attended at the scene."

"They might not have discovered it until it was time to dispense the morning's medications. But they should have called by now if they realized that he had broken in." Kenzie looked at the clock on the wall. They probably dispensed the morning meds at seven or eight o'clock. It was mid-afternoon.

"The other possibility is that he saved them up," Kenzie said. "They should check, but he could be cheeking them or even regurgitating them. He would have to find a place to stash them, somewhere they wouldn't search regularly."

"There should be protocols in place to ensure that patients can't do that. And with patients at higher risk, they should be doing blood tests to ensure that the concentrations are where they should be."

"And you would think that they would notice if he were off his meds for a month."

"You would think," Dr. Wiltshire agreed.

Kenzie caught a movement out of the corner of her eye and turned to see the homicide detective writing in his notepad. Questions to follow up on, areas to investigate based on their discussion. He looked at her. Kenzie nodded awkwardly and looked down at the pile of pills.

"What else should we do? This is pretty conclusively the cause of death."

"I would suggest weighing the pills to get an idea of how many he consumed. It won't be accurate, since some have dissolved and some have soaked up liquid, but it will give us a ballpark. Identify exactly what they are. Markings have worn off, but we can get a pretty good idea by comparing color and shape to an identification chart, then talk to the hospital and run a couple of tests to verify. And we need to check other organs for pathology. See if there was anything else going on. Was he self-medicating for pain? Were they any tumors or brain abnormalities? Examine and weigh the heart and lungs. Slides of the kidney and liver."

Kenzie nodded. Even with a case that was so clearly suicide, they needed to dot all the i's and cross all the t's. Sometimes there were still surprises or additional factors in the death.

She proceeded with the autopsy carefully, following Dr. Wiltshire's instructions step by step. A couple of times, he stopped her to offer advice or to show her a technique. Even though she had watched him do dozens of autopsies, she didn't always notice the finer points or better ways to do things.

After completing the autopsy, Kenzie was rubbing her shoulders and neck, which were definitely feeling the effects of her work. Dr. Wiltshire frowned.

"You're sore?"

"Yes." Kenzie dug her fingers into the muscles and tendons, searching out the sore spots. She would need a heating pad in the evening before bed.

"Show me where."

Kenzie's face warmed as she demonstrated the movements that were painful. Mostly the ones requiring her to lift her hands and arms to chest level or higher. She was worried that Dr. Wiltshire was going to offer to massage the sore muscles and wasn't sure how she felt about that. Dr. Wiltshire had always treated her with respect and had never made any romantic overtures or suggested anything to make her uncomfortable in that way, but she wasn't sure she wanted him rubbing any part of her body.

But he did not. "The table is too high for you," he observed.

"Oh… yes," Kenzie admitted. She always left it adjusted to the level that Dr. Wiltshire used it at, as he was the lead on the autopsies. She hadn't expected to be the one doing most of the physical work this time and had not adjusted the table once she had started. "I didn't think…"

"Next time we'll have to remember to lower it for your work. It's very quick to adjust it to the level most comfortable to you. And it will save you a lot of pain and having to load up on ibuprofen after an autopsy."

Kenzie nodded. "Yeah. I'll do that next time."

He demonstrated how to find the table level that was ergonomically correct for her, and they raised and lowered it a few times for practice.

"You'll find the most comfortable height for you after a few times. It's different for everybody, just depends on your individual skeletal structure. Once you know the best height, we can always set it to that exact height."

"Great. Thank you."

Dr. Wiltshire nodded. "If you don't take care of your body, you could end up with crippling stress injuries. You don't want to have to retire from a career you enjoy just because you didn't take the time to figure out the right table height and use it."

Kenzie nodded her agreement. She took a sip of her coffee, which had gone cold several hours earlier, and looked over the samples to be processed and sent out for testing.

"You go type up your notes on the autopsy," Dr. Wiltshire advised. "Get your thoughts down while it is still fresh in your mind. I will get these sent out."

"Oh, I can still do it," Kenzie protested. That was part of her job description, not his.

"You are sore enough already. We don't want to inflame those muscles any more. Do your computer work, check the email, and go home. Take ibuprofen and put some heat on those muscles."

Kenzie made one more protest and he again instructed her to go do her computer work while he sent out the samples. Kenzie nodded and obeyed.

36

Kenzie relieved Julie of her duties and sent her back up to her administrative tasks on one of the upper floors. She sat down at her desk and realized that the threatening letter had been set to the side and not yet taken care of. She slid it into a plastic folder as she had the previous one and shot a text off to Agent Menendez so that she didn't actually have to talk to her.

She created a new document to jot down her notes on the autopsy. They would have the dictated notes back the next day, but thought processes were important too. There were things that might need to be followed up on or investigated further, feelings about their findings, maybe a small observation or two that hadn't seemed important enough to comment on while they were in the midst of the autopsy but started to niggle at her later. Normally, this was Dr. Wiltshire's job, and she would just review his notes to see whether she had anything to add, but since she had been the primary doctor doing the work on the Kennedy autopsy, this time it was her job.

She noted Mr. Kennedy's name, file number, and statistics. She started to write out an introductory note giving the circumstances of the death, and realized with some embarrassment that there was a lump in her throat that would not go away. She swallowed a few times, took a drink of water, and tried to go on. As she wrote about his being a patient in the psychiatric unit, tears started to leak out of the corners of her eyes. She wiped them away a few times, then stopped typing and covered her face with her hands, breathing slowly and trying to center herself and get back her composure.

Kenzie had performed the autopsy without getting emotionally caught up in it. She had properly maintained a professional detachment and demeanor. She didn't understand why she was suddenly fighting waves of sorrow over a man she had never met before.

She stopped and started several times, writing what she could and then dealing with the emotions that consumed her. Not just sorrow, but anger too, unaccountably furious at somebody for Mr. Kennedy's death. It was suicide, and she knew it was no one's fault but his own. His family and friends and the doctors had undoubtedly done their best for him, but sometimes that wasn't enough. Sometimes, no matter what everyone did to head it off, a suicide simply couldn't be prevented.

Kenzie wiped her eyes and blew her nose and looked back at her screen to see where she had left off.

"How's it coming along?" Dr. Wiltshire asked gently.

Kenzie startled slightly at his words, not having realized that he was there, watching her. She sniffled.

"I'll be done before long." She used a tissue to wipe her eyes. She was going through a lot of tissue for one day.

"I understand it's hard."

"You don't do this when you write up your notes," she pointed out.

"Well, I've been at it a lot longer than you have. You can bet that there have been some cases that really hit me hard. Sometimes it is the death of a child, a particularly brutal murder, or someone dying of the same thing that Aunt Jayne died of a month ago. You never know what it's going to be, but some of them will hit you hard. It's just part of the job. Don't beat yourself up over it."

"I was fine for the autopsy."

"You did a great job on the autopsy. But one of the reasons that I had you do the work was to keep you focused on the mechanics, rather than the patient's circumstances."

Kenzie looked at Dr. Wiltshire for a moment before the light went on. "Because of Zachary, you mean? Is that why you think I'm so emotional over it?"

"Isn't it?"

Kenzie felt a huge sense of relief, as if a burden had been taken off her shoulders. Of course it was because of Zachary. Dr. Wiltshire knew very well that the suicide of someone in the same unit that Zachary was in would be difficult for her. She couldn't help but compare the two cases. To think about Zachary and put him in Mr. Kennedy's place. To think, as she had so many times before, about how she would feel if Zachary did harm himself one day, and if it were his body on the autopsy table.

Of course she thought of his bottles of pills and his sweeping all the knives in the fridge onto the floor in frustration. He was fighting his illness the best that he could, but what if one day he was no longer able to resist the impulses or deal with the fact that he would be fighting depression for the rest of his life?

Kenzie dabbed at her eyes as the tears flowed faster and a sob escaped her throat. Grief for Mr. Kennedy, a stranger to her, and for Zachary, fighting his lonely fight, and for herself, worrying that one day she might lose him. There were a lot of emotions to unpack.

"Sorry," she apologized to Dr. Wiltshire. "This is so silly."

"It's not silly at all. You've done a fine job, and you're going through some very difficult stuff in your life right now. There's nothing wrong with letting yourself feel your emotions instead of bottling them up."

"Sure, but not at the workplace."

"You will always be free to cry in my office," he told her sternly. "And if you should ever join a medical examiner's office where you are forbidden to feel emotion over the work that we do... you should find another office. These people deserve our sympathy just as much as anyone else in our lives."

Kenzie nodded and blew her nose. "Okay." The tears were starting to slow a little, as if acknowledging and allowing them took away their power over her.

"Never let the job take your humanity."

Kenzie managed a weak smile. She looked at the document on her screen, determined. She only needed another five or ten minutes to finish it, and then she could go home and relax for a while before visiting Zachary at the hospital.

"All right. I can do this."

"I never doubted it."

Dr. Wiltshire nodded and headed down the hallway toward his own office.

———

The long day and the emotion over Kennedy's suicide had taken a lot of energy. She was tired after eating supper and didn't really want to go out again, but she knew it was what she had to do.

She couldn't avoid seeing Zachary just because of the day she had been through. He still needed her support just as much as any other day. Maybe more. He would know that there had been a suicide in the ward and it was bound to be weighing on his mind. It wouldn't be easy to avoid his own suicidal thoughts when that's what everyone around him was talking about. Or being careful not to talk about.

Kenzie allowed herself one small scoop of ice cream to soothe her battered soul, and then forced herself to get up and get ready to go. It would be nice to go out in her baby, her cherry red convertible. It was too cold to put the top down, of course, but she always enjoyed going for a spin.

Then she would be able to see Zachary, and then she could relax for the night. All good things.

The nurse at the check-in desk for the ward handed Kenzie a printed notice.

"We want to make sure that our visitors know before going in that we had… an unfortunate incident last night. It is important that we acknowledge what has happened and not pretend that it didn't. Your loved one may need to talk about it."

Kenzie glanced down at the notice, outlining the bare facts of the discovery of Kennedy's death.

"Thanks. I appreciate that, and I'm sure your patients do too."

"There is extra counseling available for everyone, and that includes family members, not just the patients. Something like this can hit close to home for everyone, and we encourage open discussion and getting the help and counseling we need."

Kenzie nodded. She didn't bother to advise the nurse that she already knew far more about the case than anyone else in the ward, including the doctors. They would not get the Medical Examiner's report for a few more days.

She was escorted by a sympathetic-looking nurse to the common room. Kenzie could feel a shift in the energy and activity from the last couple of times that she had visited. It had been fairly calm and relaxed on her previous visits. There might be minor disruptions by individual patients, but overall, the ward was kept quiet and peaceful.

Without being able to put her finger on exactly what the difference was, Kenzie sensed the patients' agitation and restlessness. The air was charged with emotion. As she approached the table where Zachary sat, Kenzie folded the printed notice into quarters and then eighths, and pushed it into her coat pocket. She greeted Zachary as usual and sat down.

"How are you?" she asked, her lifted eyebrow and eye contact indicating that it was an important question and that she knew the answer was not "fine."

Zachary looked around. His eyes returned to hers, lines of stress radiating outward from them. "It's been pretty rough," he admitted. "They told you what happened?"

"I could tell them more than they could tell me."

Zachary frowned, then nodded. "I guess he would be taken to the ME's office."

Kenzie nodded. "I performed the autopsy."

His eyes got wider. "Yourself?"

"Not alone, but I was the lead."

"It seems… cruel to make that the first autopsy you were in charge of."

"Actually, it helped to keep my focus on the work. It was a good call by Dr. Wiltshire."

Zachary looked doubtful. He shook his head slightly but didn't argue the point.

"So…" he seemed uncomfortable with his question before posing it. "It really was suicide, wasn't it?"

"Yes. Definitely. He swallowed a lot of pills." She remembered the discussion with Dr. Wiltshire. "Do you know, did he break into the dispensary?"

"They're not telling us anything like that. Nothing about the 'how.' Which is probably good." He shrugged one shoulder. "Telling us how to get away with it would not be the smartest idea."

Kenzie chuckled uncomfortably. "No, probably not," she agreed. "That's okay, we'll be asking questions through the proper channels."

"You don't think it's the hospital's fault, do you?"

"There is always the chance that they are partially liable if they are negligent in the way that they store medications, dispense them, or supervise patients. But that's not for us to determine. We do our best to determine exactly what happened, and then let the police and courts take over from there."

Zachary's eyes roamed around the room, moving from one person or group to another, evaluating them all, aware of all the movements and dynamics around him. Years spent in institutions had taught him to watch everything.

37

S omething doesn't feel right," Zachary said.

Kenzie considered the comment. "What does that mean? Are you talking about your symptoms?"

"No. About… here. Something is not right here."

"Okay. Can you describe what?"

Kenzie was prepared for it to be anything, from an actual administrative problem to a delusion caused by the increase Dr. B had made in his antidepressants. Zachary looked at her, weighing his words.

"I'm not really sure. That's why I asked whether you thought it was the hospital's fault. I get the feeling that… they're worried about something. Not trying to cover it up, exactly, but maybe to *spin*…"

"Well, Kennedy should not have been able to get his hands on that many pills, so I imagine they have reason to be worried about the optics, even if they didn't do anything wrong or negligent."

"So you don't think I'm imagining it?"

"No."

Zachary looked relieved at that. "I worry sometimes about paranoia. Whether I'm being suspicious of something when I shouldn't be."

"Well, I think usually you're pretty close to the mark. Times when I've wondered if you're just imagining things, you've turned out to be right. So I think you can trust your instincts on most things."

Zachary scratched at a mark on the table.

"Has someone said something?" Kenzie asked. "One thing in particular that made you suspicious?"

"No, I don't think so… I've been places other times where there have been attempted suicides or deaths. And they mostly say the same things. They're better now about offering therapy rather than just telling you not to talk about it, like they did when I was a kid. They're saying all the usual things. It's just… I don't know. Body language? Nonverbal signals?"

"Sure. That makes sense. People who are worried act a certain way, give off a vibe." Kenzie looked around. The medical staff she could see seemed watchful and stressed, but not guilty. How would she expect them to look after they had been unable to prevent a suicide? How would she have felt? She didn't see anything that seemed out of place.

As she looked around, a movement that didn't fit attracted her attention. She focused in on a young black man and older black woman being escorted in. The boy was moving jerkily, as if angry and agitated. The orderly was trying to hold him by the arm, and the boy was pulling away.

When he saw Zachary at the table, he broke away from the orderly and charged toward them. It all happened within a second or two, and in that time, Kenzie recognized Zachary's teenage friend, Rhys Salter, and his grandmother Vera.

The orderly followed close behind, determined to quash whatever disruption Rhys was going to cause. Kenzie shook her head and motioned him back. The orderly stopped and watched, scowling.

Rhys made his way to Zachary. He flapped a white piece of paper in his hand, the notice of Kennedy's suicide. His expression was upset and worried.

Vera lagged several steps behind Rhys, unable to keep up with his long legs and energetic movements.

Zachary stood up. "It's okay," he told Rhys. He reached out his arms to engulf Rhys in a hug. "It's okay. It's okay."

Rhys clasped him tightly and pounded him on the back. Zachary pulled back after a minute so that they could look each other in the face.

Rhys pointed at the notice and then at Zachary, his movements still jerky and agitated.

"You thought this was me?" Zachary asked.

Rhys nodded.

With his own set of traumatic childhood events, Rhys was mostly mute, speaking only a word or two at a time now and then. He communicated mostly with gestures, supplemented by graphics and a few typed words on his phone. Despite all the therapy that Kenzie assumed he had been through, he did not use any standardized communication set. While he could read and write, it was only a few words at a time, and long sentences and paragraphs defeated him.

Clearly, he had been able to grasp just enough of what was written on the paper that was handed to him to understand that a patient had committed suicide, and he had thought they were telling him about Zachary.

Zachary motioned to the table. "Sit?"

Rhys slid into one of the unoccupied chairs. Zachary shook Vera's hand and received a wrinkled cheek pressed against his in return. He pulled out a chair for Vera, and she sat down.

Zachary sat down. He reached across the table and grasped Rhys's hand. He squeezed it tightly.

"I'm sorry they scared you. I'm okay, you can see that."

Rhys nodded. He crumpled the notice into a ball and threw it away from him angrily.

"Rhys!" Vera said, exasperated. "You go pick that up and throw it in a garbage can."

Rhys folded his arms over his chest and shook his head.

Kenzie got up and disposed of the paper. She could understand both of their positions. Vera's that he needed to behave properly in public and not throw garbage around no matter how frustrated he was, and Rhys's that they had just scared the crap out of him making him think that his friend was dead. They were both right, and it was easiest to just pick it up herself and not let them have an argument over it.

Vera made a face that told Kenzie she should not have interfered. Kenzie ignored it. As Dr. Wiltshire had said earlier, people needed to be allowed to show their feelings and not to be forced to stuff them down just because their emotions made others feel uncomfortable.

"How is school?" Zachary asked Rhys, choosing to focus on something other than who had committed suicide and how.

Rhys rolled his eyes dramatically and looked at Vera. He mimed writing and writing and then shaking his hand out in pain.

"Yes, he had had lots of work to do," Vera acknowledged. "There are a lot more demands as they try to get kids ready for college."

Rhys pointed at himself and shook his head firmly. *Not me.*

"Well, college isn't for everyone," Zachary said.

Rhys pointed at him, raising his brows. *You?*

Zachary shook his head. "No, I never got a college degree. But I have done other training. On private investigation, photographic techniques, that kind of stuff. As I could afford to."

Rhys nodded. He looked at Vera and jerked his thumb toward Zachary.

"I know not everyone goes to college," his grandmother said. "But try asking Kenzie the same thing."

Rhys tilted his head to the side slightly. He knew the answer to that question without asking. He put a couple of fingers over the pulse point on his wrist and shrugged. Doctors of course had to do lots of post-secondary schooling. But Rhys didn't have any plans to become a doctor.

"I did a little bit of general studies at university after I graduated," Kenzie said. "I didn't really know what I wanted to do, and I figured that was enough. I wasn't until a few years later that I decided to go into medicine. So then I was one of the oldest students in my classes."

Rhys scratched his chin, nodding.

"Sometimes it takes a while to decide what you want to do," Kenzie said.

"I really couldn't get a degree," Zachary offered. "I didn't have anyone to help support me once I turned eighteen. I would have needed a full scholarship or to join the armed forces. I never got good marks at school and didn't really want to do night school. I didn't want a degree just for the sake of having a degree. Too much work for a piece of paper."

Rhys pointed at him and made a pulling-the-trigger motion. *You got it.*

38

The visit with Rhys and Vera was brief. Conversations with Rhys were taxing on both sides and, after the first few questions, Rhys didn't want to discuss school or any of the other topics Kenzie or Vera tried to raise. He watched Zachary carefully, and Vera carried the conversation for a while, then decided it was time to go.

"I'm sorry to cut it so short," she said. "I'm an old woman and I go to bed early. And Rhys has school tomorrow. I'm sure he probably still has homework to do."

She looked at Rhys. He shook his head and moved his hands together as if brushing dust from them. *All done.*

Vera looked as if she doubted it was the truth, but she didn't pursue it. Maybe she would in the car or after they were home. There was no need to have an argument about it in front of Kenzie and Zachary.

Zachary and Kenzie said goodbye and watched the two of them head out. Kenzie turned back to Zachary. "I should be going too. But I wanted to make sure that you're okay today. This suicide… I'm sure it doesn't help your state of mind."

Zachary shook his head. "No. But I'm okay. I haven't been saving up pills, and you can bet that security here just got a whole lot tighter. They'll be watching all of us like hawks for the next little while."

"I suppose they will. And the nurse at the front desk said that if anyone needs extra therapy to deal with it, that's available. So if it's bothering you and you need to talk to someone…"

"Yeah. I could get in to see someone."

"Okay." Kenzie gave him a kiss goodbye. "Try not to think about it too much. I know it's hard not to obsess over it, but... it wasn't you. Mr. Kennedy had his own problems. Just because he failed, that doesn't mean that you can't succeed."

He stared past her; eyes unfocused. "But this will never be over. It's not something that they're suddenly going to cure."

"No. Not like that. But you'll get through your time here, and after Christmas, you'll feel better and be able to carry on with your life. I know that fighting depression and everything else sucks, but... you've got a good life." She raised her brows, encouraging him to think about it and count his blessings.

"Sure," Zachary agreed, too fast. He didn't want to hurt her feelings, of course, or to argue about it. But that didn't mean that he agreed. He was too far down the hole to see things clearly. "I just mean... it's discouraging. Knowing that there's only one way this will ever end."

Kenzie squeezed him tightly. "You're wrong," she whispered in his ear. "It will end after a long, happy, satisfying life. You're going to feel better. I promise."

He gave her a gentle hug and didn't argue the point. He was an avoider, not an arguer. He'd rather just coast past any hint of conflict. Kenzie kissed him again and got herself out of there.

There wasn't any way to argue him out of his depression.

Kenzie was relieved to get out of the ward. It would have been great to have a long, satisfying visit with Zachary in a pleasant environment, but the psychiatric unit was even more dark and oppressive than usual. Zachary was right about it feeling *off*. It was probably just the shock waves of Kennedy's death, and it would go back to normal after a few days.

She saw a small cluster of people stopped to talk in the corridor, and it wasn't until she was nearly upon them that she realized it was Rhys and Vera, stopped to talk to a second set of visitors, Zachary's sister Jocelyn and Luke, the teen that she was helping to look after. Zachary had been instrumental in rescuing Luke from his life on the streets, an addict controlled by human traffickers in his role of bringing new, younger girls and boys into the sex trade. Joss had some experience in the trade herself and had agreed to take Luke under her wing to help him rehabilitate.

The boy was not supposed to be back in Roxboro where he might be recognized by someone from his past life. As far as the cartel knew, he was dead. Showing up again could cause some real problems.

Not only that, but Rhys had developed something of a crush on Luke and none of them thought it was a particularly good idea for the two of them to get together. If Luke slipped back into the life, Rhys would be a good asset to bring back to the traffickers.

The two boys had their heads together, Rhys with his phone out to facilitate communication. Vera stood to the side watching them uncertainly. Joss did not engage with her, as the two parents of younger children who were friends might have done.

Joss was a thin, angular woman, all sharp edges in Kenzie's mind. Her tone was frequently biting and sarcastic. Zachary said that she had softened a lot upon taking Luke in, but Kenzie was not encouraged by her expression as she stood there watching the two boys.

"Joss!" Kenzie called out.

Joss turned her head and saw Kenzie. She didn't look excited to see her. She moved about two inches in Kenzie's direction, but made no other move to greet her.

"Hi," Kenzie greeted, trying to keep her voice warm and welcoming. "I didn't know you were coming tonight."

"We had some time, so I thought it would be a good idea to pop in," Joss said, her tone defensive. "Since he *is* my little brother."

"Of course. I'm sure he'll be happy to see you."

Joss snorted, as if she doubted the fact. Why would she come to visit him, if she thought that he wouldn't even be happy to see her? Because it was expected? Kenzie didn't get the feeling that Joss did anything just because it was the socially expected thing. She'd been through too much in her life to give a care what anyone else thought of her.

"He might be tired, though," Kenzie warned. "Since he's already had visitors." She indicated Rhys and Vera. "And he's feeling pretty low tonight. You should know… they had a suicide last night. So it's a difficult time. Hard for him to get away from his own suicidal thoughts under the circumstances."

"They had a suicide?" Joss repeated. "Well, that gives me confidence in the people looking after my brother. How did that happen?"

"It's under investigation. I'm not sure how he got his hands on so many pills. But Zachary said that he is okay, and they're taking stronger security measures in the wake of this incident…"

"I would certainly hope so. If they don't want anyone suing their butts off. Isn't there any kind of oversight? Guidelines to make sure that kind of thing doesn't happen? Inspections by some higher authority?"

"There are guidelines, and I'm not sure what happened. The man may have broken into a locked facility to get the pills he took. It's unclear right now. And it is the case that… someone who is really intent on committing suicide… it is impossible to prevent every possible thing they could do."

Joss stared at her, a deep crease between her eyebrows.

"Then what is the point in Zachary being here?"

"He's safer here than he is at home. I can't keep him under twenty-four-hour supervision. He knew he needed more intense therapy and a safer environment. So he checked himself in."

Joss grunted, dissatisfied. She looked over at the two boys with their heads together.

"Luke, I'm going in. Are you coming?"

Luke looked at Rhys.

Rhys shrugged. He slid his phone into his pocket and looked at Vera, nodding that he was ready to go. Luke slapped him on the shoulder in a friendly goodbye and followed Joss. Joss broke away from her conversation with Kenzie.

"Thanks for the warning."

"Okay. Take care. Have a nice visit."

Kenzie looked at Luke once more, wishing that Joss hadn't brought him along. Joss had undoubtedly made the choice that she thought the best. Maybe leaving Luke alone would have been a bad idea. But they could have made other arrangements. Kenzie could have brought a tablet with her and let Zachary visit with his sister over a video call instead of their coming into town where Luke might be seen.

39

Kenzie awoke with a start, and sat bolt upright in bed, breathing hard. She was soaked with sweat. She looked around the room for Zachary, feeling in the bed beside her and wondering whether he were asleep on the couch before remembering that he was in the hospital.

She turned on the lamp on the side table, knowing that it wasn't going to wake anyone up. She was the only one there.

It helped to see the familiar surroundings. Her racing heart started to slow.

It had been a weird dream, but one clearly born of the stressful events in recent days. In it, Agent Menendez was at the hospital with Zachary, trying to get him to agree with her injecting something into his arm, telling him that he would feel better and be able to rest if she did. Kenzie shuddered.

She picked up her phone and browsed her mail and social networks, waiting for the adrenaline to subside and her brain to remember that it was time to sleep. She was getting caught up on her sleep; she didn't want to take a step back with only a few hours under her belt.

There was an email back from Agent Menendez, who hadn't picked up the new threatening letter before the end of Kenzie's workday, but had promised to pick it up the next morning. There was nothing in her email to indicate that she thought it would be any help. Kenzie felt sort of like Menendez thought she was just being dramatic and that the note was inconsequential.

And maybe it was. Kenzie had heard that people who wrote poison pen letters didn't generally resort to actual violence. Like peeping toms, they were thought to be annoying, but safe.

Though Kenzie had heard a few stories on TV of serial killers who had started out as peepers. So maybe that theory didn't hold water.

There was nothing interesting going on in her social networks. Some Christmas memes and events. Things that Kenzie wouldn't be able to get to now that most of her evenings would be spent going to the hospital to visit with Zachary.

Maybe she should talk to friends about going to one or two weekend events, just so she didn't miss out on everything. While she wasn't a huge Christmas person, she did enjoy the holiday and didn't want to let it pass by without some kind of recognition. Just because Zachary couldn't celebrate the season, that didn't mean Kenzie had to isolate herself from it. He would understand if she explained that she wanted to do some Christmas stuff without him. Not that she needed to explain anything.

Kenzie blinked and rubbed her eyes, then decided maybe she was ready to go back to sleep again. She plugged her phone in, turned the lamp back off, closed her eyes, and waited for sleep.

The morning was quiet. Kenzie hadn't anticipated how much she would miss spending breakfast with Zachary. How had her eating a slice or two of toast with marmalade and his trying to force down a granola bar become such an important part of her life? It seemed completely out of proportion. A few minutes lingering over a few crumbs of breakfast should not be that big of a deal.

But she missed him. Kenzie was counting the days to Christmas. To the day when he would start to feel better and be able to return home safely to become a part of her routine again.

Agent Menendez was waiting for Kenzie when she arrived at the Medical Examiner's Office in the morning. Kenzie looked at her and shook her head.

"You're here early."

"I have a busy day," Menendez said pointedly. As if Kenzie were already keeping her from important meetings by not arriving at the office in time and taking the moment to say hello and exchange pleasantries.

"Well then…" Kenzie unlocked the double doors across the hallway and pushed them open. She went to her desk and unlocked her desk drawer to retrieve the latest letter. "Here it is."

Menendez received the letter and envelope in the plastic sheet protector and glanced over the message. "Well… she escalated, didn't she?"

"She?"

Menendez shrugged. "My best guess. I don't like to say 'they' like it is more than one person, or he/she. Chances are, it's a nurse, and most of the nurses are women." She looked down at the letter. "You wouldn't think that one woman would talk this way to another, though, would you?"

In Kenzie's experience, it was mostly men who called women sexually explicit names. But there were women who did it too; she couldn't rule out the possibility.

"It's the threats that bother me more than the language."

Menendez studied it. "Well… if it's any consolation, these Angel of Death killers don't usually attack people who are well and strong. They stick to those who are helpless and dying."

"As far as we know."

"Historically…"

"I know. But historically we only know who they have killed because they confess it. If there is someone who falls outside their pattern and they don't confess to it…"

"I really don't think you need to worry about that."

Kenzie did not feel reassured. From what she had seen, she was more familiar with the kind of killer they were looking for than Menendez was. Shouldn't an FBI agent be better trained in abnormal psychology and the profiles of serial killers than a medical examiner's assistant?

And even if it wasn't in her normal wheelhouse, then shouldn't she do the research to figure it out?

"So… how is the investigation coming along? Any progress on ruling out any of your suspects? Or figuring out which patients to focus on?"

"Not a lot of movement there," Menendez admitted. "We need more autopsies to identify which patients were even homicides. We are asking families for permission, but most are dead set against it."

Kenzie nodded.

"*Dead* set against it," Menendez repeated, with a chuckle.

Kenzie rolled her eyes. "You can understand how they would be," she said, without acknowledging the pun. "They've buried the person, mourned, put it behind them. They don't want to go back emotionally, and think it is morbid or disgusting to have to exhume the person and do an autopsy."

"They're more interested in putting it behind them than in finding out the truth," the agent said with disgust. "I would think that the truth would be more important than the inconvenience of an autopsy. It isn't like they even need to be there at the exhumation or autopsy. They can pretend it isn't even happening. If it was my grandma, I would want to know if someone had killed her!"

"For some people, that's important. Others, I think, they know grandma was going to die anyway, and even if they don't like the fact that a law was broken and grandma was hurried along, it doesn't bother them that much that she lost a few days or weeks of life."

"It would bother me; I'll tell you that."

Kenzie shrugged and didn't argue, but she wondered if it were true. Situations were often different when she was on the inside instead of outside looking in. What a person felt and did when they were battered by a spouse, when a family member committed a crime, or when they witnessed a robbery were often completely different from what they would have predicted before it happened. The primitive brain or emotional attachment took over the logical brain.

"I still like your Nurse Debbie for it," Menendez offered.

"She's not *my* Nurse Debbie. And I still think you're wrong. She wasn't even there for one of the two deaths that we know were murder. It doesn't make sense to me. Maybe she comes across as not being genuine and makes people uncomfortable with her cheery attitude, but that doesn't make her a murderer. I've seen her work and she is very good at what she does. She is not a killer. She's a healer."

"Just be glad she's not changing your grandma's bedpan," Menendez advised.

Kenzie didn't point out that Nurse Debbie was in Zachary's unit, and she wasn't worried about that. It was obviously going to take more than a few days to unwind the case and find out the identity of the murderer. In real life, things didn't come together magically at the forty-five-minute mark.

Kenzie looked at the digital clock on her desk phone. "I need to get to work here so everything is ready when Dr. Wiltshire gets in."

"Fine." Menendez nodded. "Let me know if you get any more correspondence. I'll turn this over to trace to see what they can find, if anything."

"And I guess I'll hear if you manage to talk anyone else into allowing an autopsy."

Menendez nodded. "I'll let you know."

After she had gone, Kenzie got to work with her usual routine, checking on any evidence that had been logged in during the night, making sure that all remains were properly labeled and documented, that Dr. Wiltshire's desk had been left clean, and all the other little things that she did to smooth the way for the rest of the day to unfold successfully.

Back at her desk to process her email inbox, Kenzie let her mind wander back to Agent Menendez. It had been exciting at first to be involved in an FBI case. But it had turned out to be very different from what Kenzie had imagined or the way it might have been portrayed on TV. Things moved very slowly, and Josie Menendez was no Samantha Spade. She had not even wanted to go to the hospital to do the initial inquiries, preferring to lay it on Kenzie instead.

Kenzie typed and printed and forwarded email reports, thinking it over.

What if there was a reason Menendez did not want to go to the geriatric unit? Not that she wanted an actual doctor to ask the questions, but for some other reason?

Was it possible that there was something Menendez did not want anyone to find out?

40

When Kenzie went to visit Zachary at the hospital that night, the nurse at the desk stopped her, looking apologetic.

"I'm sorry, I have to check ID's for anyone who visits," she advised.

Kenzie stopped and fished through her purse for her wallet. "I haven't had to show ID before."

"I know. We should probably have been checking before too. It seems a little silly when we recognize you and know who you're here to visit and everything, but that's the policy."

Kenzie pulled out her driver's license and handed it to the nurse, who looked at it briefly, then up at Kenzie's face. She nodded.

"Just give me one more second."

Kenzie watched as the nurse wrote down her name and driver's license number in a log.

"Why the increased security?"

"I guess there have been some issues of people going places where they are not authorized and getting into mischief. I don't know the details." She gave a little laugh. "It all sounds a little funny to me. We shouldn't have to card everyone who goes past this point."

At Kenzie's raised eyebrows, she nodded.

"Everyone. Nurses, doctors, janitorial, security, plumbers, IT, *everyone*. Picture me having to ask the security guard for *his* identification!"

It was sort of a funny image. But all things considered… maybe if they'd had such a policy in place before Mr. Michaels had been killed, they would be a lot further ahead on the investigation. As it was, they couldn't account for who had or had not been on the unit when he had died. And the same applied to Mr. Scott and any of the other deaths that they managed to connect to the potential serial killer. If they had proper logs of everyone who had been through the door before the death, it would be a lot easier to pin down the culprit.

"Well, sorry that you have to go through all the extra trouble," Kenzie said, tucking her driver's license into her wallet and pushing the wallet into her purse. "But it probably is a good idea. Especially in a unit like this."

"We really haven't had any security problems, though," the nurse said in a confidential tone. "We never have. It isn't as if people are walking in and out of here if they don't have to be here. Not like, say, the nursery, where people want to get a peek at the cute babies. Friends, family, even strangers and kidnappers." She rolled her eyes. "It isn't like anyone is trying to kidnap any of *our* patients."

"No," Kenzie agreed with a laugh. The image of someone trying to make their way off with Zachary or one of the other men or women she was used to seeing in the unit was pretty ridiculous. It wasn't going to happen. "But there are other things to be concerned about. Drugs or weapons being taken into the unit. Maybe a spouse or family member that is bad for the patient. You don't want someone coming in who you know will start a fistfight!"

The young nurse nodded her agreement. "Yeah. But we generally know who the troublemakers are. And we do leave notes for each other if there's someone who is likely to cause a disturbance, or who always disrupts a patient. I just don't see the need to card you and every other visitor and doctor who comes through here. We can use our eyes. We know who belongs and who doesn't."

"I guess you do what the bosses tell you to."

"Exactly. Well, have a good visit."

Kenzie walked by the desk and went to find Zachary. She was surprised not to find him sitting at the usual table in the common room, and she stood there for a moment, unsure what to do with herself.

"Can I help you?" asked an orderly standing nearby.

"Uh… maybe. I was just looking for Zachary Goldman. He's usually waiting for me here. Maybe he's gone to the restroom…"

"I'll check his room. You wait here."

Kenzie nodded. He walked away, and Kenzie looked around awkwardly. She didn't want to make anyone uncomfortable staring at them, but also didn't want to look like she was avoiding looking at anyone and felt as awkward as she did. It was important for her to be aware of what was going on around her. Not that the psych ward was a particularly dangerous place, but there were certainly people there who could act unpredictably.

Why wasn't Zachary there waiting for her?

In a few minutes, the orderly returned, Zachary walking beside him. Kenzie analyzed Zachary's gait and studied his face. He wasn't shuffling and seemed to be alert, not like they'd given him a sedative. He nodded a greeting at Kenzie and looked away. Maybe embarrassed that he had not been there waiting for her as she had expected. He might have fallen asleep in his room.

"Hey, Kenzie."

Kenzie leaned in to give him a brief hug. "Hi. Do you want to sit down to visit? If you were sleeping…"

"No. We can sit down."

Kenzie nodded her thanks to the orderly and headed toward their usual table. Zachary followed her, but did not sit down when she did. Kenzie looked up at him.

"Something up?" she asked.

"No."

She looked at his usual chair. Zachary looked at it, but still didn't sit down. He scratched his head and ran his fingers through his hair.

"Actually… do you think we could walk?"

"As long as it's okay with the staff."

He walked away from the table. Kenzie got up to follow him. She caught up and walked beside him in silence at first, following his lead and walking around the loop that took them all the way around the ward.

"This is nice," Kenzie commented. "Get some exercise."

"Don't feel like sitting right now."

"That's fine. I don't mind."

She was interested in seeing the layout of the psychiatric unit. She noted where everything was. The patient rooms. The common room. The dispensary. A shower room that was wheelchair accessible and contained a lift for maneuvering patients. Administrative offices. Interview or therapy rooms, some of them bare and plain and some of them with soft furniture, TV's, and toys or games. A couple of isolation rooms for patients who were out of control or needed to be monitored.

"That was his room," Zachary said, pointing to one of the patient rooms they passed.

Kenzie looked at him. "What? Whose room?"

But then she knew before he answered and kicked herself for asking.

"Kennedy's. That's where they found him."

"Oh. I'm sorry. Where is your room? Are you close?"

Zachary indicated a room three doors down. "There. I didn't hear anything. Not until early morning, when they called Dr. Wiltshire."

"Did they wake you up?"

"I don't know. With these sleep meds… I don't always know if I have been asleep or just in a sort of… twilight. I guess I was asleep. I was by myself and there is no clock, so it's hard to judge… it's disorienting."

"Makes sense."

"I saw Dr. Wiltshire come in. So… I knew what had happened before other patients did. I knew he was dead."

"Did Dr. Wiltshire see you? He didn't mention it."

"I don't know. I was there. But he had a job to do. He was probably focused on that."

Or he hadn't mentioned it to Kenzie because protecting the confidentiality of a patient was required by law. Even though he already knew that Zachary was there, and that Kenzie knew he was there, and that Kenzie knew Dr. Wiltshire knew he was there… Dr. Wiltshire would still obey the letter of the law, which said that he couldn't divulge it to Kenzie.

"What's going on?" Zachary inquired. "Did Dr. Wiltshire issue his certificate? Saying that it was suicide?"

"Yes. There are still some questions to be answered by the hospital, but I expect the police are following up on those. As far as cause of death goes, though, we know it was suicide. There wasn't anything else that showed up in the autopsy or lab tests."

"He seemed okay."

"Did you talk?"

Zachary nodded. "He'd been here before. Not last year… maybe the year before? I don't remember."

"What was he like?" Kenzie assumed that since Zachary had brought it up, he wanted to talk about Kennedy and what had happened.

"He was… kind of gruff. Irritable. He didn't get along very well with the staff."

Kenzie remembered how Nurse Val had gone on about how polite and well-behaved Zachary was, and that they appreciated him as a patient. That was the way Zachary was. He didn't want to offend people. He didn't want to bring them down and didn't whine or complain about his life or the troubles he had. He'd been brought up to be cooperative and compliant, and generally tried to follow the rules, though he didn't always succeed in that.

"I don't imagine the staff is always easy to get along with either," she said to Zachary, laughing slightly. He tried to get along, but people like Nurse Debbie with her enthusiastic *bonhomie* could be a bit much.

"Well… no," Zachary admitted, half his mouth turning upward in a smile for just a second. Then it was gone again.

Kenzie had a sudden rush of memory. Talking to Nurse Debbie that first day she had been allowed to visit Zachary. Nurse Debbie saying what a good patient Zachary was, and how grouchy another patient was in comparison.

Was that Kennedy?

Kenzie was almost sure it had been Kennedy that Nurse Debbie had mentioned. *That old grouch Kennedy.*

41

Kenzie stopped walking. Zachary looked back at her, hesitating. "Kenz?"

"Sorry." Kenzie stepped forward and fell into place beside him once more. "Sorry. Just had a thought."

He didn't ask her what it was.

"At least he's in a better place now," Zachary said in a flat tone.

Kenzie glanced sideways at him. She'd never heard him speak of any belief in an afterlife before. They'd discussed it once or twice, whether it was possible that there was anything after the mortality they knew, but both of them were of the opinion that there probably was not. When life ended on that plane, that was the end.

"In a better place?" Kenzie asked. "My morgue?" she teased.

Zachary tugged on his ear. "I mean… he's not in pain anymore. That's all gone now."

"Yes," Kenzie agreed. "For him. Not for his family, any loved ones he has left behind. For them… he's caused a lot more pain."

Maybe it was cruel of her to point this out, to remind Zachary that if he were to leave her behind, she would suffer for it. She wouldn't be happy to have him out of her life. She wouldn't be happy that he was no longer suffering. She would grieve and miss him terribly. The guilt would probably cling to her forever. Guilt that she hadn't been able to stop him. That she hadn't been enough to keep him. That she went on living when he felt there was nothing else left for him.

But she wanted to remind him how much she cared and how much it would hurt her if he did harm himself.

Zachary nodded slowly, acknowledging Kenzie's comment. Pain glistened in his eyes, and she did feel guilty for a moment for causing it. But if it brought him down to earth and reminded him that there were people who loved and cared for him who would be hurt if he were gone, it was worth the momentary stab of guilt.

"I'm sorry," Zachary said.

"Sorry for what?"

He didn't answer at first. "For everything," he said finally.

"You haven't done anything you need to be sorry for." Kenzie turned to him and met his eyes, making him stop walking and meet her gaze for a minute. His pupils seemed normal, not dilated or pin-point. She didn't think he'd taken anything. She really hoped that the apology was just guilt over making her life harder because she cared for him and he was in the hospital instead of at home. Not for having made the choice to end his own life.

Zachary dropped his gaze. They continued walking slowly along. Past the common room again. Past the dispensary. Dr. Wiltshire had said that there had been bottles of pills missing from the dispensary, but there was no sign that it had been broken into. Kenzie couldn't imagine how Kennedy had managed to walk into it or grab a bottle of pills that had been left within his reach without anyone catching him. Maybe he could pick a lock. A lot of people, including Zachary, had that ability.

"I don't want you getting sucked down because of what Kennedy did," Kenzie said. "Because you're thinking about it all the time. If you need to talk to someone about it, to work it through in therapy or whatever, you talk to someone. Okay? It doesn't have to be me. You choose who. But don't let it get you down."

Of course she knew he couldn't help it if it got him down. If his obsessive brain decided to cling to the thought of Kennedy's suicide and not let it go. No amount of therapy could *make* him stop thinking about it or letting it affect his mood.

"Who else do you talk to here?" Kenzie asked, deciding that a switch to a more cheerful topic was in order. "Is there anyone else that you already know?"

"The nurse, Val. The one you talked to."

"Right. I remember. She seems really sweet. Anyone else? Any of the patients?"

"One of the doctors. He's been here a few years. I've seen him on other stays."

Kenzie nodded. Zachary considered.

"One of the other patients. Freddy."

"Freddy. What's he like?"

"She."

"Oh, she. I just assumed. What is Freddy like?"

"She's okay. She's schizophrenic. Ends up here a lot in the winter."

Kenzie was puzzled. "Why in the winter?"

"Because it's somewhere warm and safe. Three meals a day."

"Oh. Is she homeless?"

He nodded. "Mostly, I think. So she intentionally goes off her meds, or acts like she's off, and gets herself admitted."

"Clever girl."

"She is really smart, actually. Like *rocket scientist* smart. But because of her schizophrenia…"

"She can't keep a job?"

"I know there are schizophrenics who do. Ones who manage really well. Who respond to medication and can have pretty normal lives as long as they follow the protocol. But Freddy…" He shook his head. "She's not one of those. She really goes off. Ranting, conspiracy theories, paranoia, seeing hallucinations."

"Kind of hard to get along in the outside world when you're dealing with that, isn't it?"

"Yeah. Most of the time, she lives on the street, and she's okay, people look out for her, and she manages. But when it gets too cold, she comes here."

"At least she's figured that out. She has a safe place to go."

"Yeah. I guess that's the best thing for her."

He was staring off into the distance, not seeing anything around him. Kenzie put her hand on his arm as they walked. "I'm glad you have a safe place to go, too. That they take care of you here."

"Uh-huh."

"Zachary."

He continued to stare at nothingness in front of him.

"I'm worried about you."

"Everything will be for the best," he assured her.

"Have they changed your meds?"

"No."

"You're acting different. Kind of spacey."

"No." He brought his hand up to his face and rubbed it tiredly. "No. Nothing different. Just feeling really…" He trailed off, and the silence drew out for so long that Kenzie didn't think he was going to finish his sentence. "Heavy," Zachary finished finally. "I'm just feeling… very heavy."

"You should tell your doctor that." She didn't like the change in him. She didn't know whether it was caused by Kennedy's death, or the advancing season, or something else. But it worried her.

"Same as usual," Zachary said. "Nothing has changed."

"Are you tired? Do you want me to go?"

She thought that he would immediately object, but he didn't. He turned toward the room that she now knew was his. "Maybe I'll just lie down."

Kenzie watched him walk away from her and return to his room without even a goodbye or peck on the cheek.

When Kenzie looked for someone she could talk to, she found that Nurse Debbie was on duty.

"Mackenzie!" Debbie greeted cheerfully. "How are you doing?"

"I'm good. But I'm a little worried about Zachary."

"Oh, he'll be okay," Nurse Debbie assured her. "He's coming along."

"Well, I know his history, and I know he's unlikely to get better before Christmas. Chances are, he'll continue to get worse until then. But tonight he seemed very different. He said that nothing in his med cocktail has been changed…?"

"No, not that I'm aware of." Nurse Debbie went to the computer at the nursing station and clicked the mouse a few times to bring up Zachary's chart. "No, he hasn't had any changes prescribed." She shrugged. "He could just be tired. A lot of the patients have been feeling extra stress today. After *you know.*"

"Yeah. It's been pretty tough on them, I know. It must be really difficult fighting your own suicidal ideation knowing that someone else here has just committed suicide."

Nurse Debbie nodded. "We're doing the best we can to keep things normal and upbeat. And to make sure that everyone is seeing their doctors and doing extra therapy as necessary. But sometimes, you just have to give people time. You can't rush mental health."

Kenzie nodded. She lingered there, thinking about everything that had happened. "So your Mr. Kennedy… I guess you don't know what happened?"

Nurse Debbie raised her brows. "What do you mean? Of course I know what happened."

"I mean… how he managed to get so many pills. I haven't heard word back from the hospital on where he obtained them. You know, whether he was stashing his own prescription, and if not, how they came into his possession."

"Oh, that. I don't know. They are investigating, I guess. There were pills missing from the dispensary, but how he managed to get his hands on them is a mystery."

"Aren't there surveillance cameras? I would think that the dispensary is a place you would want to position a couple of cameras, so that you can keep your eye on it even when it isn't in use. If someone picks a lock or breaks in…"

"I'm not in charge of security," Nurse Debbie laughed. "They're not going to be taking any advice from me. You'd best talk to hospital administration about that."

"But there isn't a camera there already?"

"There probably is. Umm…" Debbie looked at the computer, pursing her lips. She used the mouse to click a few times. Kenzie moved around the desk so that she could see the monitor. It wasn't a big screen and wasn't at the right angle for her to view, but she could see enough to tell that Nurse Debbie had brought up the security menu and was clicking through cameras, looking for one that pointed to the dispensary. "No… I don't see one pointing there. We do have a couple that are out," she clicked back and brought up a couple of black screens. "You see?"

"Who would know that those cameras were out? Did Mr. Kennedy know, or was he just lucky?"

"Who knows? He wasn't confiding anything in me. Why would he tell me about any security holes if he was going to steal meds?"

"He wouldn't, of course."

"He's better off where he is," the nurse said briskly, clearing the camera feeds from the monitor. "He isn't suffering anymore."

Kenzie shifted uncomfortably. "No, he's not suffering," she agreed. Kennedy was in a refrigerated drawer in the Medical Examiner's Office. Nowhere else. And that was where he would stay until his next of kin made arrangements to pick up his remains and have them interred.

"Does he have family?"

"No. Single guy, all alone. No one to look after him."

"I thought maybe parents or siblings…?"

"He didn't get any visitors. If there was any family around, then shame on them for not caring about him enough to come in now and then."

Kenzie thought about what it would be like for someone like Zachary, barely managing to hang on, to be all alone at home or in the psych ward. No one to tell his feelings to. No one who came by, even just briefly, to tell him that they hoped he would feel better soon. Zachary had seen Kennedy there before. The man would have known, like Zachary, that he likely had a lifetime of admittances in front of him. That he would never be able to completely shake the disease that plagued him. And he had chosen to cut that lifetime of pain short.

"Well… thank you for your help. Will you check in on Zachary in a bit? Make sure he's okay?"

"Of course, Mackenzie. I would check for you, even if I wasn't required to by my job! You know that he's being monitored while he's here. We are here to keep him safe."

Kenzie nodded a polite thank you and didn't bother to point out that they had failed to keep Mr. Kennedy safe. Where had they been when he was swallowing two full bottles of pills?

42

Kenzie grabbed a sandwich from the vending machine in the hall. She didn't know why she hadn't made herself lunch to bring in. She had known it would be a busy day and that she wouldn't have time to go to a grocery store or nearby restaurant over lunch. But she had not had the energy or motivation to make herself a sandwich to take in with her, even though she knew the only other option would be buying something from the vending machine, which she hated.

She had sabotaged her own lunch and she didn't know why.

She heard the elevator ding and heard footsteps in the hallway leading to her desk, so she pushed the sandwich to the side and looked attentive, watching to see who came around the corner. It was Joshua Campbell, a police sergeant that Zachary knew and who Kenzie had dealt with on various cases.

"Dr. Kirsch," Campbell greeted, a smile on his face. "It's good to see you. How is everything?"

"Well… coming along." Kenzie didn't jump right in to give him details about her life or Zachary's admission to the hospital. It was just a social inquiry, as far as she could tell, no heartfelt response required. "What can I do for you today?"

"Is Dr. Wiltshire in?"

"No. He had a lunch meeting to attend to, and as soon as he gets back here, he's performing an autopsy. We've got an exhumation in, and he'll want to take care of it right away."

"An exhumation." Campbell made a face. "Nasty business. Best to get them *before* they go into the ground."

Kenzie nodded her agreement. "That would be preferable."

"I was hoping to have some time to talk to him. Maybe ten, fifteen minutes to go over the Kennedy case. The suicide."

Kenzie hadn't known that Campbell was on the Kennedy case. He hadn't been the detective who had attended at the autopsy, but she supposed he had sent a junior to sit in on an autopsy that was expected to be ruled a suicide.

"Okay. If it's just a few minutes, then we could probably squeeze you in. But you'll have to be available as soon as I call."

"I'm going to be heading out myself." Campbell looked at his watch, thinking about it. "I would like to ask some questions at the hospital before shift changes. And then catch the next shift as well."

Kenzie glanced at the time. Between driving to the hospital and asking questions of two or three people, it would be tight for him to get there in enough time to do what he wanted to as it was.

"You really don't have enough time, then. Do you want to leave a message for Dr. Wiltshire instead?" Kenzie poised her fingers over the computer keys. "I can take down a very detailed message, if you would like."

Campbell hesitated. "Well… that may be the best option right now. I should probably just leave him a voicemail. No need to make you take it all down."

"If it is an important message, he will have me transcribe it for the file anyway."

"Oh. Then I guess that doesn't save you any trouble. Okay." Joshua paused, gathering his thoughts. "The police have… some concerns about Kennedy's death. As Dr. Wiltshire noted, he swallowed a very large number of pills."

Kenzie nodded, typing the header for the message, including Campbell's name, and Kennedy's name and identification number. She jotted down a sentence and waited.

"Having reviewed the security videos for that day, we are concerned that there may have been someone else involved in Kennedy's death."

Kenzie took this down, but she frowned, trying to understand what Campbell was saying.

"Why is that?"

"Kennedy is never seen near the dispensary that the meds came from, except to get his own pills at the appropriate times. He's never hanging around there casing it out. No sign of tampering with the lock."

"I thought that camera was broken."

Campbell raised his brows at her. "How did you hear that?"

"I was talking to one of the nurses yesterday. She looked at the camera feeds and said that one was broken."

"There were a couple of cameras that were not operational. The one that would show the door to the dispensary in particular. But we can see the room around it. Enough to tell that Kennedy only went to get his regular meds and wasn't there when he shouldn't be."

"Then...?"

"Then it appears that someone else was complicit in getting him the pills."

Kenzie's heart sank. Someone had helped Kennedy to get the pills to commit suicide? It couldn't have been someone who thought that it would be good for him. It wasn't like they were trying to give him something that would make him feel better. They had to know that it would kill him. That if Kennedy had those pills in his possession, he would inevitably give in to the temptation to kill himself.

"Oh, no."

Campbell nodded. "It's unfathomable, I know. You wouldn't think that anyone could do such a thing... but we've seen cases where people talk others into suicide. And with Mr. Kennedy, that clearly would not have been difficult."

"No. I would guess not."

"Are you familiar with the autopsy in this particular case?"

"Yes. I actually was the lead."

"Well, that's helpful. I just wanted to be sure... there was no reason for a medically assisted suicide, was there? What I mean is... it couldn't have been someone who thought that it was the best thing, that he was dealing with so much pain he was justified in... choosing to end his life?"

"No. We checked for tumors or anything else like that. Any organic reason that he might have had to kill himself. As far as we can tell, it was just the depression. No other influences." She paused. "Except now, this."

"You can pass that information on to Dr. Wiltshire for me," Campbell said, motioning to the computer. Kenzie had stopped typing as she had understood what Campbell was saying. She typed a flurry of words to summarize their discussion, and nodded.

"I'll let him know."

"I'll be at the hospital to make inquiries, so I'll be out of contact for a while. They always want you to turn your phone off, even if you're not in a unit with sensitive electronic equipment."

Kenzie nodded. Even though there were signs saying to turn off phones in the psych unit, Kenzie didn't bother. As Campbell had said, there were not heart monitors and other sensitive equipment in the ward. She wasn't worried about her phone interfering with anything. But Campbell chose to follow the rule, even though he knew it was nonsense. Or maybe he liked having to turn his phone off now and then. Sometimes being distraction-free was worth it.

"Uh…" Kenzie held her hand up to ask Campbell to wait for a moment. "I don't know whether you know, but I should probably tell you…"

He waited politely for the information.

"Zachary is there."

"At the hospital? Is he investigating something?"

Campbell had, Kenzie knew, run into Zachary at the hospital during the Salter investigation, so it was natural that his mind should jump immediately to that possibility.

"No. He's in the psych unit. Like Kennedy."

She could see that he was still confused, still trying to make the details fit with his case. Maybe he thought that Zachary was undercover there, pretending to be depressed like Kennedy, to see whether he could shake anything out.

"He's a patient," Kenzie told him slowly. "He's depressed and needs to be under a doctor's care."

"Oh! Oh, of course." Campbell shook his head. "I had heard that he suffered from that. Didn't realize that it was so bad."

"This time of year in particular."

"Yes. Christmas is a bad time for people who get depressed," he agreed. "High rate of—" He cut himself off. "Lots of depression this time of year when the days get shorter and there isn't as much sunlight. Or people seeing how happy everyone else seems to be."

"Yes," Kenzie agreed, deciding that Campbell didn't need to know any of the details around Zachary's traumatic memories. "Anyway… I thought you should know, in case you see him or his name…"

"I appreciate it. Do you think… would he mind if I looked in to say hello? Or would that embarrass him?"

"I think it would be fine. He tries to be open about it."

"All right. I'll check in if I get the chance."

He again turned his head to go. Kenzie licked her lips, trying to think of what else she should do. She stood up.

"Do you… have any suspects?"

"I don't have anyone specific yet. I have the list of staff who were on duty that evening. I'll need to get the list of those who were there earlier, too, maybe the last few days, as we don't know exactly when the pills walked off. I didn't see anyone but medical personnel walking away from the dispensary in the recordings that we have, so that would suggest that it was a doctor or nurse who stole them."

Campbell stood there, looking at Kenzie, waiting to see whether she had something else to say about it. He tilted his head slightly, analyzing her.

"You've been there visiting Zachary, I assume? Anyone who jumps out to you as being suspicious?"

43

Kenzie scratched the back of her head, thinking through everything she knew. If someone had given Kennedy the pills intentionally, then that was tantamount to murder. She was already investigating a series of murders. And one of the main suspects in that string of killings had transferred to the psychiatric unit.

She didn't believe that Nurse Debbie could have done anything. She had seen Nurse Debbie at work, knew how well she had gotten along with the patients, how much she had cared for them. A nurse like that did *not* turn to killing patients. And Debbie had left the geriatric unit before Michaels's death. That put her in the clear.

Someone from outside the unit might have visited and given the pills to Kennedy. Maybe even someone from outside the hospital. They were checking ID after that, closing the barn door after the horse was long since gone. The nurse who had been checking ID had said that there was a problem with people walking in that had not belonged there. Did they know that, or was it a guess? It could have been anyone.

Anyone with a key or the ability to pick a lock. Unless it was an electronic keypad, and then they needed to know the combination. She remembered how, on past cases, Zachary had been able to see and remember a phone number he had seen someone dial. If he could do that, then there were people who could have picked up on a four- or six-digit password after seeing it input once or twice.

It could have been another patient.

Anybody.

"Dr. Kirsch?" Campbell prompted.

"I don't know whether you're aware… that the FBI has been investigating a possible serial killer in the geriatric unit. It isn't yet proven that it is a serial killer. The body that's waiting for Dr. Wiltshire, the exhumation, that's another possible killing in that case."

"I'd heard about the FBI being called in."

Then there was Agent Menendez. She didn't seem to have gotten anywhere on the case. It was stalled and she couldn't push it forward. Kenzie had yet to hear anything that they had discovered about the threatening letters. If they couldn't even pull a fingerprint from a letter, how was she going to solve the case of an Angel of Death killer? How many bodies would have to pile up before Josie Menendez could get somewhere on the case?

Did she even want to solve it? Or was there something else going on behind the scenes that Kenzie was unaware of?

"Well…" Kenzie forced herself to go on. If there was a problem with Menendez's investigation, then her superiors would figure it out sooner or later. They wouldn't accept a report that she simply couldn't find any indication that there was a serial killer, let alone who it was.

Would they?

"There is one nurse in that case. A suspect, according to FBI Agent Menendez. And she… has recently transferred to the psychiatric unit. I don't *know* that there's any connection," Kenzie hurried to add. "I haven't seen anything suspicious, and I know her from before, from when my sister was sick. She's a good nurse. I don't see how it could be her. Not when she wasn't even around geriatrics anymore during the time we're looking at."

"But there must be a reason she is a suspect."

"I guess. You would have to talk to Agent Menendez, get her take on the case. Maybe she's moved on to other suspects. But… I just I talked to her last night. The nurse. And I wasn't comfortable with the way she was talking about Kennedy." Kenzie ran her fingers through her curls, as if that might help her to get her thoughts in order. "I don't know. She didn't say anything wrong; it just worried me. Especially with Zachary being in the unit."

"What's her name?" Campbell asked, not asking for any other explanation of what the nurse had said.

"Debbie. Nurse Debbie. I don't remember her last name. I have it written down somewhere, but…"

"I don't imagine there are multiple Nurse Debbies on the unit." Campbell pulled out his phone and started tapping it. Had he received a new message or was he typing a note to himself to follow up on Nurse Debbie?

"I see her on the staff list," Campbell said after a moment. "She was on the floor the night that Mr. Kennedy committed suicide."

"But you don't even know whether that's when the medications were stolen."

"I'm going to assume, until someone manages to prove otherwise, that they were stolen that day. Otherwise, someone should have noticed them missing. These drugs are supposed to be very carefully managed."

Kenzie nodded. "Yeah."

"I will follow up with her," Campbell assured Kenzie. "And I would have been talking to her anyway. You don't need to worry that I will mention your name. I would never say something like that."

"Thanks. I'm sure it's nothing. Like I said, I'm sure it's not her. I mean, one of the patients the FBI is investigating was killed *after* she had left the unit."

"But not killing that patient doesn't mean she didn't kill Kennedy."

"No. I guess not. And there's another nurse that I saw from the geriatric unit *near* the psychiatric unit. But I didn't see him in there; he wouldn't have had access to the drugs in the dispensary."

Campbell's eyebrows went up. He shook his head. "I should obviously have consulted you on this case before putting a bunch of time into it. Who is this other nurse?"

"A male nurse, Stevens is his name. I saw him… going into the NICU unit. But I know that he doesn't work in the NICU. He said he was going there to visit a friend."

"There was no indication that he was going up to psych?"

"No. None at all. It's just that he was close, and that he didn't belong there."

"And a medical professional jumping from one unit to another might not be noticed, if all the conditions were right."

"Yeah. I suppose."

Campbell tapped more information into his phone. Then he nodded. "Just the two of them, then?" he asked, tone ironic. "No one else?"

"No. Sorry. I've been busy with Zachary."

He smiled warmly and nodded. "I'll talk to you later, then. Let you know if either of these names seems to be connected. Enjoy your autopsy, if you're participating in the one this afternoon."

"Yes. Probably. Thanks."

Kenzie told Dr. Wiltshire about Campbell's visit as they suited up for the autopsy. Dr. Wiltshire shook his head, bemused.

"You think this is related to Dr. Philemon's deaths? Why would someone suddenly stop killing geriatrics and start killing people in psych?"

"I don't know. I can't figure it out either. I mean… I understand transferring if she thought that the FBI was getting too close. That makes sense. But… I would think she would move to another state, start over with a different name. No history. Just start over again. That's what usually happens, isn't it?"

Dr. Wiltshire pulled the drape back from the remains on the table, folding it down halfway. "People are not always logical. And despite what they tell you about serial killers in crime fiction on TV, they are not brilliant. They often have low to average intelligence. They're just lucky. They don't get caught because they are brazen and take the opportunities that present themselves. And people don't believe what they see with their own eyes, or don't want to get involved."

The detective Dr. Wiltshire was waiting for arrived. He sketched a wave and apologized for being late, then made his way to the observation area. Kenzie wondered what he'd done to be assigned an exhumation autopsy.

Dr. Wiltshire looked down at the body they were to autopsy and began recording. "The deceased is a Miss Adeline Burger. Age ninety-three. Five feet tall, reportedly ninety pounds at her death. Miss Burger was suffering from pancreatic cancer and died under the care of her physician, Dr. Philemon. Dr. Philemon requested that Miss Burger be exhumed to allow a postmortem to be performed in light of other recent deaths. Miss Burger's next of kin had consented to the procedure. The remains have been embalmed and were buried five months ago. We will begin with a gross examination of the body."

Kenzie was glad that Dr. Wiltshire took the lead on Miss Burger. While she had attended the other two exhumations, Kenzie was not yet accustomed to autopsying remains in a more advanced stage of decomposition. There were many things to be aware of. Dr. Wiltshire walked her through each step, asking questions and pointing out things she should notice. By half an hour in, she was accustomed enough to the sight and smell of the remains that she was no longer distracted by them, fully engaged in the process of the autopsy.

They didn't find anything that indicated obvious foul play in the examination, but knew that they might discover something when samples were tested for toxicity at the lab. There was a lot of bruising in her back, but Dr. Wiltshire said that it appeared to be livor mortis, the blood settling and pooling at the lowest points of gravity after death, rather than any indication of violence.

Like Mr. Michaels, Miss Burger had been on an IV at the time of her death, so there was a puncture wound in one arm, but they were unable to find any other antemortem punctures. Of course, there would be no reason for anyone to inject her somewhere else when a killer already had access to the IV tube draining into her arm.

They took various slides and samples, both for testing and so that Dr. Wiltshire could show Kenzie the effects of decomposition on the various tissues.

Kenzie looked at the clock on the wall, but she didn't need to get back home to have dinner with Zachary. She could grab something quick to eat at the hospital before she visited him.

"It is getting late," Dr. Wiltshire observed, noticing Kenzie's glance at the clock. "We will be done shortly."

"It's fine. I don't have to be anywhere."

"Perhaps not, but I don't want to wear you out too much. It's the weekend; you should be able to relax for a couple of days without being completely wiped out because I kept you too late on top of your other responsibilities."

"I'm fine. A little tired, but I've been sleeping okay most of the time. I can sleep in tomorrow."

She wouldn't be waking up early because Zachary was up. She could stay in bed as long as she liked. Pretend that she was back to her carefree young adult days before she had gone back to school. It seemed like a very long time ago.

"How are things?" Dr. Wiltshire asked. "Any improvements?"

Although he didn't say so explicitly, she knew that he was asking about Zachary.

"No. Not yet. But I don't really expect there to be before Christmas. I was… I'm a little worried about how he was yesterday. The way that he was talking, sleeping or spending more time in his room alone. I don't know. It's scary, not knowing what is going on in someone else's head."

"It might be scarier if you experienced it. I think it's best that we stay in our own heads."

"Yes. I think that his brain is a pretty dark place right now. Especially with the suicide. I thought maybe they had changed his meds, but the nurse said no."

Nurse Debbie.

She wouldn't have any reason to lie about it. If Zachary were reacting badly to a change in his protocol, she would want to know about it so that they could straighten him out again before things got too bad.

Zachary had said that he didn't want anything else changed before Christmas. Dr. B had already raised some of his dosages in hopes that she could get him stabilized. Adding a new medication or taking anything away would be tempting fate. Who knew how badly it could affect him?

"Hang in there," Dr. Wiltshire said.

He didn't tell her that he was sure it would get better or that Zachary would be all right. He had probably seen way too many deaths over the years to be able to spout platitudes to anyone. He knew how unpredictable life and death could be.

"Thanks. I'll do my best."

"That's all anyone can expect." Dr. Wiltshire looked at the tubs of samples on the counter. "Why don't you start getting those into the fridge? We'll send them out Monday when everything is open. I will close up here and put Miss Burger back where she can rest until the funeral home returns for her."

44

Kenzie cleared her desk, took another glance at her emails, and started to pack up to leave. She was getting hungry. She should probably have had something else to eat before going into the autopsy. But she didn't like to start an autopsy on a full stomach, just in case. Especially not an exhumation.

The light on her phone was blinking, and Kenzie considered whether to check her messages or just leave it and pick them up the next time she was in. If there were any emergencies, Dr. Wiltshire would have been informed, and he would let her know even if she didn't pick up her voicemail.

But it was the weekend, and she would not be back until Monday, so she should probably just make sure it wasn't anything important. Or something she could do in two minutes so that she didn't need to worry about it over the weekend.

Sighing, Kenzie tapped the message button and waited for it to cue up. It was set up to "verbose" mode, giving the exact date and time and all the other message envelope details before playing the recording. They had to keep accurate records of messages related to patient files.

Kenzie recognized Campbell's pleasant baritone. "Dr. Kirsch. I have left a message for Dr. Wiltshire as well, but I wanted to give you an update to make sure that you are up to speed. I have conducted interviews at the hospital with the last two shifts of medical personnel, as I had hoped to. Your Nurse Debbie was not on for either of those shifts. I have grabbed her shift schedule and personal information and will set up a time to meet with her, whether it is at the hospital or at her home."

There was a pause as Campbell hesitated or planned the rest of his message.

"I don't think there is anything suspicious about her not being here. As far as I can tell, there were not any recent changes made to the nursing schedule. I have also spoken with Nurse Stevens in the geriatric unit. I was lucky enough to find him there after finishing up in psych. I agree that his explanation is a bit fishy, and I will be following up with his alibi witness for the time of the Michaels homicide to see whether we can rule him out. He admits that he did not have a friend in the NICU. He just likes to go and look at the babies."

Campbell gave a grunt of disbelief, and then went on.

"But my main reason for wanting to touch base with you was Zachary."

Kenzie paused in straightening things out in her purse to look at the phone, as if that might help her to understand Campbell better or would hurry him along in his explanation.

"After my interviews were complete, I thought I would stop in to say hello. You said you thought it would be okay, and I thought maybe it would give him a boost to know that someone else was thinking about him. But he wasn't there."

Kenzie dropped her compact. It hit the floor with a smash, but she didn't look at it. She continued to stare at the phone, not believing her ears.

Zachary wasn't at the hospital?

It made no sense. He had known that he needed to be admitted. He recognized his own depression and suicidal thoughts and impulses and knew that he could not be responsible for his own actions. He needed to get help.

Then why would he leave?

She searched for a logical explanation. Campbell had been looking under the wrong name. There was a glitch in the patient records. The nurse helping him had typed in the wrong search string. But wouldn't Campbell have just walked around the unit until he spotted Zachary? It wasn't that big of a place. It wouldn't be hard to find Zachary.

Kenzie waited for Campbell's recording to resume. He had apparently been unsure what to tell her after that point. Zachary wasn't there. So...?

"I'm sorry. I don't mean that to sound dramatic or worried. There is nothing to indicate that there is anything wrong."

Except, of course, for the fact that Zachary had disappeared.

"He checked himself out today. The nurse said that he was a voluntary admission, so he is allowed to check himself out. Of course, if they had concerns about his safety, they could try to keep him here on a Title 18 hold. But he hasn't been making any threats to harm himself or anyone else, so they exercised their judgment and… let him go."

Kenzie didn't stop to pick up the broken compact. She zipped her purse shut and walked away from her desk at a quick clip as Campbell said a pleasant goodbye and wished her luck in a slightly strained voice.

She didn't think about the fact that she hadn't said goodbye to Dr. Wiltshire or locked up her desk. She just moved as quickly as she could. To get to the parking garage and her car and to find out what had happened to Zachary.

There had to be a reason he had left. But with the way he had been talking the previous evening, she was worried what the reason might be. He knew he had to stay there to protect himself. She wasn't aware of any other time that he had checked himself out early.

She said a brisk hello and goodbye to the guard in the parking garage. She would apologize the next time she saw him. He would be wondering what she was in such a hurry about or if he had done something to warrant being treated so brusquely.

Kenzie turned her key in the ignition and it roared to life. She gave it a bit too much gas as she backed out and narrowly missed bumping into a pillar.

She waited until she was under clear skies and then hit the Bluetooth button and said Zachary's name.

After a few moments of considering her request, the phone dialed out, and then the sound of the ringing phone was played over the speakers. Kenzie bit her lip and stopped for a red light. She was impatient to get to the hospital. It didn't make any sense. And she would hit every traffic light red on the way there, for sure. That was always the way it worked when she was in a hurry.

The phone continued to ring until it went to voicemail.

"Zachary, it's Kenzie. Give me a call back."

She hung up and redialed. Sometimes it took longer to get through to him. Maybe Bridget had been discharged and he felt an irresistible impulse to go see her again. He could be sitting across the street from her house now, watching the lights coming on in the dusk and straining for the sight of Bridget crossing in front of a window.

That actually made sense, and it made her feel better. That was one of the few things that she could imagine Zachary leaving his safe place at the hospital for.

The phone again rang through to voicemail. Kenzie stopped at another traffic light and had to make a decision. Continue to the hospital knowing that Zachary was not there? Go home to see whether he had returned? Or check to see if he had gone to Bridget's house?

Of course, he could be at his own apartment too. She wasn't sure why he would go there, but he still maintained his rent so that he had somewhere to retreat to on the odd occasion when he needed more space or wanted to pick something up that was stored there. He didn't have more than half a closet and a couple of drawers to keep things in at Kenzie's. Maybe she should convert the guest room to an office for him so that he didn't have to sit on the couch and would have room for his client files, photographs, and whatever else he needed to store. She had wanted to keep the guest room free in case her mother needed to stay over or a friend came to visit sometime. But maybe that was silly. And she did have her own home office as well, which she hardly ever used. She could make it into a combined office for the two of them.

There were horns blaring behind Kenzie. The light had changed and she was still sitting there trying to decide where to go. Kenzie blew out her breath. Bridget's house was probably the best bet. But she should check her own house and make sure he hadn't just gone home, expecting her to be there. Maybe he wanted to spend the weekend together and planned to go back to the hospital on Monday. Maybe he felt as though he could manage for a day or two if she were at home.

Kenzie finally took the turn for her house, but she tapped the Bluetooth button again.

"Gordon Drake, mobile."

The hands-free system dialed once more. Gordon answered after only two rings. "Kenzie?"

"Hi, Gordon. I'm sorry to bother you…"

"No, not at all. How can I help you?"

"Well, a couple of things. First, I was wondering how everyone is. Whether Bridget was able to go home…?"

"Yes. She is here. She has someone with her twenty-four hours a day until she is fully recovered. She wanted to get back to familiar surroundings."

"Of course. I'm glad that she's doing well enough to leave."

"The girls, of course, are not yet strong enough to leave the hospital. They are both off of respirators, though. Both breathing on their own."

"Oh, that's fantastic news. I'm glad to hear it. Julia will be catching up to Tricia in no time."

"I certainly hope so. And what else could I help you with?"

"Well, I seem to have misplaced Zachary," Kenzie said, aiming for humor. "He has also checked himself out of the hospital and he's not answering his phone. I'm going to check at home to see whether he is there. He probably is. But I wondered whether he had shown up over there. Maybe he heard that Bridget had gone home and wanted to make sure she was all right."

"I have not seen him," Gordon said slowly, "but the only time I was outside was when we got home this morning." There was a pause as he apparently checked out the window. "He isn't out in front, but of course he doesn't usually park where he is so visible. Perhaps I'll go for a walk."

"Thanks. I hate to bother you. And I will head over there if he isn't at home. But if you can have a look around… it would ease my stress levels a little if I knew that he was okay."

"I will see if I can see him. I'll call or message you back."

"Thanks, Gordon."

Kenzie terminated the call and drove as fast as she dared to her house.

45

There were no lights on other than the ones Kenzie knew were on timer switches. She already had a knot in her stomach as she drove into the garage. He wasn't there. She had told herself that he would be. But of course he wasn't. He had left the hospital for a reason, and it wasn't to come home and spend the weekend with her. If that had been the case, then he would have called her. He would have had her pick him up from the hospital and maybe they would go out to dinner somewhere. At a restaurant that didn't have Christmas decorations up. There were still a few that didn't go overboard on the holiday decor.

Kenzie got out of the car and hurried through the door into the house.

"Zachary? Are you here?"

There was no answer. The house was quiet and still.

The burglar alarm started beeping a warning and Kenzie punched her code into the panel to disarm it.

Of course, if the burglar alarm was still armed, then there was no one in the house. But it was always possible that Zachary had been home for a while and then left, re-arming the alarm again. So Kenzie took a quick walk through the house, looking for anything out of place. He hadn't taken anything with him to the hospital, so she couldn't judge by luggage or clothing dumped by the washing machine.

In the living room, his computer and equipment didn't appear to have been touched. His phone was still sitting attached to the charger, where he had left it. There wasn't any point in continuing to call him if he didn't even have his phone with him. Which also meant that she couldn't use it to track him. Maybe that was why he had left it there and not returned for it when he had signed himself out of the hospital.

She checked the bedroom just for good measure, and just to be sure of herself, checked the row of pill bottles lined up in his bathroom. All appeared to be untouched. Kenzie went back through the house to the garage, pausing to set the alarm again as she left. She checked the bin in the garage where she had left the knives. Zachary didn't know where she had put them, but he was smart enough to figure it out and go looking through the boxes for them if that were what he really wanted. But the knives all appeared to be present and accounted for.

Kenzie checked her phone in case she had missed a message from Gordon, but there was no text from him confirming that Zachary was at the house.

Kenzie was sure that was where he had to be. She shut her mind to all other possibilities. Particularly to the possibility that Kennedy's death had just been too much for him to handle and he had signed himself out in order to be alone to do what he felt compelled to do. He had checked himself into the hospital for just that reason. So that he would not be able to harm himself. She was sure that he wouldn't leave the psych ward to follow through on his suicidal ideations.

She had told him once how she feared being the one to find him one day if he did commit suicide. She had hoped that knowledge, the vision of her walking into his apartment to find his body, would help deter him from taking such action. He was a kind, compassionate person. He didn't want his actions to hurt others.

Kenzie drove to Bridget's house. It was, she knew, Gordon's house rather than Bridget's, but Zachary had always identified it as Bridget's. She was the person who mattered to him. His world revolved around her, not Gordon. And unfortunately, not around Kenzie.

She closed her mind to all other thoughts and focused on reaching the house. Zachary would be there. Watching from some corner or alley. Getting his fix, the positive boost his brain gave him when he watched his former lover.

Kenzie couldn't help marveling at the size and majesty of the home when she arrived. It really was stunning. Comparable to anything Kenzie's parents owned.

She tore her eyes from the building to look around. Where was he? She scanned the road for his car, but didn't see it.

Kenzie drove slowly down the streets, performing a circuit of the house.

She looked for the car, watched for Zachary's figure loitering across the street or under a tree, anywhere within sight of the house. He would want to see it. Being close by wouldn't be enough. After three circuits of the house, Kenzie finally had to admit that he wasn't there. She thumbed a quick message to Gordon that she had been unable to find Zachary at either house.

What is he driving? Gordon texted back. *Same car as before?*

Kenzie sat there, staring at the phone screen. She hadn't even stopped to think about how he would get around. She had driven straight to her garage, not even driving past the front of the house to see whether Zachary's car was still parked at the curb.

Not sure, she texted back, *will try to find out.*

She drove back to the house, slower this time, not wanting to risk getting pulled over by the police for speeding. She had been sure that he would be at Bridget's house. Now she wasn't going anywhere in a hurry. She had to figure out where else he would go.

She drove down the street in front of her house and saw the little white car still parked there. So Zachary didn't have a vehicle. He hadn't returned to the house to pick it up.

He was, of course, perfectly capable of calling a cab or Uber, renting a car, walking, or getting around town on the bus. Those were all possibilities. But she couldn't see him traveling around town without picking up his phone and his car.

Zachary's apartment was the only other place she could think of where he might have gone. His own man cave. If he needed to think by himself, needed space to just be himself or to get some quiet and have a nap, then maybe he would go to his apartment. Or maybe there was something there that he wanted to pick up. She couldn't imagine what it would be, but tried to assure herself that there was good reason for him to go back there. He did have a life separate from hers. His own identity.

She looked around the parking lot when she got there. Since Zachary's car was at her house, she didn't feel guilty about using the resident parking instead of looking for one of the rare visitor spaces. She pulled her car in and hurried into the building and up the elevator to Zachary's floor. There were decorated Christmas trees in the lobby. She remembered how much of a problem that had been for him the year before. He snuck in and out the back door to avoid having to see them.

She walked down the hall to Zachary's apartment and found a couple of flyers protruding from under his door. They should probably get someone on his floor to pick those up whenever they were delivered, so that it wasn't so obvious that he was not at home.

Hoping that Zachary had just left them there when he went in, she tried the door and found it locked. There was no TV blaring away inside. No sound of Zachary talking on the phone with a client. Which of course he wouldn't be, since his phone was still back at the house. Kenzie fit her key into the lock and let herself in. She stooped to pick up the flyers that had been shoved under the door, as well as a couple of letters addressed to him, and put them down on the kitchen counter as she entered.

"Zachary, are you home? It's Kenzie."

As if he wouldn't recognize her voice.

"Zach?"

Kenzie knew that he wasn't there without looking any farther. But she knew she had to look. She had to confirm to herself that he had not gone back there to harm himself.

The living room was empty. She walked down the short hall to the bedroom and pushed the door open. No one lying in the bed or strung up to the light fixture. Kenzie let out a long breath that she hadn't realized she'd been holding. How long had it been since she'd been able to breathe properly?

She glanced into the closet and looked for any other signs that Zachary had been there. There was a fine layer of dust over all the horizontal surfaces. He hadn't been there.

Kenzie withdrew from the bedroom and checked the bathroom. Again, no sign that anyone had been there in quite some time. Kenzie looked through the medicine cabinet. There were still a few bottles of pills there, prescriptions that Zachary no longer used or had since refilled and had at her house. Kenzie threw them into the bag in the bathroom garbage can and took it with her. There was no need for them to be left at the apartment. Zachary usually kept a dose or two of his meds on him, just in case something happened and he couldn't return home. That had happened enough times that he'd learned to be prepared for the unexpected.

She took one final glance around the living room and kitchen and left, locking the door behind her. She took the bag of prescriptions down to the dumpster and threw them away.

After returning to her car, Kenzie sat there for a few minutes, trying to decide what to do. She couldn't go home and wait. That was out of the question. She needed to find Zachary. He was out there somewhere and he didn't have his phone on him. She wasn't going to wait until he turned up in the river.

How long had it been since he had left the hospital? Had it been in the morning? Not until the afternoon when Campbell had been there questioning suspects? Campbell might have missed him by minutes. He hadn't given Kenzie any of those details.

She could call the psychiatric unit, but she figured it would probably take just as long to get ahold of someone who would help her on the phone as it would to drive over there and see them face-to-face. And a face-to-face meeting was a lot harder to ignore. It wasn't as easy to turn someone away when they were standing right in front of you. When they had gone to the effort of coming to you.

So she revved her engine and drove to the hospital.

One of the nurses sat at the reception desk as usual. Kenzie took her wallet and identification out as she was walking down the hall so she would have it ready when she got there.

"I'm looking for Zachary Goldman. Is he here?"

"Oh, Zachary." The nurse smiled and nodded and looked at her computer screen.

"I was told that he had checked out," Kenzie advised.

"Oh, really?" The young woman tapped a search string into her computer and sat looking at the screen. "Oh yes, I guess he did. That's funny, I thought he would be here longer term. Usually…"

"I know. I didn't expect him to check out either. What time did he go, can you tell me?"

"Oh, I don't know, I'm sorry."

"Doesn't it say on your records? There must be some kind of time code attached to that checkout record."

"Hmm…" The woman studied the screen, then eventually nodded. "This morning. Eleven o'clock." She looked at her watch as if she didn't know what time it was. "I actually probably shouldn't have told you that. We're supposed to be very careful of privacy."

"I'm his partner. It's okay to tell me. You can see my name on the visitor list."

"But that doesn't mean I can give you any information, I'm sorry."

"I'd like to talk to someone who saw him this morning. Are any of the nursing staff who were on then still on now?"

"No. I don't think so."

Kenzie stared at her, then nodded at the computer. "Maybe you could check?"

"I don't know whether I can access that." She started clicking around the screen, looking for the information. "Well, it looks like Nurse Val is doing a double shift…"

"Great. I'd like to talk to her."

"We really can't talk to people about private patient issues."

"I'd like to see her anyway. Please." Kenzie motioned to the hall behind the nurse. "I can go find her on my own. Or do you want her to come out here?"

"I…"

"I'll just go in, then," Kenzie said briskly, and took a step toward the unit.

"No, let me call her and see what she wants to do. I'm not sure of this…"

Kenzie waited while she had Nurse Val paged, and then a few more minutes for her to show up. Kenzie shifted and looked around anxiously. She didn't want to just hover over the nurse at the reception desk, but there wasn't really anything for her to do while she waited.

Turning partway around, she saw a man coming toward her and, for a split-second, thought that Zachary had returned.

But of course, it wasn't him. It was Tyrrell, his younger brother. They were similar in coloring and features, Tyrrell had Zachary's dark eyes and hair.

But his hair was longer and shaggier, he was taller than Zachary and was a healthy weight, not struggling to keep on the pounds like Zachary.

"Kenzie." Tyrrell smiled and gave her a little wave. "Hey, how are you doing? I tried calling earlier, but..."

Kenzie tried to remember if she had seen Tyrrell's number on her recent call list. He might have called while she was doing the autopsy, but if he had, he hadn't bothered to leave a message.

"How are you doing?" Kenzie gave him a perfunctory hug and looked him over. Something seemed a little "off." She wasn't sure what it was. Maybe he was out of sorts or worried about Zachary. Of course they were all worried about Zachary. Kenzie more than ever, with his disappearance.

"Good, good. I'm just fine."

"Did Zachary know you were coming?"

"Well... no. I thought I would talk to you, but then I didn't get to. So I figured I'd just come by."

He looked at Kenzie, and at the nurse at the reception desk. "Why? Is there something wrong? You said that he was going to put me on his visitor list."

Kenzie looked over her shoulder. Nurse Val had not yet shown up. "Well... the problem is... he checked out sometime earlier today. I don't know where he is."

Tyrrell blinked. "What?"

"Yeah. I'm sorry. I just found out. I haven't had a chance to tell everybody yet. And I don't know what I'm going to say. That I lost him? I can't believe that he did this."

"Well... he must have gone home. Isn't he at home?"

"No. Not at my place and not at his apartment. I've checked everywhere I can think of, but I can't find him."

"Can you call him on his phone?"

"No. His phone is at my house. He didn't bring it with him to the hospital. Same with his car," Kenzie said as Tyrrell took a breath, anticipating his question. "It's parked in front of my house."

Tyrrell shook his head. His dark eyes reminded her so much of Zachary's it was disconcerting. "That doesn't make any sense. Where would he go?"

"I don't know. I'm waiting to talk to a nurse who was on earlier when he checked himself out. We'll see whether there is anything she can tell us about what he might have said or planned."

Tyrrell's expression was concerned. Of course he would be just as worried as Kenzie about what Zachary might have done or be planning to do. He hadn't admitted himself to the hospital for no reason. He had known that he was a danger to himself and he needed to be under a doctor's supervision.

There were footsteps in the hallway and Kenzie looked up to see the familiar nurse walking toward her. She seemed to do a double-take when she saw Tyrrell standing there.

"Uh… hi. Is there something I can help you with?"

"Tyrrell, this is Nurse Val. Val, this is Tyrrell, Zachary's young brother."

"Oh. Well, I'm very glad to meet you," Val said politely, offering a hand. She and Tyrrell shook briefly. Val was clearly still wondering what was going on.

"Val, you were on this morning, right?"

"Yes. Long day today. I've been here the whole time."

"So you were around when Zachary decided to check himself out."

She shrugged.

"We're both really worried about Zachary. Did he tell you where he was planning to go?"

"No. He didn't say anything to me."

"It's really important. I'm not sure I understand why he was allowed to check himself out when he was having suicidal thoughts."

"He was voluntary. He checked himself in. He's allowed to check himself out. I understand your concern, of course, but… there wasn't really anything we could do about it. He said that he was feeling better, that he wouldn't do anything to harm himself, and… he had to go. So he went."

"You know his history. You know he's not going to be better before Christmas."

"Well…" She shrugged. "He said he was. I don't know what else to tell you."

"We need to find him. He isn't at home. He doesn't have a phone or a vehicle. He didn't tell anyone in the family that he was going to check himself out or what else he was going to do."

"He was depressed and suicidal," Tyrrell reiterated, his voice stronger than Kenzie's. And maybe it would carry more weight with the nurse. "Someone like that can just walk out of here?"

"Yes. I'm sorry. He has a history of admitting himself when he needs to, getting the treatment he needs, and then checking himself out. If he says that he is feeling better… I can't just decide that he's wrong. He hasn't had an involuntary admission in years. I don't know whether he ever has."

Kenzie looked at Tyrrell. He shook his head, at a loss.

"What we really need to do is to find him," Kenzie said. "Let's back up a bit…" She swallowed, took a couple of deep breaths, and tried to approach it logically. "I was here to see Zachary yesterday. He was still pretty upset about Mr. Kennedy." Kenzie looked at Tyrrell and filled him in. "Another patient in the ward who committed suicide this week."

Tyrrell nodded, his eyes big.

"He was talking… in a way I haven't heard him talk before. I was worried about him. I asked Nurse Debbie if any changes had been made to his medications because I thought he might be reacting to something. She said that nothing had been changed. So I hoped that he was just working things through, and maybe after a good night's sleep, he'd be feeling better. I was hoping that he would be doing better today."

Nurse Val nodded.

"He's really been having trouble with it," Kenzie reiterated.

"I know. A lot of them are. Things have been very stressful since… the incident. We are trying to give everyone the attention they need. Offering extra therapy. Some group sessions. The nurses are circulating and checking in on everybody, whether they are on watch or not, just to make sure that no one slips through the cracks. Everyone was very concerned, not just about Zachary, but about all the patients in the ward."

"Did you talk to him?" Kenzie asked.

"A little. Mostly just asking him how he was. Making casual observations. That kind of thing. He spent more time with Nurse Debbie."

Kenzie frowned. Zachary didn't like Nurse Debbie, so why would he be spending more time with her? "Are you sure? With Nurse Debbie?"

Val nodded. "Of course I'm sure."

"Did he… seek her out? Or was she checking in on him?"

"Well, that's hard to say. It isn't as if I was watching both of them all the time." Val considered, staring off into space and thinking it through. "It might have been more Debbie than Zachary. She was being proactive. She probably saw, as you did, that he was bothered by the events. Wanted to make sure that he was okay. Maybe because you said something to her."

Kenzie nodded. Her stomach was one giant, hard, heavy knot, but she tried to remain casual, to keep the conversation from becoming adversarial.

"But I thought that Nurse Debbie wasn't in today. Didn't I hear that?"

"No, you're right. She hasn't been in today. She's been on almost constantly since she transferred in. I'm sure she's in need of some major rest and relaxation. Especially after a suicide."

"I wonder… Nurse Debbie is kind of a friend of the family. Did you know that she treated my little sister years ago? In the nephrology unit in Burlington?"

"Did she?" Val smiled. "Debbie always has stories about all the patients she has treated over the years, all the families she has been friends with. She's such a bighearted person. Someone who really puts herself out there, her whole self."

Kenzie smiled and nodded. "My mom was hoping to be able to talk to her. Do you think I could get her phone number? After all these years, it would really mean a lot."

Kenzie could see the hesitation in Val's face. Of course they were not supposed to give out private phone numbers to their patients or the public. They were supposed to be able to keep their personal lives separate from their work, private, to avoid calls from cranks and disgruntled patients and family.

"Do you know who my mother is?" Kenzie asked. "Do you know Lisa Cole Kirsch? She does a lot of fundraising for kidney research and for the hospital."

Of course, the fundraising that Lisa did was more often for the big Burlington hospital than the Roxboro one, but Val didn't need to know that. Val nodded her head, familiar with the name.

"That's your mother? I never knew that. I never put the names together. Of course, I only know you through Zachary, so I didn't even know your last name."

"Yes. I'm sorry. I should be better at introducing myself." Kenzie pulled a business card holder out of her purse and passed a card to Val. She gave one to the nurse receptionist as well. "I'm Dr. Kenzie Kirsch. With the Medical Examiner's Office."

Val's eyes widened when Kenzie revealed that she was not only a doctor, but one with the Medical Examiner's Office.

"Oh, well. Of course… I'm sure it's all right for us to give Nurse Debbie's number to the Medical Examiner's Office," Val said, looking at the other nurse. "That's different."

The other nurse looked wide-eyed and uncertain about this, but when Val nodded at her, she tapped some more information into the computer and wrote a phone number on a little slip of paper. Like the papers they kept by the computers at the library.

"This is Nurse Debbie's number. Now, I really have other things that I should be doing. If you don't mind."

Kenzie looked down at the piece of paper. She was happy to have gotten something. The information was hard-won. But she wasn't sure it would lead anywhere.

"Let's go sit down over here," she said to Tyrrell, motioning to a couch off to the side, a place for people to rest while they were waiting to get into psych or for family members to visit.

47

Kenzie and Tyrrell sat down so that they wouldn't be hovering over the nurse at the reception desk. Nurse Val spoke with the other woman in a low voice for a minute, several looks were cast in Kenzie's direction, and then she returned to the unit.

Kenzie looked at the phone number.

"Where do you think he is?" Tyrrell asked worriedly.

"I wish I knew. I can't think of where else he would go. I've checked everywhere I can think of."

"What about… his ex-wife? He's always talking about her. How he's doing so much better now, not stalking her. Maybe… he fell off the wagon." He shrugged, ducking his head. "Sorry…"

"Don't apologize. It's the truth. I already know about Bridget and his issues there. There isn't any point in pretending they don't exist, is there?"

Tyrrell shook his head. "No. When you cover things up… they just get worse."

"That's right," Kenzie agreed. "I'm not pretending that behavior didn't happen. But I already checked, and he isn't around there. He doesn't even have his car. There's no sign of him."

Tyrrell nodded. "Well, sorry to bring it up."

Kenzie didn't tell him again that he didn't need to apologize for it. She took out her phone and started to tap the number into it. She hadn't realized how reluctant she was to call Nurse Debbie. She might be able to find something out about what was going on with Zachary. Maybe he had confided in her, and she could provide the key to finding him.

She knew that Zachary wouldn't have confided in Nurse Debbie. She drove him crazy with her ebullience and how physical she was.

But it was the only clue that she had. So she pressed the last button and placed the call on speaker so that Tyrrell would be able to hear it too. There were a few rings, and Kenzie wondered whether Nurse Debbie would answer it. A lot of people didn't bother to answer if they didn't recognize the number. Nurse Debbie would have no idea that it was Kenzie.

"Hello?"

"Oh, I'm glad I reached you. Nurse Debbie. It's Kenzie Kirsch."

"Well, isn't it a delight to hear from you! What can I do for you?"

"I was hoping that I could talk to you about Zachary. I'm in a bit of a bind. I know you're not on right now, but I really wanted to speak with you."

"What about Zachary?"

"I know I told you yesterday… but his behavior really concerns me. He's taken a turn, and I'm afraid it's for the worse. We need to keep an eye on any changes in behavior. We don't want to lose him. Like… Mr. Kennedy."

"I don't think you need to worry that much about Zachary. Why? What did he say?"

"He's been talking a lot about Kennedy. About how he is in a better place now."

Tyrrell was frowning at Kenzie. He mouthed *ask her where he is.*

Kenzie shook her head.

"Well, he *is* in a better place now," Nurse Debbie said. "I agree with that. While he was here, Mr. Kennedy was a tortured soul. He was miserable and made everyone around him miserable. I understand that losing him might have been a shock to the ward, but it really is for the better. Things are much more peaceful without him around. And where he is… he's not in pain anymore."

Kenzie looked at Tyrrell. He bit his lip. His face was very pale. Kenzie returned her gaze to her phone.

"I'm glad that you think Mr. Kennedy is at rest now. But I'm still worried about Zachary. I wouldn't want him copying Kennedy's actions."

"That's always a danger in a situation like this," Nurse Debbie acknowledged. "Copycats. Other miserable people."

"I don't want Zachary ending up like that."

"I'm sure you don't. You want him to be with you. But if he really was happier moving on… you have to consider that too."

Kenzie wrapped her arms around her stomach. She felt like she was going to throw up. She breathed shallowly, trying to keep herself together. If Nurse Debbie thought that Kenzie was upset with her viewpoint, she would stop talking, and Kenzie might need what she had to say.

"He wouldn't be happier. He would just be gone."

"I choose to believe that they go to a better place," Debbie said placidly. "You may not. But I think you are missing the big picture. When your sister died, weren't you relieved that she wasn't suffering anymore? Wasn't it better that she wasn't still sick? Hardly able to breathe? She was in so much pain. You didn't want to force her to stay, did you? Going through all of that?"

"That isn't the same," Kenzie said evenly. "Amanda was in a lot of pain. She was really sick. And I wasn't happy or relieved when she died. We were all devastated. We would have done anything for her, to keep her alive and well."

"But you couldn't, and if she had lived, she would have been in ongoing pain for months or years. You wouldn't have wanted that."

What Kenzie had wanted was for Amanda to get better. For her to be able to get another transplant, and again live a normal life, like she had after getting Kenzie's kidney. It had been miraculous, seeing her get off the machines and living a normal, vigorous life again. Kenzie had never seen anything like it. She had not wanted things to end the way that they had. No one would have wanted to see their loved one go through that ghastly process, eventually drowning in her own fluids.

"Zachary isn't going through what Amanda did," Kenzie said firmly. She didn't want to shout, but she needed to speak up against the nurse. "He is going through a depressive episode. And if you know his history at all, you know that when he gets past Christmas, he'll start to feel better. He isn't dying. He's just going through a dark patch and needs everyone's support."

"Would you want to keep going through that every year, over and over again?" Nurse Debbie challenged.

"Yes. His life is good. He's happy. He has a family again. He is in a relationship. He has his own business and is doing well enough to support himself. He has a good life, and he doesn't want to lose that because of cyclical depression. That's why he goes to the hospital. Because he wants to live!"

There was no response from Nurse Debbie. Kenzie stared down at the phone, blood pounding in her ears. She was furious with Nurse Debbie for insinuating that Zachary would be better off dead. Was that the way that she had been talking to Zachary when Val had seen them together? Not a nurse trying to cheer up her sick patient, but a poisonous serpent whispering in his ear, driving him closer to suicide just like a cyberbully had done the year before?

What was wrong with people?

"Did you talk to Zachary today?" Kenzie asked.

"I haven't been on shift today."

"I know that. But he could have called you on the phone. Said that he needed to ask you something or that you had told him it would be okay to call when you weren't there."

"Now, I haven't talked to him today."

"Did the two of you talk last night? After I left?"

"I checked in on him. That's my duty, and you said that you were concerned about him. So of course I went in to see how he was doing. Of course I talked to him to gauge how he was feeling."

"And…?"

"I think you have reason to be worried. He is very depressed. But that was last night. You've visited with him today. You know his state of mind better than I would."

"I haven't visited with him today."

"Didn't you go to the hospital? I thought you went every day."

"I went to the hospital to see him, but he wasn't there."

"He wasn't there?" Nurse Debbie echoed, sounding stunned.

"He checked himself out."

"But… why?"

"We're still trying to understand it. He checked himself out and he didn't go home. We don't know where he is."

"Oh goodness. I had no idea, Mackenzie. You must be so upset. Do you want me to call someone for you? Or to come visit you? I'm so sorry this has happened."

"No. I don't need you to come visit me. I'm still trying to figure out what to do. Where to look. I haven't given up on him."

"No, of course not. Here I am, going on about how he could be at peace, and you don't even know where he is. You should have told me earlier. I didn't mean to be so insensitive."

She sounded so sincere. But Kenzie was changing her mind about Nurse Debbie. She was starting to see that maybe she wasn't the woman she pretended to be. What if Agent Menendez's suspicions were true? What if Nurse Debbie had been killing patients in geriatrics? What if she had been doing it for years before that? And what if transferring out of the geriatric unit wasn't just a way to escape suspicion, but looking for new excitement? People who were not old, sick, and dying, but people in good physical health but suffering mental pain?

Someone had taken pills out of the dispensary. Someone who had legitimate access to the dispensary. And those pills had killed someone. Maybe Nurse Debbie had not forced the pills down his throat, but if she had talked Kennedy into killing himself, encouraged him to do it, and given him the pills, then she was just as guilty as if she had done it herself.

"Did Zachary talk about going anywhere? Did he say anything about going home or to someone else's house or some other place where he would be happier?" Kenzie asked, hoping to get something more from the woman.

If Nurse Debbie thought that Zachary had checked himself out to harm himself, then she might be as eager to find out where he had gone as Kenzie was.

But for very different reasons.

"No, I can't think of anywhere," the nurse said slowly. "I'm sorry."

"Did he talk about… Lorne and Pat? Going back to a place he'd known in childhood? Searching for the rest of his family…?" Kenzie dug desperately for clues as to where he might have gone. They needed to find him.

"He didn't have much to say to me," Nurse Debbie said. "I'm sorry. About the only thing I ever heard him talk about was those babies."

"Babies?" Tyrrell echoed.

"Who is that?" Nurse Debbie asked.

"Zachary's brother. He's helping me."

"Oh. Yes. The babies. The twins. He kept talking about Bridget and the twins. Who is she? A sister? He was always worrying about them."

"Something like that," Kenzie agreed. She thought about it. She had checked in with Gordon, done the circuit around Bridget's house several times. But she had not checked on the babies.

"I have to go now," she told Nurse Debbie. "I'll call you back if I find something."

Kenzie hit the red button to end the call. She looked at Tyrrell.

"What?" Tyrrell asked.

"The babies are just a couple of floors down. in the NICU."

"Then…"

"We should go see them."

Tyrrell cocked his head slightly, not understanding. "Okaaay…"

"Don't you remember about Zachary and Mindy?"

"What does Mindy have to do with it?"

"Zachary helped to take care of you younger kids when you were born. And Mindy didn't eat and needed lots of attention. And Zachary was the one who made sure she got enough to eat."

Tyrrell tilted his head, thinking about it. "I didn't know that. I was still pretty young when Mindy was born."

"He's been worried about Bridget's babies from the time she got pregnant. Worried that Bridget won't be able to take care of them. She's been released from the hospital and went home. Where do you think Zachary would go?"

Tyrrell looked relieved. "He would want to see the babies."

48

Kenzie led Tyrrell down to the NICU, her heart beating fast. Of course that was where Zachary would be. She should have thought of it right from the start. Of course he didn't need his car or his phone. He'd never left the hospital.

The only thing that could have persuaded him to leave the psychiatric unit where he was safe was to take care of someone else.

They walked at a brisk pace. A nurse tried to stop them as they entered. "Excuse me, can I help you?"

She followed them when they didn't stop. Kenzie led Tyrrell directly to the incubator she had previously visited with Gordon. Zachary sat in a chair next to the incubator, watching the infants with his dark, sunken eyes. He looked at Kenzie and Tyrrell as they entered, sat up straighter, surprised, and looked around at his surroundings.

"Zachary!" Kenzie kept her voice to a low whisper. She hurried to his side and bent down to give him a hug and a kiss. "We've been so worried! You should have let me know what was going on. Where you were going."

He looked uncertain. "What time is it?"

"It's almost nine. I've been looking everywhere for you."

"Oh." He looked around again. "There's no clock or window in here. I didn't realize."

Tears started falling down Kenzie's cheeks, she was so relieved to find him safe. She tried to wipe them away. "You need to let me know what you're doing!"

His eyes dropped back to the babies. "I didn't think you'd want to know that I was here. I planned to go back up to psych after a few hours, once I was sure they were safe. I didn't mean to be here so late."

"Have you had anything to eat? You've been here all day."

"No. I've just been sitting here."

The nurse was at Kenzie's shoulder, angry at being ignored. "There are too many people in here. We only want one person here at a time. And no conversation. These little ones need to sleep undisturbed."

Kenzie didn't give up her place. She put her hand on Zachary's shoulder. She wasn't leaving him alone.

"If you haven't had anything to eat, then we should go to the cafeteria," Tyrrell suggested. "I don't suppose there will still be staff there, but there are vending machines, at least. You're not going to get anything if you go back to your ward now. They'll have already had their meals."

"It's okay. I'm not hungry. I'll just stay here."

"You can't stay here all night," Kenzie told him firmly.

"They don't have visiting hours," Zachary said. "Parents can sit with their babies all night."

"There is one obvious flaw in that plan," Kenzie said, but didn't say in front of the nurse that Zachary was not a parent. "But besides that, you are exhausted. You need to eat and sleep. If you don't, you are going to feel worse. You remember what happened when you stayed up for three days. You need to take care of yourself."

Zachary gazed in at the sleeping babies. "They need someone here to look after them. Bridget went home."

"I know. And I'm sure she'll be back to visit them tomorrow and to make sure they have everything they need. They'll be okay for a few hours. They'll just sleep. And if there are any problems, they are still hooked up to monitors and the staff will know what to do."

Zachary shook his head. "I don't trust her."

It was the first time that Kenzie had heard Zachary say he didn't trust his ex-wife. He had couched his concerns in much more careful terms before. That he was worried about Bridget. Worried that she didn't have the resources. *What if* she couldn't take care of them because of her health?

"Bridget is still recovering from the birth. You know she has been somewhat frail since the cancer and this pregnancy was not easy on her. She'll sleep better in her own bed tonight, and tomorrow she will be back by to look after them."

Zachary looked sideways at Kenzie. "What?"

"Bridget. She will come back. And Gordon will make sure she has all the help she needs. He said she has someone to help her twenty-four hours a day right now."

"Bridget. I wasn't talking about her."

It was Kenzie's turn to look askance. "What?"

"Not her. I know she'll do her best. And Gordon. But they aren't here twenty-four hours a day. And someone needs to guard the twins."

Kenzie was flummoxed. She felt her way through the conversation, trying to make quick judgments and to figure out what was wrong with Zachary and how she could help him, when she felt as if she only knew half of the information she needed to.

"Maybe Tyrrell could guard the twins while I take you for something to eat," she suggested. "You'll be able to think more clearly if you've had something to eat. And you need your night meds soon too."

Kenzie looked at Tyrrell, hoping that he would understand and agree to sit with the twins while she got Zachary back on track. His brows were drawn down in a worried, confused frown. Kenzie imagined her own face looked much the same.

"Come on." She tugged on Zachary's arm. "You need food."

Zachary got rustily to his feet. He'd probably been sitting there all day, unmoving, and his muscles had all seized up. Zachary looked at Tyrrell.

"You're going to stay with them? The whole time? Make sure nothing happens to them?"

Tyrrell nodded. "Of course."

Kenzie was glad that he didn't challenge Zachary on what the infants needed to be protected from. She would be able to figure that out as they had something to eat together. He would unwind the story for her so she could understand his thought process, and then she would be able to make a judgment about how logical his concerns were. There wasn't really anything that Zachary or Tyrrell could do if Julia went into cardiac arrest again. They would just be in the way.

Zachary looked at the nurse who was still standing by, waiting for them to sort things out so that there was only one person visiting the NICU. Zachary put his arm around his brother's neck and led him off to the side, speaking earnestly in his ear. Kenzie couldn't hear what Zachary was saying. He looked back at the nurse several times. At first, Tyrrell was shaking his head, objecting to whatever it was Zachary was telling him, but eventually he stopped shaking and was still, listening. He gave a couple of nods, and Zachary finally let go of him and let him return to the incubator and take the spot that Zachary had occupied.

Tyrrell shot Kenzie a look, one that she interpreted as meaning that he thought Zachary was delusional.

Kenzie's heart sank. It was not a good sign if he were having additional symptoms on top of the depression. They might have to completely overhaul his cocktail. Again. And it could be weeks or months before he was stable again.

"Okay. Let's get something into you," she told Zachary firmly. "You'll feel a lot better once you've had some nourishment."

Zachary looked at Tyrrell, who nodded cooperatively, indicating that he would stay there with the babies and protect them from whatever evil influence Zachary had been warning him about.

The nurse looked at each of them. "Are any of you actually parents to these children?"

"Bridget asked me to look after them," Zachary explained. "You can call her and check. Though I wouldn't want to wake her up. She needs sleep to recover. I can't stay with them…" He looked like he wanted to go sit back down by the incubator, but Kenzie kept a firm grip on his arm and he didn't pull away from her. "I need to go eat, but Tyrrell will watch them until I get back."

The nurse looked uncertain about this. She looked at Zachary's face, frowning. "Did you show someone your ID when you got here?"

Obviously, she hadn't been on shift that many hours ago. Zachary began to pat his pockets.

"Zachary Goldman. The nurse who was on then took it all down. Talked to everyone to clear me."

He found his wallet and extracted his driver's license. While she looked at it and compared it to his thinner, more cadaverous face, he pulled out a business card and handed that to her as well. Her eyes went over the words on the card.

"And Kenzie is a doctor," Zachary said, pointing to her. "Do you want to show her your ID too?" he suggested.

The nurse shook her head, getting too much information at once. She handed Zachary's driver's license back to him and tried to give him the business card, but he wouldn't take the business card back. "Hang on to that. And Tyrrell—"

"No, no," the nurse waved off any further ID's. "Fine. You go get something to eat. You look like you should be in the eating disorder clinic. I'll let the other one sit here," she made an off-handed motion to Tyrrell, "until you get back."

Kenzie pulled Zachary toward the exit. "Let's go, then, and you can tell me everything."

It was like Zachary's feet were stuck to the floor, but eventually he managed to pry them loose and walk with her out of the unit and to the elevator.

49

They didn't say anything on their way down the elevator to the cafeteria.

The lights were turned out and all the food serving stations closed. It was a dim, echoing, spooky sort of place to be so late. But the vending machines were still brightly lit and Kenzie made several purchases. They carried the food over to one of the tables and sat down to eat in the dimly-lit room.

"So… what's going on?" Kenzie asked. "Why do you think you need to guard the babies if Bridget and Gordon aren't here? The nurses are there to take care of them. They are on monitors if they start to have some kind of medical problem. There isn't anything you could do even if they did. So…?"

Zachary poked at the sandwich she had bought him, as if it were something alien. It was in the refrigerated vending machine, and it looked better than the ones they stocked down the hall from the Medical Examiner's Office. If he hadn't eaten all day, then he should be getting hungry. His morning medications would have worn off, so that he shouldn't be nauseated anymore.

"Zachary?"

"I saw the way you and Tyrrell were looking at each other. I'm not crazy. And I'm not blind."

"No one said you were. But you were behaving strangely. I don't know what you said to Tyrrell; I couldn't hear it. So bring me up to speed."

"I wasn't trying to keep it from you, just from the nurse."

Kenzie nodded and waited.

Zachary looked around the room, but it was completely empty. The only other person there was Kenzie, which hopefully helped to ease his anxiety. He would see if anyone else showed up. Anything he said would be just between the two of them.

"I don't trust the nurses."

"Why not?"

Zachary picked at the edge of the plastic wrap of his sandwich, trying to unwrap it.

"Some of them… aren't who they say they are. And that friend of yours… I don't want to say anything against a friend, but…"

"Do you think… she had something to do with Mr. Kennedy's death?"

Zachary raised his eyebrows in surprise. He had obviously not expected her to make that connection.

"Maybe. Is that what you think?"

"The surveillance video shows that Kennedy was never hanging around the dispensary. He didn't steal the pills himself."

Zachary finally caught the edge of the plastic wrap and drew it back slowly, as if any tears or stretches would be unacceptable.

"Somebody else must have stolen them, then."

Kenzie nodded. "Yes. When I was talking to Nurse Debbie today… she said some things that worried me. I don't want to think that she could have anything to do with any deaths, but she's already being looked at for the deaths in geriatric. And if she also had something to do with Mr. Kennedy's death… if she was the one who provided him with the means, and possibly encouraged him to do it…" Kenzie felt sick at the thought.

"She was here?" Zachary asked immediately, looking alarmed. He glanced around as if she might be hiding in the shadows of the room. "She wasn't supposed to be on shift today!"

"No." Kenzie wondered how he happened to know that. Because she had told him that she would be off? Or had he managed to look at one of the computers the nursing staff used? "She wasn't at the hospital. I talked to her on the phone."

Zachary blew out his breath noisily and nodded. He took a bite of his sandwich and chewed it slowly as if it were some new food he'd never tried before, like eel or blood pudding.

"She's different when you're not there. When she's alone with a patient."

"How is she different?"

"It's hard to explain. She still talks the same way, all bubbly and smiles, and touches you like she's your best friend. But there's… an undertone. Something menacing."

"You said before that you thought the way she was so cheerful was bullying."

He nodded. Kenzie thought about the way that Nurse Debbie had acted each time she'd stopped to talk to Kenzie. Overbearing. Treating Zachary like he was a child. Acting so cheerful even after Kennedy's death. She did kind of demand that everybody else around her should behave a certain way, to put on a smile and act like there was nothing wrong. Like the bully who roasted someone and expected them to laugh about it.

"How does this all relate back to the babies?"

"Oh. Yeah. She's been… pushing me. Talking about how Kennedy is in a better place now. That it was painless, and now he isn't suffering. Asking questions about my depression and ideation… what I think about… how I feel."

"Isn't that what you would expect the nurses to do? They need to be aware of your frame of mind and relay any concerns back to the doctor. Especially after a death like this. Are you sure you're not just… looking for things to blame her for?"

"No. They might ask you for specifics in therapy, but not the nurses. And they don't want to know whether… you prefer cutting or pills."

Kenzie shuddered at the ghoulish question. She took a quick drink of water, trying to keep down the acid rising from her stomach. "She didn't!"

Zachary nodded. "Stuff like that… it's weird. I don't think it's right. I've had lots of therapy over the years, lots of different approaches, new ideas… but not asking me exactly what I think about, or whether I have anything to live for."

"Oh, Zachary…" Kenzie breathed his name. She was lucky to have found him unharmed. She couldn't imagine that Nurse Debbie would have been ignorant about questions and comments that might push Zachary over the edge. Had she done the same thing to Kennedy? Finding out that his preferred method of suicide was by pills? Asking him if he really had anything to live for, as a single, childless man in a dead-end job. Leaving the pills in his room for him and watching to see what would happen?

Zachary nodded. He took a couple more bites of the sandwich, chewing more vigorously now, finding it to his taste. Maybe surprised to find out that he could enjoy anything anymore.

"You do have something to live for," Kenzie pointed out. "So much. You have a good life. Your business, our relationship, your family. You've gone through some tough times, but things have been good lately. Some minor inconveniences… viruses and poisoners… but overall, you've got a good life, don't you think?"

Zachary nodded. "It's hard to see through the depression. Like looking through muddy windows. At night. But I know what's on the other side. I'm doing everything I can to hold it together, to get through this. Because I know what's on the other side, if I can just keep pushing through. I try to listen to you and Lorne when you tell me that it will get better after Christmas. That it always does. Sometimes I think that's just a myth I made up myself to trick myself into holding on when there is no hope."

"It's not. You'll feel better again. In just a little while… Christmas Eve will be past, and you'll wake up, and you will feel better."

"I'm so scared, Kenzie." He reached across the table for a moment and squeezed her hand. Kenzie squeezed back, trying to impart to him the depth of her feeling. How much she wanted and needed him, and how sure she was that things would get better again, if he just hung on.

"I know. It must be so hard."

"I'm scared for the babies."

50

Kenzie shook her head. They had circled around to it again, but she still had no better idea now than she'd had before about what Bridget's twins had to do with anything. Why was he so worried about the babies? What did that mean to him?

"Tell me why. Because of your mom? Because she couldn't take care of her newborns, so you think that Bridget won't be able to deal with hers?"

"No." Zachary sniffled and wiped his nose with the back of his hand. He took a couple of long gulps of his cola.

While Kenzie had to watch her calorie intake and stuck to water, she had aimed to give him the most calorie-dense foods she could, including a sugary drink.

"When I was talking to Nurse Debbie, and she asked what I had to live for… I told her about the babies."

Kenzie frowned, still unable to connect this up with anything else he'd said. And irritated over the fact that someone else's babies were his main reason for wanting to live.

"I told her how… precious they are. And how they were fighting for life. About Julia's cardiac event and Tricia being off the respirator." Zachary paused and looked at her. "They're both off of the respirator now."

"Yes, Gordon told me."

"She said that a hundred years ago, they wouldn't have survived. That maybe we were playing God by using all these artificial means to sustain them. They would grow up disabled, and it would be our fault, for allowing the doctors to do something they shouldn't. They would be brain-damaged. Have trouble in school. Be made fun of."

Something that Zachary could relate to, considering the number of learning disabilities and other issues he had battled throughout school. He wouldn't want to think of Bridget's precious babies going through the same thing.

Zachary swallowed. "She wondered how I would feel if one or both of them died. Why I was keeping my hopes up because of two tiny babies like that."

It was starting to dawn on Kenzie. She was starting to get what Zachary had seen during his conversation with Nurse Debbie. Her twisted sense of who should survive and who should not. It wasn't just old people in the geriatric unit who needed help leaving the mortal coil, but also the patients in the psychiatric unit, who could be nudged into committing suicide. And babies who shouldn't be receiving dramatic life-saving measures and using up precious resources. Babies who would never have survived without the modern equipment and knowledge.

"And you were worried that she would go down to the NICU. That you needed to watch over the twins, to make sure she couldn't get anywhere near them."

Zachary nodded.

"Why didn't you go to the authorities? Tell the doctor? Call the police? Why just go down there to sit with them yourself? You didn't even call me."

"They wouldn't let me near the phone. She told them that I was causing trouble and couldn't be allowed to use it. That I was making crank calls. Swatting. That I was delusional."

"But they let you check yourself out?"

"I waited until today, when she wasn't there. So it wouldn't be the same medical staff. I don't think she put anything on my chart saying about having delusions, but I was very calm and polite, and they couldn't see any reason to block me and insist on a psychiatric hold."

Zachary had eaten half of his sandwich and had lowered the level on his bottle of cola. His fingers danced over a cookie that Kenzie had bought, looking at her face to see whether she had bought it for herself or for the two of them to share.

"It's yours," Kenzie said.

He hesitated for a few more seconds, maybe waiting for her to act like a parent and tell him that he couldn't have the cookie until he had finished his sandwich. But she would be delighted if he ate the cookie.

"I should have called you this morning when they might have let me," Zachary admitted. "But I was so worried about the twins. I just wanted to get down to see them as soon as I could. I wanted to make sure that she couldn't get in there to do anything to them."

Kenzie nodded. She could understand that. It had probably been torture for him to be calm and polite to the medical staff to convince them to let him check himself out. The checkout procedure could take an hour or more, especially if they had concerns about his well-being. He must have been on pins and needles the whole time.

"I'm glad you looked after them. But we should probably call the police now and talk to them about it. Joshua Campbell was here today to talk to the medical staff about Kennedy's death. He knows that Kennedy didn't get the pills himself."

"I can't prove that it was Nurse Debbie."

"Well, you can tell him what you know. He can investigate it, and you can't."

Zachary opened his mouth to argue about this. He was a private investigator. Of course he could investigate it, he didn't need Campbell's permission. He always passed on any information that the police should have and had given Campbell leads more than once.

"I have to go back to psych," he said, sounding defeated.

"Probably. How are you feeling?"

"I can't leave the twins unguarded, though. Someone needs to watch them."

"We can talk to the police. The nursing staff. Security. It doesn't have to all fall to you."

Zachary shook his head. "I have to be sure. No one else is going to be as careful as I would be…"

"That's the same reason as Gordon gave for having you follow Bridget to see if she was having an affair. How did that work out?"

He looked down at the table and picked at a piece of dried food that the cleaners had missed. "He was right."

"But he should never have gotten you involved. And you should never have accepted."

"But this is different. They're babies. They are helpless."

"We'll work something out. Are you finished eating?" Kenzie nodded toward the half-sandwich he had not eaten. Zachary picked it up, sniffed it, and put it back down again.

"Yeah."

"Let's go upstairs, then, and we'll see."

They threw the rest of the food and wrappers into the garbage and went back up to the NICU.

51

As they got closer, Kenzie could hear Tyrrell's raised voice. She glanced at Zachary, and the two of them started running.

"Where's your ID?" Kenzie heard Tyrrell demand. "If you work here, then show me your ID."

"I showed you my security badge," a female voice responded. "Now move aside so I can check on the patients."

"No."

"Sir, you need to calm down and let the staff do their work," another voice interrupted.

Kenzie and Zachary turned the last corner to see the incubator and the people gathered around it, voices raised despite the "quiet please" signs on the walls. Tyrrell. The nurse who had earlier asked them to leave.

And Nurse Debbie.

Kenzie moved in quickly.

"Nurse Debbie does not work here," she said sharply.

The NICU nurse looked at Kenzie, frowning. She shook her head. "I know *you* don't work here. Nurse Carrie, on the other hand," she looked at Nurse Debbie, "has the correct hospital ID badge and has been volunteering here on her own time to hold infants when their parents are not here."

Kenzie shook her head. "That's not her name!" She looked at Nurse Debbie's ID badge, which indeed said Nurse Carrie. "These are fake credentials."

Nurse Debbie looked at Kenzie as if she had never seen her before in her life. "I don't know what you're talking about. You must be mistaking me for someone else." She shrugged at the NICU nurse. "I've been here before. You know me."

"There was a hospital-wide warning about people using fake badges to get into secure areas," Kenzie shot back hotly. "You must have received that. Did you check her driver's license?"

Nurse Debbie's lips compressed, making them long and thin. "I don't drive."

"You are still required to have photo ID. Where's your legal identification?"

Nurse Debbie looked back and forth at the people gathered around her intent on keeping her from accessing the twins.

"I'm volunteering," she insisted. "I'm doing a service. What's wrong with you people?"

"Like the service you did to Mr. Michaels by putting him out of his misery in geriatric?" Kenzie accused. "Or giving Mr. Kennedy the pills he needed to commit suicide? Or the wonderful advice you've been giving Zachary on how *he* has nothing left to live for?"

Nurse Debbie swore. She shoved Kenzie away from her violently, calling her an undeserved name and then making a break for it. Kenzie hit the hard, tiled floor with a crash.

"No you don't!" Tyrrell shouted and launched himself at Nurse Debbie. Zachary too tried to get a hand on her to prevent her from running away. If Nurse Debbie got away, she might flee to another state to start over, and they would never be able to prove what she had done in Vermont.

But the NICU nurse was faster and in better shape than either of them, and it was she who tripped Nurse Debbie up and got a hand twisted into her hair to force her down and hold her still.

"Where is security?" she shouted. "There should be a guard on the floor. You go get him!" She pointed at Tyrrell.

Tyrrell looked behind him as if to check to see whether she were pointing at someone else, and when it was clear that she was talking about him, he turned and hurried out of the unit and down the hallway to find a security guard.

52

It took some time for everything to get settled down. Security detained Nurse Debbie and the police were called, with patrol units getting there before Campbell. He spoke with the NICU nurse and to Zachary, Kenzie, and Tyrrell, shaking his head over how bold Nurse Debbie had been in using a false ID card and simply walking into other units.

"She would come to hold the babies or give them stimulation," the NICU nurse said. "I don't understand. Why would someone use a false ID for that? She had hospital ID, I relied on that."

"A NICU baby could be very vulnerable," Kenzie said, looking into the incubator where Bridget's twins lay, oblivious to the worry they had caused. "Did you ever have a baby go into distress while she was holding it?"

"Well… yes. But these are very fragile patients. We are careful not to move them around too much, but human touch and interaction is powerful medicine. They languish without any human touch, and improve when you can stroke them, talk to them, and hold them. So it's a balancing act, trying to judge which babies are strong enough to be held and how long we can keep them out of the incubator."

"And you didn't watch her the whole time she was holding these babies," Campbell suggested.

"No, of course not. She was a nurse. She was here to give us a break, to help us out on her own time. We wouldn't sit here and watch her any more than we would a parent. The parents we always watch to begin with, until they get used to handling their child. But once they are confident and know what they are doing… we have work to do."

Kenzie called Agent Menendez as well, since Nurse Debbie was a suspect in the Michaels death.

Kenzie had been so sure that she couldn't have had anything to do with it. But now, realizing that Nurse Debbie had gone to other units using false ID and might be implicated in other deaths, she was forced to reconsider.

Nurse Debbie had seemed like the perfect, attentive nurse. She had seemed to really care about her patients and had always been happy to help the family out. And maybe that had not been faked. But there was more to her than that. She had another side. Was she really driven by her compassion, as she had suggested to Zachary, that she just wanted to keep people from suffering? Or was that just an excuse for what she did and she got a kick out of watching her specially selected patients die?

"Did you ask the geriatric staff if Nurse Debbie ever went back there after she transferred?" Kenzie asked Agent Menendez after they all explained their pieces of the puzzle. "To volunteer or clear out her locker? To see a favorite patient?"

"We asked, but people don't necessarily remember everyone they have seen in a day. And as time passes, they are less and less confident of who was there on what day. We have the logs of who was on shift the day that Michaels died, and on the dates of other deaths on Dr. Philemon's list. But we can't be sure that she didn't just walk in, saying hello to the nurses that knew her, to pick up something she had forgotten, or her final paycheck, or on some other excuse."

"I suppose so." But the fact that they didn't have any eyewitnesses to testify to the fact that Nurse Debbie had been around at the appropriate times meant that they wouldn't be able to prosecute her for Michaels's death. Not unless she confessed. Of all the deaths that they thought she could be responsible for, the one they probably had the best chance of prosecuting was Kennedy's death. They could prove that she had been on shift in the psychiatric unit. That she had access to the dispensary. Zachary could testify about the conversations she'd had with him, both about Kennedy's death and about whether he had any reason to live himself.

"Do you think she is the one who was sending you the threatening notes?" Menendez asked.

"Yes, probably. I couldn't figure out why they were directed at me instead of at Dr. Wiltshire. I figured it was because I visited the geriatric unit and was asking questions there. But if it was Nurse Debbie, then she had reason to target me. She knew me. And she knew that I was still asking questions, getting closer to her. Someone in geriatric wouldn't have known that."

Kenzie caught Zachary's eyes on her, and she grimaced, knowing what was coming.

"Threatening notes?" he demanded.

"Yes. Just a couple. I got them at work, in the mail. I didn't think that there was anything to worry about. Some poison pen… they weren't likely to turn to real violence against me."

"Why didn't you tell me?"

"Like I said… I wasn't that worried about them."

His eyes didn't move from her. Kenzie sighed.

"Yes, I suppose it was because you had enough on your mind already. You were going through a tough time, and it didn't seem like it would be productive to add my own worries to the mix. I'm sorry."

"I still want you to tell me things."

"I know. But I have to judge whether it is the right time to tell you, or whether it is something that might trigger worse anxiety or depression."

He thought about that and clearly didn't like it. But Kenzie didn't know how she was going to get around it. She would always have to consider whether he had to know something, or if it was better to keep it from him until he was at least feeling better. Once the cat was out of the bag, she wasn't going to be able to cram it back in.

***

It was getting late, and Kenzie didn't know what Gordon's usual hours were, but she texted him anyway, letting him know that she had found Zachary and he was well and safe.

She got a text back from him almost immediately.

Good news. Where was he?

Kenzie hit the button to voice call him instead of responding by text. He was obviously still up, and it would be faster to explain the details than to try to explain over text.

"Kenzie," he answered cheerfully. "Glad to hear that you managed to track that rascal down. He's okay?"

"He was in the NICU," Kenzie explained. "With the twins."

There was a definite pause in the conversation as Gordon processed this. His voice, when he spoke again, was definitely cooler.

"What was he doing there?"

"He believed that the twins were in danger. That someone needed to be watching them. So he was there all day, at their sides."

"I don't want him near the twins."

Kenzie was taken aback by this. She had always thought it strange that Gordon didn't object to talking to Zachary or Kenzie, that he was willing to give Zachary updates on how Bridget was doing and didn't stop Bridget from reaching out to Zachary on the rare occasions when there was something she wanted from him. Zachary was more likely to stay at a distance if he had the answers he needed and he didn't have to see for himself that Bridget was okay.

And maybe that was why Gordon had been willing to talk to them about the twins, too. He had thought that it would keep Zachary away from them.

"I'm sorry. I didn't know he was there, or I would have handled it earlier. But... you should know that he was right. There has been a nurse here at the hospital who has been implicated in a number of deaths. Sort of mercy killings, what we call an Angel of Death killer."

"What?" Gordon's voice was sharp.

"We've been trying to figure out who it was, to catch her. And... it turns out she has been doing some volunteer work in the NICU. I don't know whether she has been involved in any deaths there, but she was trying to get to your twins today."

"You've caught this woman? How could something like this happen?"

"The ME's Office has been working with the FBI and with the local police. And the hospital, of course. No one was ignoring it, I promise you that. But there was nothing to indicate that the same killer might have been in the NICU. We didn't even realize there was a connection between the deaths in geriatric and the suicide in psych this week. Until... today."

"And the twins...?"

"They're fine," Kenzie assured him. "Zachary made sure of that."

"I guess I owe him my thanks. Again. I can't get over there tonight. Bridget needs me here. But we'll be there in the morning. I'll come see Zachary then."

Kenzie hesitated. She cleared her throat. Gordon had been blunt about not wanting Zachary to be near his children. She could be just as blunt.

"I don't want you talking to Zachary. And I especially don't want Bridget talking to him. He doesn't need any more setbacks."

Gordon breathed out in a huff. "Well... fair enough. I won't come talk to him. And if Bridget wants to see him... I'll tell her that he's unavailable."

"I'd appreciate that. Thanks."

"He needs to stay away from the twins. I will make sure that they are taken care of. And you have this woman in custody. So nothing will happen to them."

"I'll tell him. I can't promise anything, but I'll do my best to help him stay on track. He'll be in psych until Christmas. Then after that… hopefully he'll start to get evened out again. Stop worrying that Bridget can't take care of the twins."

"Why wouldn't Bridget be able to take care of the twins?" Gordon demanded, his tone still sharp.

"Of course she can. And I know you'll make sure she has whatever help she needs. I'm talking about Zachary's worries. They aren't necessarily logical. His own mother couldn't take care of her babies, so he's transferred those feelings to Bridget."

"I would appreciate it if he would stay out of the way. I'll give you updates, if that will keep him away. But I won't have him harassing my children."

Kenzie had a vision of Zachary lurking outside a playground, watching a pair of little girls laughing and playing on the play equipment. She could understand why Gordon didn't want him hanging around. Zachary was too obsessive. And while he'd never done anything to harm Bridget, if he thought that she couldn't take care of the children and that he could… things could go very badly for Zachary.

"No. I'll talk to his therapist about it too."

"Good." Gordon sighed. "Good night, Kenzie. Thank you for letting me know that everyone is safe."

———

After hanging up the phone with Gordon, Kenzie walked down the hall into the psychiatric unit to see if Zachary was settled. There was a quiet murmur of voices from the medical staff. Kenzie followed the noise to the nursing station and gave the nurses there, two women and a man, a nod.

"I'll just check in with Zachary, then I'll be on my way," she announced.

They appeared to be too startled by her assertion to find an objection before she walked by them and into the room she knew was Zachary's. He sat on the edge of the bed, hunched over, rubbing the muscles around his eyes.

"Hey," Kenzie said softly. "How are you doing? All settled?"

He nodded.

"Got your night meds?"

"Yeah. Will be a little bit before they start to kick in."

Kenzie nodded. "I talked to Gordon. Let him know that the twins were okay and you were back where you're supposed to be."

He rubbed his forehead, hiding his eyes from her.

"He says thank you for looking after the twins. But now that Nurse Debbie is in custody…"

"He doesn't want me to go down there again."

"No. He wants you to stay away from them. And I'm sure Bridget would say the same."

Zachary sighed. "Yeah."

"They'll be okay. They have a lot of people looking out for them."

"Okay. I'll… try."

Kenzie bent down to kiss him. "And one other thing. If you're going to check out… please let me know. You don't know how much of a panic I was in when I couldn't find you."

"Sorry." He caught her hand and squeezed it. "I didn't think I'd be there all day. Just… a few hours until Gordon or Bridget got there."

"Just don't do that again."

"Okay."

53

It was too early in the morning on a Saturday for Kenzie's phone to be ringing. She pulled herself out of sleep to look at the screen, sure it would be her mother. Who else but Lisa would call her on a Saturday morning and expect her to be sitting around sipping coffee rather than either sleeping in or going in to work?

It wasn't her mother's picture on the screen, though, it was Dr. Wiltshire. Kenzie fumbled, swiping several times before she managed to answer the call. But at least she managed to get it before it went to voicemail.

"Doctor."

"Kenzie? I'm sorry to disturb you. I know that you have today off."

"Did something happen?" Kenzie rubbed her eyes, trying to force herself to wake up and be alert faster.

"I have a few messages on my phone this morning. No new bodies, you don't need to come in, but I thought I would give you a call and fill you in before items start showing up in the news. After you've worked a case, you don't want to find out the developments in the news."

"Oh." Kenzie suddenly realized what he was talking about. "I should probably have called you last night. Or sent you a message."

Dr. Wiltshire chuckled. "Does that mean you already know everything? I suppose Agent Menendez reached out to you."

"Actually, no. I called her."

"You called her." Wiltshire's voice registered surprise. "How were you involved in this?"

"It was Zachary, mostly. He was in psych, and Nurse Debbie was in psych. He had his suspicions about her after Kennedy's death. He disappeared on me, and when I tracked him down… well, he was—I told you that our friends had twins? Zachary was with the twins, because he was afraid that Nurse Debbie was going to go after them next."

"I see." Dr. Wiltshire sounded baffled, not as if he understood Kenzie's explanation. "And Nurse Debbie is who Menendez has arrested."

"She was already a suspect on Agent Menendez's list. I didn't think that it could be her. I knew her, and she had left the geriatric unit before Michaels died."

"Then it seems a bit of a stretch that she could be involved in his case."

"She was still in the hospital. She could have gone back down and said that she had forgotten something or wanted to check in on one of her old patients. No one would have thought anything of it. Or necessarily have remembered when we started trying to put together a list of everyone who had been there. We were focused on their records, who we could prove had been there. Anyone else who happened to walk through the unit—that's a lot harder."

"But if witnesses don't remember her, the FBI will not be able to put her in that room. And unless there is something else to tie her to Michaels's murder, there is no way to convict her."

"Unless she confesses. Many of these killers do, because they feel that they've done the right thing. A kind, humanitarian thing."

"It should never be up to the doctor or nurse to decide to take a life."

"No," Kenzie agreed soberly. "But I think there's a good chance that they can get her for Kennedy's murder. She had access to the dispensary. And the way she was talking about him, how his life was worthless, and the way she was encouraging Zachary to do the same."

Dr. Wiltshire didn't say anything at first. Eventually, he spoke. "I can't call Kennedy's death anything but suicide, Kenzie. Not unless there is evidence that this nurse force-fed him those pills. I don't know if there is anything the police can charge him with in Vermont in connection with inciting suicide."

"Then we'll get her for the others," Kenzie resolved. "We'll keep going through Dr. Philemon's list of suspicious deaths, and tie as many as we can to her. Once a jury sees how many deaths she was connected to…"

"Don't get your hopes up. The FBI will continue to work on it and to see whether they can tie more deaths to her, but there are a lot of challenges in getting enough proof in cases like this."

54

The last couple of weeks until Christmas passed quickly.

Kenzie woke up early. She hadn't been so excited about Christmas morning since she had been a kid. She could remember that feeling of anticipation. Trying to go to sleep with the knowledge that in the morning, it would be Christmas Day, and she would be getting presents and spending a wonderful day with her family. Everyone together, happy, enjoying each other's company. The house would be festooned with decorations and tiny white lights, transforming it into a Christmas fairyland. There would be food so good she would stuff her stomach until it hurt, and then lie around for hours afterward complaining about it. And then they would eat again.

This time, it was different. She wasn't a kid anymore, eagerly anticipating presents. But she knew that they had finally passed Christmas Eve, and Zachary's anxiety over the season would begin to fade. Even though he knew that it wouldn't happen again, he was always anxious about the fire that had destroyed his home. That somehow, something would happen again on the anniversary and he would lose everything he loved. Now that the anniversary of the fire was past, he could take a deep breath and begin to recover again.

Kenzie called Lisa first. There was no point in rushing to the hospital and getting there before visiting hours. So she lay in bed and listened to the ringing phone and waited to hear her mother's voice.

"Mackenzie?" Lisa's voice was faint and far away, slurred with sleep.

Kenzie laughed about waking up before her mother. Just like on all those

Christmases gone past. Lisa knew that she didn't get up early in the morning, but this time Kenzie had turned the tables and was the excited kid once more.

"Hello, Mother. Merry Christmas!"

"Merry Christmas to you too, dear. What are you doing up so early?"

"It's Christmas!"

"Yes, it is," Lisa agreed dryly. "Have you already opened all your presents from Santa?"

"Not yet. I'm still in bed. But I wanted to say Merry Christmas to you first."

"Not to Zachary?"

"He is still in the hospital," Kenzie reminded her. "I'll see him later."

"Oh, I thought you said that he would be doing better now."

"Today, yes. But we'll need to wait until he's stabilized for sure before bringing him home. He should be feeling a lot better today, but that doesn't mean everything is okay. They'll need to see how he is feeling and if he is stable on these meds. Then… when he starts gaining weight and showing an improvement, he'll be released or sign himself out."

"Good. Well, do tell him Merry Christmas for me."

"I will. And you have a good one today. Do you have plans?"

"Your father may come by later. I'll just have a quiet day at home. It's… not like it was when you were little. It's just another holiday. Christmas is for children."

"Tell Dad Merry Christmas for me. I'll probably call him later."

Kenzie took a long shower and lingered over her breakfast of toast and a Christmas orange, but it still wasn't time to go to the hospital. She admired the Christmas magnets on the fridge and twinkle lights she could see glowing softly in the living room. The minutes seemed to be crawling by excruciatingly slowly. She thought about calling Zachary's brother and sisters to wish them a Merry Christmas, but it would be better if she could call them while she was with Zachary. He was the one that they would want to talk to.

Her phone vibrated, and Kenzie pulled it out to look at it. She thought it might be a text from her father. Like Kenzie, he wasn't an early riser, but she expected he would be up by now.

But it was, weirdly enough, a text from Josie Menendez. Kenzie's phone was set not to display text messages on the lock screen, so she had to unlock it to see what the message was. Hopefully, Agent Menendez had not decided that now that they were no longer working the Michaels case together—there didn't seem to be any more exhumations on the horizon—that she and Kenzie could be friends. Or whatever other relationship Menendez wanted. She had always seemed just a bit too up-close-and-personal for Kenzie's comfort.

I have a special Christmas present for you

Kenzie's worst fears were being realized. She decided that ignorance was her best defense against any advances by Menendez.

Really? What is it?

There was no answer. Kenzie put her dish in the dishwasher and looked at the phone again, in case an answer had come in without it vibrating. Sometimes that happened if she already had the text app in the foreground. Still nothing. Kenzie shifted uncomfortably. "Come on, Agent Menendez," she said aloud, frustrated.

Almost ten minutes passed, and Kenzie had decided that it was either supposed to be a joke, or Menendez had been interrupted and had forgotten that she'd even been texting with Kenzie.

She could probably start getting ready to go to the hospital. If she didn't get ready or drive too fast, she should be there right before visiting hours opened up, and she could get in right away.

The phone vibrated again. Kenzie picked it up. Agent Menendez again.

Nurse Debbie confessed

Kenzie blew out her breath in relief. She browsed through gifs, looking for an appropriate one, and selected a Christmas picture to send to Menendez.

Hallelujah!

Kenzie was not the first person to arrive at the psych ward. In fact, the hallway was buzzing with visitors, eager to get in to see their loved ones. Many of them were faces that Kenzie recognized from visiting with Zachary, but others were new, maybe people who had traveled longer distances to visit their friend or family member on the special day.

"Kenzie!"

Kenzie turned, looking for the source of the voice. Lorne and Pat walked toward her. "Hi! Merry Christmas!" Kenzie gave them each a hug and a kiss. "You must have left early."

"We didn't have to get up too early. But we wanted to be here to see Zach. And we have Pat's family later in the day."

Kenzie nodded. "Say hi and Merry Christmas to Gretta and Suzanne for me. I'm glad you're getting the chance to see them."

"If you don't have anywhere to go later, you'd be welcome to join us," Pat invited, smiling warmly.

"No, I'm good, thanks. Maybe sometime in the next few weeks, when Zachary is feeling better, we can get together."

"Absolutely."

The big double doors were opened, and everyone who was in line shifted and prepared to enter. Kenzie knew that it wouldn't be a race. Everyone would need their ID checked and their names checked against the patient visitor list before being escorted in. With the number of people in front of them, it would be a while.

Talking with Lorne and Pat made the wait go quickly and, eventually, they reached the front of the line and showed their driver's licenses and waited while the nurse compared them against the computer. She already knew Kenzie from her previous visits there, but dutifully checked her ID and the computer record anyway.

"Okay, you're all good to go. If you'll wait for someone to escort you in…"

"I know the way," Kenzie offered. "We don't really need directions."

The nurse looked at the next people in line. "Well, I suppose. These folks will need to be shown in."

She nodded, and Kenzie didn't wait for any further instructions. She, Lorne, and Pat walked in without an escort.

The common room was already buzzing with excitement. A lot more people than Kenzie usually saw when she visited. Hopefully, it wouldn't hamper their discussion too much. They found Zachary in his usual seat and sat down. Kenzie kissed him and studied his face. Less lined and weary today. Still hollow-cheeked and pale, but she would take that, if he was on the mend mentally.

"How are you?" She didn't usually ask, letting him pick his own time to discuss his mental well-being.

"Good. It's…" He grasped for words. "It's like my life starts over. It has been so hard, and so dark, and then… it's a new day. One that hasn't been written yet. Anything could happen."

They all smiled. Although Kenzie knew that he *should* start feeling better on Christmas Day as he usually did, she had been afraid that it would be different this year.

"Glad to hear it, Zachary," Lorne approved. "A couple of weeks ago, you weren't doing so well."

Zachary nodded. Even the night before he had been in rough shape. Knowing his history, the doctor had prescribed a strong sedative that would knock him out so that he wouldn't sit up all night, waiting for disaster to strike.

"I think before..." Zachary pursed his lips. "You remember asking whether they had changed any of my meds?" he asked Kenzie.

Kenzie nodded. "Sure. And I even had them check your chart to see. You had changed a lot in just a couple of days. I know it was probably just your reaction to Kennedy's death, and maybe Nurse Debbie's *inspiring* comments, but... you did have me worried."

"I think that she might have been slipping me something extra."

Kenzie raised her brows. "You're pretty knowledgeable about what you take. I think you would have noticed if she gave you anything different."

"Yeah, I know. But... I still think she was. I was foggier than usual. Even with my night meds, they don't make me so... slow."

"Yeah. It worried me."

"You would have noticed if she gave you the wrong pills," Pat said. "But what if she gave you an injection while you were sleeping?"

Zachary shook his head slowly. "No... I think I would have noticed a needle mark."

"Did you take them with something? Water or juice?"

"Usually water," Zachary said. "But she insisted on juice. Said that the doctor wanted me to get more calories." He shrugged. "The doctors *always* want me to get more calories."

"Maybe she put something into the juice, then," Kenzie said, picking up on Pat's suggestion. "And she was hiding the taste with juice, because you might have been able to detect it with water."

"Yeah. Maybe she did. All I know is... I felt a lot better after she was gone."

"Well, I think the two of you have had enough contact with serial killers," Lorne said firmly. "How about you stay away from them after this?"

Kenzie laughed. "That sounds like a good idea."

55

Kenzie had enjoyed the visit with Zachary, but it was obvious after a while that he was getting tired and the movement and conversation of the people around him was wearing on him. For someone who was as hypervigilant as he was, it had to be exhausting to feel as if he had to watch and monitor everyone in the room while he visited with Kenzie, Lorne, and Pat. Once they were gone, he would be able to retire to his room and not have to spend so much energy watching everyone else.

"He does seem like he's doing better," Pat remarked.

"It's amazing how much of a difference a day can make. I wish he could be desensitized to the calendar as much as he was to fire. But…"

"But having a 'Groundhog's Day' where every day was Christmas Eve would just be cruel?" Lorne filled in.

Kenzie smiled and nodded. "That would be horrible. I don't think *I* could manage that."

As they got off the elevator, Kenzie saw two more familiar faces. Gordon and Bridget.

Lorne and Pat didn't know Gordon, but they certainly knew Bridget, and she knew them. She looked anxiously at Gordon, holding tightly to his arm, as if she were afraid that the men would attack her.

Nothing could be further from the truth. Kenzie didn't know two kinder men. Though even they spoke of Bridget in clipped tones when they had to mention her.

"Kenzie," Gordon greeted with a smile, not noticing Bridget's reaction to the two men. "Merry Christmas. Have you been to see Zachary?"

"Yes. He's doing a lot better today."

"Good to hear," he approved. He looked at Bridget, as if expecting a "Merry Christmas" from her, but she said nothing to Kenzie.

"Gordon, I assume you haven't met Lorne Peterson and Pat Parker before?" Kenzie said politely. "Zachary's foster father and… stepfather."

"Oh." Gordon nodded. "I've heard so much about you. It's wonderful to meet you."

He extended a hand. Both Lorne and Pat leaned forward to shake briefly. Lorne nodded to Bridget.

"Bridget. Congratulations on your new arrivals. They are doing well, I hope?"

Bridget nodded jerkily.

"We're here to pick them up," Gordon said, smiling broadly. "They go home on Christmas Day. What better present could we ask for?"

Kenzie said her goodbyes to Pat and Lorne and got into her car. It was cold, and she sat for a few minutes waiting for it to warm up so that the windows wouldn't fog once she started to drive. The phone rang. More Merry Christmas wishers, of course.

Kenzie clicked the button to answer the call on Bluetooth without looking to see who it was.

"Merry Christmas."

"Merry Christmas, Kenzie!" Kenzie recognized Heather's voice.

"I hope you're having a good day today."

"Well, yes," Heather agreed. "It's been a nice morning, and we've talked to the children. We are planning a visit to Zachary this afternoon, the three of us siblings."

"He'll enjoy that." Kenzie was glad that he would have a good break between the Christmas visitors so that he wouldn't be too overwhelmed.

"The thing is… I can't seem to get ahold of Tyrrell to coordinate with him."

"Oh. That's odd."

"I know. He's not usually hard to get. He always has his phone with him. He answers. Unless he doesn't have a signal for some reason."

"Right."

"I was just wondering… whether you had talked to him today or seen him at the hospital. Maybe we got our wires crossed and he decided to go visit Zachary on his own or with the kids."

"No, I haven't heard from him. We had talked about me looking after the kids for an hour or two when he went to visit today, but I haven't heard from him. I thought maybe Tyrrell's plans had changed and he ended up working or didn't end up getting the children."

"He's been pretty quiet the last couple of weeks. I haven't heard much from him."

Kenzie remembered how Tyrrell had looked the last time she had seen him at the hospital, the day that he had helped to guard the twins while Kenzie asked Zachary what was going on. He had looked rough that day. Not terrible, but enough that it had crossed Kenzie's mind that he might be drinking again. He had denied it previously, when they'd been at the Lodge, but he wasn't likely to tell her if he'd fallen off the wagon.

"Maybe you should call his ex."

"I already did," Heather sighed. "He didn't show up to pick up the kids."

Kenzie's heart sank as she thought about how disappointed Mason and Alisha would be. Like Zachary, Mason had some behavioral challenges. Maybe just ADHD, maybe more. Kenzie didn't know if he had any official diagnoses.

"Oh, dear. I hope everything is okay."

"Me too," Heather agreed quietly. "Well… have a Merry Christmas. Joss and I will be over later to see Zachary, even if we can't catch up with Tyrrell."

"You too. Merry Christmas."

The call ended, and Kenzie put the car into gear.

She was going to surprise Lisa by going home to spend some of Christmas Day with her.

She didn't voluntarily spend much time with her mother, so she knew Lisa would be happy to see her. Christmas might not be like it was in the old days, but they could still have a pleasant afternoon together.

She was sure Lisa wouldn't mind.

Did you enjoy this book? Reviews and recommendations are vital to making a book successful.

Please leave a review at your favorite book store or review site and share it with your friends.

Don't miss the following bonus material:
Sign up for mailing list to get a free ebook
Read a sneak preview chapter
Other books by P.D. Workman
Learn more about the author

Sign up for my mailing list at pdworkman.com and get
Gluten-Free Murder for free!

PREVIEW OF SHE WORE MOURNING

The next volume in the Kenzie Kirsch Medical Thrillers series not not yet ready to go!

Have you read the Zachary Goldman Mysteries series? If not, read how Kenzie and Zachary met in She Wore Mourning. A preview follows.

CHAPTER 1

Zachary Goldman stared down the telephoto lens at the subjects before him. It was one of those days that left tourists gaping over the gorgeous scenery. Dark trees against crisp white snow, with the mountains as a backdrop. Like the picture on a Christmas card.

The thought made Zachary feel sick.

But he wasn't looking at the scenery. He was looking at the man and the woman in a passionate embrace. The pretty young woman's cheeks were flushed pink, more likely with her excitement than the cold, since she had barely stepped out of her car to greet the man. He had a swarthier complexion and a thin black beard, and was currently turned away from Zachary's camera.

Zachary wasn't much to look at himself. Average height, black hair cut too short, his own three-day growth of beard not hiding how pinched and pale his face was. He'd never considered himself a good catch.

He waited patiently for them to move, to look around at their surroundings so that he could get a good picture of their faces.

They thought they were alone; that no one could see them without being seen. They hadn't counted on the fact that Zachary had been surveilling them for a couple of weeks and had known where they would go. They gave him lots of warning so that he could park his car out of sight, camouflage himself in the trees, and settle in to wait for their appearance. He was no amateur; he'd been a private investigator since she had been choosing wedding dresses for her Barbie dolls.

He held down the shutter button to take a series of shots as they came up for air and looked around at the magnificent surroundings, smiling at each other, eyes shining.

All the while, he was trying to keep the negative thoughts at bay. Why had he fallen into private detection? It was one of the few ways he could make a living using his skill with a camera. He could have chosen another profession. He didn't need to spend his whole life following other people, taking pictures of their most private moments. What was the real point of his job? He destroyed lives, something he'd had his fill of long ago. When was the last time he'd brought a smile to a client's face? A real, genuine smile? He had wanted to make a difference in people's lives; to exonerate the innocent.

Zachary's phone started to buzz in his pocket. He lowered the camera and turned around, walking farther into the grove of trees. He had the pictures he needed. Anything else would be overkill.

He pulled out his phone and looked at it. Not recognizing the number, he swiped the screen to answer the call.

"Goldman Investigations."

"Uh… yes… Is this Mr. Goldman?" a voice inquired. Older, female, with a tentative quaver.

"Yes, this is Zachary," he confirmed, subtly nudging her away from the 'mister.'

"Mr. Goldman, my name is Molly Hildebrandt."

He hoped she wasn't calling her about her sixty-something-year-old husband and his renewed interest in sex. If it was another infidelity case, he was going to have to turn it down for his own sanity. He would even take a lost dog or wedding ring. As long as the ring wasn't on someone else's finger now.

"Mrs. Hildebrandt. How can Goldman Investigations help you?"

Of course, she had probably already guessed that Goldman Investigations consisted of only one employee. Most people seemed to sense that from the size of his advertisements. From the fact that he listed a post office box number instead of a business suite downtown or in one of the newer commercial areas. It wasn't really a secret.

"I don't know whether you have been following the news at all about Declan Bond, the little boy who drowned…?"

Zachary frowned. He trudged back toward his car.

"I'm familiar with the basics," he hedged. A four- or five-year-old boy whose round face and feathery dark hair had been pasted all over the news after a search for a missing child had ended tragically.

"They announced a few weeks ago that it was determined to be an accident."

Zachary ground his teeth. "Yes…?"

"Mr. Goldman, I was Declan's grandma." Her voice cracked. Zachary waited, listening to her sniffles and sobs as she tried to get herself under control. "I'm sorry. This has been very difficult for me. For everyone."

"Yes."

"Mr. Goldman, I don't believe that it was an accident. I'm looking for someone who would investigate the matter privately."

Zachary breathed out. A homicide investigation? Of a child? He'd told himself that he would take anything that wasn't infidelity, but if there was one thing that was more depressing than couples cheating on each other, it was the death of a child.

"I'm sure there are private investigators that would be more qualified for a homicide case than I am, Mrs. Hildebrandt. My schedule is pretty full right now."

Which, of course, was a lie. He had the usual infidelities, insurance investigations, liabilities, and odd requests. The dregs of the private investigation business. Nothing substantial like a homicide. It was a high-profile case. A lot of volunteers had shown up to help, expecting to find a child who had wandered out of his own yard, expecting to find him dirty and crying, not floating face down in a pond. A lot of people had mourned the death of a child they hadn't even known existed before his disappearance.

"I need your help, Mr. Goldman. Zachary. I can't afford a big name, but you've got good references. You've investigated deaths before. Can't you help me?"

He wondered who she had talked to. It wasn't like there were a lot of people who would give him a bad reference. He was competent and usually got the job done, but he wasn't a big name.

"I could meet with you," he finally conceded. "The first consultation is free. We'll see what kind of a case you have and whether I want to take it. I'm not making any promises at this point. Like I said, my schedule is pretty full already."

She gave a little half-sob. "Thank you. When are you able to come?"

After he had hung up, Zachary climbed into his car, putting his camera down on the floor in front of the passenger seat where it couldn't fall, and started the car. For a while, he sat there, staring out the front windshield at the magical, sparkling, Christmas-card scene. Every year, he told himself it would be better. He would get over it and be able to move on and to enjoy the holiday season like everyone else. Who cared about his crappy childhood experiences? People moved on.

And when he had married Bridget, he had thought he was going to achieve it. They would have a fairy-tale Christmas. They would have hot chocolate after skating at the public rink. They would wander down Main Street looking at the lights and the crèche in front of the church. They would open special, meaningful presents from each other.

But they'd fought over Christmas. Maybe it was Zachary's fault. Maybe he had sabotaged it with his gloom. The season brought with it so much baggage. There had been no skating rink. No hot chocolate, only hot tempers. No walks looking at the lights or the nativity. They had practically thrown their gifts at each other, flouncing off to their respective corners to lick their wounds and pout away the holiday.

He'd still cherished the thought that perhaps the next year there would be a baby. What could be more perfect than Christmas with a baby? It would unite them. Make them a real family. Just like Zachary had longed for since he'd lost his own family. He and Bridget and a baby. Maybe even twins. Their own little family in their own little happy bubble.

But despite a positive pregnancy test, things had gone horribly wrong.

Zachary stared at the bright white scenery and blinked hard, trying to shake off the shadows of the past. The past was past. Over and done. This year he was back to baching it for Christmas. Just him and a beer and *It's a Wonderful Life* on TV.

He put the car in reverse and didn't look into the rear-view mirror as he backed up, even knowing about the precipice behind him. He'd deliberately parked where he'd have to back up toward the cliff when he was done. There was a guardrail, but if he backed up too quickly, the car would go right through it, and who could say whether it had been accidental or deliberate? He had been cold-stone sober and had been out on a job. Mrs. Hildebrandt could testify that he had been calm and sober during their call. It would be ruled an accident.

But his bumper didn't even touch the guardrail before he shifted into drive and pulled forward onto the road.

He'd meet with the grandmother. Then, assuming he did not take the case, there would always be another opportunity.

Life was full of opportunities.

CHAPTER 2

Molly Hildebrandt was much as Zachary expected her to be. A woman in her sixties who looked ten or twenty years older with the stress of the high-profile death of her grandchild. Gray, curling hair. Pale, wrinkled skin. She wasn't hunched over, though. She sat up straight and tall as if she'd gone to a finishing school where she'd been forced to walk and sit with an encyclopedia on her head. Did they still do that? Had they ever done it?

"Mr. Goldman, thank you for seeing me so quickly," she greeted formally, holding her hand out for him to shake when he arrived at her door.

"Please, call me Zachary, ma'am. I'm not really comfortable with Mr. Goldman."

Telling her that he wasn't comfortable with it meant that she would be a bad hostess if she continued to address him that way, instead of her seeing it as a way of showing him respect. He hadn't done anything to deserve respect and was much happier if she would talk to him like the gardener or her next-door neighbor.

Not that there was any gardener. Molly lived in a small apartment in an old, dark brick building that was sturdy enough, but had been around longer than Zachary had been alive. The interior, when she invited him in, was bright and cozy. She had made coffee, and he breathed in the aroma in the air appreciatively. It wasn't hot chocolate after skating, but he could use a cup or two of coffee to warm him up after his surveillance. Standing around in the snow for a couple of hours had chilled him, even though he'd dressed for the weather.

Molly escorted him to the tiny living room.

"And you must call me Molly," she insisted.

She eyed the big camera case as he put it down. Zachary gave a grimace.

"Sorry. I didn't come to take your picture; I just don't like to leave expensive equipment in the car."

"Oh," she nodded politely. She didn't ask him who he had been taking pictures of. That wouldn't be gracious. She would have to imagine instead, and she would probably be correct in her guess.

They fussed for a few minutes with their coffees. Zachary wrapped his fingers around his mug, waiting for the coffee to cool and his fingers to warm. It felt good. Comforting. He waited for Molly to begin her story.

"You probably think that I'm just being a fussy old lady," she said. "Imagining something sinister when it was just an accident."

"Not at all. Why don't you tell me why you don't think it was an accident?"

"I'm not *sure* at all," she clarified. "Maybe they're right. Maybe it was an accident. It isn't that I doubt their findings..." she trailed off. "Not really. I know they had to do an autopsy and all that. We waited for months for them to come back with the manner of death. I thought that once they ruled, everyone would feel better."

"But you still have doubts?"

"I'm worried for my daughter."

Zachary blinked at her and waited for more.

"She's not well. I had hoped that once they released the body... and after the memorial... and after the manner of death was announced... each milestone, I thought, it would get better. It would be easier for her, but..." Molly shook her head. "She's getting worse and worse. Time isn't helping."

"Your daughter was Declan's mother."

"Yes. Of course."

"What's her name?"

"Isabella Hildebrandt," Molly said, her brows drawn down like he should have known that. "You know. *The Happy Artist.*"

Zachary had heard of *The Happy Artist.* She was on TV and was popular among the locals. Zachary didn't know whether she was syndicated nationally or just on one of the local stations. She had a painting instruction show every Sunday morning, and people awaited her next show like a popular soap. Most of the people Zachary knew who watched the show didn't paint and never intended to take it up. She was an institution.

"Oh, yes," Zachary agreed. "Of course, I know *The Happy Artist*. I didn't put the names together."

"When it was in the news, they said who she was. They said it was *The Happy Artist's* child."

"Sure. Of course," Zachary agreed. He rubbed the dark stubble along his jaw. He should have gone home to shave and clean up before meeting with Molly. He looked like he'd been on a three-day stakeout. He *had* been on a three-day stakeout. "I'm sorry. I didn't follow the story very closely. That's good for you; it means I don't have a lot of preconceived ideas about the case."

She looked at him for a minute, frowning. Reconsidering whether she really wanted to hire him? That wouldn't hurt his feelings.

"You were going to tell me about your daughter?" Zachary prompted. "I can understand how devastated she must be by her son's death."

"No. I don't think you can," Molly said flatly.

Zachary was taken aback. He shrugged and nodded, and waited for her to go on.

"Isabella has a history of… mental health issues. She was the one supervising Declan when he disappeared, and the guilt has been overwhelming for her."

That made perfect sense. Zachary sipped at his coffee, which had cooled enough not to scald him.

Molly went on. "I think… as horrible as it may sound… that it would be a relief for her if it turned out that Declan was taken from the yard, instead of just having wandered away."

"That may be, but how likely is that? Surely the police must have considered the possibility, and I can't manufacture evidence for your daughter, even if it would ease her mind."

"No… I realize that. I'm not expecting you to do anything dishonest. Just to investigate it. Read over the police reports. Interview witnesses again. Just see… if there's any possibility that there was… foul play. A third-party interfering, even if it was nothing malicious."

"I assume you know most of the details surrounding the case."

"Yes, of course."

"How likely do you think it is that the police missed something? Did they seem sloppy or like they didn't care? Did you think there were signs of foul play that they brushed off?"

"No." Molly gave a little shrug. "They seemed perfectly competent."

Zachary was silent. It wouldn't be difficult to read over the police reports and talk to the family. Was there any point?

"The only thing is…" Molly trailed off.

As impatient as Zachary was to get out of there, he knew it was no good pushing Molly to give it up any faster. She already knew she sounded crazy for asking him to reinvestigate a case where he wasn't going to be able to turn up anything new. For no reason, other than that it might help her daughter to come to terms with the child's death. He looked around the room. There were no pictures of Molly's husband, even old ones. There was no sign she had raised Isabella or any other children there. There were several pictures of a couple with a little child. Declan and Isabella and whatever the father's name was. There was one picture of Declan himself, occupying its own space, a little memorial to her lost grandson. There were no pictures of anyone else, so Zachary could only assume Isabella was an only child and Declan the only grandchild.

"Declan was afraid of water."

Zachary turned his eyes back to her. He considered. It wasn't totally inconceivable that a child afraid of the water would drown. He wouldn't know how to swim. If he fell in, he would panic, flail, and swallow water, rather than staying calm enough to float. Molly wiped at a tear.

"How afraid of the water was he?" Zachary asked.

"He wouldn't go near the water. He was terrified. He wouldn't have gone to the pond by himself."

"How tall was he?"

Molly gave a little shrug. "He was almost five years old. Three feet?"

"How steep were the banks of the pond and what was the terrain and foliage like?" He knew he would have to look at it for himself.

"I don't know what you want to know… there wasn't any shore to speak of. Just the pond. There were bulrushes. Cattails. Some trees. The ground is… uneven, but not hilly."

Zachary tried to visualize it. A child wouldn't be able to see the pond as far away as an adult would because of his short stature. If his view were further screened by the plant life, the banks steep and crumbly, he might not be able to see it until he was right on top of it. Or in it.

"It's not a lot to go on," he said. "The fact that he was afraid of water."

"I know." Molly used both hands to wipe her eyes. "I know that." She looked around the apartment, swallowing hard to get control of her emotions. "I just want the best for my baby. A parent always wants what's best. Growing up… I wasn't able to give her that. She didn't have an easy life. I wonder if…" She didn't have to finish the sentence this time. Zachary already knew what she was going to say. She wondered if that rough upbringing had caused Isabella's mental fragility. Whether things would have turned out differently if she'd been able to provide a stable environment. Molly sniffled. "Do you have children, Mr.—Zachary?"

Zachary felt that familiar pain in his chest. Like she'd plunged a knife into it. He cleared his throat and shook his head. "No. My marriage just recently ended. We didn't have any children."

"Oh." Her eyes searched his for the truth. Zachary looked away. "I'm sorry. I guess we all have our losses."

Although hers, the death of her grandson, was clearly more permanent than any relationship issues Zachary might have.

In the end, he agreed to do the preliminaries. Get the police reports. Walk the area around the house and pond. Talk to the parents. He gave her his lowest hourly fee. She clearly couldn't afford more. He wasn't even sure she'd be able to pay on receipt of his invoice. He might have to allow her a payment plan, something he normally didn't do, but something about the frail woman had gotten to him.

He put in an appearance at the police station, requesting a copy of the information available to the public, and handing over Molly Hildebrandt's request that he be provided as much information as possible for an independent evaluation.

"You got a new case?" Bowman grunted as he tapped through a few computer screens, getting a feel for how many files there were on the Declan Bond accident investigation file and how much of it he would be able to provide to Zachary.

"Yes," Zachary agreed. Obviously. He didn't encourage small talk; he really didn't want Bowman to start asking personal questions. They weren't friends, but they were friendly. Bowman had helped Zachary track down missing documents before. He knew the right people to ask for permission and the best way to ask.

Bowman dug into his pocket and pulled out a pack of gum. He unwrapped a piece and popped it into his mouth, then offered one to Zachary as an afterthought.

"No, I'm good."

Bowman chewed vigorously as he studied each screen. He was a middle-aged man, with a middle-age spread, his belly sagging over his belt. His hairline had started receding, and occasionally he put on a pair of glasses for a moment and then took them off again, jamming them into his breast pocket.

"How's Bridget?" he asked.

Zachary swallowed. He took a deep breath and steeled himself for the conversation. Bowman looked away from his screen and at Zachary's face, eyebrows up.

"She's good. In remission."

"Good to hear." Bowman looked back at his computer again. "Good to hear. It's been a tough time for the two of you." His eyes flicked back to Zachary, and he backtracked. "I mean it's been tough for her. And for you."

"Yeah," Zachary agreed. He waved away any further fumbling explanation from Bowman. "So, what have we got? On the Bond case?"

"Right!" Bowman looked back at his screen. "I've got press releases and public statements for you. medical examiner's report. The cop in charge of the file was Eugene. He likes red."

Zachary blinked at Bowman, more baffled than usual by his abbreviated language. "What?"

"Eugene Taft. I know, it's a preposterous name, but he's never had a nickname that stuck. Eugene Taft."

"And he likes red."

"Wine," Bowman said as if Zachary was dense. "He likes red wine. You know, if you want to help things along, have a better chance of getting a look at the rest of that file, the officers' notes and all the background and interviews. If you have to apply some leverage."

"And for Eugene Taft, it's red wine."

"Has to be red," Bowman confirmed.

"Okay." Zachary looked at his watch. "Can you start that stuff printing for me? Is there anyone downstairs?" He knew he would have to run down to the basement to order a copy of the medical examiner's report. Just one of those bureaucratic things.

"Sure. Kenzie should be down there still."

Zachary paused. "Kenzie. Not Bradley?"

"Kenzie," Bowman confirmed. "She's new."

"How new?"

"I don't know." Bowman gave a heavy shrug. "How long since you were down there last? Less than that."

Zachary snorted and went down the hall to the elevator.

As he waited for it, Joshua Campbell, an officer he'd worked with on an insurance fraud case several months previous, approached and hit the up button. He did a double-take, looking at Zachary.

"Zach Goldman! How are you, man? Haven't seen you around here lately."

"Good." Zachary shook hands with him. Joshua's hands were hard and rough like he'd grown up working on a farm instead of in the city. Zachary wondered what he did in his spare time that left them so rough and scarred. He wasn't boxing after work; Zachary would have been able to tell that by his knuckles. "Hey, how's Bridget doing? Did everything turn out okay…?" He trailed off and shifted uncomfortably.

"Yeah, great. She's in remission."

"Oh, good. That's great, Zach. Good to hear."

Zachary nodded politely. His elevator arrived with a ding and a flashing down indicator. Zachary sketched a quick goodbye to Joshua and jumped on. He was starting to regret agreeing to look into the Bond case.

The girl at the desk had dark, curly hair, red-lipsticked lips, and a tight, slim form. She was working through some forms, those red lips pursed in concentration, and she didn't look up at him.

"Hang on," she said. "Just let me finish this part up, before I lose my train of thought."

Zachary stood there as patiently as possible, which wasn't too hard with a pretty girl to look at. She finally filled in the last space and looked up at him. She raised an eyebrow.

"You must be Kenzie," Zachary said.

"I don't know if I must be, but I am. Kenzie Kirsch. And you are?"

"Zachary Goldman. From Goldman Investigations."

"A private investigator?"

"Yes."

He didn't usually introduce himself that way because it gave people funny ideas about the kind of life he lived and how he spent his time. Most people did not think about mounds of paperwork or painstaking accident scene reconstructions when they thought about private investigation. They thought about Dick Tracy and Phillip Marlowe and all the old hardboiled detectives. When really most of a private investigator's life was mind-numbingly boring, and he didn't need to carry a gun.

"And what can I do for you today, Mr. Private Investigator?"

"Zachary."

"Zachary," she repeated, losing the teasing tone and giving him a warm smile. "What can I do for you?"

"I need to order a copy of a medical examiner's report. Declan Bond."

"Bond. That's the boy? The drowning victim?"

"That's the one."

She looked at him, shaking her head slightly. "Why do you need that one? It's closed. A determination was made that it was an accident."

"I know. The family would like someone else to look at it. Just to set their minds at ease."

"You're not going to find anything. It's an open-and-shut case."

"That's fine. They just want someone to take a look. It's not a reflection on the medical examiner. You know how families are. They need to be able to move on. They're not quite ready to let it go yet. One last attempt to understand…"

Kenzie gave a little shrug. "Okay, then… there's a form…" She bent over and searched through a drawer full of files to find the right one. Zachary had filled them out before. Usually, he could manage to do an end-run and Bradley would just pull the file for him. Officially, he was supposed to fill one out. He didn't want to end up in hot water with the new administrator, so he leaned on the counter and filled the form out carefully.

She went on with her own forms and filing, not trying to fill the silence with small talk. Which Zachary thought was nice. When he was finished, he put the pen back in its holder and handed the form to Kenzie. To the side of the work she was doing. Not right in front of her face. She again ignored him while she finished the section she was on, then picked it up to look it over.

"You have nice printing," she observed, her voice going up slightly. She laughed at herself. "No reason why you shouldn't," she said quickly. "It's just that the majority of the forms that get submitted here are… well, to say they were chicken scratch would be insulting to chickens."

Zachary chuckled. "That's the difference between a cop and a private investigator."

"Neat handwriting?"

"Yeah. Cops have to fill out so many forms, they don't care. You can just call them if you need something clarified. Me… I know if I don't fill it out right, it's just going to go in the circular file." He nodded in the direction of the garbage can.

"I wouldn't throw it out," she protested.

"If you couldn't read it? What else would you do?"

"I would at least try to call you."

Zachary indicated the form. "That's why I printed my phone number so neatly."

Kenzie smiled and nodded. "It's very clear," she approved.

"You'll call me?"

"I'll let you know when it's ready to be picked up."

Zachary hovered there for an extra few seconds. He was enjoying the give-and-take of his conversation with her but didn't want her to accuse him of being creepy. He wasn't the type who asked a girl out the first time he saw her.

He gave her another smile and walked away from the desk. Maybe next time.

She Wore Mourning, Book #1 of the *Zachary Goldman Mysteries* series by P.D. Workman can be purchased at pdworkman.com

ABOUT THE AUTHOR

Award-winning and USA Today bestselling author P.D. (Pamela) Workman writes riveting mystery/suspense and young adult books dealing with mental illness, addiction, abuse, and other real-life issues. For as long as she can remember, the blank page has held an incredible allure and from a very young age she was trying to write her own books.

Workman wrote her first complete novel at the age of twelve and continued to write as a hobby for many years. She started publishing in 2013. She has won several literary awards from Library Services for Youth in Custody for her young adult fiction. She currently has over 80 published titles and can be found at pdworkman.com.

Born and raised in Alberta, Workman has been married for over 25 years and has one son.

Please visit P.D. Workman at pdworkman.com to see what else she is working on, to join her mailing list, and to link to her social networks.

If you enjoyed this book, please take the time to recommend it to other purchasers with a review or star rating and share it with your friends!

facebook.com/pdworkmanauthor

twitter.com/pdworkmanauthor

instagram.com/pdworkmanauthor

amazon.com/author/pdworkman

bookbub.com/authors/p-d-workman

goodreads.com/pdworkman

linkedin.com/in/pdworkman

pinterest.com/pdworkmanauthor

youtube.com/pdworkman